THE DIARY

OF

SAMUEL PEPYS, M.A., F.R.S.

LONDON: G. BELL & SONS, LIMITED,
PORTUGAL ST. LINCOLN'S INN, W.C.

THE DIARY
OF
SAMUEL PEPYS

M.A., F.R.S.; CLERK OF THE ACTS AND
SECRETARY TO THE ADMIRALTY

TRANSCRIBED BY THE LATE REV. MYNORS BRIGHT, M.A.
FROM THE SHORTHAND MANUSCRIPT IN THE
PEPYSIAN LIBRARY, MAGDALENE
COLLEGE, CAMBRIDGE

EDITED WITH ADDITIONS
BY
HENRY B. WHEATLEY, F.S.A.

VOLS. IV–VI.

1664–1667

LONDON
G. BELL AND SONS LTD.
1962

This edition was first published in 10 *vols., demy* 8*vo*, 1893–1899, *in which form it has been frequently reprinted.*

Reissued in 8 *vols., crown* 8*vo*, 1904.
Reprinted 1913, 1916, 1919, 1923.

India Paper Edition, 1923.
Reprinted 1924 (*Jan., April, and July*), 1926, 1928, 1938, 1942.

Thin paper Edition, 1946, 1949, 1952, 1962

PRINTED IN GREAT BRITAIN BY
WILLIAM CLOWES AND SONS, LIMITED, LONDON AND BECCLES.

THE

DIARY OF SAMUEL PEPYS.

January 1st, 1663–64.

WENT to bed between 4 and 5 in the morning with my mind in good temper of satisfaction and slept till about 8, that many people came to speak with me. Among others one came with the best New Year's gift that ever I had, namely from Mr. Deering, with a bill of exchange drawn upon himself for the payment of £50 to Mr. Luellin. It being for my use with a letter of compliment. I am not resolved what or how to do in this business, but I conclude it is an extraordinary good new year's gift, though I do not take the whole, or if I do then give some of it to Luellin. By and by comes Captain Allen and his son Jowles[1] and his wife, who continues pretty still. They would have had me set my hand to a certificate for his loyalty, and I know not what his ability for any employment. But I did not think it fit, but did give them a pleasing denial, and after sitting with me an hour they went away. Several others came to me about business, and then being to dine at my uncle Wight's I went to the Coffee-house, sending my wife by Will, and there staid talking an hour with Coll. Middleton, and others, and among other things about a very rich widow, young and handsome, of one Sir Nicholas

[1] Rebecca Alleyn, spinster (about eighteen), daughter of John Alleyn, was married to Henry Jowles, of Chatham, Kent, bachelor (about twenty-four), in August, 1662 (Chester's "London Marriage Licences," ed. Foster, col. 779).

Gold's,[1] a merchant, lately fallen, and of great courtiers that already look after her: her husband not dead a week yet. She is reckoned worth £80,000. Thence to my uncle Wight's, where Dr. of ——, among others, dined, and his wife, a seeming proud conceited woman, I know not what to make of her, but the Dr's. discourse did please me very well about the disease of the stone, above all things extolling Turpentine, which he told me how it may be taken in pills with great ease. There was brought to table a hot pie made of a swan I sent them yesterday, given me by Mr. Howe, but we did not eat any of it. But my wife and I rose from table, pretending business, and went to the Duke's house, the first play I have been at these six months, according to my last vowe, and here saw the so much cried-up play of "Henry the Eighth;" which, though I went with resolution to like it, is so simple a thing made up of a great many patches, that, besides the shows and processions in it, there is nothing in the world good or well done. Thence mightily dissatisfied back at night to my uncle Wight's, and supped with them, but against my stomach out of the offence the sight of my aunt's hands gives me, and ending supper with a mighty laugh, the greatest I have had these many months, at my uncle's being out in his grace after meat, we rose and broke up, and my wife and I home and to bed, being sleepy since last night.

2nd. Up and to the office, and there sitting all the morning, and at noon to the 'Change, in my going met with Luellin and told him how I had received a letter and bill for £50 from Mr. Deering, and delivered it to him, which he told me he would receive for me. To which I consented, though professed not to desire it if he do not consider himself sufficiently able by the service I have done, and that it is rather my desire to have nothing till he be further sensible of my service. From the 'Change I brought him home and dined with us, and after dinner I took my wife out, for I do find that I am not able to conquer myself as to going to plays till I come to some new vowe concerning it, and that I am now come, that is to say,

[1] Sir Nicholas Gold, or Gould, created a baronet in 1660, married Elizabeth, daughter of Sir John Garrard, Bart., of Lamers, Herts. She remarried Thomas Neal. See June 20th, 1664.—B.

that I will not see above one in a month at any of the publique theatres till the sum of 50*s.* be spent, and then none before New Year's Day next, unless that I do become worth £1,000 sooner than then, and then am free to come to some other terms, and so leaving him in Lombard Street I took her to the King's house, and there met Mr. Nicholson, my old colleague, and saw "The Usurper,"[1] which is no good play, though better than what I saw yesterday. However, we rose unsatisfied, and took coach and home, and I to the office late writing letters, and so to supper and to bed.

3rd (Lord's day). Lay long in bed, and then rose and with a fire in my chamber staid within all day, looking over and settling my accounts in good order, by examining all my books, and the kitchen books, and I find that though the proper profit of my last year was but £305, yet I did by other gain make it up £444, which in every part of it was unforeseen of me, and therefore it was a strange oversight for lack of examining my expenses that I should spend £690 this year, but for the time to come I have so distinctly settled all my accounts in writing and the particulars of all my several layings out, that I do hope I shall hereafter make a better judgment of my spendings than ever. I dined with my wife in her chamber, she in bed, and then down again and till 11 at night, and broke up and to bed with great content, but could not make an end of writing over my vows as I purposed, but I am agreed in every thing how to order myself for the year to come, which I trust in God will be much for my good. So up to prayers and to bed. This evening Sir W. Pen came to invite me against next Wednesday, being Twelfth day, to his usual feast, his wedding day.

4th. Up betimes, and my wife being ready, and her mayd Besse and the girl, I carried them by coach and set them all down in Covent Garden and there left them, and I to my Lord Sandwich's lodgings, but he not being up, I to the Duke's chamber, and there by and by to his closett,

[1] A tragedy by the Hon. Edward Howard, now first acted, but not published until 1668. Oliver Cromwell was alluded to under the name of Damocles the Syracusan, and Hugh Peters is introduced as Hugo de Petra.

where since his lady was ill, a little red bed of velvet is brought for him to lie alone, which is a very pretty one. After doing business here, I to my Lord's again, and there spoke with him, and he seems now almost friends again as he used to be. Here meeting Mr. Pierce, the chyrurgeon, he told me among other Court newes, how the Queene is very well again, and the King lay with her on Saturday night last; and that she speaks now very pretty English, and makes her sense out now and then with pretty phrazes: as among others this is mightily cried up; that, meaning to say that she did not like such a horse so well as the rest, he being too prancing and full of tricks, she said he did make too much vanity. Thence to the Tennis Court, after I had spent a little time in Westminster Hall, thinking to have met with Mrs. Lane, but I could not and am glad of it, and there saw the King play at Tennis and others: but to see how the King's play was extolled without any cause at all, was a loathsome sight, though sometimes, indeed, he did play very well and deserved to be commended; but such open flattery is beastly. Afterwards to St. James's Parke, being unwilling to go to spend money at the ordinary, and there spent an hour or two, it being a pleasant day, seeing people play at Pell Mell; where it pleased me mightily to hear a gallant, lately come from France, swear at one of his companions for suffering his man (a spruce blade) to be so saucy as to strike a ball while his master was playing on the Mall.[1] Thence took coach at White Hall and took up my wife, who is mighty sad to think of her father, who is going into Germany against the Turkes; but what will become of her brother I know not. He is so idle, and out of all capacity, I think, to earn his bread. Home and at my office till 12 at night making my solemn vowes for the next year, which I trust in the Lord I shall keep, but I fear I have a little too severely bound myself in some things and in too many, for I fear I may forget some. But however, I know the worst, and shall by the blessing of God observe to perform or pay my

[1] When Egerton was Bishop of Durham, he often played at bowls with his guests on the public days. On an occasion of this sort, a visitor happening to cross the lawn, one of the chaplains exclaimed, "You must not shake the green, for the bishop is going to bowl." — B.

forfeits punctually. So home and to bed with my mind at rest.

5th. Up and to our office, where we sat all the morning, where my head being willing to take in all business whatever, I am afraid I shall overclogg myself with it. But however, it is my desire to do my duty and shall the willinger bear it. At noon home and to the 'Change, where I met with Luellin, who went off with me and parted to meet again at the Coffee-house, but missed. So home and found him there, and Mr. Barrow came to speak with me, so they both dined with me alone, my wife not being ready, and after dinner I up in my chamber with Barrow to discourse about matters of the yard with him, and his design of leaving the place, which I am sorry for, and will prevent if I can. He being gone then Luellin did give me the £50 from Mr. Deering, which he do give me for my pains in his business and what I may hereafter take for him, though there is not the least word or deed I have yet been guilty of in his behalf but what I am sure has been to the King's advantage and the profit of the service, nor ever will. And for this money I never did condition with him or expected a farthing at the time when I did do him the service, nor have given any receipt for it, it being brought me by Luellin, nor do purpose to give him any thanks for it, but will wherein I can faithfully endeavour to see him have the privilege of his Patent as the King's merchant. I did give Luellin two pieces in gold for a pair of gloves for his kindness herein. Then he being gone, I to my office, where busy till late at night, that through my room being over confounded in business I could stay there no longer, but went home, and after a little supper to bed.

6th (Twelfth day). Up and to my office, where very busy all the morning, being indeed over loaded with it through my own desire of doing all I can. At noon to the 'Change, but did little, and so home to dinner with my poor wife, and after dinner read a lecture to her in Geography, which she takes very prettily and with great pleasure to her and me to teach her, and so to the office again, where as busy as ever in my life, one thing after another, and answering people's business, particularly drawing up things about Mr. Wood's masts, which I expect to have a quarrel about with Sir W. Batten before it be ended, but I care not. At night home to my wife, to supper, discourse, prayers, and to bed. This morning I began a practice which I find by the ease I do it with that I shall continue, it saving me money and time; that is, to trimme myself with a razer: which pleases me mightily.

7th. Up, putting on my best clothes and to the office, where all the morning we sat busy, among other things upon Mr. Wood's performance of his contract for masts, wherein I was mightily concerned, but I think was found all along in the right, and shall have my desire in it to the King's advantage. At noon, all of us to dinner to Sir W. Pen's, where a very handsome dinner, Sir J. Lawson among others, and his lady and his daughter, a very pretty lady and of good deportment, with looking upon whom I was greatly pleased, the rest of the company of the women were all of our own house, of no satisfaction or pleasure at all. My wife was not there, being not well enough, nor had any great mind. But to see how Sir W. Pen imitates me in everything, even in his having his chimney piece in his dining room the same with that in my wife's closett, and in every thing else I perceive wherein he can. But to see again how he was out in one compliment: he lets alone drinking any of the ladies' healths that were there, my Lady Batten and Lawson, till he had begun with my Lady Carteret, who was absent, and that was well enough, and then Mr. Coventry's mistresse, at which he was ashamed, and would not have had him have drunk it, at least before the ladies present, but his policy, as he thought, was such that he would do it. After dinner by coach with Sir G. Carteret and Sir J. Minnes by appointment to Auditor Beale's in Salisbury Court, and there we did with great content look over some old ledgers to see in what manner they were kept, and indeed it was in an extraordinary good method, and such as (at least out of design to keep them employed) I do persuade Sir J. Minnes to go upon, which will at least do as much good it may be to keep them for want of something to do from envying those that do something. Thence calling to see whether Mrs. Turner was returned, which she is, and I spoke one word only to her, and away again by coach home and to my office, where late, and then home to supper and bed.

8th. Up and all the morning at my office and with Sir J. Minnes, directing him and Mr. Turner about keeping of their books according to yesterday's work, wherein I shall make them work enough. At noon to the 'Change, and there long, and from thence by appointment took Luellin, Mount, and W. Symons, and Mr. Pierce, the chirurgeon, home to dinner with me and were merry. But, Lord! to hear how W. Symons do commend and look sadly and then talk bawdily and merrily, though his wife was dead but the other day, would make a dogg laugh. After dinner I did go in further part of kindness to Luellin for his kindness about Deering's £50 which he procured me the other day of him. We spent all the afternoon together and then they to cards with my wife, who this day put on her Indian blue gowne which is very pretty, where I left them for an hour, and to my office, and then to them again, and by and by they went away at night, and so I again to my office to perfect a letter to Mr. Coventry about Department Treasurers, wherein I please myself and hope to give him content and do the King service therein. So having done, I home and to teach my wife a new lesson in the globes, and to supper, and to bed. We had great pleasure this afternoon; among other things, to talk of our old passages together in Cromwell's time; and how W. Symons did make me laugh and wonder to-day when he told me how he had made shift to keep in, in good esteem and employment, through eight governments in one year (the year 1659, which were indeed, and he did name them all), and then failed unhappy in the ninth, viz. that of the King's coming in. He made good to me the story which Luellin did tell me the other day, of his wife upon her death-bed; how she dreamt of her uncle Scobell, and did foretell, from some discourse she had with him, that she should die four days thence, and not sooner, and did all along say so, and did so. Upon the 'Change a great talke there was of one Mr. Tryan, an old man, a merchant in Lyme-Streete, robbed last night (his man and mayde being gone out after he was a-bed), and gagged and robbed of £1,050 in money and about £4,000 in jewells, which he had in his house as security for money. It is believed by many circumstances that his man is guilty of confederacy, by their ready going to his secret till in his desk, wherein the key of his cash-chest lay.

9th. Up (my underlip being mightily swelled, I know not how but by overrubbing it, it itching) and to the office, where we sat all the morning, and at noon I home to dinner, and by discourse with my wife thought upon inviting my Lord Sandwich to a dinner shortly. It will cost me at least ten or twelve pounds; but, however, some arguments of prudence I have, which however I shall think again upon before I proceed to that expence. After dinner by coach I carried my wife and Jane to Westminster, leaving her at Mr. Hunt's, and I to Westminster Hall, and there visited Mrs. Lane, and by appointment went out and met her at the Trumpet, Mrs. Hare's, but the room being damp we went to the Bell tavern, and there I had her company, but could not do as I used to do (yet nothing but what was honest). . . . . So I to talk about her having Hawley, she told me flatly no, she could not love him. I took occasion to enquire of Howlett's daughter, with whom I have a mind to meet a little to see what mettle the young wench is made of, being very pretty, but she tells me she is already betrothed to Mrs. Michell's son, and she in discourse tells me more, that Mrs. Michell herself had a daughter before marriage, which is now near thirty years old, a thing I could not have believed. Thence leading her to the Hall, I took coach and called my wife and her mayd, and so to the New Exchange, where we bought several things of our pretty Mrs. Dorothy Stacy, a pretty woman, and has the modestest look that ever I saw in my life and manner of speech. Thence called at Tom's and saw him pretty well again, but has not been currant. So homeward, and called at Ludgate, at Ashwell's uncle's, but she was not within, to have spoke to her to have come to dress my wife at the time my Lord dines here. So straight home, calling for Walsingham's Manual[1] at my bookseller's to read but not to buy, recommended for a pretty book by Sir W. Warren, whose warrant however I do not much take till I do read it. So home to supper and to

[1] Said to be written or translated by Francis Walsingham, the Jesuit. "Arcana Aulica; or, Walsingham's Manual of Prudential Maxims for the Statesman and the Courtier," London, 1652, 1655.

bed, my wife not being very well since she came home, being troubled with a fainting fit, which she never yet had before since she was my wife.

10th (Lord's day). Lay in bed with my wife till 10 or 11 o'clock, having been very sleepy all night. So up, and my brother Tom being come to see me, we to dinner, he telling me how Mrs. Turner found herself discontented with her late bad journey, and not well taken by them in the country, they not desiring her coming down, nor the buriall of Mr. Edward Pepys's corps there.[1] After dinner I to the office, where all the afternoon, and at night my wife and I to my uncle Wight's, and there eat some of their swan pie, which was good, and I invited them to my house to eat a roasted swan on Tuesday next, which after I was come home did make a quarrell between my wife and I, because she had appointed a wash to-morrow. But, however, we were friends again quickly. So to bed. All our discourse to-night was Mr. Tryan's late being robbed; and that Collonell Turner (a mad, swearing, confident fellow, well known by all, and by me), one much indebted to this man for his very livelihood, was the man that either did or plotted it; and the money and things are found in his hand, and he and his wife now in Newgate for it; of which we are all glad, so very a known rogue he was.

11th. Waked this morning by 4 o'clock by my wife to call the mayds to their wash, and what through my sleeping so long last night and vexation for the lazy sluts lying so long again and their great wash, neither my wife nor I could sleep one winke after that time till day, and then I rose and by coach (taking Captain Grove with me and three bottles of Tent, which I sent to Mrs. Lane by my promise on Saturday night last) to White Hall, and there with the rest of our company to the Duke and did our business, and thence to the Tennis Court till noon, and there saw several great matches played, and so by invitation to St. James's; where, at Mr. Coventry's chamber, I dined with my Lord Barkeley, Sir G. Carteret, Sir Edward Turner,[2] Sir Ellis

[1] He was buried in the church of Tattersett (St. Andrew), Norfolk. — B.

[2] Sir Edward Turnour, born in Threadneedle Street in 1617; Speaker of the House of Commons, 1661-71; Solicitor-General, 1670; and Lord Chief Baron, 1671. Died March 4th, 1675-76.

Layton,[1] and one Mr. Seymour, a fine gentleman; where admirable good discourse of all sorts, pleasant and serious. Thence after dinner to White Hall, where the Duke being busy at the Guinny business, the Duke of Albemarle, Sir W. Rider, Povy, Sir J. Lawson and I to the Duke of Albemarle's lodgings, and there did some business, and so to the Court again, and I to the Duke of York's lodgings, where the Guinny company are choosing their assistants for the next year by ballotting. Thence by coach with Sir J. Robinson, Lieutenant of the Tower, he set me down at Cornhill, but, Lord! the simple discourse that all the way we had, he magnifying his great undertakings and cares that have been upon him for these last two years, and how he commanded the city to the content of all parties, when the loggerhead knows nothing almost that is sense. Thence to the Coffee-house, whither comes Sir W. Petty and Captain Grant, and we fell in talke (besides a young gentleman, I suppose a merchant, his name Mr. Hill, that has travelled and I perceive is a master in most sorts of musique and other things) of musique; the universal character; art of memory; Granger's counterfeiting of hands and other most excellent discourses to my great content, having not been in so good company a great while, and had I time I should covet the acquaintance of that Mr. Hill. This morning I stood by the King arguing with a pretty Quaker woman, that delivered to him a desire of hers in writing. The King showed her Sir J. Minnes, as a man the fittest for her quaking religion, saying that his beard was the stiffest thing about him, and again merrily said, looking upon the length of her paper, that if all she desired was of that length she

[1] The real name of the knight was Elisha Leighton, whose brother Robert, Bishop of Dumblane, became, soon afterwards, the excellent Archbishop of Glasgow, and as such is more generally known. Their father, Alexander Leighton, was a rank Puritan, author of "Zion's Plea against Prelacy," for writing which he had his ears cut off, and was exposed in the pillory in that state, with his nose also slit. *Elisha* was apparently euphonized into Ellis by the courtier son, who is described by Le Neve as one of the Duke of York's servants. Pepys speaks of him as Secretary of the Prize Office, and adds, that he had been a mad, freaking fellow. See January 25th, 1664-65. — B. Sir Ellis Leighton was elected a Fellow of the Royal Society, December 9th, 1663, and admitted on December 16th.

might lose her desires; she modestly saying nothing till he begun seriously to discourse with her, arguing the truth of his spirit against hers; she replying still with these words, "O King!" and thou'd him all along. The general talke of the towne still is of Collonell Turner, about the robbery; who, it is thought, will be hanged. I heard the Duke of York tell to-night, how letters are come that fifteen are condemned for the late plot by the Judges at York; and, among others, Captain Oates, against whom it was proved that he drew his sword at his going out, and flinging away the scabbard, said that he would either return victor or be hanged. So home, where I found the house full of the washing and my wife mighty angry about Will's being here to-day talking with her mayds, which she overheard, idling of their time, and he telling what a good mayd my old Jane was, and that she would never have her like again. At which I was angry, and after directing her to beat at least the little girl, I went to the office and there reproved Will, who told me that he went thither by my wife's order, she having commanded him to come thither on Monday morning. Now God forgive me! how apt I am to be jealous of her as to this fellow, and that she must needs take this time, when she knows I must be gone out to the Duke, though methinks had she that mind she would never think it discretion to tell me this story of him, to let me know that he was there, much less to make me offended with him, to forbid him coming again. But this cursed humour I cannot cool in myself by all the reason I have, which God forgive me for, and convince me of the folly of it, and the disquiet it brings me. So home, where, God be thanked, when I came to speak to my wife my trouble of mind soon vanished, and to bed. The house foul with the washing and quite out of order against to-morrow's dinner.

12th. Up and to the office, where we sat all the morning, and at noon to the 'Change awhile, and so home, getting things against dinner ready, and anon comes my uncle Wight and my aunt, with their cozens Mary and Robert, and by chance my uncle Thomas Pepys. We had a good dinner, the chief dish a swan roasted, and that excellent meate. At dinner and all day very merry. After dinner to cards, where till evening, then to the office a little, and to cards again with them, and lost half-a-crowne. They being gone, my wife did tell me how my uncle did this day accost her alone, and spoke of his hoping she was with child, and kissing her earnestly told her he should be very glad of it, and from all circumstances methinks he do seem to have some intention of good to us, which I shall endeavour to continue more than ever I did yet. So to my office till late, and then home to bed, after being at prayers, which is the first time after my late vowe to say prayers in my family twice in every week.

13th. Up and to my office a little, and then abroad to many several places about business, among others to the geometrical instrument makers, and through Bedlam (calling by the way at an old bookseller's and there fell into looking over Spanish books and pitched upon some, till I thought of my oathe when I was going to agree for them, and so with much ado got myself out of the shop glad at my heart and so away) to the African House to look upon their book of contracts for several commodities for my information in the prices we give in the Navy. So to the Coffee-[house] where extraordinary good discourse of Dr. Whistler's [1] upon my question concerning the keeping of masts, he arguing against keeping them dry, by showing the nature of corruption in bodies and the several ways thereof. So to the 'Change, and thence with Sir W. Rider to the Trinity House to dinner, and then home and to my office till night, and then with Mr. Bland to Sir T. Viner's about pieces of eight for Sir J. Lawson, and so back to my office, and there late upon business, and so home to supper and to bed.

14th. Up and to the office, where all the morning, and at noon all of us, viz., Sir G. Carteret and Sir W. Batten at one end, and Mr. Coventry, Sir J. Minnes and I (in the middle at the other end, being taught how to sit there all three by my sitting so much the backwarder) at the other end, to Sir G. Carteret's, and there dined well. Here I saw Mr. Scott, the bastard that married his youngest daughter.[2] Much pleasant talk at table, and then up and to the

[1] Daniel Whistler, M.D., was elected a Fellow of the Royal Society, May 20th, 1663.

[2] See *ante*, July 30th, 1663 (note).

office, where we sat long upon our design of dividing the Controller's work into some of the rest of our hands for the better doing of it, but he would not yield to it, though the simple man knows in his heart that he do not do one part of it. So he taking upon him to do it all we rose, I vexed at the heart to see the King's service run after this manner, but it cannot be helped. Thence to the Old James to the reference about Mr. Bland's business. Sir W. Rider being now added to us, and I believe we shall soon come to some determination in it. So home and to my office, did business, and then up to Sir W. Pen and did express my trouble about this day's business, he not being there, and plainly told him what I thought of it, and though I know him a false fellow yet I adventured, as I have done often, to tell him clearly my opinion of Sir W. Batten and his design in this business, which is very bad. Hence home, and after a lecture to my wife in her globes, to prayers and to bed.

15th. Up and to my office, where all the morning, and among other things Mr. Turner with me, and I did tell him my mind about the Controller his master and all the office, and my mind touching himself too, as he did carry himself either well or ill to me and my clerks, which I doubt not but it will operate well. Thence to the 'Change, and there met my uncle Wight, who was very kind to me, and would have had me home with him, and so kind that I begin to wonder and think something of it of good to me. Thence home to dinner, and after dinner with Mr. Hater by water, and walked thither and back again from Deptford, where I did do something checking the iron business, but my chief business was my discourse with Mr. Hater about what had passed last night and to-day about the office business, and my resolution to do him all the good I can therein. So home, and my wife tells me that my uncle Wight hath been with her, and played at cards with her, and is mighty inquisitive to know whether she is with child or no, which makes me wonder what his meaning is, and after all my thoughts, I cannot think, unless it be in order to the making his will, that he might know how to do by me, and I would to God my wife had told him that she was.

16th. Up, and having paid some money in the morning

to my uncle Thomas on his yearly annuity, to the office, where we sat all the morning. At noon I to the 'Change about some pieces of eight for Sir J. Lawson. There I hear that Collonell Turner is found guilty of felony at the Sessions in Mr. Tryan's business, which will save his life. So home and met there J. Hasper come to see his kinswoman our Jane. I made much of him and made him dine with us, he talking after the old simple manner that he used to do. He being gone, I by water to Westminster Hall, and there did see Mrs. Lane. . . . So by coach home and to my office, where Browne of the Minerys brought me an Instrument made of a Spyral line very pretty for all questions in Arithmetique almost, but it must be some use that must make me perfect in it. So home to supper and to bed, with my mind un peu troubled pour ce que fait to-day, but I hope it will be la dernier de toute ma vie.[1]

17th (Lord's day). Up, and I and my wife to church, where Pembleton appeared, which, God forgive me, did vex me, but I made nothing of it. So home to dinner, and betimes my wife and I to the French church and there heard a good sermon, the first time my wife and I were there ever together. We sat by three sisters, all pretty women. It was pleasant to hear the reader give notice to them, that the children to be catechized next Sunday were them of Hounsditch and Blanche Chapiton.[2] Thence home, and there found Ashwell come to see my wife (we having called at her lodging the other day to speak with her about dressing my wife when my Lord Sandwich dines here), and is as merry as ever, and speaks as disconcerned for any difference between us on her going away as ever. She

[1] Four lines in a different cipher.

[2] Blanch Apleton, in Aldgate Ward, is said by Stow to have been a manor belonging, in the reign of Richard II., to Sir Thomas Roos, of Hamelake, and that in 3 Edw. IV. all basket-makers, wire-drawers, and other foreigners were permitted to have shops in this manor and not elsewhere within the city or suburbs. It is enumerated (9 Hen. V.) in "The Partition of the inheritance of Humphrey de Bohun, Earl of Hereford and Essex," under the head of "London-Blaunch-Appulton." Hall, in his "Chronicle" (ed. 1548), writes it Blanchechapelton. Stow says that in the 13th of Edward I. a lane behind Blanch Apleton was granted by the king to be enclosed and shut up. The name was continued in a corrupted form as Blind Chapel Court.

being gone, my wife and I to see Sir W. Pen and there supped with him much against my stomach, for the dishes were so deadly foule that I could not endure to look upon them. So after supper home to prayers and to bed.

18th. Up, being troubled to find my wife so ready to have me go out of doors. God forgive me for my jealousy! but I cannot forbear, though God knows I have no reason to do so, or to expect her being so true to me as I would have her. I abroad to White Hall, where the Court all in mourning for the Duchesse of Savoy. We did our business with the Duke, and so I to W. Howe at my Lord's lodgings, not seeing my Lord, he being abroad, and there I advised with W. Howe about my having my Lord to dinner at my house, who likes it well, though it troubles me that I should come to need the advice of such a boy, but for the present it is necessary. Here I found Mr. Mallard, and had from him a common tune set by my desire to the Lyra Vyall, which goes most admirably. Thence home by coach to the 'Change, after having been at the Coffee-house, where I hear Turner[1] is found guilty of felony and burglary; and strange stories of his confidence at the barr, but yet great indiscretion in his argueing. All desirous of his being hanged. So home and found that Will had been with my wife. But, Lord! why should I think any evil of that; and yet I cannot forbear it. But upon enquiry, though I found no reason of doubtfulness, yet I could not bring my nature to any quiet or content in my wife all day and night, nor though I went with her to divert myself at my uncle Wight's, and there we played at cards till 12 at night and went home in a great shower of rain, it having not rained a great while before. Here was one Mr. Benson, a Dutchman, played and supped with us, that pretends to sing well, and I expected great matters but found nothing to be pleased with at all. So home and to bed, yet troubled in my mind.

19th. Up, without any kindness to my wife, and so to the office, where we sat all the morning, and at noon I to the 'Change, and thence to Mr. Cutler's with Sir W. Rider to

[1] James Turnor, a solicitor, commonly called Colonel Turnor, was hanged on January 21st, 1663-64, at Lime Street end, for robbing Mr. Fr. Fryon (*sic*), merchant (Smyth's "Obituary," p. 59). See *ante*, January 11th.

dinner, and after dinner with him to the Old James upon our reference of Mr. Bland's, and, having sat there upon the business half an hour, broke up, and I home and there found Madame Turner and her sister Dike come to see us, and staid chatting till night, and so away, and I to my office till very late, and my eyes began to fail me, and be in pain which I never felt to now-a-days, which I impute to sitting up late writing and reading by candle-light. So home to supper and to bed.

20th. Up and by coach to my Lord Sandwich's, and after long staying till his coming down (he not sending for me up, but it may be he did not know I was there), he came down, and I walked with him to the Tennis Court, and there left him, seeing the King play. At his lodgings this morning there came to him Mr. W. Montague's fine lady, which occasioned my Lord's calling me to her about some business for a friend of hers preferred to be a midshipman at sea. My Lord recommended the whole matter to me. She is a fine confident lady, I think, but not so pretty as I once thought her. My Lord did also seal a lease for the house he is now taking in Lincoln's Inn Fields, which stands him in £250 per annum rent. Thence by water to my brother's, whom I find not well in bed, sicke, they think, of a consumption, and I fear he is not well, but do not complain, nor desire to take anything. From him I visited Mr. Honiwood, who is lame, and to thank him for his visit to me the other day, but we were both abroad. So to Mr. Commander's in Warwicke Lane, to speak to him about drawing up my will, which he will meet me about in a day or two. So to the 'Change and walked home, thence with Sir Richard Ford, who told me that Turner is to be hanged to-morrow, and with what impudence he hath carried out his trial; but that last night, when he brought him newes of his death, he began to be sober and shed some tears, and he hopes will die a penitent; he having already confessed all the thing, but says it was partly done for a joke, and partly to get an occasion of obliging the old man by his care in getting him his things again, he having some hopes of being the better by him in his estate at his death. Home to dinner, and after dinner my wife and I by water, which we have not done together many a day, that is not since last summer, but the weather is now very warm, and left her at Axe Yard, and I to White Hall, and meeting Mr. Pierce walked with him an hour in the Matted Gallery; among other things he tells me that my Lady Castlemaine is not at all set by by the King, but that he do doat upon Mrs. Stewart only; and that to the leaving of all business in the world, and to the open slighting of the Queene; that he values not who sees him or stands by him while he dallies with her openly; and then privately in her chamber below, where the very sentrys observe his going in and out; and that so commonly, that the Duke or any of the nobles, when they would ask where the King is, they will ordinarily say, "Is the King above, or below?" meaning with Mrs. Stewart: that the King do not openly disown my Lady Castlemaine, but that she comes to Court; but that my Lord FitzHarding and the Hambletons,[1] and sometimes my Lord Sandwich, they say, have their snaps at her. But he says my Lord Sandwich will lead her from her lodgings in the darkest and obscurest manner, and leave her at the entrance into the Queene's lodgings, that he might be the least observed; that the Duke of Monmouth the King do still doat on beyond measure, insomuch that the King only, the Duke of York, and Prince Rupert, and the Duke of Monmouth, do now wear deep mourning, that is, long cloaks, for the Duchesse of Savoy; so that he mourns as a Prince of the Blood, while the Duke of York do no more, and all the nobles of the land not so much; which gives great offence, and he says the Duke of York do consider. But that the Duke of York do give himself up to business, and is like to prove a noble Prince; and so indeed I do from my heart think he will. He says that it is believed, as well as hoped, that care is taken to lay up a hidden treasure of money by the King against a bad day. I pray God it be so! but I should be more glad that the King himself would look after business, which it seems he do not in the least. By and by came by Mr. Coventry, and so we broke off, and he and I took a turn or two and so parted, and then my Lord Sandwich came upon me, to speak with whom my business of coming again to-night to this ende of the town chiefly was, in order

[1] The three brothers, George Hamilton, James Hamilton, and the Count Antoine Hamilton, author of the "Mémoires de Grammont."

to the seeing in what manner he received me, in order to my inviting him to dinner to my house, but as well in the morning as now, though I did wait upon him home and there offered occasion of talk with him, yet he treated me, though with respect, yet as a stranger, without any of the intimacy or friendship which he used to do, and which I fear he will never, through his consciousness of his faults, ever do again. Which I must confess do trouble me above anything in the world almost, though I neither do need at present nor fear to need to be so troubled, nay, and more, though I do not think that he would deny me any friendship now if I did need it, but only that he has not the face to be free with me, but do look upon me as a remembrancer of his former vanity, and an espy upon his present practices, for I perceive that Pickering to-day is great with him again, and that he has done a great courtesy for Mr. Pierce, the chirurgeon, to a good value, though both these and none but these did I mention by name to my Lord in the business which has caused all this difference between my Lord and me. However, I am resolved to forbear my laying out my money upon a dinner till I see him in a better posture, and by grave and humble, though high deportment, to make him think I do not want him, and that will make him the readier to admit me to his friendship again, I believe the soonest of anything but downright impudence, and thrusting myself, as others do, upon him, which yet I cannot do, nor will not endeavour. So home, calling with my wife to see my brother again, who was up, and walks up and down the house pretty well, but I do think he is in a consumption. Home, troubled in mind for these passages with my Lord, but am resolved to better my case in my business to make my stand upon my owne legs the better and to lay up as well as to get money, and among other ways I will have a good fleece out of Creed's coat ere it be long, or I will have a fall. So to my office and did some business, and then home to supper and to bed, after I had by candlelight shaved myself and cut off all my beard clear, which will make my worke a great deal the less in shaving.

21st. Up, and after sending my wife to my aunt Wight's to get a place to see Turner hanged, I to the office, where we sat all the morning, and at noon going to the 'Change;

and seeing people flock in the City, I enquired, and found that Turner was not yet hanged. And so I went among them to Leadenhall Street, at the end of Lyme Street, near where the robbery was done; and to St. Mary Axe, where he lived. And there I got for a shilling to stand upon the wheel of a cart, in great pain, above an houre before the execution was done; he delaying the time by long discourses and prayers one after another, in hopes of a reprieve; but none came, and at last was flung off the ladder in his cloake. A comely-looked man he was, and kept his countenance to the end: I was sorry to see him. It was believed there were at least 12 or 14,000 people in the street. So I home all in a sweat, and dined by myself, and after dinner to the Old James, and there found Sir W. Rider and Mr. Cutler at dinner, and made a second dinner with them, and anon came Mr. Bland and Custos, and Clerke, and so we fell to the business of reference, and upon a letter from Mr. Povy to Sir W. Rider and I telling us that the King is concerned in it, we took occasion to fling off the business from off our shoulders and would have nothing to do with it, unless we had power from the King or Commissioners of Tangier, and I think it will be best for us to continue of that mind, and to have no hand, it being likely to go against the King. Thence to the Coffee-house, and heard the full of Turner's discourse on the cart,[1] which was chiefly to clear himself of all things laid to his charge but this fault, for which he now suffers, which he confesses. He deplored the condition of his family, but his chief design was to lengthen time, believing still a reprieve would come, though the sheriff advised him to expect no such thing, for the King was resolved to grant none. After that I had good discourse with a pretty young merchant with mighty content. So to my office and did a little business, and then to my aunt Wight's to fetch my wife home, where Dr. Burnett did tell me how poorly the sheriffs did endeavour to get one jewell returned by Turner, after he was convicted, as a due to them, and not to give it to Mr. Tryan, the true owner, but ruled against them, to their great dishonour. Though they plead it might be another jewell for ought they

[1] Sir Richard Ford was one of the sheriffs. Turnor's speech at his execution has been printed. London, 8vo, 1663.

know and not Tryan's. After supper home, and my wife tells me mighty stories of my uncle's fond and kind discourses to her to-day, which makes me confident that he has thoughts of kindness for us, he repeating his desire for her to be with child, for it cannot enter into my head that he should have any unworthy thoughts concerning her. After doing some business at my office, I home to supper, prayers, and to bed.

22nd. Up, and it being a brave morning, with a gally to Woolwich, and there both at the Ropeyarde and the other yarde did much business, and thence to Greenwich to see Mr. Pett and others value the carved work of the "Henrietta" (God knows in an ill manner for the King), and so to Deptford, and there viewed Sir W. Petty's vessel; which hath an odd appearance, but not such as people do make of it, for I am of the opinion that he would never have discoursed so much of it, if it were not better than other vessels, and so I believe that he was abused the other day, as he is now, by tongues that I am sure speak before they know anything good or bad of her. I am sorry to find his ingenuity discouraged so. So home, reading all the way a good book, and so home to dinner, and after dinner a lesson on the globes to my wife, and so to my office till 10 or 11 o'clock at night, and so home to supper and to bed.

23rd. Up, and to the office, where we sat all the morning. At noon home to dinner, where Mr. Hawly came to see us and dined with us, and after we had dined came Mr. Mallard, and after he had eat something, I brought down my vyall, which he played on, the first maister that ever touched her yet, and she proves very well and will be, I think, an admirable instrument. He played some very fine things of his owne, but I was afeard to enter too far in their commendation for fear he should offer to copy them for me out, and so I be forced to give or lend him something. So to the office in the evening, whither Mr. Commander came to me, and we discoursed about my will, which I am resolved to perfect the next week by the grace of God. He being gone, I to write letters and other business late, and so home to supper and to bed.

24th (Lord's day). Lay long in bed, and then up, and being desirous to perform my vowes that I lately made, among others, to be performed this month, I did go to my office, and there fell on entering, out of a bye-book, part of my second journall-book, which hath lain these two years and more unentered. Upon this work till dinner, and after dinner to it again till night, and then home to supper, and after supper to read a lecture to my wife upon the globes, and so to prayers and to bed. This evening also I drew up a rough draught of my last will to my mind.

25th. Up and by coach to Whitehall to my Lord's lodgings, and seeing that knowing that I was in the house, my Lord did not nevertheless send for me up, I did go to the Duke's lodgings, and there staid while he was making ready, in which time my Lord Sandwich came, and so all into his closet and did our common business, and so broke up, and I homeward by coach with Sir W. Batten, and staid at Warwicke Lane and there called upon Mr. Commander and did give him my last will and testament to write over in form, and so to the 'Change, where I did several businesses. So home to dinner, and after I had dined Luellin came and we set him something to eat, and I left him there with my wife, and to the office upon a particular meeting of the East India Company, where I think I did the King good service against the Company in the business of their sending our ships home empty from the Indies contrary to their contract, and yet, God forgive me! I found that I could be willing to receive a bribe if it were offered me to conceal my arguments that I found against them, in consideration that none of my fellow officers, whose duty it is more than mine, had ever studied the case, or at this hour do understand it, and myself alone must do it. That being done Mr. Povy and Bland came to speak with me about their business of the reference, wherein I shall have some more trouble, but cannot help it, besides I hope to make some good use of Mr. Povy to my advantage. So home after business done at my office, to supper, and then to the globes with my wife, and so to bed. Troubled a little in mind that my Lord Sandwich should continue this strangeness to me that methinks he shows me now a days more than while the thing was fresh.

26th. Up and to the office, where we sat all the morning. At noon to the 'Change, after being at the Coffee-house, where I sat by Tom Killigrew, who told us of a fire last night in my Lady Castlemaine's lodging, where she bid £40 for one to adventure the fetching of a cabinet out, which at last was got to be done; and the fire at last quenched without doing much wrong. To 'Change and there did much business, so home to dinner, and then to the office all the afternoon. And so at night my aunt Wight and Mrs. Buggin came to sit with my wife, and I in to them all the evening, my uncle coming afterward, and after him Mr. Benson the Dutchman, a frank, merry man. We were very merry and played at cards till late, and so broke up and to bed in good hopes that this my friendship with my uncle and aunt will end well.

27th. Up and to the office, and at noon to the Coffee-house, where I sat with Sir G. Ascue [1] and Sir William Petty, who in discourse is, methinks, one of the most rational men that ever I heard speak with a tongue, having all his notions the most distinct and clear, and, among other things (saying, that in all his life these three books were the most esteemed and generally cried up for wit in the world — "Religio Medici," "Osborne's Advice to a Son," [2] and "Hudibras"), — did say that in these — in the two first principally — the wit lies, and confirming some pretty sayings, which are generally like paradoxes, by some argument smartly and pleasantly urged, which takes with people who do not trouble themselves to examine the force of an argument, which pleases them in the delivery, upon a subject which they like; whereas, as by many particular instances of mine, and others, out of Osborne, he did really find fault and weaken the strength of many of Osborne's arguments, so as that in downright disputation they would not bear weight; at least, so far, but that they might be weakened, and better found in their rooms to confirm what is there said. He shewed finely whence it

[1] Sir George Ayscue or Askew, see note *ante*, September 6th, 1661. After his return from his imprisonment he declined to go to sea again, although he was twice afterwards formally appointed. He sat on the court-martial on the loss of the "Defiance" in 1668.

[2] Francis Osborne, an English writer of considerable abilities and popularity, was the author of "Advice to a Son," in two parts, Oxford, 1656–8, 8vo. He died in 1659. He is the same person mentioned as "*My Father* Osborne," October 19th, 1661. — B.

happens that good writers are not admired by the present age; because there are but few in any age that do mind anything that is abstruse and curious; and so longer before any body do put the true praise, and set it on foot in the world, the generality of mankind pleasing themselves in the easy delights of the world, as eating, drinking, dancing, hunting, fencing, which we see the meanest men do the best, those that profess it. A gentleman never dances so well as the dancing master, and an ordinary fiddler makes better musique for a shilling than a gentleman will do after spending forty, and so in all the delights of the world almost. Thence to the 'Change, and after doing much business, home, taking Commissioner Pett with me, and all alone dined together. He told me many stories of the yard, but I do know him so well, and had his character given me this morning by Hempson, as well as my own too of him before, that I shall know how to value any thing he says either of friendship or other business. He was mighty serious with me in discourse about the consequence of Sir W. Petty's boat, as the most dangerous thing in the world, if it should be practised by endangering our losse of the command of the seas and our trade, while the Turkes and others shall get the use of them, which, without doubt, by bearing more sayle will go faster than any other ships, and, not being of burden, our merchants cannot have the use of them and so will be at the mercy of their enemies. So that I perceive he is afeard that the honour of his trade will down, though (which is a truth) he pretends this consideration to hinder the growth of this invention. He being gone my wife and I took coach and to Covent Garden, to buy a maske at the French House, Madame Charett's,[1] for my wife; in the way observing the streete full of coaches at the new play, "The Indian Queene;"[2] which for show, they say, exceeds "Henry the Eighth." Thence back to Mrs.

[1] Mrs. Mary Cherrett, called also Madame Cherrett, lived in the Piazza. (Rate Books of St. Paul's, Covent Garden.) Mr. George Cherrett, milliner, and Susan, his wife, were living in the Piazza in 1689. (Ib.) — B.

[2] "The Indian Queen," a tragedy in heroic verse, by Sir Robert Howard and John Dryden. It was produced with great splendour, with music composed by Purcell.

Turner's and sat a while with them talking of plays and I know not what, and so called to see Tom, but not at home, though they say he is in a deep consumption, and Mrs. Turner and Dike and they say he will not live two months to an end. So home and to the office, and then to supper and to bed.

28th. Up and to the office, where all the morning sitting, and at noon upon several things to the 'Change, and thence to Sir G. Carteret's to dinner of my own accord, and after dinner with Mr. Wayth down to Deptford doing several businesses, and by land back again, it being very cold, the boat meeting me after my staying a while for him at an alehouse by Redriffe stairs. So home, and took Will coming out of my doors, at which I was a little moved, and told my wife of her keeping him from the office (though God knows my base jealous head was the cause of it), which she seemed troubled at, and that it was only to discourse with her about finding a place for her brother. So I to my office late, Mr. Commander coming to read over my will in order to the engrossing it, and so he being gone I to other business, among others chiefly upon preparing matters against Creed for my profit, and so home to supper and bed, being mightily troubled with my left eye all this evening from some dirt that is got into it.

29th. Up, and after shaving myself (wherein twice now, one after another, I have cut myself much, but I think it is from the bluntness of the razor) there came Mr. Deane to me and staid with me a while talking about masts, wherein he prepared me in several things against Mr. Wood, and also about Sir W. Petty's boat, which he says must needs prove a folly, though I do not think so unless it be that the King will not have it encouraged. At noon, by appointment, comes Mr. Hartlibb and his wife, and a little before them Messrs. Langley and Bostocke (old acquaintances of mine at Westminster, clerks), and after shewing them my house and drinking they set out by water, my wife and I with them down to Wapping on board the "Crowne," a merchantman, Captain Floyd, a civil person. Here was Vice-Admiral Goodson, whom the more I know the more I value for a serious man and staunch. Here was Whistler the flagmaker, which vexed me, but it mattered not. Here was other sorry company and the discourse poor, so that we had no pleasure there at all, but only to see and bless God to find the difference that is now between our condition and that heretofore, when we were not only much below Hartlibb in all respects, but even these two fellows above named, of whom I am now quite ashamed that ever my education should lead me to such low company, but it is God's goodness only, for which let him be praised. After dinner I broke up and with my wife home, and thence to the Fleece[1] in Cornhill, by appointment, to meet my Lord Marlborough, a serious and worthy gentleman, who, after doing our business, about the company, he and they began to talk of the state of the Dutch in India, which is like to be in a little time without any controll; for we are lost there, and the Portuguese as bad. Thence to the Coffee-house, where good discourse, specially of Lt.-Coll. Baron touching the manners of the Turkes' Government, among whom he lived long. So to my uncle Wight's, where late playing at cards, and so home.

30th. Up, and a sorry sermon of a young fellow I knew at Cambridge; but the day kept solemnly for the King's murder, and all day within doors making up my Brampton papers, and in the evening Mr. Commander came and we made perfect and signed and sealed my last will and testament, which is so to my mind, and I hope to the liking of God Almighty, that I take great joy in myself that it is done, and by that means my mind in a good condition of quiett. At night to supper and to bed. This evening, being in a humour of making all things even and clear in the world, I tore some old papers; among others, a romance which (under the title of "Love a Cheate") I begun ten years ago at Cambridge; and at this time reading it over to-night I liked it very well, and wondered a little at myself at my vein at that time when I wrote it, doubting that I cannot do so well now if I would try.

31st (Lord's day). Up, and in my chamber all day long (but a little at dinner) settling all my Brampton accounts to this day in very good order, I having obliged

[1] There is a token of this house extant: "Will Hinton at ye Golden fleece on Corne Hill 1666" ("Boyne's Tokens," ed. Williamson, vol. i., p. 573).

myself by oathe to do that and some other things within this month, and did also perfectly prepare a state of my estate and annexed it to my last will and testament, which now is perfect, and, lastly, I did make up my monthly accounts, and find that I have gained above £50 this month clear, and so am worth £858 clear, which is the greatest sum I ever yet was master of, and also read over my usual vowes, as I do every Lord's day, but with greater seriousness than ordinary, and I do hope that every day I shall see more and more the pleasure of looking after my business and laying up of money, and blessed be God for what I have already been enabled by his grace to do. So to supper and to bed with my mind in mighty great ease and content, but my head very full of thoughts and business to dispatch this next month also, and among others to provide for answering to the Exchequer for my uncle's being Generall-Receiver in the year 1647, which I am at present wholly unable to do, but I must find time to look over all his papers.

February 1st. Up (my maids rising early this morning to washing), and being ready I found Mr. Strutt the purser below with 12 bottles of sacke, and tells me (which from Sir W. Batten I had heard before) how young Jack Davis has railed against Sir W. Batten for his endeavouring to turn him out of his place, at which for the fellow's sake, because it will likely prove his ruin, I am sorry, though I do believe he is a very arch rogue. I took Strutt by coach with me to White Hall, where I set him down, and I to my Lord's, but found him gone out betimes to the Wardrobe, which I am glad to see that he so attends his business, though it troubles me that my counsel to my prejudice must be the cause of it. They tell me that he goes into the country next week, and that the young ladies come up this week before the old lady. Here I hear how two men last night, justling for the wall about the New Exchange, did kill one another, each thrusting the other through; one of them of the King's Chappell, one Cave, and the other a retayner of my Lord Generall Middleton's.[1] Thence to White Hall; where, in the Duke's chamber, the King came and stayed an hour or two laughing at Sir W. Petty, who

[1] John Middleton, Earl of Middleton, general of the forces in Scotland. — B.

was there about his boat; and at Gresham College in general; at which poor Petty was, I perceive, at some loss; but did argue discreetly, and bear the unreasonable follies of the King's objections and other bystanders with great discretion; and offered to take oddes against the King's best boates; but the King would not lay, but cried him down with words only. Gresham College he mightily laughed at, for spending time only in weighing of ayre, and doing nothing else since they sat.[1] Thence to Westminster Hall, and there met with diverse people, it being terme time. Among others I spoke with Mrs. Lane, of whom I doubted to hear something of the effects of our last meeting about a fortnight or three weeks ago, but to my content did not. Here I met with Mr. Pierce, who tells me of several passages at Court, among others how the King, coming the other day to his Theatre to see "The Indian Queene" (which he commends for a very fine thing), my Lady Castlemaine was in the next box before he came; and leaning over other ladies awhile to whisper to the King, she rose out of the box and went into the King's, and set herself on the King's right hand, between the King and the Duke of York; which, he swears, put the King himself, as well as every body else, out of countenance; and believes that she did it only to show the world that she is not out of favour yet, as was believed. Thence with Alderman Maynell[2] by his coach to the 'Change, and there with several people busy, and so home to dinner, and took my wife out immediately to the King's Theatre, it being a new month, and once a month I may go, and there saw "The Indian Queene" acted; which indeed is a most pleasant show, and beyond my expectation; the play good, but spoiled with the ryme, which breaks the sense. But above my expectation most, the eldest Marshall[3] did do

[1] The king was greatly interested in the work of the Royal Society, but he liked to have his joke. An examination of Birch's "History of the Royal Society" will show how much was done, and how many important investigations were opened up in the early years of the society's history.

[2] Francis Menhil (Meynell or Maynell), goldsmith, was sheriff in 1661. (See note *ante*, September 18th, 1662.)

[3] Anne Marshall, a celebrated actress, and her younger sister Beck, are frequently mentioned by Pepys, who erroneously states that they

her part most excellently well as I ever heard woman in my life; but her voice not so sweet as Ianthe's;[1] but, however, we came home mightily contented. Here we met Mr. Pickering and his mistress, Mrs. Doll Wilde;[2] he tells me that the business runs high between the Chancellor and my Lord Bristoll against the Parliament; and that my Lord Lauderdale and Cooper[3] open high against the Chancellor; which I am sorry for. In my way home I 'light and to the Coffee-house, where I heard Lt.-Coll. Baron tell very good stories of his travels over the high hills in Asia above the clouds, how clear the heaven is above them, how thicke like a mist the way is through the cloud that wets like a sponge one's clothes, the ground above the clouds all dry and parched, nothing in the world growing, it being only a dry earth, yet not so hot above as below the clouds. The stars at night most delicate bright and a fine clear blue sky, but cannot see the earth at any time through the clouds, but the clouds look like a world below you. Thence home and to supper, being hungry, and so to the office, did business, specially about Creed, for whom I am now pretty well fitted, and so home to bed. This day in Westminster Hall W. Bowyer told me that his father is dead lately, and died by being drowned in the river, coming over in the night; but he says he had not been drinking. He was taken with his stick in his hand and cloake over his shoulder, as ruddy as before he died. His horse was

were the daughters of a Presbyterian minister; Colonel Chester proved conclusively that this was not the case. Stephen Marshall, the eminent preacher, died November 19th, 1655, and at the date of his will five of his daughters were already married, three of them at least to clergymen; his remaining daughter, who proved the will and was unmarried, was named Susan ("Westminster Abbey Registers," 1876, p. 149). See note on Mrs. Davenport, February 18th, 1661–62.

[1] Mrs. Betterton, see note *ante*, April 2nd, 1662.

[2] Apparently from the following licence they were already married: "Edward Pickering (Pykering), of St. Andrew's, Holborn, bachelor, about 35, and Mrs. Dorothy Weld, of St. Giles in the Fields, spinster, about 30, and at own dispose—at St. Giles in the Fields, 28 Sept. 1663" (Chester's "London Marriage Licences," 1521–1869, ed. Foster, 1887, col. 1057).

[3] Sir Anthony Ashley Cooper (1621–1683) had been created Baron Ashley of Wimborne St. Giles in 1661, and therefore it was not correct to designate him Cooper at this date.

taken overnight in the water, hampered in the bridle, but they were so silly as not to look for his master till the next morning, that he was found drowned.

2nd. Up and to the office, where, though Candlemas day, Mr. Coventry and Sir W. Pen and I all the morning, the others being at a survey at Deptford. At noon by coach to the 'Change with Mr. Coventry, thence to the Coffee-house with Captain Cocke, who discoursed well of the good effects in some kind of a Dutch warr and conquest (which I did not consider before, but the contrary), that is, that the trade of the world is too little for us two, therefore one must down: 2ndly, that though our merchants will not be the better husbands by all this, yet our wool will bear a better price by vaunting of our cloths, and by that our tenants will be better able to pay rents, and our lands will be more worth, and all our owne manufactures, which now the Dutch outvie us in; that he thinks the Dutch are not in so good a condition as heretofore because of want of men always, and now from the warrs against the Turke more than ever. Then to the 'Change again, and thence off to the Sun Taverne with Sir W. Warren, and with him discoursed long, and had good advice, and hints from him, and among other things he did give me a payre of gloves for my wife wrapt up in paper, which I would not open, feeling it hard; but did tell him that my wife should thank him, and so went on in discourse. When I came home, Lord! in what pain I was to get my wife out of the room without bidding her go, that I might see what these gloves were; and, by and by, she being gone, it proves a payre of white gloves for her and forty pieces in good gold, which did so cheer my heart, that I could eat no victuals almost for dinner for joy to think how God do bless us every day more and more, and more yet I hope he will upon the increase of my duty and endeavours. I was at great losse what to do, whether tell my wife of it or no, which I could hardly forbear, but yet I did and will think of it first before I do, for fear of making her think me to be in a better condition, or in a better way of getting money, than yet I am. After dinner to the office, where doing infinite of business till past 10 at night to the comfort of my mind, and so home with joy to supper and to bed. This evening Mr. Hempson came and told me how Sir W. Batten his master will not hear of continuing him in his employment as Clerk of the Survey at Chatham, from whence of a sudden he has removed him without any new or extraordinary cause, and I believe (as he himself do in part write, and J. Norman do confess) for nothing but for that he was twice with me the other day and did not wait upon him. So much he fears me and all that have to do with me. Of this more in the Mem. Book of my office upon this day, there I shall find it.

3rd. Up, and after a long discourse with my cozen Thomas Pepys, the executor, I with my wife by coach to Holborn, where I 'light, and she to her father's, I to the Temple and several places, and so to the 'Change, where much business, and then home to dinner alone, and so to the Mitre Taverne by appointment (and there met by chance with W. Howe come to buy wine for my Lord against his going down to Hinchingbroke, and I private with him a great while discoursing of my Lord's strangeness to me; but he answers that I have no reason to think any such thing, but that my Lord is only in general a more reserved man than he was before) to meet Sir W. Rider and Mr. Clerke, and there after much ado made an end, giving Mr. Custos £202 against Mr. Bland, which I endeavoured to bring down but could not, and think it is well enough ended for Mr. Bland for all that. Thence by coach to fetch my wife from her brother's, and found her gone home. Called at Sir Robert Bernard's about surrendering my estate in reversion to the use of my life, which will be done, and at Roger Pepys, who was gone to bed in pain of a boyle that he could not sit or stand. So home, where my wife is full of sad stories of her good-natured father and roguish brother, who is going for Holland and his wife, to be a soldier. And so after a little at the office to bed. This night late coming in my coach, coming up Ludgate Hill, I saw two gallants and their footmen taking a pretty wench, which I have much eyed, lately set up shop upon the hill, a seller of riband and gloves. They seek to drag her by some force, but the wench went, and I believe had her turn served, but, God forgive me! what thoughts and wishes I had of being in their place. In Covent Garden to-night, going to fetch home my wife, I stopped at the great Coffee-house[1] there, where I never was before; where Dryden the poet (I knew at Cambridge), and all the wits of the town, and Harris the player, and Mr. Hoole of our College. And had I had time then, or could at other times, it will be good coming thither, for there, I perceive, is very witty and pleasant discourse. But I could not tarry, and as it was late, they were all ready to go away.

4th. Up and to the office, where after a while sitting, I left the board upon pretence of serious business, and by coach to Paul's School, where I heard some good speeches of the boys that were to be elected this year. Thence by and by with Mr. Pullen and Barnes (a great Non-Conformist) with several others of my old acquaintance to the Nag's Head Taverne, and there did give them a bottle of sacke, and away again and I to the School, and up to hear the upper form examined; and there was kept by very many of the Mercers, Clutterbucke,[2] Barker, Harrington, and others; and with great respect used by them all, and had a noble dinner. Here they tell me, that in Dr. Colett's[3] will he says that he would have a Master found for the School that hath good skill in Latin, and (if it could be) one that had some knowledge of the Greeke; so little was Greeke known here at that time. Dr. Wilkins[4] and one Mr. Smallwood, Posers. After great pleasure there, and specially to Mr.

[1] This was the Rose, afterwards known as Will's Coffee-House, after William Urwin, the landlord, where Dryden had a chair reserved for him near the fireplace in winter, which was carried into the balcony for him in summer. It was on the west side of Bow Street, and at the corner of Russell Street. In earlier passages of the Diary Pepys speaks of going to Will's, but as he here says that he went to this coffee-house for the first time, that must have been some other place.

[2] Probably Alderman Clutterbuck, one of the proposed knights of the Royal Oak for Middlesex. There was a Sir Thomas Clutterbuck of London, *circiter* 1670. — B.

[3] John Colet, dean of St. Paul's and founder of the school; born 1466, died 1519.

[4] John Wilkins, born 1614, joined the Solemn League and Covenant, 1648. He married Robinia Cromwell, sister of the Protector, in 1659. Warden of Wadham College, Oxford, 1648-59; Master of Trinity College, Cambridge, 1659; consecrated Bishop of Chester, 1668; died November 19th, 1672. He was one of the founders of the Royal Society.

Crumlum, so often to tell of my being a benefactor to the School, I to my bookseller's and there spent an hour looking over Theatrum Urbium and Flandria illustrata, with excellent cuts, with great content. So homeward, and called at my little milliner's, where I chatted with her, her husband out of the way, and a mad merry slut she is. So home to the office, and by and by comes my wife home from the burial of Captain Grove's wife at Wapping (she telling me a story how her mayd Jane going into the boat did fall down and show her arse in the boat) and alone comes my uncle Wight and Mr. Maes with the state of their case, which he told me very discreetly, and I believe is a very hard one, and so after drinking a bottle of ale or two they gone, and I a little more to the office, and so home to prayers and to bed. This evening I made an end of my letter to Creed about his pieces of eight, and sent it away to him. I pray God give good end to it to bring me some money, and that duly as from him.

5th. Up, and down by water, a brave morning, to Woolwich, and there spent an houre or two to good purpose, and so walked to Greenwich and thence to Deptford, where I found (with Sir W. Batten upon a survey) Sir J. Minnes, Sir W. Pen, and my Lady Batten come down and going to dinner. I dined with them, and so after dinner by water home, all the way going and coming reading "Faber Fortunæ,"[1] which I can never read too often. At home a while with my wife, and so to my office, where till 8 o'clock, and then home to look over some Brampton papers, and my uncle's accounts as Generall-Receiver of the County for 1647 of our monthly assessment, which, contrary to my expectation, I found in such good order and so thoroughly that I did not expect, nor could have thought, and that being done, having seen discharges for every farthing of money he received, I went to bed late with great quiett.

6th. Up, and to the office, where we sat all the morning, and so at noon to the 'Change, where I met Mr. Coventry, the first time I ever saw him there, and after a little talke with him and other merchants, I up and down about several businesses, and so home, whither came one Father Fogourdy, an Irish priest, of my wife's and her mother's

[1] See note *ante*, July 20th, 1663.

acquaintance in France, a sober, discreet person, but one that I would not have converse with my wife for fear of meddling with her religion, but I like the man well. Thence with my wife abroad, and left her at Tom's, while I abroad about several businesses and so back to her, myself being vexed to find at my first coming Tom abroad, and all his books, papers, and bills loose upon the open table in the parlour, and he abroad, which I ranted at him for when he came in. Then by coach home, calling at my cozen Scott's, who (she) lies dying, they say, upon a miscarriage. My wife could not be admitted to see her, nor any body. At home to the office late writing letters, and then home to supper and to bed. Father Fogourdy confirms to me the newes that for certain there is peace between the Pope and King of France.

7th (Lord's day). Up and to church, and thence home, my wife being ill . . . kept her bed all day, and I up and dined by her bedside, and then all the afternoon till late at night writing some letters of business to my father stating of matters to him in general of great import, and other letters to ease my mind in the week days that I have not time to think of, and so up to my wife, and with great mirth read Sir W. Davenant's two speeches in dispraise of London and Paris, by way of reproach one to another,[1] and so to prayers and to bed.

8th. Up, and by coach called upon Mr. Phillips, and after a little talk with him away to my Lord Sandwich's, but he being gone abroad, I staid a little and talked with Mr. Howe, and so to Westminster in term time, and there met Mr. Pierce, who told me largely how the King still do doat upon his women, even beyond all shame; and that the good Queen will of herself stop before she goes sometimes into her dressing-room, till she knows whether the King be there, for fear he should be, as she hath sometimes taken

[1] These two speeches are in the "Entertainment at Rutland House," with which Sir William Davenant tried in 1656 to revive dramatic performances. We read, "The curtains are suddenly opened, and in the Rostras appear sitting a Parisian and a Londoner in the livery robes of both cities, who declaim concerning the pre-eminence of Paris and London." After the Parisian has declaimed, and "after a concert of Music, imitating the Waits of London, the Londoner rises and answers."

him, with Mrs. Stewart; and that some of the best parts of the Queen's joynture are, contrary to faith, and against the opinion of my Lord Treasurer and his Council, bestowed or rented, I know not how, to my Lord FitzHarding and Mrs. Stewart, and others of that crew: that the King do doat infinitely upon the Duke of Monmouth, apparently as one that he intends to have succeed him. God knows what will be the end of it! After he was gone I went and talked with Mrs. Lane about persuading her to Hawly, and think she will come on, which I wish were done, and so to Mr. Howlett and his wife, and talked about the same, and they are mightily for it, and I bid them promote it, for I think it will be for both their goods and my content. But I was much pleased to look upon their pretty daughter, which is grown a pretty mayd, and will make a fine modest woman. Thence to the 'Change by coach, and after some business done, home to dinner, and thence to Guildhall, thinking to have heard some pleading, but there were no Courts, and so to Cade's, the stationer, and there did look upon some pictures which he promised to give me the buying of, but I found he would have played the Jacke with me, but at last he did proffer me what I expected, and I have laid aside £10 or £12 worth, and will think of it, but I am loth to lay out so much money upon them. So home a little vexed in my mind to think how to-day I was forced to compliment W. Howe and admit myself to an equality with Mr. Moore, which is come to challenge in his discourse with me, but I will admit it no more, but let me stand or fall, I will show myself as strange to them as my Lord do himself to me. After at the office till 9 o'clock, I home in fear of some pain by taking cold, and so to supper and to bed.

9th. Up and to the office, where sat all the morning. At noon by coach with Mr. Coventry to the 'Change, where busy with several people. Great talke of the Dutch proclaiming themselves in India, Lords of the Southern Seas, and deny traffick there to all ships but their owne, upon pain of confiscation; which makes our merchants mad. Great doubt of two ships of ours, the "Greyhound" and another, very rich, coming from the Streights, for fear of the Turkes. Matters are made up between the Pope and the King of France; so that now all the doubt is, what the French will do with their armies. Thence home, and there found Captain Grove in mourning for his wife, and Hawly, and they dined with me. After dinner, and Grove gone, Hawly and I talked of his mistress, Mrs. Lane, and I seriously advising him and inquiring his condition, and do believe that I shall bring them together. By and by comes Mr. Moore, with whom much good discourse of my Lord, and among other things told me that my Lord is mightily altered, that is, grown very high and stately, and do not admit of any to come into his chamber to him, as heretofore, and that I must not think much of his strangeness to me, for it was the same he do to every body, and that he would not have me be solicitous in the matter, but keep off and give him now and then a visit and no more, for he says he himself do not go to him now a days but when he sends for him, nor then do not stay for him if he be not there at the hour appointed, for, says he, I do find that I can stand upon my own legs and I will not by any over submission make myself cheap to any body and contemptible, which was the doctrine of the world that I lacked most, and shall follow it. I discoursed with him about my money that my Lord hath, and the £1,000 that I stand bound with him in, to my cozen Thomas Pepys, in both which I will get myself at liberty as soon as I can; for I do not like his being angry and in debt both together to me; and besides, I do not perceive he looks after paying his debts, but runs farther and farther in. He being gone, my wife and I did walk an houre or two above in our chamber, seriously talking of businesses. I told her my Lord owed me £700, and shewed her the bond, and how I intended to carry myself to my Lord. She and I did cast about how to get Captain Grove for my sister, in which we are mighty earnest at present, and I think it would be a good match, and will indeavour it. So to my office a while, then home to supper and to bed.

10th. Up, and by coach to my Lord Sandwich, to his new house, a fine house, but deadly dear, in Lincoln's Inne Fields, where I found and spoke a little to him. He is high and strange still, but did ask me how my wife did, and at parting remembered him to his cozen, which I thought was pretty well, being willing to flatter myself that in time he will be well again. Thence home straight and busy all the forenoon, and at noon with Mr. Bland to Mr. Povy's, but he being at dinner and full of company we retreated and went into Fleet Street to a friend of his, and after a long stay, he telling me the long and most perplexed story of Coronell and Bushell's business of sugars, wherein Parke and Green and Mr. Bland and 40 more have been so concerned about the King of Portugal's duties, wherein every party has laboured to cheat another, a most pleasant and profitable story to hear, and in the close made me understand Mr. Maes' business better than I did before. By and by dinner came, and after dinner and good discourse that and such as I was willing for improvement sake to hear, I went away too to White Hall to a Committee of Tangier, where I took occasion to demand of Creed whether he had received my letter, and he told me yes, and that he would answer it, which makes me much wonder what he means to do with me, but I will be even with him before I have done, let him make as light of it as he will. Thence to the Temple, where my cozen Roger Pepys did show me a letter my Father wrote to him last Terme to shew me, proposing such things about Sturtlow and a portion for Pall, and I know not what, that vexes me to see him plotting how to put me to trouble and charge, and not thinking to pay our debts and legacys, but I will write him a letter will persuade him to be wiser. So home, and finding my wife abroad (after her coming home from being with my aunt Wight to-day to buy Lent provisions) gone with Will to my brother's, I followed them by coach, but found them not, for they were newly gone home from thence, which troubled me. I to Sir Robert Bernard's chamber, and there did surrender my reversion in Brampton lands to the use of my will, which I was glad to have done, my will being now good in all parts. Thence homewards, calling a little at the Coffee-house, where a little merry discourse, and so home, where I found my wife, who says she went to her father's to be satisfied about her brother, who I found at my house with her. He is going this next tide with his wife into Holland to seek his fortune. He had taken his leave of us this morning. I did give my wife 10*s.* to give him, and a coat that I had by me, a close-bodied light-coloured cloth coat, with a gold edgeing in each seam, that was the lace of my wife's best petty-coat that she had when I married her. I staid not there, but to my office, where Stanes the glazier was with me till 10 at night making up his contract, and, poor man, I made him almost mad through a mistake of mine, but did afterwards reconcile all, for I would not have the man that labours to serve the King so cheap above others suffer too much. He gone I did a little business more, and so home to supper and to bed, being now pretty well again, the weather being warm. My pain do leave me without coming to any great excesse, but my cold that I had got I suppose was not very great, it being only the leaving of my wastecoat unbuttoned one morning.

11th. Up, after much pleasant discourse with my wife, and to the office, where we sat all the morning, and did much business, and some much to my content by prevailing against Sir W. Batten for the King's profit. At noon home to dinner, my wife and I hand to fist to a very fine pig. This noon Mr. Falconer came and visited my wife, and brought her a present, a silver state-cup and cover, value about £3 or £4, for the courtesy I did him the other day. He did not stay dinner with me. I am almost sorry for this present, because I would have reserved him for a place to go in summer a-visiting at Woolwich with my wife.

12th. Up, and ready, did find below Mr. Creed's boy with a letter from his master for me. So I fell to reading it, and it is by way of stating the case between S. Pepys and J. Creed most excellently writ, both showing his stoutness and yet willingness to peace, reproaching me yet flattering me again, and in a word in as good a manner as I think the world could have wrote, and indeed put me to a greater stand than ever I thought I could have been in this matter. All the morning thinking how to behave myself in the business, and at noon to the Coffee-house; thence by his appointment met him upon the 'Change, and with him back to the Coffee-house, where with great seriousness and strangeness on both sides he said his part and I mine, he sometimes owning my favour and assistance, yet endeavouring to lessen it, as that the success of his business was not wholly or very much to be imputed to that assistance: I to alledge the contrary, and plainly to tell him that from the beginning I never had it in my mind to do him all that kindnesse for nothing, but he gaining 5 or £600, I did expect a share of it, at least a real and not a complimentary acknowledgment of it. In fine I said nothing all the while that I need fear he can do me more hurt with them than before I spoke them. The most I told him was after we were come to a peace, which he asked me whether he should answer the Board's letter or no. I told him he might forbear it a while and no more. Then he asked how the letter could be signed by them without their much enquiry. I told him it was as I worded it and nothing at all else of any moment, whether my words be ever hereafter spoken of again or no. So that I have the same neither better nor worse force over him that I had before, if he should not do his part. And the peace between us was this: Says he after all, well, says he, I know you will expect, since there must be some condescension, that it do become me to begin it, and therefore, says he, I do propose (just like the interstice between the death of the old and the coming in of the present king, all the time is swallowed up as if it had never been) so our breach of friendship may be as if it had never been, that I should lay aside all misapprehensions of him or his first letter, and that he would reckon himself obliged to show the same ingenuous acknowledgment of my love and service to him as at the beginning he ought to have done, before by my first letter I did (as he well observed) put him out of a capacity of doing it, without seeming to do it servilely, and so it rests, and I shall expect how he will deal with me. After that I began to be free, and both of us to discourse of other things, and he went home with me and dined with me and my wife and very pleasant, having a good dinner and the opening of my lampry (cutting a notch on one side), which proved very good. After dinner he and I to Deptford, walking all the way, where we met Sir W. Petty and I took him back, and I got him to go with me to his vessel and discourse it over to me, which he did very well, and then walked back together to the waterside at Redriffe, with good discourse all the way.

So Creed and I by boat to my house, and thence to coach with my wife and called at Alderman Backewell's and there changed Mr. Falconer's state-cup, that he did give us the other day, for a fair tankard. The cup weighed with the fashion £5 16*s.*, and another little cup that Joyce Norton did give us 17*s.*, both £6 13*s.*; for which we had the tankard, which came to £6 10*s.*, at 5*s.* 7*d.* per oz., and 3*s.* in money, and with great content away thence to my brother's, Creed going away there, and my brother bringing me the old silk standard that I lodged there long ago, and then back again home, and thence, hearing that my uncle Wight had been at my house, I went to him to the Miter, and there with him and Maes, Norbury, and Mr. Rawlinson till late eating some pot venison (where the Crowne earthen pot pleased me mightily), and then homewards and met Mr. Barrow, so back with him to the Miter and sat talking about his business of his discontent in the yard, wherein sometimes he was very foolish and pettish, till 12 at night, and so went away, and I home and up to my wife a-bed, with my mind ill at ease whether I should think that I had by this made myself a bad end by missing the certainty of £100 which I proposed to myself so much, or a good one by easing myself of the uncertain good effect but the certain trouble and reflection which must have fallen on me if we had proceeded to a public dispute, ended besides embarking myself against my Lord, who (which I had forgot) had given him his hand for the value of the pieces of eight at his rates which were all false, which by the way I shall take heed to the giving of my Lord notice of it hereafter whenever he goes out again.

13th. Up, and after I had told my wife in the morning in bed the passages yesterday with Creed my head and heart was mightily lighter than they were before, and so up and to the office, and thence, after sitting, at 11 o'clock with Mr. Coventry to the African House, and there with Sir W. Ryder by agreement we looked over part of my Lord Peterborough's accounts, these being by Creed and Vernaty. Anon down to dinner to a table which Mr. Coventry keeps here, out of his £300 per annum as one of the Assistants to the Royall Company, a very pretty dinner, and good company, and excellent discourse, and so up again to our work for an hour till the Company came to having a meeting of their own, and so we broke up and Creed and I took coach and to Reeves, the perspective glass maker, and there did indeed see very excellent microscopes, which did discover a louse or mite or sand most perfectly and largely. Being sated with that we went away (yet with a good will were it not for my obligation to have bought one) and walked to the New Exchange, and after a turn or two and talked I took coach and home, and so to my office, after I had been with my wife and saw her day's work in ripping the silke standard, which we brought home last night, and it will serve to line a bed, or for twenty uses, to our great content. And there wrote fair my angry letter to my father upon that that he wrote to my cozen Roger Pepys, which I hope will make him the more carefull to trust to my advice for the time to come without so many needless complaints and jealousys, which are troublesome to me because without reason.

14th (Lord's day). Up and to church alone, where a lazy sermon of Mr. Mills, upon a text to introduce catechizing in his parish, which I perceive he intends to begin. So home and very pleasant with my wife at dinner. All the afternoon at my office alone doing business, and then in the evening after a walk with my wife in the garden, she and I to my uncle Wight's to supper, where Mr. Norbury, but my uncle out of tune, and after supper he seemed displeased mightily at my aunt's desiring [to] put off a copper kettle, which it seems with great study he had provided to boil meat in, and now she is put in the head that it is not wholesome, which vexed him, but we were very merry about it, and by and by home, and after prayers to bed.

15th. Up, and carrying my wife to my Lord's lodgings left her, and I to White Hall, to the Duke; where he first put on a periwigg to-day;[1] but methought his hair cut short in order thereto did look very prettily of itself, before he put on his periwigg. Thence to his closet and there did our business, and thence Mr. Coventry and I down to his chamber and spent a little time, and so parted, and I took my wife homeward, I stopping at the Coffee-house,

[1] Charles II. followed his brother in the use of the periwig in the following April.

and thence a while to the 'Change, where great newes of the arrivall of two rich ships, the Greyhound and another, which they were mightily afeard of, and great insurance given, and so home to dinner, and after an houre with my wife at her globes, I to the office, where very busy till 11 at night, and so home to supper and to bed. This afternoon Sir Thomas Chamberlin[1] came to the office to me, and showed me several letters from the East Indys, showing the height that the Dutch are come to there, showing scorn to all the English, even in our only Factory there of Surat, beating several men, and hanging the English Standard St. George under the Dutch flagg in scorn;[2] saying, that whatever their masters do or say at home, they will do what they list, and will be masters of all the world there; and have so proclaimed themselves Soveraigne of all the South Seas; which certainly our King cannot endure, if the Parliament will give him money. But I doubt and yet do hope they will not yet, till we are more ready for it.

16th. Up and to the office, where very busy all the morning, and most with Mr. Wood, I vexing him about his masts. At noon to the 'Change a little and thence brought Mr. Barrow to dinner with me, where I had a haunch of venison roasted, given me yesterday, and so had a pretty dinner, full of discourse of his business, wherein the poor man is mightily troubled, and I pity him in it, but hope to get him some ease. He being gone I to the office, where very busy till night, that my uncle Wight and Mr. Maes came to me, and after discourse about Maes' business to supper very merry, but my mind upon my business, and so they being gone I to my Vyall a little, which I have not done some months, I think, before, and then a little to my office, at 11 at night, and so home and to bed.

17th. Up, and with my wife, setting her down by her father's in Long Acre, in so ill looked a place, among all the whore houses, that I was troubled at it, to see her go thither. Thence I to White Hall and there walked up and

[1] Eldest son of Sir Thomas Chamberlayne, Chief Justice of Chester. He was created a baronet in 1642.

[2] Sir George Oxenden (died 1669) was then the chief factor of the East India Company. The chief seat of government was removed from Surat to Bombay in 1686.

down talking with Mr. Pierce, who tells me of the King's giving of my Lord FitzHarding two leases which belong indeed to the Queene, worth £20,000 to him; and how people do talk of it, and other things of that nature which I am sorry to hear. He and I walked round the Park with great pleasure, and back again, and finding no time to speak with my Lord of Albemarle, I walked to the 'Change and there met my wife at our pretty Doll's, and so took her home, and Creed also whom I met there, and sent her home, while Creed and I staid on the 'Change, and by and by home and dined, where I found an excellent mastiffe, his name Towser, sent me by a chyrurgeon. After dinner I took my wife again by coach (leaving Creed by the way going to Gresham College, of which he is now become one of the virtuosos[1]) and to White Hall, where I delivered a paper about Tangier to my Lord Duke of Albemarle in the council chamber, and so to Mrs. Hunt's to call my wife, and so by coach straight home, and at my office till 3 o'clock in the morning, having spent much time this evening in discourse with Mr. Cutler, who tells me how the Dutch deal with us abroad and do not value us any where, and how he and Sir W. Rider have found reason to lay aside Captain Cocke in their company, he having played some indiscreet and unfair tricks with them, and has lost himself every where by his imposing upon all the world with the conceit he has of his own wit, and so has, he tells me, Sir R. Ford also, both of whom are very witty men. He being gone Sir W. Rider came and staid with me till about 12 at night, having found ourselves work till that time, about understanding the measuring of Mr. Wood's masts, which though I did so well before as to be thought to deal very hardly against Wood, yet I am ashamed I understand it no better, and do hope yet, whatever be thought of me, to save the King some more money, and out of an impatience to breake up with my head full of confused confounded notions, but nothing brought to a clear comprehension, I was resolved to sit up and did till now it is ready to strike 4 o'clock, all alone, cold, and my candle not enough left to light me to my owne house, and so, with my business

[1] John Creed was elected and admitted a Fellow of the Royal Society, December 16th, 1663.

however brought to some good understanding, and set it down pretty clear, I went home to bed with my mind at good quiet, and the girl sitting up for me (the rest all a-bed). I eat and drank a little, and to bed, weary, sleepy, cold, and my head akeing.

18th. Called up to the office and much against my will I rose, my head aching mightily, and to the office, where I did argue to good purpose for the King, which I have been fitting myself for the last night against Mr. Wood about his masts, but brought it to no issue. Very full of business till noon, and then with Mr. Coventry to the African House, and there fell to my Lord Peterborough's accounts, and by and by to dinner, where excellent discourse, Sir G. Carteret and others of the African Company with us, and then up to the accounts again, which were by and by done, and then I straight home, my head in great pain, and drowsy, so after doing a little business at the office I wrote to my father about sending him the mastiff was given me yesterday. I home and by daylight to bed about 6 o'clock and fell to sleep, wakened about 12 when my wife came to bed, and then to sleep again and so till morning, and then:

19th. Up in good order in my head again and shaved myself, and then to the office, whither Mr. Cutler came, and walked and talked with me a great while; and then to the 'Change together; and it being early, did tell me several excellent examples of men raised upon the 'Change by their great diligence and saving; as also his owne fortune, and how credit grew upon him; that when he was not really worth £1,100, he had credit for £100,000: of Sir W. Rider how he rose; and others. By and by joyned with us Sir John Bankes;[1] who told us several passages of the East India Company; and how in his very case, when there was due to him and Alderman Mico £64,000 from the Dutch for injury done to them in the East Indys, Oliver presently after the peace, they delaying to pay them the money, sent them word, that if they did not pay them by such a day, he would grant letters of mark to those merchants against

[1] An opulent East India merchant, residing in Lincoln's Inn Fields. Evelyn dined with him there August 25th, 1676 (see his Diary). He says Sir John "was a merchant of small beginning, but had amassed £100,000."

them; by which they were so fearful of him, they did presently pay the money every farthing. By and by, the 'Change filling, I did many businesses, and about 2 o'clock went off with my uncle Wight to his house, thence by appointment we took our wives (they by coach with Mr. Mawes) and we on foot to Mr. Jaggard, a salter, in Thames Street, for whom I did a courtesy among the poor victuallers, his wife, whom long ago I had seen, being daughter to old Day, my uncle Wight's master, is a very plain woman, but pretty children they have. They live methought at first in but a plain way, but afterward I saw their dinner, all fish, brought in very neatly, but the company being but bad I had no great pleasure in it. After dinner I to the office, where we should have met upon business extraordinary, but business not coming we broke up, and I thither again and took my wife; and taking a coach, went to visit my Ladys Jemimah and Paulina Montagu, and Mrs. Elizabeth Pickering, whom we find at their father's new house[1] in Lincolne's Inn Fields; but the house all in dirt. They received us well enough; but I did not endeavour to carry myself over familiarly with them; and so after a little stay, there coming in presently after us my Lady Aberguenny[2] and other ladies, we back again by coach, and visited, my wife did, my she cozen Scott, who is very ill still, and thence to Jaggard's again, where a very good supper and great store of plate, and above all after supper Mrs. Jaggard did at my entreaty play on the Vyall, but so well as I did not think any woman in England could and but few Maisters, I must confess it did mightily surprise me, though I knew heretofore that she could play, but little thought so well. After her I set Maes to singing, but he did it so like a coxcomb that I was sick of him. About 11 at night I carried my aunt home by coach, and then home myself, having set my wife down at home by the way. My aunt tells me they are counted very rich people, worth at least 10 or £12,000, and their country house all the yeare long and all things live-

[1] The Earl of Sandwich had just moved to a house in Lincoln's Inn Fields. Elizabeth Pickering, who afterwards married John Creed, was niece to Lord Sandwich.

[2] Mary, daughter of Henry Giffard, M.D., wife to George Nevill, ninth Earl of Abergavenny.

able, which mightily surprises me to think for how poore a man I took him when I did him the courtesy at our office. So after prayers to bed, pleased at nothing all the day but Mrs. Jaggard playing on the Vyall, and that was enough to make me bear with all the rest that did not content me.

20th. Up and to the office, where we sat all the morning, and at noon to the 'Change with Mr. Coventry and thence home to dinner, after dinner by a gally down to Woolwich, where with Mr. Falconer, and then at the other yard doing some business to my content, and so walked to Greenwich, it being a very fine evening and brought right home with me by water, and so to my office, where late doing business, and then home to supper and to bed.

21st (Lord's day). Up, and having many businesses at the office to-day I spent all the morning there drawing up a letter to Mr. Coventry about preserving of masts, being collections of my own, and at noon home to dinner, whither my brother Tom comes, and after dinner I took him up and read my letter lately of discontent to my father, and he is seemingly pleased at it, and cries out of my sister's ill nature and lazy life there. He being gone I to my office again, and there made an end of my morning's work, and then, after reading my vows of course, home and back again with Mr. Maes and walked with him talking of his business in the garden, and he being gone my wife and I walked a turn or two also, and then my uncle Wight fetching of us, she and I to his house to supper, and by the way calling on Sir G. Carteret to desire his consent to my bringing Maes to him, which he agreed to. So I to my uncle's, but staid a great while vexed both of us for Maes not coming in, and soon he came, and I with him from supper to Sir G. Carteret, and there did largely discourse of the business, and I believe he may expect as much favour as he can do him, though I fear that will not be much. So back, and after sitting there a good while, we home, and going my wife told me how my uncle when he had her alone did tell her that he did love her as well as ever he did, though he did not find it convenient to show it publicly for reasons on both sides, seeming to mean as well to prevent my jealousy as his wife's, but I am apt to think that he do mean us well, and to give us something if he should die without children.

So home to prayers and to bed. My wife called up the people to washing by four o'clock in the morning; and our little girl Susan is a most admirable Slut and pleases us mightily, doing more service than both the others and deserves wages better.

22nd. Up and shaved myself, and then my wife and I by coach out, and I set her down by her father's, being vexed in my mind and angry with her for the ill-favoured place, among or near the whore houses, that she is forced to come to him. So left her there, and I to Sir Ph. Warwick's but did not speak with him. Thence to take a turn in St. James's Park, and meeting with Anth. Joyce walked with him a turn in the Pell Mell and so parted, he St. James's ward and I out to Whitehall ward, and so to a picture-seller's by the Half Moone in the street over against the Exchange, and there looked over the maps of several cities and did buy two books of cities stitched together cost me *9s. 6d.*, and when I came home thought of my vowe, and paid *5s.* into my poor box for it, hoping in God that I shall forfeit no more in that kind. Thence, meeting Mr. Moore, and to the Exchange and there found my wife at pretty Doll's, and thence by coach set her at my uncle Wight's, to go with my aunt to market once more against Lent, and I to the Coffee-house, and thence to the 'Change, my chief business being to enquire about the manner of other countries keeping of their masts wet or dry, and got good advice about it, and so home, and alone ate a bad, cold dinner, my people being at their washing all day, and so to the office and all the afternoon upon my letter to Mr. Coventry about keeping of masts, and ended it very well at night and wrote it fair over. This evening came Mr. Alsopp the King's brewer, with whom I spent an houre talking and bewailing the posture of things at present; the King led away by half-a-dozen men, that none of his serious servants and friends can come at him. These are Lauderdale, Buckingham, Hamilton, FitzHarding (to whom he hath, it seems, given £12,000 per annum in the best part of the King's estate); and that that the old Duke of Buckingham could never get of the King. Progers is another, and Sir H. Bennett. He loves not the Queen at all, but is rather sullen to her; and she, by all reports, incapable of children. He is so fond of the Duke of Monmouth, that every body admires it; and he says the Duke hath said, that he would be the death of any man that says the King was not married to his mother: though Alsopp says, it is well known that she was a common whore before the King lay with her. But it seems, he says, that the King is mighty kind to these his bastard children; and at this day will go at midnight to my Lady Castlemaine's nurses, and take the child and dance it in his arms: that he is not likely to have his tables up again in his house,[1] for the crew that are about him will not have him come to common view again, but keep him obscurely among themselves. He hath this night, it seems, ordered that the Hall (which there is a ball to be in to-night before the King) be guarded, as the Queen-Mother's is, by his Horse Guards; whereas heretofore they were by the Lord Chamberlain or Steward, and their people. But it is feared they will reduce all to the soldiery, and all other places taken away; and what is worst of all, that he will alter the present militia, and bring all to a flying army. That my Lord Lauderdale, being Middleton's[2] enemy, and one that scorns the Chancellor even to open affronts before the King, hath got the whole power of Scotland into his hand; whereas the other day he was in a fair way to have had his whole estate, and honour, and life, voted away from him. That the King hath done himself all imaginable wrong in the business of my Lord Antrim,[3] in Ireland; who, though he was the head of rebels, yet he by his letter owns to have acted by his father's and mother's, and his commissions; but it seems the truth is, he hath obliged himself, upon the clearing of his estate, to settle it upon a daughter of the Queene-Mother's (by my Lord Germin,[4] I suppose,) in marriage, be it to whom the Queene pleases; which is a sad story. It seems a daughter of the Duke of Lenox's was, by force, going to be married the other day at Somerset House, to Harry Germin; but she got away and run to the King, and he says he will protect her. She is, it seems, very near

[1] The tables at which the king dined in public. — B.

[2] See *ante*, February 1st, 1663–64.

[3] Randall Macdonnel, second Earl and first Marquis of Antrim. Died 1673. — B.

[4] The Earl of St. Alban's.

akin to the King. Such mad doings there are every day among them! The rape upon a woman at Turnstile the other day, her husband being bound in his shirt, they both being in bed together, it being night, by two Frenchmen, who did not only lye with her but abused her with a linke, is hushed up for £300, being the Queen-Mother's servants. There was a French book in verse, the other day, translated and presented to the Duke of Monmouth in such a high stile, that the Duke of York, he tells me, was mightily offended at it.[1] The Duke of Monmouth's mother's brother hath a place at Court; and being a Welchman[2] (I think he told me) will talk very broad of the King's being married to his sister. The King did the other day, at the Council, commit my Lord Digby's[3] chaplin, and steward, and another servant, who went upon the process begun there against their lord, to swear that they saw him at church, and receive the Sacrament as a Protestant, (which, the Judges said, was sufficient to prove him such in the eye of the law);[4] the King, I say, did commit them all to the Gate-house, notwithstanding their pleading their dependance upon him, and the faith they owed him as their lord, whose bread they

[1] It was reported that the "Handsome" Sidney was the father of the Duke of Monmouth, an opinion which was confirmed by the fact that each had a mole on the upper lip.

[2] Lord Braybrooke notes that this was Mr. Justice Waters, said to be "of the Temple" by Thurloe, but Mr. Steinman in his account of Lucy Waters ("Althorp Memoirs") says that no brother of Lucy was alive in February, 1663-64. In the Prerogative Court entry, dated December, 1658, Anna Busfield, wife of John Busfield and aunt of Lucy Waters, is given as her next-of-kin. William Walter, who in 1663 was in the list of Gentlemen of the Privy Chamber, is not known to have been any connection, and he certainly was not brother to Lucy Waters.

[3] George, Lord Digby, second Earl of Bristol, who had been Secretary of State 1643-49; but by changing his religion while abroad, at the instigation of Don John of Austria, incapacitated himself from being restored to that office; and in consequence of the disappointment, which he imputed to the interference of the Lord Chancellor, conspired and effected his ruin. Charles II. gave him the K.G. in 1653, the year in which Lord Digby succeeded his father as Earl of Bristol. He died March 20th, 1678. The feuds between Lords Bristol and Clarendon are frequently mentioned in the Diary.

[4] See the letter of the Comte de Comminges to Louis XIV. dated January 25th, 1663-64, printed in the Appendix to this edition.

eat. And that the King should say, that he would soon see whether he was King, or Digby. That the Queene-Mother hath outrun herself in her expences, and is now come to pay very ill, or run in debt; the money being spent that she received for leases. He believes there is not any money laid up in bank, as I told him some did hope; but he says, from the best informers he can assure me there is no such thing, nor any body that should look after such a thing; and that there is not now above £80,000 of the Dunkirke money left in stock. That Oliver in the year when he spent £1,400,000 in the Navy, did spend in the whole expence of the kingdom £2,600,000. That all the Court are mad for a Dutch war; but both he and I did concur, that it was a thing rather to be dreaded than hoped for; unless by the French King's falling upon Flanders, they and the Dutch should be divided. That our Embassador[1] had, it is true, an audience; but in the most dishonourable way that could be; for the Princes of the Blood (though invited by our Embassador, which was the greatest absurdity that ever Embassador committed these 400 years) were not there; and so were not said to give place to our King's Embassador. And that our King did openly say, the other day in the Privy Chamber, that he would not be hectored out of his right and preeminencys by the King of France, as great as he was. That the Pope is glad to yield to a peace with the French (as the newes-book says), upon the basest terms that ever was. That the talke which these people about our King, that I named before, have, is to tell him how neither privilege of Parliament nor City is any thing; but his will is all, and ought to be so: and their discourse, it seems, when they are alone, is so base and sordid, that it makes the eares of the very gentlemen of the back-stairs (I think he called them) to tingle to hear it spoke in the King's hearing; and that must be very bad indeed. That my Lord Digby did send to Lisbon a couple of priests, to search out what they could against the Chancellor concerning the match, as to the point of his knowing before-hand that the Queene was not capable of bearing children; and that something was given her to make her

[1] Denzil, Lord Holles: see *ante*, May 24th, 1660, and December 14th, 1663.

so. But as private as they were, when they came thither they were clapped up prisoners. That my Lord Digby endeavours what he can to bring the business into the House of Commons, hoping there to master the Chancellor, there being many enemies of his there; but I hope the contrary. That whereas the late King did mortgage Clarendon[1] to somebody for £20,000, and this to have given it to the Duke of Albemarle, and he sold it to my Lord Chancellor, whose title of Earldome is fetched from thence; the King hath this day sent his order to the Privy Seale for the payment of this £20,000 to my Lord Chancellor, to clear the mortgage.[2] Ireland in a very distracted condition about the hard usage which the Protestants meet with, and the too good which the Catholiques. And from altogether, God knows my heart, I expect nothing but ruine can follow, unless things are better ordered in a little time. He being gone my wife came and told me how kind my uncle Wight had been to her to-day, and that though she says that all his kindness comes from respect to her she discovers nothing but great civility from him, yet but what she says he otherwise will tell me, but to-day he told her plainly that had she a child it should be his heir, and that should I or she want he would be a good friend to us, and did give my wife instructions to consent to all his wife says at any time, she being a pettish woman, which argues a design I think he has of keeping us in with his wife in order to our good sure, and he declaring her jealous of him that so he dares not come to see my wife as otherwise he would do and will endeavour to do. It looks strange putting all together, but yet I am in hopes he means well. My aunt also is mighty open to my wife and tells her mighty plain how her husband did intend to double her portion to her at his death as a jointure. That he will give presently £100 to her niece Mary and a good legacy at his death, and it seems did as much to the other sister, which vexed [me] to think that he should bestow so much upon his wife's friends daily as he do, but it cannot be helped for the time past, and I will endeavour to remedy it for the time to come. After

[1] Clarendon Park, near Salisbury. See August 19th, 1661.

[2] See note, July 14th, 1664.

all this discourse with my wife at my office alone, she home to see how the wash goes on and I to make an end of my work, and so home to supper and to bed.

23rd. Up, it being Shrove Tuesday, and at the office sat all the morning, at noon to the 'Change and there met with Sir W. Rider, and of a sudden knowing what I had at home, brought him and Mr. Cutler and Mr. Cooke, clerk to Mr. Secretary Morrice, a sober and pleasant man, and one that I knew heretofore, when he was my Lord ——'s secretary at Dunkirke. I made much of them and had a pretty dinner for a sudden. We talked very pleasantly, and they many good discourses of their travels abroad. After dinner they gone, I to my office, where doing many businesses very late, but to my good content to see how I grow in estimation every day more and more, and have things given more oftener than I used to have formerly, as to have a case of very pretty knives with agate shafts by Mrs. Russell. So home and to bed. This day, by the blessing of God, I have lived thirty-one years in the world; and, by the grace of God, I find myself not only in good health in every thing, and particularly as to the stone, but only pain upon taking cold, and also in a fair way of coming to a better esteem and estate in the world, than ever I expected. But I pray God give me a heart to fear a fall, and to prepare for it!

24th (Ash-Wednesday). Up and by water, it being a very fine morning, to White Hall, and there to speak with Sir Ph. Warwicke, but he was gone out to chappell, so I spent much of the morning walking in the Park, and going to the Queene's chappell, where I staid and saw their masse, till a man came and bid me go out or kneel down: so I did go out. And thence to Somerset House; and there into the chappell, where Monsieur d'Espagne[1] used to preach. But now it is made very fine, and was ten times more crouded than the Queene's chappell at St. James's; which I wonder at. Thence down to the garden of Somerset House, and up and down the new building, which in every respect will be mighty magnificent and costly. I staid a great while talking

[1] There is a small volume in the Pepysian Library called "Shibboleth, ou, Reformation de quelques Passages de la Bible, par Jean d'Espagne; Ministre du St. Evangile," printed 1653, and dedicated to Cromwell. — B.

with a man in the garden that was sawing of a piece of marble, and did give him 6*d.* to drink. He told me much of the nature and labour of the worke, how he could not saw above 4 inches of the stone in a day, and of a greater not above one or two, and after it is sawed, then it is rubbed with coarse and then with finer and finer sand till they come to putty, and so polish it as smooth as glass. Their saws have no teeth, but it is the sand only which the saw rubs up and down that do the thing. Thence by water to the Coffee-house, and there sat with Alderman Barker talking of hempe and the trade, and thence to the 'Change a little, and so home and dined with my wife, and then to the office till the evening, and then walked a while merrily with my wife in the garden, and so she gone, I to work again till late, and so home to supper and to bed.

25th. Up and to the office, where we sat, and thence with Mr. Coventry by coach to the glasshouse and there dined, and both before and after did my Lord Peterborough's accounts. Thence home to the office, and there did business till called by Creed, and with him by coach (setting my wife at my brother's) to my Lord's, and saw the young ladies, and talked a little with them, and thence to White Hall, a while talking but doing no business, but resolved of going to meet my Lord to-morrow, having got a horse of Mr. Coventry to-day. So home, taking up my wife, and after doing something at my office home, God forgive me, disturbed in my mind out of my jealousy of my wife to-morrow when I am out of town, which is a hell to my mind, and yet without all reason. God forgive me for it, and mend me. So home, and getting my things ready for me, weary to bed.

26th. Up, and after dressing myself handsomely for riding, I out, and by water to Westminster, to Mr. Creed's chamber, and after drinking some chocolate, and playing on the vyall, Mr. Mallard being there, upon Creed's new vyall, which proves, methinks, much worse than mine, and, looking upon his new contrivance of a desk and shelves for books, we set out from an inne hard by, whither Mr. Coventry's horse was carried, and round about the bush through bad ways to Highgate. Good discourse in the way had between us, and it being all day a most admirable pleasant day, we, upon consultation, had stopped at the Cocke, a mile on this side Barnett, being unwilling to put ourselves to the charge or doubtful acceptance of any provision against my Lord's coming by, and there got something and dined, setting a boy to look towards Barnett Hill, against their coming; and after two or three false alarms, they come, and we met the coach very gracefully, and I had a kind receipt from both Lord and Lady as I could wish, and some kind discourse, and then rode by the coach a good way, and so fell to discoursing with several of the people, there being a dozen attending the coach, and another for the mayds and parson. Among others talking with W. Howe, he told me how my Lord in his hearing the other day did largely tell my Lord Peterborough and Povy (who went with them down to Hinchinbrooke) how and when he discarded Creed, and took me to him, and that since the Duke of York has several times thanked him for me, which did not a little please me, and anon I desiring Mr. Howe to tell me upon [what] occasion this discourse happened, he desired me to say nothing of it now, for he would not have my Lord to take notice of our being together, but he would tell me another time, which put me into some trouble to think what he meant by it. But when we came to my Lord's house, I went in; and whether it was my Lord's neglect, or general indifference, I know not, but he made me no kind of compliment there; and, methinks, the young ladies look somewhat highly upon me. So I went away without bidding adieu to anybody, being desirous not to be thought too servile. But I do hope and believe that my Lord do yet value me as high as ever, though he dare not admit me to the freedom he once did, and that my Lady is still the same woman. So rode home and there found my uncle Wight. 'Tis an odd thing as my wife tells me his caressing her and coming on purpose to give her visits, but I do not trouble myself for him at all, but hope the best and very good effects of it. He being gone I eat something and my wife. I told all this day's passages, and she to give me very good and rational advice how to behave myself to my Lord and his family, by slighting every body but my Lord and Lady, and not to seem to have the least society or fellowship with them, which I am resolved to do, knowing that it is my high carriage that must do me good there, and to appear in good clothes and garbe. To the office, and being weary, early home to bed.

27th. Up, but weary, and to the office, where we sat all the morning. Before I went to the office there came Bagwell's wife to me to speak for her husband. I liked the woman very well and stroked her under the chin, but could not find in my heart to offer anything uncivil to her, she being, I believe, a very modest woman. At noon with Mr. Coventry to the African house, and to my Lord Peterborough's business again, and then to dinner, where, before dinner, we had the best oysters I have seen this year, and I think as good in all respects as ever I eat in my life. I eat a great many. Great, good company at dinner, among others Sir Martin Noell, who told us the dispute between him, as farmer of the Additional Duty, and the East India Company, whether callicos be linnen or no; which he says it is, having been ever esteemed so: they say it is made of cotton woole, and grows upon trees, not like flax or hempe. But it was carried against the Company, though they stand out against the verdict. Thence home and to the office, where late, and so home to supper and to bed, and had a very pleasing and condescending answer from my poor father to-day in answer to my angry discontentful letter to him the other day, which pleases me mightily.

28th (Lord's day). Up and walked to Paul's; and by chance it was an extraordinary day for the Readers of the Inns of Court and all the Students to come to church, it being an old ceremony not used these twenty-five years, upon the first Sunday in Lent. Abundance there was of Students, more than there was room to seat but upon forms, and the Church mighty full. One Hawkins preached, an Oxford man. A good sermon upon these words: "But the wisdom from above is first pure, then peaceable." Both before and after sermon I was most impatiently troubled at the Quire, the worst that ever I heard. But what was extraordinary, the Bishop of London,[1] who sat there in a pew, made a'purpose for him by the pulpitt, do give the last blessing to

[1] Humfrey Henchman, Bishop of Salisbury, succeeded Dr. Sheldon as Bishop of London, September, 1663. He died October 7th, 1675, aged eighty-three years.

the congregation; which was, he being a comely old man, a very decent thing, methought. The Lieutenant of the Tower, Sir J. Robinson, would needs have me by coach home with him, and sending word home to my house I did go and dine with him, his ordinary table being very good, and his lady a very high-carriaged but comely big woman;[1] I was mightily pleased with her. His officers of his regiment dined with him. No discourse at table to any purpose, only after dinner my Lady would needs see a boy which was represented to her to be an innocent country boy brought up to towne a day or two ago, and left here to the wide world, and he losing his way fell into the Tower, which my Lady believes, and takes pity on him, and will keep him; but though a little boy and but young, yet he tells his tale so readily and answers all questions so wittily, that for certain he is an arch rogue, and bred in this towne; but my Lady will not believe it, but ordered victuals to be given him, and I think will keep him as a footboy for their eldest son. After dinner to chappell in the Tower with the Lieutenant, with the keyes carried before us, and the Warders and Gentleman-porter going before us. And I sat with the Lieutenant in his pew, in great state, but slept all the sermon. None, it seems, of the prisoners in the Tower that are there now, though they may, will come to prayers there. Church being done, I back to Sir John's house and there left him and home, and by and by to Sir W. Pen, and staid a while talking with him about Sir J. Minnes his folly in his office, of which I am sicke and weary to speak of it, and how the King is abused in it, though Pen, I know, offers the discourse only like a rogue to get it out of me, but I am very free to tell my mind to him, in that case being not unwilling he should tell him again if he will or any body else. Thence home, and walked in the garden by brave moonshine with my wife above two hours, till past 8 o'clock, then to supper, and after prayers to bed.

29th. Up and by coach with Sir W. Pen to Charing Cross, and there I 'light, and to Sir Phillip Warwick to visit him and discourse with him about navy business,

[1] Lady Robinson was Anne, daughter of Alderman Sir George Whitmore, of Barnes, Surrey, Lord Mayor 1631.

which I did at large and he most largely with me, not only about the navy but about the general Revenue of England, above two hours, I think, many staying all the while without, but he seemed to take pains to let me either understand the affairs of the Revenue or else to be a witness of his pains and care in stating it. He showed me indeed many excellent collections of the State of the Revenue in former Kings and the late times, and the present. He showed me how the very Assessments between 1643 and 1659, which were taxes (besides Excise, Customes, Sequestrations, Decimations, King and Queene's and Church Lands, or any thing else but just the Assessments), come to above fifteen millions. He showed me a discourse of his concerning the Revenues of this and foreign States. How that of Spayne was great, but divided with his kingdoms, and so came to little. How that of France did, and do much exceed ours before for quantity; and that it is at the will of the Prince to tax what he will upon his people; which is not here. That the Hollanders have the best manner of tax, which is only upon the expence of provisions, by an excise; and do conclude that no other tax is proper for England but a pound-rate, or excise upon the expence of provisions. He showed me every particular sort of payment away of money, since the King's coming in, to this day; and told me, from one to one, how little he hath received of profit from most of them; and I believe him truly. That the £1,200,000 which the Parliament with so much ado did first vote to give the King, and since hath been re-examined by several committees of the present Parliament, is yet above £300,000 short of making up really to the King the £1,200,000, as by particulars he showed me.[1] And in my Lord Treasurer's excellent letter

[1] A committee was appointed in September, 1660, to consider the subject of the King's revenue, and they "reported to the Commons that the average revenue of Charles I., from 1637 to 1641 inclusive, had been £895,819, and the average expenditure about £1,110,000. At that time prices were lower and the country less burthened with navy and garrisons, among which latter Dunkirk alone now cost more than £100,000 a year. It appeared, therefore, that the least sum to which the King could be expected to 'conform his expense' was £1,200,000." Burnet writes, "It was believed that if two millions had been asked he could have carried it. But he (Clarendon) had no mind to put the

to the King upon this subject, he tells the King how it was the spending more than the revenue that did give the first occasion of his father's ruine, and did since to the rebels; who, he says, just like Henry the Eighth, had great and sudden increase of wealth, but yet, by overspending, both died poor; and further tells the King how much of this £1,200,000 depends upon the life of the Prince, and so must be renewed by Parliament again to his successor; which is seldom done without parting with some of the prerogatives of the Crowne; or if denied and he persists to take it of the people, it gives occasion to a civill war, which may, as it did in the late business of tonnage and poundage, prove fatal to the Crowne. He showed me how many ways the Lord Treasurer did take before he moved the King to farme the Customes in the manner he do, and the reasons that moved him to do it. He showed me a very excellent argument to prove, that our importing lesse than we export, do not impoverish the kingdom, according to the received opinion: which, though it be a paradox, and that I do not remember the argument, yet methought there was a great deale in what he said. And upon the whole I find him a most exact and methodicall man, and of great industry: and very glad that he thought fit to show me all this; though I cannot easily guess the reason why he should do it to me, unless from the plainness that he sees I use to him in telling him how much the King may suffer for our want of understanding the case of our Treasury. Thence to White Hall (where my Lord Sandwich was, and gave me a good countenance, I thought), and before the Duke did our usual business, and so I about several businesses in the house, and then out to the Mewes with Sir W. Pen. But in my way first did meet with W. Howe, who did of himself advise me to appear more free with my Lord and to come to him, for my own strangeness he tells me he thinks do make my Lord the worse. At the Mewes Sir W. Pen and Mr. Baxter did shew me several good horses, but Pen, which Sir W. Pen did give the Duke of York, was given away by the Duke the other day to a Frenchman, which Baxter is cruelly vexed at, saying

King out of the necessity of having recourse to his Parliament." — Lister's *Life of Clarendon*, vol. ii., pp. 22, 23.

that he was the best horse that he expects a great while to have to do with. Thence I to the 'Change, and thence to a Coffee-house with Sir W. Warren, and did talk much about his and Wood's business, and thence homewards, and in my way did stay to look upon a fire in an Inneyard in Lumbard Streete. But, Lord! how the mercers and merchants who had warehouses there did carry away their cloths and silks. But at last it was quenched, and I home to dinner, and after dinner carried my wife and set her and her two mayds in Fleete Streete to buy things, and I to White Hall to little purpose, and so to Westminster Hall, and there talked with Mrs. Lane and Howlett, but the match with Hawly I perceive will not take, and so I am resolved wholly to avoid occasion of further ill with her. Thence by water to Salsbury Court, and found my wife, by agreement, at Mrs. Turner's, and after a little stay and chat set her and young Armiger down in Cheapside, and so my wife and I home. Got home before our mayds, who by and by came with a great cry and fright that they had like to have been killed by a coach; but, Lord! to see how Jane did tell the story like a foole and a dissembling fanatique, like her grandmother, but so like a changeling, would make a man laugh to death almost, and yet be vexed to hear her. By and by to the office to make up my monthly accounts, which I make up to-night, and to my great content find myself worth eight hundred and ninety and odd pounds, the greatest sum I ever yet knew, and so with a heart at great ease to bed.

March 1st. Up and to the office, where we sat all the morning, and at noon to the 'Change, and after much business and meeting my uncle Wight, who told me how Mr. Maes had like to have been trapanned yesterday, but was forced to run for it; so with Creed and Mr. Hunt home to dinner, and after a good and pleasant dinner, Mr. Hunt parted, and I took Mr. Creed and my wife and down to Deptford, it being most pleasant weather, and there till night discoursing with the officers there about several things, and so walked home by moonshine, it being mighty pleasant, and so home, and I to my office, where late about getting myself a thorough understanding in the business of masts, and so home to bed, my left eye being mightily troubled with rheum.

2nd. Up, my eye mightily out of order with the rheum that is fallen down into it, however, I by coach endeavoured to have waited on my Lord Sandwich, but meeting him in Chancery Lane going towards the City I stopped and so fairly walked home again, calling at St. Paul's Churchyarde, and there looked upon a pretty burlesque poem, called "Scarronides, or Virgile Travesty;"[1] extraordinary good. At home to the office till dinner, and after dinner my wife cut my hair short, which is growne pretty long again, and then to the office, and there till 9 at night doing business. This afternoon we had a good present of tongues and bacon from Mr. Shales, of Portsmouth. So at night home to supper, and, being troubled with my eye, to bed. This morning Mr. Burgby, one of the writing clerks belonging to the Council, was with me about business, a knowing man, he complains how most of the Lords of the Council do look after themselves and their own ends, and none the publique, unless Sir Edward Nicholas. Sir G. Carteret is diligent, but all for his own ends and profit. My Lord Privy Seale, a destroyer of every body's business, and do no good at all to the publique. The Archbishop of Canterbury[2] speaks very little, nor do much, being now come to the highest pitch that he can expect. He tells me, he believes that things will go very high against the Chancellor by Digby, and that bad things will be proved. Talks much of his neglecting the King; and making the King to trot every day to him, when he is well enough to go to visit his cozen Chief-Justice Hide, but not to the Council or King. He commends my Lord of Ormond mightily in Ireland; but cries out cruelly of Sir G. Lane for his corruption;[3] and that he hath done my Lord great dishonour by selling of places here, which are now all taken away, and the poor wretches ready to starve. That nobody almost understands or judges of business better than the King, if he would not be guilty of his father's fault to be doubtfull of himself, and easily be removed

[1] By Charles Cotton, a voluminous author, but known now chiefly as the continuator of Walton's "Complete Angler." His "Scarronides" was first published in 1664.

[2] Gilbert Sheldon.

[3] See *ante*, October 12th, 1663.

from his own opinion. That my Lord Lauderdale is never from the King's eare nor council, and that he is a most cunning fellow. Upon the whole, that he finds things go very bad every where; and even in the Council nobody minds the publique.

3rd. Up pretty early and so to the office, where we sat all the morning making a very great contract with Sir W. Warren for provisions for the yeare coming, and so home to dinner, and there was W. Howe come to dine with me, and before dinner he and I walked in the garden, and we did discourse together, he assuring me of what he told me the other day of my Lord's speaking so highly in my commendation to my Lord Peterborough and Povy, which speaks my Lord having yet a good opinion of me, and also how well my Lord and Lady both are pleased with their children's being at my father's, and when the bigger ladies were there a little while ago, at which I am very glad. After dinner he went away, I having discoursed with him about his own proceedings in his studies, and I observe him to be very considerate and to mind his book in order to preferring himself by my Lord's favour to something, and I hope to the outing of Creed in his Secretaryship. For he tells me that he is confident my Lord do not love him nor will trust him in any secret matter, he is so cunning and crafty in all he do. So my wife and I out of doors thinking to have gone to have seen a play, but when we came to take coach, they tell us there are none this week, being the first of Lent. But, Lord! to see how impatient I found myself within to see a play, I being at liberty once a month to see one, and I think it is the best method I could have taken. But to my office, did very much business with several people till night, and so home, being unwilling to stay late because of my eye which is not yet well of the rheum that is fallen down into it, but to supper and to bed.

4th. Up, my eye being pretty well, and then by coach to my Lord Sandwich, with whom I spoke, walking a good while with him in his garden, which and the house is veiy fine, talking of my Lord Peterborough's accounts, wherein he is concerned both for the foolery as also inconvenience which may happen upon my Lord Peterborough's ill-stating of his matters, so as to have his gaine discovered unnecessarily. We did talk long and freely that I hope the worst is past and all will be well. There were several people by trying a new-fashion gun[1] brought my Lord this morning, to shoot off often, one after another, without trouble or danger, very pretty. Thence to the Temple, and there taking White's boat down to Woolwich, taking Mr. Shish at Deptford in my way, with whom I had some good discourse of the Navy business. At Woolwich discoursed with him and Mr. Pett about iron worke and other businesses, and then walked home, and at Greenwich did observe the foundation laying of a very great house for the King, which will cost a great deale of money.[2] So home to dinner, and my uncle Wight coming in he along with my wife and I by coach, and setting him down by the way going to Mr. Maes we two to my Lord Sandwich's to visit my Lady, with whom I left my wife discoursing, and I to White Hall, and there being met by the Duke of Yorke, he called me to him and discoursed a pretty while with me about the new ship's dispatch building at Woolwich, and talking of the charge did say that he finds always the best the most cheape, instancing in French guns, which in France you may buy for 4 pistoles, as good to look to as

[1] Many attempts to produce a satisfactory revolver were made in former centuries, but it was not till the present one that Colt's revolver was invented. On February 18th, 1661, Edward, Marquis of Worcester, obtained Letters Patent for "an invencõn to make certeyne guns or pistolls which in the tenth parte of one minute of an houre may, with a flaske contrived to that purpose, be re-charged the fourth part of one turne of the barrell which remaines still fixt, fastening it as forceably and effectually as a dozen thrids of any scrue, which in the ordinary and usual way require as many turnes." On March 3rd, 1664, Abraham Hill obtained Letters Patent for a "gun or pistoll for small shott, carrying seaven or eight charges of the same in the stocke of the gun."

[2] Building by John Webb; now a part of Greenwich Hospital. Evelyn wrote in his Diary, October 19th, 1661: "I went to London to visite my Lord of Bristoll, having been with Sir John Denham (his Maties surveyor) to consult with him about the placing of his palace at Greenwich, which I would have had built between the river and the Queene's house, so as a large cutt should have let in ye Thames like a bay; but Sir John was for setting it in piles at the very brink of the water, which I did not assent to and so came away, knowing Sir John to be a better poet than architect, tho' he had Mr. Webb (Inigo Jones's man) to assist him."

others of 16, but not the service. I never had so much discourse with the Duke before, and till now did ever fear to meet him. He found me and Mr. Prin together talking of the Chest money,[1] which we are to blame not to look after. Thence to my Lord's, and took up my wife, whom my Lady hath received with her old good nature and kindnesse, and so homewards, and she home, I 'lighting by the way, and upon the 'Change met my uncle Wight and told him my discourse this afternoon with Sir G. Carteret in Maes' business, but much to his discomfort, and after a dish of coffee home, and at my office a good while with Sir W. Warren talking with great pleasure of many businesses, and then home to supper, my wife and I had a good fowle to supper, and then I to the office again and so home, my mind in great ease to think of our coming to so good a respect with my Lord again, and my Lady, and that my Lady do so much cry up my father's usage of her children, and the goodness of the ayre there, found in the young ladies' faces at their return thence, as she says, as also my being put into the commission of the Fishery,[2] for which I must give my Lord thanks, and so home to bed, having a great cold in my head and throat to-night from my late cutting my hair so close to my head, but I hope it will be soon gone again.

5th. Up and to the office, where, though I had a great cold, I was forced to speak much upon a publique meeting of the East India Company, at our office; where our own company was full, and there was also my Lord George Barkeley,[3] in behalfe of the company of merchants (I sup-

[1] See note, July 3rd, 1662. On November 13th, 1662, Pepys mentions the names of the members of the Commission.

[2] There had been recently established, under the Great Seal of England, a Corporation for the Royal Fishing, of which the Duke of York was Governor, Lord Craven Deputy-Governor, and the Lord Mayor and Chamberlain of London, for the time being, Treasurers, in which body was vested the sole power of licensing lotteries ("The Newes," October 6th, 1664). The original charter (dated April 8th, 1664), incorporating James, Duke of York, and thirty-six assistants as Governor and Company of the Royal Fishing of Great Britain and Ireland, is among the State Papers. The duke was to be Governor till February 26th, 1665 (see "Calendar," 1663-64, p. 549).

[3] George, nineteenth Lord Berkeley of Berkeley, afterwards Earl of Berkeley.

pose he is on that company), who, hearing my name, took notice of me, and condoled my cozen Edward Pepys's death, not knowing whose son I was, nor did demand it of me. We broke up without coming to any conclusion, for want of my Lord Marlborough. We broke up and I to the 'Change, where with several people and my uncle Wight to drink a dish of coffee, and so home to dinner, and then to the office all the afternoon, my eye and my throat being very bad, and my cold increasing so as I could not speak almost at all at night. So at night home to supper, that is a posset, and to bed.

6th (Lord's day). Up, and my cold continuing in great extremity I could not go out to church, but sat all day (a little time at dinner excepted) in my closet at the office till night drawing up a second letter to Mr. Coventry about the measure of masts to my great satisfaction, and so in the evening home, and my uncle and aunt Wight came to us and supped with us, where pretty merry, but that my cold put me out of humour. At night with my cold, and my eye also sore still, to bed.

7th. Up betimes, and the Duke being gone abroad to-day, as we heard by a messenger, I spent the morning at my office writing fair my yesterday's work till almost 2 o'clock (only Sir G. Carteret coming I went down a little way by water towards Deptford, but having more mind to have my business done I pretended business at the 'Change, and so went into another boat), and then, eating a bit, my wife and I by coach to the Duke's house, where we saw "The Unfortunate Lovers;"[1] but I know not whether I am grown more curious than I was or no, but I was not much pleased with it, though I know not where to lay the fault, unless it was that the house was very empty, by reason of a new play at the other house. Yet here was my Lady Castlemayne in a box, and it was pleasant to hear an ordinary lady hard by us, that it seems did not know her before, say, being told who she was, that "she was well enough." Thence home, and I ended and sent away my letter to Mr. Coventry (having first read it and had the opinion of Sir W. Warren in the case), and so home to

[1] A tragedy by Sir William Davenant, first acted at the Blackfriars Theatre, licensed 1635, printed 1643.

supper and to bed, my cold being pretty well gone, but my eye remaining still soare and rhumey, which I wonder at, my right eye ayling nothing.

8th. Up with some little discontent with my wife upon her saying that she had got and used some puppy-dog water, being put upon it by a desire of my aunt Wight to get some for her, who hath a mind, unknown to her husband, to get some for her ugly face. I to the office, where we sat all the morning, doing not much business through the multitude of counsellors, one hindering another. It was Mr. Coventry's own saying to me in his coach going to the 'Change, but I wonder that he did give me no thanks for my letter last night, but I believe he did only forget it. Thence home, whither Luellin came and dined with me, but we made no long stay at dinner; for "Heraclius"[1] being acted, which my wife and I have a mighty mind to see, we do resolve, though not exactly agreeing with the letter of my vowe, yet altogether with the sense, to see another this month, by going hither instead of that at Court, there having been none conveniently since I made my vowe for us to see there, nor like to be this Lent, and besides we did walk home on purpose to make this going as cheap as that would have been, to have seen one at Court, and my conscience knows that it is only the saving of money and the time also that I intend by my oaths, and this has cost no more of either, so that my conscience before God do after good consultation and resolution of paying my forfeit, did my conscience accuse me of breaking my vowe, I do not find myself in the least apprehensive that I have done any violence to my oaths. The play hath one very good passage well managed in it, about two persons pretending, and yet denying themselves, to be son to the tyrant Phocas, and yet heire of Mauricius to the crowne. The garments like Romans very well. The little girle[2] is come to act very prettily, and spoke the epilogue

[1] "Heraclius; or, the Emperor of the East," translated from the French of Corneille, by Ludovic Carlell. Pepys saw it again, February 4th, 1666–67, at the Duke s Theatre. Carlell's translation (4to, 1664) was, it is said, never acted. The play which Pepys saw was probably never printed. He saw it at the Duke's Theatre. — B.

[2] Her dancing in "The Slighted Maid" is mentioned February 23rd, 1662–63.

most admirably. But at the beginning, at the drawing up of the curtaine, there was the finest scene of the Emperor and his people about him, standing in their fixed and different postures in their Roman habitts, above all that ever I yet saw at any of the theatres. Walked home, calling to see my brother Tom, who is in bed, and I doubt very ill of a consumption. To the office a while, and so home to supper and to bed.

9th. Up pretty betimes to my office, where all day long, but a little at home at dinner, at my office finishing all things about Mr. Wood's contract for masts, wherein I am sure I shall save the King £400 before I have done. At night home to supper and to bed.

10th. Up and to the office, where all the morning doing business, and at noon to the 'Change and there very busy, and so home to dinner with my wife, to a good hog's harslet,[1] a piece of meat I love, but have not eat of I think these seven years, and after dinner abroad by coach set her at Mrs. Hunt's and I to White Hall, and at the Privy Seale I enquired, and found the Bill come for the Corporation of the Royall Fishery; whereof the Duke of Yorke is made present Governor, and several other very great persons, to the number of thirty-two, made his assistants for their lives: whereof, by my Lord Sandwich's favour, I am one; and take it not only as a matter of honour, but that, that may come to be of profit to me, and so with great content went and called my wife, and so home and to the office, where busy late, and so home to supper and to bed.

11th. Up and by coach to my Lord Sandwich's, who not being up I staid talking with Mr. Moore till my Lord was ready and come down, and went directly out without calling for me or seeing any body. I know not whether he knew I was there, but I am apt to think not, because if he would have given me that slighting yet he would not have done it to others that were there. So I went back again doing nothing but discoursing with Mr. Moore, who I find by discourse to be grown rich, and indeed not to use me at all with the respect he used to do, but as his equal. He made me known to their Chaplin, who is a worthy, able

[1] Harslet or haslet, the entrails of an animal, especially of a hog, as the heart, liver, &c.

man. Thence home, and by and by to the Coffee-house, and thence to the 'Change, and so home to dinner, and after a little chat with my wife to the office, where all the afternoon till very late at the office busy, and so home to supper and to bed, hoping in God that my diligence, as it is really very useful for the King, so it will end in profit to myself. In the meantime I have good content in mind to see myself improve every day in knowledge and being known.

12th. Lay long pleasantly entertaining myself with my wife, and then up and to the office, where busy till noon, vexed to see how Sir J. Minnes deserves rather to be pitied for his dotage and folly than employed at a great salary to ruin the King's business. At noon to the 'Change, and thence home to dinner, and then down to Deptford, where busy a while, and then walking home it fell hard a raining. So at Halfway house put in, and there meeting Mr. Stacy[1] with some company of pretty women, I took him aside to a room by ourselves, and there talked with him about the several sorts of tarrs, and so by and by parted, and I walked home and there late at the office, and so home to supper and to bed.

13th (Lord's day). Lay long in bed talking with my wife, and then up in great doubt whether I should not go see Mr. Coventry or no, who hath not been well these two or three days, but it being foul weather I staid within, and so to my office, and there all the morning reading some Common Law, to which I will allot a little time now and then, for I much want it. At noon home to dinner, and then after some discourse with my wife, to the office again, and by and by Sir W. Pen came to me after sermon and walked with me in the garden, and then one comes to tell me that Anthony and Will Joyce were come to see me, so I in to them and made mighty much of them, and very pleasant we were, and most of their business I find to be to advise about getting some woman to attend my brother Tom, whom they say is very ill and seems much to want one. To which I agreed, and desired them to get their wives to enquire out one. By and by they bid me good night, but immediately as they were gone out of doors

[1] Mr. Stacy, the tar merchant (see July 16th, 1663).

comes Mrs. Turner's boy with a note to me to tell me that my brother Tom was so ill as they feared he would not long live, and that it would be fit I should come and see him. So I sent for them back, and they came, and Will Joyce desiring to speak with me alone I took him up, and there he did plainly tell me to my great astonishment that my brother is deadly ill, and that their chief business of coming was to tell me so, and what is worst that his disease is the pox, which he hath heretofore got, and hath not been cured, but is come to this, and that this is certain, though a secret told his father Fenner by the Doctor which he helped my brother to. This troubled me mightily, but however I thought fit to go see him for speech of people's sake, and so walked along with them, and in our way called on my uncle Fenner (where I have not been these 12 months and more) and advised with him, and then to my brother, who lies in bed talking idle. He could only say that he knew me, and then fell to other discourse, and his face like a dying man, which Mrs. Turner, who was here, and others conclude he is. The company being gone, I took the mayde, which seems a very grave and serious woman, and in W. Joyce's company did inquire how things are with her master. She told me many things very discreetly, and said she had all his papers and books, and key of his cutting house, and showed me a bag which I and Wm. Joyce told, coming to £5 14*s.* 0*d.*, which we left with her again, after giving her good counsel, and the boys, and seeing a nurse there of Mrs. Holden's choosing, I left them, and so walked home greatly troubled to think of my brother's condition, and the trouble that would arise to me by his death or continuing sick. So at home, my mind troubled, to bed.

14th. Up, and walked to my brother's, where I find he hath continued talking idly all night, and now knows me not, which troubles me mightily. So I walked down and discoursed a great while alone with the mayde, who tells me many passages of her master's practices, and how she concludes that he has run behind hand a great while and owes money, and has been dunned by several people, among others by one Cave,[1] both husband and wife, but

[1] See April 6th, *post*.

whether it was for money or something worse she knows not, but there is one Cranburne, I think she called him, in Fleete Lane with whom he hath many times been mighty private, but what their dealings have been she knows not, but believes these were naught, and then his sitting up two Saturday nights one after another when all were a-bed doing something to himself, which she now suspects what it was, but did not before, but tells me that he hath been a very bad husband as to spending his time, and hath often told him of it, so that upon the whole I do find he is, whether he lives or dies, a ruined man, and what trouble will befall me by it I know not. Thence to White Hall; and in the Duke's chamber, while he was dressing, two persons of quality that were there did tell his Royal Highness how the other night, in Holborne, about midnight, being at cards, a link-boy come by and run into the house, and told the people the house was a-falling. Upon this the whole family was frighted, concluding that the boy had said that the house was a-fire: so they left their cards above, and one would have got out of the balcone, but it was not open; the other went up to fetch down his children, that were in bed; so all got clear out of the house. And no sooner so, but the house fell down indeed, from top to bottom.[1] It seems my Lord Southampton's canaille[2] did come too near their foundation, and so weakened the house, and down it came; which, in every respect, is a most extraordinary passage. By and by into his closet and did our business with him. But I did not speed as I expected in a business about the manner of buying hemp for this year, which troubled me, but it proceeds only from my pride, that I must needs expect every thing to be ordered just as I apprehend, though it was not I think from my errour, but their not being willing to hear and consider all that I had to propose. Being broke up I followed my Lord Sandwich and thanked him for his putting me into

[1] "The Intelligencer" of March 12th, 1663–64, notices the fall of the house here mentioned. — B.

[2] Probably the sewer from old Southampton House, which was situated on the south side of Holborn, a little above Holborn Bars. The house was pulled down about 1652, and its site is marked by Southampton Buildings.

the Fishery, which I perceive he expected, and cried "Oh!" says he, "in the Fishery you mean. I told you I would remember you in it," but offered no other discourse. But demanding whether he had any commands for me, methought he cried "No!" as if he had no more mind to discourse with me, which still troubles me and hath done all the day, though I think I am a fool for it, in not pursuing my resolution of going handsome in clothes and looking high, for that must do it when all is done with my Lord. Thence by coach with Sir W. Batten to the city, and his son Castle, who talks mighty highly against Captain Tayler, calling him knave, and I find that the old doating father is led and talks just as the son do, or the son as the father would have him. 'Light and to Mr. Moxon's, and there saw our office globes in doing, which will be very handsome but cost money. So to the Coffee-house, and there very fine discourse with Mr. Hill the merchant, a pretty, gentile, young, and sober man. So to the 'Change, and thence home, where my wife and I fell out about my not being willing to have her have her gowne laced, but would lay out the same money and more on a plain new one. At this she flounced away in a manner I never saw her, nor which I could ever endure. So I away to the office, though she had dressed herself to go see my Lady Sandwich. She by and by in a rage follows me, and coming to me tells me in spitefull manner like a vixen and with a look full of rancour that she would go buy a new one and lace it and make me pay for it, and then let me burn it if I would after she had done it, and so went away in a fury. This vexed me cruelly, but being very busy I had not hand to give myself up to consult what to do in it, but anon, I suppose after she saw that I did not follow her, she came again to the office, where I made her stay, being busy with another, half an houre, and her stomach[1] coming down we were presently friends, and so after my business being over at the office we out and by coach to my

[1] Pride, haughtiness, only used now as a quotation.

"He was a man
Of an unbounded stomach, ever ranking
Himself with princes."
Shakespeare, *Henry VIII.*, act iv., sc. 2.

Lady Sandwich's, with whom I left my wife, and I to White Hall, where I met Mr. Delsety, and after an hour's discourse with him met with nobody to do other business with, but back again to my Lady, and after half an hour's discourse with her to my brother's, who I find in the same or worse condition. The doctors give him over and so do all that see him. He talks no sense two words together now; and I confess it made me weepe to see that he should not be able, when I asked him, to say who I was. I went to Mrs. Turner's, and by her discourse with my brother's Doctor, Mr. Powell, I find that she is full now of the disease which my brother is troubled with, and talks of it mightily, which I am sorry for, there being other company, but methinks it should be for her honour to forbear talking of it, the shame of this very thing I confess troubles me as much as anything. Back to my brother's and took my wife, and carried her to my uncle Fenner's and there had much private discourse with him. He tells me of the Doctor's thoughts of my brother's little hopes of recovery, and from that to tell me his thoughts long of my brother's bad husbandry, and from that to say that he believes he owes a great deal of money, as to my cozen Scott I know not how much, and Dr. Thos. Pepys £30, but that the Doctor confesses that he is paid £20 of it, and what with that and what he owes my father and me I doubt he is in a very sad condition, that if he lives he will not be able to show his head, which will be a very great shame to me. After this I went in to my aunt and my wife and Anthony Joyce and his wife, who were by chance there, and drank and so home, my mind and head troubled, but I hope it will [be] over in a little time one way or other. After doing a little at my office of business I home to supper and to bed. From notice that my uncle Fenner did give my father the last week of my brother's condition, my mother is coming up to towne, which also do trouble me. The business between my Lords Chancellor and Bristoll, they say, is hushed up; and the latter gone or going, by the King's licence, to France.

15th. Up and to the office, where we sat all the morning, and at noon comes Madam Turner and her daughter The., her chief errand to tell me that she had got Dr. Wiverly, her Doctor, to search my brother's mouth, where Mr. Powell says there is an ulcer, from thence he concludes that he hath had the pox. But the Doctor swears that there is not, nor ever was any, and my brother being very sensible, which I was glad to hear, he did talk with him about it, and he did wholly disclaim that ever he had the disease, or that ever he said to Powell that he had it. All which did put me into great comfort as to the reproach which was spread against him. So I sent for a barrel of oysters, and they dined, and we were very merry, I being willing to be so upon this news. After dinner we took coach and to my brother's, where contrary to my expectation he continues as bad or worse, talking idle, and now not at all knowing any of us as before. Here we staid a great while, I going up and down the house looking after things. In the evening Dr. Wiverley came again, and I sent for Mr. Powell (the Doctor and I having first by ourselves searched my brother again at his privities, where he was as clear as ever he was born, and in the Doctor's opinion had been ever so), and we three alone discoursed the business, where the coxcomb did give us his simple reasons for what he had said, which the Doctor fully confuted, and left the fellow only saying that he should cease to report any such thing, and that what he had said was the best of his judgment from my brother's words and ulcer, as he supposed, in his mouth. I threatened him that I would have satisfaction if I heard any more such discourse, and so good night to them two, giving the Doctor a piece for his fee, but the other nothing. I to my brother again, where Madam Turner and her company, and Mrs. Croxton, my wife, and Mrs. Holding. About 8 o'clock my brother began to fetch his spittle with more pain, and to speak as much but not so distinctly, till at last the phlegm getting the mastery of him, and he beginning as we thought to rattle, I had no mind to see him die, as we thought he presently would, and so withdrew and led Mrs. Turner home, but before I came back, which was in half a quarter of an hour, my brother was dead. I went up and found the nurse holding his eyes shut, and he poor wretch lying with his chops fallen, a most sad sight, and that which put me into a present very great transport of grief and cries, and indeed it was a most sad sight to see the poor wretch lie now still and dead, and pale like a stone. I staid till he was almost cold, while Mrs. Croxton, Holden, and the rest did strip and lay him out, they observing his corpse, as they told me afterwards, to be as clear as any they ever saw, and so this was the end of my poor brother, continuing talking idle and his lips working even to his last that his phlegm hindered his breathing, and at last his breath broke out bringing a flood of phlegm and stuff out with it, and so he died. This evening he talked among other talk a great deal of French very plain and good, as, among others: *quand un homme boit quand il n'a poynt d'inclination a boire il ne luy fait jamais de bien.* I once begun to tell him something of his condition, and asked him whither he thought he should go. He in distracted manner answered me—"Why, whither should I go? there are but two ways: If I go to the bad way I must give God thanks for it, and if I go the other way I must give God the more thanks for it; and I hope I have not been so undutifull and unthankfull in my life but I hope I shall go that way." This was all the sense, good or bad, that I could get of him this day. I left my wife to see him laid out, and I by coach home carrying my brother's papers, all I could find, with me, and having wrote a letter to my father telling him what hath been said I returned by coach, it being very late, and dark, to my brother's, but all being gone, the corpse laid out, and my wife at Mrs. Turner's, I thither, and there after an hour's talk, we up to bed, my wife and I in the little blue chamber, and I lay close to my wife, being full of disorder and grief for my brother that I could not sleep nor wake with satisfaction, at last I slept till 5 or 6 o'clock.

16th. And then I rose and up, leaving my wife in bed, and to my brother's, where I set them on cleaning the house, and my wife coming anon to look after things, I up and down to my cozen Stradwicke's and uncle Fenner's about discoursing for the funeral, which I am resolved to put off till Friday next. Thence home and trimmed myself, and then to the 'Change, and told my uncle Wight of my brother's death, and so by coach to my cozen Turner's and there dined very well, but my wife . . . . in great pain we were forced to rise in some disorder, and in Mrs. Turner's coach carried her home and put her to bed. Then back again with my cozen Norton[1] to Mrs. Turner's, and there staid a while talking with Dr. Pepys, the puppy, whom I had no patience to hear. So I left them and to my brother's to look after things, and saw the coffin brought; and by and by Mrs. Holden came and saw him nailed up. Then came W. Joyce to me half drunk, and much ado I had to tell him the story of my brother's being found clear of what was said, but he would interrupt me by some idle discourse or other, of his crying what a good man, and a good speaker my brother was, and God knows what. At last weary of him I got him away, and I to Mrs. Turner's, and there, though my heart is still heavy to think of my poor brother, yet I could give way to my fancy to hear Mrs. The. play upon the Harpsicon, though the musique did not please me neither. Thence to my brother's and found them with my mayd Elizabeth taking an inventory of the goods of the house, which I was well pleased at, and am much beholden to Mr. Honeywood's man in doing of it. His name is Herbert, one that says he knew me when he lived with Sir Samuel Morland, but I have forgot him. So I left them at it, and by coach home and to my office, there to do a little business, but God knows my heart and head is so full of my brother's death, and the consequences of it, that I can do very little or understand it. So home to supper, and after looking over some business in my chamber I to bed to my wife, who continues in bed in some pain still. This day I have a great barrel of oysters given me by Mr. Barrow, as big as 16 of others, and I took it in the coach with me to Mrs. Turner's, and give them to her. This day the Parliament met again, after a long prorogation, but what they have done I have not been in the way to hear.

17th. Up and to my brother's, where all the morning doing business against to-morrow, and so to my cozen Stradwicke's about the same business, and to the 'Change, and thence home to dinner, where my wife in bed sick still, but not so bad as yesterday. I dined by her, and so to the office, where we sat this afternoon, having changed this day our sittings from morning to afternoons, because of the Parliament which returned yesterday; but was adjourned

[1] Joyce Norton (see note *ante*, January 7th, 1659-60).

till Monday next,[1] upon pretence that many of the members were said to be upon the road; and also the King had other affairs, and so desired them to adjourn till then. But the truth is, the King is offended at my Lord of Bristoll, as they say, whom he hath found to have been all this while (pretending a desire of leave to go into France, and to have all the difference between him and the Chancellor made up,) endeavouring to make factions in both Houses to the Chancellor. So the King did this to keep the Houses from meeting; and in the meanwhile sent a guard and a herald last night to have taken him at Wimbleton,[2] where he was in the morning, but could not find him: at which the King was and is still mightily concerned, and runs up and down to and from the Chancellor's like a boy: and it seems would make Digby's articles against the Chancellor to be treasonable reflections against his Majesty. So that the King is very high, as they say; and God knows what will follow upon it! After office I to my brother's again, and thence to Madam Turner's, in both places preparing things against to-morrow; and this night I have altered my resolution of burying him in the churchyarde among my young brothers and sisters, and bury him in the church, in the middle isle, as near as I can to my mother's pew. This costs me *20s.* more. This being all, home by coach, bringing my brother's silver tankard for safety along with me, and so to supper, after writing to my father, and so to bed.

18th. Up betimes, and walked to my brother's, where a

[1] Parliament met on March 16th, and was at once adjourned until the 21st.

[2] The manor-house of Wimbledon was purchased of Sir Christopher Hatton by Sir Thomas Cecil (afterwards Earl of Exeter), who rebuilt it in 1588. He bequeathed it to his third son, Sir Edward Cecil (afterwards Viscount Wimbledon), at whose death in 1638 it was sold to Queen Henrietta Maria. The estate was seized during the Civil Wars, and a survey was taken by order of Parliament in 1649 (printed in "Archæologia," vol. x.). At the Restoration it again came into the possession of the Queen Dowager, who in 1661 sold it to George Digby, Earl of Bristol. On his death in 1676 it was sold by his widow to Lord Treasurer Danby (afterwards Duke of Leeds). Wimbledon House, designed by John Thorpe, was a very remarkable building, thought by some (according to Fuller) to be equal, if not to exceed Nonsuch. There is a view of the front in Lysons' "Environs of London."

great while putting things in order against anon; then to Madam Turner's and eat a breakfast there, and so to Wotton, my shoemaker, and there got a pair of shoes blacked on the soles against anon for me; so to my brother's and to church, and with the grave-maker chose a place for my brother to lie in, just under my mother's pew. But to see how a man's tombes are at the mercy of such a fellow, that for sixpence he would, (as his owne words were,) "I will justle them together but I will make room for him;" speaking of the fulness of the middle isle, where he was to lie; and that he would, for my father's sake, do my brother that is dead all the civility he can; which was to disturb other corps that are not quite rotten, to make room for him; and methought his manner of speaking it was very remarkable; as of a thing that now was in his power to do a man a courtesy or not. At noon my wife, though in pain, comes, but I being forced to go home, she went back with me, where I dressed myself, and so did Besse; and so to my brother's again: whither, though invited, as the custom is, at one or two o'clock, they came not till four or five. But at last one after another they come, many more than I bid: and my reckoning that I bid was one hundred and twenty; but I believe there was nearer one hundred and fifty. Their service was six biscuits a-piece, and what they pleased of burnt claret. My cosen Joyce Norton kept the wine and cakes above; and did give out to them that served, who had white gloves given them. But above all, I am beholden to Mrs. Holden, who was most kind, and did take mighty pains not only in getting the house and every thing else ready, but this day in going up and down to see the house filled and served, in order to mine, and their great content, I think; the men sitting by themselves in some rooms, and women by themselves in others, very close, but yet room enough. Anon to church,[1] walking out into the streete to the Conduit, and so across the streete, and had a very good company along with the corps. And being come to the grave as above, Dr. Pierson, the minister of the parish, did read the service for buriall: and so I saw my poor brother

[1] St. Bride's, of which Richard Pierson, D.D., the vicar, officiated at the funeral. "March 18, 1663-4, Mr. Thomas Pepys" ("Burial Register of St. Bride's, Fleet Street"). — B.

laid into the grave; and so all broke up; and I and my wife and Madam Turner and her family to my brother's, and by and by fell to a barrell of oysters, cake, and cheese, of Mr. Honiwood's, with him, in his chamber and below, being too merry for so late a sad work. But, Lord! to see how the world makes nothing of the memory of a man, an houre after he is dead! And, indeed, I must blame myself; for though at the sight of him dead and dying, I had real grief for a while, while he was in my sight, yet presently after, and ever since, I have had very little grief indeed for him. By and by, it beginning to be late, I put things in some order in the house, and so took my wife and Besse (who hath done me very good service in cleaning and getting ready every thing and serving the wine and things to-day, and is indeed a most excellent good-natured and faithful wench, and I love her mightily), by coach home, and so after being at the office to set down the day's work home to supper and to bed.

19th. Up and to the office, where all the morning, and at noon my wife and I alone, having a good hen, with eggs, to dinner, with great content. Then by coach to my brother's, where I spent the afternoon in paying some of the charges of the buriall, and in looking over his papers, among which I find several letters of my brother John's to him speaking very foule words of me and my deportment to him here, and very crafty designs about Sturtlow land and God knows what, which I am very glad to know, and shall make him repent them. Anon my father and my brother John came to towne by coach. I sat till night with him, giving him an account of things. He, poor man, very sad and sickly. I in great pain by a simple compressing of my cods to-day by putting one leg over another as I have formerly done, which made me hasten home, and after a little at the office in great disorder home to bed.

20th (Lord's day). Kept my bed all the morning, having laid a poultice to my cods last night to take down the tumour there which I got yesterday, which it did do, being applied pretty warm, and soon after the beginning of the swelling, and the pain was gone also. We lay talking all the while, among other things of religion, wherein I am sorry so often to hear my wife talk of her being and resolving to die a Catholique,[1] and indeed a small matter, I believe, would absolutely turn her, which I am sorry for. Up at noon to dinner, and then to my chamber with a fire till late at night looking over my brother Thomas's papers, sorting of them, among which I find many base letters of my brother John's to him against me, and carrying on plots against me to promote Tom's having of his Banbury[2] Mistress, in base slighting terms, and in worse of my sister Pall, such as I shall take a convenient time to make my father know, and him also to his sorrow. So after supper to bed, our people rising to wash to-morrow.

21st. Up, and it snowing this morning a little, which from the mildness of the winter and the weather beginning to be hot and the summer to come on apace, is a little strange to us. I did not go abroad for fear of my tumour, for fear it shall rise again, but staid within, and by and by my father came, poor man, to me, and my brother John. After much talke and taking them up to my chamber, I did there after some discourse bring in my business of anger with John, and did before my father read all his roguish letters, which troubled my father mightily, especially to hear me say what I did, against my allowing any thing for the time to come to him out of my owne purse, and other words very severe, while he, like a simple rogue, made very silly and churlish answers to me, not like a man of any goodness or witt, at which I was as much disturbed as the other, and will be as good as my word in making him to his cost know that I will remember his carriage to me in this particular the longest day I live. It troubled me to see my poor father so troubled, whose good nature did make him, poor wretch, to yield, I believe, to comply with my brother Tom and him in part of their designs, but without any ill intent to me, or doubt of me or my good intentions to him or them, though it do trouble me a little that he should in any manner do it. They dined with me, and after dinner abroad with my wife to buy some things for her,

[1] Mrs. Pepys's leaning towards Roman Catholicism was a constant trouble to her husband; but, in spite of his fears, she died a Protestant (see Dr. Milles's certificate, printed in vol. i., p. xxxvi).

[2] The young lady whom Thomas Pepys courted lived at Banbury (see September 30th, 1662)

and I to the office, where we sat till night, and then, after doing some business at my closet, I home and to supper and to bed. This day the Houses of Parliament met; and the King met them, with the Queene with him. And he made a speech to them:[1] among other things, discoursing largely of the plots abroad against him and the peace of the kingdom; and, among other things, that the dissatisfied party had great hopes upon the effect of the Act for a Triennial Parliament granted by his father, which he desired them to peruse, and, I think, repeal. So the Houses did retire to their own House, and did order the Act to be read to-morrow before them; and I suppose it will be repealed, though I believe much against the will of a good many that sit there.

22nd. Up, and spent the whole morning and afternoon at my office, only in the evening, my wife being at my aunt Wight's, I went thither, calling at my own house, going out found the parlour curtains drawn, and inquiring the reason of it, they told me that their mistress had got Mrs. Buggin's fine little dog and our little bitch, which is proud at this time, and I am apt to think that she was helping him to line her, for going afterwards to my uncle Wight's, and supping there with her, where very merry with Mr. Woolly's drollery, and going home I found the little dog so little that of himself he could not reach our bitch, which I am sorry for, for it is the finest dog that ever I saw in my life, as if he were painted the colours are so finely mixed and shaded. God forgive me, it went against me to have my wife and servants look upon them while they endeavoured to do something. . . .

23rd. Up, and going out saw Mrs. Buggin's dog, which proves as I thought last night so pretty that I took him and

[1] March 16th, 1663–64. This day both Houses met, and on the 21st the king opened the session with a speech from the throne, in which occurs this passage: "I pray, Mr. Speaker, and you, gentlemen of the House of Commons, give that Triennial Bill once a reading in your house, and then, in God's name, do what you think fit for me and yourselves and the whole kingdom. I need not tell you how much I love parliaments. Never king was so much beholden to parliaments as I have been, nor do I think the crown can ever be happy without frequent parliaments" (Cobbett's "Parliamentary History," vol. iv., cc. 290, 291).

the bitch into my closet below, and by holding down the bitch helped him to line her, which he did very stoutly, so as I hope it will take, for it is the prettiest dog that ever I saw. So to the office, where very busy all the morning, and so to the 'Change, and off hence with Sir W. Rider to the Trinity House, and there dined very well: and good discourse among the old men of Islands now and then rising and falling again in the Sea, and that there is many dangers of grounds and rocks that come just up to the edge almost of the sea, that is never discovered and ships perish without the world's knowing the reason of it. Among other things, they observed, that there are but two seamen in the Parliament house, viz., Sir W. Batten and Sir W. Pen, and not above twenty or thirty merchants; which is a strange thing in an island, and no wonder that things of trade go no better nor are better understood. Thence home, and all the afternoon at the office, only for an hour in the evening my Lady Jemimah, Paulina, and Madam Pickering come to see us, but my wife would not be seen, being unready.[1] Very merry with them; they mightily talking of their thrifty living for a fortnight before their mother came to town, and other such simple talk, and of their merry life at Brampton, at my father's, this winter. So they being gone, to the office again till late, and so home and to supper and to bed.

24th. Called up by my father, poor man, coming to advise with me about Tom's house and other matters, and he being gone I down by water to Greenwich, it being very foggy, and I walked very finely to Woolwich, and there did very much business at both yards, and thence walked back, Captain Grove with me talking, and so to Deptford and did the like there, and then walked to Redriffe (calling and eating a bit of collops and eggs at Half-way house), and so home to the office, where we sat late, and home weary to supper and to bed.

25th (Lady-day). Up and by water to White Hall, and there to chappell; where it was most infinite full to hear Dr. Critton.[2] Being not knowne, some great persons in the pew I pretended to, and went in, did question my coming

[1] Undressed. See note *ante*, October 12th, 1662.

[2] Dr. Robert Creighton. See March 7th, 1661-62.

in. I told them my pretence; so they turned to the orders of the chappell, which hung behind upon the wall, and read it, and were satisfied; but they did not demand whether I was in waiting or no; and so I was in some fear lest he that was in waiting might come and betray me. The Doctor preached upon the thirty-first of Jeremy, and the twenty-first and twenty-second verses, about a woman compassing a man; meaning the Virgin conceiving and bearing our Saviour. It was the worst sermon I ever heard him make, I must confess; and yet it was good, and in two places very bitter, advising the King to do as the Emperor Severus did, to hang up a Presbyter John (a short coat and a long gowne interchangeably) in all the Courts of England. But the story of Severus was pretty, that he hanged up forty senators before the Senate-house, and then made a speech presently to the Senate in praise of his owne lenity; and then decreed that never any senator after that time should suffer in the same manner without consent of the Senate: which he compared to the proceeding of the Long Parliament against my Lord Strafford. He said the greatest part of the lay magistrates in England were Puritans, and would not do justice; and the Bishopps, their powers were so taken away and lessened, that they could not exercise the power they ought. He told the King and the ladies plainly, speaking of death and of the skulls and bones of dead men and women,[1] how there is no difference; that nobody could tell that of the great Marius or Alexander from a pyoneer; nor, for all the pains the ladies take with their faces, he that should look in a charnell-house could not distinguish which was Cleopatra's, or fair Rosamond's, or Jane Shoare's. Thence by water home. After dinner to the office, thence with my wife to see my father and discourse how he finds Tom's matters, which he do very ill, and that he finds him to have been so negligent, that he used to trust his servants with cutting out of clothes, never hardly cutting out any thing himself; and, by the abstract of his accounts, we find him to owe above £290, and to be coming to him under £200. Thence home with my wife, it being very dirty on foot,

[1] The preacher appears to have had the grave scene in "Hamlet" in his mind, as he gives the same illustration of Alexander as Hamlet does.

and bought some fowl in Gracious Street[1] and some oysters against our feast to-morrow. So home, and after at the office a while, home to supper and to bed.

26th. Up very betimes and to my office, and there read over some papers against a meeting by and by at this office of Mr. Povy, Sir W. Rider, Creed, and Vernaty,[2] and Mr. Gauden about my Lord Peterborough's accounts for Tangier, wherein we proceeded a good way; but, Lord! to see how ridiculous Mr. Povy is in all he says or do; like a man not more fit for to be in such employments as he is, and particularly that of Treasurer (paying many and very great sums without the least written order) as he is to be King of England, and seems but this day, after much discourse of mine, to be sensible of that part of his folly, besides a great deal more in other things. This morning in discourse Sir W. Rider [said] that he hath kept a journall of his life for almost these forty years, even to this day and still do, which pleases me mightily. That being done Sir J. Minnes and I sat all the morning, and then I to the 'Change, and there got away by pretence of business with my uncle Wight to put off Creed, whom I had invited to dinner, and so home, and there found Madam Turner, her daughter The., Joyce Norton, my father and Mr. Honywood, and by and by come my uncle Wight and aunt. This being my solemn feast for my cutting of the stone,[3] it being now, blessed be God! this day six years since the time; and I bless God I do in all respects find myself free from that disease or any signs of it, more than that upon the least cold I continue to have pain in making water, by gathering of wind and growing costive, till which be removed I am at no ease, but without that I am very well. One evil more I have, which is that upon the least squeeze almost my cods begin to swell and come to great pain, which is very strange and troublesome to me, though upon the speedy applying of a poultice it goes down again, and in two days I am well again. Dinner

[1] Gracechurch Street.

[2] There are some letters of M. Vernatti or Vernatty (dated 1654, 1656, 1657) among the Rawlinson MSS. in the Bodleian Library. This man appears to have turned out a cheat, and fled the country in 1666 (see *post*, October 27th, 1667).

[3] The successful operation for the stone took place on March 26th, 1658.

not being presently ready I spent some time myself and shewed them a map of Tangier[1] left this morning at my house by Creed, cut by our order, the Commissioners, and drawn by Jonas Moore, which is very pleasant, and I purpose to have it finely set out and hung up. Mrs. Hunt coming to see my wife by chance dined here with us. After dinner Sir W. Batten sent to speak with me, and told me that he had proffered our bill to-day in the House, and that it was read without any dissenters, and he fears not but will pass very well, which I shall be glad of. He told me also how Sir [Richard] Temple hath spoke very discontentfull words in the House about the Tryennial Bill;[2] but it hath been read the second time to-day, and committed; and, he believes, will go on without more ado, though there are many in the House are displeased at it, though they dare not say much. But above all expectation, Mr. Prin is the man against it, comparing it to the idoll whose head was of gold, and his body and legs and feet of different metal. So this Bill had several degrees of calling of Parliaments, in case the King, and then the Council, and then the Lord Chancellor, and then the Sheriffes, should fail to do it. He tells me also, how, upon occasion of some 'prentices being put in the pillory to-day for beating of their masters,[3] or some such like thing, in Cheapside, a company of 'prentices came and rescued them, and pulled down the pillory; and they being set up again, did the like again. So that the Lord Mayor and Major Generall Browne was fain to come and stay there, to keep the peace; and

[1] In Pepys's General Collection of Prints in the Pepysian Library are some coloured engravings of Tangier and the Mole, before they were demolished, and in their ruins, by Thomas Phillips; but Jonas Moore's map does not appear to be there.

[2] On March 23rd, 1663–64, a Bill for the repeal of the Act entituled "An Act for the preventing the inconveniences happening by the long intermission of Parliaments, and for the provision for the calling and holding of Parliaments once in three years at least," was read the first time. The question being put that the Bill be read on Tuesday was passed in the negative (yeas 42, noes 129), and it was resolved that the Bill be read the second time on the following morning. Sir Richard Temple was one of the tellers for the yeas ("Journal of the House of Commons," vol. viii., p. 526).

[3] Two servants of one Ireland, a cooper upon Bread Street Hill ("The Intelligencer," March 28th, 1664). — B.

drums, all up and down the city, was beat to raise the trained bands, for to quiett the towne, and by and by, going out with my uncle and aunt Wight by coach with my wife through Cheapside (the rest of the company after much content and mirth being broke up), we saw a trained band stand in Cheapside upon their guard. We went, much against my uncle's will, as far almost as Hyde Park, he and my aunt falling out all the way about it, which vexed me, but by this I understand my uncle more than ever I did, for he was mighty soon angry, and wished a pox take her, which I was sorry to hear. The weather I confess turning on a sudden to rain did make it very unpleasant, but yet there was no occasion in the world for his being so angry, but she bore herself very discreetly, and I must confess she proves to me much another woman than I thought her, but all was peace again presently, and so it raining very fast, we met many brave coaches coming from the Parke and so we turned and set them down at home, and so we home ourselves, and ended the day with great content to think how it hath pleased the Lord in six years time to raise me from a condition of constant and dangerous and most painfull sicknesse and low condition and poverty to a state of constant health almost, great honour and plenty, for which the Lord God of heaven make me truly thankfull. My wife found her gowne come home laced, which is indeed very handsome, but will cost me a great deal of money, more than ever I intended, but it is but for once. So to the office and did business, and then home and to bed.

27th (Lord's day). Lay long in bed wrangling with my wife about the charge she puts me to at this time for clothes more than I intended, and very angry we were, but quickly friends again. And so rising and ready I to my office, and there fell upon business, and then to dinner, and then to my office again to my business, and by and by in the afternoon walked forth towards my father's, but it being church time, walked to St. James's,[1] to try if I could see the belle Butler, but could not; only saw her sister, who indeed is

[1] The church of St. James's, Clerkenwell, which Pepys visited, was built in 1625 on the site of an older church. The present church was erected 1788–92. The Diarist went to church to see the fair Butlers on August 11th, 1661.

pretty, with a fine Roman nose. Thence walked through the ducking-pond fields; but they are so altered since my father used to to carry us to Islington,[1] to the old man's, at the King's Head, to eat cakes and ale (his name was Pitts) that I did not know which was the ducking-pond nor where I was. So through F[l]ee[t] lane to my father's, and there met Mr. Moore, and discoursed with him and my father about who should administer for my brother Tom, and I find we shall have trouble in it, but I will clear my hands of it, and what vexed me, my father seemed troubled that I should seem to rely so wholly upon the advice of Mr. Moore, and take nobody else, but I satisfied him, and so home; and in Cheapside, both coming and going, it was full of apprentices, who have been here all this day, and have done violence, I think, to the master of the boys that were put in the pillory yesterday. But, Lord! to see how the train-bands are raised upon this: the drums beating every where as if an enemy were upon them; so much is this city subject to be put into a disarray upon very small occasions. But it was pleasant to hear the boys, and particularly one little one, that I demanded the business. He told me that that had never been done in the city since it was a city, two prentices put in the pillory, and that it ought not to be so. So I walked home, and then it being fine moonshine with my wife an houre in the garden, talking of her clothes against Easter and about her mayds, Jane being to be gone, and the great dispute whether Besse, whom we both love, should be raised to be chamber-mayde or no. We have both a mind to it, but know not whether we should venture the making her proud and so make a bad chamber-mayde of a very good-natured and sufficient cook-mayde. So to my office a little, and then to supper, prayers and to bed.

[1] In Ben Jonson's "Every Man in his Humour," there is an allusion to the "Citizens that come a-ducking to Islington Ponds" (act i., sc. 1). The piece of ground, long since built upon, was called "Ducking-pond Field," from the pool in which the unfortunate ducks were hunted by dogs, to amuse the Cockneys, who went to Islington to breathe fresh air and drink cream. "On the north side of White Conduit House, now Albert Street, and at the south end of Claremont Place, there existed a deep and dangerous pool called Wheal Pond, which until a late period was famous for this inhuman sport" (Pinks's "History of Clerkenwell," p. 543). The King's Head Tavern stood opposite the church.

28th. This is the first morning that I have begun, and I hope shall continue to rise betimes in the morning, and so up and to my office, and thence about 7 o'clock to T. Trice, and advised with him about our administering to my brother Tom, and I went to my father and told him what to do; which was to administer and to let my cozen Scott have a letter of Atturny to follow the business here in his absence for him, who by that means will have the power of paying himself (which we cannot however hinder) and do us a kindness we think too. But, Lord! what a shame, methinks, to me, that, in this condition, and at this age, I should know no better the laws of my owne country! Thence to Westminster Hall, and spent till noon, it being Parliament time, and at noon walked with Creed into St. James's Parke, talking of many things, particularly of the poor parts and great unfitness for business of Mr. Povy, and yet what a show he makes in the world. Mr. Coventry not being come to his chamber, I walked through the house with him for an hour in St. James's fields[1] talking of the same subject, and then parted, and back and with great impatience, sometimes reading, sometimes walking, sometimes thinking that Mr. Coventry, though he invited us to dinner with him, was gone with the rest of the office without a dinner. At last, at past 4 o'clock I heard that the Parliament was not up yet, and so walked to Westminster Hall, and there found it so, and meeting with Sir J. Minnes, and being very hungry, went over with him to the Leg, and before we had cut a bit, the House rises, however we eat a bit and away to St. James's and there eat a second part of our dinner with Mr. Coventry and his brother Harry,[2] Sir W. Batten and Sir W. Pen.

[1] St. James's Fields consisted of an open space west of the Haymarket, and north of Pall Mall, now occupied by St. James's Square and the adjacent streets. The square was planned about this time by the Earl of St. Albans.

[2] Henry, third son of Thomas, first Lord Coventry; after the Restoration made a Groom of the Bedchamber, and elected M.P. for Droitwich. In 1664 he was sent Envoy Extraordinary to Sweden, where he remained two years, and was again employed on an embassy to the same court in 1671. He also succeeded in negotiating the peace at Breda in 1667, and in 1672 became Secretary of State, which office he resigned in 1679, on account of ill health. He died unmarried, December 7th, 1686. — B.

The great matter to-day in the House hath been, that Mr. Vaughan,[1] the great speaker, is this day come to towne, and hath declared himself in a speech of an houre and a half, with great reason and eloquence, against the repealing of the Bill for Triennial Parliaments; but with no successe: but the House have carried it that there shall be such Parliaments, but without any coercive power upon the King, if he will bring this Act. But, Lord! to see how the best things are not done without some design; for I perceive all these gentlemen that I was with to-day were against it (though there was reason enough on their side); yet purely, I could perceive, because it was the King's mind to have it; and should he demand any thing else, I believe they would give it him. But this the discontented Presbyters, and the faction of the House will be highly displeased with; but it was carried clearly against them in the House. We had excellent good table-talke, some of which I have entered in my book of stories. So with them by coach home, and there find [by] my wife, that Father Fogourdy hath been with her to-day, and she is mightily for our going to hear a famous Reulé preach at the French Embassador's house: I pray God he do not tempt her in any matters of religion, which troubles me; and also, she had messages from her mother to-day, who sent for her old morning-gown, which was almost past wearing; and I used to call it her kingdom,[2] from the ease and content she used to have in the wearing of it. I am glad I do not hear of her begging any thing of more value, but I do not like that these messages should now come all upon Monday morning, when my wife expects of course I should be abroad at the Duke's. To the office, where Mr. Nor-

[1] John Vaughan, appointed Chief Justice of the Common Pleas, and knighted, 1668. He died December 10th, 1674.

[2] Apparently an allusion to the charming poem attributed to Sir Edward Dyer, the friend of Spenser and Sidney:

"My minde to me a kingdome is,
Such perfect joy therein I finde."

It was set to music by the celebrated William Byrd, and published in his "Psalmes, Sonets, and Songs of Sadness and Pietie," 1588. A black-letter edition of this poem is found in the Pepys Collection of Ballads.

man[1] came and showed me a design of his for the store-keeper's books, for the keeping of them regular in order to a balance, which I am mightily satisfied to see, and shall love the fellow the better, as he is in all things sober, so particularly for his endeavour to do something in this thing so much wanted. So late home to supper and to bed, weary with walking so long to no purpose in the Park to-day.

29th. Was called up this morning by a messenger from Sir G. Carteret to come to him to Sir W. Batten's, and so I rose and thither to him, and with him and Sir J. Minnes to Sir G. Carteret's to examine his accounts, and there we sat at it all the morning. About noon Sir W. Batten came from the House of Parliament and told us our Bill for our office was read the second time to-day, with great applause, and is committed. By and by to dinner, where good cheere, and Sir G. Carteret in his humour a very good man, and the most kind father and pleased father in his children that ever I saw. Here is now hung up a picture of my Lady Carteret, drawn by Lilly, a very fine picture, but yet not so good as I have seen of his doing. After dinner to the business again without any intermission till almost night, and then home, and took coach to my father to see and discourse with him, and so home again and to my office, where late, and then home to bed.

30th. Up very betimes to my office, and thence at 7 o'clock to Sir G. Carteret, and there with Sir J. Minnes made an end of his accounts, but staid not dinner, my Lady having made us drink our morning draft there of several wines, but I drank nothing but some of her coffee, which was poorly made, with a little sugar in it. Thence to the 'Change a great while, and had good discourse with Captain Cocke at the Coffee-house about a Dutch warr, and it seems the King's design is by getting underhand the merchants to bring in their complaints to the Parliament, to make them in honour begin a warr, which he cannot in honour declare first, for fear they should not second him with money. Thence homewards, staying a pretty while with my little she milliner at the end of Birchin Lane,

[1] James Norman, clerk to Sir William Batten.

talking and buying gloves of her, and then home to dinner, and in the afternoon had a meeting upon the Chest business, but I fear unless I have time to look after it nothing will be done, and that I fear I shall not. In the evening comes Sir W. Batten, who tells us that the Committee have approved of our bill with very few amendments in words, not in matter. So to my office, where late with Sir W. Warren, and so home to supper and to bed.

31st. Up betimes, and to my office, where by and by comes Povy, Sir W. Rider, Mr. Bland, Creed, and Vernatty, about my Lord Peterborough's accounts, which we now went through, but with great difficulty, and many high words between Mr. Povy and I; for I could not endure to see so many things extraordinary put in, against truthe and reason. He was very angry, but I endeavoured all I could to profess my satisfaction in my Lord's part of the accounts, but not in those foolish idle things, they say I said, that others had put in. Anon we rose and parted, both of us angry, but I contented, because I knew all of them must know I was in the right. Then with Creed to Deptford, where I did a great deal of business enquiring into the business of canvas and other things with great content, and so walked back again, good discourse between Creed and I by the way, but most upon the folly of Povy, and at home found Luellin, and so we to dinner, and thence I to the office, where we sat all the afternoon late, and being up and my head mightily crowded with business, I took my wife by coach to see my father. I left her at his house and went to him to an alehouse hard by, where my cozen Scott was, and my father's new tenant, Langford, a tailor, to whom I have promised my custom, and he seems a very modest, carefull young man. Thence my wife coming with the coach to the alley end I home, and after supper to the making up my monthly accounts, and to my great content find myself worth above £900, the greatest sum I ever yet had. Having done my accounts, late to bed. My head of late mighty full of business, and with good content to myself in it, though sometimes it troubles me that nobody else but I should bend themselves to serve the King with that diligence, whereby much of my pains proves ineffectual.

April 1st. Up and to my office, where busy till noon, and then to the 'Change, where I found all the merchants concerned with the presenting their complaints to the Committee of Parliament appointed to receive them this afternoon against the Dutch. So home to dinner, and thence by coach, setting my wife down at the New Exchange, I to White Hall; and coming too soon for the Tangier Committee walked to Mr. Blagrave for a song I left long ago there, and here I spoke with his kinswoman, he not being within, but did not hear her sing, being not enough acquainted with her, but would be glad to have her, to come and be at my house a week now and then. Back to White Hall, and in the Gallery met the Duke of Yorke (I also saw the Queene going to the Parke, and her Mayds of Honour: she herself looks ill, and methinks Mrs. Stewart is grown fatter, and not so fair as she was); and he called me to him, and discoursed a good while with me; and after he was gone, twice or thrice staid and called me again to him, the whole length of the house: and at last talked of the Dutch; and I perceive do much wish that the Parliament will find reason to fall out with them. He gone, I by and by found that the Committee of Tangier met at the Duke of Albemarle's, and so I have lost my labour. So with Creed to the 'Change, and there took up my wife and left him, and we two home, and I to walk in the garden with W. Howe, whom we took up, he having been to see us, he tells me how Creed has been questioned before the Council about a letter that has been met with, wherein he is mentioned by some fanatiques as a serviceable friend to them, but he says he acquitted himself well in it, but, however, something sticks against him, he says, with my Lord, at which I am not very sorry, for I believe he is a false fellow. I walked with him to Paul's, he telling me how my Lord is little at home, minds his carding and little else, takes little notice of any body; but that he do not think he is displeased, as I fear, with me, but is strange to all, which makes me the less troubled. So walked back home, and late at the office. So home and to bed. This day Mrs. Turner did lend me, as a rarity, a manuscript of one Mr. Wells, writ long ago, teaching the method of building a ship, which pleases me mightily. I was at it to-night, but durst not stay long at it, I being come to have a great pain and water in my eyes after candle-light.

2nd. Up and to my office, and afterwards sat, where great contest with Sir W. Batten and Mr. Wood, and that doating fool Sir J. Minnes, that says whatever Sir W. Batten says, though never minding whether to the King's profit or not. At noon to the Coffee-house, where excellent discourse with Sir W. Petty, who proposed it as a thing that is truly questionable, whether there really be any difference between waking and dreaming, that it is hard not only to tell how we know when we do a thing really or in a dream, but also to know what the difference [is] between one and the other. Thence to the 'Change, but having at this discourse long afterwards with Sir Thomas Chamberlin,[1] who tells me what I heard from others, that the complaints of most Companies were yesterday presented to the Committee of Parliament against the Dutch, excepting that of the East India, which he tells me was because they would not be said to be the first and only cause of a warr with Holland, and that it is very probable, as well as most necessary, that we fall out with that people. I went to the 'Change, and there found most people gone, and so home to dinner, and thence to Sir W. Warren's, and with him past the whole afternoon, first looking over two ships[2] of Captain Taylor's and Phin. Pett's now in building, and am resolved to learn something of the art, for I find it is not hard and very usefull, and thence to Woolwich, and after seeing Mr. Falconer, who is very ill, I to the yard, and there heard Mr. Pett tell me several things of Sir W. Batten's ill managements, and so with Sir W. Warren walked to Greenwich, having good discourse, and thence by water, it being now moonshine and 9 or 10 o'clock at night, and landed at Wapping, and by him and his man safely brought to my door, and so he home, having spent the day with him very well. So home and eat something, and then to my office a while, and so home to prayers and to bed.

[1] Sir Thomas Chamberlayne (see *ante*, February 15th, 1663-64).

[2] These ships may have been the "Adventure" and the "Providence," which were ready to launch at this time (see "Calendar of State Papers," Domestic, 1663-64, p. 499).

3rd (Lord's day). Being weary last night lay long, and called up by W. Joyce. So I rose, and his business was to ask advice of me, he being summonsed to the House of Lords to-morrow, for endeavouring to arrest my Lady Peters[1] for a debt. I did give him advice, and will assist him. He staid all the morning, but would not dine with me. So to my office and did business. At noon home to dinner, and being set with my wife in the kitchen my father comes and sat down there and dined with us. After dinner gives me an account of what he had done in his business of his house and goods, which is almost finished, and he the next week expects to be going down to Brampton again, which I am glad of because I fear the children of my Lord that are there for fear of any discontent. He being gone I to my office, and there very busy setting papers in order till late at night, only in the afternoon my wife sent for me home, to see her new laced gowne, that is her gown that is new laced; and indeed it becomes her very nobly, and is well made. I am much pleased with it. At night to supper, prayers, and to bed.

4th. Up, and walked to my Lord Sandwich's; and there spoke with him about W. Jocye, who told me he would do what was fit in so tender a point. I can yet discern a coldness in him to admit me to any discourse with him. Thence to Westminster, to the Painted Chamber, and there met the two Joyces. Will in a very melancholy taking. After a little discourse I to the Lords' House before they sat; and stood within it a good while, while the Duke of York came to me and spoke to me a good while about the new ship[2] at Woolwich. Afterwards I spoke with my Lord Barkeley and my Lord Peterborough about it.[3] And so staid without a good while, and saw my Lady

[1] Elizabeth, daughter of John Savage, second Earl Rivers, and first wife to William, fourth Lord Petre, who was, in 1678, impeached by the Commons of high treason, and died under confinement in the Tower, January 5th, 1683, *s. p.* — B.

[2] There are several references to a new ship building about this time at Woolwich among the State Papers. On February 29th, 1663-64, Commissioner Pett, writing to Pepys, expresses his opinion that "the demands of joiners and carvers for work on the new ship at Woolwich [are] exorbitant" ("Calendar," Domestic, 1663-64, p. 498).

[3] W. Joyce's business.

Peters, an impudent jade, soliciting all the Lords on her behalf. And at last W. Joyce was called in; and by the consequences, and what my Lord Peterborough told me, I find that he did speak all he said to his disadvantage, and so was committed to the Black Rod: which is very hard, he doing what he did by the advice of my Lord Peters' own steward. But the Sergeant of the Black Rod did direct one of his messengers to take him in custody, and so he was peaceably conducted to the Swan with two Necks, in Tuttle Street, to a handsome dining-room; and there was most civilly used, my uncle Fenner, and his brother Anthony, and some other friends being with him. But who would have thought that the fellow that I should have sworn could have spoken before all the world should in this be so daunted, as not to know what he said, and now to cry like a child. I protest, it is very strange to observe. I left them providing for his stay there to-night and getting a petition against to-morrow, and so away to Westminster Hall, and meeting Mr. Coventry, he took me to his chamber, with Sir William Hickeman,[1] a member of their House, and a very civill gentleman. Here we dined very plentifully, and thence to White Hall to the Duke's, where we all met, and after some discourse of the condition of the Fleete, in order to a Dutch warr, for that, I perceive, the Duke hath a mind it should come to, we away to the office, where we sat, and I took care to rise betimes, and so by water to Halfway House, talking all the way good discourse with Mr. Wayth, and there found my wife, who was gone with her mayd Besse to have a walk. But, Lord! how my jealous mind did make me suspect that she might have some appointment to meet somebody. But I found the poor souls coming away thence, so I took them back, and eat and drank, and then home, and after at the office a while, I home to supper and to bed. It was a sad sight, methought, to-day to see my Lord Peters coming out of the House fall out with his lady (from whom he is parted) about this business, saying that she disgraced him. But she hath been a handsome woman, and is, it seems, not only a lewd woman, but very high-spirited.

[1] Only son of Sir Willoughby Hickman, of Gainsborough, who had been created a baronet in 1643, and whom he succeeded in his title and estates. He was M.P. for East Retford. — B.

5th. Up very betimes, and walked to my cozen Anthony Joyce's, and thence with him to his brother Will, in Tuttle Street, where I find him pretty cheery over [what] he was yesterday (like a coxcomb), his wife being come to him, and having had his boy with him last night. Here I staid an hour or two and wrote over a fresh petition, that which was drawn by their solicitor not pleasing me, and thence to the Painted chamber, and by and by away by coach to my Lord Peterborough's, and there delivered the petition into his hand, which he promised most readily to deliver to the House to-day. Thence back, and there spoke to several Lords, and so did his solicitor (one that W. Joyce hath promised £5 to if he be released). Lord Peterborough presented a petition to the House from W. Joyce: and a great dispute, we hear, there was in the House for and against it. At last it was carried that he should be bayled till the House meets again after Easter, he giving bond for his appearance. This was not so good as we hoped, but as good as we could well expect. Anon comes the King and passed the Bill for repealing the Triennial Act,[1] and another about Writs of Errour. I crowded in and heard the King's speech to them; but he speaks the worst that ever I heard man in my life: worse than if he read it all, and he had it in writing in his hand. Thence, after the House was up, and I inquired what the order of the House was, I to W. Joyce,[2] with his brother, and told them all. Here was Kate come, and is a comely fat woman. I would not stay dinner, thinking to go home to dinner, and did go by water as far as the bridge, but thinking that they would take it kindly my being there, to be bayled for him if there was need, I returned, but finding

[1] April 5th, 1664. In compliance with the King's expressed wish "the House immediately set about repealing the obnoxious Triennial Bill, which they stigmatized as derogatory to the prerogative of the Crown, and as a short compensation prepared another short one, which provided that parliaments should not be intermitted above three years" (Cobbett's "Parliamentary History," vol. iv., col. 292).

[2] The two sisters Fenner were married to the two brothers Joyce: Kate to Anthony, and Mary to William. There is a token extant of Anthony Joyce's house (The Three Stags) "at Hoborn Conded." The initials "A K I" on the token stand for Anthony and Kate Joyce (see "Boyne's Tokens," ed. Williamson, vol. i., p. 633).

them gone out to look after it, only Will and his wife and sister left and some friends that came to visit him, I to Westminster Hall, and by and by by agreement to Mrs. Lane's lodging, whither I sent for a lobster, and with Mr. Swayne and his wife eat it, and argued before them mightily for Hawly, but all would not do, although I made her angry by calling her old, and making her know what herself is. Her body was out of temper for any dalliance, and so after staying there 3 or 4 hours, but yet taking care to have my oath safe of not staying a quarter of an hour together with her, I went to W. Joyce, where I find the order come, and bayle (his father and brother) given; and he paying his fees, which come to above £12, besides £5 he is to give one man, and his charges of eating and drinking here, and 10*s.* a-day as many days as he stands under bayle: which, I hope, will teach him hereafter to hold his tongue better than he used to do. Thence with Anth. Joyce's wife alone home talking of Will's folly, and having set her down, home myself, where I find my wife dressed as if she had been abroad, but I think she was not, but she answering me some way that I did not like I pulled her by the nose, indeed to offend her, though afterwards to appease her I denied it, but only it was done in haste. The poor wretch took it mighty ill, and I believe besides wringing her nose she did feel pain, and so cried a great while, but by and by I made her friends, and so after supper to my office a while, and then home to bed. This day great numbers of merchants came to a Grand Committee of the House to bring in their claims against the Dutch. I pray God guide the issue to our good!

6th. Up and to my office, whither by and by came John Noble, my father's old servant, to speake with me. I smelling the business, took him home; and there, all alone, he told me how he had been serviceable to my brother Tom, in the business of his getting his servant, an ugly jade, Margaret, with child. She was brought to bed in St. Sepulchre's parish of two children; one is dead, the other is alive; her name Elizabeth, and goes by the name of Taylor, daughter to John Taylor. It seems Tom did a great while trust one Crawly with the business, who daily got money of him; and at last, finding himself abused, he broke the matter to J. Noble, upon a vowe of secresy. Tom's first plott was to go on the other side the water and give a beggar woman something to take the child. They did once go, but did nothing, J. Noble saying that seven years hence the mother might come to demand the child and force him to produce it, or to be suspected of murder. Then I think it was that they consulted, and got one Cave, a poor pensioner in St. Bride's parish to take it, giving him £5, he thereby promising to keepe it for ever without more charge to them. The parish hereupon indite the man Cave for bringing this child upon the parish, and by Sir Richard Browne he is sent to the Counter. Cave thence writes to Tom to get him out. Tom answers him in a letter of his owne hand, which J. Noble shewed me, but not signed by him, wherein he speaks of freeing him and getting security for him, but nothing as to the business of the child, or anything like it: so that forasmuch as I could guess, there is nothing therein to my brother's prejudice as to the main point, and therefore I did not labour to tear or take away the paper. Cave being released, demands £5 more to secure my brother for ever against the child; and he was forced to give it him and took bond of Cave in £100, made at a scrivener's, one Hudson, I think, in the Old Bayly, to secure John Taylor, and his assigns, &c. (in consideration of £10 paid him), from all trouble, or charge of meat, drink, clothes, and breeding of Elizabeth Taylor; and it seems, in the doing of it, J. Noble was looked upon as the assignee of this John Taylor. Noble says that he furnished Tom with this money, and is also bound by another bond to pay him 20*s.* more this next Easter Monday; but nothing for either sum appears under Tom's hand. I told him how I am like to lose a great sum by his death, and would not pay any more myself, but I would speake to my father about it against the afternoon. So away he went, and I all the morning in my office busy, and at noon home to dinner mightily oppressed with wind, and after dinner took coach and to Paternoster Row, and there bought a pretty silke for a petticoate for my wife, and thence set her down at the New Exchange, and I leaving the coat at Unthanke's, went to White Hall, but the Councell meeting at Worcester House

I went thither, and there delivered to the Duke of Albemarle a paper touching some Tangier business, and thence to the 'Change for my wife, and walked to my father's, who was packing up some things for the country. I took him up and told him this business of Tom, at which the poor wretch was much troubled, and desired me that I would speak with J. Noble, and do what I could and thought fit in it without concerning him in it. So I went to Noble, and saw the bond that Cave did give and also Tom's letter that I mentioned above, and upon the whole I think some shame may come, but that it will be hard from any thing I see there to prove the child to be his. Thence to my father and told what I had done, and how I had quieted Noble by telling him that, though we are resolved to part with no more money out of our own purses, yet if he can make it appear a true debt that it may be justifiable for us to pay it, we will do our part to get it paid, and said that I would have it paid before my own debt. So my father and I both a little satisfied, though vexed to think what a rogue my brother was in all respects. I took my wife by coach home, and to my office, where late with Sir W. Warren, and so home to supper and to bed. I heard to-day that the Dutch have begun with us by granting letters of marke against us; but I believe it not.

7th. Up and to my office, where busy, and by and by comes Sir W. Warren and old Mr. Bond in order to the resolving me some questions about masts and their proportions, but he could say little to me to my satisfaction, and so I held him not long but parted. So to my office busy till noon and then to the 'Change, where high talke of the Dutch's protest against our Royall Company in Guinny,[1] and their granting letters of marke against us there, and every body expects a warr, but I hope it will not yet be so, nor that this is true. Thence to dinner, where my wife got me a pleasant French fricassee of veal for dinner, and thence to the office, where vexed to see how Sir W. Batten ordered things this afternoon (vide my office book, for about this time I have begun, my notions and informations encreasing now greatly every day, to enter all occurrences

[1] The African or Guinea Company, which had a house in Broad Street.

extraordinary in my office in a book by themselves), and so in the evening after long discourse and eased my mind by discourse with Sir W. Warren, I to my business late, and so home to supper and to bed.

8th. Up betimes and to the office, and anon, it begunn to be fair after a great shower this morning, Sir W. Batten and I by water (calling his son Castle by the way, between whom and I no notice at all of his letter the other day to me) to Deptford, and after a turn in the yard, I went with him to the Almes'-house to see the new building which he, with some ambition, is building of there, during his being Master of Trinity House; and a good worke it is, but to see how simply he answered somebody concerning setting up the arms of the corporation upon the door, that and any thing else he did not deny it, but said he would leave that to the master that comes after him. There I left him and to the King's yard again, and there made good inquiry into the business of the poop lanterns, wherein I found occasion to correct myself mightily for what I have done in the contract with the platerer, and am resolved, though I know not how, to make them to alter it, though they signed it last night, and so I took Stanes[1] home with me by boat and discoursed it, and he will come to reason when I can make him to understand it. No sooner landed but it fell a mighty storm of rain and hail, so I put into a cane shop and bought one to walk with, cost me 4*s.* 6*d.*, all of one joint. So home to dinner, and had an excellent Good Friday dinner of peas porridge and apple pye. So to the office all the afternoon preparing a new book for my contracts, and this afternoon come home the office globes done to my great content. In the evening a little to visit Sir W. Pen, who hath a feeling this day or two of his old pain. Then to walk in the garden with my wife, and so to my office a while, and then home to the only Lenten supper I

[1] Among the State Papers is a petition of Thomas Staine to the Navy Commissioners "for employment as plateworker in one or two dockyards. Has incurred illwill by discovering abuses in the great rates given by the king for several things in the said trade. Begs the appointment, whereby it will be seen who does the work best and cheapest, otherwise he and all others will be discouraged from discovering abuses in future, with order thereon for a share of the work to be given to him" ("Calendar," Domestic, 1663-64, p. 395).

have had of wiggs[1] and ale, and so to bed. This morning betimes came to my office to me boatswain Smith of Woolwich, telling me a notable piece of knavery of the officers of the yard and Mr. Gold in behalf of a contract made for some old ropes by Mr. Wood, and I believe I shall find Sir W. Batten of the plot (vide my office daybook[2]).

9th. The last night, whether it was from cold I got to-day upon the water I know not, or whether it was from my mind being over concerned with Stanes's business of the platery of the navy, for my minde was mighty troubled with the business all night long, I did wake about one o'clock in the morning, a thing I most rarely do, and pissed a little with great pain, continued sleepy, but in a high fever all night, fiery hot, and in some pain. Towards morning I slept a little and waking found myself better, but . . . . with some pain, and rose I confess with my clothes sweating, and it was somewhat cold too, which I believe might do me more hurt, for I continued cold and apt to shake all the morning, but that some trouble with Sir J. Minnes and Sir W. Batten kept me warm. At noon home to dinner upon tripes, and so though not well abroad with my wife by coach to her Tailor's and the New Exchange, and thence to my father's and spoke one word with him, and thence home, where I found myself sick in my stomach and vomited, which I do not use to do. Then I drank a glass or two of Hypocras, and to the office to dispatch some business, necessary, and so home and to bed, and by the help of Mithrydate[3] slept very well.

10th (Lord's day). Lay long in bed, and then up and my wife dressed herself, it being Easter day, but I not being so well as to go out, she, though much against her will, staid at home with me; for she had put on her new best gowne, which indeed is very fine now with the lace; and this morning her taylor brought home her other new laced silke gowne with a smaller lace, and new petticoate, I

[1] Buns or tea cakes. See March 6th, 1660–61. "*Eschaudé*, a kind of wigg or symnell."—Cotgrave.

[2] These note-books referred to in the Diary are not known to exist now.

[3] Mithridate is understood to denote an antidote, and not, as here, an opiate.

bought the other day: both very pretty. We spent the day in pleasant talke and company one with another, reading in Dr. Fuller's book[1] what he says of the family of the Cliffords and Kingsmills, and at night being myself better than I was by taking a glyster, which did carry away a great deal of wind, I after supper at night went to bed and slept well.

11th. Lay long talking with my wife, then up and to my chamber preparing papers against my father comes to lie here for discourse about country business. Dined well with my wife at home, being myself not yet thorough well, making water with some pain, but better than I was, and all my fear of an ague gone away. In the afternoon my father came to see us, and he gone I up to my morning's work again, and so in the evening a little to the office and to see Sir W. Batten, who is ill again, and so home to supper and to bed.

12th. Up, and after my wife had dressed herself very fine in her new laced gown, and very handsome indeed, W. Howe also coming to see us, I carried her by coach to my uncle Wight's and set her down there, and W. Howe and I to the Coffee-house, where we sat talking about getting of him some place under my Lord of advantage if he should go to sea, and I would be glad to get him secretary and to out Creed if I can, for he is a crafty and false rogue. Thence a little to the 'Change, and thence took him to my uncle Wight's, where dined my father, poor melancholy man, that used to be as full of life as anybody, and also my aunt's brother, Mr. Sutton, a merchant in Flanders, a very sober, fine man, and Mr. Cole and his lady; but, Lord! how I used to adore that man's talke, and now methinks he is but an ordinary man, his son a pretty boy indeed, but his nose unhappily awry. Other good company and an indifferent, and but indifferent dinner for so much company, and after dinner got a coach, very dear,

[1] Pepys had been mistaken in fancying that Fuller's "Worthies" was to be a history of all the families in England (see *ante*, January 22nd, 1660–61, and February 10th, 1661–62), and hence his disappointment, when the work came out, some months after the author's decease, at there being no mention in it of his ancestors. He then looked for the Cliffords, in hopes of finding his wife's lineage; but with no better success. — B.

it being Easter time and very foul weather, to my Lord's, and there visited my Lady, and leaving my wife there I and W. Howe to Mr. Pagett's, and there heard some musique not very good, but only one Dr. Walgrave, an Englishman bred at Rome, who plays the best upon the lute that I ever heard man. Here I also met Mr. Hill[1] the little merchant, and after all was done we sung. I did well enough a Psalm or two of Lawes; he I perceive has good skill and sings well, and a friend of his sings a good base. Thence late walked with them two as far as my Lord's, thinking to take up my wife and carry them home, but there being no coach to be got away they went, and I staid a great while, it being very late, about 10 o'clock, before a coach could be got. I found my Lord and ladies and my wife at supper. My Lord seems very kind. But I am apt to think still the worst, and that it is only in show, my wife and Lady being there. So home, and find my father come to lie at our house, and so supped, and saw him, poor man, to bed, my heart never being fuller of love to him, nor admiration of his prudence and pains heretofore in the world than now, to see how Tom hath carried himself in his trade; and how the poor man hath his thoughts going to provide for his younger children and my mother. But I hope they shall never want. So myself and wife to bed.

13th. Though late, past 12, before we went to bed, yet I heard my poor father up, and so I rang up my people, and I rose and got something to eat and drink for him, and so abroad, it being a mighty foul day, by coach, setting my father down in Fleet Streete and I to St. James's, where I found Mr. Coventry (the Duke being now come thither for the summer) with a goldsmith, sorting out his old plate to change for new; but, Lord! what a deale he hath! I staid and had two or three hours discourse with him, talking about the disorders of our office, and I largely to tell him how things are carried by Sir W. Batten and Sir J. Minnes to my great grief. He seems much concerned also, and for all the King's matters that are done after the same rate

[1] Thomas Hill, a man whose taste for music caused him to be a very acceptable companion to Pepys. In January, 1664–65, he became assistant to the secretary of the Prize Office.

every where else, and even the Duke's household matters too, generally with corruption, but most indeed with neglect and indifferency. I spoke very loud and clear to him my thoughts of Sir J. Minnes and the other, and trust him with the using of them. Then to talk of our business with the Dutch; he tells me fully that he believes it will not come to a warr; for first, he showed me a letter from Sir George Downing, his own hand, where he assures him that the Dutch themselves do not desire, but above all things fear it, and that they neither have given letters of marke against our shipps in Guinny, nor do De Ruyter[1] stay at home with his fleet with an eye to any such thing, but for want of a wind, and is now come out and is going to the Streights. He tells me also that the most he expects is that upon the merchants' complaints, the Parliament will represent them to the King, desiring his securing of his subjects against them, and though perhaps they may not directly see fit, yet even this will be enough to let the Dutch know that the Parliament do not oppose the King, and by that means take away their hopes, which was that the King of England could not get money or do anything towards a warr with them, and so thought themselves free from making any restitution, which by this they will be deceived in. He tells me also that the Dutch states are in no good condition themselves, differing one with another, and that for certain none but the states of Holland and Zealand will contribute towards a warr, the others reckoning themselves, being inland, not concerned in the profits of warr or peace. But it is pretty to see what he says, that those here that are forward for a warr at Court, they are reported in the world to be only

[1] Michael De Ruyter, the Dutch admiral, was born 1607. He served under Tromp in the war against England in 1653, and was Lieutenant Admiral General of Holland in 1665. He died April 26th, 1676, of wounds received in a battle with the French off Syracuse. Among the State Papers is a news letter (dated July 14th, 1664) containing information as to the views of the Dutch respecting a war with England. "They are preparing many ships, and raising 6,000 men, and have no doubt of conquering by sea." "A wise man says the States know how to master England by sending moneys into Scotland for them to rebel, and also to the discontented in England, so as to place the King in the same straits as his father was, and bring him to agree with Holland" ("Calendar," 1663–64, p. 642).

designers of getting money into the King's hands, they that elsewhere are for it have a design to trouble the kingdom and to give the Fanatiques an opportunity of doing hurt, and lastly those that are against it (as he himself for one is very cold therein) are said to be bribed by the Dutch. After all this discourse he carried me in his coach, it raining still, to Charing Cross, and there put me into another, and I calling my father and brother carried them to my house to dinner, my wife keeping bed all day. . . . . All the afternoon at the office with W. Boddam [1] looking over his particulars about the Chest of Chatham, which shows enough what a knave Commissioner Pett hath been all along, and how Sir W. Batten hath gone on in getting good allowance to himself and others out of the poors' money. Time will show all. So in the evening to see Sir W. Pen, and then home to my father to keep him company, he being to go out of town, and up late with him and my brother John till past 12 at night to make up papers of Tom's accounts fit to leave with my cozen Scott. At last we did make an end of them, and so after supper all to bed.

14th. Up betimes, and after my father's eating something, I walked out with him as far as Milk Streete, he turning down to Cripplegate to take coach; and at the end of the streete I took leave, being much afeard I shall not see him here any more, he do decay so much every day, and so I walked on, there being never a coach to be had till I came to Charing Cross, and there Col. Froud took me up and carried me to St. James's, where with Mr. Coventry and Povy, &c., about my Lord Peterborough's accounts, but, Lord! to see still what a puppy that Povy is with all his show is very strange. Thence to Whitehall and W. C[oventry] and I and Sir W. Rider resolved upon a day to meet and make an end of all the business. Thence walked with Creed to the Coffee-house in Covent Garden, where no company, but he told me many fine experiments at Gresham College,[2] and some demonstration that the heat and cold of

[1] William Bodham about this time was appointed clerk of the Ropeyard at Woolwich.

[2] These demonstrations by Robert Hooke at the Royal Society are described in the minutes as follows: "April 6, 1664. The experiment of stretching glass was made by Mr. Hooke, who was desired to give an

the weather do rarify and condense the very body of glasse, as in a bolt head[1] with cold water in it put into hot water, shall first by rarifying the glasse make the water sink, and then when the heat comes to the water makes that rise again, and then put into cold water makes the water by condensing the glass to rise, and then when the cold comes to the water makes it sink, which is very pretty and true, he saw it tried. Thence by coach home, and dined above with my wife by her bedside, she keeping her bed. . . . . . So to the office, where a great conflict with Wood and Castle about their New England masts.[2] So in the evening my mind a little vexed, but yet without reason, for I shall prevail, I hope, for the King's profit, and so home to supper and to bed.

15th. Up and all the morning with Captain Taylor at my house talking about things of the Navy, and among other things I showed him my letters to Mr. Coventry, wherein he acknowledges that nobody to this day did ever understand so much as I have done, and I believe him, for I perceive he did very much listen to every article as things new to him, and is contented to abide by my opinion therein in his great contest with us about his and Mr. Wood's masts. At noon to the 'Change, where I met with Mr. Hill, the little merchant, with whom, I perceive, I shall contract a musical acquaintance; but I will make it as little troublesome as I can. Home and dined, and then with my wife by coach to the Duke's house, and there saw "The German

account of the manner and success thereof in writing." "April 13. An account in writing was brought by Mr. Hooke of two experiments tried before the Society at the preceding meeting . . . 2 of the stretching and shrinking of glass upon heating and cooling; both of which were ordered to be registered" (Birch's "History of the Royal Society," vol. i., pp. 409, 411).

[1] A long straight-necked glass vessel used for chemical distillation.

[2] On September 10th, 1663, Sir William Warren contracted with the Navy Commissioners to deliver Gottenburg and Norway masts at the several dockyards. The contract, among the State Papers, has annexed to it: "Tender by Sir William Warren of 150 Gottenburg and 300 Norway masts, with three ships loads of New England masts, to be delivered free of charge at Portsmouth, Chatham, and Deptford," and "Account of the difference of price between the tenders of Sir William Warren and —— Wood, the former being the cheaper" ("Calendar of State Papers," Domestic, 1663–64, p. 270).

Princess"[1] acted, by the woman herself; but never was any thing so well done in earnest, worse performed in jest upon the stage; and indeed the whole play, abating the drollery of him that acts her husband, is very simple, unless here and there a witty sprinkle or two. We met and sat by Dr. Clerke. Thence homewards, calling at Madam Turner's, and thence set my wife down at my aunt Wight's and I to my office till late, and then at 10 at night fetched her home, and so again to my office a little, and then to supper and to bed.

16th. Up and to the office, where all the morning upon the dispute of Mr. Wood's masts, and at noon with Mr. Coventry to the African House; and after a good and pleasant dinner, up with him, Sir W. Rider, the simple Povy, of all the most ridiculous foole that ever I knew to attend to business, and Creed and Vernatty, about my Lord Peterborough's accounts; but the more we look into them, the more we see of them that makes dispute, which made us break off, and so I home, and there found my wife and Besse gone over the water to Half-way house, and after them, thinking to have gone to Woolwich, but it was too late, so eat a cake and home, and thence by coach to have spoke with Tom Trice about a letter I met with this afternoon from my cozen Scott, wherein he seems to deny proceeding as my father's attorney in administering for him in my brother Tom's estate, but I find him gone out of town, and so returned vexed home and to the office, where late writing a letter to him, and so home and to bed.

17th (Lord's day). Up, and I put on my best cloth black suit and my velvet cloake, and with my wife in her best laced suit to church, where we have not been these nine or ten weeks. The truth is, my jealousy hath hindered it, for fear she should see Pembleton. He was here to-day, but I think sat so as he could not see her, which did please me, God help me! mightily, though I know well enough that in reason this is nothing but my ridiculous folly. Home to dinner, and in the afternoon, after long consulting whether to go to Woolwich or no to see Mr. Falconer, but indeed to prevent my wife going to church, I did how ever go to church with her, where a young simple fellow did preach: I slept soundly all the sermon, and thence to Sir

[1] See note *ante*, May 29th, 1663.

W. Pen's, my wife and I, there she talking with him and his daughter, and thence with my wife walked to my uncle Wight's and there supped, where very merry, but I vexed to see what charges the vanity of my aunt puts her husband to among her friends and nothing at all among ours. Home and to bed. Our parson, Mr. Mills, his owne mistake in reading of the service was very remarkable, that instead of saying, "We beseech thee to preserve to our use the kindly fruits of the earth," he cries, "Preserve to our use our gracious Queen Katherine."

18th. Up and by coach to Westminster, and there solicited W. Joyce's business again; and did speake to the Duke of Yorke about it, who did understand it very well. I afterwards did without the House fall in company with my Lady Peters, and endeavoured to mollify her; but she told me she would not, to redeem her from hell, do any thing to release him; but would be revenged while she lived, if she lived the age of Methusalem. I made many friends, and so did others. At last it was ordered by the Lords that it should be referred to the Committee of Privileges to consider. So I, after discoursing with the Joyces, away by coach to the 'Change; and there, among other things, do hear that a Jew hath put in a policy of four per cent. to any man, to insure him against a Dutch warr for four months; I could find in my heart to take him at this offer, but however will advise first, and to that end took coach to St. James's, but Mr. Coventry was gone forth, and I thence to Westminster Hall, where Mrs. Lane was gone forth, and so I missed of my intent to be with her this afternoon, and therefore meeting Mr. Blagrave, went home with him, and there he and his kinswoman sang, but I was not pleased with it, they singing methought very ill, or else I am grown worse to please than heretofore. Thence to the Hall again, and after meeting with several persons, and talking there, I to Mrs. Hunt's (where I knew my wife and my aunt Wight were about business), and they being gone to walk in the parke I went after them with Mrs. Hunt, who staid at home for me, and finding them did by coach, which I had agreed to wait for me, go with them all and Mrs. Hunt and a kinswoman of theirs, Mrs. Steward, to Hide Parke, where I have not been since last year; where I saw the King with his periwigg, but not altered at all; and my Lady Castlemayne in a coach by herself, in yellow satin and a pinner on; and many brave persons. And myself being in a hackney and full of people, was ashamed to be seen by the world, many of them knowing me. Thence in the evening home, setting my aunt at home, and thence we sent for a joynt of meat to supper, and thence to the office at 11 o'clock at night, and so home to bed.

19th. Up and to St. James's, where long with Mr. Coventry, Povy, &c., in their Tangier accounts, but such the folly of that coxcomb Povy that we could do little in it, and so parted for the time, and I to walk with Creed and Vernaty in the Physique Garden in St. James's Parke; where I first saw orange-trees,[1] and other fine trees. So to Westminster Hall, and thence by water to the Temple, and so walked to the 'Change, and there find the 'Change full of news from Guinny, some say the Dutch have sunk our ships and taken our fort, and others say we have done the same to them. But I find by our merchants that something is done, but is yet a secret among them. So home to dinner, and then to the office, and at night with Captain Tayler consulting how to get a little money by letting him the Elias[2] to fetch masts from New England. So home to supper and to bed.

20th. Up and by coach to Westminster, and there solicited W. Joyce's business all the morning, and meeting in the Hall with Mr. Coventry, he told me how the Committee for Trade[3]

[1] John Evelyn mentions in his Diary (Sept. 25th, 1679) the excellence of the China oranges grown on his own trees, and later on he writes: "20 September, 1700. I went to Beddington, the ancient seate of the Carews, heretofore adorned with ample gardens and the first orange trees that had been seen in England planted in the open ground." William Bray, the editor, says that oranges were eaten in this kingdom in the time of King James I., if not earlier, as appears by the accounts of a student in the Temple, which he had seen.

[2] Captain William Badiley wrote to the Navy Commissioners, February 9th, 1663–64, requesting "a warrant to enter 12 or 14 men to the Elias, which is now afloat." On March 1st he wrote: "The Elias is ready to take in provisions, but wants men to stow them;" and on April 6th, 1664, he asked for "an order to remove the Elias" ("Calendar of State Papers," Domestic, 1663–64, pp. 474, 502, 546).

[3] "Proceedings in the House of Commons on the reading by Mr. Clifford of the report of the Committee for Trade, at which it was

have received now all the complaints of the merchants against the Dutch, and were resolved to report very highly the wrongs they have done us (when, God knows! it is only our owne negligence and laziness that hath done us the wrong): and this to be made to the House to-morrow. I went also out of the Hall with Mrs. Lane to the Swan at Mrs. Herbert's in the Palace Yard to try a couple of bands, and did (though I had a mind to be playing the fool with her) purposely stay but a little while, and kept the door open, and called the master and mistress of the house one after another to drink and talk with me, and showed them both my old and new bands. So that as I did nothing so they are able to bear witness that I had no opportunity there to do anything. Thence by coach with Sir W. Pen home, calling at the Temple for Lawes's Psalms, which I did not so much (by being against my oath) buy as only lay down money till others be bound better for me, and by that time I hope to get money of the Treasurer of the Navy by bills, which, according to my oath, shall make me able to do it. At home dined, and all the afternoon at a Committee of the Chest, and at night comes my aunt and uncle Wight and Nan Ferrers and supped merrily with me, my uncle coming in an hour after them almost foxed. Great pleasure by discourse with them, and so, they gone, late to bed.

21st. Up pretty betimes and to my office, and thither came by and by Mr. Vernaty and staid two hours with me, but Mr. Gauden did not come, and so he went away to meet again anon. Then comes Mr. Creed, and, after some discourse, he and I and my wife by coach to Westminster (leaving her at Unthanke's, her tailor's) Hall, and there at the Lords' House heard that it is ordered, that, upon submission upon the knee both to the House and my Lady Peters, W. Joyce shall be released. I forthwith made him

resolved to represent to the House and to his Majesty the injuries done by the Dutch in India, Africa, and America, as the greatest obstruction to trade, and to request some course for redress and prevention. The House adopted the report, and added their resolution to support the King with life and fortune against all opposition; also a conference was desired with the Lords thereon, and Mr. Clifford and others were appointed to manage it" ("Calendar of State Papers," Domestic, 1663–64, p. 562).

submit, and aske pardon upon his knees; which he did before several Lords. But my Lady would not hear it; but swore she would post the Lords, that the world might know what pitifull Lords the King hath; and that revenge was sweeter to her than milk; and that she would never be satisfied unless he stood in a pillory, and demand pardon there. But I perceive the Lords are ashamed of her, and so I away calling with my wife at a place or two to inquire after a couple of mayds recommended to us, but we found both of them bad. So set my wife at my uncle Wight's and I home, and presently to the 'Change, where I did some business, and thence to my uncle's and there dined very well, and so to the office, we sat all the afternoon, but no sooner sat but news comes my Lady Sandwich was come to see us, so I went out, and running up (her friend however before me) I perceive by my dear Lady blushing that in my dining-room she was doing something upon the pott, which I also was ashamed of, and so fell to some discourse, but without pleasure through very pity to my Lady. She tells me, and I find true since, that the House this day have voted that the King be desired to demand right for the wrong done us by the Dutch,[1] and that they will stand by him with their lives and fortunes: which is a very high vote, and more than I expected. What the issue will be, God knows! My Lady, my wife not being at home, did not stay, but, poor, good woman, went away, I being mightily taken with her dear visitt, and so to the office, where all the afternoon till late, and so to my office, and then to supper and to bed, thinking to rise betimes to-morrow.

22nd. Having directed it last night, I was called up this

[1] "April 22nd, 1664. The following resolution passed both houses, viz.: 'That the wrongs, dishonours, and indignities done to his Majesty by the subjects of the United Provinces, by invading his rights in India, Africa, and elsewhere, and the damages, affronts, and injuries done by them to our merchants, are the greatest obstructions of our Foreign Trade, and that the same be humbly and speedily presented to his Majesty, and that he be most humbly moved to take some speedy and effectual course for redress thereof, and all other of the like nature, and for prevention of the like in future: and in prosecution thereof, they will, with their lives and fortunes, assist his Majesty against all opposition whatsoever'" (Cobbett's "Parliamentary History," vol. iv., col. 292).

morning before four o'clock. It was full light enough to dress myself, and so by water against tide, it being a little coole, to Greenwich; and thence, only that it was somewhat foggy till the sun got to some height, walked with great pleasure to Woolwich, in my way staying several times to listen to the nightingales. I did much business both at the Ropeyarde and the other, and on floate I discovered a plain cheat which in time I shall publish of Mr. Ackworth's. Thence, having visited Mr. Falconer[1] also, who lies still sick, but hopes to be better, I walked to Greenwich, Mr. Deane with me. Much good discourse, and I think him a very just man, only a little conceited, but yet very able in his way, and so he by water also with me also to towne. I home, and immediately dressing myself, by coach with my wife to my Lord Sandwich's, but they having dined we would not 'light but went to Mrs. Turner's, and there got something to eat, and thence after reading part of a good play, Mrs. The., my wife and I, in their coach to Hide Parke, where great plenty of gallants, and pleasant it was, only for the dust. Here I saw Mrs. Bendy, my Lady Spillman's faire daughter that was, who continues yet very handsome. Many others I saw with great content, and so back again to Mrs. Turner's, and then took a coach and home. I did also carry them into St. James's Park and shewed them the garden. To my office awhile while supper was making ready, and so home to supper and to bed.

23rd (Coronation day). Up, and after doing something at my office, and, it being a holiday, no sitting likely to be, I down by water to Sir W. Warren's, who hath been ill, and there talked long with him good discourse, especially about Sir W. Batten's knavery and his son Castle's ill language of me behind my back, saying that I favour my fellow traytours, but I shall be even with him. So home and to the 'Change, where I met with Mr. Coventry, who himself is now full of talke of a Dutch warr; for it seems the Lords have concurred in the Commons' vote about it; and so the next week it will be presented to the King, insomuch that

[1] The following entry in the "Calendar of State Papers" (1663–64, p. 560), illustrates this: "April 18th, 1664. John Falkener to Sam. Pepys. Mr. [William] Acworth cannot supply deals for the ropeyard, having only eight score; so more will be wanting."

he do desire we would look about to see what stores we lack, and buy what we can. Home to dinner, where I and my wife much troubled about my money that is in my Lord Sandwich's hand, for fear of his going to sea and be killed; but I will get what of it out I can. All the afternoon, not being well, at my office, and there doing much business, my thoughts still running upon a warr and my money. At night home to supper and to bed.

24th (Lord's day). Up, and all the morning in my chamber setting some of my private papers in order, for I perceive that now publique business takes up so much of my time that I must get time a-Sundays or a-nights to look after my owne matters. Dined and spent all the afternoon talking with my wife, at night a little to the office, and so home to supper and to bed.

25th. Up, and with Sir W. Pen by coach to St. James's and there up to the Duke, and after he was ready to his closet, where most of our talke about a Dutch warr, and discoursing of things indeed now for it. The Duke, which gives me great good hopes, do talk of setting up a good discipline in the fleete. In the Duke's chamber there is a bird, given him by Mr. Pierce, the surgeon, comes from the East Indys, black the greatest part, with the finest collar of white about the neck;[1] but talks many things and neyes

[1] The description is insufficient to enable the bird to be determined with certainty, but Professor Newton informs the editor that it is most likely to have been a grackle of some kind. The *Gracula religiosa*, or mina, has a yellow collar, is easily tamed, and learns to talk and whistle with great facility. Professor Newton kindly contributes the following two interesting quotations, showing that minas were brought from India early in the eighteenth century; and he believes that, as the mina is a favourite cage-bird in India, it was brought over as soon as direct trade with that country was established. One of the earliest figures of the bird is by Eleazer Albin ("Natural History of Birds," vol. ii., pl. 38), in 1738, who writes: "This bird imitates a human voice, speaking very articulately. I drew this bird at Mr. Mere's coffee-house in King Street, Bloomsbury. Sir Hans Sloan had one of these birds that spoke very prettily, which he presented to Her Majesty Queen Carolina. They are brought from East India." George Edwards ("Natural History of Uncommon Birds," vol. i., pl. 17), whose plate is dated September 25th, 1740, gives two figures, one from a bird he saw at a dealer's in White Hart Yard, in the Strand, and the other from a bird which belonged to Dr. George Wharton, treasurer of the College of Physicians, adding: "For whistling, singing, and talking,

like the horse, and other things, the best almost that ever I heard bird in my life. Thence down with Mr. Coventry and Sir W. Rider, who was there (going along with us from the East Indya house to-day) to discourse of my Lord Peterborough's accounts, and then walked over the Parke, and in Mr. Cutler's coach with him and Rider as far as the Strand, and thence I walked to my Lord Sandwich's, where by agreement I met my wife, and there dined with the young ladies; my Lady, being not well, kept her chamber. Much simple discourse at table among the young ladies. After dinner walked in the garden, talking with Mr. Moore about my Lord's business. He told me my Lord runs in debt every day more and more, and takes little care how to come out of it. He counted to me how my Lord pays use now for above £9,000, which is a sad thing, especially considering the probability of his going to sea, in great danger of his life, and his children, many of them, to provide for. Thence, the young ladies going out to visit, I took my wife by coach out through the city, discoursing how to spend the afternoon; and conquered, with much ado, a desire of going to a play; but took her out at White Chapel, and to Bednal Green; so to Hackney, where I have not been many a year, since a little child I boarded there. Thence to Kingsland, by my nurse's house, Goody Lawrence, where my brother Tom and I was kept when young. Then to Newington Green, and saw the outside of Mrs. Herbert's house, where she lived, and my Aunt Ellen with her; but, Lord! how in every point I find myself to over-value things when a child. Thence to Islington, and so to St. John's to the Red Bull,[1] and there saw the latter part of a rude prize

it is accounted in the first rank, expressing words with an accent nearer human than parrots, or any other bird usually taught to talk. They are said to come from the Island of Borneo, and 'tis likely they come from thence and the adjacent parts. They are brought to us by the India Company's ships."

[1] In Sir W. Davenant's "The Playhouse to be Let" (supposed to have been acted in 1663), we find an allusion to the Red Bull:

"Tell 'em the Red Bull stands empty for fencers;
There are no tenants in it but old spiders.
Go bid the men of wrath allay their heat
With prizes there."

J. Payne Collier was in possession of a printed challenge and acceptance fought, but with good pleasure enough; and thence back to Islington, and at the King's Head, where Pitts lived, we 'light and eat and drunk for remembrance of the old house sake; and so through Kingsland again, and so to Bishopsgate, and so home with great pleasure. The country mighty pleasant, and we with great content home, and after supper to bed, only a little troubled at the young ladies leaving my wife so to-day, and from some passages fearing my Lady might be offended. But I hope the best.

26th. Up, and to my Lord Sandwich's, and coming a little too early, I went and saw W. Joyce, and by and by comes in Anthony, they both owning a great deal of kindness received from me in their late business, and indeed I did what I could, and yet less I could not do. It has cost the poor man above £40; besides, he is likely to lose his debt. Thence to my Lord's, and by and by he comes down, and with him (Creed with us) I rode in his coach to St. James's, talking about W. Joyce's business mighty merry, and my Lady Peters, he says, is a drunken jade, he himself having seen her drunk in the lobby of their House. I went up with him to the Duke, where methought the Duke did not shew him any so great fondness as he was wont; and methought my Lord was not pleased that I should see the Duke made no more of him, not that I know any thing of any unkindnesse, but I think verily he is not as he was with him in his esteem. By and by the Duke went out and we with him through the Parke, and there I left him going into White Hall, and Creed and I walked round the Parke, a pleasant walk, observing the birds, which is very pleasant; and so walked to the New Exchange, and there had a most delicate dish of curds and creame, and discourse with the good woman of the house, a discreet well-bred woman, and a place with great delight I shall make it now and then to go thither. Thence up, and after a turn or two in the

of a trial at eight several weapons to be performed betwixt two scholars of Benjamin Dobson and William Wright, masters of the noble science of defence. The trial was to come off "at the Red Bull at the upper end of St. John's Street, on Whitsun Monday, the 30th of May, 1664, beginning exactly at three of the clock in the afternoon, and the best man is to take all." The weapons were "back-sword, single rapier, sword and dagger, rapier and dagger, sword and buckler, half pike, sword and gauntlet, single faulchion."

'Change, home to the Old Exchange by coach, where great newes and true, I saw by written letters, of strange fires seen at Amsterdam in the ayre, and not only there, but in other places thereabout. The talke of a Dutch warr is not so hot, but yet I fear it will come to it at last. So home and to the office, where we sat late. My wife gone this afternoon to the buriall of my she-cozen Scott,[1] a good woman; and it is a sad consideration how the Pepys's decay, and nobody almost that I know in a present way of encreasing them. At night late at my office, and so home to my wife to supper and to bed.

27th. Up, and all the morning very busy with multitude of clients, till my head began to be overloaded. Towards noon I took coach and to the Parliament house door, and there staid the rising of the House, and with Sir G. Carteret and Mr. Coventry discoursed of some tarr that I have been endeavouring to buy, for the market begins apace to rise upon us, and I would be glad first to serve the King well, and next if I could I find myself now begin to cast how to get a penny myself. Home by coach with Alderman Backewell in his coach, whose opinion is that the Dutch will not give over the business without putting us to some trouble to set out a fleete; and then, if they see we go on well, will seek to salve up the matter. Upon the 'Change busy. Thence home to dinner, and thence to the office till my head was ready to burst with business, and so with my wife by coach, I sent her to my Lady Sandwich and myself to my cozen Roger Pepys's chamber, and there he did advise me about our Exchequer business, and also about my brother John, he is put by my father upon interceding for him, but I will not yet seem the least to pardon him nor can I in my heart. However, he and I did talk how to get him a mandamus for a fellowship, which I will endeavour. Thence to my Lady's, and in my way met Mr. Sanchy, of Cambridge, whom I have not met a great while. He seems a simple fellow, and tells me their master, Dr. Rainbow,[2] is newly made Bishop of Carlisle. To my Lady's, and she not being well did not see her, but straight home with my

[1] Judith Pepys, daughter of Richard Pepys, Lord Chief Justice of Ireland, and wife of J. Scott.

[2] Bishop Rainbow (see note *ante*, April 8th, 1663).

wife, and late to my office, concluding in the business of Wood's masts, which I have now done and I believe taken more pains in it than ever any Principall officer in this world ever did in any thing to no profit to this day. So, weary, sleepy, and hungry, home and to bed. This day the Houses attended the King, and delivered their votes to him upon the business of the Dutch; and he thanks them, and promises an answer in writing.

28th. Up and close at my office all the morning. To the 'Change busy at noon, and so home to dinner, and then in the afternoon at the office till night, and so late home quite tired with business, and without joy in myself otherwise than that I am by God's grace enabled to go through it and one day hope to have benefit by it. So home to supper and to bed.

29th. Up betimes, and with Sir W. Rider and Cutler to White Hall. Rider and I to St. James's, and there with Mr. Coventry did proceed strictly upon some fooleries of Mr. Povy's in my Lord Peterborough's accounts, which will touch him home, and I am glad of it, for he is the most troublesome impertinent man that ever I met with. Thence to the 'Change, and there, after some business, home to dinner, where Luellin and Mount came to me and dined, and after dinner my wife and I by coach to see my Lady Sandwich, where we find all the children and my Lord removed, and the house so melancholy that I thought my Lady had been dead, knowing that she was not well; but it seems she hath the meazles, and I fear the small pox, poor lady. It grieves me mightily; for it will be a sad houre to the family should she miscarry. Thence straight home and to the office, and in the evening comes Mr. Hill the merchant and another with him that sings well, and we sung some things, and good musique it seemed to me, only my mind too full of business to have much pleasure in it. But I will have more of it. They gone, and I having paid Mr. Moxon[1] for the work he has done for the office upon the

[1] Joseph Moxon, hydrographer to King Charles II., author of "Mechanick Dyalling," "Mechanick Exercises," etc. In 1668 his shop was on Ludgate Hill, at the sign of the Atlas. In 1693 he had removed to Warwick Lane. He was elected a Fellow of the Royal Society on November 30th, 1678, and admitted the same day.

King's globes, I to my office, where very late busy upon Captain Tayler's bills for his masts, which I think will never off my hand. Home to supper and to bed.

30th. Up and all the morning at the office. At noon to the 'Change, where, after business done, Sir W. Rider and Cutler took me to the Old James and there did give me a good dish of mackerell, the first I have seen this year, very good, and good discourse. After dinner we fell to business about their contract for tarr, in which and in another business of Sir W. Rider's, canvas, wherein I got him to contract with me, I held them to some terms against their wills, to the King's advantage, which I believe they will take notice of to my credit. Thence home, and by water by a gally down to Woolwich, and there a good while with Mr. Pett upon the new ship discoursing and learning of him. Thence with Mr. Deane to see Mr. Falconer, and there find him in a way to be well. So to the water (after much discourse with great content with Mr. Deane) and home late, and so to the office, wrote to my father among other things my continued displeasure against my brother John, so that I will give him nothing more out of my own purse, which will trouble the poor man, but however it is fit that I should take notice of my brother's ill carriage to me. Then home and till 12 at night about my month's accounts, wherein I have just kept within compass, this having been a spending month. So my people being all abed I put myself to bed very sleepy. All the newes now is what will become of the Dutch business, whether warr or peace. We all seem to desire it, as thinking ourselves to have advantages at present over them; for my part I dread it. The Parliament promises to assist the King with lives and fortunes, and he receives it with thanks and promises to demand satisfaction of the Dutch. My poor Lady Sandwich is fallen sick three days since of the meazles. My Lord Digby's business is hushed up, and nothing made of it; he is gone, and the discourse quite ended. Never more quiet in my family all the days of my life than now, there being only my wife and I and Besse and the little girl Susan, the best wenches to our content that we can ever expect.

May 1st (Lord's day). Lay long in bed. Went not to

church, but staid at home to examine my last night's accounts, which I find right, and that I am £908 creditor in the world, the same I was last month. Dined, and after dinner down by water with my wife and Besse with great pleasure as low as Greenwich and so back, playing as it were leisurely upon the water to Deptford, where I landed and sent my wife up higher to land below Half-way house. I to the King's yard and there spoke about several businesses with the officers, and so with Mr. Wayth consulting about canvas, to Half-way house where my wife was, and after eating there we broke and walked home before quite dark. So to supper, prayers, and to bed.

2nd. Lay pretty long in bed. So up and by water to St. James's, and there attended the Duke with Sir W. Batten and Sir J. Minnes, and having done our work with him walked to Westminster Hall, and after walking there and talking of business met Mr. Rawlinson and by coach to the 'Change, where I did some business, and home to dinner, and presently by coach to the King's Play-house to see "The Labyrinth,"[1] but, coming too soon, walked to my Lord's to hear how my Lady do, who is pretty well; at least past all fear. There by Captain Ferrers meeting with an opportunity of my Lord's coach, to carry us to the Parke anon, we directed it to come to the play-house door; and so we walked, my wife and I and Madamoiselle. I paid for her going in, and there saw "The Labyrinth," the poorest play, methinks, that ever I saw, there being nothing in it but the odd accidents that fell out, by a lady's being bred up in man's apparel, and a man in a woman's. Here was Mrs. Stewart, who is indeed very pretty, but not like my Lady Castlemayne, for all that. Thence in the coach to the Parke, where no pleasure; there being much dust, little company, and one of our horses almost spoiled by falling down, and getting his leg over the pole; but all mended presently, and after riding up and down, home. Set Madamoiselle at home, and we home, and to my office, whither comes Mr. Bland, and pays me the debt he acknowledged he owed me for my service in his business of the Tangier Merchant,[2] twenty pieces of new gold, a

[1] Or "The Fatal Embarrassment," taken from Corneille. — B.

[2] The "Tangiers Merchant" was a ship freighted by the Navy Office (see *ante*, January 21st, 1662–63).

pleasant sight. It cheered my heart; and he being gone, I home to supper, and shewed them my wife; and she, poor wretch, would fain have kept them to look on, without any other design but a simple love to them; but I thought it not convenient, and so took them into my own hand. So, after supper, to bed.

3rd. Up, and being ready, went by agreement to Mr. Bland's and there drank my morning draft in good chocollatte, and slabbering my band sent home for another, and so he and I by water to White Hall, and walked to St. James's, where met Creed and Vernatty, and by and by Sir W. Rider, and so to Mr. Coventry's chamber, and there upon my Lord Peterborough's accounts, where I endeavoured to shew the folly and punish it as much as I could of Mr. Povy; for, of all the men in the world, I never knew any man of his degree so great a coxcomb in such imployments. I see I have lost him for ever, but I value it not; for he is a coxcomb, and, I doubt, not over honest, by some things which I see; and yet, for all his folly, he hath the good lucke, now and then, to speak his follies in as good words, and with as good a show, as if it were reason, and to the purpose, which is really one of the wonders of my life. Thence walked to Westminster Hall; and there, in the Lord's House, did in a great crowd, from ten o'clock till almost three, hear the cause of Mr. Roberts,[1] my Lord

[1] In this case, Robartes *v.* Wynne, the plaintiff's bill was in the end dismissed with costs. The following is found among the State Papers: "Jan. 21, 1664. Order in the case of Rob. and Sara Robartes and their second child Chas. Bodville Robartes *v.* Sir Rich. Wynne, Bart., and others, relative to the will of John Bodville, who settled a large estate in cos. Carnarvon, Anglesea, and Merioneth, on his daughter Sara Robartes, and her son Charles, whom he educated, on which the Lord Privy Seal [Lord Robartes] settled £3,000 a year on Mr. and Mrs. Robartes; but Bodville was induced by the defendants, when his mind was impaired, to make a will in their favour. The order condemns the conduct of the defendants, but postpones for a year the reparation to be given to the plaintiffs, the case not being ripe for a final decree" ("Calendar of State Papers," Domestic, 1663–64, p. 450). On March 6th, 1664, Robartes petitioned the House of Lords. The House took the case up, and ordered the Lord Chancellor to make a speedy decree in the High Court of Chancery. Some protests followed this action (see Thorold Rogers's "Protests of the Lords," vol. i., p. 30). For account of the case, see "Reports in Chancery, Charles I. to 20 Charles II.," London, 1693, p. 236; also "Lords' Journals," vol. xi., pp. 606, 608, 609, 630, 631.

Privy Seal's son, against Win, who by false ways did get the father of Mr. Roberts's wife (Mr. Bodvill) to give him the estate and disinherit his daughter. The cause was managed for my Lord Privy Seal by Finch the Solicitor [General]; but I do really think that he is truly a man of as great eloquence as ever I heard, or ever hope to hear in all my life. Thence, after long staying to speak with my Lord Sandwich, at last he coming out to me and speaking with me about business of my Lord Peterborough, I by coach home to the office, where all the afternoon, only stept home to eat one bit and to the office again, having eaten nothing before to-day. My wife abroad with my aunt Wight and Norbury. I in the evening to my uncle Wight's, and not finding them come home, they being gone to the Parke and the Mulberry garden, I went to the 'Change, and there meeting with Mr. Hempson,[1] whom Sir W. Batten has lately turned out of his place, merely because of his coming to me when he came to town before he went to him, and there he told me many rogueries of Sir W. Batten, how he knows and is able to prove that Captain Cox of Chatham did give him £10 in gold to get him to certify for him at the King's coming in, and that Tom Newborne did make [the] poor men give him £3 to get Sir W. Batten to cause them to be entered in the yard, and that Sir W. Batten had oftentimes said: "by God, Tom, you shall get something and I will have some on't." His present clerk that is come in Norman's[2] room has given him something for his place; that they live high and (as Sir Francis Clerk's lady told his wife) do lack money as well as other people, and have bribes of a piece of sattin and cabinetts and other things from people that deal with him, and that hardly any body goes to see or hath anything done by Sir W. Batten but it comes with a bribe, and that this is publickly true that his wife was a whore, and that

[1] It appears that it was not only Sir William Batten who was dissatisfied with Hempson. The following is among the State Papers: "Jan. 21, 1664. Commissioner Peter Pett to Sam. Pepys. Has sent Capt. Taylor's bills. The price of Nath. London's timber is too great. Fears Mr. Hempson is lost to the service; it is not the king's interest to give such busy officers so great a liberty [of absence]" ("Calendar of State Papers," Domestic, 1663–64, p. 449).

[2] James Norman was clerk to Sir William Batten.

he had libells flung within his doors for a cuckold as soon as he was married; that he received £100 in money and in other things to the value of £50 more of Hempson, and that he intends to give him back but £50; that he hath abused the Chest and hath now some £1,000 by him of it. I met also upon the 'Change with Mr. Cutler, and he told me how for certain Lawson hath proclaimed warr again with Argier, though they had at his first coming given back the ships which they had taken, and all their men; though they refused afterwards to make him restitution for the goods which they had taken out of them. Thence to my uncle Wight's, and he not being at home I went with Mr. Norbury near hand to the Fleece, a mum house[1] in Leadenhall, and there drunk mum and by and by broke up, it being about 11 o'clock at night, and so leaving them also at home, went home myself and to bed.

4th. Up, and my new Taylor, Langford, comes and takes measure of me for a new black cloth suit and cloake, and I think he will prove a very carefull fellow and will please me well. Thence to attend my Lord Peterborough in bed and give him an account of yesterday's proceeding with Povy. I perceive I labour in a business will bring me little pleasure; but no matter, I shall do the King some service. To my Lord's lodgings, where during my Lady's sickness he is, there spoke with him about the same business. Back and by water to my cozen Scott's. There condoled with him the loss of my cozen, his wife, and talked about his matters, as atturney to my father, in his administering to my brother Tom. He tells me we are like to receive some shame about the business of his bastarde with Jack Noble; but no matter, so it cost us no money. Thence to the Coffee-house and to the 'Change a while. News uncertain how the Dutch proceed. Some say for, some against a war. The plague increases at Amsterdam. So home to dinner, and after dinner to my office, where very late, till my eyes (which begin to fail me nowadays by candle-light) begin to trouble me. Only in the afternoon comes Mr.

[1] There were several mum houses in various parts of London. One of Andrew Yarranton's wild schemes, at this time, was to bring the mum trade from Brunswick, and fix it on Stratford-on-Avon. See his "England's Improvement."

Peter Honiwood to see me and gives me 20*s.*, his and his friends' pence for my brother John, which, God forgive my pride, methinks I think myself too high to take of him; but it is an ungratefull pitch of pride in me, which God forgive. Home at night to supper and to bed.

5th. Up betimes to my office, busy, and so abroad to change some plate for my father to send to-day by the carrier to Brampton, but I observe and do fear it may be to my wrong that I change spoons of my uncle Robert's into new and set a P upon them that thereby I cannot claim them hereafter, as it was my brother Tom's practice. However, the matter of this is not great, and so I did it. So to the 'Change, and meeting Sir W. Warren, with him to a taverne, and there talked, as we used to do, of the evils the King suffers in our ordering of business in the Navy, as Sir W. Batten now forces us by his knavery. So home to dinner, and to the office, where all the afternoon, and thence betimes home, my eyes beginning every day to grow less and less able to bear with long reading or writing, though it be by daylight; which I never observed till now. So home to my wife, and after supper to bed.

6th. This morning up and to my office, where Sympson my joyner came to work upon altering my closet, which I alter by setting the door in another place, and several other things to my great content. Busy at it all day, only in the afternoon home, and there, my books at the office being out of order, wrote letters and other businesses. So at night with my head full of the business of my closet home to bed, and strange it is to think how building do fill my mind and put out all other things out of my thoughts.

7th. Betimes at my office with the joyners, and giving order for other things about it. By and by we sat all the morning. At noon to dinner, and after dinner comes Deane of Woolwich, and I spent, as I had appointed, all the afternoon with him about instructions which he gives me to understand the building of a ship, and I think I shall soon understand it. In the evening a little to my office to see how the work goes forward there, and then home and spent the evening also with Mr. Deane, and had a good supper, and then to bed, he lying at my house.

8th (Lord's day). This day my new tailor, Mr. Langord, brought me home a new black cloth suit and cloake ined with silk moyre, and he being gone, who pleases me ery well with his work and I hope will use me pretty well, hen Deane and I to my chamber, and there we repeated ny yesterday's lesson about ships all the morning, and I ope I shall soon understand it. At noon to dinner, and trange how in discourse he cries up chymistry from some alk he has had with an acquaintance of his, a chymist, vhen, poor man, he understands not one word of it. But discern very well that it is only his good nature, but in his of building ships he hath taken great pains, more than nost builders I believe have. After dinner he went away, nd my wife and I to church, and after church to Sir W. Pen, and there sat and talked with him, and the perfidious ogue seems, as he do always, mightily civil to us, though know he hates and envies us. So home to supper, rayers, and to bed.

9th. Up and to my office all the morning, and there saw everal things done in my work to my great content, and t noon home to dinner, and after dinner in Sir W. Pen's oach he set my wife and I down at the New Exchange, nd after buying some things we walked to my Lady Sandvich's, who, good lady, is now, thanks be to God! so well s to sit up, and sent to us, if we were not afeard, to come p to her. So we did; but she was mightily against my vife's coming so near her; though, poor wretch! she is s well as ever she was, as to the meazles, and nothing can see upon her face. There we sat talking with her above hree hours, till six o'clock, of several things with great leasure and so away, and home by coach, buying several hings for my wife in our way, and so after looking what ad been done in my office to-day, with good content home o supper and to bed. But, strange, how I cannot get any hing to take place in my mind while my work lasts at my ffice. This day my wife and I in our way to Paternoster Row to buy things called upon Mr. Hollyard to advise upon er drying up her issue in her leg, which inclines of itself o dry up, and he admits of it that it should be dried up.

10th. Up and at my office looking after my workmen all he morning, and after the office was done did the same at ight, and so home to supper and to bed.

11th. Up and all day, both forenoon and afternoon, a my office to see it finished by the joyners and washed and every thing in order, and indeed now my closet is ver convenient and pleasant for me. My uncle Wight cam to me to my office this afternoon to speak with me abou Mr. Maes's business again, and from me went to my house to see my wife, and strange to think that my wife should by and by send for me after he was gone to tell me that h should begin discourse of her want of children and hi also, and how he thought it would be best for him and he to have one between them, and he would give her £500 either in money or jewells beforehand, and make th child his heir. He commended her body, and discoursed that for all he knew the thing was lawful. She says she did give him a very warm answer, such as he did not ex cuse himself by saying that he said this in jest, but told he that since he saw what her mind was he would say no more to her of it, and desired her to make no words of it. I seemed he did say all this in a kind of counterfeit laugh but by all words that passed, which I cannot now so wel set down, it is plain to me that he was in good earnest, and that I fear all his kindness is but only his lust to her What to think of it of a sudden I know not, but I think no to take notice yet of it to him till I have thought better of it So with my mind and head a little troubled I received a letter from Mr. Coventry about a mast for the Duke's yacht,[1] which with other business makes me resolve to go betimes to Woolwich to-morrow. So to supper and to bed.

12th. Up by 4 o'clock and by water to Woolwich, where did some business and walked to Greenwich, good dis course with Mr. Deane best part of the way; there met by appointment Commissioner Pett, and with him to Dept ford, where did also some business, and so home to my office, and at noon Mrs. Hunt and her cozen's child and mayd came and dined with me. My wife sick . . . . in bed. I was troubled with it, but, however, could not help it, but attended them till after dinner, and then to the office and there sat all the afternoon, and by a letter to me

[1] The Duke of York's yacht built by Christopher Pett was named the "Anne."

ıis afternoon from Mr. Coventry I saw the first appear-
nce of a warr with Holland. So home, and betimes to
ed because of rising to-morrow.

13th. Up before three o'clock, and a little after upon
ıe water, it being very light as at noon, and a bright sun-
ising; but by and by a rainbow appeared, the first that
ver in a morning I saw, and then it fell a-raining a little,
ut held up again, and I to Woolwich, where before all the
ıen came to work I with Mr. Deane spent two hours upon
ıe new ship, informing myself in the names and natures of
ıany parts of her to my great content, and so back again,
ithout doing any thing else, and after shifting myself
way to Westminster, looking after Mr. Maes's business
nd others. In the Painted Chamber I heard a fine con-
erence between some of the two Houses upon the Bill for
onventicles. The Lords would be freed from having
heir houses searched by any but the Lord Lieutenant of
he County; and upon being found guilty, to be tried only
y their peers; and thirdly, would have it added, that
hereas the Bill says, "That that, among other things, shall
e a conventicle wherein any such meeting is found doing
ny thing contrary to the Liturgy of the Church of Eng-
and," they would have it added, "or practice." The
ommons to the Lords said, that they knew not what might
ereafter be found out which might be called the practice
f the Church of England; for there are many things may
e said to be the practice of the Church, which were never
stablished by any law, either common, statute, or canon;
s singing of psalms, binding up prayers at the end of the
ible, and praying extempore before and after sermon:
nd though these are things indifferent, yet things for aught
hey at present know may be started, which may be said to
e the practice of the Church which would not be fit to
llow. For the Lord's priviledges, Mr. Waller told them
ow tender their predecessors had been of the priviledges
f the Lords; but, however, where the peace of the king-
lom stands in competition with them, they apprehend
hose priviledges must give place. He told them that he
hought, if they should owne all to be the priviledges of
he Lords which might be demanded, they should be led
ike the man (who granted leave to his neighbour to pull

off his horse's tail, meaning that he could not do it at once that hair by hair had his horse's tail pulled off indeed: s the Commons, by granting one thing after another, migh be so served by the Lords. Mr. Vaughan,[1] whom I coul not to my grief perfectly hear, did say, if that they shoul be obliged in this manner to exempt the Lords from ever thing, it would in time come to pass that whatever (be [it never so great) should be voted by the Commons as a thin penall for a commoner, the contrary should be thought priviledge to the Lords: that also in this business, th work of a conventicle being but the work of an hour, th cause of a search would be over before a Lord Lieutenant who may be many miles off, can be sent for; and that a this dispute is but about £100; for it is said in the Act that it shall be banishment or payment of £100. I there upon heard the Duke of Lenox say, that there might b Lords who could not always be ready to lose £100, c some such thing. They broke up without coming to an end in it. There was also in the Commons' House a grea quarrel about Mr. Prin,[2] and it was believed that he shoul have been sent to the Towre, for adding something to Bill (after it was ordered to be engrossed) of his own hea —a Bill for measures for wine and other things of tha sort, and a Bill of his owne bringing in; but it appeare he could not mean any hurt in it. But, however, th King was fain to write in his behalf, and all was passe over. But it is worth my remembrance, that I saw ol Ryly the Herald,[3] and his son; and spoke to his son, wh

[1] See *ante*, March 28th, 1664.

[2] "May 13, 1664. Mr. Prynne having taken the liberty to alter th draught of a Bill relating to Public-houses, having urged in his excus 'that he did not do it out of any ill intent, but to rectify some matte mistaken in it, and to make the Bill agree with the sense of the house; the house ordered him to withdraw, and after debate being again calle in, the Speaker acquainted him, 'That the house was very sensible this great mistake in so ancient and knowing a member as he was, t break so material and essential an order of the house, as to alte amend, or interline a bill after commitment, but the house had con sidered of his answer and submission, and were content at this time, i respect thereof, to remit the offence'" (Cobbett's "Parliamentary His tory," vol. iv., col. 293).

[3] At the Restoration William Ryley had been deprived of all his post including the office of Clerk of the Tower Records, which was given t

told me in very bad words concerning Mr. Prin, that the King had given him an office of keeping the Records; but that he never comes thither, nor had been there these six months: so that I perceive they expect to get his imployment from him. Thus every body is liable to be envied and supplanted. At noon over to the Leg, where Sir G. Ascue, Sir Robt. Parkhurst and Sir W. Pen dined. A good dinner and merry. Thence to White Hall walking up and down a great while, but the Council not meeting soon enough I went homeward, calling upon my cozen Roger Pepys, with whom I talked and heard so much from him of his desire that I would see my brother's debts paid, and things still of that nature tending to my parting with what I get with pain to serve others' expenses that I was cruelly vexed. Thence to Sir R. Bernard, and there heard something of Pigott's delay of paying our money, that that also vexed me mightily. So home and there met with a letter from my cozen Scott, which tells me that he is resolved to meddle no more with our business, of administering for my father, which altogether makes me almost distracted to think of the trouble that I am like to meet with by other folks' business more than ever I hope to have by my owne. So with great trouble of mind to bed.

14th. Up, full of pain, I believe by cold got yesterday. So to the office, where we sat, and after office home to dinner, being in extraordinary pain. After dinner my pain increasing I was forced to go to bed, and by and by my pain rose to be as great for an hour or two as ever I remember it was in any fit of the stone, both in the lower part of my belly and in my back also. No wind could I break. I took a glyster, but it brought away but a little, and my height of pain followed it. At last after two hours lying thus in most extraordinary anguish, crying and roar-

Prynne. Ryley was originally made Lancaster Herald by Charles I., but he sided with the Parliament, and devoted himself to Oliver Cromwell. He was fortunate in being afterwards restored to the post of Lancaster Herald, which he held till his death in 1667, though he failed in getting back Prynne's appointment. By his wife Elizabeth, daughter of Sir Anthony Chester, Bart., of Chichley, Bucks, Ryley had a numerous issue. Perhaps the son here mentioned was William Ryley, described by Prynne as of the Inner Temple in 1662 (see note to December 7th, 1661).—B.

ing, I know not what, whether it was my great sweatin that may do it, but upon getting by chance, among m other tumblings, upon my knees, in bed, my pain bega to grow less and less, till in an hour after I was in ver little pain, but could break no wind, nor make any water and so continued, and slept well all night.

15th (Lord's day). Rose, and as I had intended withou reference to this pain, took physique, and it wrought wel with me, my wife lying from me to-night, the first time sh did in the same house ever since we were married, I thin (unless while my father was in town, that he lay with me) She took physique also to-day, and both of our physique wrought well, so we passed our time to-day, our physiqu having done working, with some pleasure talking, but was not well, for I could make no water yet, but a drop o two with great pain, nor break any wind. In the evenin came Mr. Vernatty to see me and discourse about my Lor Peterborough's business, and also my uncle Wight an Norbury, but I took no notice nor showed any differen countenance to my uncle Wight, or he to me, for all tha he carried himself so basely to my wife the last week, bu will take time to make my use of it. So, being exceedin hot, to bed, and slept well.

16th. Forced to rise because of going to the Duke t St. James's, where we did our usual business, and thence b invitation to Mr. Pierce's the chyrurgeon, where I saw hi wife, whom I had not seen in many months before. Sh holds her complexion still, but in everything else, even i this her new house and the best rooms in it, and her close which her husband with some vainglory took me to sho me, she continues the veriest slattern that ever I knew i my life. By and by we to see an experiment of killing dogg by letting opium into his hind leg.[1] He and Dr Clerke did fail mightily in hitting the vein, and in effec did not do the business after many trials; but with the littl

[1] Pepys does not say whether this experiment was in any way con nected with the work of the Royal Society. About this time the mi utes contain the following reference: "May 4, 1664. It was ordere that Dr. Croune, Dr. Balle, and Mr. Hooke take care at the next mee ing to cut off some skin of a dog; and that the operator provide a do for that purpose." Several experiments at subsequent meetings ar reported (Birch's "History of the Royal Society," vol. i., p. 422).

ıey got in, the dogg did presently fall asleep, and so lay .ll we cut him up, and a little dogg also, which they put it own his throate; he also staggered first, and then fell sleep, and so continued. Whether he recovered or no, fter I was gone, I know not, but it is a strange and sudden ffect. Thence walked to Westminster Hall, where the ̇ing was expected to come to prorogue the House, but it eems, afterwards I hear, he did not come. I promised to o again to Mr. Pierce's, but my pain grew so great, besides bruise I got to-day in my right testicle, which now vexes ıe as much as the other, that I was mighty melancholy, and o by coach home and there took another glyster, but find ittle good by it, but by sitting still my pain of my bruise vent away, and so after supper to bed, my wife and I aving talked and concluded upon sending my father an ffer of having Pall come to us to be with us for her preferment, if by any means I can get her a husband here,[1] which, hough it be some trouble to us, yet it will be better than o have her stay there till nobody will have her and then be ung upon my hands.

17th. Slept well all night and lay long, then rose and vrote my letter to my father about Pall, as we had resolved ast night. So to dinner and then to the office, finding nyself better than I was, and making a little water, but not et breaking any great store of wind, which I wonder at, or I cannot be well till I do do it. After office home and o supper and with good ease to bed, and endeavoured to ie my hands that I might not lay them out of bed, by vhich I believe I have got cold, but I could not endure it.

18th. Up and within all the morning, being willing to eep as much as I could within doors, but receiving a very vakening letter from Mr. Coventry about fitting of ships, vhich speaks something like to be done, I went forth to the office, there to take order in things, and after dinner to Vhite Hall to a Committee of Tangier, but did little. So ome again and to Sir W. Pen, who, among other things of aaste in this new order for ships, is ordered to be gone presently to Portsmouth to look after the work there. I staid to

[1] Pepys tried hard to get a husband for his sister Paulina, but for a ime without success. Eventually she married John Jackson of Brampon.

discourse with him, and so home to supper, where upon fine couple of pigeons, a good supper; and here I met pretty cabinet sent me by Mr. Shales,[1] which I give m wife, the first of that sort of goods I ever had yet, and ver conveniently it comes for her closett. I staid up late finc ing out the private boxes, but could not do some of them and so to bed, afraid that I have been too bold to-day i venturing in the cold. This day I begun to drink butte milke and whey, and I hope to find great good by it.

19th. Up, and it being very rayny weather, which make it cooler than it was, by coach to Charing Cross with Si W. Pen, who is going to Portsmouth this day, and left hir going to St. James's to take leave of the Duke, and I t White Hall to a Committee of Tangier; where God forgiv how our Report of my Lord Peterborough's accounts wa read over and agreed to by the Lords, without one of ther understanding it! And had it been what it would, it ha gone: and, besides, not one thing touching the King' profit in it minded or hit upon. Thence by coach hom again, and all the morning at the office, sat, and all th afternoon till 9 at night, being fallen again to business, an I hope my health will give me leave to follow it. So hom to supper and to bed, finding myself pretty well. A prett good stool, which I impute to my whey to-day, and brok wind also.

20th. Up and to my office, whither by and by comes Mı Cholmely, and staying till the rest of the company come h told me how Mr. Edward Montagu is turned out of th Court, not [to] return again. His fault, I perceive, wa his pride, and most of all his affecting to seem great wit the Queene:[2] and it seems indeed had more of her ear

[1] Captain John Shales.

[2] See December 23rd, 1662. Boyer, in his "Life of Queen Anne, says that he was dismissed for offending her majesty by squeezing he hand. He is mentioned in the "State Poems":

"Montagu, by court disaster,
Dwindled into the wooden horse's master."
Advice to a Painter, part i.

It is said that the Duke of York obtained for Edward Montagu th appointment of Master of the Horse to the Queen (see "Grammon Memoirs").

than any body else, and would be with her talking alone two or three hours together; insomuch that the Lords about the King, when he would be jesting with them about their wives, would tell the King that he must have a care of his wife too, for she hath now the gallant: and they say the King himself did once ask Montagu how his mistress (meaning the Queene) did. He grew so proud, and despised every body, besides suffering nobody, he or she, to get or do any thing about the Queene, that they all laboured to do him a good turn. They also say that he did give some affront to the Duke of Monmouth, which the King himself did speak to him of. But strange it is that this man should, from the greatest negligence in the world, come to be the miracle of attendance, so as to take all offices from every body, either men or women, about the Queene. Insomuch that he was observed as a miracle, but that which is the worst, that which in a wise manner performed [would] turn to his greatest advantage, was by being so observed employed to his greatest wrong, the world concluding that there must be something more than ordinary to cause him to do this. So he is gone, nobody pitying but laughing at him; and he pretends only that he is gone to his father, that is sick in the country. By and by comes Povy, Creed, and Vernatty, and so to their accounts, wherein more trouble and vexation with Povy. That being done, I sent them going and myself fell to business till dinner. So home to dinner very pleasant. In the afternoon to my office, where busy again, and by and by came a letter from my father so full of trouble for discontents there between my mother and servants, and such troubles to my father from hence from Cave that hath my brother's bastard that I know not what in the world to do, but with great trouble, it growing night, spent some time walking, and putting care as much as I could out of my head, with my wife in the garden, and so home to supper and to bed.

21st. Up, called by Mr. Cholmely, and walked with him in the garden till others came to another Committee of Tangier, as we did meet as we did use to do, to see more of Povy's folly, and so broke up, and at the office sat all the morning, Mr. Coventry with us, and very hot we are getting out some ships. At noon to the 'Change, and there did some business, and thence home to dinner, and so abroad with my wife by coach to the New Exchange, and there laid out almost 40*s*. upon her, and so called to see my Lady Sandwich, whom we found in her dining-room, which joyed us mightily; but she looks very thin, poor woman, being mightily broke. She told us that Mr. Montagu is to return to Court, as she hears, which I wonder at, and do hardly believe. So home and to my office, where late, and so home to supper and to bed.

22nd (Lord's day). Up and by water to White Hall to my Lord's lodgings, and with him walked to White Hall without any great discourse, nor do I find that he do mind business at all. Here the Duke of Yorke called me to him, to ask me whether I did intend to go with him to Chatham or no. I told him if he commanded, but I did believe there would be business here for me, and so he told me then it would be better to stay, which I suppose he will take better than if I had been forward to go. Thence, after staying and seeing the throng of people to attend the King to Chappell (but, Lord! what a company of sad, idle people they are) I walked to St. James's with Colonell Remes,[1] where staid a good while and then walked to White Hall with Mr. Coventry, talking about business. So meeting Creed, took him with me home and to dinner, a good dinner, and thence by water to Woolwich, where mighty kindly received by Mrs. Falconer and her husband, who is now pretty well again, this being the first time I ever carried my wife thither. I walked to the Docke, where I met Mrs. Ackworth alone at home, and God forgive me! what thoughts I had, but I had not the courage to stay, but went to Mr. Pett's and walked up and down the yard with him and Deane talking about the dispatch of the ships now in haste, and by and by Creed and my wife and a friend of Mr. Falconer's came with the boat and called me, and so by water to Deptford, where I landed, and after talking with others walked to Half-way house with Mr. Wayth talking about the business of his supplying us with canvas,

[1] Colonel Bullen Reymes, M.P. for Weymouth, is referred to in a communication of Rich. Yardley, Mayor of Weymouth, January 2nd, 1664 ("Calendar of State Papers," Domestic, 1663–64, p. 427). He died in 1673.

and he told me in discourse several instances of Sir W. Batten's cheats. So to Half-way house, whither my wife and them were gone before, and after drinking there we walked, and by water home, sending Creed and the other with the boat home. Then wrote a letter to Mr. Coventry, and so a good supper of pease, the first I eat this year, and so to bed.

23rd. Up and to the office, where Sir J. Minnes, Sir W. Batten, and myself met and did business, we being in a mighty hurry. The King is gone down with the Duke and a great crew this morning by break of day to Chatham. Towards noon I and my wife by water to Woolwich, leaving my wife at Mr. Falconer's, and Mr. Hater and I with some officers of the yard on board to see several ships how ready they are. Then to Mr. Falconer's to a good dinner, having myself carried them a vessel of sturgeon and a Lamprey pie, and then to the Yarde again, and among other things did at Mr. Ackworth's obtain a demonstration of his being a knave; but I did not discover it, till it be a little more seasonable. So back to the Ropeyard and took my wife and Mr. Hater back, it raining mighty hard of a sudden, but we with the tilt[1] kept ourselves dry. So to Deptford, did some business there; but, Lord! to see how in both places the King's business, if ever it should come to a warr, is likely to be done, there not being a man that looks or speaks like a man that will take pains, or use any forecast to serve the King, at which I am heartily troubled. So home, it raining terribly, but we still dry, and at the office late discoursing with Sir J. Minnes and Sir W. Batten, who like a couple of sots receive all I say but to little purpose. So late home to supper and to bed.

24th. Up and to the office, where Sir J. Minnes and I sat all the morning, and after dinner thither again, and all the afternoon hard at the office till night, and so tired home to supper and to bed. This day I heard that my uncle Fenner is dead, which makes me a little sad, to see with what speed a great many of my friends are gone, and more, I fear, for my father's sake, are going.

[1] Tilt (A.S. teld) represents a tent or awning. It was used for a cloth covering for a cart or waggon, or for a canopy or awning over a portion of a boat.

25th. Took physique betimes and to sleep, then up, in working all the morning. At noon dined, and in the afternoon in my chamber spending two or three hours to look over some unpleasant letters and things of trouble to answer my father in, about Tom's business and others, that vexed me, but I did go through it and by that means eased my mind very much. This afternoon also came Tom and Charles Pepys[1] by my sending for, and received of me £40 in part towards their £70 legacy of my uncle's. Spent the evening talking with my wife, and so to bed.

26th. Up to the office, where we sat, and I had some high words with Sir W. Batten about canvas, wherein I opposed him and all his experience, about seams in the middle, and the profit of having many breadths and narrow, which I opposed to good purpose, to the rejecting of the whole business. At noon home to dinner, and thence took my wife by coach, and she to my Lady Sandwich to see her. I to Tom Trice, to discourse about my father's giving over his administration to my brother, and thence to Sir R. Bernard, and there received £19 in money, and took up my father's bond of £21, that is £40, in part of Piggot's £209 due to us, which £40 he pays for 7 roods of meadow in Portholme. Thence to my wife, and carried her to the Old Bayly, and there we were led to the Quest House,[2] by the church, where all the kindred were by themselves at the buriall of my uncle Fenner; but, Lord! what a pitiful rout of people there was of them, but very good service and great company the whole was. And so anon to church, and a good sermon, and so home, having for ease put my £19 into W. Joyce's hand, where I left it. So to supper and to bed, being in a little pain from some cold got last night lying without anything upon my feet.

[1] Sons of Thomas Pepys, elder brother of Samuel's father. Charles Pepys was subsequently master joiner at Chatham Dockyard.

[2] The parish church of St. Sepulchre's was known as St. Sepulchre's in the Bailey. The Quest House was rebuilt by Dr. William Bell, vicar from 1662 to 1683. Strype writes of this: "A new house, free to Dr. Bell's successors, with a yard thereto. The use of a parlour, kitchen, and washhouse under the Quest-house that belonged to the parish for the said Bell's time, he being at the trouble to build it, and brought £200 towards it; the use thereof reserved to the parish on public occasions of quest or burials."

27th. Up, not without some pain by cold, which makes me mighty melancholy, to think of the ill state of my health. To the office, where busy till my brains ready to drop with variety of business, and vexed for all that to see the service like to suffer by other people's neglect. Vexed also at a letter from my father with two troublesome ones enclosed from Cave and Noble, so that I know not what to do therein. At home to dinner at noon. But to comfort my heart, Captain Taylor this day brought me £20 he promised me for my assistance to him about his masts. After dinner to the office again, and thence with Mr. Wayth to St. Catherine's to see some variety of canvas's, which indeed was worth my seeing, but only I was in some pain, and so took not the delight I should otherwise have done. So home to the office, and there busy till late at night, and so home to supper and to bed. This morning my taylor brought me a very tall mayde to be my cook-mayde; she asked £5, but my wife offered her but £3 10*s.* — whether she will take it or no I know not till to-morrow, but I am afeard she will be over high for us, she having last been a chamber mayde, and holds up her head, as my little girle Su observed.

28th. Up pretty well as to pain and wind, and to the office, where we sat close and did much business. At noon I to the 'Change, and thence to Mr. Cutler's, where I heard Sir W. Rider was, where I found them at dinner and dined with them, he having yesterday and to-day a fit of a pain like the gout, the first time he ever had it. A good dinner. Good discourse, Sir W. Rider especially much fearing the issue of a Dutch warr, wherein I very highly commend him. Thence home, and at the office a while, and then with Mr. Deane to a second lesson upon my Shipwrightry, wherein I go on with great pleasure. He being gone I to the office late, and so home to supper and to bed. But, Lord! to see how my very going to the 'Change, and being without my gowne, presently brought me wind and pain, till I came home and was well again; but I am come to such a pass that I shall not know what to do with myself, but I am apt to think that it is only my legs that I take cold in from my having so long worn a gowne constantly.

29th (Whitsunday. King's Birth and Restauration day). Up, and having received a letter last night desiring it from

Mr. Coventry, I walked to St. James's, and there he and I did long discourse together of the business of the office, and the warr with the Dutch; and he seemed to argue mightily with the little reason that there is for all this. For first, as to the wrong we pretend they have done us: that of the East Indys, for their not delivering of Poleron,[1] it is not yet known whether they have failed or no; that of their hindering the Leopard cannot amount to above £3,000 if true; that of the Guinny Company, all they had done us did not amount to above £200 or £300 he told me truly; and that now, from what Holmes, without any commission, hath done in taking an island and two forts, hath set us much in debt to them; and he believes that Holmes will have been so puffed up with this, that he by this time hath been enforced with more strength than he had then, hath, I say, done a great deale more wrong to them. He do, as to the effect of the warr, tell me clearly that it is not any skill of the Dutch that can hinder our trade if we will, we having so many advantages over them, of winds, good ports, and men; but it is our pride, and the laziness of the merchant. He seems to think that there may be some negotiation which may hinder a warr this year, but that he speaks doubtfully as unwilling I perceive to be thought to discourse any such thing. The main thing he desired to speake with me about was, to know whether I do understand my Lord Sandwich's intentions as to going to sea with this fleete; saying, that the Duke, if he desires it, is most willing to it; but thinking that twelve ships is not a fleete fit for my Lord to be troubled to go out with, he is not willing to offer it to him till he hath some intimations of his mind to go, or not. He spoke this with very great respect as to my Lord, though methinks it is strange they should not

[1] One of the Banda Islands, which had acknowledged James I. as its sovereign, but was afterwards forcibly seized by the Dutch. A series of letters from Sir George Downing to Lord Chancellor Clarendon (written at this time) is printed in Lister's "Life of Clarendon," vol. iii. These letters contain references to the "Leopard," and on May 13th we read the plea of the United Provinces: "We have taken nothing from the king nor his subjects, nor hath he taken anything from us, nor do demand anything of us, and why then should we ingage ourselves, and spend our monies, to maintain the insolvencies of the East India Companies?" (p. 322).

understand one another better at this time than to need another's mediation. Thence walked over the Parke to White Hall, Mr. Povy with me, and was taken in a very great showre in the middle of the Parke that we were very wet. So up into the house and with him to the King's closett, whither by and by the King came, my Lord Sandwich carrying the sword. A Bishopp preached, but he speaking too low for me to hear behind the King's closett, I went forth and walked and discoursed with Colonell Reames, who seems a very willing man to be informed in his business of canvas, which he is undertaking to strike in with us to serve the Navy. By and by my Lord Sandwich came forth, and called me to him: and we fell into discourse a great while about his business, wherein he seems to be very open with me, and to receive my opinion as he used to do; and I hope I shall become necessary to him again. He desired me to think of the fitness, or not, for him to offer himself to go to sea; and to give him my thoughts in a day or two. Thence after sermon among the ladies on the Queene's side; where I saw Mrs. Stewart, very fine and pretty, but far beneath my Lady Castlemayne. Thence with Mr. Povy[1] home to dinner; where extraordinary cheer. And after dinner up and down to see his house. And in a word, methinks, for his perspective upon his wall in his garden, and the springs rising up with the perspective in the little closett; his room floored above with woods of several colours, like but above the best cabinet-work I ever saw; his grotto and vault, with his bottles of wine, and a well therein to keep them cool; his furniture of all sorts; his bath at the top of his house, good pictures, and his manner of eating and drinking; do surpass all that ever I did see of one man in all my life. Thence walked home and found my uncle Wight and Mr. Rawlinson, who supped with me. They being gone, I to bed, being in some pain from my being so much abroad to-day, which is a most strange thing that in such warm weather the least ayre should get cold and wind in me. I confess it makes me mighty sad and out of all content in the world.

[1] Evelyn refers to Mr. Povy's house in Lincoln's Inn Fields, and particularly mentions the prospective painted by Streeter, as well as the ranging of the wine bottles in the cellar (July 1st, 1664).

30th. Lay long, the bells ringing, it being holiday, and then up and all the day long in my study at home studying of shipmaking with great content till the evening, and then came Mr. Howe and sat and then supped with me. He is a little conceited, but will make a discreet man. He being gone, a little to my office, and then home to bed, being in much pain from yesterday's being abroad, which is a consideration of mighty sorrow to me.

31st. Up, and called upon Mr. Hollyard, with whom I advised and shall fall upon some course of doing something for my disease of the wind, which grows upon me every day more and more. Thence to my Lord Sandwich's, and while he was dressing I below discoursed with Captain Cooke, and I think if I do find it fit to keep a boy at all I had as good be supplied from him with one as any body. By and by up to my Lord, and to discourse about his going to sea, and the message I had from Mr. Coventry to him. He wonders, as he well may, that this course should be taken, and he every day with the Duke, who, nevertheless, seems most friendly to him, who hath not yet spoke one word to my Lord of his desire to have him go to sea. My Lord do tell me clearly that were it not that he, as all other men that were of the Parliament side, are obnoxious to reproach, and so is forced to bear what otherwise he would not, he would never suffer every thing to be done in the Navy, and he never be consulted; and it seems, in the naming of all these commanders for this fleete, he hath never been asked one question. But we concluded it wholly inconsistent with his honour not to go with this fleete, nor with the reputation which the world hath of his interest at Court; and so he did give me commission to tell Mr. Coventry that he is most willing to receive any commands from the Duke in this fleete, were it less than it is, and that particularly in this service. With this message I parted, and by coach to the office, where I found Mr. Coventry, and told him this. Methinks, I confess, he did not seem so pleased with it as I expected, or at least could have wished, and asked me whether I had told my Lord that the Duke do not expect his going, which I told him I had. But now whether he means really that the Duke, as he told me the other day, do think the Fleete too small for him to take or that he would not have him go, I swear I cannot tell. But methinks other ways might have been used to put him by without going in this manner about it, and so I hope it is out of kindness indeed. Dined at home, and so to the office, where a great while alone in my office, nobody near, with Bagwell's wife of Deptford, but the woman seems so modest that I durst not offer any courtship to her, though I had it in my mind when I brought her in to me. But I am resolved to do her husband a courtesy, for I think he is a man that deserves very well. So abroad with my wife by coach to St. James's, to one Lady Poultny's,[1] where I found my Lord, I doubt, at some vain pleasure or other. I did give him a short account of what I had done with Mr. Coventry, and so left him, and to my wife again in the coach, and with her to the Parke, but the Queene being gone by the Parke to Kensington, we staid not but straight home and to supper (the first time I have done so this summer), and so to my office doing business, and then to my monthly accounts, where to my great comfort I find myself better than I was still the last month, and now come to £930. I was told to-day, that upon Sunday night last, being the King's birth-day, the King was at my Lady Castlemayne's lodgings (over the hither-gate[2] at Lambert's lodgings) dancing with fiddlers all night almost; and all the world coming by taking notice of it, which I am sorry to hear. The discourse of the town is only whether a warr with Holland or no, and we are preparing for it all we can, which is but little. Myself subject more than ordinary to pain by winde, which makes me very sad, together with the trouble which at present lies upon me in my father's behalf, rising from the death of my brother, which are many and great. Would to God they were over!

June 1st. Up, having lain long, going to bed very late after the ending of my accounts. Being up Mr. Hollyard

[1] Grace, youngest daughter of Sir John Corbet of Stoke, Salop, who married Sir William Poulteney or Pulteney, of Mesterton, co. Leicester, who was knighted at Whitehall, June 4th, 1660. He was grandfather to William, first Earl of Bath.

[2] This was the gatehouse designed by Holbein, which had formerly been occupied as the residence of General Lambert. It was now appropriated to Lady Castlemaine.

came to me and to my great sorrow, after his great assuring me that I could not possibly have the stone again, he tells me that he do verily fear that I have it again, and has brought me something to dissolve it, which do make me very much troubled, and pray to God to ease me. He gone, I down by water to Woolwich and Deptford to look after the dispatch of the ships, all the way reading Mr. Spencer's Book of Prodigys,[1] which is most ingeniously writ, both for matter and style. Home at noon, and my little girl got me my dinner, and I presently out by water and landed at Somerset stairs, and thence through Covent Garden, where I met with Mr. Southwell[2] (Sir W. Pen's friend), who tells me the very sad newes of my Lord Tiviott's and nineteen more commission officers being killed at Tangier by the Moores,[3] by an ambush of the enemy upon them, while they were surveying their lines; which is very sad, and, he says, afflicts the King much. Thence to W. Joyce's, where by appointment I met my wife (but neither of them at home), and she and I to the King's house, and saw "The Silent Woman;" but methought not so well done or so good a play as I formerly thought it to be, or else I am now-a-days out of humour. Before the play was done, it fell such a storm of hayle, that we in the middle of the pit were fain to rise;[4] and all the house in a disorder, and so

[1] John Spencer, D.D., who died in 1695, was also the author of a celebrated work, "De Legibus Hebræorum." His "Discourse concerning Prodigies" first appeared in 1663; the second edition, of 1665, contains likewise a "Discourse concerning Vulgar Prophecies." — B.

[2] Robert Southwell (born at Kinsale, Ireland, in 1635) was educated at Queen's College, Oxford, and afterwards entered at Lincoln's Inn. On September 27th, 1664, he was sworn one of the clerks of the Privy Council, and was knighted November 20th, 1665. He was employed on several diplomatic missions, and retired from public business in 1681. William III. appointed him principal Secretary of State for Ireland; and on December 1st, 1690, he was elected President of the Royal Society, an office which he held for five years. He died at his seat, King's Weston, Gloucestershire, in 1702. There is a portrait of Southwell by Kneller at the Royal Society.

[3] Particulars of the loss at Tangiers is given in "The Intelligencer," June 6th, 1664.

[4] The stage was covered in by a tiled roof, but the pit was open to the sky. "The pit lay open to the weather for sake of light, but was subsequently covered in with a glazed cupola, which, however, only imperfectly protected the audience, so that in stormy weather the house

my wife and I out and got into a little alehouse, and staid there an hour after the play was done before we could get a coach, which at last we did (and by chance took up Joyce Norton and Mrs. Bowles and set them at home), and so home ourselves, and I, after a little to my office, so home to supper and to bed.

2nd. Up and to the office, where we sat all the morning, and then to the 'Change, where after some stay by coach with Sir J. Minnes and Mr. Coventry to St. James's, and there dined with Mr. Coventry very finely, and so over the Parke to White Hall to a Committee of Tangier about providing provisions, money, and men for Tangier. At it all the afternoon, but it is strange to see how poorly and brokenly things are done of the greatest consequence, and how soon the memory of this great man is gone, or, at least, out of mind by the thoughts of who goes next, which is not yet knowne. My Lord of Oxford, Muskerry, and several others are discoursed of. It seems my Lord Tiviott's design was to go a mile and half out of the towne, to cut down a wood in which the enemy did use to lie in ambush. He had sent several spyes; but all brought word that the way was clear, and so might be for any body's discovery of an enemy before you are upon them. There they were all snapt, he and all his officers, and about 200 men, as they say; there being left now in the garrison but four captains. This happened the 3d of May last, being not before that day twelvemonth of his entering into his government there: but at his going out in the morning he said to some of his officers, "Gentlemen, let us look to ourselves, for it was this day three years that so many brave Englishmen were knocked on the head by the Moores, when Fines[1] made his sally out." Here till almost night, and then home with Sir J. Minnes by coach, and so to my office a while, and home to supper and bed, being now in constant pain in my back, but whether it be only wind or what it is the Lord knows, but I fear the worst.

3rd. Up, still in a constant pain in my back, which

was thrown into disorder, and the people in the pit were fain to rise" (Cunningham's "Story of Nell Gwyn," ed. 1893, p. 13).

[1] Major Fiennes, whose regiment formed part of the garrison of Tangiers.

much afflicts me with fear of the consequence of it. All the morning at the office, we sat at the office extraordinary upon the business of our stores, but, Lord! what a pitiful account the Surveyor makes of it grieves my heart. This morning before I came out I made a bargain with Captain Taylor for a ship for the Commissioners for Tangier, wherein I hope to get £40 or £50. To the 'Change, and thence home and dined, and then by coach to White Hall, sending my wife to Mrs. Hunt's. At the Committee for Tangier all the afternoon, where a sad consideration to see things of so great weight managed in so confused a manner as it is, so as I would not have the buying of an acre of land bought by — the Duke of York and Mr. Coventry, for aught I see, being the only two that do anything like men; Prince Rupert do nothing but swear and laugh a little, with an oathe or two, and that's all he do. Thence called my wife and home, and I late at my office, and so home to supper and to bed, pleased at my hopes of gains by to-day's work, but very sad to think of the state of my health.

4th. Up and to St. James's by coach, after a good deal of talk before I went forth with J. Noble, who tells me that he will secure us against Cave, that though he knows, and can prove it, yet nobody else can prove it, to be Tom's child; that the bond was made by one Hudson, a scrivener, next to the Fountaine taverne, in the Old Bayly; that the children were born, and christened, and entered in the parish-book of St. Sepulchre's, by the name of Anne and Elizabeth Taylor; and he will give us security against Cave if we pay him the money. And then up to the Duke, and was with him giving him an account how matters go, and of the necessity there is of a power to presse seamen, without which we cannot really raise men for this fleete of twelve sayle, besides that it will assert the King's power of pressing, which at present is somewhat doubted, and will make the Dutch believe that we are in earnest. Thence by water to the office, where we sat till almost two o'clock. This morning Captain Ferrer came to the office to tell me that my Lord hath given him a promise of Young's place in the Wardrobe, and hearing that I pretend a promise to it he comes to ask my consent, which I denied him, and told him my Lord may do what he pleases with his promise to me, but my father's condition is not so as that I should let it go if my [Lord] will stand to his word, and so I sent him going, myself being troubled a little at it. After office I with Mr. Coventry by water to St. James's and dined with him, and had excellent discourse from him. So to the Committee for Tangier all afternoon, where still the same confused doings, and my Lord Fitz-Harding now added to the Committee, which will signify much. It grieves me to see how brokenly things are ordered. So by coach home, and at my office late, and so to supper and to bed, my body by plenty of breaking of wind being just now pretty well again, having had a constant akeing in my back these 5 or 6 days. Mr. Coventry discoursing this noon about Sir W. Batten (what a sad fellow he is!) told me how the King told him the other day how Sir W. Batten, being in the ship with him and Prince Rupert when they expected to fight with Warwick,[1] did walk up and down sweating with a napkin under his throat to dry up his sweat; and that Prince Rupert being a most jealous man, and particularly of Batten, do walk up and down swearing bloodily to the King, that Batten had a mind to betray them to-day, and that the napkin was a signal; "but, by God," says he, "if things go ill, the first thing I will do is to shoot him." He discoursed largely and bravely to me concerning the different sort of valours, the active and passive valour. For the latter, he brought as an instance General Blake,[2] who, in the defending of Taunton and Lime for the Parliament, did through his stubborn sort of valour defend it the most *opiniastrément*[3] that ever any man did any thing; and yet never was the man that ever made any attaque by land or sea, but rather

[1] Robert Rich, Earl of Warwick, Lord High Admiral for the Parliament, 1643–45, 1648–49. See June 29th, 1667, where this incident is again alluded to.

[2] Colonel Robert Blake took Taunton by surprise in 1644, and held it against two sieges by the Royalists until July, 1645, when it was relieved by Fairfax. Lyme Regis declared for the Parliament, and withstood a siege of seven weeks by Prince Maurice until relieved by the Earl of Essex.

[3] In a letter of Sir George Downing to the Earl of Clarendon, dated May 20th, 1664, he says "that he does not find Peter de Groot *opiniatrative*" (Lister's "Life of Clarendon," vol. ii., p. 331).

avoyded it on all, even fair occasions. On the other side, Prince Rupert, the boldest attaquer in the world for personal courage; and yet, in the defending of Bristol, no man ever did anything worse, he wanting the patience and seasoned head to consult and advise for defence, and to bear with the evils of a siege. The like he says is said of my Lord Tiviott, who was the boldest adventurer of his person in the world, and from a mean man in a few years was come to this greatness of command and repute only by the death of all his officers, he many times having the luck of being the only survivor of them all, by venturing upon services for the King of France that nobody else would; and yet no man upon a defence, he being all fury and no judgment in a fight. He tells me above all of the Duke of Yorke, that he is more himself and more of judgment is at hand in him in the middle of a desperate service, than at other times, as appeared in the business of Dunkirke, wherein no man ever did braver things, or was in hotter service in the close of that day, being surrounded with enemies; and then, contrary to the advice of all about him, his counsel carried himself and the rest through them safe, by advising that he might make his passage with but a dozen with him; "For," says he, "the enemy cannot move after me so fast with a great body, and with a small one we shall be enough to deal with them;" and though he is a man naturally martiall to the highest degree, yet a man that never in his life talks one word of himself or service of his owne, but only that he saw such or such a thing, and lays it down for maxime that a Hector can have no courage. He told me also, as a great instance of some men, that the Prince of Condé's excellence is, that there not being a more furious man in the world, danger in fight never disturbs him more than just to make him civill, and to command in words of great obligation to his officers and men; but without any the least disturbance in his judgment or spirit.

5th (Lord's day). About one in the morning I was knocked up by my mayds to come to my wife who is very ill. I rose, and from some cold she got to-day, or from something else, she is taken with great gripings, a looseness, and vomiting. I lay a while by her upon the bed, she being in great pain, poor wretch, but that being a little over I to bed again, and lay, and then up and to my office all the morning, setting matters to rights in some accounts and papers, and then to dinner, whither Mr. Shepley, late come to town, came to me, and after dinner and some pleasant discourse he went his way, being to go out of town to Huntington again to-morrow. So all the afternoon with my wife discoursing and talking, and in the evening to my office doing business, and then home to supper and to bed.

6th. Up and found my wife very ill again, which troubles me, but I was forced to go forth. So by water with Mr. Gauden and others to see a ship hired by me for the Commissioners of Tangier, and to give order therein. So back to the office, and by coach with Mr. Gauden to White Hall, and there to my Lord Sandwich, and here I met Mr. Townsend very opportunely and Captain Ferrer, and after some discourse we did accommodate the business of the Wardrobe place, that he shall have the reversion if he will take it out by giving a covenant that if Mr. Young[1] dyes before my father my father shall have the benefit of it [for] his life. So home, and thence by water to Deptford, and there found our Trinity Brethren come from their election to church, where Dr. Britton[2] made, methought, an indifferent sermon touching the decency that we ought to observe in God's house, the church, but yet to see how ridiculously some men will carry themselves. Sir W. Batten did at open table anon in the name of the whole Society desire him to print his sermon, as if the Doctor could think that they were fit judges of a good sermon. Then by barge with Sir W. Batten to Trinity House. It seems they have with much ado carried it for Sir G. Carteret against Captain Harrison,[3] poor man, who by succession ought to have been it, and most hands were for him,

[1] For mention of the previous agreement that Pepys should have the refusal of Mr. Young's place at the Wardrobe for his father, see June 3rd, 1661.

[2] Robert Bretton, D.D., vicar of St. Nicholas, Deptford (see note *ante*, June 5th, 1663).

[3] Mark Harrison was captain of the "Elias" in the fleet at Scheveningattending Charles II. on his return to England.

but only they were forced to fright the younger Brethren by requiring them to set their hands (which is an ill course) and then Sir G. Carteret carryed it. Here was at dinner my Lord Sandwich, Mr. Coventry, my Lord Craven, and others. A great dinner, and good company. Mr. Prin[1] also, who would not drink any health, no, not the King's, but sat down with his hat on all the while; but nobody took notice of it to him at all; but in discourse with the Doctor he did declare himself that he ever was, and has expressed himself in all his books for mixt communion against the Presbyterian examination. Thence after dinner by water, my Lord Sandwich and all us Tangier men, where at the Committee busy till night with great confusion, and then by coach home, with this content, however, that I find myself every day become more and more known, and shall one day hope to have benefit by it. I found my wife a little better. A little to my office, then home to supper and to bed.

7th. Up and to the office (having by my going by water without any thing upon my legs yesterday got some pain upon me again), where all the morning. At noon a little to the 'Change, and thence home to dinner, my wife being ill still in bed. Thence to the office, where busy all the afternoon till 9 at night, and so home to my wife, to supper, and to bed.

8th. All day before dinner with Creed, talking of many things, among others, of my Lord's going so often to Chelsy, and he, without my speaking much, do tell me that his daughters do perceive all, and do hate the place, and the young woman there, Mrs. Betty Becke; for my Lord, who sent them thither only for a disguise for his going

[1] William Prynne had published in 1628 a small book against the drinking of healths, entitled, "Healthes, Sicknesse; or a compendious and briefe Discourse, prouing, the Drinking and Pledging of Healthes to be sinfull and utterly unlawfull unto Christians . . . . wherein all those ordinary objections, excuses or pretences, which are made to justifie, extenuate, or excuse the drinking or pledging of Healthes are likewise cleared and answered." The pamphlet was dedicated to Charles I. as "more interessed in the theame and subject of this compendious discourse then any other that I know," and "because your Majestie of all other persons within your owne dominions, are most dishonoured, prejudiced, and abused by these Healthes."

ither, will come under pretence to see them, and pack hem out of doors to the Parke, and stay behind with her; ut now the young ladies are gone to their mother to Kenington. To dinner, and after dinner till 10 at night in y study writing of my old broken office notes in short-and all in one book, till my eyes did ake ready to drop ut. So home to supper and to bed.

9th. Up and at my office all the morning. At noon ined at home, Mr. Hunt and his kinswoman (wife in the ountry), after dinner I to the office, where we sat all the fternoon. Then at night by coach to attend the Duke of Albemarle about the Tangier ship. Coming back my wife pied me going home by coach from Mr. Hunt's, with whom she hath gained much in discourse to-day concerning W. Howe's discourse of me to him. That he was the nan that got me to be secretary to my Lord, and all that I ave thereby, and that for all this I never did give him 6*d.* n my life. Which makes me wonder that this rogue dare alk after this manner, and I think all the world is grown alse. But I hope I shall make good use of it. So home o supper and to bed, my eyes aching mightily since last ight.

10th. Up and by water to White Hall, and there to a Committee of Tangier, and had occasion to see how my Lord Ashworth[1] deports himself, which is very fine indeed, nd it joys my heart to see that there is any body looks so ear into the King's business as I perceive he do in this usiness of my Lord Peterborough's accounts. Thence nto the Parke, and met and walked with Captain Sylas Taylor, my old acquaintance while I was of the Exchequer, nd Dr. Whore, talking of musique, and particularly of Mr. Berckenshaw's[2] way, which Taylor magnifies mightily, and erhaps but what it deserves, but not so easily to be unlerstood as he and others make of it. Thence home by vater, and after dinner abroad to buy several things, as a

[1] Lord Ashworth is probably a miswriting for Lord Ashley (aftervards Earl of Shaftesbury).

[2] John Berkinshaw (see note *ante*, January 13th, 1661–62). In the ninutes of the Royal Society there is the following entry: "Nov. 12, 662. Mr. Berckenshaw's paper on music was presented by Dr. Charlton; and Lord Viscount Brouncker was desired to examine it" Birch's "History of the Royal Society," vol. i., p. 125).

map, and powder, and other small things, and so home my office, and in the evening with Captain Taylor by wat to our Tangier ship, and so home, well pleased, havi received £26 profit to-day of my bargain for this shi which comforts me mightily, though I confess my hear what with my being out of order as to my health, and t fear I have of the money my Lord oweth me and I sta indebted to him in, is much cast down of late. In t evening home to supper and to bed.

11th. Up and to the office, where we sat all the mor ing, where some discourse arose from Sir G. Carteret an Mr. Coventry, which gives me occasion to think that som thing like a war is expected now indeed, though upon t 'Change afterwards I hear too that an Embassador is lande from Holland, and one from their East India Company to treat with ours about the wrongs we pretend to. M Creed dined with me, and thence after dinner by coac with my wife only to take the ayre, it being very warm an pleasant, to Bowe and Old Ford; and thence to Hackne There 'light, and played at shuffle-board, eat cream an good cherries; and so with good refreshment home. The to my office vexed with Captain Taylor about the delay carrying down the ship hired by me for Tangier, and la about that and other things at the office. So home to su per and to bed.

12th (Lord's day). All the morning in my chamb consulting my lesson of ship building, and at noon M Creed by appointment came and dined with us, and s talking all the afternoon till, about church time, my wi and I began our great dispute about going to Griffin child's christening, where I was to have been godfathe but Sir J. Minnes refusing, he wanted an equal for me an my Lady Batten, and so sought for other. Then the que tion was whether my wife should go, and she having dresse herself on purpose, was very angry, and began to ta openly of my keeping her within doors before Creed, whic vexed me to the guts, but I had the discretion to keep my self without passion, and so resolved at last not to go, b

[1] See *ante*, May 29th. The ambassador sent from the States Gener was Herr Van Goch (see "Calendar of State Papers," Domesti 1663–64, pp. 620, 670, 674).

go down by water, which we did by H. Russell[1] to the alf-way house, and there eat and drank, and upon a very nall occasion had a difference again broke out, where ithout any the least cause she had the cunning to cry a eat while, and talk and blubber, which made me mighty igry in mind, but said nothing to provoke her because reed was there, but walked home, being troubled in my ind also about the knavery and neglect of Captain Fudge id Taylor, who were to have had their ship for Tangier ady by Thursday last, and now the men by a mistake are ome on board, and not any master or man or boy of the iip's company on board with them when we came by her de this afternoon, and also received a letter from Mr. oventry this day in complaint of it. We came home, id after supper Creed went home, and I to bed. My ife made great means to be friends, coming to my bed-de and doing all things to please me, and at last I could ot hold out, but seemed pleased, and so parted, and I with uch ado to sleep, but was easily wakened by extraordi-ary great rain, and my mind troubled the more to think hat the soldiers would do on board to-night in all this eather.

13th. So up at 5 o'clock, and with Captain Taylor on oard her at Deptford, and found all out of order, only ie soldiers civil, and Sir Arthur Bassett a civil person. I ited at Captain Taylor, whom, contrary to my expecta-ion, I found a lying and a very stupid blundering fellow, ood for nothing, and yet we talk of him in the Navy as if e had been an excellent officer, but I find him a lying nave, and of no judgment or dispatch at all. After find-ng the condition of the ship, no master, not above four ien, and many ship's provisions, sayls, and other things anting, I went back and called upon Fudge, whom I ound like a lying rogue unready to go on board, but I did o jeer him that I made him get every thing ready, and left aylor and H. Russell to quicken him, and so away and I y water on to White Hall, where I met his Royal High-iesse at a Tangier Committee about this very thing, and id there satisfy him how things are, at which all was paci-ied without any trouble, and I hope may end well, but I

[1] Henry Russell, a waterman.

confess I am at a real trouble for fear the rogue should n do his work, and I come to shame and losse of the mon I did hope justly to have got by it. Thence walked wi Mr. Coventry to St. James's, and there spent by his desi the whole morning reading of some old Navy books give him of old Sir John Cooke's[1] by the Archbishop of Ca terbury that now is; wherein the order that was observe in the Navy then, above what it is now, is very observabl and fine things we did observe in our reading. Anon t dinner, after dinner to discourse of the business of th Dutch warr, wherein he tells me the Dutch do in eve particular, which are but few and small things that we ca demand of them, whatever cry we unjustly make, do see to offer at an accommodation, for they do owne that it not for their profit to have warr with England. We di also talk of a History of the Navy of England, how fit were to be writ; and he did say that it hath been in h mind to propose to me the writing of the History of th late Dutch warr, which I am glad to hear, it being a thin I much desire, and sorts mightily with my genius; and, well done, may recommend me much. So he says he wi get me an order for making of searches to all records, &c. in order thereto, and I shall take great delight in doing it. Thence by water down to the Tower, and thither se for Mr. Creed to my house, where he promised to be, an he and I down to the ship, and find all things in prett good order, and I hope will end to my mind. Thenc having a gally down to Greenwich, and there saw th King's works, which are great, a-doing there, and so t the Cherry Garden,[2] and so carried some cherries hom and after supper to bed, my wife lying with me, whic

[1] Sir John Coke (1563–1644) in 1618 was one of a special commi sion appointed for the examination of the state of the navy. He w rewarded for his work in the reform of the naval administration by grant of £300 a year, charged on the funds of the navy, and express stated to be given "for his service in several marine causes, and for th office of ordnance, which he had long attended far remote from h family and to his great charge" (November, 1621). — *Dictionary o National Biography.*

[2] The Cherry Garden was a place of public entertainment at Rothe hithe. The site is marked by Cherry Garden Stairs, a landing-pier f Thames steamers and small boats.

om my not being thoroughly well, nor she, we have not one above once these two or three weeks.

14th. Up and to the office, where we sat all the morn-ıg, and had great conflict about the flags again, and am exed methought to see my Lord Berkely not satisfied with hat I said, but however I stop the King's being abused y the flag makers for the present. I do not know how it ıay end, but I will do my best to preserve it. So home) dinner, and after dinner by coach to Kensington. In ıe way overtaking Mr. Laxton, the apothecary, with his 'ife and daughters, very fine young lasses, in a coach; and) both of us to my Lady Sandwich, who hath lain this ɔrtnight here at Deane Hodges's.[1] Much company came ither to-day, my Lady Carteret, &c., Sir William Wheeler nd his lady, and, above all, Mr. Becke, of Chelsy, and 'ife and daughter, my Lord's mistress, and one that hath ot one good feature in her face, and yet is a fine lady, of fine taille,[2] and very well carriaged, and mighty discreet. took all the occasion I could to discourse with the young ıdies in her company to give occasion to her to talk, 'hich now and then she did, and that mighty finely, and s, I perceive, a woman of such an ayre, as I wonder the ess at my Lord's favour to her, and I dare warrant him he hath brains enough to entangle him. Two or three ıoures we were in her company, going into Sir H. 'inche's[3] garden, and seeing the fountayne, and singing here with the ladies, and a mighty fine cool place it is, vith a great laver[4] of water in the middle and the bravest ılace for musique I ever heard. After much mirthe, dis-ıoursing to the ladies in defence of the city against the

[1] Dr. Thomas Hodges, vicar of Kensington and rector of St. Peter's, Cornhill. He had been, in September, 1661, preferred to the deanery f Hereford, which he held with his two livings till his death, August 2nd, 1672. — B.

[2] "*Taille*, the proportion, size, or stature of a man." — Cotgrave's *French Dictionary*.

[3] The house, afterwards known as Nottingham House and Kensing-on Palace, was at this time the seat of Sir Heneage Finch, created Earl of Nottingham, 1681. It was sold by his son to King William, who greatly improved it.

[4] Laver denotes a pond, cistern, trough, or conduit. "Laver, to vashe at, *lavoyr*" (Palsgrave).

country or court, and giving them occasion to invite them selves to-morrow to me to dinner, to my venison past I got their mother's leave, and so good night, very we pleased with my day's work, and, above all, that I hav seen my Lord's mistresse. So home to supper, and a litt at my office, and to bed.

15th. Up, and by appointment with Captain Witham (the Captain that brought the newes of the disaster Tangier, where my Lord Tiviott was slain) and Mr. Took to Beares Quay,[2] and there saw and more afterward at th several grannarys several parcels of oates, and strange it to hear how it will heat itself if laid up green and not ofte turned. We came not to any agreement, but did cheape several parcels, and thence away, promising to send agai to them. So to the Victualling office, and then hom And in our garden I got Captain Witham to tell me th whole story of my Lord Tiviott's misfortune; for he wa upon the guard with his horse neare the towne, when at distance he saw the enemy appear upon a hill, a mile an a half off, and made up to them, and with much ad escaped himself; but what became of my Lord he neith knows nor thinks that any body but the enemy can tel Our losse was about four hundred. But he tells me th the greater wonder is that my Lord Tiviott met no soon with such a disaster; for every day he did commit himse to more probable danger than this, for now he had th assurance of all his scouts that there was no enemy there abouts; whereas he used every day to go out with two c three with him, to make his discoveries, in greater dange and yet the man that could not endure to have anybod else to go a step out of order to endanger himself. H concludes him to be the man of the hardest fate to lose s much honour at one blow that ever was. His relation be ing done he parted; and so I home to look after things fc dinner. And anon at noon comes Mr. Creed by chance and by and by the three young ladies:[3] and very merry w

[1] Among the State Papers is a petition of Captain Edward Withai (1663?) for half-pay or employment, his troop of horse at Tangie being disbanded and he in poverty, and the other officers being on hal pay ("Calendar," 1663-64, p. 422).

[2] Bear's Quay was a market for corn near Billingsgate.

[3] Lord Sandwich's daughters

ere with our pasty, very well baked; and a good dish of ›asted chickens; pease, lobsters, strawberries. And after inner to cards: and about five o'clock, by water down to reenwich; and up to the top of the hill, and there played pon the ground at cards. And so to the Cherry Garden, ıd then by water singing finely to the Bridge, and there .nded; and so took boat again, and to Somersett House. nd by this time, the tide being against us, it was past ten f the clock; and such a troublesome passage, in regard of ıy Lady Paulina's fearfullness, that in all my life I never id see any poor wretch in that condition. Being come ither, there waited for them their coach; but it being so ıte, I doubted what to do how to get them home. After alf an hour's stay in the street, I sent my wife home by oach with Mr. Creed's boy; and myself and Creed in the oach home with them. But, Lord! the fear that my .ady Paulina was in every step of the way; and indeed at ıis time of the night it was no safe thing to go that road; ɔ that I was even afeard myself, though I appeared otherise.[1] We came safe, however, to their house, where all ere abed; we knocked them up, my Lady and all the amily being in bed. So put them into doors; and leavng them with the mayds, bade them good night, and then nto the towne,[2] Creed and I, it being about twelve o'clock nd past; and to several houses, inns, but could get no lodgng, all being in bed. At the last house, at last, we found ome people drinking and roaring; and there got in, and fter drinking, got an ill bed, where

16th. I lay in my drawers and stockings and wastecoate ill five of the clock, and so up; and being well pleased ʼith our frolique, walked to Knightsbridge, and there eat messe of creame, and so to St. James's, and there walked little, and so I to White Hall, and took coach, and found ıy wife well got home last night, and now in bed. So I o the office, where all the morning, and at noon to the

[1] We have here a curious picture of the dreadful state of the streets n London in 1664. No improvement of what they were a century efore, when they were described as "very foul, full of pits and sloughs, ery perilous and noxious" (Knight's "London," vol. i., p. 26), appears o have taken place. The alarm of Lady Paulina and Pepys at night ʼas not surprising. — B.

[2] Kensington.

'Change, so home and to my office, where Mr. Ackwort came to me (though he knows himself and I know him t be a very knave), yet he came to me to discover the knav ery of other people like the most honest man in the world However, good use I shall make of his discourse, for i this he is much in the right. He being gone I to th 'Change, Mr. Creed with me, after we had been by wate to see a vessell we have hired to carry more soldiers t Tangier, and also visited a rope ground, wherein I learn several useful things. The talk upon the 'Change is, tha De Ruyter[1] is dead, with fifty men of his own ship, of th plague, at Cales: that the Holland Embassador here d endeavour to sweeten us with fair words; and things likel to be peaceable. Home after I had spoke with my coze Richard Pepys upon the 'Change, about supplying us wit bewpers from Norwich, which I should be glad of, if cheap So home to supper and bed.

17th. Up, and to my office, where I dispatched mucl business, and then down by water to Woolwich to make discovery of a cheate providing for us in the working o some of our own ground Tows into new cordage, to be sol to us for Riga cordage. Thence to Mr. Falconer's, wher I met Sir W. Batten and Lady, and Captain Tinker, an there dined with them, and so to the Dockyarde and t Deptford by water, and there very long informing myself i the business of flags and bewpers and other things, and s home late, being weary, and full of good information to-day, but I perceive the corruptions of the Navy are of so man kinds that it is endless to look after them, especially whil such a one as Sir W. Batten discourages every man that i honest. So home to my office, there very late, and then t supper and to bed mightily troubled in my mind to hea how Sir W. Batten and Sir J. Minnes do labour all they ca to abuse or enable others to abuse the King.

18th. From morning till 11 at night (only a little a dinner at home) at my office very busy, setting many businesses in order to my great trouble, but great content in the end. So home to supper and to bed. Strange to see how pert Sir W. Pen is to-day newly come from Portsmouth

[1] Reports of De Ruyter's death were frequently abroad. He did not die till 1676.

ith his head full of great reports of his service and the ate of the ships there. When that is over he will be just ; another man again or worse. But I wonder whence Mr. oventry should take all this care for him, to send for him ɔ only to look after his Irish business with my Lord rmond and to get the Duke's leave for him to come with › much officiousness, when I am sure he knows him as well ; I do as to his little service he do.

19th (Lord's day). Up, and all the morning and after- oon (only at dinner at home) at my office doing many usinesses for want of time on the week days. In the fternoon the greatest shower of rain of a sudden and the reatest and most continued thunder that ever I heard I iink in my life. In the evening home to my wife, and iere talked seriously of several of our family concernments, nd among others of bringing Pall out of the country to us ere to try to put her off, which I am very desirous, and my ife also, of. So to supper, prayers, which I have of late ɔo much omitted. So to bed.

20th. It having been a very cold night last night I had ot some cold, and so in pain by wind, and a sure precursor f pain is sudden letting off farts, and when that stops, then ay passages stop and my pain begins. Up and did several usinesses, and so with my wife by water to White Hall, he to her father's, I to the Duke, where we did our usual usiness. And among other discourse of the Dutch, he was nerrily saying how they print that Prince Rupert, Duke of lbemarle, and my Lord Sandwich, are to be Generalls; nd soon after is to follow them "Vieux Pen;" and so the)uke called him in mirth Old Pen. They have, it seems, ately wrote to the King, to assure him that their setting- ut ships were only to defend their fishing-trade, and to tay near home, not to annoy the King's subjects; and to lesire that he would do the like with his ships: which the King laughs at, but yet is troubled they should think him uch a child, to suffer them to bring home their fish and East India Company's ships, and then they will not care a art for us. Thence to Westminster Hall, it being term ime, meeting Mr. Pickering, he tells me how my Lady last veek went to see Mrs. Becke, the mother; and by and by he daughter came in, but that my Lady do say herself, as he says, that she knew not for what reason, for she nev knew they had a daughter, which I do not believe. S was troubled, and her heart did rise as soon as she appeare and seems the most ugly woman that ever she saw. This true were strange, but I believe it is not. Thence to n Lord's lodgings; and were merry with the young ladie who make a great story of their appearing before the mother the morning after we carried them, the last wee home so late; and that their mother took it very well, least without any anger. Here I heard how the rich wido my Lady Gold, is married to one Neale,[1] after he h received a box on the eare by her brother (who was there sentinel, in behalf of some courtier) at the door; but ma him draw, and wounded him. She called Neale up to he and sent for a priest, married presently, and went to be The brother sent to the Court, and had a serjeant sent f Neale; but Neale sent for him up to be seen in bed, a she owned him for her husband: and so all is past. seems Sir H. Bennet did look after her. My Lady ve pleasant. After dinner came in Sir Thomas Crew and M Sidney[2] lately come from France, who is growne a littl and a pretty youth he is; but not so improved as they d give him out to be, but like a child still. But yet I ca perceive he hath good parts and good inclinations. Then with Creed, who dined here, to Westminster to find o Mr. Hawly, and did, but he did not accept of my offer his being steward to my Lord at sea. Thence alone several places about my law businesses, and with goo success; at last I to Mr. Townsend at the Wardrobe, an received kind words from him to be true to me again Captain Ferrers his endeavours to get the place from m father as my Lord hath promised him. Here met Wil Howe, and he went forth with me; and by water back White Hall to wait on my Lord, who is come back fro Hinchinbroke, where he has been about 4 or 5 days. B I was never more vexed to see how an over-officious visi

[1] Lady Gold married Thomas Neale (see note, January 1st, 1663-64 She had four brothers.

[2] Sidney Montagu, second son of the Earl of Sandwich, who afte wards assumed the name of Wortley, and was father of Edward Wortle Montagu (husband of the celebrated Lady Mary Wortley Montagu).

received, for he received me with as little concernment in the middle of his discontent, and a fool I am to be of servile a humour, and vexed with that consideration I ɔk coach home, and could not get it off my mind all ght. To supper and to bed, my wife finding fault with sse for her calling upon Jane that lived with us, and there ard Mrs. Harper and her talk ill of us and not told us of With which I was also vexed, and told her soundly of till she cried, poor wench, and I hope without dissimulaɔn, and yet I cannot tell; however, I was glad to see in ıat manner she received it, and so to sleep.

21st. Being weary yesterday with walking I sleep long, .d at last up and to the office, where all the morning. At ɔme to dinner, Mr. Deane with me. After dinner I to hite Hall (setting down my wife by the way) to a Comittee of Tangier, where the Duke of Yorke, I perceive, do tend the business very well, much better than any man ere or most of them, and my [mind] eased of some ɔuble I lay under for fear of his thinking ill of me from .e bad successe in the setting forth of these crew men to angier. Thence with Mr. Creed, and walked in the Parke, ıd so to the New Exchange, meeting Mr. Moore, and he ith us. I shewed him no friendly look, but he took no ɔtice to me of the Wardrobe business, which vexes me. I erceive by him my Lord's business of his family and estate ɔes very ill, and runs in debt mightily. I would to God were clear of it, both as to my owne money and the bond f £1,000, which I stand debtor for him in, to my cozen homas Pepys. Thence by coach home and to my office little, and so to supper and to bed.

22nd. Up and I found Mr. Creed below, who staid with ıe a while, and then I to business all the morning. At oon to the 'Change and Coffee-house, where great talke of ıe Dutch preparing of sixty sayle of ships. The plague rows mightily among them, both at sea and land.[1] From

[1] "There dyed this last weeke at Amsterdam 730, but they feare an ıcrease this weeke; and the plague is scattered generally over the hole country, even to Little Dorps and Villages; and it is gott to ntwerp and Bruxells, so that they will not suffer any ships or vessells f Holland or Zeland to come to Antwerp; and 2 severall shipps are eturned out of Spaine for that they would not suffer them to have any

the 'Change to dinner to Trinity House with Sir W. Rid and Cutler, where a very good dinner. Here Sir G. Asc dined also, who I perceive desires to make himself know among the seamen. Thence home, there coming to me n Lord Peterborough's Sollicitor with a letter from him desire present dispatch in his business of freight, an promises me £50, which is good newes, and I hope to d his business readily for him. This much rejoiced me. A the afternoon at his business, and late at night comes th Sollicitor again, and I with him at 9 o'clock to Mr. Povy' and there acquainted him with the business. The mone he won't pay without warrant, but that will be got done i a few days. So home by coach and to bed.

23rd. Up, and to the office, and there we sat all th morning. So to the 'Change, and then home to dinner an to my office, where till 10 at night very busy, and so hom to supper and to bed. My cozen, Thomas Pepys, was wit me yesterday and I took occasion to speak to him about th bond I stand bound for my Lord Sandwich to him i £1,000. I did very plainly, obliging him to secrecy, te him how the matter stands, yet with all duty to my Lord m resolution to be bound for whatever he desires me for hin yet that I would be glad he had any other security. perceive by Mr. Moore to-day that he hath been with m Lord, and my Lord how he takes it I know not, but he i looking after other security and I am mighty glad of i W. Howe was with me this afternoon to desire some thing to be got ready for my Lord against his going down to hi ship, which will be soon; for it seems the King and bot the Queenes intend to visit him. The Lord knows how m Lord will get out of this charge; for Mr. Moore tells m to-day that he is £10,000 in debt: and this will, with man other things that daily will grow upon him (while he minc his pleasure as he do), set him further backward. But was pretty this afternoon to hear W. Howe mince the matte and say that he do believe that my Lord is in debt £2,oo or £3,000, and then corrected himself and said, No, nc so, but I am afraid he is in debt £1,000. I pray God ge me well rid of his Lordship as to his debt, and I care no

trade at all there" (Sir George Downing's letter to Lord Clarendo July 29th, 1664). — Lister's *Life of Clarendon*, vol. iii., p. 331.

24th. Up and out with Captain Witham in several places gain to look for oats for Tangier, and among other places the City granarys, where it seems every company have eir granary[1] and obliged to keep such a quantity of corne ways there or at a time of scarcity to issue so much at so uch a bushell: and a fine thing it is to see their stores of l sorts, for piles for the bridge, and for pipes, a thing I ever saw before. Thence to the office, and there busy all e morning. At noon to my uncle Wight's, and there ined, my wife being there all the morning. After dinner White Hall; and there met with Mr. Pierce, and he owed me the Queene's bed-chamber, and her closett, here she had nothing but some pretty pious pictures, and ooks of devotion; and her holy water at her head as she eeps, with her clock by her bed-side, wherein a lamp burns at tells her the time of the night at any time. Thence ith him to the Parke, and there met the Queene coming om Chappell, with her Mayds of Honour, all in silver-lace owns again: which is new to me, and that which I did not iink would have been brought up again. Thence he arried me to the King's closett: where such variety of ictures, and other things of value and rarity, that I was roperly confounded and enjoyed no pleasure in the sight f them; which is the only time in my life that ever I was at a loss for pleasure, in the greatest plenty of objects give it me. Thence home, calling in many places and oing abundance of errands to my great content, and at ight weary home, where Mr. Creed waited for me, and he nd I walked in the garden, where he told me he is now in hurry fitting himself for sea, and that it remains that he eals as an ingenuous man with me in the business I wot f, which he will do before he goes. But I perceive he vill have me do many good turns for him first, both as to his

[1] From the commencement of the reign of Henry VIII., or perhaps arlier, it was the custom of the City of London to provide against carcity, by requiring each of the chartered Companies to keep in store certain quantity of corn, which was to be renewed from time to time, nd when required for that purpose, produced in the market for sale, t such times and prices, and in such quantities, as the Lord Mayor r Common Council should direct. See the report of a case in the Court of Chancery, "Attorney-General *v.* Haberdashers' Company" Mylne and Keen's "Reports," vol. i., p. 420). — B.

bills coming to him in this office, and also in his absen at the Committee of Tangier, which I promise, and as acquits himself to me I will willingly do. I would I kn the worst of it, what it is he intends, that so I may eith quit my hands of him or continue my kindness still to hi

25th. We staid late, and he lay with me all night a rose very merry talking, and excellent company he is, th is the truth of it, and a most cunning man. He being go I to the office, where we sat all the morning. At noon dinner, and then to my office busy, and by and by hor with Mr. Deane to a lesson upon raising a Bend of Timber and he being gone I to the office, and there came Capta Taylor, and he and I home, and I have done all very w with him as to the business of the last trouble, so that cor what will come my name will be clear of any false deali with him. So to my office again late, and then to bed.

26th (Lord's day). Up, and Sir J. Minnes set me dov at my Lord Sandwich's, where I waited till his comi down, when he came, too, could find little to say to me b only a general question or two, and so good-bye. Here h little daughter, my Lady Katharine was brought, who lately come from my father's at Brampton, to have h cheek looked after, which is and hath long been sore. B my Lord will rather have it be as it is, with a scarr in h face, than endanger it being worse by tampering.[2] H being gone, I went home, a little troubled to see he min me no more, and with Creed called at several churche which, God knows, are supplied with very young men, a the churches very empty; so home and at our owne chur looked in, and there heard one preach whom Sir W. Pe brought, which he desired us yesterday to hear, that ha been his chaplin in Ireland, a very silly fellow. So hon and to dinner, and after dinner a frolique took us, we wou

[1] This seems to refer to knee timber, of which there was not a su cient supply (see note, October 6th, 1663). A proposal was made produce this bent wood artificially: "June 22, 1664. Sir Willia Petty intimated that it seemed by the scarcity and greater rate of kn timber that nature did not furnish crooked wood enough for buildin wherefore he thought it would be fit to raise by art, so much of it proportion, as to reduce it to an equal rate with strait timbe (Birch's "History of the Royal Society," vol. i., p. 443).

[2] See September 3rd, 1661.

this afternoon to the Hope; so my wife dressed herself, .d, with good victuals and drink, we took boat presently ıd the tide with us got down, but it was night, and the tide ent by the time we got to Gravesend; so there we stopped, ıt went not on shore, only Creed, to get some cherries,[1] ıd send a letter to the Hope, where the Fleete lies. And , it being rainy, and thundering mightily, and lightning, e returned. By and by the evening turned mighty clear ıd moonshine; we got with great pleasure home, about velve o'clock, which did much please us, Creed telling etty stories in the boat. He lay with me all night.

27th. Up, and he and I walked to Paul's Church yard, ıd there saw Sir Harry Spillman's book,[2] and I bespoke and others, and thence we took coach, and he to my ord's and I to St. James's, where we did our usual busiess, and thence I home and dined, and then by water to Voolwich, and there spent the afternoon till night under retence of buying Captain Blackman's house and grounds, ıd viewing the ground took notice of Clothiers' cordage ith which he, I believe, thinks to cheat the King. That eing done I by water home, it being night first, and there find our new mayd Jane come, a cook mayd. So to bed.

28th. Up, and this day put on a half shirt first this summer, it being very hot; and yet so ill-tempered I am grown, ıat I am afeard I shall catch cold, while all the world is eady to melt away. To the office all the morning, at noon dinner at home, then to my office till the evening, then ut about several businesses and then by appointment to ıe 'Change, and thence with my uncle Wight to the Mum ouse, and there drinking, he do complain of his wife most ruel as the most troublesome woman in the world, and how

[1] Pliny tells us that cherries were introduced into Britain by the omans, and Lydgate alludes to them as sold in the London streets. ichard Haines, fruiterer to Henry VIII., imported a number of cherry ees from Flanders, and planted them at Tenham, in Kent. Hence ıe fame of the Kentish cherries.

[2] "Glossarium Archaiologicum," of which only the first part, to the etter L, was published by Spelman himself, 1626; the work was ompleted in 1664 by Sir William Dugdale from the author's papers. ir Henry Spelman died, October, 1641, at the house of his son-in-law, ir Ralph Whitfield, in the Barbican, and was buried in Westminster bbey.

she will have her will, saying she brought him a portion ar God knows what. By which, with many instances more, perceive they do live a sad life together. Thence to tl Mitre and there comes Dr. Burnett to us and Mr. Maes, b the meeting was chiefly to bring the Doctor and me togethe and there I began to have his advice about my disease, ar then invited him to my house: and I am resolved to p myself into his hands. Here very late, but I drank notl ing, nor will, though he do advise me to take care of co drinks. So home and to bed.

29th. Up, and Mr. Shepley came to me, who is latel come to town; among other things I hear by him how th children are sent for away from my father's, but he say without any great discontent. I am troubled there shoul be this occasion of difference, and yet I am glad they ar gone, lest it should have come to worse. He tells me ho my brave dogg I did give him, going out betimes on morning to Huntington, was set upon by five other dogg and worried to pieces, of which I am a little, and he th most sorry I ever saw man for such a thing. Forth wit him and walked a good way talking, then parted and I t the Temple, and to my cozen Roger Pepys, and thence b water to Westminster to see Dean Honiwood, whom I ha not visited a great while. He is a good-natured, but a ver weak man, yet a Dean, and a man in great esteem. Thenc walked to my Lord Sandwich's, and there dined, my Lor there. He was pleasant enough at table with me, but ye without any discourse of business, or any regard to m when dinner was over, but fell to cards, and my Lady an I sat two hours alone, talking of the condition of he family's being greatly in debt, and many children nov coming up to provide for. I did give her my sense ver plain of it, which she took well and carried further than my self, to the bemoaning their condition, and remembering how finely things were ordered about six years ago, when I lived there and my Lord at sea every year. Thence home, doing several errands by the way. So to my office, and there till late at night, Mr. Comander coming to me for me to sign and seal the new draft of my will, which I did do, I having altered something upon the death of my brother Tom. So home to supper and to bed.

30th. Up, and to the office, where we sat all the morning. t noon home to dinner, Mr. Wayth with me, and by and y comes in Mr. Falconer and his wife and dined with us, he first time she was ever here. We had a pretty good inner, very merry in discourse, sat after dinner an hour r two, then down by water to Deptford and Woolwich bout getting of some business done which I was bound to y my oath this month, and though in some things I have ot come to the height of my vow of doing all my business n paying all my petty debts and receipt of all my petty nonies due to me, yet I bless God I am not conscious of ny neglect in me that they are not done, having not ninded my pleasure at all, and so being resolved to take o manner of pleasure till it be done, I doubt not God will orgive me for not forfeiting the £10 I promised. Walked ack from Woolwich to Greenwich all alone, save a man hat had a cudgell in his hand, and, though he told me he aboured in the King's yarde, and many other good arguments that he is an honest man, yet, God forgive me! I lid doubt he might knock me on the head behind with his club. But I got safe home. Then to the making up my nonth's accounts, and find myself still a gainer and rose o £951, for which God be blessed. I end the month vith my mind full of business and some sorrow that I have not exactly performed all my vowes, though my not doing is not my fault, and shall be made good out of my first eisure. Great doubts yet whether the Dutch warr go on or no. The Fleet ready in the Hope, of twelve sayle. The King and Queenes go on board, they say, on Saturday next. Young children of my Lord Sandwich gone with their mayds from my mother's, which troubles me, it being, I hear from Mr. Shepley, with great discontent, saying, that though they buy good meate, yet can never have it before it stinks, which I am ashamed of.

July 1st. Up and within all the morning, first bringing down my Tryangle to my chamber below, having a new frame made proper for it to stand on. By and by comes Dr. Burnett, who assures me that I have an ulcer either in the kidneys or bladder, for my water, which he saw yesterday, he is sure the sediment is not slime gathered by heat, but is a direct pusse. He did write me down some direction[1] what to do for it, but not with the satisfaction I expected. I did give him a piece, with good hopes, however, that his advice will be of use to me, though it is strange that Mr. Hollyard should never say one word of this ulcer in all his life to me. He being gone, I to the 'Change, and thence home to dinner, and so to my office busy till the evening, and then by agreement came Mr. Hill and Andrews and one Cheswicke, a maister who plays very well upon the Spinette, and we sat singing Psalms till 9 at night, and so broke up with great pleasure, and very good company it is, and I hope I shall now and then have their company. They being gone, I to my office till towards twelve o'clock, and then home and to bed. Upon the 'Change, this day, I saw how uncertain the temper of the people is, that, from our discharging of about 200 that lay idle, having nothing to do, upon some of our ships which were ordered to be fitted for service, and their works are now done, the towne do talk that the King discharges all his men, 200 yesterday and 800 to-day, and that now he hath got £100,000 in his hand, he values not a Dutch warr. But I undeceived a great many, telling them how it is.

2nd. Up and to the office, where all the morning. At noon to the 'Change, and there, which is strange, I could

[1] Dr. Burnett's advice to mee.

The Originall is fyled among my letters.

Take of ye Rootes of Marsh-Mallows foure ounces, of Cumfry, of Liquorish, of each two ounces, of ye fflowers of St. John's Wort two Handsfull, of ye Leaves of Plantan, of Alehoofe, of each three handfulls, of Selfeheale, of Red Roses, of each one Handfull, of Cynamon, of Nutmegg, of each halfe an ounce. Beate them well, then powr upon them one Quart of old Rhenish wine, and about Six houres after strayne it and clarify it with y white of an Egge, and with a sufficient quantity of sugar, boyle it to ye consistence of a Syrrup and reserve it for use.

Dissolve one spoonefull of this Syrrup in every draught of Ale or beere you drink.

Morning and evening swallow ye quantity of an hazle-nutt of Cyprus Terebintine.

If you are bound or have a fit of ye Stone eate an ounce of Cassia new drawne, from ye poynt of a knife.

Old Canary or Malaga wine you may drinke to three or 4 glasses, but noe new wine, and what wine you drinke, lett it bee at meales.—[From a slip of paper inserted in the Diary at this place.]

eet with nobody that I could invite home to my venison asty, but only Mr. Alsopp and Mr. Lanyon, whom I inted last night, and a friend they brought along with them.) home and with our venison pasty we had other good meat ıd good discourse. After dinner sat close to discourse)out our business of the victualling of the garrison of Tanıer, taking their prices of all provisions, and I do hope to rder it so that they and I also may get something by it, hich do much please me, for I hope I may get nobly and onestly with profit to the King. They being gone came Sir /. Warren, and he and I discoursed long about the busiess of masts, and then in the evening to my office, where te writing letters, and then home to look over some rampton papers, which I am under an oathe to dispatch efore I spend one half houre in any pleasure or go to bed efore 12 o'clock, to which, by the grace of God, I will be ue. Then to bed. When I came home I found that toıorrow being Sunday I should gain nothing by doing it)-night, and to-morrow I can do it very well and better ıan to-night. I went to bed before my time, but with a esolution of doing the thing to better purpose to-morrow.

3rd (Lord's day). Up and ready, and all the morning in ıy chamber looking over and settling some Brampton usinesses. At noon to dinner, where the remains of yeserday's venison and a couple of brave green geese, which /e are fain to eat alone, because they will not keepe, which roubled us. After dinner I close to my business, and beore the evening did end it with great content, and my nind eased by it. Then up and spent the evening walkng with my wife talking, and it thundering and lightning ll the evening, and this yeare have had the most of thunler and lightning they say of any in man's memory, and o it is, it seems, in France and everywhere else. So to rayers and to bed.

4th. Up, and many people with me about business, and hen out to several places, and so at noon to my Lord Crew's, and there dined and very much made of there by ıim. He offered me the selling of some land of his in Cambridgeshire, a purchase of about £1,000, and if I can compass it I will. After dinner I walked homeward, still loing business by the way, and at home find my wife this day of her owne accord to have lain out 25*s.* upon a pa of pendantes for her eares, which did vex me and broug both me and her to very high and very foule words fro her to me, such as trouble me to think she should have her mouth, and reflecting upon our old differences, whi I hate to have remembered. I vowed to breake them, that she should go and get what she could for them agai I went with that resolution out of doors; the poor wret afterwards in a little while did send out to change the for her money again. I followed Besse her messenger the 'Change, and there did consult and sent her back; would not have them changed, being satisfied that sh yielded. So went home, and friends again as to that bus ness; but the words I could not get out of my mind, an so went to bed at night discontented, and she came to be to me, but all would not make me friends, but sleep an rise in the morning angry. This day the King and Queen went to visit my Lord Sandwich and the fleete, going fort in the Hope.[1]

5th. Up and to the office, where all the morning. A noon to the 'Change a little, then with W. Howe home an dined. So after dinner to my office, and there busy ti late at night, having had among other things much di course with young Gregory about the Chest busines wherein Sir W. Batten is so great a knave, and also wit Alsop and Lanyon about the Tangier victualling, wherei I hope to get something for myself. Late home to supp and to bed, being full of thoughts of a sudden resolutio this day taken upon the 'Change of going down to-morro to the Hope.

6th. Up very betimes, and my wife also, and got u ready; and about eight o'clock, having got some bottles o wine and beer and neat's tongues, we went to our barge a the Towre, where Mr. Pierce and his wife, and a kins woman and his sister, and Mrs. Clerke and her sister an cozen were to expect us; and so set out for the Hope, a

[1] "Their Majesties were treated at Tilbury Hope by the Earl o Sandwich, returning the same day, abundantly satisfied both with th dutiful respects of that honourable person and with the excellent con dition of all matters committed to his charge" ("The Newes," Jul 7th, 1664). — B.

e way down playing at cards and other sports, spending r time pretty merry. Come to the Hope about one and ere showed them all the ships, and had a collacion of chovies, gammon, &c., and after an houre's stay or more, nbarked again for home; and so to cards and other sports ll we came to Greenwich, and there Mrs. Clerke and my ife and I on shore to an alehouse, for them to do their isiness, and so to the barge again, having shown them e King's pleasure boat; and so home to the Bridge, inging night home with us; and it rained hard, but we ot them on foot to the Beare, and there put them into a oat, and I back to my wife in the barge, and so to the ower Wharf and home, being very well pleased to-day ith the company, especially Mrs. Pierce, who continues er complexion as well as ever, and hath, at this day, I ink, the best complexion that ever I saw on any woman, oung or old, or child either, all days of my life. Also Irs. Clerke's kinswoman sings very prettily, but is very onfident in it; Mrs. Clerke herself witty, but spoils all in eing so conceited and making so great a flutter with a few ne clothes and some bad tawdry things worne with them. ut the charge of the barge lies heavy upon me, which oubles me, but it is but once, and I may make Pierce do e some courtesy as great. Being come home, I weary to ed with sitting. The reason of Dr. Clerke's not being ere was the King's being sicke last night and let blood, nd so he durst not come away to-day.

7th. Up, and this day begun, the first day this year, to ut off my linnen waistcoat, but it happening to be a cool ay I was afraid of taking cold, which troubles me, and is ne greatest pain I have in the world to think of my bad emper of my health. At the office all the morning. Dined at home, to my office to prepare some things against Committee of Tangier this afternoon. So to White Hall, nd there found the Duke and twenty more reading their ommission (of which I am, and was also sent to, to come) or the Royall Fishery, which is very large, and a very erious charter it is; but the company generally so ill fitted or so serious a worke that I do much fear it will come to ittle. That being done, and not being able to do any hing for lacke of an oathe for the Governor and Assistants to take, we rose. Then our Committee for the Tangi victualling met and did a little, and so up, and I and M Coventry walked in the garden half an hour, talking the business of our masts, and thence away and with Cre walked half an hour or more in the Park, and thence the New Exchange to drink some creame, but missed and so parted, and I home, calling by the way for my ne bookes, viz., Sir H. Spillman's "Whole Glossary," "Sc pula's Lexicon," and Shakespeare's plays, which I ha got money out of my stationer's bills to pay for. So hon and to my office a while, and then home and to bed, fin ing myself pretty well for all my waistecoate being put c to-day. The king is pretty well to-day, though let bloc the night before yesterday.

8th. Up, and called out by my Lord Peterborough gentleman to Mr. Povy's to discourse about getting of h money, wherein I am concerned in hopes of the £50 m Lord hath promised me, but I dare not reckon myself su of it till I have it in my main,[1] for these Lords are har to be trusted. Though I well deserve it. I staid at Povy for his coming in, and there looked over his stables an every thing, but notwithstanding all the times I have bee there I do yet find many fine things to look on. Thenc to White Hall a little, to hear how the King do, he nc having been well these three days. I find that he is prett well again. So to Paul's Churchyarde about my book and to the binder's and directed the doing of my Chaucer though they were not full neate enough for me, but prett well it is; and thence to the clasp-maker's to have i clasped and bossed. So to the 'Change and home to dir ner, and so to my office till 5 o'clock, and then came M Hill and Andrews, and we sung an houre or two. The broke up and Mr. Alsop and his company came and con sulted about our Tangier victualling and brought it to good head. So they parted, and I to supper and to bed.

9th. Up, and at the office all the morning. In th afternoon by coach with Sir J. Minnes to White Hall, an

[1] Main=hand.

[2] This was Speght's edition of 1602, which is still in the Pepysia Library. The book is bound in calf, with brass clasps and bosses. is not lettered.

here to a Committee for Fishing; but the first thing was swearing to be true to the Company, and we were all sworne; but a great dispute we had, which, methought, is very ominous to the Company; some, that we should swear to be true to the best of our power, and others to the best of our understanding; and carried in the last, though in that we are the least able to serve the Company, because we would not be obliged to attend the business when we can, but when we list. This consideration did displease me, but it was voted and so went. We did nothing else, but broke up till a Committee of Guinny was set and ended, and then met again for Tangier, and there I did my business about my Lord Peterborough's order and my own for my expenses for the garrison lately. So home, by the way calling for my Chaucer and other books, and that is well done to my mind, which pleased me well. So to my office till late writing letters, and so home to my wife to supper and to bed, where we have not lain together because of the heat of the weather a good while, but now against her going into the country.

10th (Lord's day). Up and by water, towards noon, to Somersett House, and walked to my Lord Sandwich's, and there dined with my Lady and the Children. And after some ordinary discourse with my Lady, after dinner took our leaves and my wife her's, in order to her going to the country to-morrow. But my Lord took not occasion to speak one word of my father or mother about the children at all, which I wonder at, and begin I will not. Here my Lady showed us my Lady Castlemayne's[1] picture, finely done; given my Lord; and a most beautiful picture it is. Thence with my Lady Jemimah and Mr. Sidney to St. Gyles's Church, and there heard a long, poore sermon. Thence set them down and in their coach to Kate Joyce's christening, where much company, good service of sweetmeates; and after an houre's stay, left them, and in my Lord's coach — his noble, rich coach — home, and there my wife fell to putting things in order against her going to-morrow, and I to read, and so to bed, where I not well, and so had no pleasure at all with my poor wife.

[1] This fine portrait is still at Hinchingbroke, and in very good preservation. — B.

11th. But betimes up this morning, and, getting read we by coach to Holborne, where, at nine o'clock, they se out, and I and my man Will on horseback, by my wife, t Barnett; a very pleasant day; and there dined with he company, which was very good; a pretty gentlewoman wit her, that goes but to Huntington, and a neighbour to us i towne. Here we staid two hours and then parted for a together, and my poor wife I shall soon want I am sure Thence I and Will to see the Wells,[1] half a mile off, an there I drank three glasses, and went and walked and cam back and drunk two more; the woman would have had m drink three more; but I could not, my belly being full, bu this wrought very well, and so we rode home, round b Kingsland, Hackney, and Mile End till we were quit weary, and my water working at least 7 or 8 times upon th road, which pleased me well, and so home weary, and no being very well, I betimes to bed, and there fell into a mos mighty sweat in the night, about eleven o'clock, and there knowing what money I have in the house and hearing noyse, I begun to sweat worse and worse, till I melte almost to water. I rung, and could not in half an hour make either of the wenches hear me, and this made me fea the more, lest they might be gag'd; and then I begun t think that there was some design in a stone being flung a the window over our stayres this evening, by which th thiefes meant to try what looking there would be after then and know our company. These thoughts and fears I had, and do hence apprehend the fears of all rich men that are covetous and have much money by them. At last Jane rose, and then I understand it was only the dogg wants a lodging and so made a noyse. So to bed, but hardly slept, at las did, and so till morning,

12th. And so rose, called up by my Lord Peterborough's gentleman about getting his Lord's money to-day of Mr.

[1] The mineral springs at Barnet Common, nearly a mile to the west of High Barnet. The discovery of the wells was announced in the "Perfect Diurnall" of June 5th, 1652, and Fuller, writing in 1662, says that there are hopes that the waters may "save as many lives as were lost in the fatal battle at Barnet" ("Worthies," Herts). A pamphlet on "The Barnet Well Water" was published by the Rev. W. M Trinder, M.D., as late as the year 1800, but in 1840 the old well-house was pulled down.

ɔvy, wherein I took such order, that it was paid, and I had y £50 brought me, which comforts my heart. We sat at .e office all the morning, then at home. Dined alone; d for want of company and not being very well, and know ɔt how to eat alone. After dinner down with Sir G. arteret, Sir J. Minnes, and Sir W. Batten to view, and did ke a place by Deptford yard to lay masts in. By and by ɔmes Mr. Coventry, and after a little stay he and I down Blackwall, he having a mind to see the yarde, which we id, and fine storehouses there are and good docks, but of ɔ great profit to him that oweth[1] them for ought we see. ɔ home by water with him, having good discourse by the ay, and so I to the office a while, and late home to supper nd to bed.

13th. Up and to my office, at noon (after having at an le-house hard by discoursed with one Mr. Tyler, a neighour, and one Captain Sanders about the discovery of some ursers that have sold their provisions) I to my Lord Sandich, thinking to have dined there, but they not dining at ome, I with Captain Ferrers to Mr. Barwell the King's quire Sadler, where about this time twelvemonths I dined efore at a good venison pasty. The like we had now, and ery good company, Mr. Tresham and others. Thence to Vhite Hall to the Fishery, and there did little. So by ater home, and there met Lanyon, &c., about Tangier natters, and so late to my office, and thence home and to ed. Mr. Moore was with me late to desire me to come to ny Lord Sandwich to-morrow morning, which I shall, but wonder what my business is.

14th. My mind being doubtful what the business should e, I rose a little after four o'clock, and abroad. Walked o my Lord's, and nobody up, but the porter rose out of ɔed to me: so I back again to Fleete Streete, and there ought a little book of law; and thence, hearing a psalm ung, I went into St. Dunstan's, and there heard prayers ead, which, it seems, is done there every morning at six ɔ'clock; a thing I never did do at a chappell, but the

[1] For "owneth." This sense is very common in Shakespeare. In he original edition of the authorized version of the Bible we read: "So shall the Jews at Jerusalem bind the man that *oweth* this girdle" (Acts xxi. 11). — Nares's *Glossary*.

College Chappell, in all my life. Thence to my Lor again, and my Lord being up, was sent for up, and he a I alone. He did begin with a most solemn profession the same confidence in and love for me that he ever ha and then told me what a misfortune was fallen upon me a him: on me, by a displeasure which my Lord Chancell did show to him last night against me, in the highest a most passionate manner that ever any man did speak, ev to the not hearing of any thing to be said to him: but told me, that he did say all that could be said for a man to my faithfullnesse and duty to his Lordship, and did n the greatest right imaginable. And what should the bu ness be, but that I should be forward to have the trees Clarendon Park[1] marked and cut down, which he, it seem hath bought of my Lord Albemarle; when, God knows! am the most innocent man in the world in it, and d nothing of myself, nor knew of his concernment therei but barely obeyed my Lord Treasurer's warrant for t doing thereof. And said that I did most ungentlemanli with him, and had justified the rogues in cutting down tree of his; and that I had sent the veriest Fanatiq [Deane] that is in England to mark them, on purpose nose[2] him. All which, I did assure my Lord, was mo properly false, and nothing like it true; and told my Lo the whole passage. My Lord do seem most nearly affecte

[1] Near Salisbury, granted by Edward VI. to Sir W. Herbert, Earl Pembroke, for two lives, which lease determined in 1601, when it r verted to the Crown, and was conferred on the Duke of Albemar whose family got the estate after Lord Clarendon's fall; for, accordi to Britton, Clarendon Park was alienated by Christopher, second Du of Albemarle, to the Earl of Bath, from whom it passed, by purchas to the ancestor of Sir Frederic Hervey Bathurst, Bart., the prese possessor. In Lister's "Life of Lord Clarendon" (vol. iii., p. 34 there is a letter of Sir Robert Hyde to Clarendon on the complaint r specting the trees, and in a note the author examines the complaint the Chancellor. He writes: "There was, however (as appears from th letter), more reason for complaint than is admitted by Pepys; for the very time the Commissioners sent down a person to mark standi timber for felling, there was a good deal of timber, the property of th Crown, lying on the estate unappropriated, which had been 'felle divers years' before, and till this was used, the felling of other timb there was evidently unnecessary."

[2] To provoke or affront a man to his face (Bailey's "Dictionary").

is partly, I believe, for me, and partly for himself. So advised me to wait presently upon my Lord, and clear 'self in the most perfect manner I could, with all sub-ssion and assurance that I am his creature both in this d all other things; and that I do owne that all I have, is rived through my Lord Sandwich from his Lordship. , full of horror, I went, and found him busy in tryals of v in his great room; and it being Sitting-day, durst not .y, but went to my Lord and told him so: whereupon directed me to take him after dinner; and so away I me, leaving my Lord mightily concerned for me. I to e office, and there sat busy all the morning. At noon to e 'Change, and from the 'Change over with Alsopp and the hers to the Pope's Head tavern, and there staid a quarter an hour, and concluded upon this, that in case I got em no more than 3*s.* 1½ *d.* per week per man I should have them but £150 per ann., but to have it without any venture or charge, but if I got them 3*s.* 2*d.*, then they uld give me £300 in the like manner. So I directed em to draw up their tender in a line or two against the ternoon, and to meet me at White Hall. So I left them, d I to my Lord Chancellor's; and there coming out after nner I accosted him, telling him that I was the unhappy epys that had fallen into his high displeasure, and come desire him to give me leave to make myself better derstood to his Lordship, assuring him of my duty and rvice. He answered me very pleasingly, that he was nfident upon the score of my Lord Sandwich's character me, but that he had reason to think what he did, and esired me to call upon him some evening: I named to-night, d he accepted of it. So with my heart light I to White all, and there after understanding by a stratagem, and yet pearing wholly desirous not to understand Mr. Gauden's ice when he desired to show it me, I went down and dered matters in our tender so well that at the meeting y and by I was ready with Mr. Gauden's and his, both irected in a letter to me to give the board their two nders, but there being none but the Generall Monk and Ir. Coventry and Povy and I, I did not think fit to expose em to view now, but put it off till Saturday, and so with ood content rose Thence I to the Half Moone, against the 'Change, to acquaint Lanyon and his friends of c proceedings, and thence to my Lord Chancellor's, and th heard several tryals, wherein I perceive my Lord is a m able and ready man. After all done, he himself calle "Come, Mr. Pepys, you and I will take a turn in t garden." So he was led down stairs, having the goute, a there walked with me, I think, above an houre, talking m friendly, yet cunningly. I told him clearly how thir were; how ignorant I was of his Lordship's concernme in it; how I did not do nor say one word singly, but wh was done was the act of the whole Board. He told me name that he was more angry with Sir G. Carteret than wi me, and also with the whole body of the Board. But thir ing who it was of the Board that knew him least, he d place his fear upon me; but he finds that he is indebted none of his friends there. I think I did thoroughly appea him, till he thanked me for my desire and pains to satis him; and upon my desiring to be directed who I should his servants advise with about this business, he told r nobody, but would be glad to hear from me himself. I told me he would not direct me in any thing, that it mig not be said that the Lord Chancellor did labour to abu the King; or (as I offered) direct the suspending the Repc of the Purveyors: but I see what he means, and I will ma it my worke to do him service in it. But, Lord! to s how he is incensed against poor Deane, as a fanatiq rogue, and I know not what: and what he did was done spite to his Lordship, among all his friends and tenant He did plainly say that he would not direct me in a thing, for he would not put himself into the power of a man to say that he did so and so; but plainly told me as he would be glad I did something. Lord! to see how w poor wretches dare not do the King good service for fear the greatness of these men. He named Sir G. Carteret, ar Sir J. Minnes, and the rest; and that he was as angry wi them all as me. But it was pleasant to think that, while l was talking to me, comes into the garden Sir G. Cartere and my Lord avoided speaking with him, and made hi and many others stay expecting him, while I walked up ar down above an houre, I think; and would have me wa with my hat on. And yet, after all this, there has been s

le ground for this his jealousy of me, that I am some-
ıes afeard that he do this only in policy to bring me to his
e by scaring me; or else, which is worse, to try how faith-
l I would be to the King; but I rather think the former of
two. I parted with great assurance how I acknowledged
I had to come from his Lordship; which he did not
m to refuse, but with great kindness and respect parted.
I by coach home, calling at my Lord's, but he not
thin. At my office late, and so home to eat something,
ing almost starved for want of eating my dinner to-day,
d so to bed, my head being full of great and many busi-
sses of import to me.

15th. Up, and to my Lord Sandwich's; where he sent for
up, and I did give my Lord an account of what had
ssed with my Lord Chancellor yesterday; with which he
s well pleased, and advised me by all means to study in
best manner I could to serve him in this business.
ter this discourse ended, he begun to tell me that he had
w pitched upon his day of going to sea upon Monday
xt, and that he would now give me an account how
atters are with him. He told me that his work now in
e world is only to keep up his interest at Court, having
tle hopes to get more considerably, he saying that he hath
w about £8,000 per annum. It is true, he says, he
veth about £10,000; but he hath been at great charges in
tting things to this pass in his estate; besides his build-
g and good goods that he hath bought. He says he hath
w evened his reckonings at the Wardrobe till Michael-
as last, and hopes to finish it to Lady-day before he goes.
e says now there is due, too, £7,000 to him there, if he
new how to get it paid, besides £2,000 that Mr. Montagu
owe him. As to his interest, he says that he hath had
l the injury done him that ever man could have by
nother bosom friend that knows all his secrets, by Mr.
ontagu; but he says that the worst of it all is past, and he
ne out and hated, his very person by the King, and he
lieves the more upon the score of his carriage to him;
ay, that the Duke of Yorke did say a little while since in
s closett, that he did hate him because of his ungratefull
rriage to my Lord of Sandwich. He says that he is as
eat with the Chancellor, or greater, than ever in his life.

That with the King he is the like; and told me an instan that whereas he formerly was of the private council to King before he was last sicke, and that by the sickness interruption was made in his attendance upon him; King did not constantly call him, as he used to do, to private council, only in businesses of the sea and the lik but of late the King did send a message to him by Harry Bennet, to excuse the King to my Lord that he h not of late sent for him as he used to do to his priv council, for it was not out of any distaste, but to avc giving offence to some others whom he did not name; my Lord supposes it might be Prince Rupert, or it may only that the King would rather pass it by an excuse, th be thought unkind: but that now he did desire him attend him constantly, which of late he hath done, and t King never more kind to him in his life than now. T Duke of Yorke, as much as is possible; and in the busin of late, when I was to speak to my Lord about his going sea, he says that he finds the Duke did it with the great ingenuity and love in the world; "and whereas," says Lord, "here is a wise man hard by that thinks himself s and would be thought so, and it may be is in a degree (naming by and by my Lord Crew), would have had r condition with him that neither Prince Rupert nor a body should come over his head, and I know not what The Duke himself hath caused in his commission, that be made Admirall of this and what other ships or fle shall hereafter be put out after these; which is very nob He tells me in these cases, and that of Mr. Montagu's, a all others, he finds that bearing of them patiently is his be way, without noise or trouble, and things wear out of the selves and come fair again. But, says he, take it from m never to trust too much to any man in the world, for y put youself into his power; and the best seeming friend a real friend as to the present may have or take occasion fall out with you, and then out comes all. Then he to me of Sir Harry Bennet, though they were always kind, y now it is become to an acquaintance and familiarity abo ordinary, that for these months he hath done no busine but with my Lord's advice in his chamber, and promis all faithfull love to him and service upon all occasion

y Lord says, that he hath the advantage of being able by
s experience to helpe and advise him; and he believes that
at chiefly do invite Sir Harry to this manner of treating
m. "Now," says my Lord, "the only and the greatest
ıbarras that I have in the world is, how to behave myself
Sir H. Bennet and my Lord Chancellor, in case that
ere do lie any thing under the embers about my Lord
istoll, which nobody can tell; for then," says he, "I
ıst appear for one or other, and I will lose all I have in
e world rather than desert my Lord Chancellor: so that,"
ys he, "I know not for my life what to do in that case."
or Sir H. Bennet's love is come to the height, and his
nfidence, that he hath given my Lord a character,[1] and
ill oblige my Lord to correspond with him. "This,"
ys he, "is the whole condition of my estate and interest;
hich I tell you, because I know not whether I shall see you
ain or no." Then as to the voyage, he thinks it will be
charge to him, and no profit; but that he must not now
ok after nor think to encrease, but study to make good
hat he hath, that what is due to him from the Wardrobe
elsewhere may be paid, which otherwise would fail, and
l a man hath be but small content to him. So we seemed
take leave one of another; my Lord of me, desiring me
at I would write to him and give him information upon
l occasions in matters that concern him; which, put
gether with what he preambled with yesterday, makes me
ink that my Lord do truly esteem me still, and desires to
reserve my service to him; which I do bless God for. In
e middle of our discourse my Lady Crew came in to bring
y Lord word that he hath another son,[2] my Lady being
rought to bed just now, I did not think her time had been
nigh, but she's well brought to bed, for which God be
raised! and send my Lord to study the laying up of some-
ing the more! Then with Creed to St. James's, and
issing Mr. Coventry, to White Hall; where, staying for
im in one of the galleries, there comes out of the chayre-
oom Mrs. Stewart, in a most lovely form, with her hair
ll about her eares, having her picture taking there. There
as the King and twenty more, I think, standing by all the

[1] A cipher.

[2] Their sixth son, James Montagu, who died unmarried.

while, and a lovely creature she in this dress seemed to b Thence to the 'Change by coach, and so home to dinn and then to my office. In the evening Mr. Hill, Andre and I to my chamber to sing, which we did very plea antly, and then to my office again, where very late and home, with my mind I bless God in good state of ease ar body of health, only my head at this juncture very full business, how to get something. Among others what th rogue Creed will do before he goes to sea, for I wou fain be rid of him and see what he means to do, for will then declare myself his firm friend or enemy.

16th. Up in the morning, my head mightily confounde with the great deale of business I have upon me to d But to the office, and there dispatched Mr. Creed's bus ness pretty well about his bill; but then there comes W Howe for my Lord's bill of Imprest for £500 to car with him this voyage, and so I was at a loss how to car myself in it, Creed being there, but there being no help delivered it to them both, and let them contend, when perceive they did both endeavour to have it, but W. How took it, and the other had the discretion to suffer it. Bu I think I cleared myself to Creed that it past not from an practice of mine. At noon rose and did some necessar business at the 'Change. Thence to Trinity House to dinner which Sir G. Carteret makes there as Maister th year. Thence to White Hall to the Tangier Committe and there, above my expectation, got the business of ou contract for the victualling carried for my people, viz. Alsopp, Lanyon, and Yeabsly; and by their promise I d thereby get £300 per annum to myself, which do overjo me; and the matter is left to me to draw up. Mr. Lewe was in the gallery and is mightily amazed at it, and I be lieve Mr. Gauden will make some stir about it, for h wrote to Mr. Coventry to-day about it to argue why h should for the King's convenience have it, but Mr. Cov entry most justly did argue freely for them that serve cheapest. Thence walked a while with Mr. Coventry i the gallery, and first find that he is mighty cold in his pres ent opinion of Mr. Peter Pett for his flagging and doin things so lazily there, and he did also surprise me with question why Deane did not bring in their report of th timber of Clarendon. What he means thereby I know not, but at present put him off; nor do I know how to steer myself: but I must think of it, and advise with my Lord Sandwich. Thence with Creed by coach to my Lord Sandwich's, and there I got Mr. Moore to give me my Lord's hand for my receipt of £109 more of my money of Sir G. Carteret, so that then his debt to me will be under £500, I think. This do ease my mind also. Thence carried him and W. Howe into London, and set them down at Sir G. Carteret's to receive some money, and I home and there busy very late, and so home to supper and to bed, with my mind in pretty good ease, my business being in a pretty good condition every where.

17th (Lord's day). All the morning at my office doing business there, it raining hard. So dined at home alone. After dinner walked to my Lord's, and there found him and much other guests at table at dinner, and it seems they have christened his young son to-day — called him James. I got a piece of cake. I got my Lord to signe and seale my business about my selling of Brampton land, which though not so full as I would, yet is as full as I can at present. Walked home again, and there fell to read, and by and by comes my uncle Wight, Dr. Burnett, and another gentleman, and talked and drank, and the Doctor showed me the manner of eating Turpentine, which pleases me well, for it is with great ease. So they being gone, I to supper and to bed.

18th. Up, and walked to my Lord's, and there took my leave of him, he seeming very friendly to me in as serious a manner as ever in his life, and I believe he is very confident of me. He sets out this morning for Deale. Thence to St. James's to the Duke, and there did our usual business. He discourses very freely of a warr with Holland, to begin about winter, so that I believe we shall come to it. Before we went up to the Duke, Sir G. Carteret and I did talk together in the Parke about my Lord Chancellor's business of the timber; he telling me freely that my Lord Chancellor was never so angry with him in all his life, as he was for this business, in great passion; and that when he saw me there, he knew what it was about. And plots now with me how we may serve my Lord, which I am mightily glad of; and I hope together we may do it. Thence to Westminster to my barber's, to have my Periwigg he lately made me cleansed of its nits, which vexed me cruelly that he should put such a thing into my hands. Here meeting his mayd Jane, that has lived with them so long, I talked with her, and sending her of an errand to Dr. Clerk's, did meet her, and took her into a little alehouse in Brewers Yard,[1] and there did sport with her, without any knowledge of her though, and a very pretty innocent girl she is. Thence to my Lord Chancellor's, but he being busy I went away to the 'Change, and so home to dinner. By and by comes Creed, and I out with him to Fleet Street, and he to Mr. Povy's, I to my Lord Chancellor's, and missing him again walked to Povy's, and there saw his new perspective in his closet. Povy, to my great surprise and wonder, did here attacque me in his own and Mr. Bland's behalf that I should do for them both for the new contractors for the victualling of the garrison. Which I am ashamed that he should ask of me, nor did I believe that he was a man that did seek benefit in such poor things. Besides that he professed that he did not believe that I would have any hand myself in the contract, and yet here declares that he himself would have profit by it, and himself did move me that Sir W. Rider might join, and Ford with Gauden. I told him I had no interest in them, but I fear they must do something to him, for he told me that those of the Mole did promise to consider him. Thence home and Creed with me, and there he took occasion to owne his obligations to me, and did lay down twenty pieces in gold upon my shelf in my closett, which I did not refuse, but wish and expected should have been more. But, however, this is better than nothing, and now I am out of expectation, and shall henceforward know how to deal with him. After discourse of settling his matters here, we went out by coach, and he 'light at the Temple, and there took final leave of me, in order to his following my Lord to-morrow. I to my Lord Chancellor, and discoursed his business with him. I perceive, and he says plainly, that he will not have any man to have it in his

[1] There were several Brewer's Yards in London. This was probably the one by King Street, Westminster.

power to say that my Lord Chancellor did contrive the wronging the King of his timber; but yet I perceive, he would be glad to have service done him therein; and told me Sir G. Carteret hath told him that he and I would look after his business to see it done in the best manner for him. Of this I was glad, and so away. Thence home, and late with my Tangier men about drawing up their agreement with us, wherein I find much trouble, and after doing as much as we could to-night, broke up and I to bed.

19th. Up, and to the office, where we sat all the morning. At noon dined alone at home. After dinner Sir W. Batten and I down by water to Woolwich, where coming to the ropeyarde we are told that Mr. Falconer, who hath been ill of a relapse these two days, is just now dead. We went up to his widow, who is sicke in bed also. The poor woman in great sorrow, and entreats our friendship, which we shall, I think, in every thing do for her. I am sure I will. Thence to the Docke, and there in Sheldon's garden eat some fruit; so to Deptford a little, and thence home, it raining mightily, and being cold I doubted my health after it. At the office till 9 o'clock about Sir W. Warren's contract for masts, and then at home with Lanyon and Yeabsly till 12 and past about their contract for Tangier, wherein they and I differed, for I would have it drawn to the King's advantage, as much as might be, which they did not like, but parted good friends; however, when they were gone, I wished that I had forborne any disagreement till I had had their promise to me in writing. They being gone, I to bed.

20th. Up, and a while to my office, and then home with Mr. Deane till dinner, discoursing upon the business of my Lord Chancellor's timber in Clarendon Parke, and how to make a report therein without offending him; which at last I drew up, and hope it will please him. But I would to God neither I nor he ever had had any thing to have done with it! Dined together with a good pig, and then out by coach to White Hall, to the Committee for Fishing; but nothing done, it being a great day to-day there upon drawing at the Lottery[1] of Sir Arthur Slingsby. I got in

[1] Evelyn attended this lottery, which he seems to have held was a complete imposition. He wrote: "To London to see the event of the

and stood by the two Queenes and the Duchesse of Yorke, and just behind my Lady Castlemayne, whom I do heartily adore; and good sport it was to see how most that did give their ten pounds did go away with a pair of globes only for their lot, and one gentlewoman, one Mrs. Fish, with the only blanke. And one I staid to see drew a suit of hangings valued at £430, and they say are well worth the money, or near it. One other suit there is better than that; but very many lots of three and fourscore pounds. I observed the King and Queenes did get but as poor lots as any else. But the wisest man I met with was Mr. Cholmley, who insured as many as would, from drawing of the one blank for 12*d.*; in which case there was the whole number of persons to one, which I think was three or four hundred. And so he insured about 200 for 200 shillings, so that he could not have lost if one of them had drawn it, for there was enough to pay the £10; but it happened another drew it, and so he got all the money he took. I left the lottery, and went to a play, only a piece of it, which was at the Duke's house, "Worse and Worse;"[1] just the same manner of play, and writ, I believe, by the same man as "The Adventures of Five Hours;"[2] very pleasant it was, and I begin to admire Harris more than ever. Thence to Westminster to see Creed, and he and I took a walk in the Parke. He is ill, and not able yet to set out after my Lord, but will do to-morrow. So home, and late at my office, and so home to bed. This evening being moonshine I played a little late upon my flageolette in the garden. But being at Westminster Hall I met with great news that Mrs. Lane is married to one Martin, one that serves Captain Marsh. She is gone abroad with him

lottery which his Majesty had permitted Sir Arthur Slingsby to set up for one day in the Banqueting House at Whitehall. I gained only a trifle, as well as did the King, Queene Consort and Queene Mother for neere 30 lotts; which was thought to be contriv'd very unhandsomely by the master of it, who was, in truth, a meer shark" (July 19th, 1664).

[1] A comedy adapted from the Spanish by George Digby, Earl of Bristol, which was not printed.

[2] This was not so, as the "Adventures of Five Hours" was by Sir Samuel Tuke, although Downes ("Roscius Anglicanus") says that the Earl of Bristol had a hand in this play.

to-day, very fine. I must have a bout with her very shortly to see how she finds marriage.

21st. Up, and to the office, where we sat all the morning, among other things making a contract with Sir W. Warren[1] for almost 1,000 Gottenburg masts, the biggest that ever was made in the Navy, and wholly of my compassing and a good one I hope it is for the King. Dined at Sir W. Batten's, where I have not eat these many months. Sir G. Carteret, Mr. Coventry, Sir J. Minnes, and myself there only, and my Lady. A good venison pasty, and very merry, and pleasant I made myself with my Lady, and she as much to me. This morning to the office comes Nicholas Osborne, Mr. Gauden's clerke, to desire of me what piece of plate I would choose to have a £100, or thereabouts, bestowed upon me in, he having order to lay out so much; and, out of his freedom with me, do of himself come to make this question. I a great while urged my unwillingnesse to take any, not knowing how I could serve Mr. Gauden, but left it wholly to himself; so at noon I find brought home in fine leather cases a pair of the noblest flaggons that ever I saw all the days of my life; whether I shall keepe them or no I cannot tell; for it is to oblige me to him in the business of the Tangier victualling, wherein I doubt I shall not; but glad I am to see that I shall be sure to get something on one side or other, have it which will: so, with a merry heart, I looked upon them, and locked them up. After dinner to [give] my Lord Chancellor a good account of his business, and he is very well pleased therewith, and carries himself with great discretion to me, without seeming over glad or beholding to me; and yet I know that he do think himself very well served by me. Thence to Westminster and to Mrs. Lane's lodgings, to give her joy, and there suffered me to deal with her as I hoped to do, and by and by her husband

[1] Among the State Papers is a receipt by Thomas Harper, of Gottenburg deals, &c., from Sir William Warren, dated "Deptford, July 27, 1664" ("Calendar," 1663–64, p. 653). Complaints, promoted by Sir William Batten, were subsequently made respecting this contract with Sir William Warren; and Pepys alludes to them in his "Defence" (dated November 27th, 1669), which is contained in one of the Pepysian manuscripts (No. 2554).

comes, a sorry, simple fellow, and his letter to her which she proudly showed me a simple, nonsensical thing. A man of no discourse, and I fear married her to make a prize of, which he is mistaken in, and a sad wife I believe she will prove to him, for she urged me to appoint a time as soon as he is gone out of town to give her a meeting next week. So by water with a couple of cozens of Mrs. Lane's, and set them down at Queenhive, and I through Bridge home, and there late at business, and so home to supper and to bed.

22nd. Up and to my office, where busy all the morning. At noon to the 'Change, and so home to dinner, and then down by water to Deptford, where coming too soon, I spent an houre in looking round the yarde, and putting Mr. Shish[1] to measure a piece or two of timber, which he did most cruelly wrong, and to the King's losse 12 or 13*s.* in a piece of 28 feet in contents. Thence to the Clerke of the Cheques, from whose house Mr. Falconer was buried to-day; Sir J. Minnes and I the only principall officers that were there. We walked to church with him, and then I left them without staying the sermon and straight home by water, and there find as I expected, Mr. Hill, and Andrews, and one slovenly and ugly fellow, Seignor Pedro, who sings Italian songs to the theorbo most neatly, and they spent the whole evening in singing the best piece of musique counted of all hands in the world, made by Seignor Charissimi,[2] the famous master in Rome. Fine it was, indeed, and too fine for me to judge of. They have spoke

[1] Jonas Shish, master-shipwright at Deptford. There are several papers of his among the State Papers. "I was at the funeral of old Mr. Shish, Master Shipwright of His Majesty's Yard here, an honest and remarkable man, and his death a public loss, for his excellent success in building ships (though altogether illiterate) and for bringing up so many of his children to be able artists. I held up the pall with three knights who did him that honour, and he was worthy of it. It was the custom of this good man to rise in the night and pray, kneeling in his own coffin, which he had lying by him for many years. He was born that famous year, the Gunpowder-plot, 1605" (Evelyn's "Diary," May 13th, 1680).

[2] Giacomo Carissimi, maestro di capella of St. Apollinare, in the German College at Rome, one of the most excellent of the Italian musicians. He lived to be ninety years old, composed much, and died very rich (Hawkins's "Hist. of Music"). — B.

to Pedro to meet us every weeke, and I fear it will grow a trouble to me if we once come to bid judges to meet us, especially idle Masters, which do a little displease me to consider. They gone comes Mr. Lanyon, who tells me Mr. Alsopp is now become dangerously ill, and fears his recovery, which shakes my expectation of £300 per annum by the business; and, therefore, bless God for what Mr. Gauden hath sent me, which, from some discourse to-day with Mr. Osborne, swearing that he knows not any thing of this business of the victualling; but, the contrary, that it is not that moves Mr. Gauden to send it me, for he hath had order for it any time these two months. Whether this be true or no, I know not; but I shall hence with the more confidence keepe it. To supper and to the office a little, and to walk in the garden, the moon shining bright, and fine warm fair weather, and so home to bed.

23rd. Up, and all the morning at the office. At noon to the 'Change, where I took occasion to break the business of my Lord Chancellor's timber to Mr. Coventry in the best manner I could. He professed to me, that, till Sir G. Carteret did speake of it at the table, after our officers were gone to survey it, he did not know that my Lord Chancellor had any thing to do with it; but now he says that he had been told by the Duke that Sir G. Carteret had spoke to him about it, and that he had told the Duke that, were he in my Lord Chancellor's case, if he were his father, he would rather fling away the gains of two or £3,000, than have it said that the timber, which should have been the King's, if it had continued the Duke of Albemarle's, was concealed by us in favour of my Lord Chancellor; for, says he, he is a great man, and all such as he, and he himself particularly, have a great many enemies that would be glad of such an advantage against him. When I told him it was strange that Sir J. Minnes and Sir G. Carteret, that knew my Lord Chancellor's concernment therein, should not at first inform us, he answered me that for Sir J. Minnes, he is looked upon to be an old good companion, but by nobody at the other end of the towne as any man of business, and that my Lord Chancellor, he dares say, never did tell him of it, only Sir G. Carteret, he do believe, must needs know it, for he and Sir J. Shaw are the greatest confidants he hath in the world. So for himself, he said, he would not mince the matter, but was resolved to do what was fit, and stand upon his owne legs therein, and that he would speak to the Duke, that he and Sir G. Carteret might be appointed to attend my Lord Chancellor in it. All this disturbs me mightily. I know not what to say to it, nor how to carry myself therein; for a compliance will discommend me to Mr. Coventry, and a discompliance to my Lord Chancellor. But I think to let it alone, or at least meddle in it as little more as I can. From thence walked toward Westminster, and being in an idle and wanton humour, walked through Fleet Alley, and there stood a most pretty wench at one of the doors, so I took a turn or two, but what by sense of honour and conscience I would not go in, but much against my will took coach and away, and away to Westminster Hall, and there 'light of Mrs. Lane, and plotted with her to go over the water. So met at White's stairs in Chanel Row, and over to the old house at Lambeth Marsh, and there eat and drank, and had my pleasure of her twice, she being the strangest woman in talk of love to her husband sometimes, and sometimes again she do not care for him, and yet willing enough to allow me a liberty of doing what I would with her. So spending 5*s.* or 6*s.* upon her, I could do what I would, and after an hour's stay and more back again and set her ashore there again, and I forward to Fleet Street, and called at Fleet Alley, not knowing how to command myself, and went in and there saw what formerly I have been acquainted with, the wickedness of these houses, and the forcing a man to present expense. The woman indeed is a most lovely woman, but I had no courage to meddle with her for fear of her not being wholesome, and so counterfeiting that I had not money enough, it was pretty to see how cunning she was, would not suffer me to have to do in any manner with her after she saw I had no money, but told me then I would not come again, but she now was sure I would come again, but I hope in God I shall not, for though she be one of the prettiest women I ever saw, yet I fear her abusing me. So desiring God to forgive me for this vanity, I went home, taking some books from my bookseller, and taking his lad home with me, to whom I paid £10 for books I have laid up money for, and laid out within these three weeks, and shall do no more a great while I hope. So to my office writing letters, and then home and to bed, weary of the pleasure I have had to-day, and ashamed to think of it.

24th (Lord's day). Up, in some pain all day from yesterday's passages, having taken cold, I suppose. So staid within all day reading of two or three good plays. At night to my office a little, and so home, after supper to bed.

25th. Up, and with Sir J. Minnes and Sir W. Batten by coach to St. James's, but there the Duke being gone out we to my Lord Berkeley's chamber, Mr. Coventry being there, and among other things there met with a printed copy of the King's commission for the repair of Paul's,[1] which is very large, and large power for collecting money, and recovering of all people that had bought or sold formerly any thing belonging to the Church. And here I find my Lord Mayor of the City set in order before the Archbishopp or any nobleman, though all the greatest officers of state are there. But yet I do not hear by my Lord Berkeley, who is one of them, that any thing is like to come of it. Thence back again homewards, and Sir W. Batten and I to the Coffee-house, but no newes, only the plague is very hot still, and encreases among the Dutch. Home to dinner, and after dinner walked forth, and do what I could I could not keep myself from going through Fleet Lane, but had the sense of safety and honour not to go in, and the rather being a holiday I feared I might meet with some people that might know me. Thence to Charing Cross, and there called at Unthanke's to see what I owed, but found nothing, and here being a couple of pretty ladies, lodgers in the kitchen, I staid a little there. Thence to my barber Gervas, who this day buries his child, which it seems was born without a passage behind, so that it never voided any thing

[1] "I went to St. Paul's church, where, with Dr. Wren, Mr. Pratt, Mr. May, Mr. Thomas Chicheley, Mr. Slingsby, the Bishop of London, the Dean of St. Paul's (Dr. Sancroft), and several expert workmen, we went about to survey the general decays of that ancient and venerable church, and to set down in writing the particulars of what was fit to be done, with the charge thereof, giving our opinion from article to article" (Evelyn's "Diary," August 27th, 1666). — M. B.

in the week or fortnight that it has been born. Thence to Mr. Reeves, it coming just now in my head to buy a microscope, but he was not within, so I walked all round that end of the town among the loathsome people and houses, but, God be thanked! had no desire to visit any of them. So home, where I met Mr. Lanyon, who tells me Mr. Alsop is past hopes, which will mightily disappoint me in my hopes there, and yet it may be not. I shall think whether it will be safe for me to venture myself or no, and come in as an adventurer. He gone, Mr. Cole (my old Jack Cole) comes to see and speak with me, and his errand in short to tell me that he is giving over his trade; he can do no good in it, and will turn what he has into money and go to sea, his father being dead and leaving him little, if any thing. This I was sorry to hear, he being a man of good parts, but, I fear, debauched. I promised him all the friendship I can do him, which will end in little, though I truly mean it, and so I made him stay with me till 11 at night, talking of old school stories, and very pleasing ones, and truly I find that we did spend our time and thoughts then otherwise than I think boys do now, and I think as well as methinks that the best are now. He supped with me, and so away, and I to bed. And strange to see how we are all divided that were bred so long at school together, and what various fortunes we have run, some good, some bad.

26th. All the morning at the office, at noon to Anthony Joyce's, to our gossip's dinner. I had sent a dozen and a half of bottles of wine thither, and paid my double share besides, which is 18*s.* Very merry we were, and when the women were merry and rose from table, I above with them, ne'er a man but I, I began discourse of my not getting of children, and prayed them to give me their opinions and advice, and they freely and merrily did give me these ten, among them — (1) Do not hug my wife too hard nor too much; (2) eat no late suppers; (3) drink juyce of sage; (4) tent and toast; (5) wear cool holland drawers; (6) keep stomach warm and back cool; (7) upon query whether it was best to do at night or morn, they answered me neither one nor other, but when we had most mind to it; (8) wife not to go too straight laced; (9) myself to drink mum and sugar; (10) Mrs. Ward did give me, to change my place. The 3rd, 4th, 6th, 7th, and 10th they all did seriously declare, and lay much stress upon them as rules fit to be observed indeed, and especially the last, to lie with our heads where our heels do, or at least to make the bed high at feet and low at head. Very merry all, as much as I could be in such sorry company. Great discourse of the fray yesterday in Moorefields, how the butchers at first did beat the weavers (between whom there hath been ever an old competition for mastery), but at last the weavers rallied and beat them. At first the butchers knocked down all for weavers that had green or blue aprons, till they were fain to pull them off and put them in their breeches. At last the butchers were fain to pull off their sleeves, that they might not be known, and were soundly beaten out of the field, and some deeply wounded and bruised; till at last the weavers went out tryumphing, calling £100 for a butcher. I to Mr. Reeves to see a microscope, he having been with me to-day morning, and there chose one which I will have. Thence back and took up young Mrs. Harman, a pretty bred and pretty humoured woman whom I could love well, though not handsome, yet for her person and carriage, and black. By the way met her husband going for her, and set them both down at home, and so home to my office a while, and so to supper and bed.

27th. Up, and after some discourse with Mr. Duke, who is to be Secretary to the Fishery,[1] and is now Secretary to the Committee for Trade, who I find a very ingenious man, I went to Mr. Povy's, and there heard a little of his empty discourse, and fain he would have Mr. Gauden been the victualler for Tangier, which none but a fool would say to me when he knows he hath made it his request to me to get him something of these men that now do it. Thence to St. James's, but Mr. Coventry being ill and in bed I did not stay, but to White Hall a little, walked up and down, and so home to fit papers against this afternoon, and after dinner

[1] "March 14, 1664. The King to the Duke of York, Governor, and the Assistants of the Royal Fishing Company. Recommends George Duke, late Secretary of the Committee for Trade, to be entertained by them in the same post, for which he is particularly fitted" ("Calendar of State Papers," 1663–64, p. 515).

to the 'Change a little, and then to White Hall, where anon the Duke of Yorke came, and a Committee we had of Tangier, where I read over my rough draught of the contract for Tangier victualling, and acquainted them with the death of Mr. Alsopp, which Mr. Lanyon had told me this morning, which is a sad consideration to see how uncertain a thing our lives are, and how little to be presumed of in our greatest undertakings. The words of the contract approved of, and I home and there came Mr. Lanyon to me and brought my neighbour, Mr. Andrews, to me, whom he proposes for his partner in the room of Mr. Alsopp, and I like well enough of it. We read over the contract together, and discoursed it well over and so parted, and I am glad to see it once over in this condition again, for Mr. Lanyon and I had some discourse to-day about my share in it, and I hope if it goes on to have my first hopes of £300 per ann. They gone, I to supper and to bed. This afternoon came my great store of Coles in, being 10 Chaldron, so that I may see how long they will last me.

28th. At the office all the morning, dined, after 'Change, at home, and then abroad, and seeing "The Bondman"[1] upon the posts, I consulted my oaths and find I may go safely this time without breaking it; I went thither, notwithstanding my great desire to have gone to Fleet Alley, God forgive me, again. There I saw it acted. It is true, for want of practice, they had many of them forgot their parts a little; but Betterton and my poor Ianthe outdo all the world. There is nothing more taking in the world with me than that play. Thence to Westminster to my barbers, and strange to think how when I find that Jervas himself did intend to bring home my periwigg, and not Jane his maid, I did desire not to have it at all, for I had a mind to have her bring it home. I also went to Mr. Blagrave's about speaking to him for his kinswoman to come live with my wife, but they are not come to town, and so I home by coach and to my office, and then to supper and to bed. My present posture is thus: my wife in the country and my mayde Besse with her and all quiett there. I am endeavouring to find a woman for her to my mind, and above all

[1] Massinger's tragedy, first acted before the Court at Whitehall, 1623.

one that understands musique, especially singing. I am the willinger to keepe one because I am in good hopes to get 2 or £300 per annum extraordinary by the business of the victualling of Tangier, and yet Mr. Alsopp, my chief hopes, is dead since my looking after it, and now Mr. Lanyon, I fear, is falling sicke too. I am pretty well in health, only subject to wind upon any cold, and then immediate and great pains. All our discourse is of a Dutch warr, and I find it is likely to come to it, for they are very high and desire not to compliment us at all, as far as I hear, but to send a good fleete to Guinny to oppose us there. My Lord Sandwich newly gone to sea, and I, I think, fallen into his very good opinion again, at least he did before his going, and by his letter since, show me all manner of respect and confidence. I am over-joyed in hopes that upon this month's account I shall find myself worth £1,000, besides the rich present of two silver and gilt flaggons which Mr. Gauden did give me the other day. I do now live very prettily at home, being most seriously, quietly, and neatly served by my two mayds Jane and the girle Su, with both of whom I am mightily well pleased. My greatest trouble is the settling of Brampton Estate, that I may know what to expect, and how to be able to leave it when I die, so as to be just to my promise to my uncle Thomas and his son. The next thing is this cursed trouble my brother Tom is likely to put us to by his death, forcing us to law with his creditors, among others Dr. Tom Pepys, and that with some shame as trouble, and the last how to know in what manner as to saving or spending my father lives, lest they should run me in debt as one of my uncle's executors, and I never the wiser nor better for it. But in all this I hope shortly to be at leisure to consider and inform myself well.

29th. At the office all the morning dispatching of business, at noon to the 'Change after dinner, and thence to Tom Trice about Dr. Pepys's business, and thence it raining turned into Fleet Alley, and there was with Cocke an hour or so. The jade, whether I would not give her money or not enough, she would not offer to invite to do anything, but on the contrary saying she had no time, which I was glad of, for I had no mind to meddle with her, but had my end to see what a cunning jade she was, to see her impudent tricks and ways of getting money and raising the reckoning by still calling for things, that it come to 6 or 7 shillings presently. So away home, glad I escaped without any inconvenience, and there came Mr. Hill, Andrews and Seignor Pedro, and great store of musique we had, but I begin to be weary of having a master with us, for it spoils, methinks, the ingenuity of our practice. After they were gone comes Mr. Bland to me, sat till 11 at night with me, talking of the garrison of Tangier and serving them with pieces of eight. A mind he hath to be employed there, but dares not desire any courtesy of me, and yet would fain engage me to be for him, for I perceive they do all find that I am the busy man to see the King have right done him by inquiring out other bidders. Being quite tired with him, I got him gone, and so to bed.

30th. All the morning at the office; at noon to the 'Change, where great talke of a rich present brought by an East India ship from some of the Princes of India, worth to the King £70,000 in two precious stones. After dinner to the office, and there all the afternoon making an end of several things against the end of the month, that I may clear all my reckonings to-morrow; also this afternoon, with great content, I finished the contracts for victualling of Tangier with Mr. Lanyon and the rest, and to my comfort got him and Andrews to sign to the giving me £300 per annum, by which, at least, I hope to be a £100 or two the better. Wrote many letters by the post to ease my mind of business and to clear my paper of minutes, as I did lately oblige myself to clear every thing against the end of the month. So at night with my mind quiet and contented to bed. This day I sent a side of venison and six bottles of wine to Kate Joyce.

31st (Lord's day). Up, and to church, where I have not been these many weeks. So home, and thither, inviting him yesterday, comes Mr. Hill, at which I was a little troubled, but made up all very well, carrying him with me to Sir J. Minnes, where I was invited and all our families to a venison pasty. Here good cheer and good discourse. After dinner Mr. Hill and I to my house, and there to musique all the afternoon. He being gone, in the evening I to my accounts, and to my great joy and with great thanks to Almighty God, I do find myself most clearly worth £1,014, the first time that ever I was worth £1,000 before, which is the height of all that ever I have for a long time pretended to. But by the blessing of God upon my care I hope to lay up something more in a little time, if this business of the victualling of Tangier goes on as I hope it will. So with praise to God for this state of fortune that I am brought to as to wealth, and my condition being as I have at large set it down two days ago in this book, I home to supper and to bed, desiring God to give me the grace to make good use of what I have and continue my care and diligence to gain more.

August 1st. Up, my mind very light from my last night's accounts, and so up and with Sir J. Minnes, Sir W. Batten, and Sir W. Pen to St. James's, where among other things having prepared with some industry every man a part this morning and no sooner (for fear they should either consider of it or discourse of it one to another) Mr. Coventry did move the Duke and obtain it that one of the clerkes of the Clerke of the Acts should have an addition of £30 a year, as Mr. Turner hath, which I am glad of, that I may give T. Hater £20 and keep £10 towards a boy's keeping. Thence Mr. Coventry and I to the Attorney's chamber at the Temple, but not being there we parted, and I home, and there with great joy told T. Hater what I had done, with which the poor wretch was very glad, though his modesty would not suffer him to say much. So to the Coffee-house, and there all the house full of the victory Generall Soushe[1] (who is a Frenchman, a soldier of fortune, commanding part of the German army) hath had against the Turke; killing 4,000 men, and taking most extraordinary spoil. Thence taking up Harman and his wife, carried them to Anthony Joyce's, where we had my venison in a pasty well done; but, Lord! to see how much they made of it, as if they had never eat any before, and very merry we were, but Will most troublesomely so, and I find he and his wife have a most wretched life one with another, but we took no notice, but were very merry as I could be in such company. But Mrs. Harman is a very pretty-

[1] General Soushe was Louis Ratuit, Comte de Souches. The battle was fought at Lewenz (or Leva), in Hungary. — B.

humoured wretch, whom I could love with all my heart, being so good and innocent company. Thence to Westminster to Mr. Blagrave's, and there, after singing a thing or two over, I spoke to him about a woman for my wife, and he offered me his kinswoman, which I was glad of, but she is not at present well, but however I hope to have her. Thence to my Lord Chancellor's, and thence with Mr. Coventry, who appointed to meet me there, and with him to the Attorney General, and there with Sir Ph. Warwicke consulted of a new commission to be had through the Broad Seale to enable us to make this contract for Tangier victualling. So home, and there talked long with Will about the young woman of his family which he spoke of for to live with my wife, but though she hath very many good qualitys, yet being a neighbour's child and young and not very staid, I dare not venture of having her, because of her being able to spread any report of our family upon any discontent among the heart of our neighbours. So that my dependance is upon Mr. Blagrave, and so home to supper and to bed. Last night, at 12 o'clock, I was waked with knocking at Sir W. Pen's door; and what was it but people's running up and down to bring him word that his brother,[1] who hath been a good while, it seems, sicke, is dead.

2nd. At the office all the morning. At noon dined, and then to the 'Change, and there walked two hours or more with Sir W. Warren, who after much discourse in general of Sir W. Batten's dealings, he fell to talk how every body must live by their places, and that he was willing, if I desired it, that I should go shares with him in anything that he deals in. He told me again and again, too, that he confesses himself my debtor £100 for my service and friendship to him in his present great contract of masts, and that between this and Christmas he shall be in

[1] George Penn, the elder brother of Sir W. Penn, was a wealthy merchant at San Lucar, the port of Seville. He was seized as a heretic by the Holy Office, and cast into a dungeon eight feet square and dark as the grave. There he remained three years, every month being scourged to make him confess his crimes. At last, after being twice put to the rack, he offered to confess whatever they would suggest. His property, £12,000, was then confiscated, his wife, a Catholic, taken from him, and he was banished from Spain for ever. — M. B.

stocke and will pay it me. This I like well, but do not desire to become a merchant, and, therefore, put it off, but desired time to think of it. Thence to the King's play-house, and there saw "Bartholomew Fayre," which do still please me; and is, as it is acted, the best comedy in the world, I believe. I chanced to sit by Tom Killigrew, who tells me that he is setting up a Nursery;[1] that is, is going to build a house in Moorefields, wherein he will have common plays acted. But four operas it shall have in the year, to act six weeks at a time; where we shall have the best scenes and machines, the best musique, and every thing as magnificent as is in Christendome; and to that end hath sent for voices and painters and other persons from Italy. Thence homeward called upon my Lord Marlborough, and so home and to my office, and then to Sir W. Pen, and with him and our fellow officers and servants of the house and none else to Church to lay his brother in the ground, wherein nothing handsome at all, but that he lays him under the Communion table in the chancel, about nine at night.[2] So home and to bed.

3rd. Up betimes and set some joyners on work to new lay my floor in our wardrobe, which I intend to make a room for musique. Thence abroad to Westminster, among other things to Mr. Blagrave's, and there had his consent for his kinswoman to come to be with my wife for her woman, at which I am well pleased and hope she may do well. Thence to White Hall to meet with Sir G. Carteret about hiring some ground to make our mast docke at Deptford, but being Council morning failed, but met with Mr. Coventry, and he and I discoursed of the likeliness of a Dutch warr, which I think is very likely now, for the Dutch do prepare a fleet to oppose us at Guinny, and he do think we shall, though neither of us have a mind to it, fall into

[1] Among the State Papers is the licence (dated March, 1664) to William Legg "to erect a nursery for breeding players in London or Westminster under the oversight and approbation of Sir Wm. Davenant and Thos. Killigrew to be disposed of for the supply of the theatres" ("Calendar," Domestic, 1663-64, p. 539).

[2] The Rev. Alfred Povah, D.D., rector of St. Olave's, Hart Street, has been so kind as to give the editor the following extract from the register of burials of that parish, in illustration of the above entry: "1664, August 3. Mr. George Penn was Buryed in ye Chancell."

it of a sudden, and yet the plague do increase among them, and is got into their fleet, and Opdam's own ship, which makes it strange they should be so high. Thence to the 'Change, and thence home to dinner, and down by water to Woolwich to the rope yard, and there visited Mrs. Falconer, who tells me odd stories of how Sir W. Pen was rewarded by her husband with a gold watch (but seems not certain of what Sir W. Batten told me, of his daughter having a life given her in £80 per ann.) for his helping him to his place, and yet cost him £150 to Mr. Coventry besides. He did much advise it seems Mr. Falconer not to marry again, expressing that he would have him make his daughter his heire, or words to that purpose, and that that makes him, she thinks, so cold in giving her any satisfaction, and that W. Boddam hath publickly said, since he came down thither to be clerke of the ropeyard, that it hath this week cost him £100, and would be glad that it would cost him but half as much more for the place, and that he was better before than now, and that if he had been to have bought it, he would not have given so much for it. Now I am sure that Mr. Coventry hath again and again said that he would take nothing, but would give all his part in it freely to him, that so the widow might have something. What the meaning of this is I know not, but that Sir W. Pen do get something by it. Thence to the Dockeyard, and there saw the new ship in great forwardness. So home and to supper, and then to the office, where late, Mr. Bland and I talking about Tangier business, and so home to bed.

4th. Up betimes and to the office, fitting myself against a great dispute about the East India Company, which spent afterwards with us all the morning. At noon dined with Sir W. Pen, a piece of beef only, and I counterfeited a friendship and mirth which I cannot have with him, yet out with him by his coach, and he did carry me to a play and pay for me at the King's house, which is "The Rivall Ladys," [1] a very innocent and most pretty witty play. I was much pleased with it, and it being given me, [2] I look upon it as no breach to my oathe. Here we hear that

[1] A tragi-comedy by Dryden, first printed in this year.

[2] His companion paid for him. — B.

Clun,[1] one of their best actors, was, the last night, going out of towne (after he had acted the Alchymist, wherein was one of his best parts that he acts) to his country-house, set upon and murdered; one of the rogues taken, an Irish fellow. It seems most cruelly butchered and bound. The house will have a great miss of him. Thence visited my Lady Sandwich, who tells me my Lord Fitz-Harding[2] is to be made a Marquis. Thence home to my office late, and so to supper and to bed.

5th. Up very betimes and set my plaisterer to work about whiting and colouring my musique roome, which having with great pleasure seen done, about ten o'clock I dressed myself, and so mounted upon a very pretty mare, sent me by Sir W. Warren, according to his promise yesterday. And so through the City, not a little proud, God knows, to be seen upon so pretty a beast, and to my cozen W. Joyce's, who presently mounted too, and he and I out of towne toward Highgate; in the way, at Kentish-towne, showing me the place and manner of Clun's being killed and laid in a ditch, and yet was not killed by any wounds, having only one in his arm, but bled to death through his struggling. He told me, also, the manner of it, of his going home so late [from] drinking with his whore, and manner of having it found out. Thence forward to Barnett, and there drank, and so by night to Stevenage, it raining a little, but not much, and there to my great trouble, find that my wife was not come, nor any Stamford coach gone down this week, so that she cannot come. So vexed and weary, and not thoroughly out of pain neither in my old parts, I after supper to bed, and after a little sleep, W. Joyce comes in his shirt into my chamber, with a note and a messenger from my wife, that she was come by Yorke coach to Bigglesworth, and would be with us to-morrow morning. So, mightily pleased at

[1] A poem upon the death of Walter Clun was published at the time, with the following title: "An Elegy upon the most execrable murder of Mr. Clun, one of the comedians of the Theatre Royal, who was robbed and most inhumanly killed on Tuesday night, being the 2nd of August, 1664, near Tatnam Court, as he was riding to his country house at Kentish Town." Clun was noted for his performance of Iago.

[2] Charles Berkeley, Viscount Fitzharding, was created Earl of Falmouth in March, 1665, and he was killed in battle in the following June. He was never made a marquis.

her discreete action in this business, I with peace to sleep again till next morning. So up, and

6th. Here lay Deane Honiwood last night. I met and talked with him this morning, and a simple priest he is, though a good, well-meaning man. W. Joyce and I to a game at bowles on the green there till eight o'clock, and then comes my wife in the coach, and a coach full of women, only one man riding by, gone down last night to meet a sister of his coming to town. So very joyful drank there, not 'lighting, and we mounted and away with them to Welling,[1] and there 'light, and dined very well and merry and glad to see my poor wife. Here very merry as being weary I could be, and after dinner, out again, and to London. In our way all the way the mightiest merry, at a couple of young gentlemen, come down to meet the same gentlewoman, that ever I was in my life, and so W. Joyce too, to see how one of them was horsed upon a hard-trotting sorrell horse, and both of them soundly weary and galled. But it is not to be set down how merry we were all the way. We 'light in Holborne, and by another coach my wife and mayde home, and I by horseback, and found all things well and most mighty neate and clean. So, after welcoming my wife a little, to the office, and so home to supper, and then weary and not very well to bed.

7th (Lord's day). Lay long caressing my wife and talking, she telling me sad stories of the ill, improvident, disquiett, and sluttish manner that my father and mother and Pall live in the country, which troubles me mightily, and I must seek to remedy it. So up and ready, and my wife also, and then down and I showed my wife, to her great admiration and joy, Mr. Gauden's present of plate, the two flaggons, which indeed are so noble that I hardly can think that they are yet mine. So blessing God for it, we down to dinner mighty pleasant, and so up after dinner for a while, and I then to White Hall, walked thither, having at home met with a letter of Captain Cooke's, with which he had sent a boy for me to see, whom he did intend to recommend to me. I therefore went and there met and spoke with him. He gives me great hopes of the boy, which pleases me, and at Chappell I there met Mr. Blagrave, who

[1] Welwyn.

gives a report of the boy, and he showed me him, and I spoke to him, and the boy seems a good willing boy to come to me, and I hope will do well. I am to speak to Mr. Townsend to hasten his clothes for him, and then he is to come. So I walked homeward and met with Mr. Spong, and he with me as far as the Old Exchange talking of many ingenuous[1] things, musique, and at last of glasses, and I find him still the same ingenuous[1] man that ever he was, and do among other fine things tell me that by his microscope of his owne making he do discover that the wings of a moth is made just as the feathers of the wing of a bird, and that most plainly and certainly. While we were talking came by several poor creatures carried by, by constables, for being at a conventicle. They go like lambs, without any resistance. I would to God they would either conform, or be more wise, and not be catched! Thence parted with him, mightily pleased with his company, and away homeward, calling at Dan Rawlinson, and supped there with my uncle Wight, and then home and eat again for form sake with her, and then to prayers and to bed.

8th. Up and abroad with Sir W. Batten, by coach to St. James's, where by the way he did tell me how Sir J. Minnes would many times arrogate to himself the doing of that that all the Board have equal share in, and more that to himself which he hath had nothing to do in, and particularly the late paper given in by him to the Duke, the translation of a Dutch print concerning the quarrel between us and them, which he did give as his own when it was Sir Richard Ford's wholly. Also he told me how Sir W. Pen (it falling in our discourse touching Mrs. Falconer) was at first very great for Mr. Coventry to bring him in guests, and that at high rates for places, and very open was he to me therein. After business done with the Duke, I home to the Coffee-house, and so home to dinner, and after dinner to hang up my fine pictures in my dining room, which makes it very pretty, and so my wife and I abroad to the King's playhouse, she giving me her time of the last month, she having not seen any then; so my vowe is not broke at all, it costing me no more money than it would have done upon her, had she gone both her times that were due to her.

[1] See note, March 14th, 1662-63.

Here we saw "Flora's Figarys."[1] I never saw it before, and by the most ingenuous performance of the young jade Flora, it seemed as pretty a pleasant play as ever I saw in my life. So home to supper, and then to my office late, Mr. Andrews and I to talk about our victualling commission, and then he being gone I to set down my four days past journalls and expenses, and so home to bed.

9th. Up, and to my office, and there we sat all the morning, at noon home, and there by appointment Mr. Blagrave came and dined with me, and brought a friend of his of the Chappell with him. Very merry at dinner, and then up to my chamber and there we sung a Psalm or two of Lawes's, then he and I a little talke by ourselves of his kinswoman that is to come to live with my wife, who is to come about ten days hence, and I hope will do well. They gone I to my office, and there my head being a little troubled with the little wine I drank, though mixed with beer, but it may be a little more than I used to do, and yet I cannot say so, I went home and spent the afternoon with my wife talking, and then in the evening a little to my office, and so home to supper and to bed. This day comes the newes that the Emperour hath beat the Turke;[2] killed the Grand Vizier and several great Bassas, with an army of 80,000 men killed and routed; with some considerable loss of his own side, having lost three generals, and the French forces all cut off almost.[3] Which is thought as good a service to the Emperour as beating the Turke almost,

[1] "Flora's Vagaries," a comedy by Richard Rhodes when a student at Oxford, was first acted by his fellow-students at Christ Church on January 8th, 1663. Sir Henry Herbert records its performance in London on November 3rd, 1663. It was printed in 1670 and 1677. The character of Flora was afterwards played by Nell Gwynn (see October 5th, 1667).

[2] This was the battle of St. Gothard, in which the Turks were defeated with great slaughter by the imperial forces under Montecuculli, assisted by the confederates from the Rhine, and by forty troops of French cavalry under Coligni. St. Gothard is in Hungary, on the river Raab, near the frontier of Styria; it is about one hundred and twenty miles south of Vienna, and thirty east of Grätz. The battle took place on the 9th Moharrem, A.H. 1075, or 23rd July, A.D. 1664 (old style), which is that used by Pepys. — B.

[3] The fact is, the Germans were beaten by the Turks, and the French won the battle for them. — B.

for had they conquered they would have been as troublesome to him.

10th. Up, and, being ready, abroad to do several small businesses, among others to find out one to engrave my tables upon my new sliding rule with silver plates, it being so small that Browne that made it cannot get one to do it. So I find out Cocker,[1] the famous writing-master, and get him to do it, and I set an hour by him to see him design it all; and strange it is to see him with his natural eyes to cut so small at his first designing it, and read it all over, without any missing, when for my life I could not, with my best skill, read one word or letter of it; but it is use. But he says that the best light for his life to do a very small thing by (contrary to Chaucer's words to the Sun, "that he should lend his light to them that small seals grave"[2]), it should be by an artificial light of a candle, set to advantage, as he could do it. I find the fellow, by his discourse, very ingenuous; and among other things, a great

[1] Edward Cocker (whose name has become proverbial) is associated in popular memory with a work in the production of which there is every probability that he had nothing to do. He was born in 1631, probably in Norfolk, and at one time he was a schoolmaster at Northampton. Between 1657 and 1675, when he died, he published a large number of works on penmanship and the rules of arithmetic. In 1657 he was living in St. Paul's Churchyard, and not long before his death he removed to "Gutter Lane near Cheapside." He was buried in St. George's Church, Southwark. In 1678, three years after his death, John Hawkins published the famous "Cocker's Arithmetick," and stated that it was printed from Cocker's own copy; but Professor De Morgan was of opinion that the work was a forgery by Hawkins. In 1685 Hawkins published what he styled "Cocker's Decimal Arithmetick." We learn something of Cocker's personality from several entries in the Diary (see article, "Who was Cocker?" "Bibliographer," July, 1884, vol. vi., p. 25).

[2] Pepys refers to the passage in "Troylus and Cryseyde" (book iii., stanza ccii., lines 1408–1414):

"Allas! what hath this lovers the agylte?
Dispitous Day, thyn be the pyne of Helle!
For many a lover hastow slayn, and wilt;
Thi pourynge in wol nowher lat hem dwelle:
What? profrestow thi light here for to selle?
Go selle it hem that smale seles grave,
We wol the nought, as nedeth no day have."

Morris's Aldine edition of Chaucer, vol. iv., p. 284.

admirer and well read in all our English poets, and undertakes to judge of them all, and that not impertinently. Well pleased with his company and better with his judgement upon my Rule, I left him and home, whither Mr. Deane by agreement came to me and dined with me, and by chance Gunner Batters's wife. After dinner Deane and I [had] great discourse again about my Lord Chancellor's timber, out of which I wish I may get well. Thence I to Cocker's again, and sat by him with good discourse again for an hour or two, and then left him, and by agreement with Captain Silas Taylor (my old acquaintance at the Exchequer) to the Post Office[1] to hear some instrument musique of Mr. Berchenshaw's before my Lord Brunkard[2] and Sir Robert Murray. I must confess, whether it be that I hear it but seldom, or that really voice is better, but so it is that I found no pleasure at all in it, and methought two voyces were worth twenty of it. So home to my office a while, and then to supper and to bed.

11th. Up, and through pain, to my great grief forced to wear my gowne to keep my legs warm. At the office all the morning, and there a high dispute against Sir W. Batten and Sir W. Pen about the breadth of canvas again, they being for the making of it narrower, I and Mr. Coventry and Sir J. Minnes for the keeping it broader. So home to dinner, and by and by comes Mr. Creed, lately come from the Downes, and dined with me. I show him a good countenance, but love him not for his base ingratitude to me. However, abroad, carried my wife to buy things at the New Exchange, and so to my Lady Sandwich's, and there merry, talking with her a great while, and so home, whither comes Cocker with my rule, which he hath engraved to admiration, for goodness and smallness of work: it cost me 14*s.* the doing, and mightily pleased I am with it. By

[1] The General Post Office was originally in Cloak Lane, Dowgate Hill, but was subsequently removed to the Black Swan, Bishopsgate. The latter place was destroyed in the Fire of London in 1666. There is no notice of these music meetings in the records of the Post Office.

[2] Lord Viscount Brouncker was the first president of the Royal Society after the charter had been obtained, but Sir Robert Moray had been appointed president when the society was first founded, and it was in his honour as a Scotsman that the anniversary meeting was fixed to take place annually on St. Andrew's Day (November 30th).

and by, he gone, comes Mr. Moore and staid talking with me a great while about my Lord's businesses, which I fear will be in a bad condition for his family if my Lord should miscarry at sea. He gone, I late to my office, and cannot forbear admiring and consulting my new rule, and so home to supper and to bed. This day, for a wager before the King, my Lords of Castlehaven and Arran (a son of my Lord of Ormond's), they two alone did run down and kill a stoute bucke in St. James's parke.

12th. Up, and all the morning busy at the office with Sir W. Warren about a great contract for New England masts, where I was very hard with him, even to the making him angry, but I thought it fit to do it as well as just for my owne [and] the King's behalf. At noon to the 'Change a little, and so to dinner and then out by coach, setting my wife and mayde down, going to Stevens the silversmith to change some old silver lace and to go buy new silke lace for a petticoat; I to White Hall and did much business at a Tangier Committee; where, among other things, speaking about propriety of the houses there, and how we ought to let the Portugeses[1] have right done them, as many of them as continue, or did sell the houses while they were in possession, and something further in their favour, the Duke in an anger I never observed in him before, did cry, says he, "All the world rides us, and I think we shall never ride anybody." Thence home, and, though late, yet Pedro being there, he sang a song and parted. I did give him 5*s*., but find it burdensome and so will break up the meeting. At night is brought home our poor Fancy, which to my great grief continues lame still, so that I wish she had not been brought ever home again, for it troubles me to see her.

13th. Up, and before I went to the office comes my Taylor with a coate I have made to wear within doors, purposely to come no lower than my knees, for by my wearing a gowne within doors comes all my tenderness about my

[1] Portuguese has frequently been treated as a plural, and a false singular, Portuguee, formed from it. See an interesting paper by Mr. Danby P. Fry, "On the words Chinee, Maltee, Portuguee, Yankee, Pea, Cherry, Sherry, and Shay" ("Philological Society's Transactions," 1873-74, p. 253).

legs. There comes also Mr. Reeve, with a microscope and scotoscope.[1] For the first I did give him £5 10*s*., a great price, but a most curious bauble it is, and he says, as good, nay, the best he knows in England, and he makes the best in the world. The other he gives me, and is of value; and a curious curiosity it is to look objects in a darke room with. Mightly pleased with this I to the office, where all the morning. There offered by Sir W. Pen his coach to go to Epsum and carry my wife, I stept out and bade my wife make her ready, but being not very well and other things advising me to the contrary, I did forbear going, and so Mr. Creed dining with me I got him to give my wife and me a play this afternoon, lending him money to do it, which is a fallacy that I have found now once, to avoyde my vowe with, but never to be more practised I swear, and to the new play, at the Duke's house, of "Henry the Fifth;"[2] a most noble play, writ by my Lord Orrery; wherein Betterton, Harris, and Ianthe's parts are most incomparably wrote and done, and the whole play the most full of height and raptures of wit and sense, that ever I heard; having but one incongruity, or what did not please me in it, that is, that King Harry promises to plead for Tudor to their Mistresse, Princesse Katherine of France, more than when it comes to it he seems to do; and Tudor refused by her with some kind of indignity, not with a difficulty and honour that it ought to have been done in to him. Thence home and to my office, wrote by the post, and then to read a little in Dr. Power's book of discovery[3] by the Microscope to enable me a little how to use and what to expect from my glasse. So to supper and to bed.

[1] An optical instrument used to enable objects to be seen in the dark. The name is derived from the Greek words σκότος and σκοπέω.

[2] King Henry was acted by Harris and Owen Tudor by Betterton. Downes says that the "play was splendidly cloath'd. The King in the Duke of York's coronation suit, Owen Tudor in King Charles's, Duke of Burgundy (Smith) in the Lord of Oxford's, and the rest all new." Mrs. Betterton (Ianthe) acted as Princess Katharine. Mrs. Long was the Queen of France, and Mrs. Davis, Anne of Burgundy.

[3] "Experimental Philosophy in three books, containing New Experiments, Microscopical, Mercurial, Magnetical; London, 1664," by Henry Power (sm. 4to, pp. 192). Mr. F. C. S. Roper, who printed privately in 1865 a "Catalogue of Works on the Microscope," described this as the earliest work on the microscope in the English language which he had met with.

14th (Lord's day). After long lying discoursing with my wife, I up, and comes Mr. Holliard to see me, who concurs with me that my pain is nothing but cold in my legs breeding wind, and got only by my using to wear a gowne, and that I am not at all troubled with any ulcer, but my thickness of water comes from my overheat in my back. He gone, comes Mr. Herbert, Mr. Honiwood's man, and dined with me, a very honest, plain, well-meaning man, I think him to be; and by his discourse and manner of life, the true embleme of an old ordinary serving-man. After dinner up to my chamber and made an end of Dr. Power's booke of the Microscope, very fine and to my content, and then my wife and I with great pleasure, but with great difficulty before we could come to find the manner of seeing any thing by my microscope. At last did with good content, though not so much as I expect when I come to understand it better. By and by comes W. Joyce, in his silke suit, and cloake lined with velvett: staid talking with me, and I very merry at it. He supped with me; but a cunning, crafty fellow he is, and dangerous to displease, for his tongue spares nobody. After supper I up to read a little, and then to bed.

15th. Up, and with Sir J. Minnes by coach to St. James's, and there did our business with the Duke, who tells us more and more signs of a Dutch warr, and how we must presently set out a fleete for Guinny, for the Dutch are doing so, and there I believe the warr will begin. Thence home with him again, in our way he talking of his cures abroad, while he was with the King as a doctor, and above all men the pox. And among others, Sir J. Denham he told me he had cured, after it was come to an ulcer all over his face, to a miracle. To the Coffee-house I, and so to the 'Change a little, and then home to dinner with Creed, whom I met at the Coffee-house, and after dinner by coach set him down at the Temple, and I and my wife to Mr. Blagrave's. They being none of them at home, I to the Hall, leaving her there, and thence to the Trumpett, whither came Mrs. Lane, and there begins a sad story how her husband, as I feared, proves not worth a farthing, and that she is with child and undone, if I do not get him a place. I had my pleasure here of her, and she, like an impudent jade, depends upon my kindness to her husband, but I will have no more to do with her, let her brew as she has baked, seeing she would not take my counsel about Hawly. After drinking we parted, and I to Blagrave's, and there discoursed with Mrs. Blagrave about her kinswoman, who it seems is sickly even to frantiqueness sometimes, and among other things chiefly from love and melancholy upon the death of her servant,[1] insomuch that she telling us all most simply and innocently I fear she will not be able to come to us with any pleasure, which I am sorry for, for I think she would have pleased us very well. In comes he, and so to sing a song and his niece with us, but she sings very meanly. So through the Hall and thence by coach home, calling by the way at Charing Crosse, and there saw the great Dutchman that is come over, under whose arm I went with my hat on, and could not reach higher than his eyebrowes with the tip of my fingers, reaching as high as I could. He is a comely and well-made man, and his wife a very little, but pretty comely Dutch woman. It is true, he wears pretty high-heeled shoes, but not very high, and do generally wear a turbant, which makes him show yet taller than really he is, though he is very tall, as I have said before. Home to my office, and then to supper, and then to my office again late, and so home to bed, my wife and I troubled that we do not speed better in this business of her woman.

16th. Wakened about two o'clock this morning with the noise of thunder, which lasted for an houre, with such continued lightnings, not flashes, but flames, that all the sky and ayre was light; and that for a great while, not a minute's space between new flames all the time; such a thing as I never did see, not could have believed had ever been in nature. And being put into a great sweat with it, could not sleep till all was over. And that accompanied with such a storm of rain as I never heard in my life. I expected to find my house in the morning overflowed with the rain breaking in, and that much hurt must needs have been done in the city with this lightning; but I find not one drop of rain in my house, nor any newes of hurt done. But it seems it has been here and all up and down the

[1] Servant = lover.

countrie hereabouts the like tempest, Sir W. Batten saying much of the greatness thereof at Epsum. Up and all the morning at the office. At noon busy at the 'Change about one business or other, and thence home to dinner, and so to my office all the afternoon very busy, and so to supper anon, and then to my office again a while, collecting observations out of Dr. Power's booke of Microscopes, and so home to bed, very stormy weather to-night for winde. This day we had newes that my Lady Pen is landed and coming hither, so that I hope the family will be in better order and more neate than it hath been.

17th. Up, and going to Sir W. Batten to speak to him about business, he did give me three bottles of his Epsum water, which I drank and it wrought well with me, and did give me many good stools, and I found myself mightily cooled with them and refreshed. Thence I to Mr. Honiwood and my father's old house, but he was gone out, and there I staid talking with his man Herbert, who tells me how Langford and his wife are very foul-mouthed people, and will speak very ill of my father, calling him old rogue in reference to the hard penniworths he sold him of his goods when the rogue need not have bought any of them. So that I am resolved he shall get no more money by me, but it vexes me to think that my father should be said to go away in debt himself, but that I will cause to be remedied whatever comes of it. Thence to my Lord Crew, and there with him a little while. Before dinner talked of the Dutch war, and find that he do much doubt that we shall fall into it without the money or consent of Parliament, that is expected or the reason of it that is fit to have for every warr. Dined with him, and after dinner talked with Sir Thomas Crew, who told me how Mr. Edward Montagu is for ever blown up, and now quite out with his father again;[1] to whom he pretended that his going down was, not that he was cast out of the Court, but that he had leave to be

[1] Among the State Papers is a letter from Edward Montagu to Secretary Bennet, dated August 29th, 1664, in which he writes, "If his last proposal do not succeed, will rather choose what is worst for himself than trouble his friends any longer; and if unable to serve him another way, will do it by ridding him of his importunity" ("Calendar," Domestic, 1663-64, p. 675).

absent a month; but now he finds the truth. Thence to my Lady Sandwich, where by agreement my wife dined, and after talking with her I carried my wife to Mr. Pierce's and left her there, and so to Captain Cooke's, but he was not at home, but I there spoke with my boy Tom Edwards, and directed him to go to Mr. Townsend (with whom I was in the morning) to have measure taken of his clothes to be made him there out of the Wardrobe, which will be so done, and then I think he will come to me. Thence to White Hall, and after long staying there was no Committee of the Fishery as was expected. Here I walked long with Mr. Pierce, who tells me the King do still sup every night with my Lady Castlemayne, who he believes has lately slunk a great belly away, for from very big she is come to be down again. Thence to Mrs. Pierce's, and with her and my wife to see Mrs. Clarke, where with him and her very merry discoursing of the late play of Henry the 5th, which they conclude the best that ever was made, but confess with me that Tudor's being dismissed in the manner he is is a great blemish to the play. I am mightily pleased with the Doctor, for he is the only man I know that I could learn to pronounce by, which he do the best that ever I heard any man. Thence home and to the office late, and so to supper and to bed. My Lady Pen came hither first to-night to Sir W. Pen's lodgings.

18th. Lay too long in bed, till 8 o'clock, then up and Mr. Reeve came and brought an anchor and a very fair loadstone. He would have had me bought it, and a good stone it is, but when he saw that I would not buy it he said he [would] leave it for me to sell for him. By and by he comes to tell me that he had present occasion for £6 to make up a sum, and that he would pay me in a day or two, but I had the unusual wit to deny him, and so by and by we parted, and I to the office, where busy all the morning sitting. Dined alone at home, my wife going to-day to dine with Mrs. Pierce, and thence with her and Mrs. Clerke to see a new play, "The Court Secret."[1] I busy all the

[1] A tragi-comedy by James Shirley, "written when the stage was interdicted," and first performed after the Restoration. Before the publication of this notice in Pepys, Langbaine's statement was the only evidence that it had ever been acted.— B.

afternoon, toward evening to Westminster, and there in the Hall a while, and then to my barber, willing to have any opportunity to speak to Jane, but wanted it. So to Mrs. Pierce's, who was come home, and she and Mrs. Clerke busy at cards, so my wife being gone home, I home, calling by the way at the Wardrobe and met Mr. Townsend, Mr. Moore and others at the Taverne thereby, and thither I to them and spoke with Mr. Townsend about my boy's clothes, which he says shall be soon done, and then I hope I shall be settled when I have one in the house that is musicall. So home and to supper, and then a little to my office, and then home to bed. My wife says the play she saw is the worst that ever she saw in her life.

19th. Up and to the office, where Mr. Coventry and Sir W. Pen and I sat all the morning hiring of ships to go to Guinny, where we believe the warr with Holland will first break out. At noon dined at home, and after dinner my wife and I to Sir W. Pen's, to see his Lady,[1] the first time, who is a well-looked, fat, short, old Dutchwoman, but one that hath been heretofore pretty handsome, and is now very discreet, and, I believe, hath more wit than her husband. Here we staid talking a good while, and very well pleased I was with the old woman at first visit. So away home, and I to my office, my wife to go see my aunt Wight, newly come to town. Creed came to me, and he and I out, among other things, to look out a man to make a case, for to keep my stone, that I was cut of, in, and he to buy Daniel's history,[2] which he did, but I missed of my end. So parted upon Ludgate Hill, and I home and to the office, where busy till supper, and home to supper to a good dish of fritters, which I bespoke, and were done much to my mind. Then to the office a while again, and so home to bed. The newes of the Emperour's victory over the Turkes is by some doubted, but by most confessed to be very small (though great) of what was talked, which was 80,000 men to be killed and taken of the Turke's side.

[1] Pepys notices Sir W. Penn's feast on the anniversary of his wedding-day, when he had been married eighteen years (January 6th, 1661–62).

[2] The fourth edition of Samuel Daniel's "Collection of the History of England" was published in 1650, and the fifth edition in 1685. The first part was originally published in 1612.

20th. Up and to the office a while, but this day the Parliament meeting only to be adjourned to November (which was done, accordingly), we did not meet, and so I forth to bespeak a case to be made to keep my stone in, which will cost me 25*s*. Thence I walked to Cheapside, there to see the effect of a fire there this morning, since four o'clock; which I find in the house of Mr. Bois, that married Dr. Fuller's niece, who are both out of towne, leaving only a mayde and man in towne. It begun in their house, and hath burned much and many houses backward, though none forward; and that in the great uniform pile of buildings in the middle of Cheapside. I am very sorry for them, for the Doctor's sake. Thence to the 'Change, and so home to dinner. And thence to Sir W. Batten's, whither Sir Richard Ford came, the Sheriffe, who hath been at this fire all the while; and he tells me, upon my question, that he and the Mayor[1] were there, as it is their dutys to be, not only to keep the peace, but they have power of commanding the pulling down of any house or houses, to defend the whole City. By and by comes in the Common Cryer of the City to speak with him; and when he was gone, says he, "You may see by this man the constitution of the Magistracy of this City; that this fellow's place, I dare give him (if he will be true to me) £1,000 for his profits every year, and expect to get £500 more to myself thereby. When," says he, "I in myself am forced to spend many times as much." By and by came Mr. Coventry, and so we met at the office, to hire ships for Guinny, and that done broke up. I to Sir W. Batten's, there to discourse with Mrs. Falconer,[2] who hath been with Sir W. Pen, this evening, after Mr. Coventry had promised her half what W. Bodham had given him for his place, but Sir W. Pen, though he knows that, and that Mr. Bodham hath said that his place hath cost him £100 and would £100 more, yet is he so high against the poor woman that he will not

[1] Sir Anthony Bateman.

[2] Elizabeth Falkener, wife of John Falkener, announced to Pepys the death of "her dear and loving husband" in a letter dated July 19th, 1664—"begs interest that she may be in something considered by the person succeeding her husband in his employment, which has occasioned great expenses" ("Calendar of State Papers," Domestic, 1663–64, p. 646).

hear to give her a farthing, but it seems do listen after a lease where he expects Mr. Falconer hath put in his daughter's life, and he is afraid that that is not done, and did tell Mrs. Falconer that he would see it and know what is done therein in spite of her, when, poor wretch, she neither do nor can hinder him the knowing it. Mr. Coventry knows of this business of the lease, and I believe do think of it as well as I. But the poor woman is gone home without any hope, but only Mr. Coventry's own nobleness. So I to my office and wrote many letters, and so to supper and to bed.

21st (Lord's day). Waked about 4 o'clock with my wife, having a looseness, and peoples coming in the yard to the pump to draw water several times, so that fear of this day's fire made me fearful, and called Besse and sent her down to see, and it was Griffin's maid for water to wash her house. So to sleep again, and then lay talking till 9 o'clock. So up and drunk three bottles of Epsum water, which wrought well with me. I all the morning and most of the afternoon after dinner putting papers to rights in my chamber, and the like in the evening till night at my office, and renewing and writing fair over my vowes. So home to supper, prayers, and to bed. Mr. Coventry told us the Duke was gone ill of a fit of an ague to bed; so we sent this morning to see how he do.

22nd. Up and abroad, doing very many errands to my great content which lay as burdens upon my mind and memory. Home to dinner, and so to White Hall, setting down my wife at her father's, and I to the Tangier Committee, where several businesses I did to my mind, and with hopes thereby to get something. So to Westminster Hall, where by appointment I had made I met with Dr. Tom Pepys, but avoided all discourse of difference with him, though much against my will, and he like a doating coxcomb as he is, said he could not but demand his money, and that he would have his right, and that let all anger be forgot, and such sorry stuff, nothing to my mind, but only I obtained this satisfaction, that he told me about Sturbridge[1] last was 12 months or 2 years he was at Brampton,

[1] Sturbridge Fair, which is still held, is of great antiquity. The first trace of it is to be found in a charter granted about 1211 by King John to the Lepers of the Hospital of St. Mary Magdalen at Sturbridge by

and there my father did tell him that what he had done for my brother in giving him his goods and setting him up as he had done was upon condition that he should give my brother John £20 per ann., which he charged upon my father, he tells me in answer, as a great deal of hard measure that he should expect that with him that had a brother so able as I am to do that for him. This is all that he says he can say as to my father's acknowledging that he had given Tom his goods. He says his brother Roger will take his oath that my father hath given him thanks for his counsel for his giving of Tom his goods and setting him up in the manner that he hath done, but the former part of this he did not speak fully so bad nor as certain what he could say. So we walked together to my cozen Joyce's, where my wife staid for me, and then I home and her by coach, and so to my office, then to supper and to bed.

23rd. Lay long talking with my wife, and angry a while about her desiring to have a French mayde all of a sudden, which I took to arise from yesterday's being with her mother. But that went over and friends again, and so she be well qualitied, I care not much whether she be French or no, so a Protestant. Thence to the office, and at noon to the 'Change, where very busy getting ships for Guinny and for Tangier. So home to dinner, and then abroad all the afternoon doing several errands, to comply with my oath of ending many businesses before Bartholomew's day, which is two days hence. Among others I went into New Bridewell, in my way to Mr. Cole, and there I saw the new model, and it is very handsome. Several at work, among others, one pretty whore brought in last night, which works very lazily. I did give them *6d.* to drink, and so away. To Graye's Inn, but missed Mr. Cole, and so homeward called at Harman's, and there bespoke some chairs for a room, and so home, and busy late, and then to supper and to bed. The Dutch East India Fleete are now come home safe, which we are sorry for. Our Fleets on both sides are hastening out to Guinny.

24th. Up by six o'clock, and to my office with Tom

Cambridge. The fair was to be held in the close of the hospital on the vigil and feast of the Holy Cross. The name is derived from the little river of *Stere* or *Sture*, flowing into the Cam near Cambridge.

Hater dispatching business in haste. At nine o'clock to White Hall about Mr. Maes's business at the Council, which stands in an ill condition still. Thence to Graye's Inn, but missed of Mr. Cole the lawyer, and so walked home, calling among the joyners in Wood Streete to buy a table and bade in many places, but did not buy it till I come home to see the place where it is to stand, to judge how big it must be. So after 'Change home and a good dinner, and then to White Hall to a Committee of the Fishery, where my Lord Craven and Mr. Gray mightily against Mr. Creed's being joined in the warrant for Secretary with Mr. Duke. However I did get it put off till the Duke of Yorke was there, and so broke up doing nothing. So walked home, first to the Wardrobe, and there saw one suit of clothes made for my boy and linen set out, and I think to have him the latter end of this week, and so home, Mr. Creed walking the greatest part of the way with me advising what to do in his case about his being Secretary to us in conjunction with Duke, which I did give him the best I could, and so home and to my office, where very much business, and then home to supper and to bed.

25th. Up and to the office after I had spoke to my taylor, Langford (who came to me about some work), desiring to know whether he knew of any debts that my father did owe of his own in the City. He tells me, "No, not any." I did on purpose try him because of what words he and his wife have said of him (as Herbert told me the other day), and further did desire him, that if he knew of any or could hear of any that he should bid them come to me, and I would pay them, for I would not that because he do not pay my brother's debts that therefore he should be thought to deny the payment of his owne All the morning at the office busy. At noon to the 'Change, among other things busy to get a little by the hire of a ship for Tangier. So home to dinner, and after dinner comes Mr. Cooke to see me; it is true he was kind to me at sea in carrying messages to and fro to my wife from sea, but I did do him kindnesses too, and therefore I matter not much to compliment or make any regard of his thinking me to slight him as I do for his folly about my brother Tom's mistress. After dinner and some talk with him, I to my office; there busy, till by and by Jacke Noble came to me to tell me that he had Cave in prison, and that he would give me and my father good security that neither we nor any of our family should be troubled with the child; for he could prove that he was fully satisfied for him; and that if the worst came to the worst, the parish must keep it; that Cave did bring the child to his house, but they got it carried back again, and that thereupon he put him in prison. When he saw that I would not pay him the money, nor made anything of being secured against the child, he then said that then he must go to law, not himself, but come in as a witness for Cave against us. I could have told him that he could bear witness that Cave is satisfied, or else there is no money due to himself; but I let alone any such discourse, only getting as much out of him as I could. I perceive he is a rogue, and hath inquired into everything and consulted with Dr. Pepys, and that he thinks as Dr. Pepys told him that my father if he could would not pay a farthing of the debts, and yet I made him confess that in all his lifetime he never knew my father to be asked for money twice, nay, not once, all the time he lived with him, and that for his own debts he believed he would do so still, but he meant only for those of Tom. He said now that Randall and his wife and the midwife could prove from my brother's own mouth that the child was his, and that Tom had told them the circumstances of time, upon November 5th at night, that he got it on her. I offered him if he would secure my father against being forced to pay the money again I would pay him, which at first he would do, give his own security, and when I asked more than his own he told me yes he would, and those able men, subsidy men, but when we came by and by to discourse of it again he would not then do it, but said he would take his course, and joyne with Cave and release him, and so we parted. However, this vexed me so as I could not be quiet, but took coach to go speak with Mr. Cole, but met him not within, so back, buying a table by the way, and at my office late, and then home to supper and to bed, my mind disordered about this roguish business — in every thing else, I thank God, well at ease.

26th. Up by 5 o'clock, which I have not been many a

day, and down by water to Deptford, and there took in Mr. Pumpfield the rope-maker, and down with him to Woolwich to view Clothier's cordage, which I found bad and stopped the receipt of it. Thence to the ropeyard, and there among other things discoursed with Mrs. Falconer, who tells me that she has found the writing, and Sir W. Pen's daughter is not put into the lease for her life as he expected, and I am glad of it. Thence to the Dockyarde, and there saw the new ship in very great forwardness, and so by water to Deptford a little, and so home and shifting myself, to the 'Change, and there did business, and thence down by water to White Hall, by the way, at the Three Cranes, putting into an alehouse and eat a bit of bread and cheese. There I could not get into the Parke, and so was fain to stay in the gallery over the gate to look to the passage into the Parke, into which the King hath forbid of late anybody's coming, to watch his coming that had appointed me to come, which he did by and by with his lady and went to Guardener's Lane,[1] and there instead of meeting with one that was handsome and could play well, as they told me, she is the ugliest beast and plays so basely as I never heard anybody, so that I should loathe her being in my house. However, she took us by and by and showed us indeed some pictures at one Hiseman's,[2] a picture drawer, a Dutchman, which is said to exceed Lilly, and indeed there is both of the Queenes and Mayds of Honour (particularly Mrs. Stewart's[3] in a buff doublet like a soldier) as good pictures, I think, as ever I saw. The Queene is drawn in one like a shepherdess, in the other like St. Katharin,[4] most like and most admirably. I was mightily pleased with this sight indeed, and so back again to their

[1] Gardener's Lane, Westminster, between King Street and Duke Street.

[2] James Huysman (1656–96). In Walpole's "Anecdotes of Painting" he is said to have "rivalled Lely, and with reason."

[3] In the Royal Collection. "The dress is that of a cavalier about the time of the Civil War, buff with blue ribands" (Walpole's "Anecdotes of Painting," ed. Dallaway, vol. ii., p. 122, note).

[4] Huysman is said by Walpole to have been himself most partial to his picture of Queen Catherine. "He created himself the queen's painter, and to justify it, made her sit for every Madonna or Venus that he drew."

lodgings, where I left them, but before I went this man that carried me, whose name I know not but that they call him Sir John, a pitiful fellow, whose face I have long known but upon what score I know not, but he could have the confidence to ask me to lay down money for him to renew the lease of his house, which I did give eare to there because I was there receiving a civility from him, but shall not part with my money. There I left them, and I by water home, where at my office busy late, then home to supper, and so to bed. This day my wife tells me Mr. Pen,[1] Sir William's son, is come back from France, and come to visit her. A most modish person, grown, she says, a fine gentleman.

27th. Up and to the office, where all the morning. At noon to the 'Change, and there almost made my bargain about a ship for Tangier, which will bring me in a little profit with Captain Taylor. Off the 'Change with Mr. Cutler and Sir W. Rider to Cutler's house, and there had a very good dinner, and two or three pretty young ladies of their relations there. Thence to my case-maker for my stone case, and had it to my mind, and cost me *24s.*, which is a great deale of money, but it is well done and pleases me. So doing some other small errands I home, and there find my boy, Tom Edwards,[2] come, sent me by Captain

[1] William Penn, afterwards the famous Quaker. P. Gibson, writing to him in March, 1711-12, says: "I remember your honour very well, when you newly came out of France and wore pantaloon breeches."

[2] Tom Edwards made love to Mrs. Pepys's chambermaid Jane (see February 11th, 1667-68), and Jane had a fit of jealousy on August 19th, 1668, but the two were married on March 26th, 1669. There is some confusion in the Diary between the Pepys's chambermaids named Jane, for reference is made to Jane Wayneman and to Jane Gentleman, but it appears from the marriage licence that Tom's wife was Jane Birch. The licence is as follows: "Thomas Edwards, of St. Olave, Hart Street, London, gent., bachelor, about 25, and Jane Birch, of same, spinster, about 24, and at own disposal, at St. Olave aforesaid, 19 March, 1668-69" (Chester's "London Marriage Licences," ed. Foster, col. 443). Tom Edwards's death is referred to in a letter from Pepys to Sir Richard Haddock, dated August 20th, 1681 (Rawlinson, A. 194, fol. 256, Bodleian Library). In the following year Pepys got his orphan son into Christ's Hospital, as appears by a letter dated April 7th, 1682: "This will be brought by the widow Jane Edwards, mother of the boy Samuel Edwards, for whom Sir John Frederick has been pleased by your hand to send me a paper for his admission into the hospital. His father was

Cooke, having been bred in the King's Chappell these four years. I propose to make a clerke of him, and if he deserves well, to do well by him. Spent much of the afternoon to set his chamber in order, and then to the office leaving him at home, and late at night after all business was done I called Will and told him my reason of taking a boy, and that it is of necessity, not out of any unkindness to him, nor should be to his injury, and then talked about his landlord's daughter to come to my wife, and I think it will be. So home and find my boy a very schoole boy, that talks innocently and impertinently, but at present it is a sport to us, and in a little time he will leave it. So sent him to bed, he saying that he used to go to bed at eight o'clock, and then all of us to bed, myself pretty well pleased with my choice of a boy. All the newes this day is, that the Dutch are, with twenty-two sayle of ships of warr, crewsing up and down about Ostend; at which we are alarmed. My Lord Sandwich is come back into the Downes with only eight sayle, which is or may be a prey to the Dutch, if they knew our weakness and inability to set out any more speedily.

28th (Lord's day). Up, and with my boy alone to church — the first time I have had anybody to attend me to church a great while. Home to dinner, and there met Creed, who dined, and we merry together, as his learning is such and judgment that I cannot but be pleased with it. After dinner I took him to church, into our gallery, with me, but slept the best part of the sermon, which was a most silly one. So he and I to walk to the 'Change a while, talking from one pleasant discourse to another, and so home, and thither came my uncle Wight and aunt, and supped with us mighty merry. And Creed lay with us all night, and so to bed, very merry to think how Mr. Holliard (who came in this evening to see me) makes nothing, but proving as a most clear thing that Rome is Antichrist.

his Majesty's servant in the Navy for near twenty years past, and lately died an officer therein, leaving this poor woman with two small children (whereof this, being between nine and ten years old, is the eldest), and without aught more towards her and their support (through his and her long and chargeable sickness) than what she can earn in service" (Pepys's "Life, Journals, and Correspondence," 1841, vol. i., p. 284).

29th. Up betimes, intending to do business at my office, by 5 o'clock, but going out met at my door Mr. Hughes come to speak with me about office business, and told me that as he came this morning from Deptford he left the King's yarde a-fire. So I presently took a boat and down, and there found, by God's providence, the fire out; but if there had been any wind it must have burned all our stores, which is a most dreadfull consideration. But leaving all things well I home, and out abroad doing many errands, Mr. Creed also out, and my wife to her mother's, and Creed and I met at my Lady Sandwich's and there dined; but my Lady is become as handsome, I think, as ever she was; and so good and discreet a woman I know not in the world. After dinner I to Westminster to Jervas's a while, and so doing many errands by the way, and necessary ones, I home, and thither came the woman with her mother which our Will recommends to my wife. I like her well, and I think will please us. My wife and they agreed, and she is to come the next week. At which I am very well contented, for then I hope we shall be settled, but I must remember that, never since I was housekeeper, I ever lived so quietly, without any noise or one angry word almost, as I have done since my present mayds Besse, Jane, and Susan came and were together. Now I have taken a boy and am taking a woman, I pray God we may not be worse, but I will observe it. After being at my office a while, home to supper and to bed.

30th. Up and to the office, where sat long, and at noon to dinner at home; after dinner comes Mr. Pen to visit me, and staid an houre talking with me. I perceive something of learning he hath got, but a great deale, if not too much, of the vanity of the French garbe and affected manner of speech and gait. I fear all real profit he hath made of his travel will signify little. So, he gone, I to my office and there very busy till late at night, and so home to supper and to bed.

31st. Up by five o'clock and to my office, where T. Hater and Will met me, and so we dispatched a great deal of my business as to the ordering my papers and books which were behindhand. All the morning very busy at my office. At noon home to dinner, and there my wife hath got me some pretty good oysters, which is very soon and the soonest, I think, I ever eat any. After dinner I up to hear my boy play upon a lute, which I have this day borrowed of Mr. Hunt; and indeed the boy would, with little practice, play very well upon the lute, which pleases me well. So by coach to the Tangier Committee, and there have another small business by which I may get a little small matter of money. Staid but little there, and so home and to my office, where late casting up my monthly accounts, and, blessed be God! find myself worth £1,020, which is still the most I ever was worth. So home and to bed. Prince Rupert I hear this day is to go to command this fleete going to Guinny against the Dutch. I doubt few will be pleased with his going, being accounted an unhappy[1] man. My mind at good rest, only my father's troubles with Dr. Pepys and my brother Tom's creditors in general do trouble me. I have got a new boy that understands musique well, as coming to me from the King's Chappell, and I hope will prove a good boy, and my wife and I are upon having a woman, which for her content I am contented to venture upon the charge of again, and she is one that our Will finds out for us, and understands a little musique, and I think will please us well, only her friends live too near us. Pretty well in health, since I left off wearing of a gowne within doors all day, and then go out with my legs into the cold, which brought me daily pain.

Sept. 1st. A sad rainy night, up and to the office, where busy all the morning. At noon to the 'Change and thence brought Mr. Pierce, the Surgeon, and Creed, and dined very merry and handsomely; but my wife not being well of those she not with us; and we cut up the great cake Moorcocke lately sent us, which is very good. They gone I to my office, and there very busy till late at night, and so home to supper and to bed.

2nd. Up very betimes and walked (my boy with me) to Mr. Cole's, and after long waiting below, he being under the barber's hands, I spoke with him, and he did give me much hopes of getting my debt that my brother owed me, and also that things would go well with my father. But

[1] Unlucky (*infelix*).

going to his attorney's, that he directed me to, they tell me both that though I could bring my father to a confession of a judgment, yet he knowing that there are specialties out against him he is bound to plead his knowledge of them to me before he pays me, or else he must do it in his own wrong. I took a great deal of pains this morning in the thorough understanding hereof, and hope that I know the truth of our case, though it be but bad, yet better than to run spending money and all to no purpose. However, I will inquire a little more. Walked home, doing very many errands by the way to my great content, and at the 'Change met and spoke with several persons about serving us with pieces of eight at Tangier. So home to dinner above stairs, my wife not being well of those in bed. I dined by her bedside, but I got her to rise and abroad with me by coach to Bartholomew Fayre, and our boy with us, and there shewed them and myself the dancing on the ropes, and several other the best shows; but pretty it is to see how our boy carries himself so innocently clownish as would make one laugh. Here till late and dark, then up and down, to buy combes for my wife to give her mayds, and then by coach home, and there at the office set down my day's work, and then home to bed.

3rd. I have had a bad night's rest to-night, not sleeping well, as my wife observed, and once or twice she did wake me, and I thought myself to be mightily bit with fleas, and in the morning she chid her mayds for not looking the fleas a-days. But, when I rose, I found that it is only the change of the weather from hot to cold, which, as I was two winters ago, do stop my pores, and so my blood tingles and itches all day all over my body, and so continued to-day all the day long just as I was then, and if it continues to be so cold I fear I must come to the same pass, but sweating cured me then, and I hope, and am told, will this also. At the office sat all the morning, dined at home, and after dinner to White Hall, to the Fishing Committee, but not above four of us met, which could do nothing, and a sad thing it is to see so great a work so ill followed, for at this pace it can come to nothing but disgrace to us all. Broke up and did nothing. So I walked to Westminster, and there at my barber's had good luck to find Jane alone, and there talked with her, and got the poor wretch to promise to meet me in the Abbey on to-morrow come sennight, telling me that her master and mistress have a mind to get her a husband, and so will not let her go abroad without them, but only in sermon time on Sundays she do go out. I would I could get a good husband for her, for she is one I always thought a good-natured as well as a well-looked girl. Thence home, doing errands by the way, and so to my office, whither Mr. Holliard came to me to discourse about the privileges of the Surgeons' Hall, as to our signing of bills, wherein I did give him a little, and but a little, satisfaction; for we won't lose our power of recommending them once approved of by the Hall. He gone I late to send by the post, &c., and so to supper and to bed. My itching and tickling continuing still, the weather continuing cold, and Mr. Holliard tells me that sweating will cure me at any time.

4th (Lord's day). Lay long in bed, then up and took physique, Mr. Holliard's, but it being cold weather and myself negligent of myself, I fear I took cold and stopped the working of it, but I feel myself pretty well. All the morning looking over my old wardrobe and laying by things for my brother John and my father, by which I shall leave myself very bare in clothes, but yet as much as I need, and the rest would but spoile in the keeping. Dined, my wife and I very well. All the afternoon my wife and I above, and then the boy and I to singing of psalms, and then came in Mr. Hill, and he sung with us awhile; and, he being gone, the boy and I again to the singing of Mr. Porter's[1] mottets, and it is a great joy to me that I am come to this condition to maintain a person in the house able to give me such pleasure as this boy do by his thorough knowledge of musique, as he sings any thing at first sight. Mr. Hill came to tell me that he had got a gentlewoman for my wife, one Mrs. Ferrabosco,[2] that sings most admirably. I seemed glad of it; but I hear she is

[1] Walter Porter published "Mottets of two Voices for Treble or Tenor and Basse, &c., to be performed to an Organ, Harpischord, Lute or Base-Viol. *London* 1657."

[2] Mrs. Ferrabosco was probably the daughter of Alphonso Ferrabosco, himself the son of Ben Jonson's friend.

too gallant for me, and I am not sorry that I misse her. Thence to the office, setting some papers right, and so home to supper and to bed, after prayers.

5th. Up and to St. James's, and there did our business with the Duke; where all our discourse of warr in the highest measure. Prince Rupert was with us; who is fitting himself to go to sea in the Heneretta.[1] And afterwards in White Hall I met him and Mr. Gray, and he spoke to me, and in other discourse, says he, "God damn me, I can answer but for one ship, and in that I will do my part; for it is not in that as in an army, where a man can command every thing." By and by to a Committee for the Fishery, the Duke of Yorke there, where, after Duke was made Secretary, we fell to name a Committee, whereof I was willing to be one, because I would have my hand in the business, to understand it and be known in doing something in it; and so, after cutting out work for the Committee, we rose, and I to my wife to Unthanke's, and with her from shop to shop, laying out near £10 this morning in clothes for her. And so I to the 'Change, where a while, and so home and to dinner, and thither came W. Bowyer and dined with us; but strange to see how he could not endure onyons in sauce to lamb, but was overcome with the sight of it, and so was forced to make his dinner of an egg or two. He tells us how Mrs. Lane is undone, by her marrying so bad, and desires to speak with me, which I know is wholly to get me to do something for her to get her husband a place, which he is in no wise fit for. After dinner down to Woolwich with a gally, and then to Deptford, and so home, all the way reading Sir J. Suck[l]ing's "Aglaura,"[2] which, methinks, is but a mean play; nothing of design in it. Coming home it is strange to see how I was troubled to find my wife, but in a necessary compliment, expecting Mr. Pen to see her, who had been there and was by her people denied, which, he having been three times, she thought not fit he should be any more. But yet even this did raise my jeal-

[1] The "Henrietta" (previously the "Langport") was a third-rate of fifty guns, built at Horselydown in 1654 by Mr. Bright ("Archæologia," vol. xlviii., p. 170).

[2] Pepys referred to this same play on September 24th. 1662.

ousy presently and much vex me. However, he did not come, which pleased me, and I to supper, and to the office till 9 o'clock or thereabouts, and so home to bed. My aunt James had been here to-day with Kate Joyce twice to see us. The second time my wife was at home, and they it seems are going down to Brampton, which I am sorry for, for the charge that my father will be put to. But it must be borne with, and my mother has a mind to see them, but I do condemn myself mightily for my pride and contempt of my aunt and kindred that are not so high as myself, that I have not seen her all this while, nor invited her all this while.

6th. Up and to the office, where we sat all the morning. At noon home to dinner, then to my office and there waited, thinking to have had Bagwell's wife come to me about business, that I might have talked with her, but she came not. So I to White Hall by coach with Mr. Andrews, and there I got his contract for the victualling of Tangier signed and sealed by us there, so that all the business is well over, and I hope to have made a good business of it and to receive £100 by it the next weeke, for which God be praised! Thence to W. Joyce's and Anthony's, to invite them to dinner to meet my aunt James at my house, and the rather because they are all to go down to my father the next weeke, and so I would be a little kind to them before they go. So home, having called upon Doll, our pretty 'Change woman, for a pair of gloves trimmed with yellow ribbon, to [match the] petticoate my wife bought yesterday, which cost me 20*s.*; but she is so pretty, that, God forgive me! I could not think it too much — which is a strange slavery that I stand in to beauty, that I value nothing near it. So going home, and my coach stopping in Newgate Market over against a poulterer's shop, I took occasion to buy a rabbit, but it proved a deadly old one when I came to eat it, as I did do after an hour being at my office, and after supper again there till past 11 at night. So home, and to bed. This day Mr. Coventry did tell us how the Duke did receive the Dutch Embassador[1] the other day; by telling him that, whereas they think us in jest, he

[1] Herr Van Goch, ambassador from the States-General (see *ante*, June 11th).

believes that the Prince (Rupert) which goes in this fleete to Guinny[1] will soon tell them that we are in earnest, and that he himself will do the like here, in the head of the fleete here at home, and that for the *meschants*, which he told the Duke there were in England, which did hope to do themselves good by the King's being at warr, says he, the English have ever united all this private difference to attend foraigne, and that Cromwell, notwithstanding the *meschants* in his time, which were the Cavaliers, did never find them interrupt him in his foraigne businesses, and that he did not doubt but to live to see the Dutch as fearfull of provoking the English, under the government of a King, as he remembers them to have been under that of a *Coquin*. I writ all this story to my Lord Sandwich to-night into the Downes, it being very good and true, word for word from Mr. Coventry to-day.

7th. Lay long to-day, pleasantly discoursing with my wife about the dinner we are to have for the Joyces, a day or two hence. Then up and with Mr. Margetts[2] to Limehouse to see his ground and ropeyarde there, which is very fine, and I believe we shall employ it for the Navy, for the King's grounds are not sufficient to supply our defence if a warr comes. Thence back to the 'Change, where great talke of the forwardnesse of the Dutch, which puts us all to a stand, and particularly myself for my Lord Sandwich, to think him to lie where he is for a sacrifice, if they should begin with us. So home and Creed with me, and to dinner, and after dinner I out to my office taking in Bagwell's wife, who I knew waited for me, but company came to me so soon that I could have no discourse with her, as I intended, of pleasure. So anon abroad with Creed walked to Bartholomew Fayre, this being the last day, and there saw the best dancing on the ropes that I think I ever saw in my life, and

[1] At a meeting of the Royal Society on September 14th, 1664, it was resolved that "Prince Rupert be desired by Sir Robert Moray to try in his expedition to Guinea the sounding of depths without a line and the fetching up of water from the bottom of the sea" (Birch's "History of the Royal Society," vol. i., p. 467).

[2] Mr. Margets, a rope merchant near the Custom House, is mentioned in the examination of Eliz. Oldroyd, July 12th, 1664 ("Calendar of State Papers," Domestic, 1663-64, p. 639).

so all say, and so by coach home, where I find my wife hath had her head dressed by her woman, Mercer, which is to come to her to-morrow, but my wife being to go to a christening to-morrow, she came to do her head up to-night. So a while to my office, and then to supper and to bed.

8th. Up and to the office, where busy all the morning. At noon dined at home, and I by water down to Woolwich by a galley, and back again in the evening. All haste made in setting out this Guinny fleete, but yet not such as will ever do the King's business if we come to a warr. My [wife] this afternoon being very well dressed by her new woman, Mary Mercer, a decayed merchant's daughter that our Will helps us to, did go to the christening of Mrs. Mills, the parson's wife's child, where she never was before. After I was come home Mr. Povey came to me and took me out to supper to Mr. Bland's, who is making now all haste to be gone for Tangier. Here pretty merry, and good discourse, fain to admire the knowledge and experience of Mrs. Bland, who I think as good a merchant as her husband. I went home and there find Mercer, whose person I like well, and I think will do well, at least I hope so. So to my office a while and then to bed.

9th. Up, and to put things in order against dinner. I out and bought several things, among others, a dozen of silver salts; home, and to the office, where some of us met a little, and then home, and at noon comes my company, namely, Anthony and Will Joyce and their wives, my aunt James newly come out of Wales, and my cozen Sarah Gyles.[1] Her husband did not come, and by her I did understand afterwards, that it was because he was not yet able to pay me the 40*s.* she had borrowed a year ago of me. I was as merry as I could, giving them a good dinner; but W. Joyce did so talk, that he made every body else dumb, but only laugh at him. I forgot there was Mr. Harman and his wife, my aunt, a very good harmlesse woman. All their talke is of her and my two she-cozen Joyces and Will's little boy

[1] Pepys would have been more proud of his cousin had he anticipated her husband's becoming a knight, for she was probably the same person whose burial is recorded in the register of St. Helen's, Bishopsgate, September 4th, 1704: "Dame Sarah Gyles, widow, relict of Sir John Gyles." — B.

Will (who was also here to-day), down to Brampton to my father's next week, which will be trouble and charge to them, but however my father and mother desire to see them, and so let them. They eyed mightily my great cupboard of plate, I this day putting my two flaggons upon my table; and indeed it is a fine sight, and better than ever I did hope to see of my owne. Mercer dined with us at table, this being her first dinner in my house. After dinner left them and to White Hall, where a small Tangier Committee, and so back again home, and there my wife and Mercer and Tom and I sat till eleven at night, singing and fiddling, and a great joy it is to see me master of so much pleasure in my house, that it is and will be still, I hope, a constant pleasure to me to be at home. The girle plays pretty well upon the harpsicon, but only ordinary tunes, but hath a good hand; sings a little, but hath a good voyce and eare. My boy, a brave boy, sings finely, and is the most pleasant boy at present, while his ignorant boy's tricks last, that ever I saw. So to supper, and with great pleasure to bed.

10th. Up and to the office, where we sate all the morning, and I much troubled to think what the end of our great sluggishness will be, for we do nothing in this office like people able to carry on a warr. We must be put out, or other people put in. Dined at home, and then my wife and I and Mercer to the Duke's house, and there saw "The Rivalls,"[1] which is no excellent play, but good acting in it; especially Gosnell comes and sings and dances finely, but, for all that, fell out of the key, so that the musique could not play to her afterwards, and so did Harris also go out of the tune to agree with her. Thence home and late writing letters, and this night I received, by Will, £105, the first-fruits of my endeavours in the late contract for victualling of Tangier, for which God be praised! for I can with a safe conscience say that I have therein saved the King £5,000 per annum, and yet got myself a hope of £300

[1] A comedy by Sir William Davenant, first published in 1668. It is an alteration of "The Two Noble Kinsmen." Harris played Theocles; Betterton, Philander. Gosnell is not mentioned in the cast by Downes. The character of Celania was afterwards acted by Mrs. Davis, who captivated Charles II. in this part.

per annum without the least wrong to the King. So to supper and to bed.

11th (Lord's day). Up and to church in the best manner I have gone a good while, that is to say, with my wife, and her woman, Mercer, along with us, and Tom, my boy, waiting on us. A dull sermon. Home, dined, left my wife to go to church alone, and I walked in haste being late to the Abbey at Westminster, according to promise to meet Jane Welsh, and there wearily walked, expecting her till 6 o'clock from three, but no Jane came, which vexed me, only part of it I spent with Mr. Blagrave walking in the Abbey, he telling me the whole government and discipline of White Hall Chappell, and the caution now used against admitting any debauched persons, which I was glad to hear, though he tells me there are persons bad enough. Thence going home went by Jarvis's, and there stood Jane at the door, and so I took her in and drank with her, her master and mistress being out of doors. She told me how she could not come to me this afternoon, but promised another time. So I walked home contented with my speaking with her, and walked to my uncle Wight's, where they were all at supper, and among others comes fair Mrs. Margarett Wight, who indeed is very pretty. So after supper home to prayers and to bed. This afternoon, it seems, Sir J. Minnes fell sicke at church, and going down the gallery stairs fell down dead, but came to himself again and is pretty well.

12th. Up, and to my cozen Anthony Joyce's, and there took leave of my aunt James, and both cozens, their wives, who are this day going down to my father's by coach. I did give my Aunt 20*s*., to carry as a token to my mother, and 10*s*. to Pall.[1] Thence by coach to St. James's, and there did our business as usual with the Duke; and saw him with great pleasure play with his little girle,[2] like an ordinary private father of a child. Thence walked to Jervas's, where I took Jane in the shop alone, and there heard of her, her master and mistress were going out. So I went away and came again half an hour after. In the meantime went to the Abbey, and there went in to see the

[1] Pepys's sister Paulina,

[2] Afterwards Queen Mary II.

tombs with great pleasure. Back again to Jane, and there upstairs and drank with her, and staid two hours with her kissing her, but nothing more. Anon took boat and by water to the Neat Houses over against Fox Hall to have seen Greatorex dive, which Jervas and his wife were gone to see, and there I found them (and did it the rather for a pretence for my having been so long at their house), but being disappointed of some necessaries to do it I staid not, but back to Jane, but she would not go out with me. So I to Mr. Creed's lodgings, and with him walked up and down in the New Exchange, talking mightily of the convenience and necessity of a man's wearing good clothes, and so after eating a messe of creame I took leave of him, he walking with me as far as Fleete Conduit, he offering me upon my request to put out some money for me into Backewell's hands at 6 per cent. interest, which he seldom gives, which I will consider of, being doubtful of trusting any of these great dealers because of their mortality, but then the convenience of having one's money at an houre's call is very great. Thence to my uncle Wight's, and there supped with my wife, having given them a brave barrel of oysters of Povy's giving me. So home and to bed.

13th. Up and to the office, where sat busy all morning, dined at home and after dinner to Fishmonger's Hall, where we met the first time upon the Fishery Committee, and many good things discoursed of concerning making of farthings, which was proposed as a way of raising money for this business, and then that of lotterys,[1] but with great confusion; but I hope we shall fall into greater order. So home again and to my office, where after doing business home and to a little musique, after supper, and so to bed.

14th. Up, and wanting some things that should be laid ready for my dressing myself I was angry, and one thing after another made my wife give Besse warning to be gone, which the jade, whether out of fear or ill-nature or simplicity I know not, but she took it and asked leave to go forth

[1] Among the State Papers is a "Statement of Articles in the Covenant proposed by the Commissioners for the Royal Fishing to Sir Ant. Desmarces & Co. in reference to the regulation of lotteries, which are very unreasonable, and of the objections thereto" ("Calendar of State Papers," Domestic, 1663–64, p. 576).

to look a place, and did, which vexed me to the heart, she being as good a natured wench as ever we shall have, but only forgetful. At the office all the morning and at noon to the 'Change, and there went off with Sir W. Warren and took occasion to desire him to lend me £100, which he said he would let me have with all his heart presently, as he had promised me a little while ago to give me for my pains in his two great contracts for masts £100, and that this should be it. To which end I did move it to him, and by this means I hope to be possessed of the £100 presently within 2 or 3 days. So home to dinner, and then to the office, and down to Blackwall by water to view a place found out for laying of masts, and I think it will be most proper. So home and there find Mr. Pen come to visit my wife, and staid with them till sent for to Mr. Bland's, whither by appointment I was to go to supper, and against my will left them together, but, God knows, without any reason of fear in my conscience of any evil between them, but such is my natural folly. Being thither come they would needs have my wife, and so Mr. Bland and his wife (the first time she was ever at my house or my wife at hers) very civilly went forth and brought her and W. Pen, and there Mr. Povy and we supped nobly and very merry, it being to take leave of Mr. Bland, who is upon going soon to Tangier. So late home and to bed.

15th. At the office all the morning, then to the 'Change, and so home to dinner, where Luellin dined with us, and after dinner many people came in and kept me all the afternoon, among other the Master and Wardens of Chyrurgeon's Hall, who staid arguing their cause with me; I did give them the best answer I could, and after there being two hours with me parted, and I to my office to do business, which is much on my hands, and so late home to supper and to bed.

16th. Up betimes and to my office, where all the morning very busy putting papers to rights. And among other things Mr. Gauden coming to me, I had a good opportunity to speak to him about his present, which hitherto hath been a burden to me, that I could not do it, because I was doubtfull that he meant it as a temptation to me to stand by him in the business of Tangier victualling; but he clears me it was not, and that he values me and my proceedings therein very highly, being but what became me, and that what he did was for my old kindnesses to him in dispatching of his business, which I was glad to hear, and with my heart in good rest and great joy parted, and to my business again. At noon to the 'Change, where by appointment I met Sir W. Warren, and afterwards to the Sun taverne, where he brought to me, being all alone, a £100 in a bag, which I offered him to give him my receipt for, but he told me, no, it was my owne, which he had a little while since promised me and was glad that (as I had told him two days since) it would now do me courtesy, and so most kindly he did give it me, and I as joyfully, even out of myself, carried it home in a coach, he himself expressly taking care that nobody might see this business done, though I was willing enough to have carried a servant with me to have received it, but he advised me to do it myself. So home with it and to dinner; after dinner I forth with my boy to buy severall things, stools and andirons and candlesticks, &c., household stuff, and walked to the mathematical instrument maker in Moorefields and bought a large pair of compasses, and there met Mr. Pargiter, and he would needs have me drink a cup of horse-radish ale, which he and a friend of his troubled with the stone have been drinking of, which we did and then walked into the fields as far almost as Sir G. Whitmore's,[1] all the way talking of Russia, which, he says, is a sad place; and, though Moscow is a very great city, yet it is from the distance between house and house, and few people compared with this, and poor, sorry houses, the Emperor himself living in a wooden house, his exercise only flying a hawk at pigeons and carrying pigeons ten or twelve miles off and then laying wagers which pigeon shall come soonest home to her house. All the winter within doors, some few playing at chesse, but most drinking their time away. Women live very slavishly

[1] Baulmes, at Hoxton, belonged to Sir George Whitmore, of Barnes, in Surrey, who was Lord Mayor in 1631, and a great sufferer for the royal cause. His daughter Anne, mentioned by Pepys, February 28th, 1663–64, *ante*, married Sir John Robinson, Lieutenant of the Tower. Baulmes is described as an old square mansion, with two storeys in the roof: it was afterwards converted into a madhouse, and demolished in the year 1852. — B.

there, and it seems in the Emperor's court no room hath above two or three windows, and those the greatest not a yard wide or high, for warmth in winter time; and that the general cure for all diseases there is their sweating houses, or people that are poor they get into their ovens, being heated, and there lie. Little learning among things of any sort. Not a man that speaks Latin, unless the Secretary of State by chance. Mr. Pargiter and I walked to the 'Change together and there parted, and so I to buy more things and then home, and after a little at my office, home to supper and to bed. This day old Hardwicke came and redeemed a watch he had left with me in pawne for 40*s.* seven years ago, and I let him have it. Great talk that the Dutch will certainly be out this week, and will sail directly to Guinny, being convoyed out of the Channel with 42 sail of ships.

17th. Up and to the office, where Mr. Coventry very angry to see things go so coldly as they do, and I must needs say it makes me fearful every day of having some change of the office, and the truth is, I am of late a little guilty of being remiss myself of what I used to be, but I hope I shall come to my old pass again, my family being now settled again. Dined at home, and to the office, where late busy in setting all my businesses in order, and I did a very great and a very contenting afternoon's work. This day my aunt Wight sent my wife a new scarfe, with a compliment for the many favours she had received of her, which is the several things we have sent her. I am glad enough of it, for I see my uncle is so given up to the Wights that I hope for little more of them. So home to supper and to bed.

18th (Lord's day). Up and to church all of us. At noon comes Anthony and W. Joyce (their wives being in the country with my father) and dined with me very merry as I can be in such company. After dinner walked to Westminster (tiring them by the way, and so left them, Anthony in Cheapside and the other in the Strand), and there spent all the afternoon in the Cloysters as I had agreed with Jane Welsh, but she came not, which vexed me, staying till 5 o'clock, and then walked homeward, and by coach to the old Exchange, and thence to my aunt Wight's, and invited her and my uncle to supper, and so home, and by and by they came, and we eat a brave barrel of oysters Mr. Povy sent me this morning, and very merry at supper, and so to prayers and to bed. Last night it seems my aunt Wight did send my wife a new scarfe, laced, as a token for her many givings to her. It is true now and then we give them some toys, as oranges, &c., but my aime is to get myself something more from my uncle's favour than this.

19th. Up, my wife and I having a little anger about her woman already, she thinking that I take too much care of her at table to mind her (my wife) of cutting for her, but it soon over, and so up and with Sir W. Batten and Sir W. Pen to St. James's, and there did our business with the Duke, and thence homeward straight, calling at the Coffee-house, and there had very good discourse with Sir — Blunt and Dr. Whistler about Ægypt and other things. So home to dinner, my wife having put on to-day her winter new suit of moyre, which is handsome, and so after dinner I did give her £15 to lay out in linen and necessaries for the house and to buy a suit for Pall, and I myself to White Hall to a Tangier Committee, where Colonell Reames hath brought us so full and methodical an account of all matters there, that I never have nor hope to see the like of any publique business while I live again. The Committee up, I to Westminster to Jervas's, and spoke with Jane, who I find cold and not so desirous of a meeting as before, and it is no matter, I shall be the freer from the inconvenience that might follow thereof, besides offending God Almighty and neglecting my business. So by coach home and to my office, where late, and so to supper and to bed. I met with Dr. Pierce to-day, who, speaking of Dr. Frazier's[1] being so earnest to have such a one (one Collins) go chyrurgeon to the Prince's person will have him go in his terms and with so much money put into his hands, he tells me (when I was wondering that Frazier should order things with the Prince in that confident manner) that Frazier is so great with my Lady Castlemayne, and Stewart, and all the ladies at Court, in helping to slip their calfes when there is occasion, and with the great men in curing of their claps that he can do what he please with the King, in spite of any

[1] Sir Alexander Fraizer (see note, December 26th, 1660).

man, and upon the same score with the Prince; they all having more or less occasion to make use of him. Sir G. Carteret tells me this afternoon that the Dutch are not yet ready to set out, and by that means do lose a good wind which would carry them out and keep us in, and moreover he says that they begin to boggle in the business, and he thinks may offer terms of peace for all this, and seems to argue that it will be well for the King too, and I pray God send it. Colonell Reames did, among other things, this day tell me how it is clear that, if my Lord Tiviott had lived, he would have quite undone Tangier, or designed himself to be master of it. He did put the King upon most great, chargeable, and unnecessary works there, and took the course industriously to deter all other merchants but himself to deal there, and to make both King and all others pay what he pleased for all that was brought thither.

20th. Up and to the office, where we sat all the morning, at noon to the 'Change, and there met by appointment with Captain Poyntz, who hath some place, or title to a place, belonging to gameing, and so I discoursed with him about the business of our improving of the Lotterys, to the King's benefit, and that of the Fishery, and had some light from him in the business, and shall, he says, have more in writing from him. So home to dinner and then abroad to the Fishing Committee at Fishmongers' Hall, and there sat and did some business considerable, and so up and home, and there late at my office doing much business, and I find with great delight that I am come to my good temper of business again. God continue me in it. So home to supper, it being washing day, and to bed.

21st. Up, and by coach to Mr. Povy's, and there got him to signe the payment of Captain Tayler's bills for the remainder of freight for the Eagle, wherein I shall be gainer about £30, thence with him to Westminster by coach to Houseman's [Huysman] the great picture drawer, and saw again very fine pictures, and have his promise, for Mr. Povy's sake, to take pains in what picture I shall set him about, and I think to have my wife's. But it is a strange thing to observe and fit for me to remember that I am at no time so unwilling to part with money as when I am concerned in the getting of it most, as I thank God of late

I have got more in this month, viz., near £250, than ever I did in half a year before in my life, I think. Thence to White Hall with him, and so walked to the old Exchange and back to Povy's to dinner, where great and good company; among others Sir John Skeffington,[1] whom I knew at Magdalen College, a fellow-commoner, my fellow-pupil, but one with whom I had no great acquaintance, he being then, God knows, much above me. Here I was afresh delighted with Mr. Povy's house and pictures of perspective, being strange things to think how they do delude one's eye, that methinks it would make a man doubtful of swearing that ever he saw any thing. Thence with him to St. James's, and so to White Hall to a Tangier Committee, and hope I have light of another opportunity of getting a little money if Sir W. Warren will use me kindly for deales to Tangier, and with the hopes went joyfully home, and there received Captain Tayler's money, received by Will to-day, out of which (as I said above) I shall get above £30. So with great comfort to bed, after supper. By discourse this day I have great hopes from Mr. Coventry that the Dutch and we shall not fall out.

22nd. Up and at the office all the morning. To the 'Change at noon, and among other things discoursed with Sir William Warren what I might do to get a little money by carrying of deales to Tangier, and told him the opportunity I have there of doing it, and he did give me some advice, though not so good as he would have done at any other time of the year, but such as I hope to make good use of, and get a little money by. So to Sir G. Carteret's to dinner, and he and I and Captain Cocke all alone, and good discourse, and thence to a Committee of Tangier

[1] Magd: Coll: Register Book Septr 19° 1649.

Mem: eū in ordinem cōmensaliū cooptatū fuisse Apr: 17° 1651, Tutore hoc tempore D^{no} Morland.	Joannes Skeffington filius Ricardi Skeffington, equitis, de coventriâ, annum agens decimum septimum, admissus est Pensionarius, Tutore M^{ro} Merryweather. — M. B.

Sir John Skeffington married Mary, only daughter and heir of Sir John Clotworthy, who was in 1660 created Viscount Massareene of Ireland, with remainder to his son-in-law, Sir John Skeffington, who succeeded as second Viscount in 1665, and died in 1695. — B.

at White Hall, and so home, where I found my wife not well, and she tells me she thinks she is with child, but I neither believe nor desire it. But God's will be done! So to my office late, and home to supper and to bed; having got a strange cold in my head, by flinging off my hat[1] at dinner, and sitting with the wind in my neck.

23rd. My cold and pain in my head increasing, and the palate of my mouth falling, I was in great pain all night. My wife also was not well, so that a mayd was fain to sit up by her all night. Lay long in the morning, at last up, and amongst others comes Mr. Fuller, that was the wit of Cambridge, and Prævaricator[2] in my time, and staid all the morning with me discoursing, and his business to get a man discharged, which I did do for him. Dined with little heart at noon, in the afternoon against my will to the office, where Sir G. Carteret and we met about an order of the Council for the hiring him a house, giving him £1,000 fine, and £70 per annum for it. Here Sir J. Minnes took occasion, in the most childish and most unbeseeming manner, to reproach us all, but most himself, that he was not valued as Comptroller among us, nor did anything but only set his hand to paper, which is but too true; and every body had a palace, and he no house to lie in, and wished he had but as much to build him a house with, as we have laid out in carved worke. It was to no end to oppose, but all bore it, and after laughed at him for it. So home, and late reading "The Siege of Rhodes" to my wife, and then

[1] In Lord Clarendon's Essay, "On the decay of respect paid to Age," he says that in his younger days he never kept his hat on before those older than himself, except at dinner. — B.

[2] At the Commencement (Comitia Majora) in July, the Prævaricator, or Varier, held a similar position to the Tripos at the Comitia Minora. He was so named from *varying* the question which he proposed, either by a play upon the words or by the transposition of the terms in which it was expressed. Under the pretence of maintaining some philosophical question, he poured out a medley of absurd jokes and personal ridicule, which gradually led to the abolition of the office. In Thoresby's "Diary" we read, "Tuesday, July 6th. The Prævaricator's speech was smart and ingenious, attended with vollies of hurras" (see Wordsworth's "University Life in the Eighteenth Century"). — M. B.

In Dean Peacock's work on the "Statutes of the University of Cambridge," Appendix A, p. xxvi, there is an interesting account of the Varier or Prævaricator. — B.

to bed, my head being in great pain and my palate still down.

24th. Up and to the office, where all the morning busy, then home to dinner, and so after dinner comes one Phillips, who is concerned in the Lottery, and from him I collected much concerning that business. I carried him in my way to White Hall and set him down at Somersett House. Among other things he told me that Monsieur Du Puy,[1] that is so great a man at the Duke of Yorke's, and this man's great opponent, is a knave and by quality but a tailor. To the Tangier Committee, and there I opposed Colonell Legg's estimate of supplies of provisions to be sent to Tangier till all were ashamed of it, and he fain after all his good husbandry and seeming ignorance and joy to have the King's money saved, yet afterwards he discovered all his design to be to keep the furnishing of these things to the officers of the Ordnance, but Mr. Coventry seconded me, and between us we shall save the King some money in the year. In one business of deales in £520, I offer to save £172, and yet purpose getting money to myself by it. So home and to my office, and business being done home to supper and so to bed, my head and throat being still out of order mightily. This night Prior of Brampton came and paid me £40, and I find this poor painful man is the only thriving and purchasing man in the town almost. We were told to-day of a Dutch ship of 3 or 400 tons, where all the men were dead of the plague, and the ship cast ashore at Gottenburgh.

25th (Lord's day). Up, and my throat being yet very sore, and my head out of order, we went not to church, but I spent all the morning reading of "The Madd Lovers,"[2] a very good play, and at noon comes Harman and his wife, whom I sent for to meet the Joyces, but they came not. It seems Will has got a fall off his horse and broke his face. However, we were as merry as I could in their company, and we had a good chine of beef, but I had no taste nor stomach through my cold, and therefore little pleased with my dinner. It raining, they sat talking with us all

[1] Apparently Lawrence Dupuy, who was associated with other projectors in the promotion of lotteries.

[2] See note on following page.

the afternoon. So anon they went away, and then I to read another play, "The Custome of the Country,"[1] which is a very poor one, methinks. Then to supper, prayers, and bed.

26th. Up pretty well again, but my mouth very scabby, my cold being going away, so that I was forced to wear a great black patch, but that would not do much good, but it happens we did not go to the Duke to-day, and so I staid at home busy all the morning. At noon, after dinner, to the 'Change, and thence home to my office again, where busy, well employed till 10 at night, and so home to supper and to bed, my mind a little troubled that I have not of late kept up myself so briske in business, but mind my ease a little too much and my family upon the coming of Mercer and Tom. So that I have not kept company, nor appeared very active with Mr. Coventry, but now I resolve to settle to it again, not that I have idled all my time, but as to my ease something. So I have looked a little too much after Tangier and the Fishery, and that in the sight of Mr. Coventry, but I have good reason to love myself for serving Tangier, for it is one of the best flowers in my garden.

27th. Lay long, sleeping, it raining and blowing very hard. Then up and to the office, my mouth still being scabby and a patch on it. At the office all the morning. At noon dined at home, and so after dinner (Lewellin dining with me and in my way talking about Deering) to the Fishing Committee, and had there very many fine things argued, and I hope some good will come of it. So home, where my wife having (after all her merry discourse of being with child) her months upon her is gone to bed. I to my office very late doing business, then home to supper and to bed. To-night Mr. T. Trice and Piggot came to see me, and desire my going down to Brampton Court, where for Piggot's sake, for whom it is necessary, I should go, I would be glad to go, and will, contrary to my purpose, endeavour it, but having now almost £1,000, if not above, in my house, I know not what to do with it, and that will trouble my mind to leave in the house, and I not at home.

28th. Up and by water with Mr. Tucker down to Woolwich, first to do several businesses of the King's, then

[1] Both these plays were by Beaumont and Fletcher, or probably by Fletcher alone.

on board Captain Fisher's ship, which we hire to carry goods to Tangier. All the way going and coming I reading and discoursing over some papers of his which he, poor man, having some experience, but greater conceit of it than is fit, did at the King's first coming over make proposals of, ordering in a new manner the whole revenue of the kingdom, but, God knows, a most weak thing; however, one paper I keep wherein he do state the main branches of the publick revenue fit to consider and remember. So home, very cold, and fearfull of having got some pain, but, thanks be to God! I was well after it. So to dinner, and after dinner by coach to White Hall, thinking to have met at a Committee of Tangier, but nobody being there but my Lord Rutherford, he would needs carry me and another Scotch Lord to a play, and so we saw, coming late, part of "The Generall," my Lord Orrery's (Broghill)[1] second play; but, Lord! to see how no more either in words, sense, or design, it is to his "Harry the 5th" is not imaginable, and so poorly acted, though in finer clothes, is strange. And here I must confess breach of a vowe in appearance, but I not desiring it, but against my will, and my oathe being to go neither at my own charge nor at another's, as I had done by becoming liable to give them another, as I am to Sir W. Pen and Mr. Creed; but here I neither know which of them paid for me, nor, if I did, am I obliged ever to return the like, or did it by desire or with any willingness. So that with a safe conscience I do think my oathe is not broke and judge God Almighty will not think it other wise. Thence to W. Joyce's, and there found my aunt and cozen Mary come home from my father's with great pleasure and content, and thence to Kate's and

[1] Roger Boyle, Lord Broghill, created Earl of Orrery, 1660. Died October 16th, 1679. A tragi-comedy with the same title has been attributed to Shirley. The Rev. T. Morrice, in his memoirs of Lord Orrery, says that Charles II. "was the first to put my Lord upon writing plays, which his Majesty did on occasion of a dispute that arose in his royal presence about writing plays in rhyme; some affirmed it was not to be done, others said it would spoil the fancy to be so confined, but Lord Orrery was of another opinion, and his Majesty being willing a trial should be made, commanded his Lordship to employ some of his leisure that way, which my Lord readily did, and upon that occasion composed the 'Black Prince'" (Orrery's "State Letters," vol. i., p. 81).

found her also mighty pleased with her journey and their good usage of them, and so home, troubled in my conscience at my being at a play. But at home I found Mercer playing on her Vyall, which is a pretty instrument, and so I to the Vyall and singing till late, and so to bed. My mind at a great losse how to go down to Brampton this weeke, to satisfy Piggott; but what with the fears of my house, my money, my wife, and my office, I know not how in the world to think of it, Tom Hater being out of towne, and I having near £1,000 in my house.

29th. Up and to the office, where all the morning, dined at home and Creed with me; after dinner I to Sir G. Carteret, and with him to his new house he is taking in Broad Streete, and there surveyed all the rooms and bounds, in order to the drawing up a lease thereof; and that done, Mr. Cutler, his landlord, took me up and down, and showed me all his ground and house, which is extraordinary great, he having bought all the Augustine Fryers,[1] and many, many a £1,000 he hath and will bury there. So home to my business, clearing my papers and preparing my accounts against to-morrow for a monthly and a great auditt. So to supper and to bed. Fresh newes come of our beating the Dutch at Guinny quite out of all their castles almost, which will make them quite mad here at home sure. And Sir G. Carteret did tell me, that the King do joy mightily at it; but asked him laughing, "But," says ne, "how shall I do to answer this to the Embassador when he comes?" Nay they say that we have beat them out of the New Netherlands[2] too; so that we have been doing them mischief for

[1] Austin Friars, Old Broad Street. At the dissolution of the monasteries the house and grounds of the Augustine Friars were bestowed on William Paulet, first Marquis of Winchester. In 1602 the necessities of William, fourth marquis, compelled him to sell his property to John Swinnerton, afterwards Lord Mayor.

[2] Captain (afterwards Sir Robert) Holmes' expedition to attack the Dutch settlements in Africa eventuated in an important exploit. Holmes suddenly left the coast of Africa, sailed across the Atlantic, and reduced the Dutch settlement of New Netherlands to English rule, under the title of New York. "The short and true state of the matter is this: the country mentioned was part of the province of Virginia, and, as there is no settling an extensive country at once, a few Swedes crept in there, who surrendered the plantations they could not defend to the Dutch, who, having bought the charts and papers of one Hudson, a seaman, who, by

a great while in several parts of the world, without publique knowledge or reason. Their fleete for Guinny is now, they say, ready, and abroad, and will be going this week. Coming home to-night, I did go to examine my wife's house accounts, and finding things that seemed somewhat doubtful, I was angry though she did make it pretty plain, but confessed that when she do misse a sum, she do add something to other things to make it, and, upon my being very angry, she do protest she will here lay up something for herself to buy her a necklace with, which madded me and do still trouble me, for I fear she will forget by degrees the way of living cheap and under sense of want.

30th. Up, and all day, both morning and afternoon, at my accounts, it being a great month, both for profit and layings out, the last being £89 for kitchen and clothes for myself and wife, and a few extraordinaries for the house; and my profits, besides salary, £239; so that I have this weeke, notwithstanding great layings out, and preparations for laying out, which I make as paid this month, my balance to come to £1,203, for which the Lord's name be praised! Dined at home at noon, staying long looking for Kate Joyce and my aunt James and Mary, but they came not. So my wife abroad to see them, and took Mary Joyce to a play. Then in the evening came and sat working by me at the office, and late home to supper and to bed, with my heart in good rest for this day's work, though troubled to think that my last month's negligence besides the making me neglect business and spend money, and lessen myself both as to business and the world and myself, I am fain to preserve my vowe by paying 20*s*. dry[1] money into the poor's box, because I had not fulfilled all my memoran-

the commission from the crown of England, discovered a river, to which he gave his name, conceited they had purchased a province. Sometimes, when he had strength in those parts, they were English subjects; at others, when that strength declined, they were subjects of the United Provinces. However, upon King Charles's claim the States disowned the title, but resumed it during our confusions. On March 12th, 1663–64, Charles II. granted it to the Duke of York. . . . The King sent Holmes, when he returned, to the Tower, and did not discharge him, till he made it evidently appear that he had not infringed the law of nations" (Campbell's "Naval History," vol. ii., p. 89). How little did the King or Holmes himself foresee the effects of the capture. — B.

[1] Dry = hard, as "hard cash."

dums and paid all my petty debts and received all my petty credits, of the last month, but I trust in God I shall do so no more.

October 1st. Up and at the office both forenoon and afternoon very busy, and with great pleasure in being so. This morning Mrs. Lane (now Martin) like a foolish woman came to the Horseshoe[1] hard by, and sent for me while I was at the office, to come to speak with her by a note sealed up, I know to get me to do something for her husband, but I sent her an answer that I would see her at Westminster, and so I did not go, and she went away, poor soul. At night home to supper, weary, and my eyes sore with writing and reading, and to bed. We go now on with great vigour in preparing against the Dutch, who, they say, will now fall upon us without doubt upon this high newes come of our beating them so wholly in Guinny.[2]

2nd (Lord's day). My wife not being well to go to church I walked with my boy through the City, putting in at several churches, among others at Bishopsgate, and there saw the picture[3] usually put before the King's book, put up in the church but very ill painted, though it were a pretty piece to set up in a church. I intended to have seen the Quakers, who, they say, do meet every Lord's day at the Mouth[4] at Bishopsgate; but I could see none stir-

[1] There were several houses in the neighbourhood of the Navy House with the sign of the Horseshoe; one was in St. Dunstan's in the East and another on Great Tower Hill.

[2] See "Poems on State Affairs," vol. i., p. 32. — B.

[3] "The picture usually placed before the king's book, which Pepys says he saw 'put up in Bishopsgate church,' was not engraved for the Εἰκων Βασιλικὴ, but relates to the frontispiece of the large folio Common Prayer book of 1661, which consists of a sort of pattern altar piece, which it was intended should generally be placed in the churches. The design is a sort of classical affair, derived in type from the ciborium of the ancient and continental churches; a composition of two Corinthian columns, engaged or disengaged, with a pediment. It occurs very frequently in the London churches, and may be occasionally remarked in country-town churches, especially those restored at the king's coming in. Anyone who has ever seen the great Prayer Book of 1661, will at once recognize the allusion; and it is a well-known fact that the frontispiece was drawn and engraved for the purpose mentioned above" ("Gentleman's Magazine," March, 1849, p. 226). — B.

[4] There is a token, "At the Mouth Tavern without Bishop Gate. R.K.S." ("Boyne's Trade Tokens," ed. Williamson, vol. i., 1889, p. 540).

ring, nor was it fit to aske for the place, so I walked over Moorefields, and thence to Clerkenwell church, and there, as I wished, sat next pew to the fair Butler, who indeed is a most perfect beauty still; and one I do very much admire myself for my choice of her for a beauty, she having the best lower part of her face that ever I saw all days of my life. After church I walked to my Lady Sandwich's, through my Lord Southampton's new buildings[1] in the fields behind Gray's Inn; and, indeed, they are a very great and a noble work. So I dined with my Lady, and the same innocent discourse that we used to have, only after dinner, being alone, she asked me my opinion about Creed, whether he would have a wife or no, and what he was worth, and proposed Mrs. Wright[2] for him, which, she says, she heard he was once inquiring after. She desired I would take a good time and manner of proposing it, and I said I would, though I believed he would love nothing but money, and much was not to be expected there, she said. So away back to Clerkenwell Church, thinking to have got sight of la belle Boteler again, but failed, and so after church walked all over the fields home, and there my wife was angry with me for not coming home, and for gadding abroad to look after beauties, she told me plainly, so I made all peace, and to supper. This evening came Mrs. Lane (now Martin) with her husband to desire my helpe about a place for him. It seems poor Mr. Daniel is dead of the Victualling Office, a place too good for this puppy to follow him in. But I did give him the best words I could, and so after drinking a glasse of wine sent them going, but with great kindnesse. So to supper, prayers, and to bed.

3rd. Up with Sir J. Minnes, by coach to St. James's; and there all the newes now of very hot preparations for the Dutch: and being with the Duke, he told us he was resolved to make a tripp himself, and that Sir W. Pen should go in the same ship with him. Which honour, God forgive me! I could grudge him, for his knavery and dissim-

[1] This refers to the buildings erected by Lord Treasurer Southampton in what is now Bloomsbury Square. His mansion, afterwards known as Bedford House, occupied the whole north side of that square.

[2] Nan Wright, afterwards Mrs. Markham (see August 16th, 1666).

ulation, though I do not envy much the having the same place myself. Talke also of great haste in the getting out another fleete, and building some ships; and now it is likely we have put one another by each other's dalliance past a retreate. Thence with our heads full of business we broke up, and I to my barber's, and there only saw Jane and stroked her under the chin, and away to the Exchange, and there long about several businesses, hoping to get money by them, and thence home to dinner and there found Hawly. But meeting Bagwell's wife at the office before I went home I took her into the office and there kissed her only. She rebuked me for doing it, saying that did I do so much to many bodies else it would be a stain to me. But I do not see but she takes it well enough, though in the main I believe she is very honest. So after some kind discourse we parted, and I home to dinner, and after dinner down to Deptford, where I found Mr. Coventry, and there we made an experiment of Holland's and our cordage, and ours outdid it a great deale, as my book of observations tells particularly. Here we were late, and so home together by water, and I to my office, where late, putting things in order. Mr. Bland came this night to me to take his leave of me, he going to Tangier, wherein I wish him good successe. So home to supper and to bed, my mind troubled at the businesses I have to do, that I cannot mind them as I ought to do and get money, and more that I have neglected my frequenting and seeming more busy publicly than I have done of late in this hurry of business, but there is time left to recover it, and I trust in God I shall.

4th. Up and to the office, where we sat all the morning, and this morning Sir W. Pen went to Chatham to look after the ships now going out thence, and particularly that wherein the Duke and himself go. He took Sir G. Ascue with him, whom, I believe, he hath brought into play. At noon to the 'Change and thence home, where I found my aunt James and the two she Joyces. They dined and were merry with us. Thence after dinner to a play, to see "The Generall;" which is so dull and so ill-acted, that I think it is the worst I ever saw or heard in all my days. I happened to sit near to Sir Charles Sidly;[1] who I find a very

[1] The witty Sir Charles Sedley is frequently referred to by Pepys in the Diary.

witty man, and he did at every line take notice of the dullness of the poet and badness of the action, that most pertinently; which I was mightily taken with; and among others where by Altemire's command Clarimont, the Generall, is commanded to rescue his Rivall, whom she loved, Lucidor, he, after a great deal of demurre, broke out, "Well, I'le save my Rivall and make her confess, that I deserve, while he do but possesse." "Why, what, pox," says Sir Charles Sydly, "would he have him have more, or what is there more to be had of a woman than the possessing her?" Thence setting all them at home, I home with my wife and Mercer, vexed at my losing my time and above *20s.* in money, and neglecting my business to see so bad a play. To-morrow they told us should be acted, or the day after, a new play, called "The Parson's Dreame,"[1] acted all by women. So to my office, and there did business, and so home to supper and to bed.

5th. Up betimes and to my office, and thence by coach to New Bridewell to meet with Mr. Poyntz to discourse with him (being Master of the Workhouse there) about making of Bewpers for us. But he was not within; however his clerke did lead me up and down through all the house, and there I did with great pleasure see the many pretty works, and the little children employed, every one to do something, which was a very fine sight, and worthy encouragement. I cast away a crowne among them, and so to the 'Change and among the Linnen Wholesale Drapers to enquire about Callicos, to see what can be done with them for the supplying our want of Bewpers for flaggs, and I think I shall do something therein to good purpose for the King. So to the Coffee-house, and there fell in discourse with the Secretary of the Virtuosi of Gresham College,[2] and had very fine discourse with him. He tells me of a new invented instrument to be tried before the College anon, and I intend to see it. So to Trinity House, and

[1] There does not appear to have been any play with this title. It evidently was the "Parson's Wedding," referred to October 11th.

[2] Henry Oldenburg was secretary of the Royal Society from 1663 to 1677. Mr. Herbert Rix, assistant-secretary to the Royal Society, has contributed to "Nature," November 2nd, 1893 (vol. xlix., p. 9), an interesting account of Oldenburg.

there I dined among the old dull fellows, and so home and to my office a while, and then comes Mr. Cocker to see me, and I discoursed with him about his writing and ability of sight, and how I shall do to get some glasse or other to helpe my eyes by candlelight; and he tells me he will bring me the helps he hath within a day or two, and shew me what he do. Thence to the Musique-meeting at the Post-office, where I was once before. And thither anon come all the Gresham College, and a great deal of noble company: and the new instrument was brought called the Arched Viall,[1] where being tuned with lute-strings, and played on with kees like an organ, a piece of parchment is always kept moving; and the strings, which by the kees are pressed down upon it, are grated in imitation of a bow, by the parchment; and so it is intended to resemble several vyalls played on with one bow, but so basely and harshly, that it will never do. But after three hours' stay it could not be fixed in tune; and so they were fain to go to some other musique of instruments, which I am grown quite out of love with, and so I, after some good discourse with Mr. Spong, Hill, Grant, and Dr. Whistler, and others by turns, I home to my office and there late, and so home, where I understand my wife has spoke to Jane and ended matters of difference between her and her, and she stays with us, which I am glad of; for her fault is nothing but sleepiness and forgetfulness, otherwise a good-natured, quiet, well-meaning, honest servant, and one that will do as she is bid, so one called upon her and will see her do it. This morning, by three o'clock, the Prince[2] and King, and Duke with him, went down the River, and the Prince under sail the next tide after, and so is gone from the Hope. God give him better successe than he used to have! This

[1] "There seems to be a curious fate reigning over the instruments which have the word 'arch' prefixed to their name. They have no vitality, and somehow or other come to grief. Even the famous archlute, which was still a living thing in the time of Handel, has now disappeared from the concert room and joined Mr. Pepys's 'Arched Viall' in the limbo of things forgotten. . . . Mr. Pepys's verdict that it would never do . . . has been fully confirmed by the event, as his predictions usually were, being indeed always founded on calm judgment and close observation."— F. Hueffer's *Italian and other Studies* 1883, p. 263.

[2] Rupert.

day Mr. Bland went away hence towards his voyage to Tangier. This day also I had a letter from an unknown hand that tells me that Jacke Angier, he believes, is dead at Lisbon, for he left him there ill.

6th. Up and to the office, where busy all the morning, among other things about this of the flags and my bringing in of callicos to oppose Young and Whistler. At noon by promise Mr. Pierce and his wife and Madam Clerke and her niece came and dined with me to a rare chine of beefe and spent the afternoon very pleasantly all the afternoon, and then to my office in the evening, they being gone, and late at business, and then home to supper and to bed, my mind coming to itself in following of my business.

7th. Lay pretty while with some discontent abed, even to the having bad words with my wife, and blows too, about the ill-serving up of our victuals yesterday; but all ended in love, and so I rose and to my office busy all the morning. At noon dined at home, and then to my office again, and then abroad to look after callicos for flags, and hope to get a small matter by my pains therein and yet save the King a great deal of money, and so home to my office, and there came Mr. Cocker, and brought me a globe of glasse, and a frame of oyled paper, as I desired, to show me the manner of his gaining light to grave by, and to lessen the glaringnesse of it at pleasure by an oyled paper. This I bought of him, giving him a crowne for it; and so, well satisfied, he went away, and I to my business again, and so home to supper, prayers, and to bed.

8th. All the morning at the office, and after dinner abroad, and among other things contracted with one Mr. Bridges, at the White Bear[1] on Cornhill, for 100 pieces of Callico to make flaggs; and as I know I shall save the King money, so I hope to get a little for my pains and venture of my own money myself. Late in the evening doing business, and then comes Captain Tayler, and he and I till 12 o'clock at night arguing about the freight of his ship Eagle, hired formerly by me to Tangier, and at last we made an end, and I hope to get a little money, some small matter

[1] There is a token of the "Beare tavern in Cornhill, 1656. R.W.D." ("Boyne's Trade Tokens," ed. Williamson, vol. i., p. 573).

by it. So home to bed, being weary and cold, but contented that I have made an end of that business.

9th (Lord's day). Lay pretty long, but however up time enough with my wife to go to church. Then home to dinner, and Mr. Fuller, my Cambridge acquaintance, coming to me about what he was with me lately, to release a waterman, he told me he was to preach at Barking Church;[1] and so I to heare him, and he preached well and neatly. Thence, it being time enough, to our owne church, and there staid wholly privately at the great doore to gaze upon a pretty lady, and from church dogged her home, whither she went to a house near Tower hill, and I think her to be one of the prettiest women I ever saw. So home, and at my office a while busy, then to my uncle Wight's, whither it seems my wife went after sermon and there supped, but my aunt and uncle in a very ill humour one with another, but I made shift with much ado to keep them from scolding, and so after supper home and to bed without prayers, it being cold, and to-morrow washing day.

10th. Up and, it being rainy, in Sir W. Pen's coach to St. James's, and there did our usual business with the Duke, and more and more preparations every day appear against the Dutch, and (which I must confess do a little move my envy) Sir W. Pen do grow every day more and more regarded by the Duke,[2] because of his service heretofore in the Dutch warr, which I am confident is by some strong obligations he hath laid upon Mr. Coventry; for Mr. Coventry must needs know that he is a man of very mean parts, but only a bred seaman. Going home in coach with

[1] The church of Allhallows Barking, situated at the east end of Great Tower Street.

[2] "The duke had decided that the English fleet should consist of three squadrons to be commanded by himself, Prince Rupert, and Lord Sandwich, from which arrangement the two last, who were land admirals, had concluded that Penn would have no concern in this fleet. Neither the duke, Rupert, nor Sandwich had ever been engaged in an encounter of fleets. . . . Penn alone of the four was familiar with all these things. By the duke's unexpected announcement that he should take Penn with him into his own ship, Rupert and Sandwich at once discovered that they would be really and practically under Penn's command in everything that regarded the conduct of the fleet in an encounter with the enemy."—Granville Penn's *Memorials of Sir William Penn*, vol. ii., p. 295.

Sir W. Batten he told me how Sir J. Minnes by the means of Sir R. Ford was the last night brought to his house and did discover the reason of his so long discontent with him, and now they are friends again, which I am sorry for, but he told it me so plainly that I see there is no thorough understanding between them, nor love, and so I hope there will be no great combination in any thing, nor do I see Sir J. Minnes very fond as he used to be. But Sir W. Batten do raile still against Mr. Turner and his wife, telling me he is a false fellow, and his wife a false woman, and has rotten teeth and false, set in with wire, and as I know they are so, so I am glad he finds it so. To the Coffee-house, and thence to the 'Change, and there with Sir W. Warren to the Coffee-house behind the 'Change, and sat alone with him till 4 o'clock talking of his businesses first and then of business in general, and discourse how I might get money and how to carry myself to advantage to contract no envy and yet make the world see my pains; which was with great content to me, and a good friend and helpe I am like to find him, for which God be thanked! So home to dinner at 4 o'clock, and then to the office, and there late, and so home to supper and to bed, having sat up till past twelve at night to look over the account of the collections for the Fishery, and the loose and base manner that monies so collected are disposed of in, would make a man never part with a penny in that manner, and, above all, the inconvenience of having a great man, though never so seeming pious as my Lord Pembroke[1] is. He is too great to be called to an account, and is abused by his servants, and yet obliged to defend them for his owne sake. This day, by the blessing of God, my wife and I have been married nine years: but my head being full of business, I did not think of it to keep it in any extraordinary manner. But bless God for our long lives and loves and health together, which the same God long continue, I wish, from my very heart!

11th. Up and to the office, where we sat all the morning. My wife this morning went, being invited, to my Lady Sandwich, and I alone at home at dinner, till by and

[1] Philip Herbert, who succeeded as fifth Earl of Pembroke in 1650. He died December 11th, 1669.

by Luellin comes and dines with me. He tells me what a bawdy loose play this "Parson's Wedding"[1] is, that is acted by nothing but women at the King's house, and I am glad of it. Thence to the Fishery in Thames Street, and there several good discourses about the letting of the Lotterys, and, among others, one Sir Thomas Clifford,[2] whom yet I knew not, do speak very well and neatly. Thence I to my cozen Will Joyce to get him to go to Brampton with me this week, but I think he will not, and I am not a whit sorry for it, for his company both chargeable and troublesome. So home and to my office, and then to supper and then to my office again till late, and so home, with my head and heart full of business, and so to bed. My wife tells me the sad news of my Lady Castlemayne's being now become so decayed, that one would not know her; at least far from a beauty, which I am sorry for. This day with great joy Captain Titus told us the particulars of the French's expedition against Gigery upon the Barbary Coast,[3] in the Straights, with 6,000 chosen men. They have taken the Fort of Gigery, wherein were five men and

[1] A comedy written by Thomas Killigrew in Switzerland, published in 1663. It is included in Dodsley's Old Plays, ed. Hazlitt, vol. xiv.

[2] Thomas Clifford, born at Ugbrooke, Devon, August 1st, 1630, and educated at Exeter College, Oxford. He attended Charles II. in exile, and represented Totnes in the Convention Parliament and in that of 1661. He was knighted as a reward for the delivery of several speeches on behalf of the royal prerogative. After having distinguished himself at sea and acting as Envoy Extraordinary to the courts of Denmark and Sweden, he was, on November 8th, 1666, made Comptroller of the Household, and on December 5th he was sworn of the Privy Council. In 1672 he was made Secretary of State, on April 22nd created Baron Clifford, and in November raised to the post of Lord High Treasurer, which he held till June, 1673. Died September, 1673, in the forty-fourth year of his age.

[3] Colbert, in his desire to establish French colonies, wished to found one on the Mediterranean coast of Africa. For this purpose the Duc de Beaufort, High Admiral of France, took possession, on July 22nd, 1664, of Gigeri, in the province of Bugia, and he placed a garrison there under the command of Lieutenant-General Guadagni. The duke had scarcely retired before the Moors attacked the place in great force, and with such success, that Guadagni thought himself happy in evacuating it with safety. He embarked on the night of the 29th October, abandoning his artillery and stores. The regiment of Picardy perished by shipwreck. — B.

three guns, which makes the whole story of the King of France's policy and power to be laughed at.

12th. This morning all the morning at my office ordering things against my journey to-morrow. At noon to the Coffee-house, where very good discourse. For newes, all say De Ruyter is gone to Guinny before us. Sir J. Lawson is come to Portsmouth; and our fleete is hastening all speed: I mean this new fleete. Prince Rupert with his is got into the Downs. At home dined with me W. Joyce and a friend of his. W. Joyce will go with me to Brampton. After dinner I out to Mr. Bridges, the linnen draper, and evened with [him] for 100 pieces of callico, and did give him £208 18*s*., which I now trust the King for, but hope both to save the King money and to get a little by it to boot. Thence by water up and down all the timber yards to look out some Dram timber, but can find none for our turne at the price I would have, and so I home, and there at my office late doing business against my journey to clear my hands of everything for two days. So home and to supper and bed.

13th. After being at the office all the morning, I home and dined, and taking leave of my wife with my mind not a little troubled how she would look after herself or house in my absence, especially, too, leaving a considerable sum of money in the office, I by coach to the Red Lyon in Aldersgate Street, and there, by agreement, met W. Joyce and Tom Trice, and mounted, I upon a very fine mare that Sir W. Warren helps me to, and so very merrily rode till it was very darke, I leading the way through the darke to Welling,[1] and there, not being very weary, to supper and to bed. But very bad accommodation at the Swan. In this day's journey I met with Mr. White,[2] Cromwell's chaplin that was, and had a great deale of discourse with him. Among others, he tells me that Richard is, and hath long been, in France, and is now going into Italy. He owns publiquely that he do correspond, and return him all his money. That Richard hath been in some straits at the beginning; but relieved by his friends. That he goes by another name, but do not disguise himself, nor deny

[1] Welwyn.

[2] Jeremiah White, see note, September 19th, 1660.

himself to any man that challenges him. He tells me, for certain, that offers had been made to the old man, of marriage between the King and his daughter, to have obliged him, but he would not.[1] He thinks (with me) that it never was in his power to bring in the King with the consent of any of his officers about him; and that he scorned to bring him in as Monk did, to secure himself and deliver every body else. When I told him of what I found writ in a French book of one Monsieur Sorbiere,[2]

[1] The Protector wished the Duke of Buckingham to marry his daughter Frances. She married, 1. Robert Rich, grandson and heir to Robert, Earl of Warwick, on November 11th, 1657, who died in the following February; 2. Sir John Russell, Bart. She died January 27th, 1721–22, aged eighty-four.

In T. Morrice's life of Roger, Earl of Orrery, prefixed to Orrery's "State Letters" (Dublin, 1743, vol. i., p. 40), there is a circumstantial account of an interview between Orrery (then Lord Broghill) and Cromwell, in which the former suggested to the latter that Charles II. should marry Frances Cromwell. Cromwell gave great attention to the reasons urged, "but walking two or three turns, and pondering with himself, he told Lord Broghill the king would never forgive him the death of his father. His lordship desired him to employ somebody to sound the king in this matter, to see how he would take it, and offered himself to mediate in it for him. But Cromwell would not consent, but again repeated, 'The king cannot and will not forgive the death of his father;' and so he left his lordship, who durst not tell him he had already dealt with his majesty in that affair. Upon this my lord withdrew, and meeting Cromwell's wife and daughter, they inquired how he had succeeded; of which having given them an account, he added they must try their interest in him, but none could prevail."

[2] Samuel Sorbière published his "Voyage to England" at Paris in 1664, but a translation into English does not appear to have been published until 1709. The work created a great sensation, and Louis XIV. showed his displeasure by a temporary banishment of the author. It is, however, entertaining, and can be read with advantage as a picture of the time. Sorbière died in 1670. It is not clear whether Sorbière invented or only repeated the story here related, which has been disposed of by the discovery of Charles I.'s coffin in 1813; and, indeed, how any doubt upon this subject could have arisen, seems extraordinary, considering that several persons were present at the interment, and that we have Sir T. Herbert's testimony as to the fact in his published "Memoirs." See also Diary, February 26th, 1665–66, when Pepys was shown the place where the late king was buried in St. George's Chapel, and Fuller's "Church History," book xi., p. 327. Sir Henry Halford published, in 1813, "An Account of what appeared on opening the Coffin of K. Charles I. at Windsor," which was reprinted in "Essays and Orations," 1831, 1842.

that gives an account of his observations here in England; among other things he says, that it is reported that Cromwell did, in his life-time, transpose many of the bodies of the Kings of England from one grave to another, and that by that means it is not known certainly whether the head that is now set up upon a post be that of Cromwell, or of one of the Kings; Mr. White tells me that he believes he never had so poor a low thought in him to trouble himself about it. He says the hand of God is much to be seen; that all his children are in good condition enough as to estate, and that their relations that betrayed their family are all now either hanged or very miserable.

14th. Up by break of day, and got to Brampton by three o'clock, where my father and mother overjoyed to see me, my mother ready to weepe every time she looked upon me. After dinner my father and I to the Court, and there did all our business to my mind, as I have set down in a paper particularly expressing our proceedings at this court. So home, where W. Joyce full of talk and pleased with his journey, and after supper I to bed and left my father, mother, and him laughing.

15th. My father and I up and walked alone to Hinchingbroke; and among the other late chargeable works that my Lord hath done there, we saw his water-works and the Ora,[1] which is very fine; and so is the house all over, but I am sorry to think of the money at this time spent therein. Back to my father's (Mr. Sheply being out of town) and there breakfasted, after making an end with Barton about his businesses, and then my mother called me into the garden, and there but all to no purpose desiring me to be friends with John, but I told her I cannot, nor indeed easily shall, which afflicted the poor woman, but I cannot help it. Then taking leave, W. Joyce and I set out, calling T. Trice at Bugden, and thence got by night to Stevenage, and there mighty merry, though I in bed more weary than the other two days, which, I think, proceeded from our galloping so much, my other weariness being almost all over; but I find that a coney skin in my breeches preserves me perfectly from galling, and that eating after I come to

[1] No clue to the meaning of the word *ora* in this position has been found.

my Inne, without drinking, do keep me from being stomach sick, which drink do presently make me. We lay all in several beds in the same room, and W. Joyce full of his impertinent tricks and talk, which then made us merry, as any other fool would have done. So to sleep.

16th (Lord's day). It raining, we set out, and about nine o'clock got to Hatfield in church-time; and I 'light and saw my simple Lord Salsbury[1] sit there in his gallery. Staid not in the Church, but thence mounted again and to Barnett by the end of sermon, and there dined at the Red Lyon very weary again, but all my weariness yesterday night and to-day in my thighs only, the rest of my weariness in my shoulders and arms being quite gone. Thence home, parting company at my cozen Anth. Joyce's, by four o'clock, weary, but very well, to bed at home, where I find all well. Anon my wife came to bed, but for my ease rose again and lay with her woman.

17th. Rose very well and not weary, and with Sir W. Batten to St. James's; there did our business. I saw Sir J. Lawson since his return from sea first this morning, and hear that my Lord Sandwich is come from Portsmouth to town. Thence I to him, and finding him at my Lord Crew's, I went with him home to his house and much kind discourse. Thence my Lord to Court, and I with Creed to the 'Change, and thence with Sir W. Warren to a cook's shop and dined, discoursing and advising him about his great contract he is to make to-morrow, and do every day receive great satisfaction in his company, and a prospect of a just advantage by his friendship. Thence to my office doing some business, but it being very cold, I, for fear of getting cold, went early home to bed, my wife not being come home from my Lady Jemimah, with whom she hath been at a play and at Court to-day.

18th. Up and to the office, where among other things we made a very great contract with Sir W. Warren for 3,000 loade of timber. At noon dined at home. In the

[1] William Cecil, second Earl of Salisbury, K.G., who took the side of the Parliament during the Civil Wars. He died December 3rd, 1668, aged seventy-seven. See his character, "despicable to all men," drawn by Lord Clarendon, "History of the Rebellion," book vi., ed. Macray, 1888, vol. ii., p. 542.

afternoon to the Fishery, where, very confused and very ridiculous, my Lord Craven's proceedings, especially his finding fault with Sir J. Collaton[1] and Colonell Griffin's[2] report in the accounts of the lottery-men. Thence I with Mr. Gray in his coach to White Hall, but the King and Duke being abroad, we returned to Somersett House. In discourse I find him a very worthy and studious gentleman in the business of trade, and among other things he observed well to me, how it is not the greatest wits, but the steady man, that is a good merchant: he instanced in Ford and Cocke, the last of whom he values above all men as his oracle, as Mr. Coventry do Mr. Jolliffe. He says that it is concluded among merchants, that where a trade hath once been and do decay, it never recovers again, and therefore that the manufacture of cloath of England will never come to esteem again; that, among other faults, Sir Richard Ford cannot keepe a secret, and that it is so much the part of a merchant to be guilty of that fault that the Duke of Yorke is resolved to commit no more secrets to the merchants of the Royall Company; that Sir Ellis Layton is, for a speech of forty words, the wittiest man that ever he knew in his life, but longer he is nothing, his judgment being nothing at all, but his wit most absolute. At Somersett House he carried me in, and there I saw the Queene's new rooms, which are most stately and nobly furnished; and there I saw her, and the Duke of Yorke and Duchesse were there. The Duke espied me, and came to me, and talked with me a very great while about our contract this day with Sir W. Warren, and among other things did with some contempt ask whether we did except Polliards, which Sir W.

[1] Sir John Colladon, M.D., of St. Martin's in the Fields, see note, September 22nd, 1663.

[2] Edward Griffin, of Braybrooke, in Northamptonshire, at this time Lieutenant-Colonel in the Duke of York's Regiment of Foot Guards, now called the Coldstream; he was raised to the peerage in 1688 by the title of Lord Griffin, and followed the fortunes of his royal master after the Revolution, and was outlawed. Being taken prisoner in the attempted invasion of Scotland in 1708, he was committed to the Tower, and died there in confinement in November, 1710. He married Lady Essex Howard, eldest daughter, and one of the two co-heirs of James Howard, third Earl of Suffolk. Their grandson, Edward, third Lord Griffin, dying s. p. m., in 1742, the barony became extinct.—B.

Batten did yesterday (in spite, as the Duke I believe by my Lord Barkely do well enough know) among other things in writing propose. Thence home by coach, it raining hard, and to my office, where late, then home to supper and to bed. This night the Dutch Embassador desired and had an audience of the King. What the issue of it was I know not. Both sides I believe desire peace, but neither will begin, and so I believe a warr will follow. The Prince is with his fleet at Portsmouth, and the Dutch are making all preparations for warr.

19th. Up and to my office all the morning. At noon dined at home; then abroad by coach to buy for the office "Herne upon the Statute of Charitable Uses,"[1] in order to the doing something better in the Chest than we have done, for I am ashamed to see Sir W. Batten possess himself so long of so much money as he hath done. Coming home, weighed my two silver flaggons at Stevens's. They weigh 212 oz. 27 dwt., which is about £50, at 5*s.* per oz., and then they judge the fashion to be worth above 5*s.* per oz. more — nay, some say 10*s.* an ounce the fashion. But I do not believe, but yet am sorry to see that the fashion is worth so much, and the silver come to no more. So home and to my office, where very busy late. My wife at Mercer's mother's, I believe, W. Hewer with them, which I do not like, that he should ask my leave to go about business, and then to go and spend his time in sport, and leave me here busy. To supper and to bed, my wife coming in by and by, which though I know there was no hurt in it, I do not like.

20th. Up and to the office, where all the morning. At noon my uncle Thomas came, dined with me, and received some money of me. Then I to my office, where I took in with me Bagwell's wife, and there I caressed her, and find her every day more and more coming with good words and promises of getting her husband a place, which I will do. So we parted, and I to my Lord Sandwich at his lodgings, and after a little stay away with Mr. Cholmely to Fleet Streete, in the way he telling me that Tangier is like to be

[1] "The Law of Charitable Uses: wherein the Statute of 43 Eliz. chap. 4, is set forth and explained. . . . London, 1660," by John Herne. A second edition, "much enlarged," was published in 1663.

in a bad condition with this same Fitzgerald, he being a man of no honour, nor presence, nor little honesty, and endeavours to raise the Irish and suppress the English interest there, and offend every body, and do nothing that I hear of well, which I am sorry for. Thence home, by the way taking two silver tumblers home, which I have bought, and so home, and there late busy at my office, and then home to supper and to bed.

21st. Up and by coach to Mr. Cole's, and there conferred with him about some law business, and so to Sir W. Turner's, and there bought my cloth, coloured, for a suit and cloake, to line with plush the cloake, which will cost me money, but I find that I must go handsomely, whatever it costs me, and the charge will be made up in the fruit it brings. Thence to the Coffee-house and 'Change, and so home to dinner, and then to the office all the afternoon, whither comes W. Howe to see me, being come from, and going presently back to sea with my Lord. Among other things he tells me Mr. Creed is much out of favour with my Lord from his freedom of talke and bold carriage, and other things with which my Lord is not pleased, but most I doubt his not lending my Lord money, and Mr. Moore's reporting what his answer was I doubt in the worst manner. But, however, a very unworthy rogue he is, and, therefore, let him go for one good for nothing, though wise to the height above most men I converse with. In the evening (W. Howe being gone) comes Mr. Martin, to trouble me again to get him a Lieutenant's place, for which he is as fit as a foole can be. But I put him off like an asse, as he is, and so setting my papers and books in order I home to supper and to bed.

22nd. Up and to the office, where we sat all the morning. At noon comes my uncle Thomas and his daughter Mary[1] about getting me to pay them the £30 due now, but payable in law to her husband. I did give them the best answer I could, and so parted, they not desiring to stay to dinner. After dinner I down to Deptford, and there did business, and so back to my office, where very late busy, and so home to supper and to bed.

[1] Mary Pepys's husband is mentioned again on December 11th of this year, but his name is not given. She died in December, 1667.

23rd (Lord's day). Up and to church. At noon comes unexpected Mr. Fuller, the minister, and dines with me, and also I had invited Mr. Cooper with one I judge come from sea, and he and I spent the whole afternoon together, he teaching me some things in understanding of plates. At night to the office, doing business, and then home to supper. Then a psalm, to prayers, and to bed.

24th. Up and in Sir J. Minnes' coach (alone with Mrs. Turner as far as Paternoster Row, where I set her down) to St. James's, and there did our business, and I had the good lucke to speak what pleased the Duke about our great contract in hand with Sir W. Warren against Sir W. Batten, wherein the Duke is very earnest for our contracting. Thence home to the office till noon, and then dined and to the 'Change and off with Sir W. Warren for a while, consulting about managing his contract. Thence to a Committee at White Hall of Tangier, where I had the good lucke to speak something to very good purpose about the Mole at Tangier, which was well received even by Sir J. Lawson and Mr. Cholmely, the undertakers, against whose interest I spoke; that I believe I shall be valued for it. Thence into the galleries to talk with my Lord Sandwich; among other things, about the Prince's writing up to tell us of the danger he and his fleete lie in at Portsmouth, of receiving affronts from the Dutch; which, my Lord said, he would never have done, had he lain there with one ship alone: nor is there any great reason for it, because of the sands. However, the fleete will be ordered to go and lay themselves up at the Cowes. Much beneath the prowesse of the Prince, I think, and the honour of the nation, at the first to be found to secure themselves. My Lord is well pleased to think, that, if the Duke and the Prince go, all the blame of any miscarriage will not light on him; and that if any thing goes well, he hopes he shall have the share of the glory, for the Prince is by no means well esteemed of by any body. Thence home, and though not very well yet up late about the Fishery business, wherein I hope to give an account how I find the Collections to have been managed, which I did finish to my great content, and so home to supper and to bed. This day the great O'Neale[1] died; I

[1] Daniel O'Neale, third husband of Lady Catherine Stanhope, created

believe, to the content of all the Protestant pretenders in Ireland.

25th. Up and to the office, where we sat all the morning, and finished Sir W. Warren's great contract for timber, with great content to me, because just in the terms I wrote last night to Sir W. Warren and against the terms proposed by Sir W. Batten. At noon home to dinner, and there found Creed and Hawley. After dinner comes in Mrs. Ingram, the first time to make a visit to my wife. After a little stay I left them and to the Committee of the Fishery, and there did make my report of the late public collections for the Fishery, much to the satisfaction of the Committee, and I think much to my reputation, for good notice was taken of it and much it was commended. So home, in my way taking care of a piece of plate for Mr. Christopher Pett, against the launching of his new great ship to-morrow at Woolwich, which I singly did move to His Royall Highness, and did obtain it for him, to the value of twenty pieces. And he, under his hand, do acknowledge to me that he did never receive so great a kindness from any man in the world as from me herein. So to my office, and then to supper, and then to my office again, where busy late, being very full now a days of business to my great content, I thank God, and so home to bed, my house being full of a design, to go to-morrow, my wife and all her servants, to see the new ship launched.

26th. Up, my people rising mighty betimes, to fit themselves to go by water; and my boy, he could not sleep, but wakes about four o'clock, and in bed lay playing on his lute, till daylight, and, it seems, did the like last night till

Countess of Chesterfield after her first husband's death. "Mr. O'Neale, of the Bedchamber, dyed yesterday, very rich, and left his old lady all" (Ed. Savage to Dr. Sancroft, October 25th, 1664, Harl. MS. 3785, fol. 19). See note, July 3rd, 1662, where the monumental inscription quoted must be incorrect as to date. It is impossible to verify this, as the Rev. Howard A. Watson, rector of Boughton Malherbe, informs the editor that the monument no longer exists in the church. It appears, from a description in Hasted's "Kent," that the monument was injudiciously placed within the altar rails, where it was found so inconvenient that it was removed in the last century to allow room for the service of the altar. The Countess of Chesterfield died in 1666 (see "Letters of Philip, second Earl of Chesterfield," p. 33).

twelve o'clock. About eight o'clock, my wife, she and her woman, and Besse and Jane, and W. Hewer and the boy, to the water-side, and there took boat, and by and by I out of doors, to look after the flaggon, to get it ready to carry to Woolwich. That being not ready, I stepped aside and found out Nellson, he that Whistler buys his bewpers of, and did there buy 5 pieces at their price, and am in hopes thereby to bring them down or buy ourselves all we spend of Nellson at the first hand. This jobb was greatly to my content, and by and by the flaggon being finished at the burnisher's, I home, and there fitted myself, and took a hackney-coach I hired, it being a very cold and foule day, to Woolwich, all the way reading in a good book touching the fishery, and that being done, in the book upon the statute of charitable uses, mightily to my satisfaction. At Woolwich; I there up to the King and Duke, and they liked the plate well. Here I staid above with them while the ship[1] was launched, which was done with great success, and the King did very much like the ship, saying, she had the best bow that ever he saw. But, Lord! the sorry talke and discourse among the great courtiers round about him, without any reverence in the world, but with so much disorder. By and by the Queene comes and her Mayds of Honour; one whereof, Mrs. Boynton,[2] and the Duchesse of Buckingham,[3] had been very sicke coming by water in the

[1] "The Royal Catharine, of eighty-two guns. It was observed, that just upon her launching there appeared a fair rainbow, once the sign of a covenant betwixt God and the world, that it should never perish by water; and we hope it will prove as auspicious to this vessel" ("The Newes," October 27th, 1664). See also Appendix for the French ambassador's letter describing the launch. — B.

On this day there was a meeting of the Royal Society, but the "greatest part of the members were absent, being gone to Woolwich, together with the King and Council and most of the Court, to see the great ship St. Catharine launched" (Birch's "History of the Royal Society," vol. i., p. 477, note).

[2] Katharine Boynton, daughter of Matthew, second son to Sir Matthew Boynton, Bart., of Barnston, Yorkshire. She became the first wife of Richard Talbot, afterwards Duke of Tyrconnel.

[3] Mary, daughter of Thomas, third Lord Fairfax, born 1639; married to George Villiers, Duke of Buckingham, September 6th, 1657. She has been described as "a most virtuous and pious lady in a vicious age and court." Died 1705.

barge (the water being very rough); but what silly sport they made with them in very common terms, methought, was very poor, and below what people think these great people say and do. The launching being done, the King and company went down to take barge; and I sent for Mr. Pett,[1] and put the flaggon into the Duke's hand, and he, in the presence of the King, did give it, Mr. Pett taking it upon his knee. This Mr. Pett is wholly beholding to me for, and he do know and I believe will acknowledge it. Thence I to Mr. Ackworth, and there eat and drank with Commissioner Pett and his wife, and thence to Shelden's, where Sir W. Batten and his Lady were. By and by I took coach after I had enquired for my wife or her boat, but found none. Going out of the gate, an ordinary woman prayed me to give her room to London, which I did, but spoke not to her all the way, but read, as long as I could see, my book again. Dark when we came to London, and a stop of coaches in Southwarke. I staid above half an houre and then 'light, and finding Sir W. Batten's coach, heard they were gone into the Beare at the Bridge foot, and thither I to them. Presently the stop is removed, and then going out to find my coach, I could not find it, for it was gone with the rest; so I fain to go through the darke and dirt over the bridge, and my leg fell in a hole broke on the bridge, but, the constable standing there to keep people from it, I was catched up, otherwise I had broke my leg; for which mercy the Lord be praised! So at Fanchurch I found my coach staying for me, and so home, where the little girle hath looked to the house well, but no wife come home, which made me begin to fear [for] her, the water being very rough, and cold and darke. But by and by she and her company come in all well, at which I was glad, though angry. Thence I to Sir W. Batten's, and there sat late with him, Sir R. Ford, and Sir John Robinson; the last of whom continues still the same foole he was, crying up what power he has in the City, in knowing their temper, and being able to do what he will with them. It seems the City did last night very freely lend the King £100,000 without any security but the King's word, which was very noble. But this loggerhead and Sir R. Ford would make

[1] He had built the ship.

us believe that they did it. Now Sir R. Ford is a cunning man, and makes a foole of the other, and the other believes whatever the other tells him. But, Lord! to think that such a man should be Lieutenant of the Tower, and so great a man as he is, is a strange thing to me. With them late and then home and with my wife to bed, after supper.

27th. Up and to the office, where all the morning busy. At noon, Sir G. Carteret, Sir J. Minnes, Sir W. Batten, Sir W. Pen, and myself, were treated at the Dolphin by Mr. Foly,[1] the ironmonger, where a good plain dinner, but I expected musique, the missing of which spoiled my dinner, only very good merry discourse at dinner. Thence with Sir G. Carteret by coach to White Hall to a Committee of Tangier, and thence back to London, and 'light in Cheapside and I to Nellson's, and there met with a rub at first, but took him out to drink, and there discoursed to my great content so far with him that I think I shall agree with him for Bewpers to serve the Navy with. So with great content home and to my office, where late, and having got a great cold in my head yesterday home to supper and to bed.

28th. Slept ill all night, having got a very great cold the other day at Woolwich in [my] head, which makes me full of snot. Up in the morning, and my tailor brings me home my fine, new, coloured cloth suit, my cloake lined with plush, as good a suit as ever I wore in my life, and mighty neat, to my great content. To my office, and there all the morning. At noon to Nellson's, and there bought 20 pieces more of Bewpers, and hope to go on with him to a contract. Thence to the 'Change a little, and thence home with Luellin to dinner, where Mr. Deane met me by appointment, and after dinner he and I up to my chamber, and there hard at discourse, and advising him what to do in his business at Harwich, and then to discourse of our old business of ships and taking new rules of him to my great pleasure, and he being gone I to my office a little, and then to see Sir W. Batten, who is sick of a greater cold

[1] Thomas Foley, afterwards of Witley Court. He was the grandfather of the first Lord Foley, and died October 1st, 1677, aged fifty-nine. His portrait is engraved in Nash's "History of Worcestershire." —B.

than I, and thither comes to me Mr. Holliard, and into the chamber to me, and, poor man (beyond all I ever saw of him), was a little drunk, and there sat talking and finding acquaintance with Sir W. Batten and my Lady by relations on both sides, that there we staid very long. At last broke up, and he home much overcome with drink, but well enough to get well home. So I home to supper and to bed.

29th. Up, and it being my Lord Mayor's show,[1] my boy and three mayds went out; but it being a very foule, rainy day, from morning till night, I was sorry my wife let them go out. All the morning at the office. At dinner at home. In the afternoon to the office again, and about 4 o'clock by appointment to the King's Head tavern upon Fish Street Hill, whither Mr. Wolfe (and Parham by his means) met me to discourse about the Fishery, and great light I had by Parham, who is a little conceited, but a very knowing man in his way, and in the general fishing trade of England. Here I staid three hours, and eat a barrel of very fine oysters of Wolfe's giving me, and so, it raining hard, home and to my office, and then home to bed. All the talke is that De Ruyter is come over-land home with six or eight of his captaines to command here at home, and their ships kept abroad in the Straights; which sounds as if they had a mind to do something with us.

30th (Lord's day). Up, and this morning put on my new, fine, coloured cloth suit, with my cloake lined with plush, which is a dear and noble suit, costing me about £17. To church, and then home to dinner, and after dinner to a little musique with my boy, and so to church with my wife, and so home, and with her all the evening reading and at musique with my boy with great pleasure, and so to supper, prayers, and to bed.

31st. Very busy all the morning, at noon Creed to me and dined with me, and then he and I to White Hall, there to a Committee of Tangier, where it is worth remembering when Mr. Coventry proposed the retrenching some of the charge of the horse, the first word asked by the Duke of Albemarle was, "Let us see who commands them," there

[1] Sir John Laurence, afterwards distinguished for his great benevolence during the period of the great plague. The king and queen were present at the banquet ("The Intelligencer," October 31st, 1664).

being three troops. One of them he calls to mind was by Sir Toby Bridges.[1] "Oh!" says he, "there is a very good man. If you must reform [2] two of them, be sure let him command the troop that is left." Thence home, and there came presently to me Mr. Young and Whistler, who find that I have quite overcome them in their business of flags, and now they come to intreat my favour, but I will be even with them. So late to my office and there till past one in the morning making up my month's accounts, and find that my expense this month in clothes has kept me from laying up anything; but I am no worse, but a little better than I was, which is £1,205, a great sum, the Lord be praised for it! So home to bed, with my mind full of content therein, and vexed for my being so angry in bad words to my wife to-night, she not giving me a good account of her layings out to my mind to-night. This day I hear young Mr. Stanly, a brave young [gentleman], that went out with young Jermin, with Prince Rupert, is already dead of the small-pox, at Portsmouth. All preparations against the Dutch; and the Duke of Yorke fitting himself with all speed to go to the fleete which is hastening for him; being now resolved to go in the Charles.

November 1st. Up and to the office, where busy all the morning, at noon (my wife being invited to my Lady Sandwich's) all alone dined at home upon a good goose with Mr. Wayth, discussing of business. Thence I to the Committee of the Fishery, and there we sat with several good discourses and some bad and simple ones, and with great disorder, and yet by the men of businesse of the towne. But my report in the business of the collections is mightily commended and will get me some reputation, and indeed is the only thing looks like a thing well done since we sat. Then with Mr. Parham to the tavern, but I drank no wine, only he did give me another barrel of oysters, and he brought one Major Greene, an able fishmonger, and good

[1] Perhaps we should read Sir Thomas Bridges, who was made a K.B. at the Restoration (Kennett's "Chronicle"). — B.

[2] Reform, *i.e.* disband. See "Memoirs of Sir John Reresby," September 2nd, 1651. "A great many younger brothers and reformed officers of the King's army depended upon him for their meat and drink." So *reformado*, a discharged or disbanded officer. — M. B.

discourse to my information. So home and late at business at my office. Then to supper and to bed.

2nd. Up betimes, and down with Mr. Castle to Redriffe, and there walked to Deptford to view a parcel of brave knees[1] of his, which indeed are very good, and so back again home, I seeming very friendly to him, though I know him to be a rogue, and one that hates me with his heart. Home and to dinner, and so to my office all the afternoon, where in some pain in my backe, which troubled me, but I think it comes only with stooping, and from no other matter. At night to Nellson's, and up and down about business, and so home to my office, then home to supper and to bed.

3rd. Up and to the office, where strange to see how Sir W. Pen is flocked to by people of all sorts against his going to sea. At the office did much business, among other an end of that that has troubled me long, the business of the bewpers and flags. At noon to the 'Change, and thence by appointment was met with Bagwell's wife, and she followed me into Moorfields, and there into a drinking house, and all alone eat and drank together. I did there caress her, but though I did make some offer did not receive any compliance from her in what was bad, but very modestly she denied me, which I was glad to see and shall value her the better for it, and I hope never tempt her to any evil more. Thence back to the town, and we parted and I home, and then at the office late, where Sir W. Pen came to take his leave of me, being to-morrow, which is very sudden to us, to go on board to lie on board, but I think will come ashore again before the ship, the Charles,[2] can go away. So home to supper and to bed. This night Sir W. Batten did, among other things, tell me strange newes, which troubles me, that my Lord Sandwich will be sent Governor to Tangier, which, in some respects, indeed, I

[1] Knees of timber (see note, October 6th, 1663).

[2] "The Royal Charles" was the Duke of York's ship, and Sir William Penn, who hoisted his flag in the "Royal James" on November 8th, shifted to the "Royal Charles" on November 30th. The duke gave Penn the command of the fleet immediately under himself. On Penn's monument he is styled "Great Captain Commander under His Royal Highness" (Penn's "Memorials of Sir William Penn," vol. ii., p. 296).

should be glad of, for the good of the place and the safety of his person; but I think his honour will suffer, and, it may be, his interest fail by his distance.

4th. Waked very betimes and lay long awake, my mind being so full of business. Then up and to St. James's, where I find Mr. Coventry full of business, packing up for his going to sea with the Duke. Walked with him, talking, to White Hall, where to the Duke's lodgings, who is gone thither to lodge lately. I appeared to the Duke, and thence Mr. Coventry and I an hour in the Long Gallery, talking about the management of our office, he tells me the weight of dispatch will lie chiefly on me, and told me freely his mind touching Sir W. Batten and Sir. J. Minnes, the latter of whom, he most aptly said, was like a lapwing; that all he did was to keepe a flutter, to keepe others from the nest that they would find. He told me an old story of the former about the light-houses, how just before he had certified to the Duke against the use of them, and what a burden they are to trade, and presently after, at his being at Harwich, comes to desire that he might have the setting one up there, and gets the usefulness of it certified also by the Trinity House. After long discoursing and considering all our stores and other things, as how the King hath resolved upon Captain Taylor[1] and Colonell Middleton,[2] the first to be Commissioner for Harwich and the latter for Portsmouth, I away to the 'Change, and there did very much business, so home to dinner, and Mr. Duke, our Secretary for the Fishery, dined with me. After dinner to discourse of our business, much to my content, and then

[1] Captain John Taylor was appointed Commissioner for Harwich, March 23rd, 1664–65, and he held the office until 1668. Sir William Coventry, writing to Secretary Bennet (November 14th, 1664), refers to the objections made to Taylor, and adds: "Thinks the King will not easily consent to his rejection, as he is a man of great abilities and dispatch, and was formerly laid aside at Chatham on the Duchess of Albemarle's earnest interposition for another. He is a fanatic, it is true, but all hands will be needed for the work cut out; there is less danger of them in harbour than at sea, and profit will convert most of them" ("Calendar of State Papers," Domestic, 1664–65, p. 68).

[2] Thomas Middleton, whose title of Colonel appears to be due to his having held office in the Parliamentary army. He was appointed Commissioner for Portsmouth, January 3rd, 1664–65, which office he held until 1667, when he became Surveyor of the Navy. He retired in 1672.

he away, and I by water among the smiths on the other side, and to the alehouse with one and was near buying 4 or 5 anchors, and learned something worth my knowing of them, and so home and to my office, where late, with my head very full of business, and so away home to supper and to bed.

5th. Up and to the office, where all the morning, at noon to the 'Change, and thence home to dinner, and so with my wife to the Duke's house to a play, "Macbeth,"[1] a pretty good play, but admirably acted. Thence home; the coach being forced to go round by London Wall home, because of the bonefires; the day being mightily observed in the City. To my office late at business, and then home to supper, and to bed.

6th (Lord's day). Up and with my wife to church. Dined at home. And I all the afternoon close at my office drawing up some proposals to present to the Committee for the Fishery to-morrow, having a great good intention to be serviceable in the business if I can. At night, to supper with my uncle Wight, where very merry, and so home. To prayers and to bed.

7th. Up and with Sir W. Batten to White Hall, where mighty thrusting about the Duke now upon his going. We were with him long. He advised us to follow our business close, and to be directed in his absence by the Committee of the Council for the Navy.[2] By and by a meeting of the Fishery, where the Duke was, but in such haste, and things looked so superficially over, that I had not a fit opportunity to propose my paper that I wrote yesterday, but I had shewed it to Mr. Gray and Wren before, who did like it most highly, as they said, and I think they would not dissemble in that manner in a business of this nature, but I see the greatest businesses are done so superficially that I wonder anything succeeds at all among us, that is publique. Thence somewhat vexed to see myself frustrated in the

[1] This was Sir William Davenant's alteration of Shakespeare's play, which was described by Downes "as being in the nature of an opera." Malone says that it was first acted in 1663. It was not printed until 1673.

[2] This was a Committee of the Privy Council appointed to superintend navy affairs.

good I hoped to have done and a little reputation to have gained, and thence to my barber's, but Jane not being in the way I to my Lady Sandwich's, and there met my wife and dined, but I find that I dine as well myself, that is, as neatly, and my meat as good and well-dressed, as my good Lady do, in the absence of my Lord. Thence by water I to my barber's again, and did meet in the street my Jane, but could not talk with her, but only a word or two, and so by coach called my wife, and home, where at my office late, and then, it being washing day, to supper and to bed.

8th. Up and to the office, where by and by Mr. Coventry come, and after doing a little business, took his leave of us, being to go to sea with the Duke to-morrow. At noon, I and Sir J. Minnes and Lord Barkeley (who with Sir J. Duncum,[1] and Mr. Chichly, are made Masters of the Ordnance), to the office of the Ordnance, to discourse about wadding for guns. Thence to dinner, all of us to the Lieutenant's of the Tower; where a good dinner, but disturbed in the middle of it by the King's coming into the Tower: and so we broke up, and to him, and went up and down the store-houses and magazines; which are, with the addition of the new great store-house, a noble sight. He gone, I to my office, where Bagwell's wife staid for me and together with her a good while, to meet again shortly. So all the afternoon at my office till late, and then to bed, joyed in my love and ability to follow my business. This day, Mr. Lever sent my wife a pair of silver candlesticks, very pretty ones. The first man that ever presented me, to whom I have not only done little service, but apparently

[1] The warrant for a commission appointing John, Lord Berkeley of Stratton, Sir John Duncombe, and Thomas Chicheley to execute the office of Master of Ordnance, void by death of Sir William Compton, is dated October 24th, 1664 ("Calendar of State Papers," Domestic, 1664–65, p. 41). Sir John Duncombe was the son of Sir Edward Duncombe of Battlesden. He was knighted by Charles I. while the king was a prisoner at Carisbrooke Castle. He was M.P. for Bury St. Edmunds in the parliaments of 1660 and 1661, and was appointed a Commissioner of the Treasury in 1667. In 1672 he became, on the resignation of Ashley, Chancellor of the Exchequer. Burnet describes him as "a judicious man, but very haughty, and apt to raise enemies. He was an able Parliament man, but could not go into all the designs of the Court; for he had a sense of religion and a zeal for the liberty of his country" ("Own Time," vol. i., p. 437, ed. 1833).

did him the greatest disservice in his business of accounts, as Purser-Generall, of any man at the board.

9th. Called up, as I had appointed, by H. Russell, between two and three o'clock, and I and my boy Tom by water with a gally down to the Hope, it being a fine starry night. Got thither by eight o'clock, and there, as expected, found the Charles, her mainmast setting. Commissioner Pett aboard. I up and down to see the ship I was so well acquainted with, and a great worke it is, the setting so great a mast. Thence the Commissioner and I on board Sir G. Ascue, in the Henery,[1] who lacks men mightily, which makes me think that there is more believed to be in a man that hath heretofore been employed than truly there is; for one would never have thought, a month ago, that he would have wanted 1,000 men at his heels. Nor do I think he hath much of a seaman in him: for he told me, says he, "Heretofore, we used to find our ships clear and ready, everything to our hands in the Downes. Now I come, and must look to see things done like a slave, things that I never minded, nor cannot look after." And by his discourse I find that he hath not minded anything in her at all. Thence not staying, the wind blowing hard, I made use of the Jemmy yacht and returned to the Tower in her, my boy being a very droll boy and good company. Home and eat something, and then shifted myself, and to White Hall, and there the King being in his Cabinet Council (I desiring to speak with Sir G. Carteret), I was called in, and demanded by the King himself many questions, to which I did give him full answers. There were at this Council my Lord Chancellor, Archbishop of Canterbury, Lord Treasurer, the two Secretarys, and Sir G. Carteret. Not a little contented at this chance of being made known to these persons, and called often by my name by the King, I to Mr. Pierce's to take leave of him, but he not within, but saw her and made very little stay, but straight home to my office, where I did business, and then to supper and to bed. The Duke of York is this day gone away to Portsmouth.

10th. Up, and not finding my things ready, I was so angry with Besse as to bid my wife for good and all to bid

[1] Sir William Penn, writing to Coventry, November 16th, 1664, says that one hundred and six men were put on board the "Henry."

her provide herself a place, for though she be very good-natured, she hath no care nor memory of her business at all. So to the office, where vexed at the malice of Sir W. Batten and folly of Sir J. Minnes against Sir W. Warren, but I prevented, and shall do, though to my own disquiet and trouble. At noon dined with Sir W. Batten and the Auditors of the Exchequer at the Dolphin by Mr. Wayth's desire, and after dinner fell to business relating to Sir G. Carteret's account, and so home to the office, where Sir W. Batten begins, too fast, to shew his knavish tricks in giving what price he pleases for commodities. So abroad, intending to have spoke with my Lord Chancellor about the old business of his wood at Clarendon, but could not, and so home again, and late at my office, and then home to supper and bed. My little girle Susan is fallen sicke of the meazles, we fear, or, at least, of a scarlett feavour.

11th. Up, and with Sir J. Minnes and Sir W. Batten to the Council Chamber at White Hall, to the Committee of the Lords for the Navy, where we were made to wait an houre or two before called in.[1] In that time looking upon some books of heraldry of Sir Edward Walker's making, which are very fine, there I observed the Duke of Monmouth's armes are neatly done, and his title, "The most noble and high-born Prince, James Scott, Duke of Monmouth, &c.;" nor could Sir J. Minnes, nor any body there, tell whence he should take the name of Scott.[2] And then I found my Lord Sandwich, his title under his armes is, "The most noble and mighty Lord, Edward, Earl of Sandwich, &c." Sir Edward Walker afterwards coming in, in discourse did say that there was none of the families of princes in Christendom that do derive themselves so high as Julius Cæsar, nor so far by 1,000 years, that can directly prove their rise; only some in Germany do derive themselves from the patrician familys of Rome, but that uncertainly; and, among other things, did much inveigh against the writing of romances, that 500 years hence being wrote of matters in general, true as the romance of Cleo-

[1] See *ante*, November 7th.

[2] The Duke of Monmouth took the name of Scott in 1663 on his marriage to Lady Anne Scott, daughter and sole heir of Francis, Earl of Buccleuch.

patra,[1] the world will not know which is the true and which the false. Here was a gentleman attending here that told us he saw the other day (and did bring the draught of it to Sir Francis Prigeon) of a monster born of an hostler's wife at Salisbury, two women children perfectly made, joyned at the lower part of their bellies, and every part perfect as two bodies, and only one payre of legs coming forth on one side from the middle where they were joined. It was alive 24 hours, and cried and did as all hopefull children do; but, being showed too much to people, was killed. By and by we were called in, where a great many lords: Annesly[2] in the chair. But, Lord! to see what work they will make us, and what trouble we shall have to inform men in a business they are to begin to know, when the greatest of our hurry is, is a thing to be lamented; and I fear the consequence will be bad to us. Thence I by coach to the 'Change, and thence home to dinner, my head akeing mightily with much business. Our little girl better than she was yesterday. After dinner out again by coach to my Lord Chancellor's, but could not speak with him, then up and down to seek Sir Ph. Warwicke, Sir G. Carteret, and my Lord Berkely, but failed in all, and so home and there late at business. Among other things Mr. Turner making his complaint to me how my clerks do all the worke and get all the profit, and he hath no comfort, nor cannot subsist, I did make him apprehend how he is beholding to me more than to any body for my suffering him to act as Pourveyour of petty provisions, and told him so largely my little value of any body's favour, that I believe he will make no complaints again a good while. So home to supper and to bed, after prayers, and having my boy and Mercer give me some, each of them some, musique.

12th. Up, being frighted that Mr. Coventry was come to towne and now at the office, so I run down without eating

[1] The publication of the romance of "Cleopatra," by Gautier de Costes, Seigneur de la Calprenede, was commenced in 1646. Dunlop says of it: "The basis is historical, but few of the incidents are consistent with historical truth."

[2] Arthur Annesley (1614–86) succeeded his father as second Viscount Valentia in November, 1660, and was created Baron Annesley and Earl of Anglesey in April, 1661.

or drinking or washing to the office and it proved my Lord Berkeley. There all the morning, at noon to the 'Change, and so home to dinner, Mr. Wayth with me, and then to the office, where mighty busy till very late, but I bless God I go through with it very well and hope I shall.

13th (Lord's day). This morning to church, where mighty sport, to hear our clerke sing out of tune, though his master sits by him that begins and keeps the tune aloud for the parish. Dined at home very well, and spent all the afternoon with my wife within doors, and getting a speech out of Hamlett, "To bee or not to bee,"[1] without book. In the evening to sing psalms, and in come Mr. Hill to see me, and then he and I and the boy finely to sing, and so anon broke up after much pleasure, he gone I to supper, and so prayers and to bed.

14th. Up, and with Sir W. Batten to White Hall, to the Lords of the Admiralty, and there did our business betimes. Thence to Sir Philip Warwicke about Navy business: and my Lord Ashly; and afterwards to my Lord Chancellor, who is very well pleased with me, and my carrying of his business. And so to the 'Change, where mighty busy; and so home to dinner, where Mr. Creed and Moore: and after dinner I to my Lord Treasurer's, to Sir Philip Warwicke there, and then to White Hall, to the Duke of Albemarle, about Tangier; and then homeward to the Coffee-house to hear newes. And it seems the Dutch, as I afterwards found by Mr. Coventry's letters, have stopped a ship of masts of Sir W. Warren's, coming for us in a Swede's ship, which they will not release upon Sir G. Downing's claiming her: which appears as the first act of hostility; and is looked upon as so by Mr. Coventry. The Elias,[2] coming from New England (Captain Hill, commander), is sunk; only the captain and a few men saved. She foundered in the sea. So home, where infinite busy till 12 at night, and so home to supper and to bed.

[1] Pepys had "To be or not to be" set to music, and it will be found in his collection of "Songs and other Compositions" (No. 2591), in the volume devoted to "Compositions, Grave."

[2] The "Elias" frigate foundered one hundred and forty leagues from shore on the coast of New England. One hundred and twenty men were lost, and only twenty-one saved by the "Martin."

15th. That I might not be too fine for the business I intend this day, I did leave off my fine new cloth suit lined with plush and put on my poor black suit, and after office done (where much business, but little done), I to the 'Change, and thence Bagwell's wife with much ado followed me through Moorfields to a blind alehouse, and there I did caress her and eat and drink, and many hard looks and sooth the poor wretch did give me, and I think verily was troubled at what I did, but at last after many protestings by degrees I did arrive at what I would, with great pleasure, and then in the evening, it raining, walked into town to where she knew where she was, and then I took coach and to White Hall to a Committee of Tangier, where, and every where else, I thank God, I find myself growing in repute; and so home, and late, very late, at business, nobody minding it but myself, and so home to bed, weary and full of thoughts. Businesses grow high between the Dutch and us on every side.

16th. My wife not being well, waked in the night, and strange to see how dead sleep our people sleep that she was fain to ring an hour before any body would wake. At last one rose and helped my wife, and so to sleep again. Up and to my business, and then to White Hall, there to attend the Lords Commissioners, and so directly home and dined with Sir W. Batten and my Lady, and after dinner had much discourse tending to profit with Sir W. Batten, how to get ourselves into the prize office[1] or some other fair way of obliging the King to consider us in our extraordinary pains. Then to the office, and there all the afternoon very busy, and so till past 12 at night, and so home to bed. This day my wife went to the burial of a little boy of W. Joyce's.

17th. Up and to my office, and there all the morning mighty busy, and taking upon me to tell the Comptroller how ill his matters were done, and I think indeed if I continue thus all the business of the office will come upon

[1] The Calendars of State Papers are full of references to applications for Commissionerships of the Prize Office. In December, 1664, the Navy Committee appointed themselves the Commissioners for Prize Goods, Sir Henry Bennet being appointed comptroller, and Lord Ashley treasurer.

me whether I will or no. At noon to the 'Change, and then home with Creed to dinner, and thence I to the office, where close at it all the afternoon till 12 at night, and then home to supper and to bed. This day I received from Mr. Foley,[1] but for me to pay for it, if I like it, an iron chest, having now received back some money I had laid out for the King, and I hope to have a good sum of money by me, thereby, in a few days, I think above £800. But when I come home at night, I could not find the way to open it; but, which is a strange thing, my little girle Susan could carry it alone from one table clear from the ground and set upon another, when neither I nor anyone in my house but Jane the cook-mayde could do it.

18th. Up and to the office, and thence to the Committee of the Fishery at White Hall, where so poor simple doings about the business of the Lottery, that I was ashamed to see it, that a thing so low and base should have any thing to do with so noble an undertaking. But I had the advantage this day to hear Mr. Williamson discourse, who come to be a contractor with others for the Lotterys, and indeed I find he is a very logicall man and a good speaker. But it was so pleasant to see my Lord Craven, the chaireman, before many persons of worth and grave, use this comparison in saying that certainly these that would contract for all the lotteries would not suffer us to set up the Virginia lottery for plate before them, "For," says he, "if I occupy a wench first, you may occupy her again your heart out you can never have her maidenhead after I have once had it," which he did more loosely, and yet as if he had fetched a most grave and worthy instance. They made mirth, but I and others were ashamed of it. Thence to the 'Change and thence home to dinner, and thence to the office a good while, and thence to the Council chamber at White Hall to speake with Sir G. Carteret, and here by accident heard a great and famous cause between Sir G. Lane[2] and one Mr. Phill. Whore, an Irish business about Sir G. Lane's endeavouring to reverse a decree of the late

[1] Thomas Foley, the ironmonger (see *ante*, October 27th).

[2] Sir George Lane was secretary to the Duke of Ormonde, and his name frequently appears in the Carte Papers. He was created Viscount Lanesborough in the peerage of Ireland in 1676.

Commissioners of Ireland in a Rebells case for his land, which the King had given as forfeited to Sir G. Lane, for whom the Sollicitor did argue most angell like, and one of the Commissioners, Baron ——, did argue for the other and for himself and his brethren who had decreed it. But the Sollicitor do so pay the Commissioners, how four all along did act for the Papists, and three only for the Protestants, by which they were overvoted, but at last one word (which was omitted in the Sollicitor's repeating of an Act of Parliament in the case) being insisted on by the other part, the Sollicitor was put to a great stop, and I could discern he could not tell what to say, but was quite out. Thence home well pleased with this accident, and so home to my office, where late, and then to supper and to bed. This day I had a letter from Mr. Coventry, that tells me that my Lord Brunkard[1] is to be one of our Commissioners, of which I am very glad, if any more must be.

19th. All the morning at the office, and without dinner down by galley up and down the river to visit the yards and ships now ordered forth with great delight, and so home to supper, and then to office late to write letters, then home to bed.

20th (Lord's day). Up, and with my wife to church, where Pegg Pen very fine in her new coloured silk suit laced with silver lace. Dined at home, and Mr. Sheply, lately come to town, with me. A great deal of ordinary discourse with him. Among other things praying him to speak to Stankes to look after our business. With him and in private with Mr. Bodham talking of our ropeyarde stores at Woolwich, which are mighty low, even to admiration. They gone, in the evening comes Mr. Andrews and sings with us, and he gone, I to Sir W. Batten's, where Sir J. Minnes and he and I to talk about our letter to my Lord Treasurer, where his folly and simple confidence so great in a report so ridiculous that he hath drawn up to present to my Lord, nothing of it being true, that I was ashamed, and did roundly and in many words for an houre together talk boldly to him, which pleased Sir W. Batten

[1] William, second Viscount Brouncker of Castle Lyons in the peerage of Ireland, was appointed an extra Commissioner of the Navy on December 7th, 1664.

and my Lady, but I was in the right, and was the willinger to do so before them, that they might see that I am somebody, and shall serve him so in his way another time. So home vexed at this night's passage, for I had been very hot with him, so to supper and to bed, out of order with this night's vexation.

21st. Up, and with them to the Lords at White Hall, where they do single me out to speak to and to hear, much to my content, and received their commands, particularly in several businesses. Thence by their order to the Attorney General's about a new warrant for Captain Taylor[1] which I shall carry for him to be Commissioner in spite of Sir W. Batten, and yet indeed it is not I, but the ability of the man, that makes the Duke and Mr. Coventry stand by their choice. I to the 'Change and there staid long doing business, and this day for certain newes is come that Teddiman[2] hath brought in eighteen or twenty Dutchmen, merchants, their Bourdeaux fleete, and two men of warr to Portsmouth. And I had letters this afternoon, that three are brought into the Downes and Dover; so that the warr is begun: God give a good end to it! After dinner at home all the afternoon busy, and at night with Sir W. Batten and Sir J. Minnes looking over the business of stating the accounts of the navy charge to my Lord Treasurer, where Sir J. Minnes's paper served us in no stead almost, but was all false, and after I had done it with great pains, he being by, I am confident he understands not one word in it. At it till 10 at night almost. Thence by coach to Sir Philip Warwicke's, by his desire to have conferred with him, but he being in bed, I to White Hall to the Secretaries, and there wrote to Mr. Coventry, and so home by coach again, a fine clear moonshine night, but very cold. Home to my office a while, it being past 12 at night, and so to supper and to bed.

[1] See *ante*, November 4th, for Coventry's opinion of the objection to Taylor.

[2] Captain Sir Thomas Teddiman (or Tyddiman) had been appointed Rear-Admiral of Lord Sandwich's squadron of the English fleet. In a letter from Sir William Coventry to Secretary Bennet, dated November 13th, 1664, we read, "Rear Admiral Teddeman with four or five ships has gone to course in the Channel, and if he meet any refractory Dutchmen will teach them their duty" ("Calendar of State Papers," Domestic, 1664–65, p. 66).

22nd. At the office all the morning. Sir G. Carteret, upon a motion of Sir W. Batten's, did promise, if he would write a letter to him, to shew it to the King on our behalf touching our desire of being Commissioners of the Prize office.[1] I wrote a letter to my mind and, after eating a bit at home (Mr. Sheply dining and taking his leave of me), abroad and to Sir G. Carteret with the letter and thence to my Lord Treasurer's; where with Sir Philip Warwicke long studying all we could to make the last year swell as high as we could. And it is much to see how he do study for the King, to do it to get all the money from the Parliament all he can: and I shall be serviceable to him therein, to help him to heads upon which to enlarge the report of the expense. He did observe to me how obedient this Parliament was for awhile, and the last sitting how they begun to differ, and to carp at the King's officers; and what they will do now, he says, is to make agreement for the money, for there is no guess to be made of it. He told me he was prepared to convince the Parliament that the Subsidys are a most ridiculous tax (the four last not rising to £40,000), and unequall. He talks of a tax of Assessment of £70,000 for five years; the people to be secured that it shall continue no longer than there is really a warr; and the charges thereof to be paid. He told me, that one year of the late Dutch warr cost £1,623,000. Thence to my Lord Chancellor's, and there staid long with Sir W. Batten and Sir J. Minnes, to speak with my lord about our Prize Office business; but, being sicke and full of visitants, we could not speak with him, and so away home. Where Sir Richard Ford did meet us with letters from Holland this day, that it is likely the Dutch fleete will not come out this year; they have not victuals to keep them out, and it is likely they will be frozen before they can get back.[2] Captain Cocke[3] is made Steward for sick and wounded seamen. So home to supper, where troubled to hear my poor boy Tom has a fit of the stone, or some other pain like it. I must consult Mr. Holliard for him. So at one in the morning home to bed.

[1] See *ante*, Nov. 16th. [2] If they made the attempt to put to sea. — B.

[3] Captain George Cocke was officially styled Receiver for Sick and Wounded and Prisoners. Evelyn refers to him as "our Treasurer."

23rd. Up and to my office, where close all the morning about my Lord Treasurer's accounts, and at noon home to dinner, and then to the office all the afternoon very busy till very late at night, and then to supper and to bed. This evening Mr. Hollyard came to me and told me that he hath searched my boy, and he finds he hath a stone in his bladder, which grieves me to the heart, he being a good-natured and well-disposed boy, and more that it should be my misfortune to have him come to my house. Sir G. Carteret was here this afternoon; and strange to see how we plot to make the charge of this warr to appear greater than it is, because of getting money.

24th. Up and to the office, where all the morning busy answering of people. About noon out with Commissioner Pett, and he and I to a Coffee-house, to drink jocolatte,[1] very good; and so by coach to Westminster, being the first day of the Parliament's meeting. After the House had received the King's speech, and what more he had to say, delivered in writing, the Chancellor being sicke, it rose, and I with Sir Philip Warwicke home and conferred our matters about the charge of the Navy, and have more to give him in the excessive charge of this year's expense. I dined with him, and Mr. Povy with us and Sir Edmund Pooly, a fine gentleman, and Mr. Chichly, and fine discourse we had and fine talke, being proud to see myself accepted in such company and thought better than I am. After dinner Sir Philip and I to talk again, and then away home to the office, where sat late; beginning our sittings now in the afternoon, because of the Parliament; and they being rose, I to my office, where late till almost one o'clock, and then home to bed.

25th. Up and at my office all the morning, to prepare an account of the charge we have been put to extraordinary by the Dutch already; and I have brought it to appear £852,700; but God knows this is only a scare to the Parliament, to make them give the more money. Thence to the Parliament House, and there did give it to Sir Philip Warwicke; the House being hot upon giving the King a supply of money, and I by coach to the 'Change and took up Mr. Jenings along with me (my old acquaint-

[1] Chocolate (see note *ante*, April 24th, 1661).

ance), he telling me the mean manner that Sir Samuel Morland lives near him,[1] in a house he hath bought and laid out money upon, in all to the value of £1,200, but is believed to be a beggar; and so I ever thought he would be. From the 'Change with Mr. Deering and Luellin to the White Horse tavern in Lombard Street, and there dined with them, he giving me a dish of meat to discourse in order to my serving Deering, which I am already obliged to do, and shall do it, and would be glad he were a man trusty that I might venture something along with him. Thence home, and by and by in the evening took my wife out by coach, leaving her at Unthanke's while I to White Hall and to Westminster Hall, where I have not been to talk a great while, and there hear that Mrs. Lane and her husband live a sad life together, and he is gone to be a paymaster to a company to Portsmouth to serve at sea. She big with child. Thence I home, calling my wife, and at Sir W. Batten's hear that the House have given the King £2,500,000 to be paid for this warr, only for the Navy, in three years' time; which is a joyfull thing to all the King's party I see, but was much opposed by Mr. Vaughan[2] and others, that it should be so much. So home and to supper and to bed.

26th. Up and to the office, where busy all the morning. Home a while to dinner and then to the office, where very late busy till quite weary, but contented well with my dispatch of business, and so home to supper and to bed.

27th (Lord's day). To church in the morning, then dined at home, and to my office, and there all the afternoon setting right my business of flaggs, and after all my pains find reason not to be sorry, because I think it will bring me considerable profit. In the evening come Mr. Andrews and Hill, and we sung, with my boy, Ravenscroft's 4-part psalms,[3] most admirable musique. Then (Andrews not staying) we to supper, and after supper fell into the rarest

[1] This was probably at Vauxhall, where Morland lived for several years.

[2] John Vaughan, M.P. (see *ante*, March 28th).

[3] "Psalms and Hymns, with the music in iv. Parts by Tho. Ravenscroft," was published at London in 1621.

discourse with Mr. Hill[1] about Rome and Italy; but most pleasant that I ever had in my life. At it very late and then to bed.

28th. Up, and with Sir J. Minnes and W. Batten to White Hall, but no Committee of Lords (which is like to do the King's business well). So to Westminster, and there to Jervas's and was a little while with Jane, and so to London by coach and to the Coffee-house, where certain news of our peace made by Captain Allen with Argier, which is good news; and that the Dutch have sent part of their fleete round by Scotland; and resolve to pay off the rest half-pay, promising the rest in the Spring, hereby keeping their men. But how true this, I know not. Home to dinner, then come Dr. Clerke to speak with me about sick and wounded men, wherein he is like to be concerned. After him Mr. Cutler, and much talk with him, and with him to White Hall, to have waited on the Lords by order, but no meeting, neither to-night, which will spoil all. I think I shall get something by my discourse with Cutler. So home, and after being at my office an hour with Mr. Povy talking about his business of Tangier, getting him some money allowed him for freight of ships, wherein I hope to get something too. He gone, home hungry and almost sick for want of eating, and so to supper and to bed.

29th. Up, and with Sir W. Batten to the Committee of Lords at the Council Chamber, where Sir G. Carteret told us what he had said to the King, and how the King inclines to our request of making us Commissioners of the Prize office, but meeting him anon in the gallery, he tells me that my Lord Barkely is angry we should not acquaint him with it, so I found out my Lord and pacified him, but I know not whether he was so in earnest or no, for he looked very frowardly. Thence to the Parliament House, and with Sir W. Batten home and dined with him, my wife being gone to my Lady Sandwich's, and then to the office, where we sat all the afternoon, and I at my office till past 12 at night, and so home to bed. This day I hear that the King should say that the Dutch do begin to comply with him. Sir John

[1] Thomas Hill, a merchant, whom Pepys describes, in his "Collection of Signs Manual," as "my friend, who died at Lisbon in 1675." — B.

Robinson told Sir W. Batten that he heard the King say so. I pray God it may be so.

30th. Up, and with Sir W. Batten and Sir J. Minnes to the Committee of the Lords, and there did our business; but, Lord! what a sorry dispatch these great persons give to business. Thence to the 'Change, and there hear the certainty and circumstances of the Dutch having called in their fleete and paid their men half-pay, the other to be paid them upon their being ready upon beat of drum to come to serve them again, and in the meantime to have half-pay. This is said. Thence home to dinner, and so to my office all the afternoon. In the evening my wife and Sir W. Warren with me to White Hall, sending her with the coach to see her father and mother. He and I up to Sir G. Carteret, and first I alone and then both had discourse with him about things of the Navy, and so I and he calling my wife at Unthanke's, home again, and long together talking how to order things in a new contract for Norway goods, as well to the King's as to his advantage. He gone, I to my monthly accounts, and, bless God! I find I have increased my last balance, though but little; but I hope ere long to get more. In the meantime praise God for what I have, which is £1,209. So, with my heart glad to see my accounts fall so right in this time of mixing of monies and confusion, I home to bed.

December 1st. Up betimes and to White Hall to a Committee of Tangier, and so straight home and hard to my business at my office till noon, then to dinner, and so to my office, and by and by we sat all the afternoon, then to my office again till past one in the morning, and so home to supper and to bed.

2nd. Lay long in bed. Then up and to the office, where busy all the morning. At home dined. After dinner with my wife and Mercer to the Duke's House, and there saw "The Rivalls,"[1] which I had seen before; but the play not good, nor anything but the good actings of Betterton and his wife and Harris. Thence homeward, and the coach broke with us in Lincoln's Inn Fields, and so walked to Fleete Streete, and there took coach and home, and to my office, whither by and by comes Captain Cocke, and then

[1] See *ante*, September 10th, 1664.

Sir W. Batten, and we all to Sir J. Minnes, and I did give them a barrel of oysters I had given to me, and so there sat and talked, where good discourse of the late troubles, they knowing things, all of them, very well; and Cocke, from the King's own mouth, being then entrusted himself much, do know particularly that the King's credulity to Cromwell's promises, private to him, against the advice of his friends and the certain discovery of the practices and discourses of Cromwell in council (by Major Huntington[1]) did take away his life and nothing else. Then to some loose atheisticall discourse of Cocke's, when he was almost drunk, and then about 11 o'clock broke up, and I to my office, to fit up an account for Povy, wherein I hope to get something. At it till almost two o'clock, then to supper and to bed.

3rd. Up, and at the office all the morning, and at noon to Mr. Cutler's, and there dined with Sir W. Rider and him, and thence Sir W. Rider and I by coach to White Hall to a Committee of the Fishery; there only to hear Sir Edward Ford's proposal about farthings, wherein, O God! to see almost every body interested for him; only my Lord Annesly,[2] who is a grave, serious man. My Lord Barkeley was there, but is the most hot, fiery man in discourse, without any cause, that ever I saw, even to breach of civility to my Lord Anglesey, in his discourse opposing to my Lord's. At last, though without much satisfaction to me, it was voted that it should be requested of the King, and that Sir Edward Ford's proposal is the best yet made. Thence by coach home. The Duke of Yorke being expected to-night with great joy from Portsmouth, after his having

[1] According to Clarendon the officer here alluded to was a major in Cromwell's own regiment of horse, and employed by him to treat with Charles I. whilst at Hampton Court; but being convinced of the insincerity of the proceeding, communicated his suspicions to that monarch, and immediately gave up his commission. We hear no more of Huntington till the Restoration, when his name occurs with those of many other officers, who tendered their services to the king. His reasons for laying down his commission are printed in Thurloe's "State Papers" and Maseres's "Tracts." — B.

[2] Lord Annesly is an incorrect description of Arthur Annesley, first Earl of Anglesey, although in addition to his earldom he bore the title of Baron Annesley of Newport Paganel (see *ante*, November 11th)

been abroad at sea three or four days with the fleete; and the Dutch are all drawn into their harbours. But it seems like a victory: and a matter of some reputation to us it is, and blemish to them; but in no degree like what it is esteemed at, the weather requiring them to do so. Home and at my office late, and then to supper and to bed.

4th (Lord's day). Lay long in bed, and then up and to my office, there to dispatch a business in order to the getting something out of the Tangier business, wherein I have an opportunity to get myself paid upon the score of freight. I hope a good sum. At noon home to dinner, and then in the afternoon to church. So home, and by and by comes Mr. Hill and Andrews, and sung together long and with great content. Then to supper and broke up. Pretty discourse, very pleasant and ingenious, and so to my office a little, and then home (after prayers) to bed. This day I hear the Duke of Yorke is come to towne, though expected last night, as I observed, but by what hindrance stopped I can't tell.

5th. Up, and to White Hall with Sir J. Minnes; and there, among an infinite crowd of great persons, did kiss the Duke's hand; but had no time to discourse. Thence up and down the gallery, and got my Lord of Albemarle's hand to my bill for Povy, but afterwards was asked some scurvy questions by Povy about my demands, which troubled [me], but will do no great hurt I think. Thence vexed home, and there by appointment comes my cozen Roger Pepys and Mrs. Turner, and dined with me, and very merry we were. They staid all the afternoon till night, and then after I had discoursed an hour with Sir W. Warren plainly declaring my resolution to desert him if he goes on to join with Castle, who and his family I, for great provocation, love not, which he takes with some trouble, but will concur in every thing with me, he says. Now I am loth, I confess, to lose him, he having been the best friend I have had ever in this office. So he being gone, we all, it being night, in Madam Turner's coach to her house, there to see, as she tells us, how fat Mrs. The. is grown, and so I find her, but not as I expected, but mightily pleased I am to hear the mother commend her daughter Betty that she is like to be a great beauty, and she sets much by her. Thence I to White

Hall, and there saw Mr. Coventry come to towne, and, with all my heart, am glad to see him, but could have no talke with him, he being but just come. Thence back and took up my wife, and home, where a while, and then home to supper and to bed.

6th. Up, and in Sir W. Batten's coach to White Hall, but the Duke being gone forth, I to Westminster Hall, and there spent much time till towards noon to and fro with people. So by and by Mrs. Lane comes and plucks me by the cloak to speak to me, and I was fain to go to her shop, and pretending to buy some bands made her go home, and by and by followed her, and there did what I would with her, and so after many discourses and her intreating me to do something for her husband, which I promised to do, and buying a little band of her, which I intend to keep to, I took leave, there coming a couple of footboys to her with a coach to fetch her abroad I know not to whom. She is great with child, and she says I must be godfather, but I do not intend it. Thence by coach to the Old Exchange, and there hear that the Dutch are fitting their ships out again, which puts us to new discourse, and to alter our thoughts of the Dutch, as to their want of courage or force. Thence by appointment to the White Horse Taverne in Lumbard Streete, and there dined with my Lord Rutherford, Povy, Mr. Gauden, Creed, and others, and very merry, and after dinner among other things Povy and I withdrew, and I plainly told him that I was concerned in profit, but very justly, in this business of the Bill that I have been these two or three days about, and he consents to it, and it shall be paid. He tells me how he believes, and in part knows, Creed to be worth £10,000; nay, that now and then he [Povy] hath three or £4,000 in his hands, for which he gives the interest that the King gives, which is ten per cent., and that Creed do come and demand it every three months the interest to be paid him, which Povy looks upon as a cunning and mean tricke of him; but for all that, he will do and is very rich. Thence to the office, where we sat and where Mr. Coventry came the first time after his return from sea, which I was glad of. So after office to my office, and then home to supper, and to my office again, and then late home to bed.

7th. Lay long, then up, and among others Bagwell's wife coming to speak with me put new thoughts of folly into me which I am troubled at. Thence after doing business at my office, I by coach to my Lady Sandwich's, and there dined with her, and found all well and merry. Thence to White Hall, and we waited on the Duke, who looks better than he did, methinks, before his voyage; and, I think, a little more stern than he used to do. Thence to the Temple to my cozen Roger Pepys, thinking to have met the Doctor to have discoursed our business, but he came not, so I home, and there by agreement came my Lord Rutherford, Povy, Gauden, Creed, Alderman Backewell, about Tangier business of accounts between Rutherford and Gauden. Here they were with me an hour or more, then after drinking away, and Povy and Creed staid and eat with me; but I was sorry I had no better cheer for Povy; for the foole may be useful, and is a cunning fellow in his way, which is a strange one, and that, that I meet not in any other man, nor can describe in him. They late with me, and when gone my boy and I to musique, and then to bed.

8th. Up, and to my office, where all the morning busy. At noon dined at home, and then to the office, where we sat all the afternoon. In the evening comes my aunt and uncle Wight, Mrs. Norbury,[1] and her daughter, and after them Mr. Norbury, where no great pleasure, my aunt[2] being out of humour in her fine clothes, and it raining hard. Besides, I was a little too bold with her about her doating on Dr. Venner. Anon they went away, and I till past 12 at night at my office, and then home to bed.

9th. Up betimes and walked to Mr. Povy's, and there, not without some few troublesome questions of his, I got a note, and went and received £117 5*s.* of Alderman Viner upon my pretended freight of the "William"[3] for Tangier, which overbears me on one side with joy and on the other to think of my condition if I shall be called into examina-

[1] On May 27th, 1666, Pepys refers to Mr. and Mrs. Norbury as his uncle and aunt.

[2] The word aunt may either refer to Mrs. Wight or to Mrs. Norbury.

[3] The "William" is frequently mentioned in the "Calendar of State Papers," 1664–65. In November, 1664, Captain George Erwin was appointed commander of the ship.

tion about it, and (though in strictness it is due) not be able to give a good account of it. Home with it, and there comes Captain Taylor to me, and he and I did set even the business of the ship Union lately gone for Tangier, wherein I hope to get £50 more, for all which the Lord be praised. At noon home to dinner, Mr. Hunt and his wife with us, and very pleasant. Then in the afternoon I carried them home by coach, and I to Westminster Hall, and thence to Gervas's, and there find I cannot prevail with Jane to go forth with me, but though I took a good occasion of going to the Trumpet she declined coming, which vexed me. *Je avait grande envie envers elle, avec vrai amour et passion.* Thence home and to my office till one in the morning, setting to rights in writing this day's two accounts of Povy and Taylor, and then quietly to bed. This day I had several letters from several places, of our bringing in great numbers of Dutch ships.

10th. Lay long, at which I am ashamed, because of so many people observing it that know not how late I sit up, and for fear of Sir W. Batten's speaking of it to others, he having staid for me a good while. At the office all the morning, where comes my Lord Brunkard with his patent in his hand, and delivered it to Sir J. Minnes and myself, we alone being there all the day, and at noon I in his coach with him to the 'Change, where he set me down; a modest civil person he seems to be, but wholly ignorant in the business of the Navy as possible, but I hope to make a friend of him, being a worthy man. Thence after hearing the great newes of so many Dutchmen being brought in to Portsmouth and elsewhere, which it is expected will either put them upon present revenge or despair, I with Sir W. Rider and Cutler to dinner all alone to the Great James, where good discourse, and, I hope, occasion of getting something hereafter. After dinner to White Hall to the Fishery, where the Duke was with us. So home, and late at my office, writing many letters, then home to supper and to bed. Yesterday come home, and this night I visited Sir W. Pen, who dissembles great respect and love to me, but I understand him very well. Major Holmes is come from Guinny, and is now at Plymouth with great wealth, they say.

11th (Lord's day). Up and to church alone in the morning. Dined at home, mighty pleasantly. In the afternoon I to the French church,[1] where much pleased with the three sisters of the parson, very handsome, especially in their noses, and sing prettily. I heard a good sermon of the old man, touching duty to parents. Here was Sir Samuel Morland and his lady very fine, with two footmen in new liverys (the church taking much notice of them), and going into their coach after sermon with great gazeing. So I home, and my cozen, Mary Pepys's husband, comes after me, and told me that out of the money he received some months since he did receive 18*d.* too much, and did now come and give it me, which was very pretty. So home, and there found Mr. Andrews and his lady, a well-bred and a tolerable pretty woman, and by and by Mr. Hill and to singing, and then to supper, then to sing again, and so good night. To prayers and to night [bed]. It is a little strange how these Psalms of Ravenscroft[2] after 2 or 3 times singing prove but the same again, though good. No diversity appearing at all almost.

12th. Up, and with Sir W. Batten by coach to White Hall, where all of us with the Duke; Mr. Coventry privately did tell me the reason of his advice against our pretences to the Prize Office (in his letter from Portsmouth), because he knew that the King and the Duke had resolved to put in some Parliament men that have deserved well, and that would needs be obliged, by putting them in. Thence home-

[1] The French Protestant Church in Threadneedle Street (originally St. Anthony's Hospital), burnt in the Great Fire.

[2] See *ante*, November 27th. Dr. Hueffer wrote (" Italian and other Studies "), " Ravenscroft belonged to an earlier generation of musicians, and Mr. Pepys might well find his style a trifle monotonous compared with the Italian and French songs he was wont to listen to. But apart from this, and looking upon Ravenscroft in connection with the writers of his own time, the modest censure of the diarist will not be found without some show of reason. Thomas Ravenscroft was a theorist and a pedant of the deepest dye, as the very title of his absurd attempt at reviving obsolete practices of bygone days is sufficient to show. Here it is: 'A Briefe Discourse of the True (but neglected) use of charact'ring the Degrees by their perfection, imperfection, and diminution in measurable Musicke against the common practise and custome of these times; examples whereof are exprest in the Harmony of 4 voyces concerning the Pleasure of 5 usuall recreations, 1 Hunting, 2 Hawking, 3 Dancing, 4 Drinking, 5 Enamouring,' 1614."

ward, called at my bookseller's and bespoke some books against the year's out, and then to the 'Change, and so home to dinner, and then to the office, where my Lord Brunkard comes and reads over part of our Instructions in the Navy,[1] and I expounded it to him, so he is become my disciple. He gone, comes Cutler to tell us that the King of France hath forbid any canvass to be carried out of his kingdom, and I to examine went with him to the East India house to see a letter, but came too late. So home again, and there late till 12 at night at my office, and then home to supper and to bed. This day (to see how things are ordered in the world), I had a command from the Earle of Sandwich, at Portsmouth, not to be forward with Mr. Cholmly and Sir J. Lawson about the Mole at Tangier, because that what I do therein will (because of his friendship to me known) redound against him, as if I had done it upon his score. So I wrote to my Lord my mistake, and am contented to promise never to pursue it more, which goes against my mind with all my heart.

13th. Lay long in bed, then up, and many people to speak with me. Then to my office, and dined at noon at home, then to the office again, where we sat all the afternoon, and then home at night to a little supper, and so after my office again at 12 at night home to bed.

14th. Up, and after a while at the office, I abroad in several places, among others to my bookseller's, and there spoke for several books against New Year's day, I resolving to lay out about £7 or £8, God having given me some profit extraordinary of late; and bespoke also some plate, spoons, and forks. I pray God keep me from too great expenses, though these will still be pretty good money. Then to the 'Change, and I home to dinner, where Creed and Mr. Cæsar,[2] my boy's lute master, who plays indeed mighty finely, and after dinner I abroad, parting from Creed, and away to and fro, laying out or preparing for

[1] The Duke of York's Instructions for the Government of the Navy Office (see note *ante*, February 5th, 1661–62).

[2] William Cæsar, musical composer and teacher of the lute, is frequently mentioned in the Diary. Some of his songs are found in different collections of the time under the name of William Cæsar *alias* Smegergill.

laying out more money, but I hope and resolve not to exceed therein, and to-night spoke for some fruit for the country for my father against Christmas, and where should I do it, but at the pretty woman's, that used to stand at the doore in Fanchurch Streete, I having a mind to know her. So home, and late at my office, evening reckonings with Shergoll, hoping to get money by the business, and so away home to supper and to bed, not being very well through my taking cold of late, and so troubled with some wind.

15th. Called up very betimes by Mr. Cholmly, and with him a good while about some of his Tangier accounts; and, discoursing of the condition of Tangier, he did give me the whole account of the differences between Fitzgerald and Norwood, which were very high on both sides, but most imperious and base on Fitzgerald's, and yet through my Lord FitzHarding's[1] means, the Duke of York is led rather to blame Norwood and to speake that he should be called home, than be sensible of the other. He is a creature of FitzHarding's, as a fellow that may be done with what he will, and, himself certainly pretending to be Generall of the King's armies, when Monk dyeth, desires to have as few great or wise men in employment as he can now, but such as he can put in and keep under, which he do this coxcomb Fitzgerald. It seems, of all mankind there is no man so led by another as the Duke is by Lord Muskerry[2] and this FitzHarding. Insomuch, as when the King would have him to be Privy-Purse, the Duke wept, and said, "But, Sir, I must have your promise, if you will have my dear Charles from me, that if ever you have occasion for an army again, I may have him with me; believing him to be the best commander of an army in the world." But Mr. Cholmly thinks, as all other men I meet

[1] Charles Berkeley, created Baron Berkeley of Rathdown in 1661, Viscount Fitzharding of Bearhaven in 1663, and Earl of Falmouth in 1665. He was appointed Keeper of the Privy Purse to Charles II. in October, 1662.

[2] Eldest son of the Earl of Clancarty and nephew of the Duke of Ormonde. He had served with distinction in Flanders, as colonel of an infantry regiment, and was killed on board the Duke of York's ship in the sea-fight, 1665. Ormonde, writing to his mother to announce the sad news, says, "his death is a great loss to his friends and family, and is as generally lamented here (Whitehall) as anybody's."

with do, that he is a very ordinary fellow. It is strange how the Duke also do love naturally, and affect the Irish above the English.[1] He, of the company he carried with him to sea, took above two-thirds Irish and French. He tells me the King do hate my Lord Chancellor; and that they, that is the King and my Lord FitzHarding, do laugh at him for a dull fellow; and in all this business of the Dutch war do nothing by his advice, hardly consulting him. Only he is a good minister in other respects, and the King cannot be without him; but, above all, being the Duke's father-in-law, he is kept in; otherwise FitzHarding were able to fling down two of him. This, all the wise and grave lords see, and cannot help it; but yield to it. But he bemoans what the end of it may be, the King being ruled by these men, as he hath been all along since his coming; to the razing all the strong-holds in Scotland, and giving liberty to the Irish in Ireland, whom Cromwell had settled all in one corner; who are now able, and it is feared every day a massacre again among them. He being gone I abroad to the carrier's, to see some things sent away to my father against Christmas, and thence to Moorfields, and there up and down to several houses to drink to look for a place *pour rencontrer la femme de je sais quoi* against next Monday, but could meet none. So to the Coffee-house, where great talke of the Comet[2] seen in several places; and among our men at sea, and by my Lord Sandwich, to whom I intend to write about it to-night. Thence home to dinner, and then to the office, where all the afternoon, and in the evening home to supper, and then to the office late, and so to bed. This night I begun to burn wax candles in my closett at the office, to try the charge, and to see whether the smoke offends like that of tallow candles.

16th. Up, and by water to Deptford, thinking to have met *la femme de* Bagwell, but failed, and having done some business at the yard, I back again, it being a fine fresh morning to walk. Back again, Mr. Wayth walking with

[1] Because so many of the Irish were Roman Catholics. — B.

[2] This comet produced a large amount of literature. The eminent astronomer, Mr. J. R. Hind, F.R.S., has a short anonymous article on it in "Nature," February 7th, 1884, p. 345.

me to Half-Way House talking about Mr. Castle's fine knees[1] lately delivered in. In which I am well informed that they are not as they should be to make them knees, and I hope shall make good use of it to the King's service. Thence home, and having dressed myself, to the 'Change, and thence home to dinner, and so abroad by coach with my wife, and bought a looking-glasse by the Old Exchange, which costs me £5 5*s*., and 6*s*. for the hooks. A very fair glasse. So toward my cozen Scott's, but meeting my Lady Sandwich's coach, my wife turned back to follow them, thinking they might, as they did, go to visit her, and I 'light and to Mrs. Harman, and there staid and talked in her shop with her, and much pleased I am with her. We talked about Anthony Joyce's giving over trade and that he intends to live in lodgings, which is a very mad, foolish thing. She tells me she hears and believes it is because he, being now begun to be called on offices, resolves not to take the new oathe, he having formerly taken the Covenant or Engagement, but I think he do very simply and will endeavour for his wife's sake to advise him therein. Thence to my cozen Scott's, and there met my cozen Roger Pepys, and Mrs. Turner, and The. and Joyce, and prated all the while, and so with the "corps" to church and heard a very fine sermon of the Parson of the parish, and so homeward with them in their coach, but finding it too late to go home with me, I took another coach and so home, and after a while at my office, home to supper and to bed.

17th. Up and to the office, where we sat all the morning. At noon I to the 'Change, and there, among others, had my first meeting with Mr. L'Estrange,[2] who hath endeavoured several times to speak with me. It is to get, now and then, some newes of me, which I shall, as I see cause, give him. He is a man of fine conversation, I think, but I am sure most courtly and full of compliments. Thence home to dinner, and then come the looking-glass man to set up the looking-glass I bought yesterday, in my dining-room, and very handsome it is. So abroad by coach to White Hall, and there to the Committee of Tan-

[1] See *ante*, November 2nd.

[2] Roger L'Estrange, Licenser of the Press and pamphleteer. See note, September 4th, 1663.

gier, and then the Fishing. Mr. Povy did in discourse give me a rub about my late bill for money that I did get of him, which vexed me and stuck in my mind all this evening, though I know very well how to cleare myself at the worst. So home and to my office, where late, and then home to bed. Mighty talke there is of this Comet that is seen a'nights; and the King and Queene did sit up last night to see it, and did, it seems. And to-night I thought to have done so too; but it is cloudy, and so no stars appear. But I will endeavour it. Mr. Gray did tell me to-night, for certain, that the Dutch, as high as they seem, do begin to buckle;[1] and that one man in this Kingdom did tell the King that he is offered £40,000 to make a peace, and others have been offered money also. It seems the taking of their Bourdeaux fleete thus, arose from a printed Gazette of the Dutch's boasting of fighting, and having beaten the English: in confidence whereof (it coming to Bourdeaux), all the fleete comes out, and so falls into our hands.

18th (Lord's day). To church, where, God forgive me! I spent most of my time in looking [on] my new Morena[2] at the other side of the church, an acquaintance of Pegg Pen's. So home to dinner, and then to my chamber to read Ben Johnson's Cataline,[3] a very excellent piece, and so to church again, and thence we met at the office to hire ships, being in great haste and having sent for several masters of ships to come to us. Then home, and there Mr. Andrews and Hill come and we sung finely, and by and by Mr. Fuller, the Parson, and supped with me, he and a friend of his, but my musique friends would not stay supper. At and after supper Mr. Fuller and I [told] many storys of apparitions and delusions thereby, and I out with my storys of Tom Mallard. He gone, I a little to my office, and then to prayers and to bed.

19th. Going to bed betimes last night we waked betimes,

[1] To buckle = to give way or to prepare to give assent.

[2] A brunette.

[3] Jonson's "Catiline" was not revived until December 19th, 1668, when it was acted by the King's Company. Hart took the character of Catiline; Mohun, Cathegus; and Burt, Cicero. Mrs. Corey was Sempronia.

and from our people's being forced to take the key to go out to light a candle, I was very angry and begun to find fault with my wife for not commanding her servants as she ought. Thereupon she giving me some cross answer I did strike her over her left eye such a blow as the poor wretch did cry out and was in great pain, but yet her spirit was such as to endeavour to bite and scratch me. But I coying[1] with her made her leave crying, and sent for butter and parsley, and friends presently one with another, and I up, vexed at my heart to think what I had done, for she was forced to lay a poultice or something to her eye all day, and is black, and the people of the house observed it. But I was forced to rise, and up and with Sir J. Minnes to White Hall, and there we waited on the Duke. And among other things Mr. Coventry took occasion to vindicate himself before the Duke and us, being all there, about the choosing of Taylor[2] for Harwich. Upon which the Duke did clear him, and did tell us that he did expect, that, after he had named a man, none of us shall then oppose or find fault with the man; but if we had anything to say, we ought to say it before he had chose him. Sir G. Carteret thought himself concerned, and endeavoured to clear himself: and by and by Sir W. Batten did speak, knowing himself guilty, and did confess, that being pressed by the Council he did say what he did, that he was accounted a fanatique; but did not know that at that time he had been appointed by his Royal Highness. To which the Duke [replied] that it was impossible but he must know that he had appointed him; and so it did appear that the Duke did mean all this while Sir W. Batten. So by and by we parted, and Mr. Coventry did privately tell me that he did this day take this occasion to mention the business to give the Duke an opportunity of speaking his mind to Sir W. Batten in this business, of which I was heartily glad. Thence home, and not finding Bagwell's wife as I expected, I to the 'Change and there walked up and down, and then home, and she being come I bid her go and stay at Mooregate for me, and after going up to my wife (whose eye is very bad, but she is in very good temper to me), and

[1] Coying = stroking or caressing with the hand.

[2] Captain John Taylor, see *ante*, November 4th, 1664.

after dinner I to the place and walked round the fields again and again, but not finding her I to the 'Change, and there found her waiting for me and took her away, and to an alehouse, and there made I much of her, and then away thence and to another and endeavoured to caress her, but *elle ne voulait pas*, which did vex me, but I think it was chiefly not having a good easy place to do it upon. So we broke up and parted and I to the office, where we sat hiring of ships an hour or two, and then to my office, and thence (with Captain Taylor home to my house) to give him instructions and some notice of what to his great satisfaction had happened to-day. Which I do because I hope his coming into this office will a little cross Sir W. Batten and may do me good. He gone, I to supper with my wife, very pleasant, and then a little to my office and to bed. My mind, God forgive me, too much running upon what I can *ferais avec la femme de Bagwell demain*, having promised to go to Deptford and *a aller a sa maison avec son mari* when I come thither.

20th. Up and walked to Deptford, where after doing something at the yard I walked, without being observed, with Bagwell home to his house, and there was very kindly used, and the poor people did get a dinner for me in their fashion, of which I also eat very well. After dinner I found occasion of sending him abroad, and then alone *avec elle je tentais a faire ce que je voudrais et contre sa force je le faisais bien que passe a mon contentment.* By and by he coming back again I took leave and walked home, and then there to dinner, where Dr. Fayrebrother come to see me and Luellin. We dined, and I to the office, leaving them, where we sat all the afternoon, and I late at the office. To supper and to the office again very late, then home to bed.

21st. Up, and after evening reckonings to this day with Mr. Bridges, the linnen draper, for callicos, I out to Doctors' Commons, where by agreement my cozen Roger and I did meet my cozen Dr. Tom Pepys, and there a great many and some high words on both sides, but I must confess I was troubled; first, to find my cozen Roger such a simple but well-meaning man as he is; next to think that my father, out of folly and vain glory, should now and then (as by their words I gather) be speaking how he had set up his son Tom with his goods and house, and now these words are brought against him — I fear to the depriving him of all the profit the poor man intended to make of the lease of his house and sale of his owne goods. I intend to make a quiet end if I can with the Doctor, being a very foul-tounged fool and of great inconvenience to be at difference with such a one that will make the base noise about it that he will. Thence, very much vexed to find myself so much troubled about other men's matters, I to Mrs. Turner's, in Salisbury Court, and with her a little, and carried her, the porter staying for me, our eagle, which she desired the other day, and we were glad to be rid of her, she fouling our house of office mightily. They are much pleased with her. And thence I home and after dinner to the office, where Sir W. Rider and Cutler come, and in dispute I very high with them against their demands, I hope to no hurt to myself, for I was very plain with them to the best of my reason. So they gone I home to supper, then to the office again and so home to bed. My Lord Sandwich this day writes me word that he hath seen (at Portsmouth) the Comet, and says it is the most extraordinary thing that ever he saw.

22nd. Up and betimes to my office, and then out to several places, among others to Holborne to have spoke with one Mr. Underwood about some English hemp, he lies against Gray's Inn. Thereabouts I to a barber's shop to have my hair cut, and there met with a copy of verses, mightily commended by some gentlemen there, of my Lord Mordaunt's,[1] in excuse of his going to sea this late expedition, with the Duke of Yorke. But, Lord! they are but sorry things; only a Lord made them. Thence to the 'Change; and there, among the merchants, I hear fully the news of our being beaten to dirt at Guinny, by De Ruyter with his fleete. The particulars, as much as by Sir G. Carteret afterwards I heard, I have said in a letter to my Lord Sandwich this day at Portsmouth; it being most wholly to the utter ruine of our Royall Company, and reproach and shame to the whole nation, as well as justification to them

[1] John Mordaunt, second son of John, first Earl of Peterborough, born June 18th, 1626; created Baron Mordaunt of Reigate and Viscount Mordaunt of Avalon, July 10th, 1659. Died June 5th, 1675.

in their doing wrong to no man as to his private [property], only takeing whatever is found to belong to the Company, and nothing else. Dined at the Dolphin, Sir G. Carteret, Sir J. Minnes, Sir W. Batten, and I, with Sir W. Boreman and Sir Theophilus Biddulph[1] and others, Commissioners of the Sewers, about our place below to lay masts in. But coming a little too soon, I out again, and tooke boat down to Redriffe; and just in time within two minutes, and saw the new vessel of Sir William Petty's launched,[2] the King and Duke being there. It swims and looks finely, and I believe will do well. The name I think is Twilight, but I do not know certainly. Coming away back immediately to dinner, where a great deal of good discourse, and Sir G. Carteret's discourse of this Guinny business, with great displeasure at the losse of our honour there, and do now confess that the trade brought all these troubles upon us between the Dutch and us. Thence to the office and there sat late, then I to my office and there till 12 at night, and so home to bed weary.

23rd. Up and to my office, then come by appointment cozen Tom Trice to me, and I paid him the £20 remaining due to him upon the bond of £100 given him by agreement November, 1663, to end the difference between us about my aunt's, his mother's, money. And here, being willing to know the worst, I told him, "I hope now there is nothing remaining between you and I of future dispute." "No," says he, "nothing at all that I know of, but only a small matter of about 20 or 30*s*. that my father Pepys received for me of rent due to me in the country, which I will in a day or two bring you an account of," and so we parted. Dined at home upon a good turkey which Mr. Sheply sent us, then to the office all the afternoon, Mr. Cutler and others coming to me about business. I hear that the Dutch have prepared a fleete to go the backway to the Streights, where without doubt they will master our fleete. This put to that

[1] Sir Theophilus Biddulph, of Westcombe, Kent, who had been previously knighted, was made a baronet, November 2nd, 1664. He was then serving in parliament for Lichfield. — B.

[2] Pepys was wrong as to the name of Sir William Petty's new double-keeled boat. On February 13th, 1664-65, he gives the correct title, which was "The Experiment."

of Guinny makes me fear them mightily, and certainly they are a most wise people, and careful of their business. The King of France, they say, do declare himself obliged to defend them, and lays claim by his Embassador to the wines we have taken from the Dutch Bourdeaux men, and more, it is doubted whether the Swede will be our friend or no. Pray God deliver us out of these troubles! This day Sir W. Batten sent and afterwards spoke to me, to have me and my wife come and dine with them on Monday next: which is a mighty condescension in them, and for some great reason I am sure, or else it pleases God by my late care of business to make me more considerable even with them than I am sure they would willingly owne me to be. God make me thankfull and carefull to preserve myself so, for I am sure they hate me and it is hope or fear that makes them flatter me. It being a bright night, which it has not been a great while, I purpose to endeavour to be called in the morning to see the Comet, though I fear we shall not see it, because it rises in the east but 16 degrees, and then the houses will hinder us.

24th. Having sat up all night to past two o'clock this morning, our porter, being appointed, comes and tells us that the bellman tells him that the star is seen upon Tower Hill; so I, that had been all night setting in order all my old papers in my chamber, did leave off all, and my boy and I to Tower Hill, it being a most fine, bright moonshine night, and a great frost; but no Comet to be seen. So after running once round the Hill, I and Tom, we home and then to bed. Rose about 9 o'clock and then to the office, where sitting all the morning. At noon to the 'Change, to the Coffee-house; and there heard Sir Richard Ford tell the whole story of our defeat at Guinny.[1] Wherein our men are guilty of the most horrid cowardice and perfidiousness, as he says and tells it, that ever Englishmen were. Captain

[1] Sir George Downing wrote to Lord Chancellor Clarendon from the Hague on the 29th December, "I need not tell your Lordshipp what a noise the business of De Ruyter's success in Guiny hath made here, and how much it hath putt life into ye co̅mon people; on the other hand, those that looke higher and neerer into businesse say that this doth justifie, beyond all dispute, what his Majestie hath done here in ye Channell" (Lister's "Life of Clarendon," vol. iii., p. 358).

Raynolds, that was the only commander of any of the King's ships there, was shot at by De Ruyter, with a bloody flag flying. He, instead of opposing (which, indeed, had been to no purpose, but only to maintain honour), did poorly go on board himself, to ask what De Ruyter would have; and so yielded to whatever Ruyter would desire. The King and Duke are highly vexed at it, it seems, and the business deserves it. Thence home to dinner, and then abroad to buy some things, and among others to my bookseller's, and there saw several books I spoke for, which are finely bound and good books to my great content. So home and to my office, where late. This evening I being informed did look and saw the Comet,[1] which is now, whether worn away or no I know not, but appears not with a tail, but only is larger and duller than any other star, and is come to rise betimes, and to make a great arch, and is gone quite to a new place in the heavens than it was before: but I hope in a clearer night something more will be seen. So home to bed.

25th (Lord's day and Christmas day). Up (my wife's eye being ill still of the blow I did in a passion give her on Monday last) to church alone, where Mr. Mills, a good sermon. To dinner at home, where very pleasant with my wife and family. After dinner I to Sir W. Batten's, and there received so much good usage (as I have of late done) from him and my Lady, obliging me and my wife, according to promise, to come and dine with them to-morrow with our neighbours, that I was in pain all the day, and night too after, to know how to order the business of my wife's not going, and by discourse receive fresh instances of Sir J. Minnes's folly in complaining to Sir G. Carteret of Sir W. Batten and me for some family offences, such as my having of a stopcock to keepe the water from them, which vexes me, but it would more but that Sir G. Carteret knows him very well. Thence to the French church, but coming too late I returned and to Mr. Rawlinson's church, where I heard a good sermon of one that I remember was at Paul's with me, his name Maggett;[2] and very great

[1] It is one of the twenty-four comets of which the observations have been collected in Halley's "Astronomiæ Cometicæ Synopsis." — B.

[2] St. Dionis Backchurch. The rector in 1664 was John Castilion, D.D., afterwards Bishop of Exeter. The preacher may have been

store of fine women there is in this church, more than I know anywhere else about us. So home and to my chamber, looking over and setting in order my papers and books, and so to supper, and then to prayers and to bed.

26th. Up, and with Sir W. Pen to White Hall, and there with the rest did our usual business before the Duke, and then with Sir W. Batten back and to his house, where I by sicknesse excused my wife's coming to them to-day. Thence I to the Coffee-house, where much good discourse, and all the opinion now is that the Dutch will avoid fighting with us at home, but do all the hurte they can to us abroad; which it may be they may for a while, but that, I think, cannot support them long. Thence to Sir W. Batten's, where Mr. Coventry and all our families here, women and all, and Sir R. Ford and his, and a great feast and good discourse and merry, there all the afternoon and evening till late, only stepped in to see my wife, then to my office to enter my day's work, and so home to bed, where my people and wife innocently at cards very merry, and I to bed, leaving them to their sport and blindman's buff.

27th. My people came to bed, after their sporting, at four o'clock in the morning; I up at seven, and to Deptford and Woolwich in a gally; the Duke calling to me out of the barge in which the King was with him going down the river, to know whither I was going. I told him to Woolwich, but was troubled afterward I should say no farther, being in a gally, lest he think me too profuse in my journeys. Did several businesses, and then back again by two o'clock to Sir J. Minnes's to dinner by appointment, where all yesterday's company but Mr. Coventry, who could not come. Here merry, and after an hour's chat I down to the office, where busy late, and then home to supper and to bed. The Comet appeared again to-night, but duskishly. I went to bed, leaving my wife and all her folks, and Will also, too, come to make Christmas gambolls to-night.

28th. I waked in the morning about 6 o'clock and my wife not come to bed; I lacked a pot, but there was none,

Richard Meggot, D.D., who was appointed Canon of Windsor in 1677 and Dean of Winchester in 1679. He died December 7th, 1692, and was buried in St. George's Chapel, Windsor.

and bitter cold, so was forced to rise and piss in the chimney, and to bed again. Slept a little longer, and then hear my people coming up, and so I rose, and my wife to bed at eight o'clock in the morning, which vexed me a little, but I believe there was no hurt in it all, but only mirthe, therefore took no notice. I abroad with Sir W. Batten to the Council Chamber, where all of us to discourse about the way of measuring ships and the freight fit to give for them by the tun, where it was strange methought to hear so poor discourses among the Lords themselves, and most of all to see how a little empty matter delivered gravely by Sir W. Pen was taken mighty well, though nothing in the earth to the purpose. But clothes, I perceive more and more every day, is a great matter. Thence home with Sir W. Batten by coach, and I home to dinner, finding my wife still in bed. After dinner abroad, and among other things visited my Lady Sandwich, and was there, with her and the young ladies, playing at cards till night. Then home and to my office late, then home to bed, leaving my wife and people up to more sports, but without any great satisfaction to myself therein.

29th. Up and to the office, where we sat all the morning. Then whereas I should have gone and dined with Sir W. Pen (and the rest of the officers at his house), I pretended to dine with my Lady Sandwich and so home, where I dined well, and began to wipe and clean my books in my chamber in order to the settling of my papers and things there thoroughly, and then to the office, where all the afternoon sitting, and in the evening home to supper, and then to my work again.

30th. Lay very long in bed with my wife, it being very cold, and my wife very full of a resolution to keepe within doors, not so much as to go to church or see my Lady Sandwich before Easter next, which I am willing enough to, though I seem the contrary. This and other talke kept me a-bed till almost 10 a'clock. Then up and made an end of looking over all my papers and books and taking everything out of my chamber to have all made clean. At noon dined, and after dinner forth to several places to pay away money, to clear myself in all the world, and, among others, paid my bookseller £6 for books I had from him this day, and the silversmith £22 18*s*. for spoons, forks, and sugar box, and being well pleased with seeing my business done to my mind as to my meeting with people and having my books ready for me, I home and to my office, and there did business late, and then home to supper, prayers, and to bed.

31st. At the office all the morning, and after dinner there again, dispatched first my letters, and then to my accounts, not of the month but of the whole yeare also, and was at it till past twelve at night, it being bitter cold; but yet I was well satisfied with my worke, and, above all, to find myself, by the great blessing of God, worth £1,349, by which, as I have spent very largely, so I have laid up above £500 this yeare above what I was worth this day twelvemonth. The Lord make me for ever thankful to his holy name for it! Thence home to eat a little and so to bed. Soon as ever the clock struck one, I kissed my wife in the kitchen by the fireside, wishing her a merry new yeare, observing that I believe I was the first proper wisher of it this year, for I did it as soon as ever the clock struck one.

So ends the old yeare, I bless God, with great joy to me, not only from my having made so good a yeare of profit, as having spent £420 and laid up £540 and upwards; but I bless God I never have been in so good plight as to my health in so very cold weather as this is, nor indeed in any hot weather, these ten years, as I am at this day, and have been these four or five months. But I am at a great losse to know whether it be my hare's foote,[1] or taking every morning of a pill of turpentine, or my having left off the wearing of a gowne. My family is, my wife, in good health, and happy with her; her woman Mercer, a pretty, modest, quiett mayde; her chamber-mayde Besse, her cook mayde Jane, the little girl Susan, and my boy which I have had about half a yeare, Tom Edwards, which I took from the King's chappell, and a pretty and loving quiett family I have as any man in England. My credit in the world and my office grows daily, and I am in good esteeme with everybody, I think. My troubles of my uncle's estate pretty well over; but it comes to be but of little profit to us, my father being much supported by my purse. But

[1] As a charm against the colic, see *post*, January 20th, 1664-65.

great vexations remain upon my father and me from my brother Tom's death and ill condition, both to our disgrace and discontent, though no great reason for either. Publique matters are all in a hurry about a Dutch warr. Our preparations great; our provocations against them great; and, after all our presumption, we are now afeard as much of them, as we lately contemned them. Every thing else in the State quiett, blessed be God! My Lord Sandwich at sea with the fleete at Portsmouth; sending some about to cruise for taking of ships, which we have done to a great number. This Christmas I judged it fit to look over all my papers and books; and to tear all that I found either boyish or not to be worth keeping, or fit to be seen, if it should please God to take me away suddenly. Among others, I found these two or three notes, which I thought fit to keep —

AGE OF MY GRANDFATHER'S CHILDREN.[1]

Thomas, 1595.
Mary, March 16, 1597.
Edith, October 11, 1599.
John (my Father), January 14, 1601.

My father and mother marryed at Newington, in Surry, Octob. 15, 1626.

THEYR CHILDREN'S AGES.

Mary, July 24, 1627. *mort.*[2]
Paulina, Sept. 18, 1628. *mort.*
Esther, March 27, 1630. *mort.*
John, January 10, 1631. *mort.*
Samuel,[3] Febr. 23, 1632.
Thomas, June 18, 1634. *mort.*
Sarah, August 25, 1635. *mort.*
Jacob, May 1, 1637. *mort.*
Robert, Nov. 18, 1638. *mort.*
Paulina, Oct. 18, 1640.
John, Novemb. 26, 1641. *mort.*

December 31, 1664.

[1] This family register is written in long-hand.

[2] The word "mort" must have been in some instances added long after the entry was first made. — B.

[3] To this name is affixed in shorthand the following note: "Went to reside in Magd. Coll. Camb. and did put on my gown first, March 5, 1650–51." — B.

CHARMES.[1]

1. FOR STENCHING OF BLOOD.

Sanguis mane in te,
Sicut Christus fuit in se;
Sanguis mane in tuâ venâ
Sicut Christus in suâ pœnâ;
Sanguis mane fixus,
Sicut Christus quando fuit crucifixus.

2. A THORNE.

Jesus, that was of a Virgin born,
Was pricked both with nail and thorn;
It neither wealed nor belled, rankled, nor boned;
In the name of Jesus no more shall this.

Or, thus: —

Christ was of a Virgin born,
And he was pricked with a thorn;
And it did neither bell, nor swell;
And I trust in Jesus this never will.

3. A CRAMP.

Cramp be thou faintless,
As our Lady was sinless,
When she bare Jesus.

4. A BURNING.

There came three Angells out of the East;
The one brought fire, the other brought frost —
Out fire; in frost.
In the name of the Father, and Son, and Holy Ghost.
AMEN.

1664–65.

January 1st (Lord's day). Lay long in bed, having been busy late last night, then up and to my office, where upon ordering my accounts and papers with respect to my under-

[1] The first of these charms is written in long-hand, but the remainder are in shorthand.

standing my last year's gains and expense, which I find very great, as I have already set down yesterday. Now this day I am dividing my expense, to see what my clothes and every particular hath stood me in: I mean all the branches of my expense. At noon a good venison pasty and a turkey to ourselves without any body so much as invited by us, a thing unusuall for so small a family of my condition: but we did it and were very merry. After dinner to my office again, where very late alone upon my accounts, but have not brought them to order yet, and very intricate I find it, notwithstanding my care all the year to keep things in as good method as any man can do. Past 11 o'clock home to supper and to bed.

2nd. Up, and it being a most fine hard frost I walked a good way toward White Hall, and then being overtaken with Sir W. Pen's coach, went into it, and with him thither, and there did our usual business with the Duke. Thence, being forced to pay a great deale of money away in boxes (that is, basins at White Hall), I to my barber's, Gervas, and there had a little opportunity of speaking with my Jane alone, and did give her something, and of herself she did tell me a place where I might come to her on Sunday next, which I will not fail, but to see how modestly and harmlessly she brought it out was very pretty. Thence to the Swan, and there did sport a good while with Herbert's young kinswoman without hurt, though they being abroad, the old people. Then to the Hall, and there agreed with Mrs. Martin, and to her lodgings which she has now taken to lie in, in Bow Streete, pitiful poor things, yet she thinks them pretty, and so they are for her condition I believe good enough. Here I did *ce que je voudrais avec* her most freely, and it having cost 2*s*. in wine and cake upon her, I away sick of her impudence, and by coach to my Lord Brunker's, by appointment, in the Piazza, in Covent-Guarding; where I occasioned much mirth with a ballet[1] I

[1] There can be no reasonable cause for doubting this to refer to the famous song, "To all you ladies now at land," written by Lord Buckhurst (afterwards Earl of Dorset), and the reference has therefore a very distinct literary value, because it proves that the song was not "made the night before the engagement" of June 3rd, 1665, an opinion which was universally held until this passage was printed. There

brought with me, made from the seamen at sea to their ladies in town; saying Sir W. Pen, Sir G. Ascue, and Sir J. Lawson made them. Here a most noble French dinner and banquet, the best I have seen this many a day and good discourse. Thence to my bookseller's and at his binder's saw Hooke's book of the Microscope,[1] which is so pretty that I presently bespoke it, and away home to the office, where we met to do something, and then though very late

is nothing in the song itself to indicate any particular time when it was written, and it appears that the first to fix the exact period was Prior the poet (who was born in 1664). In the dedication of his poems to Lionel, Earl of Dorset and Middlesex, Prior states that the earl's father wrote the celebrated sea song "the night before the engagement with the Dutch in 1665." Dr. Johnson, in his "Lives of the Poets," says, "seldom any splendid story is wholly true," and adds that Lord Orrery told him that Lord Buckhurst had been a week employed upon it, and only retouched or finished it on the memorable evening. Lord Braybrooke was criticised for supposing that Pepys referred to Buckhurst's song, and therefore he entered fully into his own defence, summing up as follows: "In the absence of certain evidence, we cannot decide upon the fact; but all accounts agree in representing Buckhurst as having served as a volunteer under the Duke of York, whose *first cruise took place* in *November*, 1664. Perhaps, then, the ballad was written at this time, when an action between the two fleets was only delayed by the Dutch retiring to port. Thus Pepys might well have seen the song in January, 1664-65; and it still may have been retouched, and brought out with *éclat* during the excitement consequent upon the victory of June 3rd following. Nor is it, indeed, easy to imagine that anyone ever wrote a ballad when about to take part in a great naval conflict; or that, if two songs had been contemporaneously composed on the same subject, with titles so nearly identical, one only should be known to exist." The song became popular immediately, and has never lost its popularity. An immense number of imitations have appeared, and reference to some of these is made by the Rev. J. W. Ebsworth in his valuable edition of the "Bagford Ballads" (p. 615).

[1] "Micrographia: or some physiological descriptions of minute bodies made by Magnifying Glasses. London, 1665," a very remarkable work with elaborate plates, some of which have been used for lecture illustrations almost to our own day. On November 23rd, 1664, the President of the Royal Society was "desired to sign a licence for printing of Mr. Hooke's microscopical book." At this time the book was mostly printed, but it was delayed, much to Hooke's disgust, by the examination of several Fellows of the Society. In spite of this examination the council were anxious that the author should make it clear that he alone was responsible for any theory put forward, and they gave him notice to that effect. Hooke made this clear in his dedication (see Birch's "History," vol. i., pp. 490-491).

by coach to Sir Ph. Warwicke's, but having company with him could not speak with him. So back again home, where thinking to be merry was vexed with my wife's having looked out a letter in Sir Philip Sidney about jealousy for me to read, which she industriously and maliciously caused me to do, and the truth is my conscience told me it was most proper for me, and therefore was touched at it, but tooke no notice of it, but read it out most frankly, but it stucke in my stomach, and moreover I was vexed to have a dog brought to my house to line our little bitch, which they make him do in all their sights, which, God forgive me, do stir my jealousy again, though of itself the thing is a very immodest sight. However, to cards with my wife a good while, and then to bed.

3rd. Up, and by coach to Sir Ph. Warwicke's,[1] the streete being full of footballs, it being a great frost, and found him and Mr. Coventry walking in St. James's Parke. I did my errand to him about the felling of the King's timber in the forests, and then to my Lord of Oxford,[2] Justice in Eyre, for his consent thereto, for want whereof my Lord Privy Seale stops the whole business. I found him in his lodgings, in but an ordinary furnished house and roome where he was, but I find him to be a man of good discreet replys. Thence to the Coffee-house, where certain newes that the Dutch have taken some of our colliers to the North; some say four, some say seven. Thence to the 'Change a while, and so home to dinner and to the office, where we sat late, and then I to write my letters, and then to Sir W. Batten's, who is going out of towne to Harwich to-morrow to set up a light-house there, which he hath lately got a patent from the King to set up, that will turne much to his profit. Here very merry, and so to my office again, where very late, and then home to supper and to bed, but sat up with my wife at cards till past two in the morning.

[1] Sir Philip Warwick lived in the Outer Spring Garden, and the site of his house is marked by Warwick Street, Cockspur Street. Warwick House was the residence of the Princess Charlotte of Wales at the beginning of the present century.

[2] Aubrey, Earl of Oxford, was Warden and Chief Justice in Eyre of the Royal Forests, Parks, Chaces, and Warrens, South of Trent, from 1660 to 1673. He was then living in the Piazza, Covent Garden.

4th. Lay long, and then up and to my Lord of Oxford's, but his Lordshipp was in bed at past ten o'clock: and, Lord helpe us! so rude a dirty family I never saw in my life. He sent me out word my business was not done, but should against the afternoon. I thence to the Coffee-house, there but little company, and so home to the 'Change, where I hear of some more of our ships lost to the Northward. So to Sir W. Batten's, but he was set out before I got thither. I sat long talking with my lady, and then home to dinner. Then come Mr. Moore to see me, and he and I to my Lord of Oxford's, but not finding him within Mr. Moore and I to "Love in a Tubb,"[1] which is very merry, but only so by gesture, not wit at all, which methinks is beneath the House. So walked home, it being a very hard frost, and I find myself as heretofore in cold weather to begin to burn within and pimples and pricks all over my body, my pores with cold being shut up. So home to supper and to cards and to bed.

5th. Up, it being very cold and a great snow and frost to-night. To the office, and there all the morning. At noon dined at home, troubled at my wife's being simply angry with Jane, our cook mayde (a good servant, though perhaps hath faults and is cunning), and given her warning to be gone. So to the office again, where we sat late, and then I to my office, and there very late doing business. Home to supper and to the office again, and then late home to bed.

6th. Lay long in bed, but most of it angry and scolding with my wife about her warning Jane our cooke-mayde to be gone and upon that she desires to go abroad to-day to look a place. A very good mayde she is and fully to my mind, being neat, only they say a little apt to scold, but I hear her not. To my office all the morning busy. Dined at home. To my office again, being pretty well reconciled to my wife, which I did desire to be, because she had designed much mirthe to-day to end Christmas with among her servants. At night home, being twelfenight, and there

[1] "The Comical Revenge, or Love in a Tub," a comedy by Sir George Etherege; licensed for printing, July 8th, 1664, but not published till 1669. It was acted by the Duke's Company, and the Bettertons and Harris were in it.

chose my piece of cake, but went up to my viall, and then to bed, leaving my wife and people up at their sports, which they continue till morning, not coming to bed at all.

7th. Up and to the office all the morning. At noon dined alone, my wife and family most of them a-bed. Then to see my Lady Batten and sit with her a while, Sir W. Batten being out of town, and then to my office doing very much business very late, and then home to supper and to bed.

8th (Lord's day). Up betimes, and it being a very fine frosty day, I and my boy walked to White Hall, and there to the Chappell, where one Dr. Beaumont[1] preached a good sermon, and afterwards a brave anthem upon the 150 Psalm, where upon the word "trumpet" very good musique was made. So walked to my Lady's and there dined with her (my boy going home), where much pretty discourse, and after dinner walked to Westminster, and there to the house where Jane Welsh had appointed me, but it being sermon time they would not let me in, and said nobody was there to speak with me. I spent the whole afternoon walking into the Church and Abbey, and up and down, but could not find her, and so in the evening took a coach and home, and there sat discoursing with my wife, and by and by at supper, drinking some cold drink I think it was, I was forced to go make water, and had very great pain after it, but was well by and by and continued so, it being only I think from the drink, or from my straining at stool to do more than my body would. So after prayers to bed.

9th. Up and walked to White Hall, it being still a brave frost, and I in perfect good health, blessed be God! In my way saw a woman that broke her thigh, in her heels slipping up upon the frosty streete. To the Duke, and there did our usual worke. Here I saw the Royal Society bring their new book, wherein is nobly writ their charter[2]

[1] Joseph Beaumont, D.D., Prebendary of Ely, 1651, but not installed until 1660; Master of Jesus College, Cambridge, 1662-63, and of Peterhouse, 1663-1699, Regius Professor of Divinity, Cambridge, 1674. He died November 23rd, 1699.

[2] The Charter-book of the Royal Society, which contains the signatures of the Fellows of the Society from the foundation, is a volume of the greatest interest. At the meeting on January 11th, 1664-65, "The Charter-book of the Society was produced, wherein his Majesty, on the

and laws, and comes to be signed by the Duke as a Fellow; and all the Fellows' hands are to be entered there, and lie as a monument; and the King hath put his with the word Founder. Thence I to Westminster, to my barber's, and found occasion to see Jane, but in presence of her mistress, and so could not speak to her of her failing me yesterday, and then to the Swan to Herbert's girl, and lost time a little with her, and so took coach, and to my Lord Crew's and dined with him, who receives me with the greatest respect that could be, telling me that he do much doubt of the successe of this warr with Holland, we going about it, he doubts, by the instigation of persons that do not enough apprehend the consequences of the danger of it, and therein I do think with him. Holmes was this day sent to the Tower,[1] but I perceive it is made matter of jest only; but if the Dutch should be our masters, it may come to be of earnest to him, to be given over to them for a sacrifice, as Sir W. Rawly [Raleigh] was. Thence to White Hall to a Tangier Committee, where I was accosted and most highly complimented by my Lord Bellasses,[2] our new governor, beyond my expectation, or measure I could imagine he would have given any man, as if I were the only person of business that he intended to rely on, and desires my correspondence with him. This I was not only surprised at, but am well pleased with, and may make good use of it. Our patent is renewed, and he and my Lord Barkeley, and Sir Thomas Ingram[3] put in as

9th of January, had written himself CHARLES R., FOUNDER, and his Highness the Duke of York, JAMES, Fellow; the Duke of Albemarle also having entered his name at the same time. The President was desired to kiss his Majesty's hand for this honour" (Birch's "History," vol. ii., p. 4).

[1] For taking New York from the Dutch, see note *ante*, September 29th.

[2] John Belasyse, second son of Thomas, first Viscount Fauconberg, created Baron Belasyse of Worlaby, January 27th, 1644, Lord Lieutenant of the East Riding of Yorkshire, and Governor of Hull. He was appointed Governor of Tangier, and Captain of the Band of Gentlemen Pensioners. He was a Roman Catholic, and therefore was deprived of all his appointments in 1672 by the provisions of the Test Act, but in 1684 James II. made him First Commissioner of the Treasury. He died 1689.

[3] Chancellor of the Duchy of Lancaster, and a Privy Councillor. Died 1671. — B.

commissioners. Here some business happened which may bring me some profit. Thence took coach and calling my wife at her tailor's (she being come this afternoon to bring her mother some apples, neat's tongues, and wine); I home, and there at my office late with Sir W. Warren, and had a great deal of good discourse and counsel from him, which I hope I shall take being all for my good in my deportment in my office, yet with all honesty. He gone I home to supper and to bed.

10th. Lay long, it being still very cold, and then to the office, where till dinner, and then home, and by and by to the office, where we sat and were very late, and I writing letters till twelve at night, and then after supper to bed.

11th. Up, and very angry with my boy for lying long a bed and forgetting his lute. To my office all the morning. At noon to the 'Change, and so home to dinner. After dinner to Gresham College to my Lord Brunker [1] and Commissioner Pett, taking Mr. Castle with me there to discourse over his draught of a ship he is to build for us. Where I first found reason to apprehend Commissioner Pett to be a man of an ability extraordinary in any thing, for I found he did turn and wind Castle like a chicken in his business, and that most pertinently and master-like, and great pleasure it was to me to hear them discourse, I of late having studied something thereof, and my Lord Brunker is a very able person also himself in this sort of business, as owning himself to be a master in the business of all lines and Conicall Sections. Thence home, where very late at my office doing business to my content, though [God] knows with what ado it was that when I was out I could get myself to come home to my business, or when I was there though late would stay there from going abroad again. To supper and to bed. This evening, by a letter from Plymouth, I hear that two of our ships, the Leopard and another, [2] in the Straights, are lost by running aground;

[1] These consultations must have been extra-official, as they are not mentioned in Birch's "History of the Royal Society." The spelling of the name Brouncker appears to have offered great difficulty to Pepys, for he sometimes writes it Brunker and sometimes Brunkard.

[2] See entry on January 14th, where the names of the ships are given as "Phœnix" and "Nonsuch." The "Phœnix" was a fourth-rate, of thirty-eight guns, built at Woolwich in 1647 by Peter Pett, Jun.

and that three more had like to have been so, but got off, whereof Captain Allen one: and that a Dutch fleete are gone thither; which if they should meet with our lame ships, God knows what would become of them. This I reckon most sad newes; God make us sensible of it! This night, when I come home, I was much troubled to hear my poor canary bird, that I have kept these three or four years, is dead.

12th. Up, and to White Hall about getting a privy seal for felling of the King's timber for the navy, and to the Lords' House to speak with my Lord Privy Seale about it, and so to the 'Change, where to my last night's ill news I met more. Spoke with a Frenchman who was taken, but released, by a Dutch man-of-war of thirty-six guns (with seven more of the like or greater ships), off the North Foreland, by Margett. Which is a strange attempt, that they should come to our teeth; but the wind being easterly, the wind that should bring our force from Portsmouth, will carry them away home. God preserve us against them, and pardon our making them in our discourse so contemptible an enemy! So home and to dinner, where Mr. Hollyard with us dined. So to the office, and there late till 11 at night and more, and then home to supper and to bed.

13th. Up betimes and walked to my Lord Bellasses's lodgings in Lincolne's Inne Fieldes, and there he received and discoursed with me in the most respectfull manner that could be, telling me what a character of my judgment, and care, and love to Tangier he had received of me, that he desired my advice and my constant correspondence, which he much valued, and in my courtship, in which, though I understand his designe very well, and that it is only a piece of courtship, yet it is a comfort to me that I am become so considerable as to have him need to say that to me, which, if I did not do something in the world, would never have been. Here well satisfied I to Sir Ph. Warwicke, and there did some business with him; thence to Jervas's and there spent a little idle time with him, his wife, Jane, and a sweetheart of hers. So to the Hall awhile and thence to the Exchange, where yesterday's newes confirmed, though in a little different manner; but a couple of ships in the Straights we have lost, and the Dutch have been in

Margaret [Margate] Road. Thence home to dinner and so abroad and alone to the King's house, to a play, "The Traytor,"[1] where, unfortunately, I met with Sir W. Pen, so that I must be forced to confess it to my wife, which troubles me. Thence walked home, being ill-satisfied with the present actings of the House, and prefer the other House before this infinitely. To my Lady Batten's, where I find Pegg Pen, the first time that ever I saw her to wear spots. Here very merry, Sir W. Batten being looked for to-night, but is not yet come from Harwich. So home to supper and to bed.

14th. Up and to White Hall, where long waited in the Duke's chamber for a committee intended for Tangier, but none met, and so I home and to the office, where we met a little, and then to the 'Change, where our late ill newes confirmed in loss of two ships in the Straights, but are now the Phœnix and Nonsuch.[2] Home to dinner, thence with my wife to the King's house, there to see "Vulpone,"[3] a most excellent play; the best I think I ever saw, and well acted. So with Sir W. Pen home in his coach, and then to the office. So home, to supper, and bed, resolving by the grace of God from this day to fall hard to my business again, after some weeke or fortnight's neglect.

15th (Lord's day). Up, and after a little at my office to prepare a fresh draught of my vows for the next yeare, I to church, where a most insipid young coxcomb preached. Then home to dinner, and after dinner to read in "Rushworth's Collections"[4] about the charge against the late Duke of Buckingham, in order to the fitting me to speak and understand the discourse anon before the King about the suffering the Turkey merchants to send out their fleete at this dangerous time, when we can neither spare them ships to go, nor men, nor King's ships to convoy them. At four o'clock with Sir W. Pen in his coach to my Lord Chancellor's, where by and by Mr. Coventry, Sir W. Pen, Sir J.

[1] A tragedy by Shirley, licensed May 4th, 1631, and published 1635. Genest does not mention the acting of this play till 1692.

[2] See entry for January 11th.

[3] Ben Jonson's comedy, "Volpone, or the Fox," published 1605.

[4] Rushworth's "Historical Collections of private passages in state," &c., first appeared in 1659. Rushworth was born 1607, and died 1690. The reference is to the duke's expedition to the Isle of Rhé.

Lawson, Sir G. Ascue, and myself were called in to the King, there being several of the Privy Council, and my Lord Chancellor lying at length upon a couch (of the goute I suppose); and there Sir W. Pen begun, and he had prepared heads in a paper, and spoke pretty well to purpose, but with so much leisure and gravity as was tiresome; besides, the things he said were but very poor to a man in his trade after a great consideration, but it was to purpose, indeed to dissuade the King from letting these Turkey ships to go out: saying (in short) the King having resolved to have 130 ships out by the spring, he must have above 20 of them merchantmen. Towards which, he in the whole River could find but 12 or 14, and of them the five ships taken up by these merchants were a part, and so could not be spared. That we should need 30,000 [sailors] to man these 130 ships, and of them in service we have not above 16,000; so we shall need 14,000 more. That these ships will with their convoys carry above 2,000 men, and those the best men that could be got; it being the men used to the Southward that are the best men for warr, though those bred in the North among the colliers are good for labour. That it will not be safe for the merchants, nor honourable for the King, to expose these rich ships with his convoy of six ships to go, if not being enough to secure them against the Dutch, who, without doubt, will have a great fleete in the Straights. This, Sir J. Lawson enlarged upon. Sir G. Ascue he chiefly spoke that the warr and trade could not be supported together, and, therefore, that trade must stand still to give way to them. This Mr. Coventry seconded, and showed how the medium of the men the King hath one year with another employed in his Navy since his coming, hath not been above 3,000 men, or at most 4,000 men; and now having occasion of 30,000, the remaining 26,000 must be found out of the trade of the nation. He showed how the cloaths, sending by these merchants to Turkey, are already bought and paid for to the workmen, and are as many as they would send these twelve months or more; so the poor do not suffer by their not going, but only the merchant, upon whose hands they lie dead; and so the inconvenience is the less. And yet for them he propounded, either the King should, if his

Treasure would suffer it, buy them, and showed the losse would not be so great to him: or, dispense with the Act of Navigation, and let them be carried out by strangers; and ending that he doubted not but when the merchants saw there was no remedy, they would and could find ways of sending them abroad to their profit. All ended with a conviction (unless future discourse with the merchants should alter it) that it was not fit for them to go out, though the ships be loaded. The King in discourse did ask me two or three questions about my newes of Allen's loss in the Streights, but I said nothing as to the business, nor am not much sorry for it, unless the King had spoke to me as he did to them, and then I could have said something to the purpose I think. So we withdrew, and the merchants were called in. Staying without, my Lord FitzHarding come thither, and fell to discourse of Prince Rupert, and made nothing to say that his disease was the pox and that he must be fluxed, telling the horrible degree of the disease upon him with its breaking out on his head. But above all I observed how he observed from the Prince, that courage is not what men take it to be, a contempt of death; for, says he, how chagrined the Prince was the other day when he thought he should die, having no more mind to it than another man. But, says he, some men are more apt to think they shall escape than another man in fight, while another is doubtfull he shall be hit. But when the first man is sure he shall die, as now the Prince is, he is as much troubled and apprehensive of it as any man else; for, says he, since we told [him] that we believe he would overcome his disease, he is as merry, and swears and laughs and curses, and do all the things of a [man] in health, as ever he did in his life; which, methought, was a most extraordinary saying before a great many persons there of quality. So by and by with Sir W. Pen home again, and after supper to the office to finish my vows, and so to bed.

16th. Up and with Sir W. Batten and Sir W. Pen to White Hall, where we did our business with the Duke. Thence I to Westminster Hall and walked up and down. Among others Ned Pickering met me and tells me how active my Lord is at sea, and that my Lord Hinchingbroke is now at Rome, and, by all report, a very noble and hopefull gentleman. Thence to Mr. Povy's, and there met Creed, and dined well after his old manner of plenty and curiosity. But I sat in pain to think whether he would begin with me again after dinner with his enquiry after my bill, but he did not, but fell into other discourse, at which I was glad, but was vexed this morning meeting of Creed at some bye questions that he demanded of me about some such thing, which made me fear he meant that very matter, but I perceive he did not. Thence to visit my Lady Sandwich and so to a Tangier Committee, where a great company of the new Commissioners, Lords, that in behalfe of my Lord Bellasse, are very loud and busy and call for Povy's accounts, but it was a most sorrowful thing to see how he answered to questions so little to the purpose, but to his owne wrong. All the while I sensible how I am concerned in my bill of £100 and somewhat more. So great a trouble is fear, though in a case that at the worst will bear enquiry. My Lord Barkeley was very violent against Povy. But my Lord Ashly, I observe, is a most clear man in matters of accounts, and most ingeniously did discourse and explain all matters. We broke up, leaving the thing to a Committee of which I am one. Povy, Creed, and I staid discoursing, I much troubled in mind seemingly for the business, but indeed only on my own behalf, though I have no great reason for it, but so painfull a thing is fear. So after considering how to order business, Povy and I walked together as far as the New Exchange and so parted, and I by coach home. To the office a while, then to supper and to bed. This afternoon Secretary Bennet read to the Duke of Yorke his letters, which say that Allen[1] has met with the Dutch Smyrna fleet at Cales,[2] and sunk one and taken three. How true or what these ships are time will show, but it is good newes and the newes of our ships being lost is doubted at Cales[2] and Malaga. God send it false!

[1] Among the State Papers is a letter from Captain Thomas Allin to Sir Richard Fanshaw, dated from "The Plymouth, Cadiz Bay," December 25th, 1664, in which he writes: "On the 19th attacked with his seven ships left, a Dutch fleet of fourteen, three of which were men-of-war; sunk two vessels and took two others, one a rich prize from Smyrna; the others retired much battered. Has also taken a Dutch prize laden with iron and planks, coming from Lisbon" ("Calendar," Domestic, 1664-65, p. 122).

[2] The old form of the name Cadiz.

17th. Up and walked to Mr. Povy's by appointment, where I found him and Creed busy about fitting things for the Committee, and thence we to my Lord Ashly's, where to see how simply, beyond all patience, Povy did again, by his many words and no understanding, confound himself and his business, to his disgrace, and rendering every body doubtfull of his being either a foole or knave, is very wonderfull. We broke up all dissatisfied, and referred the business to a meeting of Mr. Sherwin and others to settle, but here it was mighty strange methought to find myself sit here in Committee with my hat on, while Mr. Sherwin stood bare as a clerke, with his hat off to his Lord Ashly and the rest, but I thank God I think myself never a whit the better man for all that. Thence with Creed to the 'Change and Coffee-house, and so home, where a brave dinner, by having a brace of pheasants and very merry about Povy's folly. So anon to the office, and there sitting very late, and then after a little time at Sir W. Batten's, where I am mighty great and could if I thought it fit continue so, I to the office again, and there very late, and so home to the sorting of some of my books, and so to bed, the weather becoming pretty warm, and I think and hope the frost will break.

18th. Up and by and by to my bookseller's, and there did give thorough direction for the new binding of a great many of my old books, to make my whole study of the same binding, within very few. Thence to my Lady Sandwich's, who sent for me this morning. Dined with her, and it was to get a letter of hers conveyed by a safe hand to my Lord's owne hand at Portsmouth, which I did undertake. Here my Lady did begin to talk of what she had heard concerning Creed, of his being suspected to be a fanatique and a false fellow. I told her I thought he was as shrewd and cunning a man as any in England, and one that I would feare first should outwit me in any thing. To which she readily concurred. Thence to Mr. Povy's by agreement, and there with Mr. Sherwin, Auditor Beale, and Creed and I hard at it very late about Mr. Povy's accounts, but such accounts I never did see, or hope again to see in my days. At night, late, they gone, I did get him to put out of this account our sums that are in posse only yet, which he approved of when told, but would never have stayed it if I had been gone. Thence at 9 at night home, and so to supper vexed and my head akeing and to bed.

19th. Up, and it being yesterday and to-day a great thaw it is not for a man to walk the streets, but took coach and to Mr. Povy's, and there meeting all of us again agreed upon an answer to the Lords by and by, and thence we did come to Exeter House,[1] and there was a witness of most [base] language against Mr. Povy, from my Lord Peterborough, who is most furiously angry with him, because the other, as a foole, would needs say that the £26,000 was my Lord Peterborough's account, and that he had nothing to do with it. The Lords did find fault also with our answer, but I think really my Lord Ashly would fain have the outside of an Exchequer,[2] but when we come better to be examined. So home by coach, with my Lord Barkeley, who, by his discourse, I find do look upon Mr. Coventry as an enemy, but yet professes great justice and pains. I at home after dinner to the office, and there sat all the afternoon and evening, and then home to supper and to bed. *Memorandum*. This day and yesterday, I think it is the change of the weather, I have a great deal of pain, but nothing like what I used to have. I can hardly keep myself loose, but on the contrary am forced to drive away my pain. Here I am so sleepy I cannot hold open my eyes, and therefore must be forced to break off this day's passages more shortly than I would and should have done. This day was buried (but I could not be there) my cozen Percivall Angier; and yesterday I received the newes that Dr. Tom Pepys is dead, at Impington, for which I am but little sorry, not only because he would have been troublesome to us, but a shame to his family and profession; he was such a coxcomb.

20th. Up and to Westminster, where having spoke with Sir Ph. Warwicke, I to Jervas', and there I find them all in great disorder about Jane, her mistress telling me secretly that she was sworn not to reveal anything, but she was

[1] Lord Ashley lived for several years at Exeter House (on the north side of the Strand), on the site of the present Burleigh and Exeter Streets.

[2] This word is blotted, and the whole sentence is confused.

undone. At last for all her oath she told me that she had made herself sure to a fellow that comes to their house that can only fiddle for his living, and did keep him company, and had plainly told her that she was sure to him never to leave him for anybody else. Now they were this day contriving to get her presently to marry one Hayes that was there, and I did seem to persuade her to it. And at last got them to suffer me to advise privately, and by that means had her company and think I shall meet her next Sunday, but I do really doubt she will be undone in marrying this fellow. But I did give her my advice, and so let her do her pleasure, so I have now and then her company. Thence to the Swan at noon, and there sent for a bit of meat and dined, and had my *baiser* of the *fille* of the house there, but nothing *plus*. So took coach and to my Lady Sandwich's, and so to my bookseller's, and there took home Hooke's book of microscopy, a most excellent piece, and of which I am very proud. So home, and by and by again abroad with my wife about several businesses, and met at the New Exchange, and there to our trouble found our pretty Doll is gone away to live they say with her father in the country, but I doubt something worse. So homeward, in my way buying a hare and taking it home, which arose upon my discourse to-day with Mr. Batten, in Westminster Hall, who showed me my mistake that my hare's foote hath not the joynt to it; and assures me he never had his cholique since he carried it about him: and it is a strange thing how fancy works, for I no sooner almost handled his foote but my belly began to be loose and to break wind, and whereas I was in some pain yesterday and tother day and in fear of more to-day, I became very well, and so continue. At home to my office a while, and so to supper, read, and to cards, and to bed.

21st. At the office all the morning. Thence my Lord Brunker carried me as far as Mr. Povy's, and there I 'light and dined, meeting Mr. Sherwin, Creed, &c., there upon his accounts. After dinner they parted and Mr. Povy carried me to Somersett House, and there showed me the Queene-Mother's chamber and closett, most beautiful places for furniture and pictures; and so down the great stone stairs to the garden, and tried the brave echo upon the stairs; which continues a voice so long as the singing three notes, concords, one after another, they all three shall sound in consort together a good while most pleasantly. Thence to a Tangier Committee at White Hall, where I saw nothing ordered by judgment, but great heat and passion and faction now in behalf of my Lord Bellasses, and to the reproach of my Lord Tiviott, and dislike as it were of former proceedings. So away with Mr. Povy, he carrying me homeward to Mark Lane in his coach, a simple fellow I now find him, to his utter shame in his business of accounts, as none but a sorry foole would have discovered himself; and yet, in little, light, sorry things very cunning; yet, in the principal, the most ignorant man I ever met with in so great trust as he is. To my office till past 12, and then home to supper and to bed, being now mighty well, and truly I cannot but impute it to my fresh hare's foote. Before I went to bed I sat up till two o'clock in my chamber reading of Mr. Hooke's Microscopicall Observations, the most ingenious book that ever I read in my life.

22nd (Lord's day). Up, leaving my wife in bed, being sick of her months, and to church. Thence home, and in my wife's chamber dined very merry, discoursing, among other things, of a design I have come in my head this morning at church of making a match between Mrs. Betty Pickering and Mr. Hill,[1] my friend the merchant, that loves musique and comes to me a' Sundays, a most ingenious and sweet-natured and highly accomplished person. I know not how their fortunes may agree, but their disposition and merits are much of a sort, and persons, though different, yet equally, I think, acceptable. After dinner walked to Westminster, and after being at the Abbey and heard a good anthem well sung there, I as I had appointed to the Trumpett, there expecting when Jane Welsh should come, but anon comes a maid of the house to tell me that her mistress and master would not let her go forth, not knowing of my being here, but to keep her from her sweetheart. So being defeated, away by coach home, and there

[1] Thomas Hill married in the following year, and on July 14th, 1666, Pepys refers to the "young wife, and a blithe young woman she is."

spent the evening prettily in discourse with my wife and Mercer, and so to supper, prayers, and to bed.

23rd. Up, and with Sir W. Batten and Sir W. Pen to White Hall; but there finding the Duke gone to his lodgings at St. James's for alltogether, his Duchesse being ready to lie in, we to him, and there did our usual business. And here I met the great newes confirmed by the Duke's own relation, by a letter from Captain Allen. First, of our own loss of two ships, the Phœnix and Nonesuch, in the Bay of Gibraltar: then of his, and his seven ships with him, in the Bay of Cales, or thereabouts, fighting with the 34 Dutch Smyrna fleete; sinking the King Salamon, a ship worth a £150,000 or more, some say £200,000, and another; and taking of three merchant-ships. Two of our ships were disabled, by the Dutch unfortunately falling against their will against them; the Advice, Captain W. Poole, and Antelope, Captain Clerke. The Dutch men-of-war did little service. Captain Allen did receive many shots at distance before he would fire one gun, which he did not do till he come within pistol-shot of his enemy. The Spaniards on shore at Cales did stand laughing at the Dutch, to see them run away and flee to the shore, 34 or thereabouts, against eight Englishmen at most. I do purpose to get the whole relation, if I live, of Captain Allen himself. In our loss of the two ships in the Bay of Gibraltar, it is observable how the world do comment upon the misfortune of Captain Moone[1] of the Nonesuch (who did lose, in the same manner, the Satisfaction), as a person that hath ill-luck attending him; without considering that the whole fleete was ashore. Captain Allen led the way, and Captain Allen himself writes that all the masters of the fleete, old and young, were mistaken, and did carry their ships aground. But I think I heard the Duke say that Moone, being put into the Oxford, had in this conflict regained his credit, by sinking one and taking another. Captain Seale of the Milford hath done his part very well, in boarding the King Salamon, which held out half an hour after she was boarded; and his men kept her an hour after they did master her, and then she sunk, and drowned about

[1] Captain Robert Mohun, who eminently distinguished himself in the Dutch war, 1666.

17 of her men. Thence to Jervas's, my mind, God forgive me, running too much after some folly, but *elle* not being within I away by coach to the 'Change, and thence home to dinner. And finding Mrs. Bagwell waiting at the office after dinner, away she and I to a cabaret where she and I have eat before, and there I had her company *tout* and had *mon plaisir* of *elle*. But strange to see how a woman, notwithstanding her greatest pretences of love *a son mari* and religion, may be *vaincue*. Thence to the Court of the Turkey Company at Sir Andrew Rickard's to treat about carrying some men of ours to Tangier, and had there a very civil reception, though a denial of the thing as not practicable with them, and I think so too. So to my office a little and to Jervas's again, thinking *avoir rencontrais* Jane, *mais elle n'etait pas dedans*. So I back again and to my office, where I did with great content *ferais* a vow to mind my business, and *laisser aller les femmes* for a month, and am with all my heart glad to find myself able to come to so good a resolution, that thereby I may follow my business, which and my honour thereby lies a bleeding. So home to supper and to bed.

24th. Up and by coach to Westminster Hall and the Parliament House, and there spoke with Mr. Coventry and others about business and so back to the 'Change, where no news more than that the Dutch have, by consent of all the Provinces, voted no trade to be suffered for eighteen months, but that they apply themselves wholly to the warr.[1] And they say it is very true, but very strange, for we use to believe they cannot support themselves without trade. Thence home to dinner and then to the office, where all the afternoon, and at night till very late, and then home to

[1] This statement of a total prohibition of all trade, and for so long a period as eighteen months, by a government so essentially commercial as that of the United Provinces, seems extraordinary. The fact was, that when in the beginning of the year 1665 the States General saw that the war with England was become inevitable, they took several vigorous measures, and determined to equip a formidable fleet, and with a view to obtain a sufficient number of men to man it, prohibited all navigation, especially in the great and small fisheries as they were then called, and in the whale fishery. This measure appears to have resembled the embargoes so commonly resorted to in this country on similar occasions, rather than a total prohibition of trade. — B.

supper and bed, having a great cold, got on Sunday last, by sitting too long with my head bare, for Mercer to comb my hair and wash my eares.

25th. Up, and busy all the morning, dined at home upon a hare pye, very good meat, and so to my office again, and in the afternoon by coach to attend the Council at White Hall, but come too late, so back with Mr. Gifford, a merchant, and he and I to the Coffee-house, where I met Mr. Hill, and there he tells me that he is to be Assistant to the Secretary of the Prize Office (Sir Ellis Layton), which is to be held at Sir Richard Ford's, which, methinks, is but something low, but perhaps may bring him something considerable; but it makes me alter my opinion of his being so rich as to make a fortune for Mrs. Pickering. Thence home and visited Sir J. Minnes, who continues ill, but is something better; there he told me what a mad freaking fellow Sir Ellis Layton hath been, and is, and once at Antwerp was really mad. Thence to my office late, my cold troubling me, and having by squeezing myself in a coach hurt my testicles, but I hope will cease its pain without swelling. So home out of order, to supper and to bed.

26th. Lay, being in some pain, but not much, with my last night's bruise, but up and to my office, where busy all the morning, the like after dinner till very late, then home to supper and to bed. My wife mightily troubled with the tooth ake, and my cold not being gone yet, but my bruise yesterday goes away again, and it chiefly occasioned I think now from the sudden change of the weather from a frost to a great rayne on a sudden.

27th. Called up by Mr. Creed to discourse about some Tangier business, and he gone I made me ready and found Jane Welsh, Mr. Jervas his mayde, come to tell me that she was gone from her master, and is resolved to stick to this sweetheart of hers, one Harbing (a very sorry little fellow, and poor), which I did in a word or two endeavour to dissuade her from, but being unwilling to keep her long at my house, I sent her away and by and by followed her to the Exchange, and thence led her about down to the 3 Cranes, and there took boat for the Falcon, and at a house looking into the fields there took up and sat an hour or two talking and discoursing. . . . Thence having endeavoured to make her think of making herself happy by staying out her time with her master and other counsels, but she told me she could not do it, for it was her fortune to have this man, though she did believe it would be to her ruine, which is a strange, stupid thing, to a fellow of no kind of worth in the world and a beggar to boot. Thence away to boat again and landed her at the Three Cranes again, and I to the Bridge, and so home, and after shifting myself, being dirty, I to the 'Change, and thence to Mr. Povy's and there dined, and thence with him and Creed to my Lord Bellasses', and there debated a great while how to put things in order against his going, and so with my Lord in his coach to White Hall, and with him to my Lord Duke of Albemarle, finding him at cards. After a few dull words or two, I away to White Hall again, and there delivered a letter to the Duke of Yorke about our Navy business, and thence walked up and down in the gallery, talking with Mr. Slingsby, who is a very ingenious person, about the Mint and coynage of money. Among other things, he argues that there being £700,000 coined in the Rump time, and by all the Treasurers of that time, it being their opinion that the Rump money was in all payments, one with another, about a tenth part of all their money. Then, says he, to my question, the nearest guess we can make is, that the money passing up and down in business is £7,000,000. To another question of mine he made me fully understand that the old law of prohibiting bullion to be exported, is, and ever was a folly and an injury, rather than good. Arguing thus, that if the exportations exceed importations, then the balance must be brought home in money, which, when our merchants know cannot be carried out again, they will forbear to bring home in money, but let it lie abroad for trade, or keepe in foreign banks: or if our importations exceed our exportations, then, to keepe credit, the merchants will and must find ways of carrying out money by stealth, which is a most easy thing to do, and is every where done; and therefore the law against it signifies nothing in the world. Besides, that it is seen, that where money is free, there is great plenty; where it is restrained, as here, there is a great want, as in Spayne. These and many other fine discourses I had from him. Thence by coach home (to see Sir J. Minnes first), who is still sick, and I doubt worse than he seems to be. Mrs. Turner here took me into her closet, and there did give me a glass of most pure water, and shewed me her Rocke, which indeed is a very noble thing, but a very bawble. So away to my office, where late, busy, and then home to supper and to bed.

28th. Up and to my office, where all the morning, and then home to dinner, and after dinner abroad, walked to Paul's Churchyard, but my books not bound, which vexed me. So home to my office again, where very late about business, and so home to supper and to bed, my cold continuing in a great degree upon me still. This day I received a good sum of money due to me upon one score or another from Sir G. Carteret, among others to clear all my matters about Colours,[1] wherein a month or two since I was so embarrassed and I thank God I find myself to have got clear, by that commodity, £50 and something more; and earned it with dear pains and care and issuing of my owne money, and saved the King near £100 in it.

29th (Lord's day). Up and to my office, where all the morning, putting papers to rights which now grow upon my hands. At noon dined at home. All the afternoon at my business again. In the evening come Mr. Andrews and Hill, and we up to my chamber and there good musique, though my great cold made it the less pleasing to me. Then Mr. Hill (the other going away) and I to supper alone, my wife not appearing, our discourse upon the particular vain humours of Mr. Povy, which are very extraordinary indeed. After supper I to Sir W. Batten's, where I found him, Sir W. Pen, Sir J. Robinson, Sir R. Ford and Captain Cocke and Mr. Pen junior. Here a great deal of sorry disordered talk about the Trinity House men, their being exempted from land service. But, Lord! to see how void of method and sense their discourse was, and in what heat, insomuch as Sir R. Ford (who we judged, some of us, to be a little foxed) fell into very high terms with Sir W. Batten, and then with Captain Cocke. So

[1] Flags.

that I see that no man is wise at all times. Thence home to prayers and to bed.

30th. This is solemnly kept as a Fast[1] all over the City, but I kept my house, putting my closett to rights again, having lately put it out of order in removing my books and things in order to being made clean. At this all day, and at night to my office, there to do some business, and being late at it, comes Mercer to me, to tell me that my wife was in bed, and desired me to come home; for they hear, and have, night after night, lately heard noises over their head upon the leads. Now it is strange to think how, knowing that I have a great sum of money in my house, this puts me into a most mighty affright, that for more than two hours, I could not almost tell what to do or say, but feared this and that, and remembered that this evening I saw a woman and two men stand suspiciously in the entry, in the darke; I calling to them, they made me only this answer, the woman said that the men came to see her; but who she was I could not tell. The truth is, my house is mighty dangerous, having so many ways to be come to; and at my windows, over the stairs, to see who goes up and down; but, if I escape to-night, I will remedy it. God preserve us this night safe! So at almost two o'clock, I home to my house, and, in great fear to bed, thinking every running of a mouse really a thiefe; and so to sleep, very brokenly, all night long, and found all safe in the morning.

31st. Up and with Sir W. Batten to Westminster, where to speak at the House with my Lord Bellasses, and am cruelly vexed to see myself put upon businesses so uncertainly about getting ships for Tangier being ordered, a servile thing, almost every day. So to the 'Change, back by coach with Sir W. Batten, and thence to the Crowne, a taverne hard by, with Sir W. Rider and Cutler, where we alone, a very good dinner. Thence home to the office, and there all the afternoon late. The office being up, my wife sent for me, and what was it but to tell me how Jane carries herself, and I must put her away presently. But I did hear both sides and find my wife much in fault, and the grounds of all the difference is my wife's fondness of Tom,

[1] Kept in commemoration of the martyrdom of Charles I.

to the being displeased with all the house beside to defend the boy, which vexes me, but I will cure it. Many high words between my wife and I, but the wench shall go, but I will take a course with the boy, for I fear I have spoiled him already. Thence to the office, to my accounts, and there at once to ease my mind I have made myself debtor to Mr. Povy for the £117 5*s.* got with so much joy the last month, but seeing that it is not like to be kept without some trouble and question, I do even discharge my mind of it, and so if I come now to refund it, as I fear I shall, I shall now be ne'er a whit the poorer for it, though yet it is some trouble to me to be poorer by such a sum than I thought myself a month since. But, however, a quiet mind and to be sure of my owne is worth all. The Lord be praised for what I have, which is this month come down to £1,257. I staid up about my accounts till almost two in the morning.

February 1st. Lay long in bed, which made me, going by coach to St. James's by appointment to have attended the Duke of Yorke and my Lord Bellasses, lose the hopes of my getting something by the hire of a ship to carry men to Tangier. But, however, according to the order of the Duke this morning, I did go to the 'Change, and there after great pains did light of a business with Mr. Gifford and Hubland[1] [Houblon] for bringing me as much as I hoped for, which I have at large expressed in my stating the case of the "King's Fisher," which is the ship that I have hired, and got the Duke of Yorke's agreement this after-

[1] James Houblon, an eminent London merchant, remarkable for his piety and plainness. Two of his sons rose to great wealth, and became knights and aldermen. Sir James Houblon served in parliament for his native city. Sir John was Lord Mayor in 1695, and at the same time a Lord of the Admiralty and Governor of the Bank. The best account of the father is to be found in the subjoined epitaph, said to be written by Pepys.

Jacobus Houblon,
Londinas Petri filius,
Ob fidem Flandriâ exulantis:
Ex C. Nepotibus habuit LXX superstites:
Filios V. videns mercatores florentissimos:
Ipse Londinensis Bursæ Pater
Piissimè obiit Nonagenarius,
A.D. MDCLXXXII. — B.

noon after much pains and not eating a bit of bread till about 4 o'clock. Going home I put in to an ordinary by Temple Barr and there with my boy Tom eat a pullet, and thence home to the office, being still angry with my wife for yesterday's foolery. After a good while at the office, I with the boy to the Sun behind the Exchange, by agreement with Mr. Young the flag-maker, and there was met by Mr. Hill, Andrews, and Mr. Hubland, a pretty serious man. Here two very pretty savoury dishes and good discourse. After supper a song, or three or four (I having to that purpose carried Lawes's book), and staying here till 12 o'clock got the watch to light me home, and in a continued discontent to bed. After being in bed, my people come and say there is a great stinke of burning, but no smoake. We called up Sir J. Minnes's and Sir W. Batten's people, and Griffin, and the people at the madhouse, but nothing could be found to give occasion to it. At this trouble we were till past three o'clock, and then the stinke ceasing, I to sleep, and my people to bed, and lay very long in the morning.

2nd. Then up and to my office, where till noon and then to the 'Change, and at the Coffee-house with Gifford, Hubland, the Master of the ship, and I read over and approved a charter-party for carrying goods for Tangier, wherein I hope to get some money. Thence home, my head akeing for want of rest and too much business. So to the office. At night comes Povy, and he and I to Mrs. Bland's to discourse about my serving her to helpe her to a good passage for Tangier. Here I heard her kinswoman sing 3 or 4 very fine songs and in good manner, and then home and to supper. My cook mayd Jane and her mistresse parted, and she went away this day. I vexed to myself, but was resolved to have no more trouble, and so after supper to my office and then to bed.

3rd. Up, and walked with my boy (whom, because of my wife's making him idle, I dare not leave at home) walked first to Salsbury court, there to excuse my not being at home at dinner to Mrs. Turner, who I perceive is vexed, because I do not serve her in something against the great feasting[1] for her husband's Reading in helping her

[1] On his appointment as Reader in Law. See March 3rd, 1664-65.

to some good penn'eths, but I care not. She was dressing herself by the fire in her chamber, and there took occasion to show me her leg, which indeed is the finest I ever saw, and she not a little proud of it. Thence to my Lord Bellasses; thence to Mr. Povy's, and so up and down at that end of the town about several businesses, it being a brave frosty day and good walking. So back again on foot to the 'Change, in my way taking my books from binding from my bookseller's. My bill for the rebinding of some old books to make them suit with my study, cost me, besides other new books in the same bill, £3; but it will be very handsome. At the 'Change did several businesses, and here I hear that newes is come from Deale, that the same day my Lord Sandwich sailed thence with the fleete, that evening some Dutch men of warr were seen on the back side of the Goodwin, and, by all conjecture, must be seen by my Lord's fleete; which, if so, they must engage. Thence, being invited, to my uncle Wight's, where the Wights all dined; and, among the others, pretty Mrs. Margaret, who indeed is a very pretty lady; and though by my vowe it costs me 12*d.* a kiss after the first, yet I did adventure upon a couple. So home, and among other letters found one from Jane, that is newly gone, telling me how her mistress won't pay her her Quarter's wages, and withal tells me how her mistress will have the boy sit 3 or 4 hours together in the dark telling of stories, but speaks of nothing but only her indiscretion in undervaluing herself to do it, but I will remedy that, but am vexed she should get some body to write so much because of making it publique. Then took coach and to visit my Lady Sandwich, where she discoursed largely to me her opinion of a match, if it could be thought fit by my Lord, for my Lady Jemimah, with Sir G. Carteret's eldest son; but I doubt he hath yet no settled estate in land. But I will inform myself, and give her my opinion. Then Mrs. Pickering (after private discourse ended, we going into the other room) did, at my Lady's command, tell me the manner of a masquerade[1] before the King and

[1] The masquerade at Court took place on the 2nd, and is referred to by Evelyn, who was present, in his Diary. Some amusing incidents connected with the entertainment are related in the "Grammont Memoirs" (chapter vii.).

Court the other day. Where six women (my Lady Castlemayne and Duchesse of Monmouth being two of them) and six men (the Duke of Monmouth and Lord Arran[1] and Monsieur Blanfort,[2] being three of them) in vizards, but most rich and antique dresses, did dance admirably and most gloriously. God give us cause to continue the mirthe! So home, and after awhile at my office to supper and to bed.

4th. Lay long in bed discoursing with my wife about her mayds, which by Jane's going away in discontent and against my opinion do make some trouble between my wife and me. But these are but foolish troubles and so not to be set to heart, yet it do disturb me mightily these things. To my office, and there all the morning. At noon being invited, I to the Sun behind the 'Change, to dinner to my Lord Belasses, where a great deal of discourse with him, and some good, among others at table he told us a very handsome passage of the King's sending him his message about holding out the town of Newarke, of which he was then governor for the King. This message he sent in a slugg-bullet, being writ in cypher, and wrapped up in lead and swallowed. So the messenger come to my Lord and told him he had a message from the King but it was yet in his belly; so they did give him some physique, and out it come. This was a month before the King's flying to the Scotts; and therein he told him that at such a day, being the 3d or 6th of May, he should hear of his being come to the Scotts, being assured by the King of France that in coming to them he should be used with all the liberty, honour, and safety, that could be desired. And at the just day he did come to the Scotts. He told us another odd passage: how the King having newly put out Prince Rupert

[1] Richard Butler, second surviving son of James, Duke of Ormond, born July 15th, 1639. He was created Earl of Arran in Ireland in 1662, when his father was appointed Lord Lieutenant of Ireland, and Baron Butler of Weston in the peerage of England in 1673. He died January 25th, 1685–86, and was buried in Westminster Abbey.

[2] Louis de Duras, Marquis de Blanquefort in France, born 1638, naturalized in England, October, 1665, in which year he was a volunteer with the English fleet. Created Baron Duras of Holdenby, January, 1672–73; and succeeded his father-in-law, George Sondes, as Earl of Feversham, in 1677; K.G., July 30th, 1685; Master of St. Catherine's Hospital, 1698; and died April 19th, 1709.

of his generallshipp, upon some miscarriage at Bristoll, and Sir Richard Willis[1] of his governorship of Newarke, at the entreaty of the gentry of the County, and put in my Lord Bellasses, the great officers of the King's army mutinyed, and come in that manner with swords drawn, into the market-place of the towne where the King was; which the King hearing, says, "I must to horse." And there himself personally, when every body expected they should have been opposed, the King come, and cried to the head of the mutineers, which was Prince Rupert, "Nephew, I command you to be gone." So the Prince, in all his fury and discontent, withdrew, and his company scattered, which they say was the greatest piece of mutiny in the world. Thence after dinner home to my office, and in the evening was sent to by Jane that I would give her her wages. So I sent for my wife to my office, and told her that rather than be talked on I would give her all her wages for this Quarter coming on, though two months is behind, which vexed my wife, and we begun to be angry, but I took myself up and sent her away, but was cruelly vexed in my mind that all my trouble in this world almost should arise from my disorders in my family and the indiscretion of a wife that brings me nothing almost (besides a comely person) but only trouble and discontent. She gone I late at my business, and then home to supper and to bed.

5th (Lord's day). Lay in bed most of the morning, then up and down to my chamber, among my new books, which is now a pleasant sight to me to see my whole study almost of one binding. So to dinner, and all the afternoon with W. Hewer at my office endorsing of papers there, my business having got before me much of late. In the evening comes to see me Mr. Sheply, lately come out of the country, who goes away again to-morrow, a good and a very kind man to me. There come also Mr. Andrews and Hill, and we sang very pleasantly; and so, they being gone, I and my wife to supper, and to prayers and bed.

6th. Up with Sir J. Minnes and Sir W. Pen to St.

[1] Sir Richard Willis, the betrayer of the Royalists, was one of the "Sealed Knot." When the Restoration had become a certainty, he wrote to Clarendon imploring him to intercede for him with the king (see Lister's "Life of Clarendon," vol. iii., p. 87).

James's, but the Duke is gone abroad. So to White Hall to him, and there I spoke with him, and so to Westminster, did a little business, and then home to the 'Change, where also I did some business, and went off and ended my contract with the "Kingfisher"[1] hired for Tangier, and I hope to get something by it. Thence home to dinner, and visited Sir W. Batten, who is sick again, worse than he was, and I am apt to think is very ill. So to my office, and among other things with Sir W. Warren 4 hours or more till very late, talking of one thing or another, and have concluded a firm league with him in all just ways to serve him and myself all I can, and I think he will be a most usefull and thankfull man to me. So home to supper and to bed. This being one of the coldest days, all say, they ever felt in England; and I this day, under great apprehensions of getting an ague from my putting a suit on that hath lain by without arying a great while, and I pray God it do not do me hurte.

7th. Up and to my office, where busy all the morning, and at home to dinner. It being Shrove Tuesday, had some very good fritters. All the afternoon and evening at the office, and at night home to supper and to bed. This day, Sir W. Batten, who hath been sicke four or five days, is now very bad, so as people begin to fear his death; and I am at a loss whether it will be better for me to have him die, because he is a bad man, or live, for fear a worse should come.

8th. Up and by coach to my Lord Peterborough's, where anon my Lord Ashly and Sir Thomas Ingram met, and Povy about his accounts, who is one of the most unhappy accountants that ever I knew in all my life, and one that if I were clear in reference to my bill of £117 he should be hanged before I would ever have to do with him, and as he understands nothing of his business himself, so he hath not one about him that do. Here late till I was weary, having business elsewhere, and thence home by coach, and after dinner did several businesses and very late at my office, and so home to supper and to bed.

[1] On May 10th, 1665, Symond Emison wrote to the Navy Commissioners, sending a list of twelve men on board the "Kingfisher" at Harwich ("Calendar of State Papers," Domestic, 1664–65, p. 359).

9th. Up and to my office, where all the morning very busy. At noon home to dinner, and then to my office again, where Sir William Petty come, among other things to tell me that Mr. Barlow[1] is dead; for which, God knows my heart, I could be as sorry as is possible for one to be for a stranger, by whose death he gets £100 per annum, he being a worthy, honest man; but after having considered that when I come to consider the providence of God by this means unexpectedly to give me £100 a year more in my estate, I have cause to bless God, and do it from the bottom of my heart. So home late at night, after twelve o'clock, and so to bed.

10th. Up and abroad to Paul's Churchyard, there to see the last of my books new bound: among others, my "Court of King James,"[2] and "The Rise and Fall of the Family of the Stewarts;"[3] and much pleased I am now with my study; it being, methinks, a beautifull sight. Thence (in Mr. Grey's coach, who took me up), to Westminster, where I heard that yesterday the King met the Houses to pass the great bill for the £2,500,000. After doing a little business I home, where Mr. Moore dined with me, and evened our reckonings on my Lord Sandwich's bond to me for principal and interest. So that now on both there is remaining due to me £257 7*s*., and I bless God it is no more. So all the afternoon at my office, and late home to supper, prayers, and to bed.

11th. Up and to my office, where all the morning. At noon to 'Change by coach with my Lord Brunkard, and thence after doing much business home to dinner, and so

[1] Thomas Barlow, Pepys's predecessor as Clerk of the Acts, to whom he paid part of the salary. Barlow held the office jointly with Dennis Fleming.

[2] "The Court and Character of King James, written and taken by Sir Anthony Weldon, being an eye and eare witnesse," was published in 1650, and reprinted in 1651 under the title of "Truth brought to Light." Weldon's book was answered in a work entitled "Aulicus Coquinariæ." Both the original book and the answer were reprinted in "The Secret History of the Court of King James," Edinburgh, 1811, two vols. (edited by Sir Walter Scott).

[3] "The Divine Catastrophe of the kingly family of the House of Stuarts; or a short History of the Rise, Reign and Ruine thereof." By Sir Edward Peyton. London, 1652. Reprinted in "The Secret History of the Court of King James," 1811.

to my office all the afternoon till past 12 at night very busy. So home to bed.

12th (Lord's day). Up and to church to St. Lawrence[1] to hear Dr. Wilkins, the great scholar, for curiosity, I having never heard him: but was not satisfied with him at all, only a gentleman sat in the pew I by chance sat in, that sang most excellently, and afterward I found by his face that he had been a Paul's scholler, but know not his name, and I was also well pleased with the church, it being a very fine church. So home to dinner, and then to my office all the afternoon doing of business, and in the evening comes Mr. Hill (but no Andrews) and we spent the evening very finely, singing, supping and discoursing. Then to prayers and to bed.

13th. Up and to St. James's, did our usual business before the Duke. Thence I to Westminster and by water (taking Mr. Stapely the rope-maker by the way), to his rope-ground and to Limehouse, there to see the manner of stoves and did excellently inform myself therein, and coming home did go on board Sir W. Petty's "Experiment," which is a brave roomy vessel, and I hope may do well. So went on shore to a Dutch [house] to drink some mum, and there light upon some Dutchmen, with whom we had good discourse touching stoveing[2] and making of cables. But to see how despicably they speak of us for our using so many hands more to do anything than they do, they closing a cable with 20, that we use 60 men upon. Thence home and eat something, and then to my office, where very late, and then to supper and to bed. Captain Stokes, it seems, is at last dead at Portsmouth.

14th (St. Valentine). This morning comes betimes Dicke Pen,[3] to be my wife's Valentine, and come to our

[1] St. Lawrence Jewry. Dr. John Wilkins was vicar from 1662 to 1668, when he was appointed Bishop of Chester. He died November 19th, 1672, in Chancery Lane, and was buried, December 12th, in the church of St. Lawrence, under the north wall of the chancel. At this time the great Tillotson was lecturer at this church. Bishop Wilkins died at the house of Tillotson, who married his stepdaughter.

[2] Stoveing, in sail-making, is the heating of the bolt-ropes, so as to make them pliable. — B.

[3] Richard Penn, second son to Sir William Penn, who died in April, 1673, and was buried at Walthamstow.

bedside. By the same token, I had him brought to my side, thinking to have made him kiss me; but he perceived me, and would not; so went to his Valentine: a notable, stout, witty boy. I up about business, and, opening the door, there was Bagwell's wife, with whom I talked afterwards, and she had the confidence to say she came with a hope to be time enough to be my Valentine, and so indeed she did, but my oath preserved me from loosing any time with her, and so I and my boy abroad by coach to Westminster, where did two or three businesses, and then home to the 'Change, and did much business there. My Lord Sandwich is, it seems, with his fleete at Alborough Bay. So home to dinner and then to the office, where till 12 almost at night, and then home to supper and to bed.

15th. Up and to my office, where busy all the morning. At noon with Creed to dinner to Trinity-house, where a very good dinner among the old sokers, where an extraordinary discourse of the manner of the loss of the "Royall Oake"[1] coming home from Bantam, upon the rocks of Scilly, many passages therein very extraordinary, and if I can I will get it in writing. Thence with Creed to Gresham College, where I had been by Mr. Povy the last week proposed to be admitted a member;[2] and was this day admitted, by signing a book and being taken by the hand by the President, my Lord Brunkard, and some words of admittance said to me. But it is a most acceptable thing to hear their discourse, and see their experiments; which were this day upon the nature of fire, and how it goes out in a place where the ayre is not free, and sooner out where the ayre is exhausted, which they showed by an engine on purpose. After this being done, they to the Crowne Taverne, behind the 'Change, and there my Lord and most of the company to a club supper; Sir P. Neale,[3] Sir R. Mur-

[1] For relation of the loss of the "Royal Oak," see Rawlinson MSS., A. 195, fol. 180 (Bodleian Library). — B.

[2] According to the minutes of the Royal Society for February 15th, 1664-65, "Mr. Pepys was unanimously elected and admitted." Notes of the experiments shown by Hooke and Boyle are given in Birch's "History of the Royal Society," vol. ii., p. 15.

[3] Sir Paul Neile, of White Waltham, Berks, eldest son to Richard Neile, Archbishop of York (see March 2nd, 1660-61).

rey,[1] Dr. Clerke, Dr. Whistler,[2] Dr. Goddard,[3] and others of most eminent worth. Above all, Mr. Boyle to-day was at the meeting, and above him Mr. Hooke,[4] who is the most, and promises the least, of any man in the world that ever I saw. Here excellent discourse till ten at night, and then home, and to Sir W. Batten's, where I hear that Sir Thos. Harvy[5] intends to put Mr. Turner out of his house and come in himself, which will be very hard to them, and though I love him not, yet for his family's sake I pity him. So home and to bed.

16th. Up, and with Mr. Andrews to White Hall, where a Committee of Tangier, and there I did our victuallers' business for some more money, out of which I hope to get a little, of which I was glad; but, Lord! to see to what a degree of contempt, nay, scorn, Mr. Povy, through his prodigious folly, hath brought himself in his accounts, that if he be not a man of a great interest, he will be kicked out of his employment for a foole, is very strange, and that most deservedly that ever man was, for never any man, that understands accounts so little, ever went through so much, and yet goes through it with the greatest shame and yet with confidence that ever I saw man in my life. God deliver me in my owne business of my bill out of his hands and if ever I foul my fingers with him again let me suffer

[1] Sir Robert Moray, one of the founders of the Royal Society, and President before the charter was obtained. He was made a Privy Councillor for Scotland after the Restoration.

[2] Daniel Whistler, Fellow of Merton College, Oxford, took the degree of M.D. at Leyden, 1645; and after practising in London, went as physician to the embassy, with Bulstrode Whitlock, into Sweden. On his return he became Fellow, and at length President, of the College of Physicians. He was Professor of Geometry at Gresham College, 1648-57, and died May 11th, 1684.

[3] Jonathan Goddard, M.D., F.R.S., born at Greenwich about 1617. He had been physician to Cromwell, who appointed him one of the Council of State. Professor of Physic at Gresham College, 1655. Member of the first Council of the Royal Society. Died March 24th, 1674-75.

[4] Dr. Robert Hooke, Professor of Geometry at Gresham College, and Curator of the Experiments to the Royal Society, of which he was one of the earliest and most distinguished members. He died March 3rd, 1702-3.

[5] Sir Thomas Harvey was appointed Extra Commissioner of the Navy in January, 1664-65, and succeeded Lord Berkeley.

for it! Back to the 'Change, and thence home to dinner, where Mrs. Hunt dined with me, and poor Mrs. Batters,[1] who brought her little daughter with her, and a letter from her husband, wherein, as a token, the foole presents me very seriously with his daughter for me to take the charge of bringing up for him, and to make my owne. But I took no notice to her at all of the substance of the letter, but fell to discourse, and so went away to the office, where all the afternoon till almost one in the morning, and then home to bed.

17th. Up, and it being bitter cold, and frost and snow, which I had thought had quite left us, I by coach to Povy's, where he told me, as I knew already, how he was handled the other day, and is still, by my Lord Barkeley, and among other things tells me, what I did not know, how my Lord Barkeley will say openly, that he hath fought more set fields[2] than any man in England hath done. I did my business with him, which was to get a little sum of money paid, and so home with Mr. Andrews, who met me there, and there to the office. At noon home and there found Lewellin, which vexed me out of my old jealous humour. So to my office, where till 12 at night, being only a little while at noon at Sir W. Batten's to see him, and had some high words with Sir J. Minnes about Sir W. Warren, he calling him cheating knave, but I cooled him, and at night to Sir W. Pen's, he being to go to Chatham to-morrow. So home to supper and to bed.

18th. Up, and to the office, where sat all the morning; at noon to the 'Change, and thence to the Royall Oake taverne in Lumbard Streete, where Sir William Petty and the owners of the double-bottomed boat (the Experiment) did entertain my Lord Brunkard, Sir R. Murrey, myself, and others, with marrow bones and a chine of beefe of the victuals they have made for this ship; and excellent company and good discourse: but, above all, I do value Sir W. Petty. Thence home; and took my Lord Sandwich's draught of the harbour of Portsmouth down to Ratcliffe, to one Burston, to make a plate for the King, and another for

[1] Apparently the wife of Christopher Battars, gunner of the "Santa Maria."

[2] Battles or actions.

the Duke, and another for himself; which will be very neat. So home, and till almost one o'clock in the morning at my office, and then home to supper and to bed. My Lord Sandwich, and his fleete of twenty-five ships in the Downes, returned from cruising, but could not meet with any Dutchmen.

19th. Lay in bed, it being Lord's day, all the morning talking with my wife, sometimes pleased, sometimes displeased, and then up and to dinner. All the afternoon also at home, and Sir W. Batten's, and in the evening comes Mr. Andrews, and we sung together, and then to supper, he not staying, and at supper hearing by accident of my mayds their letting in a rogueing Scotch woman that haunts the office, to helpe them to washe and scoure in our house, and that very lately, I fell mightily out, and made my wife, to the disturbance of the house and neighbours, to beat our little girle, and then we shut her down into the cellar, and there she lay all night. So we to bed.

20th. Up, and with Sir J. Minnes to attend the Duke, and then we back again and rode into the beginning of my Lord Chancellor's new house,[1] near St. James's; which common people have already called Dunkirke-house, from their opinion of his having a good bribe for the selling of that towne. And very noble I believe it will be. Near that is my Lord Barkeley[2] beginning another on one side, and Sir J. Denham on the other. Thence I to the House of Lords and spoke with my Lord Bellasses, and so to the 'Change, and there did business, and so to the Sun taverne, having in the morning had some high words with Sir J. Lawson about his sending of some bayled goods to Tangier,

[1] "Oct. 8, 1667. The Lord Chancellor's House, called 'Clarendon House,' is now almost finished. The chapel is quite completed, and was consecrated, when His Honour gave a rich Bible, the cover of which was of silver, and the Book of Common Prayer with the same covering, together with bowls and other vessels for the Sacrament, to the value of £1,000. A Sermon was preached that day by a Bishop." — Rugge's *Diurnal*. — B.

[2] Clarendon House was situated where Albemarle Street now stands; on the west side was Berkeley House, where Devonshire House now is. The house on the east side, said to have been built by Sir J. Denham, was Burlington House. These three houses were the first buildings in this part of Piccadilly.

wherein the truth is I did not favour him, but being conscious that some of my profits may come out by some words that fell from him, and to be quiet, I have accommodated it. Here we dined merry; but my club and the rest come to 7*s.* 6*d.*, which was too much. Thence to the office, and there found Bagwell's wife, whom I directed to go home, and I would do her business, which was to write a letter to my Lord Sandwich for her husband's advance into a better ship as there should be occasion. Which I did, and by and by did go down by water to Deptford, and then down further, and so landed at the lower end of the town, and it being dark *entrer en la maison de la femme de Bagwell*, and there had *sa compagnie*, though with a great deal of difficulty, *néanmoins en fin j'avais ma volonté d'elle*, and being sated therewith, I walked home to Redriffe, it being now near nine o'clock, and there I did drink some strong waters and eat some bread and cheese, and so home. Where at my office my wife comes and tells me that she hath hired a chamber mayde, one of the prettiest maydes that ever she saw in her life, and that she is really jealous of me for her, but hath ventured to hire her from month to month, but I think she means merrily. So to supper and to bed.

21st. Up, and to the office (having a mighty pain in my forefinger of my left hand, from a strain that it received last night) in struggling *avec la femme que je* mentioned yesterday, where busy till noon, and then my wife being busy in going with her woman to a hot-house to bathe herself, after her long being within doors in the dirt, so that she now pretends to a resolution of being hereafter very clean. How long it will hold I can guess. I dined with Sir W. Batten and my Lady, they being now a'days very fond of me. So to the 'Change, and off of the 'Change with Mr. Wayth to a cook's shop, and there dined again for discourse with him about Hamaccos[1] and the abuse now practised in tickets, and more like every day to be. Also of the great profit Mr. Fen[2] makes of his place, he being, though he demands but ½ per cent. of all he pays, and that is easily computed,

[1] Or hammock-battens: cleats or battens nailed to the sides of a vessel's beams, from which to suspend the seamen's hammocks.

[2] Paymaster John Fenn, with whom Pepys was afterwards so familiar as to call him Jack.

but very little pleased with any man that gives him no more. So to the office, and after office my Lord Brunkerd carried me to Lincolne's Inne Fields, and there I with my Lady Sandwich (good lady) talking of innocent discourse of good housewifery and husbands for her daughters, and the luxury and looseness of the times and other such things till past 10 o'clock at night, and so by coach home, where a little at my office, and so to supper and to bed. My Lady tells me how my Lord Castlemayne is coming over from France, and is believed will be made friends with his Lady again. What mad freaks the Mayds of Honour at Court have: that Mrs. Jenings,[1] one of the Duchesse's mayds, the other day dressed herself like an orange wench, and went up and down and cried oranges; till falling down, or by such accident, though in the evening, her fine shoes were discerned, and she put to a great deale of shame;[2] that such as these tricks being ordinary, and worse among them, thereby few will venture upon them for wives: my Lady Castlemayne will in merriment say that her daughter (not above a year old or two) will be the first mayde in the Court that will be married. This day my Lord Sandwich writ me word from the Downes, that he is like to be in towne this week.

22nd. Lay last night alone, my wife after her bathinge lying alone in another bed. So cold all night. Up and to the office, where busy all the morning. At noon at the 'Change, busy; where great talk of a Dutch ship in the North put on shore, and taken by a troop of horse. Home to dinner and Creed with me. Thence to Gresham College,[3] where very noble discourse, and thence home busy till past 12 at night, and then home to supper and to bed.

[1] Frances Jenyns, eldest daughter of Richard Jenyns, of Holywell House, St. Albans, born in 1648, maid of honour to Anne, Duchess of York, married 1st, George Hamilton, second son of Sir George Hamilton and brother of Count Hamilton (author of the "Memoirs of Grammont"); he was killed in battle, June, 1676; and 2ndly, Colonel Richard Talbot, created Earl of Tyrconnel in 1685. In 1689 the unacknowledged dukedom of Tyrconnel was conferred on him. He died August 14th, 1691. She died at Dublin, March 6th, 1730–31.

[2] This adventure is related in the "Grammont Memoirs," chap. x.

[3] Philip Carteret was elected a Fellow at this meeting. Hooke and Boyle exhibited several experiments.

Mrs. Bland come this night to take leave of me and my wife, going to Tangier.

23rd. This day, by the blessing of Almighty God, I have lived thirty-two years in the world, and am in the best degree of health at this minute that I have been almost in my life time, and at this time in the best condition of estate that ever I was in — the Lord make me thankfull. Up, and to the office, where busy all the morning. At noon to the 'Change, where I hear the most horrid and astonishing newes that ever was yet told in my memory, that De Ruyter with his fleete in Guinny hath proceeded to the taking of whatever we have, forts, goods, ships, and men, and tied our men back to back, and thrown them all into the sea, even women and children also. This a Swede or Hamburgher is come into the River and tells that he saw the thing done.[1] But, Lord! to see the consternation all our merchants are in is observable, and with what fury and revenge they discourse of it. But I fear it will like other things in a few days cool among us. But that which I fear most is the reason why he that was so kind to our men at first should afterward, having let them go, be so cruel when he went further. What I fear is that there he was informed (which he was not before) of some of Holmes's dealings with his countrymen, and so was moved to this fury. God grant it be not so! But a more dishonourable thing was never suffered by Englishmen, nor a more barbarous done by man, as this by them to us. Home to dinner, and then to the office, where we sat all the afternoon, and then at night to take my finall leave of Mrs. Bland, who sets out to-morrow for Tangier, and then I back to my office till past 12, and so home to supper and to bed.

24th. Up, and to my office, where all the morning upon advising again with some fishermen and the water bayliffe of the City, by Mr. Coventry's direction, touching the protections which are desired for the fishermen upon the River, and I am glad of the occasion to make me understand

[1] Similar reports of the cruelty of the English to the Dutch in Guinea were credited in Holland, and were related by Downing in a letter to Clarendon from the Hague, dated April 14th, 1665 (Lister's "Life of Clarendon," vol. iii., p. 374).

something of it. At noon home to dinner, and all the afternoon till 9 at night in my chamber, and Mr. Hater with me (to prevent being disturbed at the office), to perfect my contract book, which, for want of time, hath a long time lain without being entered in as I used to do from month to month. Then to my office, where till almost 12, and so home to bed.

25th. Up, and to the office, where all the morning. At noon to the 'Change; where just before I come, the Swede that had told the King and the Duke so boldly this great lie of the Dutch flinging our men back to back into the sea at Guinny, so particularly, and readily, and confidently, was whipt round the 'Change: he confessing it a lie, and that he did it in hopes to get something. It is said the Judges, upon demand, did give it their opinion that the law would judge him to be whipt, to lose his eares, or to have his nose slit: but I do not hear that anything more is to be done to him. They say he is delivered over to the Dutch Embassador to do what he pleased with him. But the world do think that there is some design on one side or other, either of the Dutch or French, for it is not likely a fellow would invent such a lie to get money whereas he might have hoped for a better reward by telling something in behalf of us to please us. Thence to the Sun taverne, and there dined with Sir W. Warren and Mr. Gifford, the merchant: and I hear how Nich. Colborne, that lately lived and got a great estate there, is gone to live like a prince in the country, and that this Wadlow,[1] that did the like at the Devil by St. Dunstane's, did go into the country, and there spent almost all he had got, and hath now choused this Colborne out of his house, that he might come to his old trade again. But, Lord! to see how full the house is, no room for any company almost to come into it. Thence home to the office, where dispatched much business; at night late home, and to clean myself with warm water; my wife will have me, because she do herself, and so to bed.

26th (Sunday). Up and to church, and so home to dinner, and after dinner to my office, and there busy all the afternoon, till in the evening comes Mr. Andrews and Hill,

[1] See note, April 22nd, 1661.

and so home and to singing. Hill staid and supped with me, and very good discourse of Italy, where he was, which is always to me very agreeable. After supper, he gone, we to prayers and to bed.

27th. Up and to St. James's, where we attended the Duke as usual. This morning I was much surprized and troubled with a letter from Mrs. Bland, that she is left behind, and much trouble it cost me this day to find out some way to carry her after the ships to Plymouth, but at last I hope I have done it. At noon to the 'Change to inquire what wages the Dutch give in their men-of-warr at this day, and I hear for certain they give but twelve guilders at most, which is not full 24*s*., a thing I wonder at. At home to dinner, and then in Sir J. Minnes's coach, my wife and I with him, and also Mercer, abroad, he and I to White Hall, and he would have his coach to wait upon my wife on her visits, it being the first time my wife hath been out of doors (but the other day to bathe her) several weeks. We to a Committee of the Council to discourse concerning pressing of men; but, Lord! how they meet; never sit down: one comes, now another goes, then comes another; one complaining that nothing is done, another swearing that he hath been there these two hours and nobody come. At last it come to this, my Lord Annesly, says he, "I think we must be forced to get the King to come to every committee; for I do not see that we do any thing at any time but when he is here." And I believe he said the truth: and very constant he is at the council table on council-days; which his predecessors, it seems, very rarely did; but thus I perceive the greatest affair in the world at this day is likely to be managed by us. But to hear how my Lord Barkeley and others of them do cry up the discipline of the late times here, and in the former Dutch warr is strange, wishing with all their hearts that the business of religion were not so severely carried on as to discourage the sober people to come among us, and wishing that the same law and severity were used against drunkennesse as there was then, saying that our evil living will call the hand of God upon us again. Thence to walk alone a good while in St. James's Parke with Mr. Coventry, who I perceive is grown a little melancholy and displeased to see things go as they do so carelessly. Thence I by coach to Ratcliffe highway, to the plate-maker's, and he has begun my Lord Sandwich's plate very neatly, and so back again. Coming back I met Colonell Atkins, who in other discourse did offer to give me a piece to receive of me 20 when he proves the late news of the Dutch, their drowning our men, at Guinny, and the truth is I find the generality of the world to fear that there is something of truth in it, and I do fear it too. Thence back by coach to Sir Philip Warwicke's; and there he did contract with me a kind of friendship and freedom of communication, wherein he assures me to make me understand the whole business of the Treasurer's business of the Navy, that I shall know as well as Sir G. Carteret what money he hath; and will needs have me come to him sometimes, or he meet me, to discourse of things tending to the serving the King: and I am mighty proud and happy in becoming so known to such a man. And I hope shall pursue it. Thence back home to the office a little tired and out of order, and then to supper and to bed.

28th. At the office all the morning. At noon dined at home. After dinner my wife and I to my Lady Batten's, it being the first time my wife hath been there, I think, these two years, but I had a mind in part to take away the strangenesse, and so we did, and all very quiett and kind. Come home, I to the taking my wife's kitchen accounts at the latter end of the month, and there find 7*s.* wanting, which did occasion a very high falling out between us, I indeed too angrily insisting upon so poor a thing, and did give her very provoking high words, calling her beggar, and reproaching her friends, which she took very stomachfully and reproached me justly with mine, and I confess, being myself, I cannot see what she could have done less. I find she is very cunning, and when she least shews it hath her wit at work; but it is an ill one, though I think not so bad but with good usage I might well bear with it, and the truth is I do find that my being over-solicitous and jealous and froward and ready to reproach her do make her worse. However, I find that now and then a little difference do no hurte, but too much of it will make her know her force too much. We parted after many high words very angry, and I to my office to my month's accounts, and find myself worth

£1,270, for which the Lord God be praised! So at almost 2 o'clock in the morning I home to supper and to bed, and so ends this month, with great expectation of the Hollanders coming forth, who are, it seems, very high and rather more ready than we. God give a good issue to it!

March 1st. Up, and this day being the day that by a promise, a great while ago, made to my wife, I was to give her £20 to lay out in clothes against Easter, she did, notwithstanding last night's falling out, come to peace with me and I with her, but did boggle mightily at the parting with my money, but at last did give it her, and then she abroad to buy her things, and I to my office, where busy all the morning. At noon I to dinner at Trinity House, and thence to Gresham College, where Mr. Hooke[1] read a second very curious lecture about the late Comett; among other things proving very probably that this is the very same Comet, that appeared before in the year 1618, and that in such a time probably it will appear again, which is a very new opinion; but all will be in print. Then to the meeting, where Sir G. Carteret's two sons, his owne, and Sir N. Slaning,[2] were admitted of the society: and this day I did pay my admission money, 40*s*. to the society. Here was very fine discourses and experiments, but I do lacke philosophy enough to understand them, and so cannot remember them. Among others, a very particular account of the making of the several sorts of bread in France, which is accounted the best place for bread in the world.[3] So home, where

[1] Hooke's lecture was probably delivered by him as Professor at Gresham College. Mr. J. R. Hind, F.R.S., writes ("Nature," February 7th, 1884, p. 345): "We do not remember to have met with other reference to this opinion of Hooke's, though probably such must exist, and it is not easy to explain upon what grounds he founded the idea. . . . The comet referred to was the third of 1618. It was observed by Harriot at Sion House, Isleworth." At the meeting of the Royal Society, a letter from Huyghens was read, in which that philosopher referred to "his agreement with Dr. Wren about the place of the comet." In reference to this it was resolved, "That Mr. Hooke should extract out of his lecture a discourse upon the late comet, and fit it for the press" (Birch's "History," vol. ii., p. 19).

[2] Philip Carteret and Sir Nicholas Slaning, K.B., who married a daughter of Sir George Carteret.

[3] At the meeting of the Royal Society on March 1st, "Mr. Evelyn's paper, intitled 'Panificium; or the several manners of making bread in

very busy getting an answer to some question of Sir Philip Warwicke touching the expense of the navy, and that being done I by coach at 8 at night with my wife and Mercer to Sir Philip's and discoursed with him (leaving them in the coach), and then back with them home and to supper and to bed.

2nd. Begun this day to rise betimes before six o'clock, and, going down to call my people, found Besse and the girle with their clothes on, lying within their bedding upon the ground close by the fireside, and a candle burning all night, pretending they would rise to scoure. This vexed me, but Besse is going and so she will not trouble me long. Up, and by water to Burston about my Lord's plate, and then home to the office, so there all the morning sitting. At noon dined with Sir W. Batten (my wife being gone again to-day to buy things, having bought nothing yesterday for lack of Mrs. Pierce's company), and thence to the office again, where very busy till 12 at night, and vexed at my wife's staying out so late, she not being at home at 9 o'clock, but at last she is come home, but the reason of her stay I know not yet. So shut up my books, and home to supper and to bed.

3rd. Up, and abroad about several things, among others to see Mr. Peter Honiwood, who was at my house the other day, and I find it was for nothing but to pay me my brother John's Quarterage. Thence to see Mrs. Turner, who takes it mighty ill I did not come to dine with the Reader, her husband, which, she says, was the greatest feast that ever was yet kept by a Reader, and I believe it was well. But I am glad I did not go, which confirms her in an opinion that I am growne proud. Thence to the 'Change, and to several places, and so home to dinner and to my office, where till 12 at night writing over a discourse of mine to Mr. Coventry touching the Fishermen of the Thames upon a reference of the business by him to me concerning their being protected from presse. Then home to supper and to bed.

4th. Up very betimes, and walked, it being bitter cold, to Ratcliffe, to the plate-maker's and back again. To

France, &c., where by general consent the best bread is eaten,' was read, and ordered to be registered" (Birch's "History," vol. ii., p. 19).

the office, where we sat all the morning, I, with being empty and full of ayre and wind, had some pain to-day. Dined alone at home, my wife being gone abroad to buy some more things. All the afternoon at the office. William Howe come to see me, being come up with my Lord from sea: he is grown a discreet, but very conceited fellow. He tells me how little respectfully Sir W. Pen did carry it to my Lord on board the Duke's ship at sea; and that Captain Minnes, a favourite of Prince Rupert's, do shew my Lord little respect; but that every body else esteems my Lord as they ought. I am sorry for the folly of the latter, and vexed at the dissimulation of the former. At night home to supper and to bed. This day was proclaimed at the 'Change the war with Holland.

5th (Lord's day). Up, and Mr. Burston bringing me by order my Lord's plates, which he has been making this week. I did take coach and to my Lord Sandwich's and dined with my Lord; it being the first time he hath dined at home since his coming from sea: and a pretty odd demand it was of my Lord to my Lady before me: "How do you, sweetheart? How have you done all this week?" himself taking notice of it to me, that he had hardly seen her the week before. At dinner he did use me with the greatest solemnity in the world, in carving for me, and nobody else, and calling often to my Lady to cut for me; and all the respect possible. After dinner looked over the plates, liked them mightily, and indeed I think he is the most exact man in what he do in the world of that kind. So home again, and there after a song or two in the evening with Mr. Hill, I to my office, and then home to supper and to bed.

6th. Up, and with Sir J. Minnes by coach, being a most lamentable cold day as any this year, to St. James's, and there did our business with the Duke. Great preparations for his speedy return to sea. I saw him try on his buff coat and hat-piece covered with black velvet. It troubles me more to think of his venture, than of anything else in the whole warr. Thence home to dinner, where I saw Besse go away; she having of all wenches that ever lived with us received the greatest love and kindnesse and good clothes, besides wages, and gone away with the greatest ingratitude.

I then abroad to look after my Hamaccoes, and so home, and there find our new chamber-mayde, Mary, come, which instead of handsome, as my wife spoke and still seems to reckon, is a very ordinary wench, I think, and therein was mightily disappointed. To my office, where busy late, and then home to supper and to bed, and was troubled all this night with a pain in my left testicle, that run up presently into my left kidney and there kept akeing all night. In great pain.

7th. Up, and was pretty well, but going to the office, and I think it was sitting with my back to the fire, it set me in a great rage again, that I could not continue till past noon at the office, but was forced to go home, nor could sit down to dinner, but betook myself to my bed, and being there a while my pain begun to abate and grow less and less. Anon I went to make water, not dreaming of any thing but my testicle that by some accident I might have bruised as I used to do, but in pissing there come from me two stones, I could feel them, and caused my water to be looked into; but without any pain to me in going out, which makes me think that it was not a fit of the stone at all; for my pain was asswaged upon my lying down a great while before I went to make water. Anon I made water again very freely and plentifully. I kept my bed in good ease all the evening, then rose and sat up an hour or two, and then to bed and lay till 8 o'clock, and then,

8th. Though a bitter cold day, yet I rose, and though my pain and tenderness in my testicle remains a little, yet I do verily think that my pain yesterday was nothing else, and therefore I hope my disease of the stone may not return to me, but void itself in pissing, which God grant, but I will consult my physitian. This morning is brought me to the office the sad newes of "The London," in which Sir J. Lawson's men were all bringing her from Chatham to the Hope, and thence he was to go to sea in her; but a little a' this side the buoy of the Nower, she suddenly blew up. About 24 [men] and a woman that were in the round-house and coach saved; the rest, being above 300, drowned: the ship breaking all in pieces, with 80 pieces of brass ordnance. She lies sunk, with her round-house above water. Sir J. Lawson hath a great loss in this of so many good chosen men, and many relations among them. I went to the

'Change, where the news taken very much to heart. So home to dinner, and Mr. Moore with me. Then I to Gresham College, and there saw several pretty experiments, and so home and to my office, and at night about 11 home to supper and to bed.

9th. Up and to the office, where we sat all the afternoon. At noon to dinner at home, and then abroad with my wife, left her at the New Exchange and I to Westminster, where I hear Mrs. Martin is brought to bed of a boy and christened Charles, which I am very glad of, for I was fearful of being called to be a godfather to it. But it seems it was to be done suddenly, and so I escaped. It is strange to see how a liberty and going abroad without purpose of doing anything do lead a man to what is bad, for I was just upon going to her, where I must of necessity [have] broken my oath or made a forfeit. But I did not, company being (I heard by my porter) with her, and so I home again, taking up my wife, and was set down by her at Paule's Schoole, where I visited Mr. Crumlum at his house; and, Lord! to see how ridiculous a conceited pedagogue he is, though a learned man, he being so dogmaticall in all he do and says. But among other discourse, we fell to the old discourse of Paule's Schoole; and he did, upon my declaring my value of it, give me one of Lilly's grammars of a very old impression, as it was in the Catholique times, which I shall much set by. And so, after some small discourse, away and called upon my wife at a linen draper's shop buying linen, and so home, and to my office, where late, and home to supper and to bed. This night my wife had a new suit of flowered ash-coloured silke, very noble.

10th. Up, and to the office all the morning. At noon to the 'Change, where very hot, people's proposal of the City giving the King[1] another ship for "The London," that is lately blown up, which would be very handsome, and if well managed, might be done; but I fear if it be put into ill hands, or that the courtiers do solicit it, it will never be done. Home to dinner, and thence to the Committee

[1] In a letter to Secretary Bennet, dated March 9th, reference is made of "a rumour in the City that the aldermen and several companies will build the king a ship to be called the London" ("Calendar of State Papers," Domestic, 1664-65, p. 247).

of Tangier at White Hall, where my Lord Barkely and Craven and others; but, Lord! to see how superficially things are done in the business of the Lottery, which will be the disgrace of the Fishery, and without profit. Home, vexed at my loss of time, and there to my office. Late at night come the two Bellamys, formerly petty warrant Victuallers of the Navy, to take my advice about a navy debt of theirs for the compassing of which they offer a great deal of money, and the thing most just. Perhaps I may undertake it, and get something by it, which will be a good job. So home late to bed.

11th. Up and to the office, at noon home to dinner, and to the office again, where very late, and then home to supper and to bed. This day returned Sir W. Batten and Sir J. Minnes from Lee Roade, where they have been to see the wrecke of "The London," out of which, they say, the guns may be got, but the hull of her will be wholly lost, as not being capable of being weighed.

12th (Lord's day). Up, and borrowing Sir J. Minnes's coach, to my Lord Sandwich's, but he was gone abroad. I sent the coach back for my wife, my Lord a second time dining at home on purpose to meet me, he having not dined once at home but those times since his coming from sea. I sat down and read over the Bishop of Chichester's[1] sermon upon the anniversary of the King's death, much cried up, but, methinks, but a mean sermon. By and by comes in my Lord, and he and I to talke of many things in the Navy, one from another, in general, to see how the greatest things are committed to very ordinary men, as to parts and experience, to do; among others, my Lord Barkeley. We talked also of getting W. Howe[2] to be put into the Muster-Mastershipp in the roome of Creed, if Creed will give way, but my Lord do it without any great gusto, calling Howe a proud coxcomb in passion. Down to dinner, where my wife in her new lace whiske, which, indeed, is very noble, and I much pleased with it, and so my Lady also. Here very pleasant my Lord was at dinner, and after dinner did look over his plate,[3] which Burston

[1] Dr. Henry King. See note, July 8th, 1660.

[2] William Howe obtained the Muster-mastership.

[3] Of the harbour of Portsmouth. See February 18th, 1664–65.

hath brought him to-day, and is the last of the three that he will have made. After satisfied with that, he abroad, and I after much discourse with my Lady about Sir G. Carteret's son, of whom she hath some thoughts for a husband for my Lady Jemimah, we away home by coach again, and there sang a good while very pleasantly with Mr. Andrews and Hill. They gone, we to supper, and betimes to bed.

13th. Up betimes, this being the first morning of my promise upon a forfeite not to lie in bed a quarter of an hour after my first waking. Abroad to St. James's, and there much business, the King also being with us a great while. Thence to the 'Change, and thence with Captain Tayler and Sir W. Warren dined at a house hard by for discourse sake, and so I home, and there meeting a letter from Mrs. Martin desiring to speak with me, I (though against my promise of visiting her) did go, and there found her in her childbed dress desiring my favour to get her husband a place. I staid not long, but taking Sir W. Warren up at White Hall home, and among other discourse fell to a business which he says shall if accomplished bring me £100. He gone, I to supper and to bed. This day my wife begun to wear light-coloured locks, quite white almost, which, though it makes her look very pretty, yet not being natural, vexes me, that I will not have her wear them. This day I saw my Lord Castlemayne at St. James's, lately come from France.

14th. Up before six, to the office, where busy all the morning. At noon dined with Sir W. Batten and Sir J. Minnes, at the Tower, with Sir J. Robinson, at a farewell dinner which he gives Major Holmes at his going out of the Tower,[1] where he hath for some time, since his coming from Guinny, been a prisoner, and, it seems, had presented the Lieutenant with fifty pieces yesterday. Here a great deale of good victuals and company. Thence home to my office, where very late, and home to supper and to bed weary of business.

15th. Up and by coach with Sir. W. Batten to St. James's, where among other things before the Duke, Captain Taylor

[1] Holmes's imprisonment in the Tower is mentioned by Pepys on January 9th, 1664-65 (see note, September 29th, 1664).

was called in, and, Sir J. Robinson his accuser not appearing, was acquitted quite from his charge, and declared that he should go to Harwich, which I was very well pleased at. Thence I to Mr. Coventry's chamber, and there privately an houre with him in discourse of the office, and did deliver to him many notes of things about which he is to get the Duke's command, before he goes, for the putting of business among us in better order. He did largely owne his dependance as to the office upon my care, and received very great expressions of love from him, and so parted with great satisfaction to myself. So home to the 'Change, and thence home to dinner, where my wife being gone down upon a sudden warning from my Lord Sandwich's daughters to the Hope with them to see "The Prince," I dined alone. After dinner to the office, and anon to Gresham College, where, among other good discourse, there was tried the great poyson of Maccassa upon a dogg,[1] but it had no effect all the time we sat there. We anon broke up and I home, where late at my office, my wife not coming home. I to bed, troubled, about 12 or past.

16th. Up and to the office, where we sat all the morning, my wife coming home from the water this morning, having lain with them on board "The Prince" all night. At noon home to dinner, where my wife told me the unpleasant journey she had yesterday among the children, whose fear upon the water and folly made it very unpleasing to her. A good dinner, and then to the office again. This afternoon Mr. Harris,[2] the sayle-maker, sent me a noble present of two large silver candlesticks and snuffers, and a slice to keep them upon, which indeed is very handsome. At night come Mr. Andrews with £36, the further fruits of my Tangier contract, and so to bed late and weary with business, but in good content of mind, blessing God for these his benefits.

[1] "The experiment of trying to poison a dog with some of the Macassar powder in which a needle had been dipped was made, but without success." Pepys himself made a communication at this meeting of the information he had received from the master of the Jersey ship, who had been in company of Major Holmes in the Guinea voyage, concerning the pendulum watches (Birch's "History," vol. ii., p. 23).

[2] John Harris, who supplied sails to the Navy Office. His contracts are referred to in the "Calendars of State Papers."

17th. Up and to my office, and then with Sir W. Batten to St. James's, where many come to take leave, as was expected, of the Duke, but he do not go till Monday. This night my Lady Wood died of the small-pox, and is much lamented among the great persons for a good-natured woman and a good wife, but for all that it was ever believed she was as others are. The Duke did give us some commands, and so broke up, not taking leave of him. But the best piece of newes is, that instead of a great many troublesome Lords, the whole business is to be left with the Duke of Albemarle to act as Admirall in his stead; which is a thing that do cheer my heart. For the other would have vexed us with attendance, and never done the business. Thence to the Committee of Tangier, where the Duke a little, and then left us and we staid. A very great Committee, the Lords Albemarle, Sandwich, Barkely, Fitzharding, Peterborough, Ashley, Sir Thos. Ingram, Sir G. Carteret and others. The whole business was the stating of Povy's accounts, of whom to say no more, never could man say worse himself nor have worse said of him than was by the company to his face; I mean, as to his folly and very reflecting words to his honesty. Broke up without any thing but trouble and shame, only I got my businesses done to the signing of two bills for the Contractors and Captain Taylor, and so come away well pleased, and home, taking up my wife at the 'Change, to dinner. After dinner out again bringing my wife to her father's again at Charing Cross, and I to the Committee again, where a new meeting of trouble about Povy, who still makes his business worse and worse, and broke up with the most open shame again to him, and high words to him of disgrace that they would not trust him with any more money till he had given an account of this. So broke up. Then he took occasion to desire me to step aside, and he and I by water to London together. In the way, of his owne accord, he proposed to me that he would surrender his place of Treasurer[1] to me to have half the profit. The thing is new to me; but the more I think the more I like it, and do put him upon getting it done by the Duke. Whether it takes or no I

[1] For Tangier.

care not, but I think at present it may have some convenience in it. Home, and there find my wife come home and gone to bed, of a cold got yesterday by water. At the office Bellamy come to me again, and I am in hopes something may be got by his business. So late home to supper and bed.

18th. Up and to the office, where all the morning. At noon to the 'Change, and took Mr. Hill along with me to Mr. Povy's, where we dined, and shewed him the house to his good content, and I expect when we meet we shall laugh at it. But I having business to stay, he went away, and Povy and Creed and I to do some business upon Povy's accounts all the afternoon till late at night, where, God help him! never man was so confounded, and all his people about him in this world as he and his are. After we had done something [to the] purpose we broke up, and Povy acquainted me before Creed (having said something of it also this morning at our office to me) what he had done in speaking to the Duke and others about his making me Treasurer, and has carried it a great way, so as I think it cannot well be set back. Creed, I perceive, envies me in it, but I think as that will do me no hurte, so if it did I am at a great losse to think whether it were not best for me to let it wholly alone, for it will much disquiett me and my business of the Navy, which in this warr will certainly be worth all my time to me. Home, continuing in this doubtfull condition what to think of it, but God Almighty do his will in it for the best. To my office, where late, and then home to supper and to bed.

19th (Lord's day). Mr. Povy sent his coach for me betimes, and I to him, and there to our great trouble do find that my Lord FitzHarding do appear for Mr. Brunkard[1] to be Paymaster upon Povy's going out, by a former promise of the Duke's, and offering to give as much as any

[1] Henry Brouncker, younger brother of William, Viscount Brouncker, President of the Royal Society. He was Groom of the Bedchamber to the Duke of York, and succeeded to the office of Cofferer on the death of William Ashburnham in 1671. His character was bad, and his conduct in the sea-fight of 1665 was impugned. He was expelled from the House of Commons, but succeeded to his brother's title in 1684. He died in January, 1687.

for it. This put us all into a great dumpe, and so we went to Creed's new lodging in the Mewes, and there we found Creed with his parrot upon his shoulder, which struck Mr. Povy coming by just by the eye, very deep, which, had it hit his eye, had put it out. This a while troubled us, but not proving very bad, we to our business consulting what to do; at last resolved, and I to Mr. Coventry, and there had his most friendly and ingenuous advice, advising me not to decline the thing, it being that that will bring me to be known to great persons, while now I am buried among three or four of us, says he, in the Navy; but do not make a declared opposition to my Lord FitzHarding. Thence I to Creed, and walked talking in the Park an hour with him, and then to my Lord Sandwich's to dinner, and after dinner to Mr. Povy's, who hath been with the Duke of Yorke, and, by the mediation of Mr. Coventry, the Duke told him that the business shall go on, and he will take off Brunkerd, and my Lord Fitz-Harding is quiett too. But to see the mischief, I hear that Sir G. Carteret did not seem pleased, but said nothing when he heard me proposed to come in Povy's room, which may learn me to distinguish between that man that is a man's true and false friend. Being very glad of this news Mr. Povy and I in his coach to Hyde Parke, being the first day of the tour there. Where many brave ladies; among others, Castlemayne lay impudently upon her back in her coach asleep, with her mouth open. There was also my Lady Kerneguy,[1] once my Lady Anne Hambleton, that is said to have given the Duke a clap upon his first coming over. Here I saw Sir J. Lawson's daughter and husband, a fine couple, and also Mr. Southwell and his new lady, very pretty. Thence back, putting in at Dr. Whore's, where I saw his lady, a very fine woman. So home, and thither by my desire comes by and by Creed and lay with me, very merry and full of discourse, what to do to-morrow, and the conveniences that will attend my having of this place, and I do think they may be very great.

[1] Daughter of William, Duke of Hamilton, wife of Lord Carnegy, who became Earl of Southesk on his father's death. She is frequently mentioned in the "Mémoires de Grammont," and in the letters of the second Earl of Chesterfield. — B.

20th. Up, Creed and I, and had Mr. Povy's coach sent for us, and we to his house; where we did some business in order to the work of this day. Povy and I to my Lord Sandwich, who tells me that the Duke is not only a friend to the business, but to me, in terms of the greatest love and respect and value of me that can be thought, which overjoys me. Thence to St. James's, and there was in great doubt of Brunkerd, but at last I hear that Brunkerd desists. The Duke did direct Secretary Bennet, who was there, to declare his mind to the Tangier Committee, that he approves of me for Treasurer; and with a character of me to be a man whose industry and discretion he would trust soon as any man's in England: and did the like to my Lord Sandwich. So to White Hall to the Committee of Tangier, where there were present, my Lord of Albemarle, my Lord Peterborough, Sandwich, Barkeley, FitzHarding, Secretary Bennet, Sir Thomas Ingram, Sir John Lawson, Povy and I. Where, after other business, Povy did declare his business very handsomely; that he was sorry he had been so unhappy in his accounts, as not to give their Lordships the satisfaction he intended, and that he was sure his accounts are right, and continues to submit them to examination, and is ready to lay down in ready money the fault of his account; and that for the future, that the work might be better done and with more quiet to him, he desired, by approbation of the Duke, he might resign his place to Mr. Pepys. Whereupon, Secretary Bennet did deliver the Duke's command, which was received with great content and allowance beyond expectation; the Secretary repeating also the Duke's character of me. And I could discern my Lord FitzHarding was well pleased with me, and signified full satisfaction, and whispered something seriously of me to the Secretary. And there I received their constitution under all their hands presently; so that I am already confirmed their Treasurer, and put into a condition of striking of tallys;[1] and

[1] The practice of striking tallies at the Exchequer was a curious survival of an ancient method of keeping accounts. The method adopted is described in Hubert Hall's "Antiquities and Curiosities of the Exchequer," 1891. The following account of the use of tallies, so frequently alluded to in the Diary, was supplied by Lord Braybrooke. Formerly accounts were kept, and large sums of money paid and

all without one harsh word or word of dislike, but quite the contrary; which is a good fortune beyond all imagination. Here we rose, and Povy and Creed and I, all full of joy, thence to dinner, they setting me down at Sir J. Winter's, by promise, and dined with him; and a worthy fine man he seems to be, and of good discourse, our business was to discourse of supplying the King with iron for anchors, if it can be judged good enough, and a fine thing it is to see myself come to the condition of being received by persons of this rank, he being, and having long been, Secretary to the Queene-Mother. Thence to Povy's, and there sat and considered of business a little and then home, where late at it, W. Howe being with me about his business of accounts for his money laid out in the fleet, and he gone, I home to supper and to bed. Newes is this day come of Captain Allen's being come home from the Straights, as far as Portland, with eleven of the King's ships, and about twenty-two of merchantmen.

21st. Up, and my taylor coming to me, did consult all my wardrobe how to order my clothes against next summer. Then to the office, where busy all the morning. At noon to the 'Change, and brought home Mr. Andrews, and there with Mr. Sheply dined and very merry, and a good dinner. Thence to Mr. Povy's to discourse about settling our business of Treasurer, and I think all things will go very fayre between us and to my content, but the more I see the more silly the man seems to me. Thence by coach to the Mewes, but Creed was not there. In our way the coach drove through a lane by Drury Lane, where abundance of

received, by the King's Exchequer, with little other form than the exchange or delivery of tallies, pieces of wood notched or scored, corresponding blocks being kept by the parties to the account; and from this usage one of the head officers of the Exchequer was called the tallier, or teller. These tallies were often negotiable; Adam Smith, in his "Wealth of Nations," book ii., ch. xi., says that "in 1696 tallies had been at forty, and fifty, and sixty per cent. discount, and bank-notes at twenty per cent." The system of tallies was discontinued in 1824; and the destruction of the Old Houses of Parliament, in the night of October 16th, 1834, is thought to have been occasioned by the overheating of the flues, when the furnaces were employed to consume the tallies rendered useless by the alteration in the mode of keeping the Exchequer accounts.

loose women stood at the doors, which, God forgive me, did put evil thoughts in me, but proceeded no further, blessed be God. So home, and late at my office, then home and there found a couple of state cups, very large, coming, I suppose, each to about £6 a piece, from Burrows[1] the slopseller.

22nd. Up, and to Mr. Povy's about our business, and thence I to see Sir Ph. Warwicke, but could not meet with him. So to Mr. Coventry, whose profession of love and esteem for me to myself was so large and free that I never could expect or wish for more, nor could have it from any man in England, that I should value it more. Thence to Mr. Povy's, and with Creed to the 'Change and to my house, but, it being washing day, dined not at home, but took him (I being invited) to Mr. Hubland's, the merchant, where Sir William Petty, and abundance of most ingenious men, owners and freighters of "The Experiment," now going with her two bodies to sea. Most excellent discourse. Among others, Sir William Petty did tell me that in good earnest he hath in his will[2] left such parts of his estate to him that could invent such and such things. As among others, that could discover truly the way of milk coming into the breasts of a woman; and he that could invent proper characters to express to another the mixture of relishes and tastes. And says, that to him that invents gold, he gives nothing for the philosopher's stone; for (says he) they that find out that, will be able to pay themselves. But, says he, by this means it is better than to give to a lecture; for here my executors, that must part with this, will be sure to be well convinced of the invention before they do part with their money. After dinner Mr. Hill took me with Mrs. Hubland,[3] who is a fine gentlewoman, into another room, and there made her sing, which she do very well, to my great content. Then to Gresham College, and there did see a kitling killed almost quite,[4] but that we

[1] John Burrowes, Navy slopseller to the Navy Commissioners.

[2] A copy of Sir William Petty's will, dated 1685, is in the British Museum (Add. MSS., No. 15,858, fol. 109). — B.

[3] Mary Ducane, wife of James Houblon. They were married November 11th, 1620, and had twelve children. — B.

[4] "Two experiments were made for the finding out a way to breathe under water, useful for divers." The first was on a bird and the second on "a kitling" (Birch's "History," vol. ii., p. 25).

could not quite kill her, with such a way; the ayre out of a receiver, wherein she was put, and then the ayre being let in upon her revives her immediately; nay, and this ayre is to be made by putting together a liquor and some body that ferments, the steam of that do do the work. Thence home, and thence to White Hall, where the house full of the Duke's going to-morrow, and thence to St. James's, wherein these things fell out: (1) I saw the Duke, kissed his hand, and had his most kind expressions of his value and opinion of me, which comforted me above all things in the world, (2) the like from Mr. Coventry most heartily and affectionately. (3) Saw, among other fine ladies, Mrs. Middleton,[1] a very great beauty I never knew or heard of before; (4) I saw Waller[2] the poet, whom I never saw before. So, very late, by coach home with W. Pen, who was there. To supper and to bed, with my heart at rest, and my head very busy thinking of my several matters now on foot, the new comfort of my old navy business, and the new one of my employment on Tangier.

23rd. Up and to my Lord Sandwich, who follows the Duke this day by water down to the Hope, where "The Prince" lies. He received me, busy as he was, with mighty kindness and joy at my promotions; telling me most largely how the Duke hath expressed on all occasions his good opinion of my service and love for me. I paid my thanks and acknowledgement to him; and so back home, where at the office all the morning. At noon to the 'Change. Home, and Lewellin dined with me. Thence abroad, carried my wife to Westminster by coach, I to the Swan, Herbert's, and there had much of the good company of Sarah and to my wish, and then to see Mrs. Martin, who was very kind, three weeks of her month of lying in is over. So took up my wife and home, and at my office a while, and thence to supper and to bed. Great talk of noises of guns heard at Deale, but nothing particularly whether in earnest or not.

[1] Jane, daughter to Sir Robert Needham, is frequently mentioned in the "Grammont Memoirs," and Evelyn calls her "that famous and indeed incomparable beauty" ("Diary," August 2nd, 1683). Her portrait is in the Royal Collection amongst the beauties of Charles II.'s Court. Sir Robert Needham was related to John Evelyn.

[2] Edmund Waller, born March 3rd, 1605, died October 21st, 1687.

24th. Up betimes, and by agreement to the Globe taverne in Fleet Street to Mr. Clerke, my sollicitor, about the business of my uncle's accounts, and we went with one Jefferys to one of the Barons (Spelman[1]), and there my accounts were declared and I sworn to the truth thereof to my knowledge, and so I shall after a few formalities be cleared of all. Thence to Povy's, and there delivered him his letters of greatest import to him that is possible, yet dropped by young Bland, just come from Tangier, upon the road by Sittingburne, taken up and sent to Mr. Pett, at Chatham. Thus every thing done by Povy is done with a fatal folly and neglect. Then to our discourse with him, Creed, Mr. Viner, myself and Poyntz about the business of the Workehouse at Clerkenwell, and after dinner went thither and saw all the works there, and did also consult the Act concerning the business and other papers in order to our coming in to undertake it with Povy, the management of the House, but I do not think we can safely meddle with it, at least I, unless I had time to look after it myself, but the thing is very ingenious and laudable. Thence to my Lady Sandwich's, where my wife all this day, having kept Good Friday very strict with fasting. Here we supped, and talked very merry. My Lady alone with me, very earnest about Sir G. Carteret's son, with whom I perceive they do desire my Lady Jemimah may be matched. Thence home and to my office, and then to bed.

25th (Lady day). Up betimes and to my office, where all the morning. At noon dined alone with Sir W. Batten, where great discourse of Sir. W. Pen, Sir W. Batten being, I perceive, quite out of love with him, thinking him too great and too high, and began to talk that the world do question his courage, upon which I told him plainly I have been told that he was articled against for it, and that Sir H. Vane was his great friend therein. This he was, I perceive, glad to hear. Thence to the office, and there very late, very busy, to my great content. This afternoon of a sudden is come home Sir W. Pen from the fleete, but upon what score I know not. Late home to supper and to bed.

[1] Clement Spelman, son of Sir Henry Spelman the antiquary. He was appointed Cursitor Baron of the Exchequer in 1663, and occupied the office till March, 1679. He died in the following June.

26th (Lord's day and Easter day). Up (and with my wife, who has not been at church a month or two) to church. At noon home to dinner, my wife and I (Mercer staying to the Sacrament) alone. This is the day seven years which, by the blessing of God, I have survived of my being cut of the stone, and am now in very perfect good health and have long been; and though the last winter hath been as hard a winter as any have been these many years, yet I never was better in my life, nor have not, these ten years, gone colder in the summer than I have done all this winter, wearing only a doublet, and a waistcoate cut open on the back; abroad, a cloake and within doors a coate I slipped on. Now I am at a losse to know whether it be my hare's foot which is my preservative against wind, for I never had a fit of the collique since I wore it, and nothing but wind brings me pain, and the carrying away of wind takes away my pain, or my keeping my back cool; for when I do lie longer than ordinary upon my back in bed, my water the next morning is very hot, or whether it be my taking of a pill of turpentine every morning, which keeps me always loose, or all together, but this I know, with thanks to God Almighty, that I am now as well as ever I can wish or desire to be, having now and then little grudgings of wind, that brings me a little pain, but it is over presently, only I do find that my backe grows very weak, that I cannot stoop to write or tell money without sitting but I have pain for a good while after it. Yet a week or two ago I had one day's great pain; but it was upon my getting a bruise on one of my testicles, and then I did void two small stones, without pain though, and, upon my going to bed and bearing up of my testicles, I was well the next. But I did observe that my sitting with my back to the fire at the office did then, as it do at all times, make my back ake, and my water hot, and brings me some pain. I sent yesterday an invitation to Mrs. Turner and her family to come to keep this day with me, which she granted, but afterward sent me word that it being Sunday and Easter day she desired to choose another and put off this. Which I was willing enough to do; and so put it off as to this day, and will leave it to my own convenience when to choose another, and perhaps shall escape a feast by it. At my office all the afternoon drawing up my agreement with Mr. Povy for me to sign to him to-morrow morning. In the evening spent an hour in the garden walking with Sir J. Minnes, talking of the Chest business, wherein Sir W. Batten deals so unfairly, wherein the old man is very hot for the present, but that zeal will not last nor is to be trusted. So home to supper, prayers, and to bed.

27th. Up betimes to Mr. Povy's, and there did sign and seal my agreement with him about my place of being Treasurer for Tangier, it being the greatest part of it drawn out of a draught of his own drawing up, only I have added something here and there in favour of myself. Thence to the Duke of Albemarle, the first time that we officers of the Navy have waited upon him since the Duke of Yorke's going, who hath deputed him to be Admirall[1] in his absence. And I find him a quiet heavy man, that will help business when he can, and hinder nothing, and am very well pleased with our attendance on him. I did afterwards alone give him thanks for his favour to me about my Tangier business, which he received kindly, and did speak much of his esteem of me. Thence, and did the same to Sir H. Bennet, who did the like to me very fully, and did give me all his letters lately come from hence for me to read, which I returned in the afternoon to him. Thence to Mrs. Martin, who, though her husband is gone away, as he writes, like a fool into France, yet is as simple and wanton as ever she was, with much I made myself merry and away. So to my Lord Peterborough's; where Povy, Creed, Williamson, Auditor Beale, and myself, and mighty merry to see how plainly my Lord and Povy did abuse one another about their accounts, each thinking the other a foole, and I thinking they were not either of them, in that point, much in the wrong, though in everything, and even in this manner of reproaching one another, very witty and pleasant. Among other things, we had here the genteelest

[1] In a letter of March 22nd, 1664–65, from the Duke of York to the Duke of Albemarle, on the power he assigns to him in his absence, printed in "Memoirs of Naval Affairs, &c.," 8vo, 1729, p. 51. On the 23rd the Duke of York assumed the command of the fleet against the Dutch. — B.

dinner and the neatest house that I have seen many a day, and the latter beyond anything I ever saw in a nobleman's house. Thence visited my Lord Barkeley, and did sit discoursing with him in his chamber a good while, and [he] mighty friendly to me about the same business of Tangier. From that to other discourse of the times and the want of money, and he said that the Parliament must be called again soon, and more money raised, not by tax, for he said he believed the people could not pay it, but he would have either a general excise upon everything, or else that every city incorporate should pay a toll into the King's revenue, as he says it is in all the cities in the world; for here a citizen hath no more laid on them than their neighbours in the country, whereas, as a city, it ought to pay considerably to the King for their charter; but I fear this will breed ill blood. Thence to Povy, and after a little talk home to my office late. Then to supper and to bed.

28th. Up betimes and to the office, where we sat all the morning, and I did most of the business there, God wot. Then to the 'Change, and thence to the Coffee-house with Sir W. Warren, where much good discourse for us both till 4 o'clock with great pleasure and content, and then parted and I home to dinner, having eat nothing, and so to my office. At night supped with my wife at Sir W. Pen's, who is to go back for good and all to the fleete to-morrow. Took leave and to my office, where till 12 at night, and then home to bed.

29th. Up betimes and to Povy's, where a good while talking about our business; thence abroad into the City, but upon his tally could not get any money in Lumbard Streete, through the disrepute which he suffers, I perceive, upon his giving up his place, which people think was not choice, but necessity, as indeed it was. So back to his house, after we had been at my house to taste my wine, but my wife being abroad nobody could come at it, and so we were defeated. To his house, and before dinner he and I did discourse of the business of freight, wherein I am so much concerned, above £100 for myself, and in my over hasty making a bill out for the rest for him, but he resolves to move Creed in it. Which troubled me much, and Creed by and by comes, and after dinner he did, but in the most cunning ingenious manner, do his business with Creed by bringing it in by the by, that the most subtile man in the world could never have done it better, and I must say that he is a most witty, cunning man and one that I [am] most afeard of in my conversation, though in all serious matters of business the veriest foole that ever I met with. The bill was produced and a copy given Creed, whereupon he wrote his *Intratur* upon the originall, and I hope it will pass, at least I am now put to it that I must stand by it and justify it, but I pray God it may never come to that test. Thence between vexed and joyed, not knowing what yet to make of it, home, calling for my Lord Cooke's[1] 3 volumes at my bookseller's, and so home, where I found a new cook mayd, her name is [2] that promises very little. So to my office, where late about drawing up a proposal for Captain Taylor, for him to deliver to the City about his building the new ship, which I have done well, and I hope will do the business, and so home to supper and to bed.

30th. Up, and to my Lord Ashly, but did nothing, and to Sir Ph. Warwicke and spoke with him about business, and so back to the office, where all the morning. At noon home to dinner, and thence to the Tangier Committee, where, Lord! to see how they did run into the giving of Sir J. Lawson (who is come to towne to-day to get this business done) £4,000 about his Mole business, and were going to give him 4*s.* per yarde more, which arises in the whole Mole to £36,000, is a strange thing, but the latter by chance was stopped, the former was given. Thence to see Mrs. Martin, whose husband being it seems gone away, and as she is informed he hath another woman whom he uses, and has long done, as a wife, she is mighty reserved and resolved to keep herself so till the return of her husband, which a pleasant thing to think of her. Thence home, and to my office, where late, and to bed.

31st. Up betimes and walked to my Lord Ashly, and there with Creed after long waiting spoke with him, and

[1] This was probably the "Reports from 14 Elizabeth to 13 James I." of Sir Edward Coke, and not his "Institutes of the Laws of England."
[2] Blank in MS.

was civilly used by him; thence to Sir Ph. Warwicke, and then to visit my Lord of Falmouth,[1] who did also receive me pretty civilly, but not as I expected; he, I perceive, believing that I had undertaken to justify Povy's accounts, taking them upon myself, but I rectified him therein. So to my Lady Sandwich's to dinner, and up to her chamber after dinner, and there discoursed about Sir G. Carteret's son, in proposition between us two for my Lady Jemimah. So to Povy, and with him spent the afternoon very busy, till I was weary of following this and neglecting my navy business. So at night called my wife at my Lady's, and so home. To my office and there made up my month's account, which, God be praised! rose to £1,300. Which I bless God for. So after 12 o'clock home to supper and to bed. I find Creed mightily transported by my Lord of Falmouth's kind words to him, and saying that he hath a place in his intention for him, which he believes will be considerable. A witty man he is in every respect, but of no good nature, nor a man ordinarily to be dealt with. My Lady Castlemayne is sicke again, people think, slipping her filly.[2]

April 1st. All the morning very busy at the office preparing a last half-year's account for my Lord Treasurer.[3] At noon eat a bit and stepped to Sir Ph. Warwicke, by coach to my Lord Treasurer's, and after some private conference and examining of my papers with him I did return into the City and to Sir G. Carteret, whom I found with the Commissioners of Prizes dining at Captain Cocke's, in Broad Streete, very merry. Among other tricks, there did come a blind fiddler to the doore, and Sir G. Carteret did go to the doore and lead the blind fiddler by the hand in. Thence with Sir G. Carteret to my Lord Treasurer, and by and by come Sir W. Batten and Sir J. Minnes, and anon we come to my Lord, and there did lay open the expence for the six months past, and an estimate of the seven months to come, to November next: the first arising to

[1] Sir Charles Berkeley, Viscount Fitzharding (1663), and Earl of Falmouth (1665), killed in the sea-fight, June, 1665.

[2] This rumour was probably unfounded, as her son George Fitzroy (created Duke of Northumberland, 1683) was born December 28th of this year.

[3] See *post*, April 12th.

above £500,000, and the latter will, as we judge, come to above £1,000,000. But to see how my Lord Treasurer did bless himself, crying he could do no more than he could, nor give more money than he had, if the occasion and expence were never so great, which is but a sad story. And then to hear how like a passionate and ignorant asse Sir G. Carteret did harangue upon the abuse of Tickets did make me mad almost and yet was fain to hold my tongue. Thence home, vexed mightily to see how simply our greatest ministers do content themselves to understand and do things, while the King's service in the meantime lies a-bleeding. At my office late writing letters till ready to drop down asleep with my late sitting up of late, and running up and down a-days. So to bed.

2nd (Lord's day). At my office all the morning, renewing my vowes in writing and then home to dinner. All the afternoon, Mr. Tasborough, one of Mr. Povy's clerks, with me about his master's accounts. In the evening Mr. Andrews and Hill sang, but supped not with me, then after supper to bed.

3rd. Up and to the Duke of Albemarle and White Hall, where much business. Thence home and to dinner, and then with Creed, my wife, and Mercer to a play at the Duke's, of my Lord Orrery's, called "Mustapha,"[1] which being not good, made Betterton's part and Inathe's but ordinary too, so that we were not contented with it at all. Thence home and to the office a while, and then home to supper and to bed. All the pleasure of the play was, the King and my Lady Castlemayne were there; and pretty witty Nell,[2] at the King's house, and the younger Marshall[3] sat next us; which pleased me mightily.

4th. All the morning at the office busy, at noon to the 'Change, and then went up to the 'Change to buy a pair of cotton stockings, which I did at the husband's shop of the most pretty woman there, who did also invite me to buy some linnen of her, and I was glad of the occasion, and

[1] Now first acted. Betterton took the character of Solyman the Magnificent, and Mrs. Betterton, Roxolana. There was an earlier tragedy of this name, by Fulk Greville, Lord Brooke.

[2] Nell Gwynne.

[3] Rebecca Marshall.

bespoke some bands of her, intending to make her my seamstress, she being one of the prettiest and most modest looked women that ever I did see. Dined at home and to the office, where very late till I was ready to fall down asleep, and did several times nod in the middle of my letters.

5th. This day was kept publiquely by the King's command, as a fast day against the Dutch warr, and I betimes with Mr. Tooker,[1] whom I have brought into the Navy to serve us as a husband to see goods timely shipped off from hence to the Fleete and other places, and took him with me to Woolwich and Deptford, where by business I have been hindered a great while of going, did a very great deale of business, and then home, and there by promise find Creed, and he and my wife, Mercer and I by coach to take the ayre; and, where we had formerly been, at Hackney, did there eat some pullets we carried with us, and some things of the house; and after a game or two at shuffle-board, home, and Creed lay with me; but, being sleepy, he had no mind to talk about business, which indeed I intended, by inviting him to lie with me, but I would not force it on him, and so to bed, he and I, and to sleep, being the first time I have been so much at my ease and taken so much fresh ayre these many weeks or months.

6th. At the office sat all the morning, where, in the absence of Sir W. Batten, Sir G. Carteret being angry about the business of tickets, spoke of Sir W. Batten for speaking some words about the signing of tickets, and called Sir W. Batten in his discourse at the table to us (the clerks being withdrawn) "shitten foole," which vexed me. At noon to the 'Change, and there set my business of lighters' buying for the King, to Sir W. Warren, and I think he will do it for me to very great advantage, at which I am mightily rejoiced. Home and after a mouthfull of dinner to the office, where till 6 o'clock, and then to White Hall, and there with Sir G. Carteret and my Lord Brunkerd attended the Duke of Albemarle about the business of money. I also went to Jervas's, my barber, for my periwigg that was mending there, and there do hear that Jane is quite undone,

[1] John Tooker, messenger to the Navy Commissioners.

taking the idle fellow for her husband yet not married, and lay with him several weeks that had another wife and child, and she is now going into Ireland. So called my wife at the 'Change and home, and at my office writing letters till one o'clock in the morning, that I was ready to fall down asleep again. Great talke of a new Comett; and it is certain one do now appear as bright as the late one at the best; but I have not seen it myself.

7th. Up betimes to the Duke of Albemarle about money to be got for the Navy, or else we must shut up shop. Thence to Westminster Hall and up and down, doing not much; then to London, but to prevent Povy's dining with me (who I see is at the 'Change) I went back again and to Herbert's at Westminster, there sent for a bit of meat and dined, and then to my Lord Treasurer's, and there with Sir Philip Warwicke, and thence to White Hall in my Lord Treasurer's chamber with Sir Philip Warwicke till dark night, about fower hours talking of the business of the Navy Charge, and how Sir G. Carteret do order business, keeping us in ignorance what he do with his money, and also Sir Philip did shew me nakedly the King's condition for money for the Navy; and he do assure me, unless the King can get some noblemen or rich money-gentlemen to lend him money, or to get the City to do it, it is impossible to find money: we having already, as he says, spent one year's share of the three-years' tax, which comes to £2,500,000. Being very glad of this day's discourse in all but that I fear I shall quite lose Sir G. Carteret, who knows that I have been privately here all this day with Sir Ph. Warwicke. However, I will order it so as to give him as little offence as I can. So home to my office, and then to supper and to bed.

8th. Up, and all the morning full of business at the office. At noon dined with Mr. Povy, and then to the getting some business looked over of his, and then I to my Lord Chancellor's, where to have spoke with the Duke of Albemarle, but the King and Council busy, I could not; then to the Old Exchange and there of my new pretty seamstress bought four bands, and so home, where I found my house mighty neat and clean. Then to my office late, till past 12, and so home to bed. The French Embassadors[1] are come incognito before their train, which will hereafter be very pompous. It is thought they come to get our King to joyne with the King of France in helping him against Flanders, and they to do the like to us against Holland. We have laine a good while with a good fleete at Harwich. The Dutch not said yet to be out. We, as high as we make our shew, I am sure, are unable to set out another small fleete, if this should be worsted. Wherefore, God send us Peace! I cry.

9th (Lord's day). To church with my wife in the morning, in her new light-coloured silk gowne, which is, with her new point, very noble. Dined at home, and in the afternoon to Fanchurch,[2] the little church in the middle of Fanchurch Streete, where a very few people and few of any rank. Thence, after sermon, home, and in the evening walking in the garden, my Lady Pen and her daughter walked with my wife and I, and so to my house to eat with us, and very merry, and so broke up and to bed.

10th. Up, and to the Duke of Albemarle's, and thence to White Hall to a Committee for Tangier, where new disorder about Mr. Povy's accounts, that I think I shall never be settled in my business of Treasurer for him. Here Captain Cooke met me, and did seem discontented about my boy Tom's having no time to mind his singing nor lute, which I answered him fully in, that he desired me that I would baste his coate. So home and to the 'Change, and thence to the "Old James" to dine with Sir W. Rider, Cutler, and Mr. Deering, upon the business of hemp, and so hence to White Hall to have attended the King and Lord Chancellor about the debts of the navy and to get some money, but the meeting failed. So my Lord Brunkard took me and Sir Thomas Harvy in his coach to the Parke, which is very troublesome with the dust; and ne'er a great beauty there to-day but Mrs. Middleton, and so home to my office,

[1] The French ambassadors were Henri de Bourbon, Duc de Verneuil, natural son of Henry IV. and brother of Henrietta Maria, and M. de Courtin. — B.

[2] St. Gabriel's Fenchurch, "in the midst of Fenchurch Street," opposite Cullum Street. The ground on which it stood was laid into the highway or street. The church was destroyed in the Great Fire, and was not rebuilt.

where Mr. Warren proposed my getting of £100 to get him a protection for a ship to go out, which I think I shall do. So home to supper and to bed.

11th. Up and betimes to Alderman Cheverton to treat with him about hempe, and so back to the office. At noon dined at the Sun, behind the 'Change, with Sir Edward Deering[1] and his brother and Commissioner Pett, we having made a contract with Sir Edward this day about timber. Thence to the office, where late very busy, but with some trouble have also some hopes of profit too. So home to supper and to bed.

12th. Up, and to White Hall to a Committee of Tangier, where, contrary to all expectation, my Lord Ashly, being vexed with Povy's accounts, did propose it as necessary that Povy should be still continued Treasurer of Tangier till he had made up his accounts; and with such arguments as, I confess, I was not prepared to answer, but by putting off of the discourse, and so, I think, brought it right again; but it troubled me so all the day after, and night too, that I was not quiet, though I think it doubtfull whether I shall be much the worse for it or no, if it should come to be so. Dined at home and thence to White Hall again (where I lose most of my time now-a-days to my great trouble, charge, and loss of time and benefit), and there, after the Council rose, Sir G. Carteret, my Lord Brunkard, Sir Thomas Harvy, and myself, down to my Lord Treasurer's chamber to him and the Chancellor, and the Duke of Albemarle; and there I did give them a large account of the charge of the Navy, and want of money. But strange to see how they held up their hands crying, "What shall we do?" Says my Lord Treasurer,[2] "Why, what means all this, Mr. Pepys? This is true, you say; but what would you have me to do? I have given all I can for my life. Why will not people lend their money? Why will they not trust the King as well as Oliver? Why do our prizes come to nothing, that yielded so much heretofore?" And this

[1] Sir Edward Dering, of Surrenden Dering, Kent, which county he represented frequently in parliament. He was the second baronet of his family, and some time one of the Lords of the Treasury. He died in 1684. — B.

[2] The Earl of Southampton.

was all we could get, and went away without other answer, which is one of the saddest things that, at such a time as this, with the greatest action on foot that ever was in England, nothing should be minded, but let things go on of themselves do as well as they can. So home, vexed, and going to my Lady Batten's, there found a great many women with her, in her chamber merry, my Lady Pen and her daughter, among others; where my Lady Pen flung me down upon the bed, and herself and others, one after another, upon me, and very merry we were, and thence I home and called my wife with my Lady Pen to supper, and very merry as I could be, being vexed as I was. So home to bed.

13th. Lay long in bed, troubled a little with wind, but not much. So to the office, and there all the morning. At noon to Sheriff Waterman's[1] to dinner, all of us men of the office in towne, and our wives, my Lady Carteret and daughters, and Ladies Batten, Pen, and my wife, &c., and very good cheer we had and merry; musique at and after dinner, and a fellow danced a jigg; but when the company begun to dance, I came away lest I should be taken out; and God knows how my wife carried herself, but I left her to try her fortune. So home, and late at the office, and then home to supper and to bed.

14th. Up, and betimes to Mr. Povy, being desirous to have an end of my trouble of mind touching my Tangier business, whether he hath any desire of accepting what my Lord Ashly offered, of his becoming Treasurer again; and there I did, with a seeming most generous spirit, offer him to take it back again upon his owne terms; but he did answer to me that he would not above all things in the world, at which I was for the present satisfied; but, going away thence and speaking with Creed, he puts me in doubt that the very nature of the thing will require that he be put in again; and did give me the reasons of the auditors, which, I confess, are so plain, that I know not how to withstand them. But he did give me most ingenious advice what to do in it, and anon, my Lord Barkeley and some of the Commissioners coming together, though not in a meet-

[1] George Waterman, Sheriff of London, afterwards knighted, and Lord Mayor, 1672. — B.

ing, I did procure that they should order Povy's payment of his remain of accounts to me; which order if it do pass will put a good stop to the fastening of the thing upon me. At noon Creed and I to a cook's shop at Charing Cross, and there dined and had much discourse, and his very good upon my business, and upon other things, among the rest upon Will Howe's dissembling with us, we discovering one to another his carriage to us, present and absent, being a very false fellow. Thence to White Hall again, and there spent the afternoon, and then home to fetch a letter for the Council, and so back to White Hall, where walked an hour with Mr. Wren, of my Lord Chancellor's, and Mr. Ager, and then to Unthanke's and called my wife, and with her through the city to Mile-End Greene, and eat some creame and cakes and so back home, and I a little at the office, and so home to supper and to bed. This morning I was saluted with newes that the fleetes, ours and the Dutch, were engaged, and that the guns were heard at Walthamstow to play all yesterday, and that Captain Teddiman's[1] legs were shot off in the Royall Katherine. But before night I hear the contrary, both by letters of my owne and messengers thence, that they were all well of our side and no enemy appears yet, and that the Royall Katherine is come to the fleete, and likely to prove as good a ship as any the King hath, of which I am heartily glad, both for Christopher Pett's sake and Captain Teddiman that is in her.

15th. Up, and to White Hall about several businesses, but chiefly to see the proposals of my warrants about Tangier under Creed, but to my trouble found them not finished. So back to the office, where all the morning, busy, then home to dinner, and then all the afternoon till very late at my office, and then home to supper and to bed, weary.

16th (Lord's day). Lay long in bed, then up and to my chamber and my office, looking over some plates which I find necessary for me to understand pretty well, because of the Dutch warr. Then home to dinner, where Creed dined with us, and so after dinner he and I walked to the

[1] Rear-Admiral Sir Thomas Tyddiman was attached to Lord Sandwich's squadron. This report turned out to be a canard. He died in 1668.

Rolls' Chappell, expecting to hear the great Stillingfleete[1] preach, but he did not; but a very sorry fellow, which vexed me. The sermon done, we parted, and I home, where I find Mr. Andrews, and by and by comes Captain Taylor,[2] my old acquaintance at Westminster, that understands musique very well and composes mighty bravely; he brought us some things of two parts to sing, very hard; but that that is the worst, he is very conceited of them, and that though they are good makes them troublesome to one, to see him every note commend and admire them. He supped with me, and a good understanding man he is and a good scholler, and, among other things, a great antiquary, and among other things he can, as he says, show the very originall Charter[3] to Worcester, of King Edgar's, wherein he stiles himself, Rex Marium Brittanniæ, &c.; which is the great text that Mr. Selden and others do quote, but imperfectly and upon trust. But he hath the very originall, which he says he will shew me. He gone we to bed. This night I am told that newes is come of our taking of three Dutch men-of-warr, with the loss of one of our Captains.

17th. Up and to the Duke of Albemarle's, where he shewed me Mr. Coventry's letters, how three Dutch privateers are taken, in one whereof Everson's[4] son is captaine.

[1] Edward Stillingfleet. He was then Preacher of the Rolls Chapel, and was this year presented to the rectory of St. Andrew's, Holborn; Dean of St. Paul's, 1678; Bishop of Worcester, 1689. He died of the gout, March 27th, 1699.

[2] Captain Silas Taylor.

[3] This is the celebrated "Charta Eadgari R. de Oswaldeslawe," dat. Gloucester, December 28th, 964, mentioning not only the dominion of the sea, but also that Edgar had subdued the greatest part of Ireland, a piece of history which rests solely on the authority of this instrument. It is cited by Coke, Selden, Ussher, Dugdale, and Spelman, not to mention inferior names. Three copies existed; the finest and most complete, and probably the same which is here mentioned by Taylor, is now in the Harleian Collection in the British Museum. It is fully described in the "Dissertatio Epistolaris" (p. 86), prefixed by Hickes to his "Thesaurus Linguarum Septentrionalium," and an engraved facsimile of the whole is given by him at the end. It is right to say that the charter is now generally considered to be a forgery executed in later times. — B.

[4] Evertsen. There were two admirals of this name, John and Cornelius.

But they have killed poor Captaine Golding[1] in The Diamond. Two of them, one of 32 and the other of 20 odd guns, did stand stoutly up against her, which hath 46, and the Yarmouth that hath 52 guns, and as many more men as they. So that they did more than we could expect, not yielding till many of their men were killed. And Everson, when he was brought before the Duke of Yorke, and was observed to be shot through the hat, answered, that he wished it had gone through his head, rather than been taken. One thing more is written: that two of our ships the other day appearing upon the coast of Holland, they presently fired their beacons round the country to give notice. And newes is brought the King, that the Dutch Smyrna fleete is seen upon the back of Scotland; and thereupon the King hath wrote to the Duke, that he do appoint a fleete to go to the Northward to try to meet them coming home round: which God send! Thence to White Hall; where the King seeing me, did come to me, and calling me by name, did discourse with me about the ships in the River: and this is the first time that ever I knew the King did know me personally; so that hereafter I must not go thither, but with expectation to be questioned, and to be ready to give good answers. So home, and thence with Creed, who come to dine with me, to the Old James, where we dined with Sir W. Rider and Cutler, and, by and by, being called by my wife, we all to a play, "The Ghosts,"[2] at the Duke's house, but a very simple play. Thence up and down, with my wife with me, to look [for] Sir Ph. Warwicke (Mr. Creed going from me), but missed of him and so home, and late and busy at my office. So home to supper and to bed. This day was left at my house a very neat silver watch, by one Briggs, a scrivener and sollicitor, at which I was angry with my wife for receiving, or, at least, for opening the box wherein it was, and so far witnessing our receipt of it, as to give the messenger 5*s.* for bringing it; but it can't be helped, and I will endeavour to do the man a kindnesse, he being a friend of my uncle Wight's.

[1] Captain John Golding and nine of his men were killed.

[2] A comedy, on the authority of Downes (p. 26) attributed to a Mr. Holden, and probably never printed. — B.

18th. Up and to Sir Philip Warwicke, and walked with him an houre with great delight in the Parke about Sir G. Carteret's accounts, and the endeavours that he hath made to bring Sir G. Carteret to show his accounts and let the world see what he receives and what he pays. Thence home to the office, where I find Sir J. Minnes come home from Chatham, and Sir W. Batten both this morning from Harwich, where they have been these 7 or 8 days. At noon with my wife and Mr. Moore by water to Chelsey about my Privy Seale for Tangier, but my Lord Privy Seale was gone abroad, and so we, without going out of the boat, forced to return, and found him not at White Hall. So I to Sir Philip Warwicke and with him to my Lord Treasurer, who signed my commission for Tangier-Treasurer and the docquet of my Privy Seale, for the monies to be paid to me. Thence to White Hall to Mr. Moore again, and not finding my Lord I home, taking my wife and woman up at Unthanke's. Late at my office, then to supper and to bed.

19th. Up by five o'clock, and by water to White Hall; and there took coach, and with Mr. Moore to Chelsy; where, after all my fears what doubts and difficulties my Lord Privy Seale[1] would make at my Tangier Privy Seale, he did pass it at first reading, without my speaking with him. And then called me in, and was very civil to me. I passed my time in contemplating (before I was called in) the picture of my Lord's son's lady, a most beautiful woman,[2] and most like to Mrs. Butler. Thence very much joyed to London back again, and found out Mr. Povy; told him this; and then went and left my Privy Seale at my Lord Treasurer's; and so to the 'Change, and thence to Trinity-House; where a great dinner of Captain Crisp, who is made an Elder Brother. And so, being very pleasant at dinner, away home, Creed with me; and there met Povy; and we to Gresham College, where we saw some experiments upon a hen, a dogg, and a cat, of the Florence poyson.[3] The first it made for a time drunk, but it come

[1] John, Lord Robartes, Lord Privy Seal, 1661–73: created Earl of Radnor, 1679. Died July 17th, 1685.

[2] Sara Bodville, wife of Robert Robartes. See note, May 3rd, 1664.

[3] "Sir Robert Moray presented the Society from the King with a

to itself again quickly; the second it made vomitt mightily, but no other hurt. The third I did not stay to see the effect of it, being taken out by Povy. He and I walked below together, he giving me most exceeding discouragements in the getting of money (whether by design or no I know not, for I am now come to think him a most cunning fellow in most things he do, but his accounts), and made it plain to me that money will be hard to get, and that it is to be feared Backewell hath a design in it to get the thing forced upon himself. This put me into a cruel melancholy to think I may lose what I have had so near my hand; but yet something may be hoped for which to-morrow will shew. He gone, Creed and I together a great while consulting what to do in this case, and after all I left him to do what he thought fit in his discourse to-morrow with my Lord Ashly. So home, and in my way met with Mr. Warren, from whom my hopes I fear will fail of what I hoped for, by my getting him a protection. But all these troubles will if not be over, yet we shall see the worst of them in a day or two. So to my office, and thence to supper, and my head akeing, betimes, that is by 10 or 11 o'clock, to bed.

20th. Up, and all the morning busy at the office. At noon dined, and Mr. Povy by agreement with me (where his boldness with Mercer, poor innocent wench, did make both her and me blush, to think how he were able to debauch a poor girl if he had opportunity) at a dish or two of plain meat of his own choice. After dinner comes Creed and then Andrews, where want of money to Andrews the main discourse, and at last in confidence of Creed's judgement I am resolved to spare him 4 or £500 of what lies by me upon the security of some Tallys. This went against my heart to begin, but when obtaining Mr. Creed to joyne with me we do resolve to assist Mr. Andrews. Then anon we parted, and I to my office, where late, and then home to supper and to bed. This night I am told the first play is played in White Hall noon-hall, which

phial of Florentine poison sent for by his Majesty from Florence, on purpose to have those experiments related of the efficacy thereof, tried by the Society." The poison had little effect upon the kitten (Birch's "History," vol. ii., p. 31).

is now turned to a house of playing. I had a great mind, but could not go to see it.

21st. Up and to my office about business. Anon comes Creed and Povy, and we treat about the business of our lending money, Creed and I, upon a tally for the satisfying of Andrews, and did conclude it as in papers is expressed, and as I am glad to have an opportunity of having 10 per cent. for my money, so I am as glad that the sum I begin this trade with is no more than £350. We all dined at Andrews' charge at the Sun behind the 'Change, a good dinner the worst dressed that ever I eat any, then home, and there found Kate Joyce and Harman come to see us. With them, after long talk, abroad by coach, a tour in the fields, and drunk at Islington, it being very pleasant, the dust being laid by a little rain, and so home very well pleased with this day's work. So after a while at my office to supper and to bed. This day we hear that the Duke and the fleete are sailed yesterday. Pray God go along with them, that they have good speed in the beginning of their worke.

22nd. Up, and Mr. Cæsar, my boy's lute-master, being come betimes to teach him, I did speak with him seriously about the boy, what my mind was, if he did not look after his lute and singing that I would turn him away; which I hope will do some good upon the boy. All the morning busy at the office. At noon dined at home, and then to the office again very busy till very late, and so home to supper and to bed. My wife making great preparation to go to Court to Chappell to-morrow. This day I have newes from Mr. Coventry that the fleete is sailed yesterday from Harwich to the coast of Holland to see what the Dutch will do. God go along with them!

23rd (Lord's day). Mr. Povy, according to promise, sent his coach betimes, and I carried my wife and her woman to White Hall Chappell and set them in the Organ Loft, and I having left to untruss went to the Harp and Ball and there drank also, and entertained myself in talke with the mayde of the house, a pretty mayde and very modest. Thence to the Chappell and heard the famous young Stillingfleete, whom I knew at Cambridge, and is now newly admitted one of the King's chaplains; and was presented, they say, to my Lord Treasurer for St. Andrew's, Holborne, where he is now minister, with these words: that they (the Bishops of Canterbury, London, and another) believed he is the ablest young man to preach the Gospel of any since the Apostles. He did make the most plain, honest, good, grave sermon, in the most unconcerned and easy yet substantial manner, that ever I heard in my life, upon the words of Samuell to the people, "Fear the Lord in truth with all your heart, and remember the great things that he hath done for you." It being proper to this day, the day of the King's Coronation. Thence to Mr. Povy's, where mightily treated, and Creed with us. But Lord! to see how Povy overdoes every thing in commending it, do make it nauseous to me, and was not (by reason of my large praise of his house) over acceptable to my wife. Thence after dinner Creed and we by coach took the ayre in the fields beyond St. Pancras, it raining now and then, which it seems is most welcome weather, and then all to my house, where comes Mr. Hill, Andrews, and Captain Taylor, and good musique, but at supper to hear the arguments[1] we had against Taylor concerning a Corant, he saying that the law of a dancing Corant is to have every barr to end in a pricked crochet and quaver, which I did deny, was very strange. It proceeded till I vexed him, but all parted friends, for Creed and I to laugh at when he was gone. After supper, Creed and I together to bed, in Mercer's bed, and so to sleep.

24th. Up and with Creed in Sir W. Batten's coach to White Hall. Sir W. Batten and I to the Duke of Albemarle, where very busy. Then I to Creed's chamber, where I received with much ado my two orders about receiving Povy's monies and answering his credits, and it is

[1] Dr. Hueffer wrote respecting this passage: "If one may at this day decide such a question it would appear that Mr. Pepys had decidedly the best of the argument. We all know that the courante is a lively dance in 3-4 or 3-2 time, beginning with a short note at the end of the bar, and expressing, as Mattheson, writing a good many years after Pepys, discovered, 'sweet hope, and in fact a combination of confidence, desire, and joy.' But neither the Italian *corrente* of Corelli, nor yet the French *courante*, as developed by Couperin and the great Bach, seems to bear out the law laid down by Captain Taylor" ("Italian and other Studies," p. 252).

strange how he will preserve his constant humour of delaying all business that comes before him. Thence he and I to London to my office, and back again to my Lady Sandwich's to dinner, where my wife by agreement. After dinner alone, my Lady told me, with the prettiest kind of doubtfullnesse, whether it would be fit for her with respect to Creed to do it, that is, in the world, that Creed had broke his desire to her of being a servant to Mrs. Betty Pickering, and placed it upon encouragement which he had from some discourse of her ladyship, commending of her virtues to him, which, poor lady, she meant most innocently. She did give him a cold answer, but not so severe as it ought to have been; and, it seems, as the lady since to my Lady confesses, he had wrote a letter to her, which she answered slightly, and was resolved to contemn any motion of his therein. My Lady takes the thing very ill, as it is fit she should; but I advise her to stop all future occasions of the world's taking notice of his coming thither so often as of late he hath done. But to think that he should have this devilish presumption to aime at a lady so near to my Lord is strange, both for his modesty and discretion. Thence to the Cockepitt, and there walked an houre with my Lord Duke of Albemarle alone in his garden, where he expressed in great words his opinion of me; that I was the right hand of the Navy here, nobody but I taking any care of any thing therein; so that he should not know what could be done without me. At which I was (from him) not a little proud. Thence to a Committee of Tangier, where because not a quorum little was done, and so away to my wife (Creed with me) at Mrs. Pierce's, who continues very pretty and is now great with child. I had not seen her a great while. Thence by coach to my Lord Treasurer's, but could not speak with Sir Ph. Warwicke. So by coach with my wife and Mercer to the Parke; but the King being there, and I now-a-days being doubtfull of being seen in any pleasure, did part from the tour, and away out of the Parke to Knightsbridge, and there eat and drank in the coach, and so home, and after a while at my office, home to supper and to bed, having got a great cold I think by my pulling off my periwigg so often.

25th. At the office all the morning, and the like after

dinner, at home all the afternoon till very late, and then to bed, being very hoarse with a cold I did lately get with leaving off my periwigg. This afternoon W. Pen, lately come from his father in the fleete, did give me an account how the fleete did sayle, about 103 in all, besides small catches, they being in sight of six or seven Dutch scouts, and sent ships in chase of them.

26th. Up very betimes, my cold continuing and my stomach sick with the buttered ale that I did drink the last night in bed, which did lie upon me till I did this morning vomitt it up. So walked to Povy's, where Creed met me, and there I did receive the first parcel of money as Treasurer of Tangier, and did give him my receipt for it, which was about £2,800 value in Tallys; we did also examine and settle several other things, and then I away to White Hall, talking, with Povy alone, about my opinion of Creed's indiscretion in looking after Mrs. Pickering, desiring him to make no more a sport of it, but to correct him, if he finds that he continues to owne any such thing. This I did by my Lady's desire, and do intend to pursue the stop of it. So to the Carrier's by Cripplegate, to see whether my mother be come to towne or no, I expecting her to-day, but she is not come. So to dinner to my Lady Sandwich's, and there after dinner above in the dining-room did spend an houre or two with her talking again about Creed's folly; but strange it is that he should dare to propose this business himself of Mrs. Pickering to my Lady, and to tell my Lady that he did it for her virtue sake, not minding her money, for he could have a wife with more, but, for that, he did intend to depend upon her Ladyshipp to get as much of her father and mother for her as she could; and that, what he did, was by encouragement from discourse of her Ladyshipp's: he also had wrote to Mrs. Pickering, but she did give him a slighting answer back again. But I do very much fear that Mrs. Pickering's honour, if the world comes to take notice of it, may be wronged by it. Thence home, and all the afternoon till night at my office, then home to supper and to bed.

27th. Up, and to my office, where all the morning, at noon Creed dined with me; and, after dinner, walked in the garden, he telling me that my Lord Treasurer now begins to be scrupulous, and will know what becomes of the £26,000 saved by my Lord Peterborough, before he parts with any more money, which puts us into new doubts, and me into a great fear, that all my cake will be doe[1] still. But I am well prepared for it to bear it, being not clear whether it will be more for my profit to have it, or go without it, as my profits of the Navy are likely now to be. All the afternoon till late hard at the office. Then to supper and to bed. This night William Hewer is returned from Harwich, where he hath been paying off of some ships this fortnight, and went to sea a good way with the fleete, which was 96 in company then, men of warr, besides some come in, and following them since, which makes now above 100, whom God bless!

28th. Up at 5 o'clock, and by appointment with Creed by 6 at his chamber, expecting Povy, who come not. Thence he and I out to Sir Philip Warwicke's, but being not up we took a turn in the garden hard by, and thither comes Povy to us. After some discourse of the reason of the difficulty that Sir Philip Warwicke makes in issuing a warrant for my striking of tallys, namely, the having a clear account of the £26,000 saved by my Lord of Peterborough, we parted, and I to Sir P. Warwicke, who did give me an account of his demurr, which I applied myself to remove by taking Creed with me to my Lord Ashly, from whom, contrary to all expectation, I received a very kind answer, just as we could have wished it, that he would satisfy my Lord Treasurer. Thence very well satisfied I home, and down the river to visit the victualling-ships, where I find all out of order. And come home to dinner, and then to write a letter to the Duke of Albemarle about the victualling-ships, and carried it myself to the Council-chamber, where it was read; and when they rose, my Lord Chancellor passing by stroked me on the head, and told me that the Board had read my letter, and taken order for the punishing of the watermen for not appearing on board

[1] An obsolete proverb, signifying to lose one's hopes, a cake coming out of the oven in a state of dough being considered spoiled.

"My cake is dough; but I'll in among the rest;
Out of hope of all, but my share in the feast."
Shakespeare, *Taming of the Shrew*, act v., sc. 1. — M. B.

the ships.[1] And so did the King afterwards, who do now know me so well, that he never sees me but he speaks to me about our Navy business. Thence got my Lord Ashly to my Lord Treasurer below in his chamber, and there removed the scruple, and by and by brought Mr. Sherwin to Sir Philip Warwicke and did the like, and so home, and after a while at my office, to bed.

29th. All the morning busy at the office. In the afternoon to my Lord Treasurer's, and there got my Lord Treasurer to sign the warrant for my striking of tallys, and so doing many jobbs in my way home, and there late writeing letters, being troubled in my mind to hear that Sir W. Batten and Sir J. Minnes do take notice that I am now-a-days much from the office upon no office business, which vexes me, and will make me mind my business the better, I hope in God; but what troubles me more is, that I do omit to write, as I should do, to Mr. Coventry, which I must not do, though this night I minded it so little as to sleep in the middle of my letter to him, and committed forty blotts and blurrs in my letter to him, but of this I hope never more to be guilty, if I have not already given him sufficient offence. So, late home, and to bed.

30th (Lord's day). Up and to my office alone all the morning, making up my monthly accounts, which though it hath been very intricate, and very great disbursements and receipts and odd reckonings, yet I differed not from the truth; viz.: between my first computing what my profit ought to be and then what my cash and debts do really make me worth, not above 10*s.*, which is very much, and I do much value myself upon the account, and herein I with great joy find myself to have gained this month above £100 clear, and in the whole to be worth above £1,400, the greatest sum I ever yet was worth. Thence home to dinner, and there find poor Mr. Spong walking at my door, where he had knocked, and being told I was at the office

[1] Among the State Papers are lists of watermen impressed and put on board the victualling ships. Attached to one of these is a "note of their unfitness and refractory conduct; also that many go ashore to sleep, and are discontent that they, as masters of families, are pressed, while single men are excused on giving money to the pressmen" ("Calendar," Domestic, 1664–65, p. 323).

staid modestly there walking because of disturbing me, which methinks was one of the most modest acts (of a man that hath no need of being so to me) that ever I knew in my life. He dined with me, and then after dinner to my closet, where abundance of mighty pretty discourse, wherein, in a word, I find him the man of the world that hath of his own ingenuity obtained the most in most things, being withall no scholler. He gone, I took boat and down to Woolwich and Deptford, and made it late home, and so to supper and to bed. Thus I end this month in great content as to my estate and gettings: in much trouble as to the pains I have taken, and the rubs I expect yet to meet with, about the business of Tangier. The fleete, with about 106 ships upon the coast of Holland, in sight of the Dutch, within the Texel. Great fears of the sickenesse here in the City, it being said that two or three houses are already shut up. God preserve us all!

May 1st. Up and to Mr. Povy's, and by his bedside talked a good while. Among other things he do much insist I perceive upon the difficulty of getting of money, and would fain have me to concur in the thinking of some other way of disposing of the place of Treasurer to one Mr. Bell, but I did seem slight of it, and resolved to try to do the best or to give it up. Thence to the Duke of Albemarle, where I was sorry to find myself to come a little late, and so home, and at noon going to the 'Change I met my Lord Brunkard, Sir Robert Murry, Deane Wilkins, and Mr. Hooke, going by coach to Colonell Blunt's[1] to dinner.

[1] At Wricklesmarsh, in the parish of Charlton, which belonged in 1617 to Edward Blount, whose family alienated it towards the end of the seventeenth century. The old mansion was pulled down by Sir Gregory Page, Bart., who erected a magnificent stone structure on the site; which, devolving to his great-nephew, Sir Gregory Page Turner, shared the same fate as the former house, having been sold in lots in 1784. The site of Colonel Blount's house is now covered with villas, and is called Blackheath Park. — B.

"Col. Blount produced another model of a chariot with four springs, esteemed by him very easy both to the rider and horse, and at the same time cheap. It was ordered that the committee formerly appointed, viz., the President, Sir Robert Moray, Sir William Petty, Dr. Wilkins, Col. Blount, and Mr. Hooke, should be desired to meet at Col. Blount's house at Writlemarsh, about this matter, on the Monday

So they stopped and took me with them. Landed at the Tower-wharf, and thence by water to Greenwich; and there coaches met us; and to his house, a very stately sight for situation and brave plantations; and among others, a vineyard, the first that ever I did see. No extraordinary dinner, nor any other entertainment good; but only after dinner to the tryall of some experiments about making of coaches easy. And several we tried; but one did prove mighty easy (not here for me to describe, but the whole body of the coach lies upon one long spring), and we all, one after another, rid in it; and it is very fine and likely to take. These experiments were the intent of their coming, and pretty they are. Thence back by coach to Greenwich, and in his pleasure boat to Deptford, and there stopped and into Mr. Evelyn's,[1] which is a most beautiful place; but it being dark and late, I staid not; but Deane Wilkins and Mr. Hooke and I walked to Redriffe; and noble discourse all day long did please me, and it being late did take them to my house to drink, and did give them some sweetmeats, and thence sent them with a lanthorn home, two worthy persons as are in England, I think, or the world. So to my Lady Batten, where my wife is to-night, and so after some merry talk home and to bed.

2nd. Up and to the office all day, where sat late, and then to the office again, and by and by Sir W. Batten and my Lady and my wife and I by appointment yesterday (my Lady Pen failed us, who ought to have been with us) to the Rhenish winehouse at the Steelyard, and there eat a couple of lobsters and some prawns, and pretty merry, specially to see us four together, while my wife and my Lady did never intend ever to be together again after a year's distance between one another. Hither by and by come Sir Richard Ford and also Mrs. Esther, that lived formerly with my Lady Batten, now well married to a priest, come to see my Lady. Thence toward evening home, and to my office, where late, and then home to supper and to bed.

3rd. Up betimes and walked to Sir Ph. Warwicke's,

following, and give an account of what they had done there at the next meeting of the Society." On May 3rd Hooke reported (Birch's "History," vol. ii., pp. 41, 45).

[1] Sayes Court, the well-known residence of John Evelyn.

where a long time with him in his chamber alone talking of Sir G. Carteret's business, and the abuses he puts on the nation by his bad payments to both our vexations, but no hope of remedy for ought I see. Thence to my Lord Ashly to a Committee of Tangier for my Lord Rutherford's accounts, and that done we to my Lord Treasurer's, where I did receive my Lord's warrant to Sir R. Long for drawing a warrant for my striking of tallys. So to the Inne again by Cripplegate, expecting my mother's coming to towne, but she is not come this weeke neither, the coach being too full. So to the 'Change and thence home to dinner, and so out to Gresham College, and saw a cat killed with the Duke of Florence's poyson, and saw it proved that the oyle of tobacco[1] drawn by one of the Society do the same effect, and is judged to be the same thing with the poyson both in colour and smell and effect. I saw also an abortive child preserved fresh in spirits of salt. Thence parted, and to White Hall to the Council-chamber about an order touching the Navy (our being empowered to commit seamen or Masters that do not, being hired or pressed, follow their worke), but they could give us none. So a little vexed at that, because I put in the memorial to the Duke of Albemarle alone under my own hand, home, and after some time at the office home to bed. My Lord Chief-Justice Hide[2] did die suddenly this week a day or two ago, of an apoplexy.

4th. Up, and to the office, where we sat busy all the morning. At noon home to dinner, and then to the office again all day till almost midnight, and then, weary, home to supper and to bed.

5th. Up betimes, and by water to Westminster, there to speak the first time with Sir Robert Long, to give him my

[1] "Mr. Daniel Coxe read an account of the effects of tobacco-oil distilled in a retort, by one drop of which given at the mouth he had killed a lusty cat, which being opened, smelled strongly of the oil, and the blood of the heart more strongly than the rest. . . . One drop of the Florentine *oglio di tobacco* being again given to a dog, it proved stupefying and vomitive, as before" (Birch's "History of the Royal Society," vol. ii., pp. 42, 43).

[1] Sir Robert Hyde, cousin of the Earl of Clarendon, appointed Chief Justice of the King's Bench, October 10th, 1663. Born 1595, died May 1st, 1665. He was buried in Salisbury Cathedral.

Privy Seal and my Lord Treasurer's order for Tangier Tallys; he received me kindly enough. Thence home by water, and presently down to Woolwich and back to Blackewall, and there viewed the Breach, in order to a Mast Docke,[1] and so to Deptford to the Globe, where my Lord Brunkard, Sir J. Minnes, Sir W. Batten, and Commissioner Pett were at dinner, having been at the Breach also, but they find it will be too great charge to make use of it. After dinner to Mr. Evelyn's; he being abroad, we walked in his garden, and a lovely noble ground he hath indeed. And among other rarities, a hive of bees, so as being hived in glass, you may see the bees making their honey and combs mighty pleasantly. Thence home, and I by and by to Mr. Povy's to see him, who is yet in his chamber not well, and thence by his advice to one Lovett's, a varnisher, to see his manner of new varnish, but found not him at home, but his wife, a very beautiful woman, who shewed me much variety of admirable work, and is in order to my having of some papers fitted with his lines for my use for tables and the like. I know not whether I was more pleased with the thing, or that I was shewed it by her, but resolved I am to have some made. So home to my office late, and then to supper and to bed. My wife tells me that she hears that my poor aunt James hath had her breast cut off here in town, her breast having long been out of order. This day, after I had suffered my owne hayre to grow long, in order to wearing it, I find the convenience of periwiggs is so great, that I have cut off all short again, and will keep to periwiggs.

6th. Up, and all day at the office, but a little at dinner, and there late till past 12. So home to bed, pleased as I always am after I have rid a great deal of work, it being very satisfactory to me.

7th (Lord's day). Up, and to church with my wife. Home and dined. After dinner come Mr. Andrews and spent the afternoon with me, about our Tangier business of the victuals, and then parted, and after sermon comes Mr.

[1] Christopher Pett wrote to Pepys from Woolwich on April 22nd, 1665, and begged for "allowance for two divers employed when the estimate for the mast dock at Blackwall was made" ("Calendar of State Papers," Domestic, 1664–65, p. 324).

Hill and a gentleman, a friend of his, one Mr. Scott, that sings well also, and then comes Mr. Andrews, and we all sung and supped, and then to sing again and passed the Sunday very pleasantly and soberly, and so I to my office a little, and then home to prayers and to bed. Yesterday begun my wife to learn to limn of one Browne,[1] which Mr. Hill helps her to, and, by her beginning upon some eyes, I think she will [do] very fine things, and I shall take great delight in it.

8th. Up very betimes, and did much business before I went out with several persons, among others Captain Taylor, who would leave the management of most of his business now he is going to Harwich, upon me, and if I can get money by it, which I believe it will, I shall take some of it upon me. Thence with Sir W. Batten to the Duke of Albemarle's and there did much business, and then to the 'Change, and thence off with Sir W. Warren to an ordinary, where we dined and sat talking of most usefull discourse till 5 in the afternoon, and then home, and very busy till late, and so home and to bed.

9th. Up betimes, and to my business at the office, where all the morning. At noon comes Mrs. The. Turner, and dines with us, and my wife's painting-master staid and dined, and I take great pleasure in thinking that my wife will really come to something in that business. Here dined also Luellin. So after dinner to my office, and there very busy till almost midnight, and so home to supper and to bed. This day we have newes of eight ships being taken by some of ours going into the Texel, their two men of warr, that convoyed them, running in. They come from about Ireland, round to the north.

10th. Up betimes, and abroad to the Cocke-pitt, where the Duke [of Albemarle] did give Sir W. Batten and me an account of the late taking of eight ships, and of his intent to come back to the Gunfleete[2] with the fleete presently; which creates us much work and haste therein, against the fleete comes. So to Mr. Povy, and after discourse with him

[1] Alexander Browne, a printseller, who taught drawing, and practised it with success. He published in 1669, "Ars Pictoria, or an Academy treating of Drawing, Painting, Limning and Etching."

[2] The Gunfleet Sand off the Essex coast.

home, and thence to the Guard in Southwarke, there to get some soldiers, by the Duke's order, to go keep pressmen on board our ships. So to the 'Change and did much business, and then home to dinner, and there find my poor mother come out of the country to-day in good health, and I am glad to see her, but my business, which I am sorry for, keeps me from paying the respect I ought to her at her first coming, she being grown very weak in her judgement, and doating again in her discourse, through age and some trouble in her family. I left her and my wife to go abroad to buy something, and then I to my office. In the evening by appointment to Sir W. Warren and Mr. Deering at a taverne hard by with intent to do some good upon their agreement in a great bargain of planks. So home to my office again, and then to supper and to bed, my mother being in bed already.

11th. Up betimes, and at the office all the morning. At home dined, and then to the office all day till late at night, and then home to supper, weary with business, and to bed.

12th. Up betimes, and find myself disappointed in my receiving presently of my £50 I hoped for sure of Mr. Warren upon the benefit of my press warrant, but he promises to make it good. So by water to the Exchequer, and there up and down through all the offices to strike my tallys for £17,500, which methinks is so great a testimony of the goodness of God to me, that I, from a mean clerke there, should come to strike tallys myself for that sum, and in the authority that I do now, is a very stupendous mercy to me. I shall have them struck to-morrow. But to see how every little fellow looks after his fees, and to get what he can for everything, is a strange consideration; the King's fees that he must pay himself for this £17,500 coming to above £100. Thence called my wife at Unthanke's to the New Exchange and elsewhere to buy a lace band for me, but we did not buy, but I find it so necessary to have some handsome clothes that I cannot but lay out some money thereupon. To the 'Change and thence to my watchmaker, where he has put it [*i.e.* the watch] in order, and a good and brave piece it is, and he tells me worth £14, which is a greater present than I valued it. So home to dinner, and after dinner comes several people, among others my cozen, Thomas Pepys,[1] of Hatcham, to receive some money of my Lord Sandwich's, and there I paid him what was due to him upon my uncle's score, but, contrary to my expectation, did get him to sign and seale to my sale of lands for payment of debts. So that now I reckon myself in better condition by £100 in my content than I was before, when I was liable to be called to an account and others after me by my uncle Thomas or his children for every foot of land we had sold before. This I reckon a great good fortune in the getting of this done. He gone, come Mr. Povy, Dr. Twisden, and Mr. Lawson about settling my security in the paying of the £4,000 ordered to Sir J. Lawson. So a little abroad and then home, and late at my office and closet settling this day's disordering of my papers, then to supper and to bed.

13th. Up, and all day in some little gruntings of pain, as I used to have from winde, arising I think from my fasting so long, and want of exercise, and I think going so hot in clothes, the weather being hot, and the same clothes I wore all winter. To the 'Change after office, and received my watch from the watchmaker, and a very fine [one] it is, given me by Briggs, the Scrivener. Home to dinner, and then I abroad to the Atturney Generall, about advice upon the Act for Land Carriage, which he desired not to give me before I had received the King's and Council's order therein, going home bespoke the King's works, will cost me 50*s.*, I believe. So home and late at my office. But, Lord! to see how much of my old folly and childishnesse hangs upon me still that I cannot forbear carrying my watch in my hand in the coach all this afternoon, and seeing what o'clock it is one hundred times, and am apt to think with myself, how could I be so long without one; though I remember since, I had one, and found it a trouble, and resolved to carry one no more about me while I lived. So home to supper and to bed, being troubled at a letter from Mr. Cholmly from Tangier, wherein he do advise me how people are at worke to overthrow our Victualling business, by which I shall lose £300 per annum. I am much obliged to him for this secret kindnesse, and concerned

[1] Thomas Pepys, of Hatcham Barnes, Surrey, Master of the Jewel House to Charles II. and James II.

to repay it him in his own concernments and look after this.

14th (Lord's day). Up, and with my wife to church, it being Whitsunday; my wife very fine in a new yellow bird's-eye hood, as the fashion is now. We had a most sorry sermon; so home to dinner, my mother having her new suit brought home, which makes her very fine. After dinner my wife and she and Mercer to Thomas Pepys's wife's christening of his first child, and I took a coach, and to Wanstead, the house where Sir H. Mildmay died, and now Sir Robert Brookes[1] lives, having bought it of the Duke of Yorke, it being forfeited to him. A fine seat, but an old-fashioned house; and being not full of people looks desolately. Thence to Walthamstow, where (failing at the old place) Sir W. Batten by and by come home, I walking up and down the house and garden with my Lady very pleasantly, then to supper very merry, and then back by coach by dark night. I all the afternoon in the coach reading the treasonous book of the Court of King James, printed a great while ago, and worth reading, though ill intended. As soon as I come home, upon a letter from the Duke of Albemarle, I took boat at about 12 at night, and down the River in a gally, my boy and I, down to the Hope and so up again, sleeping and waking, with great pleasure, my business to call upon every one of

15th. Our victualling ships to set them agoing, and so home, and after dinner to the King's playhouse, all alone, and saw "Love's Maistresse."[2] Some pretty things and good variety in it, but no or little fancy in it. Thence to the Duke of Albemarle to give him account of my day's works, where he shewed me letters from Sir G. Downing, of four days' date, that the Dutch are come out and joyned, well-manned, and resolved to board our best ships, and fight for certain they will. Thence to the Swan at Herbert's, and there the company of Sarah a little while, and so away and called at the Harp and Ball, where the mayde, Mary, is very *formosa*;[3] but, Lord! to see in what readiness I

[1] For note on Sir Robert Brooke, Lord of the Manor of Wanstead, see vol. i., p. xxvii.

[2] "Loves Maistresse, or The Queen's Masque," by Thomas Heywood, printed 1636, 1640.

[3] Formosa = handsome (*Italian*).

am, upon the expiring of my vowes this day, to begin to run into all my pleasures and neglect of business. Thence home, and being sleepy to bed.

16th. Up betimes, and to the Duke of Albemarle with an account of my yesterday's actions in writing. So back to the office, where all the morning very busy. After dinner by coach to see and speak with Mr. Povy, and after little discourse back again home, where busy upon letters till past 12 at night, and so home to supper and to bed, weary.

17th. Up, and by appointment to a meeting of Sir John Lawson and Mr. Cholmly's atturney and Mr. Povy at the Swan taverne at Westminster to settle their business about my being secured in the payment of money to Sir J. Lawson in the other's absence. Thence at Langford's, where I never was since my brother died there. I find my wife and Mercer, having with him agreed upon two rich silk suits for me, which is fit for me to have, but yet the money is too much, I doubt, to lay out altogether; but it is done, and so let it be, it being the expense of the world that I can the best bear with and the worst spare. Thence home, and after dinner to the office, where late, and so home to supper and to bed. Sir J. Minnes and I had an angry bout this afternoon with Commissioner Pett about his neglecting his duty and absenting himself, unknown to us, from his place at Chatham, but a most false man I every day find him more and more, and in this very full of equivocation. The fleete we doubt not come to Harwich by this time. Sir W. Batten is gone down this day thither, and the Duchesse of Yorke went down yesterday to meet the Duke.

18th. Up, and with Sir J. Minnes to the Duke of Albemarle, where we did much business, and I with good content to myself; among other things we did examine Nixon and Stanesby,[1] about their late running from two Dutch-

[1] Captain Edward Nixon, of the "Elizabeth," and Captain John Stanesby, of the "Eagle." John Lanyon wrote to the Navy Commissioners from Plymouth, May 16th: "Understands from the seamen that the conduct of Captains Nixon and Stanesby in their late engagement with two Dutch capers was very foul; the night they left the Dutch, no lights were put out as formerly, and though in sight of them in the morning, they still kept on their way; the Eagle lay by some time, and both the enemy's ships plied on her, but finding the Elizabeth nearly

men; for which they are committed to a vessel to carry them to the fleete to be tried. A most fowle unhandsome thing as ever was heard, for plain cowardice on Nixon's part. Thence with the Duke of Albemarle in his coach to my Lord Treasurer, and there was before the King (who ever now calls me by my name) and Lord Chancellor, and many other great Lords, discoursing about insuring of some of the King's goods, wherein the King accepted of my motion that we should; and so away, well pleased. To the office, and dined, and then to the office again, and abroad, to speak with Sir G. Carteret; but, Lord! to see how fraile a man I am, subject to my vanities, that can hardly forbear, though pressed with never so much business, my pursuing of pleasure, but home I got, and there very busy very late. Among other things consulting with Mr. Andrews about our Tangier business, wherein we are like to meet with some trouble, and my lord Bellasses's endeavour to supplant us, which vexes my mind; but, however, our undertaking is so honourable that we shall stand a tug for it I think. So home to supper and to bed.

19th. Up, and to White Hall, where the Committee for Tangier met, and there, though the case as to the merit of it was most plain and most of the company favourable to our business, yet it was with much ado that I got the business not carried fully against us, but put off to another day, my Lord Arlington being the great man in it, and I was sorry to be found arguing so greatly against him. The business I believe will in the end be carried against us, and the whole business fall; I must therefore endeavour the most I can to get money another way. It vexed me to see Creed so hot against it, but I cannot much blame him, having never declared to him my being concerned in it. But that that troubles me most is my Lord Arlington calls to me privately and asks me whether I had ever said to any body that I desired to leave this employment, hav-

out of sight she also made sail; it is true the wind and sea were high, but there were no sufficient reasons for such endeavours to get from them" ("Calendar of State Papers," Domestic, 1664–65, p. 367). Both captains were tried; Nixon was condemned to be shot, but Stanesby was cleared, and Charnock asserts that he was commander of the "Happy Return" in 1672.

ing not time to look after it. I told him, No, for that the thing being settled it will not require much time to look after it. He told me then he would do me right to the King, for he had been told so, which I desired him to do, and by and by he called me to him again and asked me whether I had no friend about the Duke, asking me (I making a stand) whether Mr. Coventry was not my friend. I told him I had received many friendships from him. He then advised me to procure that the Duke would in his next letter write to him to continue me in my place and remove any obstruction; which I told him I would, and thanked him. So parted, vexed at the first and amazed at this business of my Lord Arlington's. Thence to the Exchequer, and there got my tallys for £17,500, the first payment I ever had out of the Exchequer, and at the Legg spent 14*s.* upon my old acquaintance, some of them the clerks, and away home with my tallys in a coach, fearful every step of having one of them fall out, or snatched from me. Being come home, I much troubled out again by coach (for company taking Sir W. Warren with me), intending to have spoke to my Lord Arlington to have known the bottom of it, but missed him, and afterwards discoursing the thing as a confidant to Sir W. Warren, he did give me several good hints and principles not to do anything suddenly, but consult my pillow upon that and every great thing of my life, before I resolve anything in it. Away back home, and not being fit for business I took my wife and Mercer down by water to Greenwich at 8 at night, it being very fine and cool and moonshine afterward. Mighty pleasant passage it was; there eat a cake or two, and so home by 10 or 11 at night, and then to bed, my mind not settled what to think.

20th. Up, and to my office, where busy all the morning. At noon dined at home, and to my office, very busy.

21st. Till past one, Lord's day, in the morning writing letters to the fleete and elsewhere, and my mind eased of much business, home to bed and slept till 8. So up, and this day is brought home one of my new silk suits, the plain one, but very rich camelott and noble. I tried it and it pleases me, but did not wear it, being I would not go out to-day to church. So laid it by, and my mind changed, thinking to go see my Lady Sandwich, and I did go a little way, but stopped and returned home to dinner, after dinner up to my chamber to settle my Tangier accounts, and then to my office, there to do the like with other papers. In the evening home to supper and to bed.

22nd. Up, and down to the ships, which now are hindered from going down to the fleete (to our great sorrow and shame) with their provisions, the wind being against them. So to the Duke of Albemarle, and thence down by water to Deptford, it being Trinity Monday, and so the day of choosing the Master of Trinity House for the next yeare, where, to my great content, I find that, contrary to the practice and design of Sir W. Batten, to breake the rule and custom of the Company in choosing their Masters by succession, he would have brought in Sir W. Rider or Sir W. Pen, over the head of Hurleston[1] (who is a knave too besides, I believe), the younger brothers did all oppose it against the elder, and with great heat did carry it for Hurleston, which I know will vex him to the heart. Thence, the election being over, to church, where an idle sermon from that conceited fellow, Dr. Britton, saving that his advice to unity, and laying aside all envy and enmity among them was very apposite. Thence walked to Redriffe, and so to the Trinity House, and a great dinner, as is usual, and so to my office, where busy all the afternoon till late, and then home to bed, being much troubled in mind for several things, first, for the condition of the fleete for lacke of provisions, the blame this office lies under and the shame that they deserve to have brought upon them for the ships not being gone out of the River, and then for my business of Tangier which is not settled, and lastly for fear that I am not observed to have attended the office business of late as much as I ought to do, though there has been nothing but my attendance on Tangier that has occasioned my absence, and that of late not much.

23rd. Up, and at the office busy all the morning. At noon dined alone, my wife and mother being gone by invitation to dine with my mother's old servant Mr. Cordery, who made them very welcome. So to Mr. Povy's, where

[1] Nicholas Hurleston, Master of the Trinity House. He died in November of this year.

after a little discourse about his business I home again, and late at the office busy. Late comes Sir Arthur Ingram[1] to my office, to tell me that, by letters from Amsterdam of the 28th of this month (their style[2]), the Dutch fleete, being about 100 men-of-war, besides fire-ships, &c., did set out upon the 23rd and 24th inst. Being divided into seven squadrons,[3] viz., 1. Generall Opdam. 2. Cottenar, of Rotterdam. 3. Trump. 4. Schram, of Horne. 5. Stillingworth, of Freezland. 6. Everson. 7. One other, not named, of Zealand.

24th. Up, and by 4 o'clock in the morning, and with W. Hewer, there till 12 without intermission putting some papers in order. Thence to the Coffee-house with Creed, where I have not been a great while, where all the newes is of the Dutch being gone out, and of the plague growing upon us in this towne; and of remedies against it: some saying one thing, some another. So home to dinner, and after dinner Creed and I to Colvill's, thinking to shew him all the respect we could by obliging him in carrying him 5 tallys of £5,000 to secure him for so much credit he has formerly given Povy to Tangier, but he, like an impertinent fool, cavills at it, but most ignorantly that ever I heard man in my life. At last Mr. Viner by chance comes, who I find a very moderate man, but could not persuade the fool to reason, but brought away the tallys again, and so

[1] Sir Arthur Ingram, knight, of Knottingley, Surveyor of the Customs at Hull. He lived in Fenchurch Street, and was a liberal benefactor to the parish of St. Dionis Backchurch after the Great Fire. The site of his mansion is marked by Ingram Court.

[2] The new style was adopted by most of the countries of Europe long before it was legalized in England, although Russia still retains the old style.

[3] A list of the Dutch fleet, May 23rd, 1665, is printed in Penn's "Memorials of Sir William Penn," vol. ii., p. 318, from which Pepys's lists of the commanders of the seven squadrons can be corrected. The first squadron was under Jacob van Wassenaer, Baron d'Opdam, Great Admiral of Holland and West Frieseland; the second under Lieut.-Admiral John Evertsen; the third under Lieut.-Admiral Egbert Meeuswisz Cortenaer (who died of his wounds after the sea-fight of June 3rd); the fourth under Lieut.-Admiral Stellingwerf; the fifth under Vice-Admiral Cornelius Tromp (son of the great Martin H. Tromp); the sixth under Vice-Admiral Cornelius Evertsen, and the seventh under Vice-Admiral Wouter Schram.

vexed to my office, where late, and then home to my supper and to bed.

25th. Up, and to the office, where all the morning. At noon dined at home, and then to the office all the afternoon, busy till almost 12 at night, and then home to supper and to bed.

26th. Up at 4 o'clock, and all the morning in my office with W. Hewer finishing my papers that were so long out of order, and at noon to my bookseller's, and there bespoke a book or two, and so home to dinner, where Creed dined with me, and he and I afterwards to Alderman Backewell's to try him about supplying us with money, which he denied at first and last also, saving that he spoke a little fairer at the end than before. But the truth is I do fear I shall have a great deale of trouble in getting of money. Thence home, and in the evening by water to the Duke of Albemarle, whom I found mightily off the hooks, that the ships are not gone out of the River; which vexed me to see, insomuch that I am afeard that we must expect some change or addition of new officers brought upon us, so that I must from this time forward resolve to make myself appear eminently serviceable in attending at my office duly and no where else, which makes me wish with all my heart that I had never anything to do with this business of Tangier. After a while at my office, home to supper vexed, and to bed.

27th. Up, and to the office, where all the morning; at noon dined at home, and then to my office again, where late, and so to bed, with my mind full of fears for the business of this office and troubled with that of Tangier, concerning which Mr. Povy was with me, but do give me little help, but more reason of being troubled. So that were it not for our Plymouth business I would be glad to be rid of it.

28th (Lord's day). By water to the Duke of Albemarle, where I hear that Nixon is condemned to be shot to death for his cowardice, by a Council of War.[1] Went to chapel and heard a little musique, and there met with Creed, and with him a little while walking, and to Wilkinson's for me

[1] See *ante*, May 18th.

to drink, being troubled with winde, and at noon to Sir Philip Warwicke's to dinner, where abundance of company come in unexpectedly; and here I saw one pretty piece of household stuff, as the company increaseth, to put a larger leaf upon an ovall table. After dinner much good discourse with Sir Philip, who I find, I think, a most pious, good man, and a professor of a philosophicall manner of life and principles like Epictetus,[1] whom he cites in many things. Thence to my Lady Sandwich's, where, to my shame I had not been a great while before. Here, upon my telling her a story of my Lord Rochester's[2] running away on Friday night last with Mrs. Mallett,[3] the great beauty and fortune of the North, who had supped at White Hall with Mrs. Stewart, and was going home to her lodgings with her grandfather, my Lord Haly,[4] by coach; and was at Charing Cross seized on by both horse and foot men, and forcibly taken from him, and put into a coach with six horses, and two women provided to receive her, and carried away. Upon immediate pursuit, my Lord of Rochester (for whom the King had spoke to the lady often, but with no successe) was taken at Uxbridge; but the lady is not yet heard of, and the King mighty angry, and the Lord sent to the Tower. Hereupon my Lady did confess to me, as a great secret, her being concerned in this story. For if this match breaks between my Lord Rochester and her, then, by the consent of all her friends, my Lord Hinchingbroke stands fair, and is invited for her. She is worth, and will be at her mother's death (who keeps but a little from her), £2,500 per annum. Pray God give a good success to it! But my poor Lady, who is afeard of the sickness, and resolved to be gone into

[1] For note on Pepys's quotation from Epictetus, see September 9th, 1662.

[2] John Wilmot, second Earl of Rochester, celebrated for his wit and notorious for his profligacy. Born April 10th, 1648; died July 26th, 1680.

[3] Elizabeth, daughter of John Malet, of Enmere, co. Somerset; married to the Earl of Rochester in 1667.

[4] Sir Francis Hawley of Buckland House, co. Somerset, created a baronet, 1642, and in 1646 an Irish peer, by the title of Baron Hawley of Donamore; in 1671 he was chosen M.P. for St. Michael's, and in 1673 became a Gentleman of the Bedchamber to the Duke of York. He died 1684, aged seventy-six. His daughter Elizabeth was Elizabeth Malet's mother.

the country, is forced to stay in towne a day or two, or three about it, to see the event of it. Thence home and to see my Lady Pen, where my wife and I were shown a fine rarity: of fishes[1] kept in a glass of water, that will live so for ever; and finely marked they are, being foreign. So to supper at home and to bed, after many people being with me about business, among others the two Bellamys about their old debt due to them from the King for their victualling business, out of which I hope to get some money.

29th. Lay long in bed, being in some little pain of the wind collique, then up and to the Duke of Albemarle, and so to the Swan, and there drank at Herbert's, and so by coach home, it being kept a great holiday through the City, for the birth and restoration of the King. To my office, where I stood by and saw Symson the joyner do several things, little jobbs, to the rendering of my closet handsome and the setting up of some neat plates that Burston has for my money made me, and so home to dinner, and then with my wife, mother, and Mercer in one boat, and I in another, down to Woolwich. I walking from Greenwich, the others going to and fro upon the water till my coming back, having done but little business. So home and to supper, and, weary, to bed. We have every where taken some prizes. Our merchants have good luck to come home safe: Colliers from the North, and some Streights' men just now. And our Hambrough ships, of whom we were so much afeard, are safe in Hambrough. Our fleete resolved to sail out again from Harwich in a day or two.

30th. Lay long, and very busy all the morning, at noon to the 'Change, and thence to dinner to Sir G. Carteret's, to talk upon the business of insuring our goods upon the Hambrough [ships]. Here a very fine, neat French dinner, without much cost, we being all alone with my Lady and one of the house with her; thence home and wrote letters, and then in the evening, by coach, with my wife and mother and Mercer, our usual tour by coach, and eat at the old house at Islington; but, Lord! to see how my mother found herself talk upon every object to think of old stories. Here I met with one that tells me that Jack Cole,[2] my old schoole-

[1] Gold fish introduced from China.

[2] See June 18th, 1661.

fellow, is dead and buried lately of a consumption, who was a great crony of mine. So back again home, and there to my closet to write letters. Hear to my great trouble that our Hambrough ships,[1] valued of the King's goods and the merchants' (though but little of the former) to £200,000 [are lost]. By and by, about 11 at night, called into the garden by my Lady Pen and daughter, and there walked with them and my wife till almost twelve, and so in and closed my letters, and home to bed.

31st. Up, and to my office, and to Westminster, doing business till noon, and then to the 'Change, where great the noise and trouble of having our Hambrough ships lost; and that very much placed upon Mr. Coventry's forgetting to give notice to them of the going away of our fleete from the coast of Holland. But all without reason, for he did; but the merchants not being ready, staid longer than the time ordered for the convoy to stay, which was ten days. Thence home with Creed and Mr. Moore to dinner. Anon we broke up, and Creed and I to discourse about our Tangier matters of money, which vex me. So to Gresham College, staid a very little while, and away and I home busy, and busy late, at the end of the month, about my month's accounts, but by the addition of Tangier it is rendered more intricate, and so (which I have not done these 12 months, nor would willingly have done now) failed of having it done, but I will do it as soon as I can. So weary and sleepy to bed. I endeavoured but missed of seeing Sir Thomas Ingram at Westminster, so went to Houseman's[2] the Painter, who I intend shall draw my wife, but he was not within, but I saw several very good pictures.

June 1st. Up and to the office, where sat all the morning, at noon to the 'Change, and there did some business, and home to dinner, whither Creed comes, and after dinner I put on my new silke camelott sute; the best that ever I wore in my life, the sute costing me above £24. In this I

[1] On May 29th Sir William Coventry wrote to Lord Arlington: "Capt. Langhorne has arrived with seven ships, and reports the taking of the Hamburg fleet with the man of war their convoy; mistaking the Dutch fleet for the English, he fell into it" ("Calendar of State Papers," Domestic, 1664–65, p. 393).

[2] Huysman.

went with Creed to Goldsmiths' Hall, to the burial of Sir Thomas Viner;[1] which Hall, and Haberdashers' also, was so full of people, that we were fain for ease and coolness to go forth to Pater Noster Row, to choose a silke to make me a plain ordinary suit. That done, we walked to Cornehill, and there at Mr. Cade's[2] stood in the balcon and saw all the funeral, which was with the blue-coat boys and old men, all the Aldermen, and Lord Mayor, &c., and the number of the company very great; the greatest I ever did see for a taverne. Hither come up to us Dr. Allen, and then Mr. Povy and Mr. Fox. The show being over, and my discourse with Mr. Povy, I took coach and to Westminster Hall, where I took the fairest flower, and by coach to Tothill Fields for the ayre till it was dark. I 'light, and in with the fairest flower to eat a cake, and there did do as much as was safe with my flower, and that was enough on my part. Broke up, and away without any notice, and, after delivering the rose where it should be, I to the Temple and 'light, and come to the middle door, and there took another coach, and so home to write letters, but very few, God knows, being by my pleasure made to forget everything that is. The coachman that carried [us] cannot know me again, nor the people at the house where we were. Home to bed, certain news being come that our fleete is in sight of the Dutch ships.

2nd. Lay troubled in mind abed a good while, thinking of my Tangier and victualling business, which I doubt will fall. Up and to the Duke of Albemarle, but missed him. Thence to the Harp and Ball and to Westminster Hall, where I visited "the flowers" in each place, and so met with Mr. Creed, and he and I to Mrs. Croft's to drink and did, but saw not her daughter Borroughes. I away home, and there dined and did business. In the afternoon went with my tallys, made a fair end with Colvill and Viner,

[1] Thomas Vyner, born 1588, Sheriff of London, 1648. When Lord Mayor, in 1654, he was knighted by Cromwell (Ludlow's "Memoirs"), and created a baronet at the Restoration, 1660. He was a goldsmith, and dying May 11th, 1665, was buried in St. Mary Woolnoth, in Lombard Street.

[2] Cade's tavern was "The Three Golden Lyons" in Cornhill. The ground floor was apparently occupied by a bookseller's shop ("Boyne's Tokens," ed. Williamson, 1889, vol. i., p. 372).

delivering them £5,000 tallys to each and very quietly had credit given me upon other tallys of Mr. Colvill for £2,000 and good words for more, and of Mr. Viner too. Thence to visit the Duke of Albemarle, and thence my Lady Sandwich and Lord Crew. Thence home, and there met an expresse from Sir W. Batten at Harwich, that the fleete is all sailed from Solebay, having spied the Dutch fleete at sea, and that, if the calmes hinder not they must needs now be engaged with them. Another letter also come to me from Mr. Hater, committed by the Council this afternoon to the Gate House, upon the misfortune of having his name used by one, without his knowledge or privity, for the receiving of some powder that he had bought. Up to Court about these two, and for the former was led up to my Lady Castlemayne's lodgings, where the King and she and others were at supper, and there I read the letter and returned; and then to Sir G. Carteret about Hater, and shall have him released to-morrow, upon my giving bail for his appearance, which I have promised to do. Sir G. Carteret did go on purpose to the King to ask this, and it was granted. So home at past 12, almost one o'clock in the morning. To my office till past two, and then home to supper and to bed.

3rd. Up and to White Hall, where Sir G. Carteret did go with me to Secretary Morris, and prevailed with him to let Mr. Hater be released upon bail for his appearance. So I at a loss how to get another besides myself, and got Mr. Hunt, who did patiently stay with me all the morning at Secretary Morris's chamber, Mr. Hater being sent for with his keeper, and at noon comes in the Secretary, and upon entering [into] recognizances, he for £200, and Mr. Hunt and I for £100 each for his appearance upon demand, he was released, it costing him, I think, above £3. I thence home, vexed to be kept from the office all the morning, which I had not been in many months before, if not some years. At home to dinner, and all the afternoon at the office, where late at night, and much business done, then home to supper and to bed. All this day by all people upon the River, and almost every where else hereabout were heard the guns, our two fleets for certain being engaged; which was confirmed by letters from Harwich, but nothing particular: and all our hearts full of concernment for the Duke, and I particularly for my Lord Sandwich and Mr. Coventry after his Royall Highnesse.

4th (Sunday). Up and at my chamber all the forenoon, at evening my accounts, which I could not do sooner, for the last month, and, blessed be God! am worth £1,400 odd money, something more than ever I was yet in the world. Dined very well at noon, and then to my office, and there and in the garden discoursed with several people about business, among others Mr. Howell, the turner, who did give me so good a discourse about the practices of the Paymaster J. Fenn that I thought fit to recollect all when he was gone, and have entered it down to be for ever remembered. Thence to my chamber again to settle my Tangier accounts against to-morrow and some other things, and with great joy ended them, and so to supper, where a good fowl and tansy, and so to bed. Newes being come that our fleete is pursuing the Dutch, who, either by cunning, or by being worsted, do give ground, but nothing more for certain. Late to bed upon my papers being quite finished.

5th. Up very betimes to look some other papers, and then to White Hall to a Committee of Tangier, where I offered my accounts with great acceptation, and so had some good words and honour by it, and one or two things done to my content in my business of Treasurer, but I do clearly see that we shall lose our business of victualling, Sir Thomas Ingram undertaking that it shall be done by persons there as cheap as we do it, and give the seamen their full allowance and themselves give good security here for performance of contract, upon which terms there is no opposing it. This would trouble me, but that I hope when that fails to spend my time to some good advantage other ways, and so shall permit it all to God Almighty's pleasure. Thence home to dinner, after 'Change, where great talke of the Dutch being fled and we in pursuit of them, and that our ship Charity[1] is lost upon our Captain's, Wilkinson, and

[1] Sir William Coventry and Sir William Penn to the Navy Commissioners, June 4th: "Engaged yesterday with the Dutch; they began to stand away at 3 p.m. Chased them all the rest of the day and night; 20 considerable ships are destroyed and taken; we have only lost the Great Charity. The Earl of Marlborough, Rear-Admiral Sansum, and

Lieutenant's yielding, but of this there is no certainty, save the report of some of the sicke men of the Charity, turned adrift in a boat out of the Charity and taken up and brought on shore yesterday to Sole Bay, and the newes hereof brought by Sir Henry Felton.[1] Home to dinner, and Creed with me. Then he and I down to Deptford, did some business, and back again at night. He home, and I to my office, and so to supper and to bed. This morning I had great discourse with my Lord Barkeley about Mr. Hater, towards whom from a great passion reproaching him with being a fanatique and dangerous for me to keepe, I did bring him to be mighty calme and to ask me pardons for what he had thought of him and to desire me to ask his pardon of Hater himself for the ill words he did give him the other day alone at White Hall (which was, that he had always thought him a man that was no good friend to the King, but did never think it would breake out in a thing of this nature), and did advise him to declare his innocence to the Council and pray for his examination and vindication. Of which I shall consider and say no more, but remember one compliment that in great kindness to me he did give me, extolling my care and diligence, that he did love me heartily for my owne sake, and more that he did will me whatsoever I thought for Mr. Coventry's sake, for though the world did think them enemies, and to have an ill aspect, one to another, yet he did love him with all his heart, which was a strange manner of noble compliment, confessing his owning me as a confidant and favourite of Mr. Coventry's.

6th. Waked in the morning before 4 o'clock with great pain to piss, and great pain in pissing by having, I think, drank too great a draught of cold drink before going to bed. But by and by to sleep again, and then rose and to the office, where very busy all the morning, and at noon

Captain Kirby are slain, and Sir John Lawson wounded" ("Calendar of State Papers," Domestic, 1664–65, p. 406).

[1] Sir Henry Felton, of Playford, Suffolk, Bart., who married Susanne, daughter of Sir Lionel Talmash, of Helmingham, Bart. Their second son, Sir Thomas Felton, married Lady Elizabeth Howard, daughter and co-heir of James, Lord Howard de Walden, and third Earl of Suffolk. — B.

to dinner with Sir G. Carteret to his house with all our Board, where a good pasty and brave discourse. But our great fear was some fresh news of the fleete, but not from the fleete, all being said to be well and beaten the Dutch, but I do not give much belief to it, and indeed the news come from Sir W. Batten at Harwich, and writ so simply that we all made good mirth of it. Thence to the office, where upon Sir G. Carteret's accounts, to my great vexation there being nothing done by the Controller to right the King therein. I thence to my office and wrote letters all the afternoon, and in the evening by coach to Sir Ph. Warwicke's about my Tangier business to get money, and so to my Lady Sandwich's, who, poor lady, expects every hour to hear of my Lord; but in the best temper, neither confident nor troubled with fear, that I ever did see in my life. She tells me my Lord Rochester is now declaredly out of hopes of Mrs. Mallett, and now she is to receive notice in a day or two how the King stands inclined to the giving leave for my Lord Hinchingbroke to look after her, and that being done to bring it to an end shortly. Thence by coach home, and to my office a little, and so before 12 o'clock home and to bed.

7th. This morning my wife and mother rose about two o'clock; and with Mercer, Mary, the boy, and W. Hewer, as they had designed, took boat and down to refresh themselves on the water to Gravesend. Lay till 7 o'clock, then up and to the office upon Sir G. Carteret's accounts again, where very busy; thence abroad and to the 'Change, no news of certainty being yet come from the fleete. Thence to the Dolphin Taverne, where Sir J. Minnes, Lord Brunkard, Sir Thomas Harvy, and myself dined, upon Sir G. Carteret's charge, and very merry we were, Sir Thomas Harvy being a very drolle. Thence to the office, and meeting Creed away with him to my Lord Treasurer's, there thinking to have met the goldsmiths, at White Hall, but did not, and so appointed another time for my Lord to speak to them to advance us some money. Thence, it being the hottest day that ever I felt in my life, and it is confessed so by all other people the hottest they ever knew in England in the beginning of June, we to the New Exchange, and there drunk whey, with much entreaty getting it for our money, and [they] would not be entreated to let us have one glasse more. So took water and to Fox-Hall,[1] to the Spring garden, and there walked an houre or two with great pleasure, saving our minds ill at ease concerning the fleete and my Lord Sandwich, that we have no newes of them, and ill reports run up and down of his being killed, but without ground. Here staid pleasantly walking and spending but 6*d.* till nine at night, and then by water to White Hall, and there I stopped to hear news of the fleete, but none come, which is strange, and so by water home, where weary with walking and with the mighty heat of the weather, and for my wife's not coming home, I staying walking in the garden till twelve at night, when it begun to lighten exceedingly, through the greatness of the heat. Then despairing of her coming home, I to bed. This day, much against my will, I did in Drury Lane see two or three houses marked with a red cross upon the doors, and "Lord have mercy upon us" writ there; which was a sad sight to me, being the first of the kind that, to my remembrance, I ever saw. It put me into an ill conception of myself and my smell, so that I was forced to buy some roll-tobacco to smell to and chaw, which took away the apprehension.

8th. About five o'clock my wife come home, it having lightened all night hard, and one great shower of rain. She come and lay upon the bed; I up and to the office, where all the morning. Alone at home to dinner, my wife, mother, and Mercer dining at W. Joyce's; I giving her a caution to go round by the Half Moone to his house, because of the plague. I to my Lord Treasurer's by appointment of Sir Thomas Ingram's, to meet the Goldsmiths; where I met with the great news at last newly come, brought by Bab May[2] from the Duke of Yorke, that we

[1] Vauxhall Gardens.

[2] Although the two Mays are so frequently mentioned in these pages, and by almost every contemporary annalist, no authentic account of their parentage has been traced; nor is it clear whether they were brothers, or in any way related. There is, however, a strong presumption that they sprung from a family of the same name, seated at Rawmere, in Sussex, one of whom, Jeffrey May, acquired property at Sutton Cheynell, in Leicestershire, in 1574, which was sold by the representatives of Baptist May, in 1712, under an Act passed for the payment of

have totally routed the Dutch; that the Duke himself, the Prince, my Lord Sandwich, and Mr. Coventry are all well: which did put me into such joy, that I forgot almost all other thoughts. The particulars I shall set down by and by. By and by comes Alderman Maynell and Mr. Viner, and there my Lord Treasurer did intreat them to furnish me with money upon my tallys, Sir Philip Warwicke before my Lord declaring the King's changing of the hand from Mr. Povy to me, whom he called a very sober person, and one whom the Lord Treasurer would owne in all things that I should concern myself with them in the business of money. They did at present declare they could not part with money at present. My Lord did press them very hard, and I hope upon their considering we shall get some of them. Thence with great joy to the Cocke-pitt; where the Duke of Albe-

his debts. But though Nichols ("History of Leicestershire," vol. iv., pt. ii., p. 548) gives a detailed pedigree of the Mays, he could not ascertain whose son Baptist May was, who held the office of Privy Purse to Charles II.; and he does not even allude to Hugh May. It is stated in Collins's "Peerage," vol. ii., p. 560, ed. 1741, that during their flight after the battle of Worcester, James, Duke of York, delivered his George, which had been a present from the queen his mother, to Mr. Hugh May, who preserved it through all difficulties, and afterwards returned it to his royal highness in Holland. Soon after 1662 Hugh May was established as an architect, and employed at Windsor, and in erecting stables at Cornbury, and in building Berkeley House, Piccadilly, and Cassiobury (Evelyn's "Diary"). He also held a place under Sir John Denham, the Surveyor of the Works, whom he expected to succeed; but the office becoming vacant, by the knight's death in 1667, was given to Sir Christopher Wren, and May was promised an annuity of £300 out of the Works, to make up for his disappointment. Whatever may have been his professional merits, he is not even named in Horace Walpole's list of architects; and we know nothing more of his career, except that in 1683 he was busy in building a house at Chiswick for Sir Stephen Fox. Baptist May's history is soon told: He was born about 1627, and after the Restoration belonged to the Duke of York's household; but he was promoted by the king to the office of Keeper of the Privy Purse, and became the confidant of Charles's amours. He was also made a Page of the Bedchamber, which place he lost, having contrived to offend his royal master. In 1689–90 we find him returned at the general election as burgess for Windsor, with Sir Christopher Wren; they were, however, both unseated by petition. Baptist died May 2nd, 1693, and lies buried in St. George's Chapel, where the slab inscribed to his memory is still to be seen. — B.

Baptist May has been supposed to be the son of Humphry May, who in early life was Vice-Chamberlain to James I.

marle, like a man out of himself with content, new-told me all; and by and by comes a letter from Mr. Coventry's own hand to him, which he never opened (which was a strange thing), but did give it me to open and read, and consider what was fit for our office to do in it, and leave the letter with Sir W. Clerke;[1] which upon such a time and occasion was a strange piece of indifference, hardly pardonable. I copied out the letter, and did also take minutes out of Sir W. Clerke's other letters; and the sum of the newes is:—

Victory Over the Dutch,[2] June 3rd, 1665.

This day they engaged; the Dutch neglecting greatly the opportunity of the wind they had of us, by which they lost the benefit of their fire-ships. The Earl of Falmouth, Muskerry, and Mr. Richard Boyle[3] killed on board the Duke's ship, the Royall Charles, with one shot: their blood and brains flying in the Duke's face; and the head of Mr. Boyle striking down the Duke, as some say. Earle of Marlborough,[4] Portland, Rear-Admirall Sansum (to Prince

[1] Sir William Clarke acted as secretary to the Duke of Albemarle. There are several of his letters among the State Papers, which are dated from the Cockpit, Whitehall. He lost his leg in the fight with the Dutch in June, 1666, and died two days after.

[2] See Sir John Denham's "Advice to a Painter" concerning the Dutch war in "Poems on State Affairs," vol. i., p. 24.—B.

[3] The Earl of Falmouth is better known as Lord FitzHarding. The Duke of Ormonde's letters to his mother (Lady Thurles) and his sister (the Countess of Clancarty), on the death of Lord Muskerry, are printed in Penn's "Memorials of Sir W. Penn," vol. ii., pp. 338, 339. Richard Boyle was the second son of the Earl of Burlington, and had been Member for Cork in 1661. Clarendon wrote of him: "He was a youth of great hope, who came newly home from travel, where he had spent his time with singular advantage, and took the first opportunity to lose his life in the king's service. There were many other gentlemen volunteers in the same ship, who had the same fate."

[4] James Ley, Earl of Marlborough, was captain of the "Old James." A letter from him to his friend, Sir Hugh Pollard, written about five weeks before the battle, is printed in Penn's "Memorials of Sir W. Penn" (vol. ii., p. 340). Charles Weston, third Earl of Portland, was a volunteer on board Lord Marlborough's ship. Robert Sansum, commander of the "Resolution," was Rear-Admiral of the White. He was captain of the "Portsmouth" in the fleet at Scheveling attending Charles II. on his return to England. Robert Kirby was captain of the "Breda." James Ableson was captain of the "Guinea."

Rupert), killed, and Capt. Kirby and Ableson. Sir John Lawson[1] wounded on the knee; hath had some bones taken out, and is likely to be well again. Upon receiving the hurt, he sent to the Duke for another to command the Royall Oake. The Duke sent Jordan[2] out of the St. George, who did brave things in her. Capt. Jer. Smith of the Mary was second to the Duke, and stepped between him and Captain Seaton of the Urania[3] (76 guns and 400 men), who had sworn to board the Duke; killed him, 200 men, and took the ship; himself losing 99 men, and never an officer saved but himself and lieutenant. His master indeed is saved, with his leg cut off. Admirall Opdam blown up, Trump killed, and said by Holmes; all the rest of their admiralls, as they say, but Everson (whom they dare not trust for his affection to the Prince of Orange), are killed: we having taken and sunk, as is believed, about 24 of their best ships; killed and taken near 8 or

[1] When Opdam's ship blew up, a shot from it mortally wounded Sir John Lawson, which is thus alluded to in the "Poems on State Affairs," vol. i., p. 28:

> "Destiny allowed
> Him his revenge, to make his death more proud.
> A fatal bullet from his side did range,
> And battered Lawson; oh, too dear exchange!
> He led our fleet that day too short a space,
> But lost his knee: since died, in glorious race:
> Lawson, whose valour beyond Fate did go,
> And still fights Opdam in the lake below."

In the same poem, Lord Falmouth's death is thus noticed:

> "Falmouth was there, I know not what to act;
> Some say 'twas to grow Duke, too, by contract.
> An untaught bullet, in its wanton scope,
> Dashes him all to pieces, and his Hope.
> Such was his rise, such was his fall, unpraised;
> A chance-shot sooner took him than chance raised:
> His shattered head the fearless Duke distains,
> And gave the last first proof that he had brains." — B.

[2] Afterwards Sir Joseph Jordan, commander of the "Royal Sovereign," and Vice-Admiral of the Red, 1672. He was knighted on July 1st, 1665. — B.

[3] Captain Sebastian Senten, of the "Orange," was attached to the second squadron of the Dutch fleet (see Penn's "Memorials of Sir W. Penn," vol. ii., p. 318).

10,000 men, and lost, we think, not above 700. A great[er] victory never known in the world. They are all fled, some 43 got into the Texell, and others elsewhere, and we in pursuit of the rest. Thence, with my heart full of joy, home, and to my office a little; then to my Lady Pen's, where they are all joyed and not a little puffed up at the good successe of their father;[1] and good service indeed is said to have been done by him. Had a great bonefire at the gate; and I with my Lady Pen's people and others to Mrs. Turner's great room, and then down into the streete. I did give the boys 4*s*. among them, and mighty merry. So home to bed, with my heart at great rest and quiett, saving that the consideration of the victory[2] is too great for me presently to comprehend.

9th. Lay long in bed, my head akeing with too much thoughts I think last night. Up and to White Hall, and my Lord Treasurer's to Sir Ph. Warwicke, about Tangier business, and in my way met with Mr. Moore, who eases me in one point wherein I was troubled; which was, that I heard of nothing said or done by my Lord Sandwich: but he tells

[1] In the royal charter granted by Charles II. in 1680 to William Penn for the government of his American province, to be styled Pennsylvania, special reference is made to "the memory and merits of Sir William Penn in divers services, and particularly his conduct, courage, and discretion under our dearest brother, James, Duke of York, in that signal battle and victory fought and obtained against the Dutch fleet commanded by Heer van Opdam in 1665" (Penn's "Memorials of Sir W. Penn," vol. ii., p. 359).

[2] Mrs. Ady (Julia Cartwright), in her fascinating life of Henrietta, Duchess of Orleans, gives an account of the receipt of the news of the great sea-fight in Paris, and quotes a letter of Charles II. to his sister, dated, "Whitehall, June 8th, 1665." The first report that reached Paris was that "the Duke of York's ship had been blown up, and he himself had been drowned." "The shock was too much for Madame . . . she was seized with convulsions, and became so dangerously ill that Lord Hollis wrote to the king, 'If things had gone ill at sea I really believe Madame would have died.'" Charles wrote: "I thanke God we have now the certayne newes of a very considerable victory over the Duch; you will see most of the particulars by the relation my Lord Hollis will shew you, though I have had as great a losse as 'tis possible in a good frinde, poore C. Barckely. It troubles me so much, as I hope you will excuse the shortnesse of this letter, haveing receaved the newes of it but two houres agoe" ("Madame," 1894, pp. 215, 216).

me that Mr. Cowling,[1] my Lord Chamberlain's secretary, did hear the King say that my Lord Sandwich had done nobly and worthily. The King, it seems, is much troubled at the fall of my Lord of Falmouth;[2] but I do not meet with any man else that so much as wishes him alive again, the world conceiving him a man of too much pleasure to do the King any good, or offer any good office to him. But I hear of all hands he is confessed to have been a man of great honour, that did show it in this his going with the Duke, the most that ever any man did. Home, where my people busy to make ready a supper against night for some guests, in lieu of my stone-feast.[3] At noon eat a small dinner at home, and so abroad to buy several things, and among others with my taylor to buy a silke suit, which though I had one lately, yet I do, for joy of the good newes we have lately had of our victory over the Dutch, which makes me willing to spare myself something extraordinary in clothes; and after long resolution of having nothing but black, I did buy a coloured silk ferrandin.[4] So to the Old Exchange, and there at my pretty seamstresse's bought a pair of stockings of her husband, and so home, where by and by comes Mr. Honiwood and Mrs. Wilde, and Roger Pepys and, after long time spent, Mrs. Turner, The. and Joyce. We had a very good venison pasty, this being instead of my stone-feast the last March, and very merry we were, and the more I know the more I like Mr. Honiwood's conversation. So after a good supper they parted, walking to the 'Change for a coach, and I with them to see them there. So home and to bed, glad it was over.

[1] Richard Cowling or Cooling. The name is usually spelt in the latter way in the Diary. The Lord Chamberlain was Edward, Earl of Manchester.

[2] For the king's expression of regret at the loss of Charles Berkeley (Earl of Falmouth), see previous note (June 8th).

[3] On March 26th, 1658, the successful operation for the stone was performed at Pepys's cousin's (Mrs. Turner's) house in Salisbury Court, and Pepys resolved to hold a commemorative feast for ever after on the anniversary of that day. On the first anniversary mentioned in the Diary, March 26th, 1660, he was at sea. In 1661 Mrs. Turner and her party dined with him at his father's. In 1662 they all dined at Pepys's house. In 1663 the dinner was postponed owing to Mrs. Pepys's illness. In 1664 the feast was held on the correct day.

[4] See note, January 28th, 1662–63.

10th. Lay long in bed, and then up and at the office all the morning. At noon dined at home, and then to the office busy all the afternoon. In the evening home to supper; and there, to my great trouble, hear that the plague is come into the City (though it hath these three or four weeks since its beginning been wholly out of the City); but where should it begin but in my good friend and neighbour's, Dr. Burnett, in Fanchurch Street: which in both points troubles me mightily. To the office to finish my letters and then home to bed, being troubled at the sicknesse, and my head filled also with other business enough, and particularly how to put my things and estate in order, in case it should please God to call me away, which God dispose of to his glory!

11th (Lord's day). Up, and expected long a new suit; but, coming not, dressed myself in my late new black silke camelott suit; and, when fully ready, comes my new one of coloured ferrandin, which my wife puts me out of love with, which vexes me, but I think it is only my not being used to wear colours which makes it look a little unusual upon me. To my chamber and there spent the morning reading. At noon, by invitation, comes my two cozen Joyces and their wives, my aunt James and he-cozen Harman,[1] his wife being ill. I had a good dinner for them, and as merry as I could be in such company. They being gone, I out of doors a little, to shew, forsooth, my new suit, and back again, and in going I saw poor Dr. Burnett's door shut; but he hath, I hear, gained great goodwill among his neighbours; for he discovered it himself first, and caused himself to be shut up of his own accord: which was very handsome. In the evening comes Mr. Andrews and his wife and Mr. Hill, and staid and played, and sung and supped, most excellent pretty company, so pleasant, ingenious, and harmless, I cannot desire better. They gone we to bed, my mind in great present ease.

12th. Up, and in my yesterday's new suit to the Duke of

[1] Harman appears to have been the son of the Mr. and Mrs. Harman referred to on September 9th, 1664. His wife, whom Pepys describes as "a very pretty, good-humoured wretch" (see August 1st, 1664), died in 1665, and Pepys then tried to get him to marry Paulina Pepys (see July 21st, 1665).

Albemarle, and after a turne in White Hall, and then in Westminster Hall, returned, and with my taylor bought some gold lace for my sleeve hands in Pater Noster Row. So home to dinner, and then to the office, and down the River to Deptford, and then back again and to my Lord Treasurer's, and up and down to look after my Tangier business, and so home to my office, then to supper and to bed. The Duke of Yorke is sent for last night and expected to be here to-morrow.

13th. Up and to the office, where all the morning doing business. At noon with Sir G. Carteret to my Lord Mayor's to dinner, where much company in a little room, and though a good, yet no extraordinary table. His name, Sir John Lawrence, whose father, a very ordinary old man, sat there at table, but it seems a very rich man. Here were at table three Sir Richard Brownes,[1] viz.: he of the Councill, a clerk, and the Alderman, and his son; and there was a little grandson also Richard, who will hereafter be Sir Richard Browne. The Alderman did here openly tell in boasting how he had, only upon suspicion of disturbances, if there had been any bad newes from sea, clapped up several persons that he was afeard of; and that he had several times done the like and would do, and take no bail where he saw it unsafe for the King. But by and by he said that he was now sued in the Exchequer by a man for false imprisonment, that he had, upon the same score, imprisoned while he was Mayor four years ago, and asked advice upon it. I told him I believed there was none, and told my story of Field, at which he was troubled, and said that it was then unsafe for any man to serve the King, and, I believed, knows not what to do therein; but that Sir Richard Browne, of the Councill, advised him to speak with my Lord Chancellor about it. My Lord Mayor very respectfull to me; and so I after dinner away and found Sir J.

[1] Alderman Sir Richard Browne, Bart., was Lord Mayor in 1660–61, and Major-General of the Trained-bands; see *ante*, February 22nd, 1659–60. His son was Sir Richard Browne, Knight. Sir Richard Browne, the Clerk of the Council, noticed January 25th, 1661–62, was of a different family. The Lord Mayor was seated at Debden Hall, in Essex, which he had purchased soon after 1660, and the estate was alienated by his son, the second baronet. — B.

Minnes ready with his coach and four horses at our office gate, for him and me to go out of towne to meet the Duke of Yorke coming from Harwich to-night, and so as far as Ilford, and there 'light. By and by comes to us Sir John Shaw and Mr. Neale,[1] that married the rich widow Gold, upon the same errand. After eating a dish of creame, we took coach again, hearing nothing of the Duke, and away home, a most pleasant evening and road. And so to my office, where, after my letters wrote, to supper and to bed. All our discourse in our way was Sir J. Minnes's telling me passages of the late King's and his father's, which I was mightily pleased to hear for information, though the pride of some persons and vice of most was but a sad story to tell how that brought the whole kingdom and King to ruine.

14th. Up, and to Sir Ph. Warwicke's and other places, about Tangier business, but to little purpose. Among others to my Lord Treasurer's, there to speak with him, and waited in the lobby three long hours for to speake with him, to the trial of my utmost patience, but missed him at last, and forced to go home without it, which may teach me how I make others wait. Home to dinner and staid Mr. Hater with me, and after dinner drew up a petition for Mr. Hater to present to the Councill about his troublesome business of powder,[2] desiring a trial that his absence may be vindicated, and so to White Hall, but it was not proper to present it to-day. Here I met with Mr. Cowling, who observed to me how he finds every body silent in the praise of my Lord Sandwich, to set up the Duke and the Prince; but that the Duke did both to the King and my Lord Chancellor write abundantly of my Lord's courage and service.[3] And I this day met with a letter of Captain Ferrers, wherein he tells [us] my Lord was with his ship in all the heat of the day, and did most worthily. Met with Creed, and he and I to Westminster; and there saw my Lord Marlborough[4] brought to be buried, several Lords of the

[1] Thomas Neale. See *ante*, January 2nd and June 20th.

[2] See *ante*, June 2nd.

[3] Charles II.'s letter of thanks to Lord Sandwich, dated "Whitehall, June 9th, 1665," written entirely in the king's hand, is printed in Ellis's "Original Letters," 1st series, vol. iii., p. 327.

[4] Of the four distinguished men who died after the late action with

Council carrying him, and with the herald in some state. Thence, vexed in my mind to think that I do so little in my Tangier business, and so home, and after supper to bed.

15th. Up, and put on my new stuff suit with close knees, which becomes me most nobly, as my wife says. At the office all day. At noon, put on my first laced band, all lace; and to Kate Joyce's to dinner, where my mother, wife, and abundance of their friends, and good usage. Thence, wife and Mercer and I to the Old Exchange, and there bought two lace bands more, one of my semstresse, whom my wife concurs with me to be a pretty woman. So down to Deptford and Woolwich, my boy and I. At Woolwich, discoursed with Mr. Sheldon[1] about my bringing my wife down for a month or two to his house, which he approves of, and, I think, will be very convenient. So late back, and to the office, wrote letters, and so home to supper and to bed. This day the Newesbook (upon Mr. Moore's showing L'Estrange[2] Captain Ferrers's letter) did do my Lord Sandwich great right as to the late victory. The Duke of Yorke not yet come to towne. The towne grows very sickly, and people to be afeard of it; there dying this last week of the plague 112,[3] from 43 the week before, whereof but [one] in Fanchurch-streete, and one in Broad-streete, by the Treasurer's office.

16th. Up and to the office, where I set hard to business, but was informed that the Duke of Yorke is come, and hath appointed us to attend him this afternoon. So after dinner, and doing some business at the office, I to White Hall, where the Court is full of the Duke and his courtiers returned from sea. All fat and lusty, and ruddy by being

the Dutch and were buried in Westminster Abbey, the Earl of Marlborough was interred on June 14th, Viscount Muskerry on the 19th, the Earl of Falmouth on the 22nd, and Sir Edward Broughton on the 26th. After the entries in the Abbey Registers is this note: "These four last Honble Persons dyed in his Ma^tyes^ service against the Dutch, excepting only that S^r^ E^d^ B^r^ received his death's wound at sea, but dyed here at home" (Chester's "Westminster Abbey Registers," p. 162).

1 William Sheldon, Clerk of the Cheque at Woolwich.

2 "The Public Intelligencer," published by Roger L'Estrange, the predecessor of the "London Gazette."

3 The number of deaths in London from all diseases, in the week ending June 13th, was 558; of these 112 died from the plague.

in the sun. I kissed his hands, and we waited all the afternoon. By and by saw Mr. Coventry, which rejoiced my very heart. Anon he and I, from all the rest of the company, walked into the Matted Gallery; where after many expressions of love, we fell to talk of business. Among other things, how my Lord Sandwich, both in his counsells and personal service, hath done most honourably and serviceably. Sir J. Lawson is come to Greenwich; but his wound in his knee yet very bad. Jonas Poole, in the Vantguard, did basely, so as to be, or will be, turned out of his ship. Captain Holmes[1] expecting upon Sansum's death to be made Rear-admirall to the Prince (but Harman[2] is put in) hath delivered up to the Duke his commission, which the Duke took and tore. He, it seems, had bid the Prince, who first told him of Holmes's intention, that he should dissuade him from it; for that he was resolved to take it if he offered it. Yet Holmes would do it, like a rash, proud coxcombe. But he is rich, and hath, it seems, sought an occasion of leaving the service. Several of our captains have done ill. The great ships are the ships do the business, they quite deadening the enemy. They run away upon sight of "The Prince."[3] It is strange to see how people do already slight Sir William Barkeley,[4]

[1] Captain Robert Holmes (afterwards knighted). Sir William Coventry, in a letter to Lord Arlington (dated from "The Royal Charles," Southwold Bay, June 13th, writes: "Capt. Holmes asked to be rear-admiral of the white squadron in place of Sansum who was killed, but the Duke gave the place to Captain Harman, on which he delivered up his commission, which the Duke received, and put Captain Langhorne in his stead" ("Calendar of State Papers," Domestic, 1664–65, p. 423).

[2] John Harman, afterwards knighted. He had served with great reputation in several naval fights, and was desperately wounded in 1673, while engaged with a Dutch man-of-war, which he captured. He survived the action some years, but never recovered his health. — B. For an account of the life of Sir John Harman, see Charnock's "Biographia Navalis," i. 97–103.

[3] "The Prince" was Lord Sandwich's ship; the captain was Roger Cuttance. It was put up at Chatham for repair at this date.

[4] **Sir William Berkeley, see note, November 9th, 1663. His behaviour after the death of his brother, Lord Falmouth, is severely commented on in "Poems on State Affairs," vol. i., p. 29:**

"Berkeley had heard it soon, and thought not good
To venture more of royal Harding's blood;

my Lord FitzHarding's brother, who, three months since, was the delight of the Court. Captain Smith[1] of "The Mary" the Duke talks mightily of; and some great thing will be done for him. Strange to hear how the Dutch do relate, as the Duke says, that they are the conquerors; and bonefires are made in Dunkirke in their behalf; though a clearer victory can never be expected. Mr. Coventry thinks they cannot have lost less than 6,000 men, and we not dead above 200, and wounded about 400; in all about 600. Thence home and to my office till past twelve, and then home to supper and to bed, my wife and mother not being yet come home from W. Hewer's chamber, who treats my mother to-night. Captain Grove,[2] the Duke told us this day, hath done the basest thing at Lowestoffe, in hearing of the guns, and could not (as others) be got out, but staid there; for which he will be tried; and is reckoned a prating coxcombe, and of no courage.

17th. My wife come to bed about one in the morning. I up and abroad about Tangier business, then back to the office, where we sat, and at noon home to dinner, and then abroad to Mr. Povy's, after I and Mr. Andrews had been with Mr. Ball and one Major Strange, who looks after the getting of money for tallys and is helping Mr. Andrews. I had much discourse with Ball, and it may be he may prove a necessary man for our turns. With Mr. Povy I spoke very freely my indifference as to my place of Treasurer, being so much troubled in it, which he took with much seeming trouble, that I should think of letting go so lightly the place, but if the place can't be held I will. So hearing that my Lord Treasurer[3] was gone out of town with his

To be immortal he was not of age,
And did e'en now the Indian Prize presage;
And judged it safe and decent, cost what cost,
To lose the day, *since his dear brother's lost.*
With his whole squadron straight away he bore,
And, like good boy, promised to fight no more." — B.

[1] Jeremy Smith, knighted June, 1665. He succeeded Penn as Comptroller of the Victualling in 1669, and held the office until September, 1675.

[2] Captain Edward Grove commanded "The Success" in 1664.

[3] The Lord Treasurer (Earl of Southampton) lived at Southampton House on the north side of Bloomsbury Square, which afterwards came

family because of the sicknesse, I returned home without staying there, and at the office find Sir W. Pen come home, who looks very well; and I am gladder to see him than otherwise I should be because of my hearing so well of him for his serviceablenesse in this late great action. To the office late, and then home to bed. It struck me very deep this afternoon going with a hackney coach from my Lord Treasurer's down Holborne, the coachman I found to drive easily and easily, at last stood still, and come down hardly able to stand, and told me that he was suddenly struck very sicke, and almost blind, he could not see; so I 'light and went into another coach, with a sad heart for the poor man and trouble for myself, lest he should have been struck with the plague, being at the end of the towne that I took him up; but God have mercy upon us all! Sir John Lawson, I hear, is worse than yesterday: the King went to see him to-day most kindly. It seems his wound is not very bad; but he hath a fever, a thrush, and a hic-kup, all three together, which are, it seems, very bad symptoms.

18th (Lord's day). Up, and to church, where Sir W. Pen was the first time [since he] come from sea, after the battle. Mr. Mills made a sorry sermon to prove that there was a world to come after this. Home and dined and then to my chamber, where all the afternoon. Anon comes Mr. Andrews to see and sing with me, but Mr. Hill not coming, and having business, we soon parted, there coming Mr. Povy and Creed to discourse about our Tangier business of money. They gone, I hear Sir W. Batten and my Lady are returned from Harwich. I went to see them, and it is pretty to see how we appear kind one to another, though neither of us care *2d.* one for another. Home to supper, and there coming a hasty letter from Commissioner Pett for pressing of some calkers (as I would ever on his Majesty's service), with all speed, I made a warrant presently and issued it. So to my office a little, and then home to bed.

19th. Up, and to White Hall with Sir W. Batten (calling at my Lord Ashly's, but to no purpose, by the way, he being not up), and there had our usual meeting before the

into the possession of the family of Russell owing to the marriage of Lady Rachael Russell, and was then known as Bedford House.

Duke with the officers of the Ordnance with us, which in some respects I think will be the better for us, for despatch sake. Thence home to the 'Change and dined alone (my wife gone to her mother's), after dinner to my little new goldsmith's,[1] whose wife indeed is one of the prettiest, modest black women that ever I saw. I paid for a dozen of silver salts £6 14*s*. 6*d*. Thence with Sir W. Pen from the office down to Greenwich to see Sir J. Lawson, who is better, but continues ill; his hickupp not being yet gone, could have little discourse with him. So thence home and to supper, a while to the office, my head and mind mightily vexed to see the multitude of papers and business before [me] and so little time to do it in. So to bed.

20th. Thankes-giving-day for victory over ye Dutch. Up, and to the office, where very busy alone all the morning till church time, and there heard a mean sorry sermon of Mr. Mills. Then to the Dolphin Taverne, where all we officers of the Navy met with the Commissioners of the Ordnance by agreement, and dined: where good musique at my direction. Our club[2] come to 34*s*. a man, nine of us. Thence after dinner, I to White Hall with Sir W. Berkely in his coach, and so walked to Herbert's and there spent a little time. . . . Thence by water to Fox-hall, and there walked an hour alone, observing the several humours of the citizens that were there this holy-day, pulling of cherries,[3] and God knows what, and so home to my office, where late, my wife not being come home with my mother, who have been this day all abroad upon the water, my

[1] John Colvill of Lombard Street, see *ante*, May 24th. He lost £85,832 17*s*. 2*d*. by the closing of the Exchequer in 1672, and he died between 1672 and 1677 (Price's "Handbook of London Bankers").

[2] Club = share.

"Next these a sort of Sots there are,
Who crave more wine than they can bear,
Yet hate, when drunk, to pay or spend
Their equal Club or Dividend,
But wrangle, when the Bill is brought,
And think they're cheated when they're not."

The Delights of the Bottle, or the Compleat Vintner, 3rd ed., 1721, p. 29.

[3] The game of bob-cherry.

mother being to go out of town speedily. So I home and to supper and to bed, my wife come home when I come from the office. This day I informed myself that there died four or five at Westminster of the plague in one alley in several houses upon Sunday last, Bell Alley, over against the Palace-gate; yet people do think that the number will be fewer in the towne than it was the last weeke.[1] The Dutch are come out again with 20 sail under Bankert;[2] supposed gone to the Northward to meete their East India fleete.

21st. Up, and very busy all the morning. At noon with Creed to the Excise Office, where I find our tallys will not be money in less than sixteen months, which is a sad thing for the King to pay all that interest for every penny he spends; and, which is strange, the goldsmiths with whom I spoke, do declare that they will not be moved to part with money upon the increase of their consideration of ten per cent. which they have, and therefore desire I would not move in it, and indeed the consequence would be very ill to the King, and have its ill consequences follow us through all the King's revenue. Home, and my uncle Wight and aunt James dined with me, my mother being to go away to-morrow. So to White Hall, and there before and after Council discoursed with Sir Thomas Ingram about our ill case as to Tangier for money. He hath got the King to appoint a meeting on Friday, which I hope will put an end one way or other to my pain. So homewards and to the Cross Keys at Cripplegate, where I find all the towne almost going out of towne, the coaches and waggons being all full of people going into the country. Here I had some of the company of the tapster's wife a while, and so home to my office, and then home to supper and to bed.

22nd. Up pretty betimes, and in great pain whether to send my mother into the country to-day or no, I hearing, by my people, that she, poor wretch, hath a mind to stay a little longer, and I cannot blame her, considering what a life she will through her own folly lead when she comes

[1] According to the Bills of Mortality there was no reduction in the number of deaths. The total number of burials in the week ending June 20th was 611, of which number 168 died from the plague.

[2] Rear-Admiral Bancquert.

home again, unlike the pleasure and liberty she hath had here. At last I resolved to put it to her, and she agreed to go, so I would not oppose it, because of the sicknesse in the towne, and my intentions of removing my wife. So I did give her money and took a kind leave of her, she, poor wretch, desiring that I would forgive my brother John, but I refused it to her, which troubled her, poor soul, but I did it in kind words and so let the discourse go off, she leaving me though in a great deal of sorrow. So I to my office and left my wife and people to see her out of town, and I at the office all the morning. At noon my wife tells me that she is with much ado gone, and I pray God bless her, but it seems she was to the last unwilling to go, but would not say so, but put it off till she lost her place in the coach, and was fain to ride in the waggon part. After dinner to the office again till night, very busy, and so home not very late to supper and to bed.

23rd. Up and to White Hall to a Committee for Tangier, where his Royal Highness was. Our great design was to state to them the true condition of this Committee for want of money, the want whereof was so great as to need some sudden help, and it was with some content resolved to see it supplied and means proposed towards the doing of it. At this Committee, unknown to me, comes my Lord of Sandwich, who, it seems, come to towne last night. After the Committee was up, my Lord Sandwich did take me aside, and we walked an hour alone together in the robe-chamber, the door shut, telling me how much the Duke and Mr. Coventry did, both in the fleete and here, make of him, and that in some opposition to the Prince; and as a more private message, he told me that he hath been with them both when they have made sport of the Prince and laughed at him: yet that all the discourse of the towne, and the printed relation, should not give him one word of honour my Lord thinks mighty strange; he assuring me, that though by accident the Prince was in the van the beginning of the fight for the first pass, yet all the rest of the day my Lord was in the van, and continued so. That notwithstanding all this noise of the Prince, he had hardly a shot in his side nor a man killed, whereas he hath above 30 in her hull, and not one mast whole nor yard; but the most battered ship of the fleet, and lost most men, saving Captain Smith of "The Mary." That the most the Duke did was almost out of gun-shot; but that, indeed, the Duke did come up to my Lord's rescue after he had a great while fought with four of them. How poorly Sir John Lawson performed, notwithstanding all that was said of him; and how his ship turned out of the way, while Sir J. Lawson himself was upon the deck, to the endangering of the whole fleete. It therefore troubles my Lord that Mr. Coventry should not mention a word of him in his relation. I did, in answer, offer that I was sure the relation was not compiled by Mr. Coventry, but by L'Estrange, out of several letters, as I could witness; and that Mr. Coventry's letter[1] that he did give the Duke of Albemarle did give him as much right as the Prince, for I myself read it first and then copied it out, which I promised to show my Lord, with which he was somewhat satisfied. From that discourse my Lord did begin to tell me how much he was concerned to dispose of his children, and would have my advice and help; and propounded to match my Lady Jemimah to Sir G. Carteret's[2] eldest son, which I approved of, and did undertake the speaking with him about it as from myself, which my Lord liked. So parted, with my head full of care about this business. Thence home to the 'Change, and so to dinner, and thence by coach to Mr. Povy's. Thence by appointment with him and Creed to one Mr. Finch,[3] one of the Commissioners for the Excise, to be informed about some things of the Excise, in order to our settling matters therein better for us for our Tangier business. I find him a very discreet, grave person. Thence well satisfied I and Creed to Mr. Fox at White Hall to speak with him about the same matter, and having some pretty satisfaction from him also, he and I took boat and to Fox Hall, where we spent two or three hours talking of several matters very

[1] Coventry's letter to the Duke of Albemarle (dated June 4th, 1665), which was transcribed by Pepys, is printed in the Rev. John Smith's "Life, Journals and Correspondence of S. Pepys," vol. i, p. 85.

[2] Philip Carteret, afterwards knighted. He perished on board Lord Sandwich's (his father-in-law) flag-ship at the battle of Solebay. — B.

[3] Daniel Finch.

soberly and contentfully to me, which, with the ayre and pleasure of the garden, was a great refreshment to me, and, methinks, that which we ought to joy ourselves in. Thence back to White Hall, where we parted, and I to find my Lord to receive his farther direction about his proposal this morning. Wherein I did that I should first by another hand break my intentions to Sir G. Carteret. I pitched upon Dr. Clerke, which my Lord liked, and so I endeavoured but in vain to find him out to-night. So home by hackney-coach, which is become a very dangerous passage now-a-days, the sickness increasing mightily, and to bed.

24th (Midsummer-day). Up very betimes, by six, and at Dr. Clerke's at Westminster by 7 of the clock, having over night by a note acquainted him with my intention of coming, and there I, in the best manner I could, broke my errand about a match between Sir G. Carteret's eldest son and my Lord Sandwich's eldest daughter, which he (as I knew he would) took with great content: and we both agreed that my Lord and he, being both men relating to the sea, under a kind aspect of His Majesty, already good friends, and both virtuous and good familys, their allyance might be of good use to us; and he did undertake to find out Sir George this morning, and put the business in execution. So being both well pleased with the proposition, I saw his niece there and made her sing me two or three songs very prettily, and so home to the office, where to my great trouble I found Mr. Coventry and the board met before I come. I excused my late coming by having been on the River about office business. So to business all the morning. At noon Captain Ferrers and Mr. Moore dined with me, the former of them the first time I saw him since his coming from sea, who do give me the best conversation in general, and as good an account of the particular service of the Prince and my Lord of Sandwich in the late sea-fight that I could desire. After dinner they parted. So I to White Hall, where I with Creed and Povy attended my Lord Treasurer, and did prevail with him to let us have an assignment for 15 or £20,000, which, I hope, will do our business for Tangier. So to Dr. Clerke, and there found that he had broke the business to Sir G. Carteret, and that he takes the thing mighty well. Thence I to Sir G. Carteret at his chamber, and in the best manner I could, and most obligingly, moved the business: he received it with great respect and content, and thanks to me, and promised that he would do what he could possibly for his son, to render him fit for my Lord's daughter, and shewed great kindness to me, and sense of my kindness to him herein. Sir William Pen told me this day that Mr. Coventry [1] is to be sworn a Privy Counsellor, at which my soul is glad. So home and to my letters by the post, and so home to supper and bed.

25th (Lord's day). Up, and several people about business come to me by appointment relating to the office. Thence I to my closet about my Tangier papers. At noon dined, and then I abroad by water, it raining hard, thinking to have gone down to Woolwich, but I did not, but back through bridge to White Hall, where, after I had again visited Sir G. Carteret, and received his (and now his Lady's) full content in my proposal, I went to my Lord Sandwich, and having told him how Sir G. Carteret received it, he did direct me to return to Sir G. Carteret, and give him thanks for his kind reception of this offer, and that he would the next day be willing to enter discourse with him about the business. Which message I did presently do, and so left the business with great joy to both sides. My Lord, I perceive, intends to give £5,000 with her, and expects about £800 *per annum* joynture. So by water home and to supper and bed, being weary with long walking at Court, but had a Psalm or two with my boy and Mercer before bed, which pleased me mightily. This night Sir G. Carteret told me with great kindnesse that the order of the Council did run for the making of Hater and Whitfield incapable of any serving the King again, but that he had stopped the entry of it, which he told me with great kindnesse, but the thing troubles me. After dinner, before I went to White Hall, I went down to Greenwich by water, thinking to have visited Sir J. Lawson, [2] where, when I come,

[1] In the "Calendar of State Papers," 1664-65 (p. 239), it is stated that Coventry was knighted on March 3rd, 1665.

[2] In his will dated April 19th, 1665, Sir John Lawson requested that the pension of £500 settled upon him for life, which was promised to his daughters if he died in the service, might be divided equally

I find that he is dead, and died this morning, at which I was much surprized; and indeed the nation hath a great loss; though I cannot, without dissembling, say that I am sorry for it, for he was a man never kind to me at all. Being at White Hall, I visited Mr. Coventry, who, among other talk, entered about the great question now in the House about the Duke's going to sea again; about which the whole House is divided. He did concur with me that, for the Duke's honour and safety, it were best, after so great a service and victory and danger, not to go again; and, above all, that the life of the Duke cannot but be a security to the Crowne; if he were away, it being more easy to attempt anything upon the King; but how the fleete will be governed without him, the Prince[1] being a man of no government and severe in council, that no ordinary man can offer any advice against his; saying truly that it had been better he had gone to Guinny, and that were he away, it were easy to say how matters might be ordered, my Lord Sandwich being a man of temper and judgment as much as any man he ever knew, and that upon good observation he said this, and that his temper must correct the Prince's. But I perceive he is much troubled what will be the event of the question. And so I left him.

26th. Up and to White Hall with Sir J. Minnes, and to the Committee of Tangier, where my Lord Treasurer was, the first and only time he ever was there, and did promise us £15,000 for Tangier and no more, which will be short. But if I can pay Mr. Andrews all his money I care for no more, and the bills of Exchange. Thence with Mr. Povy and Creed below to a new chamber of Mr. Povy's, very pretty, and there discourse about his business, not to his content, but with the most advantage I could to him, and Creed also did the like. Thence with Creed to the King's Head,[2] and there dined with him at the ordinary, and good

between his two daughters, Elizabeth and Anna Lawson. On August 4th, 1665, a warrant was issued for grants to these two of a pension of £250 a year each ("Calendar of State Papers," Domestic, 1664-65, pp. 489, 502).

[1] Prince Rupert.

[2] King's Head, corner of Chancery Lane. There is a token of "the King's Head tavern at Chancery Lane end," with a bust of Henry VIII. ("Boyne's Tokens," ed. Williamson, vol. i., p. 554).

sport with one Mr. Nicholls, a prating coxcomb, that would be thought a poet, but would not be got to repeat any of his verses. Thence I home, and there find my wife's brother[1] and his wife, a pretty little modest woman, where they dined with my wife. He did come to desire my assistance for a living, and, upon his good promises of care, and that it should be no burden to me, I did say and promise I would think of finding something for him, and the rather because his wife seems a pretty discreet young thing, and humble, and he, above all things, desirous to do something to maintain her, telling me sad stories of what she endured with him in Holland, and I hope it will not be burdensome. So down by water to Woolwich, walking to and again from Greenwich thither and back again, my business being to speak again with Sheldon, who desires and expects my wife coming thither to spend the summer, and upon second thoughts I do agree that it will be a good place for her and me too. So, weary, home, and to my office a while, till almost midnight, and so to bed. The plague encreases mightily, I this day seeing a house, at a bitt-maker's over against St. Clement's Church, in the open street, shut up; which is a sad sight.

27th. Up and to the office, where all the morning. At noon dined by chance at my Lady Batten's, and they sent for my wife, and there was my Lady Pen and Pegg. Very merry, and so I to my office again, where till 12 o'clock at night, and so home to supper and to bed.

28th. Sir J. Minnes carried me and my wife to White Hall, and thence his coach along with my wife where she would. There after attending the Duke to discourse of the navy. We did not kiss his hand, nor do I think, for all their pretence, of going away to-morrow. Yet I believe they will not go for good and all, but I did take my leave of Sir William Coventry, who, it seems, was knighted and sworn a Privy-Counsellor two days since; who with his old kindness treated me, and I believe I shall ever find [him] a noble friend. Thence by water to Blackfriars, and so to Paul's churchyard and bespoke severall books, and so home and there dined, my man William giving me a lobster sent

[1] Balthasar St. Michel (see note, February 8th, 1659–60). His wife's name was Esther.

him by my old maid Sarah. This morning I met with Sir G. Carteret, who tells me how all things proceed between my Lord Sandwich and himself to full content, and both sides depend upon having the match finished presently, and professed great kindnesse to me, and said that now we were something akin. I am mightily, both with respect to myself and much more of my Lord's family, glad of this alliance. After dinner to White Hall, thinking to speak with my Lord Ashly, but failed, and I whiled away some time in Westminster Hall against he did come, in my way observing several plague houses in King's Streete and [near] the Palace. Here I hear Mrs. Martin is gone out of town, and that her husband, an idle fellow, is since come out of France, as he pretends, but I believe not that he hath been. I was fearful of going to any house, but I did to the Swan, and thence to White Hall, giving the waterman a shilling, because a young fellow and belonging to the Plymouth. Thence by coach to several places, and so home, and all the evening with Sir J. Minnes and all the women of the house (excepting my Lady Batten) late in the garden chatting. At 12 o'clock home to supper and to bed. My Lord Sandwich is gone towards the sea to-day, it being a sudden resolution, I having taken no leave of him.

29th. Up and by water to White Hall, where the Court full of waggons and people ready to go out of towne. To the Harp and Ball, and there drank and talked with Mary, she telling me in discourse that she lived lately at my neighbour's, Mr. Knightly, which made me forbear further discourse. This end of the towne every day grows very bad of the plague. The Mortality Bill is come to 267;[1] which

[1] According to the Bills of Mortality, the total number of deaths in London for the week ending June 27th was 684, of which number 267 were deaths from the plague. The number of deaths rose week by week until September 19th, when the total was 8,297, and the deaths from the plague 7,165. On September 26th the total had fallen to 6,460, and deaths from the plague to 5,533. The number fell gradually, week by week, till October 31st, when the total was 1,388, and deaths from the plague 1,031. On November 7th there was a rise to 1,787 and 1,414 respectively. On November 14th the numbers had gone down to 1,359 and 1,050 respectively. On December 12th the total had fallen to 442, and deaths from the plague to 243. On December 19th there was a rise to 525 and 281 respectively. The total of

is about ninety more than the last: and of these but four in the City, which is a great blessing to us. Thence to Creed, and with him up and down about Tangier business, to no purpose. Took leave again of Mr. Coventry; though I hope the Duke has not gone to stay, and so do others too. So home, calling at Somersett House, where all are packing up too: the Queene-Mother setting out for France this day to drink Bourbon waters this year, she being in a consumption; and intends not to come till winter come twelvemonths.[1] So by coach home, where at the office all the morning, and at noon Mrs. Hunt dined with us. Very merry, and she a very good woman. To the office, where busy a while putting some things in my office in order, and then to letters till night. About 10 o'clock home, the days being sensibly shorter before I have once kept a summer's day by shutting up office by daylight, but my life hath been still as it was in winter almost. But I will for a month try what I can do by daylight. So home to supper and to bed.

30th. Up, and to White Hall, to the Duke of Albemarle, who I find at Secretary Bennet's, there being now no other great Statesman, I think, but my Lord Chancellor, in towne.

burials in 1665 was 97,506, of which number the plague claimed 68,596 victims.

[1] The Queen-Mother never came to England again. She retired to her chateau at Colombes, near Paris, where she died in August, 1669, after a long illness; the immediate cause of her death being an opiate ordered by her physicians. She was buried, September 12th, in the church of St. Denis. Her funeral sermon was preached by Bossuet. Sir John Reresby speaks of Queen Henrietta Maria in high terms. He says that in the winter, 1659–60, although the Court of France was very splendid, there was a greater resort to the Palais Royal, "the good humour and wit of our Queen Mother, and the beauty of the Princess [Henrietta] her daughter, giving greater invitation than the more particular humour of the French Queen, being a Spaniard." In another place he says: "Her majesty had a great affection for England, notwithstanding the severe usage she and hers had received from it. Her discourse was much with the great men and ladies of France in praise of the people and of the country; of their courage, generosity, good nature; and would excuse all their miscarriages in relation to unfortunate effects of the late war, as if it were a convulsion of some desperate and infatuated persons, rather than from the genius and temper of the kingdom" ("Memoirs of Sir John Reresby," ed. Cartwright, pp. 43, 45).

I received several commands from them; among others, to provide some bread and cheese for the garrison at Guernsey, which they promised to see me paid for. So to the 'Change, and home to dinner. In the afternoon I down to Woolwich and after me my wife and Mercer, whom I led to Mr. Sheldon's, to see his house, and I find it a very pretty place for them to be at. So I back again, walking both forward and backward, and left my wife to come by water. I straight to White Hall, late, to Secretary Bennet's to give him an account of the business I received from him to-day, and there staid weary and sleepy till past 12 at night. Then writ my mind to him, and so back by water and in the dark and against tide shot the bridge,[1] groping with their pole for the way, which troubled me before I got through. So home, about one or two o'clock in the morning, my family at a great losse what was become of me. To supper, and to bed. Thus this book of two years ends. Myself and family in good health, consisting of myself and wife, Mercer, her woman, Mary, Alce, and Susan our maids, and Tom my boy. In a sickly time of the plague growing on. Having upon my hands the troublesome care of the Treasury of Tangier, with great sums drawn upon me, and nothing to pay them with: also the business of the office great. Consideration of removing my wife to Woolwich; she lately busy in learning to paint, with great pleasure and successe. All other things well; especially a new interest I am making, by a match in hand between the eldest son of Sir G. Carteret, and my Lady Jemimah Montagu. The Duke of Yorke gone down to the fleete, but all suppose not with intent to stay there, as it is not fit, all men conceive, he should.[2]

[1] Shooting London Bridge. See note, August 8th, 1662.
[2] Here ends the third volume of the manuscript.

END OF VOL. IV.

VOL. V.

July 1st, 1665.

CALLED up betimes, though weary and sleepy, by appointment by Mr. Povy and Colonell Norwood to discourse about some payments of Tangier. They gone, I to the office and there sat all the morning. At noon dined at home, and then to the Duke of Albemarle's, by appointment, to give him an account of some disorder in the Yarde at Portsmouth, by workmen's going away of their owne accord, for lacke of money, to get work of hay-making, or any thing else to earne themselves bread.[1] Thence to Westminster, where I hear the sicknesse encreases greatly, and to the Harp and Ball with Mary talking, who tells me simply her losing of her first love in the country in Wales, and coming up hither unknown to her friends, and it seems Dr. Williams do pretend love to her, and I have found him there several times. Thence by coach and late at the office, and so to bed. Sad at the newes that seven or eight houses in Bazing Hall street, are shut up of the plague.

2nd (Sunday). Up, and all the morning dressing my closet at the office with my plates, very neatly, and a fine place now it is, and will be a pleasure to sit in, though I

[1] There are several letters among the State Papers from Commissioner Thomas Middleton relating to the want of workmen at Portsmouth Dockyard. On June 29th Middleton wrote to Pepys, "The ropemakers have discharged themselves for want of money, and gone into the country to make hay." The blockmakers, the joiners, and the sawyers all refused to work longer without money ("Calendar," 1664–65, p. 453).

thank God I needed none before. At noon dined at home, and after dinner to my accounts and cast them up, and find that though I have spent above £90 this month yet I have saved £17, and am worth in all above £1,450, for which the Lord be praised! In the evening my Lady Pen and daughter come to see, and supped with us, then a messenger about business of the office from Sir G. Carteret at Chatham, and by word of mouth did send me word that the business between my Lord and him is fully agreed on,[1] and is mightily liked of by the King and the Duke of Yorke, and that he sent me this word with great joy; they gone, we to bed. I hear this night that Sir J. Lawson[2] was buried late last night at St. Dunstan's by us, without any company at all, and that the condition of his family is but very poor, which I could be contented to be sorry for, though he never was the man that ever obliged me by word or deed.

3rd. Up and by water with Sir W. Batten and Sir J. Minnes to White Hall to the Duke of Albemarle, where, after a little business, we parted, and I to the Harp and Ball, and there staid a while talking to Mary, and so home to dinner. After dinner to the Duke of Albemarle's again, and so to the Swan, and there *demeurais un peu de temps con la fille*, and so to the Harp and Ball, and alone *demeurais un peu de temps baisant la*, and so away home and late at the office about letters, and so home, resolving from this night forwards to close all my letters, if possible, and end all my business at the office by daylight, and I shall go near to do it and put all my affairs in the world in good order, the season growing so sickly, that it is much to be feared how a man can escape having a share with others in it, for which the good Lord God bless me, or to be fitted to receive it. So after supper to bed, and mightily troubled in my sleep all night with dreams of Jacke Cole, my old schoolfellow, lately dead, who was born at the same time with me, and we reckoned our fortunes pretty equal. God fit me for his condition!

1 The arrangements for the marriage of Lady Jemimah Montagu to Philip Carteret were soon settled, for the wedding took place on July 31st.

2 In the register of the Old Church at Greenwich is the following entry: "Sir John Lawson carried away, June 27th, 1665." — B.

4th. Up, and sat at the office all the morning. At noon to the 'Change and thence to the Dolphin, where a good dinner at the cost of one Mr. Osbaston,[1] who lost a wager to Sir W. Batten, Sir W. Rider, and Sir R. Ford, a good while since and now it is spent. The wager was that ten of our ships should not have a fight with ten of the enemy's before Michaelmas. Here was other very good company, and merry, and at last in come Mr. Buckeworth,[2] a very fine gentleman, and proves to be a Huntingdonshire man. Thence to my office and there all the afternoon till night, and so home to settle some accounts of Tangier and other papers. I hear this day the Duke and Prince Rupert are both come back from sea, and neither of them go back again. The latter I much wonder at, but it seems the towne reports so, and I am very glad of it. This morning I did a good piece of work with Sir W. Warren, ending the business of the lotterys, wherein honestly I think I shall get above £100. Bankert,[3] it seems, is come home with the little fleete he hath been abroad with, without doing any thing, so that there is nobody of an enemy at sea. We are in great hopes of meeting with the Dutch East India fleete, which is mighty rich, or with De Ruyter, who is so also. Sir Richard Ford told me this day, at table, a fine account, how the Dutch were like to have been mastered by the present Prince of Orange[4] his father to be besieged in Amsterdam, having drawn an army of foot into the towne, and horse near to the towne by night, within three miles of the towne, and they never knew of it; but by chance the Hamburgh post in the night fell among the horse, and heard

[1] A Mr. Osbaldstone, grocer, clerk of St. Botolph's, Aldersgate, died of the plague on September 22nd, 1665 (Smith's "Obituary," p. 67).

[2] There are several letters of John Buckworth among the State Papers, and one of these to Secretary Williamson is dated from Crutched Friars, November 2nd, 1664. He appears to have been engaged with Sir Richard Ford in some business connected with tin.

[3] The Dutch Admiral Bancquert or Banckart.

[4] *Sic orig.* The period alluded to is 1650, when the States-General disbanded part of the forces which the Prince of Orange (William) wished to retain. The prince attempted, but unsuccessfully, to possess himself of Amsterdam. In the same year he died, at the early age of twenty-four; some say of the small-pox; others, with Sir Richard Ford, say of poison. — B.

their design, and knowing the way, it being very dark and rainy, better than they, went from them, and did give notice to the towne before the others could reach the towne, and so were saved. It seems this De Witt and another family, the Beckarts, were among the chief of the familys that were enemys to the Prince, and were afterwards suppressed by the Prince, and continued so till he was, as they say, poysoned; and then they turned all again, as it was, against the young Prince, and have so carried it to this day, it being about 12 and 14 years, and De Witt in the head of them.

5th. Up, and advised about sending of my wife's bedding and things to Woolwich, in order to her removal thither. So to the office, where all the morning till noon, and so to the 'Change, and thence home to dinner. In the afternoon I abroad to St. James's, and there with Mr. Coventry a good while, and understand how matters are ordered in the fleete: that is, my Lord Sandwich goes Admiral; under him Sir G. Ascue, and Sir T. Teddiman; Vice-Admiral, Sir W. Pen; and under him Sir W. Barkeley, and Sir Jos. Jordan: Reere-Admiral, Sir Thomas Allen; and under him Sir Christopher Mings[1] and Captain Harman. We talked in general of business of the Navy, among others how he had lately spoken to Sir G. Carteret, and professed great resolution of friendship with him and reconciliation, and resolves to make it good as well as he can, though it troubles him, he tells me, that something will come before him wherein he must give him offence, but I do find upon the whole that Mr. Coventry do not listen to these complaints of money with the readiness and resolvedness to remedy that he used to do, and I think if he begins to draw in it is high time for me to do so too. From thence walked round to White Hall, the Parke being quite locked up; and I observed a house shut up this day in the Pell Mell,[2] where heretofore in Cromwell's time we young men used to keep our weekly clubs. And so to White Hall to Sir G. Carteret, who is come this day from Chatham, and mighty glad he is to see

[1] The son of a shoemaker, bred to the sea-service; he rose to the rank of an admiral, and was killed in the fight with the Dutch, June, 1666.—B. See *post*, June 10th, 1666.

[2] Pepys refers to this place as Wood's on July 26th, 1660.

me, and begun to talk of our great business of the match, which goes on as fast as possible, but for convenience we took water and over to his coach to Lambeth, by which we went to Deptford, all the way talking, first, how matters are quite concluded with all possible content between my Lord and him and signed and sealed, so that my Lady Sandwich is to come thither to-morrow or next day, and the young lady is sent for, and all likely to be ended between them in a very little while, with mighty joy on both sides, and the King, Duke, Lord Chancellor, and all mightily pleased. Thence to newes, wherein I find that Sir G. Carteret do now take all my Lord Sandwich's business to heart, and makes it the same with his owne. He tells me how at Chatham it was proposed to my Lord Sandwich to be joined with the Prince in the command of the fleete, which he was most willing to; but when it come to the Prince, he was quite against it; saying, there could be no government, but that it would be better to have two fleetes, and neither under the command of the other, which he would not agree to. So the King was not pleased; but, without any unkindnesse, did order the fleete to be ordered as above, as to the Admirals and commands: so the Prince is come up; and Sir G. Carteret, I remember, had this word thence, that, says he, by this means, though the King told him that it would be but for this expedition, yet I believe we shall keepe him out for altogether. He tells me how my Lord was much troubled at Sir W. Pen's being ordered forth (as it seems he is, to go to Solebay, and with the best fleete he can, to go forth), and no notice taken of my Lord Sandwich going after him, and having the command over him. But after some discourse Mr. Coventry did satisfy, as he says, my Lord, so as they parted friends both in that point and upon the other wherein I know my Lord was troubled, and which Mr. Coventry did speak to him of first thinking that my Lord might justly take offence at, his not being mentioned in the relation of the fight in the news book,[1] and did clear all to my Lord how little he was concerned in it, and therewith my Lord also satisfied, which I am mightily glad of, because I should take it a very great misfortune to

[1] See note, June 23rd, 1665.

me to have them two to differ above all the persons in the world. Being come to Deptford, my Lady not being within, we parted, and I by water to Woolwich, where I found my wife come, and her two mayds, and very prettily accommodated they will be; and I left them going to supper, grieved in my heart to part with my wife, being worse by much without her, though some trouble there is in having the care of a family at home in this plague time, and so took leave, and I in one boat and W. Hewer in another home very late, first against tide, we having walked in the dark to Greenwich. Late home and to bed, very lonely.

6th. Up and forth to give order to my pretty grocer's wife's house, who, her husband tells me, is going this day for the summer into the country. I bespoke some sugar, &c., for my father, and so home to the office, where all the morning. At noon dined at home, and then by water to White Hall to Sir G. Carteret about money for the office, a sad thought, for in a little while all must go to wracke, winter coming on apace, when a great sum must be ready to pay part of the fleete, and so far we are from it that we have not enough to stop the mouths of poor people and their hands from falling about our eares here almost in the office. God give a good end to it! Sir G. Carteret told me one considerable thing: Alderman Backewell[1] is ordered abroad upon some private score with a great sum of money; wherein I was instrumental the other day in shipping him away. It seems some of his creditors have taken notice of it, and he was like to be broke yesterday in his absence; Sir G. Carteret telling me that the King and the kingdom must as good as fall with that man at this time; and that he was forced to get £4,000 himself to answer Backewell's people's occasions, or he must have broke; but committed this to me as a great secret and which I am heartily sorry to hear. Thence, after a little merry discourse of our marrying business, I parted, and by coach to several places, among others to see my Lord Brunkerd, who is not well, but was at rest when I come. I could not see him, nor had much mind, one of the great houses within two doors of

[1] Alderman Edward Backwell kept on his business until 1672, when he was ruined by the closing of the Exchequer (see note, June 23rd, 1660).

him being shut up: and, Lord! the number of houses visited, which this day I observed through the town quite round in my way by Long Lane and London Wall. So home to the office, and thence to Sir W. Batten, and spent the evening at supper; and, among other discourse, the rashness of Sir John Lawson, for breeding up his daughter so high and proud, refusing a man of great interest, Sir W. Barkeley, to match her with a melancholy fellow, Colonell Norton's[1] son, of no interest nor good nature nor generosity at all, giving her £6,000, when the other would have taken her with two; when he himself knew that he was not worth the money himself in all the world, he did give her that portion, and is since dead, and left his wife and two daughters beggars, and the other gone away with £6,000, and no content in it, through the ill qualities of her father-in-law and husband, who, it seems, though a pretty woman, contracted for her as if he had been buying a horse; and, worst of all, is now of no use to serve the mother and two little sisters in any stead at Court, whereas the other might have done what he would for her: so here is an end of this family's pride, which, with good care, might have been what they would, and done well. Thence, weary of this discourse, as the act of the greatest rashness that ever I heard of in all my little conversation, we parted, and I home to bed. Sir W. Pen, it seems, sailed last night from Sole-bay with about sixty sail of ship, and my Lord Sandwich in "The Prince" and some others, it seems, going after them to overtake them, for I am sure my Lord Sandwich will do all possible to overtake them, and will be troubled to the heart if he do it not.

7th. Up, and having set my neighbour, Mr. Hudson, wine coopers, at work drawing out a tierce of wine for the sending of some of it to my wife, I abroad, only taking notice to what a condition it hath pleased God to bring me that at this time I have two tierces of Claret, two quarter casks of Canary, and a smaller vessel of Sack; a vessel of Tent, another of Malaga, and another of white wine, all in my wine cellar together; which, I believe, none of my

[1] Norton died in August, 1666 (see *post*, August 29th, 1666). He appears to have left his widow a jointure of £800 a year.

friends of my name now alive ever had of his owne at one time. To Westminster, and there with Mr. Povy and Creed talking of our Tangier business, and by and by I drew Creed aside and acquainted him with what Sir G. Carteret did tell me about Backewell the other day, because he hath money of his in his hands. So home, taking some new books, £5 worth, home to my great content. At home all the day after busy. Some excellent discourse and advice of Sir W. Warren's in the afternoon, at night home to look over my new books, and so late to bed.

8th. All day very diligent at the office, ended my letters by 9 at night, and then fitted myself to go down to Woolwich to my wife, which I did, calling at Sir G. Carteret's at Deptford, and there hear that my Lady Sandwich is come, but not very well. By 12 o'clock to Woolwich, found my wife asleep in bed, but strange to think what a fine night I had down, but before I had been one minute on shore, the mightiest storm come of wind and rain that almost could be for a quarter of an houre and so left. I to bed, being the first time I come to her lodgings, and there lodged well.

9th (Lord's day). Very pleasant with her and among my people, while she made her ready, and, about 10 o'clock, by water to Sir G. Carteret, and there find my Lady [Sandwich] in her chamber, not very well, but looks the worst almost that ever I did see her in my life. It seems her drinking of the water at Tunbridge did almost kill her before she could with most violent physique get it out of her body again. We are received with most extraordinary kindnesse by my Lady Carteret and her children, and dined most nobly. Sir G. Carteret went to Court this morning. After dinner I took occasion to have much discourse with Mr. Ph. Carteret, and find him a very modest man; and I think verily of mighty good nature, and pretty understanding. He did give me a good account of the fight with the Dutch. My Lady Sandwich dined in her chamber. About three o'clock I, leaving my wife there, took boat and home, and there shifted myself into my black silke suit, and having promised Harman yesterday, I to his house, which I find very mean, and mean company. His wife very ill; I could not see her. Here I, with her father and Kate Joyce, who was also very ill, were godfathers and godmother to his boy, and was christened Will. Mr. Meriton[1] christened him. The most observable thing I found there to my content, was to hear him and his clerk tell me that in this parish of Michell's, Cornhill, one of the middlemost parishes and a great one of the towne, there hath, notwithstanding this sickliness, been buried of any disease, man, woman, or child, not one for thirteen months last past; which [is] very strange. And the like in a good degree in most other parishes, I hear, saving only of the plague in them, but in this neither the plague nor any other disease. So back again home and reshifted myself, and so down to my Lady Carteret's, where mighty merry and great pleasantnesse between my Lady Sandwich and the young ladies and me, and all of us mighty merry, there never having been in the world sure a greater business of general content than this match proposed between Mr. Carteret and my Lady Jemimah. But withal it is mighty pretty to think how my poor Lady Sandwich, between her and me, is doubtfull whether her daughter will like of it or no, and how troubled she is for fear of it, which I do not fear at all, and desire her not to do it, but her fear is the most discreet and pretty that ever I did see. Late here, and then my wife and I, with most hearty kindnesse from my Lady Carteret by boat to Woolwich, come thither about 12 at night, and so to bed.

10th. Up, and with great pleasure looking over a nest of puppies of Mr. Shelden's, with which my wife is most extraordinary pleased, and one of them is promised her. Anon I took my leave, and away by water to the Duke of Albemarle's, where he tells me that I must be at Hampton Court anon. So I home to look over my Tangier papers, and having a coach of Mr. Povy's attending me, by appointment, in order to my coming to dine at his country house at Brainford,[2] where he and his family is, I went and Mr. Tasbrough with me therein, it being a pretty chariot, but most inconvenient as to the horses throwing dust and dirt into one's eyes and upon one's clothes. There I staid a quarter of an houre, Creed being there, and being able to

[1] The Rev. John Meriton was instituted into the rectory of St. Michael's, Cornhill, in 1663.

[2] Brentford. Mr. Povy's country-house was The Priory, Hounslow.

do little business (but the less the better). Creed rode before, and Mr. Povy and I after him in the chariot; and I was set down by him at the Parke pale, where one of his saddle horses was ready for me, he himself not daring to come into the house or be seen, because that a servant of his, out of his house, happened to be sicke, but is not yet dead, but was never suffered to come into his house after he was ill. But this opportunity was taken to injure Povy, and most horribly he is abused by some persons hereupon, and his fortune, I believe, quite broke; but that he hath a good heart to bear, or a cunning one to conceal his evil. There I met with Sir W. Coventry, and by and by was heard by my Lord Chancellor and Treasurer about our Tangier money, and my Lord Treasurer had ordered me to forbear meddling with the £15,000 he offered me the other day, but, upon opening the case to them, they did offer it again, and so I think I shall have it, but my Lord Generall must give his consent in it, this money having been promised to him, and he very angry at the proposal. Here though I have not been in many years, yet I lacke time to stay, besides that it is, I perceive, an unpleasing thing to be at Court, everybody being fearful one of another, and all so sad, enquiring after the plague, so that I stole away by my horse to Kingston, and there with trouble was forced to press two sturdy rogues to carry me to London, and met at the waterside with Mr. Charnocke, Sir Philip Warwicke's clerke, who had been in company and was quite foxed. I took him with me in my boat, and so away to Richmond, and there, by night, walked with him to Moreclacke,[1] a very pretty walk, and there staid a good while, now and then talking and sporting with Nan the servant, who says she is a seaman's wife, and at last bade good night.

11th. And so all night down by water, a most pleasant passage, and come thither by two o'clock, and so walked from the Old Swan home, and there to bed to my Will, being very weary, and he lodging at my desire in my house. At 6 o'clock up and to Westminster (where and all the towne besides, I hear, the plague encreases), and, it being too soon to go to the Duke of Albemarle, I to the Harp and

[1] Mortlake.

Ball, and there made a bargain with Mary to go forth with me in the afternoon, which she with much ado consented to. So I to the Duke of Albemarle's, and there with much ado did get his consent in part to my having the money promised for Tangier, and the other part did not concur. So being displeased with this, I back to the office and there sat alone a while doing business, and then by a solemn invitation to the Trinity House, where a great dinner and company, Captain Dobbin's[1] feast for Elder Brother. But I broke up before the dinner half over and by water to the Harp and Ball, and thence had Mary meet me at the New Exchange, and there took coach and I with great pleasure took the ayre to Highgate, and thence to Hampstead, much pleased with her company, pretty and innocent, and had what pleasure almost I would with her, and so at night, weary and sweaty, it being very hot beyond bearing, we back again, and I set her down in St. Martin's Lane, and so I to the evening 'Change, and there hear all the towne full that Ostend is delivered to us, and that Alderman Backewell[2] did go with £50,000 to that purpose. But the truth of it I do not know, but something I believe there is extraordinary in his going. So to the office, where I did what I could as to letters, and so away to bed, shifting myself, and taking some Venice treakle, feeling myself out of order, and thence to bed to sleep.

12th. After doing what business I could in the morning, it being a solemn fast-day[3] for the plague growing upon us,

[1] Captain Joseph Dobbins.

[2] Among the State Papers is a letter from the king to the Lord General (dated August 8th, 1665): "Alderman Backwell being in great straits for the second payment he has to make for the service in Flanders, as much tin is to be transmitted to him as will raise the sum. Has authorized him and Sir George Carteret to treat with the tin farmers for 500 tons of tin to be speedily transported under good convoy; but if, on consulting with Alderman Backwell, this plan of the tin seems insufficient, then without further difficulty he is to dispose for that purpose of the £10,000 assigned for pay of the Guards, not doubting that before that comes due, other ways will be found for supplying it; the payment in Flanders is of such importance that some means must be found of providing for it" ("Calendar," Domestic, 1664–65, pp. 508, 509).

[3] "A form of Common Prayer; together with an order for fasting for the averting of God's heavy visitation upon many places of this realm. The fast to be observed within the cities of London and Westminster

I took boat and down to Deptford, where I stood with great pleasure an houre or two by my Lady Sandwich's bedside, talking to her (she lying prettily in bed) of my Lady Jemimah's being from my Lady Pickering's when our letters come to that place; she being at my Lord Montagu's, at Boughton. The truth is, I had received letters of it two days ago, but had dropped them, and was in a very extraordinary straite what to do for them, or what account to give my Lady, but sent to every place; I sent to Moreclacke, where I had been the night before, and there they were found, which with mighty joy come safe to me; but all ending with satisfaction to my Lady and me, though I find my Lady Carteret not much pleased with this delay, and principally because of the plague, which renders it unsafe to stay long at Deptford. I eat a bit (my Lady Carteret being the most kind lady in the world), and so took boat, and a fresh boat at the Tower, and so up the river, against tide all the way, I having lost it by staying prating to and with my Lady, and, from before one, made it seven ere we got to Hampton Court; and when I come there all business was over, saving my finding Mr. Coventry at his chamber, and with him a good while about several businesses at his chamber, and so took leave, and away to my boat, and all night upon the water, staying a while with Nan at Moreclacke, very much pleased and merry with her, and so on homeward, and come home by two o'clock, shooting the bridge at that time of night, and so to bed, where I find Will is not, he staying at Woolwich to come with my wife to dinner to-morrow to my Lady Carteret's. Heard Mr. Williamson repeat at Hampton Court to-day how the King of France hath lately set out a most high arrest[1] against the Pope, which is reckoned very lofty and high.

and places adjacent, on Wednesday the twelfth of this instant July, and both there and in all parts of this realm on the first Wednesday in every month during the visitation" ("Calendar of State Papers," Domestic, 1664–65, p. 466).

[1] *Arrêt.* The rupture between Alexander VII. and Louis XIV. was healed in 1664, by the treaty signed at Pisa, on February 12th. On August 9th, the pope's nephew, Cardinal Chigi, made his entry into Paris, as legate, to give the king satisfaction for the insult offered at Rome by the Corsican guard to the Duc de Créqui, the French ambassador: see January 25th, 1662–63. Cardinal Imperiali, Governor of

13th. Lay long, being sleepy, and then up to the office, my Lord Brunker (after his sickness) being come to the office, and did what business there was, and so I by water, at night late, to Sir G. Carteret's,[1] but there being no oars to carry me, I was fain to call a skuller that had a gentleman already in it, and he proved a man of love to musique, and he and I sung together the way down with great pleasure, and an incident extraordinary to be met with. There come to dinner, they haveing dined, but my Lady caused something to be brought for me, and I dined well and mighty merry, especially my Lady Slaning and I about eating of creame and brown bread, which she loves as much as I. Thence after long discourse with them and my Lady alone, I and [my] wife, who by agreement met here, took leave, and I saw my wife a little way down (it troubling me that this absence makes us a little strange instead of more fond), and so parted, and I home to some letters, and then home to bed. Above 700 died of the plague this week.

14th. Up, and all the morning at the Exchequer endeavouring to strike tallys for money for Tangier, and mightily vexed to see how people attend there, some out of towne, and others drowsy, and to others it was late, so that the King's business suffers ten times more than all their service is worth. So I am put off to to-morrow. Thence to the Old Exchange, by water, and there bespoke two fine shirts of my pretty seamstress, who, she tells me, serves Jacke Fenn. Upon the 'Change all the news is that guns have been heard and that news is come by a Dane that my Lord

Rome, asked pardon of the king in person, and all the hard conditions of the treaty were fulfilled. But no *arrêt* against the pope was set forth in 1665. On the contrary, Alexander, now wishing to please the king, issued a constitution on February 2nd, 1665, ordering all the clergy of France, without any exception, to sign a formulary condemning the famous five propositions extracted from the works of Jansenius and on April 29th, the king in person ordered the parliament to register the bull. The Jansenist party, of course, demurred to this proceeding: the Bishops of Alais, Angers, Beauvais, and Pamiers, issuing mandates calling upon their clergy to refuse. It was against these mandates, as being contrary to the king's declaration and the pope's intentions, that the *arrêt* was directed. — B.

[1] At the Treasurer's house at Deptford, Sir G. Carteret's official residence.

was in view of De Ruyter, and that since his parting from my Lord of Sandwich he hath heard guns, but little of it do I think true. So home to dinner, where Povy by agreement, and after dinner we to talk of our Tangier matters, about keeping our profit at the pay and victualling of the garrison, if the present undertakers should leave it, wherein I did [not] nor will do any thing unworthy me and any just man, but they being resolved to quit it, it is fit I should suffer Mr. Povy to do what he can with Mr. Gauden about it to our profit. Thence to the discoursing of putting some sums of money in order and tallys, which we did pretty well. So he in the evening gone, I by water to Sir G. Carteret's, and there find my Lady Sandwich and her buying things for my Lady Jem.'s wedding; and my Lady Jem. is beyond expectation come to Dagenhams,[1] where Mr. Carteret is to go to visit her to-morrow; and my proposal of waiting on him, he being to go alone to all persons strangers to him, was well accepted, and so I go with him. But, Lord! to see how kind my Lady Carteret is to her! Sends her most rich jewells, and provides bedding and things of all sorts most richly for her, which makes my Lady and me out of our wits almost to see the kindnesse she treats us all with, as if they would buy the young lady. Thence away home and, foreseeing my being abroad two days, did sit up late making of letters ready against to-morrow, and other things, and so to bed, to be up betimes by the helpe of a larum watch, which by chance I borrowed of my watchmaker to-day, while my owne is mending.

15th. Up, and after all business done, though late, I to Deptford, but before I went out of the office saw there young

[1] Dagnams, about four miles from Romford, the seat of Lady Wright, widow of Sir Henry Wright, and sister of Lady Sandwich. In 1454 Henry Percy, Earl of Northumberland, died seised of the manors of Dagnams and Cockerells. In 1637 it belonged to Lawrence Wright, M.D., whose son Henry was created baronet by Cromwell in 1658, and by Charles II. in 1660. The estate was devised by Anne (daughter of Sir Henry and Lady Wright), widow, first, of Sir Robert Pye, and afterwards of William Rider, to her cousin Edward Carteret, Postmaster-General, third son of Sir Philip and Lady Jemimah Carteret. The manor was sold in 1749 to Henry Muilman, and again in 1772 to Sir Richard Neave, who pulled down the old house (built by Sir Henry Wright), and built the present mansion on a new site. The present proprietor is Sir Thomas Neave, Bart.

Bagwell's wife returned, but could not stay to speak to her, though I had a great mind to it, and also another great lady, as to fine clothes, did attend there to have a ticket signed; which I did do, taking her through the garden to my office, where I signed it and had a salute of her, and so I away by boat to Redriffe, and thence walked, and after dinner, at Sir G. Carteret's, where they stayed till almost three o'clock for me, and anon took boat, Mr. Carteret and I to the ferry-place at Greenwich, and there staid an hour crossing the water to and again to get our coach and horses over; and by and by set out, and so toward Dagenhams. But, Lord! what silly discourse we had by the way as to love-matters, he being the most awkerd man I ever met with in my life as to that business. Thither we come, by that time it begun to be dark, and were kindly received by Lady Wright and my Lord Crew. And to discourse they went, my Lord discoursing with him, asking of him questions of travell, which he answered well enough in a few words; but nothing to the lady from him at all. To supper, and after supper to talk again, he yet taking no notice of the lady. My Lord would have had me have consented to leaving the young people together to-night, to begin their amours, his staying being but to be little. But I advised against it, lest the lady might be too much surprised. So they led him up to his chamber, where I staid a little, to know how he liked the lady, which he told me he did mightily; but, Lord! in the dullest insipid manner that ever lover did. So I bid him good night, and down to prayers with my Lord Crew's family, and after prayers, my Lord, and Lady Wright, and I, to consult what to do; and it was agreed at last to have them go to church together, as the family used to do, though his lameness was a great objection against it. But at last my Lady Jem. sent me word by my Lady Wright that it would be better to do just as they used to do before his coming; and therefore she desired to go to church, which was yielded then to.

16th (Lord's day). I up, having lain with Mr. Moore in the chaplin's chamber. And having trimmed myself, down to Mr. Carteret; and he being ready we down and walked in the gallery an hour or two, it being a most noble and pretty house that ever, for the bigness, I saw. Here I taught him what to do: to take the lady always by the hand to lead her, and telling him that I would find opportunity to leave them two together, he should make these and these compliments, and also take a time to do the like to Lord Crew and Lady Wright. After I had instructed him, which he thanked me for, owning that he needed my teaching him, my Lord Crew come down and family, the young lady among the rest; and so by coaches to church four miles off; where a pretty good sermon, and a declaration of penitence of a man that had undergone the Churche's censure for his wicked life. Thence back again by coach, Mr. Carteret having not had the confidence to take his lady once by the hand, coming or going, which I told him of when we come home, and he will hereafter do it. So to dinner. My Lord excellent discourse. Then to walk in the gallery, and to sit down. By and by my Lady Wright and I go out (and then my Lord Crew, he not by design), and lastly my Lady Crew come out, and left the young people together. And a little pretty daughter of my Lady Wright's most innocently come out afterward, and shut the door to, as if she had done it, poor child, by inspiration; which made us without, have good sport to laugh at. They together an hour, and by and by church-time, whither he led her into the coach and into the church, and so at church all the afternoon, several handsome ladies at church. But it was most extraordinary hot that ever I knew it. So home again and to walk in the gardens, where we left the young couple a second time; and my Lady Wright and I to walk together, who to my trouble tells me that my Lady Jem. must have something done to her body by Scott before she can be married, and therefore care must be had to send him, also that some more new clothes must of necessity be made her, which and other things I took care of. Anon to supper, and excellent discourse and dispute between my Lord Crew and the chaplin, who is a good scholler, but a nonconformist. Here this evening I spoke with Mrs. Carter, my old acquaintance, that hath lived with my Lady these twelve or thirteen years, the sum of all whose discourse and others for her, is, that I would get her a good husband; which I have promised, but know not when I shall perform. After Mr. Carteret was carried to his chamber, we to prayers again and then to bed.

17th. Up all of us, and to billiards; my Lady Wright, Mr. Carteret, myself, and every body. By and by the young couple left together. Anon to dinner; and after dinner Mr. Carteret took my advice about giving to the servants, and I led him to give £10 among them, which he did, by leaving it to the chief man-servant, Mr. Medows, to do for him. Before we went, I took my Lady Jem. apart, and would know how she liked this gentleman, and whether she was under any difficulty concerning him. She blushed, and hid her face awhile; but at last I forced her to tell me. She answered that she could readily obey what her father and mother had done; which was all she could say, or I expect. So anon I took leave, and for London. But, Lord! to see, among other things, how all these great people here are afeard of London, being doubtfull of anything that comes from thence, or that hath lately been there, that I was forced to say that I lived wholly at Woolwich. In our way Mr. Carteret did give me mighty thanks for my care and pains for him, and is mightily pleased, though the truth is, my Lady Jem. hath carried herself with mighty discretion and gravity, not being forward at all in any degree, but mighty serious in her answers to him, as by what he says and I observed, I collect. To London to my office, and there took letters from the office, where all well, and so to the Bridge, and there he and I took boat and to Deptford, where mighty welcome, and brought the good newes of all being pleased to them. Mighty mirth at my giving them an account of all; but the young man could not be got to say one word before me or my Lady Sandwich of his adventures, but, by what he afterwards related to his father and mother and sisters, he gives an account that pleases them mightily. Here Sir G. Carteret would have me lie all night, which I did most nobly, better than ever I did in my life, Sir G. Carteret being mighty kind to me, leading me to my chamber; and all their care now is, to have the business ended, and they have reason, because the sicknesse puts all out of order, and they cannot safely stay where they are.

18th. Up and to the office, where all the morning, and so to my house and eat a bit of victuals, and so to the 'Change, where a little business and a very thin Exchange; and so walked through London to the Temple, where I took water for Westminster to the Duke of Albemarle, to wait on him, and so to Westminster Hall, and there paid for my newes-books, and did give Mrs. Michell, who is going out of towne because of the sicknesse, and her husband, a pint of wine, and so Sir W. Warren coming to me by appointment we away by water home, by the way discoursing about the project I have of getting some money and doing the King good service too about the mast docke at Woolwich, which I fear will never be done if I do not go about it. After dispatching letters at the office, I by water down to Deptford, where I staid a little while, and by water to my wife, whom I have not seen 6 or 5 days, and there supped with her, and mighty pleasant, and saw with content her drawings, and so to bed mighty merry. I was much troubled this day to hear at Westminster how the officers do bury the dead in the open Tuttle-fields, pretending want of room elsewhere; whereas the New Chappell[1] church-yard was walled-in at the publick charge in the last plague-time, merely for want of room and now none, but such as are able to pay dear for it, can be buried there.

19th. Up and to the office, and thence presently to the Exchequer, and there with much trouble got my tallys, and afterwards took Mr. Falconer, Spicer, and another or two to the Leg and there give them a dinner, and so with my tallys and about 30 dozen of bags, which it seems are my due, having paid the fees as if I had received the money I away home, and after a little stay down by water to Deptford, where I find all full of joy, and preparing to go to Dagenhams to-morrow. To supper, and after supper to talk without end. Very late I went away, it raining, but I had a design *pour aller à la femme de Bagwell* and did so. . . . So away about 12, and it raining hard I back to Sir G. Carteret and there called up the page, and to bed there, being all in a most violent sweat.

[1] The erection of New Chapel, Broadway, Westminster, is ascribed to Dr. Darrell, prebendary of St. Peter's, who in 1631 left £400 for the purpose ; Sir Robert Pye, who added £500 to complete and furnish it; and Archbishop Laud, who contributed £1,000 and some painted glass. It was not completed till 1636. Whitelocke mentions the burying ground under the year 1649. Christ Church (dedicated December 14th, 1843) has now taken the place of the New Chapel.

20th. Up, in a boat among other people to the Tower, and there to the office, where we sat all the morning. So down to Deptford and there dined, and after dinner saw my Lady Sandwich and Mr. Carteret and his two sisters over the water, going to Dagenhams, and my Lady Carteret towards Cranburne.[1] So all the company broke up in most extraordinary joy, wherein I am mighty contented that I have had the good fortune to be so instrumental, and I think it will be of good use to me. So walked to Redriffe, where I hear the sickness is, and indeed is scattered almost every where, there dying 1,089 of the plague this week. My Lady Carteret did this day give me a bottle of plague-water home with me. So home to write letters late, and then home to bed, where I have not lain these 3 or 4 nights. I received yesterday a letter from my Lord Sandwich, giving me thanks for my care about their marriage business, and desiring it to be dispatched, that no disappointment may happen therein, which I will help on all I can. This afternoon I waited on the Duke of Albemarle, and so to Mrs. Croft's, where I found and saluted Mrs. Burrows,[2] who is a very pretty woman for a mother of so many children. But, Lord! to see how the plague spreads. It being now all over King's Streete, at the Axe, and next door to it, and in other places.

21st. Up and abroad to the goldsmiths, to see what money I could get upon my present tallys upon the advance of the Excise, and I hope I shall get £10,000. I went also and had them entered at the Excise Office. Alderman Backewell is at sea. Sir R. Viner come to towne but this morning. So Colvill was the only man I could yet speak withal to get any money of. Met with Mr. Povy, and I with him and dined at the Custom House Taverne, there to talk of our Tangier business, and Stockedale[3] and Hewet with us. So abroad to several places, among others to Anthony Joyce's, and there broke to him my desire to have Pall married to Harman, whose wife, poor woman, is lately dead, to my

[1] The royal lodge of that name in Windsor Forest, occupied by Sir George Carteret as Vice-Chamberlain to the King. — B.

[2] Probably Mrs. Burrows, of Westminster, whose husband, Lieutenant Burrows, died in the following December (see December 21st, 1665).

[3] Apparently Robert Stockdale, a contractor for naval stores.

trouble, I loving her very much, and he will consider it. So home and late at my chamber, setting some papers in order; the plague growing very raging, and my apprehensions of it great. So very late to bed.

22nd. As soon as up I among my goldsmiths, Sir Robert Viner and Colvill, and there got £10,000 of my new tallys accepted, and so I made it my work to find out Mr. Mervin and sent for others to come with their bills of Exchange, as Captain Hewett, &c., and sent for Mr. Jackson, but he was not in town. So all the morning at the office, and after dinner, which was very late, I to Sir R. Viner's, by his invitation in the morning, and got near £5,000 more accepted, and so from this day the whole, or near £15,000, lies upon interest. Thence I by water to Westminster, and the Duke of Albemarle being gone to dinner to my Lord of Canterbury's, I thither, and there walked and viewed the new hall,[1] a new old-fashion hall, as much as possible. Begun, and means left for the ending of it, by Bishop Juxon. Not coming proper to speak with him, I to Foxhall, where to the Spring garden; but I do not see one guest there, the town being so empty of any body to come thither. Only, while I was there, a poor woman come to scold with the master of the house that a kinswoman, I think, of her's, that was newly dead of the plague, might be buried in the church-yard; for, for her part, she should not be buried in the commons, as they said she should. Back to White Hall, and by and by comes the Duke of Albemarle, and there, after a little discourse, I by coach home, not meeting with but two coaches, and but two carts from White Hall to my own house, that I could observe; and the streets mighty thin of people. I met this noon with Dr. Burnett, who told me, and I find in the news-book this week that he posted upon the 'Change, that whoever did spread the report that, instead of the plague, his servant was by him killed, it was forgery, and shewed me the acknowledgment of the master of the pest-house, that his servant died of a bubo on his right groine, and two spots on his right thigh, which is the plague. To my office, where late writing letters, and getting myself

[1] The hall here spoken of was converted into the archiepiscopal library by Archbishop Howley.

prepared with business for Hampton Court to-morrow, and so having caused a good pullet to be got for my supper, all alone, I very late to bed. All the news is great: that we must of necessity fall out with France, for He will side with the Dutch against us. That Alderman Backewell is gone over (which indeed he is) with money, and that Ostend is in our present possession. But it is strange to see how poor Alderman Backewell is like to be put to it in his absence, Mr. Shaw his right hand being ill. And the Alderman's absence gives doubts to people, and I perceive they are in great straits for money, besides what Sir G. Carteret told me about fourteen days ago. Our fleet under my Lord Sandwich being about the latitude 55½ (which is a great secret) to the Northward of the Texell. So to bed very late. In my way I called upon Sir W. Turner, and at Mr. Shelcrosse's (but he was not at home, having left his bill with Sir W. Turner), that so I may prove I did what I could as soon as I had money to answer all bills.

23rd (Lord's day). Up very betimes, called by Mr. Cutler, by appointment, and with him in his coach and four horses over London Bridge to Kingston, a very pleasant journey, and at Hampton Court by nine o'clock, and in our way very good and various discourse, as he is a man, that though I think he be a knave, as the world thinks him, yet a man of great experience and worthy to be heard discourse. When we come there, we to Sir W. Coventry's chamber, and there discoursed long with him, he and I alone, the others being gone away, and so walked together through the garden to the house, where we parted, I observing with a little trouble that he is too great now to expect too much familiarity with, and I find he do not mind me as he used to do, but when I reflect upon him and his business I cannot think much of it, for I do not observe anything but the same great kindness from him. I followed the King to chappell, and there hear a good sermon; and after sermon with my Lord Arlington, Sir Thomas Ingram and others, spoke to the Duke about Tangier, but not to much purpose. I was not invited any whither to dinner, though a stranger, which did also trouble me; but yet I must remember it is a Court, and indeed where most are strangers; but, however,

Cutler carried me to Mr. Marriott's [1] the house-keeper, and there we had a very good dinner and good company, among others Lilly, the painter. Thence to the councill-chamber, where in a back room I sat all the afternoon, but the councill begun late to sit, and spent most of the time upon Morisco's Tarr businesse.[2] They sat long, and I forced to follow Sir Thomas Ingram, the Duke, and others, so that when I got free and come to look for Cutler, he was gone with his coach, without leaving any word with any body to tell me so; so that I was forced with great trouble to walk up and down looking of him, and at last forced to get a boat to carry me to Kingston, and there, after eating a bit at a neat inne, which pleased me well, I took boat, and slept all the way, without intermission, from thence to Queenhive,[3] where, it being about two o'clock, too late and too soon to go home to bed, I lay and slept till about four.

24th. And then up and home, and there dressed myself, and by appointment to Deptford, to Sir G. Carteret's, between six and seven o'clock, where I found him and my Lady almost ready, and by and by went over to the ferry, and took coach and six horses nobly for Dagenhams, himself and lady and their little daughter, Louisonne,[4] and myself in the coach; where, when we come, we were bravely entertained and spent the day most pleasantly with the young ladies, and I so merry as never more. Only for want of sleep, and drinking of strong beer had a rheum in one of my eyes, which troubled me much. Here with great content all the day, as I think I ever passed a day in my life, because of the contentfulnesse of our errand, and the noblenesse of the company and our manner of going. But I find Mr. Carteret yet as backward almost in his caresses, as he was the first day. At night, about seven o'clock, took coach again; but, Lord! to see in what a pleasant humour Sir G. Carteret hath been both coming and going; so light,

[1] James Marriott, "Keeper of the standing Wardrobe and privy lodgings at Hampton Court," who succeeded to this post in December, 1664, on the death of Richard Marriott. Richard Marriott is referred to on May 12th, 1662.

[2] Mr. Morris had contracts for tar with the Navy office.

[3] Queenhithe is usually written "Queenhive" by our old dramatists.

[4] Louisa Marguerite Carteret, afterwards married to Sir Robert Atkins.

so fond, so merry, so boyish (so much content he takes in this business), it is one of the greatest wonders I ever saw in my mind. But once in serious discourse he did say that, if he knew his son to be a debauchee, as many and most are now-a-days about the Court, he would tell it, and my Lady Jem. should not have him; and so enlarged both he and she about the baseness and looseness of the Court, and told several stories of the Duke of Monmouth, and Richmond, and some great person, my Lord of Ormond's second son,[1] married to a lady of extraordinary quality (fit and that might have been made a wife for the King himself), about six months since, that this great person hath given the pox to ——;[2] and discoursed how much this would oblige the Kingdom if the King would banish some of these great persons publiquely from the Court, and wished it with all their hearts. We set out so late that it grew dark, so as we doubted the losing of our way; and a long time it was, or seemed, before we could get to the water-side, and that about eleven at night, where, when we come, all merry (only my eye troubled me, as I said), we found no ferry-boat was there, nor no oares to carry us to Deptford. However, afterwards oares was called from the other side at Greenwich; but, when it come, a frolique, being mighty merry, took us, and there we would sleep all night in the coach in the Isle of Doggs. So we did, there being now with us my Lady Scott,[3] and with great pleasure drew up the glasses, and slept till daylight, and then some victuals and wine being brought us, we ate a bit, and so up and took boat, merry as might be; and when come to Sir G. Carteret's, there all to bed.

25th. Our good humour in every body continuing, and there I slept till seven o'clock. Then up and to the office, well refreshed, my eye only troubling me, which by keeping a little covered with my handkercher and washing now and

[1] Richard Butler, Earl of Arran (see note, *ante*, February 3rd, 1664–65). He married, firstly, Lady Mary Stuart, daughter of James, first Duke of Richmond and fourth of Lenox, who died in 1667 without issue (apparently the lady referred to in the text), and, secondly, Dorothy, daughter of John Ferrers, of Tamworth Castle, co. Warwick.

[2] The name is not given in the manuscript.

[3] Sir G. Carteret's daughter. See note, July 30th, 1663.

then with cold water grew better by night. At noon to the 'Change, which was very thin, and thence homeward, and was called in by Mr. Rawlinson, with whom I dined and some good company very harmlessly merry. But sad the story of the plague in the City, it growing mightily. This day my Lord Brunker did give me Mr. Grant's[1] book upon the Bills of Mortality, new printed and enlarged. Thence to my office awhile, full of business, and thence by coach to the Duke of Albemarle's, not meeting one coach going nor coming from my house thither and back again, which is very strange. One of my chief errands was to speak to Sir W. Clerke[2] about my wife's brother,[3] who importunes me, and I doubt he do want mightily, but I can do little for him there as to employment in the army, and out of my purse I dare not for fear of a precedent, and letting him come often to me is troublesome and dangerous too, he living in the dangerous part of the town, but I will do what I can possibly for him and as soon as I can. Mightily troubled all this afternoon with masters coming to me about Bills of Exchange and my signing them upon my Goldsmiths, but I did send for them all and hope to ease myself this weeke of all the clamour. These two or three days Mr. Shaw at Alderman Backewell's hath lain sick, like to die, and is feared will not live a day to an end. At night home and to bed, my head full of business, and among others, this day come a letter to me from Paris from my Lord Hinchingbroke, about his coming over; and I have sent this night an order from the Duke of Albemarle for a ship of 36 guns[4] to [go] to Calais to fetch him.

26th. Up, and after doing a little business, down to Deptford with Sir W. Batten, and there left him, and I to Greenwich to the Park, where I hear the King and Duke are come by water this morn from Hampton Court. They asked me several questions. The King mightily pleased with his new

[1] For note on Captain John Graunt and his work on the Bills of Mortality, see March 24th, 1661–62.

[2] Sir William Clarke. See note, *ante*, June 8th, 1665.

[3] Balthasar St. Michel.

[4] Pepys wrote to Lord Hinchingbroke from the Navy Office on July 25th, 1665, to inform him that a ship of 36 guns would be at Calais on August 1st to take him to Dover.

buildings there. I followed them to Castle's ship in building, and there met Sir W. Batten, and thence to Sir G. Carteret's, where all the morning with them; they not having any but the Duke of Monmouth, and Sir W. Killigrew,[1] and one gentleman, and a page more. Great variety of talk, and was often led to speak to the King and Duke. By and by they to dinner, and all to dinner and sat down to the King saving myself, which, though I could not in modesty expect, yet, God forgive my pride! I was sorry I was there, that Sir W. Batten should say that he could sit down where I could not, though he had twenty times more reason than I, but this was my pride and folly. I down and walked with Mr. Castle, who told me the design of Ford and Rider to oppose and do all the hurt they can to Captain Taylor in his new ship "The London,"[2] and how it comes, and that they are a couple of false persons, which I believe, and withal that he himself is a knave too. He and I by and by to dinner mighty nobly, and the King having dined, he come down, and I went in the barge with him, I sitting at the door. Down to Woolwich (and there I just saw and kissed my wife, and saw some of her painting, which is very curious; and away again to the King) and back again with him in the barge, hearing him and the Duke talk, and seeing and observing their manner of discourse. And God forgive me! though I admire them with all the duty possible, yet the more a man considers and observes them, the less he finds of difference between them and other men, though (blessed be God!) they are both princes of great nobleness and spirits. The barge put me into another boat that come to our side, Mr. Holder with a bag of gold to the Duke, and so they away and I home to the office. The Duke of Monmouth is the most skittish leaping gallant that ever I saw, always in action, vaulting or leaping, or clambering. Thence mighty full of the honour of this day, I took coach and to Kate Joyce's, but she not within, but

[1] Sir William Killigrew, elder brother of Tom Killigrew. He was made a baronet about 1661. He wrote some verses and plays, and became Vice-Chamberlain to the Queen. He died about 1694.

[2] The new "London" being built to replace the old "London" by Captain John Taylor, Navy Commissioner at Harwich (see April 21st, 1666).

spoke with Anthony, who tells me he likes well of my proposal for Pall to Harman, but I fear that less than £500 will not be taken, and that I shall not be able to give, though I did not say so to him. After a little other discourse and the sad news of the death of so many in the parish of the plague, forty last night, the bell always going, I back to the Exchange, where I went up and sat talking with my beauty, Mrs. Batelier,[1] a great while, who is indeed one of the finest women I ever saw in my life. After buying some small matter, I home, and there to the office and saw Sir J. Minnes now come from Portsmouth, I home to set my Journall for these four days in order, they being four days of as great content and honour and pleasure to me as ever I hope to live or desire, or think any body else can live. For methinks if a man would but reflect upon this, and think that all these things are ordered by God Almighty to make me contented, and even this very marriage now on foot is one of the things intended to find me content in, in my life and matter of mirth, methinks it should make one mightily more satisfied in the world than he is. This day poor Robin Shaw at Backewell's died, and Backewell himself now in Flanders. The King himself asked about Shaw, and being told he was dead, said he was very sorry for it. The sicknesse is got into our parish this week, and is got, indeed, every where; so that I begin to think of setting things in order, which I pray God enable me to put both as to soul and body.

27th. Called up at 4 o'clock. Up and to my preparing some papers for Hampton Court, and so by water to Fox Hall, and there Mr. Gauden's coach took me up, and by and by I took up him, and so both thither, a brave morning to ride in and good discourse with him. Among others he begun with me to speak of the Tangier Victuallers resigning their employment, and his willingness to come on. Of which I was glad, and took the opportunity to answer him with all kindness and promise of assistance. He told me a while since my Lord Berkeley did speak of it to him, and yesterday a message from Sir Thomas Ingram. When I come to Hampton Court I find Sir T. Ingram and Creed

[1] Mary Batelier, the beauty, who kept a linendraper's shop in the Royal Exchange. She and her brother William are frequently mentioned in the Diary.

ready with papers signed for the putting of Mr. Gawden in, upon a resignation signed to by Lanyon and sent to Sir Thos. Ingram. At this I was surprized but yet was glad, and so it passed but with respect enough to those that are in, at least without any thing ill taken from it. I got another order signed about the boats, which I think I shall get something by. So dispatched all my business, having assurance of continuance of all hearty love from Sir W. Coventry, and so we staid and saw the King and Queene set out toward Salisbury, and after them the Duke and Duchesse, whose hands I did kiss. And it was the first time I did ever, or did see any body else, kiss her hand, and it was a most fine white and fat hand. But it was pretty to see the young pretty ladies dressed like men, in velvet coats, caps with ribbands, and with laced bands, just like men. Only the Duchesse herself it did not become. They gone, we with great content took coach again, and hungry come to Clapham about one o'clock, and Creed there too before us, where a good dinner, the house having dined, and so to walk up and down in the gardens, mighty pleasant. By and by comes by promise to me Sir G. Carteret, and viewed the house [1] above and below, and sat and drank there, and I had a little opportunity to kiss and spend some time with the ladies above, his daughter, a buxom lass, and his sister Fissant, a serious lady, and a little daughter of hers, that begins to sing prettily. Thence, with mighty pleasure, with Sir G. Carteret by coach, with great discourse of kindnesse with him to my Lord Sandwich, and to me also; and I every day see more good by the alliance. Almost at Deptford I 'light and walked over to Half-way House, and so home, in my way being shown my cozen Patience's house, which seems, at distance, a pretty house. At home met the weekly Bill, where above 1,000 encreased in the Bill, and of them, in all about 1,700 of the plague, which hath made the officers this day resolve of sitting at Deptford, which puts me to some consideration what to do. Therefore home to think and consider of every thing about it, and without determining any thing eat a little supper and to bed, full of the pleasure of these 6 or 7 last days.

[1] Mr. Gauden's house at Clapham (see note, July 25th, 1663).

28th. Up betimes, and down to Deptford, where, after a little discourse with Sir G. Carteret, who is much displeased with the order of our officers yesterday to remove the office to Deptford, pretending other things, but to be sure it is with regard to his own house (which is much because his family is going away). I am glad I was not at the order making, and so I will endeavour to alter it. Set out with my Lady all alone with her with six horses to Dagenhams; going by water to the Ferry. And a pleasant going, and good discourse; and when there, very merry, and the young couple now well acquainted. But, Lord! to see in what fear all the people here do live would make one mad, they are afeard of us that come to them, insomuch that I am troubled at it, and wish myself away. But some cause they have; for the chaplin, with whom but a week or two ago we were here mighty high disputing, is since fallen into a fever and dead, being gone hence to a friend's a good way off. A sober and a healthful man. These considerations make us all hasten the marriage, and resolve it upon Monday next, which is three days before we intended it. Mighty merry all of us, and in the evening with full content took coach again and home by daylight with great pleasure, and thence I down to Woolwich, where find my wife well, and after drinking and talking a little we to bed.

29th. Up betimes, and after viewing some of my wife's pictures, which now she is come to do very finely to my great satisfaction beyond what I could ever look for, I went away and by water to the office, where nobody to meet me, but busy all the morning. At noon to dinner, where I hear that my Will is come in thither and laid down upon my bed, ill of the headake, which put me into extraordinary fear; and I studied all I could to get him out of the house, and set my people to work to do it without discouraging him, and myself went forth to the Old Exchange to pay my fair Batelier for some linnen, and took leave of her, they breaking up shop for awhile; and so by coach to Kate Joyce's, and there used all the vehemence and rhetorique I could to get her husband to let her go down to Brampton, but I could not prevail with him; he urging some simple reasons, but most that of profit, minding the house, and the distance, if either of them should be ill. However, I did my best, and more than I had a mind to do, but that I saw him so resolved against it, while she was mightily troubled at it. At last he yielded she should go to Windsor, to some friends there. So I took my leave of them, believing that it is great odds that we ever all see one another again; for I dare not go any more to that end of the towne. So home, and to writing of letters hard, and then at night home, and fell to my Tangier papers till late, and then to bed, in some ease of mind that Will is gone to his lodging, and that he is likely to do well, it being only the headake.

30th (Lord's day). Up, and in my night gowne, cap and neckcloth, undressed all day long, lost not a minute, but in my chamber, setting my Tangier accounts to rights. Which I did by night to my very heart's content, not only that it is done, but I find every thing right, and even beyond what, after so long neglecting them, I did hope for. The Lord of Heaven be praised for it! Will was with me to-day, and is very well again. It was a sad noise to hear our bell to toll and ring so often to-day, either for deaths or burials; I think five or six times. At night weary with my day's work, but full of joy at my having done it, I to bed, being to rise betimes to-morrow to go to the wedding at Dagenhams. So to bed, fearing I have got some cold sitting in my loose garments all this day.

31st. Up, and very betimes by six o'clock at Deptford, and there find Sir G. Carteret, and my Lady ready to go: I being in my new coloured silk suit, and coat trimmed with gold buttons and gold broad lace round my hands, very rich and fine. By water to the Ferry, where, when we come, no coach there; and tide of ebb so far spent as the horse-boat could not get off on the other side the river to bring away the coach. So we were fain to stay there in the unlucky Isle of Doggs, in a chill place, the morning cool, and wind fresh, above two if not three hours to our great discontent. Yet being upon a pleasant errand, and seeing that it could not be helped, we did bear it very patiently; and it was worth my observing, I thought, as ever any thing, to see how upon these two scores, Sir G. Carteret, the most passionate man in the world, and that was in greatest haste to be gone, did bear with it, and very pleasant all the while, at least not troubled much so as to fret and storm at it.

Anon the coach comes: in the mean time there coming a News thither with his horse to go over, that told us he did come from Islington this morning; and that Proctor[1] the vintner of the Miter in Wood-street, and his son, are dead this morning there, of the plague; he having laid out abundance of money there, and was the greatest vintner for some time in London for great entertainments. We, fearing the canonicall hour would be past before we got thither, did with a great deal of unwillingness send away the license and wedding ring. So that when we come, though we drove hard with six horses, yet we found them gone from home; and going towards the church, met them coming from church, which troubled us. But, however, that trouble was soon over; hearing it was well done: they being both in their old cloaths; my Lord Crew giving her, there being three coach fulls of them. The young lady mighty sad, which troubled me; but yet I think it was only her gravity in a little greater degree than usual. All saluted her, but I did not till my Lady Sandwich did ask me whether I had saluted her or no. So to dinner, and very merry we were; but yet in such a sober way as never almost any wedding was in so great families: but it was much better. After dinner company divided, some to cards, others to talk. My Lady Sandwich and I up to settle accounts, and pay her some money. And mighty kind she is to me, and would fain have had me gone down for company with her to Hinchingbroke; but for my life I cannot. At night to supper, and so to talk; and which, methought, was the most extraordinary thing, all of us to prayers as usual, and the young bride and bridegroom too: and so after prayers, soberly to bed; only I got into the bridegroom's chamber while he undressed himself, and there was very merry, till he was called to the bride's chamber, and into bed they went. I kissed the bride in bed, and so the curtaines drawne with the greatest gravity that could be, and so good night. But the modesty and gravity of this business was so decent, that it was to me indeed ten times more delightfull than if it had been twenty times more merry and joviall.

[1] "1665, Aug. 1. Mr. Wm. Proctor, vintner, at ye Mitre, in Wood Street, with his young son, died at Islington (insolvent). *Ex Peste.*" — Smith's *Obituary*, p. 64.

Whereas I feared I must have sat up all night, we did here all get good beds, and I lay in the same I did before with Mr. Brisband, who is a good scholler and sober man; and we lay in bed, getting him to give me an account of Rome, which is the most delightfull talke a man can have of any traveller: and so to sleep. My eyes much troubled already with the change of my drink. Thus I ended this month with the greatest joy that ever I did any in my life, because I have spent the greatest part of it with abundance of joy, and honour, and pleasant journeys, and brave entertainments, and without cost of money; and at last live to see the business ended with great content on all sides.[1] This evening with Mr. Brisband, speaking of enchantments and spells, I telling him some of my charms; he told me this of his owne knowledge, at Bourdeaux in France.[2] The words these:

Voyci un Corps mort,
Royde come un Baston,
Froid comme Marbre,
Leger come un esprit,
Levons te au nom de Jesus Christ.

He saw four little girls, very young ones, all kneeling, each of them, upon one knee; and one begun the first line, whispering in the eare of the next, and the second to the third, and the third to the fourth, and she to the first.

[1] The marriage licence of Philip Carteret, of St. Peter-le-Poor, bachelor, aged 24, and Dame Jemima Montagu, spinster, aged 17, is dated July 29th, 1665 (Chester's "London Marriage Licences," ed. Foster, 1887, col. 249). Pepys wrote to Lord Sandwich on August 7th, and in his letter he says, "After a fortnight's acquaintance between the young people their marriage was completed on Monday, July 31st; present Sir G. Carteret, my Lady, and my Lady Slaning on their side, with my Lord Crew, Lady Sandwich, Lady Wright and all her family on your Lordship's, and is the only occurrence of all my life I ever met with, begun, proceeded on, and finished with the same uninterrupted excess of satisfaction to all parties." The letter is printed in Smith's "Life, Journals, and Correspondence of S. Pepys," vol. i., pp. 95–100.

[2] This curious experiment is referred to in most books of games and tricks, and a full account will be found in Brewster's "Natural Magic," p. 256. Lord Braybrooke added a note on the authority of Dr. S. R. Maitland respecting an experiment once tried in Gloucestershire on a very stout gentleman, the information respecting which he obtained from the late Mr. W. J. Thoms, founder of "Notes and Queries."

Then the first begun the second line, and so round quite through, and, putting each one finger only to a boy that lay flat upon his back on the ground, as if he was dead; at the end of the words, they did with their four fingers raise this boy as high as they could reach, and he [Mr. Brisband] being there, and wondering at it, as also being afeard to see it, for they would have had him to have bore a part in saying the words, in the roome of one of the little girles that was so young that they could hardly make her learn to repeat the words, did, for feare there might be some sleight used in it by the boy, or that the boy might be light, call the cook of the house, a very lusty fellow, as Sir G. Carteret's cook, who is very big, and they did raise him in just the same manner. This is one of the strangest things I ever heard, but he tells it me of his owne knowledge, and I do heartily believe it to be true. I enquired of him whether they were Protestant or Catholique girles; and he told me they were Protestant, which made it the more strange to me. Thus we end this month, as I said, after the greatest glut of content that ever I had; only under some difficulty because of the plague, which grows mightily upon us, the last week being about 1,700 or 1,800 of the plague. My Lord Sandwich at sea with a fleet of about 100 sail, to the Northward, expecting De Ruyter, or the Dutch East India fleet. My Lord Hinchingbroke coming over from France, and will meet his sister at Scott's-hall.[1] Myself having obliged both these families in this business very much; as both my Lady, and Sir G. Carteret and his Lady do confess exceedingly, and the latter do also now call me cozen, which I am glad of. So God preserve us all friends long, and continue health among us.

August 1st. Slept, and lay long; then up and my Lord [Crew] and Sir G. Carteret being gone abroad, I first to see the bridegroom and bride, and found them both up, and he

[1] Lady Jemimah. "This evening I accompanied Mr. Treasurer and Vice-Chamberlin Carteret to his lately married son-in-law's, Sir Thomas Scott, to Scott's Hall. We took barge as far as Gravesend, thence by post to Rochester, whence in coach and six horses to Scott's Hall, a right noble seat, uniformly built, with a handsome gallery. It stands in a park well stor'd, the land fat and good."—Evelyn's *Diary*, August 2nd, 1663.

gone to dress himself. Both red in the face, and well enough pleased this morning with their night's lodging. Thence down and Mr. Brisband and I to billiards: anon come my Lord and Sir G. Carteret in, who have been looking abroad and visiting some farms that Sir G. Carteret hath thereabouts, and, among other things, report the greatest stories of the bigness of the calfes they find there, ready to sell to the butchers, as big, they say, as little cowes, and that they do give them a piece of chalke to licke, which they hold makes them white in the flesh within. Very merry at dinner, and so to talk and laugh after dinner, and up and down, some to [one] place, some to another, full of content on all sides. Anon about five o'clock, Sir G. Carteret and his lady and I took coach with the greatest joy and kindnesse that could be from the two familys or that ever I saw with so much appearance, and, I believe, reality in all my life. Drove hard home, and it was night ere we got to Deptford, where, with much kindnesse from them to me, I left them, and home to the office, where I find all well, and being weary and sleepy, it being very late, I to bed.

2nd. Up, it being a publique fast, as being the first Wednesday of the month, for the plague;[1] I within doors all day, and upon my monthly accounts late, and there to my great joy settled almost all my private matters of money in my books clearly, and allowing myself several sums which I had hitherto not reckoned myself sure of, because I would not be over sure of any thing, though with reason I might do it, I did find myself really worth £1,900, for which the great God of Heaven and Earth be praised! At night to the office to write a few letters, and so home to bed, after fitting myself for to-morrow's journey.

3rd. Up, and betimes to Deptford to Sir G. Carteret's, where, not liking the horse that had been hired by Mr. Uthwayt for me, I did desire Sir G. Carteret to let me ride his new £40 horse, which he did, and so I left my *hacquenée*[2] behind, and so after staying a good while in their bedchamber while they were dressing themselves, discoursing merrily, I parted and to the ferry, where I was forced to

[1] See note, *ante*, July 12th.
[2] Haquenée = an ambling nag fitted for ladies' riding.

stay a great while before I could get my horse brought over, and then mounted and rode very finely to Dagenhams; all the way people, citizens, walking to and again to enquire how the plague is in the City this week by the Bill; which by chance, at Greenwich, I had heard was 2,020 of the plague, and 3,000 and odd of all diseases; but methought it was a sad question to be so often asked me. Coming to Dagenhams, I there met our company coming out of the house, having staid as long as they could for me; so I let them go a little before, and went and took leave of my Lady Sandwich, good woman, who seems very sensible of my service in this late business, and having her directions in some things, among others, to get Sir G. Carteret and my Lord to settle the portion, and what Sir G. Carteret is to settle, into land, soon as may be, she not liking that it should lie long undone, for fear of death on either side. So took leave of her, and then down to the buttery, and eat a piece of cold venison pie, and drank and took some bread and cheese in my hand; and so mounted after them, Mr. Marr very kindly staying to lead me the way. By and by met my Lord Crew returning, after having accompanied them a little way, and so after them, Mr. Marr telling me by the way how a mayde servant of Mr. John Wright's (who lives thereabouts) falling sick of the plague, she was removed to an out-house, and a nurse appointed to look to her; who, being once absent, the mayde got out of the house at the window, and run away. The nurse coming and knocking, and having no answer, believed she was dead, and went and told Mr. Wright so; who and his lady were in great strait what to do to get her buried. At last resolved to go to Burntwood[1] hard by, being in the parish, and there get people to do it. But they would not; so he went home full of trouble, and in the way met the wench walking over the common, which frighted him worse than before; and was forced to send people to take her, which he did; and they got one of the pest coaches and put her into it to carry her to a pest house. And passing in a narrow lane, Sir Anthony Browne,[2] with his brother and some friends in the coach,

[1] Brentwood, Essex, is still locally called Burntwood.
[2] He commanded a troop of horse in the Train-bands, 1662. — B.

met this coach with the curtains drawn close. The brother being a young man, and believing there might be some lady in it that would not be seen, and the way being narrow, he thrust his head out of his own into her coach, and to look, and there saw somebody look very ill, and in a sick dress, and stunk mightily; which the coachman also cried out upon. And presently they come up to some people that stood looking after it, and told our gallants that it was a mayde of Mr. Wright's carried away sick of the plague; which put the young gentleman into a fright had almost cost him his life, but is now well again. I, overtaking our young people, 'light, and into the coach to them, where mighty merry all the way; and anon come to the Blockehouse,[1] over against Gravesend, where we staid a great while, in a little drinking-house. Sent back our coaches to Dagenhams. I, by and by, by boat to Gravesend, where no newes of Sir G. Carteret come yet; so back again, and fetched them all over, but the two saddle-horses that were to go with us, which could not be brought over in the horse-boat, the wind and tide being against us, without towing; so we had some difference with some watermen, who would not tow them over under 20*s*., whereupon I swore to send one of them to sea and will do it. Anon some others come to me and did it for 10*s*. By and by comes Sir G. Carteret, and so we set out for Chatham: in my way overtaking some company, wherein was a lady, very pretty, riding singly, her husband in company with her. We fell into talke, and I read a copy of verses which her husband showed me, and he discommended, but the lady commended: and I read them, so as to make the husband turn to commend them. By and by he and I fell into acquaintance, having known me formerly at the Exchequer. His name is Nokes, over against Bow Church. He was servant to Alderman Dashwood. We promised to meet, if ever we come both to London again; and, at parting, I had a fair salute on horseback, in Rochester streets, of the lady, and so parted. Come to Chatham mighty merry, and anon to supper, it being near 9 o'clock ere we come thither. My Lady Carteret come thither in a coach, by herself, before us. Great

[1] Tilbury fort.

mind they have to buy a little *hacquenée* that I rode on from Greenwich, for a woman's horse. Mighty merry, and after supper, all being withdrawn, Sir G. Carteret did take an opportunity to speak with much value and kindness to me, which is of great joy to me. So anon to bed. Mr. Brisband and I together to my content.

4th. Up at five o'clock, and by six walked out alone, with my Lady Slanning,[1] to the Docke Yard, where walked up and down, and so to Mr. Pett's, who led us into his garden, and there the lady, the best humoured woman in the world, and a devout woman (I having spied her on her knees half an houre this morning in her chamber), clambered up to the top of the banquetting-house to gather nuts, and mighty merry, and so walked back again through the new rope house, which is very usefull; and so to the Hill-house to breakfast and mighty merry. Then they took coach, and Sir G. Carteret kissed me himself heartily, and my Lady several times, with great kindnesse, and then the young ladies, and so with much joy, bade "God be with you!" and an end I think it will be to my mirthe for a great while, it having been the passage of my whole life the most pleasing for the time, considering the quality and nature of the business, and my noble usage in the doing of it, and very many fine journys, entertainments and great company. I returned into the house for a while to do business there with Commissioner Pett, and there with the officers of the Chest, where I saw more of Sir W. Batten's business than ever I did before, for whereas he did own once under his hand to them that he was accountable for £2,200, of which he had yet paid but £1,600, he writes them a letter lately that he hath but about £150 left that is due to the Chest, but I will do something in it and that speedily. That being done I took horse, and Mr. Barrow[2] with me bore me company to Gravesend, discoursing of his business, wherein I vexed him, and he me, I seeing his frowardness, but yet that he is in my conscience a very honest man, and some good things he told me, which I shall remember to the

[1] Sir G. Carteret's eldest daughter, Anne, married in 1663 to Sir Nicholas Slaning, K.B. — B.

[2] This was probably Phil. Barrow, who was storekeeper at Chatham.

King's advantage. There I took boat alone, and, the tide being against me, landed at Blackwall and walked to Wapping, Captain Bowd whom I met with talking with me all the way, who is a sober man. So home, and found all things well, and letters from Dover that my Lord Hinchingbroke is arrived at Dover, and would be at Scott's hall this night, where the whole company will meet. I wish myself with them. After writing a few letters I took boat and down to Woolwich very late, and there found my wife and her woman upon the key hearing a fellow in a barge, that lay by, fiddle. So I to them and in, very merry, and to bed, I sleepy and weary.

5th. In the morning up, and my wife showed me several things of her doing, especially one fine woman's Persian head mighty finely done, beyond what I could expect of her; and so away by water, having ordered in the yarde six or eight bargemen to be whipped, who had last night stolen some of the King's cordage from out of the yarde. I to Deptford, and there by agreement met with my Lord Bruncker, and there we kept our office, he and I, and did what there was to do, and at noon parted to meet at the office next week. Sir W. Warren and I thence did walk through the rain to Half-Way House, and there I eat a piece of boiled beef and he and I talked over several businesses, among others our design upon the mast docke, which I hope to compass and get 2 or £300 by. Thence to Redriffe, where we parted, and I home, where busy all the afternoon. Stepped to Colvill's to set right a business of money, where he told me that for certain De Ruyter is come home, with all his fleete, which is very ill newes, considering the charge we have been at in keeping a fleete to the northward so long, besides the great expectation of snapping him, wherein my Lord Sandwich will I doubt suffer some dishonour. I am told also of a great ryott upon Thursday last in Cheapside; Colonell Danvers,[1] a delinquent, having been taken, and in his way to the Tower was rescued from the captain of the guard, and carried away; only one of the rescuers being taken. I am told also that the Duke of Buckingham

[1] The rescue of Colonel Danvers in Cheapside is mentioned in a letter from Sir William Coventry to Lord Arlington, dated August 7th, 1665 ("Calendar of State Papers," 1664-65, p. 506).

is dead,[1] but I know not of a certainty. So home and very late at letters, and then home to supper and to bed.

6th (Lord's day). Dressed and had my head combed by my little girle, to whom I confess que je sum demasiado kind, nuper ponendo mes mains in su des choses de son breast, mais il faut que je leave it lest it bring me to alcun major inconvenience. So to my business in my chamber, look over and settling more of my papers than I could the two last days I have spent about them. In the evening, it raining hard, down to Woolwich, where after some little talk to bed.

7th. Up, and with great pleasure looking over my wife's pictures, and then to see my Lady Pen, whom I have not seen since her coming hither, and after being a little merry with her, she went forth and I staid there talking with Mrs. Pegg and looking over her pictures, and commended them; but, Lord! so far short of my wife's, as no comparison. Thence to my wife, and there spent, talking, till noon, when by appointment Mr. Andrews come out of the country to speake with me about their Tangier business, and so having done with him and dined, I home by water, where by appointment I met Dr. Twisden, Mr. Povy, Mr. Lawson, and Stockdale about settling their business of money; but such confusion I never met with, nor could anything be agreed on, but parted like a company of fools, I vexed to lose so much time and pains to no purpose. They gone, comes Rayner, the boat-maker, about some business, and brings a piece of plate with him, which I refused to take of him, thinking indeed that the poor man hath no reason nor encouragement from our dealings with him to give any of us any presents. He gone, there comes Luellin, about Mr. Deering's business of planke, to have the contract perfected, and offers me twenty pieces in gold, as Deering had done some time since himself, but I both then and now refused it, resolving not to be bribed to dispatch business, but will have it done however out of hand forthwith. So he gone, I to supper and to bed.

8th. Up and to the office, where all the morning we sat. At noon I home to dinner alone, and after dinner Bagwell's

[1] The Duke of Buckingham did not die till 1687.

wife waited at the door, and went with me to my office. . . . So parted, and I to Sir W. Batten's, and there sat the most of the afternoon talking and drinking too much with my Lord Bruncker, Sir G. Smith, G. Cocke and others very merry. I drunk a little mixed, but yet more than I should do. So to my office a little, and then to the Duke of Albemarle's about some business. The streets mighty empty all the way, now even in London, which is a sad sight. And to Westminster Hall, where talking, hearing very sad stories from Mrs. Mumford; among others, of Mrs. Michell's son's family. And poor Will, that used to sell us ale at the Hall-door, his wife and three children died, all, I think, in a day. So home through the City again, wishing I may have taken no ill in going; but I will go, I think, no more thither. Late at the office, and then home to supper, having taken a pullet home with me, and then to bed. The news of De Ruyter's coming home is certain; and told to the great disadvantage of our fleete, and the praise of De Ruyter; but it cannot be helped, nor do I know what to say to it.

9th. Up betimes to my office, where Tom Hater to the writing of letters with me, which have for a good while been in arreare, and we close at it all day till night, only made a little step out for half an houre in the morning to the Exchequer about striking of tallys, but no good done therein, people being most out of towne. At noon T. Hater dined with me, and so at it all the afternoon. At night home and supped, and after reading a little in Cowley's poems, my head being disturbed with overmuch business to-day, I to bed.

10th. Up betimes, and called upon early by my she-cozen Porter, the turner's wife, to tell me that her husband was carried to the Tower, for buying of some of the King's powder, and would have my helpe, but I could give her none, not daring any more to appear in the business, having too much trouble lately therein. By and by to the office, where we sat all the morning; in great trouble to see the Bill this week rise so high, to above 4,000 in all, and of them above 3,000 of the plague. And an odd story of Alderman Bence's[1] stumbling at night over a dead corps in

[1] Alderman J. Bence was secretary to the Royal African Society.

the streete, and going home and telling his wife, she at the fright, being with child, fell sicke and died of the plague. We sat late, and then by invitation my Lord Brunker, Sir J. Minnes, Sir W. Batten and I to Sir G. Smith's to dinner, where very good company and good cheer. Captain Cocke was there and Jacke Fenn, but to our great wonder Alderman Bence, and tells us that not a word of all this is true, and others said so too, but by his owne story his wife hath been ill, and he fain to leave his house and comes not to her, which continuing a trouble to me all the time I was there. Thence to the office and, after writing letters, home, to draw over anew my will, which I had bound myself by oath to dispatch by to-morrow night; the town growing so unhealthy, that a man cannot depend upon living two days to an end. So having done something of it, I to bed.

11th. Up, and all day long finishing and writing over my will twice, for my father and my wife, only in the morning a pleasant rencontre happened in having a young married woman brought me by her father, old Delkes, that carries pins always in his mouth, to get her husband off that he should not go to sea, une contre pouvait avoir done any cose cum elle, but I did nothing, *si ni biasser* her. After they were gone my mind run upon having them called back again, and I sent a messenger to Blackwall, but he failed. So I lost my expectation. I to the Exchequer, about striking new tallys, and I find the Exchequer, by proclamation, removing to Nonesuch.[1] Back again and at my papers, and putting up my books into chests, and settling my house and all things in the best and speediest order I can, lest it should please God to take me away, or force me to leave my house. Late up at it, and weary and full of wind, finding perfectly that so long as I keepe myself in company at meals and do there eat lustily (which I cannot do alone, having no love to eating, but my mind runs upon my business), I am as well as can be, but when I come to be alone, I do not eat in time, nor enough, nor with any good heart, and I immediately begin to be full of wind, which brings my pain, till I come to fill my belly adays again, then am presently well.

[1] Nonsuch Palace, near Epsom, where the Exchequer money was kept during the time of the plague. See note, *ante*, July 26th, 1663.

12th. The office now not sitting, but only hereafter on Thursdays at the office, I within all the morning about my papers and setting things still in order, and also much time in settling matters with Dr. Twisden. At noon am sent for by Sir G. Carteret, to meet him and my Lord Hinchingbroke at Deptford, but my Lord did not come thither, he having crossed the river at Gravesend to Dagenhams, whither I dare not follow him, they being afeard of me; but Sir G. Carteret says, he is a most sweet youth in every circumstance. Sir G. Carteret being in haste of going to the Duke of Albemarle and the Archbishop, he was pettish, and so I could not fasten any discourse, but take another time. So he gone, I down to Greenwich and sent away the Bezan, thinking to go with my wife to-night to come back again to-morrow night to the Soveraigne at the buoy off the Nore. Coming back to Deptford, old Bagwell walked a little way with me, and would have me in to his daughter's, and there he being gone dehors, ego had my volunté de su hiza. Eat and drank and away home, and after a little at the office to my chamber to put more things still in order, and late to bed. The people die so, that now it seems they are fain to carry the dead to be buried by day-light, the nights not sufficing to do it in. And my Lord Mayor commands people to be within at nine at night all, as they say, that the sick may have liberty to go abroad for ayre. There is one also dead out of one of our ships at Deptford, which troubles us mightily; the Providence fire-ship, which was just fitted to go to sea. But they tell me to-day no more sick on board. And this day W. Bodham tells me that one is dead at Woolwich, not far from the Rope-yard.[1] I am told, too, that a wife of one of the groomes at Court is dead at Salsbury; so that the King and Queene are speedily to be all gone to Milton.[2] God preserve us!

13th (Lord's day). Up betimes and to my chamber, it being a very wet day all day, and glad am I that we did not

[1] Christopher Pett wrote to the Navy Commissioners from Woolwich on August 15th, and in his letter he says, "It has pleased God to send the infection of the plague into the town, and two houses are already visited; fear it will be very mortal, will take every care to prevent it spreading to the yard" ("Calendar of State Papers," 1664–65, p. 519).

[2] The court went in the following month from Salisbury to Oxford. This Milton may be intended for Milton Lilbourne, a parish in Wiltshire.

go by water to see "The Soveraigne"[1] to-day, as I intended, clearing all matters in packing up my papers and books, and giving instructions in writing to my executors, thereby perfecting the whole business of my will, to my very great joy; so that I shall be in much better state of soul, I hope, if it should please the Lord to call me away this sickly time. At night to read, being weary with this day's great work, and then after supper to bed, to rise betimes to-morrow, and to bed with a mind as free as to the business of the world as if I were not worth £100 in the whole world, every thing being evened under my hand in my books and papers, and upon the whole I find myself worth, besides Brampton estate, the sum of £2,164, for which the Lord be praised!

14th. Up, and my mind being at mighty ease from the dispatch of my business so much yesterday, I down to Deptford to Sir G. Carteret, where with him a great while, and a great deale of private talke concerning my Lord Sandwich's and his matters, and chiefly of the latter, I giving him great deale of advice about the necessity of his having caution concerning Fenn, and the many ways there are of his being abused by any man in his place, and why he should not bring his son in to look after his business, and more, to be a Commissioner of the Navy, which he listened to and liked, and told me how much the King was his good Master, and was sure not to deny him that or any thing else greater than that, and I find him a very cunning man, whatever at other times he seems to be, and among other things he told me he was not for the fanfaroone[2] to make a show with a great title, as he might have had long since, but the main thing to get an estate; and another thing, speaking of minding of business, "By God," says he, "I will and have already almost brought it to that pass, that the King shall

[1] "The Sovereign of the Seas" was built at Woolwich in 1637 of timber which had been stripped of its bark while growing in the spring, and not felled till the second autumn afterwards; and it is observed by Dr. Plot ("Phil. Trans." for 1691), in his discourse on the most seasonable time for felling timber, written by the advice of Pepys, that after forty-seven years, "all the ancient timber then remaining in her, it was no easy matter to drive a nail into it" ("Quarterly Review," vol. viii., p. 35). — B.

[2] *Fanfaron*, French, from *fanfare*, a sounding of trumpets; hence, a swaggerer, or empty boaster.

not be able to whip a cat, but I must be at the tayle of it." Meaning so necessary he is, and the King and my Lord Treasurer and all do confess it; which, while I mind my business, is my own case in this office of the Navy, and I hope shall be more, if God give me life and health. Thence by agreement to Sir J. Minnes's lodgings, where I found my Lord Bruncker, and so by water to the ferry, and there took Sir W. Batten's coach that was sent for us, and to Sir W. Batten's, where very merry, good cheer, and up and down the garden with great content to me, and, after dinner, beat Captain Cocke at billiards, won about 8*s*. of him and my Lord Bruncker. So in the evening after much pleasure back again and I by water to Woolwich, where supped with my wife, and then to bed betimes, because of rising to-morrow at four of the clock in order to the going out with Sir G. Carteret toward Cranborne to my Lord Hinchingbrooke in his way to Court. This night I did present my wife with the dyamond ring, awhile since given me by Mr. Dicke Vines's brother, for helping him to be a purser, valued at about £10, the first thing of that nature I did ever give her. Great fears we have that the plague will be a great Bill this weeke.

15th. Up by 4 o'clock and walked to Greenwich, where called at Captain Cocke's and to his chamber, he being in bed, where something put my last night's dream into my head, which I think is the best that ever was dreamt, which was that I had my Lady Castlemayne in my armes and was admitted to use all the dalliance I desired with her, and then dreamt that this could not be awake, but that it was only a dream; but that since it was a dream, and that I took so much real pleasure in it, what a happy thing it would be if when we are in our graves (as Shakespeere resembles it) we could dream, and dream but such dreams as this, that then we should not need to be so fearful of death, as we are this plague time. Here I hear that news is brought Sir G. Carteret that my Lord Hinchingbrooke is not well, and so cannot meet us at Cranborne to-night. So I to Sir G. Carteret's; and there was sorry with him for our disappointment. So we have put off our meeting there till Saturday next. Here I staid talking with Sir G. Carteret, he being mighty free with me in his business, and among other things hath ordered Rider and Cutler to put into my hands copper to the value of £5,000 (which Sir G. Carteret's share it seems come to in it), which is to raise part of the money he is to lay out for a purchase for my Lady Jemimah. Thence he and I to Sir J. Minnes's by invitation, where Sir W. Batten and my Lady, and my Lord Bruncker, and all of us dined upon a venison pasty and other good meat, but nothing well dressed. But my pleasure lay in getting some bills signed by Sir G. Carteret, and promise of present payment from Mr. Fenn, which do rejoice my heart, it being one of the heaviest things I had upon me, that so much of the little I have should lie (viz. near £1,000) in the King's hands. Here very merry and (Sir G. Carteret being gone presently after dinner) to Captain Cocke's, and there merry, and so broke up and I by water to the Duke of Albemarle, with whom I spoke a great deale in private, they being designed to send a fleete of ships privately to the Streights. No news yet from our fleete, which is much wondered at, but the Duke says for certain guns have been heard to the northward very much. It was dark before I could get home, and so land at Church-yard stairs,[1] where, to my great trouble, I met a dead corps of the plague, in the narrow ally just bringing down a little pair of stairs. But I thank God I was not much disturbed at it. However, I shall beware of being late abroad again.

16th. Up, and after doing some necessary business about my accounts at home, to the office, and there with Mr. Hater wrote letters, and I did deliver to him my last will, one part of it to deliver to my wife when I am dead. Thence to the Exchange, where I have not been a great while. But, Lord! how sad a sight it is to see the streets empty of people, and very few upon the 'Change. Jealous of every door that one sees shut up, lest it should be the plague; and about us two shops in three, if not more, generally shut up. From the 'Change to Sir G. Smith's[2] with Mr. Fenn, to whom I am nowadays very complaisant, he being under payment of my bills to me, and some other

[1] Churchyard Alley, Upper Thames Street, close by London Bridge.

[2] Sir George Smith, of St. Bartholomew, by the Exchange. He married Martha, daughter of John Swift, of London, merchant. — B.

sums at my desire, which he readily do. Mighty merry with Captain Cocke and Fenn at Sir G. Smith's, and a brave dinner, but I think Cocke is the greatest epicure that is, eats and drinks with the greatest pleasure and liberty that ever man did. Very contrary newes to-day upon the 'Change, some that our fleete hath taken some of the Dutch East India ships, others that we did attaque it at Bergen and were repulsed, others that our fleete is in great danger after this attaque by meeting with the great body now gone out of Holland, almost 100 sayle of men of warr. Every body is at a great losse and nobody can tell. Thence among the goldsmiths to get some money, and so home, settling some new money matters, and to my great joy have got home £500 more of the money due to me, and got some more money to help Andrews first advanced. This day I had the ill news from Dagenhams, that my poor lord of Hinchingbroke his indisposition is turned to the small-pox. Poor gentleman! that he should be come from France so soon to fall sick, and of that disease too, when he should be gone to see a fine lady, his mistresse. I am most heartily sorry for it. So late setting papers to rights, and so home to bed.

17th. Up and to the office, where we sat all the morning, and at noon dined together upon some victuals I had prepared at Sir W. Batten's upon the King's charge, and after dinner, I having dispatched some business and set things in order at home, we down to the water and by boat to Greenwich to the Bezan yacht, where Sir W. Batten, Sir J. Minnes, my Lord Bruncker and myself, with some servants (among others Mr. Carcasse,[1] my Lord's clerk, a very civil

[1] James Carcasse (or Carkesse) was one of the four clerks of the Ticket Office, and in a paper of Pepys's at Magdalene College he is described as the clerk to attend on Sir John Minnes for the signing of tickets. He was dismissed from the office for irregularities, principally through the action of Pepys. He published a quarto volume of poems in 1679, called "Lucida Intervalla," the following extract from which, strongly reflecting upon Pepys, has been printed in "Notes and Queries" (1st series), vol. ii., p. 87:—

"Get thee behind me, then, dumb devil, begone,
The Lord hath Eppthatha said to my tongue.
Him I must praise who open'd hath my lips,
Sent me from Navy to the Ark by Pepys;
By Mr. Pepys, who hath my rival been
For the Duke's favour, more than years thirteen;

gentleman), embarked in the yacht and down we went most pleasantly, and noble discourse I had with my Lord Bruncker, who is a most excellent person. Short of Gravesend it grew calme, and so we come to an anchor, and to supper mighty merry, and after it, being moonshine, we out of the cabbin to laugh and talk, and then, as we grew sleepy, went in and upon velvet cushions of the King's that belong to the yacht fell to sleep, which we all did pretty well till 3 or 4 of the clock, having risen in the night to look for a new comet which is said to have lately shone, but we could see no such thing.

18th. Up about 5 o'clock and dressed ourselves, and to sayle again down to the Soveraigne at the buoy of the Nore, a noble ship, now rigged and fitted and manned; we did not stay long, but to enquire after her readinesse and thence to Sheernesse, where we walked up and down, laying out the ground to be taken in for a yard to lay provisions for cleaning and repairing of ships, and a most proper place it is for the purpose.[1] Thence with great pleasure up the Meadeway, our yacht contending with Commissioner Pett's, wherein he met us from Chatham, and he had the best of it. Here I come by, but had not tide enough to stop at Quinbrough,[2] with mighty pleasure spent the day in doing all and seeing these places, which I had never done before. So to the Hill house at Chatham and there dined, and after dinner spent some time discoursing of business. Among others arguing with the Commissioner about his proposing the laying out so much money upon Sheerenesse unless it be to the slighting of Chatham yarde, for it is much a better

But I excluded, he high and fortunate,
This Secretary I could never mate.
But Clerk of th' Acts, if I'm a parson, then
I shall prevail, the voice outdoes the pen;
Though in a gown, the challenge I may make,
And wager win, save, if you can, your stake.
To th' Admiral I all submit, and vail ——"

The concluding line cut off and imperfect.

[1] The yard and fortifications of Sheerness were designed and first "staked out" by Sir Bernard de Gomme (see March 24th, 1667). The original plan is in the British Museum. — B.

[2] Queenborough, a parish and town in Kent, in the Isle of Sheppey, two miles south of Sheerness.

place than Chatham, which however the King is not at present in purse to do, though it were to be wished he were. Thence in Commissioner Pett's coach (leaving them there). I late in the darke to Gravesend, where great is the plague, and I troubled to stay there so long for the tide. At 10 at night, having supped, I took boat alone, and slept well all the way to the Tower docke about three o'clock in the morning. So knocked up my people, and to bed.

19th. Slept till 8 o'clock, and then up and met with letters from the King and Lord Arlington, for the removal of our office to Greenwich. I also wrote letters, and made myself ready to go to Sir G. Carteret, at Windsor; and having borrowed a horse of Mr. Blackbrough,[1] sent him to wait for me at the Duke of Albemarle's door: when, on a sudden, a letter comes to us from the Duke of Albemarle,[2] to tell us that the fleete is all come back to Solebay, and are presently to be dispatched back again. Whereupon I presently by water to the Duke of Albemarle to know what news; and there I saw a letter from my Lord Sandwich to the Duke of Albemarle, and also from Sir W. Coventry and Captain Teddiman; how my Lord having commanded Teddiman with twenty-two ships[3] (of which but fifteen

[1] Peter Blackborow, or Blackbery, held contracts with the Navy Commissioners for the supply of timber.

[2] This letter of the Duke of Albemarle to the Navy Commissioners is among the State Papers, it orders a supply of provisions to be sent forthwith to the Gunfleet, and thence convoyed to Southwold Bay. "Ammunition is wanted also, and as many men as can be obtained" ("Calendar." 1664–65, p. 524).

[3] A news letter of August 19th (Salisbury), gives the following account of this affair: — "The Earl of Sandwich being on the Norway coast, ordered Sir Thomas Teddeman with 20 ships to attack 50 Dutch merchant ships in Bergen harbour; six convoyers had so placed themselves that only four or five of the ships could be reached at once. The Governor of Bergen fired on our ships, and placed 100 pieces of ordnance and two regiments of foot on the rocks to attack them, but they got clear without the loss of a ship, only 500 men killed or wounded, five or six captains among them. The fleet has gone to Sole Bay to repair losses and be ready to encounter the Dutch fleet, which is gone northward" ("Calendar of State Papers," 1664–65, pp. 526, 527). Medals were struck in Holland, the inscription in Dutch on one of these is thus translated: "Thus we arrest the pride of the English, who extend their piracy even against their friends, and who insulting the forts of Norway, violate the rights of the harbours of King Frederick; but, for the re-

could get thither, and of those fifteen but eight or nine could come up to play) to go to Bergen; where, after several messages to and fro from the Governor of the Castle, urging that Teddiman ought not to come thither with more than five ships, and desiring time to think of it, all the while he suffering the Dutch ships to land their guns to their best advantage; Teddiman on the second pretence, began to play at the Dutch ships, (wherof ten East India-men,) and in three hours' time (the town and castle, without any provocation, playing on our ships,) they did cut all our cables, so as the wind being off the land, did force us to go out, and rendered our fire-ships useless; without doing any thing, but what hurt of course our guns must have done them: we having lost five commanders,[1] besides Mr. Edward Mon-

ward of their audacity, see their vessels destroyed by the balls of the Dutch" (Hawkins's "Medallic Illustrations of the History of Great Britain and Ireland," ed. Franks and Grueber, 1885, vol. i., p. 508). Sir Gilbert Talbot's "True Narrative of the Earl of Sandwich's Attempt upon Bergen with the English Fleet on the 3rd of August, 1665, and the Cause of his Miscarriage thereupon," is in the British Museum (Harl. MS., No. 6859). It is printed in "Archæologia," vol. xxii., p. 33. The Earl of Rochester also gave an account of the action in a letter to his mother (Wordsworth's "Ecclesiastical Biography," fourth edition, vol. iv., p. 611). Sir John Denham, in his "Advice to a Painter," gives a long satirical account of the affair. A coloured drawing of the attack upon Bergen, on vellum, showing the range of the ships engaged, is in the British Museum. Shortly after the Bergen affair forty of the Dutch merchant vessels, on their way to Holland, fell into the hands of the English, and in Penn's "Memorials of Sir William Penn," vol. ii., p. 364, is a list of the prizes taken on the 3rd and 4th September. The troubles connected with these prizes and the disgrace into which Lord Sandwich fell are fully set forth in subsequent pages of the Diary. Evelyn writes in his Diary (November 27th, 1665): "There was no small suspicion of my Lord Sandwich having permitted divers commanders who were at ye taking of ye East India prizes to break bulk and take to themselves jewels, silkes, &c., tho' I believe some whom I could name fill'd their pockets, my Lo. Sandwich himself had the least share. However, he underwent the blame, and it created him enemies, and prepossess'd ye Lo. Generall [Duke of Albemarle], for he spake to me of it with much zeale and concerne, and I believe laid load enough on Lo. Sandwich at Oxford."

[1] The captains killed in the unfortunate attack upon Bergen were Captain Seale of the "Breda," Captain Utber, jun., of the "Guernsey," Captain Hayward of the "Prudent Mary," Captain Lawson, "Coast" frigate, Captain Cadman of "Hamburgh Merchant," Captain Price of the "Briar."

tagu,[1] and Mr. Windham.[2] Our fleete is come home to our great grief with not above five weeks' dry, and six days' wet provisions: however, must out again; and the Duke hath ordered the Soveraigne, and all other ships ready, to go out to the fleete to strengthen them. This news troubles us all, but cannot be helped. Having read all this news, and received commands of the Duke with great content, he giving me the words which to my great joy he hath several times said to me, that his greatest reliance is upon me. And my Lord Craven also did come out to talk with me, and told me that I am in mighty esteem with the Duke, for which I bless God. Home, and having given my fellow-officers an account thereof, to Chatham, and wrote other letters, I by water to Charing-Cross, to the post-house, and there the people tell me they are shut up; and so I went to the new post-house, and there got a guide and horses to Hounslow, where I was mightily taken with a little girle, the daughter of the master of the house (Betty Gysby), which, if she lives, will make a great beauty. Here I met with a fine fellow who, while I staid for my horses, did enquire newes, but I could not make him remember Bergen in Norway, in 6 or 7 times telling, so ignorant he was. So to Stanes, and there by this time it was dark night, and got a guide who lost his way in the forest, till by help of the moone (which recompences me for all the pains I ever took about studying of her motions,) I led my guide into the way back again; and so we made a man rise that kept a gate, and so he carried us to Cranborne. Where in the dark I perceive an old house new building with a great deal of rubbish, and was fain to go up a ladder to Sir G. Carteret's chamber. And there in his bed I sat down, and told him all my bad newes, which troubled him mightily; but yet we were very merry, and made the best of it; and being myself

[1] Mr. Edward Montagu was killed in the action at Bergen, and is much lamented by his friends (Earl of Arlington's "Letters," vol. ii., p. 87). — B.

[2] This Mr. Windham had entered into a formal engagement with the Earl of Rochester, "not without ceremonies of religion, that if either of them died, he should appear, and give the other notice of the future state, if there was any." He was probably one of the brothers of Sir William Wyndham, Bart. See Wordsworth's "Ecclesiastical Biography," fourth edition, vol. iv., p. 615. — B.

weary did take leave, and after having spoken with Mr. Fenn[1] in bed, I to bed in my Lady's chamber that she uses to lie in, and where the Duchesse of York, that now is, was born. So to sleep; being very well, but weary, and the better by having carried with me a bottle of strong water, whereof now and then a sip did me good.

20th (Lord's day). Sir G. Carteret come and walked by my bedside half an houre, talking and telling me how my Lord is in this unblameable in all this ill-successe, he having followed orders; and that all ought to be imputed to the falsenesse of the King of Denmarke, who, he told me as a secret, had promised to deliver up the Dutch ships to us, and we expected no less; and swears it will, and will easily, be the ruine of him and his kingdom, if we fall out with him, as we must in honour do; but that all that can be, must be to get the fleete out again to intercept De Witt, who certainly will be coming home with the East India ships, he being gone thither. He being gone, I up and with Fenn, being ready to walk forth to see the place; and I find it to be a very noble seat in a noble forest, with the noblest prospect towards Windsor, and round about over many countys, that can be desired; but otherwise a very melancholy place, and little variety save only trees. I had thoughts of going home by water, and of seeing Windsor Chappell and Castle, but finding at my coming in that Sir G. Carteret did prevent me in speaking for my sudden return to look after business, I did presently eat a bit off the spit about 10 o'clock, and so took horse for Stanes, and thence to Brainford to Mr. Povy's, the weather being very pleasant to ride in. Mr. Povy not being at home I lost my labour, only eat and drank there with his lady, and told my bad newes, and hear the plague is round about them there. So away to Brainford; and there at the inn that goes down to the water-side, I 'light and paid off my post-horses, and so slipped on my shoes, and laid my things by, the tide not serving, and to church, where a dull sermon, and many Londoners. After church to my inn, and eat and drank, and so about seven o'clock by water, and got between nine and ten to Queen-

[1] It is not clear whether the Mr. Fenn mentioned several times about this period was Pepys's old friend Jack Fenn, or Nicholas Fenn who was at a later date Commissioner of the Victualling Office.

hive, very dark. And I could not get my waterman to go elsewhere for fear of the plague. Thence with a lanthorn, in great fear of meeting of dead corpses, carried to be buried; but, blessed be God, met none, but did see now and then a linke (which is the mark of them) at a distance. So got safe home about 10 o'clock, my people not all abed, and after supper I weary to bed.

21st. Called up, by message from Lord Bruncker and the rest of my fellows, that they will meet me at the Duke of Albemarle's this morning; so I up, and weary, however, got thither before them, and spoke with my Lord, and with him and other gentlemen to walk in the Parke, where, I perceive, he spends much of his time, having no whither else to go; and here I hear him speake of some Presbyter people that he caused to be apprehended yesterday, at a private meeting in Covent Garden, which he would have released upon paying £5 per man to the poor, but it was answered, they would not pay anything; so he ordered them to another prison from the guard. By and by comes my fellow-officers, and the Duke walked in, and to counsel with us; and that being done we departed, and Sir W. Batten and I to the office, where, after I had done a little business, I to his house to dinner, whither comes Captain Cocke, for whose epicurisme a dish of partriges was sent for, and still gives me reason to think is the greatest epicure in the world. Thence, after dinner, I by water to Sir W. Warren's and with him two hours, talking of things to his and my profit, and particularly good advice from him what use to make of Sir G. Carteret's kindnesse to me and my interest in him, with exceeding good cautions for me not using it too much nor obliging him to fear by prying into his secrets, which it were easy for me to do. Thence to my Lord Bruncker, at Greenwich, and Sir J. Minnes by appointment, to looke after the lodgings appointed for us there for our office, which do by no means please me, they being in the heart of all the labourers and workmen there, which makes it as unsafe as to be, I think, at London. Mr. Hugh May, who is a most ingenuous man, did show us the lodgings, and his acquaintance I am desirous of. Thence walked, it being now dark, to Sir J. Minnes's, and there staid at the door talking with him an hour while messengers went to get a boat for me, to carry me to Woolwich, but all to no purpose; so I was forced to walk it in the darke, at ten o'clock at night, with Sir J. Minnes's George with me, being mightily troubled for fear of the doggs at Coome farme, and more for fear of rogues by the way, and yet more because of the plague which is there, which is very strange, it being a single house, all alone from the towne, but it seems they use to admit beggars, for their owne safety, to lie in their barns, and they brought it to them; but I bless God I got about eleven of the clock well to my wife, and giving 4*s*. in recompence to George, I to my wife, and having first viewed her last piece of drawing since I saw her, which is seven or eight days, which pleases me beyond any thing in the world, to bed with great content but weary.

22nd. Up, and after much pleasant talke and being importuned by my wife and her two mayds, which are both good wenches, for me to buy a necklace of pearle for her, and I promising to give her one of £60 in two years at furthest, and in less if she pleases me in her painting, I went away and walked to Greenwich, in my way seeing a coffin with a dead body therein, dead of the plague, lying in an open close belonging to Coome farme, which was carried out last night, and the parish have not appointed any body to bury it; but only set a watch there day and night, that nobody should go thither or come thence, which is a most cruel thing: this disease making us more cruel to one another than if we are doggs. So to the King's House, and there met my Lord Bruncker and Sir J. Minnes, and to our lodgings again that are appointed for us, which do please me better to day than last night, and are set a doing. Thence I to Deptford, where by appointment I find Mr. Andrews come, and to the Globe, where we dined together and did much business as to our Plymouth gentlemen; and after a good dinner and good discourse, he being a very good man, I think verily, we parted and I to the King's yard, walked up and down, and by and by out at the back gate, and there saw the Bagwell's wife's mother and daughter, and went to them, and went in to the daughter's house with the mother, and faciebam le cose que ego tenebam a mind to con elle, and drinking and talking, by and by away, and so walked to Redriffe, troubled to go through the little lane, where the plague is, but did and took water and home, where all well; but Mr. Andrews not coming to even accounts, as I expected, with relation to something of my own profit, I was vexed that I could not settle to business, but home to my viall, though in the evening he did come to my satisfaction. So after supper (he being gone first) I to settle my journall and to bed.

23rd. Up, and whereas I had appointed Mr. Hater and Will to come betimes to the office to meet me about business there, I was called upon as soon as ready by Mr. Andrews to my great content, and he and I to our Tangier accounts, where I settled, to my great joy, all my accounts with him, and, which is more, cleared for my service to the contractors since the last sum I received of them £222 13*s.* profit to myself, and received the money actually in the afternoon. After he was gone comes by a pretence of mine yesterday old Delks the waterman, with his daughter Robins, and several times to and again, he leaving her with me, about the getting of his son Robins off, who was pressed yesterday again. . . . All the afternoon at my office mighty busy writing letters, and received a very kind and good one from my Lord Sandwich of his arrival with the fleete at Solebay, and the joy he has at my last newes he met with, of the marriage of my Lady Jemimah; and he tells me more, the good newes that all our ships, which were in such danger that nobody would insure upon them, from the Eastland,[1] were all safe arrived, which I am sure is a great piece of good luck, being in much more danger than those of Hambrough which were lost, and their value much greater at this time to us. At night home, much contented with this day's work, and being at home alone looking over my papers, comes a neighbour of ours hard by to speak with me about business of the office, one Mr. Fuller, a great merchant, but not my acquaintance, but he come drunk, and would have had me gone and drunk with him at home,

[1] Eastland was a name given to the eastern countries of Europe. The Eastland Company, or Company of Merchants trading to the East Country, was incorporated in Queen Elizabeth's reign (anno 21), and the charter was confirmed 13 Car. II. They were also called "The Merchants of Elbing."

or have let him send for wine hither, but I would do neither, nor offered him any, but after some sorry discourse parted, and I up to [my] chamber and to bed.

24th. Up betimes to my office, where my clerks with me, and very busy all the morning writing letters. At noon down to Sir J. Minnes and Lord Bruncker to Greenwich to sign some of the Treasurer's books, and there dined very well; and thence to look upon our rooms again at the King's house, which are not yet ready for us. So home and late writing letters, and so, weary with business, home to supper and to bed.

25th. Up betimes to the office, and there, as well as all the afternoon, saving a little dinner time, all alone till late at night writing letters and doing business, that I may get beforehand with my business again, which hath run behind a great while, and then home to supper and to bed. This day I am told that Dr. Burnett,[1] my physician, is this morning dead of the plague; which is strange, his man dying so long ago, and his house this month open again. Now himself dead. Poor unfortunate man!

26th. Up betimes, and prepared to my great satisfaction an account for the board of my office disbursements, which I had suffered to run on to almost £120. That done I down by water to Greenwich, where we met the first day my Lord Bruncker, Sir J. Minnes, and I, and I think we shall do well there, and begin very auspiciously to me by having my account abovesaid passed, and put into a way of having it presently paid. When we rose I find Mr. Andrews and Mr. Yeabsly, who is just come from Plymouth, at the door,

[1] Alexander Burnett, M.D. (Camb., 1648), admitted an Honorary Fellow of the College of Physicians in December, 1664. His house was in Fenchurch Street. He was reported to have fallen a victim to his zeal. "Dr. Burnett, Dr. Glover, and one or two more of the College of Physicians, with Dr. O'Dowd, which was licensed by my Lord's Grace of Canterbury, some surgeons, apothecaries, and Johnson, the chemist, died all very suddenly. Some say (but God forbid that I should report it for truth) that these, in a consultation together, if not all, yet the greatest part of them, attempted to open a dead corpse which was full of the tokens; and being in hand with the dissected body, some fell down dead immediately, and others did not outlive the next day at noon" (J. Tillison to Dr. Sancroft, September 14th, 1665, in Ellis's "Original Letters," second series, vol. iv., p. 37).

and we walked together toward my Lord Brunker's, talking about their business, Yeabsly being come up on purpose to discourse with me about it, and finished all in a quarter of an hour, and is gone again. I perceive they have some inclination to be going on with their victualling business for a while longer before they resign it to Mr. Gauden, and I am well contented, for it brings me very good profit with certainty, yet with much care and some pains. We parted at my Lord Bruncker's doore, where I went in, having never been there before, and there he made a noble entertainment for Sir J. Minnes, myself, and Captain Cocke, none else saving some painted lady that dined there, I know not who she is.[1] But very merry we were, and after dinner into the garden, and to see his and her chamber, where some good pictures, and a very handsome young woman for my lady's woman. Thence I by water home, in my way seeing a man taken up dead, out of the hold of a small catch that lay at Deptford. I doubt it might be the plague, which, with the thought of Dr. Burnett, did something disturb me, so that I did not what I intended and should have done at the office, as to business, but home sooner than ordinary, and after supper, to read melancholy alone, and then to bed.

27th (Lord's day). Very well in the morning, and up and to my chamber all the morning to put my things and papers yet more in order, and so to dinner. Thence all the afternoon at my office till late making up my papers and letters there into a good condition of order, and so home to supper, and after reading a good while in the King's works,[2] which is a noble book, to bed.

28th. Up, and being ready I out to Mr. Colvill, the goldsmith's, having not for some days been in the streets; but now how few people I see, and those looking like people that had taken leave of the world. I there, and made even all accounts in the world between him and I, in a very good condition, and I would have done the like with Sir Robert Viner, but he is out of towne, the sicknesse being every where thereabouts. I to the Exchange, and I think there

[1] Mrs. Williams, Lord Brouncker's mistress, frequently mentioned in the Diary after this date.

[2] For note on the copy of Charles I.'s Works, now in the Pepysian Library, see June 10th, 1662.

was not fifty people upon it, and but few more like to be as they told me, Sir G. Smith and others. Thus I think to take adieu to-day of the London streets, unless it be to go again to Viner's. Home to dinner, and there W. Hewer brings me £119 he hath received for my office disbursements, so that I think I have £1,800 and more in the house, and, blessed be God! no money out but what I can very well command and that but very little, which is much the best posture I ever was in in my life, both as to the quantity and the certainty I have of the money I am worth; having most of it in my own hand. But then this is a trouble to me what to do with it, being myself this day going to be wholly at Woolwich; but for the present I am resolved to venture it in an iron chest, at least for a while. In the afternoon I sent down my boy to Woolwich with some things before me, in order to my lying there for good and all, and so I followed him. Just now comes newes that the fleete is gone, or going this day, out again, for which God be praised! and my Lord Sandwich hath done himself great right in it, in getting so soon out again. I pray God, he may meet the enemy. Towards the evening, just as I was fitting myself, comes W. Hewer and shows me a letter which Mercer had wrote to her mother about a great difference between my wife and her yesterday, and that my wife will have her go away presently. This, together with my natural jealousy that some bad thing or other may be in the way, did trouble me exceedingly, so as I was in a doubt whether to go thither or no, but having fitted myself and my things I did go, and by night got thither, where I met my wife walking to the waterside with her paynter, Mr. Browne, and her mayds. There I met Commissioner Pett, and my Lord Brunker, and the lady at his house had been there to-day, to see her. Commissioner Pett staid a very little while, and so I to supper with my wife and Mr. Shelden, and so to bed with great pleasure.

29th. In the morning waking, among other discourse my wife begun to tell me the difference between her and Mercer, and that it was only from restraining her to gad abroad to some Frenchmen that were in the town, which I do not wholly yet in part believe, and for my quiet would not enquire into it. So rose and dressed myself, and away by land walking a good way, then remembered that I had promised Commissioner Pett to go with him in his coach, and therefore I went back again to him, and so by his coach to Greenwich, and called at Sir Theophilus Biddulph's,[1] a sober, discreet man, to discourse of the preventing of the plague in Greenwich, and Woolwich, and Deptford, where in every place it begins to grow very great. We appointed another meeting, and so walked together to Greenwich and there parted, and Pett and I to the office, where all the morning, and after office done I to Sir J. Minnes and dined with him, and thence to Deptford thinking to have seen Bagwell, but did not, and so straight to Redriffe, and home, and late at my business to dispatch away letters, and then home to bed, which I did not intend, but to have staid for altogether at Woolwich, but I made a shift for a bed for Tom, whose bed is gone to Woolwich, and so to bed.

30th. Up betimes and to my business of settling my house and papers, and then abroad and met with Hadley, our clerke, who, upon my asking how the plague goes, he told me it encreases much, and much in our parish; for, says he, there died nine this week, though I have returned but six: which is a very ill practice, and makes me think it is so in other places; and therefore the plague much greater than people take it to be. Thence, as I intended, to Sir R. Viner's, and there found not Mr. Lewes ready for me, so I went forth and walked towards Moorefields to see (God forbid my presumption!) whether I could see any dead corps going to the grave; but, as God would have it, did not. But, Lord! how every body's looks, and discourse in the street is of death, and nothing else, and few people going up and down, that the towne is like a place distressed and forsaken. After one turne there back to Viner's, and there found my business ready for me, and evened all reckonings with them to this day to my great content. So home, and all day till very late at night setting my Tangier and private accounts in order, which I did in both, and in the latter to my great joy do find myself yet in the much best condition that ever I was in, finding myself worth £2,180

[1] Theophilus Biddulph, of Westcombe, co. Kent, was created a baronet in October, 1664.

and odd, besides plate and goods, which I value at £250 more, which is a very great blessing to me. The Lord make me thankfull! and of this at this day above £1,800 in cash in my house, which speaks but little out of my hands in desperate condition, but this is very troublesome to have in my house at this time. So late to bed, well pleased with my accounts, but weary of being so long at them.

31st. Up; and, after putting several things in order to my removal, to Woolwich; the plague having a great encrease this week, beyond all expectation of almost 2,000, making the general Bill 7,000, odd 100; and the plague above 6,000. I down by appointment to Greenwich, to our office, where I did some business, and there dined with our company and Sir W. Boreman, and Sir The. Biddulph, at Mr. Boreman's, where a good venison pasty, and after a good merry dinner I to my office, and there late writing letters, and then to Woolwich by water, where pleasant with my wife and people, and after supper to bed. Thus this month ends with great sadness upon the publick, through the greatness of the plague every where through the kingdom almost. Every day sadder and sadder news of its encrease. In the City died this week 7,496, and of them 6,102 of the plague. But it is feared that the true number of the dead this week is near 10,000; partly from the poor that cannot be taken notice of, through the greatness of the number, and partly from the Quakers and others that will not have any bell ring for them. Our fleete gone out to find the Dutch, we having about 100 sail in our fleete, and in them the Soveraigne one; so that it is a better fleete than the former with the Duke was. All our fear is that the Dutch should be got in before them; which would be a very great sorrow to the publick, and to me particularly, for my Lord Sandwich's sake. A great deal of money being spent, and the kingdom not in a condition to spare, nor a parliament without much difficulty to meet to give more. And to that; to have it said, what hath been done by our late fleetes? As to myself I am very well, only in fear of the plague, and as much of an ague by being forced to go early and late to Woolwich, and my family to lie there continually. My late gettings have been very great to my great content, and am likely to have yet a few more profitable jobbs in a little while; for which Tangier and Sir W. Warren I am wholly obliged to.

Sept. 1st. Up, and to visit my Lady Pen and her daughter at the Ropeyarde where I did breakfast with them and sat chatting a good while. Then to my lodging at Mr. Shelden's, where I met Captain Cocke and eat a little bit of dinner, and with him to Greenwich by water, having good discourse with him by the way. After being at Greenwich a little while, I to London, to my house, there put many more things in order for my totall remove, sending away my girle Susan and other goods down to Woolwich, and I by water to the Duke of Albemarle, and thence home late by water. At the Duke of Albemarle's I overheard some examinations of the late plot that is discoursed of and a great deale of do there is about it. Among other discourses, I heard read, in the presence of the Duke, an examination and discourse of Sir Philip Howard's,[1] with one of the plotting party. In many places these words being, "Then," said Sir P. Howard, "if you so come over to the King, and be faithfull to him, you shall be maintained, and be set up with a horse and armes," and I know not what. And then said such a one, "Yes, I will be true to the King." "But, damn me," said Sir Philip, "will you so and so?" And thus I believe twelve times Sir P. Howard answered him a "damn me," which was a fine way of rhetorique to persuade a Quaker or Anabaptist from his persuasion. And this was read in the hearing of Sir P. Howard, before the Duke and twenty more officers, and they make sport of it, only without any reproach, or he being anything ashamed of it.[2] But it ended, I remember, at last, "But such a one (the plotter) did at last bid them remember that he had not told them what King he would be faithfull to."

2nd. This morning I wrote letters to Mr. Hill and Andrews to come to dine with me to-morrow, and then I to the office, where busy, and thence to dine with Sir J.

[1] Seventh son of Thomas Howard, first Earl of Berkshire; he was the direct ancestor of the present Earl of Suffolk, to whom both the titles descended. — B.

[2] This republican plot was described by the Lord Chancellor in a speech delivered on October 9th, when parliament met at Oxford.

Minnes, where merry, but only that Sir J. Minnes who hath lately lost two coach horses, dead in the stable, has a third now a dying. After dinner I to Deptford, and there took occasion to entrar a la casa de la gunaica de ma Minusier, and did what I had a mind. . . . To Greenwich, where wrote some letters, and home in pretty good time.

3rd (Lord's day). Up; and put on my coloured silk suit very fine, and my new periwigg, bought a good while since, but durst not wear, because the plague was in Westminster when I bought it; and it is a wonder what will be the fashion after the plague is done, as to periwiggs, for nobody will dare to buy any haire, for fear of the infection, that it had been cut off of the heads of people dead of the plague. Before church time comes Mr. Hill (Mr. Andrews failing because he was to receive the Sacrament), and to church, where a sorry dull parson, and so home and most excellent company with Mr. Hill and discourse of musique. I took my Lady Pen home, and her daughter Pegg, and merry we were; and after dinner I made my wife show them her pictures, which did mad Pegg Pen, who learns of the same man and cannot do so well.[1] After dinner left them and I by water to Greenwich, where much ado to be suffered to come into the towne because of the sicknesse, for fear I should come from London, till I told them who I was. So up to the church, where at the door I find Captain Cocke in my Lord Brunker's coach, and he come out and walked with me in the church-yarde till the church was done, talking of the ill government of our Kingdom, nobody setting to heart the business of the Kingdom, but every body minding their particular profit or pleasures, the King himself minding nothing but his ease, and so we let things go to wracke. This arose upon considering what we shall do for money when the fleete comes in, and more if the fleete should not meet with the Dutch, which will put a disgrace upon the King's actions, so as the Parliament and Kingdom will have the less mind to give more money, besides so bad an account of the last money, we fear, will be given, not half of it being spent, as it ought to be, upon the Navy. Be-

[1] Alexander Browne, the limner, who taught Mrs. Pepys drawing.

sides, it is said that at this day our Lord Treasurer cannot tell what the profit of Chimney money[1] is, what it comes to per annum, nor looks whether that or any other part of the revenue be duly gathered as it ought; the very money that should pay the City the £200,000 they lent the King, being all gathered and in the hands of the Receiver and hath been long and yet not brought up to pay the City, whereas we are coming to borrow 4 or £500,000 more of the City, which will never be lent as is to be feared. Church being done, my Lord Bruncker, Sir J. Minnes, and I up to the Vestry at the desire of the Justices of the Peace, Sir Theo. Biddulph and Sir W. Boreman and Alderman Hooker,[2] in order to the doing something for the keeping of the plague from growing; but Lord! to consider the madness of the people of the town, who will (because they are forbid) come in crowds along with the dead corps to see them buried; but we agreed on some orders for the prevention thereof. Among other stories, one was very passionate, methought, of a complaint brought against a man in the towne for taking a child from London from an infected house. Alderman Hooker told us it was the child of a very able citizen in Gracious Street, a saddler, who had buried all the rest of his children of the plague, and himself and wife now being shut up and in despair of escaping, did desire only to save the life of this little child; and so prevailed to have it received stark-naked into the arms of a friend, who brought it (having put it into new fresh clothes) to Greenwich; where upon hearing the story, we did agree it should be permitted to be received and kept in the towne. Thence with my Lord Bruncker to Captain Cocke's, where we mighty merry and supped, and very late I by water to Woolwich, in great apprehensions of an ague. Here was my Lord Bruncker's lady of pleasure, who, I perceive, goes every where with him; and he, I find, is obliged to carry her, and make all the courtship to her that can be.

4th. Writing letters all the morning, among others to my Lady Carteret, the first I have wrote to her, telling her the state of the city as to health and other sorrowfull stories,

[1] See note, *ante*, March 3rd, 1661–62.

[2] Alderman Sir William Hooker was Sheriff in 1665 and Lord Mayor in 1673. He contracted to supply tallow to the Navy Commissioners

and thence after dinner to Greenwich, to Sir J. Minnes, where I found my Lord Bruncker, and having staid our hour for the Justices by agreement, the time being past we to walk in the Park with Mr. Hammond and Turner, and there eat some fruit out of the King's garden and walked in the Parke, and so back to Sir J. Minnes, and thence walked home, my Lord Bruncker giving me a very neat cane to walk with; but it troubled me to pass by Coome farme where about twenty-one people have died of the plague, and three or four days since I saw a dead corps in a coffin lie in the Close unburied, and a watch is constantly kept there night and day to keep the people in, the plague making us cruel, as doggs, one to another.

5th. Up, and walked with some Captains and others talking to me to Greenwich, they crying out upon Captain Teddiman's management of the business of Bergen, that he staid treating too long while he saw the Dutch fitting themselves, and that at first he might have taken every ship, and done what he would with them. How true I cannot tell. Here we sat very late and for want of money, which lies heavy upon us, did nothing of business almost. Thence home with my Lord Bruncker to dinner where very merry with him and his doxy. After dinner comes Colonell Blunt in his new chariot made with springs;[1] as that was of wicker, wherein a while since we rode at his house. And he hath rode, he says, now this journey, many miles in it with one horse, and out-drives any coach, and out-goes any horse, and so easy, he says. So for curiosity I went into it to try it, and up the hill[2] to the heath, and over the cart-rutts and found it pretty well, but not so easy as he pretends, and so back again, and took leave of my Lord and drove myself in the chariot to the office, and there ended my letters and home pretty betimes and there found W. Pen, and he staid supper with us and mighty merry talking of his travells and the French humours, etc., and so parted and to bed.

6th. Busy all the morning writing letters to several, so to dinner, to London, to pack up more things thence; and

[1] See, on Colonel Blunt's carriage, note, *ante*, May 1st, 1665.

[2] Shooter's Hill, Blackheath.

there I looked into the street and saw fires burning in the street, as it is through the whole City, by the Lord Mayor's order. Thence by water to the Duke of Albemarle's: all the way fires on each side of the Thames, and strange to see in broad daylight two or three burials upon the Bankeside, one at the very heels of another: doubtless all of the plague; and yet at least forty or fifty people going along with every one of them. The Duke mighty pleasant with me; telling me that he is certainly informed that the Dutch were not come home upon the 1st instant, and so he hopes our fleete may meet with them, and here to my great joy I got him to sign bills for the several sums I have paid on Tangier business by his single letter, and so now I can get more hands to them. This was a great joy to me. Home to Woolwich late by water, found wife in bed, and yet late as [it] was to write letters in order to my rising betimes to go to Povy to-morrow. So to bed, my wife asking me to-night about a letter of hers I should find, which indeed Mary did the other day give me as if she had found it in my bed, thinking it had been mine, brought to her from a man without name owning great kindness to her and I know not what. But looking it over seriously, and seeing it bad sense and ill writ, I did believe it to be her brother's and so had flung it away, but finding her now concerned at it and vexed with Mary about it, it did trouble me, but I would take no notice of it to-night, but fell to sleep as if angry.

7th. Up by 5 of the clock, mighty full of fear of an ague, but was obliged to go, and so by water, wrapping myself up warm, to the Tower, and there sent for the Weekely Bill, and find 8,252 dead in all, and of them 6,978 of the plague; which is a most dreadfull number, and shows reason to fear that the plague hath got that hold that it will yet continue among us. Thence to Brainford, reading "The Villaine," a pretty good play, all the way. There a coach of Mr. Povy's stood ready for me, and he at his house ready to come in, and so we together merrily to Swakely,[1] Sir R.

[1] Swakeley House, in the parish of Ickenham, Middlesex, was built in 1638 by Sir Edmund Wright (Lord Mayor 1641), whose daughter married Sir James Harrington, one of Charles I.'s judges. The property was sold in 1665 by Lady Harrington to Sir Robert Vyner (Lord Mayor

Viner's. A very pleasant place, bought by him of Sir James Harrington's lady. He took us up and down with great respect, and showed us all his house and grounds; and it is a place not very moderne in the garden nor house, but the most uniforme in all that ever I saw; and some things to excess. Pretty to see over the screene of the hall (put up by Sir J. Harrington, a Long Parliament-man) the King's head, and my Lord of Essex on one side, and Fairfax on the other; and upon the other side of the screene, the parson of the parish, and the lord of the manor and his sisters. The window-cases, door-cases, and chimnys of all the house are marble. He showed me a black boy that he had, that died of a consumption, and being dead, he caused him to be dried in an oven, and lies there entire in a box. By and by to dinner, where his lady I find yet handsome, but hath been a very handsome woman;[1] now is old. Hath brought him near £100,000 and now he lives, no man in England in greater plenty, and commands both King and Council with his credit he gives them. Here was a fine lady a merchant's wife at dinner with us, and who should be here in the quality of a woman but Mrs. Worship's daughter, Dr. Clerke's niece, and after dinner Sir Robert led us up to his long gallery, very fine, above stairs (and better, or such, furniture I never did see), and there Mrs. Worship did give us three or four very good songs, and sings very neatly, to my great delight. After all this, and ending the chief business to my content about getting a promise of some money of him, we took leave, being exceedingly well treated here, and a most pleasant journey we had back, Povy and I, and his company most excellent in anything but business, he here giving me an account of as many persons at Court as I had a mind or thought of enquiring after. He tells me by a letter he showed me, that the King is not, nor hath been of late, very well, but quite out of humour; and, as some think, in a consumption, and weary of every thing. He showed me my Lord

1674). Benjamin Lethieullier bought the manor in 1741 from the Vyner family and sold it to Thomas Clarke in 1750. The manor belonged to Robert Swaklyve in the early part of the fourteenth century.

[1] Mary, daughter of John Whitchurch, Esq., and widow of Sir Thomas Hyde, Bart., of Albury, Herts.

Arlington's house[1] that he was born in, in a towne called Harlington:[2] and so carried me through a most pleasant country to Brainford, and there put me into my boat, and good night. So I wrapt myself warm, and by water got to Woolwich about one in the morning, my wife and all in bed.

8th. Waked, and fell in talk with my wife about the letter, and she satisfied me that she did not know from whence it come, but believed it might be from her cozen Franke Moore lately come out of France. The truth is the thing I think cannot have much in it, and being unwilling (being in other things so much at ease) to vex myself in a strange place at a melancholy time, passed all by and were presently friends. Up, and several with me about business. Anon comes my Lord Bruncker, as I expected, and we to the enquiring into the business of the late desertion of the Shipwrights from worke, who had left us for three days together for want of money, and upon this all the morning, and brought it to a pretty good issue, that they, we believe, will come to-morrow to work. To dinner, having but a mean one, yet sufficient for him, and he well enough pleased, besides that I do not desire to vye entertainments with him or any else. Here was Captain Cocke also, and Mr. Wayth. We staid together talking upon one business or other all the afternoon. In the evening my Lord Bruncker hearing that Mr. Ackeworth's clerke, the Dutchman who writes and draws so well, was transcribing a book of Rates and our ships for Captain Millet a gallant of his mistress's, we sent for him for it. He would not deliver it, but said it was his mistress's and had delivered it to her. At last we were forced to send to her for it; she would come herself, and indeed the book was a very neat one and worth keeping as a rarity, but we did think fit, and though much against my will, to cancell all that he had finished of it, and did give her the rest, which vexed her, and she bore it discretely enough, but with a cruel deal of malicious rancour

[1] Dawley House, long the seat of the Bennet family.

[2] Harlington is a village in Middlesex, about a mile from Uxbridge. The manor was sold by Francis Coppinger in 1607 to Sir John Bennet, whose son, Sir Henry Bennet, took his title from the place under the cocknified form of Arlington. It was alienated by Ford Grey, Earl of Tankerville, to Viscount Bolingbroke.

in her looks. I must confess I would have persuaded her to have let us have it to the office, and it may be the board would not have censured too hardly of it, but my intent was to have had it as a Record for the office, but she foresaw what would be the end of it and so desired it might rather be cancelled, which was a plaguy deal of spite. My Lord Bruncker being gone and company, and she also, afterwards I took my wife and people and walked into the fields about a while till night, and then home, and so to sing a little and then to bed. I was in great trouble all this day for my boy Tom who went to Greenwich yesterday by my order and come not home till to-night for fear of the plague, but he did come home to-night, saying he staid last night by Mr. Hater's advice hoping to have me called as I come home with my boat to come along with me.

9th. Up and walked to Greenwich, and there we sat and dispatched a good deal of business I had a mind to. At noon, by invitation, to my Lord Bruncker's, all of us, to dinner, where a good venison pasty, and mighty merry. Here was Sir W. Doyly,[1] lately come from Ipswich about the sicke and wounded, and Mr. Evelyn and Captain Cocke. My wife also was sent for by my Lord Bruncker, by Cocke, and was here. After dinner, my Lord and his mistress would see her home again, it being a most cursed rainy afternoon, having had none a great while before, and I, forced to go to the office on foot through all the rain, was almost wet to my skin, and spoiled my silke breeches almost. Rained all the afternoon and evening, so as my letters being done, I was forced to get a bed at Captain Cocke's, where I find Sir W. Doyly, and he, and Evelyn at supper; and I with them full of discourse of the neglect of our masters, the great officers of State, about all business, and especially that of money: having now some thousands, prisoners, kept to no purpose at a great charge, and no money provided almost for the doing of it. We fell to talk largely of the want of some persons understanding to look

[1] Sir William Doyly, of Shottisham, Norfolk, knighted 1642, created a baronet 1663. M.P. for Yarmouth. Died 1677. He and Mr. Evelyn were at this time appointed commissioners for the care of the sick and wounded seamen and prisoners of war. — B.

after businesses, but all goes to rack. "For," says Captain Cocke, "my Lord Treasurer, he minds his ease, and lets things go how they will: if he can have his £8,000 per annum, and a game at l'ombre,[1] he is well. My Lord Chancellor he minds getting of money and nothing else; and my Lord Ashly will rob the Devil and the Alter, but he will get money if it be to be got." But that that put us into this great melancholy, was newes brought to-day, which Captain Cocke reports as a certain truth, that all the Dutch fleete, men-of-war and merchant East India ships, are got every one in from Bergen the 3d of this month, Sunday last; which will make us all ridiculous. The fleete come home with shame to require a great deale of money, which is not to be had, to discharge many men that must get the plague then or continue at greater charge on shipboard, nothing done by them to encourage the Parliament to give money, nor the Kingdom able to spare any money, if they would, at this time of the plague, so that, as things look at present, the whole state must come to ruine. Full of these melancholy thoughts, to bed; where, though I lay the softest I ever did in my life, with a downe bed,[2] after the Danish manner, upon me, yet I slept very ill, chiefly through the thoughts of my Lord Sandwich's concernment in all this ill successe at sea.

10th (Lord's day). Walked home; being forced thereto by one of my watermen falling sick yesterday, and it was God's great mercy I did not go by water with them yesterday, for he fell sick on Saturday night, and it is to be feared of the plague. So I sent him away to London with his fellow; but another boat come to me this morning, whom I sent to Blackewall for Mr. Andrews. I walked to Woolwich, and there find Mr. Hill, and he and I all the morning at musique and a song he hath set of three parts, methinks,

[1] Ombre is a Spanish game of cards, and the name is derived from the Spanish word *hombre*, a man. It is said that the game was introduced into England by Queen Katharine of Braganza. Waller wrote an epigram "On a card that her Majesty tore at Ombre." Mr. H. Hucks Gibbs published anonymously in 1873 an interesting little volume, with coloured plates, entitled, "The Game of Ombre."

[2] The practice of having a down coverlet like a bed is not confined to Denmark, as all travellers in Germany and Switzerland know.

very good. Anon comes Mr. Andrews, though it be a very ill day, and so after dinner we to musique and sang till about 4 or 5 o'clock, it blowing very hard, and now and then raining, and wind and tide being against us, Andrews and I took leave and walked to Greenwich. My wife before I come out telling me the ill news that she hears that her father is very ill, and then I told her I feared of the plague, for that the house is shut up. And so she much troubled she did desire me to send them something; and I said I would, and will do so. But before I come out there happened newes to come to me by an expresse from Mr. Coventry, telling me the most happy news of my Lord Sandwich's meeting with part of the Dutch; his taking two of their East India ships, and six or seven others, and very good prizes:[1] and that he is in search of the rest of the fleet, which he hopes to find upon the Wellbancke, with the loss only of the Hector,[2] poor Captain Cuttle. This newes do so overjoy me that I know not what to say enough to express it, but the better to do it I did walk to Greenwich, and there sending away Mr. Andrews, I to Captain Cocke's, where I find my Lord Bruncker and his mistress, and Sir J. Minnes. Where we supped (there was also Sir W. Doyly and Mr. Evelyn); but the receipt of this newes did put us all into such an extacy of joy, that it inspired into Sir J. Minnes and Mr. Evelyn such a spirit of mirth, that in all my life I never met with so merry a two hours as our company this night was. Among other humours, Mr. Evelyn's repeating of some verses made up of nothing but the various acceptations of *may* and *can*, and doing it so aptly upon occasion of something of that nature, and so fast, did make us all die almost with laughing, and did so stop the mouth of Sir J. Minnes in the middle of all his mirth (and in a thing agreeing with his own manner of genius), that I never saw any man so out-done in all my life; and Sir J. Minnes's mirth too to see himself out-done, was the crown of all our mirth. In this humour we sat till

[1] See *ante*, August 19th, for note respecting these prizes.

[2] "'The Hector' is lost, with most of her crew, and her captain, a gallant man, who had brought in the Vice-Admiral of the East India fleet. Captains Lambert and Langhorne have also fallen." ("Calendar of State Papers," 1664–65, p. 562.)

about ten at night, and so my Lord and his mistress home, and we to bed, it being one of the times of my life wherein I was the fullest of true sense of joy.

11th. Up and walked to the office, there to do some business till ten of the clock, and then by agreement my Lord, Sir J. Minnes, Sir W. Doyly, and I took boat and over to the ferry, where Sir W. Batten's coach was ready for us, and to Walthamstow drove merrily, excellent merry discourse in the way, and most upon our last night's revells; there come we were very merry, and a good plain venison dinner. After dinner to billiards, where I won an angel,[1] and among other sports we were merry with my pretending to have a warrant to Sir W. Hickes[2] (who was there, and was out of humour with Sir W. Doyly's having lately got a warrant for a leash of buckes, of which we were now eating one) which vexed him, and at last would compound with me to give my Lord Bruncker half a buck now, and me a Doe for it a while hence when the season comes in, which we agreed to and had held, but that we fear Sir W. Doyly did betray our design, which spoiled all; however, my Lady Batten invited herself to dine with him this week, and she invited us all to dine with her there, which we agreed to, only to vex him, he being the most niggardly fellow, it seems, in the world. Full of good victuals and mirth we set homeward in the evening, and very merry all the way. So to Greenwich, where when come I find my Lord Rutherford and Creed come from Court, and among other things have brought me several orders for money to pay for Tangier; and, among the rest £7,000 and more, to this Lord, which is an excellent thing to consider, that, though they can do nothing else, they can give away the King's money upon their progresse. I did give him the best answer I could to pay him with tallys, and that is all they could get from me. I was not in humour to spend much time with them, but walked a little before Sir J. Minnes's door and then took leave, and

[1] A gold coin, so called because it bore the image of an angel, varying in value from six shillings and eightpence to ten shillings.

[2] Sir William Hickes, created a baronet 1619. Died 1680, aged eighty-four. His country seat was called Ruckholts, or Rookwood, at Layton, in Essex, where he entertained King Charles II. after hunting. — B.

I by water to Woolwich, where with my wife to a game at tables,[1] and to bed.

12th. Up, and walked to the office, where we sat late, and thence to dinner home with Sir J. Minnes, and so to the office, where writing letters, and home in the evening, where my wife shews me a letter from her brother speaking of their father's being ill, like to die, which, God forgive me! did not trouble me so much as it should, though I was indeed sorry for it. I did presently resolve to send him something in a letter from my wife, viz. 20*s*. So to bed.

13th. Up, and walked to Greenwich, taking pleasure to walk with my minute watch in my hand, by which I am come now to see the distances of my way from Woolwich to Greenwich, and do find myself to come within two minutes constantly to the same place at the end of each quarter of an houre. Here we rendezvoused at Captain Cocke's, and there eat oysters, and so my Lord Bruncker, Sir J. Minnes, and I took boat, and in my Lord's coach to Sir W. Hickes's, whither by and by my Lady Batten and Sir William comes. It is a good seat, with a fair grove of trees by it, and the remains of a good garden; but so let to run to ruine, both house and every thing in and about it, so ill furnished and miserably looked after, I never did see in all my life. Not so much as a latch to his dining-room door; which saved him nothing, for the wind blowing into the room for want thereof, flung down a great bow pott that stood upon the side-table, and that fell upon some Venice glasses, and did him a crown's worth of hurt. He did give us the meanest dinner (of beef, shoulder and umbles of venison[2] which he takes away from the keeper of the

[1] The old name for backgammon, used by Shakespeare and others. The following lines are from an epitaph entirely made up of puns on backgammon: —

> "Man's life's a game at tables, and he may
> Mend his bad fortune by his wiser play."
>
> *Wit's Recre.*, i. 250, reprint, 1817.

[2] Dr. Johnson was puzzled by the following passage in "The Merry Wives of Windsor," act v., sc. 3: "Divide me like a bribe-buck, each a haunch. I will keep the sides to myself; *my shoulders for the fellow of this walk.*" If he could have read the account of Sir William Hickes's dinner, he would at once have understood the allusion to the keeper's perquisites of the shoulders of all deer killed in his walk. — B.

Forest,[1] and a few pigeons, and all in the meanest manner) that ever I did see, to the basest degree. After dinner we officers of the Navy stepped aside to read some letters and consider some business, and so in again. I was only pleased at a very fine picture of the Queene-Mother, when she was young, by Van-Dike; a very good picture, and a lovely sweet face. Thence in the afternoon home, and landing at Greenwich I saw Mr. Pen walking my way, so we walked together, and for discourse I put him into talk of France, when he took delight to tell me of his observations, some good, some impertinent, and all ill told, but it served for want of better, and so to my house, where I find my wife abroad, and hath been all this day, nobody knows where, which troubled me, it being late and a cold evening. So being invited to his mother's to supper, we took Mrs. Barbara,[2] who was mighty finely dressed, and in my Lady's coach, which we met going for my wife, we thither, and there after some discourse went to supper. By and by comes my wife and Mercer, and had been with Captain Cocke all day, he coming and taking her out to go see his boy at school at Brumly [Bromley], and brought her home again with great respect. Here pretty merry, only I had no stomach, having dined late, to eat. After supper Mr. Pen and I fell to discourse about some words in a French song my wife was saying, "D'un air tout interdict," wherein I laid twenty to one against him which he would not agree with me, though I know myself in the right as to the sense of the word, and almost angry we were, and were an houre and more upon the dispute, till at last broke up not satisfied, and so home in their coach and so to bed. H. Russell did this day deliver my *20s.* to my wife's father or mother, but has not yet told us how they do.

14th. Up, and walked to Greenwich, and there fitted myself in several businesses to go to London, where I have not been now a pretty while. But before I went from the office newes is brought by word of mouth that letters are now just now brought from the fleete of our taking a great many more of the Dutch fleete, in which I did never more plainly

[1] Epping Forest, of which he was Ranger.

[2] Daughter of William Sheldon.

see my command of my temper in my not admitting myself to receive any kind of joy from it till I had heard the certainty of it, and therefore went by water directly to the Duke of Albemarle, where I find a letter of the 12th from Solebay, from my Lord Sandwich, of the fleete's meeting with about eighteen more of the Dutch fleete, and his taking of most of them; and the messenger says, they had taken three after the letter was wrote and sealed; which being twenty-one, and the fourteen took the other day, is forty-five[1] sail; some of which are good, and others rich ships, which is so great a cause of joy in us all that my Lord and everybody is highly joyed thereat. And having taken a copy of my Lord's letter, I away back again to the Beare at the Bridge foot, being full of wind and out of order, and there called for a biscuit and a piece of cheese and gill of sacke, being forced to walk over the Bridge, toward the 'Change, and the plague being all thereabouts. Here my news was highly welcome, and I did wonder to see the 'Change so full, I believe 200 people; but not a man or merchant of any fashion, but plain men all. And Lord! to see how I did endeavour all I could to talk with as few as I could, there being now no observation of shutting up of houses infected, that to be sure we do converse and meet with people that have the plague upon them. I to Sir Robert Viner's, where my main business was about settling the business of Debusty's £5,000 tallys, which I did for the present to enable me to have some money, and so home, buying some things for my wife in the way. So home, and put up several things to carry to Woolwich, and upon serious thoughts I am advised by W. Griffin to let my money and plate rest there, as being as safe as any place, nobody imagining that people would leave money in their houses now, when all their families are gone. So for the present that being my opinion, I did leave them there still. But, Lord! to see the trouble that it puts a man to, to keep safe what with pain a man hath been getting together, and there is good reason for it. Down to the office, and there wrote letters to and again about this good newes of our victory, and so by water home late. Where, when I come home I spent

[1] A mistake for thirty-five.

some thoughts upon the occurrences of this day, giving matter for as much content on one hand and melancholy on another, as any day in all my life. For the first; the finding of my money and plate, and all safe at London, and speeding in my business of money this day. The hearing of this good news to such excess, after so great a despair of my Lord's doing anything this year; adding to that, the decrease of 500 and more, which is the first decrease we have yet had in the sickness since it begun: and great hopes that the next week it will be greater. Then, on the other side, my finding that though the Bill in general is abated, yet the City within the walls is encreased, and likely to continue so, and is close to our house there. My meeting dead corpses of the plague, carried to be buried close to me at noon-day through the City in Fanchurch-street. To see a person sick of the sores, carried close by me by Gracechurch in a hackney coach. My finding the Angell tavern [1] at the lower end of Tower-hill, shut up, and more than that, the alehouse at the Tower-stairs, and more than that, the person was then dying of the plague when I was last there, a little while ago, at night, to write a short letter there, and I overheard the mistresse of the house sadly saying to her husband somebody was very ill, but did not think it was of the plague. To hear that poor Payne, my waiter, hath buried a child, and is dying himself. To hear that a labourer I sent but the other day to Dagenhams, to know how they did there, is dead of the plague; and that one of my own watermen, that carried me daily, fell sick as soon as he had landed me on Friday morning last, when I had been all night upon the water (and I believe he did get his infection that day at Brainford), and is now dead of the plague. To hear that Captain Lambert and Cuttle [2] are killed in the taking these ships; and that Mr. Sidney Montague [3] is sick of a desperate fever at my Lady Carteret's, at

[1] There is a token of the Angel Tavern at Tower Hill, dated 1649. The alehouse was probably the Rose and Crown at Tower Stairs, of which there is also a token. (See "Boyne's Tokens," ed. Williamson, vol. i., p. 775.)

[2] See *ante*, September 10th.

[3] Sidney Montagu, brother of Edward, Earl of Sandwich, was with his niece, Lady Jemima Carteret. Scot's Hall belonged to her husband's brother-in-law, Sir Thomas Scott.

Scott's-hall. To hear that Mr. Lewes hath another daughter sick. And, lastly, that both my servants, W. Hewer and Tom Edwards, have lost their fathers, both in St. Sepulchre's parish, of the plague this week, do put me into great apprehensions of melancholy, and with good reason. But I put off the thoughts of sadness as much as I can, and the rather to keep my wife in good heart and family also. After supper (having eat nothing all this day) upon a fine tench of Mr. Shelden's taking, we to bed.

15th. Up, it being a cold misling morning, and so by water to the office, where very busy upon several businesses. At noon got the messenger, Marlow, to get me a piece of bread and butter and cheese and a bottle of beer and ale, and so I went not out of the office but dined off that, and my boy Tom, but the rest of my clerks went home to dinner. Then to my business again, and by and by sent my waterman to see how Sir W. Warren do, who is sicke, and for which I have reason to be very sorry, he being the friend I have got most by of most friends in England but the King: who returns me that he is pretty well again, his disease being an ague. I by water to Deptford, thinking to have seen my valentine, but I could not, and so come back again, and to the office, where a little business, and thence with Captain Cocke, and there drank a cup of good drink, which I am fain to allow myself during this plague time, by advice of all, and not contrary to my oathe, my physician being dead, and chyrurgeon out of the way, whose advice I am obliged to take, and so by water home and eat my supper, and to bed, being in much pain to think what I shall do this winter time; for go every day to Woolwich I cannot, without endangering my life; and staying from my wife at Greenwich is not handsome.

16th. Up, and walked to Greenwich reading a play, and to the office, where I find Sir J. Minnes gone to the fleete, like a doating foole, to do no good, but proclaim himself an asse; for no service he can do there, nor inform my Lord, who is come in thither to the buoy of the Nore, in anything worth his knowledge. At noon to dinner to my Lord Bruncker, where Sir W. Batten and his Lady come, by invitation, and very merry we were, only that the discourse of the likelihood of the increase of the plague this weeke makes us a little sad, but then again the thoughts of the late prizes make us glad. After dinner, by appointment, comes Mr. Andrews, and he and I walking alone in the garden talking of our Tangier business, and I endeavoured by the by to offer some encouragements for their continuing in the business, which he seemed to take hold of, and the truth is my profit is so much concerned that I could wish they would, and would take pains to ease them in the business of money as much as was possible. He being gone (after I had ordered him £2,000, and he paid me my quantum out of it) I also walked to the office, and there to my business; but find myself, through the unfitness of my place to write in, and my coming from great dinners, and drinking wine, that I am not in the good temper of doing business now a days that I used to be and ought still to be. At night to Captain Cocke's, meaning to lie there, it being late, and he not being at home, I walked to him to my Lord Bruncker's, and there staid a while, they being at tables; and so by and by parted, and walked to his house; and, after a mess of good broth, to bed, in great pleasure, his company being most excellent.

17th (Lord's day). Up, and before I went out of my chamber did draw a musique scale, in order to my having it at any time ready in my hand to turn to for exercise, for I have a great mind in this Vacation to perfect myself in my scale, in order to my practising of composition, and so that being done I down stairs, and there find Captain Cocke under the barber's hands, the barber that did heretofore trim Commissioner Pett, and with whom I have been. He offered to come this day after dinner with his violin to play me a set of Lyra-ayres upon it, which I was glad of, hoping to be merry thereby. Being ready we to church, where a company of fine people to church, and a fine Church, and very good sermon, Mr. Plume[1] being a very excellent scholler and preacher. Coming out of the church I met Mrs. Pierce, whom I was ashamed to see, having not been with her since my coming to town, but promised to visit her. Thence with Captain Cocke, in his coach, home to dinner, whither

[1] Thomas Plume, D.D., vicar of Greenwich, 1662, and installed Archdeacon of Rochester, 1679. Died November 20th, 1704, and buried in Longfield churchyard.

comes by invitation my Lord Bruncker and his mistresse and very good company we were, but in dinner time comes Sir J. Minnes from the fleete, like a simple weak man, having nothing to say of what he hath done there, but tells of what value he imagines the prizes to be, and that my Lord Sandwich is well, and mightily concerned to hear that I was well. But this did put me upon a desire of going thither; and, moving of it to my Lord, we presently agreed upon it to go this very tide, we two and Captain Cocke. So every body prepared to fit himself for his journey, and I walked to Woolwich to trim and shift myself, and by the time I was ready they come down in the Bezan yacht, and so I aboard and my boy Tom, and there very merrily we sailed to below Gravesend, and there come to anchor for all night, and supped and talked, and with much pleasure at last settled ourselves to sleep having very good lodging upon cushions in the cabbin.

18th. By break of day we come to within sight of the fleete, which was a very fine thing to behold, being above 100 ships, great and small; with the flag-ships of each squadron, distinguished by their several flags on their main, fore, or mizen masts. Among others, the Soveraigne, Charles, and Prince; in the last of which my Lord Sandwich was. When we called by her side his Lordshipp was not stirring, so we come to anchor a little below his ship, thinking to have rowed on board him, but the wind and tide was so strong against us that we could not get up to him, no, though rowed by a boat of the Prince's that come to us to tow us up; at last however he brought us within a little way, and then they flung out a rope to us from the Prince and so come on board, but with great trouble and time and patience, it being very cold; we find my Lord newly up in his night-gown very well. He received us kindly; telling us the state of the fleet, lacking provisions, having no beer at all, nor have had most of them these three weeks or month, and but few days' dry provisions. And indeed he tells us that he believes no fleete was ever set to sea in so ill condition of provision, as this was when it went out last. He did inform us in the business of Bergen,[1] so as to let us

[1] Lord Sandwich was not so successful in convincing other people as to the propriety of his conduct at Bergen as he was with Pepys.

see how the judgment of the world is not to be depended on in things they know not; it being a place just wide enough, and not so much hardly, for ships to go through to it, the yard-armes sticking in the very rocks. He do not, upon his best enquiry, find reason to except against any part of the management of the business by Teddiman; he having staid treating no longer than during the night, whiles he was fitting himself to fight, bringing his ship a-breast, and not a quarter of an hour longer (as is said); nor could more ships have been brought to play, as is thought. Nor could men be landed, there being 10,000 men effectively always in armes of the Danes; nor, says he, could we expect more from the Dane than he did, it being impossible to set fire on the ships but it must burn the towne. But that wherein the Dane did amisse is, that he did assist them, the Dutch, all the while, while he was treating with us, while he should have been neutrall to us both. But, however, he did demand but the treaty of us; which is, that we should not come with more than five ships. A flag of truce is said, and confessed by my Lord, that he believes it was hung out; but while they did hang it out, they did shoot at us; so that it was not either seen perhaps, or fit to cease upon sight of it, while they continued actually in action against us. But the main thing my Lord wonders at, and condemns the Dane for, is, that the blockhead, who is so much in debt to the Hollander, having now a treasure more by much than all his Crowne was worth, and that which would for ever have beggared the Hollanders, should not take this time to break with the Hollander, and thereby paid his debt which must have been forgiven him, and got the greatest treasure into his hands that ever was together in the world. By and by my Lord took me aside to discourse of his private matters, who was very free with me touching the ill condition of the fleete that it hath been in, and the good fortune that he hath had, and nothing else that these prizes are to be imputed to. He also talked with me about Mr. Coventry's dealing with him in sending Sir W. Pen away before him, which was not fair nor kind; but that he hath mastered and cajoled Sir W. Pen, that he hath been able to do nothing in the fleete, but been obedient to him; but withal tells me he is a man that is but of very mean parts, and a fellow not to be lived with, so false and base he is; which I know well enough to be very true, and did, as I had formerly done, give my Lord my knowledge of him. By and by was called a Council of Warr on board, when come Sir W. Pen there, and Sir Christopher Mings, Sir Edward Spragg, Sir Jos. Jordan, Sir Thomas Teddiman, and Sir Roger Cuttance, and so the necessity of the fleete for victuals, clothes, and money was discoursed, but by the discourse there of all but my Lord, that is to say, the counterfeit grave nonsense of Sir W. Pen and the poor mean discourse of the rest, methinks I saw how the government and management of the greatest business of the three nations is committed to very ordinary heads, saving my Lord, and in effect is only upon him, who is able to do what he pleases with them, they not having the meanest degree of reason to be able to oppose anything that he says, and so I fear it is ordered but like all the rest of the King's publique affayres. The council being up they most of them went away, only Sir W. Pen who staid to dine there and did so, but the wind being high the ship (though the motion of it was hardly discernible to the eye) did make me sick, so as I could not eat any thing almost. After dinner Cocke did pray me to helpe him to £500 of W. How, who is deputy Treasurer, wherein my Lord Bruncker and I am to be concerned and I did aske it my Lord, and he did consent to have us furnished with £500, and I did get it paid to Sir Roger Cuttance and Mr. Pierce in part for above £1,000 worth of goods, Mace, Nutmegs, Cynamon, and Cloves, and he tells us we may hope to get £500 by it, which God send! Great spoil, I hear, there hath been of the two East India ships, and that yet they will come in to the King very rich: so that I hope this journey will be worth £100 to me.[1] After having paid this money, we took leave of my Lord and so to our Yacht again, having seen many of my friends there. Among others I hear that W. Howe will grow very rich by this last business and grows very proud and insolent by it; but it is what I ever expected. I hear by every body how much my poor Lord of Sandwich was concerned for me during my

[1] There is a shorthand journal of proceedings relating to Pepys's purchase of some East India prize goods among the Rawlinson MSS. in the Bodleian Library.

silence a while, lest I had been dead of the plague in this sickly time. No sooner come into the yacht, though overjoyed with the good work we have done to-day, but I was overcome with sea sickness so that I begun to spue soundly, and so continued a good while, till at last I went into the cabbin and shutting my eyes my trouble did cease that I fell asleep, which continued till we come into Chatham river where the water was smooth, and then I rose and was very well, and the tide coming to be against us we did land before we come to Chatham and walked a mile, having very good discourse by the way, it being dark and it beginning to rain just as we got thither. At Commissioner Pett's we did eat and drink very well and very merry we were, and about 10 at night, it being moonshine and very cold, we set out, his coach carrying us, and so all night travelled to Greenwich, we sometimes sleeping a little and then talking and laughing by the way, and with much pleasure, but that it was very horrible cold, that I was afeard of an ague. A pretty passage was that the coach stood of a sudden and the coachman come down and the horses stirring, he cried, Hold! which waked me, and the coach[man] standing at the boote to [do] something or other and crying, Hold! I did wake of a sudden and not knowing who he was, nor thinking of the coachman between sleeping and waking I did take up the heart to take him by the shoulder, thinking verily he had been a thief. But when I waked I found my cowardly heart to discover a fear within me and that I should never have done it if I had been awake.

19th. About 4 or 5 of the clock we come to Greenwich, and, having first set down my Lord Bruncker, Cocke and I went to his house, it being light, and there to our great trouble, we being sleepy and cold, we met with the ill newes that his boy Jacke was gone to bed sicke, which put Captain Cocke and me also into much trouble, the boy, as they told us, complaining of his head most, which is a bad sign it seems. So they presently betook themselves to consult whither and how to remove him. However I thought it not fit for me to discover too much fear to go away, nor had I any place to go to. So to bed I went and slept till 10 of the clock and then comes Captain Cocke to wake me and tell me that his boy was well again. With great joy I heard the newes and he told it, so I up and to the office where we did a little, and but a little business. At noon by invitation to my Lord Bruncker's where we staid till four of the clock for my Lady Batten and she not then coming we to dinner and pretty merry but disordered by her making us stay so long. After dinner I to the office, and there wrote letters and did business till night and then to Sir J. Minnes's, where I find my Lady Batten come, and she and my Lord Bruncker and his mistresse, and the whole house-full there at cards. But by and by my Lord Bruncker goes away and others of the company, and when I expected Sir J. Minnes and his sister should have staid to have made Sir W. Batten and Lady sup, I find they go up in snuffe to bed without taking any manner of leave of them, but left them with Mr. Boreman. The reason of this I could not presently learn, but anon I hear it is that Sir J. Minnes did expect and intend them a supper, but they without respect to him did first apply themselves to Boreman, which makes all this great feude. However I staid and there supped, all of us being in great disorder from this, and more from Cocke's boy's being ill, where my Lady Batten and Sir W. Batten did come to town with an intent to lodge, and I was forced to go seek a lodging which my W. Hewer did get me, viz., his own chamber in the towne, whither I went and found it a very fine room, and there lay most excellently.

20th. Called up by Captain Cocke (who was last night put into great trouble upon his boy's being rather worse than better, upon which he removed him out of his house to his stable), who told me that to my comfort his boy was now as well as ever he was in his life. So I up, and after being trimmed, the first time I have been touched by a barber these twelvemonths, I think, and more, went to Sir J. Minnes's, where I find all out of order still, they having not seen one another till by and by Sir J. Minnes and Sir W. Batten met, to go into my Lord Bruncker's coach, and so we four to Lambeth, and thence to the Duke of Albemarle, to inform him what we have done as to the fleete, which is very little, and to receive his direction. But, Lord! what a sad time it is to see no boats upon the River; and grass grows all up and down White Hall court, and nobody but poor wretches in the streets! And, which is worst of all, the Duke showed us the number of the plague this week, brought in the last night from the Lord Mayor; that it is encreased about 600 more than the last, which is quite contrary to all our hopes and expectations, from the coldness of the late season. For the whole general number is 8,297, and of them the plague 7,165; which is more in the whole by above 50, than the biggest Bill yet; which is very grievous to us all. I find here a design in my Lord Bruncker and Captain Cocke to have had my Lord Bruncker chosen as one of us to have been sent aboard one of the East India-men, and Captain Cocke as a merchant to be joined with him, and Sir J. Minnes for the other, and Sir G. Smith to be joined with him. But I did order it so that my Lord Bruncker and Sir J. Minnes were ordered, but I did stop the merchants to be added, which would have been a most pernicious thing to the King I am sure. In this I did, I think, a very good office, though I cannot acquit myself from some envy of mine in the business to have the profitable business done by another hand while I lay wholly imployed in the trouble of the office. Thence back again by my Lord's coach to my Lord Bruncker's house, where I find my Lady Batten, who is become very great with Mrs. Williams (my Lord Bruncker's whore), and there we dined and were mighty merry. After dinner I to the office there to write letters, to fit myself for a journey to-morrow to Nonsuch to the Exchequer by appointment. That being done I to Sir J. Minnes where I find Sir W. Batten and his Lady gone home to Walthamstow in great snuffe as to Sir J. Minnes, but yet with some necessity, hearing that a mayde-servant of theirs is taken ill. Here I staid and resolved of my going in my Lord Bruncker's coach which he would have me to take, though himself cannot go with me as he intended, and so to my last night's lodging to bed very weary.

21st. Up between five and six o'clock; and by the time I was ready, my Lord's coach comes for me; and taking Will Hewer with me, who is all in mourning for his father, who is lately dead of the plague, as my boy Tom's is also, I set out, and took about £100 with me to pay the fees there, and so I rode in some fear of robbing. When I come thither, I find only Mr. Ward, who led me to Burgess's bedside, and Spicer's, who, watching of the house, as it is their turns every night, did lie long in bed to-day, and I find nothing at all done in my business, which vexed me. But not seeing how to helpe it I did walk up and down with Mr. Ward to see the house; and by and by Spicer and Mr. Falconbrige come to me and he and I to a towne near by, Yowell[1] there drink and set up my horses and also bespoke a dinner, and while that is dressing went with Spicer and walked up and down the house and park; and a fine place it hath heretofore been, and a fine prospect about the house.[2] A great walk of an elme and a walnutt set one after another in order. And all the house on the outside filled with figures of stories, and good painting of Rubens' or Holben's doing. And one great thing is, that most of the house is covered, I mean the posts, and quarters in the walls, covered with lead, and gilded. I walked into the ruined garden, and there found a plain little girle, kinswoman of Mr. Falconbridge, to sing very finely by the eare only, but a fine way of singing, and if I come ever to lacke a girle again I shall think of getting her. Thence to the towne, and there Spicer, Woodruffe, and W. Bowyer and I dined together and a friend of Spicer's, and a good dinner I had for them. Falconbrige dined somewhere else, by appointment. Strange to see how young W. Bowyer looks at 41 years; one would not take him for 24 or more, and is one of the greatest wonders I ever did see. After dinner, about 4 of the clock we broke up, and I took coach and home (in fear for the money I had with me, but that this friend of Spicer's, one of the Duke's guard did ride along the best part of the way with us). I got to my Lord Bruncker's before night, and there I sat and supped with him and his mistresse, and Cocke whose boy is yet ill. Thence, after losing a crowne betting at Tables, we walked home, Cocke seeing me at my new lodging, where I went to bed. All my worke this day in the coach going and coming was to refresh myself in my musique scale, which I would fain have perfecter than ever I had yet.

22nd. Up betimes and to the office, meaning to have

[1] Ewell.

[2] This was Nonsuch. When proclamation was made, September 26th, that the courts were to be removed from Westminster to Oxford, it was announced that the Exchequer was to remain at Nonsuch. There is no authority for attributing any of the work to either Holbein or Rubens. See *ante*, August 11th, 1665, and July 26th, 1663.

entered my last 5 or 6 days' Journall, but was called away by my Lord Bruncker and Sir J. Minnes, and to Blackwall, there to look after the storehouses in order to the laying of goods out of the East India ships when they shall be unloaden. That being done, we into Johnson's house, and were much made of, eating and drinking. But here it is observable what he tells us, that in digging his late Docke, he did 12 foot under ground find perfect trees over-covered with earth. Nut trees, with the branches and the very nuts upon them; some of whose nuts he showed us. Their shells black with age, and their kernell, upon opening, decayed, but their shell perfectly hard as ever. And a yew tree he showed us (upon which, he says, the very ivy was taken up whole about it), which upon cutting with an addes [adze], we found to be rather harder than the living tree usually is.[1] They say, very much, but I do not know how hard a yew tree naturally is. The armes, they say, were taken up at first whole, about the body, which is very strange. Thence away by water, and I walked with my Lord Bruncker home, and there at dinner comes a letter from my Lord Sandwich to tell me that he would this day be at Woolwich, and desired me to meet him. Which fearing might have lain in Sir J. Minnes' pocket a while, he sending it me, did give my Lord Bruncker, his mistress, and I occasion to talk of him as the most unfit man for business in the world. Though at last afterwards I found that he was not in this faulty, but hereby I have got a clear evidence of my Lord Bruncker's opinion of him. My Lord Bruncker presently ordered his coach to be ready and we to Woolwich, and my Lord Sandwich not being come, we took a boat and about a mile off met him in his Catch, and boarded him, and come up with him; and, after making a little halt at my house, which I ordered, to have my wife see him, we all together by coach to Mr. Boreman's, where Sir J. Minnes did receive him very handsomely, and there he is to lie; and Sir J. Minnes did give him on the sudden, a very handsome supper and brave discourse, my Lord Bruncker, and Captain Cocke, and Captain Herbert being there, with

[1] The same discovery was made in 1789, in digging the Brunswick Dock, also at Blackwall, and elsewhere in the neighbourhood. See "Notes and Queries," 1st series, vol. viii., p. 263. — M. B.

myself. Here my Lord did witness great respect to me, and very kind expressions, and by other occasions, from one thing to another did take notice how I was overjoyed at first to see the King's letter to his Lordship, and told them how I did kiss it, and that, whatever he was, I did always love the King. This my Lord Bruncker did take such notice [of] as that he could not forbear kissing me before my Lord, professing his finding occasion every day more and more to love me, and Captain Cocke has since of himself taken notice of that speech of my Lord then concerning me, and may be of good use to me. Among other discourse concerning long life, Sir J. Minnes saying that his great-grandfather was alive in Edward the Vth's time; my Lord Sandwich did tell us how few there have been of his family since King Harry the VIIIth; that is to say, the then Chiefe Justice,[1] and his son the Lord Montagu,[2] who

[1] Sir Edward Montagu, Chief Justice of the King's Bench, 1539–45; Chief Justice of the Common Pleas, 1545–53. He died February 10th, 1556–57.

[2] These are the words in the MS., and not "his son *and* the Lord Montagu," as in some former editions. Pepys seems to have written Lord Montagu by mistake for Sir Edward Montagu.

PEDIGREE OF THE EARL OF SANDWICH.

EDWARD MONTAGU,
Lord Chief Justice, temp. Henry VIII., died 1557.

EDWARD MONTAGU, Knt.,
"A worthy patriot in the reign of Queen Elizabeth," died 1602.

EDWD. MONTAGU, Knt., First Lord Montagu of Boughton.	WALTER, Knt.	HENRY, Lord Montagu, First Earl of Manchester.	CHARLES, Knt.	JAMES, Bishop of Bath 1605, and Winchester 1616.	SIDNEY, Knt., M.P. for Huntingdon in the Long Parliament, whence he was expelled. MAR. PAULINA, daughter of John Pepys, of Cottenham, Camb., died 1644.

HENRY, drowned at sea.	EDWARD, a distinguished Parliamentary Captain. M.P. for Huntingdon, Admiral. *First Earl of Sandwich*, died 1672.	ELIZABETH, mar. Sir Gilbert Pyckering, of Titchmarsh.

—M. B.

was father to Sir Sidney,[1] who was his father. And yet, what is more wonderfull, he did assure us from the mouth of my Lord Montagu himself, that in King James's time ([when he] had a mind to get the King to cut off the entayle of some land which was given in Harry the VIIIth's time to the family, with the remainder in the Crowne); he did answer the King in showing how unlikely it was that ever it could revert to the Crown, but that it would be a present convenience to him; and did show that at that time there were 4,000 persons derived from the very body of the Chiefe Justice. It seems the number of daughters in the family having been very great, and they too had most of them many children, and grandchildren, and great-grandchildren. This he tells as a most known and certain truth. After supper, my Lord Bruncker took his leave, and I also did mine, taking Captain Herbert home to my lodging to lie with me, who did mighty seriously inquire after who was that in the black dress with my wife yesterday, and would not believe that it was my wife's mayde, Mercer, but it was she.

23rd. Up, and to my Lord Sandwich, who did advise alone with me how far he might trust Captain Cocke in the business of the prize-goods,[2] my Lord telling me that he

Lord Sandwich speaks of five [four?] generations in which the number of descendants might have multiplied *ad infinitum*. "When King James came into England," observes Ward, in his "Diary," p. 170, "he was ffeasted at Boughton, by Sir Edward Montagu, and his six sonnes brought upp the six first dishes; three of them after were lords, and three more knights— Sir Walter Montagu, Sir Sydney, and Sir Charles, whose daughter Lady Hatton is." Fuller, also, in his "Worthies," records that "Hester Sandys, the wife of Sir Thomas Temple, of Stowe, Bart., had four sons and nine daughters, which lived to be married, and so exceedingly multiplied, that she saw seven hundred extracted from her body. Besides, there was a new generation of marriageable females just at her death" (see Collins's "Peerage," vol. ii., p. 411). When Charles, thirteenth Duke of Norfolk, had completed his restoration of Arundel Castle, he proposed to entertain all the descendants of his ancestor, Jock of Norfolk, who fell at Bosworth Field; but gave up his intention on finding that he should have to invite upwards of six thousand persons. — B.

[1] Master of the Requests to Charles I.

[2] In the British Museum, Egerton MS., 861, is an account showing the value of all prizes taken during the war with the Dutch; distinguishing the vessels, their goods, the ports at which they were condemned, and the parties to whose accounts the amounts were debited. — B.

hath taken into his hands 2 or £3,000 value of them: it being a good way, he says, to get money, and afterwards to get the King's allowance thereof, it being easier, he observes, to keepe money when got of the King than to get it when it is too late. I advised him not to trust Cocke too far, and did therefore offer him ready money for a £1,000 or two, which he listens to and do agree to, which is great joy to me, hoping thereby to get something! Thence by coach to Lambeth, his Lordship, and all our office, and Mr. Evelyn, to the Duke of Albemarle, where, after the compliment with my Lord very kind, we sat down to consult of the disposing and supporting of the fleete with victuals and money, and for the sicke men and prisoners; and I did propose the taking out some goods out of the prizes, to the value of £10,000, which was accorded to, and an order, drawn up and signed by the Duke and my Lord, done in the best manner I can, and referred to my Lord Bruncker and Sir J. Minnes, but what inconveniences may arise from it I do not yet see, but fear there may be many. Here we dined, and I did hear my Lord Craven whisper, as he is mightily possessed with a good opinion of me, much to my advantage, which my good Lord did second, and anon my Lord Craven did speak publiquely of me to the Duke, in the hearing of all the rest; and the Duke did say something of the like advantage to me; I believe, not much to the satisfaction of my brethren; but I was mightily joyed at it. Thence took leave, leaving my Lord Sandwich to go visit the Bishop of Canterbury, and I and Sir W. Batten down to the Tower, where he went further by water, and I home, and among other things took out all my gold to carry along with me to-night with Captain Cocke downe to the fleete, being £180 and more, hoping to lay out that and a great deal more to good advantage. Thence down to Greenwich to the office, and there wrote several letters, and so to my Lord Sandwich, and mighty merry and he mighty kind to me in the face of all, saying much in my favour, and after supper I took leave and with Captain Cocke set out in the yacht about ten o'clock at night, and after some discourse, and drinking a little, my mind full of what we are going about and jealous of Cocke's outdoing me. So to sleep upon beds brought by Cocke on board mighty handsome, and never slept better than upon this bed upon the floor in the Cabbin.

24th (Lord's day). Waked, and up and drank, and then to discourse; and then being about Grayes, and a very calme, curious morning, we took our wherry, and to the fishermen, and bought a great deal of fine fish, and to Gravesend to White's, and had part of it dressed; and, in the meantime, we to walk about a mile from the towne, and so back again; and there, after breakfast, one of our watermen told us he had heard of a bargain of cloves for us, and we went to a blind alehouse at the further end of the towne to a couple of wretched, dirty seamen, who, poor wretches, had got together about 37 lb. of cloves and 10 lb. of nutmeggs, and we bought them of them, the first at 5*s.* 6*d.* per lb. and the latter at 4*s.*, and paid them in gold; but, Lord! to see how silly these men are in the selling of it, and easily to be persuaded almost to anything, offering a bag to us to pass as 20 lbs. of cloves, which upon weighing proved 25 lbs. But it would never have been allowed by my conscience to have wronged the poor wretches, who told us how dangerously they had got some, and dearly paid for the rest of these goods. This being done we with great content herein on board again and there Captain Cocke and I to discourse of our business, but he will not yet be open to me, nor am I to him till I hear what he will say and do with Sir Roger Cuttance. However, this discourse did do me good, and got me a copy of the agreement made the other day on board for the parcel of Mr. Pierce and Sir Roger Cuttance, but this great parcel is of my Lord Sandwich's. By and by to dinner about 3 o'clock and then I in the cabbin to writing down my journall for these last seven days to my great content, it having pleased God that in this sad time of the plague everything else has conspired to my happiness and pleasure more for these last three months than in all my life before in so little time. God long preserve it and make me thankfull for it! After finishing my Journall, then to discourse and to read, and then to supper and to bed, my mind not being at full ease, having not fully satisfied myself how Captain Cocke will deal with me as to the share of the profits.

25th. Found ourselves come to the fleete, and so aboard

the Prince; and there, after a good while in discourse, we did agree a bargain of £5,000 with Sir Roger Cuttance for my Lord Sandwich for silk, cinnamon, nutmeggs, and indigo. And I was near signing to an undertaking for the payment of the whole sum; but I did by chance escape it; having since, upon second thoughts, great cause to be glad of it, reflecting upon the craft and not good condition, it may be, of Captain Cocke. I could get no trifles for my wife. Anon to dinner and thence in great haste to make a short visit to Sir W. Pen, where I found them and his lady and daughter and many commanders at dinner. Among others Sir G. Askue, of whom whatever the matter is, the world is silent altogether. But a very pretty dinner there was, and after dinner Sir W. Pen made a bargain with Cocke for ten bales of silke, at 16*s*. per lb., which, as Cocke says, will be a good pennyworth, and so away to the Prince and presently comes my Lord on board from Greenwich, with whom, after a little discourse about his trusting of Cocke, we parted and to our yacht; but it being calme, we to make haste, took our wherry toward Chatham; but, it growing darke, we were put to great difficultys, our simple, yet confident waterman, not knowing a step of the way; and we found ourselves to go backward and forward, which, in the darke night and a wild place, did vex us mightily. At last we got a fisher boy by chance, and took him into the boat, and being an odde kind of boy, did vex us too; for he wou'd not answer us aloud when we spoke to him, but did carry us safe thither, though with a mistake or two; but I wonder they were not more. In our way I was [surprised] and so were we all, at the strange nature of the sea-water in a darke night, that it seemed like fire upon every stroke of the oare, and, they say, is a sign of winde. We went to the Crowne Inne, at Rochester, and there to supper, and made ourselves merry with our poor fisher-boy, who told us he had not been in a bed in the whole seven years since he came to 'prentice, and hath two or three more years to serve. After eating something, we in our clothes to bed.

26th. Up by five o'clock and got post horses and so set out for Greenwich, calling and drinking at Dartford. Being come to Greenwich and shifting myself I to the office, from whence by and by my Lord Bruncker and Sir J.

Minnes set out toward Erith to take charge of the two East India shipps, which I had a hand in contriving for the King's service and may do myself a good office too thereby. I to dinner with Mr. Wright to his father-in-law in Greenwich, one of the most silly, harmless, prating old men that ever I heard in my life. Creed dined with me, and among other discourses got of me a promise of half that he could get my Lord Rutherford to give me upon clearing his business, which should not be less, he says, than £50 for my half, which is a good thing, though cunningly got of him. By and by Luellin comes, and I hope to get something of Deering shortly. They being gone, Mr. Wright and I went into the garden to discourse with much trouble for fear of losing all the profit and principal of what we have laid out in buying of prize goods, and therefore puts me upon thoughts of flinging up my interest, but yet I shall take good advice first. Thence to the office, and after some letters down to Woolwich, where I have not lain with my wife these eight days I think, or more. After supper, and telling her my mind in my trouble in what I have done as to buying of these goods, we to bed.

27th. Up, and saw and admired my wife's picture of our Saviour,[1] now finished, which is very pretty. So by water to Greenwich, where with Creed and Lord Rutherford, and there my Lord told me that he would give me £100 for my pains, which pleased me well, though Creed, like a cunning rogue, hath got a promise of half of it from me. We to the King's Head, the great musique house, the first time I was ever there, and had a good breakfast, and thence parted, I being much troubled to hear from Creed, that he was told at Salsbury[2] that I am come to be a great swearer and drinker, though I know the contrary; but, Lord! to see how my late little drinking of wine is taken notice of by envious men to my disadvantage. I thence to Captain Cocke's, [and] (he not yet come from town) to Mr. Evelyn's, where much company; and thence in his coach with him to the Duke of Albemarle by Lambeth, who was in a mighty pleas-

[1] This picture by Mrs. Pepys may have given trouble when Pepys was unjustifiably attacked for having Popish pictures in his house.

[2] The Court was then held at Salisbury, where the King and Queen removed on July 27th.

ant humour; there the Duke tells us that the Dutch do stay abroad, and our fleet must go out again, or to be ready to do so. Here we got several things ordered as we desired for the relief of the prisoners, and sick and wounded men. Here I saw this week's Bill of Mortality, wherein, blessed be God! there is above 1,800 decrease, being the first considerable decrease we have had. Back again the same way and had most excellent discourse of Mr. Evelyn touching all manner of learning; wherein I find him a very fine gentleman, and particularly of paynting, in which he tells me the beautifull Mrs. Middleton is rare, and his own wife do brave things. He brought me to the office, whither comes unexpectedly Captain Cocke, who hath brought one parcel of our goods by waggons, and at first resolved to have lodged them at our office; but then the thoughts of its being the King's house altered our resolution, and so put them at his friend's, Mr. Glanvill's, and there they are safe. Would the rest of them were so too! In discourse, we come to mention my profit, and he offers me £500 clear, and I demand £600 for my certain profit. We part to-night, and I lie there at Mr. Glanvill's house, there being none there but a mayde-servant and a young man; being in some pain, partly from not knowing what to do in this business, having a mind to be at a certainty in my profit, and partly through his having Jacke sicke still, and his blackemore now also fallen sicke. So he being gone, I to bed.

28th. Up, and being mightily pleased with my night's lodging drank a cup of beer, and went out to my office, and there did some business, and so took boat and down to Woolwich (having first made a visit to Madam Williams, who is going down to my Lord Bruncker) and there dined, and then fitted my papers and money and every thing else for a journey to Nonsuch to-morrow. That being done I walked to Greenwich, and there to the office pretty late expecting Captain Cocke's coming, which he did, and so with me to my new lodging (and there I chose rather to lie because of my interest in the goods that we have brought there to lie), but the people were abed, so we knocked them up, and so I to bed, and in the night was mightily troubled with a looseness (I suppose from some fresh damp linen that I put on this night), and feeling for a chamber-pott, there was none, I having called the mayde up out of her bed, she had forgot I suppose to put one there; so I was forced in this strange house to rise and shit in the chimney twice; and so to bed and was very well again, and

29th. To sleep till 5 o'clock, when it is now very dark, and then rose, being called up by order by Mr. Marlow, and so up and dressed myself, and by and by comes Mr. Lashmore on horseback, and I had my horse I borrowed of Mr. Gillthropp, Sir W. Batten's clerke, brought to me, and so we set out and rode hard and was at Nonsuch by about eight o'clock, a very fine journey and a fine day. There I come just about chappell time and so I went to chappell with them and thence to the several offices about my tallys, which I find done, but strung for sums not to my purpose, and so was forced to get them to promise me to have them cut into other sums. But, Lord! what ado I had to persuade the dull fellows to it, especially Mr. Warder,[1] Master of the Pells, and yet without any manner of reason for their scruple. But at last I did, and so left my tallies there against another day, and so walked to Yowell, and there did spend a peece upon them, having a whole house full, and much mirth by a sister of the mistresse of the house, an old mayde lately married to a lieutenant of a company that quarters there, and much pleasant discourse we had and, dinner being done, we to horse again and come to Greenwich before night, and so to my lodging, and there being a little weary sat down and fell to order some of my pocket papers, and then comes Captain Cocke, and after a great deal of discourse with him seriously upon the disorders of our state through lack of men to mind the public business and to understand it, we broke up, sitting up talking very late. We spoke a little of my late business propounded of taking profit for my money laid out for these goods, but he finds I rise in my demand, he offering me still £500 certain. So we did give it over, and I to bed. I hear for certain this night upon the road that Sir Martin Noell[2] is this day dead of the plague in London, where he hath lain sick of it these eight days.

[1] William Wardour was appointed Clerk of the Pells in 1660.

[2] He had been a farmer of the excise and customs before the Restoration (see note, *ante*, September 5th, 1662).

30th. Up and to the office, where busy all the morning, and at noon with Sir W. Batten to Coll. Cleggat to dinner, being invited, where a very pretty dinner to my full content and very merry. The great burden we have upon us at this time at the office, is the providing for prisoners and sicke men that are recovered, they lying before our office doors all night and all day, poor wretches. Having been on shore, the captains won't receive them on board, and other ships we have not to put them on, nor money to pay them off, or provide for them. God remove this difficulty! This made us followed all the way to this gentleman's house and there are waited for our coming out after dinner. Hither come Luellin to me and would force me to take Mr. Deering's 20 pieces in gold he did offer me a good while since, which I did, yet really and sincerely against my will and content, I seeing him a man not likely to do well in his business, nor I to reap any comfort in having to do with, and be beholden to, a man that minds more his pleasure and company than his business. Thence mighty merry and much pleased with the dinner and company and they with me I parted and there was set upon by the poor wretches, whom I did give good words and some little money to, and the poor people went away like lambs, and in good earnest are not to be censured if their necessities drive them to bad courses of stealing or the like, while they lacke wherewith to live. Thence to the office, and there wrote a letter or two and dispatched a little business, and then to Captain Cocke's, where I find Mr. Temple,[1] the fat blade, Sir Robert Viner's chief man. And we three and two companions of his in the evening by agreement took ship in the Bezan and the tide carried us no further than Woolwich about 8 at night, and so I on shore to my wife, and there to my great trouble find my wife out of order, and she took me downstairs and there alone did tell me her falling out with both her mayds and particularly Mary, and how Mary had to her teeth told her she would tell me of something that should stop her mouth and words of that sense. Which I suspect may be about Brown, but my wife prays me to call it to

[1] John Temple and John Seale were goldsmiths at the Three Tuns in Lombard Street (see "A Collection of the Names of the Merchants living in and about the City of London, 1677." 12mo.).

examination, and this, I being of myself jealous, do make me mightily out of temper, and seeing it not fit to enter into the dispute did passionately go away, thinking to go on board again. But when I come to the stairs I considered the Bezan would not go till the next ebb, and it was best to lie in a good bed and, it may be, get myself into a better humour by being with my wife. So I back again and to bed and having otherwise so many reasons to rejoice and hopes of good profit, besides considering the ill that trouble of mind and melancholly may in this sickly time bring a family into, and that if the difference were never so great, it is not a time to put away servants, I was resolved to salve up the business rather than stir in it, and so become pleasant with my wife and to bed, minding nothing of this difference. So to sleep with a good deal of content, and saving only this night and a day or two about the same business a month or six weeks ago, I do end this month with the greatest content, and may say that these last three months, for joy, health, and profit, have been much the greatest that ever I received in all my life in any twelve months almost in my life, having nothing upon me but the consideration of the sicklinesse of the season during this great plague to mortify mee. For all which the Lord God be praised!

October 1st (Lord's day). Called up about 4 of the clock and so dressed myself and so on board the Bezan, and there finding all my company asleep I would not wake them, but it beginning to be break of day I did stay upon the decke walking, and then into the Maister's cabbin and there laid and slept a little, and so at last was waked by Captain Cocke's calling of me, and so I turned out, and then to chat and talk and laugh, and mighty merry. We spent most of the morning talking and reading of "The Siege of Rhodes," which is certainly (the more I read it the more I think so) the best poem that ever was wrote. We breakfasted betimes and come to the fleete about two of the clock in the afternoon, having a fine day and a fine winde. My Lord received us mighty kindly, and after discourse with us in general left us to our business, and he to his officers, having called a council of warr, we in the meantime settling of papers with Mr. Pierce and everybody else, and by and by with Captain

Cuttance. Anon called down to my Lord, and there with him till supper talking and discourse; among other things, to my great joy, he did assure me that he had wrote to the King and Duke about these prize-goods, and told me that they did approve of what he had done, and that he would owne what he had done, and would have me to tell all the world so, and did, under his hand, give Cocke and me his certificate of our bargains, and giving us full power of disposal of what we have so bought. This do ease my mind of all my fear, and makes my heart lighter by £100 than it was before. He did discourse to us of the Dutch fleete being abroad, eighty-five of them still, and are now at the Texell, he believes, in expectation of our Eastland ships coming home with masts and hempe, and our loaden Hambrough ships going to Hambrough. He discoursed against them that would have us yield to no conditions but conquest over the Dutch, and seems to believe that the Dutch will call for the protection of the King of France and come under his power, which were to be wished they might be brought to do under ours by fair means, and to that end would have all Dutch men and familys, that would come hither and settled, to be declared denizens; and my Lord did whisper to me alone that things here must break in pieces, nobody minding any thing, but every man his owne business of profit or pleasure, and the King some little designs of his owne, and that certainly the kingdom could not stand in this condition long, which I fear and believe is very true. So to supper and there my Lord the kindest man to me, before all the table talking of me to my advantage and with tenderness too that it overjoyed me. So after supper Captain Cocke and I and Temple on board the Bezan, and there to cards for a while and then to read again in "Rhodes" and so to sleep. But, Lord! the mirth which it caused me to be waked in the night by their snoaring round about me; I did laugh till I was ready to burst, and waked one of the two companions of Temple, who could not a good while tell where he was that he heard one laugh so, till he recollected himself, and I told him what it was at, and so to sleep again, they still snoaring.

2nd. We having sailed all night (and I do wonder how they in the dark could find the way) we got by morning to

Gillingham, and thence all walked to Chatham; and there with Commissioner Pett viewed the Yard; and among other things, a teame of four horses come close by us, he being with me, drawing a piece of timber that I am confident one man could easily have carried upon his back. I made the horses be taken away, and a man or two to take the timber away with their hands. This the Commissioner did see, but said nothing, but I think had cause to be ashamed of. We walked, he and I and Cocke, to the Hill-house, where we find Sir W. Pen in bed and there much talke and much dissembling of kindnesse from him, but he is a false rogue, and I shall not trust him, but my being there did procure his consent to have his silk carried away before the money received, which he would not have done for Cocke I am sure. Thence to Rochester, walked to the Crowne, and while dinner was getting ready, I did there walk to visit the old Castle ruines, which hath been a noble place, and there going up I did upon the stairs overtake three pretty mayds or women and took them up with me, and I did *baiser sur mouches et toucher leur mains* and necks to my great pleasure: but, Lord! to see what a dreadfull thing it is to look down the precipices, for it did fright me mightily, and hinder me of much pleasure which I would have made to myself in the company of these three, if it had not been for that. The place hath been very noble and great and strong in former ages. So to walk up and down the Cathedral, and thence to the Crowne, whither Mr. Fowler, the Mayor of the towne, was come in his gowne, and is a very reverend magistrate. After I had eat a bit, not staying to eat with them, I went away, and so took horses and to Gravesend, and there staid not, but got a boat, the sicknesse being very much in the towne still, and so called on board my Lord Bruncker and Sir John Minnes, on board one of the East Indiamen at Erith, and there do find them full of envious complaints for the pillageing of the ships, but I did pacify them, and discoursed about making money of some of the goods, and do hope to be the better by it honestly. So took leave (Madam Williams being here also with my Lord), and about 8 o'clock got to Woolwich and there supped and mighty pleasant with my wife, who is, for ought I see, all friends with her mayds, and so in great joy and content to bed.

3rd. Up, and to my great content visited betimes by Mr. Woolly, my uncle Wight's cozen, who comes to see what work I have for him about these East India goods, and I do find that this fellow might have been of great use, and hereafter may be of very great use to me, in this trade of prize goods, and glad I am fully of his coming hither. While I dressed myself, and afterwards in walking to Greenwich we did discourse over all the business of the prize goods, and he puts me in hopes I may get some money in what I have done, but not so much as I expected, but that I may hereafter do more. We have laid a design of getting more, and are to talk again of it a few days hence. To the office, where nobody to meet me, Sir W. Batten being the only man and he gone this day to meet to adjourne the Parliament to Oxford. Anon by appointment comes one to tell me my Lord Rutherford is come; so I to the King's Head to him, where I find his lady,[1] a fine young Scotch lady, pretty handsome and plain. My wife also, and Mercer, by and by comes, Creed bringing them; and so presently to dinner and very merry; and after to even our accounts, and I to give him tallys, where he do allow me £100, of which to my grief the rogue Creed has trepanned me out of £50. But I do foresee a way how it may be I may get a greater sum of my Lord to his content by getting him allowance of interest upon his tallys. That being done, and some musique and other diversions, at last away goes my Lord and Lady, and I sent my wife to visit Mrs. Pierce, and so I to my office, where wrote important letters to the Court, and at night (Creed having clownishly left my wife), I to Mrs. Pierce's, and brought her and Mrs. Pierce to the King's Head and there spent a piece upon a supper for her and mighty merry and pretty discourse, she being as pretty as ever, most of our mirth being upon "my Cozen" (meaning my Lord Bruncker's ugly mistress, whom he calls cozen), and to my trouble she tells me that the fine Mrs. Middleton is noted for carrying about her body a continued sour base smell, that is very offensive, especially if she be a little hot. Here some bad musique to close the night and so away and all of us saw Mrs. Belle Pierce (as pretty as ever she was

[1] Christian, daughter of Sir Alexander Urquhart of Cromarty. — B.

almost) home, and so walked to Will's lodging where I used to lie, and there made shift for a bed for Mercer, and mighty pleasantly to bed. This night I hear that of our two watermen that use to carry our letters, and were well on Saturday last, one is dead, and the other dying sick of the plague. The plague, though decreasing elsewhere, yet being greater about the Tower and thereabouts.

4th. Up and to my office, where Mr. Andrews comes, and reckoning with him I get £64 of him. By and by comes Mr. Gawden, and reckoning with him he gives me £60 in his account, which is a great mercy to me. Then both of them met and discoursed the business of the first man's resigning and the others taking up the business of the victualling of Tangier, and I do not think that I shall be able to do as well under Mr. Gawden as under these men, or within a little as to profit and less care upon me. Thence to the King's Head to dinner, where we three and Creed and my wife and her woman dined mighty merry and sat long talking, and so in the afternoon broke up, and I led my wife to our lodging again, and I to the office where did much business, and so to my wife. This night comes Sir George Smith[1] to see me at the office, and tells me how the plague is decreased this week 740, for which God be praised! but that it encreases at our end of the town still, and says how all the towne is full of Captain Cocke's being in some ill condition about prize-goods, his goods being taken from him, and I know not what. But though this troubles me to have it said, and that it is likely to be a business in Parliament, yet I am not much concerned at it, because yet I believe this newes is all false, for he would have wrote to me sure about it. Being come to my wife, at our lodging, I did go to bed, and left my wife with her people to laugh and dance and I to sleep.

5th. Lay long in bed talking among other things of my sister Pall, and my wife of herself is very willing that I should give her £400 to her portion, and would have her married soon as we could; but this great sicknesse time do make it unfit to send for her up. I abroad to the office and thence to the Duke of Albemarle, all my way reading a book

[1] See August 16th, 1665.

of Mr. Evelyn's translating and sending me as a present, about directions for gathering a Library;[1] but the book is above my reach, but his epistle to my Lord Chancellor is a very fine piece. When I come to the Duke it was about the victuallers' business, to put it into other hands, or more hands, which I do advise in, but I hope to do myself a jobb of work in it. So I walked through Westminster to my old house the Swan, and there did pass some time with Sarah, and so down by water to Deptford and there to my Valentine.[2] Round about and next door on every side is the plague, but I did not value it, but there did what I would *con elle*, and so away to Mr. Evelyn's to discourse of our confounded business of prisoners, and sick and wounded seamen, wherein he and we are so much put out of order.[3] And here he showed me his gardens, which are for variety of evergreens, and hedge of holly, the finest things I ever saw in my life.[4] Thence in his coach to Greenwich, and there to my office, all the way having fine discourse of trees and the nature of vegetables. And so to write letters, I very late to Sir W. Coventry of great concernment, and so to my last night's lodging, but my wife is gone home to Wool-

[1] "Instructions concerning erecting of a Library, presented to my Lord the President De Mesme by Gilbert Naudeus, and now interpreted by Jo. Evelyn, Esquire. London, 1661." This little book was dedicated to Lord Clarendon by the translator. It was printed while Evelyn was abroad, and is full of typographical errors; these are corrected in a copy mentioned in Evelyn's "Miscellaneous Writings," 1825, p. xii., where a letter to Dr. Godolphin on the subject is printed.

[2] Mrs. Bagwell. See *ante*, February 14th, 1664–65

[3] Each of the Commissioners for the Sick and Wounded was appointed to a particular district, and Evelyn's district was Kent and Sussex. On September 25th, 1665, Evelyn wrote in his Diary: "My Lord Admiral being come from ye fleete to Greenewich, I went thence with him to ye Cockpit to consult with the Duke of Albemarle. I was peremptory that unlesse we had £10,000 immediately, the prisoners would starve, and 'twas proposed it should be rais'd out of the E. India prizes now taken by Lord Sandwich. They being but two of ye Commission, and so not impower'd to determine, sent an expresse to his Majesty and Council to know what they should do."

[4] Evelyn purchased Sayes Court, Deptford, in 1653, and laid out his gardens, walks, groves, enclosures, and plantations, which afterwards became famous for their beauty. When he took the place in hand it was nothing but an open field of one hundred acres, with scarcely a hedge in it.

wich. The Bill, blessed be God! is less this week by 740 of what it was the last week. Being come to my lodging I got something to eat, having eat little all the day, and so to bed, having this night renewed my promises of observing my vowes as I used to do; for I find that, since I left them off, my mind is run a' wool-gathering and my business neglected.

6th. Up, and having sent for Mr. Gawden he come to me, and he and I largely discoursed the business of his Victualling, in order to the adding of partners to him or other ways of altering it, wherein I find him ready to do anything the King would have him do. So he and I took his coach and to Lambeth and to the Duke of Albemarle about it, and so back again, where he left me. In our way discoursing of the business and contracting a great friendship with him, and I find he is a man most worthy to be made a friend, being very honest and gratefull, and in the freedom of our discourse he did tell me his opinion and knowledge of Sir W. Pen to be, what I know him to be, as false a man as ever was born, for so, it seems, he hath been to him. He did also tell me, discoursing how things are governed as to the King's treasure, that, having occasion for money in the country, he did offer Alderman Maynell to pay him down money here, to be paid by the Receiver in some county in the country, upon whom Maynell had assignments, in whose hands the money also lay ready. But Maynell refused it, saying that he could have his money when he would, and had rather it should lie where it do than receive it here in towne this sickly time, where he hath no occasion for it. But now the evil is that he hath lent this money upon tallys which are become payable, but he finds that nobody looks after it, how long the money is unpaid, and whether it lies dead in the Receiver's hands or no, so the King he pays Maynell 10 per cent. while the money lies in his Receiver's hands to no purpose but the benefit of the Receiver. I to dinner to the King's Head with Mr. Woolly, who is come to instruct me in the business of my goods, but gives me not so good comfort as I thought I should have had. But, however, it will be well worth my time though not above 2 or £300. He gone I to my office, where very busy drawing up a letter by way of discourse to the Duke of Albemarle about my conception how the business of the Victualling should be ordered, wherein I have taken great pains, and I think have hitt the right if they will but follow it. At this very late and so home to our lodgings to bed.

7th. Up and to the office along with Mr. Childe, whom I sent for to discourse about the victualling business, who will not come into partnership (no more will Captain Beckford[1]), but I do find him a mighty understanding man, and one I will keep a knowledge of. Did business, though not much, at the office; because of the horrible crowd and lamentable moan of the poor seamen that lie starving in the streets for lack of money. Which do trouble and perplex me to the heart; and more at noon when we were to go through them, for then a whole hundred of them followed us; some cursing, some swearing, and some praying to us. And that that made me more troubled was a letter come this afternoon from the Duke of Albemarle, signifying the Dutch to be in sight, with 80 sayle, yesterday morning, off of Solebay, coming right into the bay. God knows what they will and may do to us, we having no force abroad able to oppose them, but to be sacrificed to them. Here come Sir W. Rider to me, whom I sent for about the victualling business also, but he neither will not come into partnership, but desires to be of the Commission if there be one. Thence back the back way to my office, where very late, very busy. But most of all when at night come two waggons from Rochester with more goods from Captain Cocke; and in houseing them at Mr. Tooker's[2] lodgings come two of the Custome-house to seize them and did

[1] Apparently Thomas Beckford the slopseller, who was afterwards knighted (see note, January 5th, 1660–61). Mr. Frank Cundall has written a valuable article on the Beckfords in the "Journal of the Institute of Jamaica," vol. i., no. 8, p. 349. Mr. Cundall suggested to the editor that this may be Captain Edward Beckford, who is mentioned in a deposition dated December 18th, 1668, calendared by Mr. W. Noel Sainsbury in the "Calendar of State Papers," Colonial Series (America and West Indies, 1661–68, p. 635). Thomas Beckford, however, is referred to in August, 1666, as Major Beckford, and therefore he may well have been a captain in 1665.

[2] John Tooker, Navy Office messenger. See *ante*, April 5th.

seize them: but I showed them my *Transire*. However, after some hot and angry words, we locked them up, and sealed up the key, and did give it to the constable to keep till Monday, and so parted. But, Lord! to think how the poor constable come to me in the dark going home; "Sir," says he, "I have the key, and if you would have me do any service for you, send for me betimes to-morrow morning, and I will do what you would have me." Whether the fellow do this out of kindness or knavery, I cannot tell; but it is pretty to observe. Talking with him in the high way, come close by the bearers with a dead corpse of the plague; but, Lord! to see what custom is, that I am come almost to think nothing of it. So to my lodging, and there, with Mr. Hater and Will, ending a business of the state of the last six months' charge of the Navy, which we bring to £1,000,000 and above, and I think we do not enlarge much in it if anything. So to bed.

8th (Lord's day). Up and, after being trimmed, to the office, whither I upon a letter from the Duke of Albemarle to me, to order as many ships forth out of the river as I can presently, to joyne to meet the Dutch; having ordered all the Captains of the ships in the river to come to me, I did some business with them, and so to Captain Cocke's to dinner, he being in the country. But here his brother Solomon was, and, for guests, myself, Sir. G. Smith, and a very fine lady, one Mrs. Penington,[1] and two more gentlemen. But, both [before] and after dinner, most witty discourse with this lady, who is a very fine witty lady, one of the best I ever heard speake, and indifferent handsome. There after dinner an houre or two, and so to the office, where ended my business with the Captains; and I think of twenty-two ships we shall make shift to get out seven. (God helpe us! men being sick, or provisions lacking.)

[1] Judith Penington was daughter of the Parliamentarian Alderman Isaac Penington, and sister of Isaac Penington the Quaker, and of Arthur Penington, who became a Roman Catholic priest. A letter to Judith Penington from her brother Isaac, in which he addresses her on her religious state, is printed in Maria Webb's "The Penns and Peningtons of the Seventeenth Century," 1867, p. 311: "Is thy soul in unity with God, or art thou separated from Him? Whither art thou travelling? oh, whither art thou travelling?"

And so to write letters to Sir Ph. Warwicke, Sir W. Coventry, and Sir G. Carteret to Court about the last six months' accounts, and sent away by an express to-night. This day I hear the Pope is dead;[1] and one said, that the newes is, that the King of France is stabbed, but that the former is very true, which will do great things sure, as to the troubling of that part of the world, the King of Spayne being so lately dead.[2] And one thing more, Sir Martin Noell's lady is dead with griefe for the death of her husband and nothing else, as they say, in the world; but it seems nobody can make anything of his estate, whether he be dead worth anything or no, he having dealt in so many things, publique and private, as nobody can understand whereabouts his estate is, which is the fate of these great dealers at everything. So after my business being done I home to my lodging and to bed.

9th. Up, my head full of business, and called upon also by Sir John Shaw, to whom I did give a civil answer about our prize goods, that all his dues as one of the Farmers of the Customes are paid, and showed him our *Transire;* with which he was satisfied, and parted, ordering his servants to see the weight of them. I to the office, and there found an order for my coming presently to the Duke of Albemarle, and what should it be, but to tell me, that, if my Lord Sandwich do not come to towne, he do resolve to go with the fleete to sea himself, the Dutch, as he thinks, being in the Downes, and so desired me to get a pleasure boat for to take him in to-morrow morning, and do many other things, and with a great liking of me, and my management especially, as that coxcombe my Lord Craven do tell me, and I perceive it, and I am sure take pains enough to deserve it. Thence away and to the office at London, where I did some business about my money and private accounts, and there eat a bit of goose of Mr. Griffin's, and so by water, it raining most miserably, to Greenwich, calling on several vessels in my passage. Being come there I hear another seizure hath been made of our goods by one Captain Fisher that hath been at Chat-

[1] A false report. Alexander VII. did not die till 1667.

[2] Philip IV., King of Spain, who succeeded to the throne in 1621, died in 1665. He was succeeded by his son Charles II.

ham by warrant of the Duke of Albemarle, and is come in my absence to Tooker's and viewed them, demanding the key of the constable, and so sealed up the door. I to the house, but there being no officers nor constable could do nothing, but back to my office full of trouble about this, and there late about business, vexed to see myself fall into this trouble and concernment in a thing that I want instruction from my Lord Sandwich whether I should appear in it or no, and so home to bed, having spent two hours, I and my boy, at Mr. Glanvill's removing of faggots to make room to remove our goods to, but when done I thought it not fit to use it. The newes of the killing of the [King of] France is wholly untrue, and they say that of the Pope too.

10th. Up, and receive a stop from the Duke of Albemarle of setting out any more ships, or providing a pleasure boat for himself, which I am glad of, and do see, what I thought yesterday, that this resolution of his was a sudden one and silly. By and by comes Captain Cocke's Jacob to tell me that he is come from Chatham this morning, and that there are four waggons of goods at hand coming to towne, which troubles me. I directed him to bring them to his master's house. But before I could send him away to bring them thither, newes is brought me that they are seized on in the towne by this Captain Fisher and they will carry them to another place. So I to them and found our four waggons in the streete stopped by the church by this Fisher and company and 100 or 200 people in the streetes gazing. I did give them good words, and made modest desires of carrying the goods to Captain Cocke's, but they would have them to a house of their hiring, where in a barne the goods were laid. I had *transires* to show for all, and the tale was right, and there I spent all the morning seeing this done. At which Fisher was vexed that I would not let it be done by any body else for the merchant, and that I must needs be concerned therein, which I did not think fit to owne. So that being done, I left the goods to be watched by men on their part and ours, and so to the office by noon, whither by and by comes Captain Cocke, whom I had with great care sent for by expresse the last night, and so I with him to his house and there eat a bit, and so by coach to Lambeth, and I took occasion first to go to the Duke of Albemarle to acquaint him with some thing of what had been done this morning in behalf of a friend absent, which did give a good entrance and prevented their possessing the Duke with anything of evil of me by their report, and by and by in comes Captain Cocke and tells his whole story. So an order was made for the putting him in possession upon giving security to be accountable for the goods, which for the present did satisfy us, and so away, giving Locke that drew the order a piece. (Lord! to see how unhappily a man may fall into a necessity of bribing people to do him right in a thing, wherein he hath done nothing but fair, and bought dear.) So to the office, there to write my letters, and Cocke comes to tell me that Fisher is come to him, and that he doubts not to cajole Fisher and his companion and make them friends with drink and a bribe. This night comes Sir Christopher Mings to towne, and I went to see him, and by and by he being then out of the town comes to see me. He is newly come from Court,[1] and carries direction for the making a show of getting out the fleete again to go fight the Dutch, but that it will end in a fleete of 20 good sayling frigates to go to the Northward or Southward, and that will be all. I enquired, but he would not be to know that he had heard any thing at Oxford about the business of the prize goods, which I did suspect, but he being gone, anon comes Cocke and tells me that he hath been with him a great while, and that he finds him sullen and speaking very high what disrespect he had received of my Lord, saying that he hath walked 3 or 4 hours together at that Earle's cabbin door for audience and could not be received, which, if true, I am sorry for. He tells me that Sir G. Ascue says, that he did from the beginning declare against these [prize] goods, and would not receive his dividend; and that he and Sir W. Pen are at odds about it, and that he fears Mings hath been doing ill offices to my Lord. I did to-night give my Lord an account of all this, and so home and to bed.

11th. Up, and so in my chamber staid all the morning doing something toward my Tangier accounts, for the stat-

[1] The King and Court removed to Oxford from Salisbury on September 23rd.

ing of them, and also comes up my landlady, Mrs. Clerke, to make an agreement for the time to come; and I, for the having room enough, and to keepe out strangers, and to have a place to retreat to for my wife, if the sicknesse should come to Woolwich, am contented to pay dear; so for three rooms and a dining-room, and for linen and bread and beer and butter, at nights and mornings, I am to give her £5 10*s*. per month, and I wrote and we signed to an agreement. By and by comes Cocke to tell me that Fisher and his fellow were last night mightily satisfied and promised all friendship, but this morning he finds them to have new tricks and shall be troubled with them. So he being to go down to Erith with them this afternoon about giving security, I advised him to let them go by land, and so he and I (having eat something at his house) by water to Erith, but they got thither before us, and there we met Mr. Seymour, one of the Commissioners for Prizes, and a Parliament-man, and he was mighty high, and had now seized our goods on their behalf; and he mighty imperiously would have all forfeited, and I know not what. I thought I was in the right in a thing I said and spoke somewhat earnestly, so we took up one another very smartly, for which I was sorry afterwards, shewing thereby myself too much concerned, but nothing passed that I valued at all. But I could not but think [it odd] that a Parliament-man, in a serious discourse before such persons as we and my Lord Bruncker, and Sir John Minnes, should quote Hudibras, as being the book I doubt he hath read most They I doubt will stand hard for high security, and Cocke would have had me bound with him for his appearing, but I did stagger at it, besides Seymour do stop the doing it at all till he has been with the Duke of Albemarle. So there will be another demurre. It growing late, and I having something to do at home, took my leave alone, leaving Cocke there for all night, and so against tide and in the darke and very cold weather to Woolwich, where we had appointed to keepe the night merrily; and so, by Captain Cocke's coach, had brought a very pretty child, a daughter of one Mrs. Tooker's, next door to my lodging, and so she, and a daughter and kinsman of Mrs. Pett's made up a fine company at my lodgings at Woolwich, where my wife and Mercer, and Mrs. Barbara danced, and mighty merry we were, but especially at Mercer's dancing a jigg, which she does the best I ever did see, having the most natural way of it, and keeps time the most perfectly I ever did see. This night is kept in lieu of yesterday, for my wedding day of ten years; for which God be praised! being now in an extreme good condition of health and estate and honour, and a way of getting more money, though at this houre under some discomposure, rather than damage, about some prize goods that I have bought off the fleete, in partnership with Captain Cocke; and for the discourse about the world concerning my Lord Sandwich, that he hath done a thing so bad; and indeed it must needs have been a very rash act; and the rather because of a Parliament now newly met to give money, and will have some account of what hath already been spent, besides the precedent for a General to take what prizes he pleases, and the giving a pretence to take away much more than he intended, and all will lie upon him; and not giving to all the Commanders, as well as the Flaggs, he displeases all them, and offends even some of them, thinking others to be better served than themselves; and lastly, puts himself out of a power of begging anything again a great while of the King. Having danced with my people as long as I saw fit to sit up, I to bed and left them to do what they would. I forgot that we had W. Hewer there, and Tom, and Golding, my barber at Greenwich, for our fiddler, to whom I did give 10*s*.

12th. Called up before day, and so I dressed myself and down, it being horrid cold, by water to my Lord Bruncker's ship, who advised me to do so, and it was civilly to show me what the King had commanded about the prize-goods, to examine most severely all that had been done in the taking out any with or without order, without respect to my Lord Sandwich at all, and that he had been doing of it, and find him examining one man, and I do find that extreme ill use was made of my Lord's order. For they did toss and tumble and spoil and breake things in hold to a great losse and shame to come at the fine goods, and did take a man that knows where the fine goods were, and did this over and over again for many days, Sir W. Berkeley being the chief hand that did it, but others did the like at other times, and they did say in doing it that my Lord Sandwich's back was broad enough to bear it. Having learned as much as I could, which was, that the King and Duke were very severe in this point, whatever order they before had given my Lord in approbation of what he had done, and that all will come out and the King see, by the entries at the Custome House, what all do amount to that had been taken, and so I took leave, and by water, very cold, and to Woolwich where it was now noon, and so I staid dinner and talking part of the afternoon, and then by coach, Captain Cocke's, to Greenwich, taking the young lady home, and so to Cocke, and he tells me that he hath cajolled with Seymour, who will be our friend; but that, above all, Seymour tells him, that my Lord Duke did shew him to-day an order from Court, for having all respect paid to the Earle of Sandwich, and what goods had been delivered by his order, which do overjoy us, and that to-morrow our goods shall be weighed, and he doubts not possession to-morrow or next day. Being overjoyed at this I to write my letters, and at it very late. Good newes this week that there are about 600 less dead of the plague than the last. So home to bed.

13th. Lay long, and this morning comes Sir Jer. Smith[1] to see me in his way to Court, and a good man he is, and one that I must keep fair with, and will, it being I perceive my interest to have kindnesse with the Commanders. So to the office, and there very busy till about noon comes Sir W. Warren, and he goes and gets a bit of meat ready at the King's Head for us, and I by and by thither, and we dined together, and I am not pleased with him about a little business of Tangier that I put to him to do for me, but however, the hurt is not much, and his other matters of profit to me continue very likely to be good. Here we spent till 2 o'clock, and so I set him on shore, and I by water to the Duke of Albemarle, where I find him with Lord Craven and Lieutenant of the Tower about him; among other things, talking of ships to get of the King to fetch coles for the poore of the city, which is a good worke.

[1] Captain Jeremiah Smith (or Smyth), knighted June, 1665; Admiral of the Blue in 1666. He succeeded Sir William Penn as Comptroller of the Victualling Accounts in 1669, and held the office until 1675.

But, Lord! to hear the silly talke between these three great people! Yet I have no reason to find fault, the Duke and Lord Craven being my very great friends. Here did the business I come about, and so back home by water, and there Cocke comes to me and tells me that he is come to an understanding with Fisher, and that he must give him £100, and that he shall have his goods in possession to-morrow, they being all weighed to-day, which pleases me very well. This day the Duke tells me that there is no news heard of the Dutch, what they do or where they are, but believes that they are all gone home, for none of our spyes can give us any tideings of them. Cocke is fain to keep these people, Fisher and his fellow, company night and day to keep them friends almost and great troubles withal. My head is full of settling the victualling business also, that I may make some profit out of it, which I hope justly to do to the King's advantage. To-night come Sir J. Bankes to me upon my letter to discourse it with him, and he did give me the advice I have taken almost as fully as if I had been directed by him what to write. The business also of my Tangier accounts to be sent to Court is upon my hands in great haste; besides, all my owne proper accounts are in great disorder, having been neglected now above a month, which grieves me, but it could not be settled sooner. These together and the feare of the sicknesse and providing for my family do fill my head very full, besides the infinite business of the office, and nobody here to look after it but myself. So late from my office to my lodgings, and to bed.

14th. Up, and to the office, where mighty busy, especially with Mr. Gawden, with whom I shall, I think, have much to do, and by and by comes the Lieutenant of the Tower by my invitation yesterday, but I had got nothing for him, it is to discourse about the Cole shipps. So he went away to Sheriffe Hooker's, and I staid at the office till he sent for me at noon to dinner, I very hungry. When I come to the Sheriffe's he was not there, nor in many other places, nor could I find him at all, so was forced to come to the office and get a bit of meat from the taverne, and so to my business. By and by comes the Lieutenant and reproaches me with my not treating him as I ought.

but all in jest, he it seemed dined with Mr. Adrian May. Very late writing letters at the office, and much satisfied to hear from Captain Cocke that he had got possession of some of his goods to his own house, and expected to have all to-night. The towne, I hear, is full of talke that there are great differences in the fleete among the great Commanders, and that Mings at Oxford did impeach my Lord of something, I think about these goods, but this is but talke. But my heart and head to-night is full of the Victualling business, being overjoyed and proud at my success in my proposal about it, it being read before the King, Duke, and the Caball with complete applause and satisfaction. This Sir G. Carteret and Sir W. Coventry both writ me, besides Sir W. Coventry's letter to the Duke of Albemarle, which I read yesterday, and I hope to find my profit in it also. So late home to bed.

15th (Lord's day). Up, and while I staid for the barber, tried to compose a duo of counterpoint, and I think it will do very well, it being by Mr. Berckenshaw's rule. By and by by appointment comes Mr. Povy's coach, and, more than I expected, him himself, to fetch me to Brainford: so he and I immediately set out, having drunk a draft of mulled sacke; and so rode most nobly, in his most pretty and best contrived charriott in the world, with many new conveniences, his never having till now, within a day or two, been yet finished; our discourse upon Tangier business, want of money, and then of publique miscarriages, nobody minding the publique, but every body himself and his lusts. Anon we come to his house, and there I eat a bit, and so with fresh horses, his noble fine horses, the best confessedly in England, the King having none such, he sent me to Sir Robert Viner's,[1] whom I met coming just from church, and so after having spent half-an-hour almost looking upon the horses with some gentlemen that were in company, he and I into his garden to discourse of money, but none is to be had, he confessing himself in great straits, and I believe it. Having this answer, and that I could not get better, we fell to publique talke, and to think how the fleete and seamen will be paid, which he protests he do not think it

[1] At Swakeley House. See September 7th, 1665.

possible to compass, as the world is now: no money got by trade, nor the persons that have it by them in the City to be come at. The Parliament, it seems, have voted the King £1,250,000 at £50,000 per month, tax for the war; and voted to assist the King against the Dutch, and all that shall adhere to them; and thanks to be given him for his care of the Duke of Yorke, which last is a very popular vote on the Duke's behalf. He tells me how the taxes of the last assessment, which should have been in good part gathered, are not yet laid, and that even in part of the City of London; and the Chimny-money comes almost to nothing, nor any thing else looked after. Having done this I parted, my mind not eased by any money, but only that I had done my part to the King's service. And so in a very pleasant evening back to Mr. Povy's, and there supped, and after supper to talke and to sing, his man Dutton's wife singing very pleasantly (a mighty fat woman), and I wrote out one song from her and pricked the tune, both very pretty. But I did never heare one sing with so much pleasure to herself as this lady do, relishing it to her very heart, which was mighty pleasant.

16th. Up about seven o'clock; and, after drinking, and I observing Mr. Povy's being mightily mortifyed in his eating and drinking, and coaches and horses, he desiring to sell his best, and every thing else, his furniture of his house, he walked with me to Syon,[1] and there I took water, in our way he discoursing of the wantonnesse of the Court, and how it minds nothing else, and I saying that that would leave the King shortly if he did not leave it, he told me "No," for the King do spend most of his time in feeling and kissing them naked. . . . But this lechery will never leave him. Here I took boat (leaving him there) and down to the Tower, where I hear the Duke of Albemarle is, and I to Lumbard Streete, but can get no money. So upon the Exchange, which is very empty, God knows! and but mean people there. The newes for certain that

[1] Sion House, granted by Edward VI. to his uncle, the Duke of Somerset. After his execution, 1552, it was forfeited, and given to John Dudley, Duke of Northumberland. The duke being beheaded in 1553, it reverted to the Crown, and was granted in 1604 to Henry Percy, Earl of Northumberland. It still belongs to the Duke of Northumberland.

the Dutch are come with their fleete before Margett, and some men were endeavouring to come on shore when the post come away, perhaps to steal some sheep. But, Lord! how Colvill talks of the businesse of publique revenue like a madman, and yet I doubt all true; that nobody minds it, but that the King and Kingdom must speedily be undone, and rails at my Lord about the prizes, but I think knows not my relation to him. Here I endeavoured to satisfy all I could, people about Bills of Exchange from Tangier, but it is only with good words, for money I have not, nor can get. God knows what will become of all the King's matters in a little time, for he runs in debt every day, and nothing to pay them looked after. Thence I walked to the Tower; but, Lord! how empty the streets are and melancholy, so many poor sick people in the streets full of sores; and so many sad stories overheard as I walk, every body talking of this dead, and that man sick, and so many in this place, and so many in that. And they tell me that, in Westminster, there is never a physician and but one apothecary left, all being dead; but that there are great hopes of a great decrease this week: God send it! At the Tower found my Lord Duke[1] and Duchesse at dinner; so I sat down. And much good cheer, the Lieutenant and his lady, and several officers with the Duke. But, Lord! to hear the silly talk that was there, would make one mad; the Duke having none almost but fools about him. Much of their talke about the Dutch coming on shore, which they believe they may some of them have been and steal sheep, and speak all in reproach of them in whose hands the fleete is; but, Lord helpe him, there is something will hinder him and all the world in going to sea, which is want of victuals; for we have not wherewith to answer our service; and how much better it would have been if the Duke's advice had been taken for the fleete to have gone presently out; but, God helpe the King! while no better counsels are given, and what is given no better taken. Thence after dinner receiving many commands from the Duke, I to our office on the Hill, and there did a little business and to Colvill's again, and so took water at the Tower, and there

[1] Monk, Duke of Albemarle.

met with Captain Cocke, and he down with me to Greenwich, I having received letters from my Lord Sandwich to-day, speaking very high about the prize goods, that he would have us to fear nobody, but be very confident in what we have done, and not to confess any fault or doubt of what he hath done; for the King hath allowed it, and do now confirm it, and sent orders, as he says, for nothing to be disturbed that his Lordshipp hath ordered therein as to the division of the goods to the fleete; which do comfort us, but my Lord writes to me that both he and I may hence learn by what we see in this business. But that which pleases me best is that Cocke tells me that he now understands that Fisher was set on in this business by the design of some of the Duke of Albemarle's people, Warcupp and others, who lent him money to set him out in it, and he has spent high. Who now curse him for a rogue to take £100 when he might have had as well £1500, and they are mightily fallen out about it. Which in due time shall be discovered, but that now that troubles me afresh is, after I am got to the office at Greenwich that some new troubles are come, and Captain Cocke's house is beset before and behind with guards, and more, I do fear they may come to my office here to search for Cocke's goods and find some small things of my clerk's. So I assisted them in helping to remove their small trade, but by and by I am told that it is only the Custome House men who came to seize the things that did lie at Mr. Glanville's, for which they did never yet see our *Transire*, nor did know of them till to-day. So that my fear is now over, for a *transire* is ready for them. Cocke did get a great many of his goods to London to-day. To the Still Yarde, which place, however, is now shut up of the plague; but I was there, and we now make no bones of it. Much talke there is of the Chancellor's speech and the King's at the Parliament's meeting, which are very well liked; and that we shall certainly, by their speeches, fall out with France at this time, together with the Dutch, which will find us work. Late at the office entering my Journall for 8 days past, the greatness of my business hindering me of late to put it down daily, but I have done it now very true and particularly, and hereafter will, I hope, be able to fall into my old way of doing it daily. So to my lodging, and there had a good pullet to my supper, and so to bed, it being very cold again, God be thanked for it!

17th. Up, and all day long busy at the office, mighty busy, only stepped to my lodging and had a fowl for my dinner, and at night my wife and Mercer comes to me, which troubled me a little because I am to be mighty busy to-morrow all day seriously about my accounts. So late from my office to her, and supped, and so to bed.

18th. Up, and after some pleasant discourse with my wife (though my head full of business) I out and left her to go home, and myself to the office, and thence by water to the Duke of Albemarle's, and so back again and find my wife gone. So to my chamber at my lodgings, and to the making of my accounts up of Tangier, which I did with great difficulty, finding the difference between short and long reckonings where I have had occasion to mix my moneys, as I have of late done my Tangier treasure upon other occasions, and other moneys upon that. However, I was at it late and did it pretty perfectly, and so, after eating something, to bed, my mind eased of a great deal of figures and castings.

19th. Up, and to my accounts again, and stated them very clear and fair, and at noon dined at my lodgings with Mr. Hater and W. Hewer at table with me, I being come to an agreement yesterday with my landlady for £6 per month, for so many rooms for myself, them, and my wife and mayde, when she shall come, and to pay besides for my dyett. After dinner I did give them my accounts and letters to write against I went to the Duke of Albemarle's this evening, which I did; and among other things, spoke to him for my wife's brother, Balty, to be of his guard, which he kindly answered that he should. My business of the Victualling goes on as I would have it; and now my head is full how to make some profit of it to myself or people. To that end, when I came home, I wrote a letter to Mr. Coventry, offering myself to be the Surveyor Generall, and am apt to think he will assist me in it, but I do not set my heart much on it, though it would be a good helpe. So back to my office, and there till past one before I could get all these letters and papers copied out, which vexed me, but so sent them away without hopes of saving the post, and so to my lodging to bed.

20th. Up, and had my last night's letters brought back to me, which troubles me, because of my accounts, lest they should be asked for before they come, which I abhorr, being more ready to give than they can be to demand them: so I sent away an expresse to Oxford with them, and another to Portsmouth, with a copy of my letter to Mr. Coventry about my victualling business, for fear he should be gone from Oxford, as he intended, thither. So busy all the morning and at noon to Cocke, and dined there. He and I alone, vexed that we are not rid of all our trouble about our goods, but it is almost over, and in the afternoon to my lodging, and there spent the whole afternoon and evening with Mr. Hater, discoursing of the business of the office, where he tells me that among others Thomas Willson do now and then seem to hint that I do take too much business upon me, more than I can do, and that therefore some do lie undone. This I confess to my trouble is true, but it arises from my being forced to take so much on me, more than is my proper task to undertake. But for this at last I did advise to him to take another clerk if he thinks fit, I will take care to have him paid. I discoursed also much with him about persons fit to be put into the victualling business, and such as I could spare something out of their salaries for them, but without trouble I cannot, I see, well do it, because Thomas Willson must have the refusal of the best place which is London of £200 per annum, which I did intend for Tooker, and to get £50 out of it as a help to Mr. Hater. How[ever], I will try to do something of this kind for them. Having done discourse with him late, I to enter my Tangier accounts fair, and so to supper and to bed.

21st. Up, and to my office, where busy all the morning, and then with my two clerks home to dinner, and so back again to the office, and there very late very busy, and so home to supper and to bed.

22nd (Lord's day). Up, and after ready and going to Captain Cocke's, where I find we are a little further safe in some part of our goods, I to Church, in my way was meeting with some letters, which made me resolve to go after church to my Lord Duke of Albemarle's, so, after sermon, I took Cocke's chariott, and to Lambeth; but, in going and getting over the water, and through White Hall, I spent so much time, the Duke had almost dined. However, fresh meat was brought for me to his table, and there I dined, and full of discourse and very kind. Here they are again talking of the prizes, and my Lord Duke did speake very broad that my Lord Sandwich and Pen should do what they would, and answer for themselves. For his part, he would lay all before the King. Here he tells me the Dutch Embassador at Oxford is clapped up, but since I hear it is not true. Thence back again, it being evening before I could get home, and there Cocke not being within, I and Mr. Salomon to Mr. Glanville's, and there we found Cocke and sat and supped, and was mighty merry with only Madam Penington,[1] who is a fine, witty lady. Here we spent the evening late with great mirth, and so home and to bed.

23rd. Up, and after doing some business I down by water, calling to see my wife, with whom very merry for ten minutes, and so to Erith, where my Lord Bruncker and I kept the office, and dispatched some business by appointment on the Bezan. Among other things about the slop-sellers, who have trusted us so long, they are not able, nor can be expected to trust us further, and I fear this winter the fleete will be undone by that particular. Thence on board the East India ship, where my Lord Bruncker had provided a great dinner, and thither comes by and by Sir John Minnes and before him Sir W. Warren and anon a Perspective glasse maker, of whom we, every one, bought a pocket glasse. But I am troubled with the much talke and conceitedness of Mrs. Williams and her impudence, in case she be not married to my Lord. They are getting themselves ready to deliver the goods all out to the East India Company, who are to have the goods in their possession and to advance two thirds of the moderate value thereof and sell them as well as they can and the King to give them 6 per cent. for the use of the money they shall so advance. By this means the company will not suffer by

[1] Judith Penington. See *ante*, October 8th.

the King's goods bringing down the price of their own. Thence in the evening back again with Sir W. Warren and Captain Taylor in my boat, and the latter went with me to the office, and there he and I reckoned; and I perceive I shall get £100 profit by my services of late to him, which is a very good thing. Thence to my lodging, where I find my Lord Rutherford, of which I was glad. We supped together and sat up late, he being a mighty wanton man with a daughter in law of my landlady's, a pretty conceited woman big with child, and he would be handling her breasts, which she coyly refused. But they gone, my Lord and I to business, and he would have me forbear paying Alderman Backewell the money ordered him, which I, in hopes to advantage myself, shall forbear, but do not think that my Lord will do any thing gratefully more to me than he hath done, not that I shall get any thing as I pretended by helping him to interest for his last £7,700, which I could do, and do him a courtesy too. Discourse being done, he to bed in my chamber and I to another in the house.

24th. Lay long, having a cold. Then to my Lord and sent him going to Oxford, and I to my office, whither comes Sir William Batten now newly from Oxford. I can gather nothing from him about my Lord Sandwich about the business of the prizes, he being close, but he shewed me a bill which hath been read in the House making all breaking of bulke for the time to come felony, but it is a foolish Act, and will do no great matter, only is calculated to my Lord Sandwich's case. He shewed me also a good letter printed from the Bishopp of Munster to the States of Holland shewing the state of their case. Here we did some business and so broke up and I to Cocke, where Mr. Evelyn was, to dinner, and there merry, yet vexed again at publique matters, and to see how little heed is had to the prisoners and sicke and wounded. Thence to my office, and no sooner there but to my great surprise am told that my Lord Sandwich is come to towne; so I presently to Boreman's, where he is and there found him: he mighty kind to me, but no opportunity of discourse private yet, which he tells me he must have with me; only his business is sudden to go to the fleete, to get out a few ships to drive away the Dutch. I left him in discourse with Sir W. Batten and others, and myself to the office till about 10 at night and so, letters being done, I to him again to Captain Cocke's, where he supped, and lies, and never saw him more merry, and here is Charles Herbert,[1] who the King hath lately knighted. My Lord, to my great content, did tell me before them, that never anything was read to the King and Council, all the chief Ministers of State being there, as my letter about the Victualling was, and no more said upon it than a most thorough consent to every word was said, and directed, that it be pursued and practised. After much mirth, and my Lord having travelled all night last night, he to bed, and we all parted, I home.

25th. Up, and to my Lord Sandwich's, where several Commanders, of whom I took the state of all their ships, and of all could find not above four capable of going out. The truth is, the want of victuals being the whole overthrow of this yeare both at sea, and now at the Nore here and Portsmouth, where all the fleete lies. By and by comes down my Lord, and then he and I an houre together alone upon private discourse. He tells me that Mr. Coventry and he are not reconciled, but declared enemies: the only occasion of it being, he tells me, his ill usage from him about the first fight, wherein he had no right done him, which, methinks, is a poor occasion, for, in my conscience, that was no design of Coventry's. But, however, when I asked my Lord whether it were not best, though with some

[1] This person, erroneously called by Pepys Sir C. Herbert, will be best defined by subjoining the inscription on his monument in Westminster Abbey: "Sir Charles Harbord, Knight, third son of Sir Charles Harbord, Knight, Surveyor-General, and First Lieutenant of the Royall James, under the most noble and illustrious Captaine, Edward, Earle of Sandwich, Vice-Admirall of England, which, after a terrible fight, maintained to admiration against a squadron of the Holland fleet, above six hours, neere the Suffolk coast, having put off two fire-ships; at last, being utterly disabled, and few of her men remaining unhurt, was, by a third, unfortunately set on fire. But he (though he swome well) neglected to save himselfe, as some did, and out of perfect love to that worthy Lord, whom, for many yeares, he had constantly accompanyed, in all his honourable employments, and in all the engagements of the former warre, dyed with him, at the age of xxxii., much bewailed by his father, whom he never offended; and much beloved by all for his knowne piety, vertue, loyalty, fortitude, and fidelity." — B

condescension, to be friends with him, he told me it was not possible, and so I stopped. He tells me, as very private, that there are great factions at the Court between the King's party and the Duke of Yorke's, and that the King, which is a strange difficulty, do favour my Lord in opposition to the Duke's party; that my Lord Chancellor, being, to be sure, the patron of the Duke's, it is a mystery whence it should be that Mr. Coventry is looked upon by him [Clarendon] as an enemy to him; that if he had a mind himself to be out of this employment, as Mr. Coventry, he believes, wishes, and himself and I do incline to wish it also, in many respects, yet he believes he shall not be able, because of the King, who will keepe him in on purpose, in opposition to the other party; that Prince Rupert and he are all possible friends in the world; that Coventry hath aggravated this business of the prizes, though never so great plundering in the world as while the Duke and he were at sea; and in Sir John Lawson's time he could take and pillage, and then sink a whole ship in the Streights, and Coventry say nothing to it; that my Lord Arlington is his fast friend; that the Chancellor is cold to him, and though I told him that I and the world do take my Lord Chancellor, in his speech the other day, to have said as much as could be wished, yet he thinks he did not. That my Lord Chancellor do from hence begin to be cold to him, because of his seeing him and Arlington so great: that nothing at Court is minded but faction and pleasure, and nothing intended of general good to the kingdom by anybody heartily; so that he believes with me, in a little time confusion will certainly come over all the nation. He told me how a design was carried on a while ago, for the Duke of Yorke to raise an army in the North, and to be the Generall of it, and all this without the knowledge or advice of the Duke of Albemarle, which when he come to know, he was so vexed, they were fain to let it fall to content him: that his matching with the family of Sir G. Carteret do make the difference greater between Coventry and him, they being enemies; that the Chancellor did, as every body else, speak well of me the other day, but yet was, at the Committee for Tangier, angry that I should offer to suffer a bill of exchange to be protested. So my Lord did bid me take heed, for that I might easily suppose I could not want enemies, no more than others. In all he speaks with the greatest trust and love and confidence in what I say or do, that a man can do. After this discourse ended we sat down to dinner and mighty merry, among other things, at the Bill brought into the House to make it felony to break bulke, which, as my Lord says well, will make that no prizes shall be taken, or, if taken, shall be sunke after plundering; and the Act for the method of gathering this last £1,250,000 now voted, and how paid wherein are several strange imperfections. After dinner my Lord by a ketch down to Erith, where the Bezan was, it blowing these last two days and now both night and day very hard southwardly, so that it has certainly drove the Dutch off the coast. My Lord being gone I to the office, and there find Captain Ferrers, who tells me his wife is come to town to see him, having not seen him since 15 weeks ago at his first going to sea last. She is now at a Taverne and stays all night, so I was obliged to give him my house and chamber to lie in, which he with great modesty and after much force took, and so I got Mr. Evelyn's coach to carry her thither, and the coach coming back, I with Mr. Evelyn to Deptford, where a little while with him doing a little business, and so in his coach back again to my lodgings, and there sat with Mrs. Ferrers two hours, and with my little girle, Mistress Frances Tooker, and very pleasant. Anon the Captain comes, and then to supper very merry, and so I led them to bed. And so to bed myself, having seen my pretty little girle home first at the next door.

26th. Up, and, leaving my guests to make themselves ready, I to the office, and thither comes Sir Jer. Smith and Sir Christopher Mings to see me, being just come from Portsmouth and going down to the Fleete. Here I sat and talked with them a good while and then parted, only Sir Christopher Mings and I together by water to the Tower; and I find him a very witty well-spoken fellow, and mighty free to tell his parentage, being a shoemaker's son, to whom he is now going, and I to the 'Change, where I hear how the French have taken two and sunk one of our merchant-men in the Streights, and carried the ships to Toulon; so that there is no expectation but we must fall out with them.

The 'Change pretty full, and the town begins to be lively again, though the streets very empty, and most shops shut. So back again I and took boat and called for Sir Christopher Mings at St. Katharine's, who was followed with some ordinary friends, of which, he says, he is proud, and so down to Greenwich, the wind furious high, and we with our sail up till I made it be taken down. I took him, it being 3 o'clock, to my lodgings and did give him a good dinner and so parted, he being pretty close to me as to any business of the fleete, knowing me to be a servant of my Lord Sandwich's. He gone I to the office till night, and then they come and tell me my wife is come to towne, so I to her vexed at her coming, but it was upon innocent business, so I was pleased and made her stay, Captain Ferrers and his lady being yet there, and so I left them to dance, and I to the office till past nine at night, and so to them and there saw them dance very prettily, the Captain and his wife, my wife and Mrs. Barbary, and Mercer and my landlady's daughter, and then little Mistress Frances Tooker and her mother, a pretty woman come to see my wife. Anon to supper, and then to dance again (Golding being our fiddler, who plays very well and all tunes) till past twelve at night, and then we broke up and every one to bed, we make shift for all our company, Mrs. Tooker being gone.

27th. Up, and after some pleasant discourse with my wife, I out, leaving her and Mrs. Ferrers there, and I to Captain Cocke's, there to do some business, and then away with Cocke in his coach through Kent Streete, a miserable, wretched, poor place, people sitting sicke and muffled up with plasters at every 4 or 5 doors. So to the 'Change, and thence I by water to the Duke of Albemarle's, and there much company, but I staid and dined, and he makes mighty much of me; and here he tells us the Dutch are gone, and have lost above 160 cables and anchors, through the last foule weather. Here he proposed to me from Mr. Coventry, as I had desired of Mr. Coventry, that I should be Surveyor-Generall of the Victualling business, which I accepted. But, indeed, the terms in which Mr. Coventry proposes it for me are the most obliging that ever I could expect from any man, and more; it saying me to be the fittest man in England, and that he is sure, if I will undertake, I will perform it; and that it will be also a very desirable thing that I might have this encouragement, my encouragement in the Navy alone being in no wise proportionable to my pains or deserts. This, added to the letter I had three days since from Mr. Southerne,[1] signifying that the Duke of Yorke had in his master's absence opened my letter, and commanded him to tell me that he did approve of my being the Surveyor-General, do make me joyful beyond myself that I cannot express it, to see that as I do take pains, so God blesses me, and hath sent me masters that do observe that I take pains. After having done here, I back by water and to London, and there met with Captain Cocke's coach again, and I went in it to Greenwich and thence sent my wife in it to Woolwich, and I to the office, and thence home late with Captain Taylor, and he and I settled all accounts between us, and I do find that I do get above £120 of him for my services for him within these six months. At it till almost one in the morning, and after supper he away and I to bed, mightily satisfied in all this, and in a resolution I have taken to-night with Mr. Hater to propose the port of London for the victualling business for Thomas Willson, by which it will be better done and I at more ease, in case he should grumble.[2] So to bed.

28th. Up, and sent for Thomas Willson, and broke the victualling business to him and he is mightily contented, and so am I that I have bestowed it on him, and so I to Mr. Boreman's, where Sir W. Batten is, to tell him what I had proposed to Thomas Willson, and the newes also I have this morning from Sir W. Clerke, which is, that notwithstanding all the care the Duke of Albemarle hath taken about the putting the East India prize goods into the East India Company's hands, and my Lord Bruncker and Sir J. Minnes having laden out a great part of the goods, an order is come from Court to stop all, and to have the goods delivered to

[1] James Sotherne, secretary to Sir W. Coventry, and afterwards himself Secretary of the Admiralty (see note, *ante*, January 24th, 1659-60).

[2] The Duke of York's letter appointing Thomas Wilson Surveyor of the Victualling of His Majesty's Navy in the Port of London, and referring to Pepys as Surveyor-General of the Victualling Affairs, is printed in "Memoirs of the English Affairs, chiefly Naval, 1660-73," by James, Duke of York, 1729, p. 131.

the Sub-Commissioners of prizes. At which I am glad, because it do vex this simple weake man, and we shall have a little reparation for the disgrace my Lord Sandwich has had in it. He tells me also that the Parliament hath given the Duke of Yorke £120,000,[1] to be paid him after the £1,250,000 is gathered upon the tax which they have now given the King. He tells me that the Dutch have lately launched sixteen new ships; all which is great news. Thence by horsebacke with Mr. Deane to Erith, and so aboard my Lord Bruncker and dined, and very merry with him and good discourse between them about ship building, and, after dinner and a little pleasant discourse, we away and by horse back again to Greenwich, and there I to the office very late, offering my persons for all the victualling posts much to my satisfaction. Also much other business I did to my mind, and so weary home to my lodging, and there after eating and drinking a little I to bed. The King and Court, they say, have now finally resolved to spend nothing upon clothes, but what is of the growth of England; which, if observed, will be very pleasing to the people, and very good for them.

29th (Lord's day). Up, and being ready set out with Captain Cocke in his coach toward Erith, Mr. Deane riding along with us, where we dined and were very merry. After dinner we fell to discourse about the Dutch, Cocke undertaking to prove that they were able to wage warr with us three years together, which, though it may be true, yet, not being satisfied with his arguments, my Lord and I did oppose the strength of his arguments, which brought us to a great heate, he being a conceited man, but of no Logique in his head at all, which made my Lord and I mirth. Anon we parted, and back again, we hardly having a word all the way, he being so vexed at our not yielding to his persuasion. I was set down at Woolwich towne end, and walked through the towne in the darke, it being now night. But in the streete did overtake and almost run upon two women crying and carrying a man's coffin between them. I suppose the husband of one of them, which, methinks, is a sad

[1] This sum was granted by the Commons to Charles, with a request that he would bestow it on his brother. — B.

thing. Being come to Shelden's, I find my people in the darke in the dining room, merry and laughing, and, I thought, sporting one with another, which, God helpe me! raised my jealousy presently. Come in the darke, and one of them touching me (which afterward I found was Susan) made them shreeke, and so went out up stairs, leaving them to light a candle and to run out. I went out and was very vexed till I found my wife was gone with Mr. Hill and Mercer this day to see me at Greenwich, and these people were at supper, and the candle on a sudden falling out of the candlesticke (which I saw as I come through the yarde) and Mrs. Barbary being there I was well at ease again, and so bethought myself what to do, whether to go to Greenwich or stay there; at last go I would, and so with a lanthorne, and 3 or 4 people with me, among others Mr. Browne, who was there, would go, I walked with a lanthorne and discoursed with him about paynting and the several sorts of it. I came in good time to Greenwich, where I found Mr. Hill with my wife, and very glad I was to see him. To supper and discourse of musique and so to bed, I lying with him talking till midnight about Berckenshaw's musique rules, which I did to his great satisfaction inform him in, and so to sleep.

30th. Up, and to my office about business. At noon to dinner, and after some discourse of musique, he and I to the office awhile, and he to get Mr. Coleman, if he can, against night. By and by I back again home, and there find him returned with Mr. Coleman (his wife being ill)[1] and Mr. Laneare,[2] with whom with their Lute we had excellent

[1] Edward Coleman, musical composer and singer, who undertook the character of Alphonso when the first part of D'Avenant's "The Siege of Rhodes" was acted at Rutland House in 1656. His wife represented the character of Ianthe at the same time.

[2] Nicholas Lanier, composer of the symphonies to several of the masques written by Ben Jonson, and performed at Court, had died, æt. 78, November 4th, 1646, and was buried at St. Martin's-in-the-Fields ("Somerset House Gazette," vol. i., p. 57). The Letters-Patent under which the Society of Musicians was incorporated at the Restoration, mention a Lanier, possibly a son of Nicholas, as first Marshal, and four others of his name as Wardens or Assistants of the Company. There is an engraved portrait of him in the British Museum (Addit. MS. 15,858, fol. 55), and a letter to his niece, Mrs. Richards, "at her house in the Old Aumery, Westminster." — B.

company and good singing till midnight, and a good supper I did give them, but Coleman's voice is quite spoiled, and when he begins to be drunk he is excellent company, but afterward troublesome and impertinent. Laneare sings in a melancholy method very well, and a sober man he seems to be. They being gone, we to bed, Captain Ferrers coming this day from my Lord is forced to lodge here, and I put him to Mr. Hill.

31st. Up, and to the office, Captain Ferrers going back betimes to my Lord. I to the office, where Sir W. Batten met me, and did tell me that Captain Cocke's black was dead of the plague, which I had heard of before, but took no notice. By and by Captain Cocke come to the office, and Sir W. Batten and I did send to him that he would either forbear the office, or forbear going to his owne office. However, meeting yesterday the Searchers with their rods in their hands coming from Captain Cocke's house, I did overhear them say that the fellow did not die of the plague, but he had I know been ill a good while, and I am told that his boy Jack is also ill. At noon home to dinner, and then to the office again, leaving Mr. Hill if he can to get Mrs. Coleman at night. About nine at night I come home, and there find Mrs. Pierce come and little Fran. Tooker, and Mr. Hill, and other people, a great many dancing, and anon comes Mrs. Coleman with her husband and Laneare. The dancing ended and to sing, which Mrs. Coleman do very finely, though her voice is decayed as to strength but mighty sweet though soft, and a pleasant jolly woman, and in mighty good humour was to-night. Among other things Laneare did, at the request of Mr. Hill, bring two or three the finest prints for my wife to see that ever I did see in all my life. But for singing, among other things, we got Mrs. Coleman to sing part of the Opera, though she won't owne that ever she did get any of it without book in order to the stage; but, above all, her counterfeiting of Captain Cooke's part, in his reproaching his man with cowardice, "Base slave," &c., she do it most excellently. At it till past midnight, and then broke up and to bed. Hill and I together again, and being very sleepy we had little discourse as we had the other night. Thus we end the month merrily; and the more for that, after some fears that the plague would have increased again this week, I hear for certain that there is above 400 [less], the whole number being 1,388, and of them of the plague, 1,031. Want of money in the Navy puts every thing out of order. Men grow mutinous; and nobody here to mind the business of the Navy but myself. At least Sir W. Batten for the few days he has been here do nothing. I in great hopes of my place of Surveyor-Generall of the Victualling, which will bring me £300 per annum.

November 1st. Lay very long in bed discoursing with Mr. Hill of most things of a man's life, and how little merit do prevail in the world, but only favour; and that, for myself, chance without merit brought me in; and that diligence only keeps me so, and will, living as I do among so many lazy people that the diligent man becomes necessary, that they cannot do anything without him, and so told him of my late business of the victualling, and what cares I am in to keepe myself having to do with people of so different factions at Court, and yet must be fair with them all, which was very pleasant discourse for me to tell, as well as he seemed to take it, for him to hear. At last up, and it being a very foule day for raine and a hideous wind, yet having promised I would go by water to Erith, and bearing sayle was in danger of oversetting, but ordered them take down their sayle, and so cold and wet got thither, as they had ended their dinner. How[ever], I dined well, and after dinner all on shore, my Lord Bruncker with us to Mrs. Williams's lodgings, and Sir W. Batten, Sir Edmund Pooly,[1] and others; and there, it being my Lord's birth-day, had every one a green riband tied in our hats very foolishly; and methinks mighty disgracefully for my Lord to have his folly so open to all the world with this woman. But by and by Sir W. Batten and I took coach, and home to Boreman, and so going home by the backside I saw Captain Cocke 'lighting out of his coach (having been at Erith also with her but not on board) and so he would come along with me to my lodging, and there sat and supped and talked with us, but we were angry a little a while about our message to him the

[1] M.P. for Bury St. Edmunds, and in the list of proposed Knights of the Royal Oak for Suffolk. — B.

other day about bidding him keepe from the office or his owne office, because of his black dying. I owned it and the reason of it, and would have been glad he had been out of the house, but I could not bid him go, and so supped, and after much other talke of the sad condition and state of the King's matters we broke up, and my friend and I to bed. This night coming with Sir W. Batten into Greenwich we called upon Coll. Cleggatt, who tells us for certaine that the King of Denmark hath declared to stand for the King of England, but since I hear it is wholly false.

2nd. Up, left my wife and to the office, and there to my great content Sir W. Warren come to me to settle the business of the Tangier boates, wherein I shall get above £100, besides £100 which he gives me in the paying for them out of his owne purse. He gone, I home to my lodgings to dinner, and there comes Captain Wager[1] newly returned from the Streights, who puts me in great fear for our last ships that went to Tangier with provisions, that they will be taken. A brave, stout fellow this Captain is, and I think very honest. To the office again after dinner and there late writing letters, and then about 8 at night set out from my office and fitting myself at my lodgings intended to have gone this night in a Ketch down to the Fleete, but calling in my way at Sir J. Minnes's, who is come up from Erith about something about the prizes, they persuaded me not to go till the morning, it being a horrible darke and a windy night. So I back to my lodging and to bed.

3rd. Was called up about four o'clock and in the darke by lanthorne took boat and to the Ketch and set sayle, sleeping a little in the Cabbin till day and then up and fell to reading of Mr. Evelyn's book about Paynting,[2] which is a very pretty book. Carrying good victuals and Tom with me I to breakfast about 9 o'clock, and then to read again

[1] Charles Wager was captain of the "Yarmouth" in the fleet at Scheveningen attending Charles on his return to England. He died at Deal, February 24th, 1665–66. Pepys says that even the Moors mentioned him with tears (see *post*, March 27th, 1668).

[2] This must surely have been Evelyn's "Sculptura, or the History and Art of Chalcography and Engraving in Copper," published in 1662. The translation of Freart's "Idea of the Perfection of Painting demonstrated" was not published until 1668.

and come to the Fleete about twelve, where I found my Lord (the Prince being gone in) on board the Royall James, Sir Thomas Allen commander, and with my Lord an houre alone discoursing what was my chief and only errand about what was adviseable for his Lordship to do in this state of things, himself being under the Duke of Yorke's and Mr. Coventry's envy, and a great many more and likely never to do anything honourably but he shall be envied and the honour taken as much as can be from it. His absence lessens his interest at Court, and what is worst we never able to set out a fleete fit for him to command, or, if out, to keepe them out or fit them to do any great thing, or if that were so yet nobody at home minds him or his condition when he is abroad, and lastly the whole affairs of state looking as if they would all on a sudden break in pieces, and then what a sad thing it would be for him to be out of the way. My Lord did concur in every thing and thanked me infinitely for my visit and counsel, telling me that in every thing he concurs, but puts a query, what if the King will not think himself safe, if any man should go but him. How he should go off then? To that I had no answer ready, but the making the King see that he may be of as good use to him here while another goes forth. But for that I am not able to say much. We after this talked of some other little things and so to dinner, where my Lord infinitely kind to me, and after dinner I rose and left him with some Commanders at the table taking tobacco and I took the Bezan back with me, and with a brave gale and tide reached up that night to the Hope, taking great pleasure in learning the seamen's manner of singing when they sound the depths, and then to supper and to sleep, which I did most excellently all night, it being a horrible foule night for wind and raine.

4th. They sayled from midnight, and come to Greenwich about 5 o'clock in the morning. I however lay till about 7 or 8, and so to my office, my head a little akeing, partly for want of natural rest, partly having so much business to do to-day, and partly from the newes I hear that one of the little boys at my lodging is not well; and they suspect, by their sending for plaister and fume, that it may be the plague; so I sent Mr. Hater and W. Hewer to speake with the mother; but they returned to me, satisfied that there is no hurt nor danger, but the boy is well, and offers to be searched, however, I was resolved myself to abstain coming thither for a while. Sir W. Batten and myself at the office all the morning. At noon with him to dinner at Boreman's, where Mr. Seymour with us, who is a most conceited fellow and not over much in him. Here Sir W. Batten told us (which I had not heard before) that the last sitting day his cloake was taken from Mingo he going home to dinner, and that he was beaten by the seamen and swears he will come to Greenwich, but no more to the office till he can sit safe. After dinner I to the office and there late, and much troubled to have 100 seamen all the afternoon there, swearing below and cursing us, and breaking the glasse windows, and swear they will pull the house down on Tuesday next. I sent word of this to Court, but nothing will helpe it but money and a rope. Late at night to Mr. Glanville's there to lie for a night or two, and to bed.

5th (Lord's day). Up, and after being trimmed, by boat to the Cockpitt, where I heard the Duke of Albemarle's chaplin[1] make a simple sermon: among other things, reproaching the imperfection of humane learning, he cried: "All our physicians cannot tell what an ague is, and all our arithmetique is not able to number the days of a man;" which, God knows, is not the fault of arithmetique, but that our understandings reach not the thing. To dinner, where a great deale of silly discourse, but the worst is I hear that the plague increases much at Lambeth, St. Martin's and Westminster, and fear it will all over the city. Thence I to the Swan, thinking to have seen Sarah but she was at church, and so I by water to Deptford, and there made a visit to Mr. Evelyn, who, among other things, showed me most excellent painting in little; in distemper, Indian incke, water colours: graveing; and, above all, the whole secret of mezzo-tinto, and the manner of it, which is very pretty, and good things done with it.[2] He read to me very

[1] The Duke of Albemarle had more than one chaplain. Thomas Gumble, D.D., who wrote the life of his patron (1671), was one of these.

[2] Evelyn described the new art of mezzotint in his "Sculptura." He published several works on gardening, and left MSS. on the same subject. We have no record of the plays referred to by Pepys.

much also of his discourse, he hath been many years and now is about, about Guardenage; which will be a most noble and pleasant piece. He read me part of a play or two of his making, very good, but not as he conceits them, I think, to be. He showed me his Hortus Hyemalis; leaves laid up in a book of several plants kept dry, which preserve colour, however, and look very finely, better than any Herball. In fine, a most excellent person he is, and must be allowed a little for a little conceitedness; but he may well be so, being a man so much above others. He read me, though with too much gusto, some little poems of his own, that were not transcendant, yet one or two very pretty epigrams; among others, of a lady looking in at a grate, and being pecked at by an eagle that was there. Here comes in, in the middle of our discourse Captain Cocke, as drunk as a dogg, but could stand, and talk and laugh. He did so joy himself in a brave woman that he had been with all the afternoon, and who should it be but my Lady Robinson, but very troublesome he is with his noise and talke, and laughing, though very pleasant. With him in his coach to Mr. Glanville's, where he sat with Mrs. Penington and myself a good while talking of this fine woman again and then went away. Then the lady and I to very serious discourse and, among other things, of what a bonny lasse my Lady Robinson is, who is reported to be kind to the prisoners, and has said to Sir G. Smith, who is her great crony, "Look! there is a pretty man, I would be content to break a commandment with him," and such loose expressions she will have often. After an houre's talke we to bed, the lady mightily troubled about a pretty little bitch she hath, which is very sicke, and will eat nothing, and the worst was, I could hear her in her chamber bemoaning the bitch, and by and by taking her into bed with her. The bitch pissed and shit a bed, and she was fain to rise and had coals out of my chamber to dry the bed again. This night I had a letter that Sir G. Carteret would be in towne to-morrow, which did much surprize me.

6th. Up, and to my office, where busy all the morning and then to dinner to Captain Cocke's with Mr. Evelyn, where very merry, only vexed after dinner to stay too long for our coach. At last, however, to Lambeth and thence the Cockpitt, where we found Sir G. Carteret come, and in with the Duke and the East India Company about settling the business of the prizes, and they have gone through with it. Then they broke up, and Sir G. Carteret come out, and thence through the garden to the water side and by water I with him in his boat down with Captain Cocke to his house at Greenwich, and while supper was getting ready Sir G. Carteret and I did walk an houre in the garden before the house, talking of my Lord Sandwich's business; what enemies he hath, and how they have endeavoured to bespatter him: and particularly about his leaving of 30 ships of the enemy, when Pen would have gone, and my Lord called him back again: which is most false. However, he says, it was purposed by some hot-heads in the House of Commons, at the same time when they voted a present to the Duke of Yorke, to have voted £10,000 to the Prince, and half-a-crowne to my Lord of Sandwich; but nothing come of it.[1] But, for all this, the King is most firme to my Lord, and so is my Lord Chancellor, and my Lord Arlington. The Prince, in appearance, kind; the Duke of Yorke silent, says no hurt; but admits others to say it in his hearing. Sir W. Pen, the falsest rascal that ever was in the world; and that this afternoon the Duke of Albemarle did tell him that Pen was a very cowardly rogue, and one that hath brought all these rogueish fanatick Captains into the fleete, and swears he should never go out with the fleete again. That Sir W. Coventry is most kind to Pen still; and says nothing nor do any thing openly to the prejudice of my Lord. He agrees with me, that it is impossible for the King [to] set out a fleete again the next year; and that he fears all will come to ruine, there being no money in prospect but these prizes, which will bring, it may be, £20,000, but that will signify nothing in the world for it. That this late Act of Parliament for bringing the money into the Exchequer, and making of it payable out there, intended as a prejudice to him and will be his convenience hereafter and ruine the King's business, and so I fear it will and do wonder Sir W. Coventry would be led

[1] The tide of popular indignation ran high against Lord Sandwich, and he was sent to Spain as ambassador to get him honourably out of the way (see *post*, December 6th, p. 154).

by Sir G. Downing to persuade the King and Duke to have it so, before they had thoroughly weighed all circumstances; that for my Lord, the King has said to him lately that I was an excellent officer, and that my Lord Chancellor do, he thinks, love and esteem of me as well as he do of any man in England that he hath no more acquaintance with. So having done and received from me the sad newes that we are like to have no money here a great while, not even of the very prizes, I set up my rest[1] in giving up the King's service to be ruined and so in to supper, where pretty merry, and after supper late to Mr. Glanville's, and Sir G. Carteret to bed. I also to bed, it being very late.

7th. Up, and to Sir G. Carteret, and with him, he being very passionate to be gone, without staying a minute for breakfast, to the Duke of Albemarle's and I with him by water and with Fen: but, among other things, Lord! to see how he wondered to see the river so empty of boats, nobody working at the Custome-house keys; and how fearful he is, and vexed that his man, holding a wine-glasse in his hand for him to drinke out of, did cover his hands, it being a cold, windy, rainy morning, under the waterman's coate, though he brought the waterman from six or seven miles up the river, too. Nay, he carried this glasse with him for his man to let him drink out of at the Duke of Albemarle's, where he intended to dine, though this he did to prevent sluttery, for, for the same reason he carried a napkin with him to Captain Cocke's, making him believe that he should eat with foule linnen. Here he with the Duke walked a good while in the Parke, and I with Fen, but cannot gather that he intends to stay with us, nor thinks any thing at all of ever paying one farthing of money more to us here, let what will come of it. Thence in, and Sir W. Batten comes in by and by, and so staying till noon, and there being a great deal of company there, Sir W. Batten and I took leave of the Duke and Sir G. Carteret, there being no good to be done more for money, and so

[1] The phrase "set up my rest" is a metaphor from the once fashionable game of Primero, meaning, to stand upon the cards you have in your hand, in hopes they may prove better than those of your adversary. Hence, to make up your mind, to be determined (see Nares's "Glossary").

over the River and by coach to Greenwich, where at Boreman's we dined, it being late. Thence my head being full of business and mind out of order for thinking of the effects which will arise from the want of money, I made an end of my letters by eight o'clock, and so to my lodging and there spent the evening till midnight talking with Mrs. Penington, who is a very discreet, understanding lady and very pretty discourse we had and great variety, and she tells me with great sorrow her bitch is dead this morning, died in her bed. So broke up and to bed.

8th. Up, and to the office, where busy among other things to looke my warrants for the settling of the Victualling business, the warrants being come to me for the Surveyors of the ports and that for me also to be Surveyor-Generall. I did discourse largely with Tom Willson about it and doubt not to make it a good service to the King as well, as the King gives us very good salarys. It being a fast day, all people were at church and the office quiett; so I did much business, and at noon adventured to my old lodging, and there eat, but am not yet well satisfied, not seeing of Christopher, though they say he is abroad. Thence after dinner to the office again, and thence am sent for to the King's Head by my Lord Rutherford, who, since I can hope for no more convenience from him, his business is troublesome to me, and therefore I did leave him as soon as I could and by water to Deptford, and there did order my matters so, walking up and down the fields till it was dark night, that je allais a la maison of my valentine,[1] and there je faisais whatever je voudrais avec her, and, about eight at night, did take water, being glad I was out of the towne; for the plague, it seems, rages there more than ever, and so to my lodgings, where my Lord had got a supper and the mistresse of the house and her daughters, and here staid Mrs. Pierce to speake with me about her husband's business, and I made her sup with us, and then at night my Lord and I walked with her home, and so back again. My Lord and I ended all we had to say as to his business over-night, and so I took leave, and went again to Mr. Glanville's and so to bed, it being very late.

[1] This was Bagwell's wife. See February 14th, 1664-65.

9th. Up, and did give the servants something at Mr. Glanville's and so took leave, meaning to lie to-night at my owne lodging. To my office, where busy with Mr. Gawden running over the Victualling business, and he is mightily pleased that this course is taking and seems sensible of my favour and promises kindnesse to me. At noon by water, to the King's Head at Deptford, where Captain Taylor invites Sir W. Batten, Sir John Robinson (who come in with a great deale of company from hunting, and brought in a hare alive and a great many silly stories they tell of their sport, which pleases them mightily, and me not at all, such is the different sense of pleasure in mankind), and others upon the score of a survey of his new ship; and strange to see how a good dinner and feasting reconciles everybody, Sir W. Batten and Sir J. Robinson being now as kind to him, and report well of his ship and proceedings, and promise money, and Sir W. Batten is a solicitor for him, but it is a strange thing to observe, they being the greatest enemys he had, and yet, I believe, hath in the world in their hearts. Thence after dinner stole away and to my office, where did a great deale of business till midnight, and then to Mrs. Clerk's, to lodge again, and going home W. Hewer did tell me my wife will be here to-morrow, and hath put away Mary, which vexes me to the heart, I cannot helpe it, though it may be a folly in me, and when I think seriously on it, I think my wife means no ill design in it, or, if she do, I am a foole to be troubled at it, since I cannot helpe it. The Bill of Mortality, to all our griefs, is encreased 399 this week, and the encrease generally through the whole City and suburbs, which makes us all sad.[1]

10th. Up, and entered all my Journall since the 28th of October, having every day's passages well in my head, though it troubles me to remember it, and which I was forced to, being kept from my lodging, where my books and papers are, for several days. So to my office, where till two or three o'clock busy before I could go to my lodging to dinner, then did it and to my office again. In the evening newes is brought me my wife is come: so I to her,

[1] See note, *ante*, June 29th, 1665, for note on the number of deaths from the plague as given in the Bills of Mortality.

and with her spent the evening, but with no great pleasure, I being vexed about her putting away of Mary in my absence, but yet I took no notice of it at all, but fell into other discourse, and she told me, having herself been this day at my house at London, which was boldly done, to see Mary have her things, that Mr. Harrington, our neighbour, an East country merchant, is dead at Epsum of the plague, and that another neighbour of our's, Mr. Hollworthy, a very able man, is also dead by a fall in the country from his horse, his foot hanging in the stirrup, and his brains beat out. Here we sat talking, and after supper to bed.

11th. I up and to the office (leaving my wife in bed) and there till noon, then to dinner and back again to the office, my wife going to Woolwich again, and I staying very late at my office, and so home to bed.

12th (Lord's day). Up, and invited by Captain Cocke to dinner. So after being ready I went to him, and there he and I and Mr. Yard (one of the Guinny Company) dined together and very merry. After dinner I by water to the Duke of Albemarle, and there had a little discourse and business with him, chiefly to receive his commands about pilotts to be got for our Hambro' ships, going now at this time of the year convoy to the merchant ships, that have lain at great pain and charge, some three, some four months at Harwich for a convoy. They hope here the plague will be less this weeke. Thence back by water to Captain Cocke's, and there he and I spent a great deale of the evening as we had done of the day reading and discoursing over part of Mr. Stillingfleet's "Origines Sacræ,"[1] wherein many things are very good and some frivolous. Thence by and by he and I to Mrs. Penington's, but she was gone to bed. So we back and walked a while, and then to his house and to supper, and then broke up, and I home to my lodging to bed.

13th. Up, and to my office, where busy all the morning, and at noon to Captain Cocke's to dinner as we had appointed in order to settle our business of accounts. But here came in an Alderman, a merchant, a very merry man,

[1] "Origines Sacræ, or a rational Account of the Christian Faith," by Edward Stillingfleet, afterwards Dean of St. Paul's and Bishop of Worcester, was published in 1662.

and we dined, and, he being gone, after dinner Cocke and I walke into the garden, and there after a little discourse he did undertake under his hand to secure me £500 profit, for my share of the profit of what we have bought of the prize goods. We agreed upon the terms, which were easier on my side than I expected, and so with extraordinary inward joy we parted till the evening. So I to the office and among other business prepared a deed for him to sign and seale to me about our agreement, which at night I got him to come and sign and seale, and so he and I to Glanville's, and there he and I sat talking and playing with Mrs. Penington, whom we found undrest in her smocke and petticoats by the fireside, and there we drank and laughed, and she willingly suffered me to put my hand in her bosom very wantonly, and keep it there long. Which methought was very strange, and I looked upon myself as a man mightily deceived in a lady, for I could not have thought she could have suffered it, by her former discourse with me; so modest she seemed and I know not what. We staid here late, and so home after he and I had walked till past midnight, a bright moonshine, clear, cool night, before his door by the water, and so I home after one of the clock.

14th. Called up by break of day by Captain Cocke, by agreement, and he and I in his coach through Kent-streete (a sad place through the plague, people sitting sicke and with plaisters about them in the street begging) to Viner's and Colvill's about money business, and so to my house, and there I took £300 in order to the carrying it down to my Lord Sandwich in part of the money I am to pay for Captain Cocke by our agreement. So I took it down, and down I went to Greenwich to my office, and there sat busy till noon, and so home to dinner, and thence to the office again, and by and by to the Duke of Albemarle's by water late, where I find he had remembered that I had appointed to come to him this day about money, which I excused not doing sooner; but I see, a dull fellow, as he is, do sometimes remember what another thinks he mindeth not. My business was about getting money of the East India Company; but, Lord! to see how the Duke himself magnifies himself in what he had done with the Company; and my

Lord Craven what the King could have done without my Lord Duke, and a deale of stir, but most mightily what a brave fellow I am. Back by water, it raining hard, and so to the office, and stopped my going, as I intended, to the buoy of the Nore, and great reason I had to rejoice at it, for it proved the night of as great a storme as was almost ever remembered. Late at the office, and so home to bed. This day, calling at Mr. Rawlinson's to know how all did there, I hear that my pretty grocer's wife, Mrs. Beversham, over the way there, her husband is lately dead of the plague at Bow, which I am sorry for, for fear of losing her neighbourhood.

15th. Up and all the morning at the office, busy, and at noon to the King's Head taverne,[1] where all the Trinity House dined to-day, to choose a new Master in the room of Hurlestone, that is dead, and Captain Crispe[2] is chosen. But, Lord! to see how Sir W. Batten governs all and tramples upon Hurlestone, but I am confident the Company will grow the worse for that man's death, for now Batten, and in him a lazy, corrupt, doating rogue, will have all the sway there. After dinner who comes in but my Lady Batten, and a troop of a dozen women almost, and expected, as I found afterward, to be made mighty much of, but nobody minded them; but the best jest was, that when they saw themselves not regarded, they would go away, and it was horrible foule weather; and my Lady Batten walking through the dirty lane with new spicke and span white shoes, she dropped one of her galoshes in the dirt, where it stuck, and she forced to go home without one, at which she was horribly vexed, and I led her; and after vexing her a little more in mirth, I parted, and to Glanville's, where I knew Sir John Robinson, Sir G. Smith, and Captain Cocke were gone, and there, with the company of Mrs. Penington, whose father,[3] I hear, was one of the Court of Justice, and

[1] There was a once famous King's Head at the corner of Fleet Street and Chancery Lane.

[2] Captain Crispe had only been made an Elder Brother in the previous April (see April 19th, 1665).

[3] Alderman Isaac Penington, Sheriff of London 1638, was elected Member of Parliament for the City of London in 1640, and in 1642 chosen Lord Mayor, and afterwards appointed Lieutenant of the Tower. He was one of the Commissioners for the trial of Charles I., but he did

died prisoner, of the stone, in the Tower, I made them, against their resolutions, to stay from houre to houre till it was almost midnight, and a furious, darke and rainy, and windy, stormy night, and, which was best, I, with drinking small beer, made them all drunk drinking wine, at which Sir John Robinson made great sport. But, they being gone, the lady and I very civilly sat an houre by the fire-side observing the folly of this Robinson, that makes it his worke to praise himself, and all he say and do, like a heavy-headed coxcombe. The plague, blessed be God! is decreased 400; making the whole this week but 1,300 and odd; for which the Lord be praised!

16th. Up, and fitted myself for my journey down to the fleete, and sending my money and boy down by water to Eriffe,[1] I borrowed a horse of Mr. Boreman's son, and after having sat an houre laughing with my Lady Batten and Mrs. Turner, and eat and drank with them, I took horse and rode to Eriffe, where, after making a little visit to Madam Williams, who did give me information of W. Howe's having bought eight bags of precious stones taken from about the Dutch Vice-Admirall's neck, of which there were eight dyamonds which cost him £4,000 sterling, in India, and hoped to have made £12,000 here for them. And that this is told by one that sold him one of the bags, which hath nothing but rubys in it, which he had for 35*s.*; and that it will be proved he hath made £125 of one stone that he bought. This she desired, and I resolved I would give my Lord Sandwich notice of. So I on board my Lord Bruncker; and there he and Sir Edmund Pooly carried me down into the hold of the India shipp, and there did show me the greatest wealth lie in confusion that a man can see in the world. Pepper scattered through every chink, you trod upon it; and in cloves and nutmegs, I walked above

not sign the warrant for his execution, and a member of the Council of State, 1649. In 1660 he was committed to the Tower as one of the King's judges, and his estates confiscated. He died there on December 17th, 1661. "Dec. 19th, 1661. Warrant to Sir John Robinson, Lieutenant of the Tower, to deliver the corpse of Isaac Penington, who died in prison there [Dec. 17], to his relations" ("State Papers"). He had two sons: Isaac, a well-known Quaker, and Arthur, who became a Romish priest; and a daughter Judith.

[1] Erith.

the knees; whole rooms full. And silk in bales, and boxes of copper-plate, one of which I saw opened. Having seen this, which was as noble a sight as ever I saw in my life, I away on board the other ship in despair to get the pleasure-boat of the gentlemen there to carry me to the fleet. They were Mr. Ashburnham [1] and Colonell Wyndham [2]; but pleading the King's business, they did presently agree I should have it. So I presently on board, and got under sail, and had a good bedd by the shift, of Wyndham's; and so,—

17th. Sailed all night, and got down to Quinbrough water, where all the great ships are now come, and there on board my Lord, and was soon received with great content. And after some little discourse, he and I on board Sir W. Pen; and there held a council of Warr about many wants of the fleete, but chiefly how to get slopps and victuals for the fleete now going out to convoy our Hambro' ships, that have been so long detained for four or five months for want of convoy, which we did accommodate one way or other, and so, after much chatt, Sir W. Pen did give us a very good and neat dinner, and better, I think, than ever I did see at his owne house at home in my life, and so was the other I eat with him. After dinner much talke, and about other things, he and I about his money for his prize goods, wherein I did give him a cool answer, but so as we did not disagree in words much, and so let that fall, and so followed my Lord Sandwich, who was gone a little before me on board the Royall James. And there spent an houre, my Lord playing upon the gittarr, which he now commends above all musique in the world, because it is base enough for a single voice, and is so portable and manageable without much trouble. That being done, I got my Lord to be alone, and so I fell to acquaint him with W. Howe's business, which he had before heard a little of from Captain

[1] John Ashburnham, a Groom of the Bedchamber to Charles I., whom he attended during the whole of the Rebellion, and afterwards filled the same post under Charles II. He was, in 1661, M.P. for Sussex. Ob. 1671. The late Earl of Ashburnham, who was lineally descended from him, wrote an excellent vindication of his ancestor, against the insinuations of Clarendon and others.—B.

[2] Colonel Francis Wyndham, a distinguished loyalist, Governor of Dunster Castle, Somersetshire. He was created a baronet November 18th, 1673.—B.

Cocke, but made no great matter of it, but now he do, and resolves nothing less than to lay him by the heels, and seize on all he hath, saying that for this yeare or two he hath observed him so proud and conceited he could not endure him. But though I was not at all displeased with it, yet I prayed him to forbear doing anything therein till he heard from me again about it, and I had made more enquiry into the truth of it, which he agreed to. Then we fell to publique discourse, wherein was principally this: he cleared it to me beyond all doubt that Coventry is his enemy, and has been long so. So that I am over that, and my Lord told it me upon my proposal of a friendship between them, which he says is impossible, and methinks that my Lord's displeasure about the report in print of the first fight was not of his making, but I perceive my Lord cannot forget it, nor the other think he can. I shewed him how advisable it were upon almost any terms for him to get quite off the sea employment. He answers me again that he agrees to it, but thinks the King will not let him go off. He tells me he lacks now my Lord Orrery to solicit it for him, who is very great with the King. As an infinite secret, my Lord tells me, the factions are high between the King and the Duke, and all the Court are in an uproare with their loose amours; the Duke of Yorke being in love desperately with Mrs. Stewart. Nay, that the Duchesse herself is fallen in love with her new Master of the Horse, one Harry Sidney,[1] and another, Harry Savill.[2] So that God knows what will be the end of it. And that the Duke is not so obsequious as he used to be, but very high of late; and would be glad to be in the head of an army as Generall; and that it is said that he do propose to go and command under the King of Spayne, in Flanders. That his amours to Mrs. Stewart are told the King. So that all is like to be nought among them. That he knows that the Duke of Yorke do give leave to have

[1] Known as Handsome Sidney. He was fourth son of Robert, second Earl of Leicester, created Earl of Romney, 1694. He was Warden of the Cinque Ports, 1691–1702; Lord Lieutenant of Ireland, 1692–95; and Master of the Ordnance, 1693–1702. He died, unmarried, April 8th, 1704.

[2] Henry Saville, some time one of the Grooms of the Bedchamber to the Duke of York.—B.

him spoken slightly of in his owne hearing, and doth not oppose it, and told me from what time he hath observed this to begin. So that upon the whole my Lord do concur to wish with all his heart that he could with any honour get from off the imployment. After he had given thanks to me for my kind visit and good counsel, on which he seems to set much by, I left him, and so away to my Bezan againe, and there to read in a pretty French book, "La Nouvelle Allegorique," upon the strife between rhetorique and its enemies, very pleasant. So, after supper, to sleepe, and sayled all night, and came to Erith before break of day.

18th. About nine of the clock, I went on shore, there (calling by the way only to look upon my Lord Bruncker) to give Mrs. Williams an account of her matters, and so hired an ill-favoured horse, and away to Greenwich to my lodgings, where I hear how rude the souldiers have been in my absence, swearing what they would do with me, which troubled me, but, however, after eating a bit I to the office and there very late writing letters, and so home and to bed.

19th (Lord's day). Up, and after being trimmed, alone by water to Erith, all the way with my song book singing of Mr. Lawes's long recitative song [1] in the beginning of his

[1] Dr. Hueffer says that this song of Henry Lawes is evidently the one given to "Ariadne sitting upon a rock in the Island of Naxos deserted by Theseus," opening the first book of the "Ayres and Dialogues;" and he adds, "Pepys shows his keen perception of the characteristics belonging not only to a single piece, but to a whole school of music. Lawes's songs, even those of the most lyrical type, partake of the nature of the recitative in the sense that the declamatory element is never lost sight of" (Hueffer's "Italian and other Studies," 1883, p. 293).

Henry Lawes, son of William Lawes of Steeple Langford, and born at Dinton, co. Wilts. He was baptized January 1st, 1595–6, was sworn in as Pistler of the Chapel Royal January 1st, 1625–6, and afterwards became Gentleman and Clerk of the Cheque. He composed the musiç for Milton's "Comus," performed at Ludlow Castle in 1634, and performed the part of the attendant spirit. He continued in the service of Charles I. until the king's execution. He then had recourse to teaching. At the Restoration he was replaced in his offices at the Chapel Royal, and composed the Coronation Anthems for Charles II. He died October 21st, 1662, and was buried in the cloisters of Westminster Abbey (see "The Old Cheque Book of the Chapel Royal, 1561–1744," edited by Dr. Rimbault, 1872, pp. 11, 13, 49, 59, 99, 114, 128, 145, 208).

book. Being come there, on board my Lord Bruncker, I find Captain Cocke and other company, the lady not well, and mighty merry we were; Sir Edmund Pooly being very merry, and a right English gentleman, and one of the discontented Cavaliers, that think their loyalty is not considered. After dinner, all on shore to my Lady Williams, and there drank and talked; but, Lord! the most impertinent bold woman with my Lord that ever I did see. I did give her an account again of my business with my Lord touching W. Howe, and she did give me some more information about it, and examination taken about it, and so we parted and I took boat, and to Woolwich, where we found my wife not well of them, and I out of humour begun to dislike her paynting, the last things not pleasing me so well as the former, but I blame myself for my being so little complaisant. So without eating or drinking, there being no wine (which vexed me too), we walked with a lanthorne to Greenwich and eat something at his house, and so home to bed.

20th. Up before day, and wrote some letters to go to my Lord, among others that about W. Howe, which I believe will turn him out, and so took horse for Nonesuch, with two men with me, and the ways very bad, and the weather worse, for wind and rayne. But we got in good time thither, and I did get my tallys got ready, and thence, with as many as could go, to Yowell, and there dined very well, and I saw my Besse, a very well-favoured country lass there, and after being very merry and having spent a piece I took horse, and by another way met with a very good road, but it rained hard and blew, but got home very well. Here I find Mr. Deering come to trouble me about business, which I soon dispatched and parted, he telling me that Luellin[1] hath been dead this fortnight, of the plague, in St. Martin's Lane, which much surprised me.

[1] Peter Llewelyn was admitted a Clerk of the Privy Council on February 8th, 1659–60 ("Index of Proceedings of Council," "Calendar of State Papers," Domestic). He is frequently mentioned by Pepys as Luellin, but on April 26th, 1660, his Christian name is given. Mr. W. R. Lluellyn has kindly given the editor this reference to the State Papers, and has also pointed out that Peter Llewelyn was probably the "Peter Fewellin" recorded in the register of St. George's

21st. Up, and to the office, where all the morning doing business, and at noon home to dinner and quickly back again to the office, where very busy all the evening and late sent a long discourse to Mr. Coventry by his desire about the regulating of the method of our payment of bills in the Navy, which will be very good, though, it may be, he did ayme principally at striking at Sir G. Carteret. So weary but pleased with this business being over I home to supper and to bed.

22nd. Up, and by water to the Duke of Albemarle, and there did some little business, but most to shew myself, and mightily I am yet in his and Lord Craven's books, and thence to the Swan and there drank and so down to the bridge, and so to the 'Change, where spoke with many people, and about a great deale of business, which kept me late. I heard this day that Mr. Harrington is not dead of the plague, as we believed, at which I was very glad, but most of all, to hear that the plague is come very low; that is, the whole under 1,000, and the plague 600 and odd: and great hopes of a further decrease, because of this day's being a very exceeding hard frost, and continues freezing. This day the first of the Oxford Gazettes come out, which is very pretty, full of newes, and no folly in it. Wrote by Williamson.[1] Fear that our Hambro' ships at last cannot

Chapel, Windsor, as having been "borne on the 29th September and baptised on the 30th do. in the year 1636." This Peter Llewelyn was son of David Llewelyn, under-keeper of the privy lodgings and house at Windsor Castle, who died October 16th, 1661, and was buried on the 17th. In May, 1660, David petitioned for the reversion of the housekeeper's place, on the ground that he defended the lodgings and wardrobe at the hazard of his life, and was imprisoned, and ordered to be tried for his life, but the late king himself mediated for him ("Calendar of State Papers"). His son, Charles Llewellin (baptized March 30th, 1630), succeeded his father as under-keeper of the house and privy lodgings at Windsor Castle ("Calendar of State Papers," Domestic, vol. clxxxv.). Another son, David (born 22nd, and baptized 30th April, 1641), became rector of Tansor, and successively Prebendary of Lincoln and Peterborough ("Register of St. Peter's, Westminster;" Bridges' "Northamptonshire." See Chester's "Westminster Abbey Registers," p. 18). The name is variously spelt—"Fluellin" (the form adopted by Shakespeare) giving the nearest approach to the correct pronunciation.

[1] No. xxiv. of the "Oxford Gazette" was the first London Gazette. The Williamson who "wrote" it was afterwards Sir Joseph Williamson. —B.

go, because of the great frost, which we believe it is there, nor are our ships cleared at the Pillow [Pillau], which will keepe them there too all this winter, I fear. From the 'Change, which is pretty full again, I to my office and there took some things, and so by water to my lodging at Greenwich and dined, and then to the office awhile and at night home to my lodgings, and took T. Willson and T. Hater with me, and there spent the evening till midnight discoursing and settling of our Victualling business, that thereby I might draw up instructions for the Surveyours and that we might be doing something to earne our money. This done I late to bed. Among other things it pleased me to have it demonstrated, that a Purser without professed cheating is a professed loser, twice as much as he gets.

23rd. Up betimes, and so, being trimmed, I to get papers ready against Sir H. Cholmly come to me by appointment, he being newly come over from Tangier.[1] He did by and by come, and we settled all matters about his money, and he is a most satisfied man in me, and do declare his resolution to give me £200 per annum. It continuing to be a great frost, which gives us hope for a perfect cure of the plague, he and I to walk in the parke, and there discoursed with grief of the calamity of the times; how the King's service is performed, and how Tangier is governed by a man, who, though honourable, yet do mind his ways of getting and little else compared, which will never make the place flourish. I brought him and had a good dinner for him, and there come by chance Captain Cuttance, who tells me how W. Howe is laid by the heels, and confined to the Royall Katharine, and his things all seized: and how, also, for a quarrel, which indeed the other night my Lord told me, Captain Ferrers, having cut all over the back of another of my Lord's servants, is parted from my Lord. I sent for little Mrs. Frances Tooker, and after they were gone I sat dallying with her an hour, doing what I would with my hands about her. And a very pretty creature it is. So in the evening to the office, where late writing letters, and at my lodging late writing for

[1] Among the Rawlinson MSS. in the Bodleian Library is Pepys's acknowledgment of money received from Sir Hugh Cholmeley in 1665.

the last twelve days my Journall and so to bed. Great expectation what mischief more the French will do us, for we must fall out. We in extraordinary lacke of money and everything else to go to sea next year. My Lord Sandwich is gone from the fleete yesterday toward Oxford.

24th. Up, and after doing some business at the office, I to London, and there, in my way, at my old oyster shop in Gracious Streete, bought two barrels of my fine woman of the shop, who is alive after all the plague, which now is the first observation or inquiry we make at London concerning everybody we knew before it. So to the 'Change, where very busy with several people, and mightily glad to see the 'Change so full, and hopes of another abatement still the next week. Off the 'Change I went home with Sir G. Smith to dinner, sending for one of my barrels of oysters, which were good, though come from Colchester, where the plague hath been so much. Here a very brave dinner, though no invitation; and, Lord! to see how I am treated, that come from so mean a beginning, is matter of wonder to me. But it is God's great mercy to me, and His blessing upon my taking pains, and being punctual in my dealings. After dinner Captain Cocke and I about some business, and then with my other barrel of oysters home to Greenwich, sent them by water to Mrs. Penington, while he and I landed, and visited Mr. Evelyn, where most excellent discourse with him; among other things he showed me a ledger[1] of a Treasurer of the Navy, his great grandfather, just 100 years old; which I seemed mighty fond of, and he did present me with it, which I take as a great rarity; and he hopes to find me more, older than it. He also shewed us several letters of the old Lord of Leicester's,[2] in Queen Elizabeth's time, under the very handwriting of Queen Elizabeth, and Queen Mary, Queen of

[1] This ledger is now in the British Museum, amongst some of Pepys's papers, in the Ducket Collection. — B.

[2] Amongst these documents, still in the Pepysian Library — for Evelyn complains ("Correspondence," vol. iii., p. 381, edit. 1852) that he lent them to Pepys, who omitted to return them — are some letters relating to the death of Amy Robsart, Lady Robert Dudley. These letters between Lord Robert Dudley and Thomas Blount were published by Lord Braybrooke as an Appendix to the diary.

Scotts; and others, very venerable names. But, Lord! how poorly, methinks, they wrote in those days, and in what plain uncut paper. Thence, Cocke having sent for his coach, we to Mrs. Penington, and there sat and talked and eat our oysters with great pleasure, and so home to my lodging late and to bed.

25th. Up, and busy at the office all day long, saving dinner time, and in the afternoon also very late at my office, and so home to bed. All our business is now about our Hambro' fleete, whether it can go or no this yeare, the weather being set in frosty, and the whole stay being for want of Pilotts now, which I have wrote to the Trinity House about, but have so poor an account from them, that I did acquaint Sir W. Coventry with it this post.

26th (Lord's day). Up, though very late abed, yet before day to dress myself to go toward Erith, which I would do by land, it being a horrible cold frost to go by water: so borrowed two horses of Mr. Howell and his friend, and with much ado set out, after my horses being frosted[1] (which I know not what it means to this day), and my boy having lost one of my spurs and stockings, carrying them to the smith's; but I borrowed a stocking, and so got up, and Mr. Tooker with me, and rode to Erith, and there on board my Lord Bruncker, met Sir W. Warren upon his business, among others, and did a great deale, Sir J. Minnes, as God would have it, not being there to hinder us with his impertinences. Business done, we to dinner very merry, there being there Sir Edmund Pooly, a very worthy gentleman. They are now come to the copper boxes in the prizes, and hope to have ended all this weeke. After dinner took leave, and on shore to Madam Williams, to give her an account of my Lord's letter to me about Howe, who he has clapped by the heels on suspicion of having the jewells, and she did give me my Lord Bruncker's examination of the fellow, that declares his having them, and so away, Sir W. Warren riding with me, and the way being very bad, that is, hard and slippery by reason of the frost, so we could not come to past Woolwich till night. However, having a great mind to have gone to the Duke of

[1] Frosting means, having the horses' shoes turned up by the smith.

Albemarle, I endeavoured to have gone farther, but the night come on and no going, so I 'light and sent my horse by Tooker, and returned on foot to my wife at Woolwich, where I found, as I had directed, a good dinner to be made against to-morrow, and invited guests in the yarde, meaning to be merry, in order to her taking leave, for she intends to come in a day or two to me for altogether. But here, they tell me, one of the houses behind them is infected, and I was fain to stand there a great while, to have their back-door opened, but they could not, having locked them fast, against any passing through, so was forced to pass by them again, close to their sicke beds, which they were removing out of the house, which troubled me; so I made them uninvite their guests, and to resolve of coming all away to me to-morrow, and I walked with a lanthorne, weary as I was, to Greenwich; but it was a fine walke, it being a hard frost, and so to Captain Cocke's, but he I found had sent for me to come to him to Mrs. Penington's, and there I went, and we were very merry, and supped, and Cocke being sleepy he went away betimes. I stayed alone talking and playing with her till past midnight, she suffering me whatever ego voulais avec ses mamilles. . . . Much pleased with her company we parted, and I home to bed at past one, all people being in bed thinking I would have staid out of town all night.

27th. Up, and being to go to wait on the Duke of Albemarle, who is to go out of towne to Oxford to-morrow, and I being unwilling to go by water, it being bitter cold, walked it with my landlady's little boy Christopher to Lambeth, it being a very fine walke and calling at half the way and drank, and so to the Duke of Albemarle, who is visited by every body against his going; and mighty kind to me: and upon my desiring his grace to give me his kind word to the Duke of Yorke, if any occasion there were of speaking of me, he told me he had reason to do so; for there had been nothing done in the Navy without me. His going, I hear, is upon putting the sea business into order, and, as some say, and people of his owne family, that he is agog to go to sea himself the next year. Here I met with a letter from Sir. G. Carteret who is come to Cranborne, that he will be here this afternoon and desires me to be with him. So the Duke would have me dine with him. So it being not dinner time, I to the Swan, and there found Sarah all alone in the house. . . . So away to the Duke of Albemarle again, and there to dinner, he most exceeding kind to me to the observation of all that are there. At dinner comes Sir G. Carteret and dines with us. After dinner a great deal alone with Sir G. Carteret, who tells me that my Lord hath received still worse and worse usage from some base people about the Court. But the King is very kind, and the Duke do not appear the contrary; and my Lord Chancellor swore to him "by —— I will not forsake my Lord of Sandwich." Our next discourse is upon this Act for money, about which Sir G. Carteret comes to see what money can be got upon it. But none can be got, which pleases him the thoughts of, for, if the Exchequer should succeede in this, his office would faile. But I am apt to think at this time of hurry and plague and want of trade, no money will be got upon a new way which few understand. We walked, Cocke and I, through the Parke with him, and so we being to meet the Vice-Chamberlayne to-morrow at Nonesuch, to treat with Sir Robert Long about the same business, I into London, it being dark night, by a hackney coach; the first I have durst to go in many a day, and with great pain now for fear. But it being unsafe to go by water in the dark and frosty cold, and unable being weary with my morning walke to go on foot, this was my only way. Few people yet in the streets, nor shops open, here and there twenty in a place almost; though not above five or sixe o'clock at night. So to Viner's, and there heard of Cocke, and found him at the Pope's Head, drinking with Temple. I to them, where the Goldsmiths do decry the new Act, for money to be all brought into the Exchequer, and paid out thence, saying they will not advance one farthing upon it; and indeed it is their interest to say and do so. Thence Cocke and I to Sir G. Smith's, it being now night, and there up to his chamber and sat talking, and I barbing [1] against to-morrow; and anon, at nine at night, comes to us Sir G. Smith and the Lieutenant of the Tower, and there they sat talking and

[1] Shaving.

drinking till past midnight, and mighty merry we were, the Lieutenant of the Tower being in a mighty vein of singing, and he hath a very good eare and strong voice, but no manner of skill. Sir G. Smith shewed me his lady's closett, which was very fine; and, after being very merry, here I lay in a noble chamber, and mighty highly treated, the first time I have lain in London a long time.

28th. Up before day, and Cocke and I took a hackney coach appointed with four horses to take us up, and so carried us over London Bridge. But there, thinking of some business, I did 'light at the foot of the bridge, and by helpe of a candle at a stall, where some pavers were at work, I wrote a letter to Mr. Hater, and never knew so great an instance of the usefulness of carrying pen and ink and wax about one: so we, the way being very bad, to Nonesuch, and thence to Sir Robert Long's house;[1] a fine place, and dinner time ere we got thither; but we had breakfasted a little at Mr. Gawden's, he being out of towne though, and there borrowed Dr. Taylor's sermons,[2] and is a most excellent booke and worth my buying, where had a very good dinner, and curiously dressed, and here a couple of ladies, kinswomen of his, not handsome though, but rich, that knew me by report of The. Turner, and mighty merry we were. After dinner to talk of our business, the Act of Parliament, where in short I see Sir R. Long mighty fierce in the great good qualities of it. But in that and many other things he was stiff in, I think without much judgement, or the judgement I expected from him, and already they have evaded the necessity of bringing people into the Exchequer with their bills to be paid there. Sir G. Carteret is titched[3] at this, yet resolves with me to make the best use we can of this Act for the King, but all our care, we think, will not render it as it should be. He

[1] Sir Robert Long was Auditor of the Exchequer, which office was removed from Westminster to his Majesty's honour of Nonsuch, August 15th, 1665. On September 22nd, 1670, the king demised the Great Park, Great Park Meadow, and the mansion house called Worcester Park, to Sir Robert Long, Bart., for ninety-nine years (Manning and Bray's "Surrey," vol. ii., p. 606).

[2] Collections of Bishop Jeremy Taylor's Sermons were published in 1651-53 and 1657.

[3] Fretful, tetchy.

did again here alone discourse with me about my Lord, and is himself strongly for my Lord's not going to sea, which I am glad to hear and did confirm him in it. He tells me too that he talked last night with the Duke of Albemarle about my Lord Sandwich, by the by making him sensible that it is his interest to preserve his old friends, which he confessed he had reason to do, for he knows that ill offices were doing of him, and that he honoured my Lord Sandwich with all his heart. After this discourse we parted, and all of us broke up and we parted. Captain Cocke and I through Wandsworth. Drank at Sir Allen Broderick's,[1] a great friend and comrade of Cocke's, whom he values above the world for a witty companion, and I believe he is so. So to Fox-Hall and there took boat, and down to the Old Swan, and thence to Lumbard Streete, it being darke night, and thence to the Tower. Took boat and down to Greenwich, Cocke and I, he home and I to the office, where did a little business, and then to my lodgings, where my wife is come, and I am well pleased with it, only much trouble in those lodgings we have, the mistresse of the house being so deadly dear in everything we have; so that we do resolve to remove home soon as we know how the plague goes this weeke, which we hope will be a good decrease. So to bed.

29th. Up, my wife and I talking how to dispose of our goods, and resolved upon sending our two mayds Alce (who has been a day or two at Woolwich with my wife, thinking to have had a feast there) and Susan home. So my wife after dinner did take them to London with some goods, and I in the afternoon after doing other business did go also by agreement to meet Captain Cocke and from him to Sir Roger Cuttance, about the money due from Cocke to him for the late prize goods, wherein Sir Roger is troubled that he hath not payment as agreed, and the other, that he must pay without being secured in the quiett possession of

[1] Alan Broderick, son of Sir Thomas Broderick, of Richmond, Yorkshire, and Wandsworth, Surrey, was born in 1623 at Garret, near Wandsworth. After the Restoration he successively filled the offices of Provost-Marshal of Munster, Surveyor-General of Ireland, and one of the Commissioners for the settlement of the affairs of that kingdom. He was knighted by Charles II., and died in 1680.

them, but some accommodation to both, I think, will be found. But Cocke do tell me that several have begged so much of the King to be discovered out of stolen prize goods and so I am afeard we shall hereafter have trouble, therefore I will get myself free of them as soon as I can and my money paid. Thence home to my house, calling my wife, where the poor wretch is putting things in a way to be ready for our coming home, and so by water together to Greenwich, and so spent the night together.

30th. Up, and at the office all the morning. At noon comes Sir Thomas Allen, and I made him dine with me, and very friendly he is, and a good man, I think, but one that professes he loves to get and to save. He dined with my wife and me and Mrs. Barbary, whom my wife brings along with her from Woolwich for as long as she stays here. In the afternoon to the office, and there very late writing letters and then home, my wife and people sitting up for me, and after supper to bed. Great joy we have this week in the weekly Bill, it being come to 544 in all, and but 333 of the plague; so that we are encouraged to get to London soon as we can. And my father writes as great news of joy to them, that he saw Yorke's waggon go again this week to London, and was full of passengers; and tells me that my aunt Bell hath been dead of the plague these seven weeks.

December 1st. This morning to the office, full of resolution to spend the whole day at business, and there, among other things, I did agree with Poynter to be my clerke for my Victualling business, and so all alone all the day long shut up in my little closett at my office, drawing up instructions,[1] which I should long since have done for my Surveyours of the Ports, Sir W. Coventry desiring much to have them, and he might well have expected them long since. After dinner to it again, and at night had long discourse with Gibson, who is for Yarmouth, who makes me understand so much of the victualling business and the pursers' trade, that I am ashamed I should go about the concerning myself in a business which I understand so very very little of, and made me distrust all I had been doing to-day. So

[1] Instructions for the Victualling Agent in the Port of London, dated November 30th, 1665, will be found among the Rawlinson MSS. in the Bodleian.

I did lay it by till to-morrow morning to think of it afresh, and so home by promise to my wife, to have mirth there. So we had our neighbours, little Miss Tooker and Mrs. Daniels, to dance, and after supper I to bed, and left them merry below, which they did not part from till two or three in the morning.

2nd. Up, and discoursing with my wife, who is resolved to go to London for good and all this day, we did agree upon giving Mr. Sheldon £10, and Mrs. Barbary two pieces, and so I left her to go down thither to fetch away the rest of the things and pay him the money, and so I to the office, where very busy setting Mr. Poynter to write out my last night's worke, which pleases me this day, but yet it is pretty to reflect how much I am out of confidence with what I had done upon Gibson's discourse with me, for fear I should have done it sillily, but Poynter likes them, and Mr. Hater also, but yet I am afeard lest they should do it out of flattery, so conscious I am of my ignorance. Dined with my wife at noon and took leave of her, she being to go to London, as I said, for altogether, and I to the office, busy till past one in the morning.

3rd. It being Lord's day, up and dressed and to church, thinking to have sat with Sir James Bunce[1] to hear his daughter[2] and her husband sing, that are so much commended, but was prevented by being invited into Coll. Cleggatt's pew. However, there I sat, near Mr. Laneare, with whom I spoke, and in sight, by chance, and very near my fat brown beauty of our Parish, the rich merchant's lady, a very noble woman,[3] and Madame Pierce. A good sermon of Mr. Plume's, and so to Captain Cocke's, and there dined with him, and Colonell Wyndham, a worthy gentleman, whose wife was nurse to the present King,[4] and one that while she lived governed him and every thing else,

[1] Sir James Bunce was an alderman of the city of London.

[2] Mrs. Chamberlain (see December 24th).

[3] Apparently Mrs. Lethieulier, daughter of Sir William Hooker (see December 13th).

[4] Colonel Wyndham's wife was Anne, daughter and co-heir of Thomas Gerard, of Trent, Somersetshire. As to Mrs. Wyndham's influence over Charles II., when Prince of Wales, see Clarendon, vol. v., p. 153, ed. 1826. — B.

as Cocke says, as a minister of state; the old King putting mighty weight and trust upon her. They talked much of matters of State and persons, and particularly how my Lord Barkeley hath all along been a fortunate, though a passionate and but weak man as to policy; but as a kinsman brought in and promoted by my Lord of St. Alban's, and one that is the greatest vapourer in the world, this Colonell Wyndham says; and one to whom only, with Jacke Asheburne[1] and Colonel Legg,[2] the King's removal to the Isle of Wight from Hampton Court was communicated; and (though betrayed by their knavery, or at best by their ignorance, insomuch that they have all solemnly charged one another with their failures therein, and have been at daggers-drawing publickly about it), yet now none greater friends in the world. We dined, and in comes Mrs. Owen, a kinswoman of my Lord Bruncker's, about getting a man discharged, which I did for her, and by and by Mrs. Pierce to speake with me (and Mary my wife's late maid, now gone to her) about her husband's business of money, and she tells us how she prevented Captain Fisher the other day in his purchase of all her husband's fine goods, as pearls and silks, that he had seized in an Apothecary's house, a friend of theirs, but she got in and broke them open and removed all before Captain Fisher came the next day to fetch them away, at which he is starke mad. She went home, and I to my lodgings. At night by agreement I fetched her again with Cocke's coach, and he come and we sat and talked together, thinking to have had Mrs. Coleman and my songsters, her husband and Laneare, but they failed me. So we to supper, and as merry as was sufficient, and my pretty little Miss with me; and so after supper walked [with] Pierce home, and so back and to bed. But, Lord! I stand admiring of the wittinesse of her little boy, which is one of the wittiest boys, but most confident that ever I did see of a child of 9 years old or under in all my life, or indeed one twice his age almost, but all for roguish wit. So to bed.

[1] Should be Ashburnham. See Sir John Ashburnham's "Vindication," and note to November 16th, *ante*.

[2] William Legge, Groom of the Bedchamber to Charles I., and father to George Legge, first Lord Dartmouth. He was M.P. for Southampton. Died 1672.

4th. Several people to me about business, among others Captain Taylor, intended Storekeeper for Harwich, whom I did give some assistance in his dispatch by lending him money. So out and by water to London and to the 'Change, and up and down about several businesses, and after the observing (God forgive me!) one or two of my neighbour Jason's women come to towne, which did please me very well, home to my house at the office, where my wife had got a dinner for me: and it was a joyfull thing for us to meet here, for which God be praised! Here was her brother come to see her, and speake with me about business. It seems my recommending of him hath not only obtained his presently being admitted into the Duke of Albemarle's guards, and present pay, but also by the Duke's and Sir Philip Howard's direction, to be put as a right-hand man, and other marks of special respect, at which I am very glad, partly for him, and partly to see that I am reckoned something in my recommendations, but wish he may carry himself that I may receive no disgrace by him. So to the 'Change. Up and down again in the evening about business and to meet Captain Cocke, who waited for Mrs. Pierce (with whom he is mightily stricken), to receive and hide for her her rich goods she saved the other day from seizure. Upon the 'Change to-day Colvill tells me, from Oxford, that the King in person hath justified my Lord Sandwich to the highest degree; and is right in his favour to the uttermost. So late by water home, taking a barrel of oysters with me, and at Greenwich went and sat with Madam Penington . . . . and made her undress her head and sit dishevilled all night sporting till two in the morning, and so away to my lodging and so to bed. Over-fasting all the morning hath filled me mightily with wind, and nothing else hath done it, that I fear a fit of the cholique.

5th. Up and to the office, where very busy about several businesses all the morning. At noon empty, yet without stomach to dinner, having spoiled myself with fasting yesterday, and so filled with wind. In the afternoon by water, calling Mr. Stevens (who is with great trouble paying of seamen of their tickets at Deptford) and to London, to look for Captain Kingdon, whom we found at home about

5 o'clock. I tried him, and he promised to follow us presently to the East India House to sign papers to-night in order to the settling the business of my receiving money for Tangier. We went and stopt the officer there to shut up. He made us stay above an houre. I sent for him; he comes, but was not found at home, but abroad on other business, and brings a paper saying that he had been this houre looking for the Lord Ashley's order. When he looks for it, that is not the paper. He would go again to look; kept us waiting till almost 8 at night. Then was I to go home by water this weather and darke, and to write letters by the post, besides keeping the East India officers there so late. I sent for him again; at last he comes, and says he cannot find the paper (which is a pretty thing to lay orders for £100,000 no better). I was angry; he told me I ought to give people ease at night, and all business was to be done by day. I answered him sharply, that I did [not] make, nor any honest man, any difference between night and day in the King's business, and this was such, and my Lord Ashley should know. He answered me short. I told him I knew the time (meaning the Rump's time) when he did other men's business with more diligence. He cried, "Nay, say not so," and stopped his mouth, not one word after. We then did our business without the order in less than eight minutes, which he made me to no purpose stay above two hours for the doing. This made him mad, and so we exchanged notes, and I had notes for £14,000 of the Treasurer of the Company, and so away and by water to Greenwich and wrote my letters, and so home late to bed.

6th. Up betimes, it being fast-day; and by water to the Duke of Albemarle,[1] who come to towne from Oxford last night. He is mighty brisk, and very kind to me, and asks my advice principally in everything. He surprises me with the news that my Lord Sandwich goes Embassador to Spayne speedily;[2] though I know not whence this arises,

[1] At the Cockpit.

[2] Lord Sandwich's conduct at Bergen, when he captured eight Dutch ships of war and about twenty other vessels, and appropriated a portion of the cargo to his own use, caused him to be reprimanded and deprived of his command. To screen him, however, from public disgrace

FACSIMILE OF FIRST PAGE OF MS. IN THE PEPYS COLLECTION.

FACSIMILE OF FIRST PAGE OF MS. IN THE PEPYS COLLECTION.

yet I am heartily glad of it. He did give me several directions what to do, and so I home by water again and to church a little, thinking to have met Mrs. Pierce in order to our meeting at night; but she not there, I home and dined, and comes presently by appointment my wife. I spent the afternoon upon a song[1] of Solyman's words to Roxalana that I have set, and so with my wife walked and Mercer to Mrs. Pierce's, where Captain Rolt and Mrs. Knipp,[2] Mr. Coleman and his wife, and Laneare, Mrs. Worshipp[3] and her singing daughter, met; and by and by unexpectedly comes Mr. Pierce from Oxford. Here the best company for musique I ever was in, in my life, and wish I could live and die in it, both for musique and the face of Mrs. Pierce, and my wife and Knipp, who is pretty enough; but the most excellent, mad-humoured thing, and

he was appointed ambassador to Spain. Sir Richard Fanshaw, our ambassador there, was unjustly superseded. Clarendon, in his "Life," gives as the reason for Fanshaw's recall disapproval of the commercial treaty between England and Spain of December 17th, 1665, which he had signed; but we see from Pepys's words that Lord Sandwich's appointment had been decided upon before this (see Lister's "Life of Clarendon," vol. ii., p. 359).

[1] The words of this song, addressed by Solyman to Roxolana, are taken from the second part of the "Siege of Rhodes," act iv., sc. 2. Pepys's music is in the Pepysian Library.

"Beauty retire; thou doest my pitty move,
Believe my pitty, and then trust my love.
[*Exit* ROXOLANA.
Att first I thought her by our Prophet sent,
As a re-ward for valour's toiles,
More worth than all my Fa-ther's spoiles;
But now, she is become my punishment.
But thou art just, O Pow'r di-vine,
With niew and painfull arts
Of studied warr, I breake the hearts
Of half the world, and shee breakes mine."

[2] Genest, in his "History of the British Stage," vol. i., enumerates sixteen characters filled by Mrs. Knipp, at the King's House, between 1664 and 1678, when she disappears from the playbills, in which her name is spelt in six different ways. The details in the Diary respecting this lively actress and "her brute of a husband,' whom Pepys describes as a "horse jockey," are so amusing, that any particulars of their subsequent history would have been interesting.

[3] Sister of Mrs. Clerke, wife of Dr. Clerke. See February 13th, 1666-67.

sings the noblest that ever I heard in my life, and Rolt, with her, some things together most excellently. I spent the night in extasy almost; and, having invited them to my house a day or two hence, we broke up, Pierce having told me that he is told how the King hath done my Lord Sandwich all the right imaginable, by shewing him his countenance before all the world on every occasion, to remove thoughts of discontent; and that he is to go Embassador, and that the Duke of Yorke is made generall of all forces by land and sea, and the Duke of Albemarle, lieutenant-generall. Whether the two latter alterations be so, true or no, he knows not, but he is told so; but my Lord is in full favour with the King. So all home and to bed.

7th. Up and to the office, where very busy all day. Sir G. Carteret's letter tells me my Lord Sandwich is, as I was told, declared Embassador Extraordinary to Spayne, and to go with all speed away, and that his enemies have done him as much good as he could wish. At noon late to dinner, and after dinner spent till night with Mr. Gibson and Hater discoursing and making myself more fully [know] the trade of pursers, and what fittest to be done in their business, and so to the office till midnight writing letters, and so home, and after supper with my wife about one o'clock to bed.

8th. Up, well pleased in my mind about my Lord Sandwich, about whom I shall know more anon from Sir G. Carteret, who will be in towne, and also that the Hambrough [ships] after all difficulties are got out. God send them good speed! So, after being trimmed, I by water to London, to the Navy office, there to give order to my mayde to buy things to send down to Greenwich for supper to-night; and I also to buy other things, as oysters, and lemons, 6*d.* per piece, and oranges, 3*d.* That done I to the 'Change, and among many other things, especially for getting of my Tangier money, I by appointment met Mr. Gawden, and he and I to the Pope's Head Taverne, and there he did give me alone a very pretty dinner. Our business to talk of his matters and his supply of money, which was necessary for us to talk on before the Duke of Albemarle this afternoon and Sir G. Carteret. After that I offered now to pay him the £4,000 remaining of his

£8,000 for Tangier, which he took with great kindnesse, and prayed me most frankly to give him a note for £3,500 and accept the other £500 for myself, which in good earnest was against my judgement to do, for [I] expected about £100 and no more, but however he would have me do it, and ownes very great obligations to me, and the man indeed I love, and he deserves it. This put me into great joy, though with a little stay to it till we have time to settle it, for so great a sum I was fearfull any accident might by death or otherwise defeate me, having not now time to change papers. So we rose, and by water to White Hall, where we found Sir G. Carteret with the Duke, and also Sir G. Downing, whom I had not seen in many years before. He greeted me very kindly, and I him; though methinks I am touched, that it should be said that he was my master heretofore, as doubtless he will. So to talk of our Navy business, and particularly money business, of which there is little hopes of any present supply upon this new Act, the goldsmiths being here (and Alderman Backewell newly come from Flanders), and none offering any. So we rose without doing more than my stating the case of the Victualler, that whereas there is due to him on the last year's declaration £80,000, and the charge of this year's amounts to £420,-000 and odd, he must be supplied between this and the end of January with £150,000, and the remainder in 40 weeks by weekly payments, or else he cannot go through his business. Thence after some discourse with Sir G. Carteret, who, though he tells me that he is glad of my Lord's being made Embassador, and that it is the greatest courtesy his enemies could do him; yet I find he is not heartily merry upon it, and that it was no design of my Lord's friends, but the prevalence of his enemies, and that the Duke of Albemarle and Prince Rupert are like to go to sea together the next year. I pray God, when my Lord is gone, they do not fall hard upon the Vice-Chamberlain, being alone, and in so envious a place, though by this late Act and the instructions now a brewing for our office as to method of payments will destroy the profit of his place of itself without more trouble. Thence by water down to Greenwich, and there found all my company come; that is, Mrs. Knipp, and an ill, melancholy, jealous-looking fellow, her husband, that spoke not a word to us all the night, Pierce and his wife, and Rolt, Mrs. Worshipp and her daughter, Coleman and his wife, and Laneare, and, to make us perfectly happy, there comes by chance to towne Mr. Hill to see us. Most excellent musique we had in abundance, and a good supper, dancing, and a pleasant scene of Mrs. Knipp's rising sicke from table, but whispered me it was for some hard word or other her husband gave her just now when she laughed and was more merry than ordinary. But we got her in humour again, and mighty merry; spending the night, till two in the morning, with most complete content as ever in my life, it being increased by my day's work with Gawden. Then broke up, and we to bed, Mr. Hill and I, whom I love more and more, and he us.

9th. Called up betimes by my Lord Bruncker, who is come to towne from his long water worke at Erith last night, to go with him to the Duke of Albemarle, which by his coach I did. Our discourse upon the ill posture of the times through lacke of money. At the Duke's did some business, and I believe he was not pleased to see all the Duke's discourse and applications to me and every body else. Discoursed also with Sir G. Carteret about office business, but no money in view. Here my Lord and I staid and dined, the Vice-Chamberlain taking his leave. At table the Duchesse, a damned ill-looked woman, complaining of her Lord's going to sea the next year, said these cursed words: "If my Lord had been a coward he had gone to sea no more: it may be then he might have been excused, and made an Embassador" (meaning my Lord Sandwich).[1] This made me mad, and I believed she perceived my countenance change, and blushed herself very much. I was in hopes others had not minded it, but my Lord Bruncker, after we were come away, took notice of the words to me

[1] When Lord Sandwich was away a new commander had to be chosen, and rank and long service pointed out Prince Rupert for the office, it having been decided that the heir presumptive should be kept at home. It was thought, however, that the same confidence could not be placed in the prince's discretion as in his courage, and therefore the Duke of Albemarle was induced to take a joint command with him, "and so make one admiral of two persons" (see Lister's "Life of Clarendon," vol. ii., pp. 360, 361).

with displeasure. Thence after dinner away by water, calling and taking leave of Sir G. Carteret, whom we found going through at White Hall, and so over to Lambeth and took coach and home, and so to the office, where late writing letters, and then home to Mr. Hill, and sang, among other things, my song of "Beauty retire," which he likes, only excepts against two notes in the base, but likes the whole very well. So late to bed.

10th (Lord's day). Lay long talking, Hill and I, with great pleasure, and then up, and being ready walked to Cocke's for some newes, but heard none, only they would have us stay their dinner, and sent for my wife, who come, and very merry we were, there being Sir Edmund Pooly and Mr. Evelyn. Before we had dined comes Mr. Andrews, whom we had sent for to Bow, and so after dinner home, and there we sang some things, but not with much pleasure, Mr. Andrews being in so great haste to go home, his wife looking every hour to be brought to bed. He gone Mr. Hill and I continued our musique, one thing after another, late till supper, and so to bed with great pleasure.

11th. Lay long with great pleasure talking. So I left him and to London to the 'Change, and after discoursed with several people about business; met Mr. Gawden at the Pope's Head, where he brought Mr. Lewes and T. Willson to discourse about the Victualling business, and the alterations of the pursers' trade, for something must be done to secure the King a little better, and yet that they may have wherewith to live. After dinner I took him aside, and perfected to my great joy my business with him, wherein he deals most nobly in giving me his hand for the £4,000, and would take my note but for £3,500. This is a great blessing, and God make me thankfull truly for it. With him till it was darke putting in writing our discourse about victualling, and so parted, and I to Viner's, and there evened all accounts, and took up my notes setting all straight between us to this day. The like to Colvill, and paying several bills due from me on the Tangier account. Then late met Cocke and Temple[1] at the Pope's Head, and there had good discourse with Temple, who tells me that of the

[1] "Sir Robert Viner's chief man" (see September 30th, 1665).

£80,000 advanced already by the East India Company, they have had £45,000 out of their hands. He discoursed largely of the quantity of money coyned, and what may be thought the real sum of money in the kingdom. He told me, too, as an instance of the thrift used in the King's business, that the tools and the interest of the money-using to the King for the money he borrowed while the new invention of the mill money was perfected, cost him £35,000, and in mirthe tells me that the new fashion money is good for nothing but to help the Prince if he can secretly get copper plates shut up in silver it shall never be discovered, at least not in his age. Thence Cocke and I by water, he home and I home, and there sat with Mr. Hill and my wife supping, talking and singing till midnight, and then to bed. [That I may remember it the more particularly, I thought fit to insert this additional memorandum of Temple's discourse this night with me, which I took in writing from his mouth. Before the Harp and Crosse money was cried down, he and his fellow goldsmiths did make some particular trials what proportion that money bore to the old King's money, and they found that generally it come to, one with another, about £25 in every £100. Of this money there was, upon the calling of it in, £650,000 at least brought into the Tower; and from thence he computes that the whole money of England must be full £16,250,000. But for all this believes that there is above £30,000,000; he supposing that about the King's coming in (when he begun to observe the quantity of the new money) people begun to be fearfull of this money's being cried down, and so picked it out and set it a-going as fast as they could, to be rid of it; and he thinks £30,000,000 the rather, because if there were but £16,250,000 the King having £2,000,000 every year, would have the whole money of the kingdom in his hands in eight years. He tells me about £350,000 sterling was coined out of the French money, the proceeds of Dunkirke; so that, with what was coined of the Crosse money, there is new coined about £1,000,000 besides the gold, which is guessed at £500,000. He tells me, that, though the King did deposit the French money in pawn all the while for the £350,000 he was forced to borrow thereupon till the tools could be made for the new Minting in the present form, yet the interest he paid for that time came to £35,000, Viner having to his knowledge £10,000 for the use of £100,000 of it.][1]

12th. Up, and to the office, where my Lord Bruncker met, and among other things did finish a contract with Cocke for hemp, by which I hope to get my money due from him paid presently. At noon home to dinner, only eating a bit, and with much kindness taking leave of Mr. Hill who goes away to-day, and so I by water saving the tide through Bridge and to Sir G. Downing by appointment at Charing Crosse, who did at first mightily please me with informing me thoroughly the virtue and force of this Act, and indeed it is ten times better than ever I thought could have been said of it, but when he come to impose upon me that without more ado I must get by my credit people to serve in goods and lend money upon it and none could do it better than I, and the King should give me thanks particularly in it, and I could not get him to excuse me, but I must come to him though to no purpose on Saturday, and that he is sure I will bring him some bargains or other made upon this Act, it vexed me more than all the pleasure I took before, for I find he will be troublesome to me in it, if I will let him have as much of my time as he would have. So late I took leave and in the cold (the weather setting in cold) home to the office and, after my letters being wrote, home to supper and to bed, my wife being also gone to London.

13th. Up betimes and finished my Journall for five days back, and then after being ready to my Lord Bruncker by appointment, there to order the disposing of some money that we have come into the office, and here to my great content I did get a bill of imprest to Captain Cocke to pay myself in part of what is coming to me from him for my Lord Sandwich's satisfaction and my owne, and also another payment or two wherein I am concerned, and having done that did go to Mr. Pierce's, where he and his wife made me drink some tea, and so he and I by water together to London. Here at a taverne in Cornhill he and I did agree

[1] The passage between brackets is from a piece of paper inserted in this place.

upon my delivering up to him a bill of Captain Cocke's, put into my hand for Pierce's use upon evening of reckonings about the prize goods, and so away to the 'Change, and there hear the ill news, to my great and all our great trouble, that the plague is encreased again this week, notwithstanding there hath been a day or two great frosts; but we hope it is only the effects of the late close warm weather, and if the frosts continue the next week, may fall again; but the town do thicken so much with people, that it is much if the plague do not grow again upon us. Off the 'Change invited by Sheriff Hooker, who keeps the poorest, mean, dirty table in a dirty house that ever I did see any Sheriff of London; and a plain, ordinary, silly man I think he is, but rich; only his son, Mr. Lethulier,[1] I like, for a pretty, civil, understanding merchant; and the more by much, because he happens to be husband to our noble, fat, brave lady in our parish, that I and my wife admire so. Thence away to the Pope's Head Taverne, and there met first with Captain Cocke, and dispatched my business with him to my content, he being ready to sign his bill of imprest of £2,000, and gives it me in part of his payment to me, which glads my heart. He being gone, comes Sir W. Warren, who advised with me about several things about getting money, and £100 I shall presently have of him. We advised about a business of insurance, wherein something may be saved to him and got to me, and to that end he and I did take a coach at night and to the Cockepitt, there to get the Duke of Albemarle's advice for our insuring some of our Sounde goods coming home under Harman's convoy, but he proved shy of doing it without knowledge of the Duke of Yorke, so we back again and calling at my house to see my wife, who is well; though my great trouble is that our poor little parish is the greatest number this weeke in all the city within the walls, having six, from one the last weeke; and so by water to Greenwich leaving Sir W. Warren at home, and I straight to my Lord Bruncker, it being late, and concluded upon insuring something and to send to that purpose to Sir W. Warren to come to us

[1] Mr. Lethieulier's wife was Anne, daughter of Sir William Hooker (see October 14th, 1666), and his wife Mary, daughter of Thomas Gipps, or Gibbs, of London.

to-morrow morning. So I home and, my mind in great rest, to bed.

14th. Up, and to the office a while with my Lord Bruncker, where we directed Sir W. Warren in the business of the insurance as I desired, and ended some other businesses of his, and so at noon I to London, but the 'Change was done before I got thither, so I to the Pope's Head Taverne, and there find Mr. Gawden and Captain Beckford and Nick Osborne going to dinner, and I dined with them and very exceeding merry we were as I had [not] been a great while, and dinner being done I to the East India House and there had an assignment on Mr. Temple for the £2,000 of Cocke's, which joyed my heart; so, having seen my wife in the way, I home by water and to write my letters and then home to bed.

15th. Up, and spent all the morning with my Surveyors of the Ports for the Victualling, and there read to them what instructions I had provided for them and discoursed largely much of our business and the business of the pursers. I left them to dine with my people, and to my Lord Bruncker's, where I met with a great good dinner and Sir T. Teddiman, with whom my Lord and I were to discourse about the bringing of W. Howe to a tryall for his jewells, and there till almost night, and so away toward the office and in my way met with Sir James Bunce; and after asking what newes, he cried "Ah!" says he (I know [not] whether in earnest or jest), "this is the time for you," says he, "that were for Oliver heretofore; you are full of employment, and we poor Cavaliers sit still and can get nothing;" which was a pretty reproach, I thought, but answered nothing to it, for fear of making it worse. So away and I to see Mrs. Penington, but company being to come to her, I staid not, but to the office a little and so home, and after supper to bed.

16th. Up, and met at the office; Sir W. Batten with us, who come from Portsmouth on Monday last, and hath not been with us to see or discourse with us about any business till this day. At noon to dinner, Sir W. Warren with me on boat, and thence I by water, it being a fearfull cold, snowing day to Westminster to White Hall stairs and thence to Sir G. Downing, to whom I brought the happy newes of my having contracted, as we did this day with Sir W. Warren, for a ship's lading of Norway goods here and another at Harwich to the value of above £3,000, which is the first that hath been got upon the New Act, and he is overjoyed with it and tells me he will do me all the right to Court about it in the world, and I am glad I have it to write to Sir W. Coventry to-night. He would fain have me come in £200 to lend upon the Act, but I desire to be excused in doing that, it being to little purpose for us that relate to the King to do it, for the sum gets the King no courtesy nor credit. So I parted from him and walked to Westminster Hall, where Sir W. Warren, who come along with me, staid for me, and there I did see Betty Howlet come after the sicknesse to the Hall. Had not opportunity to salute her, as I desired, but was glad to see her and a very pretty wench she is. Thence back, landing at the Old Swan and taking boat again at Billingsgate, and setting ashore we home and I to the office, . . . and there wrote my letters, and so home to supper and to bed, it being a great frost. Newes is come to-day of our Sounde fleete being come, but I do not know what Sir W. Warren hath insured.

17th (Lord's day). After being trimmed word brought me that Cutler's coach is, by appointment, come to the Isle of Doggs for me, and so I over the water; and in his coach to Hackney, a very fine, cold, clear, frosty day. At his house I find him with a plain little dinner, good wine, and welcome. He is still a prating man; and the more I know him, the less I find in him. A pretty house he hath here indeed, of his owne building. His old mother was an object at dinner that made me not like it; and, after dinner, to visit his sicke wife I did not also take much joy in, but very friendly he is to me, not for any kindnesse I think he hath to any man, but thinking me, I perceive, a man whose friendship is to be looked after. After dinner back again and to Deptford to Mr. Evelyn's, who was not within, but I had appointed my cozen Thos. Pepys of Hatcham to meet me there, to discourse about getting his £1,000 of my Lord Sandwich, having now an opportunity of my having above that sum in my hands of his. I found this a dull fellow still in all his discourse, but in this he is ready enough to embrace what I counsel him to, which is, to write importunately to my Lord and me about it and I will look after it. I do again and again declare myself a man unfit to be security for such a sum. He walked with me as far as Deptford upper towne, being mighty respectfull to me, and there parted, he telling me that this towne is still very bad of the plague. I walked to Greenwich first, to make a short visit to my Lord Bruncker, and next to Mrs. Penington and spent all the evening with her with the same freedom I used to have and very pleasant company. With her till one of the clock in the morning and past, and so to my lodging to bed, and

18th. Betimes up, it being a fine frost, and walked it to Redriffe, calling and drinking at Half-way house, thinking, indeed, to have overtaken some of the people of our house, the women, who were to walk the same walke, but I could not. So to London, and there visited my wife, and was a little displeased to find she is so forward all of a spurt to make much of her brother and sister since my last kindnesse to him in getting him a place, but all ended well presently, and I to the 'Change and up and down to Kingdon and the goldsmith's to meet Mr. Stephens, and did get all my money matters most excellently cleared to my complete satisfaction. Passing over Cornhill I spied young Mrs. Daniel and Sarah, my landlady's daughter, who are come, as I expected, to towne, and did say they spied me and I dogged them to St. Martin's, where I passed by them being shy, and walked down as low as Ducke Lane and enquired for some Spanish books, and so back again and they were gone. So to the 'Change, hoping to see them in the streete, and missing them, went back again thither and back to the 'Change, but no sight of them, so went after my business again, and, though late, was sent to by Sir W. Warren (who heard where I was) to intreat me to come dine with him, hearing that I lacked a dinner, at the Pope's Head; and there with Mr. Hinton,[1] the goldsmith, and others, very merry; but, Lord! to see how Dr. Hinton[2] come in with a gallant or two from

[1] Edmund Hinton, a goldsmith in Lombard Street (Ellis's "Original Letters," 3rd series, vol. iv., p. 310).

[2] John Hinton, M.D., a strong royalist, who attended Henrietta Maria in her confinement at Exeter when she gave birth to the Princess

Court, and do so call "Cozen" Mr. Hinton, the goldsmith, but I that know him to be a beggar and a knave, did make great sport in my mind at it. After dinner Sir W. Warren and I alone in another room a little while talking about business, and so parted, and I hence, my mind full of content in my day's worke, home by water to Greenwich, the river beginning to be very full of ice, so as I was a little frighted, but got home well, it being darke. So having no mind to do any business, went home to my lodgings, and there got little Mrs. Tooker, and Mrs. Daniel, the daughter, and Sarah to my chamber to cards and sup with me, when in comes Mr. Pierce to me, who tells me how W. Howe has been examined on shipboard by my Lord Bruncker to-day, and others, and that he has charged him out of envy with sending goods under my Lord's seale and in my Lord Bruncker's name, thereby to get them safe passage, which, he tells me, is false, but that he did use my name to that purpose, and hath acknowledged it to my Lord Bruncker, but do also confess to me that one parcel he thinks he did use my Lord Bruncker's name, which do vexe me mightily that my name should be brought in question about such things, though I did not say much to him of my discontent till I have spoke with my Lord Bruncker about it. So he being gone, being to go to Oxford to-morrow, we to cards again late, and so broke up, I having great pleasure with my little girle, Mrs. Tooker.

19th. Up, and to the office, where all the morning. At noon by agreement comes Hatcham Pepys to dine with me. I thought to have had him to Sir J. Minnes to a good venison pasty with the rest of my fellows, being invited, but seeing much company I went away with him and had a good dinner at home. He did give me letters he hath wrote to my Lord and Moore about my Lord's money to get it paid to my cozen, which I will make good use of. I made mighty much of him, but a sorry dull fellow he is, fit

Henrietta. He was knighted by Charles II., and appointed physician in ordinary to the king and queen. His knighthood was a reward for having procured a private advance of money from his kinsman, the goldsmith, to enable the Duke of Albemarle to pay the army (see "Memorial to King Charles II. from Sir John Hinton, A.D. 1679," printed in Ellis's "Original Letters," 3rd series, vol. iv., p. 296).

for nothing that is ingenious, nor is there a turd of kindnesse or service to be had from him. So I shall neglect him if I could get but him satisfied about this money that I may be out of bonds for my Lord to him. To see that this fellow could desire me to helpe him to some employment if it were but of £100 per annum: when he is not worth less than, I believe, £20,000. He gone, I to Sir J. Minnes, and thence with my Lord Bruncker on board the Bezan to examine W. Howe again, who I find upon this tryall one of much more wit and ingenuity in his answers than ever I expected, he being very cunning and discreet and well spoken in them. I said little to him or concerning him; but, Lord! to see how he writes to me adays, and styles me "My Honour." So much is a man subjected and dejected under afflictions as to flatter me in that manner on this occasion. Back with my Lord to Sir J. Minnes, where I left him and the rest of a great deale of company, and so I to my office, where late writing letters and then home to bed.

20th. Up, and was trimmed, but not time enough to save my Lord Bruncker's coach or Sir J. Minnes's, and so was fain to walk to Lambeth on foot, but it was a very fine frosty walke, and great pleasure in it, but troublesome getting over the River for ice. I to the Duke of Albemarle, whither my brethren were all come, but I was not too late. There we sat in discourse upon our Navy business an houre, and thence in my Lord Bruncker's coach alone, he walking before (while I staid awhile talking with Sir G. Downing about the Act, in which he is horrid troublesome) to the Old Exchange. Thence I took Sir Ellis Layton to Captain Cocke's, where my Lord Bruncker and Lady Williams dine, and we all mighty merry; but Sir Ellis Layton one of the best companions at a meale in the world. After dinner I to the Exchange to see whether my pretty seamstress be come again or no, and I find she is, so I to her, saluted her over her counter in the open Exchange above, and mightily joyed to see her, poor pretty woman! I must confess I think her a great beauty. After laying out a little money there for two pair of thread stockings, cost 8*s.*, I to Lumbard Streete to see some business to-night there at the goldsmith's, among others paying in £1,258 to Viner for my Lord Sandwich's use upon Cocke's account. I was called by my Lord Bruncker in his coach with his mistresse, and Mr. Cottle the lawyer, our acquaintance at Greenwich, and so home to Greenwich, and thence I to Mrs. Penington, and had a supper from the King's Head for her, and there mighty merry and free as I used to be with her, and at last, late, I did pray her to undress herself into her nightgowne, that I might see how to have her picture drawne carelessly (for she is mighty proud of that conceit), and I would walk without in the streete till she had done. So I did walk forth, and whether I made too many turns or no in the darke cold frosty night between the two walls up to the Parke gate I know not, but she was gone to bed when I come again to the house, upon pretence of leaving some papers there, which I did on purpose by her consent. So I away home, and was there sat up for to be spoken with my young Mrs. Daniel, to pray me to speake for her husband to be a Lieutenant. I had the opportunity here of kissing her again and again, and did answer that I would be very willing to do him any kindnesse, and so parted, and I to bed, exceedingly pleased in all my matters of money this month or two, it having pleased God to bless me with several opportunities of good sums, and that I have them in effect all very well paid, or in my power to have. But two things trouble me; one, the sicknesse is increased above 80 this weeke (though in my owne parish not one has died, though six the last weeke); the other, most of all, which is, that I have so complexed an account for these last two months for variety of layings out upon Tangier, occasions and variety of gettings that I have not made even with myself now these 3 or 4 months, which do trouble me mightily, finding that I shall hardly ever come to understand them thoroughly again, as I used to do my accounts when I was at home.

21st. At the office all the morning. At noon all of us dined at Captain Cocke's at a good chine of beef, and other good meat; but, being all frost-bitten, was most of it unroast; but very merry, and a good dish of fowle we dressed ourselves. Mr. Evelyn there, in very good humour. All the afternoon till night pleasant, and then I took my leave of them and to the office, where I wrote my letters, and away home, my head full of business and some trouble for my letting my accounts go so far that I have made an oathe this night for the drinking no wine, &c., on such penalties till I have passed my accounts and cleared all. Coming home and going to bed, the boy tells me his sister Daniel has provided me a supper of little birds killed by her husband, and I made her sup with me, and after supper were alone a great while, and I had the pleasure of her lips, she being a pretty woman, and one whom a great belly becomes as well as ever I saw any. She gone, I to bed. This day I was come to by Mrs. Burrows, of Westminster, Lieutenant Burrows (lately dead) his wife, a most pretty woman and my old acquaintance; I had a kiss or two of her, and a most modest woman she is.

22nd. Up betimes and to my Lord Bruncker to consider the late instructions sent us for the method of our signing bills hereafter and paying them. By and by, by agreement, comes Sir J. Minnes and Sir W. Batten, and then to read them publicly and consider of putting them in execution. About this all the morning, and, it appearing necessary for the Controller to have another Clerke, I recommended Poynter to him, which he accepts, and I by that means rid of one that I fear would not have been fit for my turne, though he writes very well. At noon comes Mr. Hill to towne, and finds me out here, and brings Mr. Houbland,[1] who met him here. So I was compelled to leave my Lord and his dinner and company, and with them to the Beare, and dined with them and their brothers, of which Hill had his and the other two of his, and mighty merry and very fine company they are, and I glad to see them. After dinner I forced to take leave of them by being called upon by Mr. Andrews, I having sent for him, and by a fine glosse did bring him to desire tallys for what orders I have to pay him and his company for Tangier victualls, and I by that means cleared to myself £210 coming to me upon their two orders, which is also a noble addition to my late profits, which have been very considerable of late, but how great I know not till I come to cast up my accounts, which burdens my mind that it should be so backward, but I am resolved to settle to nothing till I have done it. He gone, I to my Lord Bruncker's, and there spent the evening by my desire

[1] James Houblon.

in seeing his Lordship open to pieces and make up again his watch, thereby being taught what I never knew before; and it is a thing very well worth my having seen, and am mightily pleased and satisfied with it. So I sat talking with him till late at night, somewhat vexed at a snappish answer Madam Williams did give me to herself, upon my speaking a free word to her in mirthe, calling her a mad jade. She answered, we were not so well acquainted yet. But I was more at a letter from my Lord Duke of Albemarle to-day, pressing us to continue our meetings for all Christmas, which, though every body intended not to have done, yet I am concluded in it, who intended nothing else. But I see it is necessary that I do make often visits to my Lord Duke, which nothing shall hinder after I have evened my accounts, and now the river is frozen I know not how to get to him. Thence to my lodging, making up my Journall for 8 or 9 days, and so my mind being eased of it, I to supper and to bed. The weather hath been frosty these eight or nine days, and so we hope for an abatement of the plague the next weeke, or else God have mercy upon us! for the plague will certainly continue the next year if it do not.

23rd. At my office all the morning and home to dinner, my head full of business, and there my wife finds me unexpectedly. But I not being at leisure to stay or talk with her, she went down by coach to Woolwich, thinking to fetch Mrs. Barbary to carry her to London to keep her Christmas with her, and I to the office. This day one come to me with four great turkies, as a present from Mr. Deane, at Harwich, three of which my wife carried in the evening home with her to London in her coach (Mrs. Barbary not being to be got so suddenly, but will come to her the next week), and I at my office late, and then to my lodgings to bed.

24th (Sunday). Up betimes, to my Lord Duke of Albemarle by water, and after some talke with him about business of the office with great content, and so back again and to dinner, my landlady and her daughters with me, and had mince-pies, and very merry at a mischance her young son had in tearing of his new coate quite down the outside of his sleeve in the whole cloth, one of the strangest mishaps that ever I saw in my life. Then to church, and placed myself in the Parson's pew under the pulpit, to hear Mrs. Chamberlain in the next pew sing, who is daughter to Sir James Bunch, of whom I have heard much, and indeed she sings very finely, and from church met with Sir W. Warren and he and I walked together talking about his and my businesses, getting of money as fairly as we can, and, having set him part of his way home, I walked to my Lord Bruncker, whom I heard was at Alderman Hooker's, hoping to see and salute Mrs. Lethulier, whom I did see in passing, but no opportunity of beginning acquaintance, but a very noble lady she is, however the silly alderman got her. Here we sat talking a great while, Sir The. Biddulph and Mr. Vaughan, a son-in-law of Alderman Hooker's. Hence with my Lord Bruncker home and sat a little with him and so home to bed.

25th (Christmas-day). To church in the morning, and there saw a wedding in the church, which I have not seen many a day; and the young people so merry one with another, and strange to see what delight we married people have to see these poor fools decoyed into our condition, every man and woman gazing and smiling at them. Here I saw again my beauty Lethulier. Thence to my Lord Bruncker's by invitation and dined there, and so home to look over and settle my papers, both of my accounts private, and those of Tangier, which I have let go so long that it were impossible for any soul, had I died, to understand them, or ever come to any good end in them. I hope God will never suffer me to come to that disorder again.

26th. Up, and to the office, where Sir J. Minnes and my Lord Bruncker and I met, to give our directions to the Commanders of all the ships in the river to bring in lists of their ships' companies, with entries, discharges, &c., all the last voyage, where young Seymour,[1] among 20 that stood bare, stood with his hat on, a proud, saucy young man. Thence with them to Mr. Cuttle's, being invited, and dined nobly and neatly; with a very pretty house and a fine turret at top, with winding stairs and the finest prospect I know about all Greenwich, save the top of the hill,

[1] Captain Hugh Seymour, of the "Foresight" (fourth rate), who was killed in the action of July, 1666 (see *post*, July 29th).

and yet in some respects better than that. Here I also saw some fine writing worke and flourishing of Mr. Hore, he one that I knew long ago, an acquaintance of Mr. Tomson's at Westminster, that is this man's clerk. It is the story of the several Archbishops of Canterbury, engrossed in vellum, to hang up in Canterbury Cathedrall in tables, in lieu of the old ones, which are almost worn out. Thence to the office a while, and so to Captain Cocke's and there talked, and home to look over my papers, and so to bed.

27th. Up, and with Cocke, by coach to London, there home to my wife, and angry about her desiring a mayde yet, before the plague is quite over. It seems Mercer is troubled that she hath not one under her, but I will not venture my family by increasing it before it be safe. Thence about many businesses, particularly with Sir W. Warren on the 'Change, and he and I dined together and settled our Tangier matters, wherein I get above £200 presently. We dined together at the Pope's Head to do this, and thence to the goldsmiths, I to examine the state of my matters there too, and so with him to my house, but my wife was gone abroad to Mrs. Mercer's, so we took boat, and it being darke and the thaw having broke the ice, but not carried it quite away, the boat did pass through so much of it all along, and that with the crackling and noise that it made me fearfull indeed. So I forced the watermen to land us on Redriffe side, and so walked together till Sir W. Warren and I parted near his house and thence I walked quite over the fields home by light of linke, one of my watermen carrying it, and I reading by the light of it, it being a very fine, clear, dry night. So to Captain Cocke's, and there sat and talked, especially with his Counsellor, about his prize goods, that hath done him good turne, being of the company with Captain Fisher, his name Godderson; here I supped and so home to bed, with great content that the plague is decreased to 152, the whole being but 330.

28th. Up and to the office, and thence with a great deal of business in my head, dined alone with Cocke. So home alone strictly about my accounts, wherein I made a good beginning, and so, after letters wrote by the post, to bed.

29th. Up betimes, and all day long within doors upon my accounts, publique and private, and find the ill effect of letting them go so long without evening, that no soul could have ever understood them but myself, and I with much ado. But, however, my regularity in all I did and spent do helpe me, and I hope to find them well. Late at them and to bed.

30th. Up and to the office, at noon home to dinner, and all the afternoon to my accounts again, and there find myself, to my great joy, a great deal worth above £4,000, for which the Lord be praised! and is principally occasioned by my getting £500 of Cocke, for my profit in his bargains of prize goods, and from Mr. Gawden's making me a present of £500 more, when I paid him £8,000 for Tangier. So to my office to write letters, then to my accounts again, and so to bed, being in great ease of mind.

31st (Lord's day). All the morning in my chamber, writing fair the state of my Tangier accounts, and so dined at home. In the afternoon to the Duke of Albemarle and thence back again by water, and so to my chamber to finish the entry of my accounts and to think of the business I am next to do, which is the stating my thoughts and putting in order my collections about the business of pursers, to see where the fault of our present constitution relating to them lies and what to propose to mend it, and upon this late and with my head full of this business to bed. Thus ends this year, to my great joy, in this manner. I have raised my estate from £1,300 in this year to £4,400. I have got myself greater interest, I think, by my diligence, and my employments encreased by that of Treasurer for Tangier, and Surveyour of the Victualls. It is true we have gone through great melancholy because of the great plague, and I put to great charges by it, by keeping my family long at Woolwich, and myself and another part of my family, my clerks, at my charge at Greenwich, and a mayde at London; but I hope the King will give us some satisfaction for that. But now the plague is abated almost to nothing, and I intending to get to London as fast as I can. My family, that is my wife and maids, having been there these two or three weeks. The Dutch war goes on very ill, by reason of lack of money; having none to hope for, all being put into disorder by a new Act that is made as an experiment to bring credit to the Exchequer, for goods and money to be advanced upon the credit of that Act. I have never lived so merrily (besides that I never got so much) as I have done this plague time, by my Lord Brouncker's and Captain Cocke's good company, and the acquaintance of Mrs. Knipp, Coleman and her husband, and Mr. Laneare, and great store of dancings we have had at my cost (which I was willing to indulge myself and wife) at my lodgings. The great evil of this year, and the only one indeed, is the fall of my Lord of Sandwich, whose mistake about the prizes hath undone him, I believe, as to interest at Court; though sent (for a little palliating it) Embassador into Spayne, which he is now fitting himself for. But the Duke of Albemarle goes with the Prince to sea this next year, and my Lord very meanly spoken of; and, indeed, his miscarriage about the prize goods is not to be excused, to suffer a company of rogues to go away with ten times as much as himself, and the blame of all to be deservedly laid upon him.[1] My whole family hath been well all this while, and all my friends I know of, saving my aunt Bell, who is dead, and some children of my cozen Sarah's, of the plague. But many of such as I know very well, dead; yet, to our great joy, the town fills apace, and shops begin to be open again. Pray God continue the plague's decrease! for that keeps the Court away from the place of business, and so all goes to rack as to publick matters, they at this distance not thinking of it.

1665–66.

January 1st (New-Yeare's Day). Called up by five o'clock, by my order, by Mr. Tooker, who wrote, while I dictated to him, my business of the Pursers; and so, without eating or drinking, till three in the afternoon, and then, to my great content, finished it. So to dinner, Gibson and he and I, and then to copying it over, Mr. Gibson reading and I writing, and went a good way in it till interrupted

[1] According to Granville Penn ("Memorials of Sir W. Penn," ii. 488 n.) £2,000 went to Lord Sandwich and £8,000 among eight others.

by Sir W. Warren's coming, of whom I always learne something or other, his discourse being very good and his brains also. He being gone we to our business again, and wrote more of it fair, and then late to bed.[1]

2nd. Up by candlelight again, and wrote the greatest part of my business fair, and then to the office, and so home to dinner, and after dinner up and made an end of my fair writing it, and that being done, set two entering while to my Lord Bruncker's, and there find Sir J. Minnes and all his company, and Mr. Boreman and Mrs. Turner, but, above all, my dear Mrs. Knipp, with whom I sang, and in perfect pleasure I was to hear her sing, and especially her little Scotch song of "Barbary Allen;"[2] and to make our mirthe the completer, Sir J. Minnes was in the highest pitch of mirthe, and his mimicall tricks, that ever I saw, and most excellent pleasant company he is, and the best mimique that ever I saw, and certainly would have made an excellent actor, and now would be an excellent teacher of actors. Thence, it being post night, against my will took leave, but before I come to my office, longing for more of her company, I returned and met them coming home in coaches, so I got into the coach where Mrs. Knipp was and got her upon my knee (the coach being full) and played with her breasts and sung, and at last set her at her house and so good night. So home to my lodgings and there endeavoured to have finished the examining my papers of Pursers' business to have sent away to-night, but I was so sleepy with my late early risings and late goings to bed that I could not do it, but was forced to go to bed and leave it to send away to-morrow by an Expresse.

[1] This document is in the British Museum (Harleian MS. 6287), and is entitled, "A Letter from Mr. Pepys, dated at Greenwich, 1 Jan. 1665-6, which he calls his New Year's Gift to his hon. friend, Sir Wm. Coventry, wherein he lays down a method for securing his Majesty in husbandly execution of the Victualling Part of the Naval Expence." It consists of nineteen closely written folio pages, and is a remarkable specimen of Pepys's business habits. — B. There are copies of several letters on the victualling of the navy, written by Pepys in 1666, among the Rawlinson MSS. in the Bodleian.

[2] The Scottish ballad is entitled, "Sir John Grehme and Barbara Allan," and the English version, "Barbara Allen's Cruelty." Both are printed in Percy's "Reliques," Series III.

3rd. Up, and all the morning till three in the afternoon examining and fitting up my Pursers' paper and sent it away by an Expresse. Then comes my wife, and I set her to get supper ready against I go to the Duke of Albemarle and back again; and at the Duke's with great joy I received the good news of the decrease of the plague this week to 70, and but 253 in all; which is the least Bill hath been known these twenty years in the City. Through the want of people in London is it, that must make it so low below the ordinary number for Bills. So home, and find all my good company I had bespoke, as Coleman and his wife, and Laneare, Knipp and her surly husband; and good musique we had, and, among other things, Mrs. Coleman sang my words I set of "Beauty retire," and I think it is a good song, and they praise it mightily. Then to dancing and supper, and mighty merry till Mr. Rolt come in, whose pain of the tooth-ake made him no company, and spoilt ours; so he away, and then my wife's teeth fell of akeing, and she to bed. So forced to break up all with a good song, and so to bed.

4th. Up, and to the office, where my Lord Bruncker and I, against Sir W. Batten and Sir J. Minnes and the whole table, for Sir W. Warren in the business of his mast contract, and overcome them and got them to do what I had a mind to, for indeed my Lord being unconcerned in what I aimed at. So home to dinner, where Mr. Sheldon come by invitation from Woolwich, and as merry as I could be with all my thoughts about me and my wife still in pain of her tooth. He anon took leave and took Mrs. Barbary his niece home with him, and seems very thankful to me for the £10 I did give him for my wife's rent of his house, and I am sure I am beholding to him, for it was a great convenience to me, and then my wife home to London by water and I to the office till 8 at night, and so to my Lord Bruncker's, thinking to have been merry, having appointed a meeting for Sir J. Minnes and his company and Mrs. Knipp again, but whatever hindered I know not, but no company come, which vexed me because it disappointed me of the glut of mirthe I hoped for. However, good discourse with my Lord and merry, with Mrs. Williams's descants upon Sir J. Minnes's and Mrs. Turner's not coming. So home and to bed.

5th. I with my Lord Bruncker and Mrs. Williams by coach with four horses to London, to my Lord's house in Covent-Guarden. But, Lord! what staring to see a nobleman's coach come to town. And porters every where bow to us; and such begging of beggars! And a delightfull thing it is to see the towne full of people again as now it is; and shops begin to open, though in many places seven or eight together, and more, all shut; but yet the towne is full, compared with what it used to be. I mean the City end; for Covent-Guarden and Westminster are yet very empty of people, no Court nor gentry being there. Set Mrs. Williams down at my Lord's house and he and I to Sir G. Carteret, at his chamber at White Hall, he being come to town last night to stay one day. So my Lord and he and I much talke about the Act, what credit we find upon it, but no private talke between him and I. So I to the 'Change, and there met Mr. Povy, newly come to town, and he and I to Sir George Smith's and there dined nobly. He tells me how my Lord Bellases complains for want of money and of him and me therein, but I value it not, for I know I do all that can be done. We had no time to talk of particulars, but leave it to another day, and I away to Cornhill to expect my Lord Bruncker's coming back again, and I staid at my stationer's house, and by and by comes my Lord, and did take me up and so to Greenwich, and after sitting with them a while at their house, home, thinking to get Mrs. Knipp, but could not, she being busy with company, but sent me a pleasant letter, writing herself "Barbary Allen." I went therefore to Mr. Boreman's for pastime, and there staid an houre or two talking with him, and reading a discourse about the River of Thames, the reason of its being choked up in several places with shelfes; which is plain is, by the encroachments made upon the River, and running out of causeways into the River at every wood-wharfe; which was not heretofore when Westminster Hall and White Hall were built, and Redriffe Church, which now are sometimes overflown with water. I had great satisfaction herein. So home and to my papers for lacke of company, but by and by comes little Mrs. Tooker and sat and supped with me, and I kept her very late talking and making her comb my head, and did what I will with her. So late to bed.

6th. Up betimes and by water to the Cockepitt, there met Sir G. Carteret and, after discourse with the Duke, all together, and there saw a letter wherein Sir W. Coventry did take notice to the Duke with a commendation of my paper about Pursers, I to walke in the Parke with the Vice-Chamberlain, and received his advice about my deportment about the advancing the credit of the Act; giving me caution to see that we do not misguide the King by making them believe greater matters from it than will be found. But I see that this arises from his great trouble to see the Act succeede, and to hear my name so much used and my letters shown at Court about goods served us in upon the credit of it. But I do make him believe that I do it with all respect to him and on his behalfe too, as indeed I do, as well as my owne, that it may not be said that he or I do not assist therein. He tells me that my Lord Sandwich do proceed on his journey with the greatest kindnesse that can be imagined from the King and Chancellor, which was joyfull newes to me. Thence with Lord Bruncker to Greenwich by water to a great dinner and much company; Mr. Cottle and his lady and others and I went, hoping to get Mrs. Knipp to us, having wrote a letter to her in the morning, calling myself "Dapper Dicky,"[1] in answer to her's of "Barbary Allen," but could not, and am told by the boy that carried my letter, that he found her crying; but I fear she lives a sad life with that ill-natured fellow her husband: so we had a great, but I a melancholy dinner, having not her there, as I hoped. After dinner to cards, and then comes notice that my wife is come unexpectedly to me to towne. So I to her. It is only to see what I do, and why I come not home; and she is in the right that I would have a little more of Mrs. Knipp's company before I go away. My wife to fetch away my things from Woolwich, and I back to cards and after cards to choose King and Queene, and a good cake there was, but no marks found; but I privately found the clove, the mark of the knave, and privately put it into Captain Cocke's piece, which made some mirthe, because of his lately being knowne by his buying

[1] A song called "Dapper Dicky" is in the British Museum; it begins, "In a barren tree." It was printed in 1710. — B.

of clove and mace of the East India prizes. At night home to my lodging, where I find my wife returned with my things, and there also Captain Ferrers is come upon business of my Lord's to this town about getting some goods of his put on board in order to his going to Spain, and Ferrers presumes upon my finding a bed for him, which I did not like to have done without my invitation because I had done [it] several times before, during the plague, that he could not provide himself safely elsewhere. But it being Twelfth Night, they had got the fiddler and mighty merry they were; and I above come not to them, but when I had done my business among my papers went to bed, leaving them dancing, and choosing King and Queene.

7th (Lord's day). Up, and being trimmed I was invited by Captain Cocke, so I left my wife, having a mind to some discourse with him, and dined with him. He tells me of new difficulties about his goods which troubles me and I fear they will be great. He tells me too what I hear everywhere how the towne talks of my Lord Craven being to come into Sir G. Carteret's place; but sure it cannot be true. But I do fear those two families, his and my Lord Sandwich's, are quite broken. And I must now stand upon my own legs. Thence to my lodging, and considering how I am hindered by company there to do any thing among my papers, I did resolve to go away to-day rather than stay to no purpose till to-morrow and so got all my things packed up and spent half an hour with W. Howe about his papers of accounts for contingencies and my Lord's accounts, so took leave of my landlady and daughters, having paid dear for what time I have spent there, but yet having been quiett and my health, I am very well contented therewith. So with my wife and Mercer took boat and away home; but in the evening, before I went, comes Mrs. Knipp, just to speake with me privately, to excuse her not coming to me yesterday, complaining how like a devil her husband treats her, but will be with us in towne a weeke hence, and so I kissed her and parted. Being come home, my wife and I to look over our house and consider of laying out a little money to hang our bedchamber better than it is, and so resolved to go and buy something to-morrow, and so after supper, with great joy in my heart for my coming once again hither, to bed.

8th. Up, and my wife and I by coach to Bennett's, in Paternoster Row, few shops there being yet open, and there bought velvett for a coate, and camelott for a cloake for myself; and thence to a place to look over some fine counterfeit damasks to hang my wife's closett, and pitched upon one, and so by coach home again, I calling at the 'Change, and so home to dinner and all the afternoon look after my papers at home and my office against to-morrow, and so after supper and considering the uselessness of laying out so much money upon my wife's closett, but only the chamber, to bed.

9th. Up, and then to the office, where we met first since the plague, which God preserve us in! At noon home to dinner, where uncle Thomas with me, and in comes Pierce lately come from Oxford, and Ferrers. After dinner Pierce and I up to my chamber, where he tells me how a great difference hath been between the Duke and Duchesse, he suspecting her to be naught with Mr. Sidney.[1] But some way or other the matter is made up; but he was banished the Court, and the Duke for many days did not speak to the Duchesse at all. He tells me that my Lord Sandwich is lost there at Court, though the King is particularly his friend. But people do speak every where slightly of him; which is a sad story to me, but I hope it may be better again. And that Sir G. Carteret is neglected, and hath great enemies at work against him. That matters must needs go bad, while all the town, and every boy in the streete, openly cries, "The King cannot go away till my Lady Castlemaine be ready to come along with him;" she

[1] "This Duchess was Chancellor Hyde's daughter, and she was a very handsome woman, and had a great deal of wit; therefore it was not without reason that Mr. Sydney, the handsomest youth of his time, of the Duke's bedchamber, was so much in love with her, as appeared to us all, and the Duchess not unkind to him, but very innocently. He was afterwards banished the Court for another reason, as was reported" (Sir John Reresby's "Memoirs," August 5th, 1664, ed. Cartwright, pp. 64, 65). "'How could the Duke of York make my mother a Papist?' said the Princess Mary to Dr. Burnet. 'The Duke caught a man in bed with her,' said the Doctor, 'and then had power to make her do anything.' The Prince, who sat by the fire, said, 'Pray, madam, ask the Doctor a few more questions'" (Spence's "Anecdotes," ed. Singer, 329).

being lately put to bed.[1] And that he visits her and Mrs. Stewart every morning before he eats his breakfast. All this put together makes me very sad, but yet I hope I shall do pretty well among them for all this, by my not meddling with either of their matters. He and Ferrers gone I paid uncle Thomas his last quarter's money, and then comes Mr. Gawden and he and I talked above stairs together a good while about his business, and to my great joy got him to declare that of the £500 he did give me the other day, none of it was for my Treasurershipp for Tangier (I first telling him how matters stand between Povy and I, that he was to have half of whatever was coming to me by that office), and that he will gratify me at 2 per cent. for that when he next receives any money. So there is £80 due to me more than I thought of. He gone I with a glad heart to the office to write my letters and so home to supper and bed, my wife mighty full of her worke she hath to do in furnishing her bedchamber.

10th. Up, and by coach to Sir G. Downing, where Mr. Gawden met me by agreement to talke upon the Act. I do find Sir G. Downing to be a mighty talker, more than is true, which I now know to be so, and suspected it before, but for all that I have good grounds to think it will succeed for goods and in time for money too, but not presently. Having done with him, I to my Lord Bruncker's house in Covent-Garden, and, among other things, it was to acquaint him with my paper of Pursers, and read it to him, and had his good liking of it. Shewed him Mr. Coventry's sense of it, which he sent me last post much to my satisfaction. Thence to the 'Change, and there hear to our grief how the plague is encreased this week from seventy to eighty-nine. We have also great fear of our Hambrough fleete, of their meeting the Dutch; as also have certain newes, that by storms Sir Jer. Smith's fleet is scattered, and three of them come without masts back to Plymouth, which is another very exceeding great disappointment,[2] and if the victualling ships

[1] December 28th, 1665. In a Fellow's chamber in Merton College, Oxford, of George Fitzroy, afterwards Duke of Northumberland. — B.

[2] Admiral Sir Jeremy Smith, mentioned October 13th, 1665, *ante*, commanded a fleet in the Streights at this time, and another in the Channel in 1668. — B.

are miscarried will tend to the losse of the garrison of Tangier. Thence home, in my way had the opportunity I longed for, of seeing and saluting Mrs. Stokes, my little goldsmith's wife in Paternoster Row, and there bespoke some thing, a silver chafing-dish for warming plates, and so home to dinner, found my wife busy about making her hangings for her chamber with the upholster. So I to the office and anon to the Duke of Albemarle, by coach at night, taking, for saving time, Sir W. Warren with me, talking of our businesses all the way going and coming, and there got his reference of my pursers' paper to the Board to consider of it before he reads it, for he will never understand it I am sure. Here I saw Sir W. Coventry's kind letter to him concerning my paper, and among others of his letters, which I saw all, and that is a strange thing, that whatever is writ to this Duke of Albemarle, all the world may see; for this very night he did give me Mr. Coventry's letter to read, soon as it come to his hand, before he had read it himself, and bid me take out of it what concerned the Navy, and many things there was in it, which I should not have thought fit for him to have let any body so suddenly see; but, among other things, find him profess himself to the Duke a friend into the inquiring further into the business of Prizes, and advises that it may be publique, for the righting the King, and satisfying the people and getting the blame to be rightly laid where it should be, which strikes very hard upon my Lord Sandwich, and troubles me to read it. Besides, which vexes me more, I heard the damned Duchesse again say to twenty gentlemen publiquely in the room, that she would have Montagu sent once more to sea, before he goes his Embassy, that we may see whether he will make amends for his cowardice, and repeated the answer she did give the other day in my hearing to Sir G. Downing, wishing her Lord had been a coward, for then perhaps he might have been made an Embassador, and not been sent now to sea. But one good thing she said, she cried mightily out against the having of gentlemen Captains with feathers and ribbands, and wished the King would send her husband to sea with the old plain sea Captains, that he served with formerly, that would make their ships swim with blood, though they could not make legs[1] as Captains now-a-days can. It grieved me to see how slightly the Duke do every thing in the world, and how the King and every body suffers whatever he will to be done in the Navy, though never so much against reason, as in the business of recalling tickets, which will be done notwithstanding all the arguments against it. So back again to my office, and there to business and so to bed.

11th. Up and to the office. By and by to the Custome House to the Farmers, there with a letter of Sir G. Carteret's for £3,000, which they ordered to be paid me. So away back again to the office, and at noon to dinner all of us by invitation to Sir W. Pen's, and much other company. Among others, Lieutenant of the Tower, and Broome, his poet,[2] and Dr. Whistler, and his (Sir W. Pen's) son-in-law Lowder,[3] servant to Mrs. Margaret Pen, and Sir Edward Spragg, a merry man, that sang a pleasant song pleasantly. Rose from table before half dined, and with Mr. Mountney of the Custome House to the East India House, and there delivered to him tallys for £3,000, and received a note for the money on Sir R. Viner. So ended the matter, and back to my company, where staid a little, and thence away with my Lord Bruncker for discourse sake, and he and I to Gresham College to have seen Mr. Hooke and a new invented chariott of Dr. Wilkins, but met with nobody at home.[4] So to Dr.

[1] Make bows, play the courtier. The reading, "make leagues," appeared in former editions till Mr. Mynors Bright corrected it.

[2] Alexander Brome.

[3] Anthony Lowther, of Marske, in Yorkshire, one of the original Fellows of the Royal Society, who shortly afterwards married Margaret Penn, was M.P. for Appleby in 1678 and 1679. He was buried at Walthamstow in 1692. William, his son by Margaret Penn, created a baronet in 1697, married the heir of Thomas Preston, of Holker, Lancashire. The second baronet married Elizabeth, daughter of William, Duke of Devonshire, and their son, dying unmarried, bequeathed Holker and other estates to his cousin, Lord George Cavendish.

[4] The Royal Society did not meet until February 21st, having had a specially long recess on account of the plague. At the previous meeting on June 28th, 1665, "Mr. Hooke was ordered to prosecute his chariot-wheels, watches, and glasses during the recess." At the meeting of March 14th, "The President inquiring into the employments in which the members of the Society had been engaged during their long recess, several of those who were present gave some account thereof, viz., Dr. Wilkins and Mr. Hooke, of the business of the chariots, viz., that after great variety of trials they conceived that they brought it to a

Wilkins's, where I never was before, and very kindly received and met with Dr. Merritt, and fine discourse among them to my great joy, so sober and so ingenious. He is now upon finishing his discourse of a universal character. So away and I home to my office about my letters, and so home to supper and to bed.

12th. By coach to the Duke of Albemarle, where Sir W. Batten and I only met. Troubled at my heart to see how things are ordered there without consideration or understanding. Thence back by coach and called at Wotton's, my shoemaker, lately come to towne, and bespoke shoes, as also got him to find me a taylor to make me some clothes, my owne being not yet in towne, nor Pym, my Lord Sandwich's taylor. So he helped me to a pretty man, one Mr. Penny, against St. Dunstan's Church. Thence to the 'Change and there met Mr. Moore, newly come to towne, and took him home to dinner with me and after dinner to talke, and he and I do conclude my Lord's case to be very bad and may be worse, if he do not get a pardon for his doings about the prizes and his business at Bergen, and other things done by him at sea, before he goes for Spayne. I do use all the art I can to get him to get my Lord to pay my cozen Pepys, for it is a great burden to my mind my being bound for my Lord in £1,000 to him. Having done discourse with him and directed him to go with my advice to my Lord expresse to-morrow to get his pardon perfected before his going, because of what I read the other night in Sir W. Coventry's letter, I to the office, and there had an extraordinary meeting of Sir J. Minnes, Sir W. Batten, and Sir W. Pen, and my Lord Bruncker and I to hear my paper read about pursers, which they did all of them with great good will and great approbation of my method and pains in all, only Sir W. Pen, who must except against every thing and remedy nothing, did except against my proposal for some reasons, which I could not understand, I confess, nor my Lord Bruncker neither, but he did detect indeed a failure or two of mine in my report about the ill condition of the present pursers, which I did magnify in one or two little

good issue, the defects found since the chariot came to London being thought easy to remedy," &c. (Birch's "History of the Royal Society," vol. ii., p. 66).

things, to which, I think, he did with reason except, but at last with all respect did declare the best thing he ever heard of this kind, but when Sir W. Batten did say, "Let us that do know the practical part of the Victualling meet Sir J. Minnes, Sir W. Pen and I and see what we can do to mend all," he was so far from offering or furthering it, that he declined it and said, he must be out of towne. So as I ever knew him never did in his life ever attempt to mend any thing, but suffer all things to go on in the way they are, though never so bad, rather than improve his experience to the King's advantage. So we broke up, however, they promising to meet to offer some thing in it of their opinions, and so we rose, and I and my Lord Bruncker by coach a little way for discourse sake, till our coach broke, and tumbled me over him quite down the side of the coach, falling on the ground about the Stockes,[1] but up again, and thinking it fit to have for my honour some thing reported in writing to the Duke in favour of my pains in this, lest it should be thought to be rejected as frivolous, I did move it to my Lord, and he will see it done to-morrow. So we parted, and I to the office and thence home to my poor wife, who works all day at home like a horse, at the making of her hangings for our chamber and the bed. So to supper and to bed.

13th. At the office all the morning, where my Lord Bruncker moved to have something wrote in my matter as I desired him last night, and it was ordered and will be done next sitting. Home with his Lordship to Mrs. Williams's, in Covent-Garden, to dinner (the first time I ever was there), and there met Captain Cocke; and pretty merry, though not perfectly so, because of the fear that there is of a great encrease again of the plague this week. And again my Lord Bruncker do tell us, that he hath it from Sir John Baber,[2] who is related to my Lord Craven, that my Lord Craven do look after Sir G. Carteret's place, and do reckon himself sure of it. After dinner Cocke and I together by coach to the Exchange, in our way talking of our matters, and do conclude that every thing must breake in pieces,

[1] On the site of the Mansion House.

[2] John Baber, M.D., Physician in Ordinary to the king, who knighted him March 19th, 1660. He died 1703-4, aged seventy-nine.

while no better counsels govern matters than there seem to do, and that it will become him and I and all men to get their reckonings even, as soon as they can, and expect all to breake. Besides, if the plague continues among us another yeare, the Lord knows what will become of us. I set him down at the 'Change, and I home to my office, where late writing letters and doing business, and thence home to supper and to bed. My head full of cares, but pleased with my wife's minding her worke so well, and busying herself about her house, and I trust in God if I can but clear myself of my Lord Sandwich's bond, wherein I am bound with him for £1,000 to T. Pepys, I shall do pretty well, come what will come.

14th (Lord's day). Long in bed, till raised by my new taylor, Mr. Penny, [who] comes and brings me my new velvet coat, very handsome, but plain, and a day hence will bring me my camelott cloak. He gone I close to my papers and to set all in order and to perform my vow to finish my journall and other things before I kiss any woman more or drink any wine, which I must be forced to do to-morrow if I go to Greenwich as I am invited by Mr. Boreman to hear Mrs. Knipp sing, and I would be glad to go, so as we may be merry. At noon eat the second of the two cygnets Mr. Shepley sent us for a new-year's gift, and presently to my chamber again and so to work hard all day about my Tangier accounts, which I am going again to make up, as also upon writing a letter to my father about Pall, whom it is time now I find to think of disposing of while God Almighty hath given me something to give with her, and in my letter to my father I do offer to give her £450 to make her own £50 given her by my uncle up £500. I do also therein propose Mr. Harman the upholster for a husband for her, to whom I have a great love and did heretofore love his former wife, and a civil man he is and careful in his way, beside, I like his trade and place he lives in, being Cornhill. Thus late at work, and so to supper and to bed. This afternoon, after sermon, comes my dear fair beauty of the Exchange, Mrs. Batelier, brought by her sister, an acquaintance of Mercer's, to see my wife. I saluted her with as much pleasure as I had done any a great while. We sat and talked together an houre, with infinite pleasure to me, and so the fair creature went away, and proves one of the modestest women, and pretty, that ever I saw in my life, and my [wife] judges her so too.

15th. Busy all the morning in my chamber in my old cloth suit, while my usuall one is to my taylor's to mend, which I had at noon again, and an answer to a letter I had sent this morning to Mrs. Pierce to go along with my wife and I down to Greenwich to-night upon an invitation to Mr. Boreman's to be merry to dance and sing with Mrs. Knipp. Being dressed, and having dined, I took coach and to Mrs. Pierce, to her new house in Covent-Garden, a very fine place and fine house. Took her thence home to my house, and so by water to Boreman's by night, where the greatest disappointment that ever I saw in my life, much company, a good supper provided, and all come with expectation of excesse of mirthe, but all blank through the waywardnesse of Mrs. Knipp, who, though she had appointed the night, could not be got to come. Not so much as her husband could get her to come; but, which was a pleasant thing in all my anger, I asking him, while we were in expectation what answer one of our many messengers would bring, what he thought, whether she would come or no, he answered that, for his part, he could not so much as thinke. By and by we all to supper, which the silly master of the feast commended, but, what with my being out of humour, and the badnesse of the meate dressed, I did never eat a worse supper in my life. At last, very late, and supper done, she came undressed, but it brought me no mirthe at all; only, after all being done, without singing, or very little, and no dancing, Pierce and I to bed together, and he and I very merry to find how little and thin clothes they give us to cover us, so that we were fain to lie in our stockings and drawers, and lay all our coates and clothes upon the bed. So to sleep.

16th. Up, and leaving the women in bed together (a pretty black and white) I to London to the office, and there forgot, through business, to bespeake any dinner for my wife and Mrs. Pierce. However, by noon they come, and a dinner we had, and Kate Joyce comes to see us, with whom very merry. After dinner she and I up to my chamber, who told me her business was chiefly for my advice about her husband's leaving off his trade, which though I wish enough, yet I did advise against, for he is a man will not know how to live idle, and employment he is fit for none. Thence anon carried her and Mrs. Pierce home, and so to the Duke of Albemarle, and mighty kind he to me still. So home late at my letters, and so to bed, being mightily troubled at the newes of the plague's being encreased, and was much the saddest news that the plague hath brought me from the beginning of it; because of the lateness of the year, and the fear, we may with reason have, of its continuing with us the next summer. The total being now 375, and the plague 158.

17th. Busy all the morning, settling things against my going out of towne this night. After dinner, late took horse, having sent for Lashmore to go with me, and so he and I rode to Dagenhams in the dark. There find the whole family well. It was my Lord Crew's desire that I should come, and chiefly to discourse with me of Lord Sandwich's matters; and therein to persuade, what I had done already, that my Lord should sue out a pardon for his business of the prizes, as also for Bergen, and all he hath done this year past, before he begins his Embassy to Spayne. For it is to be feared that the Parliament will fly out against him and particular men, the next Session. He is glad also that my Lord is clear of his sea-imployment, though sorry as I am, only in the manner of its bringing about. By and by to supper, my Lady Wright very kind. After supper up to wait on my Lady Crew, who is the same weake silly lady as ever, asking such saintly questions. Down to my Lord again and sat talking an houre or two, and anon to prayers the whole family, and then all to bed, I handsomely used, lying in the chamber Mr. Carteret formerly did, but sat up an houre talking sillily with Mr. Carteret and Mr. Marre, and so to bed.

18th. Up before day and thence rode to London before office time, where I met a note at the doore to invite me to supper to Mrs. Pierce's because of Mrs. Knipp, who is in towne and at her house. To the office, where, among other things, vexed with Major Norwood's coming, who takes it ill my not paying a bill of Exchange of his, but I have good reason for it, and so the less troubled, but yet troubled, so as at noon being carried by my Lord Bruncker to Captain Cocke's to dinner, where Mrs. Williams was, and Mrs. Knipp, I was not heartily merry, though a glasse of wine did a little cheer me. After dinner to the office. Anon comes to me thither my Lord Bruncker, Mrs. Williams, and Knipp. I brought down my wife in her night-gowne, she not being indeed very well, to the office to them and there by and by they parted all and my wife and I anon and Mercer, by coach, to Pierce's; where mighty merry, and sing and dance with great pleasure; and I danced, who never did in company in my life, and Captain Cocke come for a little while and danced, but went away, but we staid and had a pretty supper, and spent till two in the morning, but got home well by coach, though as dark as pitch, and so to bed.

19th. Up and ready, called on by Mr. Moone, my Lord Bellases' secretary, who and I good friends though I have failed him in some payments. Thence with Sir J. Minnes to the Duke of Albemarle's, and carried all well, and met Norwood but prevented him in desiring a meeting of the Commissioners for Tangier. Thence to look for Sir H. [Cholmly], but he not within, he coming to town last night. It is a remarkable thing how infinitely naked all that end of the towne, Covent-Garden, is at this day of people; while the City is almost as full again of people as ever it was. To the 'Change and so home to dinner and the office, whither anon comes Sir H. Cholmley to me, and he and I to my house, there to settle his accounts with me, and so with great pleasure we agreed and great friends become, I think, and he presented me upon the foot of our accounts for this year's service for him £100, whereof Povy must have half. Thence to the office and wrote a letter to Norwood to satisfy him about my nonpayment of his bill, for that do still stick in my mind. So at night home to supper and to bed.

20th. To the office, where upon Mr. Kinaston's coming to me about some business of Colonell Norwood's, I sent my boy home for some papers, where, he staying longer than I would have him, and being vexed at the business and to be kept from my fellows in the office longer than was fit, I become angry, and boxed my boy when he came, that I do hurt my thumb so much, that I was not able to stir all the day after, and in great pain. At noon to dinner, and then to the office again, late, and so to supper and to bed.

21st (Lord's day). Lay almost till noon merrily and with pleasure talking with my wife in bed. Then up looking about my house, and the roome which my wife is dressing up, having new hung our bedchamber with blue, very handsome. After dinner to my Tangier accounts and there stated them against to-morrow very distinctly for the Lords to see who meet to-morrow, and so to supper and to bed.

22nd. Up, and set my people to work in copying Tangier accounts, and I down the river to Greenwich to the office to fetch away some papers and thence to Deptford, where by agreement my Lord Bruncker was to come, but staid almost till noon, after I had spent an houre with W. Howe talking of my Lord Sandwich's matters and his folly in minding his pleasures too much now-a-days, and permitting himself to be governed by Cuttance to the displeasing of all the Commanders almost of the fleete, and thence we may conceive indeed the rise of all my Lord's misfortunes of late. At noon my Lord Bruncker did come, but left the keys of the chests we should open, at Sir G. Carteret's lodgings, of my Lord Sandwich's, wherein Howe's supposed jewells are;[1] so we could not, according to my Lord Arlington's order, see them to-day; but we parted, resolving to meet here at night: my Lord Bruncker being going with Dr. Wilkins, Mr. Hooke,[2] and others, to Colonell Blunt's, to consider again of the business of charriots, and to try their new invention. Which I saw here my Lord Bruncker ride in; where the coachman sits astride upon a pole over the horse, but do not touch the horse, which is a pretty odde thing; but it seems it is most easy for the horse, and, as they say, for the man also. Thence I with speede by water home and eat a bit, and took my accounts and to the Duke of Albemarle, where for all I feared of Norwood he was very civill, and Sir Thomas Ingram beyond expectation, I giving them all content and I thereby settled mightily in my mind, for I was weary of the employment, and had had thoughts of giving it over. I did also give a good step in a business of

[1] The jewels were stolen from the Dutch Vice-Admiral. See *ante*, November 16th.

[2] Dr. Robert Hooke. See note, *ante*, February 15th, 1664–65.

Mr. Hubland's, about getting a ship of his to go to Tangier, which during this strict embargo is a great matter, and I shall have a good reward for it, I hope. Thence by water in the darke down to Deptford, and there find my Lord Bruncker come and gone, having staid long for me. I back presently to the Crowne taverne behind the Exchange by appointment, and there met the first meeting of Gresham College since the plague. Dr. Goddard did fill us with talke, in defence of his and his fellow physicians going out of towne in the plague-time; saying that their particular patients were most gone out of towne, and they left at liberty; and a great deal more, &c. But what, among other fine discourse pleased me most, was Sir G. Ent[1] about Respiration; that it is not to this day known, or concluded on among physicians, nor to be done either, how the action is managed by nature, or for what use it is. Here late till poor Dr. Merriot[2] was drunk, and so all home, and I to bed.

23rd. Up and to the office and then to dinner. After dinner to the office again all the afternoon, and much business with me. Good newes beyond all expectation of the decrease of the plague, being now but 79, and the whole but 272. So home with comfort to bed. A most furious storme all night and morning.

24th. By agreement my Lord Bruncker called me up, and though it was a very foule, windy, and rainy morning, yet down to the waterside we went, but no boat could go, the storme continued so. So my Lord to stay till fairer weather carried me into the Tower to Mr. Hore's and there we staid talking an houre, but at last we found no boats yet could go, so we to the office, where we met upon an occasion extraordinary of examining abuses of our clerkes in taking money for examining of tickets, but nothing done in it. Thence my Lord and I, the weather being a little

[1] Sir George Ent, M.D., F.R.S. (1604–1689), President of the College of Physicians, 1670–75, 1682–1684. He was knighted by Charles II. in 1665, in the Harveian Museum, immediately after the delivery of his Anatomy Lectures. His last publication was entitled "Animadversiones in Malachiæ Thrustoni, M.D. Diatribam de Respirationis usu primario," London, 1672, 8vo. (Munk's "Roll of the College of Physicians," vol. i., p. 223). Died 1689.

[2] Christopher Merrett, M.D. (1614–1695).

fairer, by water to Deptford to Sir G. Carteret's house, where W. Howe met us, and there we opened the chests, and saw the poor sorry rubys which have caused all this ado to the undoing of W. Howe; though I am not much sorry for it, because of his pride and ill nature. About 200 of these very small stones, and a cod of muske (which it is strange I was not able to smell) is all we could find; so locked them up again, and my Lord and I, the wind being again very furious, so as we durst not go by water, walked to London quite round the bridge, no boat being able to stirre; and, Lord! what a dirty walk we had, and so strong the wind, that in the fields we many times could not carry our bodies against it, but were driven backwards. We went through Horsydowne, where I never was since a little boy, that I went to enquire after my father, whom we did give over for lost coming from Holland.[1] It was dangerous to walk the streets, the bricks and tiles falling from the houses that the whole streets were covered with them; and whole chimneys, nay, whole houses in two or three places, blowed down. But, above all, the pales on London-bridge on both sides were blown away, so that we were fain to stoop very low for fear of blowing off of the bridge. We could see no boats in the Thames afloat, but what were broke loose, and carried through the bridge, it being ebbing water. And the greatest sight of all was, among other parcels of ships driven here and there in clusters together, one was quite overset and lay with her masts all along in the water, and keel above water. So walked home, my Lord away to his house and I to dinner, Mr. Creed being come to towne and to dine with me, though now it was three o'clock. After dinner he and I to our accounts and very troublesome he is and with tricks which I found plainly and was vexed at; while we were together comes Sir G. Downing with Colonell

[1] From the Domestic State Papers in the Public Record Office, London. Page 327, Entry Book No. 105 of the Protector Oliver's Council of State.

Ordered by the Council, Thursday, August 7th, 1656, "That passes be graunted to goe beyond ye Seas to ye p'sons following, vizt To John Pepys and his man wth necessaryes for Holland, being on the desire of Mr Samll Pepys."

Probably this was a later journey of Pepys' father to Holland, as Pepys says here he was a little boy then. — M. B.

Norwood, Rumball,[1] and Warrupp to visit me. I made them drink good wine and discoursed above alone a good while with Sir G. Downing, who is very troublesome, and then with Colonell Norwood, who hath a great mind to have me concerned with him in everything; which I like, but am shy of adventuring too much, but will thinke of it. They gone, Creed and I to finish the settling his accounts. Thence to the office, where the Houblans and we discoursed upon a rubb which we have for one of the ships I hoped to have got to go out to Tangier for them. They being gone, I to my office-business late, and then home to supper and even sacke for lacke of a little wine, which I was forced to drink against my oathe, but without pleasure.

25th. Up and to the office, at noon home to dinner. So abroad to the Duke of Albemarle and Kate Joyce's and her husband, with whom I talked a great deale about Pall's business, and told them what portion I would give her, and they do mightily like of it and will proceed further in speak-

[1] Rumball is mentioned on several occasions in the Diary. On October 29th, 1660, Pepys praises his claret, and on December 8th, 1661, a great christening of Rumball's child (Charles) is mentioned. Since these passages were printed the editor has been obligingly informed as to this worthy by Sir Horace Rumbold, Bart., G.C.M.G., H.B.M. Minister at the Hague. The forms Rumball and Rumbell given by Pepys are corruptions of the correct name, which was Rumbold. William Rumbold entered the office of the Great Wardrobe in 1629, attended Charles I. all through the Civil War till Naseby, where he was engaged, together with his father, Thomas Rumbold, afterwards taken prisoner by the Parliamentary forces, and during the period of the Commonwealth he rendered considerable service to the royal cause. He acted as Secretary to the Secret Council which was kept up in England by Charles II. during his exile, and among the Clarendon Papers at Oxford there are numerous letters from him written to the king, Lord Chancellor Hyde, Ormonde, and others. At the Restoration he became Comptroller of the Great Wardrobe and Surveyor-General of the Customs. He died May 27th, 1667, at his house at Parson's Green, Fulham, where he is buried in the chancel of All Saints' Church with his wife Mary, daughter of William Barclay, Esquire of the Body to Charles I. This distinguished royalist was an ancestor of Sir Horace Rumbold, who has contributed to the Transactions of the Royal Historical Society "Notes on the History of the Family of Rumbold in the Seventeenth Century" (N.S., vol. vi., p. 145). Sir Horace mentions the Colonel Henry Norwood referred to in the text as one of those friends who spoke of William Rumbold with great affection.

ing with Harman, who hath already been spoke to about it, as from them only, and he is mighty glad of it, but doubts it may be an offence to me, if I should know of it, so thinks that it do come only from Joyce, which I like the better. So I do believe the business will go on, and I desire it were over. I to the office then, where I did much business, and set my people to work against furnishing me to go to Hampton Court, where the King and Duke will be on Sunday next. It is now certain that the King of France hath publickly declared war against us, and God knows how little fit we are for it. At night comes Sir W. Warren, and he and I into the garden, and talked over all our businesses. He gives me good advice not to embarke into trade (as I have had it in my thoughts about Colonell Norwood) so as to be seen to mind it, for it will do me hurte, and draw my mind off from my business and embroile my estate too soon. So to the office business, and I find him as cunning a man in all points as ever I met with in my life and mighty merry we were in the discourse of our owne trickes. So about 10 o'clock at night I home and staid with him there settling my Tangier-Boates business and talking and laughing at the folly of some of our neighbours of this office till two in the morning and so to bed.

26th. Up, and pleased mightily with what my poor wife hath been doing these eight or ten days with her owne hands, like a drudge in fitting the new hangings of our bed-chamber of blue, and putting the old red ones into my dressing-room, and so by coach to White Hall, where I had just now notice that Sir G. Carteret is come to towne. He seems pleased, but I perceive he is heartily troubled at this Act, and the report of his losing his place, and more at my not writing to him to the prejudice of the Act. But I carry all fair to him and he to me. He bemoans the Kingdom as in a sad state, and with too much reason I doubt, having so many enemys about us and no friends abroad, nor money nor love at home. Thence to the Duke of Albemarle, and there a meeting with all the officers of the Navy, where, Lord! to see how the Duke of Albemarle flatters himself with false hopes of money and victuals and all without reason. Then comes the Committee of Tangier to sit, and I there carry all before me very well. Thence with Sir J. Bankes and Mr. Gawden to the 'Change, they both very wise men. After 'Change and agreeing with Houblon about our ships, D. Gawden and I to the Pope's Head and there dined and little Chaplin (who a rich man grown). He gone after dinner, D. Gawden and I to talke of the Victualling business of the Navy in what posture it is, which is very sad also for want of money. Thence home to my chamber by oathe to finish my Journall. Here W. Hewer came to me with £320 from Sir W. Warren, whereof £220 is got clearly by a late business of insurance of the Gottenburg ships, and the other £100 which was due and he had promised me before to give me to my very extraordinary joy, for which I ought and do bless God and so to my office, where late providing a letter to send to Mr. Gawden in a manner we concluded on to-day, and so to bed.

27th. Up very betimes to finish my letter and writ it fair to Mr. Gawden, it being to demand several arrears in the present state of the victualling, partly to the King's and partly to give him occasion to say something relating to the want of money on his own behalf. This done I to the office, where all the morning. At noon after a bit of dinner back to the office and there fitting myself in all points to give an account to the Duke and Mr. Coventry in all things, and in my Tangier business, till three o'clock in the morning, and so to bed,

28th. And up again about six (Lord's day), and being dressed in my velvett coate and plain cravatte took a hackney coach provided ready for me by eight o'clock, and so to my Lord Bruncker's with all my papers, and there took his coach with four horses and away toward Hampton Court, having a great deale of good discourse with him, particularly about his coming to lie at the office, when I went further in inviting him to than I intended, having not yet considered whether it will be convenient for me or no to have him here so near us, and then of getting Mr. Evelyn or Sir Robert Murray into the Navy in the room of Sir Thomas Harvey. At Brainford I 'light, having need to shit, and went into an Inne doore that stood open, found the house of office and used it, but saw no people, only after I was in the house, heard a great dogg barke, and so was afeard how I should get safe back again, and therefore drew my sword and scabbard out of my belt to have ready in my hand, but did not need to use it, but got safe into the coach again, but lost my belt by the shift, not missing it till I come to Hampton Court. At the Wicke found Sir J. Minnes and Sir W. Batten at a lodging provided for us by our messenger, and there a good dinner ready. After dinner took coach and to Court, where we find the King, and Duke, and Lords, all in council; so we walked up and down: there being none of the ladies come, and so much the more business I hope will be done. The Council being up, out comes the King, and I kissed his hand, and he grasped me very kindly by the hand. The Duke also, I kissed his, and he mighty kind, and Sir W. Coventry. I found my Lord Sandwich there, poor man! I see with a melancholy face, and suffers his beard to grow on his upper lip more than usual. I took him a little aside to know when I should wait on him, and where: he told me, and that it would be best to meet at his lodgings, without being seen to walk together. Which I liked very well; and, Lord! to see in what difficulty I stand, that I dare not walk with Sir W. Coventry, for fear my Lord or Sir G. Carteret should see me; nor with either of them, for fear Sir W. Coventry should. After changing a few words with Sir W. Coventry, who assures me of his respect and love to me, and his concernment for my health in all this sickness, I went down into one of the Courts, and there met the King and Duke; and the Duke called me to him. And the King come to me of himself, and told me, "Mr. Pepys," says he, "I do give you thanks for your good service all this year, and I assure you I am very sensible of it." And the Duke of Yorke did tell me with pleasure, that he had read over my discourse about pursers, and would have it ordered in my way, and so fell from one discourse to another. I walked with them quite out of the Court into the fields, and then back to my Lord Sandwich's chamber, where I find him very melancholy and not well satisfied, I perceive, with my carriage to Sir G. Carteret, but I did satisfy him and made him confess to me, that I have a very hard game to play; and told me he was sorry to see it, and the inconveniences which likely may fall upon me with him; but, for all that, I am not much afeard, if I can but keepe out of harm's way in not being found too much concerned in my Lord's or Sir G. Carteret's matters, and that I will not be if I can helpe it. He hath got over his business of the prizes, so far as to have a privy seale passed for all that was in his distribution to the officers, which I am heartily glad of; and, for the rest, he must be answerable for what he is proved to have. But for his pardon for anything else, he thinks it not seasonable to aske it, and not usefull to him; because that will not stop a Parliament's mouth, and for the King, he is sure enough of him. I did aske him whether he was sure of the interest and friendship of any great Ministers of State and he told me, yes. As we were going further, in comes my Lord Mandeville, so we were forced to breake off and I away, and to Sir W. Coventry's chamber, where he not come in but I find Sir W. Pen, and he and I to discourse. I find him very much out of humour, so that I do not think matters go very well with him, and I am glad of it. He and I staying till late, and Sir W. Coventry not coming in (being shut up close all the afternoon with the Duke of Albemarle), we took boat, and by water to Kingston, and so to our lodgings, where a good supper and merry, only I sleepy, and therefore after supper I slunk away from the rest to bed, and lay very well and slept soundly, my mind being in a great delirium between joy for what the King and Duke have said to me and Sir W. Coventry, and trouble for my Lord Sandwich's concernments, and how hard it will be for me to preserve myself from feeling thereof.

29th. Up, and to Court by coach, where to Council before the Duke of Yorke, the Duke of Albemarle with us, and after Sir W. Coventry had gone over his notes that he had provided with the Duke of Albemarle, I went over all mine with good successe, only I fear I did once offend the Duke of Albemarle, but I was much joyed to find the Duke of Yorke so much contending for my discourse about the pursers against Sir W. Pen, who opposes it like a foole; my Lord Sandwich come in in the middle of the business, and, poor man, very melancholy, methought, and said little at all, or to the business, and sat at the lower end, just as he come, no roome being made for him, only I did give him my stoole, and another was reached me. After council done, I walked to and again up and down the house, discoursing with this and that man. Anon others tooke occasion to thanke the Duke of Yorke for his good opinion in general of my service, and particularly his favour in conferring on me the Victualling business. He told me that he knew nobody so fit as I for it, and next, he was very glad to find that to give me for my encouragement, speaking very kindly of me. So to Sir W. Coventry's to dinner with him, whom I took occasion to thanke for his favour and good thoughts of what little service I did, desiring he would do the last act of friendship in telling me of my faults also. He told me he would be sure he would do that also, if there were any occasion for it. So that as much as it is possible under so great a fall of my Lord Sandwich's, and difference between them, I may conclude that I am thoroughly right with Sir W. Coventry. I dined with him with a great deale of company, and much merry discourse. I was called away before dinner ended to go to my company who dined at our lodgings. Thither I went with Mr. Evelyn (whom I met) in his coach going that way, but finding my company gone, but my Lord Bruncker left his coach for me; so Mr. Evelyn and I into my Lord's coach, and rode together with excellent discourse till we come to Clapham, talking of the vanity and vices of the Court, which makes it a most contemptible thing; and indeed in all his discourse I find him a most worthy person. Particularly he entertained me with discourse of an Infirmary, which he hath projected for the sick and wounded seamen against the next year, which I mightily approve of; and will endeavour to promote it, being a worthy thing, and of use, and will save money. He set me down at Mr. Gawden's, where nobody yet come home, I having left him and his sons and Creed at Court, so I took a book and into the gardens, and there walked and read till darke with great pleasure, and then in and in comes Osborne, and he and I to talk of Mr. Jaggard, who comes from London, and great hopes there is of a decrease this week also of the plague. Anon comes in Creed, and after that Mr. Gawden and his sons, and then they bringing in three ladies, who were in the house, but I do not know them. his daughter and two nieces, daughters of Dr. Whistler's, with whom and Creed mighty sport at supper, the ladies very pretty and mirthfull. I perceive they know Creed's gut and stomach as well as I, and made as much mirthe as I with it at supper. After supper I made the ladies sing, and they have been taught, but, Lord! though I was forced to commend them, yet it was the saddest stuff I ever heard. However, we sat up late, and then I, in the best chamber like a prince, to bed, and Creed with me, and being sleepy talked but little.

30th. Lay long till Mr. Gawden was gone out being to take a little journey. Up, and Creed and I some good discourse, but with some trouble for the state of my Lord's matters. After walking a turne or two in the garden, and bid good morrow to Mr. Gawden's sons, and sent my service to the ladies, I took coach after Mr. Gawden's, and home, finding the towne keeping the day solemnly, it being the day of the King's murther, and they being at church, I presently into the church, thinking to see Mrs. Lethulier or Batelier, but did not, and a dull sermon of our young Lecturer, too bad. This is the first time I have been in this church since I left London for the plague, and it frighted me indeed to go through the church more than I thought it could have done, to see so [many] graves lie so high upon the churchyards where people have been buried of the plague.[1] I was much troubled at it, and do not think to go through it again a good while. So home to my wife, whom I find not well, in bed, and it seems hath not been well these two days. She rose and we to dinner, after dinner up to my chamber, where she entertained me with what she hath lately bought of clothes for herself, and Damask linnen, and other things for the house. I did give her a serious account how matters stand with me, of favour with the King and Duke, and of danger in reference to my

[1] The following summary of the deaths from the plague of 1665, in the parish of St. Olave's, Hart Street, was extracted from the register by the Rev. C. Murray, and printed in the "Gentleman's Magazine," October, 1845: In July, 4; August, 22; September, 63; October, 54; November, 18; December, 5. Of these, there were buried in the churchyard, 98; in the new churchyard, 42; in vaults, 12; in the church, 7; in the chancel, 1. Buried, places of interment not specified, 166. Total, 326. No wonder that Pepys felt nervous on first entering the church after the sickness abated.—B.

Lord's and Sir G. Carteret's falls, and the dissatisfaction I have heard the Duke of Albemarle hath acknowledged to somebody, among other things, against my Lord Sandwich, that he did bring me into the Navy against his desire and endeavour for another, which was our doting foole Turner. Thence from one discourse to another, and looking over my house, and other things I spent the day at home, and at night betimes to bed. After dinner this day I went down by water to Deptford, and fetched up what money there was of W. Howe's contingencies in the chest there, being £516 13*s.* 3*d.* and brought it home to dispose of.

31st. Lay pretty long in bed, and then up and to the office, where we met on extraordinary occasion about the business of tickets. By and by to the 'Change, and there did several businesses, among others brought home my cozen Pepys, whom I appointed to be here to-day, and Mr. Moore met us upon the business of my Lord's bond. Seeing my neighbour Mr. Knightly walk alone from the 'Change, his family being not yet come to town, I did invite him home with me, and he dined with me, a very sober, pretty man he is. He is mighty solicitous, as I find many about the City that live near the churchyards, to have the churchyards covered with lime, and I think it is needfull, and ours I hope will be done. Good pleasant discourse at dinner of the practices of merchants to cheate the "Customers," occasioned by Mr. Moore's being with much trouble freed of his prize goods, which he bought, which fell into the Customers' hands, and with much ado hath cleared them. Mr. Knightly being gone, my cozen Pepys and Moore and I to our business, being the clearing of my Lord Sandwich's bond wherein I am bound with him to my cozen for £1,000; I have at last by my dexterity got my Lord's consent to have it paid out of the money raised by his prizes. So the bond is cancelled, and he paid by having a note upon Sir Robert Viner, in whose hands I had lodged my Lord's money, by which I am to my extraordinary comfort eased of a liablenesse to pay the sum in case of my Lord's death, or troubles in estate, or my Lord's greater fall, which God defend! Having settled this matter at Sir R. Viner's, I took up Mr. Moore (my cozen going home) and to my Lord Chancellor's new house which he is building, only to view it, hearing so much from Mr. Evelyn of it; and, indeed, it is the finest pile I ever did see in my life, and will be a glorious house.[1] Thence to the Duke of Albemarle, who tells me Mr. Coventry is come to town and directs me to go to him about some business in hand, whether out of displeasure or desire of ease I know not; but I asked him not the reason of it but went to White Hall, but could not find him there, though to my great joy people begin to bustle up and down there, the King holding his resolution to be in towne tomorrow, and hath good encouragement, blessed be God! to do so, the plague being decreased this week to 56, and the total to 227. So after going to the Swan in the Palace, and sent for Spicer to discourse about my last Tangier tallys that have some of the words washed out with the rain, to have them new writ, I home, and there did some business and at the office, and so home to supper, and to bed.

February 1st. Up and to the office, where all the morning till late, and Mr. Coventry with us, the first time since before the plague, then hearing my wife was gone abroad to buy things and see her mother and father, whom she hath not seen since before the plague, and no dinner provided for me ready, I walked to Captain Cocke's, knowing my Lord Bruncker dined there, and there very merry, and a good dinner. Thence my Lord and his mistresse, Madam Williams, set me down at the Exchange, and I to Alderman Backewell's to set all my reckonings straight there, which I did, and took up all my notes. So evened to this day, and thence to Sir Robert Viner's, where I did the like, leaving clear in his hands just £2,000 of my owne money, to be called for when I pleased. Having done all this I home, and there to the office, did my business there by the post and so home, and spent till one in the morning in my chamber to set right all my money matters, and so to bed.

2nd. Up betimes, and knowing that my Lord Sandwich is come to towne with the King and Duke, I to wait upon him, which I did, and find him in very good humour, which

[1] Clarendon House. See note, *ante*, February 20th, 1664–65.

I am glad to see with all my heart. Having received his commands, and discoursed with some of his people about my Lord's going, and with Sir Roger Cuttance, who was there, and finds himself slighted by Sir W. Coventry, I advised him however to look after employment lest it should be said that my Lord's friends do forsake the service after he hath made them rich with the prizes. I to London, and there among other things did look over some pictures at Cade's for my house, and did carry home a silver drudger[1] for my cupboard of plate, and did call for my silver chafing dishes, but they are sent home, and the man would not be paid for them, saying that he was paid for them already, and with much ado got him to tell me by Mr. Wayth, but I would not accept of that, but will send him his money, not knowing any courtesy I have yet done him to deserve it. So home, and with my wife looked over our plate, and picked out £40 worth, I believe, to change for more usefull plate, to our great content, and then we shall have a very handsome cupboard of plate. So to dinner, and then to the office, where we had a meeting extraordinary, about stating to the Duke the present debts of the Navy, for which ready money must be had, and that being done, I to my business, where late, and then home to supper, and to bed.

3rd. Up, and to the office very busy till 3 o'clock, and then home, all of us, for half an hour to dinner, and to it

[1] The dredger was probably the *drageoir* of France; in low Latin, *dragerium*, or *drageria*, in which comfits (*dragées*) were kept. Roquefort says, "The ladies wore a little spice-box, in shape like a watch, to carry *dragées*, and it was called a *drageoir*." The custom continued certainly till the middle of the last century. Old Palsgrave, in his "Eclaircissement de la Langue Françayse," gives "dradge" as spice, rendering it by the French word *dragée*. Chaucer says, of his Doctor of Physic,

"Full ready hadde he his Apothecaries
To send him dragges, and his lattuaries."

The word sometimes may have signified the pounded condiments in which our forefathers delighted. It is worth notice, that "dragge" was applied to a grain in the eastern counties, though not exclusively there, appearing to denote mixed grain. Bishop Kennett tells us that "dredge mault is mault made up of oats, mixed with barley, of which they make an excellent, freshe, quiete sort of drinke, in Staffordshire." The dredger is still commonly used in our kitchen. — B.

again till eight at night, stating our wants of money for the Duke, but could not finish it. So broke up, and I to my office, then about letters and other businesses very late, and so home to supper, weary with business, and to bed.

4th. Lord's day; and my wife and I the first time together at church since the plague, and now only because of Mr. Mills his coming home to preach his first sermon; expecting a great excuse for his leaving the parish before any body went, and now staying till all are come home; but he made but a very poor and short excuse, and a bad sermon. It was a frost, and had snowed last night, which covered the graves in the churchyard, so as I was the less afeard for going through. Here I had the content to see my noble Mrs. Lethulier, and so home to dinner, and all the afternoon at my Journall till supper, it being a long while behindhand. At supper my wife tells me that W. Joyce has been with her this evening, the first time since the plague, and tells her my aunt James is lately dead of the stone, and what she had hath given to his and his brother's wife and my cozen Sarah. So after supper to work again, and late to bed.

5th. Up, and with Sir W. Batten (at whose lodgings calling for him, I saw his Lady the first time since her coming to towne since the plague, having absented myself designedly to shew some discontent, and that I am not at all the more suppliant because of my Lord Sandwich's fall), to my Lord Bruncker's, to see whether he goes to the Duke's this morning or no. But it is put off, and so we parted. My Lord invited me to dinner to-day to dine with Sir W. Batten and his Lady there, who were invited before, but lest he should thinke so little an invitation would serve me my turne I refused and parted, and to Westminster about business, and so back to the 'Change, and there met Mr. Hill, newly come to town, and with him the Houblands, preparing for their ship's and his going to Tangier, and agreed that I must sup with them to-night. So home and eat a bit, and then to White Hall to a Committee for Tangier, but it did not meet but was put off to to-morrow, so I did some little business and visited my Lord Sandwich, and so, it raining, went directly to the Sun, behind the Exchange, about seven o'clock, where I find all the five brothers Houblons, and mighty fine gentlemen they are all, and used me mighty respectfully. We were mighty civilly merry, and their discourses, having been all abroad, very fine. Here late and at last accompanied home with Mr. J. Houblon and Hill, whom I invited to sup with me on Friday, and so parted and I home to bed.

6th. Up, and to the office, where very busy all the morning. We met upon a report to the Duke of Yorke of the debts of the Navy, which we finished by three o'clock, and having eat one little bit of meate, I by water before the rest to White Hall (and they to come after me) because of a Committee for Tangier, where I did my business of stating my accounts perfectly well, and to good liking, and do not discern, but the Duke of Albemarle is my friend in his intentions notwithstanding my general fears. After that to our Navy business, where my fellow officers were called in, and did that also very well, and then broke up, and I home by coach, Tooker with me, and staid in Lumbard Streete at Viner's, and sent home for the plate which my wife and I had a mind to change, and there changed it, about £50 worth, into things more usefull, whereby we shall now have a very handsome cupboard of plate. So home to the office, wrote my letters by the post, and to bed.

7th. It being fast day I staid at home all day long to set things to rights in my chamber by taking out all my books, and putting my chamber in the same condition it was before the plague. But in the morning doing of it, and knocking up a nail I did bruise my left thumb so as broke a great deal of my flesh off, that it hung by a little. It was a sight frighted my wife, but I put some balsam of Mrs. Turner's to it, and though in great pain, yet went on with my business, and did it to my full content, setting every thing in order, in hopes now that the worst of our fears are over as to the plague for the next year. Interrupted I was by two or three occasions this day to my great vexation, having this the only day I have been able to set apart for this work since my coming to town. At night to supper, weary, and to bed, having had the plasterers and joiners also to do some jobbs.

8th. Up, and all the morning at the office. At noon to the 'Change, expecting to have received from Mr. Houbland, as he promised me, an assignment upon Viner, for my reward for my getting them the going of their two ships to Tangier, but I find myself much disappointed therein, for I spoke with him and he said nothing of it, but looked coldly, through some disturbance he meets with in our business through Colonell Norwood's pressing them to carry more goods than will leave room for some of their own. But I shall ease them. Thence to Captain Cocke's, where Mr. Williamson, Wren, Boldell and Madam Williams, and by and by Lord Bruncker, he having been with the King and Duke upon the water to-day, to see Greenwich house, and the yacht Castle is building of, and much good discourse. So to White Hall to see my Lord Sandwich, and then home to my business till night, and then to bed.

9th. Up, and betimes to Sir Philip Warwicke, who was glad to see me, and very kind. Thence to Colonell Norwood's lodgings, and there set about Houblons' business about their ships. Thence to Westminster, to the Exchequer, about my Tangier business to get orders for tallys, and so to the Hall, where the first day of the Terme, and the Hall very full of people, and much more than was expected, considering the plague that hath been. Thence to the 'Change, and to the Sun behind it to dinner with the Lieutenant [of the] Tower, Colonell Norwood and others, where strange pleasure they seem to take in their wine and meate, and discourse of it with the curiosity and joy that methinks was below men of worthe. Thence home, and there very much angry with my people till I had put all things in good forwardnesse about my supper for the Houblons, but that being done I was in good humour again, and all things in good order. Anon the five brothers Houblons come and Mr. Hill, and a very good supper we had, and good company and discourse, with great pleasure. My new plate sets off my cupboard very nobly. Here they were till about eleven at night with great pleasure, and a fine sight it is to see these five brothers thus loving one to another, and all industrious merchants. Our subject was principally Mr. Hill's going for them to Portugall, which was the occasion of this entertainment. They gone, we to bed.

10th. Up, and to the office. At noon, full of business, to dinner. This day comes first Sir Thomas Harvy after the plague, having been out of towne all this while. He was coldly received by us, and he went away before we rose also, to make himself appear yet a man less necessary. After dinner, being full of care and multitude of business, I took coach and my wife with me. I set her down at her mother's (having first called at my Lord Treasurer's and there spoke with Sir Ph. Warwicke), and I to the Exchequer about Tangier orders, and so to the Swan and there staid a little, and so by coach took up my wife, and at the old Exchange bought a muffe, and so home and late at my letters, and so to supper and to bed, being now-a-days, for these four or five months, mightily troubled with my snoring in my sleep, and know not how to remedy it.

11th (Lord's day). Up, and put on a new black cloth suit to an old coate that I make to be in mourning at Court, where they are all, for the King of Spayne.[1] To church I, and at noon dined well, and then by water to White Hall, carrying a captain of the Tower (who desired his freight thither); there I to the Parke, and walked two or three turnes of the Pell Mell with the company about the King and Duke; the Duke speaking to me a good deal. There met Lord Bruncker and Mr. Coventry, and discoursed about the Navy business; and all of us much at a loss that we yet can hear nothing of Sir Jeremy Smith's fleete, that went away to the Streights the middle of December, through all the storms that we have had since, that have driven back three or four of them with their masts by the board. Yesterday come out the King's Declaration of War against the French,[2] but with such mild invitations of both them and the Dutch to come over hither with promise of their protection, that every body wonders at it. Thence home with my Lord Bruncker for discourse sake, and thence by hackney coach

[1] Philip IV., who died September 17th, 1665.

[2] It was proclaimed by the Herald-at-Arms, and two of his brethren. His Majesty's Sergeants-at-Arms, with other usual officers (with his Majesty's trumpeters attending), before his royal palace at Whitehall; and afterwards (the Lord Mayor and his brethren assisting) at Temple Bar, and other the usual parts of the city ("The London Gazette," February 8th–12th, 1665–6). — B.

home, and so my wife and I mighty pleasant discourse, supped and to bed. The great wound I had Wednesday last in my thumb having with once dressing by Mrs. Turner's balsam been perfectly cured, whereas I did not hope to save my nail, whatever else ill it did give me. My wife and I are much thoughtfull now-a-days about Pall's coming up in order to a husband.

12th. Up, and very busy to perform an oathe in finishing my Journall this morning for 7 or 8 days past. Then to several people attending upon business, among others Mr. Grant and the executors of Barlow for the £25 due for the quarter before he died, which I scrupled to pay, being obliged but to pay every half year. Then comes Mr. Cæsar, my boy's lute-master, whom I have not seen since the plague before, but he hath been in Westminster all this while very well; and tells me in the height of it, how bold people there were, to go in sport to one another's burials; and in spite too, ill people would breathe in the faces (out of their windows) of well people going by. Then to dinner before the 'Change, and so to the 'Change, and then to the taverne to talk with Sir William Warren, and so by coach to several places, among others to my Lord Treasurer's, there to meet my Lord Sandwich, but missed, and met him at [my] Lord Chancellor's, and there talked with him about his accounts, and then about Sir G. Carteret, and I find by him that Sir G. Carteret has a worse game to play than my Lord Sandwich, for people are jeering at him, and he cries out of the business of Sir W. Coventry, who strikes at all and do all. Then to my bookseller's, and then received some books I have new bought, and here late choosing some more to new bind, having resolved to give myself £10 in books, and so home to the office and then home to supper, where Mr. Hill was and supped with us, and good discourse; an excellent person he still appears to me. After supper and he gone, we to bed.

13th. Up, and all the morning at the office. At noon to the 'Change, and thence after business dined at the Sheriffe's [Hooker], being carried by Mr. Lethulier, where to my heart's content I met with his wife, a most beautifull fat woman. But all the house melancholy upon the sickness of a daughter of the house in childbed, Mr. Vaughan's lady.

So all of them undressed, but however this lady a very fine woman. I had a salute of her, and after dinner some discourse the Sheriffe and I about a parcel of tallow I am buying for the office of him. I away home, and there at the office all the afternoon till late at night, and then away home to supper and to bed. Ill newes this night that the plague is encreased this week, and in many places else about the towne, and at Chatham and elsewhere. This day my wife wanting a chambermaid with much ado got our old little Jane to be found out, who come to see her and hath lived all this while in one place, but is so well that we will not desire her removal, but are mighty glad to see the poor wench, who is very well and do well.

14th (St. Valentine's day). This morning called up by Mr. Hill, who, my wife thought, had been come to be her Valentine; she, it seems, having drawne him last night, but it proved not. However, calling him up to our bed-side, my wife challenged him. I up, and made myself ready, and so with him by coach to my Lord Sandwich's by appointment to deliver Mr. Howe's accounts to my Lord. Which done, my Lord did give me hearty and large studied thanks for all my kindnesse to him and care of him and his business. I after profession of all duty to his Lordship took occasion to bemoane myself that I should fall into such a difficulty about Sir G. Carteret, as not to be for him, but I must be against Sir W. Coventry, and therefore desired to be neutrall, which my Lord approved and confessed reasonable, but desired me to befriend him privately. Having done in private with my Lord I brought Mr. Hill to kisse his hands, to whom my Lord professed great respect upon my score. My Lord being gone, I took Mr. Hill to my Lord Chancellor's new house that is building, and went with trouble up to the top of it, and there is there the noblest prospect that ever I saw in my life, Greenwich being nothing to it; and in every thing is a beautiful house, and most strongly built in every respect; and as if, as it hath, it had the Chancellor for its master. Thence with him to his paynter, Mr. Hales, who is drawing his picture, which will be mighty like him, and pleased me so, that I am resolved presently to have my wife's and mine done by him, he having a very masterly hand. So with mighty satisfaction to the 'Change and thence home, and after dinner abroad, taking Mrs. Mary Batelier with us, who was just come to see my wife, and they set me down at my Lord Treasurer's, and themselves went with the coach into the fields to take the ayre. I staid a meeting of the Duke of Yorke's, and the officers of the Navy and Ordnance. My Lord Treasurer lying in bed of the gowte. Our business was discourse of the straits of the Navy for want of money, but after long discourse as much out of order as ordinary people's, we come to no issue, nor any money promised, or like to be had, and yet the worke must be done. Here I perceive Sir G. Carteret had prepared himself to answer a choque of Sir W. Coventry, by offering of himself to shew all he had paid, and what is unpaid, and what moneys and assignments he hath in his hands, which, if he makes good, was the best thing he ever did say in his life, and the best timed, for else it must have fallen very foule on him. The meeting done I away, my wife and they being come back and staying for me at the gate. But, Lord! to see how afeard I was that Sir W. Coventry should have spyed me once whispering with Sir G. Carteret, though not intended by me, but only Sir G. Carteret come to me and I could not avoyde it. So home, they set me down at the 'Change, and I to the Crowne, where my Lord Bruncker was come and several of the Virtuosi, and after a small supper and but little good discourse I with Sir W. Batten (who was brought thither with my Lord Bruncker) home, where I find my wife gone to Mrs. Mercer's to be merry, but presently come in with Mrs. Knipp, who, it seems, is in towne, and was gone thither with my wife and Mercer to dance, and after eating a little supper went thither again to spend the whole night there, being W. Howe there, at whose chamber they are, and Lawd Crisp by chance. I to bed.

15th. Up, and my wife not come home all night. To the office, where sat all the morning. At noon to Starky's, a great cooke in Austin Friars, invited by Colonell Atkins, and a good dinner for Colonell Norwood and his friends, among others Sir Edward Spragg and others, but ill attendance. Before dined, called on by my wife in a coach, and so I took leave, and then with her and Knipp and Mercer (Mr. Hunt newly come out of the country being there also come to see us) to Mr. Hales, the paynter's, having set down Mr. Hunt by the way. Here Mr. Hales[1] begun my wife in the posture we saw one of my Lady Peters, like a St. Katharine.[2] While he painted, Knipp, and Mercer, and I, sang; and by and by comes Mrs. Pierce, with my name in her bosom for her Valentine, which will cost me money. But strange how like his very first dead colouring is, that it did me good to see it, and pleases me mightily, and I believe will be a noble picture. Thence with them all as far as Fleete Streete, and there set Mercer and Knipp down, and we home. I to the office, whither the Houblons come telling me of a little new trouble from Norwood about their ship, which troubles me, though without reason. So late home to supper and to bed. We hear this night of Sir Jeremy Smith, that he and his fleete have been seen at Malaga; which is good newes.

16th. Up betimes, and by appointment to the Exchange, where I met Messrs. Houblons, and took them up in my coach and carried them to Charing Crosse, where they to Colonell Norwood to see how they can settle matters with him, I having informed them by the way with advice to be easy with him, for he may hereafter do us service, and they and I are like to understand one another to very good purpose. I to my Lord Sandwich, and there alone with him to talke of his affairs, and particularly of his prize goods, wherein I find he is wearied with being troubled, and gives over the care of it to let it come to what it will, having the King's release for the dividend made, and for the rest he thinks himself safe from being proved to have anything more. Thence to the Exchequer, and so by coach to the 'Change, Mr. Moore with me, who tells me very odde passages of the indiscretion of my Lord in the management of his family, of his carelessnesse, &c., which troubles me, but makes me rejoice with all my heart of my being rid of the bond of £1,000, for that would have been a cruel blow to

[1] John Hayls, or Hales, a portrait-painter "remarkable for copying Vandyke well, and for being a rival of Lely." Pepys employed him to paint portraits of himself, his wife, and his father.

[2] It was the fashion at this time to be painted as St. Catherine, in compliment to the queen.

me. With Moore to the Coffee-House,[1] the first time I have been there, where very full, and company it seems hath been there all the plague time. So to the 'Change, and then home to dinner, and after dinner to settle accounts with him for my Lord, and so evened with him to this day. Then to the office, and out with Sir W. Warren for discourse by coach to White Hall, thinking to have spoke with Sir W. Coventry, but did not, and to see the Queene, but she comes but to Hampton Court to-night. Back to my office and there late, and so home to supper and bed. I walked a good while to-night with Mr. Hater in the garden, talking about a husband for my sister, and reckoning up all our clerks about us, none of which he thinks fit for her and her portion. At last I thought of young Gawden, and will thinke of it again.

17th. Up, and to the office, where busy all the morning. Late to dinner, and then to the office again, and there busy till past twelve at night, and so home to supper and to bed. We have newes of Sir Jeremy Smith's being very well with his fleete at Cales.[2]

18th (Lord's day). Lay long in bed discoursing with pleasure with my wife, among other things about Pall's coming up, for she must be here a little to be fashioned, and my wife hath a mind to go down for her, which I am not much against, and so I rose and to my chamber to settle several things. At noon comes my uncle Wight to dinner, and brings with him Mrs. Wight, sad company to me, nor was I much pleased with it, only I must shew respect to my uncle. After dinner they gone, and it being a brave day, I walked to White Hall, where the Queene and ladies are all come: I saw some few of them, but not the Queene, nor any of the great beauties. I endeavoured to have seen my Lord Hinchingbrooke, who come to town yesterday, but I could not. Met with Creed and walked with him a turne or two in the Parke, but without much content, having now designs of getting money in my head, which allow me not the leisure I used to have with him, besides an odde story lately told of him for a great truth, of his endeavouring to

[1] This is supposed to be intended for the famous Will's Coffee House in Covent Garden.

[2] Cadiz.

lie with a woman at Oxford, and her crying out saved her; and this being publickly known, do a little make me hate him. Thence took coach, and calling by the way at my bookseller's for a booke[1] writ about twenty years ago in prophecy of this year coming on, 1666, explaining it to be the marke of the beast, I home, and there fell to reading, and then to supper, and to bed.

19th. Up, and by coach to my Lord Sandwich's, but he was gone out. So I to White Hall, and there waited on the Duke of Yorke with some of the rest of our brethren, and thence back again to my Lord's, to see my Lord Hinchingbroke, which I did, and I am mightily out of countenance in my great expectation of him by others' report, though he is indeed a pretty gentleman, yet nothing what I took him for, methinks, either as to person or discourse discovered to me, but I must try him more before I go too far in censuring. Hence to the Exchequer from office to office, to set my business of my tallys in doing, and there all the morning. So at noon by coach to St. Paul's Church-yarde to my Bookseller's, and there bespoke a few more books to bring all I have lately bought to £10. Here I am told for certain, what I have heard once or twice already, of a Jew in town, that in the name of the rest do offer to give any man £10 to be paid £100, if a certain person now at Smyrna be within these two years owned by all the Princes of the East, and particularly the grand Signor as the King of the world, in the same manner we do the King of England here, and that this man is the true Messiah. One named a friend of his that had received ten pieces in gold upon this score, and says that the Jew hath disposed of £1,100 in this manner, which is very strange; and certainly this year of 1666 will be a year of great action; but what

[1] The book purchased by Pepys is entitled, "An Interpretation of the Number 666, wherein not only the manner how this Number ought to be interpreted is clearly proved and demonstrated; but it is also shewed that this number is an exquisite and perfect character, truly, exactly, and essentially describing that state of Government to which all other notes of Antichrist doe agree. With all knowne objections solidly and fully answered, that can be materially made against it." By Francis Potter, B.D., Oxford, 1642, 4to. A copy of this work in the British Museum contains the book-plate of "William Hewer, of Clapham, in the county of Surrey, Esq., 1699." See November 4th and 10th, 1666, *post*. — B.

the consequences of it will be, God knows! Thence to the 'Change, and from my stationer's thereabouts carried home by coach two books of Ogilby's, his Æsop and Coronation, which fell to my lot at his lottery.[1] Cost me £4 besides the binding. So home. I find my wife gone out to Hales, her paynter's, and I after a little dinner do follow her, and there do find him at worke, and with great content I do see it will be a very brave picture. Left her there, and I to my Lord Treasurer's, where Sir G. Carteret and Sir J. Minnes met me, and before my Lord Treasurer and Duke of Albemarle the state of our Navy debts were laid open, being very great, and their want of money to answer them openly professed, there being but £1,500,000 to answer a certaine expense and debt of £2,300,000. Thence walked with Fenn down to White Hall, and there saw the Queene at cards with many ladies, but none of our beauties were there. But glad I was to see the Queene so well, who looks prettily; and methinks hath more life than before, since it is confessed of all that she miscarryed lately; Dr. Clerke telling me yesterday at White Hall that he had the membranes and other vessels in his hands which she voided, and were perfect as ever woman's was that bore a child. Thence hoping to find my Lord Sandwich, away by coach to my Lord Chancellor's, but missed him, and so home and to office, and then to supper and my Journall, and to bed.

20th. Up, and to the office; where, among other businesses, Mr. Evelyn's proposition about publique Infirmarys was read and agreed on, he being there: and at noon I took him home to dinner, being desirous of keeping my acquaintance with him; and a most excellent humoured man I still find him, and mighty knowing. After dinner I took him by coach to White Hall, and there he and I parted, and I to my Lord Sandwich's, where coming and bolting into the dining-room, I there found Captain Ferrers going to christen a child of his born yesterday, and I come

[1] John Ogilby's "Entertainment of Charles II. in his Passage through the City of London to his Coronation" was published by the king's command in 1662 — a splendid volume with plates by Hollar. His translation of Æsop was published in 1651 and 1658; but it was probably the illustrated edition issued in 1665 which Pepys bought. The lottery took place at the old theatre between Lincoln's Inn Fields and Vere Street.

just pat to be a godfather, along with my Lord Hinchingbrooke, and Madam Pierce, my Valentine, which for that reason I was pretty well contented with, though a little vexed to see myself so beset with people to spend me money, as she of a Valentine and little Mrs. Tooker, who is come to my house this day from Greenwich, and will cost me 20*s.*, my wife going out with her this afternoon, and now this christening. Well, by and by the child is brought and christened Katharine, and I this day on this occasion drank a glasse of wine, which I have not professedly done these two years, I think, but a little in the time of the sicknesse. After that done, and gone and kissed the mother in bed, I away to Westminster Hall, and there hear that Mrs. Lane is come to town. So I staid loitering up and down till anon she comes and agreed to meet at Swayn's, and there I went anon, and she come, but staid but little, the place not being private. I have not seen her since before the plague. So thence parted and rencontrais à her last logis, and in the place did what I tenais a mind pour ferais con her. At last she desired to borrow money of me, £5, and would pawn gold with me for it, which I accepted and promised in a day or two to supply her. So away home to the office, and thence home, where little Mrs. Tooker staid all night with us, and a pretty child she is, and happens to be niece to my beauty that is dead, that lived at the Jackanapes, in Cheapside. So to bed, a little troubled that I have been at two houses this afternoon with Mrs. Lane that were formerly shut up of the plague.

21st. Up, and with Sir J. Minnes to White Hall by his coach, by the way talking of my brother John to get a spiritual promotion for him, which I am now to looke after, for as much as he is shortly to be Master in Arts, and writes me this weeke a Latin letter that he is to go into orders this Lent. There to the Duke's chamber, and find our fellows discoursing there on our business, so I was sorry to come late, but no hurte was done thereby. Here the Duke, among other things, did bring out a book of great antiquity of some of the customs of the Navy, about 100 years since, which he did lend us to read and deliver him back again. Thence I to the Exchequer, and there did strike my tallys for a quarter for Tangier and carried them home with me, and thence to Trinity-house, being invited to an Elder Brother's feast; and there met and sat by Mr. Prin, and had good discourse about the privileges of Parliament, which, he says, are few to the Commons' House, and those not examinable by them, but only by the House of Lords. Thence with my Lord Bruncker to Gresham College, the first time after the sicknesse that I was there, and the second time any met. And here a good lecture of Mr. Hooke's about the trade of felt-making, very pretty. And anon alone with me about the art of drawing pictures by Prince Rupert's rule and machine, and another of Dr. Wren's;[1] but he says nothing do like squares, or, which is the best in the world, like a darke roome,[2] which pleased me mightily. Thence with Povy home to my house, and there late settling accounts with him, which was very troublesome to me, and he gone, found Mr. Hill below, who sat with me till late talking, and so away, and we to bed.

22nd. Up, and to the office, where sat all the morning. At noon home to dinner and thence by coach with my wife for ayre principally for her. I alone stopped at Hales's and there mightily am pleased with my wife's picture that is begun there, and with Mr. Hill's, though I must [owne] I am not more pleased with it now the face is finished than I was when I saw it the second time of sitting. Thence to my Lord Sandwich's, but he not within, but goes to-morrow. My wife to Mrs. Hunt's, who is lately come to towne and grown mighty fat. I called her there, and so home and late at the office, and so home to supper and to bed. We are much troubled that the sicknesse in general (the town being so full of people) should be but three, and yet of the particular disease of the plague there should be ten encrease.

23rd. Up betimes, and out of doors by 6 of the clock, and walked (W. Howe with me) to my Lord Sandwich's, who did lie the last night at his house in Lincoln's Inne Fields. It being fine walking in the morning, and the streets full of people again. There I staid, and the house

[1] Afterwards the famous Sir Christopher Wren. He was one of the mainstays of the Royal Society.

[2] The *camera obscura*.

full of people come to take leave of my Lord, who this day goes out of towne upon his embassy towards Spayne. And I was glad to find Sir W. Coventry to come, though I know it is only a piece of courtshipp. I had much discourse with my Lord, he telling me how fully he leaves the King his friend and the large discourse he had with him the other day, and how he desired to have the business of the prizes examined before he went, and that he yielded to it, and it is done as far as it concerns himself to the full, and the Lords Commissioners for prizes did reprehend all the informers in what related to his Lordship, which I am glad of in many respects. But we could not make an end of discourse, so I promised to waite upon [him] on Sunday at Cranborne, and took leave and away hence to Mr. Hales's with Mr. Hill and two of the Houblons, who come thither to speak with me, and saw my wife's picture, which pleases me well, but Mr. Hill's picture never a whit so well as it did before it was finished, which troubled me, and I begin to doubt the picture of my Lady Peters my wife takes her posture from, and which is an excellent picture, is not of his making, it is so master-like. I set them down at the 'Change and I home to the office, and at noon dined at home and to the office again. Anon comes Mrs. Knipp to see my wife, who is gone out, so I fain to entertain her, and took her out by coach to look my wife at Mrs. Pierce's and Unthanke's, but find her not. So back again, and then my wife comes home, having been buying of things, and at home I spent all the night talking with this baggage, and teaching her my song of "Beauty retire," which she sings and makes go most rarely, and a very fine song it seems to be. She also entertained me with repeating many of her own and others' parts of the play-house, which she do most excellently; and tells me the whole practices of the play-house and players, and is in every respect most excellent company. So I supped, and was merry at home all the evening, and the rather it being my birthday, 33 years, for which God be praised that I am in so good a condition of healthe and estate, and every thing else as I am, beyond expectation, in all. So she to Mrs. Turner's to lie, and we to bed. Mightily pleased to find myself in condition to have these people come about me and to be able to entertain them, and have the pleasure of their qualities, than which no man can have more in the world.

24th. All the morning at the office till past three o'clock. At that houre home and eat a bit alone, my wife being gone out. So abroad by coach with Mr. Hill, who staid for me to speake about business, and he and I to Hales's, where I find my wife and her woman, and Pierce and Knipp, and there sung and was mighty merry, and I joyed myself in it; but vexed at first to find my wife's picture not so like as I expected; but it was only his having finished one part, and not another, of the face; but, before I went, I was satisfied it will be an excellent picture. Here we had ale and cakes and mighty merry, and sung my song, which she [Knipp] now sings bravely, and makes me proud of myself. Thence left my wife to go home with Mrs. Pierce, while I home to the office, and there pretty late, and to bed, after fitting myself for to-morrow's journey.

25th (Lord's day). My wife up between three and four of the clock in the morning to dress herself, and I about five, and were all ready to take coach, she and I and Mercer, a little past five, but, to our trouble, the coach did not come till six. Then with our coach of four horses I hire on purpose, and Leshmore to ride by, we through the City to Branford and so to Windsor, Captain Ferrers overtaking us at Kensington, being to go with us, and here drank, and so through, making no stay, to Cranborne,[1] about eleven o'clock, and found my Lord and the ladies at a sermon in the house; which being ended we to them, and all the company glad to see us, and mighty merry to dinner. Here was my Lord, and Lord Hinchingbroke, and Mr. Sidney,[2] Sir Charles Herbert,[3] and Mr. Carteret, my Lady Carteret, my Lady Jemimah, and Lady Slaning.[4] After dinner to talk to and again, and then to walke in the Parke, my Lord and I alone, talking upon these heads; first, he has left his business of the prizes as well as is possible for him, having cleared himself before the Commis-

[1] Cranbourne Lodge. Sir G. Carteret's official residence, as Vice-Chamberlain. See July 20th, 1665.

[2] Sidney Montagu, Lord Sandwich's second son.

[3] Sir Charles Harbord. See *ante*, October 24th, 1665.

[4] Sir George Carteret's daughter Caroline.

sioners by the King's commands, so that nothing or little is to be feared from that point, he goes fully assured, he tells me, of the King's favour. That upon occasion I may know, I desired to know, his friends I may trust to, he tells me, but that he is not yet in England, but continues this summer in Ireland, my Lord Orrery is his father almost in affection. He tells me my Lord of Suffolke, Lord Arlington, Archbishop of Canterbury, Lord Treasurer, Mr. Atturny Montagu, Sir Thomas Clifford in the House of Commons, Sir G. Carteret, and some others I cannot presently remember, are friends that I may rely on for him. He tells me my Lord Chancellor seems his very good friend, but doubts that he may not think him so much a servant of the Duke of Yorke's as he would have him, and indeed my Lord tells me he hath lately made it his business to be seen studious of the King's favour, and not of the Duke's, and by the King will stand or fall, for factions there are, as he tells me, and God knows how high they may come. The Duke of Albemarle's post is so great, having had the name of bringing in the King, that he is like to stand, or, if it were not for him, God knows in what troubles we might be from some private faction, if an army could be got into another hand, which God forbid! It is believed that though Mr. Coventry be in appearance so great against the Chancellor, yet that there is a good understanding between the Duke and him. He dreads the issue of this year, and fears there will be some very great revolutions before his coming back again. He doubts it is needful for him to have a pardon for his last year's actions, all which he did without commission, and at most but the King's private single word for that of Bergen; but he dares not ask it at this time, lest it should make them think that there is something more in it than yet they know; and if it should be denied, it would be of very ill consequence. He says also, if it should in Parliament be enquired into the selling of Dunkirke (though the Chancellor was the man that would have it sold to France, saying the King of Spayne had no money to give for it); yet he will be found to have been the greatest adviser of it; which he is a little apprehensive may be called upon this Parliament. He told me it would not be necessary for him to tell me his debts, because he thinks

I know them so well. He tells me, that for the match propounded of Mrs. Mallett for my Lord Hinchingbroke, it hath been lately off, and now her friends bring it on again, and an overture hath been made to him by a servant of her's, to compass the thing without consent of friends, she herself having a respect to my Lord's family, but my Lord will not listen to it but in a way of honour. The Duke hath for this weeke or two been very kind to him, more than lately, and so others, which he thinks is a good sign of faire weather again. He says the Archbishopp of Canterbury hath been very kind to him, and hath plainly said to him that he and all the world knows the difference between his judgment and brains and the Duke of Albemarle's, and then calls my Lady Duchesse the veryest slut and drudge and the foulest worde that can be spoke of a woman almost. My Lord having walked an houre with me talking thus and going in, and my Lady Carteret not suffering me to go back again to-night, my Lord to walke again with me about some of this and other discourse, and then in a-doors and to talke with all and with my Lady Carteret, and I with the young ladies and gentlemen, who played on the guittar, and mighty merry, and anon to supper, and then my Lord going away to write, the young gentlemen to flinging of cushions, and other mad sports; at this late till towards twelve at night, and then being sleepy, I and my wife in a passage-room to bed, and slept not very well because of noise.

26th. Called up about five in the morning, and my Lord up, and took leave, a little after six, very kindly of me and the whole company. Then I in, and my wife up and to visit my Lady Slaning in her bed, and there sat three hours, with Lady Jemimah with us, talking and laughing, and by and by my Lady Carteret comes, and she and I to talke, I glad to please her in discourse of Sir G. Carteret, that all will do well with him, and she is much pleased, he having had great annoyance and fears about his well doing, and I fear hath doubted that I have not been a friend to him, but cries out against my Lady Castlemaine, that makes the King neglect his business and seems much to fear that all will go to wracke, and I fear with great reason; exclaims against the Duke of Albemarle, and more the Duchesse for a filthy woman, as indeed she is. Here staid till 9 o'clock almost, and then took coach with so much love and kindnesse from my Lady Carteret, Lady Jemimah, and Lady Slaning, that it joys my heart, and when I considered the manner of my going hither, with a coach and four horses and servants and a woman with us, and coming hither being so much made of, and used with that state, and then going to Windsor and being shewn all that we were there, and had wherewith to give every body something for their pains, and then going home, and all in fine weather and no fears nor cares upon me, I do thinke myself obliged to thinke myself happy, and do look upon myself at this time in the happiest occasion a man can be, and whereas we take pains in expectation of future comfort and ease, I have taught myself to reflect upon myself at present as happy, and enjoy myself in that consideration, and not only please myself with thoughts of future wealth and forget the pleasure we at present enjoy. So took coach and to Windsor, to the Garter, and thither sent for Dr. Childe;[1] who come to us, and carried us to St. George's Chappell; and there placed us among the Knights' stalls (and pretty the observation, that no man, but a woman may sit in a Knight's place, where any brass-plates are set); and hither come cushions to us, and a young singing-boy to bring us a copy of the anthem to be sung. And here, for our sakes, had this anthem and the great service sung extraordinary, only to entertain us. It is a noble place indeed, and a good Quire of voices. Great bowing by all the people, the poor Knights particularly, to the Alter. After prayers, we to see the plate of the chappell, and the robes of Knights, and a man to shew us the banners of the several Knights in being, which hang up over the stalls. And so to other discourse very pretty, about the Order. Was shewn where

[1] William Child, Doctor of Music, born at Bristol in 1604, and educated in the choir of the cathedral under Elway Bevin. In 1636 he was appointed one of the organists of St. George's Chapel at Windsor. After the Restoration he was appointed "Chanter of the King's Chapel at Whitehall," and one of the organists. He died on March 23rd, 1696–7, in the ninety-first year of his age, and was buried in St. George's Chapel, Windsor (Rimbault's "Old Cheque Book of the Chapel Royal," p. 226).

the late [King] is buried,[1] and King Henry the Eighth, and my Lady [Jane] Seymour. This being done, to the King's house, and to observe the neatness and contrivance of the house and gates: it is the most romantique castle that is in the world. But, Lord! the prospect that is in the balcone in the Queene's lodgings, and the terrace and walk, are strange things to consider, being the best in the world, sure. Infinitely satisfied I and my wife with all this, she being in all points mightily pleased too, which added to my pleasure; and so giving a great deal of money to this and that man and woman, we to our taverne, and there dined, the Doctor with us; and so took coach and away to Eton, the Doctor with me. Before we went to Chappell this morning, Kate Joyce, in a stage-coach going toward London, called to me. I went to her and saluted her, but could not get her to stay with us, having company. At Eton I left my wife in the coach, and he and I to the College, and there find all mighty fine. The school good, and the custom pretty of boys cutting their names in the struts of the window when they go to Cambridge, by which many a one hath lived to see himself Provost and Fellow, that had his name in the window standing. To the Hall, and there find the boys' verses, "De Peste;" it being their custom to make verses at Shrove-tide. I read several, and very good ones they were, and better, I think, than ever I made when I was a boy, and in rolls as long and longer than the whole Hall, by much. Here is a picture of Venice hung up given, and a monument made of Sir H. Wotton's giving it to the College. Thence to the porter's, in the absence of the butler, and did drink of the College beer, which is very good; and went into the back fields to see the scholars play. And so to the chappell, and there saw, among other things, Sir H. Wotton's stone with this Epitaph:

> Hic jacet primus hujus sententiæ Author: —
> Disputandi pruritus fit ecclesiæ scabies.

But unfortunately the word "Author" was wrong writ, and now so basely altered that it disgraces the stone. Thence

[1] Sir Henry Halford wrote "An Account of what appeared on opening the Coffin of K. Charles I. at Windsor," 1813, which was reprinted in his "Essays and Orations," 1831, 1842.

took leave of the Doctor, and so took coach, and finely, but sleepy, away home, and got thither about eight at night, and after a little at my office, I to bed; and an houre after, was waked with my wife's quarrelling with Mercer, at which I was angry, and my wife and I fell out. But with much ado to sleep again, I beginning to practise more temper, and to give her her way.

27th. Up, and after a harsh word or two my wife and I good friends, and so up and to the office, where all the morning. At noon late to dinner, my wife gone out to Hales's about her picture, and, after dinner, I after her, and do mightily like her picture, and think it will be as good as my Lady Peters's. So home mightily pleased, and there late at business and set down my three last days' journalls, and so to bed, overjoyed to thinke of the pleasure of the last Sunday and yesterday, and my ability to bear the charge of these pleasures, and with profit too, by obliging my Lord, and reconciling Sir George Carteret's family.

28th (Ash Wednesday). Up, and after doing a little business at my office I walked, it being a most curious dry and cold morning, to White Hall, and there I went into the Parke, and meeting Sir Ph. Warwicke took a turne with him in the Pell Mall, talking of the melancholy posture of affairs, where every body is snarling one at another, and all things put together looke ominously. This new Act too putting us out of a power of raising money. So that he fears as I do, but is fearfull of enlarging in that discourse of an ill condition in every thing, and the State and all. We appointed another time to meet to talke of the business of the Navy alone seriously, and so parted, and I to White Hall, and there we did our business with the Duke of Yorke, and so parted, and walked to Westminster Hall, where I staid talking with Mrs. Michell and Howlett long and her daughter, which is become a mighty pretty woman, and thence going out of the Hall was called to by Mrs. Martin, so I went to her and bought two bands, and so parted, and by and by met at her chamber, and there did what I would, and so away home and there find Mrs. Knipp, and we dined together, she the pleasantest company in the world. After dinner I did give my wife money to lay out on Knipp, 20*s.*, and I abroad to White Hall to visit Colonell Norwood, and then Sir G. Carteret, with whom I have brought myself right again, and he very open to me; is very melancholy, and matters, I fear, go down with him, but he seems most afeard of a general catastrophe to the whole kingdom, and thinks, as I fear, that all things will come to nothing. Thence to the Palace Yard, to the Swan, and there staid till it was dark, and then to Mrs. Lane's, and there lent her £5 upon £4. 01*s.* in gold. And then did what I would with her, and I perceive she is come to be very bad, and offers any thing, that it is dangerous to have to do with her, nor will I see [her] any more a good while. Thence by coach home and to the office, where a while, and then betimes to bed by ten o'clock, sooner than I have done many a day. And thus ends this month, with my mind full of resolution to apply myself better from this time forward to my business than I have done these six or eight days, visibly to my prejudice both in quiett of mind and setting backward of my business, that I cannot give a good account of it as I ought to do.

March 1st. Up, and to the office and there all the morning sitting and at noon to dinner with my Lord Bruncker, Sir W. Batten and Sir W. Pen at the White Horse in Lumbard Streete, where, God forgive us! good sport with Captain Cocke's having his mayde sicke of the plague a day or two ago and sent to the pest house, where she now is, but he will not say anything but that she is well. But blessed be God! a good Bill this week we have; being but 237 in all, and 42 of the plague, and of them but six in the City: though my Lord Bruncker says, that these six are most of them in new parishes where they were not the last week. Here was with us also Mr. Williamson, who the more I know, the more I honour. Hence I slipt after dinner without notice home and there close to my business at my office till twelve at night, having with great comfort returned to my business by some fresh vowes in addition to my former, and more severe, and a great joy it is to me to see myself in a good disposition to business. So home to supper and to my Journall and to bed.

2nd. Up, as I have of late resolved before 7 in the morning and to the office, where all the morning, among other things setting my wife and Mercer with much pleasure to worke upon the ruling of some paper for the making of books for pursers, which will require a great deale of worke and they will earn a good deale of money by it, the hopes of which makes them worke mighty hard. At noon dined and to the office again, and about 4 o'clock took coach and to my Lord Treasurer's and thence to Sir Philip Warwicke's new house by appointment, there to spend an houre in talking and we were together above an hour, and very good discourse about the state of the King as to money, and particularly in the point of the Navy. He endeavours hard to come to a good understanding of Sir G. Carteret's accounts, and by his discourse I find Sir G. Carteret must be brought to it, and what a madman he is that he do not do it of himself, for the King expects the Parliament will call upon him for his promise of giving an account of the money, and he will be ready for it, which cannot be, I am sure, without Sir G. Carteret's accounts be better understood than they are. He seems to have a great esteem of me and my opinion and thoughts of things. After we had spent an houre thus discoursing and vexed that we do but grope so in the darke as we do, because the people, that should enlighten us, do not helpe us, we resolved fitting some things for another meeting, and so broke up. He shewed me his house, which is yet all unhung, but will be a very noble house indeed. Thence by coach calling at my bookseller's and carried home £10 worth of books, all, I hope, I shall buy a great while. There by appointment find Mr. Hill come to sup and take his last leave of me, and by and by in comes Mr. James Houbland to bear us company, a man I love mightily, and will not lose his acquaintance. He told me in my eare this night what he and his brothers have resolved to give me, which is £200, for helping them out with two or three ships. A good sum and that which I did believe they would give me, and I did expect little less. Here we talked and very good company till late, and then took leave of one another, and indeed I am heartily sorry for Mr. Hill's leaving us, for he is a very worthy gentleman, as most I know. God give him a good voyage and successe in his business. Thus we parted and my wife and I to bed, heavy for the losse of our friend.

3rd. All the morning at the office, at noon to the Old James, being sent for, and there dined with Sir William Rider, Cutler, and others, to make an end with two Scots Maisters about the freight of two ships of my Lord Rutherford's. After a small dinner and a little discourse I away to the Crowne behind the Exchange to Sir W. Pen, Captain Cocke and Fenn, about getting a bill of Cocke's paid to Pen, in part for the East India goods he sold us. Here Sir W. Pen did give me the reason in my eare of his importunity for money, for that he is now to marry his daughter. God send her better fortune than her father deserves I should wish him for a false rogue. Thence by coach to Hales's, and there saw my wife sit; and I do like her picture mightily, and very like it will be, and a brave piece of work. But he do complain that her nose hath cost him as much work as another's face, and he hath done it finely indeed. Thence home and late at the office, and then to bed.

4th (Lord's day). And all day at my Tangier and private accounts, having neglected them since Christmas, which I hope I shall never do again; for I find the inconvenience of it, it being ten times the labour to remember and settle things. But I thank God I did it at last, and brought them all fine and right; and I am, I thinke, by all appears to me (and I am sure I cannot be £10 wrong), worth above £4,600, for which the Lord be praised! being the biggest sum I ever was worth yet.

5th. I was at it till past two o'clock on Monday morning, and then read my vowes, and to bed with great joy and content that I have brought my things to so good a settlement, and now having my mind fixed to follow my business again and sensible of Sir W. Coventry's jealousies, I doubt, concerning me, partly my siding with Sir G. Carteret, and partly that indeed I have been silent in my business of the office a great while, and given but little account of myself and least of all to him, having not made him one visitt since he came to towne from Oxford, I am resolved to fall hard to it again, and fetch up the time and interest I have lost or am in a fair way of doing it. Up about eight o'clock, being called up by several people, among others by Mr. Moone, with whom I went to Lumbard Streete to Colvill, and so back again and in my chamber he and I did end all our businesses together of accounts for money upon bills of Exchange, and am pleased to find myself reputed a man of business and method, as he do give me out to be. To the 'Change at noon and so home to dinner. Newes for certain of the King of Denmarke's declaring for the Dutch, and resolution to assist them. To the office, and there all the afternoon. In the evening come Mr. James and brother Houblons to agree upon share parties for their ships, and did acquaint me that they had paid my messenger, whom I sent this afternoon for it, £200 for my friendship in the business, which pleases me mightily. They being gone I forth late to Sir R. Viner's to take a receipt of them for the £200 lodged for me there with them, and so back home, and after supper to bed.

6th. Up betimes and did much business before office time. Then to the office and there till noon and so home to dinner and to the office again till night. In the evening being at Sir W. Batten's, stepped in (for I have not used to go thither a good while), I find my Lord Bruncker and Mrs. Williams, and they would of their own accord, though I had never obliged them (nor my wife neither) with one visit for many of theirs, go see my house and my wife; which I showed them and made them welcome with wine and China oranges (now a great rarity since the war, none to be had). There being also Captain Cocke and Mrs. Turner, who had never been in my house since I come to the office before, and Mrs. Carcasse, wife of Mr. Carcasse's. My house happened to be mighty clean, and did me great honour, and they mightily pleased with it. They gone I to the office and did some business, and then home to supper and to bed. My mind troubled through a doubtfulness of my having incurred Sir W. Coventry's displeasure by not having waited on him since his coming to towne, which is a mighty faulte and that I can bear the fear of the bad effects of till I have been with him, which shall be to-morrow, God willing. So to bed.

7th. Up betimes, and to St. James's, thinking Mr. Coventry had lain there; but he do not, but at White Hall; so thither I went and had as good a time as heart could wish, and after an houre in his chamber about publique business he and I walked up, and the Duke being gone abroad we walked an houre in the Matted Gallery: he of himself begun to discourse of the unhappy differences between him and my Lord of Sandwich, and from the beginning to the end did run through all passages wherein my Lord hath, at any time, gathered any dissatisfaction, and cleared himself to me most honourably; and in truth, I do believe he do as he says. I did afterwards purge myself of all partiality in the business of Sir G. Carteret, (whose story Sir W. Coventry did also run over), that I do mind the King's interest, notwithstanding my relation to him; all which he declares he firmly believes, and assures me he hath the same kindnesse and opinion of me as ever. And when I said I was jealous of myself, that having now come to such an income as I am, by his favour, I should not be found to do as much service as might deserve it; he did assure me, he thinks it not too much for me, but thinks I deserve it as much as any man in England. All this discourse did cheer my heart, and sets me right again, after a good deal of melancholy, out of fears of his disinclination to me, upon the differences with my Lord Sandwich and Sir G. Carteret; but I am satisfied throughly, and so went away quite another man, and by the grace of God will never lose it again by my folly in not visiting and writing to him, as I used heretofore to do. Thence by coach to the Temple, and it being a holy day, a fast-day, there 'light, and took water, being invited, and down to Greenwich, to Captain Cocke's, where dined, he and Lord Bruncker, and Matt. Wren,[1] Boltele, and Major Cooper, who is also a very pretty companion; but they all drink hard, and, after dinner, to gaming at cards. So I provoked my Lord to be gone, and he and I to Mr. Cottle's and met Mrs. Williams (without whom he cannot stir out of doors) and there took coach and away home. They carry me to London and set me down at the Temple, where my mind

[1] Matthew Wren, eldest son of the Bishop of Ely, of both his names, M.P. for St. Michael's, 1661, and made secretary to Lord Clarendon, after whose fall he filled a similar office under the Duke of York, till his death in 1672. According to Pepys's "Signs Manual," Wren was mortally wounded in the battle of Solebay. He was one of the earliest members of the Royal Society, and published two tracts in answer to Harrington's "Oceana." — B.

changed and I home, and to writing and heare my boy play on the lute, and a turne with my wife pleasantly in the garden by moonshine, my heart being in great peace, and so home to supper and to bed. The King and Duke are to go to-morrow to Audly End, in order to the seeing and buying of it of my Lord Suffolke.[1]

8th. Up betimes and to the office, where all the morning sitting and did discover three or four fresh instances of Sir W. Pen's old cheating dissembling tricks, he being as false a fellow as ever was born. Thence with Sir W. Batten and Lord Bruncker to the White Horse in Lumbard Streete to dine with Captain Cocke, upon particular business of canvas to buy for the King, and here by chance I saw the mistresse of the house I have heard much of, and a very pretty woman she is indeed and her husband the simplest looked fellow and old that ever I saw. After dinner I took coach and away to Hales's, where my wife is sitting; and, indeed, her face and necke, which are now finished, do so please me that I am not myself almost, nor was not all the night after in writing of my letters, in consideration of the fine picture that I shall be master of. Thence home and to the office, where very late, and so home to supper and to bed.

9th. Up, and being ready, to the Cockpitt to make a visit to the Duke of Albemarle, and to my great joy find him the same man to me that [he has been] heretofore, which I was in great doubt of, through my negligence in not visiting of him a great while; and having now set all to rights there, I am in mighty ease in my mind and I think shall never suffer matters to run so far backward again as I have done of late, with reference to my neglecting him and Sir W. Coventry. Thence by water down to Deptford, where I met my Lord Bruncker and Sir W. Batten by agreement, and to measuring Mr. Castle's new third-rate ship, which is to be called the

[1] The king took possession of Audley End the following autumn, but the conveyance of the estate was not executed till May 8th, 1699; of the purchase-money, which was £50,000, £20,000 remained on mortgage of the Hearth Tax in Ireland; and, in 1701, Henry Howard, fifth Earl of Suffolk, was allowed by the Crown, upon the debt being cancelled, to re-establish himself in the seat of his ancestors. It seems very doubtful whether the interest of the mortgage was ever received by the Suffolk family. — B.

Defyance.[1] And here I had my end in saving the King some money and getting myself some experience in knowing how they do measure ships. Thence I left them and walked to Redriffe, and there taking water was overtaken by them in their boat, and so they would have me in with them to Castle's house, where my Lady Batten and Madam Williams were, and there dined and a deale of doings. I had a good dinner and counterfeit mirthe and pleasure with them, but had but little thinking how I neglected my business. Anon, all home to Sir W. Batten's and there Mrs. Knipp coming we did spend the evening together very merry. She and I singing, and, God forgive me! I do still see that my nature is not to be quite conquered, but will esteem pleasure above all things, though yet in the middle of it, it has reluctances after my business, which is neglected by my following my pleasure. However musique and women I cannot but give way to, whatever my business is. They being gone I to the office a while and so home to supper and to bed.

10th. Up, and to the office, and there busy sitting till noon. I find at home Mrs. Pierce and Knipp come to dine with me. We were mighty merry; and, after dinner, I carried them and my wife out by coach to the New Exchange, and there I did give my valentine, Mrs. Pierce, a dozen payre of gloves, and a payre of silke stockings, and Knipp for company's sake, though my wife had, by my consent, laid out 20*s*. upon her the other day, six payre of gloves. Thence to Hales's to have seen our pictures, but could not get in, he being abroad, and so to the Cakehouse hard by, and there sat in the coach with great pleasure, and eat some fine cakes and so carried them to Pierce's and away home. It is a mighty fine witty boy, Mrs. Pierce's little boy. Thence home and to the office, where late writing letters and leaving a great deale to do on Monday, I home to supper and to bed. The truth is, I do indulge myself a little the

[1] William Castell wrote to the Navy Commissioners on February 17th, 1665-66, to inform them that the "Defiance" had gone to Longreach, and again, on February 22nd, to say that Mr. Grey had no masts large enough for the new ship. Sir William Batten on March 29th asked for the consent of the Board to bring the "Defiance" into dock ("Calendar of State Papers," Domestic, 1665-66, pp. 252, 262, 324).

more in pleasure, knowing that this is the proper age of my life to do it; and out of my observation that most men that do thrive in the world, do forget to take pleasure during the time that they are getting their estate, but reserve that till they have got one, and then it is too late for them to enjoy it with any pleasure.

11th (Lord's day). Up, and by water to White Hall, there met Mr. Coventry coming out, going along with the Commissioners of the Ordnance to the water side to take barge, they being to go down to the Hope. I returned with them as far as the Tower in their barge speaking with Sir W. Coventry and so home and to church, and at noon dined and then to my chamber, where with great pleasure about one business or other till late, and so to supper and to bed.

12th. Up betimes, and called on by abundance of people about business, and then away by water to Westminster, and there to the Exchequer about some business, and thence by coach calling at several places, to the Old Exchange, and there did much business, and so homeward and bought a silver salt for my ordinary table to use, and so home to dinner, and after dinner comes my uncle and aunt Wight, the latter I have not seen since the plague; a silly, froward, ugly woman she is. We made mighty much of them, and she talks mightily of her fear of the sickness, and so a deale of tittle tattle and I left them and to my office where late, and so home to supper and to bed. This day I hear my Uncle Talbot Pepys died the last week, and was buried. All the news now is, that Sir Jeremy Smith is at Cales[1] with his fleete, and Mings in the Elve.[2] The King is come this noon to towne from Audly End, with the Duke of Yorke and a fine train of gentlemen.

13th. Up betimes, and to the office, where busy sitting all the morning, and I begin to find a little convenience by holding up my head to Sir W. Pen, for he is come to be more supple. At noon to dinner, and then to the office again, where mighty business, doing a great deale till midnight and then home to supper and to bed. The plague encreased this week 29 from 28, though the total fallen from 238 to 207, which do never a whit please me.

[1] Cadiz. [2] Elbe.

14th. Up, and met by 6 o'clock in my chamber Mr. Povy (from White Hall) about evening reckonings between him and me, on our Tangier business, and at it hard till toward eight o'clock, and he then carried me in his chariot to White Hall, where by and by my fellow officers met me, and we had a meeting before the Duke. Thence with my Lord Bruncker towards London, and in our way called in Covent Garden, and took in Sir John (formerly Dr.) Baber; who hath this humour that he will not enter into discourse while any stranger is in company, till he be told who he is that seems a stranger to him. This he did declare openly to me, and asked my Lord who I was, giving this reason, that he has been inconvenienced by being too free in discourse till he knew who all the company were. Thence to Guildhall (in our way taking in Dr. Wilkins), and there my Lord and I had full and large discourse with Sir Thomas Player,[1] the Chamberlain of the City (a man I have much heard of for his credit and punctuality in the City, and on that score I had a desire to be made known to him), about the credit of our tallys, which are lodged there for security to such as should lend money thereon to the use of the Navy. And I had great satisfaction therein: and the truth is, I find all our matters of credit to be in an ill condition. Thence, I being in a little haste walked before and to the 'Change a little and then home, and presently to Trinity house to dinner, where Captain Cox made his Elder Brother's dinner. But it seemed to me a very poor sorry dinner. I having many things in my head rose, when my belly was full, though the dinner not half done, and home and there to do some business, and by and by out of doors and met Mr. Povy coming to me by appointment, but it being a little too late, I took a little pride in the streete not to go back with him, but prayed him to come another time, and I away to Kate Joyce's, thinking to have spoke to her husband about Pall's business, but a stranger, the Welsh Dr. Powell, being there I forebore and went away and so to Hales's, to see my wife's picture, which I like

[1] One of the City Members in the Oxford and Westminster Parliaments. See more of him in the Notes, by Scott, to "Absalom and Achitophel;" in which poem he is introduced under the designation of "railing Rabsheka." — B.

mighty well, and there had the pleasure to see how suddenly he draws the Heavens, laying a darke ground and then lightening it when and where he will. Thence to walk all alone in the fields behind Grayes Inne, making an end of reading over my dear "Faber fortunæ," of my Lord Bacon's, and thence, it growing dark, took two or three wanton turns about the idle places and lanes about Drury Lane, but to no satisfaction, but a great fear of the plague among them, and so anon I walked by invitation to Mrs. Pierce's, where I find much good company, that is to say, Mrs. Pierce, my wife, Mrs. Worshipp and her daughter, and Harris the player, and Knipp, and Mercer, and Mrs. Barbary Sheldon, who is come this day to spend a weeke with my wife; and here with musique we danced, and sung and supped, and then to sing and dance till past one in the morning; and much mirthe with Sir Anthony Apsley and one Colonell Sidney, who lodge in the house; and above all, they are mightily taken with Mrs. Knipp. Hence weary and sleepy we broke up, and I and my company homeward by coach and to bed.

15th. Lay till it was full time to rise, it being eight o'clock, and so to the office and there sat till almost three o'clock and then to dinner, and after dinner (my wife and Mercer and Mrs. Barbary being gone to Hales's before), I and my cozen Anthony Joyce, who come on purpose to dinner with me, and he and I to discourse of our proposition of marriage between Pall and Harman, and upon discourse he and I to Harman's house and took him to a taverne hard by, and we to discourse of our business, and I offered £500, and he declares most ingenuously that his trade is not to be trusted on, that he however needs no money, but would have her money bestowed on her, which I like well, he saying that he would adventure 2 or £300 with her. I like him as a most good-natured, and discreet man, and, I believe, very cunning. We come to this conclusion for us to meete one another the next weeke, and then we hope to come to some end, for I did declare myself well satisfied with the match. Thence to Hales's, where I met my wife and people; and do find the picture, above all things, a most pretty picture, and mighty like my wife; and I asked him his price: he says £14, and the truth is, I think he do deserve it. Thence toward London and home, and I to the office, where I did much, and betimes to bed, having had of late so little sleep, and there slept

16th. Till 7 this morning. Up and all the morning about the Victualler's business, passing his account. At noon to the 'Change, and did several businesses, and thence to the Crowne behind the 'Change and dined with my Lord Bruncker and Captain Cocke and Fenn, and Madam Williams, who without question must be my Lord's wife, and else she could not follow him wherever he goes and kisse and use him publiquely as she do. Thence to the office, where Sir W. Pen and I made an end of the Victualler's business, and thence abroad about several businesses, and so in the evening back again, and anon called on by Mr. Povy, and he and I staid together in my chamber till 12 at night ending our reckonings and giving him tallys for all I was to pay him and so parted, and I to make good my Journall for two or three days, and begun it till I come to the other side, where I have scratched so much, for, for want of sleep, I begun to write idle and from the purpose. So forced to breake off, and to bed.[1]

17th. Up, and to finish my Journall, which I had not sense enough the last night to make an end of, and thence to the office, where very busy all the morning. At noon home to dinner and presently with my wife out to Hales's, where I am still infinitely pleased with my wife's picture. I paid him £14 for it, and 25*s.* for the frame, and I think it is not a whit too deare for so good a picture. It is not yet quite finished and dry, so as to be fit to bring home yet. This day I begun to sit, and he will make me, I think, a very fine picture. He promises it shall be as good as my wife's, and I sit to have it full of shadows, and do almost break my neck looking over my shoulder to make the posture for him to work by. Thence home and to the office, and so home having a great cold, and so my wife and Mrs. Barbary have very great ones, we are at a loss how we all come by it together, so to bed, drinking butter-ale. This day my W. Hewer comes from Portsmouth and gives me an instance of another piece of knavery of Sir W. Pen, who wrote to Commissioner Middleton, that it was my negli-

[1] There are several erasures in the original MS.

gence the other day he was not acquainted, as the board directed, with our clerks coming down to the pay. But I need no new arguments to teach me that he is a false rogue to me and all the world besides.

18th (Lord's day). Up and my cold better, so to church, and then home to dinner, and so walked out to St. James's Church, thinking to have seen faire Mrs. Butler, but could not, she not being there, nor, I believe, lives thereabouts now. So walked to Westminster, very fine fair dry weather, but all cry out for lack of rain. To Herbert's and drank, and thence to Mrs. Martin's, and did what I would with her; her husband going for some wine for us. The poor man I do think would take pains if I can get him a purser's place, which I will endeavour. She tells me as a secret that Betty Howlet of the Hall, my little sweetheart, that I used to call my second wife, is married to a younger son of Mr. Michell's (his elder brother, who should have had her, being dead this plague), at which I am glad, and that they are to live nearer me in Thames Streete, by the Old Swan. Thence by coach home and to my chamber about some accounts, and so to bed. Sir Christopher Mings is come home from Hambro' without anything done, saving bringing home some pipestaves for us.

19th. Up betimes and upon a meeting extraordinary at the office most of the morning with Lord Bruncker, Sir W. Coventry, and Sir W. Pen, upon the business of the accounts. Where now we have got almost as much as we would have we begin to lay all on the Controller, and I fear he will be run down with it, for he is every day less and less capable of doing business. Thence with my Lord Bruncker, Sir W. Coventry to the ticket office, to see in what little order things are there, and there it is a shame to see how the King is served. Thence to the Chamberlain of London, and satisfy ourselves more particularly how much credit we have there, which proves very little. Thence to Sir Robert Long's, absent. About much the same business, but have not the satisfaction we would have there neither. So Sir W. Coventry parted, and my Lord and I to Mrs. Williams's, and there I saw her closett, where indeed a great many fine things there are, but the woman I hate. Here we dined, and Sir J. Minnes come to us, and after dinner we walked to the King's play-house, all in dirt, they being altering of the stage to make it wider. But God knows when they will begin to act again; but my business here was to see the inside of the stage and all the tiring-rooms and machines; and, indeed, it was a sight worthy seeing. But to see their clothes, and the various sorts, and what a mixture of things there was; here a wooden-leg, there a ruff, here a hobby-horse, there a crown, would make a man split himself to see with laughing; and particularly Lacy's[1] wardrobe, and Shotrell's.[2] But then again, to think how fine they show on the stage by candle-light, and how poor things they are to look now too near hand, is not pleasant at all. The machines are fine, and the paintings very pretty. Thence mightily satisfied in my curiosity I away with my Lord to see him at her house again, and so take leave and by coach home and to the office, and thence sent for to Sir G. Carteret by and by to the Broad Streete, where he and I walked two or three hours till it was quite darke in his gallery talking of his affairs, wherein I assure him all will do well, and did give him (with great liberty, which he accepted kindly) my advice to deny the Board nothing they would aske about his accounts, but rather call upon them to know whether there was anything more they desired, or was wanting. But our great discourse and serious reflections was upon the bad state of the kingdom in general, through want of money and good conduct, which we fear will undo all. Thence mightily satisfied with this good fortune of this discourse with him I home, and there walked in the darke till 10 o'clock at night in the garden with Sir W. Warren, talking of many things belonging to us particularly, and I hope to get something considerably by him before the year be over. He gives me good advice of circumspection in

[1] John Lacy, the celebrated comedian (see note, *ante*, May 21st, 1662).

[2] Robert and William Shotterel both belonged to the King's Company at the opening of their new theatre in 1663. One of them, called by Downes a good actor, had been quartermaster to the troop of horse in which Hart was serving as lieutenant and Burt as cornet under Charles I.'s standard; but nothing further is recorded of his merits or career. Pepys refers to Robert Shotterel, who, it appears, was living in Playhouse Yard, Drury Lane, 1681–84. — B.

my place, which I am now in great mind to improve; for I think our office stands on very ticklish terms, the Parliament likely to sit shortly and likely to be asked more money, and we able to give a very bad account of the expence of what we have done with what they did give before. Besides, the turning out the prize officers may be an example for the King giving us up to the Parliament's pleasure as easily, for we deserve it as much. Besides, Sir G. Carteret did tell me to-night how my Lord Bruncker himself, whose good-will I could have depended as much on as any, did himself to him take notice of the many places I have; and though I was a painful man, yet the Navy was enough for any man to go through with in his owne single place there, which much troubles me, and shall yet provoke me to more and more care and diligence than ever. Thence home to supper, where I find my wife and Mrs. Barbary with great colds, as I also at this time have. This day by letter from my father he propounds a match in the country for Pall, which pleased me well, of one that hath seven score and odd pounds land per annum in possession, and expects £1,000 in money by the death of an old aunt. He hath neither father, mother, sister, nor brother, but demands £600 down, and £100 on the birth of first child, which I had some inclination to stretch to. He is kinsman to, and lives with, Mr. Phillips, but my wife tells me he is a drunken, ill-favoured, ill-bred country fellow, which sets me off of it again, and I will go on with Harman. So after supper to bed.

20th. Up and to the office, where busy all the morning. At noon dined in haste, and so my wife, Mrs. Barbary, Mercer, and I by coach to Hales's, where I find my wife's picture now perfectly finished in all respects, and a beautiful picture it is, as almost I ever saw. I sat again, and had a great deale done, but, whatever the matter is, I do not fancy that it has the ayre of my face, though it will be a very fine picture. Thence home and to my business. being post night, and so home to supper and to bed.

21st. Up betimes, and first by coach to my Lord Generall to visitt him, and then to the Duke of Yorke, where we all met and did our usual business with him; but, Lord! how everything is yielded to presently, even by Sir W.

Coventry, that is propounded by the Duke, as now to have Troutbecke,[1] his old surgeon, and intended to go Surgeon-General of the fleete, to go Physician-General of the fleete, of which there never was any precedent in the world, and he for that to have £20 per month. Thence with Lord Bruncker to Sir Robert Long,[2] whom we found in his closett, and after some discourse of business he fell to discourse at large and pleasant, and among other things told us of the plenty of partridges in France, where he says the King of France and his company killed with their guns, in the plain de Versailles, 300 and odd partridges at one bout. Thence I to the Excise Office behind the 'Change, and there find our business of our tallys in great disorder as to payment, and thereupon do take a resolution of thinking how to remedy it, as soon as I can. Thence home, and there met Sir W. Warren, and after I had eat a bit of victuals (he staying in the office) he and I to White Hall. He to look after the business of the prize ships which we are endeavouring to buy, and hope to get money by them. So I to London by coach and to Gresham College, where I staid half an houre, and so away home to my office, and there walking late alone in the darke in the garden with Sir W. Warren, who tells me that at the Committee of the Lords for the prizes to-day, there passed very high words between my Lord Ashly and Sir W. Coventry, about our business of the prize ships. And that my Lord Ashly did snuff and talk as high to him, as he used to do to any ordinary seaman. And that Sir W. Coventry did take it very quietly, but yet for all did speak his mind soberly and with reason, and went away, saying, he had done his duty therein, and so left it to them, whether they would let so many ships go for masts or not. Here he and I talked of 1,000 businesses, all profitable discourse, and late parted, and I home to supper and to bed, troubled a little at a letter from my father, telling me how [he] is like to be sued for a debt of Tom's, by Smith, the mercer.

[1] John Troutbecke in 1661 was surgeon to the Life Guards, commanded by the Duke of Albemarle.

[2] Sir Robert Long (see notes *ante*, March 21st, 1662–63 and November 28th, 1665).

22nd. Up, and to the office all the morning. At noon my wife being gone to her father's I dined with Sir W. Batten, he inviting me. After dinner to my office close, and did very much business, and so late home to supper and to bed. The plague increased four this week, which troubles me, though but one in the whole.

23rd. Up, and going out of my dressing-room, when ready to go down stairs, I spied little Mrs. Tooker, my pretty little girle, which, it seems, did come yesterday to our house to stay a little while with us, but I did not know of it till now. I was glad of her coming, she being a very pretty child, and now grown almost a woman. I out by six o'clock by appointment to Hales's, where we fell to my picture presently very hard, and it comes on a very fine picture, and very merry, pleasant discourse we had all the morning while he was painting. Anon comes my wife and Mercer and little Tooker, and having done with me we all to a picture drawer's hard by, Hales carrying me to see some landskipps of a man's doing. But I do not [like] any of them, save only a piece of fruit, which indeed was very fine. Thence I to Westminster, to the Chequer, about a little business, and then to the Swan, and there sent for a bit of meat and dined; and after dinner had opportunity of being pleased with Sarah; and so away to Westminster Hall, and there Mrs. Michell tells me with great joy how little Betty Howlett is married to her young son Michell, which is a pretty odd thing, that he should so soon succeed in the match to his elder brother that died of the plague, and to the house and trade intended for him, and more they say that the girle has heretofore said that she did love this little one more than the other brother that was intended her all along. I am mighty glad of this match, and more that they are likely to live near me in Thames Streete, where I may see Betty now and then, whom I from a girle did use to call my second wife, and mighty pretty she is. Thence by coach to Anthony Joyce to receive Harman's answer, which did trouble me to receive, for he now demands £800, whereas he never made exception at the portion, but accepted of £500. This I do not like; but, however, I cannot much blame the man, if he thinks he can get more of another than of me. So home and hard to my business at the office, where much business, and so home to supper and to bed.

24th. Up and to the office, where all the morning. At noon home to dinner, where Anthony Joyce, and I did give my final answer, I would give but £500 with my sister, and did show him the good offer made us in the country, to which I did now more and more incline, and intend to pursue that. After dinner I to White Hall to a Committee for Tangier, where the Duke of Yorke was, and I acquitted myself well in what I had to do. After the Committee up, I had occasion to follow the Duke into his lodgings, into a chamber where the Duchesse was sitting to have her picture drawn by Lilly, who was there at work. But I was well pleased to see that there was nothing near so much resemblance of her face in his work, which is now the second, if not the third time, as there was of my wife's at the very first time. Nor do I think at last it can be like, the lines not being in proportion to those of her face. So home, and to the office, where late, and so to bed.

25th (Lady day and Sunday). Up, and to my chamber in my gowne all the morning about settling my papers there. At noon to dinner, where my wife's brother, whom I sent for to offer making him a Muster-Master and send to sea, which the poore man likes well of and will go, and it will be a good preferment to him, only hazardous. I hope he will prove a good discreet man. After dinner to my papers and Tangier accounts again till supper, and after supper again to them, but by my mixing them, I know not how, my private and publique accounts, it makes me mad to see how hard it is to bring them to be understood, and my head is confounded, that though I did sweare to sit up till one o'clock upon them, yet, I fear, it will be to no purpose, for I cannot understand what I do or have been doing of them to-day.

26th. Up, and a meeting extraordinary there was of Sir W. Coventry, Lord Bruncker, and myself, about the business of settling the ticket office, where infinite room is left for abusing the King in the wages of seamen. Our [meeting] being done, my Lord Bruncker and I to the Tower, to see the famous engraver,[1] to get him to grave a seale for

[1] One of the Rotiers (see March 9th, 1662-63).

the office. And did see some of the finest pieces of work in embossed work, that ever I did see in my life, for fineness and smallness of the images thereon, and I will carry my wife thither to shew them her. Here I also did see bars of gold melting, which was a fine sight. So with my Lord to the Pope's Head Taverne in Lumbard Streete to dine by appointment with Captain Taylor, whither Sir W. Coventry come to us, and were mighty merry, and I find reason to honour him every day more and more. Thence alone to Broade Street to Sir G. Carteret by his desire to confer with him, who is I find in great pain about the business of the office, and not a little, I believe, in fear of falling there, Sir W. Coventry having so great a pique against him, and herein I first learn an eminent instance how great a man this day, that nobody would think could be shaken, is the next overthrown, dashed out of countenance, and every small thing of irregularity in his business taken notice of, where nobody the other day durst cast an eye upon them, and next I see that he that the other day nobody durst come near is now as supple as a spaniel, and sends and speaks to me with great submission, and readily hears to advice. Thence home to the office, where busy late, and so home a little to my accounts publique and private, but could not get myself rightly to know how to dispose of them in order to passing.

27th. All the morning at the office busy. At noon dined at home, Mr. Cooke, our old acquaintance at my Lord Sandwich's, come to see and dine with me, but I quite out of humour, having many other and better things to thinke of. Thence to the office to settle my people's worke and then home to my publique accounts of Tangier, which it is strange by meddling with evening reckonings with Mr. Povy lately how I myself am become intangled therein, so that after all I could do, ready to breake my head and brains, I thought of another way, though not so perfect, yet the only one which this account is capable of. Upon this latter I sat up till past two in the morning and then to bed.

28th. Up, and with Creed, who come hither betimes to speake with me about his accounts, to White Hall by water, mighty merry in discourse, though I had been very little troubled with him, or did countenance it, having now, blessed be God! a great deale of good business to mind to better purpose than chatting with him. Waited on the Duke, after that walked with Sir W. Clerke into St. James's Parke, and by and by met with Mr. Hayes,[1] Prince Rupert's Secretary, who are mighty, both, briske blades, but I fear they promise themselves more than they expect. Thence to the Cockpitt, and dined with a great deal of company at the Duke of Albemarle's, and a bad and dirty, nasty dinner. So by coach to Hales's, and there sat again, and it is become mighty like. Hither come my wife and Mercer brought by Mrs. Pierce and Knipp, we were mighty merry and the picture goes on the better for it. Thence set them down at Pierce's, and we home, where busy and at my chamber till 12 at night, and so to bed. This night, I am told, the Queene of Portugall, the mother to our Queene, is lately dead, and newes brought of it hither this day.[2]

29th. All the morning hard at the office. At noon dined and then out to Lumbard Streete, to look after the getting of some money that is lodged there of mine in Viner's hands, I having no mind to have it lie there longer. So back again and to the office, where and at home about publique and private business and accounts till past 12 at night, and so to bed. This day, poor Jane, my old, little Jane, came to us again, to my wife's and my great content, and we hope to take mighty pleasure in her, she having all the marks and qualities of a good and loving and honest servant, she coming by force away from the other place, where she hath lived ever since she went from us, and at our desire, her late mistresse having used all the stratagems she could to keepe her.

30th. My wife and I mighty pleased with Jane's coming to us again. Up, and away goes Alce, our cooke-mayde,

[1] James Hayes.

[2] Donna Luiza, the Queen Regent of Portugal. She was daughter of the Duke de Medina Sidonia and widow of Juan IV. The Court wore the deepest mourning on this occasion. The ladies were directed to wear their hair plain, and to appear without spots on their faces, the disfiguring fashion of patching having just been introduced. — Strickland's *Queens of England*, vol. viii., p. 362.

a good servant, whom we loved and did well by her, and she an excellent servant, but would not bear being told of any faulte in the fewest and kindest words and would go away of her owne accord, after having given her mistresse warning fickly for a quarter of a yeare together. So we shall take another girle and make little Jane our cook, at least, make a trial of it. Up, and after much business I out to Lumbard Streete, and there received £2,200 and brought it home; and, contrary to expectation, received £35 for the use of £2,000 of it [for] a quarter of a year, where it hath produced me this profit, and hath been a convenience to me as to care and security of my house, and demandable at two days' warning, as this hath been. This morning Sir W. Warren come to me a second time about having £2,000 of me upon his bills on the Act to enable him to pay for the ships he is buying, wherein I shall have considerable profit. I am loth to do it, but yet speaking with Colvill I do not see but I shall be able to do it and get money by it too. Thence home and eat one mouthful, and so to Hales's, and there sat till almost quite darke upon working my gowne, which I hired to be drawn in; an Indian gowne, and I do see all the reason to expect a most excellent picture of it. So home and to my private accounts in my chamber till past one in the morning, and so to bed, with my head full of thoughts for my evening of all my accounts to-morrow, the latter end of the month, in which God give me good issue, for I never was in such a confusion in my life and that in great sums.

31st. All the morning at the office busy. At noon to dinner, and thence to the office and did my business there as soon as I could, and then home and to my accounts, where very late at them, but, Lord! what a deale of do I have to understand any part of them, and in short do what I could, I could not come to any understanding of them, but after I had throughly wearied myself, I was forced to go to bed and leave them much against my will and vowe too, but I hope God will forgive me, for I have sat up these four nights till past twelve at night to master them, but cannot. Thus ends this month, with my head and mind mighty full and disquiett because of my accounts, which I have let go too long, and confounded my publique with my private that I cannot come to any liquidating of them. However, I do see that I must be grown richer than I was by a good deale last month. Busy also I am in thoughts for a husband for my sister, and to that end my wife and I have determined that she shall presently go into the country to my father and mother, and consider of a proffer made them for her in the country, which, if she likes, shall go forward.

April 1st (Lord's day). Up and abroad, and by coach to Charing Cross, to wait on Sir Philip Howard; whom I found in bed: and he do receive me very civilly. My request was about suffering my wife's brother to go to sea, and to save his pay in the Duke's guards; which after a little difficulty he did with great respect agree to. I find him a very fine-spoken gentleman, and one of great parts, and very courteous. Much pleased with this visit I to White Hall, where I met Sir G. Downing, and to discourse with him an houre about the Exchequer payments upon the late Act, and informed myself of him thoroughly in my safety in lending £2,000 to Sir W. Warren, upon an order of his upon the Exchequer for £2,602 and I do purpose to do it. Thence meeting Dr. Allen,[1] the physician, he and I and another walked in the Parke, a most pleasant warm day, and to the Queene's chappell; where I do not so dislike the musique. Here I saw on a post an invitation to all good Catholiques to pray for the soul of such a one departed this life. The Queene, I hear, do not yet hear of the death of her mother, she being in a course of physique, that they dare not tell it her. At noon by coach home, and there by invitation met my uncle and aunt Wight and their cozen Mary, and dined with me and very merry. After dinner my uncle and I abroad by coach to White Hall, up and down the house, and I did some business and thence with him and a gentleman he met with to my Lord Chancellor's new house, and there viewed it again and again and up to the top and I like it as well as ever and think it a most noble house. So all up and down my Lord St. Albans his new building and market-house,[2] and

[1] Thomas Allen, M.D. (see note, November 3rd, 1663).

[2] Jermyn Street and St. Alban's Market, which was afterwards called St. James's Market. "A large place with a commodious Market House

the taverne under the market-house, looking to and again into every place of building, and so away and took coach and home, where to my accounts, and was at them till I could not hold open my eyes, and so to bed. I this afternoon made a visit to my Lady Carteret, whom I understood newly come to towne; and she took it mighty kindly, but I see her face and heart are dejected from the condition her husband's matters stand in. But I hope they will do all well enough. And I do comfort her as much as I can, for she is a noble lady.

2nd. Up, and to the office and thence with Mr. Gawden to Guildhall to see the bills and tallys there in the chamber (and by the way in the streete his new coach broke and we fain to take an old hackney). Thence to the Exchequer again to inform myself of some other points in the new Act in order to my lending Sir W. Warren £2,000 upon an order of his upon the Act, which they all encourage me to. There walking with Mr. Gawden in Westminster Hall, he and I to talke from one business to another and at last to the marriage of his daughter. He told me the story of Creed's pretences to his daughter, and how he would not believe but she loved him, while his daughter was in great passion on the other hand against him. Thence to talke of his son Benjamin; and I propounded a match for him, and at last named my sister, which he embraces heartily, and speaking of the lowness of her portion, that it would be less than £1,000, he tells me if everything else agrees, he will out of what he means to give me yearly, make a portion for her shall cost me nothing more than I intend freely. This did mightily rejoice me and full of it did go with him to London to the 'Change; and there did much business and at the Coffee-house with Sir W. Warren, who very wisely did shew me that my matching my sister with Mr. Gawden would undo me in all my places, everybody suspecting me in all I do; and I shall neither be able to serve him, nor free myself from imputation of being of his faction, while I am placed for

in the midst, filled with Butchers' shambles, besides the Stalls in the Market-Place for country Butchers, Higglers, and the like; being a market now (1720) grown to great account, and much resorted unto, as being well served with good provisions." — Strype, b. vi., p. 83.

his severest check. I was convinced that it would be for neither of our interests to make this alliance, and so am quite off of it again, but with great satisfaction in the motion. Thence to the Crowne tavern behind the Exchange to meet with Cocke and Fenn and did so, and dined with them, and after dinner had the intent of our meeting, which was some private discourse with Fenn, telling him what I hear and think of his business, which he takes very kindly and says he will look about him. It was about his giving of ill language and answers to people that come to him about money and some other particulars. This morning Mrs. Barbary and little Mrs. Tooker went away homeward. Thence my wife by coach calling me at White Hall to visit my Lady Carteret, and she was not within. So to Westminster Hall, where I purposely tooke my wife well dressed into the Hall to see and be seen; and, among others, [met] Howlet's daughter, who is newly married, and is she I call wife, and one I love mightily. So to Broad Streete and there met my Lady and Sir G. Carteret, and sat and talked with them a good while and so home, and to my accounts which I cannot get through with. But at it till I grew drowsy, and so to bed mightily vexed that I can come to no better issue in my accounts.

3rd. Up, and Sir W. Warren with me betimes and signed a bond, and assigned his order on the Exchequer to a blank for me to fill and I did deliver him £1,900.[1] The truth is, it is a great venture to venture so much on the Act, but thereby I hedge in £300 gift for my service about some ships that he hath bought, prizes, and good interest besides, and his bond to repay me the money at six weeks' warning. So to the office, where busy all the morning. At noon home to dinner, and there my brother Balty dined with me and my wife, who is become a good serious man, and I hope to do him good being sending him a Muster-Master on one of the squadrons of the fleete. After dinner and he gone I to my accounts hard all the afternoon till it was quite darke, and I thank God I do come to bring them very fairly to make me worth £5,000 stocke in the world,

[1] Among the Rawlinson MSS. is a memorandum of this loan of £1,900, dated April 3rd, 1666.

which is a great mercy to me. Though I am a little troubled to find £50 difference between the particular account I make to myself of my profits and loss in each month and the account which I raise from my acquittances and money which I have at the end of every month in my chest and other men's hands. However I do well believe that I am effectually £5,000, the greatest sum I ever was in my life yet, and this day I have as I have said before agreed with Sir W. Warren and got of him £300 gift. At night a while to the office and then home and supped and to my accounts again till I was ready to sleepe, there being no pleasure to handle them, if they are not kept in good order. So to bed.

4th. Up, and with Sir W. Pen in his coach to White Hall, in his way talking simply and fondly as he used to do, but I find myself to slight him and his simple talke, I thank God, and that my condition will enable me to do it. Thence, after doing our business with the Duke of Yorke, with Captain Cocke home to the 'Change in his coach. He promises me presently a dozen of silver salts, and proposes a business for which he hath promised Mrs. Williams for my Lord Bruncker a set of plate shall cost him £500 and me the like, which will be a good business indeed. After done several businesses at the 'Change I home, and being washing day dined upon cold meate, and so abroad by coach to Hales's, and there sat till night, mightily pleased with my picture, which is now almost finished. So by coach home, it being the fast day and to my chamber and so after supper to bed, consulting how to send my wife into the country to advise about Pall's marriage, which I much desire, and my father too, and two or three offers are now in hand.

5th. Up, and before office time to Lumbard Streete, and there at Viner's was shewn the silver plates, made for Captain Cocke to present my Lord Bruncker; and I chose a dozen of the same weight to be bespoke for myself, which he told me yesterday he would give me on the same occasion. To the office, where the falsenesse and impertinencies of Sir W. Pen would make a man mad to think of. At noon would have avoided, but could not, dining with my Lord Bruncker and his mistresse with Captain Cocke at the

Sun Taverne in Fish Streete, where a good dinner, but the woman do tire me, and indeed how simply my Lord Bruncker, who is otherwise a wise man, do proceed at the table in serving of Cocke, without any means of understanding in his proposal, or defence when proposed, would make a man think him a foole. After dinner home, where I find my wife hath on a sudden, upon notice of a coach going away to-morrow, taken a resolution of going in it to Brampton, we having lately thought it fit for her to go to satisfy herself and me in the nature of the fellow that is there proposed to my sister. So she to fit herself for her journey and I to the office all the afternoon till late, and so home and late putting notes to "It is decreed, nor shall thy fate, &c."[1] and then to bed. The plague is, to our great grief, encreased nine this week, though decreased a few in the total. And this encrease runs through many parishes, which makes us much fear the next year.

6th. Up mighty betimes upon my wife's going this day toward Brampton. I could not go to the coach with her, but W. Hewer did and hath leave from me to go the whole day's journey with her. All the morning upon business at the office, and at noon dined, and Mrs. Hunt coming lent her £5 on her occasions and so carried her to Axe Yard end at Westminster and there left her, a good and understanding woman, and her husband I perceive thrives mightily in his business of the Excise. Thence to Mr. Hales and there sat, and my picture almost finished, which by the word of Mr. and Mrs. Pierce (who come in accidently) is mighty like, and I am sure I am mightily pleased both in the thing and the posture. Thence with them home a little, and so to White Hall and there met by agreement with Sir Stephen Fox and Mr. Ashburnham, and discoursed the business of our Excise tallys; the former being Treasurer of the guards, and the other Cofferer of the King's household. I benefitted much by their discourse. We come to no great conclusion upon our dis-

[1] Pepys did not finish his setting of Ben Jonson's song,

"It is decreed — nor shall thy fate, O Rome!
Resist my vow, though hills were set on hills,"

until November 11th, 1666. The original is preserved in the Pepysian Library.

course, but parted, and I home, where all things, methinks, melancholy in the absence of my wife. This day great newes of the Swedes declaring for us against the Dutch, and, so far as that, I believe it. After a little supper to bed.

7th. Lay pretty long to-day, lying alone and thinking of several businesses. So up to the office and there till noon. Thence with my Lord Bruncker home by coach to Mrs. Williams's, where Bab. Allen and Dr. Charleton dined. Bab and I sang and were mighty merry as we could be there, where the rest of the company did not overplease. Thence took her by coach to Hales's, and there find Mrs. Pierce and her boy and Mary. She had done sitting the first time, and indeed her face is mighty like at first dash. Thence took them to the cakehouse, and there called in the coach for cakes and drank, and thence I carried them to my Lord Chancellor's new house to shew them that, and all mightily pleased, thence set each down at home, and so I home to the office, where about ten of the clock W. Hewer comes to me to tell me that he has left my wife well this morning at Bugden, which was great riding, and brings me a letter from her. She is very well got thither, of which I am heartily glad. After writing several letters, I home to supper and to bed. The Parliament of which I was afraid of their calling us of the Navy to an account of the expense of money and stores and wherein we were so little ready to give them a good answer [will soon meet].[1] The Bishop of Munster, every body says, is coming to peace with the Dutch, we having not supplied him with the money promised him.

8th (Lord's day). Up, and was in great trouble how to get a passage to White Hall, it raining, and no coach to be had. So I walked to the Old Swan, and there got a scull. To the Duke of Yorke, where we all met to hear the debate between Sir Thomas Allen and Mr. Wayth; the former complaining of the latter's ill usage of him at the late pay of his ship. But a very sorry poor occasion he had for it. The Duke did determine it with great judgement, chiding both, but encouraging Wayth to continue to

[1] Parliament was summoned to meet on the 23rd April.

be a check to all captains in any thing to the King's right. And, indeed, I never did see the Duke do any thing more in order, nor with more judgement than he did pass the verdict in this business. The Court full this morning of the newes of Tom Cheffin's[1] death, the King's closett-keeper. He was well last night as ever, playing at tables in the house, and not very ill this morning at six o'clock, yet dead before seven: they think, of an imposthume in his breast. But it looks fearfully among people now-a-days, the plague, as we hear, encreasing every where again. To the Chappell, but could not get in to hear well. But I had the pleasure once in my life to see an Archbishop[2] (this was of Yorke) in a pulpit. Then at a loss how to get home to dinner, having promised to carry Mrs. Hunt thither. At last got my Lord Hinchingbroke's coach, he staying at Court; and so took her up in Axe-yard, and home and dined. And good discourse of the old matters of the Protector and his family, she having a relation to them. The Protector[3] lives in France: spends about £500 per annum. Thence carried her home again and then to Court and walked over to St. James's Chappell, thinking to have heard a Jesuite preach, but come too late. So got a hackney and home, and there to business. At night had Mercer comb my head and so to supper, sing a psalm, and to bed.

9th. Up betimes, and with my Joyner begun the making of the window in my boy's chamber bigger, purposing it shall be a roome to eat and for having musique in. To the office, where a meeting upon extraordinary business,

[1] Sir E. Walker, Garter King at Arms, in 1644 gave a grant of arms *gratis* to Thomas Chiffinch, one of the pages of his Majesty's Bed-chamber, Keeper of his private Closet, and Comptroller of the Excise. His brother William (whose daughter Barbara married Edward Villiers, first Earl of Jersey) appears to have succeeded to the two first-named appointments, and became a great favourite with the king, whom he survived. He died April 6th, 1666, and was buried on the 10th in Westminster Abbey. There is a portrait of William Chiffinch at Gorhambury. — B.

[2] Richard Sterne, Bishop of Carlisle, elected Archbishop of York, 1664. Died June 18th, 1683.

[3] Richard Cromwell subsequently returned to England, and resided in strict privacy at Cheshunt for some years before his death in 1712.

at noon to the 'Change about more, and then home with Creed and dined, and then with him to the Committee of Tangier, where I got two or three things done I had a mind to of convenience to me. Thence by coach to Mrs. Pierce's, and with her and Knipp and Mrs. Pierce's boy and girle abroad, thinking to have been merry at Chelsey; but being come almost to the house by coach near the waterside, a house alone, I think the Swan, a gentleman walking by called to us to tell us that the house was shut up of the sicknesse. So we with great affright turned back, being holden to the gentleman; and went away (I for my part in great disorder) for Kensington, and there I spent about 30*s.* upon the jades with great pleasure, and we sang finely and staid till about eight at night, the night coming on apace and so set them down at Pierce's, and so away home, where awhile with Sir W. Warren about business, and then to bed.

10th. Up betimes, and many people to me about business. To the office and there sat till noon, and then home and dined, and to the office again all the afternoon, where we sat all, the first time of our resolution to sit both forenoons and afternoons. Much business at night and then home, and though late did see some work done by the plasterer to my new window in the boy's chamber plastered. Then to supper, and after having my head combed by the little girle to bed. Bad news that the plague is decreased in the general again and two increased in the sickness.

11th. To White Hall, having first set my people to worke about setting me rails upon the leads of my wife's closett, a thing I have long designed, but never had a fit opportunity till now. After having done with the Duke of Yorke, I to Hales's, where there was nothing found to be done more to my picture,[1] but the musique, which now pleases

[1] This picture was bought by Mr. Peter Cunningham at the sale of the Pepys-Cockerell collection in 1848, in the catalogue of which it was described as, "Portrait of a Musician," and was exhibited at the Manchester Art Treasures Exhibition, 1857. It was purchased by the trustees of the National Portrait Gallery in 1866. Pepys is represented in a gown "which I hired to be drawn in; a morning gowne," and holding in his left hand a piece of music, his own composition, with the words, "Beauty retire." An etching from this picture is given as the frontispiece to the Library Edition of this work (see *post*, 13th inst., where

me mightily, it being painted true. Thence home, and after dinner to Gresham College, where a great deal of do and formality in chosing of the Council and Officers. I had three votes to be of the Council, who am but a stranger, nor expected any.[1] So my Lord Bruncker being confirmed President I home, where I find to my great content my rails up upon my leads. To the office and did a little business, and then home and did a great jobb at my Tangier accounts, which I find are mighty apt to run into confusion, my head also being too full of other businesses and pleasures. This noon Bagwell's wife come to me to the office, after her being long at Portsmouth. After supper, and past 12 at night to bed.

12th. Up and to the office, where all the morning. At noon dined at home and so to my office again, and taking a turne in the garden my Lady Pen comes to me and takes me into her house, where I find her daughter and a pretty lady of her acquaintance, one Mrs. Lowder,[2] sister, I suppose, of her servant Lowder's, with whom I, notwithstanding all my resolution to follow business close this afternoon, did stay talking and playing the foole almost all the afternoon, and there saw two or three foolish sorry pictures of her doing, but very ridiculous compared to what my wife do. She grows mighty homely and looks old. Thence ashamed at myself for this losse of time, yet not able to leave it, I to the office, where my Lord Bruncker come; and he and I had a little fray, he being, I find, a very peevish man, if he be denied what he expects, and very simple in his argument in this business (about signing a warrant for paying Sir Thos. Allen £1,000 out of the groats); but we were pretty good friends before we parted, and so we broke up and I to the writing my letters by the post, and so home to supper and to bed.

13th. Up, being called up by my wife's brother, for

we are informed that the landscape background was painted out by Pepys's wish). There is a similar picture belonging to Mr. Hawes, of Kensington, which Mr. George Scharf, C.B., the Keeper of the National Portrait Gallery, thinks is either a replica or a good old copy.

[1] John Creed was selected as a member of council at this meeting.

[2] Margaret Lowther subsequently married John Holmes, afterwards knighted. — B.

whom I have got a commission from the Duke of Yorke for Muster-Master of one of the divisions, of which Harman is Rere-Admirall, of which I am glad as well as he. After I had acquainted him with it, and discoursed a little of it, I went forth and took him with me by coach to the Duke of Albemarle, who being not up, I took a walk with Balty into the Parke, and to the Queene's Chappell, it being Good Friday, where people were all upon their knees very silent; but, it seems, no masse this day. So back and waited on the Duke and received some commands of his, and so by coach to Mr. Hales's, where it is pretty strange to see that his second doing, I mean the second time of her sitting, is less like Mrs. Pierce than the first, and yet I am confident will be most like her, for he is so curious that I do not see how it is possible for him to mistake. Here he and I presently resolved of going to White Hall, to spend an houre in the galleries there among the pictures, and we did so to my great satisfaction, he shewing me the difference in the payntings, and when I come more and more to distinguish and observe the workmanship, I do not find so many good things as I thought there was, but yet great difference between the works of some and others; and, while my head and judgment was full of these, I would go back again to his house to see his pictures, and indeed, though, I think, at first sight some difference do open, yet very inconsiderably but that I may judge his to be very good pictures. Here we fell into discourse of my picture, and I am for his putting out the Landskipp, though he says it is very well done, yet I do judge it will be best without it, and so it shall be put out, and be made a plain sky like my wife's picture, which will be very noble. Thence called upon an old woman in Pannier Ally to agree for ruling of some paper for me and she will do it pretty cheap. Here I found her have a very comely black mayde to her servant, which I liked very well. So home to dinner and to see my joiner do the bench upon my leads to my great content. After dinner I abroad to carry paper to my old woman, and so to Westminster Hall, and there beyond my intention or design did see and speak with Betty Howlett, at her father's still, and it seems they carry her to her own house to begin the world with her young husband on Monday next, Easter Monday. I please myself with the thoughts of her neighbourhood, for I love the girl mightily. Thence home, and thither comes Mr. Houblon and a brother, with whom I evened for the charter parties of their ships for Tangier, and paid them the third advance on their freight to full satisfaction, and so, they being gone, comes Creed and with him till past one in the morning, evening his accounts till my head aked and I was fit for nothing, however, coming at last luckily to see through and settle all to my mind, it did please me mightily, and so with my mind at rest to bed, and he with me and hard to sleep.

14th. Up about seven and finished our papers, he and I, and I delivered him tallys and some money and so away I to the office, where we sat all the morning. At noon dined at home and Creed with me, then parted, and I to the office, and anon called thence by Sir H. Cholmley and he and I to my chamber, and there settled our matters of accounts, and did give him tallys and money to clear him, and so he being gone and all these accounts cleared I shall be even with the King, so as to make a very clear and short account in a very few days, which pleases me very well. Here he and I discoursed a great while about Tangier, and he do convince me, as things are now ordered by my Lord Bellasses and will be by Norwood (men that do only mind themselves), the garrison will never come to any thing, and he proposes his owne being governor, which in truth I do think will do very well, and that he will bring it to something. He gone I to my office, where to write letters late, and then home and looked over a little more my papers of accounts lately passed, and so to bed.

15th (Easter Day). Up and by water to Westminster to the Swan to lay down my cloak, and there found Sarah alone, with whom after I had staid awhile I to White Hall Chapel, and there coming late could hear nothing of the Bishop of London's sermon. So walked into the Park to the Queene's chappell, and there heard a good deal of their mass, and some of their musique, which is not so contemptible, I think, as our people would make it, it pleasing me very well; and, indeed, better than the anthem I heard afterwards at White Hall, at my coming back. I staid till the King went down to receive the Sacrament, and stood in his closett with a great many others, and there saw him receive it, which I did never see the manner of before. But I do see very little difference between the degree of the ceremonies used by our people in the administration thereof, and that in the Roman church, saving that methought our Chappell was not so fine, nor the manner of doing it so glorious, as it was in the Queene's chappell. Thence walked to Mr. Pierce's, and there dined, I alone with him and her and their children: very good company and good discourse, they being able to tell me all the businesses of the Court; the amours and the mad doings that are there; how for certain Mrs. Stewart do do everything with the King that a mistress should do; and that the King hath many bastard children that are known and owned, besides the Duke of Monmouth. After a great deale of this discourse I walked thence into the Parke with her little boy James with me, who is the wittiest boy and the best company in the world, and so back again through White Hall both coming and going, and people did generally take him to be my boy and some would aske me. Thence home to Mr. Pierce again; and he being gone forth, she and I and the children out by coach to Kensington, to where we were the other day, and with great pleasure stayed till night; and were mighty late getting home, the horses tiring and stopping at every twenty steps. By the way we discoursed of Mrs. Clerke, who, she says, is grown mighty high, fine, and proud, but tells me an odd story how Captain Rolt did see her the other day accost a gentleman in Westminster Hall and went with him, and he dogged them to Moorefields to a little blind bawdy house, and there staid watching three hours and they come not out, so could stay no longer but left them there, and he is sure it was she, he knowing her well and describing her very clothes to Mrs. Pierce, which she knows are what she wears. Seeing them well at home I homeward, but the horses at Ludgate Hill made a final stop; so there I 'lighted, and with a linke, it being about 10 o'clock, walked home, and after singing a Psalm or two and supped to bed.

16th. Up, and set my people, Mercer, W. Hewer, Tom

and the girle at work at ruling and stitching my ruled book for the Muster-Masters, and I hard toward the settling of my Tangier accounts. At noon dined alone, the girl Mercer taking physique can eat nothing, and W. Hewer went forth to dinner. So up to my accounts again, and then comes Mrs. Mercer and fair Mrs. Turner, a neighbour of hers that my wife knows by their means, to visit me. I staid a great while with them, being taken with this pretty woman, though a mighty silly, affected citizen woman she is. Then I left them to come to me at supper anon, and myself out by coach to the old woman in Pannyer Alley for my ruled papers, and they are done, and I am much more taken with her black maid Nan. Thence further to Westminster, thinking to have met Mrs. Martin, but could not find her, so back and called at Kirton's to borrow 10*s.* to pay for my ruled papers, I having not money in my pocket enough to pay for them. But it was a pretty consideration that on this occasion I was considering where I could with most confidence in a time of need borrow 10*s.*, and I protest I could not tell where to do it and with some trouble and fear did aske it here. So that God keepe me from want, for I shall be in a very bad condition to helpe myself if ever I should come to want or borrow. Thence called for my papers and so home, and there comes Mrs. Turner and Mercer and supped with me, and well pleased I was with their company, but especially Mrs. Turner's, she being a very pretty woman of person and her face pretty good, the colour of her haire very fine and light. They staid with me talking till about eleven o'clock and so home, W. Hewer, who supped with me, leading them home. So I to bed.

17th. Up, and to the office, where all the morning. At noon dined at home, my brother Balty with me, who is fitting himself to go to sea. So after dinner to my accounts and did proceed a good way in settling them, and thence to the office, where all the afternoon late, writing my letters and doing business, but, Lord! what a conflict I had with myself, my heart tempting me 1,000 times to go abroad about some pleasure or other, notwithstanding the weather foule. However I reproached myself with my weaknesse in yielding so much my judgment to my sense, and prevailed with difficulty and did not budge, but stayed within, and, to my great content, did a great deale of business, and so home to supper and to bed. This day I am told that Moll Davis, the pretty girle, that sang and danced so well at the Duke's house, is dead.[1]

18th. [Up] and by coach with Sir W. Batten and Sir Thos. Allen to White Hall, and there after attending the Duke as usual and there concluding of many things preparatory to the Prince and Generall's going to sea on Monday next, Sir W. Batten and Sir T. Allen and I to Mr. Lilly's, the painter's; and there saw the heads, some finished, and all begun, of the Flaggmen[2] in the late great fight with the Duke of Yorke against the Dutch. The Duke of Yorke hath them done to hang in his chamber, and very finely they are done indeed. Here is the Prince's, Sir G. Askue's, Sir Thomas Teddiman's, Sir Christopher Mings, Sir Joseph Jordan, Sir William Barkeley, Sir Thomas Allen, and Captain Harman's, as also the Duke of Albemarle's; and will be my Lord Sandwich's, Sir W. Pen's, and Sir Jeremy Smith's. Being very well satisfied with this sight, and other good pictures hanging in the house, we parted, and I left them, and [to] pass away a little time went to the printed picture seller's in the way thence to the Exchange, and there did see great plenty of fine prints; but did not buy any, only a print of an old pillar in Rome made for a Naval Triumph,[3] which for the antiquity of the shape of ships, I buy and keepe.[4] Thence to the Exchange, that is, the New Exchange, and looked over some play books and intend to get all the late new plays. So to Westminster, and there at the Swan got a bit of meat and dined alone; and so away toward King's Street, and spying out of my coach Jane that lived heretofore at Jevons, my

[1] This report of her death was not true (see March 7th, 1666–67). — M. B.

[2] These portraits of the Admirals by Sir Peter Lely are at present at Greenwich Hospital. They were exhibited at the Naval Exhibition, 1891. Pepys does not mention Sir John Lawson.

[3] The *columna rostrata* erected in the Forum to C. Duilius, who obtained a triumph for the first naval victory over the Carthaginians, B.C. 261. Part of the column was discovered in the ruins of the Forum near the arch of Septimius, and transferred to the Capitol. — B.

[4] This is the first mention of Pepys's buying prints. — B.

barber's, I went a little further and stopped, and went on foot back, and overtook her, taking water at Westminster Bridge, and spoke to her, and she telling me whither she was going I over the water and met her at Lambeth, and there drank with her; she telling me how he that was so long her servant, did prove to be a married man, though her master told me (which she denies) that he had lain with her several times in his house. There left her sans essayer alcun cose con elle, and so away by boat to the 'Change, and took coach and to Mr. Hales, where he would have persuaded me to have had the landskipp stand in my picture, but I like it not and will have it otherwise, which I perceive he do not like so well, however is so civil as to say it shall be altered. Thence away to Mrs. Pierce's, who was not at home, but gone to my house to visit me with Mrs. Knipp. I therefore took up the little girle Betty and my mayde Mary that now lives there and to my house, where they had been but were gone, so in our way back again met them coming back again to my house in Cornehill, and there stopped laughing at our pretty misfortunes, and so I carried them to Fish Streete, and there treated them with prawns and lobsters, and it beginning to grow darke we away, but the jest is our horses would not draw us up the Hill, but we were fain to 'light and stay till the coachman had made them draw down to the bottom of the Hill, thereby warming their legs, and then they came up cheerfully enough, and we got up and I carried them home, and coming home called at my paper ruler's and there found black Nan, which pleases me mightily, and having saluted her again and again away home and to bed. . . . In all my ridings in the coach and intervals my mind hath been full these three weeks of setting in musique "It is decreed, &c."

19th. Lay long in bed, so to the office, where all the morning. At noon dined with Sir W. Warren at the Pope's Head. So back to the office, and there met with the Commissioners of the Ordnance, where Sir W. Pen being almost drunk vexed me, and the more because Mr. Chichly observed it with me, and it was a disparagement to the office. They gone I to my office. Anon comes home my wife from Brampton, not looked for till Saturday, which will hinder me of a little pleasure, but I am glad of her coming. She tells me Pall's business with Ensum is like to go on, but I must give, and she consents to it, another £100. She says she doubts my father is in want of money, for rents come in mighty slowly. My mother grows very unpleasant and troublesome and my father mighty infirm through his old distemper,[1] which altogether makes me mighty thoughtfull. Having heard all this and bid her welcome I to the office, where late, and so home, and after a little more talk with my wife, she to bed and I after her.

20th. Up, and after an houre or two's talke with my poor wife, who gives me more and more content every day than other, I abroad by coach to Westminster, and there met with Mrs. Martin, and she and I over the water to Stangold,[2] and after a walke in the fields to the King's Head, and there spent an houre or two with pleasure with her, and eat a tansy and so parted, and I to the New Exchange, there to get a list of all the modern plays which I intend to collect and to have them bound up together. Thence to Mr. Hales's, and there, though against his particular mind, I had my landskipp done out, and only a heaven made in the roome of it, which though it do not please me thoroughly now it is done, yet it will do better than as it was before. Thence to Paul's Churchyarde, and there bespoke some new books, and so to my ruling woman's and there did see my work a doing, and so home and to my office a little, but was hindered of business I intended by being sent for to Mrs. Turner, who desired some discourse with me and lay her condition before me, which is bad and poor. Sir Thomas Harvey intends again to have lodgings in her house, which she prays me to prevent if I can, which I promised. Thence to talke generally of our neighbours. I find she tells me the faults of all of them, and their bad words of me and my wife, and indeed do discover more than I thought. So I told her, and so will practise that I will have nothing to do with any of them. She ended all with a promise of shells to my wife, very fine ones indeed, and seems to have great respect and honour for my wife. So home and to bed.

[1] A rupture. [2] Stangate.

21st. Up betimes and to the office, there to prepare some things against the afternoon for discourse about the business of the pursers and settling the pursers' matters of the fleete according to my proposition. By and by the office sat, and they being up I continued at the office to finish my matters against the meeting before the Duke this afternoon, so home about three to clap a bit of meate in my mouth, and so away with Sir W. Batten to White Hall, and there to the Duke, but he being to go abroad to take the ayre, he dismissed us presently without doing any thing till to-morrow morning. So my Lord Bruncker and I down to walk in the garden [at White Hall], it being a mighty hot and pleasant day; and there was the King, who, among others, talked to us a little; and among other pretty things, he swore merrily that he believed the ketch that Sir W. Batten bought the last year at Colchester was of his own getting, it was so thick to its length. Another pleasant thing he said of Christopher Pett, commending him that he will not alter his moulds of his ships upon any man's advice; "as," says he, "Commissioner Taylor I fear do of his New London, that he makes it differ, in hopes of mending the Old London, built by him." "For," says he, "he finds that God hath put him into the right, and so will keep in it while he is in." "And," says the King, "I am sure it must be God put him in, for no art of his owne ever could have done it;" for it seems he cannot give a good account of what he do as an artist. Thence with my Lord Bruncker in his coach to Hide Parke, the first time I have been there this year. There the King was; but I was sorry to see my Lady Castlemaine, for the mourning forceing all the ladies to go in black, with their hair plain and without any spots, I find her to be a much more ordinary woman than ever I durst have thought she was; and, indeed, is not so pretty as Mrs. Stewart, whom I saw there also. Having done at the Park he set me down at the Exchange, and I by coach home and there to my letters, and they being done, to writing a large letter about the business of the pursers to Sir W. Batten against to-morrow's discourse, and so home and to bed.

22nd (Lord's day). Up, and put on my new black coate, long down to my knees, and with Sir W. Batten to White

Hall, where all in deep mourning for the Queene's mother. There had great discourse, before the Duke and Sir W. Coventry begun the discourse of the day about the purser's business, which I seconded, and with great liking to the Duke, whom however afterward my Lord Bruncker and Sir W. Pen did stop by some thing they said, though not much to the purpose, yet because our proposition had some appearance of certain charge to the King it was ruled that for this year we should try another the same in every respect with ours, leaving out one circumstance of allowing the pursers the victuals of all men short of the complement. I was very well satisfied with it and am contented to try it, wishing it may prove effectual. Thence away with Sir W. Batten in his coach home, in our way he telling me the certaine newes, which was afterward confirmed to me this day by several, that the Bishopp of Munster has made a league [with] the Hollanders, and that our King and Court are displeased much at it: moreover we are not sure of Sweden. I home to my house, and there dined mighty well, my poor wife and Mercer and I. So back again walked to White Hall, and there to and again in the Parke, till being in the shoemaker's stockes[1] I was heartily weary, yet walked however to the Queene's Chappell at St. James's, and there saw a little mayde baptized; many parts and words whereof are the same with that of our Liturgy, and little that is more ceremonious than ours. Thence walked to Westminster and eat a bit of bread and drank, and so to Worster House,[2] and there staid, and saw the Council up, and then back, walked to the Cockepitt, and there took my leave of the Duke of Albemarle, who is going to-morrow to sea. He seems mightily pleased with me, which I am glad of; but I do find infinitely my concernment in being careful to appear to the King and Duke to continue my care of his business, and to be found diligent as I used to be. Thence walked wearily as far as Fleet Streete and so there met a coach and home to supper and to bed, having sat a great while with Will Joyce, who come to see me, and it is the first time I have seen him at my house

[1] A cant expression for tight shoes.

[2] In the Strand; the mansion stood where Beaufort Buildings are now; it was rented by Lord Clarendon while his house was building.

since the plague, and find him the same impertinent, prating coxcombe that ever he was.

23rd. Being mighty weary last night, lay long this morning, then up and to the office, where Sir W. Batten, Lord Bruncker and I met, and toward noon took coach and to White Hall, where I had the opportunity to take leave of the Prince, and again of the Duke of Albemarle; and saw them kiss the King's hands and the Duke's; and much content, indeed, there seems to be in all people at their going to sea, and [they] promise themselves much good from them. This morning the House of Parliament do meet, only to adjourne again till winter. The plague, I hear, encreases in the towne much, and exceedingly in the country everywhere. Thence walked to Westminster Hall, and after a little stay, there being nothing now left to keep me there, Betty Howlett being gone, I took coach and away home, in my way asking in two or three places the worth of pearles, I being now come to the time that I have long ago promised my wife a necklace. Dined at home and took Balty with me to Hales's to show him his sister's picture, and thence to Westminster, and there I to the Swan and drank, and so back again alone to Hales's and there met my wife and Mercer, Mrs. Pierce being sitting, and two or three idle people of her acquaintance more standing by. Her picture do come on well. So staid until she had done and then set her down at home, and my wife and I and the girle by coach to Islington, and there eat and drank in the coach and so home, and there find a girle sent at my desire by Mrs. Michell of Westminster Hall, to be my girle under the cooke-mayde, Susan. But I am a little dissatisfied that the girle, though young, is taller and bigger than Su, and will not, I fear, be under her command, which will trouble me, and the more because she is recommended by a friend that I would not have any unkindness with, but my wife do like very well of her. So to my accounts and journall at my chamber, there being bonfires in the streete, for being St. George's day, and the King's Coronation, and the day of the Prince and Duke's going to sea. So having done my business, to bed.

24th. Up, and presently am told that the girle that came

yesterday hath packed up her things to be gone home again to Enfield, whence she come, which I was glad of, that we might be at first rid of her altogether rather than be liable to her going away hereafter. The reason was that London do not agree with her. So I did give her something, and away she went. By and by comes Mr. Bland to me, the first time since his coming from Tangier, and tells me, in short, how all things are out of order there, and like to be; and the place never likely to come to anything while the soldiers govern all, and do not encourage trade. He gone I to the office, where all the morning, and so to dinner, and there in the afternoon very busy all day till late, and so home to supper and to bed.

25th. Up, and to White Hall to the Duke as usual, and did our business there. So I away to Westminster (Balty with me, whom I had presented to Sir W. Coventry) and there told Mrs. Michell of her kinswoman's running away, which troubled her. So home, and there find another little girle come from my wife's mother, likely to do well. After dinner I to the office, where Mr. Prin come to meet about the Chest business; and till company come, did discourse with me a good while alone in the garden about the laws of England, telling me the many faults in them; and among others, their obscurity through multitude of long statutes, which he is about to abstract out of all of a sort; and as he lives, and Parliaments come, get them put into laws, and the other statutes repealed, and then it will be a short work to know the law, which appears a very noble good thing. By and by Sir W. Batten and Sir W. Rider met with us, and we did something to purpose about the Chest, and hope we shall go on to do so. They up, I to present Balty to Sir W. Pen, who at my entreaty did write a most obliging letter to Harman to use him civilly, but the dissembling of the rogue is such, that it do not oblige me at all. So abroad to my ruler's of my books, having, God forgive me! a mind to see Nan there, which I did, and so back again, and then out again to see Mrs. Bettons, who were looking out of the window as I come through Fenchurch Streete. So that indeed I am not, as I ought to be, able to command myself in the pleasures of my eye. So home, and with my wife and Mercer spent our evening upon our new leads by our bed-chamber singing, while Mrs. Mary Batelier looked out of the window to us, and we talked together, and at last bid good night. However, my wife and I staid there talking of several things with great pleasure till eleven o'clock at night, and it is a convenience I would not want for any thing in the world, it being, methinks, better than almost any roome in my house. So having supped upon the leads, to bed. The plague, blessed be God! is decreased sixteen this week.

26th. To the office, where all the morning. At noon home to dinner, and in the afternoon to my office again, where very busy all the afternoon and particularly about fitting of Mr. Yeabsly's accounts for the view of the Lords Commissioners for Tangier. At night home to supper and to bed.

27th. Up (taking Balty with me, who lay at my house last [night] in order to his going away to-day to sea with the pursers of the Henery, whom I appointed to call him), abroad to many several places about several businesses, to my Lord Treasurer's, Westminster, and I know not where. At noon to the 'Change a little, and there bespoke some maps to hang in my new roome (my boy's roome) which will be very pretty. Home to dinner, and after dinner to the hanging up of maps, and other things for the fitting of the roome, and now it will certainly be one of the handsomest and most usefull roomes in my house. So that what with this room and the room on my leads my house is half as good again as it was. All this afternoon about this till I was so weary and it was late I could do no more but finished the room. So I did not get out to the office all the day long. At night spent a good deale of time with my wife and Mercer teaching them a song, and so after supper to bed.

28th. Up and to the office. At noon dined at home. After dinner abroad with my wife to Hales's to see only our pictures and Mrs. Pierce's, which I do not think so fine as I might have expected it. My wife to her father's, to carry him some ruling work,[1] which I have advised her

[1] For the making books of accounts for pursers see March 2nd, 1665-66.

to let him do. It will get him some money. She also is to look out again for another little girle, the last we had being also gone home the very same day she came. She was also to look after a necklace of pearle, which she is mighty busy about, I being contented to lay out £80 in one for her. I home to my business. By and by comes my wife and presently after, the tide serving, Balty took leave of us, going to sea, and upon very good terms, to be Muster-Master of a squadron, which will be worth £100 this yeare to him, besides keeping him the benefit of his pay in the Guards. He gone, I very busy all the afternoon till night, among other things, writing a letter to my brother John, the first I have done since my being angry with him, and that so sharpe a one too that I was sorry almost to send it when I had wrote it, but it is preparatory to my being kind to him, and sending for him up hither when he hath passed his degree of Master of Arts. So home to supper and to bed.

29th (Lord's day). Up, and to church, where Mr. Mills, a lazy, simple sermon upon the Devil's having no right to any thing in this world. So home to dinner, and after dinner I and my boy down by water to Redriffe and thence walked to Mr. Evelyn's, where I walked in his garden till he come from Church, with great pleasure reading Ridly's[1] discourse, all my way going and coming, upon the Civill and Ecclesiastical Law. He being come home, he and I walked together in the garden with mighty pleasure, he being a very ingenious man; and the more I know him, the more I love him. His chief business with me was to propose having my cozen Thomas Pepys in Commission of the Peace, which I do not know what to say to till I speake with him, but should be glad of it and will put him upon it. Thence walked back again reading and so took water and home, where I find my uncle and aunt Wight, and supped with them upon my leads with mighty pleasure and mirthe, and they being gone I mighty weary to bed, after having my haire of my head cut shorter, even close to my skull, for coolnesse, it being mighty hot weather.

[1] Sir Thomas Ridley, a native of Ely. He was a Master in Chancery, and author of "A View of the Civil and Ecclesiastical Law," published at Oxford in 1607, and frequently reprinted. He died 1626.—M. B.

30th. Up and, being ready, to finish my journall for four days past. To the office, where busy all the morning. At noon dined alone, my wife gone abroad to conclude about her necklace of pearle. I after dinner to even all my accounts of this month; and, bless God! I find myself, notwithstanding great expences of late; viz. £80 now to pay for a necklace; near £40 for a set of chairs and couch; near £40 for my three pictures: yet I do gather, and am now worth £5,200. My wife comes home by and by, and hath pitched upon a necklace with three rows, which is a very good one, and £80 is the price. In the evening, having finished my accounts to my full content and joyed that I have evened them so plainly, remembering the trouble my last accounts did give me by being let alone a little longer than ordinary, by which I am to this day at a loss for £50, I hope I shall never commit such an error again, for I cannot devise where the £50 should be, but it is plain I ought to be worth £50 more than I am, and blessed be God the error was no greater. In the evening with my [wife] and Mercer by coach to take the ayre as far as Bow, and eat and drank in the coach by the way and with much pleasure and pleased with my company. At night home and up to the leads, but were contrary to expectation driven down again with a stinke by Sir W. Pen's shying of a shitten pot in their house of office close by, which do trouble me for fear it do hereafter annoy me. So down to sing a little and then to bed. So ends this month with great layings-out. Good health and gettings, and advanced well in the whole of my estate, for which God make me thankful!

May 1st. Up, and all the morning at the office. At noon, my cozen Thomas Pepys did come to me, to consult about the business of his being a Justice of the Peace, which he is much against; and among other reasons, tells me, as a confidant, that he is not free to exercise punishment according to the Act against Quakers and other people, for religion. Nor do he understand Latin, and so is not capable of the place as formerly, now all warrants do run in Latin. Nor is he in Kent, though he be of Deptford parish, his house[1] standing in Surry. However, I

[1] Hatcham, near New Cross, on the Deptford Road.

did bring him to incline towards it, if he be pressed to take it. I do think it may be some repute to me to have my kinsman in Commission there, specially if he behave himself to content in the country. He gone and my wife gone abroad, I out also to and fro, to see and be seen, among others to find out in Thames Streete where Betty Howlett is come to live, being married to Mrs. Michell's son; which I did about the Old Swan, but did not think fit to go thither or see them. Thence by water to Redriffe, reading a new French book my Lord Bruncker did give me to-day, "L'Histoire Amoureuse des Gaules,"[1] being a pretty libel against the amours of the Court of France. I walked up and down Deptford yarde, where I had not been since I come from living at Greenwich, which is some months. There I met with Mr. Castle, and was forced against my will to have his company back with me. So we walked and drank at Halfway house and so to his house, where I drank a cupp of syder, and so home, where I find Mr. Norbury newly come to town to see us. After he gone my wife tells me the ill newes that our Susan is sicke and gone to bed, with great pain in her head and back, which troubles us all. However we to bed expecting what to-morrow would produce. She hath we conceive wrought a little too much, having neither maid nor girle to help her.

2nd. Up and find the girle better, which we are glad of, and with Sir W. Batten to White Hall by coach. There attended the Duke as usual. Thence with Captain Cocke, whom I met there, to London, to my office, to consult about serving him in getting him some money, he being already tired of his slavery to my Lord Bruncker, and the charge it costs him, and gets no manner of courtesy from him for it. He gone I home to dinner, find the girle yet better, so no fear of being forced to send her out of doors as we intended. After dinner I by water to White

[1] This book, which has frequently been reprinted, was written by Roger de Rabutin, Comte de Bussy, for the amusement of his mistress, Madame de Montglas, and consists of sketches of the chief ladies of the court, in which he libelled friends and foes alike. These circulated in manuscript, and were printed at Liège in 1665. Louis XIV. was so much annoyed with the book that he sent the author to the Bastille for over a year.

Hall to a Committee for Tangier upon Mr. Yeabsly's business, which I got referred to a Committee to examine. Thence among other stops went to my ruler's house, and there staid a great while with Nan idling away the afternoon with pleasure. By and by home, so to my office a little, and then home to supper with my wife, the girle being pretty well again, and then to bed.

3rd. Up, and all the morning at the office. At noon home, and contrary to my expectation find my little girle Su worse than she was, which troubled me, and the more to see my wife minding her paynting and not thinking of her house business, this being the first day of her beginning the second time to paynt. This together made me froward that I was angry with my wife, and would not have Browne to think to dine at my table with me always, being desirous to have my house to myself without a stranger and a mechanique to be privy to all my concernments. Upon this my wife and I had a little disagreement, but it ended by and by, and then to send up and down for a nurse to take the girle home and would have given anything. I offered to the only one that we could get 20*s*. per weeke, and we to find clothes, and bedding and physique, and would have given 30*s*., as demanded, but desired an houre or two's time. So I away by water to Westminster, and there sent for the girle's mother to Westminster Hall to me; she came and undertakes to get her daughter a lodging and nurse at next doore to her, though she dare not, for the parish's sake, whose sexton her husband is, to [have] her into her owne house. Thence home, calling at my bookseller's and other trifling places, and in the evening the mother come and with a nurse she has got, who demanded and I did agree at 10*s*. per weeke to take her, and so she away, and my house mighty uncouth, having so few in it, and we shall want a servant or two by it, and the truth is my heart was a little sad all the afternoon and jealous of myself. But she went, and we all glad of it, and so a little to the office, and so home to supper and to bed.

4th. Up and by water to Westminster to Charing Cross (Mr. Gregory for company with me) to Sir Ph. Warwicke's, who was not within. So I took Gregory to White Hall, and there spoke with Joseph Williamson to have leave in the next Gazette to have a general pay for the Chest at Chatham declared upon such a day in June. Here I left Gregory, and I by coach back again to Sir Philip Warwicke's, and in the Park met him walking, so discoursed about the business of striking a quarter's tallys for Tangier, due this day, which he hath promised to get my Lord Treasurer's warrant for, and so away hence, and to Mr. Hales, to see what he had done to Mrs. Pierce's picture, and whatever he pretends, I do not think it will ever be so good a picture as my wife's. Thence home to the office a little and then to dinner, and had a great fray with my wife again about Browne's coming to teach her to paynt, and sitting with me at table, which I will not yield to. I do thoroughly believe she means no hurte in it; but very angry we were, and I resolved all into my having my will done, without disputing, be the reason what it will; and so I will have it. After dinner abroad again and to the New Exchange about play books, and to White Hall, thinking to have met Sir G. Carteret, but failed. So to the Swan at Westminster, and there spent a quarter of an hour with Jane, and thence away home, and my wife coming home by and by (having been at her mother's to pray her to look out for a mayde for her) by coach into the fields to Bow, and so home back in the evening, late home, and after supper to bed, being much out of order for lack of somebody in the room of Su. This evening, being weary of my late idle courses, and the little good I shall do the King or myself in the office, I bound myself to very strict rules till Whitsunday next.

5th. At the office all the morning. After dinner upon a letter from the fleete from Sir W. Coventry I did do a great deale of worke for the sending away of the victuallers that are in the river, &c., too much to remember. Till 10 at night busy about letters and other necessary matter of the office. About 11 I home, it being a fine moonshine and so my wife and Mercer come into the garden, and, my business being done, we sang till about twelve at night, with mighty pleasure to ourselves and neighbours, by their casements opening, and so home to supper and to bed.

6th (Lord's day). To church. Home, and after dinner walked to White Hall, thinking to have seen Mr. Coventry, but failed, and therefore walked clear on foot back again. Busy till night in fitting my Victualling papers in order, which I through my multitude of business and pleasure have not examined these several months. Walked back again home, and so to the Victualling Office, where I met Mr. Gawden, and have received some satisfaction, though it be short of what I expected, and what might be expected from me. So after evened I have gone, and so to supper and to bed.

7th. Up betimes to set my Victualling papers in order against Sir W. Coventry comes, which indeed makes me very melancholy, being conscious that I am much to seeke in giving a good answer to his queries about the Victualling business. At the office mighty busy, and brought myself into a pretty plausible condition before Sir W. Coventry come, and did give him a pretty tolerable account of every thing and went with him into the Victualling office, where we sat and examined his businesses and state of the victualling of the fleete, which made me in my heart blushe that I could say no more to it than I did or could. But I trust in God I shall never be in that condition again. We parted, and I with pretty good grace, and so home to dinner, where my wife troubled more and more with her swollen cheek. So to dinner, my sister-in-law with us, who I find more and more a witty woman; and then I to my Lord Treasurer's and the Exchequer about my Tangier businesses, and with my content passed by all things and persons without so much as desiring any stay or loss of time with them, being by strong vowe obliged on no occasion to stay abroad but my publique offices. So home again, where I find Mrs. Pierce and Mrs. Ferrers come to see my wife. I staid a little with them, being full of business, and so to the office, where busy till late at night and so weary and a little conscious of my failures to-day, yet proud that the day is over without more observation on Sir W. Coventry's part, and so to bed and to sleepe soundly.

8th. Up, and to the office all the morning. At noon dined at home, my wife's cheek bad still. After dinner to the office again and thither comes Mr. Downing,[1] the

[1] John Downing.

anchor-smith, who had given me 50 pieces in gold the last month to speake for him to Sir W. Coventry, for his being smith at Deptford; but after I had got it granted to him, he finds himself not fit to go on with it, so lets it fall. So has no benefit of my motion. I therefore in honour and conscience took him home the money, and, though much to my grief, did yet willingly and forcibly force him to take it again, the poor man having no mind to have it. However, I made him take it, and away he went, and I glad to have given him so much cause to speake well of me. So to my office again late, and then home to supper to a good lobster with my wife, and then a little to my office again, and so to bed.

9th. Up by five o'clock, which I have not a long time done, and down the river by water to Deptford, among other things to examine the state of Ironworke, in order to the doing something with reference to Downing that may induce him to returne me the 50 pieces. Walked back again reading of my Civill Law Book, and so home and by coach to White Hall, where we did our usual business before the Duke, and heard the Duke commend Deane's ship "The Rupert" before "The Defyance," built lately by Castle, in hearing of Sir W. Batten, which pleased me mightily. Thence by water to Westminster, and there looked after my Tangier order, and so by coach to Mrs. Pierce's, thinking to have gone to Hales's, but she was not ready, so away home and to dinner, and after dinner out by coach to Lovett's to have forwarded what I have doing there, but find him and his pretty wife gone to my house to show me something. So away to my Lord Treasurer's, and thence to Pierce's, where I find Knipp, and I took them to Hales's to see our pictures finished, which are very pretty, but I like not hers half so well as I thought at first, it being not so like, nor so well painted as I expected, or as mine and my wife's are. Thence with them to Cornhill to call and choose a chimney-piece for Pierce's closett, and so home, where my wife in mighty pain and mightily vexed at my being abroad with these women; and when they were gone called them whores and I know not what, which vexed me, having been so innocent with them. So I with them to Mrs. Turner's and there sat with them a while, anon my wife sends for me, I come, and what was it but to scold at me and she would go abroad to take the ayre presently, that she would. So I left my company and went with her to Bow, but was vexed and spoke not one word to her all the way going nor coming, or being come home, but went up straight to bed. Half an hour after (she in the coach leaning on me as being desirous to be friends) she comes up mighty sicke with a fit of the cholique and in mighty pain and calls for me out of the bed; I rose and held her, she prays me to forgive her, and in mighty pain we put her to bed, where the pain ceased by and by, and so had some asparagus to our bed side for supper and very kindly afterward to sleepe and good friends in the morning.

10th. So up, and to the office, where all the morning. At noon home to dinner and there busy all the afternoon till past six o'clock, and then abroad with my wife by coach, who is now at great ease, her cheeke being broke inward. We took with us Mrs. Turner, who was come to visit my wife just as we were going out. A great deale of tittle tattle discourse to little purpose, I finding her, though in other things a very discreete woman, as very a gossip speaking of her neighbours as any body. Going out towards Hackney by coach for the ayre, the silly coachman carries us to Shoreditch, which was so pleasant a piece of simplicity in him and us, that made us mighty merry. So back again late, it being wondrous hot all the day and night and it lightning exceeding all the way we went and came, but without thunder. Coming home we called at a little alehouse, and had an eele pye, of which my wife eat part and brought home the rest. So being come home we to supper and to bed. This day come our new cook maid Mary, commended by Mrs. Batters.

11th. Up betimes, and then away with Mr. Yeabsly to my Lord Ashly's, whither by and by comes Sir H. Cholmly and Creed, and then to my Lord, and there entered into examination of Mr. Yeabsly's accounts, wherein as in all other things I find him one of the most distinct men that ever I did see in my life. He raised many scruples which were to be answered another day and so parted, giving me an alarme how to provide myself against the day of my passing my accounts. Thence I to Westminster to look after the striking of my tallys, but nothing done or to be done therein. So to the 'Change, to speake with Captain Cocke, among other things about getting of the silver plates[1] of him, which he promises to do; but in discourse he tells me that I should beware of my fellow-officers; and by name told me that my Lord Bruncker should say in his hearing, before Sir W. Batten, of me, that he could undo the man, if he would; wherein I think he is a foole; but, however, it is requisite I be prepared against the man's friendship. Thence home to dinner alone, my wife being abroad. After dinner to the setting some things in order in my dining-room; and by and by comes my wife home and Mrs. Pierce with her, so I lost most of this afternoon with them, and in the evening abroad with them, our long tour by coach, to Hackney, so to Kingsland, and then to Islington, there entertaining them by candle-light very well, and so home with her, set her down, and so home and to bed.

12th. Up to the office very betimes to draw up a letter for the Duke of Yorke relating to him the badness of our condition in this office for want of money. That being in good time done we met at the office and there sat all the morning. At noon home, where I find my wife troubled still at my checking her last night in the coach in her long stories out of Grand Cyrus, which she would tell, though nothing to the purpose, nor in any good manner.[2] This she took unkindly, and I think I was to blame indeed; but she do find with reason, that in the company of Pierce, Knipp, or other women that I love, I do not value her, or mind her as I ought. However very good friends by and

[1] See April 5th, 1666

[2] Sir Walter Scott observes, in his "Life of Dryden," that the romances of Calprenede and Scuderi, those ponderous and unmerciful folios, now consigned to oblivion, were, in their day, not only universally read and admired, but supposed to furnish the most perfect models of gallantry and heroism. Dr. Johnson read them all. "I have," says Mrs. Chapone, "and yet I am still alive, dragged through 'Le Grand Cyrus,' in twelve huge volumes; 'Cleopatra,' in eight or ten; 'Ibrahim,' 'Clelie,' and some others, whose names, as well as all the rest of them, I have forgotten" ("Letters to Mrs. Carter"). No wonder that Pepys sat on thorns, when his wife began to recite "Le Grand Cyrus" in the coach, "and trembled at the impending tale." — B.

by, and to dinner, and after dinner up to the putting our dining room in order, which will be clean again anon, but not as it is to be because of the pictures which are not come home. To the office and did much business, in the evening to Westminster and White Hall about business and among other things met Sir G. Downing on White Hall bridge, and there walked half an hour, talking of the success of the late new Act; and indeed it is very much, that that hath stood really in the room of £800,000[1] now since Christmas, being itself but £1,250,000. And so I do really take it to be a very considerable thing done by him; for the beginning, end, and every part of it, is to be imputed to him. So home by water, and there hard till 12 at night at work finishing the great letter to the Duke of Yorke against to-morrow morning, and so home to bed. This day come home again my little girle Susan, her sicknesse proving an ague, and she had a fit soon almost as she come home. The fleete is not yet gone from the Nore. The plague encreases in many places, and is 53 this week with us.

13th (Lord's day). Up, and walked to White Hall, where we all met to present a letter to the Duke of Yorke, complaining solemnly of the want of money, and that being done, I to and again up and down Westminster, thinking to have spent a little time with Sarah at the Swan, or Mrs. Martin, but was disappointed in both, so walked the greatest part of the way home, where comes Mr. Symons, my old acquaintance, to dine with me, and I made myself as good company as I could to him, but he was mighty impertinent methought too yet, and thereby I see the difference between myself now and what it was heretofore, when I reckoned him a very brave fellow. After dinner he and I walked together as far as Cheapside, and I quite through to Westminster again, and fell by chance into St. Margett's[2] Church, where I heard a young man play the foole upon the doctrine of purgatory. At this church I spied Betty Howlett, who indeed is mighty pretty, and struck me mightily. After church time, standing in the Church yarde,

[1] There appears to be some error in these figures. — B.
[2] St. Margaret's.

she spied me, so I went to her, her father and mother and husband being with her. They desired and I agreed to go home with Mr. Michell, and there had the opportunity to have saluted two or three times Betty and make an acquaintance which they are pleased with, though not so much as I am or they think I am. I staid here an houre or more chatting with them in a little sorry garden of theirs by the Bowling Alley, and so left them and I by water home, and there was in great pain in mind lest Sir W. Pen, who is going down to the Fleete, should come to me or send for me to be informed in the state of things, and particularly the Victualling, that by my pains he might seem wise. So after spending an houre with my wife pleasantly in her closett, I to bed even by daylight.

14th. Comes betimes a letter from Sir W. Coventry, that he and Sir G. Carteret are ordered presently down to the Fleete. I up and saw Sir W. Pen gone also after them, and so I finding it a leisure day fell to making cleane my closett in my office, which I did to my content and set up my Platts again, being much taken also with Griffin's mayde, that did cleane it, being a pretty mayde. I left her at it, and toward Westminster myself with my wife by coach and meeting took up Mr. Lovett the varnisher with us, who is a pleasant speaking and humoured man, so my wife much taken with him, and a good deale of worke I believe I shall procure him. I left my wife at the New Exchange and myself to the Exchequer, to looke after my Tangier tallys, and there met Sir G. Downing, who shewed me his present practise now begun this day to paste up upon the Exchequer door a note of what orders upon the new Act are paid and now in paying, and my Lord of Oxford coming by, also took him, and shewed him his whole method of keeping his books, and everything of it, which indeed is very pretty, and at this day there is assigned upon the Act £804,000. Thence at the New Exchange took up my wife again, and so home to dinner, and after dinner to my office again to set things in order. In the evening out with my wife and my aunt Wight, to take the ayre, and happened to have a pleasant race between our hackney-coach and a gentleman's. At Bow we eat and drank and so back again, it being very cool in the evening. Having set home my aunt and come home, I fell to examine my wife's kitchen book, and find 20*s.* mistake, which made me mighty angry and great difference between us, and so in the difference to bed.

15th. Up and to the office, where we met and sat all the morning. At noon home to dinner, and after dinner by coach to Sir Philip Warwicke's, he having sent for me, but was not within, so I to my Lord Crew's, who is very lately come to towne, and with him talking half an houre of the business of the warr, wherein he is very doubtful, from our want of money, that we shall fail. And I do concur with him therein. After some little discourse of ordinary matters, I away to Sir Philip Warwicke's again, and was come in, and gone out to my Lord Treasurer's; whither I followed him, and there my business was, to be told that my Lord Treasurer hath got £10,000 for us in the Navy, to answer our great necessities, which I did thank him for; but the sum is not considerable. So home, and there busy all the afternoon till night, and then home to supper and to bed.

16th. Up very betimes, and so down the river to Deptford to look after some business, being by and by to attend the Duke and Mr. Coventry, and so I was wiling to carry something fresh that I may look as a man minding business, which I have done too much for a great while to forfeit, and is now so great a burden upon my mind night and day that I do not enjoy myself in the world almost. I walked thither, and come back again by water, and so to White Hall, and did our usual business before the Duke, and so to the Exchequer, where the lazy rogues have not yet done my tallys, which vexes me. Thence to Mr. Hales, and paid him for my picture, and Mr. Hill's, for the first £14 for the picture, and 25*s.* for the frame, and for the other £7 for the picture, it being a copy of his only, and 5*s.* for the frame; in all, £22 10*s.* I am very well satisfied in my pictures, and so took them in another coach home along with me, and there with great pleasure my wife and I hung them up, and, that being done, to dinner, where Mrs. Barbara Sheldon come to see us and dined with us, and we kept her all the day with us, I going down to Deptford, and, Lord! to see with what itching desire I did endeavour to see Bagwell's wife, but failed, for which I am glad, only I observe the folly of my mind that cannot refrain from pleasure at a season above all others in my life requisite for me to shew my utmost care in. I walked both going and coming, spending my time reading of my Civill and Ecclesiastical Law book. Being returned home, I took my wife and Mrs. Barbary and Mercer out by coach and went our Grand Tour, and baited at Islington, and so late home about 11 at night, and so with much pleasure to bed.

17th. Up, lying long, being wearied yesterday with long walking. So to the office, where all the morning with fresh occasion of vexing at myself for my late neglect of business, by which I cannot appear half so usefull as I used to do. Home at noon to dinner, and then to my office again, where I could not hold my eyes open for an houre, but I drowsed (so little sensible I apprehend my soul is of the necessity of minding business), but I anon wakened and minded my business, and did a great deale with very great pleasure, and so home at night to supper and to bed, mightily pleased with myself for the business that I have done, and convinced that if I would but keepe constantly to do the same I might have leisure enough and yet do all my business, and by the grace of God so I will. So to bed.

18th. Up by 5 o'clock, and so down by water to Deptford and Blackewall to dispatch some business. So walked to Dickeshoare,[1] and there took boat again and home, and thence to Westminster, and attended all the morning on the Exchequer for a quarter's tallys for Tangier. But, Lord! to see what a dull, heavy sort of people they are there would make a man mad. At noon had them and carried them home, and there dined with great content with my people, and within and at the office all the afternoon and night, and so home to settle some papers there, and so to bed, being not very well, having eaten too much lobster at noon at dinner with Mr. Hollyard, he coming in and commending it so much.

[1] Dick Shore or Duck Shore, Limehouse (see note, January 15th, 1660-61.

19th. Up, and to the office all the morning. At noon took Mr. Deane (lately come to towne) home with me to dinner, and there after giving him some reprimands and good advice about his deportment in the place where by my interest he is at Harwich, and then declaring my resolution of being his friend still, we did then fall to discourse about his ship "Rupert," built by him there, which succeeds so well as he hath got great honour by it, and I some by recommending him; the King, Duke, and every body saying it is the best ship that was ever built. And then he fell to explain to me his manner of casting the draught of water which a ship will draw before-hand: which is a secret the King and all admire in him; and he is the first that hath come to any certainty before-hand, of foretelling the draught of water of a ship before she be launched. I must confess I am much pleased in his successe in this business, and do admire at the confidence of Castle who did undervalue the draught Deane sent up to me, that I was ashamed to owne it or him, Castle asking of me upon the first sight of it whether he that laid it down had ever built a ship or no, which made me the more doubtfull of him. He being gone, I to the office, where much business and many persons to speake with me. Late home and to bed, glad to be at a little quiett.

20th (Lord's day). With my wife to church in the morning. At noon dined mighty nobly, ourselves alone. After dinner my wife and Mercer by coach to Greenwich, to be gossip to Mrs. Daniel's child. I out to Westminster, and straight to Mrs. Martin's, and there did what I would with her, she staying at home all the day for me; and not being well pleased with her over free and loose company, I away to Westminster Abbey, and there fell in discourse with Mr. Blagrave, whom I find a sober politique man, that gets money and increase of places, and thence by coach home, and thence by water after I had discoursed awhile with Mr. Yeabsly, whom I met and took up in my coach with me, and who hath this day presented my Lord Ashly with £100 to bespeak his friendship to him in his accounts now before us; and my Lord hath received it, and so I believe is as bad, as to bribes, as what the world says of him. Calling on all the Victualling ships to know what they had of their complements, and so to Deptford, to enquire after a little business there, and thence by water back again, all the way coming and going reading my Lord Bacon's "Faber Fortunæ," which I can never read too often, and so back home, and there find my wife come home, much pleased with the reception she had there, and she was godmother, and did hold the child at the Font, and it is called John. So back again home, and after setting my papers in order and supping, to bed, desirous to rise betimes in the morning.

21st. Up between 4 and 5 o'clock and to set several papers to rights, and so to the office, where we had an extraordinary meeting. But, Lord! how it torments me to find myself so unable to give an account of my Victualling business, which puts me out of heart in every thing else, so that I never had a greater shame upon me in my owne mind, nor more trouble as to publique business than I have now, but I will get out of it as soon as possibly I can. At noon dined at home, and after dinner comes in my wife's brother Balty and his wife, he being stepped ashore from the fleete for a day or two. I away in some haste to my Lord Ashly, where it is stupendous to see how favourably, and yet closely, my Lord Ashly carries himself to Mr. Yeabsly, in his business, so as I think we shall do his business for him in very good manner. But it is a most extraordinary thing to observe, and that which I would not but have had the observation of for a great deal of money. Being done there, and much forwarded Yeabsly's business, I with Sir H. Cholmly to my Lord Bellassis, who is lately come from Tangier to visit him, but is not within. So to Westminster Hall a little about business and so home by water, and then out with my wife, her brother, sister, and Mercer to Islington, our grand tour, and there eat and drank. But in discourse I am infinitely pleased with Balty, his deportment in his business of Muster-Master, and hope mighty well from him, and am glad with all my heart I put him into this business. Late home and to bed, they also lying at my house, he intending to go away to-morrow back again to sea.

22nd. Up betimes and to my business of entering some Tangier payments in my book in order, and then to the office, where very busy all the morning. At noon home to dinner, Balty being gone back to sea and his wife dining with us, whom afterward my wife carried home. I after dinner to the office, and anon out on several occasions, among others to Lovett's, and there staid by him and her and saw them (in their poor conditioned manner) lay on their varnish, which however pleased me mightily to see. Thence home to my business writing letters, and so at night home to supper and to bed.

23rd. Up by 5 o'clock and to my chamber settling several matters in order. So out toward White Hall, calling in my way on my Lord Bellassis, where I come to his bedside, and did give me a full and long account of his matters, how he left them at Tangier. Declares himself fully satisfied with my care: seems cunningly to argue for encreasing the number of men there. Told me the whole story of his gains by the Turky prizes, which he owns he hath got about £5,000 by. Promised me the same profits Povy was to have had; and in fine, I find him a pretty subtle man; and so I left him, and to White Hall before the Duke and did our usual business, and eased my mind of two or three things of weight that lay upon me about Lanyon's salary, which I have got to be £150 per annum. Thence to Westminster to look after getting some little for some great tallys, but shall find trouble in it. Thence homeward and met with Sir Philip Warwicke, and spoke about this, in which he is scrupulous. After that to talk of the wants of the Navy. He lays all the fault now upon the new Act, and owns his owne folly in thinking once so well of it as to give way to others' endeavours about it, and is grieved at heart to see what passe things are like to come to. Thence to the Excise Office to the Commissioners to get a meeting between them and myself and others about our concernments in the Excise for Tangier, and so to the 'Change awhile, and thence home with Creed, and find my wife at dinner with Mr. Cooke, who is going down to Hinchinbrooke. After dinner Creed and I and wife and Mercer out by coach, leaving them at the New Exchange, while I to White Hall, and there staid at Sir G. Carteret's chamber till the Council rose, and then he and I, by agreement this morning, went forth in his coach by Tiburne, to the Parke; discoursing of the state of the Navy as to money, and the state of the Kingdom too, how ill able to raise more: and of our office as to the condition of the officers; he giving me caution as to myself, that there are those that are my enemies as well as his, and by name my Lord Bruncker, who hath said some odd speeches against me. So that he advises me to stand on my guard; which I shall do, and unless my too-much addiction to pleasure undo me, will be acute enough for any of them. We rode to and again in the Parke a good while, and at last home and set me down at Charing Crosse, and thence I to Mrs. Pierce's to take up my wife and Mercer, where I find her new picture by Hales do not please her, nor me indeed, it making no show, nor is very like, nor no good painting. Home to supper and to bed, having my right eye sore and full of humour of late, I think, by my late change of my brewer, and having of 8*s.* beer.

24th. Up very betimes, and did much business in my chamber. Then to the office, where busy all the morning. At noon rose in the pleasantest humour I have seen Sir W. Coventry and the whole board in this twelvemonth from a pleasant crossing humour Sir W. Batten was in, he being hungry, and desirous to be gone. Home, and Mr. Hunt come to dine with me, but I was prevented dining till 4 o'clock by Sir H. Cholmly and Sir J. Bankes's coming in about some Tangier business. They gone I to dinner, the others having dined. Mr. Sheply is also newly come out of the country and come to see us, whom I am glad to see. He left all well there; but I perceive under some discontent in my Lord's behalfe, thinking that he is under disgrace with the King; but he is not so at all, as Sir G. Carteret assures me. They gone I to the office and did business, and so in the evening abroad alone with my wife to Kingsland, and so back again and to bed, my right eye continuing very ill of the rheum, which hath troubled it four or five days.

25th. Up betimes and to my chamber to do business, where the greatest part of the morning. Then out to the 'Change to speake with Captain [Cocke], who tells me my silver plates are ready for me, and shall be sent me speedily; and proposes another proposition of serving us with a thousand tons of hempe, and tells me it shall bring me £500, if the bargain go forward, which is a good word. Thence to Sir G. Carteret, who is at the pay of the tickets with Sir J. Minnes this day, and here I sat with them a while, the first time I ever was there, and thence to dinner with him, a good dinner. Here come a gentleman over from France arrived here this day, Mr. Browne of St. Mellos,[1] who, among other things, tells me the meaning of the setting out of doggs every night out of the towne walls, which are said to secure the city; but it is not so, but only to secure the anchors, cables, and ships that lie dry, which might otherwise in the night be liable to be robbed. And these doggs are set out every night, and called together in every morning by a man with a horne, and they go in very orderly. Thence home, and there find Knipp at dinner with my wife, now very big, and within a fortnight of lying down. But my head was full of business and so could have no sport. So I left them, promising to return and take them out at night, and so to the Excise Office, where a meeting was appointed of Sir Stephen Fox, the Cofferer, and myself, to settle the business of our tallys, and it was so pretty well against another meeting. Thence away home to the office and out again to Captain Cocke (Mr. Moore for company walking with me and discoursing and admiring of the learning of Dr. Spencer), and there he and I discoursed a little more of our matters, and so home, and (Knipp being gone) took out my wife and Mercer to take the ayre a little, and so as far as Hackney and back again, and then to bed.

26th. Up betimes and to the office, where all the morning. At noon dined at home. So to the office again, and a while at the Victualling Office to understand matters there a little, and thence to the office and despatched much business, to my great content, and so home to supper and to bed.

27th (Lord's day). Rose betimes, and to my office till church time to write two copies of my Will fair, bearing date this day, wherein I have given my sister Pall £500, my father for his owne and my mother's support £2,000, to my wife the rest of my estate, but to have £2,500 secured to her, though by deducting out of what I have given my

[1] St. Malo.

father and my sister. I dispatched all before church time and then to church, my wife with me. Thence home to dinner, whither come my uncle Wight, and aunt and uncle Norbury, and Mr. Shepley. A good dinner and very merry. After dinner we broke up and I by water to Westminster to Mrs. Martin's, and there sat with her and her husband and Mrs. Burrows, the pretty, an hour or two, then to the Swan a while, and so home by water, and with my wife by and by by water as low as Greenwich, for ayre only, and so back again home to supper and to bed with great pleasure.

28th. Up and to my chamber to do some business there, and then to the office, where a while, and then by agreement to the Excise Office, where I waited all the morning for the Cofferer and Sir St. Foxe's coming, but they did not, so I and the Commissioners lost their labour and expectation of doing the business we intended. Thence home, where I find Mr. Lovett and his wife came to see us. They are a pretty couple, and she a fine bred woman. They dined with us, and Browne, the paynter, and she plays finely on the lute. My wife and I were well pleased with her company. After dinner broke up, I to the office and they abroad. All the afternoon I busy at the office, and down by water to Deptford. Walked back to Redriffe, and so home to the office again, being thoughtfull how to answer Sir W. Coventry against to-morrow in the business of the Victualling, but that I do trust to Tom Wilson, that he will be ready with a book for me to-morrow morning. So to bed, my wife telling me where she hath been to-day with my aunt Wight, and seen Mrs. Margaret Wight, and says that she is one of the beautifullest women that ever she saw in her life, the most excellent nose and mouth. They have been also to see pretty Mrs. Batelier, and conclude her to be a prettier woman than Mrs. Pierce, whom my wife led my aunt to see also this day.

29th (King's birth-day and Restauration day). Waked with the ringing of the bells all over the towne; so up before five o'clock, and to the office, where we met, and I all the morning with great trouble upon my spirit to think how I should come off in the afternoon when Sir W. Coventry did go to the Victualling office to see the state of matters there, and methinks by his doing of it without speaking to me, and only with Sir W. Pen, it must be of design to find my negligence. However, at noon I did, upon a small invitation of Sir W. Pen's, go and dine with Sir W. Coventry at his office, where great good cheer and many pleasant stories of Sir W. Coventry; but I had no pleasure in them. However, I had last night and this morning made myself a little able to report how matters were, and did readily go with them after dinner to the Victualling office; and there, beyond belief, did acquit myself very well to full content; so that, beyond expectation, I got over this second rub in this business; and if ever I fall on it again, I deserve to be undone. Being broke up there, I with a merry heart home to my office, and thither my wife comes to me, to tell me, that if I would see the handsomest woman in England, I shall come home presently; and who should it be but the pretty lady of our parish, that did heretofore sit on the other side of our church, over against our gallery, that is since married; she with Mrs. Anne Jones, one of this parish, that dances finely, and Mrs. —— sister did come to see her this afternoon, and so I home and there find Creed also come to me. So there I spent most of the afternoon with them, and indeed she is a pretty black woman, her name Mrs. Horsely. But, Lord! to see how my nature could not refrain from the temptation; but I must invite them to Foxhall, to Spring Gardens, though I had freshly received minutes of a great deale of extraordinary business. However I could not helpe it, but sent them before with Creed, and I did some of my business; and so after them, and find them there, in an arbour, and had met with Mrs. Pierce, and some company with her. So here I spent *20s.* upon them, and were pretty merry. Among other things, had a fellow that imitated all manner of birds, and doggs, and hogs, with his voice, which was mighty pleasant. Staid here till night: then set Mrs. Pierce in at the New Exchange, and ourselves took coach, and so set Mrs. Horsely home, and then home ourselves, but with great trouble in the streets by bonefires, it being the King's birth-day and day of Restauration; but, Lord! to see the difference how many there were on the other side, and so few ours, the City side of the Temple, would make one wonder the difference between the temper of one sort of people and the other: and the difference among all between what they do now, and what it was the night when Monk come into the City. Such a night as that I never think to see again, nor think it can be. After I come home I was till one in the morning with Captain Cocke drawing up a contract with him intended to be offered to the Duke to-morrow, which, if it proceeds, he promises me £500.

30th. Up and to my office, there to settle some business in order to our waiting on the Duke to-day. That done to White Hall to Sir W. Coventry's chamber, where I find the Duke gone out with the King to-day on hunting. So after some discourse with him, I by water to Westminster, and there drew a draught of an order for my Lord Treasurer to sign for my having some little tallys made me in lieu of two great ones, of £2,000 each, to enable me to pay small sums therewith. I shewed it to Sir R. Long and had his approbation, and so to Sir Ph. Warwicke's, and did give it him to get signed. So home to my office, and there did business. By and by toward noon word is brought me that my father and my sister are come. I expected them to-day, but not so soon. I to them, and am heartily glad to see them, especially my father, who, poor man, looks very well, and hath rode up this journey on horseback very well, only his eyesight and hearing is very bad. I staid and dined with them, my wife being gone by coach to Barnet, with W. Hewer and Mercer, to meet them, and they did come Ware way. After dinner I left them to dress themselves and I abroad by appointment to my Lord Ashly, who, it is strange to see, how prettily he dissembles his favour to Yeabsly's business, which none in the world could mistrust only I, that am privy to his being bribed. Thence to White Hall, and there staid till the Council was up, with Creed expecting a meeting of Tangier to end Yeabsly's business, but we could not procure it. So I to my Lord Treasurer's and got my warrant, and then to Lovett's, but find nothing done there. So home and did a little business at the office, and so down by water to Deptford and back again home late, and having signed some papers and given order in business, home, where my wife is come home, and so to supper with my father, and mighty pleasant we were, and my wife mighty kind to him and Pall, and so after supper to bed, myself being sleepy, and my right eye still very sore, as it has been now about five days or six, which puts me out of tune. To-night my wife tells me newes has been brought her that Balty's wife is brought to bed, by some fall or fit, before her time, of a great child but dead. If the woman do well we have no reason to be sorry, because his staying a little longer without a child will be better for him and her.

31st. Waked very betimes in the morning by extraordinary thunder and rain, which did keep me sleeping and waking till very late, and it being a holiday and my eye very sore, and myself having had very little sleep for a good while till nine o'clock, and so up, and so saw all my family up, and my father and sister, who is a pretty good-bodied woman, and not over thicke, as I thought she would have been, but full of freckles, and not handsome in face. And so I out by water among the ships, and to Deptford and Blackewall about business, and so home and to dinner with my father and sister and family, mighty pleasant all of us; and, among other things, with a sparrow that our Mercer hath brought up now for three weeks, which is so tame that it flies up and down, and upon the table, and eats and pecks, and do every thing so pleasantly, that we are mightily pleased with it. After dinner I to my papers and accounts of this month to sett all straight, it being a publique Fast-day appointed to pray for the good successe of the fleete. But it is a pretty thing to consider how little a matter they make of this keeping of a Fast, that it was not so much as declared time enough to be read in the churches the last Sunday; but ordered by proclamation since: I suppose upon some sudden newes of the Dutch being come out. To my accounts and settled them clear; but to my grief find myself poorer than I was the last by near £20, by reason of my being forced to return £50 to Downing, the smith, which he had presented me with. However, I am well contented, finding myself yet to be worth £5,200. Having done, to supper with my wife, and then to finish the writing fair of my accounts, and so to bed. This day come to town Mr. Homewood, and I took him home in the evening to my chamber, and discoursed with him about my business of the Victualling, which I have a mind to employ him in, and he is desirous of also, but do very ingenuously declare he understands it not so well as other things, and desires to be informed in the nature of it before he attempts it, which I like well, and so I carried him to Mr. Gibson to discourse with him about it, and so home again to my accounts.[1] Thus ends this month, with my mind oppressed by my defect in my duty of the Victualling, which lies upon me as a burden, till I get myself into a better posture therein, and hinders me and casts down my courage in every thing else that belongs to me, and the jealousy I have of Sir W. Coventry's being displeased with me about it; but I hope in a little time to remedy all. As to publique business; by late tidings of the French fleete being come to Rochelle (how true, though, I know not) our fleete is divided; Prince Rupert being gone with about thirty ships to the Westward as is conceived to meet the French, to hinder their coming to join with the Dutch. My Lord Duke of Albemarle lies in the Downes with the rest, and intends presently to sail to the Gunfleete.

June 1st. Being prevented yesterday in meeting by reason of the fast day, we met to-day all the morning. At noon I and my father, wife and sister, dined at Aunt Wight's here hard by at Mr. Woolly's, upon sudden warning, they being to go out of town to-morrow. Here dined the faire Mrs. Margaret Wight, who is a very fine lady, but the cast of her eye, got only by an ill habit, do her much wrong and her hands are bad; but she hath the face of a noble Roman lady. After dinner my uncle and Woolly and I out into their yarde, to talke about what may be done hereafter to all our profits by prize-goods, which did give us reason to lament the losse of the opportunity of the last yeare, which, if we were as wise as we are now, and at the peaceable end of all those troubles that we met with, all might have been such a hit as will never come again in this age, and so I do really believe it. Thence home to my office and there did much business, and at night home to my father to supper and to bed.

[1] In the margin of the MS. is this note: "This of Mr. Homewood ought to come in upon the first of June."

2nd. Up, and to the office, where certain newes is brought us of a letter come to the King this morning from the Duke of Albemarle, dated yesterday at eleven o'clock, as they were sailing to the Gunfleete, that they were in sight of the Dutch fleete, and were fitting themselves to fight them; so that they are, ere this, certainly engaged; besides, several do averr they heard the guns all yesterday in the afternoon. This put us at the Board into a tosse. Presently come orders for our sending away to the fleete a recruite of 200 soldiers. So I rose from the table, and to the Victualling-office, and thence upon the River among several vessels, to consider of the sending them away; and lastly, down to Greenwich, and there appointed two yachts to be ready for them; and did order the soldiers to march to Blackewall. Having set all things in order against the next flood, I went on shore with Captain Erwin at Greenwich, and into the Parke, and there we could hear the guns from the fleete most plainly. Thence he and I to the King's Head and there bespoke a dish of steaks for our dinner about four o'clock. While that was doing, we walked to the water-side, and there seeing the King and Duke come down in their barge to Greenwich-house, I to them, and did give them an account [of] what I was doing. They went up to the Parke to hear the guns of the fleete go off. All our hopes now are that Prince Rupert with his fleete is coming back and will be with the fleete this even: a message being sent to him to that purpose on Wednesday last; and a return is come from him this morning, that he did intend to sail from St. Ellen's point about four in the afternoon on Wednesday [Friday], which was yesterday; which gives us great hopes, the wind being very fair, that he is with them this even, and the fresh going off of the guns makes us believe the same. After dinner, having nothing else to do till flood, I went and saw Mrs. Daniel, to whom I did not tell that the fleets were engaged, because of her husband, who is in the R. Charles. Very pleasant with her half an hour, and so away and down to Blackewall, and there saw the soldiers (who were by this time gotten most of them drunk) shipped off. But, Lord! to see how the poor fellows kissed their wives and sweethearts in that simple manner at their going off, and shouted, and let off their guns, was strange sport. In the evening come up the River the Katharine yacht, Captain Fazeby, who hath brought over my Lord of Alesbury[1] and Sir Thomas Liddall[2] (with a very pretty daughter, and in a pretty travelling-dress) from Flanders, who saw the Dutch fleete on Thursday, and ran from them; but from that houre to this hath not heard one gun, nor any newes of any fight. Having put the soldiers on board, I home and wrote what I had to write by the post, and so home to supper and to bed, it being late.

3rd (Lord's-day; Whit-sunday). Up, and by water to White Hall, and there met with Mr. Coventry, who tells me the only news from the fleete is brought by Captain Elliott, of The Portland, which, by being run on board by The Guernsey, was disabled from staying abroad; so is come in to Aldbrough. That he saw one of the Dutch great ships blown up, and three on fire. That they begun to fight on Friday; and at his coming into port, he could make another ship of the King's coming in, which he judged to be the Rupert: that he knows of no other hurt to our ships. With this good newes I home by water again, and to church in the sermon-time, and with great joy told it my fellows in the pew. So home after church time to dinner, and after dinner my father, wife, sister, and Mercer by water to Woolwich, while I walked by land, and saw the Exchange as full of people, and hath been all this noon as of any other day, only for newes. I to St. Margeret's, Westminster, and there saw at church my pretty Betty Michell, and thence to the Abbey, and so to Mrs. Martin, and there did what je voudrais avec her. . . . So by and by he come in, and after some discourse with him I away to White Hall, and there met with this bad newes farther, that the Prince come to Dover but at ten o'clock last night, and there heard nothing of a fight; so that we are defeated of all our hopes of his helpe to the fleete. It is also reported by some Victuallers that the Duke of Albemarle and Holmes their flags were shot down, and both fain to come to anchor to

[1] Robert, Lord Bruce, succeeded his father as Earl of Elgin, December 21st, 1663; created Earl of Aylesbury, March 18th, 1665. Died October 20th, 1685.

[2] Of Ravensworth Castle, Durham, succeeded his grandfather, the first baronet, 1650. He had three daughters. Died 1697. — B.

renew their rigging and sails. A letter is also come this afternoon, from Harman in the Henery; which is she [that] was taken by Elliott for the Rupert; that being fallen into the body of the Dutch fleete, he made his way through them, was set on by three fire-ships one after another, got two of them off, and disabled the third; was set on fire himself; upon which many of his men leapt into the sea and perished; among others, the parson first. Have lost above 100 men, and a good many women (God knows what is become of Balty), and at last quenched his own fire and got to Aldbrough; being, as all say, the greatest hazard that ever any ship escaped, and as bravely managed by him. The mast of the third fire-ship fell into their ship on fire, and hurt Harman's leg, which makes him lame now, but not dangerous. I to Sir G. Carteret, who told me there hath been great bad management in all this; that the King's orders that went on Friday for calling back the Prince, were sent but by the ordinary post on Wednesday; and come to the Prince his hands but on Friday; and then, instead of sailing presently, he stays till four in the evening. And that which is worst of all, the Hampshire, laden with merchants' money, come from the Straights, set out with or but just before the fleete, and was in the Downes by five in the clock yesterday morning; and the Prince with his fleete come to Dover but at ten of the clock at night. This is hard to answer, if it be true. This puts great astonishment into the King, and Duke, and Court, every body being out of countenance. So meeting Creed, he and I by coach to Hide Parke alone to talke of these things, and do blesse God that my Lord Sandwich was not here at this time to be concerned in a business like to be so misfortunate. It was a pleasant thing to consider how fearfull I was of being seen with Creed all this afternoon, for fear of people's thinking that by our relation to my Lord Sandwich we should be making ill construction of the Prince's failure. But, God knows, I am heartily sorry for the sake of the whole nation, though, if it were not for that, it would not be amisse to have these high blades find some checke to their presumption and their disparaging of as good men. Thence set him down in Covent Guarden and so home by the 'Change, which is full of people still, and all talk highly of the failure of the Prince in not making more haste after his instructions did come, and of our managements here in not giving it sooner and with more care and oftener. Thence. After supper to bed.

4th. Up, and with Sir J. Minnes and Sir W. Pen to White Hall in the latter's coach, where, when we come, we find the Duke at St. James's, whither he is lately gone to lodge. So walking through the Parke we saw hundreds of people listening at the Gravell-pits,[1] and to and again in the Parke to hear the guns, and I saw a letter, dated last night, from Strowd, Governor of Dover Castle, which says that the Prince come thither the night before with his fleete, but that for the guns which we writ that we heard, it is only a mistake for thunder;[2] and so far as to yesterday it is a miraculous thing that we all Friday, and Saturday and yesterday, did hear every where most plainly the guns go off, and yet at Deale and Dover to last night they did not hear one word of a fight, nor think they heard one gun. This, added to what I have set down before the other day about the Katharine, makes room for a great dispute in philosophy, how we should hear it and they not, the same wind that brought it to us being the same that should bring it to them: but so it is. Major Halsey, however (he was sent down on purpose to hear newes), did bring newes this morning that he did see the Prince and his fleete at nine of the clock yesterday morning, four or five leagues to sea behind the Goodwin, so that by the hearing of the guns this morning we conclude he is come to the fleete. After wayting upon the Duke, Sir W. Pen (who was commanded to go to-night by water down to Harwich, to dispatch away all the ships he can) and I home, drinking two bottles of Cocke ale in the streete in his new fine coach, where no sooner come, but newes is brought me of a couple of men come to speak with me from the fleete; so I down, and who should it be but Mr. Daniel, all muffled up, and his face as black as the chimney, and covered with dirt, pitch, and tarr, and powder, and muffled with dirty clouts, and his right eye

[1] Kensington.

[2] Evelyn was in his garden when he heard the guns, and he at once set off to Rochester and the coast, but he found that nothing had been heard at Deal (see his "Diary," June 1st, 1666).

stopped with okum. He is come last night at five o'clock from the fleete, with a comrade of his that hath endangered another eye. They were set on shore at Harwich this morning, and at two o'clock, in a catch with about twenty more wounded men from the Royall Charles. They being able to ride, took post about three this morning, and were here between eleven and twelve. I went presently into the coach with them, and carried them to Somerset-House-stairs, and there took water (all the world gazing upon us, and concluding it to be newes from the fleete, and every body's face appeared expecting of newes) to the Privy-stairs, and left them at Mr. Coventry's lodging (he, though, not being there); and so I into the Parke to the King, and told him my Lord Generall was well the last night at five o'clock, and the Prince come with his fleete and joyned with his about seven. The King was mightily pleased with this newes, and so took me by the hand and talked a little of it. Giving him the best account I could; and then he bid me to fetch the two seamen to him, he walking into the house. So I went and fetched the seamen into the Vane room to him, and there he heard the whole account.

THE FIGHT.

How we found the Dutch fleete at anchor on Friday half seas over, between Dunkirke and Ostend, and made them let slip their anchors. They about ninety, and we less than sixty. We fought them, and put them to the run, till they met with about sixteen sail of fresh ships, and so bore up again. The fight continued till night, and then again the next morning from five till seven at night. And so, too, yesterday morning they begun again, and continued till about four o'clock, they chasing us for the most part of Saturday and yesterday, we flying from them. The Duke himself, then those people were put into the catch, and by and by spied the Prince's fleete coming, upon which De Ruyter called a little council (being in chase at this time of us), and thereupon their fleete divided into two squadrons; forty in one, and about thirty in the other (the fleete being at first about ninety, but by one accident or other, supposed to be lessened to about seventy); the bigger to follow the Duke, the less to meet the Prince.[1] But the Prince come up with the Generall's fleete, and the Dutch come together again and bore towards their own coast, and we with them; and now what the consequence of this day will be, at that time fighting, we know not. The Duke was forced to come to anchor on Friday, having lost his sails and rigging. No particular person spoken of to be hurt but Sir W. Clerke, who hath lost his leg, and bore it bravely. The Duke himself had a little hurt in his thigh, but signified little. The King did pull out of his pocket about twenty pieces in gold, and did give it Daniel for himself and his companion; and so parted, mightily pleased with the account he did give him of the fight, and the successe it ended with, of the Prince's coming, though it seems the Duke did give way again and again. The King did give order for care to be had of Mr. Daniel and his companion; and so we parted from him, and then met the Duke [of York], and gave him the same account: and so broke up, and I left them going to the surgeon's and I myself by water to the 'Change, and to several people did give account of the business. So home about four o'clock to dinner, and was followed by several people to be told the newes, and good newes it is. God send we may hear a good issue of this day's business! After I had eat something I walked to Gresham College, where I heard my Lord Bruncker was, and there got a promise of the receipt of the fine varnish, which I shall be glad to have. Thence back with Mr. Hooke to my house and there lent some of my tables of naval matters, the names of rigging and the timbers about a ship, in order to Dr. Wilkins' book coming out about the Universal Language.[2] Thence, he being gone, to the Crown, behind the 'Change, and there supped at the club

[1] Sir Joseph Jordan, in a letter to Sir William Penn, dated "Royal Oak, June 5th," 1666, writes: "It is believed, that if Prince Rupert had been with us the first day, the enemy could not have escaped. But we must submit to the all-seeing Providence, who knows what is best for us. It is my part to praise my God that hath delivered me and this ship wonderfully, after so many days' battle; the greatest passes, I think, that ever was fought at sea" (Penn's "Memorials of Sir William Penn," ii., 390).

[2] Bishop Wilkins's "Essay towards a Real Character and a Philosophical Language" was published in 1668.

with my Lord Bruncker, Sir G. Ent, and others of Gresham College; and all our discourse is of this fight at sea, and all are doubtful of the successe, and conclude all had been lost if the Prince had not come in, they having chased us the greatest part of Saturday and Sunday. Thence with my Lord Bruncker and Creed by coach to White Hall, where fresh letters are come from Harwich, where the Gloucester, Captain Clerke,[1] is come in, and says that on Sunday night upon coming in of the Prince, the Duke did fly; but all this day they have been fighting; therefore they did face again, to be sure. Captain Bacon[2] of The Bristoll is killed. They cry up Jenings[3] of The Ruby, and Saunders[4] of The Sweepstakes. They condemn mightily Sir Thomas Teddiman for a coward, but with what reason time must shew. Having heard all this Creed and I walked into the Parke till 9 or 10 at night, it being fine moonshine, discoursing of the unhappinesse of our fleete, what it would have been if the Prince had not come in, how much the Duke hath failed of what he was so presumptuous of, how little we deserve of God Almighty to give us better fortune, how much this excuses all that was imputed to my Lord Sandwich, and how much more he is a man fit to be trusted with all those matters than those that now command, who act by nor with any advice, but rashly and without any order. How bad we are at intelligence that should give the Prince no sooner notice of any thing but let him come to Dover without notice of any fight, or where the fleete were, or any thing else, nor give the Duke any notice that he might depend upon the Prince's reserve; and lastly, of how good use all may be to checke our pride and presumption in adventuring upon hazards upon unequal force against a people that can fight, it seems now, as well as we, and that will not be discouraged by any losses, but that they will rise again. Thence by water home, and to supper (my father, wife, and sister having been at Islington to-day at Pitt's) and to bed.

5th. Up, and to the office, where all the morning, expecting every houre more newes of the fleete and the

[1] Captain Robert Clark.
[2] Captain Philemon Bacon.
[3] Captain William Jennings, knighted soon after this engagement.
[4] Captain Francis Sanders.

issue of yesterday's fight, but nothing come. At noon, though I should have dined with my Lord Mayor[1] and Aldermen at an entertainment of Commissioner Taylor's, yet it being a time of expectation of the successe of the fleete, I did not go, but dined at home, and after dinner by water down to Deptford (and Woolwich, where I had not been since I lodged there, and methinks the place has grown natural to me), and thence down to Longreach, calling on all the ships in the way, seeing their condition for sayling, and what they want. Home about 11 of the clock, and so eat a bit and to bed, having received no manner of newes this day, but of The Rainbow's being put in from the fleete, maimed as the other ships are, and some say that Sir W. Clerke is dead of his leg being cut off.

6th. Up betimes, and vexed with my people for having a key taken out of the chamber doors and nobody knew where it was, as also with my boy for not being ready as soon as I, though I called him, whereupon I boxed him soundly, and then to my business at the office and on the Victualling Office, and thence by water to St. James's, whither he [the Duke of York] is now gone, it being a monthly fast-day for the plague. There we all met, and did our business as usual with the Duke, and among other things had Captain Cocke's proposal of East country goods read, brought by my Lord Bruncker, which I make use of as a monkey do the cat's foot. Sir W. Coventry did much oppose it, and it's likely it will not do; so away goes my hopes of £500. Thence after the Duke into the Parke, walking through to White Hall, and there every body listening for guns, but none heard, and every creature is now overjoyed and concludes upon very good grounds that the Dutch are beaten because we have heard no guns nor no newes of our fleete. By and by walking a little further, Sir Philip Frowde[2] did meet the Duke with an expresse to Sir W. Coventry (who was by) from Captain Taylor, the Storekeeper at Harwich, being the narration of Captain Hayward of The Dunkirke; who gives a very serious account, how

[1] Sir Thomas Bludworth.

[2] A loyal officer in the army of Charles I., afterwards secretary to Anne Hyde, Duchess of York. His grandson, of the same name, was author of some plays and poems, and died in 1738.—B.

upon Monday the two fleetes fought all day till seven at night, and then the whole fleete of Dutch did betake themselves to a very plain flight, and never looked back again. That Sir Christopher Mings is wounded in the leg; that the Generall is well. That it is conceived reasonably, that of all the Dutch fleete, which, with what recruits they had, come to one hundred sayle, there is not above fifty got home; and of them, few if any of their flags. And that little Captain Bell, in one of the fire-ships, did at the end of the day fire a ship of 70 guns. We were all so overtaken with this good newes, that the Duke ran with it to the King, who was gone to chappell, and there all the Court was in a hubbub, being rejoiced over head and ears in this good newes. Away go I by coach to the New Exchange, and there did spread this good newes a little, though I find it had broke out before. And so home to our own church, it being the common Fast-day, and it was just before sermon; but, Lord! how all the people in the church stared upon me to see me whisper to Sir John Minnes and my Lady Pen. Anon I saw people stirring and whispering below, and by and by comes up the sexton from my Lady Ford to tell me the newes (which I had brought), being now sent into the church by Sir W. Batten in writing, and handed from pew to pew. But that which pleased me as much as the newes, was, to have the fair Mrs. Middleton at our church, who indeed is a very beautiful lady. Here after sermon comes to our office 40 people almost of all sorts and qualities to hear the newes, which I took great delight to tell them. Then home and found my wife at dinner, not knowing of my being at church, and after dinner my father and she out to Hales's, where my father is to begin to sit to-day for his picture, which I have a desire to have. I all the afternoon at home doing some business, drawing up my vowes for the rest of the yeare to Christmas; but, Lord! to see in what a condition of happiness I am, if I would but keepe myself so; but my love of pleasure is such, that my very soul is angry with itself for my vanity in so doing. Anon took coach and to Hales's, but he was gone out, and my father and wife gone. So I to Lovett's, and there to my trouble saw plainly that my project of varnished books will not take, it not keeping colour, not being able to take polishing upon a single paper. Thence home, and my father and wife not coming in, I proceeded with my coach to take a little ayre as far as Bow all alone, and there turned back and home; but before I got home, the bonefires were lighted all the towne over, and I going through Crouched Friars, seeing Mercer at her mother's gate, stopped, and 'light, and into her mother's, the first time I ever was there, and find all my people, father and all, at a very fine supper at W. Hewer's lodging, very neatly, and to my great pleasure. After supper, into his chamber, which is mighty fine with pictures and every thing else, very curious, which pleased me exceedingly. Thence to the gate, with the women all about me, and Mrs. Mercer's son had provided a great many serpents, and so I made the women all fire some serpents. By and by comes in our faire neighbour, Mrs. Turner, and two neighbour's daughters, Mrs. Tite, the elder of whom, a long red-nosed silly jade; the younger, a pretty black girle, and the merriest sprightly jade that ever I saw. With them idled away the whole night till twelve at night at the bonefire in the streets. Some of the people thereabouts going about with musquets, and did give me two or three vollies of their musquets, I giving them a crowne to drink; and so home. Mightily pleased with this happy day's newes, and the more, because confirmed by Sir Daniel Harvy,[1] who was in the whole fight with the Generall, and tells me that there appear but thirty-six in all of the Dutch fleete left at the end of the voyage when they run home. The joy of the City was this night exceeding great.

7th. Up betimes, and to my office about business (Sir W. Coventry having sent me word that he is gone down to the fleete to see how matters stand, and to be back again speedily); and with the same expectation of congratulating ourselves with the victory that I had yesterday. But my Lord Bruncker and Sir T. H.[2] that come from Court, tell me quite contrary newes, which astonishes me: that is to say, that we are beaten, lost many ships and good commanders; have not taken one ship of the enemy's; and so can only report ourselves a victory; nor is it certain that we

[1] Ranger of Richmond Park. He was brother-in-law to the Edward Montagu killed at Bergen. — B.

[2] Sir Thomas Harvey.

were left masters of the field. But, above all, that The Prince run on shore upon the Galloper, and there stuck; was endeavoured to be fetched off by the Dutch, but could not; and so they burned her; and Sir G. Ascue is taken prisoner, and carried into Holland. This newes do much trouble me, and the thoughts of the ill consequences of it, and the pride and presumption that brought us to it. At noon to the 'Change, and there find the discourse of towne, and their countenances much changed; but yet not very plain. So home to dinner all alone, my father and people being gone all to Woolwich to see the launching of the new ship The Greenwich, built by Chr. Pett. I left alone with little Mrs. Tooker, whom I kept with me in my chamber all the afternoon, and did what I would with her. By and by comes Mr. Wayth to me; and discoursing of our ill successe, he tells me plainly from Captain Page's own mouth (who hath lost his arm in the fight), that the Dutch did pursue us two hours before they left us, and then they suffered us to go on homewards, and they retreated towards their coast: which is very sad newes. Then to my office and anon to White Hall, late, to the Duke of York to see what commands he hath and to pray a meeting to-morrow for Tangier in behalf of Mr. Yeabsly, which I did do and do find the Duke much damped in his discourse, touching the late fight, and all the Court talk sadly of it. The Duke did give me several letters he had received from the fleete, and Sir W. Coventry and Sir W. Pen, who are gone down thither, for me to pick out some works to be done for the setting out the fleete again; and so I took them home with me, and was drawing out an abstract of them till midnight. And as to newes, I do find great reason to think that we are beaten in every respect, and that we are the losers. The Prince upon the Galloper, where both the Royall Charles and Royall Katharine had come twice aground, but got off. The Essex carried into Holland; the Swiftsure missing (Sir William Barkeley) ever since the beginning of the fight. Captains Bacon, Tearne, Wood, Mootham, Whitty, and Coppin,[1] slayne. The Duke of Albemarle writes, that he

[1] John Coppin (see April 15th, 1660). He commanded the "St. George," a second-rate, in this bloody conflict.

never fought with worse officers in his life, not above twenty of them behaving themselves like men. Sir William Clerke lost his leg; and in two days died. The Loyall George, Seven Oakes, and Swiftsure, are still missing, having never, as the Generall writes himself, engaged with them. It was as great an alteration to find myself required to write a sad letter instead of a triumphant one to my Lady Sandwich this night, as ever on any occasion I had in my life. So late home and to bed.

8th. Up very betimes and to attend the Duke of York by order, all of us to report to him what the works are that are required of us and to divide among us, wherein I have taken a very good share, and more than I can perform, I doubt. Thence to the Exchequer about some Tangier businesses, and then home, where to my very great joy I find Balty come home without any hurt, after the utmost imaginable danger he hath gone through in the Henery, being upon the quarter-deck with Harman all the time; and for which service Harman I heard this day commended most seriously and most eminently by the Duke of Yorke. As also the Duke did do most utmost right to Sir Thomas Teddiman, of whom a scandal was raised, but without cause, he having behaved himself most eminently brave all the whole fight, and to extraordinary great service and purpose, having given Trump himself such a broadside as was hardly ever given to any ship. Mings is shot through the face, and into the shoulder, where the bullet is lodged. Young Holmes[1] is also ill wounded, and Atber in The Rupert. Balty tells me the case of The Henery; and it was, indeed, most extraordinary sad and desperate. After dinner Balty and I to my office, and there talked a great deal of this fight; and I am mightily pleased in him and have great content in, and hopes of his doing well. Thence out to White Hall to a Committee for Tangier, but it met not. But, Lord! to see how melancholy the Court is, under the thoughts of this last overthrow (for so it is), instead of a victory, so much and so unreasonably expected. Thence, the Committee not meeting, Creed and I down the river as low as Sir W. War-

[1] Brother of Sir Robert Holmes, and afterwards Sir John Holmes. He married Margaret Lowther.

ren's, with whom I did motion a business that may be of profit to me, about buying some lighters to send down to the fleete, wherein he will assist me. So back again, he and I talking of the late ill management of this fight, and of the ill management of fighting at all against so great a force bigger than ours, and so to the office, where we parted, but with this satisfaction that we hear the Swiftsure, Sir W. Barkeley, is come in safe to the Nore, after her being absent ever since the beginning of the fight, wherein she did not appear at all from beginning to end. But wherever she has been, they say she is arrived there well, which I pray God however may be true. At the office late, doing business, and so home to supper and to bed.

9th. Up, and to St. James's, there to wait on the Duke of Yorke, and had discourse with him about several businesses of the fleete. But, Lord! to see how the Court is divided about The Swiftsure and The Essex's being safe. And wagers and odds laid on both sides. I did tell the Duke how Sir W. Batten did tell me this morning that he was sure the Swiftsure is safe. This put them all in a great joy and certainty of it, but this I doubt will prove nothing. Thence to White Hall in expectation of a meeting of Tangier, and we did industriously labour to have it this morning; but we could not get a fifth person there, so after much pains and thoughts on my side on behalfe of Yeabsly, we were fain to breake up. But, Lord! to see with what patience Lord Ashly did stay all the morning to get a Committee, little thinking that I know the reason of his willingnesse. So I home to dinner and back again to White Hall, and, being come thither a little too soon, went to Westminster Hall, and bought a payre of gloves, and to see how people do take this late fight at sea, and I find all give over the thoughts of it as a victory and to reckon it a great overthrow. So to White Hall, and there when we were come all together in certain expectation of doing our business to Yeabsly's full content, and us that were his friends, my Lord Peterborough (whether through some difference between him and my Lord Ashly, or him and me or Povy, or through the falsenesse of Creed, I know not) do bring word that the Duke of Yorke (who did expressly bid me wait at the Committee for the dispatch of the business) would not have us go forward in this business of allowing the losse of the ships till Sir G. Carteret and Sir W. Coventry were come to towne, which was the very thing indeed which we would have avoided. This being told us, we broke up doing nothing, to my great discontent, though I said nothing, and afterwards I find by my Lord Ashly's discourse to me that he is troubled mightily at it, and indeed it is a great abuse of him and of the whole Commissioners that nothing of that nature can be done without Sir G. Carteret or Sir W. Coventry. No sooner was the Committee up, and I going [through] the Court homeward, but I am told Sir W. Coventry is come to town; so I to his chamber, and there did give him an account how matters go in our office, and with some content I parted from him, after we had discoursed several things of the haste requisite to be made in getting the fleete out again and the manner of doing it. But I do not hear that he is at all pleased or satisfied with the late fight; but he tells me more newes of our suffering, by the death of one or two captains more than I knew before. But he do give over the thoughts of the safety of The Swiftsure or Essex. Thence homewards, landed at the Old Swan, and there find my pretty Betty Michell and her husband at their doore in Thames Streete, which I was glad to find, and went into their shop, and they made me drink some of their strong water, the first time I was ever with them there. I do exceedingly love her. After sitting a little and talking with them about several things at great distance I parted and home to my business late. But I am to observe how the drinking of some strong water did immediately put my eyes into a fit of sorenesse again as they were the other day. I mean my right eye only. Late at night I had an account brought me by Sir W. Warren that he has gone through four lighters for me, which pleases me very well. So home to bed, much troubled with our disappointment at the Tangier Committee.

10th (Lord's day). Up very betimes, and down the river to Deptford, and did a good deale of business in sending away and directing several things to the Fleete. That being done, back to London to my office, and there at my office till after Church time fitting some notes to carry to Sir W. Coventry in the afternoon. At noon home to dinner, where my cozen Joyces, both of them, they and their wives and little Will, come by invitation to dinner to me, and I had a good dinner for them; but, Lord! how sicke was I of W. Joyce's company, both the impertinencies of it and his ill manners before me at my table to his wife, which I could hardly forbear taking notice of; but being at my table and for his wife's sake, I did, though I will prevent his giving me the like occasion again at my house I will warrant him. After dinner I took leave and by water to White Hall, and there spent all the afternoon in the Gallery, till the Council was up, to speake with Sir W. Coventry. Walking here I met with Pierce the surgeon, who is lately come from the fleete, and tells me that all the commanders, officers, and even the common seamen do condemn every part of the late conduct of the Duke of Albemarle: both in his fighting at all, in his manner of fighting, running among them in his retreat, and running the ships on ground; so as nothing can be worse spoken of. That Holmes, Spragg, and Smith do all the business, and the old and wiser commanders nothing. So as Sir Thomas Teddiman (whom the King and all the world speak well of) is mightily discontented, as being wholly slighted. He says we lost more after the Prince come, than before too. The Prince was so maimed, as to be forced to be towed home. He says all the fleete confess their being chased home by the Dutch; and yet the body of the Dutch that did it, was not above forty sayle at most. And yet this put us into the fright, as to bring all our ships on ground. He says, however, that the Duke of Albemarle is as high almost as ever, and pleases himself to think that he hath given the Dutch their bellies full, without sense of what he hath lost us; and talks how he knows now the way to beat them. But he says, that even Smith himself, one of his creatures, did himself condemn the late conduct from the beginning to the end. He tells me further, how the Duke of Yorke is wholly given up to his new mistresse, my Lady Denham, going at noon-day with all his gentlemen with him to visit her in Scotland Yard;[1] she

[1] Margaret Brook, married to Sir John Denham, May 25th, 1665. George Brook, third son of William Brook, Lord Cobham, was attainted and executed for his share in Raleigh's plot. He left a son, William Brook, who, having been restored in blood, and made a Knight of the

declaring she will not be his mistresse, as Mrs. Price,[1] to go up and down the Privy-stairs, but will be owned publicly; and so she is. Mr. Bruncker, it seems, was the pimp to bring it about, and my Lady Castlemaine, who designs thereby to fortify herself by the Duke; there being a falling-out the other day between the King and her: on this occasion, the Queene, in ordinary talke before the ladies in her drawing-room, did say to my Lady Castlemaine that she feared the King did take cold, by staying so late abroad at her house. She answered before them all, that he did not stay so late abroad with her, for he went betimes thence (though he do not before one, two, or three in the morning), but must stay somewhere else. The King then coming in and overhearing, did whisper in the eare aside, and told her she was a bold impertinent woman, and bid her to be gone out of the Court, and not come again till he sent for her; which she did presently, and went to a lodging in the Pell Mell, and kept there two or three days, and then sent to the King to know whether she might send for her things away out of her house. The King sent to her, she must first come and view them: and so she come, and the King went to her, and all friends again. He tells me

Bath, espoused Penelope, third daughter of Sir Moyses Hill, of Hillsborough Castle, in Ireland, the ancestor of the Marquises of Downshire, by whom he had issue three daughters: *first*, Hill, who became the wife of Sir William Boothby; the *second*, Frances, described, on the lettering of her engraved portrait, as "Lady Whitmore." She was the wife of Sir Thomas Whitmore, of Bridgenorth, second son of Sir Thomas Whitmore, of Apley, Bart. Her daughter, Frances, married William, grandson of Sir George Whitmore, of Balmes, mentioned by Pepys. See Dryden's epitaph on her in his "Works" (Scott's edit., vol. xi., p. 150): the *third* was Lady Denham.

Their mother, Lady Brook, surviving her husband, re-married Edward Russell, youngest son of Francis, fifth Earl of Bedford, whose sister was Countess of Bristol. Hence the relationship, or rather the connection, between the two families; for Hamilton ("Mém. de Grammont") mentioning that "*les Demoiselles Brook*" assisted at all Lord Bristol's fêtes, calls them "*ses parents*." — B.

The marriage of Sir John Denham to Margaret Brook took place in Westminster Abbey.

[1] Henrietta Maria Price, daughter of Colonel Sir Herbert Price, Bart., Master of the Household to Queen Henrietta Maria, and afterwards to King Charles II., maid of honour to the queen, who figures far from creditably in the Grammont memoirs.

she did, in her anger, say she would be even with the King, and print his letters to her. So putting all together, we are and are like to be in a sad condition. We are endeavouring to raise money by borrowing it of the City; but I do not think the City will lend a farthing. By and by the Council broke up, and I spoke with Sir W. Coventry about business, with whom I doubt not in a little time to be mighty well, when I shall appear to mind my business again as I used to do, which by the grace of God I will do. Gone from him I endeavoured to find out Sir G. Carteret, and at last did at Mr. Ashburnham's, in the Old Palace Yarde, and thence he and I stepped out and walked an houre in the church-yarde, under Henry the Seventh's Chappell, he being lately come from the fleete; and tells me, as I hear from every body else, that the management in the late fight was bad from top to bottom. That several said this would not have been if my Lord Sandwich had had the ordering of it. Nay, he tells me that certainly had my Lord Sandwich had the misfortune to have done as they have done, the King could not have saved him. There is, too, nothing but dis-content among the officers; and all the old experienced men are slighted. He tells me to my question (but as a great secret), that the dividing of the fleete did proceed first from a proposition from the fleete, though agreed to hence. But he confesses it arose from want of due intelli-gence, which he confesses we do want. He do, however, call the fleete's retreat on Sunday a very honourable retreat, and that the Duke of Albemarle did do well in it, and would have been well if he had done it sooner, rather than venture the loss of the fleete and crown, as he must have done if the Prince had not come. He was surprised when I told him I heard that the King did intend to borrow some money of the City, and would know who had spoke of it to me; I told him Sir Ellis Layton[1] this afternoon. He says it is a dangerous discourse, for that the City certainly will not be invited to do it, and then for the King to ask it and be denied, will be the beginning of our sorrow. He seems to fear we shall all fall to pieces among ourselves. This evening we hear that Sir Christopher Mings is dead of his

[1] Sir Ellis Layton or Elisha Leighton (see note, Jan. 11th, 1663-64).

late wounds; and Sir W. Coventry did commend him to me in a most extraordinary manner. But this day, after three days' trial in vain, and the hazard of the spoiling of the ship in lying till next spring, besides the disgrace of it, newes is brought that the Loyall London is launched at Deptford. Having talked thus much with Sir G. Carteret we parted there, and I home by water, taking in my boat with me young Michell and my Betty his wife, meeting them accidentally going to look a boat. I set them down at the Old Swan and myself went through bridge to the Tower, and so home, and after supper to bed.

11th. Up, and down by water to Sir W. Warren's (the first time I was in his new house on the other side the water since he enlarged it) to discourse about our lighters that he hath bought for me, and I hope to get £100 by this jobb. Having done with him I took boat again (being mightily struck with a woman in a hat, a seaman's mother,[1] that stood on the key) and home, where at the office all the morning with Sir W. Coventry and some others of our board hiring of fireships, and Sir W. Coventry begins to see my pains again, which I do begin to take, and I am proud of it, and I hope shall continue it. He gone, at noon I home to dinner, and after dinner my father and wife out to the painter's to sit again, and I, with my Lady Pen and her daughter, to see Harman; whom we find lame in bed. His bones of his anckle are broke, but he hopes to do well soon; and a fine person by his discourse he seems to be and my hearty [friend]; and he did plainly tell me that at the Council of War before the fight, it was against his reason to begin the fight then, and the reasons of most sober men there, the wind being such, and we to windward, that they could not use their lower tier of guns, which was a very sad thing for us to have the honour and weal of the nation ventured so foolishly. I left them there, and walked to Deptford, reading in Walsingham's Manual, a very good book, and there met with Sir W. Batten and my Lady at Uthwayt's. Here I did much business and yet had some little mirthe with my Lady, and anon we all come up together to our office, where I was very late doing much

[1] Mother or mauther, a wench.

business. Late comes Sir J. Bankes to see me, and tells me that coming up from Rochester he overtook three or four hundred seamen, and he believes every day they come flocking from the fleete in like numbers; which is a sad neglect there, when it will be impossible to get others, and we have little reason to think that these will return presently again. He gone, I to end my letters to-night, and then home to supper and to bed.

12th. Up, and to the office, where we sat all the morning. At noon to dinner, and then to White Hall in hopes of a meeting of Tangier about Yeabsly's business, but it could not be obtained, Sir G. Carteret nor Sir W. Coventry being able to be there, which still vexes [me] to see the poor man forced still to attend, as also being desirous to see what my profit is, and get it. Walking here in the galleries I find the Ladies of Honour dressed in their riding garbs, with coats and doublets with deep skirts, just for all the world like mine, and buttoned their doublets up the breast, with perriwigs and with hats; so that, only for a long petticoat dragging under their men's coats, nobody could take them for women in any point whatever; which was an odde sight, and a sight did not please me. It was Mrs. Wells and another fine lady that I saw thus. Thence down by water to Deptford, and there late seeing some things dispatched down to the fleete, and so home (thinking indeed to have met with Bagwell, but I did not) to write my letters very late, and so to supper and to bed.

13th. Up, and by coach to St. James's, and there did our business before the Duke as usual, having, before the Duke come out of his bed, walked in an ante-chamber with Sir H. Cholmly,[1] who tells me there are great jarrs between the Duke of Yorke and the Duke of Albemarle, about the latter's turning out one or two of the commanders put in by the Duke of Yorke. Among others, Captain Du Tell,[2] a

[1] Sir Hugh Cholmley (see note, August 6th. 1662).

[2] Charnock ("Biographia Navalis," p. 163) mentions a Sir John Du Tiel, said to have been of French extraction and a knight of Malta. The Duke of York took Captain Du Tell into his service as Yeoman of the Cellar and Cupbearer. This most improper step of the Duke of York is alluded to in the "Poems on State Affairs," vol. i., p. 36, ed. 1703:

> "Cashier the memory of Dutell, raised up
> To taste, instead of death, his Highness' cup."

See July 27th, 1666.

Frenchman, put in by the Duke of Yorke, and mightily defended by him; and is therein led by Monsieur Blancford,[1] that it seems hath the same command over the Duke of Yorke as Sir W. Coventry hath; which raises ill blood between them. And I do in several little things observe that Sir W. Coventry hath of late, by the by, reflected on the Duke of Albemarle and his captains, particularly in that of old Teddiman, who did deserve to be turned out this fight, and was so; but I heard Sir W. Coventry say that the Duke of Albemarle put in one as bad as he is in his room, and one that did as little. After we had done with the Duke of Yorke, I with others to White Hall, there to attend again a Committee of Tangier, but there was none, which vexed me to the heart, and makes me mighty doubtfull that when we have one, it will be prejudiced against poor Yeabsly and to my great disadvantage thereby, my Lord Peterborough making it his business, I perceive (whether in spite to me, whom he cannot but smell to be a friend to it, or to my Lord Ashly, I know not), to obstruct it, and seems to take delight in disappointing of us; but I shall be revenged of him. Here I staid a very great while, almost till noon, and then meeting Balty I took him with me, and to Westminster to the Exchequer about breaking of two tallys of £2,000 each into smaller tallys, which I have been endeavouring a good while, but to my trouble it will not, I fear, be done, though there be no reason against it, but only a little trouble to the clerks; but it is nothing to me of real profit at all. Thence with Balty to Hales's by coach, it being the seventh day from my making my late oathes, and by them I am at liberty to dispense with any of my oathes every seventh day after I had for the six days before going performed all my vowes. Here I find my father's picture begun, and so much to my content, that it joys my very heart to thinke that I should have his picture so well done; who, besides that he is my father, and a man that loves me, and hath ever done so, is also, at this day, one of the most carefull and innocent men in the world. Thence with mighty content homeward, and in my way at the Stockes

[1] Louis de Duras, Marquis de Blanquefort in France, who served with the English fleet as a volunteer; Earl of Feversham in 1677. See note, February 3rd, 1664-65.

did buy a couple of lobsters, and so home to dinner, where I find my wife and father had dined, and were going out to Hales's to sit there, so Balty and I alone to dinner, and in the middle of my grace, praying for a blessing upon (these his good creatures), my mind fell upon my lobsters: upon which I cried, Odd zooks! and Balty looked upon me like a man at a losse what I meant, thinking at first that I meant only that I had said the grace after meat instead of that before meat. But then I cried, what is become of my lobsters? Whereupon he run out of doors to overtake the coach, but could not, so came back again, and mighty merry at dinner to thinke of my surprize. After dinner to the Excise Office by appointment, and there find my Lord Bellasses and the Commissioners, and by and by the whole company come to dispute the business of our running so far behindhand there, and did come to a good issue in it, that is to say, to resolve upon having the debt due to us, and the Household and the Guards from the Excise stated, and so we shall come to know the worst of our condition and endeavour for some helpe from my Lord Treasurer. Thence home, and put off Balty, and so, being invited, to Sir Christopher Mings's funeral, but find them gone to church. However I into the church (which is a fair, large church, and a great chappell) and there heard the service, and staid till they buried him, and then out. And there met with Sir W. Coventry (who was there out of great generosity, and no person of quality there but he) and went with him into his coach, and being in it with him there happened this extraordinary case,—one of the most romantique that ever I heard of in my life, and could not have believed, but that I did see it; which was this:—About a dozen able, lusty, proper men come to the coach-side with tears in their eyes, and one of them that spoke for the rest begun and says to Sir W. Coventry, "We are here a dozen of us that have long known and loved, and served our dead commander, Sir Christopher Mings, and have now done the last office of laying him in the ground. We would be glad we had any other to offer after him, and in revenge of him. All we have is our lives; if you will please to get His Royal Highness to give us a fireship among us all, here is a dozen of us, out of all which choose you one to be commander, and the rest of us, whoever he is, will serve him; and, if possible, do that that shall show our memory of our dead commander, and our revenge." Sir W. Coventry was herewith much moved (as well as I, who could hardly abstain from weeping), and took their names, and so parted; telling me that he would move His Royal Highness as in a thing very extraordinary, which was done. Thereon see the next day in this book. So we parted. The truth is, Sir Christopher Mings was a very stout man, and a man of great parts, and most excellent tongue among ordinary men; and as Sir W. Coventry says, could have been the most useful man at such a pinch of time as this. He was come into great renowne here at home, and more abroad in the West Indys. He had brought his family into a way of being great; but dying at this time, his memory and name (his father being always and at this day a shoemaker, and his mother a Hoyman's daughter;[1] of which he was used frequently to boast) will be quite forgot in a few months as if he had never been, nor any of his name be the better by it; he having not had time to will any estate, but is dead poor rather than rich. So we left the church and crowd, and I home (being set down on Tower Hill), and there did a little business and then in the evening went down by water to Deptford, it being very late, and there I staid out as much time as I could, and then took boat again homeward, but the officers being gone in, returned and walked to Mrs. Bagwell's house, and there (it being by this time pretty dark and past ten o'clock) went into her house and did what I would. But I was not a little fearfull of what she told me but now, which is, that her servant was dead of the plague, that her coming to me yesterday was the first day of her coming forth, and that she had new whitened the house all below stairs, but that above stairs they are not so fit for me to go up to, they being not so. So I parted thence, with a very good will, but very civil, and away to the waterside, and sent for a pint of sacke and so home, drank what I would and gave the waterman the rest, and so adieu. Home about twelve at night, and so to bed, find-

[1] Professor Laughton (in the "Dict. Nat. Biog.") shows cause for doubting the correctness of this statement.

ing most of my people gone to bed. In my way home I called on a fisherman and bought three eeles, which cost me three shillings.

14th. Up, and to the office, and there sat all the morning. At noon dined at home, and thence with my wife and father to Hales's, and there looked only on my father's picture (which is mighty like); and so away to White Hall to a committee for Tangier, where the Duke of York was, and Sir W. Coventry, and a very full committee; and instead of having a very prejudiced meeting, they did, though indeed inclined against Yeabsly, yield to the greatest part of his account, so as to allow of his demands to the value of £7,000 and more, and only give time for him to make good his pretence to the rest; which was mighty joy to me: and so we rose up. But I must observe the force of money, which did make my Lord Ashly to argue and behave himself in the business with the greatest friendship, and yet with all the discretion imaginable; and [it] will be a business of admonition and instruction to me concerning him (and other men, too, for aught I know) as long as I live. Thence took Creed with some kind of violence and some hard words between us to St. James's, to have found out Sir W. Coventry to have signed the order for his payment among others that did stay on purpose to do it (and which is strange among the rest my Lord Ashly, who did cause Creed to write it presently and kept two or three of them with him by cunning to stay and sign it), but Creed's ill nature (though never so well bribed, as it hath lately in this case by twenty pieces) will not be overcome from his usual delays. Thence failing of meeting Sir W. Coventry I took leave of Creed (very good friends) and away home, and there took out my father, wife, sister, and Mercer our grand Tour in the evening, and made it ten at night before we got home, only drink at the doore at Islington at the Katherine Wheel, and so home and to the office a little, and then to bed.

15th. Up betimes, and to my Journall entries, but disturbed by many businesses, among others by Mr. Houblon's coming to me about evening their freight for Tangier, which I did, and then Mr. Bland, who presented me yesterday with a very fine African mat, to lay upon the ground under a bed of state, being the first fruits of our peace with Guyland. So to the office, and thither come my pretty widow Mrs. Burrows, poor woman, to get her ticket paid for her husband's service, which I did her myself, and did baisser her moucher, and I do hope may thereafter have some day sa company. Thence to Westminster to the Exchequer, but could not persuade the blockheaded fellows to do what I desire, of breaking my great tallys into less, notwithstanding my Lord Treasurer's order, which vexed [me] so much that I would not bestow more time and trouble among a company of dunces, and so back again home, and to dinner, whither Creed come and dined with me and after dinner Mr. Moore, and he and I abroad, thinking to go down the river together, but the tide being against me would not, but returned and walked an houre in the garden, but, Lord! to hear how he pleases himself in behalf of my Lord Sandwich, in the miscarriage of the Duke of Albemarle, and do inveigh against Sir W. Coventry as a cunning knave, but I thinke that without any manner of reason at all, but only his passion. He being gone I to my chamber at home to set my Journall right and so to settle my Tangier accounts, which I did in very good order, and then in the evening comes Mr. Yeabsly to reckon with me, which I did also, and have above £200 profit therein to myself, which is a great blessing, the God of heaven make me thankfull for it. That being done, and my eyes beginning to be sore with overmuch writing, I to supper and to bed.

16th. Up betimes and to my office, and there we sat all the morning and dispatched much business, the King, Duke of Yorke, and Sir W. Coventry being gone down to the fleete. At noon home to dinner and then down to Woolwich and Deptford to look after things, my head akeing from the multitude of businesses I had in my head yesterday in settling my accounts. All the way down and up, reading of "The Mayor of Quinborough,"[1] a simple play. At Deptford, while I am there, comes Mr. Williamson, Sir Arthur Ingram and Jacke Fen, to see the new ships, which they had done, and then I with them home in their boat,

[1] A comedy, by Thomas Middleton, acted at the Blackfriars, and published in 1661.

and a very fine gentleman Mr. Williamson is. It seems the Dutch do mightily insult of their victory, and they have great reason.[1] Sir William Barkeley was killed before his ship taken; and there he lies dead in a sugar-chest, for every body to see, with his flag standing up by him. And Sir George Ascue is carried up and down the Hague for people to see. Home to my office, where late, and then to bed.

17th (Lord's day). Being invited to Anthony Joyce's to dinner, my wife and sister and Mercer and I walked out in the morning, it being fine weather, to Christ Church, and there heard a silly sermon, but sat where we saw one of the prettiest little boys with the prettiest mouth that ever I saw in [my] life. Thence to Joyce's, where William Joyce and his wife were, and had a good dinner; but, Lord! how sicke was I of the company, only hope I shall have no more of it a good while; but am invited to Will's this week; and his wife, poor unhappy woman, cried to hear me say that I could not be there, she thinking that I slight her: so they got me to promise to come. Thence my father and I walked to Gray's Inne Fields, and there spent an houre or two walking and talking of several businesses; first, as to his estate, he told me it produced about £80 per ann., but then there goes £30 per ann. taxes and other things, certain charge, which I do promise to make good as far as this £30, at which the poor man was overjoyed and wept. As

[1] This treatment seems to have been that of the Dutch populace alone, and there does not appear to have been cause of complaint against the government. Respecting Sir W. Berkeley's body the following notice was published in the "London Gazette" of July 15th, 1666 (No. 69): "Whitehall, July 15. This day arrived a trumpet from the States of Holland, who came over from Calais in the Dover packet-boat, with a letter to his Majesty, that the States have taken order for the embalming the body of Sir William Berkeley, which they have placed in the chapel of the great church at the Hague, a civility they profess to owe to his corpse, in respect to the quality of his person, the greatness of his command, and of the high courage and valour he showed in the late engagement; desiring his Majesty to signify his pleasure about the further disposal of it." "Frederick Ruysch, the celebrated Dutch anatomist, undertook, by order of the States-General, to inject the body of the English Admiral Berkeley, killed in the sea-fight of 1666; and the body, already somewhat decomposed, was sent over to England as well prepared as if it had been the fresh corpse of

to Pall he tells me he is mightily satisfied with Ensum,[1] and so I promised to give her £500 presently, and to oblige myself to £100 more on the birth of her first child, he insuring her in £10 per ann. for every £100, and in the meantime till she do marry I promise to allow her £10 per ann. Then as to John I tell him I will promise him nothing, but will supply him as so much lent him, I declaring that I am not pleased with him yet, and that when his degree is over I will send for him up hither, and if he be good for any thing doubt not to get him preferment. This discourse ended to the joy of my father and no less to me to see that I am able to do this, we return to Joyce's and there wanting a coach to carry us home I walked out as far as the New Exchange to find one, but could not. So down to the Milke-house, and drank three glasses of whay, and then up into the Strand again, and there met with a coach, and so to Joyce's and took up my father, wife, sister, and Mercer, and to Islington, where we drank, and then our tour by Hackney home, where, after a little business at my office and then talke with my Lady and Pegg Pen in the garden, I home and to bed, being very weary.

18th. Up betimes and in my chamber most of the morning setting things to rights there, my Journall and accounts with my father and brother, then to the office a little, and so to Lumbard Streete, to borrow a little money upon a tally, but cannot. Thence to the Exchequer, and there after much wrangling got consent that I should have a great tally broken into little ones. Thence to Hales's to see how my father's picture goes on, which pleases me mighty well, though I find again, as I did in Mrs. Pierce's, that a picture may have more of a likeness in the first or second working than it shall have when finished, though this is very well and to my full content, but so it is, and certainly mine was not so like at the first, second, or third sitting as it was afterward. Thence to my Lord Bellasses, by invitation,

a child. This produced to Ruysch, on the part of the States-General, a recompense worthy of their liberality, and the merit of the anatomist" (James's "Medical Dictionary," quoted in the "Gentleman's Magazine," vol. lvii., p. 214). Sir William Berkeley was buried the following August in Westminster Abbey.

[1] Mr. Ensum died at the end of the year (see December 12th, 1666).

and there dined with him, and his lady and daughter; and at dinner there played to us a young boy, lately come from France, where he had been learning a yeare or two on the viallin, and plays finely. But impartially I do not find any goodnesse in their ayres (though very good) beyond ours when played by the same hand, I observed in several of Baptiste's[1] (the present great composer) and our Bannister's.[2] But it was pretty to see how passionately my Lord's daughter loves musique, the most that ever I saw creature in my life. Thence after dinner home and to the office and anon to Lumbard Streete again, where much talke at Colvill's, he censuring the times, and how matters are ordered, and with reason enough; but, above all, the thinking to borrow money of the City, which will not be done, but be denied, they being little pleased with the King's affairs, and that must breed differences between the King and the City. Thence down by water to Deptford, to order things away to the fleete and back again, and after some business at my office late home to supper and to bed. Sir W. Coventry is returned this night from the fleete, he being the activest man in the world, and we all (myself particularly) more afeard of him than of the King or his service, for aught I see; God forgive us! This day the great newes is come of the French, their taking the island of St. Chris-

[1] Jean Baptiste Lulli, son of a Tuscan peasant, born 1633, died 1687. He invented the dramatic overture. "But during the first years of Charles II. all musick affected by the *beau mond* run in the french way; and the rather becaus at that time the master of the court musick in France, whose name was Baptista (an Italian frenchifyed) had influenced the french style by infusing a great portion of the Italian harmony into it, whereby the ayre was exceedingly improved" (North's "Memoires of Musick," ed. Rimbault, 1846, p. 102).

[2] John Bannister, composer of "Choice Ayres and Songs" and of the incidental music to several masques, tragedies, and plays, including Shakespeare's "Tempest." He was in 1663 appointed first violin to the king, which post he is said to have lost owing to his upholding within the hearing of his Majesty the superiority of English over French players. He started successful concerts in London "over against the George Tavern in Whitefriars" (Hueffer's "Italian and other Studies," p. 247). In the "London Gazette," January 21/5, 1674, is the following entry: "Mr. John Bannister that lived in White Fryers is removed to Shandois Street, Covent Garden, and there intends to have the like entertainment as formerly on Tuesday next, and every evening for the future, Sunday excepted." Bannister died in 1679 at the age of forty-nine.

topher's[1] from us; and it is to be feared they have done the like of all those islands thereabouts: this makes the city mad.

19th. Up, and to my office, there to fit business against the rest meet, which they did by and by, and sat late. After the office rose (with Creed with me) to Wm. Joyce's to dinner, being invited, and there find my father and sister, my wife and Mercer, with them, almost dined. I made myself as complaisant as I could till I had dined, but yet much against my will, and so away after dinner with Creed to Penny's, my Tailor, where I bespoke a thin stuff suit, and did spend a little time evening some little accounts with Creed and so parted, and I to Sir G. Carteret's by appointment; where I perceive by him the King is going to borrow some money of the City; but I fear it will do no good, but hurt. He tells me how the Generall[2] is displeased, and there have been some high words between the Generall and Sir W. Coventry. And it may be so; for I do not find Sir W. Coventry so highly commending the Duke as he used to be, but letting fall now and then some little jerkes: as this day, speaking of newes from Holland, he says, "I find their victory begins to shrinke there, as well as ours here." Here I met with Captain Cocke, and he tells me that the first thing the Prince said to the King upon his coming, was complaining of the Commissioners of the Navy; that they could have been abroad in three or four days but for us; that we do not take care of them: which I am troubled at, and do fear may in violence break out upon this office some time or other; for we shall not be able to carry on the business. Thence home, and at my business till late at night, then with my wife into the garden and there sang with Mercer, whom I feel myself begin to love too much by handling of her breasts in a' morning when she dresses me, they being the finest that ever I saw in my

[1] The island of St. Christopher's or St. Kitt's, one of the Leeward Islands, was discovered in November, 1493, by Columbus, who was so pleased with it that he gave it his own Christian name. It was never colonized by the Spaniards, but in 1625 was taken possession of by a band of buccaneers consisting of English and French. Many contentions took place before it became definitely a British possession.

[2] The Duke of Albemarle.

life, that is the truth of it. So home and to supper with beans and bacon and to bed.

20th. Up, but in some pain of the collique. I have of late taken too much cold by washing my feet and going in a thin silke waistcoate, without any other coate over it, and open-breasted, but I hope it will go over. I did this morning (my father being to go away to-morrow) give my father some money to buy him a horse, and for other things to himself and my mother and sister, among them £20, besides undertaking to pay for other things for them to about £3, which the poor man takes with infinite kindnesse, and I do not thinke I can bestow it better. Thence by coach to St. James's as usual to wait on the Duke of York, after having discoursed with Collonell Fitzgerald, whom I met in my way and he returned with me to Westminster, about paying him a sum of 700 and odd pounds, and he bids me defalk[1] £25 for myself, which is a very good thing; having done with the Duke I to the Exchequer and there after much ado to get my business quite over of the difficulty of breaking a great tally into little ones and so shall have it done to-morrow. Thence to the Hall and with Mrs. Martin home and staid with her a while, and then away to the Swan and sent for a bit of meat and dined there, and thence to Faythorne,[2] the picture-seller's, and there chose two or three good Cutts to try to vernish, and so to Hales's to see my father's picture, which is now near finished and is very good, and here I staid and took a nap of an hour, thinking my father and wife would have come, but they did not; so I away home as fast as I could, fearing lest my father this day going abroad to see Mr. Honiwood at Major Russell's might meet with any trouble, and so in great pain home; but to spite me, in Cheapside I met Mrs. Williams in a coach, and she called me, so I must needs 'light and go along with her and poor Knipp (who is so big as she can tumble and looks every day to lie down) as far as Paternoster

[1] Abate from an amount.

> "And do not see how much they must defalke
> Of their accounts, to make them gree with ours."
>
> Daniel, *Philotas*, 1605.

[2] Faithorne's shop was on the north side of the Strand just outside Temple Bar, on the site of part of the Law Courts.

Row, which I did do and there staid in Bennett's shop with them, and was fearfull lest the people of the shop, knowing me, should aske after my father and give Mrs. Williams any knowledge of me to my disgrace. Having seen them done there and accompanied them to Ludgate I 'light and into my owne coach and home, where I find my father and wife had had no intent of coming at all to Hales's. So I at home all the evening doing business, and at night in the garden (it having been these three or four days mighty hot weather) singing in the evening, and then home to supper and to bed.

21st. Up, and at the office all the morning; where by several circumstances I find Sir W. Coventry and the Duke of Albemarle do not agree as they used to do; Sir W. Coventry commending Aylett[1] (in some reproach to the Duke), whom the Duke hath put out for want of courage; and found fault with Steward,[2] whom the Duke keeps in, though as much in fault as any commander in the fleete. At noon home to dinner, my father, sister, and wife dining at Sarah Giles's, poor woman, where I should have been, but my pride would not suffer me. After dinner to Mr. Debasty's to speake with Sir Robert Viner, a fine house and a great many fine ladies. He used me mighty civilly. My business was to set the matter right about the letter of credit he did give my Lord Belassis, that I may take up the tallys lodged with Viner for his security in the answering of my Lord's bills, which we did set right very well, and Sir Robert Viner went home with me and did give me the £5,000 tallys presently. Here at Mr. Debasty's I saw, in a gold frame, a picture of a fluter playing on his flute which, for a good while, I took for paynting, but at last observed it a piece of tapestry, and is the finest that ever I saw in my life for figures, and good natural colours, and a very fine thing it is indeed. So home and met Sir George Smith by the way, who tells me that this day my Lord Chancellor and some of the Court have been with the City, and the City have voted to lend the King £100,000; which, if soon paid (as he says he believes it will), will be a greater ser-

[1] Captain John Aylett of the "Portland."

[2] Captain Francis Steward.

vice than I did ever expect at this time from the City. So home to my letters and then with my wife in the garden, and then upon our leades singing in the evening and so to supper (while at supper comes young Michell, whose wife I love, little Betty Howlet, to get my favour about a ticket, and I am glad of this occasion of obliging him and give occasion of his coming to me, for I must be better acquainted with him and her), and after supper to bed.

22nd. Up, and before I went out Mr. Peter Barr sent me a tierce of claret, which is very welcome. And so abroad down the river to Deptford and there did some business, and then to Westminster, and there did with much ado get my tallys (my small ones instead of one great one of £2,000), and so away home and there all day upon my Tangier accounts with Creed, and, he being gone, with myself, in settling other accounts till past twelve at night, and then every body being in bed, I to bed, my father, wife, and sister late abroad upon the water, and Mercer being gone to her mother's and staid so long she could not get into the office, which vexed me.

23rd. My father and sister very betimes took their leave; and my wife, with all possible kindnesse, went with them to the coach, I being mightily pleased with their company thus long, and my father with his being here, and it rejoices my heart that I am in condition to do any thing to comfort him, and could, were it not for my mother, have been contented he should have stayed always here with me, he is such innocent company. They being gone, I to my papers, but vexed at what I heard but a little of this morning, before my wife went out, that Mercer and she fell out last night, and that the girle is gone home to her mother's for alltogether. This troubles me, though perhaps it may be an ease to me of so much charge. But I love the girle, and another we must be forced to keepe I do foresee and then shall be sorry to part with her. At the office all the morning, much disquiett in my mind in the middle of my business about this girle. Home at noon to dinner, and what with the going away of my father to-day and the losse of Mercer, I after dinner went up to my chamber and there could have cried to myself, had not people come to me about business. In the evening down to Tower Wharfe thinking to go by water, but could not get watermen; they being now so scarce, by reason of the great presse; so to the Custome House, and there, with great threats, got a couple to carry me down to Deptford, all the way reading Pompey the Great (a play translated from the French[1] by several noble persons; among others, my Lord Buckhurst), that to me is but a mean play, and the words and sense not very extraordinary. From Deptford I walked to Redriffe, and in my way was overtaken by Bagwell, lately come from sea in the Providence, who did give me an account of several particulars in the late fight, and how his ship was deserted basely by the York, Captain Swanly,[2] commander. So I home and there after writing my letters home to supper and to bed, fully resolved to rise betimes, and go down the river to-morrow morning, being vexed this night to find none of the officers in the yarde at 7 at night, nor any body concerned as if it were a Dutch warr. It seems Mercer's mother was here in the morning to speak with my wife, but my wife would not. In the afternoon I and my wife in writing did instruct W. Hewer in some discourse to her, and she in the evening did come and satisfy my wife, and by and by Mercer did come, which I was mighty glad of and eased of much pain about her.

24th. Sunday. Midsummer Day. Up, but, being weary the last night, not so soon as I intended. Then being dressed, down by water to Deptford, and there did a great deale of business, being in a mighty hurry, Sir W. Coventry writing to me that there was some thoughts that the Dutch fleete were out or coming out. Business being done in providing for the carrying down of some provisions to the fleete, I away back home and after dinner by water to White Hall, and there waited till the councill rose, in the boarded gallery, and there among other things I hear that Sir Francis Prujean[3] is dead, after being married to a widow about a

[1] Corneille's play ("Pompée"), one act of which was translated by Edmund Waller, and the rest by Lord Buckhurst, Sir Charles Sedley, and Sidney Godolphin. Published in 1664.

[2] Captain John Swanley, appointed to the "York" in 1664.

[3] See note, October 24th, 1663. Prujean married at Westminster, February 13th, 1664–65, Lady Margaret, daughter of Edward, Lord Gorges, and relict of Sir Thomas Fleming. She subsequently remarried Sir John Maynard, serjeant-at-law.

yeare or thereabouts. He died very rich, and had, for the last yeare, lived very handsomely, his lady bringing him to it. He was no great painstaker in person, yet died very rich; and, as Dr. Clerke says, was of a very great judgment, but hath writ nothing to leave his name to posterity. In the gallery among others met with Major Halsey, a great creature of the Duke of Albemarle's; who tells me that the Duke, by name, hath said that he expected to have the worke here up in the River done, having left Sir W. Batten and Mr. Phipps there. He says that the Duke of Albemarle do say that this is a victory we have had, having, as he was sure, killed them 8,000 men, and sunk about fourteen of their ships; but nothing like this appears true. He lays much of the little success we had, however, upon the fleete's being divided by order from above, and the want of spirit in the commanders; and that he was commanded by order to go out of the Downes to the Gun-fleete, and in the way meeting the Dutch fleete, what should he do? should he not fight them? especially having beat them heretofore at as great disadvantage. He tells me further, that having been downe with the Duke of Albemarle, he finds that Holmes and Spragge do govern most business of the Navy; and by others I understand that Sir Thomas Allen is offended thereat; that he is not so much advised with as he ought to be. He tells me also, as he says, of his own knowledge, that several people before the Duke went out did offer to supply the King with £100,000 provided he would be treasurer of it, to see it laid out for the Navy; which he refused, and so it died. But I believe none of this. This day I saw my Lady Falmouth,[1] with whom I remember now I have dined at my Lord Barkeley's heretofore, a pretty woman: she was now in her second or third mourning, and pretty pleasant in her looks. By and by the Council rises, and Sir W. Coventry comes out; and

[1] Mary, daughter of Colonel Hervey Bagot, of Pipe Hall, co. Warwick, born 1645; maid of honour to the Duchess of York, 1660; married, December 18th, 1664, Charles Berkeley, Earl of Falmouth, who was killed June 3rd, 1665, in the battle of Southwold Bay. In June, 1674, she took for a second husband Charles Sackville, Earl of Dorset and Middlesex, K.G., and died in childbed September 12th, 1679. Her name is usually given as Elizabeth, but this is a mistake.

he and I went aside, and discoursed of much business of the Navy; and afterwards took his coach, and to Hide-Parke, he and I alone: there we had much talke. First, he started a discourse of a talke he hears about the towne, which, says he, is a very bad one, and fit to be suppressed, if we knew how: which is, the comparing of the successe of the last year with that of this; saying that that was good, and that bad. I was as sparing in speaking as I could, being jealous of him and myself also, but wished it could be stopped; but said I doubted it could not otherwise than by the fleete's being abroad again, and so finding other worke for men's minds and discourse. Then to discourse of himself, saying, that he heard that he was under the lash of people's discourse about the Prince's not having notice of the Dutch being out, and for him to come back again, nor the Duke of Albemarle notice that the Prince was sent for back again: to which he told me very particularly how careful he was the very same night that it was resolved to send for the Prince back, to cause orders to be writ, and waked the Duke, who was then in bed, to sign them; and that they went by expresse that very night, being the Wednesday night before the fight, which begun on the Friday; and that for sending them by the post expresse, and not by gentlemen on purpose, he made a sport of it, and said, I knew of none to send it with, but would at least have lost more time in fitting themselves out, than any diligence of theirs beyond that of the ordinary post would have recovered. I told him that this was not so much the towne talke as the reason of dividing the fleete. To this he told me he ought not to say much; but did assure me in general that the proposition did first come from the fleete, and the resolution not being prosecuted with orders so soon as the Generall thought fit, the Generall did send Sir Edward Spragge up on purpose for them; and that there was nothing in the whole business which was not done with the full consent and advice of the Duke of Albemarle. But he did adde (as the Catholiques call *le secret de la Masse*), that Sir Edward Spragge — who had even in Sir Christopher Mings's time put in to be the great favourite of the Prince, but much more now had a mind to be the great man with him, and to that end had a mind to have the Prince at a distance from the Duke of Albemarle, that they might be doing something alone — did, as he believed, put on this business of dividing the fleete, and that thence it came.[1] He tells me as to the business of intelligence, the want whereof the world did complain much of, that for that it was not his business, and as he was therefore to have no share in the blame, so he would not meddle to lay it any where else. That de Ruyter was ordered by the States not to make it his business to come into much danger, but to preserve himself as much as was fit out of harm's way, to be able to direct the fleete. He do, I perceive, with some violence, forbear saying any thing to the reproach of the Duke of Albemarle; but, contrarily, speaks much of his courage; but I do as plainly see that he do not like the Duke of Albemarle's proceedings, but, contrarily, is displeased therewith. And he do plainly diminish the commanders put in by the Duke, and do lessen the miscarriages of any that have been removed by him. He concurs with me, that the next bout will be a fatal one to one side or other, because, if we be beaten, we shall not be able to set out our fleete again. He do confess with me that the hearts of our seamen are much saddened; and for that reason, among others, wishes Sir Christopher Mings was alive, who might inspire courage and spirit into them. Speaking of Holmes, how great a man he is, and that he do for the present, and hath done all the voyage, kept himself in good order and within bounds; but, says he, a cat will be a cat still, and some time or other out his humour must break again. He do not disowne but that the dividing of the fleete upon the presumptions that were then had (which, I suppose, was the French fleete being come this way), was a good resolution. Having had all this discourse, he and I back to White Hall; and there I left him, being [in] a little doubt whether I had behaved myself in my discourse with the policy and circumspection which ought to be used to so great a courtier as he is, and so wise and factious a man, and by water home, and so, after supper, to bed.

[1] This division of the fleet was the original cause of the disaster, and at a later period the enemies of Clarendon charged him with having advised this action, but Coventry's communication to Pepys in the text completely exonerates Clarendon.

25th. Up, and all the morning at my Tangier accounts, which the chopping and changing of my tallys make mighty troublesome; but, however, I did end them with great satisfaction to myself. At noon, without staying to eat my dinner, I down by water to Deptford, and there coming find Sir W. Batten and Sir Jeremy Smith (whom the dispatch of the Loyall London detained) at dinner at Greenwich at the Beare Taverne, and thither I to them and there dined with them. Very good company of strangers there was, but I took no great pleasure among them, being desirous to be back again. So got them to rise as soon as I could, having told them the newes Sir W. Coventry just now wrote me to tell them, which is, that the Dutch are certainly come out. I did much business at Deptford, and so home, by an old poor man, a sculler, having no oares to be got, and all this day on the water entertained myself with the play of Commenius,[1] and being come home did go out to Aldgate, there to be overtaken by Mrs. Margot Pen in her father's coach, and my wife and Mercer with her, and Mrs. Pen carried us to two gardens at Hackny, (which I every day grow more and more in love with,) Mr. Drake's one, where the garden is good, and house and the prospect admirable; the other my Lord Brooke's,[2] where the gardens are much better, but the house not so good, nor the prospect good at all. But the gardens are excellent; and here I first saw oranges grow:[3] some green, some half, some a quarter, and some full ripe, on the same tree, and one fruit of the same tree do come a year or two after the other. I pulled off a little one by stealth (the man being mighty

[1] John Amos Comenius, a learned grammarian, born in Moravia, in 1592. Amongst other works, he published the play here mentioned, entitled, "Schola Ludus seu Encyclopædia Viva (hoc est) Januæ Linguarum Praxis Scenica." This curious book contains the details of eight dramatic pieces, represented at the author's school, at Patak, in 1654. Comenius died at Amsterdam, in 1671. — B.

[2] Robert Greville, Lord Brooke, died 1676. Evelyn mentions this garden as Lady Brooke's, and describes it as "one of the neatest and most celebrated in England" (May 8th, 1654). Brooke House, at Clapton, was subsequently occupied as a private madhouse.

[3] There is some dispute as to the date of the introduction of the sweet orange into Europe. It appears that in 1492 it was cultivated in England, and in some parts of the country it has thrived in the open air even during the winter.

curious of them) and eat it, and it was just as other little green small oranges are; as big as half the end of my little finger. Here were also great variety of other exotique plants, and several labarinths, and a pretty aviary. Having done there with very great pleasure we away back again, and called at the Taverne in Hackny by the church, and there drank and eate, and so in the coole of the evening home. This being the first day of my putting on my black stuff bombazin suit, and I hope to feel no inconvenience by it, the weather being extremely hot. So home and to bed, and this night the first night of my lying without a waistcoat, which I hope I shall very well endure. So to bed. This morning I did with great pleasure hear Mr. Cæsar play some good things on his lute, while he come to teach my boy Tom, and I did give him 40*s*. for his encouragement.

26th. Up and to my office betimes, and there all the morning, very busy to get out the fleete, the Dutch being now for certain out, and we shall not, we thinke, be much behindhand with them. At noon to the 'Change about business, and so home to dinner, and after dinner to the setting my Journall to rights, and so to the office again, where all the afternoon full of business, and there till night, that my eyes were sore, that I could not write no longer. Then into the garden, then my wife and Mercer and my Lady Pen and her daughter with us, and here we sung in the darke very finely half an houre, and so home to supper and to bed. This afternoon, after a long drowth, we had a good shower of rain, but it will not signify much if no more come. This day in the morning come Mr. Chichly[1] to Sir W. Coventry, to tell him the ill successe of the guns made for the Loyall London; which is, that in the trial every one of the great guns, the whole cannon of seven (as I take it), broke in pieces, which is a strange mishap, and that which will give more occasion to people's discourse of the King's business being done ill. This night Mary my cooke-mayde, that hath been with us about three months, but find herself not able to do my worke, so

[1] Mr., afterwards Sir Thomas Chicheley, a Privy Counsellor and Commissioner of the Ordnance. — B.

is gone with great kindnesse away, and another (Luce) come, very ugly and plaine, but may be a good servant for all that.

27th. Up, and to my office awhile, and then down the river a little way to see vessels ready for the carrying down of 400 land soldiers to the fleete. Then back to the office for my papers, and so to St. James's, where we did our usual attendance on the Duke. Having done with him, we all of us down to Sir W. Coventry's chamber (where I saw his father my Lord Coventry's picture hung up, done by Stone,[1] who then brought it home. It is a good picture, drawn in his judge's robes, and the great seale by him. And while it was hanging up, "This," says Sir W. Coventry, merrily, "is the use we make of our fathers,") to discourse about the proposition of serving us with hempe, delivered in by my Lord Brouncker as from an unknown person, though I know it to be Captain Cocke's. My Lord and Sir William Coventry had some earnest words about it, the one promoting it for his private ends, being, as Cocke tells me himself, to have £500 if the bargain goes on, and I am to have as much, and the other opposing it for the unseasonableness of it, not knowing at all whose the proposition is, which seems the more ingenious of the two. I sat by and said nothing, being no great friend to the proposition, though Cocke intends me a convenience by it. But what I observed most from the discourse was this of Sir W. Coventry, that he do look upon ourselves in a desperate condition. The issue of all standing upon this one point, that by the next fight, if we beat, the Dutch will certainly be content to take eggs for their money[2] (that was his expression); or if we be beaten, we must be contented to make peace, and glad if we can have

[1] Henry Stone, painter and statuary, son of Nicholas Stone, master mason, died August 24th, 1653. If the portrait of Lord Coventry (died January 14th, 1639–40) was painted by him, the painting mentioned in the text was probably copied by Stone's brother John.

[2] A proverbial expression when a person was either awed by threats, or overreached by subtlety, to give money upon a trifling or fictitious consideration.

"*Leon.* Mine honest friend,
Will you take eggs for money?
Mam. No, my Lord, I'll fight."
Shakespeare, *Winter's Tale*, act i., sc. 2.

(Nares's Glossary.)

it without paying too dear for it. And withall we do rely wholly upon the Parliament's giving us more money the next sitting, or else we are undone. Being gone hence, I took coach to the Old Exchange, but did not go to it, but to Mr. Cade's, the stationer, stood till the shower was over, it being a great and welcome one after so much dry weather. Here I understand that Ogleby is putting out some new fables of his owne, which will be very fine and very satyricall. Thence home to dinner, and after dinner carried my wife to her sister's and I to Mr. Hales's, to pay for my father's picture, which cost me £10 the head and 25*s.* the frame. Thence to Lovett's, who has now done something towards the varnishing of single paper for the making of books, which will do, I think, very well. He did also carry me to a Knight's chamber in Graye's Inne, where there is a frame of his making, of counterfeite tortoise shell, which indeed is most excellently done. Then I took him with me to a picture shop to choose a print for him to vernish, but did not agree for one then. Thence to my wife to take her up and so carried her home, and I at the office till late, and so to supper with my wife and to bed. I did this afternoon visit my Lord Bellasses, who professes all imaginable satisfaction in me. He spoke dissatisfiedly with Creed, which I was pleased well enough with. My Lord is going down to his garrison to Hull, by the King's command, to put it in order for fear of an invasion: which course I perceive is taken upon the sea-coasts round; for we have a real apprehension of the King of France's invading us.

28th. Up, and at the office all the morning. At noon home to dinner, and after dinner abroad to Lumbard Streete, there to reckon with Sir Robert Viner for some money, and did sett all straight to my great content, and so home, and all the afternoon and evening at the office, my mind full at this time of getting my accounts over, and as much money in my hands as I can, for a great turne is to be feared in the times, the French having some great design (whatever it is) in hand, and our necessities on every side very great. The Dutch are now known to be out, and we may expect them every houre upon our coast. But our fleete is in pretty good readinesse for them.

29th. Up, and within doors most of the morning, sending a porter (Sanders) up and down to several people to pay them money to clear my month's debts every where, being mighty desirous to have all clear so soon as I can, and to that end did so much in settling my Tangier accounts clear. At noon dined, having first been down at Deptford and did a little business there and back again. After dinner to White Hall to a Committee of Tangier, but I come a little too late, they were up, so I to several places about business, among others to Westminster Hall, and there did meet with Betty Michell at her own mother's shop. I would fain have carried her home by water, but she was to sup at that end of the town. So I away to White Hall, and thence, the Council being up, walked to St. James's, and there had much discourse with Sir W. Coventry at his chamber, who I find quite weary of the warr, decries our having any warr at all, or himself to have been any occasion of it, that he hopes this will make us shy of any warr hereafter, or to prepare better for it, believes that one overthrow on the Dutch side would make them desire peace, and that one on ours will make us willing to accept of one: tells me that Commissioner Pett is fallen infinitely under the displeasure of the Prince and Duke of Albemarle, not giving them satisfaction in the getting out of the fleete, and that the complaint he believes is come to the King, and by Sir W. Coventry's discourse I find he do concur in it, and speaks of his having of no authority in the place where he is, and I do believe at least it will end in his being removed to some other yarde, and I am not sorry for it, but do fear that though he deserves as bad, yet at this time the blame may not be so well deserved. Thence home and to the office; where I met with a letter from Dover, which tells me (and it did come by expresse) that newes is brought over by a gentleman from Callice that the Dutch fleete, 130 sail, are come upon the French coast; and that the country is bringing in picke-axes, and shovells, and wheel-barrows into Callice; that there are 6,000 men armed with head, back, and breast (Frenchmen) ready to go on board the Dutch fleete, and will be followed by 12,000 more. That they pretend they are to come to Dover; and that thereupon the Governor of Dover Castle is getting the victuallers' provision out of the towne into the Castle to secure it. But I do think this is a ridiculous conceit; but a little time will show. At night home to supper and to bed.

30th. Up, and to the office, and mightily troubled all this morning with going to my Lord Mayor (Sir Thomas Budworth, a silly man,[1] I think), and other places, about getting shipped some men that they have these two last nights pressed in the City out of houses: the persons wholly unfit for sea, and many of them people of very good fashion, which is a shame to think of, and carried to Bridewell they are, yet without being impressed with money legally as they ought to be. But to see how the King's business is done; my Lord Mayor himself did scruple at this time of extremity to do this thing, because he had not money to pay the pressed-money to the men, he told me so himself; nor to take up boats to carry them down through bridge to the ships I had prepared to carry them down in; insomuch that I was forced to promise to be his paymaster, and he did send his City Remembrancer afterwards to the office, and at the table, in the face of the officers, I did there out of my owne purse disburse £15 to pay for their pressing and diet last night and this morning; which is a thing worth record of my Lord Mayor. Busy about this all the morning, at noon dined and then to the office again, and all the afternoon till twelve at night full of this business and others, and among these others about the getting off men pressed by our officers of the fleete into the service; even our owne men that are at the office, and the boats that carry us. So that it is now become impossible to have so much as a letter carried from place to place, or any message done for us: nay, out of Victualling ships full loaden to go down to the fleete, and out of the vessels of the officers of the Ordnance, they press men, so that for want of discipline in this respect I do fear all will be undone. Vexed with these things, but eased in mind by my ridding of a great deale of business from the office, I late home to supper and to bed. But before I was in bed, while I was

[1] As his conduct during the Great Fire fully proved, when he is said to have boasted that he would extinguish the flames by the same means to which Swift tells us Gulliver had recourse at Lilliput. — B.

undressing myself, our new ugly mayde, Luce, had like to have broke her necke in the darke, going down our upper stairs; but, which I was glad of, the poor girle did only bruise her head, but at first did lie on the ground groaning and drawing her breath, like one a-dying. This month I end in much hurry of business, but in much more trouble in mind to thinke what will become of publique businesses, having so many enemys abroad, and neither force nor money at all, and but little courage for ourselves, it being really true that the spirits of our seamen and commanders too are really broke by the last defeate with the Dutch, and this is not my conjecture only, but the real and serious thoughts of Sir G. Carteret and Sir W. Coventry, whom I have at distinct times heard the same thing come from with a great deale of grief and trouble. But, lastly, I am providing against a foule day to get as much money into my hands as I can, at least out of the publique hands, that so, if a turne, which I fear, do come, I may have a little to trust to. I pray God give me good successe in my choice how to dispose of what little I have, that I may not take it out of publique hands, and put it into worse.

July 1st (Sunday). Up betimes, and to the office receiving letters, two or three one after another from Sir W. Coventry, and sent as many to him, being full of variety of business and hurry, but among the chiefest is the getting of these pressed men out of the City down the river to the fleete. While I was hard at it comes Sir W. Pen to towne, which I little expected, having invited my Lady and her daughter Pegg to dine with me to-day; which at noon they did, and Sir W. Pen with them: and pretty merry we were. And though I do not love him, yet I find it necessary to keep in with him; his good service at Shearnesse in getting out the fleete being much taken notice of, and reported to the King and Duke [of York], even from the Prince and Duke of Albemarle themselves, and made the most of to me and them by Sir W. Coventry: therefore I think it discretion, great and necessary discretion, to keep in with him. After dinner to the office again, where busy, and then down to Deptford to the yard, thinking to have seen Bagwell's wife, whose husband is gone yesterday back to the fleete, but I did not see her, so missed what I went for, and so back to the Tower several times, about the business of the pressed men, and late at it till twelve at night, shipping of them. But, Lord! how some poor women did cry; and in my life I never did see such natural expression of passion as I did here in some women's bewailing themselves, and running to every parcel of men that were brought, one after another, to look for their husbands, and wept over every vessel that went off, thinking they might be there, and looking after the ship as far as ever they could by moone-light, that it grieved me to the heart to hear them. Besides, to see poor patient labouring men and housekeepers, leaving poor wives and families, taking up on a sudden by strangers, was very hard, and that without press-money, but forced against all law to be gone. It is a great tyranny.[1] Having done this I to the Lieutenant of the Tower and bade him good night, and so away home and to bed.

2nd. Up betimes, and forced to go to my Lord Mayor's, about the business of the pressed men; and indeed I find him a mean man of understanding and dispatch of any publique business. Thence out of curiosity to Bridewell to see the pressed men, where there are about 300; but so unruly that I durst not go among them: and they have reason to be so, having been kept these three days prisoners, with little or no victuals, and pressed out, and, contrary to all course of law, without press-money, and men that are not liable to it. Here I met with prating Colonel Cox, one of the City collonells, heretofore a great presbyter: but to hear how the fellow did commend himself, and the service he do the King; and, like an asse, at Paul's did take me out of my way on purpose to show me the gate (the little north gate) where he had two men shot close by him on each hand, and his own hair burnt by a bullet-shot in the insurrection of Venner, and himself escaped. Thence home and to the Tower to see the men from Bridewell shipped. Being rid of him I home to dinner, and thence to the Excise office by appointment to meet my Lord Bel-

[1] The practice of impressment was sanctioned by custom, and several acts of parliament were passed from the reign of Philip and Mary to that of George III. to regulate it. These laws have not been repealed, although they have fallen into abeyance.

lasses and the Commissioners, which we did and soon dispatched, and so I home, and there was called by Pegg Pen to her house, where her father and mother, and Mrs. Norton, the second Roxalana,[1] a fine woman, indifferent handsome, good body and hand, and good mine, and pretends to sing, but do it not excellently. However I took pleasure there, and my wife was sent for, and Creed come in to us, and so there we spent the most of the afternoon. Thence weary of losing so much time I to the office, and thence presently down to Deptford; but to see what a consternation there is upon the water by reason of this great press, that nothing is able to get a waterman to appear almost. Here I meant to have spoke with Bagwell's mother,[2] but her face was sore, and so I did not, but returned and upon the water found one of the vessels loaden with the Bridewell birds in a great mutiny, and they would not sail, not they; but with good words, and cajoling the ringleader into the Tower (where, when he was come, he was clapped up in the hole), they were got very quietly; but I think it is much if they do not run the vessel on ground. But away they went, and I to the Lieutenant of the Tower, and having talked with him a little, then home to supper very late and to bed weary.

3rd. Being very weary, lay long in bed, then to the office and there sat all the day. At noon dined at home, Balty's wife with us, and in very good humour I was and merry at dinner, and after dinner a song or two, and so I abroad to my Lord Treasurer's (sending my sister home by the coach), while I staid there by appointment to have met my Lord Bellasses and Commissioners of Excise, but they did not meet me, he being abroad. However Mr. Finch,[3] one of the Commissioners, I met there, and he and I walked two houres together in the garden, talking of many things; sometimes of Mr. Povy, whose vanity, prodigality, neglect of his business, and committing it to unfit hands hath undone him and outed him of all his publique employ-

[1] The first Roxolana was Mrs. Davenport (see note, *ante*, February 18th, 1661–62). Mrs. Norton is not mentioned in Genest's "English Stage."

[2] Mother or mauther, a wench, see *ante*, June 11th.

[3] Francis Finch was one of the "Commissioners for discharging, settling and recovering the arrears of excise due to the King."

ments, and the thing set on foot by an accidental revivall of a business, wherein he had three or four years ago, by surprize, got the Duke of Yorke to sign to the having a sum of money paid out of the Excise, before some that was due to him, and now the money is fallen short, and the Duke never likely to be paid. This being revived hath undone Povy. Then we fell to discourse of the Parliament, and the great men there: and among others, Mr. Vaughan,[1] whom he reports as a man of excellent judgement and learning, but most passionate and opiniastre. He had done himself the most wrong (though he values it not), that is, the displeasure of the King in his standing so long against the breaking of the Act for a trienniall parliament; but yet do believe him to be a most loyall gentleman. He told me Mr. Prin's character; that he is a man of mighty labour and reading and memory, but the worst judge of matters, or layer together of what he hath read, in the world; which I do not, however, believe him in; that he believes him very true to the King in his heart, but can never be reconciled to episcopacy; that the House do not lay much weight upon him, or any thing he says. He told me many fine things, and so we parted, and I home and hard to work a while at the office and then home and till midnight about settling my last month's accounts, wherein I have been interrupted by public business, that I did not state them two or three days ago, but I do now to my great joy find myself worth above £5,600, for which the Lord's name be praised! So with my heart full of content to bed. Newes come yesterday from Harwich, that the Dutch had appeared upon our coast with their fleete, and we believe did go to the Gunfleete, and they are supposed to be there now; but I have heard nothing of them to-day. Yesterday Dr. Whistler, at Sir W. Pen's, told me that Alexander Broome,[2] the great song-maker, is lately dead.

4th. Up, and visited very betimes by Mr. Sheply, who is come to town upon business from Hinchingbrooke, where

[1] John Vaughan (born 1603, died 1674) was appointed Chief Justice of the Common Pleas in 1668, when he was knighted. See March 28th, 1664.

[2] Brome died June 30th, 1666, and was buried, by his own desire, under Lincoln's Inn Chapel, by the side of Prynne. — B.

he left all well. I out and walked along with him as far as Fleet Streete, it being a fast day, the usual fast day for the plague, and few coaches to be had. Thanks be to God, the plague is, as I hear, encreased but two this week; but in the country in several places it rages mightily, and particularly in Colchester, where it hath long been, and is believed will quite depopulate the place. To St. James's, and there did our usual business with the Duke, all of us, among other things, discoursing about the places where to build ten great ships; the King and Council have resolved on none to be under third-rates; but it is impossible to do it, unless we have more money towards the doing it than yet we have in any view. But, however, the shew must be made to the world. Thence to my Lord Bellasses to take my leave of him, he being going down to the North to look after the Militia there, for fear of an invasion. Thence home and dined, and then to the office, where busy all day, and in the evening Sir W. Pen come to me, and we walked together, and talked of the late fight. I find him very plain, that the whole conduct of the late fight was ill, and that that of truth's all, and he tells me that it is not he, but two-thirds of the commanders of the whole fleete have told him so: they all saying, that they durst not oppose it at the Council of War, for fear of being called cowards, though it was wholly against their judgement to fight that day with the disproportion of force, and then we not being able to use one gun of our lower tier, which was a greater disproportion than the other. Besides, we might very well have staid in the Downs without fighting, or any where else, till the Prince could have come up to them; or at least till the weather was fair, that we might have the benefit of our whole force in the ships that we had. He says three things must [be] remedied, or else we shall be undone by this fleete. 1. That we must fight in a line, whereas we fight promiscuously, to our utter and demonstrable ruine; the Dutch fighting otherwise; and we, whenever we beat them. 2. We must not desert ships of our own in distress, as we did, for that makes a captain desperate, and he will fling away his ship, when there is no hopes left him of succour. 3. That ships, when they are a little shattered, must not take the liberty to come in of themselves, but refit themselves the best they can, and stay out — many of our ships coming in with very small disablenesses. He told me that our very commanders, nay, our very flag-officers, do stand in need of exercising among themselves, and discoursing the business of commanding a fleete; he telling me that even one of our flag-men in the fleete did not know which tacke lost the wind, or which kept it, in the last engagement. He says it was pure dismaying and fear that made them all run upon the Galloper, not having their wits about them; and that it was a miracle they were not all lost. He much inveighs upon my discoursing of Sir John Lawson's saying heretofore, that sixty sail would do as much as one hundred; and says that he was a man of no counsel at all, but had got the confidence to say as the gallants did, and did propose to himself to make himself great by them, and saying as they did; but was no man of judgement in his business, but hath been out in the greatest points that have come before them. And then in the business of fore-castles, which he did oppose, all the world sees now the use of them for shelter of men. He did talk very rationally to me, insomuch that I took more pleasure this night in hearing him discourse, than I ever did in my life in any thing that he said. He gone I to the office again, and so after some business home to supper and to bed.

5th. Up and to the office, where we sat all the morning busy, then at noon dined and Mr. Sheply with me, who come to towne the other day. I lent him £30 in silver upon 30 pieces in gold. But to see how apt every body is to neglect old kindnesses! I must charge myself with the ingratitude of being unwilling to lend him so much money without some pawne, if he should have asked it, but he did not aske it, poor man, and so no harm done. After dinner, he gone, I to my office and Lumbard Streete about money, and then to my office again, very busy, and so till late, and then a song with my wife and Mercer in the garden, and so with great content to bed.

6th. Up, and after doing some business at my office abroad to Lumbard Street, about the getting of a good sum of money, thence home, in preparation for my having some good sum in my hands, for fear of a trouble in the State, that I may not have all I have in the world out of my hands and so be left a beggar. Having put that in a way, I home to the office, and so to the Tower, about shipping of some more pressed men, and that done, away to Broad Streete, to Sir G. Carteret, who is at a pay of tickets all alone, and I believe not less than one thousand people in the streets. But it is a pretty thing to observe that both there and every where else, a man shall see many women now-a-days of mean sort in the streets, but no men; men being so afeard of the press. I dined with Sir G. Carteret, and after dinner had much discourse about our publique business; and he do seem to fear every day more and more what I do; which is, a general confusion in the State; plainly answering me to the question, who is it that the weight of the warr depends [upon]? that it is only Sir W. Coventry. He tells me, too, the Duke of Albemarle is dissatisfied, and that the Duchesse do curse Coventry as the man that betrayed her husband to the sea: though I believe that it is not so. Thence to Lumbard Streete, and received £2,000, and carried it home: whereof £1,000 in gold. The greatest quantity not only that I ever had of gold, but that ever I saw together, and is not much above half a 100lb. bag full, but is much weightier. This I do for security sake, and convenience of carriage; though it costs me above £70 the change of it, at 18½*d.* per piece. Being at home, I there met with a letter from Bab Allen,[1] to invite me to be godfather to her boy, with Mrs. Williams, which I consented to, but know not the time when it is to be. Thence down to the Old Swan, calling at Michell's, he not being within, and there I did steal a kiss or two of her, and staying a little longer, he come in, and her father, whom I carried to Westminster, my business being thither, and so back again home, and very busy all the evening. At night a song in the garden and to bed.

7th. At the office all the morning, at noon dined at home and Creed with me, and after dinner he and I two or three hours in my chamber discoursing of the fittest way for a man to do that hath money, and find all he offers of turning some into gold and leaving some in a friend's hand is nothing more than what I thought of myself, but is doubt-

[1] Mrs. Knipp. See January 5th, 1665–66.

ful, as well as I, what is best to be done of all these or other ways to be thought on. He tells me he finds all things mighty dull at Court; and that they now begin to lie long in bed; it being, as we suppose, not seemly for them to be found playing and gaming as they used to be; nor that their minds are at ease enough to follow those sports, and yet not knowing how to employ themselves (though there be work enough for their thoughts and councils and pains), they keep long in bed. But he thinks with me, that there is nothing in the world can helpe us but the King's personal looking after his business and his officers, and that with that we may yet do well; but otherwise must be undone: nobody at this day taking care of any thing, nor hath any body to call him to account for it. Thence left him and to my office all the afternoon busy, and in some pain in my back by some bruise or other I have given myself in my right testicle this morning, and the pain lies there and hath done, and in my back thereupon all this day. At night into the garden to my wife and Lady Pen and Pegg, and Creed, who staid with them till 10 at night. My Lady Pen did give us a tarte and other things, and so broke up late and I to bed. It proved the hottest night that ever I was in in my life, and thundered and lightened all night long and rained hard. But, Lord! to see in what [fear] I lay a good while, hearing of a little noise of somebody walking in the house: so rung the bell, and it was my mayds going to bed about one o'clock in the morning. But the fear of being robbed, having so much money in the house, was very great, and is still so, and do much disquiet me.

8th (Lord's day). Up, and pretty well of my pain, so that it did not trouble me at all, and I do clearly find that my pain in my back was nothing but only accompanied my bruise in my stones. To church, wife and Mercer and I, in expectation of hearing some mighty preacher to-day, Mrs. Mary Batelier sending us word so; but it proved our ordinary silly lecturer, which made me merry, and she laughed upon us to see her mistake. At noon W. Hewer dined with us, and a good dinner, and I expected to have had newes sent me of Knipp's christening to-day; but, hearing nothing of it, I did not go, though I fear it is but their forgetfulness and so I may disappoint them. To church, after dinner, again, a thing I have not done a good while before, go twice in one day. After church with my wife and Mercer and Tom by water through bridge to the Spring Garden at Fox Hall, and thence down to Deptford and there did a little business, and so back home and to bed.

9th. Up betimes, and with Sir W. Pen in his coach to Westminster to Sir G. Downing's, but missed of him, and so we parted, I by water home, where busy all the morning, at noon dined at home, and after dinner to my office, where busy till come to by Lovett and his wife, who have brought me some sheets of paper varnished on one side, which lies very white and smooth and, I think, will do our business most exactly, and will come up to the use that I intended them for, and I am apt to believe will be an invention that will take in the world. I have made up a little book of it to give Sir W. Coventry to-morrow, and am very well pleased with it. Home with them, and there find my aunt Wight with my wife come to take her leave of her, being going for the summer into the country; and there was also Mrs. Mary Batelier and her sister, newly come out of France, a black, very black woman, but mighty good-natured people both, as ever I saw. Here I made the black one sing a French song, which she did mighty innocently; and then Mrs. Lovett play on the lute, which she do very well; and then Mercer and I sang; and so, with great pleasure, I left them, having shewed them my chamber, and £1,000 in gold, which they wondered at, and given them sweetmeats, and shewn my aunt Wight my father's picture, which she admires. So I left them and to the office, where Mr. Moore come to me and talking of my Lord's family business tells me that Mr. Sheply is ignorantly, we all believe, mistaken in his accounts above £700 more than he can discharge himself of, which is a mighty misfortune, poor man, and may undo him, and yet every body believes that he do it most honestly. I am troubled for him very much. He gone, I hard at the office till night, then home to supper and to bed.

10th. Up, and to the office, where busy all the morning, sitting, and there presented Sir W. Coventry with my little book made up of Lovett's varnished paper, which he and the whole board liked very well. At noon home to dinner and then to the office; the yarde being very full of women (I believe above three hundred) coming to get money for their husbands and friends that are prisoners in Holland; and they lay clamouring and swearing and cursing us, that my wife and I were afeard to send a venison-pasty that we have for supper to-night to the cook's to be baked, for fear of their offering violence to it: but it went, and no hurt done. Then I took an opportunity, when they were all gone into the fore-yarde, and slipt into the office and there busy all the afternoon, but by and by the women got into the garden, and come all to my closett window, and there tormented me, and I confess their cries were so sad for money, and laying down the condition of their families and their husbands, and what they have done and suffered for the King, and how ill they are used by us, and how well the Dutch are used here by the allowance of their masters, and what their husbands are offered to serve the Dutch abroad, that I do most heartily pity them, and was ready to cry to hear them, but cannot helpe them. However, when the rest were gone, I did call one to me that I heard complaine only and pity her husband and did give her some money, and she blessed me and went away. Anon my business at the office being done I to the Tower to speak with Sir John Robinson about business, principally the bad condition of the pressed men for want of clothes, so it is represented from the fleete, and so to provide them shirts and stockings and drawers. Having done with him about that, I home and there find my wife and the two Mrs. Bateliers walking in the garden. I with them till almost 9 at night, and then they and we and Mrs. Mercer, the mother, and her daughter Anne, and our Mercer, to supper to a good venison-pasty and other good things, and had a good supper, and very merry, Mistresses Bateliers being both very good-humoured. We sang and talked, and then led them home, and there they made us drink; and, among other things, did show us, in cages, some birds brought from about Bourdeaux, that are all fat, and, examining one of them, they are so, almost all fat. Their name is [Ortolans],[1] which are brought over to the King for him to eat, and indeed are excellent things.

[1] There is a blank space here in the MS.

We parted from them and so home to bed, it being very late, and to bed.

11th. Up, and by water to Sir G. Downing's, there to discourse with him about the reliefe of the prisoners in Holland; which I did, and we do resolve of the manner of sending them some. So I away by coach to St. James's, and there hear that the Duchesse is lately brought to bed of a boy.[1] By and by called to wait on the Duke, the King being present; and there agreed, among other things, of the places to build the ten new great ships ordered to be built, and as to the relief of prisoners in Holland. And then about several stories of the basenesse of the King of Spayne's being served with officers: they in Flanders having as good common men as any Prince in the world, but the veriest cowards for the officers, nay for the generall officers, as the Generall and Lieutenant-generall, in the whole world. But, above all things, the King did speake most in contempt of the ceremoniousnesse of the King of Spayne, that he do nothing but under some ridiculous form or other, and will not piss but another must hold the chamber-pot. Thence to Westminster Hall and there staid a while, and then to the Swan and kissed Sarah, and so home to dinner, and after dinner out again to Sir Robert Viner, and there did agree with him to accommodate some business of tallys so as I shall get in near £2,000 into my own hands, which is in the King's, upon tallys; which will be a pleasure to me, and satisfaction to have a good sum in my own hands, whatever evil disturbances should be in the State; though it troubles me to lose so great a profit as the King's interest of ten per cent. for that money. Thence to Westminster, doing several things by the way, and there failed of meeting Mrs. Lane, and so by coach took up my wife at her sister's, and so away to Islington, she and I alone, and so through Hackney, and home late, our discourse being about laying up of some money safe in prevention to the troubles I am afeard we may have in the state, and so sleepy (for want of sleep the last night, going to bed late and rising betimes in the morning) home, but when I come to the office, I there met with a command from my Lord Arlington, to go down

[1] Charles Stuart, born on the 4th; created Duke of Kendal; died May 22nd, 1667.

to a galliott at Greenwich, by the King's particular command, that is going to carry the Savoy Envoye over, and we fear there may be many Frenchmen there on board; and so I have a power and command to search for and seize all that have not passes from one of the Secretarys of State, and to bring them and their papers and everything else in custody some whither. So I to the Tower, and got a couple of musquetiers with me, and Griffen and my boy Tom and so down; and, being come, found none on board but two or three servants, looking to horses and doggs, there on board, and, seeing no more, I staid not long there, but away and on shore at Greenwich, the night being late and the tide against us; so, having sent before, to Mrs. Clerke's and there I had a good bed, and well received, the whole people rising to see me, and among the rest young Mrs. Daniel, whom I kissed again and again alone, and so by and by to bed and slept pretty well.

12th. But was up again by five o'clock, and was forced to rise, having much business, and so up and dressed myself (enquiring, was told that Mrs. Tooker was gone hence to live at London) and away with Poundy to the Tower, and thence, having shifted myself, but being mighty drowsy for want of sleep, I by coach to St. James's, to Goring House,[1] there to wait on my Lord Arlington to give him an account of my night's worke, but he was not up, being not long since married:[2] so, after walking up and down the house below,— being the house I was once at Hartlib's[3] sister's wedding, and is a very fine house and finely furnished,— and then thinking it too much for me to lose time to wait my Lord's rising, I away to St. James's, and there to Sir W. Coventry, and wrote a letter to my Lord Arlington giving him an account of what I have done, and so with Sir W. Coventry into London, to the office. And all the way I observed him mightily to make mirth of the Duke of Albe-

[1] Goring House was afterwards named Arlington House, and stood on the site of the present Buckingham Palace.

[2] To Isabella, daughter of Louis de Nassau, Lord of Beverwaert and Count of Nassau, natural son of Prince Maurice. She was sister of the Countess of Ossory; her daughter by Lord Arlington was afterwards first Duchess of Grafton. — B.

[3] Nan Hartlib. See July 10th, 1660.

marle and his people about him, saying, that he was the happiest man in the world for doing of great things by sorry instruments. And so particularized in Sir W. Clerke, and Riggs, and Halsey, and others. And then again said that the only quality eminent in him was, that he did persevere; and indeed he is a very drudge, and stands by the King's business. And this he said, that one thing he was good at, that he never would receive an excuse if the thing was not done; listening to no reasoning for it, be it good or bad. But then I told him, what he confessed, that he would however give the man, that he employs, orders for removing of any obstruction that he thinks he shall meet with in the world, and instanced in several warrants that he issued for breaking open of houses and other outrages about the business of prizes, which people bore with either for affection or fear, which he believes would not have been borne with from the King, nor Duke, nor any man else in England, and I thinke he is in the right, but it is not from their love of him, but from something else I cannot presently say. Sir W. Coventry did further say concerning Warcupp, his kinsman, that had the simplicity to tell Sir W. Coventry, that the Duke did intend to go to sea and to leave him his agent on shore for all things that related to the sea. But, says Sir W. Coventry, I did believe but the Duke of Yorke would expect to be his agent on shore for all sea matters. And then he begun to say what a great man Warcupp was, and something else, and what was that but a great lyer; and told me a story, how at table he did, they speaking about antipathys, say, that a rose touching his skin any where, would make it rise and pimple;[1] and, by and by, the dessert coming, with roses upon it, the Duchesse[2] bid him try, and they did; but they rubbed and rubbed, but nothing would do in the world, by which his lie was found at then. He spoke contemptibly of Holmes and his mermidons, that come to take down the ships from hence, and have carried

[1] See Evelyn's "Diary," June 18th, 1670: "Lord Stafford rose from table, in some disorder, because there were roses stuck about the fruit when the discert was set on the table; such an antipathy, it seems, he had to them as once Lady Selenger also had, and to that degree that, as Sir Kenelm Digby tells us, laying but a rose upon her cheek, when she was asleep, it raised a blister; but Sir Kenelm was a teller of strange things."

[2] Of Albemarle.

them without any necessaries, or any thing almost, that they will certainly be longer getting ready than if they had staid here. In fine, I do observe, he hath no esteem nor kindnesse for the Duke's matters, but, contrarily, do slight him and them; and I pray God the Kingdom do not pay too dear by this jarring; though this blockheaded Duke I did never expect better from. At the office all the morning, at noon home and thought to have slept, my head all day being full of business and yet sleepy and out of order, and so I lay down on my bed in my gowne to sleep, but I could not, therefore about three o'clock up and to dinner and thence to the office, where Mrs. Burroughs, my pretty widow, was and so I did her business and sent her away by agreement, and presently I by coach after and took her up in Fenchurch Streete and away through the City, hiding my face as much as I could, but she being mighty pretty and well enough clad, I was not afeard, but only lest somebody should see me and think me idle. I quite through with her, and so into the fields Uxbridge way, a mile or two beyond Tyburne, and then back and then to Paddington, and then back to Lyssen green,[1] a place the coachman led me to (I never knew in my life) and there we eat and drank and so back to Charing Crosse, and there I set her down. All the way most excellent pretty company. I had her lips as much as I would, and a mighty pretty woman she is and very modest and yet kinde in all fair ways. All this time I passed with mighty pleasure, it being what I have for a long time wished for, and did pay this day 5*s.* forfeite for her company. She being gone, I to White Hall and there to Lord Arlington's, and met Mr. Williamson, and find there is no more need of my trouble about the Galliott, so with content departed, and went straight home, where at the office did the most at the office in that wearied and sleepy state I could, and so home to supper, and after supper falling to singing with Mercer did however sit up with her, she pleasing me with her singing of "Helpe, helpe,"[2] till past midnight and I not a whit drowsy, and so to bed.

[1] The manor of Lisson Green (originally Lilestone) was described at the end of the last century as "a pleasant village near Paddington." The name Lisson Grove still remains.

[2] "Help, help, O help, Divinity of Love," by Henry Lawes (see note, *ante*, May 31st, 1660).

13th. Lay sleepy in bed till 8 in the morning, then up and to the office, where till about noon, then out to the 'Change and several places, and so home to dinner. Then out again to Sir R. Viner, and there to my content settled the business of two tallys, so as I shall have £2,000 almost more of my owne money in my hand, which pleases me mightily, and so home and there to the office, where mighty busy, and then home to supper and to even my Journall and to bed. Our fleete being now in all points ready to sayle, but for the carrying of the two or three new ships, which will keepe them a day or two or three more. It is said the Dutch is gone off our coast, but I have no good reason to believe it, Sir W. Coventry not thinking any such thing.

14th. Up betimes to the office, to write fair a laborious letter I wrote as from the Board to the Duke of Yorke, laying out our want of money again; and particularly the business of Captain Cocke's tender[1] of hemp, which my Lord Bruncker brought in under an unknown hand without name. Wherein his Lordship will have no great successe, I doubt. That being done, I down to Thames-streete, and there agreed for four or five tons of corke, to send this day to the fleete, being a new device to make barricados with, instead of junke. By this means I come to see and kiss Mr. Hill's young wife, and a blithe young woman she is. So to the office and at noon home to dinner, and then sent for young Michell and employed him all the afternoon about weighing and shipping off of the corke, having by this means an opportunity of getting him 30 or 40*s*. Having set him a doing, I home and to the office very late, very busy, and did indeed dispatch much business, and so to supper and to bed. After a song in the garden, which, and after dinner, is now the greatest pleasure I take, and indeed do please me mightily, to bed, after washing my legs and feet with warm water in my kitchen. This evening I had Davila[2] brought home to me, and find it a most excellent history as ever I read.

[1] For which Pepys was to receive £500. — B.

[2] Enrico Caterino Davila (1576–1631) was one of the chief historical writers of Italy, and his "Storia delle guerre civili di Francia" covers a period of forty years, from the death of Henri II. to the Peace of Vervins in 1598.

15th (Lord's day). Up, and to church, where our lecturer made a sorry silly sermon, upon the great point of proving the truth of the Christian religion. Home and had a good dinner, expecting Mr. Hunt, but there comes only young Michell and his wife, whom my wife concurs with me to be a pretty woman, and with her husband is a pretty innocent couple. Mightily pleasant we were, and I mightily pleased in her company and to find my wife so well pleased with them also. After dinner he and I walked to White Hall, not being able to get a coach. He to the Abbey, and I to White Hall, but met with nobody to discourse with, having no great mind to be found idling there, and be asked questions of the fleete, so walked only through to the Parke, and there, it being mighty hot and I weary, lay down by the canaille, upon the grasse, and slept awhile, and was thinking of a lampoone which hath run in my head this weeke, to make upon the late fight at sea, and the miscarriages there; but other businesses put it out of my head. Having lain there a while, I then to the Abbey and there called Michell, and so walked in great pain, having new shoes on, as far as Fleete Streete and there got a coach, and so in some little ease home and there drank a great deale of small beer; and so took up my wife and Betty Michell and her husband, and away into the fields, to take the ayre, as far as beyond Hackny, and so back again, in our way drinking a great deale of milke, which I drank to take away my heartburne, wherewith I have of late been mightily troubled, but all the way home I did break abundance of wind behind, which did presage no good but a great deal of cold gotten. So home and supped and away went Michell and his wife, of whom I stole two or three salutes, and so to bed in some pain and in fear of more, which accordingly I met with, for I was in mighty pain all night long of the winde griping of my belly and making of me shit often and vomit too, which is a thing not usual with me, but this I impute to the milke that I drank after so much beer, but the cold, to my washing my feet the night before.

16th. Lay in great pain in bed all the morning and most of the afternoon, being in much pain, making little or no water, and indeed having little within to make any with.

And had great twinges with the wind all the day in my belly with wind. And a looseness with it, which however made it not so great as I have heretofore had it. A wonderful dark sky, and shower of rain this morning, which at Harwich proved so too with a shower of hail as big as walnuts. I had some broth made me to drink, which I love, only to fill up room. Up in the afternoon, and passed the day with Balty, who is come from sea for a day or two before the fight, and I perceive could be willing fairly to be out of the next fight, and I cannot much blame him, he having no reason by his place to be there; however, would not have him to be absent, manifestly to avoid being there. At night grew a little better and took a glyster of sacke, but taking it by halves it did me not much good, I taking but a little of it. However, to bed, and had a pretty good night of it.

17th. So as to be able to rise to go to the office and there sat, but now and then in pain, and without making much water, or freely. However, it grew better and better, so as after dinner believing the jogging in a coach would do me good, I did take my wife out to the New Exchange to buy things. She there while I with Balty went and bought a common riding-cloake for myself, to save my best. It cost me but 30*s.*, and will do my turne mighty well. Thence home and walked in the garden with Sir W. Pen a while, and saying how the riding in the coach do me good (though I do not yet much find it), he ordered his to be got ready while I did some little business at the office, and so abroad he and I after 8 o'clock at night, as far almost as Bow, and so back again, and so home to supper and to bed. This day I did bid Balty to agree with ——, the Dutch paynter, which he once led me to, to see landskipps, for a winter piece of snow, which indeed is a good piece, and costs me but 40*s.*, which I would not take the money again for, it being, I think, very good. After a little supper to bed, being in less pain still, and had very good rest.

18th. Up in good case, and so by coach to St. James's after my fellows, and there did our business, which is mostly every day to complain of want of money, and that only will undo us in a little time. Here, among other things, before us all, the Duke of Yorke did say, that now at length he is come to a sure knowledge that the Dutch did lose in the late engagements twenty-nine captains and thirteen ships. Upon which Sir W. Coventry did publickly move, that if his Royal Highness had this of a certainty, it would be of use to send this down to the fleete, and to cause it to be spread about the fleete, for the recovering of the spirits of the officers and seamen; who are under great dejectedness for want of knowing that they did do any thing against the enemy, notwithstanding all that they did to us. Which, though it be true, yet methought was one of the most dishonourable motions to our countrymen that ever was made; and is worth remembering. Thence with Sir W. Pen home, calling at Lilly's,[1] to have a time appointed when to be drawn among the other Commanders of Flags the last year's fight. And so full of work Lilly is, that he was fain to take his table-book out to see how his time is appointed, and appointed six days hence for him to come between seven and eight in the morning. Thence with him home; and there by appointment I find Dr. Fuller, now Bishop of Limericke, in Ireland; whom I knew in his low condition at Twittenham.[2] I had also by his desire Sir W. Pen, and with him his lady and daughter, and had a good dinner, and find the Bishop the same good man as ever; and in a word, kind to us, and, methinks, one of the comeliest and most becoming prelates in all respects that ever I saw in my life. During dinner comes an acquaintance of his, Sir Thomas Littleton;[3] whom I knew not while he was in my house, but liked his discourse; and afterwards, by Sir W. Pen, do come to know that he is one of the greatest speakers in the House of Commons, and the usual second to the great Vaughan. So was sorry I did observe him no more, and gain more of his acquaintance. After dinner, they being gone, and I

[1] This portrait is now at Greenwich Hospital, and an engraving from it is given here.

[2] Twickenham, where Dr. William Fuller kept a school. He was translated to Lincoln in 1667 (see note, January 17th, 1659–60).

[3] Afterwards made Treasurer of the Navy, in conjunction with Sir Thomas Osborne. He was the eldest son of Sir Adam Littleton, of Stoke Milburgh, Salop, who had been created a baronet in 1642. He married Anne, daughter and heir of Edward, Lord Littleton, the Lord Keeper, and died in 1681, aged fifty-seven. Sir Thomas Littleton, the only son of this match, became Speaker of the House of Commons, and deceased, s. p., in 1709. — B.

mightily pleased with my guests, I down the river to Greenwich, about business, and thence walked to Woolwich, reading "the Rivall Ladys" all the way, and find it a most pleasant and fine writ play. At Woolwich saw Mr. Shelden, it being late, and there eat and drank, being kindly used by him and Bab, and so by water to Deptford, it being 10 o'clock before I got to Deptford, and dark, and there to Bagwell's, and, having staid there a while, away home, and after supper to bed. The Duke of Yorke said this day that by the letters from the Generals they would sail with the Fleete this day or to-morrow.

19th. Up in very good health in every respect, only my late fever got by my pain do break out about my mouth. So to the office, where all the morning sitting. Full of wants of money, and much stores to buy, for to replenish the stores, and no money to do it with, nor anybody to trust us without it. So at noon home to dinner, Balty and his wife with us. By and by Balty takes his leave of us, he going away just now towards the fleete, where he will pass through one great engagement more before he be two days older, I believe. I to the office, where busy all the afternoon, late, and then home, and, after some pleasant discourse to my wife, to bed. After I was in bed I had a letter from Sir W. Coventry that tells me that the fleete is sailed this morning; God send us good newes of them!

20th. Up, and finding by a letter late last night that the fleete is gone, and that Sir W. Pen[1] is ordered to go down to Sheernesse, and finding him ready to go to St. James's this morning, I was willing to go with him to see how things go, and so with him thither (but no discourse with the Duke), but to White Hall, and there the Duke of York did bid Sir W. Pen to stay to discourse with him and the King about business of the fleete, which troubled me a little, but it was only out of envy, for which I blame myself, having no reason to expect to be called to advise in a matter I understand not. So I away to Lovett's, there to see how

[1] Sir William Penn's instructions from the Duke of York directing him to embark on his Majesty's yacht "Henrietta," and to see to the manning of such ships as had been left behind by the fleet, dated on this day, 20th July, is printed in Penn's "Memorials of Sir W. Penn," vol. ii., p. 406.

my picture goes on to be varnished (a fine Crucifix),[1] which will be very fine; and here I saw some fine prints, brought from France by Sir Thomas Crew, who is lately returned. So home, calling at the stationer's for some paper fit to varnish, and in my way home met with Lovett, to whom I gave it, and he did present me with a varnished staffe, very fine and light to walk with. So home and to dinner, there coming young Mrs. Daniel and her sister Sarah, and dined with us; and old Mr. Hawly, whose condition pities me, he being forced to turne under parish-clerke at St. Gyles's, I think at the other end of the towne. Thence I to the office, where busy all the afternoon, and in the evening with Sir W. Pen, walking with whom in the garden I am of late mighty great, and it is wisdom to continue myself so, for he is of all the men of the office at present most manifestly usefull and best thought of. He and I supped together upon the seat in the garden, and thence, he gone, my wife and Mercer come and walked and sang late, and then home to bed.

21st. Up and to the office, where all the morning sitting. At noon walked in the garden with Commissioner Pett (newly come to towne), who tells me how infinite the disorders are among the commanders and all officers of the fleete. No discipline: nothing but swearing and cursing, and every body doing what they please; and the Generalls, understanding no better, suffer it, to the reproaching of this Board, or whoever it will be. He himself hath been challenged twice to the field, or something as good, by Sir Edward Spragge and Captain Seymour. He tells me that captains carry, for all the late orders, what men they please; demand and consume what provisions they please. So that he fears, and I do no less, that God Almighty cannot bless us while we keep in this disorder that we are in: he observing to me too, that there is no man of counsel or advice in the fleete; and the truth is, the gentlemen captains will undo us, for they are not to be kept in order, their friends about the King and Duke, and their own house, is so free, that it is not for any person but the Duke himself

[1] This picture occasioned Pepys trouble long afterwards, having been brought as evidence that he was a Papist (see "Life," vol. i., p. xxxiii).

to have any command over them. He gone I to dinner, and then to the office, where busy all the afternoon. At night walked in the garden with my wife, and so home to supper and to bed. Sir W. Pen is gone down to Sheernesse to-day to see things made ready against the fleete shall come in again, which makes Pett mad, and calls him dissembling knave, and that himself takes all the pains and is blamed, while he do nothing but hinder business and takes all the honour of it to himself, and tells me plainly he will fling up his commission rather than bear it.

22nd (Lord's day). Up, and to my chamber, and there till noon mighty busy, setting money matters and other things of mighty moment to rights to the great content of my mind, I finding that accounts but a little let go can never be put in order by strangers, for I cannot without much difficulty do it myself. After dinner to them again till about four o'clock and then walked to White Hall, where saw nobody almost, but walked up and down with Hugh May, who is a very ingenious man. Among other things, discoursing of the present fashion of gardens to make them plain, that we have the best walks of gravell in the world, France having none, nor Italy; and our green of our bowling allies is better than any they have. So our business here being ayre, this is the best way, only with a little mixture of statues, or pots, which may be handsome, and so filled with another pot of such or such a flower or greene as the season of the year will bear. And then for flowers, they are best seen in a little plat by themselves; besides, their borders spoil the walks of another garden: and then for fruit, the best way is to have walls built circularly one within another, to the South, on purpose for fruit, and leave the walking garden only for that use. Thence walked through the House, where most people mighty hush and, methinks, melancholy. I see not a smiling face through the whole Court; and, in my conscience, they are doubtfull of the conduct again of the Generalls, and I pray God they may not make their fears reasonable. Sir Richard Fanshaw is lately dead[1] at Madrid. Guyland is lately overthrowne wholly in Barbary by the King of Tafiletta. The fleete

[1] He died June 16th, 1666 (see note, *ante*, June 29th, 1660).

cannot yet get clear of the River, but expect the first wind to be out, and then to be sure they fight. The Queene and Maids of Honour are at Tunbridge.

23rd. Up, and to my chamber doing several things there of moment, and then comes Sympson, the Joyner; and he and I with great pains contriving presses to put my books up in: they now growing numerous, and lying one upon another on my chairs, I lose the use to avoyde the trouble of removing them, when I would open a book. Thence out to the Excise office about business, and then homewards met Colvill, who tells me he hath £1,000 ready for me upon a tally; which pleases me, and yet I know not now what to do with it, having already as much money as is fit for me to have in the house, but I will have it. I did also meet Alderman Backewell, who tells me of the hard usage he now finds from Mr. Fen, in not getting him a bill or two paid, now that he can be no more usefull to him; telling me that what by his being abroad and Shaw's death he hath lost the ball, but that he doubts not to come to give a kicke at it still, and then he shall be wiser and keepe it while he hath it. But he says he hath a good master, the King, who will not suffer him to be undone,[1] as otherwise he must have been, and I believe him. So home and to dinner, where I confess, reflecting upon the ease and plenty that I live in, of money, goods, servants, honour, every thing, I could not but with hearty thanks to Almighty God ejaculate my thanks to Him while I was at dinner, to myself. After dinner to the office and there till five or six o'clock, and then by coach to St. James's and there with Sir W. Coventry and Sir G. Downing to take the ayre in the Parke. All full of expectation of the fleete's engagement, but it is not yet. Sir W. Coventry says they are eighty-nine men-of-warr, but one fifth-rate, and that, the Sweepstakes, which carries forty guns. They are most infinitely manned. He tells me the Loyall London, Sir J. Smith (which, by the way, he commends to be the best ship in the world, large and small), hath above eight hundred men; and moreover takes notice, which is worth notice, that the fleete hath laine now near

[1] He had reason afterwards to alter his opinion of his "good master, the King," by whom he was ruined (see note, *ante*, June 23rd, 1660). — M. B.

fourteen days without any demand for a farthing-worth of any thing of any kind, but only to get men. He also observes, that with this excesse of men, nevertheless, they have thought fit to leave behind them sixteen ships, which they have robbed of their men, which certainly might have been manned, and they been serviceable in the fight, and yet the fleete well-manned, according to the excesse of supernumeraries, which we hear they have. At least two or three of them might have been left manned, and sent away with the Gottenburgh ships. They conclude this to be much the best fleete, for force of guns, greatnesse and number of ships and men, that ever England did see; being, as Sir W. Coventry reckons, besides those left behind, eighty-nine men of warr, and twenty fire-ships, though we cannot hear that they have with them above eighteen. The French are not yet joined with the Dutch, which do dissatisfy the Hollanders, and if they should have a defeat, will undo De Witt;[1] the people generally of Holland do hate this league with France. We cannot think of any business, but lie big with expectation of the issue of this fight, but do conclude that, this fight being over, we shall be able to see the whole issue of the warr, good or bad. So homeward, and walked over the Parke (St. James's) with Sir G. Downing, and at White Hall took a coach; and there to supper with much pleasure and to bed.

24th. Up, and to the office, where little business done, our heads being full of expectation of the fleete's being engaged, but no certain notice of it, only Sheppeard in the Duke's yacht left them yesterday morning within a league of the Dutch fleete, and making after them, they standing into the sea. At noon to dinner, and after dinner with Mercer (as of late my practice is) a song and so to the office, there to set up again my frames about my Platts, which I have got to be all gilded, and look very fine, and then to my business, and busy very late, till midnight, drawing up a representation of the state of my victualling business to the Duke, I having never appeared to him doing anything yet and therefore I now do it in writing, I now having the advantage of having had two fleetes dispatched

[1] Pepys seems to have foreseen the fate of De Witt. — B.

in better condition than ever any fleetes were yet, I believe; at least, with least complaint, and by this means I shall with the better confidence get my bills out for my salary. So home to bed.

25th. Up betimes to write fair my last night's paper for the Duke, and so along with Sir W. Batten by hackney coach to St. James's, where the Duke is gone abroad with the King to the Parke, but anon come back to White Hall, and we, after an houre's waiting, walked thither (I having desired Sir W. Coventry in his chamber to read over my paper about the victualling, which he approves of, and I am glad I showed it him first, it makes it the less necessary to show it the Duke at all, if I find it best to let it alone). At White Hall we find [the Court] gone to Chappell, it being St. James's-day. And by and by, while they are at chappell, and we waiting chappell being done, come people out of the Parke, telling us that the guns are heard plain. And so every body to the Parke, and by and by the chappell done, and the King and Duke into the bowling-green, and upon the leads, whither I went, and there the guns were plain to be heard; though it was pretty to hear how confident some would be in the loudnesse of the guns, which it was as much as ever I could do to hear them. By and by the King to dinner, and I waited there his dining; but, Lord! how little I should be pleased, I think, to have so many people crowding about me; and among other things it astonished me to see my Lord Barkeshire[1] waiting at table, and serving the King drink, in that dirty pickle as I never saw man in my life. Here I met Mr. Williams, who in serious discourse told me he did hope well of this fight because of the equality of force or rather our having the advantage in number, and also because we did not go about it with the presumption that we did heretofore, when, he told me, he did before the last fight look upon us by our pride fated to be overcome. He would have me to dine where he was invited to dine, at the Backe-stayres. So after the King's meat was taken away, we thither; but he could not stay, but left me there among two or three of the King's servants, where we dined

[1] Thomas Howard, second son of Thomas, first Earl of Suffolk, created Knight of the Garter in 1625, and Earl of Berkshire in February, 1625-26. Died July 16th, 1669, aged nearly ninety.

with the meat that come from his table; which was most excellent, with most brave drink cooled in ice (which at this hot time was welcome), and I drinking no wine, had metheglin for the King's owne drinking, which did please me mightily. Thence, having dined mighty nobly, I away to Mrs. Martin's new lodgings, where I find her, and was with her close, but, Lord! how big she is already. She is, at least seems, in mighty trouble for her husband at sea, when I am sure she cares not for him, and I would not undeceive her, though I know his ship is one of those that is not gone, but left behind without men. Thence to White Hall again to hear news, but found none; so back toward Westminster, and there met Mrs. Burroughs, whom I had a mind to meet, but being undressed did appear a mighty ordinary woman. Thence by water home, and out again by coach to Lovett's to see my Crucifix, which is not done. So to White Hall again to have met Sir G. Carteret, but he is gone abroad, so back homewards, and seeing Mr. Spong took him up, and he and I to Reeves, the glass maker's, and did see several glasses and had pretty discourse with him, and so away and set down Mr. Spong in London, and so home and with my wife, late, twatling at my Lady Pen's, and so home to supper and to bed. I did this afternoon call at my woman that ruled my paper to bespeak a musique card, and there did kiss Nan. No news to-night from the fleete how matters go yet.

26th. Up, and to the office, where all the morning. At noon dined at home: Mr. Hunt and his wife, who is very gallant, and newly come from Cambridge, because of the sicknesse, with us. Very merry at table, and the people I do love mightily, but being in haste to go to White Hall I rose, and Mr. Hunt with me, and by coach thither, where I left him in the boarded gallery, and I by appointment to attend the Duke of Yorke at his closett, but being not come, Sir G. Carteret and I did talke together, and [he] advises me, that, if I could, I would get the papers of examination touching the business of the last year's prizes, which concern my Lord Sandwich, out of Warcupp's hands, who being now under disgrace and poor, he believes may be brought easily to part with them. My Lord Crew, it seems, is fearfull yet that matters may be enquired into.

This I will endeavour to do, though I do not thinke it signifies much. By and by the Duke of Yorke comes and we had a meeting and, among other things, I did read my declaration of the proceedings of the Victualling hired this yeare, and desired his Royall Highnesse to give me the satisfaction of knowing whether his Royall Highnesse were pleased therewith. He told me he was, and that it was a good account, and that the business of the Victualling was much in a better condition than it was the last yeare; which did much joy me, being said in the company of my fellows, by which I shall be able with confidence to demand my salary and the rest of the subsurveyors. Thence away mightily satisfied to Mrs. Pierce's, there to find my wife. Mrs. Pierce hath lain in of a boy about a month. The boy is dead this day. She lies in good state, and very pretty she is, but methinks do every day grow more and more great, and a little too much, unless they get more money than I fear they do. Thence with my wife and Mercer to my Lord Chancellor's new house, and there carried them up to the leads, where I find my Lord Chamberlain, Lauderdale, Sir Robert Murray,[1] and others, and do find it the most delightfull place for prospect that ever was in the world, and even ravishing me, and that is all, in short, I can say of it. Thence to Islington to our old house and eat and drank, and so round by Kingsland home, and there to the office a little and Sir W. Batten's, but no newes at all from the fleete, and so home to bed.

27th. Up and to the office, where all the morning busy. At noon dined at home and then to the office again, and there walking in the garden with Captain Cocke till 5 o'clock. No newes yet of the fleete. His great bargaine of Hempe with us by his unknown proposition is disliked by the King, and so is quite off; of which he is glad, by this means being rid of his obligation to my Lord Bruncker, which he was tired with, and especially his mistresse, Mrs. Williams, and so will fall into another way about it, wherein he will advise only with myself, which do not displease me, and will be better for him and the King too.

[1] Sir Robert Moray, one of the founders of the Royal Society, who acted frequently as president before the charter of 1662, and as vice-president afterwards.

Much common talke of publique business, the want of money, the uneasinesse that Parliament will find in raising any, and the ill condition we shall be in if they do not, and his confidence that the Swede is true to us, but poor, but would be glad to do us all manner of service in the world. He gone, I away by water from the Old Swan to White Hall. The waterman tells me that newes is come that our ship Resolution is burnt, and that we had sunke four or five of the enemy's ships. When I come to White Hall I met with Creed, and he tells me the same news, and walking with him to the Park I to Sir W. Coventry's lodging, and there he showed me Captain Talbot's letter, wherein he says that the fight begun on the 25th; that our White squadron begun with one of the Dutch squadrons, and then the Red with another so hot that we put them both to giving way, and so they continued in pursuit all the day, and as long as he stayed with them: that the Blue fell to the Zealand squadron; and after a long dispute, he against two or three great ships, he received eight or nine dangerous shots, and so come away; and says, he saw the Resolution burned by one of their fire-ships, and four or five of the enemy's. But says that two or three of our great ships were in danger of being fired by our owne fire-ships, which Sir W. Coventry, nor I, cannot understand. But upon the whole, he and I walked two or three turns in the Parke under the great trees, and do doubt that this gallant is come away a little too soon, having lost never a mast nor sayle. And then we did begin to discourse of the young gentlemen captains, which he was very free with me in speaking his mind of the unruliness of them; and what a losse the King hath of his old men, and now of this Hannam,[1] of the Resolution, if he be dead, and that there is but few old sober men in the fleete, and if these few of the Flags that are so should die, he fears some other gentlemen captains will get in, and then what a council we shall have, God knows. He told me how he is disturbed to hear the commanders at sea called cowards here on shore, and that he was yesterday concerned publiquely at a dinner to defend them, against somebody

[1] Captain Willoughby Hannam, or Hanham, greatly distinguished himself in this action. He, his officers, and crew were saved, and he lived on till 1672, when he was killed in the action off Solebay.

that said that not above twenty of them fought as they should do, and indeed it is derived from the Duke of Albemarle himself, who wrote so to the King and Duke, and that he told them how they fought four days, two of them with great disadvantage. The Count de Guiche,[1] who was on board De Ruyter, writing his narrative home in French of the fight, do lay all the honour that may be upon the English courage above the Dutch, and that he himself [Sir W. Coventry] was sent down from the King and Duke of Yorke after the fight, to pray them to spare none that they thought had not done their parts, and that they had removed but four, whereof Du Tell is one, of whom he would say nothing; but, it seems, the Duke of Yorke hath been much displeased at his removal, and hath now taken him into his service,[2] which is a plain affront to the Duke of Albemarle; and two of the others, Sir W. Coventry did speake very slenderly of their faults. Only the last, which was old Teddiman, he says, is in fault, and hath little to excuse himself with; and that, therefore, we should not be forward in condemning men of want of courage, when the Generalls, who are both men of metal, and hate cowards, and had the sense of our ill successe upon them (and by the way must either let the world thinke it was the miscarriage of the Captains or their owne conduct), have thought fit to remove no more of them, when desired by the King and Duke of Yorke to do it, without respect to any favour any of them can pretend to in either of them. At last we concluded that we never can hope to beat the Dutch with such advantage as now in number and force and a fleete in want of nothing, and he hath often repeated now and at other times industriously that many of the Captains have declared that they want nothing, and again, that they did lie ten days together at the Nore without demanding of any thing in the world but men, and of them they afterward, when they went away, the generalls themselves acknowledge that they have permitted several ships to carry supernumeraries, but that if we do not speede well, we must then play small games and spoile their trade in small parties. And so we parted, and I,

[1] Eldest son of the Duc de Grammont.

[2] Captain Du Tell, see *ante*, June 13th.

meeting Creed in the Parke again, did take him by coach and to Islington, thinking to have met my Lady Pen and wife, but they were gone, so we eat and drank and away back, setting him down in Cheapside and I home, and there after a little while making of my tune to "It is decreed," to bed.

28th. Up, and to the office, where no more newes of the fleete than was yesterday. Here we sat and at noon to dinner to the Pope's Head, where my Lord Bruncker and his mistresse dined and Commissioner Pett, Dr. Charleton,[1] and myself, entertained with a venison pasty by Sir W. Warren. Here very pretty discourse of Dr. Charleton's, concerning Nature's fashioning every creature's teeth according to the food she intends them; and that men's, it is plain, was not for flesh, but for fruit, and that he can at any time tell the food of a beast unknown by the teeth. My Lord Bruncker made one or two objections to it that creatures find their food proper for their teeth rather than that the teeth were fitted for the food, but the Doctor, I think, did well observe that creatures do naturally and from the first, before they have had experience to try, do love such a food rather than another, and that all children love fruit, and none brought to flesh, but against their wills at first. Thence with my Lord Bruncker to White Hall, where no news. So to St. James's to Sir W. Coventry, and there hear only of the Bredah's[2] being come in and gives the same small account that the other did yesterday, so that we know not what is done by the body of the fleete at all, but conceive great reason to hope well. Thence with my Lord to

[1] Walter Charleton, M.D., son of the Rev. Walter Charleton, rector of Shepton Mallet, in Somersetshire, was born in the rectory house, February 2nd, 1619, and soon after the breaking out of the Civil War he was appointed physician to the king. He was afterwards one of the travelling physicians to Charles II., and physician in ordinary to the king during his exile and after the Restoration. He was president of the College of Physicians in 1689, 1690, and 1691. He was a learned and voluminous author, and died on April 24th, 1707 (Munk's "Roll of the College of Physicians," vol. i., p. 390).

[2] In a letter from Richard Browne to Williamson, dated Aldborough, July 31st, we read, "It was the 'Breda,' not the 'Rainbow,' that was disabled, and her commander, Captain Saunders, sadly wounded" ("Calendar of State Papers," 1665–66, p. 594).

his coach-house, and there put in his six horses into his coach, and he and I alone to Highgate. All the way going and coming I learning of him the principles of Optickes, and what it is that makes an object seem less or bigger and how much distance do lessen an object, and that it is not the eye at all, or any rule in optiques, that can tell distance, but it is only an act of reason comparing of one mark with another, which did both please and inform me mightily. Being come thither we went to my Lord Lauderdale's house[1] to speake with him, about getting a man at Leith to joyne with one we employ to buy some prize goods for the King; we find [him] and his lady and some Scotch people at supper. Pretty odd company; though my Lord Bruncker tells me, my Lord Lauderdale is a man of mighty good reason and judgement. But at supper there played one of their servants upon the viallin some Scotch tunes only; several, and the best of their country, as they seemed to esteem them, by their praising and admiring them: but, Lord! the strangest ayre that ever I heard in my life, and all of one cast. But strange to hear my Lord Lauderdale say himself that he had rather hear a cat mew, than the best musique in the world; and the better the musique, the more sicke it makes him; and that of all instruments, he hates the lute most, and next to that, the baggpipe. Thence back with my Lord to his house, all the way good discourse, informing of myself about optiques still, and there left him and by a hackney home, and after writing three or four letters, home to supper and to bed.

29th (Lord's day). Up and all the morning in my chamber making up my accounts in my book with my father and brother and stating them. Towards noon before sermon was done at church comes newes by a letter to Sir W. Batten, to my hand, of the late fight, which I sent to his house, he at church. But, Lord! with what impatience I staid till sermon was done, to know the issue of the fight, with a thousand hopes and fears and thoughts about the consequences of either. At last sermon is done and he come home, and the bells immediately rung soon as the church

[1] Lauderdale House and grounds, on Highgate Hill, are now open to the public and known as Waterlow Park. The house is used for refreshment rooms.

was done. But coming to Sir W. Batten to know the newes, his letter said nothing of it; but all the towne is full of a victory. By and by a letter from Sir W. Coventry tells me that we have the victory. Beat them into the Weelings;[1] had taken two of their great ships; but by the orders of the Generalls they are burned. This being, methought, but a poor result after the fighting of two so great fleetes, and four days having no tidings of them, I was still impatient; but could know no more. So away home to dinner, where Mr. Spong and Reeves dined with me by invitation. And after dinner to our business of my microscope to be shown some of the observables of that, and then down to my office to looke in a darke room with my glasses and tube, and most excellently things appeared indeed beyond imagination. This was our worke all the afternoon trying the several glasses and several objects, among others, one of my plates, where the lines appeared so very plain that it is not possible to thinke how plain it was done. Thence satisfied exceedingly with all this we home and to discourse many pretty things, and so staid out the afternoon till it began to be dark, and then they away and I to Sir W. Batten, where the Lieutenant of the Tower[2] was, and Sir John Minnes, and the newes I find is no more or less than what I had heard before; only that our Blue squadron, it seems, was pursued the most of the time, having more ships, a great many, than its number allotted to her share. Young Seamour[3] is killed, the only captain slain. The Resolution burned; but, as they say, most of her [crew] and commander saved. This is all, only we keep the sea, which denotes a victory, or at least that we are not beaten; but no great matters to brag of, God knows. So home to supper and to bed.

30th. Up, and did some business in my chamber, then by and by comes my boy's Lute-Master, and I did direct

[1] In a letter from Richard Browne to Williamson, dated Yarmouth, July 30th, we read, "The Zealanders were engaged with the Blue squadron Wednesday and most of Thursday, but at length the Zealanders ran; the Dutch fleet escaped to the Weelings and Goree" ("Calendar of State Papers," 1665-66, p. 591).

[2] Sir John Robinson.

[3] Captain Hugh Seymour, of the "Foresight."

him hereafter to begin to teach him to play his part on the Theorbo, which he will do, and that in a little time I believe. So to the office, and there with Sir W. Warren, with whom I have spent no time a good while. We set right our business of the Lighters, wherein I thinke I shall get £100. At noon home to dinner and there did practise with Mercer one of my new tunes that I have got Dr. Childe to set me a base to and it goes prettily. Thence abroad to pay several debts at the end of the month, and so to Sir W. Coventry, at St. James's, where I find him in his new closett, which is very fine, and well supplied with handsome books. I find him speak very slightly of the late victory: dislikes their staying with the fleete up their coast, believing that the Dutch will come out in fourteen days, and then we with our unready fleete, by reason of some of the ships being maymed, shall be in bad condition to fight them upon their owne coast: is much dissatisfied with the great number of men, and their fresh demands of twenty-four victualling ships, they going out but the other day as full as they could stow. I asked him whether he did never desire an account of the number of supernumeraries, as I have done several ways, without which we shall be in great errour about the victuals; he says he has done it again and again, and if any mistake should happen they must thanke themselves. He spoke slightly of the Duke of Albemarle, saying, when De Ruyter come to give him a broadside — "Now," says he, chewing of tobacco the while, "will this fellow come and give me two broadsides, and then he will run;" but it seems he held him to it two hours, till the Duke himself was forced to retreat to refit, and was towed off, and De Ruyter staied for him till he come back again to fight. One in the ship saying to the Duke, "Sir, methinks De Ruyter hath given us more than two broadsides;" — "Well," says the Duke, "but you shall find him run by and by," and so he did, says Sir W. Coventry; but after the Duke himself had been first made to fall off. The Resolution had all brass guns, being the same that Sir J. Lawson had in her in the Straights. It is observed, that the two fleetes were even in number to one ship. Thence home; and to sing with my wife and Mercer in the garden; and coming in I find my wife plainly dissatisfied with me, that I can spend so much time with Mercer, teaching her to sing, and could never take the pains with her. Which I acknowledge; but it is because that the girl do take musique mighty readily, and she do not, and musique is the thing of the world that I love most, and all the pleasure almost that I can now take. So to bed in some little discontent, but no words from me.

31st. Good friends in the morning and up to the office, where sitting all the morning, and while at table we were mightily joyed with newes brought by Sir J. Minnes and Sir W. Batten of the death of De Ruyter, but when Sir W. Coventry come, he told us there was no such thing, which quite dashed me again, though, God forgive me! I was a little sorry in my heart before lest it might give occasion of too much glory to the Duke of Albemarle. Great bandying this day between Sir W. Coventry and my Lord Bruncker about Captain Cocke, which I am well pleased with, while I keepe from any open relyance on either side, but rather on Sir W. Coventry's. At noon had a haunch of venison boiled and a very good dinner besides, there dining with me on a sudden invitation the two mayden sisters, Bateliers, and their elder brother, a pretty man, understanding and well discoursed, much pleased with his company. Having dined myself I rose to go to a Committee of Tangier, and did come thither time enough to meet Povy and Creed and none else. The Court being empty, the King being gone to Tunbridge, and the Duke of Yorke a-hunting. I had some discourse with Povy, who is mightily discontented, I find, about his disappointments at Court; and says, of all places, if there be hell, it is here. No faith, no truth, no love, nor any agreement between man and wife, nor friends. He would have spoke broader, but I put it off to another time; and so parted. Then with Creed and read over with him the narrative of the late [fight], which he makes a very poor thing of, as it is indeed, and speaks most slightingly of the whole matter. Povy discoursed with me about my Lord Peterborough's £50 which his man did give me from him, the last year's salary I paid him, which he would have Povy pay him again; but I have not taken it to myself yet, and therefore will most heartily return him, and mark him out for a coxcomb. Povy went down to Mr. Williamson's, and brought me up this extract out of the Flanders' letters to-day come: — That Admiral Everson, and the Admiral and Vice-Admiral of Freezeland,[1] with many captains and men, are slain; that De Ruyter is safe, but lost 250 men out of his own ship; but that he is in great disgrace, and Trump in better favour; that Bankert's ship is burned, himself hardly escaping with a few men on board De Haes; that fifteen captains are to be tried the seventh of August; and that the hangman was sent from Flushing to assist the Council of Warr. How much of this is true, time will shew. Thence to Westminster Hall and walked an hour with Creed talking of the late fight, and observing the ridiculous management thereof and success of the Duke of Albemarle. Thence parted and to Mrs. Martin's lodgings, and sat with her a while, and then by water home, all the way reading the Narrative of the late fight in order, it may be, to the making some marginal notes upon it. At the Old Swan found my Betty Michell at the doore, where I staid talking with her a pretty while, it being dusky, and kissed her and so away home and writ my letters, and then home to supper, where the brother and Mary Batelier are still and Mercer's two sisters. They have spent the time dancing this afternoon, and we were very merry, and then after supper into the garden and there walked, and then home with them and then back again, my wife and I and the girle, and sang in the garden and then to bed. Colville was with me this morning, and to my great joy I could now have all my money in, that I have in the world. But the times being open again, I thinke it is best to keepe some of it abroad. Mighty well, and end this month in content of mind and body. The publique matters looking more safe for the present than they did, and we having a victory over the Dutch just such as I could have wished, and as the kingdom was fit to bear, enough to give us the name of conquerors, and leave us masters of the sea, but without any such great matters done as should give the Duke of Albemarle any honour at all, or give him cause to rise to his former insolence.

[1] Admiral John Evertsen; Michael Adrian de Ruyter, Admiral of Friezland; Adrian Banckaert, Vice-Admiral of Holland.

August 1st. Up betimes to the settling of my last month's accounts, and I bless God I find them very clear, and that I am worth £5,700, the most that ever my book did yet make out. So prepared to attend the Duke of Yorke as usual, but Sir W. Pen, just as I was going out, comes home from Sheernesse, and held me in discourse about publique business, till I come by coach too late to St. James's, and there find that every thing stood still, and nothing done for want of me. Thence walked over the Parke with Sir W. Coventry, who I clearly see is not thoroughly pleased with the late management of the fight, nor with any thing that the Generalls do; only is glad to hear that De Ruyter is out of favour, and that this fight hath cost them 5,000 men, as they themselves do report. And it is a strange thing, as he observes, how now and then the slaughter runs on one hand; there being 5,000 killed on theirs, and not above 400 or 500 killed and wounded on ours, and as many flag-officers on theirs as ordinary captains in ours; there being Everson, and the Admiral and Vice-Admiral of Freezeland on theirs, and Seamour, Martin,[1] and ———, on ours. I left him going to Chappell, it being the common fast day, and the Duke of York at Chappell. And I to Mrs. Martin's, but she abroad, so I sauntered to or again to the Abbey, and then to the parish church, fearfull of being seen to do so, and so after the parish church was ended, I to the Swan and there dined upon a rabbit, and after dinner to Mrs. Martin's, and there find Mrs. Burroughs, and by and by comes a pretty widow, one Mrs. Eastwood, and one Mrs. Fenton, a maid; and here merry kissing and looking on their breasts, and all the innocent pleasure in the world. But, Lord! to see the dissembling of this widow, how upon the singing of a certain jigg by Doll, Mrs. Martin's sister, she seemed to be sick and fainted and God knows what, because the jigg which her husband (who died this last sickness) loved. But by and by I made her as merry as is possible, and towzled and tumbled her as I pleased, and then carried her and her sober pretty kinswoman Mrs. Fenton home to their lodgings in the new market[2] of my Lord Treasurer's, and

[1] Captain William Martin. He was buried in Aldeburgh Church.

[2] Southampton Market, established in 1662, and afterwards called

there left them. Mightily pleased with this afternoon's mirth, but in great pain to ride in a coach with them, for fear of being seen. So home, and there much pleased with my wife's drawing to-day in her pictures, and so to supper and to bed very pleasant.

2nd. [Up] and to the office, where we sat, and in discourse at the table with Sir W. Batten, I was obliged to tell him it was an untruth, which did displease him mightily, and parted at noon very angry with me. At home find Lovett, who brought me some papers varnished, and showed me my crucifix, which will be very fine when done. He dined with me and Balty's wife, who is in great pain for her husband, not hearing of him since the fight; but I understand he was not in it, going hence too late, and I am glad of it. Thence to the office, and thither comes to me Creed, and he and I walked a good while, and then to the victualling office together, and there with Mr. Gawden I did much business, and so away with Creed again, and by coach to see my Lord Bruncker, who it seems was not well yesterday, but being come thither, I find his coach ready to carry him abroad, but Tom, his footman, whatever the matter was, was lothe to desire me to come in, but I walked a great while in the Piatza till I was going away, but by and by my Lord himself comes down and coldly received me. So I soon parted, having enough for my over officious folly in troubling myself to visit him, and I am apt to think that he was fearfull that my coming was out of design to see how he spent his time [rather] than to enquire after his health. So parted, and I with Creed down to the New Exchange Stairs, and there I took water, and he parted, so home, and then down to Woolwich, reading and making an end of the "Rival Ladys," and find it a very pretty play. At Woolwich, it being now night, I find my wife and Mercer, and Mr. Batelier and Mary there, and a supper getting ready. So I staid, in some pain, it being late, and post night. So supped and merrily home, but it was twelve at night first. However, sent away some letters, and home to bed.

Bloomsbury Market. It was never very successful, and was swept away about 1847, when New Oxford Street was formed. Market Street still remains.

3rd. Up and to the office, where Sir W. Batten and I sat to contract for some fire-ships. I there close all the morning. At noon home to dinner, and then abroad to Sir Philip Warwicke's at White Hall about Tangier one quarter tallys, and there had some serious discourse touching money, and the case of the Navy, where in all I could get of him was that we had the full understanding of the treasure as much as my Lord Treasurer himself, and knew what he can do, and that whatever our case is, more money cannot be got till the Parliament. So talked of getting an account ready as soon as we could to give the Parliament, and so very melancholy parted. So I back again, calling my wife at her sister's, from whose husband we do now hear that he was safe this week, and going in a ship to the fleete from the buoy of the Nore, where he has been all this while, the fleete being gone before he got down. So home, and busy till night, and then to Sir W. Pen, with my wife, to sit and chat, and a small supper, and home to bed. The death of Everson, and the report of our success, beyond expectation, in the killing of so great a number of men, hath raised the estimation of the late victory considerably; but it is only among fools: for all that was but accidental. But this morning, getting Sir W. Pen to read over the Narrative with me, he did sparingly, yet plainly, say that we might have intercepted their Zealand squadron coming home, if we had done our parts; and more, that we might have spooned[1] before the wind as well as they, and have overtaken their ships in the pursuite, in all the while.

4th. Up and to the office, where all the morning, and at noon to dinner, and Mr. Cooke dined with us, who is lately come from Hinchingbroke, [Lord Hinchingbrooke] who is also come to town. The family all well. Then I to the office, where very busy to state to Mr. Coventry the account of the victuals of the fleete, and late at it, and then home to supper and to bed. This evening, Sir W.

[1] To spoom, or spoon, is to go right before the wind, without any sail. — *Sea Dictionary*, 1708. Dryden uses the word:

"When virtue spooms before a prosperous gale,
My heaving wishes help to fill the sail."

Hind and Panther, iii. 96.

Pen come into the garden, and walked with me, and told me that he had certain notice that at Flushing they are in great distraction. De Ruyter dares not come on shore for fear of the people; nor any body open their houses or shops for fear of the tumult: which is a very good hearing.

5th (Lord's day). Up, and down to the Old Swan, and there called Betty Michell and her husband, and had two or three long salutes from her out of sight of su mari, which pleased me mightily, and so carried them by water to Westminster, and I to St. James's, and there had a meeting before the Duke of Yorke, complaining of want of money, but nothing done to any purpose, for want we shall, so that now our advices to him signify nothing. Here Sir W. Coventry did acquaint the Duke of Yorke how the world do discourse of the ill method of our books, and that we would consider how to answer any enquiry which shall be made after our practice therein, which will I think concern the Controller most, but I shall make it a memento to myself. Thence walked to the Parish Church to have one look upon Betty Michell, and so away homeward by water, and landed to go to the church, where, I believe, Mrs. Horsely goes, by Merchant-tailors' Hall, and there I find in the pulpit Elborough,[1] my old schoolfellow and a simple rogue, and yet I find him preaching a very good sermon, and in as right a parson-like manner, and in good manner too, as I have heard any body; and the church very full, which is a surprising consideration; but I did not see her. So home, and had a good dinner, and after dinner with my wife, and Mercer, and Jane by water, all the afternoon up as high as Morclacke[2] with great pleasure, and a fine day, reading over the second part of the "Siege of Rhodes," with great delight. We landed and walked at Barne-elmes, and then at the Neat Houses I landed and bought a millon, and we did also land and eat and drink at Wandsworth, and so to the Old Swan, and thence walked home. It being a mighty fine cool evening, and there being come, my wife and I spent an houre in the garden talking of our living in the country, when I shall be turned out of the office, as

[1] St. Lawrence Poultney, of which parish Thomas Elborough was curate. See September 2nd, 1666. [2] Mortlake.

I fear the Parliament may find faults enough with the office to remove us all, and I am joyed to think in how good a condition I am to retire thither, and have wherewith very well to subsist. Nan, at Sir W. Pen's, lately married to one Markeham, a kinsman of Sir W. Pen's, a pretty wench she is.

6th. Up, and to the office a while, and then by water to my Lady Montagu's, at Westminster, and there visited my Lord Hinchingbroke, newly come from Hinchingbroke, and find him a mighty sober gentleman, to my great content. Thence to Sir Ph. Warwicke and my Lord Treasurer's, but failed in my business; so home and in Fenchurch-streete met with Mr. Battersby; says he, "Do you see Dan Rawlinson's[1] door shut up?" (which I did, and wondered). "Why," says he, "after all the sickness, and himself spending all the last year in the country, one of his men is now dead of the plague, and his wife and one of his mayds sicke, and himself shut up;" which troubles me mightily. So home; and there do hear also from Mrs. Sarah Daniel, that Greenwich is at this time much worse than ever it was, and Deptford too: and she told us that they believed all the towne would leave the towne and come to London; which is now the receptacle of all the people from all infected places. God preserve us! So by and by to dinner, and after dinner in comes Mrs. Knipp, and I being at the office went home to her, and there I sat and talked with her, it being the first time of her being here since her being brought to bed. I very pleasant with her; but perceive my wife hath no great pleasure in her being here, she not being pleased with my kindnesse to her.

[1] In the church of St. Dionis Backchurch, amongst other memorials of different members of his family, is a monument on a pillar for Daniel Rawlinson, the person mentioned in the text. He was a London wine merchant, descended from the Graisdales of Lancashire, born in this parish, and died in 1679, aged sixty-five. He was the father of Sir Thomas Rawlinson, President of Bridewell Hospital, and Lord Mayor in 1706; two of whose sons, Thomas and Richard, LL.D., were well known in the literary world as eminent antiquaries and book collectors, though their extensive libraries were ultimately consigned to the hammer. Richard, who had been educated at St. John's College, Oxford, will long be remembered as a munificent benefactor to that university (see Malcolm's "London," vol. iii., p. 438, edit. 1803). — B.

However, we talked and sang, and were very pleasant. By and by comes Mr. Pierce and his wife, the first time she also hath been here since her lying-in, both having been brought to bed of boys, and both of them dead. And here we talked, and were plesant, only my wife in a chagrin humour, she not being pleased with my kindnesse to either of them, and by and by she fell into some silly discourse wherein I checked her, which made her mighty pettish, and discoursed mighty offensively to Mrs. Pierce, which did displease me, but I would make no words, but put the discourse by as much as I could (it being about a report that my wife said was made of herself and meant by Mrs. Pierce, that she was grown a gallant, when she had but so few suits of clothes these two or three years, and a great deale of that silly discourse), and by and by Mrs. Pierce did tell her that such discourses should not trouble her, for there went as bad on other people, and particularly of herself at this end of the towne, meaning my wife, that she was crooked, which was quite false, which my wife had the wit not to acknowledge herself to be the speaker of, though she has said it twenty times. But by this means we had little pleasure in their visit; however, Knipp and I sang, and then I offered them to carry them home, and to take my wife with me, but she would not go: so I with them, leaving my wife in a very ill humour, and very slighting to them, which vexed me. However, I would not be removed from my civility to them, but sent for a coach, and went with them; and, in our way, Knipp saying that she come out of doors without a dinner to us, I took them to Old Fish Streete, to the very house and woman where I kept my wedding dinner,[1] where I never was since, and there I did give them a jole of salmon, and what else was to be had. And here we talked of the ill-humour of my wife, which I did excuse as much as I could, and they seemed to admit of it, but did both confess they wondered at it; but from thence to other discourse, and among others to that of my Lord Bruncker and Mrs. Williams, who it seems do speake mighty hardly of me for my not treating

[1] The tavern was evidently selected to mark Pepys's disgust at his wife's ill-humour; but he probably did not venture to mention the circumstance on his return home. — B

them, and not giving her something to her closett, and do speake worse of my wife, and dishonourably, but it is what she do of all the world, though she be a whore herself; sc I value it not. But they told me how poorly my Lord carried himself the other day to his kinswoman, Mrs. Howard, and was displeased because she called him uncle to a little gentlewoman that is there with him, which he will not admit of; for no relation is to be challenged from others to a lord, and did treat her thereupon very rudely and ungenteely. Knipp tells me also that my Lord keeps another woman besides Mrs. Williams; and that, when I was there the other day, there was a great hubbub in the house, Mrs. Williams being fallen sicke, because my Lord was gone to his other mistresse, making her wait for him till his return from the other mistresse; and a great deale of do there was about it; and Mrs. Williams swounded at it, at the very time when I was there and wondered at the reason of my being received so negligently. I set them both at home, Knipp at her house, her husband being at the doore; and glad she was to be found to have staid out so long with me and Mrs. Pierce, and none else; and Mrs. Pierce at her house, and am mightily pleased with the discretion of her during the simplicity and offensiveness of my wife's discourse this afternoon. I perceive by the new face at Mrs. Pierce's door that our Mary is gone from her. So I home, calling on W. Joyce in my coach, and staid and talked a little with him, who is the same silly prating fellow that ever he was, and so home, and there find my wife mightily out of order, and reproaching of Mrs. Pierce and Knipp as wenches, and I know not what. But I did give her no words to offend her, and quietly let all pass, and so to bed without any good looke or words to or from my wife.

7th. Up, and to the office, where we sat all the morning, and home to dinner, and then to the office again, being pretty good friends with my wife again, no angry words passed; but she finding fault with Mercer, suspecting that it was she that must have told Mary, that must have told her mistresse of my wife's saying that she was crooked. But the truth is, she is jealous of my kindnesse to her. After dinner, to the office, and did a great deale of business. In the evening comes Mr. Reeves, with a twelve-foote glasse, so I left the office and home, where I met Mr. Batelier with my wife, in order to our going to-morrow, by agreement, to Bow to see a dancing meeting. But, Lord! to see how soon I could conceive evil fears and thoughts concerning them; so Reeves and I and they up to the top of the house, and there we endeavoured to see the moon, and Saturne and Jupiter; but the heavens proved cloudy, and so we lost our labour, having taken pains to get things together, in order to the managing of our long glasse. So down to supper and then to bed, Reeves lying at my house, but good discourse I had from him in his own trade, concerning glasses, and so all of us late to bed. I receive fresh intelligence that Deptford and Greenwich are now afresh exceedingly afflicted with the sickness more than ever.

8th. Up, and with Reeves walk as far as the Temple, doing some business in my way at my bookseller's and elsewhere, and there parted, and I took coach, having first discoursed with Mr. Hooke a little, whom we met in the streete, about the nature of sounds, and he did make me understand the nature of musicall sounds made by strings, mighty prettily; and told me that having come to a certain number of vibrations proper to make any tone, he is able to tell how many strokes a fly makes with her wings (those flies that hum in their flying) by the note that it answers to in musique during their flying. That, I suppose, is a little too much refined; but his discourse in general of sound was mighty fine. There I left them, and myself by coach to St. James's, where we attended with the rest of my fellows on the Duke, whom I found with two or three patches upon his nose and about his right eye, which come from his being struck with the bough of a tree the other day in his hunting; and it is a wonder it did not strike out his eye. After we had done our business with him, which is now but little, the want of money being such as leaves us little to do but to answer complaints of the want thereof, and nothing to offer to the Duke, the representing of our want of money being now become uselesse, I into the Park, and there I met with Mrs. Burroughs by appointment, and did agree (after discoursing of some business of her's) for her to meet me at New Exchange, while I by coach to my Lord Treasurer's, and then called at the New Exchange, and thence carried her by water to Parliament stayres, and I to the Exchequer about my Tangier quarter tallys, and that done I took coach and to the west door of the Abby, where she come to me, and I with her by coach to Lissen-greene where we were last, and staid an hour or two before dinner could be got for us, I in the meantime having much pleasure with her, but all honest. And by and by dinner come up, and then to my sport again, but still honest; and then took coach and up and down in the country toward Acton, and then toward Chelsy, and so to Westminster, and there set her down where I took her up, with mighty pleasure in her company, and so I by coach home, and thence to Bow, with all the haste I could, to my Lady Pooly's,[1] where my wife was with Mr. Batelier and his sisters, and there I found a noble supper, and every thing exceeding pleasant, and their mother, Mrs. Batelier, a fine woman, but mighty passionate upon sudden news brought her of the loss of a dog borrowed of the Duke of Albemarle's son to line a bitch of hers that is very pretty, but the dog was by and by found, and so all well again, their company mighty innocent and pleasant, we having never been here before. About ten o'clock we rose from table, and sang a song, and so home in two coaches (Mr. Batelier and his sister Mary and my wife and I in one, and Mercer alone in the other); and after being examined at Allgate, whether we were husbands and wives, home, and being there come, and sent away Mr. Batelier and his sister, I find Reeves there, it being a mighty fine bright night, and so upon my leads, though very sleepy, till one in the morning, looking on the moon and Jupiter, with this twelve-foote glasse and another of six foote, that he hath brought with him to-night, and the sights mighty pleasant, and one of the glasses I will buy, it being very usefull. So to bed mighty sleepy, but with much pleasure. Reeves lying at my house again; and mighty proud I am (and ought to be thankfull to God Almighty) that I am able to have a spare bed for my friends.

[1] Wife of Sir Edmund Pooly, mentioned before (November 1st, 1665).

9th. Up and to the office to prepare business for the Board, Reeves being gone and I having lent him £5 upon one of the glasses. Here we sat, but to little purpose, nobody coming at us but to ask for money, not to offer us any goods. At noon home to dinner, and then to the office again, being mightily pleased with a Virgin's head that my wife is now doing of. In the evening to Lumbard-streete, about money, to enable me to pay Sir G. Carteret's £3,000, which he hath lodged in my hands, in behalf of his son and my Lady Jemimah, toward their portion, which, I thank God, I am able to do at a minute's warning. In my [way] I inquired, and find Mrs. Rawlinson is dead of the sickness, and her mayde continues mighty ill. He[1] himself is got out of the house. I met also with Mr. Evelyn in the streete, who tells me the sad condition at this very day at Deptford for the plague, and more at Deale (within his precinct as one of the Commissioners for sick and wounded seamen), that the towne is almost quite depopulated. Thence back home again, and after some business at my office, late, home to supper and to bed, I being sleepy by my late want of rest, notwithstanding my endeavouring to get a nap of an hour this afternoon after dinner. So home and to bed.

10th. Up and to my chamber; there did some business and then to my office, and towards noon by water to the Exchequer about my Tangier order, and thence back again and to the Exchange, where little newes but what is in the book, and, among other things, of a man sent up for by the King and Council for saying that Sir W. Coventry did give intelligence to the Dutch of all our matters here. I met with Colvill, and he and I did agree about his lending me £1,000 upon a tally of £1,000 for Tangier. Thence to Sympson, the joyner, and I am mightily pleased with what I see of my presses for my books, which he is making for me. So homeward, and hear in Fanchurch-streete, that now the mayde also is dead at Mr. Rawlinson's; so that there are three dead in all, the wife, a man-servant, and mayde-servant. Home to dinner, where sister Balty dined with us, and met a letter come to me from him. He is well at Harwich, going to the fleete. After dinner to the

[1] Her husband, Daniel Rawlinson. — B.

office, and anon with my wife and sister abroad, left them in Paternoster Row, while Creed, who was with me at the office, and I to Westminster; and leaving him in the Strand, I to my Lord Chancellor's, and did very little business, and so away home by water, with more and more pleasure, I every time reading over my Lord Bacon's "Faber Fortunæ." So home, and there did little business, and then walked an hour talking of sundry things in the garden, and find him a cunning knave, as I always observed him to be, and so home to supper, and to bed. Pleased that this day I find, if I please, I can have all my money in that I have out of my hands, but I am at a loss whether to take it in or no, and pleased also to hear of Mrs. Barbara Sheldon's good fortune, who is like to have Mr. Wood's son, the mast-maker, a very rich man, and to be married speedily, she being already mighty fine upon it.

11th. Up and to the office, where we sat all the morning. At noon home to dinner, where mighty pleased at my wife's beginnings of a little Virgin's head. To the office and did much business, and then to Mr. Colvill's, and with him did come to an agreement about my £2,600 assignment on the Exchequer, which I had of Sir W. Warren; and, to my great joy, I think I shall get above £100 by it, but I must leave it to be finished on Monday. Thence to the office, and there did the remainder of my business, and so home to supper and to bed. This afternoon I hear as if we had landed some men upon the Dutch coasts, but I believe it is but a foolery either in the report or the attempt.

12th (Lord's day). Up and to my chamber, where busy all the morning, and my thoughts very much upon the manner of my removal of my closett things the next weeke into my present musique room, if I find I can spare or get money to furnish it. By and by comes Reeves, by appointment, but did not bring the glasses and things I expected for our discourse and my information to-day, but we have agreed on it for next Sunday. By and by, in comes Betty Michell and her husband, and so to dinner, I mightily pleased with their company. We passed the whole day talking with them, but without any pleasure, but only her being there. In the evening, all parted, and I and my wife up to her closett to consider how to order that the next summer, if we live to it; and then down to my chamber at night to examine her kitchen accounts, and there I took occasion to fall out with her for her buying a laced handkercher and pinner without my leave. Though the thing is not much, yet I would not permit her begin to do so, lest worse should follow. From this we began both to be angry, and so continued till bed, and did not sleep friends.

13th. Up, without being friends with my wife, nor great enemies, being both quiet and silent. So out to Colvill's, but he not being come to town yet, I to Paul's Church-yarde, to treat with a bookbinder, to come and gild the backs of all my books, to make them handsome, to stand in my new presses, when they come. So back again to Colvill's, and there did end our treaty, to my full content, about my Exchequer assignment of £2,600 of Sir W. Warren's, for which I give him £170 to stand to the hazard of receiving it. So I shall get clear by it £230, which is a very good jobb. God be praised for it! Having done with him, then he and I took coach, and I carried him to Westminster, and there set him down, in our way speaking of several things. I find him a bold man to say any thing of any body, and finds fault with our great ministers of state that nobody looks after any thing; and I thought it dangerous to be free with him, for I do not think he can keep counsel, because he blabs to me what hath passed between other people and him. Thence I to St. James's, and there missed Sir W. Coventry; but taking up Mr. Robinson in my coach, I towards London, and there in the way met Sir W. Coventry, and followed him to White Hall, where a little discourse very kind, and so I away with Robinson, and set him down at the 'Change, and thence I to Stokes[1] the goldsmith, and sent him to and again to get me £1,000 in gold; and so home to dinner, my wife and I friends, without any words almost of last night. After dinner, I abroad to Stokes, and there did receive £1,000 worth in gold, paying $18\frac{3}{4}$*d.* and 19*d.* for

[1] **According to the "Little London Directory" of 1677, Humphrey Stocks was a goldsmith at the Black Horse in Lombard Street; his successor was Robert Stokes.**

others exchange. Home with them, and there to my office to business, and anon home in the evening, there to settle some of my accounts, and then to supper and to bed.

14th. (Thanksgiving day.[1]) Up, and comes Mr. Foley and his man, with a box of a great variety of carpenter's and joyner's tooles, which I had bespoke, to me, which please me mightily; but I will have more. Then I abroad down to the Old Swan, and there I called and kissed Betty Michell, and would have got her to go with me to Westminster, but I find her a little colder than she used to be, methought, which did a little molest me. So I away not pleased, and to White Hall, where I find them at Chappell, and met with Povy, and he and I together, who tells me how mad my letter makes my Lord Peterborough, and what a furious letter he hath writ to me in answer, though it is not come yet. This did trouble me; for though there be no reason, yet to have a nobleman's mouth open against a man may do a man hurt; so I endeavoured to have found him out and spoke with him, but could not. So to the chappell, and heard a piece of the Dean of Westminster's[2] sermon, and a special good anthemne before the king, after a sermon, and then home by coach with Captain Cocke, who is in pain about his hempe, of which he says he hath bought great quantities, and would gladly be upon good terms with us for it, wherein I promise to assist him. So we 'light at the 'Change, where, after a small turn or two, taking no pleasure now-a-days to be there, because of answering questions that would be asked there which I cannot answer; so home and dined, and after dinner, with my wife and Mercer to the Beare-garden,[3] where I have not

1 A proclamation ordering August 14th to be observed in London and Westminster, and August 23rd in other places, as a day of thanksgiving for the late victory at sea over the Dutch, was published on August 6th.

2 John Dolben, born March 20th, 1625; educated at Westminster and Christ Church, Oxford. He was under arms for the king until the forces were disbanded. He took orders in 1656, and was made Canon of Christ Church at the Restoration; Dean of Westminster, 1662; Bishop of Rochester, 1666; Lord High Almoner, 1675; and Archbishop of York, 1683. He died of small pox at his palace, April 11th, 1686. The sermon (on Psalm xviii. 1–3) was printed, London, 1666, 4to.

3 The Bear Garden was situated on Bankside, close to the precinct of the Clinke Liberty, and very near to the old palace of the bishops of Winchester. Stow, in his "Survey," says: "There be two Bear Gar-

been, I think, of many years, and saw some good sport of the bull's tossing of the dogs: one into the very boxes. But it is a very rude and nasty pleasure. We had a great many hectors in the same box with us (and one very fine went into the pit, and played his dog for a wager, which was a strange sport for a gentleman), where they drank wine, and drank Mercer's health first, which I pledged with my hat off; and who should be in the house but Mr. Pierce the surgeon, who saw us and spoke to us. Thence home, well enough satisfied, however, with the variety of this afternoon's exercise; and so I to my chamber, till in the evening our company come to supper. We had invited to a venison pasty Mr. Batelier and his sister Mary, Mrs. Mercer, her daughter Anne, Mr. Le Brun, and W. Hewer; and so we supped, and very merry. And then about nine o'clock to Mrs. Mercer's gate, where the fire and boys expected us, and her son had provided abundance of serpents and rockets; and there mighty merry (my Lady Pen and Pegg going thither with us, and Nan Wright), till about twelve at night, flinging our fireworks, and burning one another and the people over the way. And at last our businesses being most spent, we into Mrs. Mercer's, and there mighty merry, smutting one another with candle grease and soot, till most of us were like devils. And that being done, then we broke up, and to my house; and there I made them drink, and upstairs we went, and then fell into dancing (W. Batelier dancing well), and dressing, him and I and one Mr. Banister (who with his wife come over also with us) like women; and Mercer put on a suit of Tom's, like a boy, and mighty mirth we had, and Mercer danced a jigg; and Nan Wright and my wife and Pegg Pen put on perriwigs. Thus we spent till three or four in the morning, mighty merry; and then parted, and to bed.

15th. Mighty sleepy; slept till past eight of the clock, and was called up by a letter from Sir W. Coventry, which, among other things, tells me how we have burned one hundred and sixty ships of the enemy within the Fly.[1] I

dens, the old and new Places." The name still exists in a street or lane at the foot of Southwark Bridge, and in Bear Garden Wharf.

[1] On the 8th August the Duke of Albemarle reported to Lord Arlington that he had "sent 1,000 good men under Sir R. Holmes and

up, and with all possible haste, and in pain for fear of coming late, it being our day of attending the Duke of Yorke, to St. James's, where they are full of the particulars; how they are generally good merchant ships, some of them laden and supposed rich ships. We spent five fire-ships upon them. We landed on the Schelling (Sir Philip Howard with some men, and Holmes, I think, with others, about 1,000 in all), and burned a town; and so come away. By and by the Duke of Yorke with his books showed us the very place and manner, and that it was not our design or expectation to have done this, but only to have landed on the Fly, and burned some of their store; but being come in, we spied those ships, and with our long boats, one by one, fired them, our ships running all aground, it being so shoal water. We were led to this by, it seems, a renegado captain of the Hollanders, who found himself ill used by De Ruyter for his good service, and so come over to us, and hath done us good service; so that now we trust him, and he himself did go on this expedition. The service is very great, and our joys as great for it. All this will make the Duke of Albemarle in repute again, I doubt, though there is nothing of his in this. But, Lord! to see what successe do, whether with or without reason, and making a man seem wise, notwithstanding never so late demonstration of the profoundest folly in the world. Thence walked over the Parke with Sir W. Coventry, in our way talking of the unhappy state of our office; and I took an opportunity to let him know, that though the backwardnesses of all our matters of the office may be well imputed to the known want of money, yet, perhaps, there might be personal and particular failings; and that I did, therefore, depend still upon his

Sir William Jennings to destroy the islands of Vlie and Schelling." On the 10th James Hayes wrote to Williamson: "On the 9th at noon smoke was seen rising from several places in the island of Vlie, and the 10th brought news that Sir Robert had burned in the enemy's harbour 160 outward bound valuable merchant men and three men-of-war, and taken a little pleasure boat and eight guns in four hours. The loss is computed at a million sterling, and will make great confusion when the people see themselves in the power of the English at their very doors. Sir Robert then landed his forces, and is burning the houses in Vlie and Schelling as bonfires for his good success at sea" ("Calendar of State Papers," 1666–67, pp. 21, 27).

promise of telling me whenever he finds any ground to believe any defect or neglect on my part, which he promised me still to do; and that there was none he saw, nor, indeed, says he, is there room now-a-days to find fault with any particular man, while we are in this condition for money. This, methought, did not so well please me; but, however, I am glad I have said this, thereby giving myself good grounds to believe that at this time he did not want an occasion to have said what he pleased to me, if he had had anything in his mind, which by his late distance and silence I have feared. But then again I am to consider he is grown a very great man, much greater than he was, and so must keep more distance; and, next, that the condition of our office will not afford me occasion of shewing myself so active and deserving as heretofore; and, lastly, the muchness of his business cannot suffer him to mind it, or give him leisure to reflect on anything, or shew the freedom and kindnesse that he used to do. But I think I have done something considerable to my satisfaction in doing this; and that if I do but my duty remarkably from this time forward, and not neglect it, as I have of late done, and minded my pleasures, I may be as well as ever I was. Thence to the Exchequer, but did nothing, they being all gone from their offices; and so to the Old Exchange, where the towne full of the good newes, but I did not stay to tell or hear any, but home, my head akeing and drowsy, and to dinner, and then lay down upon the couch, thinking to get a little rest, but could not. So down the river, reading "The Adventures of Five Houres," which the more I read the more I admire. So down below Greenwich, but the wind and tide being against us, I back again to Deptford, and did a little business there, and thence walked to Redriffe; and so home, and to the office a while. In the evening comes W. Batelier and his sister, and my wife, and fair Mrs. Turner into the garden, and there we walked, and then with my Lady Pen and Pegg in a-doors, and eat and were merry, and so pretty late broke up, and to bed. The guns of the Tower going off, and there being bonefires also in the street for this late good successe.

16th. Up, having slept well, and after entering my Journal, to the office, where all the morning, but of late Sir W.

Coventry hath not come to us, he being discouraged from the little we have to do but to answer the clamours of people for money. At noon home, and there dined with me my Lady Pen only and W. Hewer at a haunch of venison boiled, where pretty merry, only my wife vexed me a little about demanding money to go with my Lady Pen to the Exchange to lay out. I to the office, where all the afternoon and very busy and doing much business; but here I had a most eminent experience of the evil of being behindhand in business. I was the most backward to begin any thing, and would fain have framed to myself an occasion of going abroad, and should, I doubt, have done it, but some business coming in, one after another, kept me there, and I fell to the ridding away of a great deale of business, and when my hand was in it was so pleasing a sight to [see] my papers disposed of, and letters answered, which troubled my book and table, that I could have continued there with delight all night long, and did till called away by my Lady Pen and Pegg and my wife to their house to eat with them; and there I went, and exceeding merry, there being Nan Wright, now Mrs. Markham, and sits at table with my Lady. So mighty merry, home and to bed. This day Sir W. Batten did show us at the table a letter from Sir T. Allen, which says that we have taken ten or twelve ships (since the late great expedition of burning their ships and towne), laden with hempe, flax, tarr, deales, &c. This was good newes; but by and by comes in Sir G. Carteret, and he asked us with full mouth what we would give for good newes. Says Sir W. Batten, "I have better than you, for a wager." They laid sixpence, and we that were by were to give sixpence to him that told the best newes. So Sir W. Batten told his of the ten or twelve ships. Sir G. Carteret did then tell us that upon the newes of the burning of the ships and towne the common people of Amsterdam did besiege De Witt's house, and he was forced to flee to the Prince of Orange, who is gone to Cleve to the marriage of his sister. This we concluded all the best newes, and my Lord Bruncker and myself did give Sir G. Carteret our sixpence a-piece, which he did give Mr. Smith to give the poor. Thus we made ourselves mighty merry.

17th. Up and betimes with Captain Erwin[1] down by

[1] Captain George Erwin, of the "William."

water to Woolwich, I walking alone from Greenwich thither, making an end of the "Adventures of Five Hours," which when all is done is the best play that ever I read in my life. Being come thither I did some business there and at the Rope Yarde, and had a piece of bride-cake sent me by Mrs. Barbary[1] into the boate after me, she being here at her uncle's, with her husband, Mr. Wood's son, the mast-maker. and mighty nobly married, they say, she was, very fine, and he very rich, a strange fortune for so odd a looked mayde, though her hands and body be good, and nature very good, I think. Back with Captain Erwin, discoursing about the East Indys, where he hath often been. And among other things he tells me how the King of Syam seldom goes out without thirty or forty thousand people with him, and not a word spoke, nor a hum or cough in the whole company to be heard. He tells me the punishment frequently there for malefactors is cutting off the crowne of their head, which they do very dexterously, leaving their brains bare, which kills them presently. He told me what I remember he hath once done heretofore: that every body is to lie flat down at the coming by of the King, and nobody to look upon him upon pain of death. And that he and his fellows, being strangers, were invited to see the sport of taking of a wild elephant, and they did only kneel, and look toward the King. Their druggerman[2] did desire them to fall down, for otherwise he should suffer for their contempt of the King. The sport being ended, a messenger comes from the King, which the druggerman thought had been to have taken away his life; but it was to enquire how the strangers liked the sport. The druggerman answered that they did cry it up to be the best that ever they saw, and that they never heard of any Prince so great in every thing as this King. The messenger being gone back, Erwin and his company asked their druggerman what he had said, which he told them. "But why," say they, "would you say that without our leave, it being not true?" "It is no matter for that," says he, "I must have said it, or have been hanged, for our King do not live by meat, nor drink, but by having great lyes told him." In our way back we come by a little

[1] Mrs. Barbara Sheldon.

[2] Dragoman.

vessel that come into the river this morning, and says he left the fleete in Sole Bay, and that he hath not heard (he belonging to Sir W. Jenings, in the fleete) of any such prizes taken as the ten or twelve I inquired about, and said by Sir W. Batten yesterday to be taken, so I fear it is not true. So to Westminster, and there, to my great content, did receive my £2,000 of Mr. Spicer's telling, which I was to receive of Colvill, and brought it home with me [to] my house by water, and there I find one of my new presses for my books brought home, which pleases me mightily. As, also, do my wife's progresse upon her head that she is making. So to dinner, and thence abroad with my wife, leaving her at Unthanke's; I to White Hall, waiting at the Council door till it rose, and there spoke with Sir W. Coventry, who and I do much fear our Victuallers, they having missed the fleete in their going. But Sir W. Coventry says it is not our fault, but theirs, if they have not left ships to secure them. This he spoke in a chagrin sort of way, methought. After a little more discourse of several businesses, I away homeward, having in the gallery the good fortune to see Mrs. Stewart, who is grown a little too tall, but is a woman of most excellent features. The narrative of the late expedition[1] in burning the ships is in print, and makes it a great thing, and I hope it is so. So took up my wife and home, there I to the office, and thence with Sympson the joyner home to put together the press he hath brought me for my books this day, which pleases me exceedingly. Then to Sir W. Batten's, where Sir Richard Ford did, very understandingly, methought, give us an account of the originall of the Hollands Bank,[2] and the nature of it, and how they do never give any interest at all to any person that brings in their money, though what is brought in upon the public faith interest is given by the

[1] See August 15th, *ante*.

[2] This bank at Amsterdam is referred to in a tract entitled "An Appeal to Cæsar," 1660, p. 22. In 1640 Charles I. seized the money in the mint in the Tower entrusted to the safe keeping of the Crown. It was the practice of the London goldsmiths at this time to allow interest at the rate of six or eight per cent. on money deposited with them (J. Biddulph Martin, "The Grasshopper in Lombard Street," 1892, p. 152).

State for. The unsafe condition of a Bank under a Monarch, and the little safety to a Monarch to have any; or Corporation alone (as London in answer to Amsterdam) to have so great a wealth or credit, it is, that makes it hard to have a Bank here. And as to the former, he did tell us how it sticks in the memory of most merchants how the late King (when by the war between Holland and France and Spayne all the bullion of Spayne was brought hither, one-third of it to be coyned; and indeed it was found advantageous to the merchant to coyne most of it), was persuaded in a strait by my Lord Cottington[1] to seize upon the money in the Tower, which, though in a few days the merchants concerned did prevail to get it released, yet the thing will never be forgot. So home to supper and to bed, understanding this evening, since I come home, that our Victuallers are all come in to the fleete, which is good newes. Sir John Minnes come home to-night not well, from Chatham, where he hath been at a pay, holding it at Upnor Castle, because of the plague so much in the towne of Chatham. He hath, they say, got an ague, being so much on the water.

18th. All the morning at my office; then to the Exchange (with my Lord Bruncker in his coach) at noon, but it was only to avoid Mr. Chr. Pett's being invited by me to dinner. So home, calling at my little mercer's in Lumbard Streete, who hath the pretty wench, like the old Queene, and there cheapened some stuffs to hang my roome, that I intend to turn into a closett. So home to dinner, and after dinner comes Creed to discourse with me about several things of Tangier concernments and accounts, among others starts the doubt, which I was formerly aware of, but did wink at it, whether or no Lanyon and his partners be not paid for more than they should be, which he presses, so that

[1] Sir Francis Cottington, a younger son of Philip Cottington, of Godmanston, Somerset, was created by Charles I. Lord Cottington of Hanworth. He became successively one of the clerks of the council, Chancellor of the Exchequer, ambassador into Spain, and Lord Treasurer of England under the two elder Stuarts. He died at Valladolid in 1653, s. p., and his body was brought to England and interred under a stately monument in Westminster Abbey, erected by Charles Cottington, his nephew and heir. See December 6th, 1667, for an account of his disinheriting a nephew for a foolish speech. — B.

it did a little discompose me; but, however, I do think no harm will arise thereby. He gone, I to the office, and there very late, very busy, and so home to supper and to bed.

19th (Lord's day). Up and to my chamber, and there began to draw out fair and methodically my accounts of Tangier, in order to shew them to the Lords. But by and by comes by agreement Mr. Reeves, and after him Mr. Spong, and all day with them, both before and after dinner, till ten o'clock at night, upon opticke enquiries, he bringing me a frame he closes on, to see how the rays of light do cut one another, and in a darke room with smoake, which is very pretty. He did also bring a lanthorne with pictures in glasse, to make strange things appear on a wall, very pretty. We did also at night see Jupiter and his girdle and satellites, very fine, with my twelve-foote glasse, but could not Saturne, he being very dark. Spong and I had also several fine discourses upon the globes this afternoon, particularly why the fixed stars do not rise and set at the same houre all the yeare long, which he could not demonstrate, nor I neither, the reason of. So, it being late, after supper they away home. But it vexed me to understand no more from Reeves and his glasses touching the nature and reason of the several refractions of the several figured glasses, he understanding the acting part, but not one bit the theory, nor can make any body understand it, which is a strange dullness, methinks. I did not hear anything yesterday or at all to confirm either Sir Thos. Allen's news of the 10 or 12 ships taken, nor of the disorder at Amsterdam upon the news of the burning of the ships, that he [De Witt] should be fled to the Prince of Orange, it being generally believed that he was gone to France before.

20th. Waked this morning about six o'clock, with a violent knocking at Sir J. Minnes's doore, to call up Mrs. Hammon, crying out that Sir J. Minnes is a-dying. He come home ill of an ague on Friday night. I saw him on Saturday, after his fit of the ague, and then was pretty lusty. Which troubles me mightily, for he is a very good, harmless, honest gentleman, though not fit for the business. But I much fear a worse may come, that may be more uneasy to me. Up, and to Deptford by water, reading "Othello, Moore of Venice," which I ever heretofore esteemed a mighty good play, but having so lately read "The Adventures of Five Houres," it seems a mean thing. Walked back, and so home, and then down to the Old Swan and drank at Betty Michell's, and so to Westminster to the Exchequer about my quarter tallies, and so to Lumbard Streete to choose stuff to hang my new intended closet, and have chosen purple. So home to dinner, and all the afternoon till almost midnight upon my Tangier accounts, getting Tom Wilson to help me in writing as I read, and at night W. Hewer, and find myself most happy in the keeping of all my accounts, for that after all the changings and turnings necessary in such an account, I find myself right to a farthing in an account of £127,000. This afternoon I visited Sir J. Minnes, who, poor man, is much impatient by these few days' sickness, and I fear indeed it will kill him.

21st. Up, and to the office, where much business and Sir W. Coventry there, who of late hath wholly left us, most of our business being about money, to which we can give no answer, which makes him weary of coming to us. He made an experiment to-day, by taking up a heape of petitions that lay upon the table. They proved seventeen in number, and found them thus: one for money for reparation for clothes, four desired to have tickets made out to them, and the other twelve were for money. Dined at home, and sister Balty with us. My wife snappish because I denied her money to lay out this afternoon; however, good friends again, and by coach set them down at the New Exchange, and I to the Exchequer, and there find my business of my tallys in good forwardness. I passed down into the Hall, and there hear that Mr. Bowles, the grocer, after 4 or 5 days' sickness, is dead, and this day buried. So away, and taking up my wife, went homewards. I 'light and with Harman to my mercer's in Lumbard Streete, and there agreed for our purple serge for my closett, and so I away home. So home and late at the office, and then home, and there found Mr. Batelier and his sister Mary, and we sat chatting a great while, talking of witches and spirits, and he told me of his own knowledge, being with some others at Bourdeaux, making a bargain with another man at a taverne for some clarets, they did hire a fellow to thunder (which he had the art of doing upon a deale board) and to rain and hail, that is, make the noise of, so as did give them a pretence of undervaluing their merchants' wines, by saying this thunder would spoil and turne them. Which was so reasonable to the merchant, that he did abate two pistolls per ton for the wine in belief of that, whereas, going out, there was no such thing. This Batelier did see and was the cause of to his profit, as is above said. By and by broke up and to bed.

22nd. Up and by coach with £100 to the Exchequer to pay fees there. There left it, and I to St. James's, and there with the Duke of Yorke. I had opportunity of much talk with Sir W. Pen to-day (he being newly come from the fleete); and he do much undervalue the honour that is given to the conduct of the late business of Holmes in burning the ships and town,[1] saying it was a great thing indeed, and of great profit to us in being of great losse to the enemy, but that it was wholly a business of chance, and no conduct employed in it. I find Sir W. Pen do hold up his head at this time higher than ever he did in his life. I perceive he do look after Sir J. Minnes's place if he dies, and though I love him not nor do desire to have him in, yet I do think [he] is the first man in England for it. To the Exchequer, and there received my tallys, and paid my fees in good order, and so home, and there find Mrs. Knipp and my wife going to dinner. She tells me my song of "Beauty Retire" is mightily cried up, which I am not a little proud of; and do think I have done "It is Decreed" better, but I have not finished it. My closett is doing by upholsters, which I am pleased with, but fear my purple will be too sad for that melancholy roome. After dinner and doing something at the office, I with my wife, Knipp, and Mercer, by coach to Moorefields, and there saw "Polichinello," which pleases me mightily, and here I saw our Mary, our last chambermaid, who is gone from Mrs. Pierce's it seems. Thence carried Knipp home, calling at the Cocke alehouse at the

[1] The town burned (see August 15th, *ante*) was Brandaris, a place of 1,000 houses, on the isle of Schelling; the ships lay between that island and the Fly (*i.e.* Vlieland), the adjoining island. This attack probably provoked that by the Dutch on Chatham. See note, August 15th, and Pepys's remarks, June 30th, 1667, *post*. — B.

doore and drank, and so home, and there find Reeves, and so up to look upon the stars, and do like my glasse very well, and did even with him for it and a little perspective and the Lanthorne that shows tricks, altogether costing me £9 5*s*. 0*d*. So to bed, he lying at our house.

23rd. At the office all the morning, whither Sir W. Coventry sent me word that the Dutch fleete is certainly abroad; and so we are to hasten all we have to send to our fleete with all speed. But, Lord! to see how my Lord Bruncker undertakes the despatch of the fire-ships, when he is no more fit for it than a porter; and all the while Sir W. Pen, who is the most fit, is unwilling to displease him, and do not look after it; and so the King's work is like to be well done. At noon dined at home, Lovett with us; but he do not please me in his business, for he keeps things long in hand, and his paper do not hold so good as I expected — the varnish wiping off in a little time — a very sponge; and I doubt by his discourse he is an odde kind of fellow, and, in plain terms, a very rogue. He gone, I to the office (having seen and liked the upholsters' work in my roome — which they have almost done), and there late, and in the evening find Mr. Batelier and his sister there, and then we talked and eat and were merry, and so parted late, and to bed.

24th. Up, and dispatched several businesses at home in the morning, and then comes Sympson to set up my other new presses[1] for my books, and so he and I fell in to the furnishing of my new closett, and taking out the things out of my old, and I kept him with me all day, and he dined with me, and so all the afternoon till it was quite darke hanging things, that is my maps and pictures and draughts, and setting up my books, and as much as we could do, to my most extraordinary satisfaction; so that I think it will be as noble a closett as any man hath, and light enough — though, indeed, it would be better to have had a little more light. He gone, my wife and I to talk, and sup, and then to setting right my Tangier accounts and

[1] These presses still exist, and, according to Pepys's wish, they are placed in the second court of Magdalene College in a room which they exactly fit, and the books are arranged in the presses just as they were when presented to the college. — M. B.

enter my Journall, and then to bed with great content in my day's worke. This afternoon comes Mrs. Barbary Sheldon, now Mrs. Wood, to see my wife: I was so busy I would not see her. But she came, it seems, mighty rich in rings and fine clothes, and like a lady, and says she is matched mighty well, at which I am very glad, but wonder at her good fortune and the folly of her husband, and vexed at myself for not paying her the respect of seeing her, but I will come out of her debt another time.

25th. All the morning at the office. At noon dined at home, and after dinner up to my new closett, which pleases me mightily, and there I proceeded to put many things in order as far as I had time, and then set it in washing, and stood by myself a great while to see it washed; and then to the office, and then wrote my letters and other things, and then in mighty good humour home to supper and to bed.

26th (Lord's day). Up betimes, and to the finishing the setting things in order in my new closett out of my old, which I did thoroughly by the time sermon was done at church, to my exceeding joy, only I was a little disturbed with newes my Lord Bruncker brought me, that we are to attend the King at White Hall this afternoon, and that it is about a complaint from the Generalls against us. Sir W. Pen dined by invitation with me, his Lady and daughter being gone into the country. We very merry. After dinner we parted, and I to my office, whither I sent for Mr. Lewes and instructed myself fully in the business of the Victualling, to enable me to answer in the matter; and then Sir W. Pen and I by coach to White Hall, and there staid till the King and Cabinet were met in the Green Chamber, and then we were called in; and there the King begun with me, to hear how the victualls of the fleete stood. I did in a long discourse tell him and the rest (the Duke of Yorke, Lord Chancellor, Lord Treasurer, both the Secretarys, Sir G. Carteret, and Sir W. Coventry,) how it stood, wherein they seemed satisfied, but press mightily for more supplies; and the letter of the Generalls, which was read, did lay their not going or too soon returning from the Dutch coast, this next bout, to the want of victuals. They then proceeded to the enquiry after the fire-ships; and did all very superficially, and without any severity at all. But, however, I was in pain, after we come out, to know how I had done; and hear well enough. But, however, it shall be a caution to me to prepare myself against a day of inquisition. Being come out, I met with Mr. Moore, and he and I an houre together in the Gallery, telling me how far they are gone in getting my Lord [Sandwich's] pardon, so as the Chancellor is prepared in it; and Sir H. Bennet do promote it, and the warrant for the King's signing is drawn. The business between my Lord Hinchingbroke and Mrs. Mallett is quite broke off; he attending her at Tunbridge, and she declaring her affections to be settled; and he not being fully pleased with the vanity and liberty of her carriage. He told me how my Lord has drawn a bill of exchange from Spayne of £1,200, and would have me supply him with £500 of it, but I avoyded it, being not willing to embarke myself in money there, where I see things going to ruine. Thence to discourse of the times; and he tells me he believes both my Lord Arlington and Sir W. Coventry, as well as my Lord Sandwich and Sir G. Carteret, have reason to fear, and are afeard of this Parliament now coming on. He tells me that Bristoll's faction is getting ground apace against my Lord Chancellor. He told me that my old Lord Coventry[1] was a cunning, crafty man, and did make as many bad decrees in Chancery as any man; and that in one case, that occasioned many years' dispute, at last when the King come in, it was hoped by the party grieved, to get my Lord Chancellor to reverse a decree of his. Sir W. Coventry took the opportunity of the business between the Duke of Yorke and the Duchesse, and said to my Lord Chancellor, that he had rather be drawn up Holborne to be hanged, than live to see his father pissed upon (in these very terms) and any decree of his reversed. And so the Chancellor did not think fit to do it, but it still stands, to the undoing of one Norton, a printer, about his right to the printing of the Bible, and Grammar, &c.[2]

[1] The Lord Keeper. Died January 14th, 1639-40.

[2] The patent for printing Bibles, &c., in London was held by Bonham Norton in the early part of the seventeenth century. The printer referred to by Pepys appears to have been Roger Norton, who was Master of the Stationers' Company in 1678, 1682. 1683, 1684, and 1687.

Thence Sir W. Pen and I to Islington and there drank at the Katherine Wheele, and so down the nearest way home, where there was no kind of pleasure at all. Being come home, hear that Sir J. Minnes has had a very bad fit all this day, and a hickup do take him, which is a very bad sign, which troubles me truly. So home to supper a little and then to bed.

27th. Up, and to my new closett, which pleases me mightily, and there did a little business. Then to break open a window to the leads' side in my old closett, which will enlighten the room mightily, and make it mighty pleasant. So to the office, and then home about one thing or other, about my new closet, for my mind is full of nothing but that. So at noon to dinner, mightily pleased with my wife's picture that she is upon. Then to the office, and thither come and walked an hour with me Sir G. Carteret, who tells me what is done about my Lord's pardon, and is not for letting the Duke of Yorke know any thing of it beforehand, but to carry it as speedily and quietly as we can. He seems to be very apprehensive that the Parliament will be troublesome and inquisitive into faults, but seems not to value them as to himself. He gone, I to the Victualling Office, there with Lewes[1] and Willson setting the business of the state of the fleete's victualling even and plain, and that being done, and other good discourse about it over, Mr. Willson and I by water down the River for discourse only, about business of the office, and then back, and I home, and after a little at my office home to my new closet, and there did much business on my Tangier account and my Journall for three days. So to supper and to bed. We are not sure that the Dutch fleete is out. I have another memento from Sir W. Coventry of the want of provisions in the fleete, which troubles me, though there is no reason for it; but will have the good effect of making me more wary. So, full of thoughts, to bed.

Amongst the State Papers is a "Petition of Roger Norton, printer, to the King, to be resettled in the place of King's Printer, on his claim to which a suit is depending in Chancery. The place is now held by gentlemen who do not understand printing, and the work is done by those who were printers under Cromwell, and who, as permitted by him, still print Bibles and service books" ("Calendar," 1661–62, p. 76).

[1] Thomas Lewis, clerk in the Victualling Office.

28th. Up, and in my new closet a good while doing business. Then called on Mrs. Martin and Burroughs of Westminster about business of the former's husband. Which done, I to the office, where we sat all the morning. At noon I, with my wife and Mercer, to Philpott Lane,[1] a great cook's shop, to the wedding of Mr. Longracke, our purveyor, a good, sober, civil man, and hath married a sober, serious mayde. Here I met much ordinary company, I going thither at his great request; but there was Mr. Madden and his lady, a fine, noble, pretty lady, and he, and a fine gentleman seems to be. We four were most together; but the whole company was very simple and innocent. A good dinner, and, what was best, good musique. After dinner the young women went to dance; among others Mr. Christopher Pett his daughter, who is a very pretty, modest girle, I am mightily taken with her; and that being done about five o'clock, home, very well pleased with the afternoon's work. And so we broke up mightily civilly, the bride and bridegroom going to Greenwich (they keeping their dinner here only for my sake) to lie, and we home, where I to the office, and anon am on a sudden called to meet Sir W. Pen and Sir W. Coventry at the Victualling Office, which did put me out of order to be so surprised. But I went, and there Sir William Coventry did read me a letter from the Generalls to the King,[2] a most scurvy letter, reflecting most upon Sir W. Coventry, and then upon me for my accounts (not that they are not true, but that we do not consider the expence of the fleete), and then of the whole office, in neglecting them and the King's

[1] Philpot Lane, between Fenchurch Street and Eastcheap, where the Commissioners of the Navy had an office in 1623.

[2] The letter from Prince Rupert and the Duke of Albemarle to the king (dated August 27th, from the "Royal Charles," Sole Bay) is among the State Papers. The generals "complain of the want of supplies, in spite of repeated importunities. The demands are answered by accounts from Mr. Pepys of what has been sent to the fleet, which will not satisfy the ships, unless the provisions could be found. . . . Have not a month's provision of beer, yet Sir Wm. Coventry assures the ministers that they are supplied till Oct. 3; unless this is quickened they will have to return home too soon. . . . Want provisions according to their own computation, not Sir Wm. Coventry's, to last to the end of October" ("Calendar," 1666–67, p. 71).

service, and this in very plain and sharp and menacing terms. I did give a good account of matters according to our computation of the expence of the fleete. I find Sir W. Coventry willing enough to accept of any thing to confront the Generalls. But a great supply must be made, and shall be in grace of God! But, however, our accounts here will be found the true ones. Having done here, and much work set me, I with greater content home than I thought I should have done, and so to the office a while, and then home, and a while in my new closet, which delights me every day more and more, and so late to bed.

29th. Up betimes, and there to fit some Tangier accounts, and then, by appointment, to my Lord Bellasses, but about Paul's thought of the chant paper I should carry with me, and so fain to come back again, and did, and then met with Sir W. Pen, and with him to my Lord Bellasses, he sitting in the coach the while, while I up to my Lord and there offered him my account of the bills of exchange I had received and paid for him, wherein we agree all but one £200 bill of Vernatty's drawing, wherein I doubt he hath endeavoured to cheate my Lord; but that will soon appear. Thence took leave, and found Sir W. Pen talking to Orange Moll, of the King's house, who, to our great comfort, told us that they begun to act on the 18th of this month. So on to St. James's, in the way Sir W. Pen telling me that Mr. Norton,[1] that married Sir J. Lawson's daughter, is dead. She left £800 a year jointure, a son to inherit the whole estate. She freed from her father-in-law's tyranny, and is in condition to helpe her mother, who needs it; of which I am glad, the young lady being very pretty. To St. James's, and there Sir W. Coventry took Sir W. Pen and me apart, and read to us his answer to the Generalls' letter to the King that he read last night; wherein he is very plain, and states the matter in full defence of himself and of me with him, which he could not avoid; which is a good comfort to me, that I happen to be involved with him in the same cause. And then, speaking of the supplies which have been made to

[1] See July 6th, 1665.

this fleete, more than ever in all kinds to any, even that wherein the Duke of Yorke himself was, "Well," says he, "if this will not do, I will say, as Sir J. Falstaffe did to the Prince, 'Tell your father, that if he do not like this let him kill the next Piercy himself,' "[1] and so we broke up, and to the Duke, and there did our usual business. So I to the Parke and there met Creed, and he and I walked to Westminster to the Exchequer, and thence to White Hall talking of Tangier matters and Vernatty's knavery, and so parted, and then I homeward and met Mr. Povy in Cheapside, and stopped and talked a good while upon the profits of the place which my Lord Bellasses hath made this last year, and what share we are to have of it, but of this all imperfect, and so parted, and I home, and there find Mrs. Mary Batelier, and she dined with us; and thence I took them to Islington, and there eat a custard; and so back to Moorfields, and shewed Batelier, with my wife, "Polichinello," which I like the more I see it; and so home with great content, she being a mighty good-natured, pretty woman, and thence I to the Victualling office, and there with Mr. Lewes and Willson upon our Victualling matters till ten at night, and so I home and there late writing a letter to Sir W. Coventry, and so home to supper and to bed. No newes where the Dutch are. We begin to think they will steale through the Channel to meet Beaufort.[2] We think our fleete sayled yesterday, but we have no newes of it.

30th. Up and all the morning at the office, dined at home, and in the afternoon, and at night till two in the morning, framing my great letter to Mr. Hayes[3] about the victualling of the fleete, about which there has been so much ado and exceptions taken by the Generalls.

[1] "King Henry IV.," Part I., act v., sc. 4.

[2] François de Vendôme, Duc de Beaufort, well known in the annals of France, was born in 1616, and in 1664 and 1665 commanded a naval expedition against the African corsairs (see October 11th, 1664). The following year he had the charge of a fleet intended to act in concert with the Dutch against England, but which was merely sent out as a political demonstration. He was killed at the siege of Candia in 1669. — B.

[3] James Hayes, secretary to Prince Rupert.

31st. To bed at 2 or 3 in the morning and up again at 6 to go by appointment to my Lord Bellasses, but he out of town, which vexed me. So back and got Mr. Poynter to enter into my book while I read from my last night's notes the letter, and that being done to writing it fair. At noon home to dinner, and then the boy and I to the office, and there he read while I writ it fair, which done I sent it to Sir W. Coventry to peruse and send to the fleete by the first opportunity; and so pretty betimes to bed. Much pleased to-day with thoughts of gilding the backs of all my books alike in my new presses.

September 1st. Up and at the office all the morning, and then dined at home. Got my new closet made mighty clean against to-morrow. Sir W. Pen and my wife and Mercer and I to "Polichinelly," but were there horribly frighted to see Young Killigrew come in with a great many more young sparks; but we hid ourselves, so as we think they did not see us. By and by they went away, and then we were at rest again; and so, the play being done, we to Islington, and there eat and drank and mighty merry; and so home singing, and, after a letter or two at the office, to bed.

2nd (Lord's day). Some of our mayds sitting up late last night to get things ready against our feast to-day, Jane called us up about three in the morning, to tell us of a great fire they saw in the City. So I rose and slipped on my night-gowne, and went to her window, and thought it to be on the back-side of Marke-lane at the farthest; but, being unused to such fires as followed, I thought it far enough off; and so went to bed again and to sleep. About seven rose again to dress myself, and there looked out at the window, and saw the fire not so much as it was and further off. So to my closett to set things to rights after yesterday's cleaning. By and by Jane comes and tells me that she hears that above 300 houses have been burned down to-night by the fire we saw, and that it is now burning down all Fish-street, by London Bridge. So I made myself ready presently, and walked to the Tower, and there got up upon one of the high places, Sir J. Robinson's little son going up with me; and there I did see the houses at that end of the bridge all on fire, and an infinite great fire on this and the other side the end of the bridge; which, among other people, did trouble me for poor little Michell and our Sarah on the bridge. So down, with my heart full of trouble, to the Lieutenant of the Tower, who tells me that it begun this morning in the King's baker's[1] house in Pudding-lane, and that it hath burned St. Magnus's Church and most part of Fish-street already. So I down to the water-side, and there got a boat and through bridge, and there saw a lamentable fire. Poor Michell's house, as far as the Old Swan, already burned that way, and the fire running further, that in a very little time it got as far as the Steele-yard, while I was there. Everybody endeavouring to remove their goods, and flinging into the river or bringing them into lighters that lay off; poor people staying in their houses as long as till the very fire touched them, and then running into boats, or clambering from one pair of stairs by the water-side to another. And among other things, the poor pigeons, I perceive, were loth to leave their houses, but hovered about the windows and balconys till they were, some of them burned, their wings, and fell down. Having staid, and in an hour's time seen the fire rage every way, and nobody, to my sight, endeavouring to quench it, but to remove their goods, and leave all to the fire, and having seen it get as far as the Steele-yard, and the wind mighty high and driving it into the City; and every thing, after so long a drought, proving combustible, even the very stones of churches, and among other things the poor steeple[2] by which pretty Mrs. —— lives, and whereof my old schoolfellow Elborough is parson, taken fire in the very top, and there burned till it fell down: I to White Hall (with a gentleman with me who desired to go off from the Tower, to see the fire, in my boat); to White Hall, and there up to the King's closett in the Chappell, where people come about me, and I did give them an account dismayed them all, and word was carried in to the King. So I was called for, and did tell the King and Duke of Yorke what I saw, and that unless his Majesty did command houses to be pulled down nothing could stop the fire. They seemed much troubled, and the King com-

[1] Pudding Lane, leading from Eastcheap to Lower Thames Street. The name of the baker was Farryner.

[2] St. Lawrence Poultney. See note, *ante*, August 5th.

manded me to go to my Lord Mayor[1] from him, and command him to spare no houses, but to pull down before the fire every way. The Duke of York bid me tell him that if he would have any more soldiers he shall; and so did my Lord Arlington afterwards, as a great secret.[2] Here meeting with Captain Cocke, I in his coach, which he lent me, and Creed with me to Paul's, and there walked along Watling-street, as well as I could, every creature coming away loaden with goods to save, and here and there sicke people carried away in beds. Extraordinary good goods carried in carts and on backs. At last met my Lord Mayor in Canning-street, like a man spent, with a handkercher about his neck. To the King's message he cried, like a fainting woman, "Lord! what can I do? I am spent: people will not obey me. I have been pulling down houses; but the fire overtakes us faster than we can do it." That he needed no more soldiers; and that, for himself, he must go and refresh himself, having been up all night. So he left me, and I him, and walked home, seeing people all almost distracted, and no manner of means used to quench the fire. The houses, too, so very thick thereabouts, and full of matter for burning, as pitch and tarr, in Thames-street; and warehouses of oyle, and wines, and brandy, and other things. Here I saw Mr. Isaake Houblon, the handsome man, prettily dressed and dirty, at his door at Dowgate, receiving some of his brothers' things, whose houses were on fire; and, as he says, have been removed twice already; and he doubts (as it soon proved) that they must be in a little time removed from his house also, which was a sad consideration. And to see the churches all filling with goods by people who themselves should have been quietly there at this time. By this time it was about twelve o'clock; and so home, and there find my guests, which was Mr. Wood and his wife Barbary Sheldon, and also Mr.

[1] Sir Thomas Bludworth. See June 30th, 1666.

[2] Sir William Coventry wrote to Lord Arlington on the evening of this day, "The Duke of York fears the want of workmen and tools to-morrow morning, and wishes the deputy lieutenants and justices of peace to summon the workmen with tools to be there by break of day. In some churches and chapels are great hooks for pulling down houses, which should be brought ready upon the place to-night against the morning" ("Calendar of State Papers," 1666–67, p. 95).

Moone: she mighty fine, and her husband, for aught I see, a likely man. But Mr. Moone's design and mine, which was to look over my closett and please him with the sight thereof, which he hath long desired, was wholly disappointed; for we were in great trouble and disturbance at this fire, not knowing what to think of it. However, we had an extraordinary good dinner, and as merry as at this time we could be. While at dinner Mrs. Batelier come to enquire after Mr. Woolfe and Stanes (who, it seems, are related to them), whose houses in Fish-street are all burned, and they in a sad condition. She would not stay in the fright. Soon as dined, I and Moone away, and walked through the City, the streets full of nothing but people and horses and carts loaden with goods, ready to run over one another, and removing goods from one burned house to another. They now removing out of Canning-streete (which received goods in the morning) into Lumbard-streete, and further; and among others I now saw my little goldsmith, Stokes, receiving some friend's goods, whose house itself was burned the day after. We parted at Paul's; he home, and I to Paul's Wharf, where I had appointed a boat to attend me, and took in Mr. Carcasse[1] and his brother, whom I met in the streete, and carried them below and above bridge to and again to see the fire, which was now got further, both below and above, and no likelihood of stopping it. Met with the King and Duke of York in their barge, and with them to Queenhithe, and there called Sir Richard Browne to them. Their order was only to pull down houses apace, and so below bridge at the water-side; but little was or could be done, the fire coming upon them so fast. Good hopes there was of stopping it at the Three Cranes above, and at Buttolph's Wharf below bridge, if care be used; but the wind carries it into the City, so as we know not by the water-side what it do there. River full of lighters and boats taking in goods, and good goods swimming in the water, and only I observed that hardly one lighter or boat in three that had the goods of a house in, but there was a pair of Virginalls[2] in it. Having seen as

[1] James Carcasse. See note, *ante*, August 17th, 1665.

[2] The virginal differed from the spinet in being square instead of triangular in form. The word pair was used in the obsolete sense of a

much as I could now, I away to White Hall by appointment, and there walked to St. James's Parke, and there met my wife and Creed and Wood and his wife, and walked to my boat; and there upon the water again, and to the fire up and down, it still encreasing, and the wind great. So near the fire as we could for smoke; and all over the Thames, with one's face in the wind, you were almost burned with a shower of fire-drops. This is very true; so as houses were burned by these drops and flakes of fire, three or four, nay, five or six houses, one from another. When we could endure no more upon the water, we to a little ale-house on the Bankside, over against the Three Cranes, and there staid till it was dark almost, and saw the fire grow; and, as it grew darker, appeared more and more, and in corners and upon steeples, and between churches and houses, as far as we could see up the hill of the City, in a most horrid malicious bloody flame, not like the fine flame of an ordinary fire. Barbary and her husband away before us. We staid till, it being darkish, we saw the fire as only one entire arch of fire from this to the other side the bridge, and in a bow up the hill for an arch of above a mile long: it made me weep to see it. The churches, houses, and all on fire and flaming at once; and a horrid noise the flames made, and the cracking of houses at their ruine. So home with a sad heart, and there find every body discoursing and lamenting the fire; and poor Tom Hater come with some few of his goods saved out of his house, which is burned upon Fish-streete Hill. I invited him to lie at my house, and did receive his goods, but was deceived in his lying there, the newes coming every moment of the growth of the fire; so as we were forced to begin to pack up our owne goods, and prepare for their removal; and did by moonshine (it being brave dry, and moonshine, and warm weather) carry much of my goods into the garden, and Mr. Hater and I did remove my money and iron chests into my cellar, as thinking that the safest place. And got my bags of gold into my office, ready to carry away, and my chief papers of accounts also there, and my tallys into a box by themselves. So

set, as we read also of a pair of organs. The instrument is supposed to have obtained its name from young women playing upon it.

great was our fear, as Sir W. Batten hath carts come out of the country to fetch away his goods this night. We did put Mr. Hater, poor man, to bed a little; but he got but very little rest, so much noise being in my house, taking down of goods.

3rd. About four o'clock in the morning, my Lady Batten sent me a cart to carry away all my money, and plate, and best things, to Sir W. Rider's at Bednall-greene. Which I did, riding myself in my night-gowne in the cart; and, Lord! to see how the streets and the highways are crowded with people running and riding, and getting of carts at any rate to fetch away things. I find Sir W. Rider tired with being called up all night, and receiving things from several friends. His house full of goods, and much of Sir W. Batten's and Sir W. Pen's. I am eased at my heart to have my treasure so well secured. Then home, with much ado to find a way, nor any sleep all this night to me nor my poor wife. But then and all this day she and I, and all my people labouring to get away the rest of our things, and did get Mr. Tooker to get me a lighter to take them in, and we did carry them (myself some) over Tower Hill, which was by this time full of people's goods, bringing their goods thither; and down to the lighter, which lay at the next quay, above the Tower Docke. And here was my neighbour's wife, Mrs. ——, with her pretty child, and some few of her things, which I did willingly give way to be saved with mine; but there was no passing with any thing through the postern, the crowd was so great. The Duke of Yorke come this day by the office, and spoke to us, and did ride with his guard up and down the City to keep all quiet (he being now Generall, and having the care of all). This day, Mercer being not at home, but against her mistress's order gone to her mother's, and my wife going thither to speak with W. Hewer, met her there, and was angry; and her mother saying that she was not a 'prentice girl, to ask leave every time she goes abroad, my wife with good reason was angry, and, when she came home, bid her be gone again. And so she went away, which troubled me, but yet less than it would, because of the condition we are in, fear of coming into in a little time of being less able to keepe one in her quality. At night lay down a little upon a quilt of W.

Hewer's in the office, all my owne things being packed up or gone; and after me my poor wife did the like, we having fed upon the remains of yesterday's dinner, having no fire nor dishes, nor any opportunity of dressing any thing.

4th. Up by break of day to get away the remainder of my things; which I did by a lighter at the Iron gate:[1] and my hands so few, that it was the afternoon before we could get them all away. Sir W. Pen and I to Tower-streete, and there met the fire burning three or four doors beyond Mr. Howell's, whose goods, poor man, his trayes, and dishes, shovells, &c., were flung all along Tower-street in the kennels, and people working therewith from one end to the other; the fire coming on in that narrow streete, on both sides, with infinite fury. Sir W. Batten not knowing how to remove his wine, did dig a pit in the garden, and laid it in there; and I took the opportunity of laying all the papers of my office that I could not otherwise dispose of. And in the evening Sir W. Pen and I did dig another, and put our wine in it; and I my Parmazan cheese, as well as my wine and some other things. The Duke of Yorke was at the office this day, at Sir W. Pen's; but I happened not to be within. This afternoon, sitting melancholy with Sir W. Pen in our garden, and thinking of the certain burning of this office, without extraordinary means, I did propose for the sending up of all our workmen from Woolwich and Deptford yards (none whereof yet appeared), and to write to Sir W. Coventry to have the Duke of Yorke's permission to pull down houses, rather than lose this office, which would much hinder the King's business. So Sir W. Pen he went down this night, in order to the sending them up to-morrow morning; and I wrote to Sir W. Coventry about the business,[2] but received no answer. This night Mrs. Turner

[1] Irongate Stairs, at the bottom of Little Tower Hill.

[2] A copy of this letter, preserved among the Pepys MSS. in the author's own handwriting, is subjoined:

"SIR, — The fire is now very neere us as well on Tower Streete as Fanchurch Street side, and we little hope of our escape but by that remedy, to ye want whereof we doe certainly owe ye loss of ye City, namely, ye pulling down of houses, in ye way of ye fire. This way Sir W. Pen and myself have so far concluded upon ye practising, that he is gone to Woolwich and Deptford to supply himself with men and necessarys in order to the doeing thereof, in case at his returne our (who, poor woman, was removing her goods all this day, good goods into the garden, and knows not how to dispose of them), and her husband supped with my wife and I at night, in the office, upon a shoulder of mutton from the cook's, without any napkin or any thing, in a sad manner, but were merry. Only now and then walking into the garden, and saw how horridly the sky looks, all on a fire in the night, was enough to put us out of our wits; and, indeed, it was extremely dreadful, for it looks just as if it was at us, and the whole heaven on fire. I after supper walked in the darke down to Tower-streete, and there saw it all on fire, at the Trinity House on that side, and the Dolphin Taverne on this side, which was very near us; and the fire with extraordinary vehemence. Now begins the practice of blowing up of houses in Tower-streete, those next the Tower, which at first did frighten people more than any thing; but it stopped the fire where it was done, it bringing down the houses to the ground in the same places they stood, and then it was easy to quench what little fire was in it, though it kindled nothing almost. W. Hewer this day went to see how his mother did, and comes late home, telling us how he hath been forced to remove her to Islington, her house in Pye-corner being burned; so that the fire is got so far that way, and all the Old Bayly, and was running down to Fleete-streete; and Paul's is burned, and all Cheapside. I wrote to my father this night, but the post-house being burned, the letter could not go.[1]

condition be not bettered and that he meets with his R. H[s] approbation, which I have thus undertaken to learn of you. Pray please to let me have this night (at whatever hour it is) what his R. H[s] directions are in this particular. Sir J. Minnes and Sir W. Batten having left us, we cannot add, though we are well assured of their, as well as all y[e] neighbourhood's concurrence.

"Y[r] obedient Serv[nt],

"S. P.

"Sir W. Coventry,

"Sept[r]. 4, 1666."

[1] J. Hickes wrote to Williamson on September 3rd from the "Golden Lyon, Red Cross Street Posthouse. Sir Philip [Frowde] and his lady fled from the [letter] office at midnight for safety; stayed himself till 1 a.m. till his wife and childrens' patience could stay no longer, fearing lest they should be quite stopped up; the passage was so tedious they had much ado to get where they are. The Chester and Irish mails have come in; sends him his letters, knows not how to dispose of the business" ("Calendar of State Papers," 1666–67, p. 95).

5th. I lay down in the office again upon W. Hewer's quilt, being mighty weary, and sore in my feet with going till I was hardly able to stand. About two in the morning my wife calls me up and tells me of new cryes of fire, it being come to Barkeing Church, which is the bottom of our lane.[1] I up, and finding it so, resolved presently to take her away, and did, and took my gold, which was about £2,350, W. Hewer, and Jane, down by Proundy's boat to Woolwich; but, Lord! what a sad sight it was by moone-light to see the whole City almost on fire, that you might see it plain at Woolwich, as if you were by it. There, when I come, I find the gates shut, but no guard kept at all, which troubled me, because of discourse now begun, that there is plot in it, and that the French had done it. I got the gates open, and to Mr. Shelden's, where I locked up my gold, and charged my wife and W. Hewer never to leave the room without one of them in it, night or day. So back again, by the way seeing my goods well in the lighters at Deptford, and watched well by people. Home, and whereas I expected to have seen our house on fire, it being now about seven o'clock, it was not. But to the fyre, and there find greater hopes than I expected; for my confidence of finding our Office on fire was such, that I durst not ask any body how it was with us, till I come and saw it not burned. But going to the fire, I find by the blowing up of houses, and the great helpe given by the workmen out of the King's yards, sent up by Sir W. Pen, there is a good stop given to it, as well as at Marke-lane end as ours; it having only burned the dyall of Barking Church, and part of the porch, and was there quenched. I up to the top of Barking steeple, and there saw the saddest sight of desolation that I ever saw; every where great fires, oyle-cellars, and brimstone, and other things burning. I became afeard to stay there long, and therefore down again as fast as I could, the fire being spread as far as I could see it; and to Sir W. Pen's, and there eat a piece of cold meat, having eaten[2] nothing since Sunday, but the

[1] Allhallows Barking, in Great Tower Street, nearly opposite the end of Seething Lane. The church had a narrow escape.

[2] He forgot the shoulder of mutton from the cook's the day before. — B.

remains of Sunday's dinner. Here I met with Mr. Young and Whistler; and having removed all my things, and received good hopes that the fire at our end is stopped, they and I walked into the town, and find Fanchurch-streete, Gracious-streete, and Lumbard-streete all in dust. The Exchange a sad sight, nothing standing there, of all the statues or pillars, but Sir Thomas Gresham's picture[1] in the corner. Walked into Moorefields (our feet ready to burn, walking through the towne among the hot coles), and find that full of people, and poor wretches carrying their goods there, and every body keeping his goods together by themselves (and a great blessing it is to them that it is fair weather for them to keep abroad night and day); drank there, and paid twopence for a plain penny loaf. Thence homeward, having passed through Cheapside and Newgate Market, all burned, and seen Anthony Joyce's house in fire. And took up (which I keep by me) a piece of glasse of Mercers' Chappell in the streete, where much more was, so melted and buckled with the heat of the fire like parchment. I also did see a poor cat taken out of a hole in the chimney, joyning to the wall of the Exchange, with the hair all burned off the body, and yet alive. So home at night, and find there good hopes of saving our office; but great endeavours of watching all night, and having men ready; and so we lodged them in the office, and had drink and bread and cheese for them. And I lay down and slept a good night about midnight, though when I rose I heard that there had been a great alarme of French and Dutch being risen, which proved nothing. But it is a strange thing to see how long this time did look since Sunday, having been always full of variety of actions, and little sleep, that it looked like a week or more, and I had forgot almost the day of the week.

6th. Up about five o'clock, and there met Mr. Gawden at the gate of the office (I intending to go out, as I used, every now and then to-day, to see how the fire is) to call our men to Bishop's-gate, where no fire had yet been near,

[1] Evelyn writes in his "Diary," under date September 7th: "Sir Tho. Gresham's statue, tho' fallen from its nich in the Royal Exchange, remained intire, when all those of ye Kings since ye Conquest were broken to pieces."

and there is now one broke out: which did give great grounds to people, and to me too, to think that there is some kind of plot[1] in this (on which many by this time have been taken, and it hath been dangerous for any stranger to walk in the streets), but I went with the men, and we did put it out in a little time; so that that was well again. It was pretty to see how hard the women did work in the cannells, sweeping of water; but then they would scold for drink, and be as drunk as devils. I saw good butts of sugar broke open in the street, and people go and take handsfull out, and put into beer, and drink it. And now all being pretty well, I took boat, and over to Southwarke, and took boat on the other side the bridge, and so to Westminster, thinking to shift myself, being all in dirt from top to bottom; but could not there find any place to buy a shirt or pair of gloves, Westminster Hall being full of people's goods, those in Westminster having removed all their goods, and the Exchequer money put into vessels to carry to Nonsuch; but to the Swan, and there was trimmed; and then to White Hall, but saw nobody; and so home. A sad sight to see how the River looks: no houses nor church near it, to the Temple, where it stopped. At home, did go with Sir W. Batten, and our neighbour, Knightly (who, with one more, was the only man of any fashion left in all the neighbourhood thereabouts, they all removing their goods and leaving their houses to the mercy of the fire), to Sir R. Ford's, and there dined in an earthen platter — a fried breast of mutton; a great many of us, but very merry, and indeed as good a meal, though as ugly a one, as ever I had in my life. Thence down to Deptford, and there with great satisfaction landed all my goods at Sir G. Carteret's safe, and nothing missed I could see, or hurt. This being done to my great content, I home, and to Sir W. Batten's, and there with Sir R. Ford, Mr.

[1] The terrible disaster which overtook London was borne by the inhabitants of the city with great fortitude, but foreigners and Roman Catholics had a bad time. As no cause for the outbreak of the fire could be traced, a general cry was raised that it owed its origin to a plot. In a letter from Thomas Waade to Williamson (dated "Whitby, Sept. 14") we read, "The destruction of London by fire is reported to be a hellish contrivance of the French, Hollanders, and fanatic party" ("Calendar of State Papers," 1666–67, p. 124).

Knightly, and one Withers, a professed lying rogue, supped well, and mighty merry, and our fears over. From them to the office, and there slept with the office full of labourers, who talked, and slept, and walked all night long there. But strange it was to see Cloathworkers' Hall on fire these three days and nights in one body of flame, it being the cellar full of oyle.

7th. Up by five o'clock; and, blessed be God! find all well; and by water to Paul's Wharfe. Walked thence, and saw all the towne burned, and a miserable sight of Paul's church, with all the roofs fallen, and the body of the quire fallen into St. Fayth's;[1] Paul's school also, Ludgate, and Fleet-street, my father's house, and the church, and a good part of the Temple the like. So to Creed's lodging, near the New Exchange, and there find him laid down upon a bed; the house all unfurnished, there being fears of the fire's coming to them. There borrowed a shirt of him, and washed. To Sir W. Coventry, at St. James's, who lay without curtains, having removed all his goods; as the King at White Hall, and every body had done, and was doing. He hopes we shall have no publique distractions upon this fire, which is what every body fears, because of the talke of the French having a hand in it. And it is a proper time for discontents; but all men's minds are full of care to protect themselves, and save their goods: the militia is in armes every where. Our fleetes, he tells me, have been in sight one of another, and most unhappily by

[1] "St. Faith's under St. Paul's" was situated immediately beneath the choir of old St. Paul's. When the cathedral was lengthened eastward, about 1255, the old parish church of St. Faith was cleared away to make room for this extension. The "famous vault," as Dugdale calls it, was then appropriated as a parish church. At the Reformation the church of the parish was removed to Jesus Chapel in the cathedral, but the crypt retained its old name. Evelyn writes of the burning of St. Paul's: "It was astonishing to see what immense stones the heate had in a manner calcined, so that all ye ornaments, columns, freezes, capitals and projectures of massie Portland stone flew off, even to ye very roofe, where a sheet of lead covering a great space (no less than six akers by measure) was totally mealted; the ruines of the vaulted roofe falling broke into St. Faith's, which being fill'd with the magazines of bookes belonging to ye stationers, and carried thither for safety, they were all consumed, burning for a weeke following" ("Diary," September 7th).

fowle weather were parted, to our great losse, as in reason they do conclude; the Dutch being come out only to make a shew, and please their people; but in very bad condition as to stores, victuals, and men. They are at Bullen,[1] and our fleete come to St. Ellen's.[2] We have got nothing, but have lost one ship, but he knows not what. Thence to the Swan, and there drank: and so home, and find all well. My Lord Bruncker, at Sir W. Batten's, and tells us the Generall[3] is sent for up, to come to advise with the King about business at this juncture, and to keep all quiet; which is great honour to him, but I am sure is but a piece of dissimulation. So home, and did give orders for my house to be made clean; and then down to Woolwich, and there find all well. Dined, and Mrs. Markham come to see my wife. So I up again, and calling at Deptford for some things of W. Hewer's, he being with me, and then home and spent the evening with Sir R. Ford, Mr. Knightly, and Sir W. Pen at Sir W. Batten's. This day our Merchants first met at Gresham College, which, by proclamation,[4] is to be their

[1] Boulogne.

[2] St. Helen's, or Watch-house Point, is in the parish of St. Helen's, Isle of Wight, near Brading Harbour. St. Helen's road lies off the coast. It is a roadstead with anchorage in from three to five fathoms, but dangerous on account of the shoals and rocks.

[3] The Duke of Albemarle had been sent for, and this desire of the king and his Council to have him in London shows the unique position which he held in the popular esteem. Lord Arlington, writing to Sir Thomas Clifford on September 4th, says: "The king, with the unanimous concurrence of the Council, wishes the Lord General were there, and Sec. Morice is sounding him to know whether he would be willing to be ordered home. Is confident, could he see the condition they are in, he would think it more honour to be called home than to stay in the fleet, where he may not have an opportunity of fighting; he would have it in his hands to give the king his kingdom a second time, and the world would see the value the king sets on him. Wishes this to be urged upon him, only with the reserve that his Majesty leaves him to make the choice himself" ("Calendar of State Papers," 1666-67, p. 99).

[4] The proclamation (dated September 6th) ordered "Gresham College, Bishopsgate Street, to be used instead of the Royal Exchange, which is burnt" ("Calendar of State Papers," 1666-67, p. 104). At the meeting of the Royal Society on September 12th, "It was resolved that the society should meet the next time in Dr. Pope's lodgings in Gresham College; and by reason that the former place of meeting for the society, and other rooms also convenient for the same, were taken

Exchange. Strange to hear what is bid for houses all up and down here; a friend of Sir W. Rider's having £150 for what he used to let for £40 per annum. Much dispute where the Custome-house shall be; thereby the growth of the City again to be foreseen. My Lord Treasurer, they say, and others, would have it at the other end of the towne. I home late to Sir W. Pen's, who did give me a bed; but without curtains or hangings, all being down. So here I went the first time into a naked bed, only my drawers on; and did sleep pretty well: but still both sleeping and waking had a fear of fire in my heart, that I took little rest. People do all the world over cry out of the simplicity of my Lord Mayor in generall; and more particularly in this business of the fire, laying it all upon him. A proclamation[1] is come out for markets to be kept at Leadenhall and Mile-end-greene, and several other places about the towne; and Tower-hill, and all churches to be set open to receive poor people.

8th. Up and with Sir W. Batten and Sir W. Pen by water to White Hall and they to St. James's. I stopped with Sir G. Carteret to desire him to go with us, and to enquire after money. But the first he cannot do, and the other as little, or says, "when we can get any, or what shall we do for it?" He, it seems, is employed in the correspondence between the City and the King every day, in settling of things. I find him full of trouble, to think how things will go. I left him, and to St. James's, where we met first at Sir W. Coventry's chamber, and there did what business we can, without any books. Our discourse, as every thing else, was confused. The fleete is at Ports-

up for the use of the Lord Mayor of London and the City, it was ordered that . . . . a committee consider of another place for the future meetings" (Birch's "Hist. of the Royal Society," vol. ii., p. 113).

[1] On September 5th proclamation was made "ordering that for supply of the distressed people left destitute by the late dreadful and dismal fire . . . great proportions of bread be brought daily, not only to the former markets, but to those lately ordained; that all churches, chapels, schools, and public buildings are to be open to receive the goods of those who know not how to dispose of them." On September 6th, proclamation ordered "that as the markets are burned down, markets be held in Bishopsgate Street, Tower Hill, Smithfield, and Leadenhall Street" ("Calendar of State Papers," 1666–67, pp. 100, 104).

mouth, there staying a wind to carry them to the Downes, or towards Bullen, where they say the Dutch fleete is gone, and stays. We concluded upon private meetings for a while, not having any money to satisfy any people that may come to us. I bought two eeles upon the Thames, cost me six shillings. Thence with Sir W. Batten to the Cock-pit, whither the Duke of Albemarle is come. It seems the King holds him so necessary at this time, that he hath sent for him, and will keep him here.[1] Indeed, his interest in the City, being acquainted, and his care in keeping things quiet, is reckoned that wherein he will be very serviceable. We to him; he is courted in appearance by every body. He very kind to us; I perceive he lays by all business of the fleete at present, and minds the City, and is now hastening to Gresham College, to discourse with the Aldermen. Sir W. Batten and I home (where met by my brother John, come to town to see how things are with us), and then presently he with me to Gresham College; where infinity of people, partly through novelty to see the new place, and partly to find out and hear what is become one man of another. I met with many people undone, and more that have extraordinary great losses. People speaking their thoughts variously about the beginning of the fire, and the rebuilding of the City. Then to Sir W. Batten's, and took my brother with me, and there dined with a great company of neighbours, and much good discourse; among others, of the low spirits of some rich men in the City, in sparing any encouragement to the poor people that wrought for the saving their houses. Among others, Alderman Starling, a very rich man, without children, the fire at next door to him in our lane, after our men had saved his house, did give *2s. 6d.* among thirty of them, and did quarrel with some that would remove the rubbish out of the way of the fire, saying that they come to steal. Sir W. Coventry told me of another this morning in Holborne, which he shewed the King: that when it was offered to stop the fire near his house for such a reward that came but to *2s. 6d.* a man among the neighbours he would give but *18d.* Thence to Bednall Green by coach, my brother with me, and saw all

[1] See *ante,* September 7th.

well there, and fetched away my journall-book to enter for five days past, and then back to the office, where I find Bagwell's wife, and her husband come home. Agreed to come to their house to-morrow, I sending him away to his ship to-day. To the office and late writing letters, and then to Sir W. Pen's, my brother lying with me, and Sir W. Pen gone down to rest himself at Woolwich. But I was much frighted and kept awake in my bed, by some noise I heard a great while below stairs; and the boys not coming up to me when I knocked. It was by their discovery of people stealing of some neighbours' wine that lay in vessels in the streets. So to sleep; and all well all night.

9th (Sunday). Up; and was trimmed, and sent my brother to Woolwich to my wife, to dine with her. I to church, where our parson made a melancholy but good sermon; and many and most in the church cried, specially the women. The church mighty full; but few of fashion, and most strangers. I walked to Bednall Green, and there dined well, but a bad venison pasty at Sir W. Rider's. Good people they are, and good discourse; and his daughter, Middleton, a fine woman, discreet. Thence home, and to church again, and there preached Dean Harding;[1] but, methinks, a bad, poor sermon, though proper for the time; nor eloquent, in saying at this time that the City is reduced from a large folio to a decimo-tertio. So to my office, there to write down my journall, and take leave of my brother, whom I sent back this afternoon, though rainy; which it hath not done a good while before. But I had no room or convenience for him here till my house is fitted; but I was very kind to him, and do take very well of him his journey. I did give him 40*s.* for his pocket, and so, he being gone, and, it presently rayning, I was troubled for him, though it is good for the fyre. Anon to Sir W. Pen's to bed, and made my boy Tom to read me asleep.

10th. All the morning clearing our cellars, and breaking in pieces all my old lumber, to make room, and to prevent fire. And then to Sir W. Batten's, and dined; and there hear that Sir W. Rider says that the towne is full of the

[1] Nathaniel Hardy, installed Dean of Rochester December 10th, 1660. He died at Croydon, June 1st, 1670.

report of the wealth that is in his house, and would be glad that his friends would provide for the safety of their goods there. This made me get a cart; and thither, and there brought my money all away. Took a hackney-coach myself (the hackney-coaches now standing at Allgate). Much wealth indeed there is at his house. Blessed be God, I got all mine well thence, and lodged it in my office; but vexed to have all the world see it. And with Sir W. Batten, who would have taken away my hands before they were stowed. But by and by comes brother Balty from sea, which I was glad of; and so got him, and Mr. Tooker, and the boy, to watch with them all in the office all night, while I upon Jane's coming went down to my wife, calling at Deptford, intending to see Bagwell, but did not ouvrir la porte comme je did expect. So down late to Woolwich, and there find my wife out of humour and indifferent, as she uses upon her having much liberty abroad.

11th. Lay there, and up betimes, and by water with my gold, and laid it with the rest in my office, where I find all well and safe. So with Sir W. Batten to the New Exchange by water and to my Lord Bruncker's house, where Sir W. Coventry and Sir G. Carteret met. Little business before us but want of money. Broke up, and I home by coach round the town. Dined at home, Balty and myself putting up my papers in my closet in the office. He away, I down to Deptford and there spoke with Bagwell and agreed upon to-morrow, and come home in the rain by water. In the evening at Sir W. Pen's, with my wife, at supper: he in a mad, ridiculous, drunken humour; and it seems there have been some late distances between his lady and him, as my [wife] tells me. After supper, I home, and with Mr. Hater, Gibson,[1] and Tom alone, got all my chests and money into the further cellar with much pains, but great content to me when done. So very late and weary to bed.

12th. Up, and with Sir W. Batten and Sir W. Pen to St. James's by water, and there did our usual business with the Duke of Yorke. Thence I to Westminster, and there spoke with Michell and Howlett, who tell me how their poor young ones are going to Shadwell's. The latter told me of

[1] Richard Gibson, victualling agent in the navy, &c.

the unkindness of the young man to his wife, which is now over, and I have promised to appear a counsellor to him. I am glad she is like to be so near us again. Thence to Martin, and there did tout ce que je voudrais avec her, and drank, and away by water home and to dinner, Balty and his wife there. After dinner I took him down with me to Deptford, and there by the Bezan loaded above half my goods and sent them away. So we back home, and then I found occasion to return in the dark and to Bagwell, and there . . . did do all that I desired, but though I did intend pour avoir demeurais con elle to-day last night, yet when I had done ce que je voudrais I did hate both elle and la cose, and taking occasion from the occasion of su marido's return . . . did me lever, and so away home late to Sir W. Pen's (Balty and his wife lying at my house), and there in the same simple humour I found Sir W. Pen, and so late to bed.

13th. Up, and down to Tower Wharfe; and there, with Balty and labourers from Deptford, did get my goods housed well at home. So down to Deptford again to fetch the rest, and there eat a bit of dinner at the Globe, with the master of the Bezan with me, while the labourers went to dinner. Here I hear that this poor towne do bury still of the plague seven or eight in a day. So to Sir G. Carteret's to work, and there did to my content ship off into the Bezan all the rest of my goods, saving my pictures and fine things, that I will bring home in wherrys when the house is fit to receive them: and so home, and unload them by carts and hands before night, to my exceeding satisfaction: and so after supper to bed in my house, the first time I have lain there; and lay with my wife in my old closett upon the ground, and Balty and his wife in the best chamber, upon the ground also.

14th. Up, and to work, having carpenters come to helpe in setting up bedsteads and hangings; and at that trade my people and I all the morning, till pressed by publique business to leave them against my will in the afternoon: and yet I was troubled in being at home, to see all my goods lie up and down the house in a bad condition, and strange workmen going to and fro might take what they would almost. All the afternoon busy; and Sir W. Coventry come to me, and found me, as God would have it, in my office, and people about me setting my papers to rights; and there discoursed about getting an account ready against the Parliament, and thereby did create me infinite of business, and to be done on a sudden; which troubled me: but, however, he being gone, I about it late, and to good purpose. And so home, having this day also got my wine out of the ground again, and set in my cellar; but with great pain to keep the porters that carried it in from observing the money-chests there. So to bed as last night, only my wife and I upon a bedstead with curtains in that which was Mercer's chamber, and Balty and his wife (who are here and do us good service), where we lay last night. This day, poor Tom Pepys, the turner, was with me, and Kate Joyce, to bespeake places; one for himself, the other for her husband. She tells me he hath lost £140 per annum, but have seven houses left.

15th. All the morning at the office, Harman being come to my great satisfaction to put up my beds and hangings, so I am at rest, and followed my business all day. Dined with Sir W. Batten, mighty busy about this account, and while my people were busy, wrote near thirty letters and orders with my owne hand. At it till eleven at night; and it is strange to see how clear my head was, being eased of all the matter of all these letters; whereas one would think that I should have been dazed. I never did observe so much of myself in my life. In the evening there comes to me Captain Cocke, and walked a good while in the garden. He says he hath computed that the rents of houses lost by this fire in the City comes to £600,000 per annum; that this will make the Parliament more quiet than otherwise they would have been, and give the King a more ready supply; that the supply must be by excise, as it is in Holland; that the Parliament will see it necessary to carry on the warr; that the late storm hindered our beating the Dutch fleete, who were gone out only to satisfy the people, having no business to do but to avoid us; that the French, as late in the yeare as it is, are coming; that the Dutch are really in bad condition, but that this unhappinesse of ours do give them heart; that there was a late difference between my Lord Arlington and Sir W. Coventry about neglect in the last to send away an express of the other's in time; that it come before the King, and the Duke of Yorke concerned himself in it; but this fire hath stopped it. The Dutch fleete is not gone home, but rather to the North, and so dangerous to our Gottenburgh fleete. That the Parliament is likely to fall foul upon some persons; and, among others, on the Vice-chamberlaine,[1] though we both believe with little ground. That certainly never so great a loss as this was borne so well by citizens in the world; he believing that not one merchant upon the 'Change will break upon it. That he do not apprehend there will be any disturbances in State upon it; for that all men are busy in looking after their owne business to save themselves. He gone, I to finish my letters, and home to bed; and find to my infinite joy many rooms clean; and myself and wife lie in our own chamber again. But much terrified in the nights now-a-days with dreams of fire, and falling down of houses.

16th (Lord's day). Lay with much pleasure in bed talking with my wife about Mr. Hater's lying here and W. Hewer also, if Mrs. Mercer leaves her house. To the office, whither also all my people about this account, and there busy all the morning. At noon, with my wife, against her will, all undressed and dirty, dined at Sir W. Pen's, where was all the company of our families in towne; but, Lord! so sorry a dinner: venison baked in pans, that the dinner I have had for his lady alone hath been worth four of it. Thence, after dinner, displeased with our entertainment, to my office again, and there till almost midnight and my people with me, and then home, my head mightily akeing about our accounts.

17th. Up betimes, and shaved myself after a week's growth: but, Lord! how ugly I was yesterday and how fine to-day! By water, seeing the City all the way, a sad sight indeed, much fire being still in. To Sir W. Coventry, and there read over my yesterday's work: being a collection of the particulars of the excess of charge created by a war, with good content. Sir W. Coventry was in great pain lest the French fleete should be passed by our fleete, who had notice of them on Saturday, and were preparing to go meet them; but their minds altered, and judged them merchant-

[1] Sir G. Carteret.

men, when the same day the Success, Captain Ball,[1] made their whole fleete, and come to Brighthelmstone, and thence at five o'clock afternoon, Saturday, wrote Sir W. Coventry newes thereof; so that we do much fear our missing them. Here come in and talked with him Sir Thomas Clifford,[2] who appears a very fine gentleman, and much set by at Court for his activity in going to sea, and stoutness every where, and stirring up and down. Thence by coach over the ruines, down Fleete Streete and Cheapside to Broad Streete to Sir G. Carteret, where Sir W. Batten (and Sir J. Minnes, whom I had not seen a long time before, being his first coming abroad) and Lord Bruncker passing his accounts. Thence home a little to look after my people at work and back to Sir G. Carteret's to dinner; and thence, after some discourse with him upon our publique accounts, I back home, and all the day with Harman and his people finishing the hangings and beds in my house, and the hangings will be as good as ever, and particularly in my new closet. They gone and I weary, my wife and I, and Balty and his wife, who come hither to-day to helpe us, to a barrel of oysters I sent from the river to-day, and so to bed.

18th. Strange with what freedom and quantity I pissed this night, which I know not what to impute to but my oysters, unless the coldness of the night should cause it, for it was a sad rainy and tempestuous night. Soon as up I begun to have some pain in my bladder and belly, as usual, which made me go to dinner betimes, to fill my belly, and that did ease me, so as I did my business in the afternoon, in forwarding the settling of my house, very well. Betimes to bed, my wife also being all this day ill in the same manner. Troubled at my wife's haire coming off so much. This day the Parliament met, and adjourned till Friday, when the King will be with them.

19th. Up, and with Sir W. Pen by coach to St. James's,

[1] Captain Napthali Ball was made commander of the "Bramble" fireship in 1665, and removed to the "Success" at the end of the same year.

[2] Eldest son of Hugh Clifford, Esq., of Ugbrooke, M.P. for Totnes, 1661, and knighted for his conduct in the sea-fight, 1665. After filling several high offices, he was, in 1672, created Baron Clifford of Chudleigh, and constituted High Treasurer, which place he resigned the following year, a few months before his death. — B.

and there did our usual business before the Duke of Yorke; which signified little, our business being only complaints of lack of money. Here I saw a bastard of the late King of Sweden's come to kiss his hands; a mighty modish French-like gentleman. Thence to White Hall, with Sir W. Batten and Sir W. Pen, to Wilkes's; and there did hear the many profane stories of Sir Henry Wood[1] damning the parsons for so much spending the wine at the sacrament, cursing that ever they took the cup to themselves, and then another story that he valued not all the world's curses, for for two pence he shall get at any time the prayers of some poor body that is worth a 1,000 of all their curses; Lord Norwich drawing a tooth at a health. Another time, he and Pinchbacke and Dr. Goffe,[2] now a religious man, Pinchbacke did begin a frolick to drink out of a glass with a toad in it that he had taken up going out to shit, he did it without harm. Goffe, who knew sacke would kill the toad, called for sacke; and when he saw it dead, says he, "I will have a quick toad, and will not drink from a dead toad."[3] By that means, no other being to be found, he escaped the health. Thence home, and dined, and to Deptford and got all my pictures put into wherries, and my other fine things, and landed them all very well, and brought them home, and got Sympson to set them all up to-night; and he gone, I and the boy to finish and set up my books, and everything else in my house, till two o'clock in the morning, and then to bed; but mightily troubled, and even in my sleep, at my missing four or five of my biggest books. Speed's Chronicle and Maps, and the two parts of Waggoner,[4] and

[1] He had been Clerk of the Spicery to Charles I., and after the Restoration was Clerk to the Board of Green Cloth. Evelyn mentions his marriage ("Diary," November 17th, 1651), "I went to congratulate ye marriage of Mrs. Gardner, maid of honor lately married to that odd person Sir Hen. Wood, but riches do many things."

[2] Dr. Stephen Goffe, Clerk of the Queen's Closet, and her assistant confessor. He had been chaplain to Colonel Goring, but became, in 1641, a Roman Catholic. — B.

[3] "They swallow their own contradictions as easily as a hector can drink a frog in a glass of wine." — *Bentivoglio and Urania*, book v., p. 92, 3rd edit. — B.

[4] Apparently Wagenaer's "Speculum Nauticum," published at Leyden in 1585, and translated into English by Anthony Ashley about the year 1588. — B.

a book of cards, which I suppose I have put up with too much care, that I have forgot where they are, for sure they are not stole. Two little pictures of sea and ships, and a little gilt frame belonging to my plate of the River, I want; but my books do heartily trouble me. Most of my gilt frames are hurt, which also troubles me, but most my books. This day I put on two shirts, the first time this year, and do grow well upon it; so that my disease is nothing but wind.

20th. Up, much troubled about my books, but cannot imagine where they should be. Up, to the setting my closett to rights, and Sir W. Coventry takes me at it, which did not displease me. He and I to discourse about our accounts, and the bringing them to the Parliament, and with much content to see him rely so well on my part. He and I together to Broad Streete to the Vice-Chamberlain, and there discoursed a while and parted. My Lady Carteret come to town, but I did not see her. He tells me how the fleete is come into the Downes. Nothing done, nor French fleete seen: we drove all from our anchors. But he says newes is come that De Ruyter[1] is dead, or very near it, of a hurt in his mouth, upon the discharge of one of his own guns; which put him into a fever, and he likely to die, if not already dead. We parted, and I home to dinner, and after dinner to the setting things in order, and all my people busy about the same work. In the afternoon, out by coach, my wife with me, which we have not done several weeks now, through all the ruines, to shew her them, which frets her much, and is a sad sight indeed. Set her down at her brother's, and thence I to Westminster Hall, and there staid a little while, and called her home. She did give me an account of great differences between her mother and Balty's wife. The old woman charges her with going abroad and staying out late, and painting in the absence of her husband, and I know not what; and they grow proud, both he and she, and do not help their father and mother out of what I help them to, which I do not like, nor my wife. So home, and to the office, to even my journall, and then home, and very late up with Jane setting my books in

[1] Admiral Michael Adrian de Ruyter did not die until April 11th, 1676.

perfect order in my closet, but am mightily troubled for my great books that I miss, and I am troubled the more for fear there should be more missing than what I find, though by the room they take on the shelves I do not find any reason to think it. So to bed.

21st. Up, and mightily pleased with the setting of my books the last night in order, and that which did please me most of all is that W. Hewer tells me that upon enquiry he do find that Sir W. Pen hath a hamper more than his own, which he took for a hamper of bottles of wine, and are books in it. I was impatient to see it, but they were carried into a wine-cellar, and the boy is abroad with him at the House, where the Parliament met to-day, and the King[1] to be with them. At noon after dinner I sent for Harry, and he tells me it is so, and brought me by and by my hamper of books to my great joy, with the same books I missed, and three more great ones, and no more. I did give him 5*s.* for his pains. And so home with great joy, and to the setting of some of them right, but could not finish it, but away by coach to the other end of the town, leaving my wife at the 'Change, but neither come time enough to the Council to speak with the Duke of Yorke, nor with Sir G. Carteret, and so called my wife, and paid for some things she bought, and so home, and there after a little doing at the office about our accounts, which now draw near the time they should be ready, the House having ordered Sir G. Carteret, upon his offering them, to bring them in on Saturday next, I home, and there, with great pleasure, very late new setting all my books; and now I am in as good condition as I desire to be in all worldly respects. The Lord of Heaven make me thankfull, and continue me therein! So to bed. This day I had new stairs of main timber put to my cellar going into the yard.

22nd. To my closet, and had it new washed, and now my house is so clean as I never saw it, or any other house in my life, and every thing in as good condition as ever before the fire; but with, I believe, about £20 cost one

[1] The king made a speech in which he alluded to the Great Fire, and pointed out the immense expense of the war, asking for fresh supplies.

way or other, besides about £20 charge in removing my goods, and do not find that I have lost any thing but two little pictures of ships and sea, and a little gold frame for one of my sea-cards. My glazier, indeed, is so full of worke that I cannot get him to come to perfect my house. To the office, and there busy now for good and all about my accounts. My Lord Bruncker come thither, thinking to find an office, but we have not yet met. He do now give me a watch, a plain one, in the roome of my former watch with many motions which I did give him. If it goes well, I care not for the difference in worth, though I believe there is above £5. He and I to Sir G. Carteret to discourse about his account, but Mr. Waith not being there nothing could be done, and therefore I home again, and busy all day. In the afternoon comes Anthony Joyce to see me, and with tears told me his losse, but yet that he had something left that he can live well upon, and I doubt it not. But he would buy some place that he could have, and yet keepe his trade where he is settled in St. Jones's.[1] He gone, I to the office again, and then to Sir G. Carteret, and there found Mr. Wayth, but, Lord! how fretfully Sir G. Carteret do discourse with Mr. Wayth about his accounts, like a man that understands them not one word. I held my tongue and let him go on like a passionate foole. In the afternoon I paid for the two lighters that carried my goods to Deptford, and they cost me £8. Till past midnight at our accounts, and have brought them to a good issue, so as to be ready to meet Sir G. Carteret and Sir W. Coventry to-morrow, but must work to-morrow, which Mr. T. Hater had no mind to, it being the Lord's day, but, being told the necessity, submitted, poor man! This night writ for brother John to come to towne. Among other reasons, my estate lying in money, I am afeard of any sudden miscarriage. So to bed mightily contented in dispatching so much business, and find my house in the best condition that ever I knew it. Home to bed.

23rd (Lord's day). Up, and after being trimmed, all the morning at the office with my people about me till

[1] St. John's, Clerkenwell, which is not far from Holborn Conduit, where Anthony Joyce kept the Three Stags. St. John's is written S. Jones in Norden's map of London.

about one o'clock, and then home, and my people with me, and Mr. Wayth and I eat a bit of victuals in my old closet, now my little dining-room, which makes a pretty room, and my house being so clean makes me mightily pleased, but only I do lacke Mercer or somebody in the house to sing with. Soon as eat a bit Mr. Wayth and I by water to White Hall, and there at Sir G. Carteret's lodgings Sir W. Coventry met, and we did debate the whole business of our accounts to the Parliament; where it appears to us that the charge of the war from September 1st, 1664, to this Michaelmas, will have been but £3,200,000, and we have paid in that time somewhat about £2,200,000; so that we owe above £900,000: but our method of accounting, though it cannot, I believe, be far wide from the mark, yet will not abide a strict examination if the Parliament should be troublesome. Here happened a pretty question of Sir W. Coventry, whether this account of ours will not put my Lord Treasurer to a difficulty to tell what is become of all the money the Parliament have given in this time for the war, which hath amounted to about £4,000,000, which nobody there could answer; but I perceive they did doubt what his answer could be. Having done, and taken from Sir W. Coventry the minutes of a letter to my Lord Treasurer, Wayth and I back again to the office, and thence back down to the water with my wife and landed him in Southwarke, and my wife and I for pleasure to Fox-hall, and there eat and drank, and so back home, and I to the office till midnight drawing the letter we are to send with our accounts to my Lord Treasurer, and that being done to my mind, I home to bed.

24th. Up, and with Sir W. Batten and Sir W. Pen to St. James's, and there with Sir W. Coventry read and all approved of my letter, and then home, and after dinner, Mr. Hater and Gibson dining with me, to the office, and there very late new moulding my accounts and writing fair my letter, which I did against the evening, and then by coach, left my wife at her brother's, and I to St. James's, and up and down to look [for] Sir W. Coventry; and at last found him and Sir G. Carteret with the Lord Treasurer at White Hall, consulting how to make up my Lord Treasurer's general account, as well as that of the Navy particularly.

Here I brought the letter, but found that Sir G. Carteret had altered his account since he did give me the abstract of it: so all my letter must be writ over again, to put in his last abstract. So to Sir G. Carteret's lodgings, to speak a little about the alteration; and there looking over the book that Sir G. Carteret intends to deliver to the Parliament of his payments since September 1st, 1664, and there I find my name the very second for flags, which I had bought for the Navy, of calico, once, about 500 and odd pounds, which vexed me mightily. At last, I concluded of scraping out my name and putting in Mr. Tooker's, which eased me; though the price was such as I should have had glory by. Here I saw my Lady Carteret lately come to towne, who, good lady! is mighty kind, and I must make much of her, for she is a most excellent woman. So took up my wife and away home, and there to bed, and

25th. Up betimes, with all my people to get the letter writ over, and other things done, which I did, and by coach to Lord Bruncker's, and got his hand to it; and then to the Parliament House and got it signed by the rest, and then delivered it at the House-door to Sir Philip Warwicke; Sir G. Carteret being gone into the House with his book of accounts under his arme, to present to the House. I had brought my wife to White Hall, and leaving her with Mrs. Michell, where she sat in her shop and had burnt wine sent for her, I walked in the Hall, and among others with Ned Pickering, who continues still a lying, bragging coxcombe, telling me that my Lord Sandwich may thank himself for all his misfortune; for not suffering him and two or three good honest fellows more to take them by the throats that spoke ill of him, and told me how basely Lionell Walden[1] hath carried himself towards my Lord, by speaking slightly of him, which I shall remember. Thence took my wife home to dinner, and then to the office, where Mr. Hater all the day putting in order and entering in a book all the measures that this account of the Navy hath been made up by, and late at night to Mrs. Turner's, where she had got my wife and Lady Pen and Pegg, and supped, and after supper and the rest of the company by design

[1] M.P. for the borough of Huntingdon. Elected April 12, 1661.

gone, Mrs. Turner and her husband did lay their case to me about their lodgings, Sir J. Minnes being now gone wholly to his owne, and now, they being empty, they doubt Sir T. Harvy or Lord Bruncker may look after the lodgings. I did give them the best advice, poor people, that I could, and would do them any kindnesse, though it is strange that now they should have ne'er a friend of Sir W. Batten or Sir W. Pen to trust to but me, that they have disobliged. So home to bed, and all night still mightily troubled in my sleepe with fire and houses pulling down.

26th. Up, and with Sir J. Minnes to St. James's, where every body going to the House, I away by coach to White Hall, and after a few turns, and hearing that our accounts come into the House but to-day, being hindered yesterday by other business, I away by coach home, taking up my wife and calling at Bennet's, our late mercer, who is come into Covent Garden to a fine house looking down upon the Exchange; and I perceive many Londoners every day come; and Mr. Pierce hath let his wife's closett, and the little blind bed-chamber, and a garret to a silke man for £50 fine, and £30 per annum, and £40 per annum more for dieting the master and two prentices. So home, not agreeing for silk for a petticoat for her which she desired, but home to dinner and then back to White Hall, leaving my wife by the way to buy her petticoat of Bennet, and I to White Hall waiting all the day on the Duke of Yorke to move the King for getting Lanyon some money at Plymouth out of some oyle prizes brought in thither, but could get nothing done, but here by Mr. Dugdale[1] I hear the great loss of books in St. Paul's Church-yarde, and at their Hall also, which they value at about £150,000; some booksellers being wholly undone, and among others, they say, my poor Kirton. And Mr. Crumlum,[2] all his books and household stuff burned; they trusting to St. Fayth's, and the roof of the church falling, broke the arch down

[1] John Dugdale, born June 16th, 1628, chief gentleman of the chamber to Lord Chancellor Clarendon; Windsor Herald, 1684; Norroy King, 1686, when he was knighted. He died at Coventry, August 31st, 1700.

[2] Samuel Cromleholme, or Crumlum, head-master of St. Paul's School (see note, January 24th, 1659–60).

into the lower church, and so all the goods burned. A very great loss. His father[1] hath lost above £1,000 in books; one book newly printed, a Discourse, it seems, of Courts. Here I had the hap to see my Lady Denham: and at night went into the dining-room and saw several fine ladies; among others, Castlemayne, but chiefly Denham again; and the Duke of Yorke taking her aside and talking to her in the sight of all the world, all alone; which was strange, and what also I did not like. Here I met with good Mr. Evelyn, who cries out against it, and calls it bitchering,[2] for the Duke of Yorke talks a little to her, and then she goes away, and then he follows her again like a dog. He observes that none of the nobility come out of the country at all to help the King, or comfort him, or prevent commotions at this fire; but do as if the King were nobody; nor ne'er a priest comes to give the King and Court good council, or to comfort the poor people that suffer; but all is dead, nothing of good in any of their minds: he bemoans it, and says he fears more ruin hangs over our heads. Thence away by coach, and called away my wife at Unthanke's, where she tells me she hath bought a gowne of 15*s.* per yard; the same, before her face, my Lady Castlemayne this day bought also, which I seemed vexed for, though I do not grudge it her, but to incline her to have Mercer again, which I believe I shall do, but the girle, I hear, has no mind to come to us again, which vexes me. Being come home, I to Sir W. Batten, and there hear our business was tendered to the House to-day, and a Committee of the whole House chosen to examine our accounts, and a great many Hotspurs enquiring into it,

[1] William Dugdale, born September 12th, 1605. He early devoted himself to antiquarian and topographical pursuits, and was appointed Pursuivant Extraordinary, with the title of Blanch Lyon, in 1638. In the following year he became Rouge Croix Pursuivant, and in 1644 Chester Herald. At the Restoration he was appointed Norroy King-at-Arms, and Garter in 1677, when he was knighted. He died February 10th, 1686. His "Origines Juridiciales, or Historical Memorials of the English Laws, Courts of Justice," &c., was published in 1666, but with the exception of a few presentation copies the whole impression was destroyed in the Fire. A second edition was published in 1671, and a third in 1680.

[2] This word was apparently of Evelyn's own making.

and likely to give us much trouble and blame, and perhaps (which I am afeard of) will find faults enow to demand better officers. This I truly fear. Away with Sir W. Pen, who was there, and he and I walked in the garden by moonlight, and he proposes his and my looking out into Scotland about timber, and to use Pett there; for timber will be a good commodity this time of building the City; and I like the motion, and doubt not that we may do good in it. We did also discourse about our Privateer, and hope well of that also, without much hazard, as, if God blesses us, I hope we shall do pretty well toward getting a penny. I was mightily pleased with our discourse, and so parted, and to the office to finish my journall for three or four days, and so home to supper, and to bed. Our fleete abroad, and the Dutch too, for all we know; the weather very bad; and under the command of an unlucky man, I fear. God bless him, and the fleete under him!

27th. A very furious blowing night all the night; and my mind still mightily perplexed with dreams, and burning the rest of the town, and waking in much pain for the fleete. Up, and with my wife by coach as far as the Temple, and there she to the mercer's again, and I to look out Penny, my tailor, to speak for a cloak and cassock for my brother, who is coming to town; and I will have him in a canonical dress, that he may be the fitter to go abroad with me. I then to the Exchequer, and there, among other things, spoke to Mr. Falconbridge about his girle I heard sing at Nonsuch, and took him and some other 'Chequer men to the Sun Taverne, and there spent 2*s*. 6*d*. upon them, and he sent for the girle, and she hath a pretty way of singing, but hath almost forgot for want of practice. She is poor in clothes, and not bred to any carriage, but will be soon taught all, and if Mercer do not come again, I think we may have her upon better terms, and breed her to what we please. Thence to Sir W. Coventry's, and there dined with him and Sir W. Batten, the Lieutenant of the Tower, and Mr. Thin,[1] a pretty gentleman, going to Gottenburgh. Hav-

[1] Thomas Thynne, born 1640, Envoy Extraordinary to Sweden. He was the eldest son of Sir Thomas Thynne, Bart., of Kempsford, by Mary, daughter of Thomas, first Lord Coventry, and on the murder of his cousin, Thomas Thynne, of Longleate, succeeded to all his posses-

ing dined, Sir W. Coventry, Sir W. Batten, and I walked into his closet to consider of some things more to be done in a list to be given to the Parliament of all our ships, and time of entry and discharge. Sir W. Coventry seems to think they will soon be weary of the business, and fall quietly into the giving the King what is fit. This he hopes. Thence I by coach home to the office, and there intending a meeting, but nobody being there but myself and Sir J. Minnes, who is worse than nothing, I did not answer any body, but kept to my business in the office till night, and then Sir W. Batten and Sir W. Pen to me, and thence to Sir W. Batten's, and eat a barrel of oysters I did give them, and so home, and to bed. I have this evening discoursed with W. Hewer about Mercer, I having a mind to have her again, and I am vexed to hear him say that she hath no mind to come again, though her mother hath. No newes of the fleete yet, but that they went by Dover on the 25th towards the Gun-fleete, but whether the Dutch be yet abroad, or no, we hear not. De Ruyter is not dead, but like to do well. Most think that the gross of the French fleete are gone home again.

28th. Lay long in bed, and am come to agreement with my wife to have Mercer again, on condition she may learn this winter two months to dance, and she promises me she will endeavour to learn to sing, and all this I am willing enough to. So up, and by and by the glazier comes to finish the windows of my house, which pleases me, and the bookbinder to gild the backs of my books. I got the glass of my book-presses to be done presently, which did mightily content me, and to setting my study in a little better order; and so to my office to my people, busy about our Parliament accounts; and so to dinner, and then at them again close. At night comes Sir W. Pen, and he and I a turn in the garden, and he broke to me a proposition of his and my joining in a design of fetching timber and deals from Scotland, by the help of Mr. Pett upon the place; which, while London is building, will yield good money. I approve it. We judged a third man, that is knowing, is necessary, and

sions. He succeeded his father as second baronet in 1680, and in 1682 was created Baron Thynne of Warminster and Viscount Weymouth. He died July 18th, 1714.—B.

concluded on Sir W. Warren, and sent for him to come to us to-morrow morning. I full of this all night, and the project of our man of war; but he and I both dissatisfied with Sir W. Batten's proposing his son to be Lieutenant, which we, neither of us, like. He gone, I discoursed with W. Hewer about Mercer, having a great mind she should come to us again, and instructed him what to say to her mother about it. And so home, to supper, and to bed.

29th. A little meeting at the office by Sir W. Batten, Sir W. Pen, and myself, being the first since the fire. We rose soon, and comes Sir W. Warren, by our desire, and with Sir W. Pen and I talked of our Scotch motion, which Sir W. Warren did seem to be stumbled at, and did give no ready answer, but proposed some thing previous to it, which he knows would find us work, or writing to Mr. Pett to be informed how matters go there as to cost and ways of providing sawyers or saw-mills. We were parted without coming to any good resolution in it, I discerning plainly that Sir W. Warren had no mind to it, but that he was surprised at our motion. He gone, I to some office business, and then home to dinner, and then to office again, and then got done by night the lists that are to be presented to the Parliament Committee of the ships, number of men, and time employed since the war, and then I with it (leaving my wife at Unthanke's) to St. James's, where Sir W. Coventry staid for me, and he and I perused our lists, and find to our great joy that the wages, victuals, wear and tear, cast by the medium of the men, will come to above 3,000,000; and that the extraordinaries, which all the world will allow us, will arise to more than will justify the expence we have declared to have been at since the war, viz., £320,000, he and I being both mightily satisfied, he saying to me, that if God send us over this rubb, we must take another course for a better Comptroller. So we parted, and I to my wife [at Unthanke's], who staid for the finishing her new best gowne (the best that ever I made her), coloured tabby, flowered, and so took it and her home; and then I to my people, and having cut them out a little more work than they expected, viz., the writing over the lists in a new method, I home to bed, being in good humour, and glad of the end we have brought this matter to.

30th (Lord's day). Up, and to church, where I have not been a good while: and there the church infinitely thronged with strangers since the fire come into our parish; but not one handsome face in all of them, as if, indeed, there was a curse, as Bishop Fuller heretofore said, upon our parish. Here I saw Mercer come into the church, which I had a mind to, but she avoided looking up, which vexed me. A pretty good sermon, and then home, and comes Balty and dined with us. A good dinner; and then to have my haire cut against winter close to my head, and then to church again. A sorry sermon, and away home. [Sir] W. Pen and I to walk to talk about several businesses, and then home; and my wife and I to read in Fuller's Church History, and so to supper and to bed. This month ends with my mind full of business and concernment how this office will speed with the Parliament, which begins to be mighty severe in the examining our accounts, and the expence of the Navy this war.

END OF VOL. V.

VOL. VI.

October 1st, 1666.

Up, and all the morning at the office, getting the list of all the ships and vessels employed since the war, for the Committee of Parliament. At noon with it to Sir W. Coventry's chamber, and there dined with him and [Sir] W. Batten, and [Sir] W. Pen, and after dinner examined it and find it will do us much right in the number of men rising to near the expense we delivered to the Parliament. [Sir] W. Coventry and I (the others going before the Committee) to Lord Bruncker's for his hand, and find him simply mighty busy in a council of the Queen's. He come out and took in the papers to sign, and sent them mighty wisely out again. Sir W. Coventry away to the Committee, and I to the Mercer's, and there took a bill of what I owe of late, which comes to about £17. Thence to White Hall, and there did hear Betty Michell was at this end of the towne, and so without breach of vowe did stay to endeavour to meet with her and carry her home; but she did not come, so I lost my whole afternoon. But pretty! how I took another pretty woman for her, taking her a clap on the breech, thinking verily it had been her. Staid till [Sir] W. Batten and [Sir] W. Pen come out and so away home by water with them, and to the office to do some business, and then home, and my wife do tell me that W. Hewer tells her that Mercer hath no mind to come. So I was angry at it, and resolved with her to have Falconbridge's girle, and I think it will be better for us, and will please me better with singing. With this resolution, to supper and to bed.

2nd. Up, and am sent for to Sir G. Carteret, and to him, and there he tells me how our lists are referred to a Sub-committee to consider and examine, and that I am ordered to be there this afternoon. So I away thence to my new bookbinder to see my books gilding in the backs, and then to White Hall to the House, and spoke to Sir W. Coventry, where he told me I must attend the Committee in the afternoon, and received some hints of more work to do. So I away to the 'Chequer, and thence to an alehouse, and found Mr. Falconbridge, and agreed for his kinswoman to come to me. He says she can dress my wife, and will do anything we would have her to do, and is of a good spirit and mighty cheerful. He is much pleased therewith, and so we shall be. So agreed for her coming the next week. So away home, and eat a short dinner, and then with Sir W. Pen to White Hall, and do give his boy my book of papers to hold while he went into the Committee Chamber in the Inner Court of Wards,[1] and I walked without with Mr. Slingsby, of the Tower, who was there, and who did in walking inform me mightily in several things; among others, that the heightening or lowering of money is only a cheat, and do good to some particular men, which, I can but remember how, I am now by him fully convinced of. Anon Sir W. Pen went away, telling me that Sir W. Coventry that was within had told him that the fleete is all come into the buoy of the Nore, and that he must hasten down to them, and so went away, and I into the Committee Chamber before the Committee sat, and there heard Birch discourse highly and understandingly about the Navy business and a proposal made heretofore to farm the Navy; but Sir W. Coventry did abundantly answer him, and is a most excellent person. By and by the Committee met, and I walked out, and anon they rose and called me in, and appointed me to attend a Committee of them to-morrow at the office to examine our lists. This put me into a mighty fear and trouble, they doing it in a very ill humour, methought. So I away and called on my Lord Bruncker to desire him to be there to-morrow, and so home, having

[1] The Court of Wards and Liveries was held at the end of Westminster Hall, opposite St. Stephen's Chapel. The court was abolished 12 Car. II (see note, February 10th, 1659-60).

taken up my wife at Unthanke's, full of trouble in mind to think what I shall be obliged to answer, that am neither fully fit, nor in any measure concerned to take the shame and trouble of this office upon me, but only from the inability and folly of the Comptroller that occasions it. When come home I to Sir W. Pen's, to his boy, for my book, and there find he hath it not, but delivered it to the doore-keeper of the Committee for me. This, added to my former disquiet, made me stark mad, considering all the nakedness of the office lay open in papers within those covers. I could not tell in the world what to do, but was mad on all sides, and that which made me worse Captain Cocke was there, and he did so swear and curse at the boy that told me. So Cocke, Griffin, and the boy with me, they to find the housekeeper of the Parliament, Hughes, while I to Sir W. Coventry, but could hear nothing of it there. But coming to our rendezvous at the Swan Taverne, in King Streete, I find they have found the housekeeper, and the book simply locked up in the Court. So I staid and drank, and rewarded the doore-keeper, and away home, my heart lighter by all this, but to bed very sad notwithstanding, in fear of what will happen to-morrow upon their coming.

3rd. Waked betimes, mightily troubled in mind, and in the most true trouble that I ever was in my life, saving in the business last year of the East India prizes. So up, and with Mr. Hater and W. Hewer and Griffin to consider of our business, and books and papers necessary for this examination; and by and by, by eight o'clock, comes Birch, the first, with the lists and books of accounts delivered in. He calls me to work, and there he and I begun, when, by and by, comes Garraway,[1] the first time I ever saw him, and Sir W. Thompson and Mr. Boscawen. They to it, and I did make shift to answer them better than I expected. Sir W. Batten, Lord Bruncker, [Sir] W. Pen, come in, but presently went out; and [Sir] J. Minnes come

[1] William Garway, elected M.P. for Chichester, March 26th, 1661, and in 1674 he was appointed by the House to confer with Lord Shaftesbury respecting the charge against Pepys being popishly affected. See note to the Life, vol. i., p. xxx, and for his character, October 6th, 1666.

in, and said two or three words from the purpose, but to do hurt; and so away he went also, and left me all the morning with them alone to stand or fall. At noon Sir W. Batten comes to them to invite them (though fast day) to dinner, which they did, and good company they were, but especially Garraway. Here I have news brought me of my father's coming to town, and I presently to him, glad to see him, poor man, he being come to town unexpectedly to see us and the city. I could not stay with him, but after dinner to work again, only the Committee and I, till dark night, and by that time they cast up all the lists, and found out what the medium of men was borne all the war, of all sorts, and ended with good peace, and much seeming satisfaction; but I find them wise and reserved, and instructed to hit all our blots, as among others, that we reckon the ships full manned from the beginning. They gone, and my heart eased of a great deale of fear and pain, and reckoning myself to come off with victory, because not overcome in anything or much foiled, I away to Sir W. Coventry's chamber, but he not within, then to White Hall, and there among the ladies, and saw my Lady Castlemaine never looked so ill, nor Mrs. Stewart neither, as in this plain, natural dress. I was not pleased with either of them. Away, not finding [Sir] W. Coventry, and so home, and there find my father and my brother come to towne — my father without my expectation; but glad I am to see him. And so to supper with him, and to work again at the office; then home, to set up all my folio books, which are come home gilt on the backs, very handsome to the eye, and then at midnight to bed. This night [Sir] W. Pen told me [Sir] W. Batten swears he will have nothing to do with the Privateer if his son do not go Lieutenant, which angers me and him; but we will be even with him, one way or other.

4th. Up, and mighty betimes, to [Sir] W. Coventry, to give him an account of yesterday's work, which do give him good content. He did then tell me his speech lately to the House in his owne vindication about the report of his selling of places, he having a small occasion offered him by chance, which he did desire, and took, and did it to his content, and, he says, to the House's seeming to approve of it by their hum. He confessed how long he had done it, and how he desired to have something else; and, since then, he had taken nothing, and challenged all the world. I was glad of this also. Thence up to the Duke of York, by appointment, with fellow officers, to complaine, but to no purpose, of want of money, and so away. I to Sir G. Carteret, to his lodging, and here discoursed much of the want of money and our being designed for destruction. How the King hath lost his power, by submitting himself to this way of examining his accounts, and is become but as a private man. He says the King is troubled at it, but they talk an entry[1] shall be made, that it is not to be brought into example; that the King must, if they do not agree presently, make them a courageous speech, which he says he may do, the City of London being now burned, and himself master of an army, better than any prince before him, and so I believe. Thence home, about noon, to dinner. After dinner the bookbinder come, and I sent by him some more books to gild. I to the office all day, and spent most of it with Sir W. Warren, whom I have had no discourse with a great while, and when all is done I do find him a mighty wise man as any I know, and his counsel as much to be followed. Late with Mr. Hater upon comparing the charge and husbandry of the last Dutch war with ours now, and do find good roome to think we have done little worse than they, whereof good use may and will be made. So home to supper, and to bed.

5th. Up, and with my father talking awhile, then to the office, and there troubled with a message from Lord Peterborough about money; but I did give as kind answer as I could, though I hate him. Then to Sir G. Carteret to discourse about paying of part of the great ships come in, and so home again to compare the comparison of the two Dutch wars' charges for [Sir] W. Coventry, and then by water (and saw old Mr. Michell digging like a painfull father for his son) to him, and find him at dinner. After dinner to look over my papers, and comparing them with some notes of his and brought me, the sight of some good Navy notes of his which I shall get. Then examined and liked well my notes, and away together to White Hall, in the way

[1] In the Journals of the House of Commons. — B.

discoursing the inconvenience of the King's being thus subject to an account, but it will be remedied for the time to come, he thinks, if we can get this over, and I find he will have the Comptroller's business better done, swearing he will never be for a wit to be employed on business again. Thence I home, and back again to White Hall, and meeting Sir H. Cholmly to White Hall; there walked till night that the Committee come down, and there [Sir] W. Coventry tells me that the Sub-committee have made their report to the Grand Committee, and in pretty kind terms, and have agreed upon allowing us £4 per head, which I am sure will do the business, but he had endeavoured to have got more, but this do well, and he and I are both mighty glad it is come to this, and the heat of the present business seems almost over. But I have more worke cut out for me, to prepare a list of the extraordinaries, not to be included within the £4, against Monday. So I away from him, and met with the Vice-Chamberlain, and I told him when I had this evening in coming hither met with Captain Cocke, and he told me of a wild motion made in the House of Lords by the Duke of Buckingham for all men that had cheated the King to be declared traitors and felons, and that my Lord Sandwich was named. This put me into a great pain; so the Vice-Chamberlain, who had heard nothing of it, having been all day in the City, away with me to White Hall; and there come to me and told me that, upon Lord Ashly's asking their direction whether, being a peere, he should bring in his accounts to the Commons, which they did give way to, the Duke of Buckingham did move that, for the time to come, what I have written above might be declared by some fuller law than heretofore. Lord Ashly answered, that it was not the fault of the present laws, but want of proof; and so said the Lord Chancellor. He answered, that a better law, he thought, might be made: so the House laughing, did refer it to him to bring in a Bill to that purpose, and this was all. So I away with joyful heart home, calling on Cocke and telling him the same. So I away home to the office to clear my Journall for five days, and so home to supper and to bed, my father who had staid out late and troubled me thereat being come home well and gone to bed, which pleases me also. This day, coming home, Mr. Kirton's kinsman, my bookseller, come in my way; and so I am told by him that Mr. Kirton is utterly undone, and made 2 or £3,000 worse than nothing, from being worth 7 or £8,000. That the goods laid in the Churchyarde fired through the windows those in St. Fayth's church; and those coming to the warehouses' doors fired them, and burned all the books and the pillars of the church, so as the roof falling down, broke quite down, which it did not do in the other places of the church, which is alike pillared (which I knew not before); but being not burned, they stand still. He do believe there is above £150,000 of books burned; all the great booksellers almost undone: not only these, but their warehouses at their Hall, and under Christchurch, and elsewhere being all burned. A great want thereof there will be of books, specially Latin books and foreign books; and, among others, the Polyglottes[1] and new Bible, which he believes will be presently worth £40 a-piece.

6th. Up, and having seen my brother in his cassocke, which I am not the most satisfied in, being doubtfull at this time what course to have him profess too soon. To the office and there busy about a list of the extraordinaries of the charge of the fleete this war; and was led to go to the office of the ordnance to be satisfied in something, and find their accounts and books kept in mighty good order, but that they can give no light, nor will the nature of their affairs permit it to tell what the charge of the ordnance comes to a man a month. So home again and to dinner, there coming Creed to me; but what with business and my hatred to the man, I did not spend any time with him, but after dinner [my] wife and he and I took coach and to Westminster, but he 'light about Paul's, and set her at her tailor's, and myself to St. James's, but there missing [Sir] W. Coventry, returned and took up my wife, and calling

[1] Bishop Walton's great work, published in 1657, entitled, "Biblia Sacra Polyglotta," in six large folio volumes. Nine languages are used in it, though no one book of the Bible is printed in so many. It was printed by subscription, under the patronage of Oliver Cromwell; but the Protector dying before it was finished, the bishop cancelled two leaves of the preface commendatory of his patron, and others were printed complimentary to Charles II. Hence the distinction of *republican* and *loyal* copies. The former are the most valued. — B.

at the Exchange home, whither Sir H. Cholmly come to visit me, but my business suffered me not to stay with him. So he gone I by water to Westminster Hall and thence to St. James's, and there found [Sir] W. Coventry waiting for me, and I did give him a good account to his mind of the business he expected about extraordinaries and then fell to other talke, among others, our sad condition contracted by want of a Comptroller;[1] and it was his words, that he believes, besides all the shame and trouble he hath brought on the office, the King had better have given £100,000 than ever have had him there. He did discourse about some of these discontented Parliament-men, and says that Birch is a false rogue, but that Garraway is a man that hath not been well used by the Court, though very stout to death, and hath suffered all that is possible for the King from the beginning. But discontented as he is, yet he never knew a Session of Parliament but he hath done some good deed for the King before it rose. I told him the passage Cocke told me of — his having begged a brace of bucks of the Lord Arlington for him, and when it come to him, he sent it back again. Sir W. Coventry told me, it is much to be pitied that the King should lose the service of a man so able and faithfull; and that he ought to be brought over, but that it is always observed, that by bringing over one discontented man, you raise up three in his room; which is a State lesson I never knew before. But when others discover your fear, and that discontent procures favour, they will be discontented too, and impose on you. Thence to White Hall and got a coach and home, and there did business late, and so home and set up my little books of one of my presses come home gilt, which pleases me mightily, and then to bed. This morning my wife told me of a fine gentlewoman my Lady Pen tells her of, for £20 per annum, that sings, dances, plays on four or five instruments and many other fine things, which pleases me mightily: and she sent to have her see her, which she did this afternoon; but sings basely, and is a tawdry wench that would take £8, but [neither] my wife nor I think her fit to come.

[1] As Sir John Minnes performed the duties inefficiently, it was considered necessary to take the office from him. See January 21st.

7th (Lord's day). Up, and after visiting my father in his chamber, to church, and then home to dinner. Little Michell and his wife come to dine with us, which they did, and then presently after dinner I with Sir J. Minnes to White Hall, where met by [Sir] W. Batten and Lord Bruncker, to attend the King and Duke of York at the Cabinet; but nobody had determined what to speak of, but only in general to ask for money. So I was forced immediately to prepare in my mind a method of discoursing. And anon we were called in to the Green Room, where the King, Duke of York, Prince Rupert, Lord Chancellor, Lord Treasurer, Duke of Albemarle, [Sirs] G. Carteret, W. Coventry, Morrice. Nobody beginning, I did, and made a current, and I thought a good speech, laying open the ill state of the Navy: by the greatness of the debt; greatness of work to do against next yeare; the time and materials it would take; and our incapacity, through a total want of money. I had no sooner done, but Prince Rupert rose up and told the King in a heat, that whatever the gentleman had said, he had brought home his fleete in as good a condition as ever any fleete was brought home; that twenty boats would be as many as the fleete would want: and all the anchors and cables left in the storm might be taken up again. This arose from my saying, among other things we had to do, that the fleete was come in — the greatest fleete that ever his Majesty had yet together, and that in as bad condition as the enemy or weather could put it; and to use Sir W. Pen's words, who is upon the place taking a survey, he dreads the reports he is to receive from the Surveyors of its defects.[1] I therefore did only answer, that I was sorry for his Highness's offence, but that what I said was but the report we received from those entrusted in the fleete to inform us. He muttered and repeated what he had said; and so, after a long silence on all hands, nobody, not so much as the Duke of Albemarle, seconding the Prince, nor taking notice of what he said, we withdrew. I was not a little troubled at this passage, and the more when speaking with Jacke Fenn about it, he told me that the

[1] Sir William Coventry's letter of instructions to Sir William Penn, directing him to visit the fleet at the Nore, dated October 2nd, is printed in Penn's "Memorials of Sir W. Penn," vol. ii., p. 422.

Prince will be asking now who this Pepys is, and find him to be a creature of my Lord Sandwich's, and therefore this was done only to disparage him. Anon they broke up, and Sir W. Coventry come out; so I asked his advice. He told me he had said something to salve it, which was, that his Highnesse had, he believed, rightly informed the King that the fleete is come in good condition to have staid out yet longer, and have fought the enemy, but yet that Mr. Pepys his meaning might be, that, though in so good condition, if they should come in and lie all the winter, we shall be very loth to send them to sea for another year's service with[out] great repairs. He said it would be no hurt if I went to him, and showed him the report himself brought up from the fleete, where every ship, by the Commander's report, do need more or less, and not to mention more of Sir W. Pen for doing him a mischief. So I said I would, but do not think that all this will redound to my hurt, because the truth of what I said will soon appear. Thence, having been informed that, after all this pains, the King hath found out how to supply us with 5 or £6,000, when £100,000 were at this time but absolutely necessary, and we mentioned £50,000. This is every day a greater and greater omen of ruine. God fit us for it! Sir J. Minnes and I home (it raining) by coach, calling only on Sir G. Carteret at his lodging (who is I find troubled at my Lord Treasurer and Sir Ph. Warwicke bungling in his accounts), and come home to supper with my father, and then all to bed. I made my brother in his cassocke to say grace this day, but I like his voice so ill that I begin to be sorry he hath taken this order upon him.

8th. Up and to my office, called up by Commissioner Middleton,[1] newly come to town, but staid not with me; so I to my office busy all the morning. Towards noon, by water to Westminster Hall, and there by several hear that the Parliament do resolve to do something to retrench Sir G. Carteret's great salary; but cannot hear of any thing bad they can lay to his charge. The House did this day order to be engrossed the Bill against importing Irish cattle; a thing, it seems, carried on by the Western Parliament-men,

[1] For note on Colonel Middleton, see November 4th, 1664.

wholly against the sense of most of the rest of the House; who think if you do this, you give the Irish again cause to rebel. Thus plenty on both sides makes us mad. The Committee of the Canary Company of both factions come to me for my Cozen Roger that is of the Committee.[1] Thence with [Sir] W. Coventry when the House rose and [Sir] W. Batten to St. James's, and there agreed of and signed our paper of extraordinaries, and there left them, and I to Unthanke's, where Mr. Falconbridge's girle is, and by and by comes my wife, who likes her well, though I confess I cannot (though she be of my finding out and sings pretty well), because she will be raised from so mean a condition to so high all of a sudden; but she will be much to our profit, more than Mercer, less expense. Here we bespoke a new gowne for her, and to come to us on Friday. She being gone, my wife and I home by coach, and then I presently by water with Mr. Pierce to Westminster Hall, he in the way telling me how the Duke of York and Duke of Albemarle do not agree. The Duke of York is wholly given up to this bitch of Denham. The Duke of Albemarle and Prince Rupert do less agree. So that we are all in pieces, and nobody knows what will be done the next year. The King hath yesterday in Council declared his resolution of setting a fashion for clothes, which he will never alter.[2] It will be a vest, I know not well how; but it is to teach the nobility thrift, and will do good. By and by comes down from the Committee [Sir] W. Coventry, and I find him troubled at several things happened this

[1] The Canary Company of Merchants was incorporated by charter, bearing date March 17th, 1664, to trade with the seven islands formerly called the Fortunate Islands, and afterwards the Canary Islands. The House of Commons considered the company's patent to be illegal and a monopoly; and in December, 1666, the Houses of Lords and Commons held a conference on the subject. In the end the Commons obtained their will, and an address of both houses was presented to the king thanking his Majesty "for causing the Canary Patent to be surrendered and vacated" ("Journals of the House of Lords," vol. xii., p. 119). The trade was in consequence freed from all control.

[2] There are several references to this new fashion of dress introduced by the king. Pepys saw the Duke of York put on the vest on the 13th, and he says Charles II. himself put it on on the 15th. On November 4th Pepys dressed himself in the new vest and coat. See notes, October 15th (*post*) and Nov. 22nd.

afternoon, which vexes me also; our business looking worse and worse, and our worke growing on our hands. Time spending, and no money to set anything in hand with; the end thereof must be speedy ruine. The Dutch insult and have taken off Bruant's head,[1] which they have not dared to do (though found guilty of the fault he did die for, of something of the Prince of Orange's faction) till just now, which speaks more confidence in our being worse than before. Alderman Maynell, I hear, is dead. Thence returned in the darke by coach all alone, full of thoughts of the consequences of this ill complexion of affairs, and how to save myself and the little I have, which if I can do, I have cause to bless God that I am so well, and shall be well contented to retreat to Brampton, and spend the rest of my days there. So to my office, and did some business, and finished my Journall with resolutions, if God bless me, to apply myself soberly to settle all matters for myself, and expect the event of all with comfort. So home to supper and to bed.

9th. Up and to the office, where we sat the first day since the fire, I think. At noon home, and my uncle Thomas was there, and dined with my brother and I (my father and I were gone abroad), and then to the office again in the afternoon, and there close all day long, and did much business. At night to Sir W. Batten, where Sir R. Ford did occasion some discourse of sending a convoy to the Maderas; and this did put us upon some new thoughts of sending our privateer thither on merchants' accounts, which I have more mind to, the profit being certain and occasion honest withall. So home and to supper with my father, and then to set my remainder of my books gilt in order with much pleasure, and so late to bed.

10th (Fast-day for the fire).[2] Up with Sir W. Batten by

[1] Captain Du Buat, a Frenchman in the Dutch service, plotted with two magistrates of Rotterdam to obtain a peace with England as the readiest means of pressing the elevation of the Prince of Orange to the office of Captain-General. He was brought before the Supreme Court of Holland, condemned, and executed. He had been one of the household of the Prince of Orange who were dismissed by De Witt.

[2] "Proclamation (Whitehall, Sept. 13, 1666) ordering Oct. 10 to be observed as a day of humiliation and fasting on account of the late fire, whereby the greatest part of London within the walls, part of the

water to White Hall, and anon had a meeting before the Duke of York, where pretty to see how Sir W. Batten, that carried the surveys of all the fleete with him, to shew their ill condition to the Duke of York, when he found the Prince there, did not speak one word, though the meeting was of his asking — for nothing else. And when I asked him, he told me he knew the Prince too well to anger him, so that he was afeard to do it. Thence with him to Westminster, to the parish church,[1] where the Parliament-men, and Stillingfleete in the pulpit. So full, no standing there; so he and I to eat herrings at the Dog Taverne. And then to church again, and there was Mr. Frampton[2] in the pulpit, they cry up so much, a young man, and of a mighty ready tongue. I heard a little of his sermon, and liked it; but the crowd so great, I could not stay. So to the Swan, and blaise a fille, and drank, and then home by coach, and took father, wife, brother, and W. Hewer to Islington, where I find mine host dead. Here eat and drank, and merry; and so home, and to the office a while, and then to Sir W. Batten to talk a while, and with Captain Cocke into the office to hear his newes, who is mighty conversant with Garraway and those people, who tells me what they object as to the mal-administration of things as to money. But that they mean well, and will do well; but their reckonings are very good, and show great faults, as I will insert here. They say the king hath had towards this war expressly thus much:

suburbs, 80 parishes, with churches, chapels, hospitals, &c., are become one ruinous heap; also ordering the distressed state of the people to be earnestly recommended to general charity in collections to be distributed by the Lord Mayor of London as he sees fit" ("Calendar of State Papers," 1666–67, p. 122).

[1] St. Margaret's. Dr. Sancroft, Dean of St. Paul's, preached before his Majesty at the Cathedral; Seth Ward, Bishop of Exeter, before the House of Lords, in Westminster Abbey; and Dr. Stillingfleet and Dr. Frampton before the House of Commons at St. Margaret's, Westminster. — *The London Gazette*, No. 94. — B.

[2] Robert Frampton, a native of Pimpern, in Dorsetshire, educated at Corpus Christi College, Oxford, and afterwards a student of Christ Church, and chaplain to a man-of-war. In 1673 he became Dean of Gloucester, and in 1681 bishop of that see; but refusing to take the oaths of allegiance to William and Mary, he was deprived, Feb. 1, 1690–1, and retired into private life. He died at Standish, near Gloucester, on May 25th, 1708, aged eighty-six years.

Royal Ayde	£2,450,000
More	1,250,000
Three months' tax given the King by a power of raising a month's tax of £70,000 every year for three years .	0,210,000
Customes, out of which the King did promise to pay £240,000, which for two years comes to	0,480,000
Prizes, which they moderately reckon at	0,300,000
A debt declared by the Navy, by us	0,900,000
	5,590,000
The whole charge of the Navy, as we state it for two years and a month, hath been but	3,200,000
So what is become of all this sum? . . .	2,390,000

He and I did bemoan our public condition. He tells me the Duke of Albemarle is under a cloud, and they have a mind at Court to lay him aside. This I know not; but all things are not right with him, and I am glad of it, but sorry for the time. So home to supper, and to bed, it being my wedding night,[1] but how many years I cannot tell; but my wife says ten.

11th. Up, and discoursed with my father of my sending some money for safety into the country, for I am in pain what to do with what I have. I did give him money, poor man, and he overjoyed. So left him, and to the office, where nothing but sad evidences of ruine coming on us for want of money. So home to dinner, which was a very good dinner, my father, brother, wife and I, and then to the office again, where I was all the afternoon till very late, busy, and then home to supper and to bed.

Memorandum. I had taken my Journall during the fire and the disorders following in loose papers until this very day, and could not get time to enter them in my book till January 18, in the morning, having made my eyes sore by frequent attempts this winter to do it. But now it is done, for which I thank God, and pray never the like occasion may happen.

[1] See Life, vol. i., p. xix., where the register of St. Margaret's parish, Westminster, is quoted to the effect that Pepys was married December 1st, 1655. It seems incomprehensible that both husband and wife should have been wrong as to the date of their wedding day, but Mrs. Pepys was unquestionably wrong as to the number of years, for they had been married nearly eleven.

12th. Up, and after taking leave of my poor father, who is setting out this day for Brampton by the Cambridge coach, he having taken a journey to see the city burned, and to bring my brother to towne, I out by water; and so coach to St. James's, the weather being foul; and there, from Sir W. Coventry, do hear how the House have cut us off £150,000 of our wear and tear, for that which was saved by the King while the fleete lay in harbour in winter. However, he seems pleased, and so am I, that they have abated no more and do intend to allow of 28,000 men for the next year; and this day have appointed to declare the sum they will give the King,[1] and to propose the way of raising it; so that this is likely to be the great day. This done in his chamber, I with him to Westminster Hall, and there took a few turns, the Hall mighty full of people, and the House likely to be very full to-day about the money business. Here I met with several people, and do find that people have a mighty mind to have a fling at the Vice-Chamberlain, if they could lay hold of anything, his place being, indeed, too much for such, they think, or any single subject of no greater parts and quality than he, to enjoy. But I hope he may weather all, though it will not be by any dexterity of his, I dare say, if he do stand, but by his fate only, and people's being taken off by other things. Thence home by coach, mighty dirty weather, and then to the Treasurer's office and got a ticket paid for my little Michell, and so again by coach to Westminster, and come presently after the House rose. So to the Swan, and there sent for a piece of meat and dined alone and played with Sarah, and so to the Hall a while, and thence to Mrs. Martin's lodging and did what I would with her. She is very big, and resolves I must be godfather. Thence away by water with Cropp to Deptford. It was almost night before I got thither. So I did only give directions concerning a press that I have making there to hold my turning and joyner's tooles that were lately given me, which will be very handsome, and so away back again, it being now dark, and so home, and there find my wife come home, and hath

[1] The parliament voted this day a supply of £1,800,000 sterling. See below.

brought her new girle I have helped her to, of Mr. Falconbridge's. She is wretched poor, and but ordinary favoured; and we fain to lay out seven or eight pounds worth of clothes upon her back, which, methinks, do go against my heart; and I do not think I can ever esteem her as I could have done another that had come fine and handsome; and which is more, her voice, for want of use, is so furred, that it do not at present please me; but her manner of singing is such, that I shall, I think, take great pleasure in it. Well, she is come, and I wish us good fortune in her. Here I met with notice of a meeting of the Commissioners for Tangier to-morrow, and so I must have my accounts ready for them, which caused me to confine myself to my chamber presently and set to the making up my accounts, which I find very clear, but with much difficulty by reason of my not doing them sooner, things being out of my mind.

13th. It cost me till four o'clock in the morning, and, which was pretty to think, I was above an hour, after I had made all right, in casting up of about twenty sums, being dozed with much work, and had for forty times together forgot to carry the 60 which I had in my mind, in one denomination which exceeded 60; and this did confound me for above an hour together. At last all even and done, and so to bed. Up at seven, and so to the office, after looking over my last night's work. We sat all the morning. At noon by coach with my Lord Bruncker and 'light at the Temple, and so alone I to dinner at a cooke's, and thence to my Lord Bellasses', whom I find kind; but he had drawn some new proposal to deliver to the Lords Commissioners to-day, wherein one was, that the garrison would not be well paid without some goldsmith's undertaking the paying of the bills of exchange for Tallys. He professing so much kindness to me, and saying that he would not be concerned in the garrison without me; and that if he continued in the employment, no man should have to do with the money but myself. I did ask his Lordship's meaning of the proposition in his paper. He told me he had not much considered it, but that he meant no harm to me. I told him I thought it would render me useless; whereupon he did very frankly, after my seeming denials for a good while, cause it to be writ over again, and that clause left out, which did satisfy me abundantly. It being done, he and I together to White Hall, and there the Duke of York (who is gone over to all his pleasures again, and leaves off care of business, what with his woman, my Lady Denham, and his hunting three times a week) was just come in from hunting. So I stood and saw him dress himself, and try on his vest, which is the King's new fashion, and will be in it for good and all on Monday next, and the whole Court: it is a fashion, the King says, he will never change. He being ready, he and my Lord Chancellor, and Duke of Albemarle, and Prince Rupert, Lord Bellasses, Sir H. Cholmly, Povy, and myself, met at a Committee for Tangier. My Lord Bellasses's propositions were read and discoursed of, about reducing the garrison to less charge; and indeed I am mad in love with my Lord Chancellor, for he do comprehend and speak out well, and with the greatest easinesse and authority that ever I saw man in my life. I did never observe how much easier a man do speak when he knows all the company to be below him, than in him; for though he spoke, indeed, excellent well, yet his manner and freedom of doing it, as if he played with it, and was informing only all the rest of the company, was mighty pretty. He did call again and again upon Mr. Povy for his accounts. I did think fit to make the solemn tender of my accounts that I intended. I said something that was liked, touching the want of money, and the bad credit of our tallys. My Lord Chancellor moved, that without any trouble to any of the rest of the Lords, I might alone attend the King, when he was with his private Council, and open the state of the garrison's want of credit; and all that could be done, should. Most things moved were referred to Committees, and so we broke up. And at the end Sir W. Coventry come; so I away with him, and he discoursed with me something of the Parliament's business. They have voted giving the [King] for next year £1,800,000; which, were it not for his debts, were a great sum. He says, he thinks the House may say no more to us for the present, but that we must mend our manners against the next tryall, and mend them we will. But he thinks it not a fit time to be found making of trouble among ourselves, meaning about Sir J. Minnes, who most certainly must be removed, or made a Commissioner, and somebody else Comptroller. But he tells me that the House has a great envy at Sir G. Carteret, and that had he ever thought fit in all his discourse to have touched upon the point of our want of money and badness of payment, it would have been laid hold on to Sir G. Carteret's hurt; but he hath avoided it, though without much reason for it, most studiously, and in short did end thus, that he has never shewn so much of the pigeon[1] in all his life as in his innocence to Sir G. Carteret at this time; which I believe, and will desire Sir G. Carteret to thank him for it. So we broke up and I by coach home, calling for a new pair of shoes, and so, little being to do at the office, did go home, and after spending a little in righting some of my books, which stood out of order, I to bed.

14th (Lord's day). Lay long in bed, among other things, talking of my wife's renewing her acquaintance with Mrs. Pierce, which, by my wife's ill using her when she was here last, hath been interrupted. Herein we were a little angry together, but presently friends again; and so up, and I to church, which was mighty full, and my beauties, Mrs. Lethulier,[2] and fair Batelier both there. A very foul morning, and rained; and sent for my cloake to go out of the church with. So dined, and after dinner (a good discourse thereat to my brother) he and I by water to White Hall, and he to Westminster Abbey. Here I met with Sir Stephen Fox, who told me how much right I had done myself, and how well it is represented by the Committee to the House, my readinesse to give them satisfaction in everything when they were at the office. I was glad of this. He did further discourse of Sir W. Coventry's great abilities, and how necessary it were that I were of the House to assist him. I did not owne it, but do myself think it were not unnecessary if either he should die, or be removed to the Lords, or any thing to hinder his doing the like service the next trial, which makes me think that it were not a thing very unfit; but I will not move in it. He and

[1] The timidity of the pigeon has caused the addition of a series of words to the English language, as, pigeon, a gull; to pigeon; pigeon-hearted, and pigeon-livered, the latter expression used in "Hamlet."

[2] See December 13th, 1665.

I parted, I to Mrs. Martin's, thinking to have met Mrs. Burrows, but she was not there, so away and took my brother out of the Abbey and home, and there to set some accounts right, and to the office to even my Journall, and so home to supper and to bed.

15th. Called up, though a very rainy morning, by Sir H. Cholmley, and he and I most of the morning together evening of accounts, which I was very glad of. Then he and I out to Sir Robt. Viner's, at the African house[1] (where I had not been since he come thither); but he was not there; but I did some business with his people, and then to Colvill's, who, I find, lives now in Lyme Streete, and with the same credit as ever, this fire having not done them any wrong that I hear of at all. Thence he and I together to Westminster Hall, in our way talking of matters and passages of state, the viciousness of the Court; the contempt the King brings himself into thereby; his minding nothing, but doing all things just as his people about him will have it; the Duke of York becoming a slave to this whore Denham, and wholly minds her; that there really was amours between the Duchesse and Sidney;[2] that there is reason to fear that, as soon as the Parliament have raised this money, the King will see that he hath got all that he can get, and then make up a peace. He tells me, what I wonder at, but that I find it confirmed by Mr. Pierce, whom I met by-and-by in the Hall, that Sir W. Coventry is of the caball with the Duke of York, and Bruncker, with this Denham; which is a shame, and I am sorry for it, and that Sir W. Coventry do make her visits; but yet I hope it is not so. Pierce tells me, that as little agreement as there is between the Prince[3] and Duke of Albemarle, yet they are likely to go to sea again; for the first will not be trusted alone, and nobody will go with him but this Duke of Albemarle. He tells me much how all the commanders of the fleete and officers that are sober men do cry out upon their bad discipline, and the ruine that must follow it if it continue. But that which I wonder most at, it seems their secretaries have been the

[1] The African House of the Royal African or Guinea Company of Merchants was situated in Leadenhall Street.

[2] See note, January 9th, 1665-66.

[3] Prince Rupert.

most exorbitant in their fees to all sorts of the people, that it is not to be believed that they durst do it, so as it is believed they have got £800 apiece by the very vacancies in the fleete. He tells me that Lady Castlemayne is concluded to be with child again; and that all the people about the King do make no scruple of saying that the King do lie with Mrs. Stewart, who, he says, is a most excellent-natured lady. This day the King begins to put on his vest, and I did see several persons of the House of Lords and Commons too, great courtiers, who are in it; being a long cassocke close to the body, of black cloth, and pinked with white silke under it, and a coat over it, and the legs ruffled with black riband like a pigeon's leg; and, upon the whole, I wish the King may keep it, for it is a very fine and handsome garment.[1] Walking with Pierce in the Court of Wards out comes Sir W. Coventry, and he and I talked of business. Among others I proposed the making Sir J. Minnes a Commissioner, and make somebody else Comptroller. He tells me it is the thing he hath been thinking of, and hath spoke to the Duke of York of it. He believes it will be done; but that which I fear is that Pen will be Comptroller, which I shall grudge a little. The Duke of Buckingham called him aside and spoke a good while with him. I did presently fear it might be to discourse something of his design to blemish my Lord of Sandwich, in

[1] Evelyn describes the new fashion as "a comely dress after ye Persian mode" (see "Diary," October 18th, 1666). He adds that he had described the "comelinesse and usefulnesse" of the Persian clothing in his pamphlet entitled "Tyrannus, or the Mode." "I do not impute to this discourse the change which soone happen'd, but it was an identity I could not but take notice of."

Rugge, in his "Diurnal," thus describes the new Court costume: "1666, Oct. 11. In this month His Majestie and whole Court changed the fashion of their clothes — viz. a close coat of cloth, pinkt with a white taffety under the cutts. This in length reached the calf of the leg, and upon that a sercoat cutt at the breast, which hung loose and shorter than the vest six inches. The breeches the Spanish cut, and buskins some of cloth, some of leather, but of the same colour as the vest or garment; of never the like fashion since William the Conqueror." It is represented in a portrait of Lord Arlington, by Sir P. Lely formerly belonging to Lord de Clifford, and engraved in Lodge's "Portraits." Louis XIV. ordered his servants to wear the dress. See October 8th and November 22nd.

pursuance of the wild motion he made the other day in the House. Sir W. Coventry, when he come to me again, told me that he had wrought a miracle, which was, the convincing the Duke of Buckingham that something — he did not name what — that he had intended to do was not fit to be done, and that the Duke is gone away of that opinion. This makes me verily believe it was something like what I feared. By and by the House rose, and then we parted, and I with Sir G. Carteret, and walked in the Exchequer Court, discoursing of businesses. Among others, I observing to him how friendly Sir W. Coventry had carried himself to him in these late inquiries, when, if he had borne him any spleen, he could have had what occasion he pleased offered him, he did confess he found the same thing, and would thanke him for it. I did give him some other advices, and so away with him to his lodgings at White Hall to dinner, where my Lady Carteret is, and mighty kind, both of them, to me. Their son and my Lady Jemimah will be here very speedily. She tells me the ladies are to go into a new fashion shortly, and that is, to wear short coats, above their ancles; which she and I do not like, but conclude this long trayne to be mighty graceful. But she cries out of the vices of the Court, and how they are going to set up plays already; and how, the next day after the late great fast, the Duchesse of York did give the King and Queene a play. Nay, she told me that they have heretofore had plays at Court the very nights before the fast for the death of the late King. She do much cry out upon these things, and that which she believes will undo the whole nation; and I fear so too. After dinner away home, Mr. Brisband along with me as far as the Temple, and there looked upon a new booke, set out by one Rycault,[1] secretary to my Lord Wincheslea, of the policy and customs of

[1] Paul Rycaut (B.A. Camb., 1650) was appointed secretary to the Earl of Winchelsea when that nobleman went to Constantinople in 1661 as Ambassador Extraordinary to the Sultan Mahomet Han. He was afterwards consul at Smyrna, secretary to Henry Hyde, Earl of Clarendon, Lord Lieutenant of Ireland, 1685–87, when he was knighted, and Resident at Hamburg. He died December 16th, 1700. The book referred to appears to be "The Present State of the Ottoman Empire" (see March 20th and April 8th, 1667).

the Turks, which is, it seems, much cried up. But I could not stay, but home, where I find Balty come back, and with him some muster-books, which I am glad of, and hope he will do me credit in his employment. By and by took coach again and carried him home, and my wife to her tailor's, while I to White Hall to have found out Povy, but miss him and so call in my wife and home again, where at Sir W. Batten's I met Sir W. Pen, lately come from the fleete at the Nore; and here were many good fellows, among others Sir R. Holmes, who is exceeding kind to me, more than usual, which makes me afeard of him, though I do much wish his friendship. Thereupon, after a little stay, I withdrew, and to the office and awhile, and then home to supper and to my chamber to settle a few papers, and then to bed. This day the great debate was in Parliament, the manner of raising the £1,800,000 they voted [the King] on Friday; and at last, after many proposals, one moved that the Chimney-money might be taken from the King, and an equal revenue of something else might be found for the King, and people be enjoyned to buy off this tax of Chimney-money for ever at eight years' purchase, which will raise present money, as they think, £1,600,000 and the State be eased of an ill burthen and the King be supplied of something as good or better for his use. The House seems to like this, and put off the debate to to-morrow.

16th. Up, and to the office, where sat to do little business but hear clamours for money. At noon home to dinner, and to the office again, after hearing my brother play a little upon the Lyra viall, which he do so as to show that he hath a love to musique and a spirit for it, which I am well pleased with. All the afternoon at the office, and at night with Sir W. Batten, Sir W. Pen, [and Sir] J. Minnes, at [Sir] W. Pen's lodgings, advising about business and orders fit presently to make about discharging of ships come into the river, and which to pay first, and many things in order thereto. But it vexed me that, it being now past seven o'clock, and the businesses of great weight, and I had done them by eight o'clock, and sending them to be signed, they were all gone to bed, and Sir W. Pen, though awake, would not, being in bed, have them brought to him to sign; this made me quite angry. Late at work at the office, and then home to supper and to bed. Not come to any resolution at the Parliament to-day about the manner of raising this £1,800,000.

17th. Up, and busy about public and private business all the morning at the office. At noon home to dinner, alone with my brother, with whom I had now the first private talke I have had, and find he hath preached but twice in his life. I did give him some advice to study pronunciation; but I do fear he will never make a good speaker, nor, I fear, any general good scholar, for I do not see that he minds optickes or mathematiques of any sort, nor anything else that I can find. I know not what he may be at divinity and ordinary school-learning. However, he seems sober, and that pleases me. After dinner took him and my wife and Barker (for so is our new woman called, and is yet but a sorry girle), and set them down at Unthanke's, and so to White Hall, and there find some of my brethren with the Duke of York, but so few I put off the meeting. So staid and heard the Duke discourse, which he did mighty scurrilously, of the French, and with reason, that they should give Beaufort orders when he was to bring, and did bring, his fleete hither, that his rendezvous for his fleete, and for all sluggs to come to, should be between Calais and Dover; which did prove the taking of La Roche[lle], who, among other sluggs behind, did, by their instructions, make for that place, to rendezvous with the fleete; and Beaufort, seeing them as he was returning, took them for the English fleete, and wrote word to the King of France that he had passed by the English fleete, and the English fleete durst not meddle with him. The Court is all full of vests, only my Lord St. Albans not pinked but plain black; and they say the King says the pinking upon white makes them look too much like magpyes, and therefore hath bespoke one of plain velvet. Thence to St. James's by coach, and spoke, at four o'clock or five, with Sir W. Coventry, newly come from the House, where they have sat all this day and not come to an end of the debate how the money shall be raised. He tells me that what I proposed to him the other day was what he had himself thought on and determined, and that he believes it will speedily be done — the making Sir J. Minnes a Commissioner, and bringing somebody else to be Comptroller, and that (which do not please me, I confess, for my own particulars, so well as Sir J. Minnes) will, I fear, be Sir W. Pen, for he is the only fit man for it. Away from him and took up my wife, and left her at Temple Bar to buy some lace for a petticoat, and I took coach and away to Sir R. Viner's about a little business, and then home, and by and by to my chamber, and there late upon making up an account for the Board to pass to-morrow, if I can get them, for the clearing all my imprest[1] bills, which if I can do, will be to my very good satisfaction. Having done this, then to supper and to bed.

18th. Up, and to the office, where we sat all the morning. The waters so high in the roads, by the late rains, that our letters come not in till to-day, and now I understand that my father is got well home, but had a painful journey of it. At noon with Lord Bruncker to St. Ellen's,[2] where the master of the late Pope's Head Taverne is now set up again, and there dined at Sir W. Warren's cost, a very good dinner. Here my Lord Bruncker proffered to carry me and my wife into a play at Court to-night, and to lend me his coach home, which tempted me much; but I shall not do it. Thence rose from table before dinner ended, and homewards met my wife, and so away by coach towards Lovett's (in the way wondering at what a good pretty wench our Barker makes, being now put into good clothes, and fashionable, at my charge; but it becomes her, so that I do not now think much of it, and is an example of the power of good clothes and dress), where I stood godfather. But it was pretty, that, being a Protestant, a man stood by and was my Proxy to answer for me. A priest christened it, and the boy's name is Samuel. The ceremonies many, and some foolish. The priest in a gentleman's dress, more than my owne; but is a Capuchin, one of the Queene-mother's priests. He did give my proxy and the woman proxy (my Lady Bills,[3] absent, had a

[1] See note, November 28th, 1660.

[2] Apparently the parish of St. Helen's, Bishopsgate, which escaped the Fire.

[3] Lady Diana Fane, daughter of Mildmay Fane, second Earl of Westmoreland, widow of Edward Pellam, Esq., of Brocklesby, in Lincolnshire, remarried John Bills, Esq., of Caen Wood, Highgate.

proxy also) good advice to bring up the child, and, at the end, that he ought never to marry the child nor the godmother, nor the godmother the child or the godfather: but, which is strange, they say that the mother of the child and the godfather may marry. By and by the Lady Bills come in, a well-bred but crooked woman. The poor people of the house had good wine, and a good cake; and she a pretty woman in her lying-in dress. It cost me near 40*s.* the whole christening: to midwife 20*s.*, nurse 10*s.*, mayde 2*s.* 6*d.*, and the coach 5*s.* I was very well satisfied with what I have done, and so home and to the office, and thence to Sir W. Batten's, and there hear how the business of buying off the Chimney-money is passed in the House; and so the King to be satisfied some other way, and the King supplied with the money raised by this purchasing off of the chimnies. So home, mightily pleased in mind that I have got my bills of imprest cleared by bills signed this day, to my good satisfaction. To supper, and to bed.

19th. Up, and by coach to my Lord Ashly's, and thence (he being gone out), to the Exchequer chamber, and there find him and my Lord Bellasses about my Lord Bellasses' accounts, which was the business I went upon. This was soon ended, and then I with Creed back home to my house, and there he and I did even accounts for salary, and by that time dinner was ready, and merry at dinner, and then abroad to Povy's, who continues as much confounded in all his business as ever he was; and would have had me paid money, as like a fool as himself, which I troubled him in refusing; but I did persist in it. After a little more discourse, I left them, and to White Hall, where I met with Sir Robert Viner, who told me a little of what, in going home, I had seen; also a little of the disorder and mutiny among the seamen at the Treasurer's office, which did trouble me then and all day since, considering how many more seamen will come to towne every day, and no money for them. A Parliament sitting, and the Exchange close by, and an enemy to hear of, and laugh at it.[1] Viner

Her only child, Diana, by her second husband, died the widow of Captain Francis D'Arcy Savage, May 23rd, 1726, and is buried at Barnes. Lady Diana Bills was at this time in her thirty-sixth year.—B.

[1] The King of Denmark was induced to conclude a treaty with the

too, and Backewell, were sent for this afternoon; and was before the King and his Cabinet about money; they declaring they would advance no more, it being discoursed of in the House of Parliament for the King to issue out his privy-seals to them to command them to trust him, which gives them reason to decline trusting. But more money they are persuaded to lend, but so little that (with horrour I speake it), coming after the Council was up, with Sir G. Carteret, Sir W. Coventry, Lord Bruncker, and myself, I did lay the state of our condition before the Duke of York, that the fleete could not go out without several things it wanted, and we could not have without money, particularly rum and bread, which we have promised the man Swan to helpe him to £200 of his debt, and a few other small sums of £200 a piece to some others, and that I do foresee the Duke of York would call us to an account why the fleete is not abroad, and we cannot answer otherwise than our want of money; and that indeed we do not do the King any service now, but do rather abuse and betray his service by being there, and seeming to do something, while we do not. Sir G. Carteret asked me (just in these words, for in this and all the rest I set down the very words for memory sake, if there should be occasion) whether £50 or £60 would do us any good; and when I told him the very rum man[1] must have £200, he held up his eyes as if we had asked a million. Sir W. Coventry told the Duke of York plainly he did rather desire to have his commission called in than serve in so ill a place, where he cannot do the King service, and I did concur in saying the same. This was all very plain, and the Duke of York did confess that he did not see how he could do anything without a present supply of £20,000, and that he would speak to the King next Council day, and I promised to wait on him to put

United Provinces, a secret article of which bound him to declare war against England. The order in council for the printing and publishing a declaration of war against Denmark is dated "Whitehall, Sept. 19, 1666;" annexed is "A True Declaration of all transactions between his Majesty of Great Britain and the King of Denmark, with a declaration of war against the said king, and the motives that obliged his Majesty thereunto" ("Calendar of State Papers," 1666-67, p. 140).

[1] The contractor Swan referred to above.

him in mind of it. This I set down for my future justification, if need be, and so we broke up, and all parted, Sir W. Coventry being not very well, but I believe made much worse by this night's sad discourse. So I home by coach, considering what the consequence of all this must be in a little time. Nothing but distraction and confusion; which makes me wish with all my heart that I were well and quietly settled with what little I have got at Brampton, where I might live peaceably, and study, and pray for the good of the King and my country. Home, and to Sir W. Batten's, where I saw my Lady, who is now come down stairs after a great sickness. Sir W. Batten was at the pay to-day, and tells me how rude the men were, but did go away quietly, being promised pay on Wednesday next. God send us money for it! So to the office, and then to supper and to bed. Among other things proposed in the House to-day, to give the King in lieu of chimneys, there was the bringing up of sealed paper, such as Sir J. Minnes shewed me to-night, at Sir W. Batten's, is used in Spayne, and brings the King a great revenue; but it shows what shifts we are put to too much.

20th. Up, and all the morning at the office, where none met but myself. So I walked a good while with Mr. Gawden in the garden, who is lately come from the fleete at the buoy of the Nore, and he do tell me how all the sober commanders, and even Sir Thomas Allen himself, do complain of the ill government of the fleete. How Holmes and Jennings have commanded all the fleete this yeare, that nothing is done upon deliberation, but if a sober man give his opinion otherwise than the Prince would have it the Prince would cry, "Damn him, do you follow your orders, and that is enough for you." He tells me he hears of nothing but of swearing and drinking and whoring, and all manner of profaneness, quite through the whole fleete. He being gone, there comes to me Commissioner Middleton, whom I took on purpose to walk in the garden with me, and to learn what he observed when the fleete was at Portsmouth. He says that the fleete was in such a condition, as to discipline, as if the Devil had commanded it; so much wickedness of all sorts. Enquiring how it come to pass that so many ships miscarried this year, he tells me that he enquired; and the pilots do say, that they dare not do nor go but as the Captains will have them; and if they offer to do otherwise, the Captains swear they will run them through. He says that he heard Captain Digby[1] (my Lord of Bristoll's son, a young fellow that never was but one year, if that, in the fleete) say that he did hope he should not see a tarpaulin[2] have the command of a ship within this twelve months. He observed while he was on board the Admirall, when the fleete was at Portsmouth, that there was a faction there. Holmes commanded all on the Prince's side, and Sir Jeremy Smith on the Duke's, and every body that come did apply themselves to one side or other; and when the Duke of Albemarle was gone away to come hither, then Sir Jeremy Smith did hang his head, and walked in the Generall's ship but like a private commander. He says he was on board The Prince, when the newes come of the burning of London; and all the Prince said was, that now Shipton's prophecy was out;[3] and he heard a young commander presently swear, that now a citizen's wife that would not take under half a piece before, would be occupied for half-a-crowne: and made mighty sport of it. He says that Hubberd[4] that commanded this year the Admiral's ship is a proud conceited fellow (though I thought otherwise of him), and fit to command a single ship but not a fleete, and he do wonder that there hath not been more

[1] Francis Digby, second son of George, second Earl of Bristol. He was appointed lieutenant of the "Royal Charles" in 1666, and promoted to the command of the "Jersey" in the same year. He was killed in the sea-fight at Solebay, and Charnock ("Biographia Navalis," vol. i., pp. 222, 223) speaks highly of his intrepidity.

[2] This word (now used only in the curtailed form of tar) was once common. "The Archbishop of Bordeaux is at present general of the French Naval Forces, who though a priest is yet permitted to turn tarpaulin and soldier." — *The Turkish Spy*, Letter I. (1691).

[3] Evidently the concluding passage of "Mother Shipton's Prophecies," viz., "A ship come sayling up the Thames to London, and the master of the ship shall weepe, and the mariners shall aske him why he weepeth, being he hath made so good a voyage, and he shall say, 'Ah, what a goodlie citie this was! none in the world comparable to it; and now there is scarcely left any house that can let us have drinke for our money.'" Quoted from the edition of 1641, which Prince Rupert might have seen. — B.

[4] "John Hubbard commanded the Return, the Helversome and Lyon in succession during the year 1665; in 1666 he was made cap-

mischief this year than there hath. He says the fleete come to anchor between the Horse and the Island, so that when they came to weigh many of the ships could not turn, but run foul of the Horse, and there stuck, but that the weather was good. He says that nothing can do the King more disservice, nor please the standing officers of the ship better than these silly commanders that now we have, for they sign to anything that their officers desire of them, nor have judgment to contradict them if they would. He told me other good things, which made me bless God that we have received no greater disasters this year than we have, though they have been the greatest that ever was known in England before, put all their losses of the King's ships by want of skill and seamanship together from the beginning. He being gone, comes Sir G. Carteret, and he and I walked together awhile, discoursing upon the sad condition of the times, what need we have, and how impossible it is to get money. He told me my Lord Chancellor the other day did ask him how it come to pass that his friend Pepys do so much magnify all things to worst, as I did on Sunday last, in the bad condition of the fleete. Sir G. Carteret tells me that he answered him, that I was but the mouth of the rest, and spoke what they have dictated to me; which did, as he says, presently take off his displeasure. So that I am well at present with him, but I must have a care not to be over busy in the office again, and burn my fingers. He tells me he wishes he had sold his place at some good rate to somebody or other at the beginning of the warr, and that he would do it now, but no body will deale with him for it. He tells me the Duke of Albemarle is very much discontented, and the Duke of York do not, it seems, please

tain of the Royal Charles, the ship on board which the joint commanders in chief, Prince Rupert and the Duke of Albemarle, hoisted the standard. The very conspicuous share borne by this ship in the victory obtained over the Dutch may naturally be inferred from the known active intrepidity of those two great men. And while their extensive minds were engaged in arranging and manœuvring the fleet under their command, surely no small degree of merit ought to be attributed to the captain of the ship in which they fought, who by his conduct and gallantry enabled them to transfer their attention from an individual object to the weightier part of their charge." — Charnock's *Biographia Navalis*, vol. i., p. 168.

him. He tells me that our case as to money is not to be made good at present, and therefore wishes a good and speedy peace before it be too late, and from his discourse methinks I find that there is something moving towards it. Many people at the office, but having no more of the office I did put it off till the next meeting. Thence, with Sir G. Carteret, home to dinner, with him, my Lady and Mr. Ashburnham, the Cofferer. Here they talk that the Queene hath a great mind to alter her fashion, and to have the feet seen, which she loves mightily; and they do believe that it [will] come into it in a little time. Here I met with the King's declaration[1] about his proceedings with the King of Denmarke, and particularly the business of Bergen; but it is so well writ, that, if it be true, the King of Denmarke is one of the most absolute wickednesse in the world for a person of his quality. After dinner home, and there met Mr. Povy by appointment, and there he and I all the afternoon, till late at night, evening of all accounts between us, which we did to both our satisfaction; but that which troubles me most is, that I am to refund to the ignoble Lord Peterborough what he had given us six months ago, because we did not supply him with money; but it is no great matter. He gone I to the office, and there did some business; and so home, my mind in good ease by having done with Povy in order to the adjusting of all my accounts in a few days. So home to supper and to bed.

21st (Lord's day). Up, and with my wife to church, and her new woman Barker with her the first time. The girle will, I think, do very well. Here a lazy sermon, and so home to dinner, and took in my Lady Pen and Peg (Sir William being below with the fleete), and mighty merry we were, and then after dinner presently (it being a mighty cool day) I by coach to White Hall, and there attended the Cabinet, and was called in before the King and them to give an account of our want of money for Tangier, which troubles me that it should be my place so often and so soon after one another to come to speak there of their wants — the thing of the world that they love least to hear of, and that which is no welcome thing to be the solicitor for — and to

[1] For note on declaration of war with Denmark see *ante*, Oct. 19th.

see how like an image the King sat and could not speak one word when I had delivered myself was very strange; only my Lord Chancellor did ask me, whether I thought it was in nature at this time to help us to anything. So I was referred to another meeting of the Lords Commissioners for Tangier and my Lord Treasurer, and so went away, and by coach home, where I spent the evening in reading Stillingfleet's defence of the Archbishopp,[1] the part about Purgatory, a point I had never considered before, what was said for it or against it, and though I do believe we are in the right, yet I do not see any great matter in this book. So to supper; and my people being gone, most of them, to bed, my boy and Jane and I did get two of my iron chests out of the cellar into my closett, and the money to my great satisfaction to see it there again, and the rather because the damp cellar spoils all my chests. This being done, and I weary, to bed. This afternoon walking with Sir H. Cholmly long in the gallery, he told me, among many other things, how Harry Killigrew[2] is banished the Court lately, for saying that my Lady Castlemayne was a little lecherous girle when she was young. . . . This she complained to the King of, and he sent to the Duke of York, whose servant he is, to turn him away. The Duke of York hath done it, but takes it ill of my Lady that he was not complained to first. She attended him to excuse it, but ill blood is made by it. He told me how Mr. Williamson stood in a little place to have come into the House of Commons, and they would not choose him; they said, "No courtier."[3] And

[1] The archbishop defended by Stillingfleet was Laud, and the work referred to is entitled, "A Rational Account of the Grounds of the Protestant Religion . . . . being a Vindication of the Archbishop's Relation of a Conference from the pretended Answer of T. C[arwell]. London, 1665."

[2] Son of Thomas Killigrew by his first wife, Cecilia, daughter of Sir John Crofts, and maid of honour to Henrietta Maria. Born April 9th, 1637, and baptized in St. Martin's-in-the-Fields, April 16th. He is called "young," to distinguish him from his uncle of the same name, who was Master of the Savoy. He was Groom of the Bedchamber to the Duke of York (1656), then to the king (1662), again to the duke (1666), and again to the king (1669). He was living in 1694, when he held his father's place of Master of the Revels.

[3] Williamson stood for Morpeth, but was unsuccessful; Edward, Lord Morpeth, was elected on September 27th, 1666.

which is worse, Bab May went down in great state to Winchelsea with the Duke of York's letters, not doubting to be chosen; and there the people chose a private gentleman in spite of him, and cried out they would have no Court pimp to be their burgesse; which are things that bode very ill.[1] This afternoon I went to see and sat a good while with Mrs. Martin, and there was her sister Doll, with whom, contrary to all expectation, I did what I would, and might have done anything else.

22nd. Up, and by coach to Westminster Hall, there thinking to have met Betty Michell, who I heard yesterday staid all night at her father's, but she was gone. So I staid a little and then down to the bridge by water, and there overtook her and her father. So saluted her and walked over London Bridge with them and there parted, the weather being very foul, and so to the Tower by water, and so home, where I find Mr. Cæsar playing the treble to my boy upon the Theorbo, the first time I heard him, which pleases me mightily. After dinner I carried him and my wife towards Westminster, by coach, myself 'lighting at the Temple, and there, being a little too soon, walked in the Temple Church, looking with pleasure on the monuments and epitaphs, and then to my Lord Belasses, where Creed and Povy by appointment met to discourse of some of their Tangier accounts between my Lord and Vernatty, who will prove a very knave. That being done I away with Povy to White Hall, and thence I to Unthanke's, and there take up my wife, and so home, it being very foule and darke. Being there come, I to the settling of some of my money matters in my chests, and evening some accounts, which I was at late, to my extraordinary content, and especially to see all things hit so even and right and with an apparent profit and advantage since my last accounting, but how much I cannot particularly yet come to adjudge. Late to supper and to bed.

23rd. Up, and to the office all the morning. At noon Sir W. Batten told me Sir Richard Ford would accept of one-third of my profit of our private man-of-war, and bear

[1] Robert Austin of Tenterden was elected M.P. for Winchelsea, October 4th, 1666.

one-third of the charge, and be bound in the Admiralty, so I shall be excused being bound, which I like mightily of, and did draw up a writing, as well as I could, to that purpose and signed and sealed it, and so he and Sir R. Ford are to go to enter into bond this afternoon. Home to dinner, and after dinner, it being late, I down by water to Shadwell, to see Betty Michell, the first time I was ever at their new dwelling since the fire, and there find her in the house all alone. I find her mighty modest. But had her lips as much as I would, and indeed she is mighty pretty, that I love her exceedingly. I paid her £10 1*s*. that I received upon a ticket for her husband, which is a great kindness I have done them, and having kissed her as much as I would, I away, poor wretch, and down to Deptford to see Sir J. Minnes ordering of the pay of some ships there, which he do most miserably, and so home. Bagwell's wife, seeing me come the fields way, did get over her pales to come after and talk with me, which she did for a good way, and so parted, and I home, and to the office, very busy, and so to supper and to bed.

24th. Up, and down to the Old Swan, and there find little Michell come to his new shop that he hath built there in the room of his house that was burned. I hope he will do good here. I drank and bade him joy, for I love him and his wife well, him for his care, and her for her person, and so to White Hall, where we attended the Duke; and to all our complaints for want of money, which now we are tired out with making, the Duke only tells us that he is sorry for it, and hath spoke to the King of it, and money we shall have as soon as it can be found; and though all the issue of the war lies upon it, yet that is all the answer we can get, and that is as bad or worse than nothing. Thence to Westminster Hall, where the term is begun, and I did take a turn or two, and so away by coach to Sir R. Viner's, and there received some money, and then home and to dinner. After dinner to little business, and then abroad with my wife, she to see her brother, who is sick, and she believes is from some discontent his wife hath given him by her loose carriage, which he is told, and he hath found has been very suspicious in his absence, which I am sorry for. I to the Hall and there walked long, among others talking with Mr. Hayes, Prince Rupert's Secretary, a very ingenious man, and one, I think, fit to contract some friendship with. Here I staid late, walking to and again, hearing how the Parliament proceeds, which is mighty slowly in the settling of the money business, and great factions growing every day among them. I am told also how Holmes did last Sunday deliver in his articles to the King and Cabinet against [Sir Jeremy] Smith, and that Smith hath given in his answer, and lays his not accompanying the fleete to his pilot, who would not undertake to carry the ship further; which the pilot acknowledges. The thing is not accommodated, but only taken up, and both sides commanded to be quiet; but no peace like to be. The Duke of Albemarle is Smith's friend, and hath publiquely swore that he would never go to sea again unless Holmes's commission were taken from him.[1] I find by Hayes that they did expect great glory in coming home in so good condition as they did with the fleete, and therefore I the less wonder that the Prince was distasted with my discourse the other day about the bad state of the fleete.

[1] In the instructions given to Sir Thomas Clifford (August 5th, 1666) to be communicated to Prince Rupert and the Duke of Albemarle, we read: "to tell them that the complaint of Sir Jeremy Smith's misbehaviour in the late engagement being so universal, unless he have fully satisfied the generals he should be brought to trial by court-martial, and there purged or condemned." The Duke of Albemarle answered the king (August 14th?): "Wishes to clear a gallant man falsely accused, Sir Jeremiah Smith, who had more men killed and hurt, and his ship received more shot than any in the fleet. There is not a more spirited man serves in the fleet." On October 27th H. Muddiman wrote to Sir Edward Stradling: "Sir Jeremy Smith has got as much credit by his late examination as his enemies wished him disgrace, the King and Duke of York being fully satisfied of his valour in the engagement. It appears that he had 147 men killed and wounded, while the most eminent of his accusers had but two or three." With regard to Sir Jeremy's counter-charges, we read: "Nov. 3. The King having maturely considered the charges brought against Sir Rob. Holmes by Sir Jeremy Smith, finds no cause to suspect Sir Robert of cowardice in the fight with the Dutch of June 25 and 26, but thinks that on the night of the 26th he yielded too easily to the opinion of his pilot, without consulting those of the other ships, muzzled his ship, and thus obliged the squadron to do the same, and so the enemy, which might have been driven into the body of the king's fleet, then returning from the pursuit, was allowed to escape" ("Calendar of State Papers," 1666-67, pp. 14, 40, 222, 236).

But it pleases me to hear that he did expect great thanks, and lays the fault of the want of it upon the fire, which deadened everything, and the glory of his services. About seven at night home, and called my wife, and, it being moonshine, took her into the garden, and there layed open our condition as to our estate, and the danger of my having it [his money] all in the house at once, in case of any disorder or troubles in the State, and therefore resolved to remove part of it to Brampton, and part some whither else, and part in my owne house, which is very necessary, and will tend to our safety, though I shall not think it safe out of my owne sight. So to the office, and then to supper and to bed.

25th. Up betimes and by water to White Hall, and there with Sir G. Carteret to Sir W. Coventry, who is come to his winter lodgings at White Hall, and there agreed upon a method of paying of tickets; and so I back again home and to the office, where we sate all the morning, but to little purpose but to receive clamours for money. At noon home to dinner, where the two Mrs. Daniels come to see us, and dined with us. After dinner I out with my wife to Mrs. Pierce's, where she hath not been a great while, from some little unkindness[1] of my wife's to her when she was last here, but she received us with mighty respect and discretion, and was making herself mighty fine to go to a great ball to-night at Court, being the Queene's birthday; so the ladies for this one day do wear laces, but to put them off again to-morrow. Thence I to my Lord Bruncker's, and with him to Mrs. Williams's, where we met Knipp. I was glad to see the jade. Made her sing; and she told us they begin at both houses to act on Monday next. But I fear, after all this sorrow, their gains will be but little. Mrs. Williams says, the Duke's house will now be much the better of the two, because of their women; which I am glad to hear. Thence with Lord Bruncker to White Hall and there spoke with Sir W. Coventry about some office business, and then I away to Mrs. Pierce's, and there saw her new closet, which is mighty rich and fine. Her daughter Betty grows mighty pretty. Thence with my wife home and

[1] See August 6th, 1666.

to do business at the office. Then to Sir W. Batten's, who tells me that the House of Parliament makes mighty little haste in settling the money, and that he knows not when it will be done; but they fall into faction, and libells have been found in the House. Among others, one yesterday, wherein they reckon up divers great sums to be given away by the King, among others, £10,000 to Sir W. Coventry, for weare and teare (the point he stood upon to advance that sum by, for them to give the King); Sir G. Carteret £50,000 for something else, I think supernumerarys; and so to Matt. Wren £5,000 for passing the Canary Company's patent; and so a great many other sums to other persons. So home to supper and to bed.

26th. Up, and all the morning and most of the afternoon within doors, beginning to set my accounts in order from before this fire, I being behindhand with them ever since; and this day I got most of my tradesmen to bring in their bills and paid them. Dined at home, and busy again after dinner, and then abroad by water to Westminster Hall, where I walked till the evening, and then out, the first time I ever was abroad with Doll Lane, to the Dog tavern, and there drank with her, a bad face, but good bodied girle. Did nothing but salute and play with her and talk, and thence away by coach, home, and so to do a little more in my accounts, and then to supper and to bed. Nothing done in the House yet as to the finishing of the bill for money, which is a mighty sad thing, all lying at stake for it.

27th. Up, and there comes to see me my Lord Belasses, which was a great honour. He tells me great newes, yet but what I suspected, that Vernatty is fled, and so hath cheated him and twenty more, but most of all, I doubt, Mr. Povy. Thence to talk about publique business; he tells me how the two Houses begin to be troublesome; the Lords to have quarrels one with another. My Lord Duke of Buckingham having said to the Lord Chancellor (who is against the passing of the Bill for prohibiting the bringing over of Irish cattle), that whoever was against the Bill, was there led to it by an Irish interest, or an Irish understanding, which is as much as to say he is a foole; this bred heat from my Lord Chancellor, and something he

[Buckingham] said did offend my Lord of Ossory[1] (my Lord Duke of Ormond's son), and they two had hard words, upon which the latter sends a challenge to the former; of which the former complains to the House, and so the business is to be heard on Monday next.[2] Then as to the Commons; some ugly knives, like poignards, to stab people with, about two or three hundred of them were brought in yesterday to the House, found in one of the house's rubbish that was burned, and said to be the house of a Catholique. This and several letters out of the country, saying how high the Catholiques are everywhere and bold in the owning their religion, have made the Commons mad, and they presently voted that the King be desired to put all Catholiques out of employment, and other high things; while the business of money hangs in the hedge. So that upon the whole, God knows we are in a sad condition like to be, there being the very beginnings of the late troubles. He gone, I at the office all the morning. At noon home to dinner, where Mrs. Pierce and her boy and Knipp, who sings as well, and is the best company in the world, dined with us, and infinite merry. The playhouses begin to play next week. Towards evening I took them out to the New Exchange, and there my wife bought things, and I did give each of them a pair of Jesimy[3]

[1] Thomas, Earl of Ossory, sat in the House of Lords as Baron Butler, but his creation in 1665 is not mentioned in Courthope's "Historic Peerage" or in Solly's "Titles of Honour." In these books his creation in 1679 as Baron Butler of More Park, co. Hertford, only is mentioned. He died in 1680, and was succeeded by his son James, who himself succeeded his grandfather as second Duke of Ormonde in 1688.

[2] The proceedings on the 27th are not clearly stated. According to Clarendon, this bill was urgently pressed forward in the House of Lords by the Duke of Buckingham. The debate became most disorderly, especially on the part of its promoters. On the duke making the remark above quoted, Lord Ossory, not trusting himself with a reply in the house, challenged Buckingham privately. This the duke endeavoured to avoid, and was found in a place not fixed for the meeting. On the following morning he informed the house of the affair. Clarendon regards the whole as a "gross shift" on the part of the duke. Both parties were sent to the Tower. The bill was subsequently passed. See Lord Arlington's account of the quarrel in Brown's "Miscellanea Aulica," p. 423, &c. — B.

[3] Jessemin (Jasminum), the flowers of which are of a delicate

plain gloves, and another of white. Here Knipp and I walked up and down to see handsome faces, and did see several. Then carried each of them home, and with great pleasure and content, home myself, where, having writ several letters, I home, and there, upon some serious discourse between my wife and I upon the business, I called to us my brother, and there broke to him our design to send him into the country with some part of our money, and so did seriously discourse the whole thing, and then away to supper and to bed. I pray God give a blessing to our resolution, for I do much fear we shall meet with speedy distractions for want of money.

28th (Lord's day). Up, and to church with my wife, and then home, and there is come little Michell and his wife, I sent for them, and also comes Captain Guy to dine with me, and he and I much talk together. He cries out of the discipline of the fleete, and confesses really that the true English valour we talk of is almost spent and worn out; few of the commanders doing what they should do, and he much fears we shall therefore be beaten the next year. He assures me we were beaten home the last June fight, and that the whole fleete was ashamed to hear of our bonefires. He commends Smith, and cries out of Holmes for an idle, proud, conceited, though stout fellow. He tells me we are to owe the losse of so many ships on the sands, not to any fault of the pilots, but to the weather; but in this I have good authority to fear there was something more. He says the Dutch do fight in very good order, and we in none at all. He says that in the July fight, both the Prince and Holmes had their belly-fulls, and were fain to go aside; though, if the wind had continued, we had utterly beaten them. He do confess the whole to be governed by a company of fools, and fears our ruine. After dinner he gone, I with my brother to White Hall,

sweet smell, and often used to perfume gloves. Edmund Howes, Stow's continuator, informs us that sweet or perfumed gloves were first brought into England by the Earl of Oxford on his return from Italy, in the fifteenth year of Queen Elizabeth, during whose reign, and long afterwards, they were very fashionable. They are frequently mentioned by Shakespeare. Autolycus, in the "Winter's Tale," has among his wares — "Gloves as sweet as damask roses." — B.

and he to Westminster Abbey. I presently to Mrs. Martin's, and there met widow Burroughes and Doll, and did tumble them all the afternoon as I pleased, and having given them a bottle of wine I parted and home by boat (my brother going by land), and thence with my wife to sit and sup with my uncle and aunt Wight, and see Woolly's wife, who is a pretty woman, and after supper, being very merry, in abusing my aunt with Dr. Venner, we home, and I to do something in my accounts, and so to bed. The Revenge having her forecastle blown up with powder to the killing of some men in the River, and the Dyamond's being overset in the careening at Sheernesse,[1] are further marks of the method all the King's work is now done in. The Foresight also and another come to disasters in the same place this week in the cleaning; which is strange.

29th. Up, and to the office to do business, and thither comes to me Sir Thomas Teddiman, and he and I walked a good while in the garden together, discoursing of the disorder and discipline of the fleete, wherein he told me how bad every thing is; but was very wary in speaking any thing to the dishonour of the Prince or Duke of Albemarle, but do magnify my Lord Sandwich much before them both, for ability to serve the King, and do heartily wish for him here. For he fears that we shall be undone the next year, but that he will, however, see an end of it. To prevent the necessity of his dining with me I was forced to pretend occasion of going to Westminster, so away I went, and Mr. Barber, the clerk, having a request to make to me to get him into employment, did walk along with me, and by water to Westminster with me, he professing great love to me, and an able clerk he is. When I come thither I find the new Lord Mayor Bolton[2] a-swearing at the Exchequer, with some of the Aldermen and Livery; but, Lord! to see how meanely they now look, who upon this day used to be all little lords, is a sad sight and worthy

[1] On October 24th Sir William Penn wrote to the Navy Commissioners from Sheerness, with "particulars of the accident befallen the Diamond, Greenwich, and Foresight"—"they are now afloat and their damages repaired" ("Calendar of State Papers," 1666-67, p. 216).

[2] Sir William Bolton, Merchant Tailor; Sheriff, 1660.

consideration. And every body did reflect with pity upon the poor City, to which they are now coming to choose and swear their Lord Mayor, compared with what it heretofore was. Thence by coach (having in the Hall bought me a velvet riding cap, cost me *20s.*) to my taylor's, and there bespoke a plain vest, and so to my goldsmith to bid him look out for some gold for me; and he tells me that ginnys, which I bought 2,000 of not long ago, and cost me but 18½*d.* change, will now cost me *22d.*; and but very few to be had at any price. However, some more I will have, for they are very convenient, and of easy disposal. So home to dinner and to discourse with my brother upon his translation of my Lord Bacon's "Faber Fortunæ," which I gave him to do and he has done it, but meanely; I am not pleased with it at all, having done it only literally, but without any life at all. About five o'clock I took my wife (who is mighty fine, and with a new fair pair of locks, which vex me, though like a foole I helped her the other night to buy them), and to Mrs. Pierce's, and there staying a little I away before to White Hall and into the new play-house[1] there, the first time I ever was there, and the first play I have seen since before the great plague. By and by Mr. Pierce comes, bringing my wife and his, and Knipp. By and by the King and Queene, Duke and Duchesse, and all the great ladies of the Court; which, indeed, was a fine sight. But the play being "Love in a Tub,"[2] a silly play, and though done by the Duke's people, yet having neither Betterton nor his wife,[3] and the whole thing done ill, and being ill also, I had no manner of pleasure in the play. Besides, the House, though very fine, yet bad for the voice, for hearing. The sight of the ladies, indeed, was exceeding noble; and above all, my Lady Castlemayne. The play done by ten o'clock. I carried them all home, and then home myself, and well satisfied

[1] The "Warrant appointing Henry Glover keeper of the Royal Theatre at Whitehall, with the scenes, engines, &c., fee £30 a year from the money allowed for plays, &c.," is dated November 21st, 1666 ("Calendar of State Papers," 1666–67, p. 278).

[2] "The Comical Revenge, or Love in a Tub," a comedy by Sir George Etherege, licensed for printing in 1664, and published in 1669.

[3] See note, *ante*, April 2nd, 1662.

with the sight, but not the play, we with great content to bed.

30th. Up, and to the office, where sat all the morning, and at noon home to dinner, and then to the office again, where late, very busy, and dispatching much business. Mr. Hater staying most of the afternoon abroad, he come to me, poor man, to make excuse, and it was that he had been looking out for a little house for his family. His wife being much frightened in the country with the discourses of troubles and disorders like to be, and therefore durst not be from him, and therefore he is forced to bring her to towne that they may be together. This is now the general apprehension of all people; particulars I do not know, but my owne fears are also great, and I do think it time to look out to save something, if a storm should come. At night home to supper, and singing with my wife, who hath lately begun to learn, and I think will come to do something, though her eare is not good, nor I, I confess, have patience enough to teach her, or hear her sing now and then a note out of tune, and am to blame that I cannot bear with that in her which is fit I should do with her as a learner, and one that I desire much could sing, and so should encourage her. This I was troubled at, for I do find that I do put her out of heart, and make her fearfull to sing before me. So after supper to bed.

31st. Out with Sir W. Batten toward White Hall, being in pain in my cods by being squeezed the other night in a little coach when I carried Pierce and his wife and my people. But I hope I shall be soon well again. This day is a great day at the House, so little to do with the Duke of York, but soon parted. Coming out of the Court I met Colonell Atkins, who tells me the whole city rings to-day of Sir Jeremy Smith's killing of Holmes in a duell, at which I was not much displeased, for I fear every day more and more mischief from the man, if he lives; but the thing is not true, for in my coach I did by and by meet Sir Jer. Smith going to Court. So I by coach to my goldsmith, there to see what gold I can get, which is but little, and not under 22*d.* So away home to dinner, and after dinner to my closett, where I spent the whole afternoon till late at evening of all my accounts publique and private, and to my great satisfaction I do find that I do bring my accounts to a very near balance, notwithstanding all the hurries and troubles I have been put to by the late fire, that I have not been able to even my accounts since July last before; and I bless God I do find that I am worth more than ever I yet was, which is £6,200, for which the Holy Name of God be praised! and my other accounts of Tangier in a very plain and clear condition, that I am not liable to any trouble from them; but in fear great I am, and I perceive the whole city is, of some distractions and disorders among us, which God of his goodness prevent! Late to supper with my wife and brother, and then to bed. And thus ends the month with an ill aspect, the business of the Navy standing wholly still. No credit, no goods sold us, nobody will trust. All we have to do at the office is to hear complaints for want of money. The Duke of York himself for now three weeks seems to rest satisfied that we can do nothing without money, and that all must stand still till the King gets money, which the Parliament have been a great while about; but are so dissatisfied with the King's management, and his giving himself up to pleasures, and not minding the calling to account any of his officers, and they observe so much the expense of the war, and yet that after we have made it the most we can, it do not amount to what they have given the King for the warr, that they are backward of giving any more. However, £1,800,000 they have voted, but the way of gathering it has taken up more time than is fit to be now lost. The seamen grow very rude, and every thing out of order; commanders having no power over their seamen, but the seamen do what they please. Few stay on board, but all coming running up hither to towne and nobody can with justice blame them, we owing them so much money; and their familys must starve if we do not give them money, or they procure upon their tickets from some people that will trust them. A great folly is observed by all people in the King's giving leave to so many merchantmen to go abroad this winter, and some upon voyages where it is impossible they should be back again by the spring, and the rest will be doubtfull, but yet we let them go; what the reason of State is nobody can tell, but all condemn it.

The Prince and Duke of Albemarle have got no great credit by this year's service. Our losses both of reputation and ships having been greater than is thought have ever been suffered in all ages put together before; being beat home, and fleeing home the first fight, and then losing so many ships then and since upon the sands, and some falling into the enemy's hands, and not one taken this yeare, but the Ruby, French prize, now at the end of the yeare, by the Frenchmen's mistake in running upon us. Great folly in both Houses of Parliament, several persons falling together by the eares, among others in the House of Lords, the Duke of Buckingham and my Lord Ossory.[1] Such is our case that every body fears an invasion the next yeare; and for my part, I do methinks foresee great unhappiness coming upon us, and do provide for it by laying by something against a rainy day, dividing what I have, and laying it in several places, but with all faithfulness to the King in all respects; my grief only being that the King do not look after his business himself, and thereby will be undone both himself and his nation, it being not yet, I believe, too late if he would apply himself to it, to save all, and conquer the Dutch; but while he and the Duke of York mind their pleasure, as they do and nothing else, we must be beaten. So late with my mind in good condition of quiet after the settling all my accounts, and to bed.

November 1st. Up, and was presented by Burton, one of our smith's wives, with a very noble cake, which I presently resolved to have my wife go with to-day, and some wine, and house-warme my Betty Michell, which she readily resolved to do. So I to the office and sat all

[1] October 31st, 1666. "Humble petition of George, Duke of Bucks, shewing, 'That the displeasure of this Honourable House has been a greater trouble to him than anything could have befallen him in this business which has been the occasion of it.' Likewise the petition of Thomas, Lord Butler, was read, shewing, 'That he being heartily sorry for the occasion he hath given their Lordships to be displeased at him, in the late quarrel he had with the Duke of Buckingham . . . . humbly beseecheth their Lordships to restore him to his Liberty and their favour.' Hereupon it is ordered, That the Duke of Bucks and the Lord Butler be released and discharged from their present and respective restraints" ("Journals of the House of Lords," vol. xii., p. 22).

the morning, where little to do but answer people about want of money; so that there is little service done the King by us, and great disquiet to ourselves; I am sure there is to me very much, for I do not enjoy myself as I would and should do in my employment if my pains could do the King better service, and with the peace that we used to do it. At noon to dinner, and from dinner my wife and my brother, and W. Hewer and Barker away to Betty Michell's, to Shadwell, and I to my office, where I took in Mrs. Bagwell and did what I would with her, and so she went away, and I all the afternoon till almost night there, and then, my wife being come back, I took her and set her at her brother's, who is very sicke, and I to White Hall, and there all alone a pretty while with Sir W. Coventry at his chamber. I find him very melancholy under the same considerations of the King's service that I am. He confesses with me he expects all will be undone, and all ruined; he complains and sees perfectly what I with grief do, and said it first himself to me that all discipline is lost in the fleete, no order nor no command, and concurs with me that it is necessary we do again and again represent all things more and more plainly to the Duke of York, for a guard to ourselves hereafter when things shall come to be worse. He says the House goes on slowly in finding of money, and that the discontented party do say they have not done with us, for they will have a further bout with us as to our accounts, and they are exceedingly well instructed where to hit us. I left him with a thousand sad reflections upon the times, and the state of the King's matters, and so away, and took up my wife and home, where a little at the office, and then home to supper, and talk with my wife (with whom I have much comfort) and my brother, and so to bed.

2nd. Up betimes, and with Sir W. Batten to Woolwich, where first we went on board the Ruby,[1] French prize, the only ship of war we have taken from any of our enemies

[1] "M. de la Roche has been taken in the Ruby, a ship of 54 guns and 500 men, which was separated from Beaufort, and fell into the midst of the White Squadron, the colour of the flag deceiving him that it was French" (Letter from Jo. Hayes to Williamson, dated September 19th, "Calendar of State Papers," 1666–67, p. 139).

this year. It seems a very good ship, but with galleries quite round the sterne to walk in as a balcone, which will be taken down. She had also about forty good brass guns, but will make little amends to our loss in The Prince. Thence to the Ropeyarde and the other yards to do several businesses, he and I also did buy some apples and pork; by the same token the butcher commended it as the best in England for cloath and colour. And for his beef, says he, "Look how fat it is; the lean appears only here and there a speck, like beauty-spots." Having done at Woolwich, we to Deptford (it being very cold upon the water), and there did also a little more business, and so home, I reading all the way to make end of the "Bondman" (which the oftener I read the more I like), and begun "The Duchesse of Malfy,"[1] which seems a good play. At home to dinner, and there come Mr. Pierce, surgeon, to see me, and after I had eat something, he and I and my wife by coach to Westminster, she set us down at White Hall, and she to her brother's. I up into the House, and among other things walked a good while with the Serjeant Trumpet,[2] who tells me, as I wished, that the King's Italian here is about setting three parts for trumpets, and shall teach some to sound them, and believes they will be admirable musique. I also walked with Sir Stephen Fox an houre, and good discourse of publique business with him, who seems very much satisfied with my discourse, and desired more of my acquaintance. Then comes out the King and Duke of York from the Council, and so I spoke awhile to Sir W. Coventry about some office business, and so called my wife (her brother being now a little better than he was), and so home, and I to my chamber to do some business, and then to supper and to bed.

3rd. This morning comes Mr. Lovett, and brings me my print of the Passion, varnished by him, and the frame

[1] Massinger's "Bondman," acted before the court in 1623, and published in the following year. Webster's "Duchess of Malfy" was first published in 1623.

[2] The serjeant trumpeter was Gervase Price. The year's salary (which was not very regularly paid) for the serjeant trumpeter, sixteen trumpeters, and kettle-drummer, was £1,120 ("Calendar of State Papers," 1666–67, p. 446).

black, which indeed is very fine, though not so fine as I expected, however, pleases me exceedingly. This, and the sheets of paper he prepared for me, come to £3, which I did give him, and though it be more than is fit to lay out on pleasure, yet, it being ingenious, I did not think much of it. He gone, I to the office, where all the morning to little purpose, nothing being before us but clamours for money. So at noon home to dinner, and after dinner to hang up my new varnished picture and set my chamber in order to be made clean, and then to the office again, and there all the afternoon till late at night, and so to supper and to bed.

4th (Lord's day). Comes my taylor's man in the morning, and brings my vest home, and coate to wear with it, and belt, and silver-hilted sword. So I rose and dressed myself, and I like myself mightily in it, and so do my wife.[1] Then, being dressed, to church; and after church pulled my Lady Pen and Mrs. Markham into my house to dinner, and Sir J. Minnes he got Mrs. Pegg along with him. I had a good dinner for them, and very merry; and after dinner to the waterside, and so, it being very cold, to White Hall, and was mighty fearfull of an ague, my vest being new and thin, and the coat cut not to meet before upon my breast. Here I waited in the gallery till the Council was up, and among others did speak with Mr. Cooling, my Lord Chamberlain's secretary, who tells me my Lord Generall is become mighty low in all people's opinion, and that he hath received several slurs from the King and Duke of York. The people at Court do see the difference between his and the Prince's management, and my Lord Sandwich's. That this business which he is put upon of crying out against the Catholiques and turning them out of all employment, will undo him, when he comes to turn out the officers out of the Army, and this is a thing of his own seeking. That he is grown a drunken sot, and drinks with nobody but Troutbecke, whom nobody else will keep company with. Of whom he told me this story: That once the Duke of Albemarle in his drink taking

[1] See notes on the new costume introduced by the king, *ante*, October 8th, 15th; *post*, November 22nd.

notice as of a wonder that Nan Hide should ever come to be Duchesse of York, "Nay," says Troutbecke, "ne'er wonder at that; for if you will give me another bottle of wine, I will tell you as great, if not greater, a miracle." And what was that, but that our dirty Besse (meaning his Duchesse) should come to be Duchesse of Albemarle? Here we parted, and so by and by the Council rose, and out comes Sir G. Carteret and Sir W. Coventry, and they and my Lord Bruncker and I went to Sir G. Carteret's lodgings, there to discourse about some money demanded by Sir W. Warren, and having done that broke up. And Sir G. Carteret and I alone together a while, where he shows a long letter, all in cipher, from my Lord Sandwich to him. The contents he hath not yet found out, but he tells me that my Lord is not sent for home, as several people have enquired after of me. He spoke something reflecting upon me in the business of pursers, that their present bad behaviour is what he did foresee, and had convinced me of, and yet when it come last year to be argued before the Duke of York I turned and said as the rest did. I answered nothing to it, but let it go, and so to other discourse of the ill state of things, of which all people are full of sorrow and observation, and so parted, and then by water, landing in Southwarke, home to the Tower, and so home, and there began to read "Potters' Discourse upon 666,"[1] which pleases me mightily, and then broke off and to supper and to bed.

5th (A holyday). Lay long; then up, and to the office, where vexed to meet with people come from the fleete at the Nore, where so many ships are laid up and few going abroad, and yet Sir Thomas Allen hath sent up some Lieutenants with warrants to presse men for a few ships to go out this winter, while every day thousands appear here, to our great trouble and affright, before our office and the ticket office, and no Captains able to command one man

[1] "An Interpretation of the number 666." Oxford, 1642, 4to. The work was afterwards translated into French, Dutch, and Latin. It was written by Francis Potter, an English divine, born in Wiltshire, 1594, who died about 1678, at Kilmington, in Somersetshire, of which he was rector (Wood's "Athenæ"). See February 18th, 1665-66. — B.

aboard. Thence by water to Westminster, and there at the Swan find Sarah is married to a shoemaker yesterday, so I could not see her, but I believe I shall hereafter at good leisure. Thence by coach to my Lady Peterborough,[1] and there spoke with my Lady, who had sent to speak with me. She makes mighty moan of the badness of the times, and her family as to money. My Lord's passionateness for want thereof, and his want of coming in of rents, and no wages from the Duke of York. No money to be had there for wages nor disbursements, and therefore prays my assistance about his pension. I was moved with her story, which she largely and handsomely told me, and promised I would try what I could do in a few days, and so took leave, being willing to keep her Lord fair with me, both for his respect to my Lord Sandwich and for my owne sake hereafter, when I come to pass my accounts. Thence to my Lord Crew's, and there dined, and mightily made of, having not, to my shame, been there in 8 months before. Here my Lord and Sir Thomas Crew, Mr. John, and Dr. Crew,[2] and two strangers. The best family in the world for goodness and sobriety. Here beyond my expectation I met my Lord Hinchingbroke, who is come to towne two days since from Hinchingbroke, and brought his sister and brother Carteret with him, who are at Sir G. Carteret's. After dinner I and Sir Thomas Crew went aside to discourse of public matters, and do find by him that all the country gentlemen are publickly jealous of the courtiers in the Parliament, and that they do doubt every thing that they propose; and that the true reason why the country gentlemen are for a land-tax and against a general excise, is, because they are fearful that if the latter be granted they shall never get it down again; whereas the land-tax will be but for so much, and when the war ceases, there will be no ground got by the Court to keep it up. He do much cry out upon our accounts, and that

[1] See August 10th, 1663.

[2] John, Lord Crew (see note, January 2nd, 1659–60); Sir Thomas Crew, his eldest son, second Lord Crew, 1679 (see note, January 25th, 1659–60); John Crew, younger son of first Lord Crew; Nathaniel Crew, fifth son of the first Lord Crew, Bishop of Durham, 1674, succeeded as third Lord Crew in 1697 (see note, May 17th, 1662).

all that they have had from the King hath been but estimates both from my Lord Treasurer and us, and from all people else, so that the Parliament is weary of it. He says the House would be very glad to get something against Sir G. Carteret, and will not let their inquiries die till they have got something. He do, from what he hath heard at the Committee for examining the burning of the City, conclude it as a thing certain that it was done by plots;[1] it being proved by many witnesses that endeavours were made in several places to encrease the fire, and that both in City and country it was bragged by several Papists that upon such a day or in such a time we should find the hottest weather that ever was in England, and words of plainer sense. But my Lord Crew was discoursing at table how the Judges have determined in the case whether the landlords or the tenants (who are, in their leases, all of them generally tied to maintain and uphold their houses) shall bear the losse of the fire; and they say that tenants should against all casualties of fire beginning either in their owne or in their neighbour's; but, where it is done by an enemy, they are not to do it. And this was by an enemy, there having been one convicted and hanged upon this very score. This is an excellent salvo for the tenants, and for which I am glad, because of my father's house. After dinner and this discourse I took coach, and at the same time find my Lord Hinchingbroke and Mr. John Crew and the Doctor going out to see the ruins of the City; so I took the Doctor into my hackney coach (and he is a very fine sober gentleman), and so through the City. But, Lord! what pretty and sober observations he made of the City and its desolation; till anon we come to my house, and there I took them upon Tower Hill to shew them what houses were pulled down there since the fire; and then to my house, where I treated them with good wine of several sorts, and they took it mighty respectfully, and a fine company of gentlemen they are; but above all I was glad to see my Lord Hinchingbroke drink no wine at all. Here I got them to appoint Wednesday come se'nnight to dine here at my house, and so we broke up and all took coach

[1] See note, December 13th, *post*.

again, and I carried the Doctor to Chancery Lane, and thence I to White Hall, where I staid walking up and down till night, and then got almost into the playhouse, having much mind to go and see the play at Court this night; but fearing how I should get home, because of the bonefires and the lateness of the night to get a coach, I did not stay; but having this evening seen my Lady Jemimah, who is come to towne, and looks very well and fat, and heard how Mr. John Pickering is to be married this week, and to a fortune with £5,000, and seen a rich necklace of pearle and two pendants of dyamonds, which Sir G. Carteret hath presented her with since her coming to towne, I home by coach, but met not one bonefire through the whole town in going round by the wall, which is strange, and speaks the melancholy disposition of the City at present, while never more was said of, and feared of, and done against the Papists than just at this time. Home, and there find my wife and her people at cards, and I to my chamber, and there late, and so to supper and to bed.

6th. Up, and to the office, where all the morning sitting. At noon home to dinner, and after dinner down alone by water to Deptford, reading "Duchesse of Malfy," the play, which is pretty good, and there did some business, and so up again, and all the evening at the office. At night home, and there find Mr. Batelier, who supped with us, and good company he is, and so after supper to bed.

7th. Up, and with Sir W. Batten to White Hall, where we attended as usual the Duke of York, and there was by the folly of Sir W. Batten prevented in obtaining a bargain for Captain Cocke, which would, I think have [been] at this time (during our great want of hempe), both profitable to the King and of good convenience to me; but I matter it not, it being done only by the folly, not any design, of Sir W. Batten's. Thence to Westminster Hall, and, it being fast day, there was no shops open, but meeting with Doll Lane, did go with her to the Rose taverne, and there drank and played with her a good while. She went away, and I staid a good while after, and was seen going out by one of our neighbours near the office and two of the Hall people that I had no mind to have been seen by, but there was no hurt in it nor can be alledged from it. Therefore

I am not solicitous in it, but took coach and called at Faythorne's, to buy some prints for my wife to draw by this winter, and here did see my Lady Castlemayne's picture, done by him from Lilly's, in red chalke and other colours, by which he hath cut it in copper to be printed. The picture in chalke is the finest thing I ever saw in my life, I think; and did desire to buy it; but he says he must keep it awhile to correct his copper-plate[1] by, and when that is done he will sell it me. Thence home and find my wife gone out with my brother to see her brother. I to dinner and thence to my chamber to read, and so to the office (it being a fast day and so a holiday), and then to Mrs. Turner's, at her request to speake and advise about Sir Thomas Harvy's coming to lodge there, which I think must be submitted to, and better now than hereafter, when he gets more ground, for I perceive he intends to stay by it, and begins to crow mightily upon his late being at the payment of tickets; but a coxcombe he is and will never be better in the business of the Navy. Thence home, and there find Mr. Batelier come to bring my wife a very fine puppy of his mother's spaniel, a very fine one indeed, which my wife is mighty proud of. He staid and supped with us, and they to cards. I to my chamber to do some business, and then out to them to play and were a little merry, and then to bed. By the Duke of York his discourse to-day in his chamber, they have it at Court, as well as we here, that a fatal day is to be expected shortly, of some great mischiefe to the remainder of this day; whether by the Papists, or what, they are not certain. But the day is disputed; some say next Friday, others a day sooner, others later, and I hope all will prove a foolery. But it is observable how every body's fears are busy at this time.

8th. Up, and before I went to the office I spoke with Mr. Martin for his advice about my proceeding in the business of the private man-of-war, he having heretofore served in one of them, and now I have it in my thoughts to send him purser in ours. After this discourse I to the office, where I sat all the morning, Sir W. Coventry with

[1] See December 1st, 1666, on which day Pepys bought three copies of the engraving.

us, where he hath not been a great while, Sir W. Pen also, newly come from the Nore, where he hath been some time fitting of the ships out. At noon home to dinner and then to the office awhile, and so home for my sword, and there find Mercer come to see her mistresse. I was glad to see her there, and my wife mighty kind also, and for my part, much vexed that the jade is not with us still. Left them together, designing to go abroad to-morrow night to Mrs. Pierce's to dance; and so I to Westminster Hall, and there met Mr. Grey, who tells me the House is sitting still (and now it was six o'clock), and likely to sit till midnight; and have proceeded fair to give the King his supply presently; and herein have done more to-day than was hoped for. So to White Hall to Sir W. Coventry, and there would fain have carried Captain Cocke's business for his bargain of hemp, but am defeated and disappointed, and know hardly how to carry myself in it between my interest and desire not to offend Sir W. Coventry. Sir W. Coventry did this night tell me how the business is about Sir J. Minnes; that he is to be a Commissioner, and my Lord Bruncker and Sir W. Pen are to be Controller joyntly, which I am very glad of, and better than if they were either of them alone; and do hope truly that the King's business will be better done thereby, and infinitely better than now it is. Thence by coach home, full of thoughts of the consequence of this alteration in our office, and I think no evil to me. So at my office late, and then home to supper and to bed. Mr. Grey did assure me this night, that he was told this day, by one of the greater Ministers of State in England, and one of the King's Cabinet, that we had little left to agree on between the Dutch and us towards a peace, but only the place of treaty; which do astonish me to hear, but I am glad of it, for I fear the consequence of the war. But he says that the King, having all the money he is like to have, we shall be sure of a peace in a little time.

9th. Up and to the office, where did a good deale of business, and then at noon to the Exchange and to my little goldsmith's, whose wife[1] is very pretty and modest,

[1] Mrs. Stokes, of Paternoster Row (see January 10th, 1665–66), wife of Humphry Stokes.

that ever I saw any. Upon the 'Change, where I seldom have of late been, I find all people mightily at a losse what to expect, but confusion and fears in every man's head and heart. Whether war or peace, all fear the event will be bad. Thence home and with my brother to dinner, my wife being dressing herself against night; after dinner I to my closett all the afternoon, till the porter brought my vest back from the taylor's, and then to dress myself very fine, about 4 or 5 o'clock, and by that time comes Mr. Batelier and Mercer, and away by coach to Mrs. Pierce's, by appointment, where we find good company: a fair lady, my Lady Prettyman,[1] Mrs. Corbet,[2] Knipp; and for men, Captain Downing, Mr. Lloyd, Sir W. Coventry's clerk, and one Mr. Tripp, who dances well. After some trifling discourse, we to dancing, and very good sport, and mightily pleased I was with the company. After our first bout of dancing, Knipp and I to sing, and Mercer and Captain Downing (who loves and understands musique) would by all means have my song of "Beauty, retire:" which Knipp had spread abroad, and he extols it above any thing he ever heard, and, without flattery, I know it is good in its kind. This being done and going to dance again, comes news that White Hall was on fire; and presently more particulars, that the Horse-guard was on fire;[3] and so we run up to the garret, and find it so; a horrid great fire; and by and by we saw and heard part of it blown up with powder. The ladies begun presently to be afeard: one fell into fits. The whole town in an alarme. Drums beat and trumpets,

[1] Margaret, daughter and heir of Sir Matthew Mennes, K.B., and wife of Sir John Prettyman, Bart., M.P. for Leicester. — B.

[2] There was an actress of this name. She played Clevly, at the King's House, in the Hon. Edward Howard's "Man of Newmarket," 1678. — B.

[3] "Nov. 9th. Between seven and eight at night, there happened a fire in the Horse Guard House, in the Tilt Yard, over against Whitehall, which at first arising, it is supposed, from some snuff of a candle falling amongst the straw, broke out with so sudden a flame, that at once it seized the north-west part of that building; but being so close under His Majesty's own eye, it was, by the timely help His Majesty and His Royal Highness caused to be applied, immediately stopped, and by ten o'clock wholly mastered, with the loss only of that part of the building it had at first seized." — *The London Gazette*, No. 103. — B.

and the guards every where spread, running up and down in the street. And I begun to have mighty apprehensions how things might be at home, and so was in mighty pair to get home, and that that encreased all is that we are in expectation, from common fame, this night, or to-morrow, to have a massacre, by the having so many fires one after another, as that in the City, and at the same time begun in Westminster, by the Palace, but put out; and since in Southwarke, to the burning down some houses: and now this do make all people conclude there is something extraordinary in it; but nobody knows what. By and by comes news that the fire has slackened; so then we were a little cheered up again, and to supper, and pretty merry. But, above all, there comes in the dumb boy that I knew in Oliver's time, who is mightily acquainted here, and with Downing; and he made strange signs of the fire, and how the King was abroad, and many things they understood, but I could not, which I wondering at, and discoursing with Downing about it, "Why," says he, "it is only a little use, and you will understand him, and make him understand you with as much ease as may be." So I prayed him to tell him that I was afeard that my coach would be gone, and that he should go down and steal one of the seats out of the coach and keep it, and that would make the coachman to stay. He did this, so that the dumb boy did go down, and, like a cunning rogue, went into the coach, pretending to sleep; and, by and by, fell to his work, but finds the seats nailed to the coach. So he did all he could, but could not do it; however, stayed there, and stayed the coach till the coachman's patience was quite spent, and beat the dumb boy by force, and so went away. So the dumb boy come up and told him all the story, which they below did see all that passed, and knew it to be true. After supper, another dance or two, and then newes that the fire is as great as ever, which put us all to our wit's-end; and I mightily [anxious] to go home, but the coach being gone, and it being about ten at night, and rainy dirty weather, I knew not what to do; but to walk out with Mr. Batelier, myself resolving to go home on foot, and leave the women there. And so did; but at the Savoy got a coach, and come back and took up the women; and so, having, by people come from the fire, understood that the fire was overcome, and all well, we merrily parted, and home. Stopped by several guards and constables quite through the town, round the wall, as we went, all being in armes. We got well home. . . . Being come home, we to cards, till two in the morning, and drinking lamb's-wool.[1] So to bed.

10th. Up and to the office, where Sir W. Coventry come to tell us that the Parliament did fall foul of our accounts again yesterday; and we must arme to have them examined, which I am sorry for: it will bring great trouble to me, and shame upon the office. My head full this morning how to carry on Captain Cocke's bargain of hemp, which I think I shall by my dexterity do, and to the King's advantage as well as my own. At noon with my Lord Bruncker and Sir Thomas Harvy, to Cocke's house, and there Mrs. Williams and other company, and an excellent dinner. Mr. Temple's wife,[2] after dinner, fell to play on the harpsicon, till she tired everybody, that I left the house without taking leave, and no creature left standing by her to hear her. Thence I home and to the office, where late doing of business, and then home. Read an hour, to make an end of Potter's Discourse of the Number 666, which I like all along, but his close is most excellent; and, whether it be right or wrong, is mighty ingenious. Then to supper and to bed. This is the fatal day that every body hath discoursed for a long time to be the day that the Papists, or I know not who, had designed to commit a massacre upon;[3] but, however, I trust in God we shall rise to-morrow morning as well as ever. This afternoon Creed comes to me, and by him, as also my Lady Pen, I hear that my Lady Denham is exceeding sick, even to death, and that she says, and every body else discourses, that she is poysoned; and Creed tells me, that it is said that there hath been a design to poison the King. What the meaning of all these

[1] A beverage consisting of ale mixed with sugar, nutmeg, and the pulp of roasted apples. "A cupp of lamb's-wool they dranke unto him then." — *The King and the Miller of Mansfield* (Percy's "Reliques," Series III., book ii., No. 20).

[2] The wife of John Temple, Sir Robert Viner's chief clerk.

[3] See December 13th, 1666.

sad signs is, the Lord knows; but every day things look worse and worse. God fit us for the worst!

11th (Lord's day). Up, and to church, myself and wife, where the old dunce Meriton,[1] brother to the known Meriton, of St. Martin's, Westminster, did make a very good sermon, beyond my expectation. Home to dinner, and we carried in Pegg Pen, and there also come to us little Michell and his wife, and dined very pleasantly. Anon to church, my wife and I and Betty Michell, her husband being gone to Westminster. . . . After church home, and I to my chamber, and there did finish the putting time to my song of "It is decreed," and do please myself at last and think it will be thought a good song. By and by little Michell comes and takes away his wife home, and my wife and brother and I to my uncle Wight's, where my aunt is grown so ugly and their entertainment so bad that I am in pain to be there; nor will go thither again a good while, if sent for, for we were sent for to-night, we had not gone else. Wooly's wife, a silly woman, and not very handsome, but no spirit in her at all; and their discourse mean, and the fear of the troubles of the times hath made them not to bring their plate to town, since it was carried out upon the business of the fire, so that they drink in earth and a wooden can, which I do not like. So home, and my people to bed. I late to finish my song, and then to bed also, and the business of the firing of the city, and the fears we have of new troubles and violences, and the fear of fire among ourselves, did keep me awake a good while, considering the sad condition I and my family should be in. So at last to sleep.

12th. Lay long in bed, and then up, and Mr. Carcasse brought me near 500 tickets to sign, which I did, and by discourse find him a cunning, confident, shrewd man, but

[1] The Rev. John Meriton (1636–1704), rector of St. Michael's, Cornhill, from 1663 till his death, who is referred to on July 9th, 1665, was appointed Sunday lecturer of St. Martin's-in-the-Fields shortly before the Restoration. Miss Porter, the writer of the life of Meriton in the "Dictionary of National Biography," considers him to be the same person as he who Pepys styles "an old dunce;" but the statement in the text that the latter was brother to the known Meriton seems to throw a doubt on this statement.

one that I do doubt hath by his discourse of the ill will he hath got with my Lord Marquess of Dorchester (with whom he lived), he hath had cunning practices in his time, and would not now spare to use the same to his profit. That done I to the office, whither by and by comes Creed to me, and he and I walked in the garden a little, talking of the present ill condition of things, which is the common subject of all men's discourse and fears now-a-days, and particularly of my Lady Denham,[1] whom everybody says is poisoned, and he tells me she hath said it to the Duke of York; but is upon the mending hand, though the town says she is dead this morning. He and I to the 'Change. There I had several little errands, and going to Sir R. Viner's, I did get such a splash and spots of dirt upon my new vest, that I was out of countenance to be seen in the street. This day I received 450 pieces of gold more of Mr. Stokes, but cost me 22½*d.* change; but I am well contented with it, I having now near £2,800 in gold, and will not rest till I get full £3,000, and then will venture my fortune for the saving that and the rest. Home to dinner, though Sir R. Viner would have staid us to dine with him, he being sheriffe; but, poor man, was so out of countenance that he had no wine ready to drink to us, his butler being out of the way, though we know him to be a very liberal man. And after dinner I took my wife out, intending to have gone and have seen my Lady Jemimah, at White Hall, but so great a stop there was at the New Exchange, that we could not pass in half an houre, and therefore 'light and bought a little matter at the Exchange, and then home, and then at the office awhile, and then home to my chamber, and after my wife and all the mayds abed but Jane, whom I put confidence in — she and I, and my brother, and Tom, and W. Hewer, did bring up all the remainder of my money, and my plate-chest, out of the cellar, and placed the money in my study, with the rest, and the plate in my dressing-room; but indeed I am in great pain to think how to dispose of my money, it being wholly unsafe to keep it all in coin in one place. But now I have it all at my hand, I shall remember it better to think

[1] See January 7th and 8th, 1666–67.

of disposing of it. This done, by one in the morning to bed. This afternoon going towards Westminster, Creed and I did stop, the Duke of York being just going away from seeing of it, at Paul's, and in the Convocation House Yard[1] did there see the body of Robert Braybrooke, Bishop of London, that died 1404. He fell down in his tomb out of the great church into St. Fayth's this late fire, and is here seen his skeleton with the flesh on; but all tough and dry like a spongy dry leather, or touchwood all upon his bones. His head turned aside. A great man in his time, and Lord Chancellor; and [his skeleton] now exposed to be handled and derided by some, though admired for its duration by others. Many flocking to see it.

13th. At the office all the morning, at noon home to dinner, and out to Bishopsgate Street, and there bought some drinking-glasses, a case of knives, and other things, against to-morrow, in expectation of my Lord Hinchingbroke's coming to dine with me. So home, and having set some things in the way of doing, also against to-morrow, I to my office, there to dispatch business, and do here receive notice from my Lord Hinchingbroke that he is not well, and so not in condition to come to dine with me to-morrow, which I am not in much trouble for, because of the disorder my house is in, by the bricklayers coming to mend the chimney in my dining-room for smoking, which they were upon almost till midnight, and have now made it very pretty, and do carry smoke exceeding well. This evening come all the Houblons to me, to invite me to sup with them to-morrow night. I did take them home, and there we sat and talked a good while, and a glass of wine, and then parted till to-morrow night. So at night, well satisfied in the alteration of my chimney, to bed.

14th. Up, and by water to White Hall, and thence to Westminster, where I bought several things, as a hone, ribbon, gloves, books, and then took coach and to Knipp's lodging, whom I find not ready to go home with me. So I away to do a little business, among others to call upon Mr. Osborne for my Tangier warrant for the last quarter,

[1] The old Chapter House of St. Paul's was also styled the Convocation House. See Sparrow Simpson's "Chapters in the History of Old St. Paul's," 1881, p. 274.

and so to the Exchange for some things for my wife, and then to Knipp's again, and there staid reading of Waller's verses, while she finished dressing, her husband being by. I had no other pastime. Her lodging very mean, and the condition she lives in; yet makes a shew without doors, God bless us! I carried him along with us into the City, and set him down in Bishopsgate Street, and then home with her. She tells me how Smith,[1] of the Duke's house, hath killed a man upon a quarrel in play; which makes every body sorry, he being a good actor, and, they say, a good man, however this happens. The ladies of the Court do much bemoan him, she says. Here she and we alone at dinner to some good victuals, that we could not put off, that was intended for the great dinner of my Lord Hinchingbroke's, if he had come. After dinner I to teach her my new recitative of "It is decreed," of which she learnt a good part, and I do well like it and believe shall be well pleased when she hath it all, and that it will be found an agreeable thing. Then carried her home, and my wife and I intended to have seen my Lady Jemimah at White Hall, but the Exchange Streete was so full of coaches, every body, as they say, going thither to make themselves fine against to-morrow night, that, after half an hour's stay, we could not do any [thing], only my wife to see her brother, and I to go speak one word with Sir G. Carteret about office business, and talk of the general complexion of matters, which he looks upon, as I do, with horrour, and gives us all for an undone people. That there is no such thing as a peace in hand, nor possibility of any without our begging it, they being as high, or higher, in their terms than ever, and tells me that, just now, my Lord Hollis had been with him, and wept to think in what a condition we are fallen. He shewed me my Lord Sandwich's letter to him, complaining of the lack of money, which Sir G. Carteret is at a loss how in the world to get the King to supply him with, and wishes him, for that reason, here; for that he fears he will be brought to disgrace there, for want of supplies. He says the House is yet in a bad

[1] William Smith, originally a barrister-at-law of the Society of Gray's Inn. He was a good actor, and highly esteemed by his fellows. He died 1696.

humour; and desiring to know whence it is that the King stirs not, he says he minds it not, nor will be brought to it, and that his servants of the House do, instead of making the Parliament better, rather play the rogue one with another, and will put all in fire. So that, upon the whole, we are in a wretched condition, and I went from him in full apprehensions of it. So took up my wife, her brother being yet very bad, and doubtful whether he will recover or no, and so to St. Ellen's [St. Helen's], and there sent my wife home, and myself to the Pope's Head, where all the Houblons were, and Dr. Croone,[1] and by and by to an exceeding pretty supper, excellent discourse of all sorts, and indeed [they] are a set of the finest gentlemen that ever I met withal in my life. Here Dr. Croone told me, that, at the meeting at Gresham College to-night, which, it seems, they now have every Wednesday again, there was a pretty experiment of the blood of one dogg let out, till he died, into the body of another on one side, while all his own run out on the other side.[2] The first died upon the place, and the other very well, and likely to do well. This did give occasion to many pretty wishes, as of the blood of a Quaker to be let into an Archbishop, and such like; but, as Dr. Croone says, may, if it takes, be of

[1] William Croune, or Croone, of Emanuel College, Cambridge, chosen Rhetoric Professor at Gresham College, 1659, F.R.S. and M.D. Died October 12th, 1684, and was interred at St. Mildred's in the Poultry. He was a prominent Fellow of the Royal Society and first Registrar. In accordance with his wishes his widow (who married Sir Edwin Sadleir, Bart.) left by will one-fifth of the clear rent of the King's Head tavern in or near Old Fish Street, at the corner of Lambeth Hill, to the Royal Society for the support of a lecture and illustrative experiments for the advancement of natural knowledge on local motion. The Croonian lecture is still delivered before the Royal Society.

[2] At the meeting on November 14th, "the experiment of transfusing the blood of one dog into another was made before the Society by Mr. King and Mr. Thomas Coxe upon a little mastiff and a spaniel with very good success, the former bleeding to death, and the latter receiving the blood of the other, and emitting so much of his own, as to make him capable of receiving that of the other." On November 21st the spaniel "was produced and found very well" (Birch's "History of the Royal Society," vol. ii., pp. 123, 125). The experiment of transfusion of blood, which occupied much of the attention of the Royal Society in its early days, was revived within the last few years.

mighty use to man's health, for the amending of bad blood by borrowing from a better body. After supper, James Houblon and another brother took me aside and to talk of, some businesses of their owne, where I am to serve them and will, and then to talk of publique matters, and I do find that they and all merchants else do give over trade and the nation for lost, nothing being done with care or foresight, no convoys granted, nor any thing done to satisfaction; but do think that the Dutch and French will master us the next yeare, do what we can: and so do I, unless necessity makes the King to mind his business, which might yet save all. Here we sat talking till past one in the morning, and then home, where my people sat up for me, my wife and all, and so to bed.

15th. This [morning] come Mr. Shepley (newly out of the country) to see me; after a little discourse with him, I to the office, where we sat all the morning, and at noon home, and there dined, Shepley with me, and after dinner I did pay him £70, which he had paid my father for my use in the country. He being gone, I took coach and to Mrs. Pierce's, where I find her as fine as possible, and himself going to the ball at night at Court, it being the Queen's birth-day, and so I carried them in my coach, and having set them into the house, and gotten Mr. Pierce to undertake the carrying in my wife, I to Unthanke's, where she appointed to be, and there told her, and back again about business to White Hall, while Pierce went and fetched her and carried her in. I, after I had met with Sir W. Coventry and given him some account of matters, I also to the ball, and with much ado got up to the loft, where with much trouble I could see very well. Anon the house grew full, and the candles light, and the King and Queen and all the ladies set: and it was, indeed, a glorious sight to see Mrs. Stewart in black and white lace, and her head and shoulders dressed with dyamonds, and the like a great many great ladies more, only the Queen none; and the King in his rich vest of some rich silke and silver trimming, as the Duke of York and all the dancers were, some of cloth of silver, and others of other sorts, exceeding rich. Presently after the King was come in, he took the Queene, and about fourteen more couple there was, and begun the

Bransles.[1] As many of the men as I can remember presently, were, the King, Duke of York, Prince Rupert, Duke of Monmouth, Duke of Buckingham, Lord Douglas,[2] Mr. [George] Hamilton, Colonell Russell,[3] Mr. Griffith, Lord Ossory, Lord Rochester;[4] and of the ladies, the Queene, Duchess of York, Mrs. Stewart, Duchess of Monmouth, Lady Essex Howard,[5] Mrs. Temple,[6] Swedes Embassadress,[7] Lady Arlington,[8] Lord George Barkeley's daughter,[9] and many others I remember not; but all most excellently dressed in rich petticoats and gowns, and dyamonds, and pearls. After the Bransles, then to a Corant, and now and then a French dance; but that so rare that the Corants grew tiresome, that I wished it done. Only Mrs. Stewart danced mighty finely, and many French dances, specially one the King called the New Dance, which was very pretty; but upon the whole matter, the business of the

[1] For notes on the dances: the brawls and coranto, see December 31st, 1662.

[2] James, second Marquis of Douglas, nephew to the Duke of Hamilton.

[3] Colonel Russell, brother of William, fifth Earl of Bedford (created Duke of Bedford in 1694), and uncle of the celebrated Lord William Russell.

[4] John Wilmot, second Earl of Rochester, born April 10th, 1648, succeeded his father in 1659. He was at this time a Gentleman of the Bedchamber to the king. He died July 26th, 1680.

[5] Only daughter of James Howard, third Earl of Suffolk, by his first wife, Susannah, daughter of Henry Rich, Earl of Holland; afterwards married, March 4th, 1666–67, at St. Margaret's, Westminster, to Edward Griffin, Lord Griffin of Braybrooke. There is a very fine portrait of her at Audley End, by Lely. — B.

[6] Anne, daughter and co-heir of Thomas Temple, of Frankton, in Warwickshire, by Rebecca, daughter of Sir Nicholas Carew, of Beddington, in Surrey, became the second wife of Sir Charles Lyttelton, who had been Governor of Jamaica, and lived to be eighty-seven. His widow survived him four years, dying in 1718, and had issue by him eight daughters and five sons. From this alliance the Lords Lyttelton descend. — B.

[7] "The Lord George Flemming, the Lord Peter Julius Coyet, ambassadors-extraordinary from the crown of Sweden, made their public entry through the City of London, on the 27th June, 1666." — Pointer's *Chronological History of England*, vol. i., p. 213. The lady was the wife of one of these. — B.

[8] See July 12th, *ante*.

[9] George, Lord Berkeley, had six daughters. The one mentioned here was probably the eldest, Lady Elizabeth. — B.

dancing of itself was not extraordinary pleasing. But the clothes and sight of the persons was indeed very pleasing, and worth my coming, being never likely to see more gallantry while I live, if I should come twenty times. About twelve at night it broke up, and I to hire a coach with much difficulty, but Pierce had hired a chair for my wife, and so she being gone to his house, he and I, taking up Barker at Unthanke's, to his house, whither his wife was come home a good while ago and gone to bed. So away home with my wife, between displeased with the dull dancing, and satisfied at the clothes and persons. My Lady Castlemayne, without whom all is nothing, being there, very rich, though not dancing. And so after supper, it being very cold, to bed.

16th. Up again betimes to attend the examination of Mr. Gawden's accounts, where we all met, but I did little but fit myself for the drawing my great letter to the Duke of York of the state of the Navy for want of money. At noon to the 'Change, and thence back to the new taverne come by us, the Three Tuns, where D. Gawden did feast us all with a chine of beef and other good things, and an infinite dish of fowl, but all spoiled in the dressing. This noon I met with Mr. Hooke, and he tells me the dog which was filled with another dog's blood, at the College the other day, is very well, and like to be so as ever, and doubts not its being found of great use to men; and so do Dr. Whistler, who dined with us at the taverne. Thence home in the evening, and I to my preparing my letter, and did go a pretty way in it, staying late upon it, and then home to supper and to bed, the weather being on a sudden set in to be very cold.

17th. Up, and to the office, where all the morning. At noon home to dinner, and in the afternoon shut myself in my chamber, and there till twelve at night finishing my great letter to the Duke of York, which do lay the ill condition of the Navy so open to him, that it is impossible if the King and he minds any thing of their business, but it will operate upon them to set all matters right, and get money to carry on the war, before it be too late, or else lay out for a peace upon any termes. It was a great convenience to-night that what I had writ foule in short hand,

I could read to W. Hewer, and he take it fair in short hand, so as I can read it to-morrow to Sir W. Coventry, and then come home, and Hewer read it to me while I take it in long-hand to present, which saves me much time. So to bed.

18th (Lord's day). Up by candle-light and on foote to White Hall, where by appointment I met Lord Bruncker at Sir W. Coventry's chamber, and there I read over my great letter, and they approved it: and as I do do our business in defence of the Board, so I think it is as good a letter in the manner, and believe it is the worst in the matter of it, as ever come from any office to a Prince. Back home in my Lord Bruncker's coach, and there W. Hewer and I to write it over fair; dined at noon, and Mercer with us, and mighty merry, and then to finish my letter; and it being three o'clock ere we had done, when I come to Sir W. Batten, he was in a huffe, which I made light of, but he signed the letter, though he would not go, and liked the letter well. Sir W. Pen, it seems, he would not stay for it: so, making slight of Sir W. Pen's putting so much weight upon his hand to Sir W. Batten, I down to the Tower Wharf, and there got a sculler, and to White Hall, and there met Lord Bruncker, and he signed it, and so I delivered it to Mr. Cheving,[1] and he to Sir W. Coventry, in the cabinet, the King and councill being sitting, where I leave it to its fortune, and I by water home again, and to my chamber, to even my Journall; and then comes Captain Cocke to me, and he and I a great deal of melancholy discourse of the times, giving all over for gone, though now the Parliament will soon finish the Bill for money. But we fear, if we had it, as matters are now managed, we shall never make the best of it, but consume it all to no purpose or a bad one. He being gone, I again to my Journall and finished it, and so to supper and to bed.

19th. Lay pretty long in bed talking with pleasure with my wife, and then up and all the morning at my own chamber

[1] William Chiffinch, pimp to Charles II. and receiver of the secret pensions paid by the French Court. He succeeded his brother, Thomas Chiffinch (who died in April, 1666), as Keeper of the King's Private Closet (see note, April 8th, 1666). He is introduced by Scott into his "Peveril of the Peak."

fitting some Tangier matters against the afternoon for a meeting. This morning also came Mr. Cæsar, and I heard him on the lute very finely, and my boy begins to play well. After dinner I carried and set my wife down at her brother's, and then to Barkeshire-house,[1] where my Lord Chancellor hath been ever since the fire, but he is not come home yet, so I to Westminster Hall, where the Lords newly up and the Commons still sitting. Here I met with Mr. Robinson, who did give me a printed paper wherein he states his pretence to the post office, and intends to petition the Parliament in it. Thence I to the Bull-head tavern, where I have not been since Mr. Chetwind[2] and the time of our club, and here had six bottles of claret filled, and I sent them to Mrs. Martin, whom I had promised some of my owne, and, having none of my owne, sent her this. Thence to my Lord Chancellor's, and there Mr. Creed and Gawden, Cholmley, and Sir G. Carteret walking in the Park over against the house. I walked with Sir G. Carteret, who I find displeased with the letter I have drawn and sent in yesterday, finding fault with the account we give of the ill state of the Navy, but I said little, only will justify the truth of it. Here we walked to and again till one dropped away after another, and so I took coach to White Hall, and there visited my Lady Jemimah, at Sir G. Carteret's lodgings. Here was Sir Thomas Crew, and he told me how hot words grew again to-day in the House of Lords between my Lord Ossory and Ashly, the former saying that something said by the other was said like one of Oliver's Council. Ashly said that he must give him reparation, or he would take it his owne way. The House therefore did bring my Lord Ossory to confess his fault, and ask pardon for it, as he was also to my Lord Buckingham, for saying that something was not truth that my Lord Buckingham had said. This will render my Lord Ossory very little in a little time. By and by away, and calling

[1] Belonging to the Earl of Berkshire; afterwards purchased by Charles II., and presented to the Duchess of Cleveland, whose name is preserved in "Cleveland Row." It was then of great extent, and stood on or near the site of Bridgewater House. — B.

[2] Pepys's "old and most ingenious acquaintance," Mr. Chetwind, died at the end of 1662 (see December 5th, 1662).

my wife went home, and then a little at Sir W. Batten's to hear news, but nothing, and then home to supper, whither Captain Cocke, half foxed, come and sat with us, and so away, and then we to bed.

20th. Called up by Mr. Sheply, who is going into the country to-day to Hinchingbroke, I sent my service to my Lady, and in general for newes: that the world do think well of my Lord, and do wish he were here again, but that the publique matters of the State as to the war are in the worst condition that is possible. By and by Sir W. Warren, and with him half an hour discoursing of several businesses, and some I hope will bring me a little profit. He gone, and Sheply, I to the office a little, and then to church, it being thanksgiving-day for the cessation of the plague; but, Lord! how the towne do say that it is hastened before the plague is quite over, there dying some people still,[1] but only to get ground for plays to be publickly acted, which the Bishops would not suffer till the plague was over; and one would thinke so, by the suddenness of the notice given of the day, which was last Sunday, and the little ceremony. The sermon being dull of Mr. Minnes, and people with great indifferency come to hear him. After church home, where I met Mr. Gregory, who I did then agree with to come to teach my wife to play on the Viall, and he being an able and sober man, I am mightily glad of it. He had dined, therefore went away, and I to dinner, and after dinner by coach to Barkeshire-house, and there did get a very great meeting; the Duke of York being there, and much business done, though not in proportion to the greatness of the business, and my Lord Chancellor sleeping and snoring the greater part of the time. Among other things I declared the state of our credit as to tallys to raise money by, and there was an order for payment of £5,000 to Mr. Gawden, out of which I hope to get something against Christmas. Here we sat late, and here I did hear that there are some troubles like to be in Scotland, there being a discontented party already risen, that have seized on the Governor of Dumfreeze and

[1] According to the Bills of Mortality seven persons died in London of the plague during the week November 20th to 27th: and for some weeks after deaths continued from this cause.

imprisoned him,[1] but the story is yet very uncertain, and therefore I set no great weight on it. I home by Mr. Gawden in his coach, and so with great pleasure to spend the evening at home upon my Lyra Viall, and then to supper and to bed. With mighty peace of mind and a hearty desire that I had but what I have quietly in the country, but, I fear, I do at this day see the best that either I or the rest of our nation will ever see.

21st. Up, with Sir W. Batten to Charing Cross, and thence I to wait on Sir Philip Howard, whom I find dressing himself in his night-gown and turban like a Turke, but one of the finest persons that ever I saw in my life. He had several gentlemen of his owne waiting on him, and one playing finely on the gittar: he discourses as well as ever I heard man, in few words and handsome. He expressed all kindness to Balty, when I told him how sick he is: he says that, before he comes to be mustered again, he must bring a certificate of his swearing the oaths of Allegiance and Supremacy, and having taken the Sacrament according to the rites of the Church of England. This, I perceive, is imposed on all, and he will be ready to do. I pray God he may have his health again to be able to do it. Being mightily satisfied with his civility, I away to Westminster Hall, and there walked with several people,

[1] William Fielding, writing to Sir Phil. Musgrave from Carlisle on November 15th, says: "Major Baxter, who has arrived from Dumfries, reports that this morning a great number of horse and foot came into that town, with drawn swords and pistols, gallopped up to Sir Jas. Turner's lodgings, seized him in his bed, carried him without clothes to the market-place, threatened to cut him to pieces, and seized and put into the Tolbooth all the foot soldiers that were with him; they also secured the minister of Dumfries. Many of the party were lairds and county people from Galloway — 200 horse well mounted, one minister was with them who had swords and pistols, and 200 or 300 foot, some with clubs, others with scythes." On November 17th Rob. Meine wrote to Williamson: "On the 15th 120 fanatics from the Glenkins, Deray, and neighbouring parishes in Dumfriesshire, none worth £10 except two mad fellows, the lairds of Barscob and Corsuck, came to Dumfries early in the morning, seized Sir Jas. Turner, commander of a company of men in Dumfriesshire, and carried him, without violence to others, to a strong house in Maxwell town, Galloway, declaring they sought only revenge against the tyrant who had been severe with them for not keeping to church, and had laid their families waste" ("Calendar of State Papers," 1666-67, pp. 262, 268).

and all the discourse is about some trouble in Scotland I heard of yesterday, but nobody can tell the truth of it. Here was Betty Michell with her mother. I would have carried her home, but her father intends to go with her, so I lost my hopes. And thence I to the Excise Office about some tallies, and then to the Exchange, where I did much business, and so home to dinner, and then to the office, where busy all the afternoon till night, and then home to supper, and after supper an hour reading to my wife and brother something in Chaucer with great pleasure, and so to bed.

22nd. Up, and to the office, where we sat all the morning, and my Lord Bruncker did show me Hollar's new print of the City,[1] with a pretty representation of that part which is burnt, very fine indeed; and tells me that he was yesterday sworn the King's servant, and that the King hath commanded him to go on with his great map of the City,[2] which he was upon before the City was burned, like Gombout of Paris,[3] which I am glad of. At noon home to dinner, where my wife and I fell out, I being displeased with her cutting away a lace handkercher sewed about her neck down to her breasts almost, out of a belief, but without reason, that it is the fashion. Here

[1] "A Map or Ground Plott of the City of London, with the Suburbes thereof, so far as the Lord Mayor's jurisdiction doeth extend; by which is exactly demonstrated the present condition since the last sad accident by fire; the blanke space signifying the burnt part, and where the houses be, those places yet standing. — W. Hollar, f. 1666. Cum Privilegio Regis." — B.

[2] Hollar engraved, in 1675, "A new Map of the Citties of London, Westminster, and y[e] Borough of Southwarke, with their Suburbs; shewing the streets, lanes, alleys, courts, &c., with other remarks, as they are now truely and carefully delineated; and the prospect of London, as it was flourishing before the destruction by fire. Sold by Robert Greene at y[e] Rose and Crown in Budg Row and Robert Morden at y[e] Atlas in Cornhill." A large sheet, $23\frac{1}{4}$ in. by $17\frac{1}{2}$ in. In the Pepysian Library is a "Prospect of London and Westminster, taken at several stations to the southward thereof, by Robert Morden and Phil. Lea," in eight sheets, 1677. This map was the result of a survey by William Morgan.

[3] Gombout's Plan of Paris, on a very large scale, was engraved in 1642. It is of great rarity. A copy, which was in the possession of the Baron Walckenaer, was purchased for a royal personage, at his sale at Paris, in April, 1853, Lot 3028, for more than 1000 francs. — B.

we did give one another the lie too much, but were presently friends, and then I to my office, where very late and did much business, and then home, and there find Mr. Batelier, and did sup and play at cards awhile. But he tells me the newes how the King of France hath, in defiance to the King of England, caused all his footmen to be put into vests,[1] and that the noblemen of France will do the like; which, if true, is the greatest indignity ever done by one Prince to another, and would incite a stone to be revenged; and I hope our King will, if it be so, as he tells me it is:[2] being told by one that come over from Paris with my Lady Fanshaw, who is come over with the dead body of her husband,[3] and that saw it before he come away. This makes me mighty merry, it being an ingenious kind of affront;

[1] It is possible that some tradition of this proceeding of Louis XIV. may have given to Steele the hint for his story of the rival ladies, Brunetta and Phillis, in the "Spectator," No. 80; a subject which has been well treated by Stothard: as also in a clever picture by Mr. A. Solomon, exhibited at the Royal Academy in the year 1853. — B.

[2] Planché throws some doubt on this story in his "Cyclopædia of Costume" (vol. ii., p. 240), and asks the question, "Was Mr. Batelier hoaxing the inquisitive secretary, or was it the idle gossip of the day, as untrustworthy as such gossip is in general?" But the same statement was made by the author of the "Character of a Trimmer," who wrote from actual knowledge of the Court: "About this time a general humour, in opposition to France, had made us throw off their fashion, and put on vests, that we might look more like a distinct people, and not be under the servility of imitation, which ever pays a greater deference to the original than is consistent with the equality all independent nations should pretend to. France did not like this small beginning of ill humours, at least of emulation; and wisely considering, that it is a natural introduction, first to make the world their apes, that they may be afterwards their slaves. It was thought, that one of the instructions Madame [Henrietta, Duchess of Orleans] brought along with her, was to laugh us out of these vests; which she performed so effectually, that in a moment, like so many footmen who had quitted their master's livery, we all took it again, and returned to our old service; so that the very time of doing it gave a very critical advantage to France, since it looked like an evidence of our returning to her interest, as well as to their fashion." — *The Character of a Trimmer* ("Miscellanies by the Marquis of Halifax," 1704, p. 164). Evelyn reports that when the king expressed his intention never to alter this fashion, "divers courtiers and gentlemen gave his Majesty gold by way of wager that he would not persist in this resolution" ("Diary," October 18th, 1666).

[3] Sir Richard Fanshawe. See note, June 29th, 1660.

but yet it makes me angry, to see that the King of England is become so little as to have the affront offered him. So I left my people at cards, and so to my chamber to read, and then to bed. Batelier did bring us some oysters to-night, and some bottles of new French wine of this year, mighty good, but I drank but little. This noon Bagwell's wife was with me at the office, and I did what I would, and at night comes Mrs. Burroughs, and appointed to meet upon the next holyday and go abroad together.

23rd. Up, and with Sir J. Minnes to White Hall, where we and the rest attended the Duke of York, where, among other things, we had a complaint of Sir William Jennings[1] against his lieutenant, Le Neve,[2] one that had been long the Duke's page, and for whom the Duke of York hath great kindness. It was a drunken quarrel, where one was as blameable as the other. It was referred to further examination, but the Duke of York declared, that as he would not favour disobedience, so neither drunkenness, and therein he said very well. Thence with Sir W. Coventry to Westminster Hall, and there parted, he having told me how Sir J. Minnes do disagree from the proposition of resigning his place, and that so the whole matter is again at a stand, at which I am sorry for the King's sake, but glad that Sir W. Pen is again defeated, for I would not have him come to be Comptroller if I could help it, he will be so cruel proud. Here I spoke with Sir G. Downing about our prisoners in Holland, and their being released; which he is concerned in, and most of them are. Then, discoursing of matters of the House of Parliament, he tells me that it is not the fault of the House, but the King's own party, that have hindered the passing of the Bill for money, by their popping in of new projects for raising it: which

[1] Captain of the "Lyon." He was a distinguished sea-officer, and brother of Sir Robert Jennings, of Ripon. He attended James II. after his abdication, and served as a captain in the French navy (see Charnock's "Biographia Navalis," vol. i., p. 106).

[2] Richard Le Neve, lieutenant of the "Lyon." He was made captain of the "Phœnix" in 1671, of the "Plymouth" in 1672, and of the "Edgar" in 1673. He was killed in the engagement with the Dutch on August 11th, 1673, and was buried in Westminster Abbey, where there is a monument to his memory. He was only twenty-seven years of age at the date of his death.

is a strange thing; and mighty confident he is, that what money is raised, will be raised and put into the same form that the last was, to come into the Exchequer; and, for aught I see, I must confess I think it is the best way. Thence down to the Hall, and there walked awhile, and all the talk is about Scotland, what news thence; but there is nothing come since the first report, and so all is given over for nothing. Thence home, and after dinner to my chamber with Creed, who come and dined with me, and he and I to reckon for his salary, and by and by comes in Colonel Atkins, and I did the like with him, and it was Creed's design to bring him only for his own ends, to seem to do him a courtesy, and it is no great matter. The fellow I hate, and so I think all the world else do. Then to talk of my report I am to make of the state of our wants of money to the Lord Treasurer, but our discourse come to little. However, in the evening, to be rid of him, I took coach and saw him to the Temple and there 'light, and he being gone, with all the haste back again and to my chamber late to enter all this day's matters of account, and to draw up my report to my Lord Treasurer, and so to bed. At the Temple I called at Playford's, and there find that his new impression of his ketches[1] are not yet out, the fire having hindered it, but his man tells me that it will be a very fine piece, many things new being added to it.

24th. Up, and to the office, where we sat all the morning. At noon rose and to my closet, and finished my report to my Lord Treasurer of our Tangier wants, and then with Sir J. Minnes by coach to Stepney to the Trinity House,[2] where it is kept again now since the burning of their other house in London. And here a great many met at Sir Thomas Allen's feast, of his being made an Elder Brother; but he is sick, and so could not be there. Here

[1] John Hilton's "Catch that catch can, or a Choice Collection of Catches, Rounds and Canons for 3 or 4 voyces," was first published by Playford in 1651 or 1652. The book was republished "with large additions by John Playford" in 1658. The edition referred to in the text was published in 1667 with a second title of "The Musical Companion." The book was republished in 1672–73.

[2] Sir Thomas Spert, Comptroller of the Navy in the reign of Henry VIII., and founder of the Trinity House, was buried in the parish church of Stepney.

was much good company, and very merry; but the discourse of Scotland, it seems, is confirmed, and that they are 4,000 of them in armes, and do declare for King and Covenant, which is very ill news.[1] I pray God deliver us from the ill consequences we may justly fear from it. Here was a good venison pasty or two and other good victuals; but towards the latter end of the dinner I rose, and without taking leave went away from the table, and got Sir J. Minnes' coach and away home, and thence with my report to my Lord Treasurer's, where I did deliver it to Sir Philip Warwicke for my Lord, who was busy, my report for him to consider against to-morrow's council. Sir Philip Warwicke, I find, is full of trouble in his mind to see how things go, and what our wants are; and so I have no delight to trouble him with discourse, though I honour the man with all my heart, and I think him to be a very able and right-honest man. So away home again, and there to my office to write my letters very late, and then home to supper, and then to read the late printed discourse of witches by a member of Gresham College,[2] and then to bed; the discourse being well writ, in good stile, but methinks not very convincing. This day Mr. Martin is come to tell me his wife is brought to bed of a girle, and I promised to christen it next Sunday.

[1] See November 20th for note respecting the commencement of the troubles at Dumfries. On November 22nd Ro. Meine wrote from Edinburgh to Williamson: "A proclamation is issued ordering all to submit within twenty-four hours, on promise of pardon, or then to be declared rebels, with all their abettors. An oath is to be tendered to all the county pledging them to aid in quelling this or any other insurrection; 800 are said to be near Glasgow, but they call every 20, 120. . . . They profess to fight for King and Covenant; their leader is James Wallace of Athens, whom they call the good man. Most of their captains are deposed ministers" ("Calendar of State Papers," 1666-67, p. 280).

[2] The Rev. Joseph Glanvill (1636-1680) was elected a Fellow of the Royal Society on the 14th December, 1664. He published in 1666 "Philosophical Considerations touching Witches and Witchcraft," and most part of the impression was destroyed in the Great Fire. The book was reissued in 1667, and a fourth edition appeared in 1668 under the title of "A Blow at Modern Sadducism." It was reprinted in 1681 as "Sadducismus Triumphatus." One of the appendixes is an "Account of the famed disturbance by the drummer at the house of Mr. Mompesson."

25th (Lord's day). Up, and with Sir J. Minnes by coach to White Hall, and there coming late, I to rights to the chapel, where in my usual place I heard one of the King's chaplains, one Mr. Floyd, preach. He was out two or three times in his prayer, and as many in his sermon, but yet he made a most excellent good sermon, of our duty to imitate the lives and practice of Christ and the saints departed, and did it very handsomely and excellent stile; but was a little overlarge in magnifying the graces of the nobility and prelates, that we have seen in our memorys in the world, whom God hath taken from us. At the end of the sermon an excellent anthem; but it was a pleasant thing, an idle companion in our pew, a prating, bold counsellor that hath been heretofore at the Navy Office, and noted for a great eater and drinker, not for quantity, but of the best, his name Tom Bales, said, "I know a fitter anthem for this sermon," speaking only of our duty of following the saints, and I know not what. "Cooke should have sung, 'Come, follow, follow me.'"[1] After sermon up into the gallery, and then to Sir G. Carteret's to dinner; where much company. Among others, Mr. Carteret and my Lady Jemimah, and here was also Mr. [John] Ashburnham, the great man, who is a pleasant man, and that hath seen much of the world, and more of the Court. After dinner Sir G. Carteret and I to another room, and he tells me more and more of our want of money and in how ill condition we are likely to be soon in, and that he believes we shall not have a fleete at sea the next year. So do I believe; but he seems to speak it as a thing expected by the King and as if their matters were laid accordingly. Thence into the Court and there delivered copies of my report to my Lord Treasurer, to the Duke of York, Sir W. Coventry, and others, and attended there till the Council met, and then was called in, and I read my letter. My Lord Treasurer declared that the King had nothing to give till the Parliament did give him some money. So the

[1] This is the first line of "The Fairy Queen," a song first printed in a book entitled "A Description of the King and Queen of the Fayries," 1635. It is included in Percy's "Reliques," Series III., book ii., No. 25, and with the air is printed in the "Musical Miscellany," London, 1729, vol. ii., p. 22.

King did of himself bid me to declare to all that would take our tallys for payment, that he should, soon as the Parliament's money do come in, take back their tallys, and give them money: which I giving him occasion to repeat to me, it coming from him against the *gré*,[1] I perceive, of my Lord Treasurer, I was content therewith, and went out, and glad that I have got so much. Here staid till the Council rose, walking in the gallery. All the talke being of Scotland, where the highest report, I perceive, runs but upon three or four hundred in armes; but they believe that it will grow more, and do seem to apprehend it much, as if the King of France had a hand in it. My Lord Lauderdale do make nothing of it, it seems, and people do censure him for it, he from the beginning saying that there was nothing in it, whereas it do appear to be a pure rebellion; but no persons of quality being in it, all do hope that it cannot amount to much. Here I saw Mrs. Stewart this afternoon, methought the beautifullest creature that ever I saw in my life, more than ever I thought her so, often as I have seen her; and I begin to think do exceed my Lady Castlemayne, at least now. This being St. Catherine's day, the Queene was at masse by seven o'clock this morning; and Mr. Ashburnham do say that he never saw any one have so much zeale in his life as she hath: and, the question being asked by my Lady Carteret, much beyond the bigotry that ever the old Queen-mother had, I spoke with Mr. May,[2] who tells me that the design of building the City do go on apace,[3] and by his description it will be mighty handsome, and to the satisfaction of the people; but I pray God it come not out too late. The Council up, after speaking with Sir W. Coventry a little, away home with Captain Cocke in his coach, discourse about the forming of his contract he made with us lately for hempe, and so home, where we parted, and I find my

[1] Apparently a translation of the French *contre le gré*, and presumably an expression in common use. "Against the grain" is generally supposed to have its origin in the use of a plane against the grain of the wood.

[2] Hugh May.

[3] The first brick laid after the fire was in Fleet Street, at the house of a plumber, to cast his lead in, only one room (Rugge's "Diurnal"). — B.

uncle Wight and Mrs. Wight and Woolly, who staid and supped, and mighty merry together and then I to my chamber to even my Journal, and then to bed. I will remember that Mr. Ashburnham to-day at dinner told how the rich fortune Mrs. Mallett reports of her servants;[1] that my Lord Herbert[2] would have had her; my Lord Hinchingbroke was indifferent to have her;[3] my Lord John Butler[4] might not have her; my Lord of Rochester would have forced her;[5] and Sir —— Popham,[6] who nevertheless is likely to have her, would kiss her breach to have her.

26th. Up, and to my chamber to do some business. Then to speak with several people, among others with Mrs. Burroughs, whom I appointed to meet me at the New Exchange in the afternoon. I by water to Westminster,

[1] Elizabeth, daughter of John Malet of Enmore, co. Somerset, and her lovers. She died July, 1681, a year after her husband, Lord Rochester.

[2] William, Lord Herbert, succeeded his father as sixth Earl of Pembroke, 1669. Died, unmarried, 1674. — B.

[3] They had quarrelled (see August 26th, *ante*). She, perhaps, was piqued at Lord Hinchingbroke's refusal "to compass the thing without consent of friends" (see February 25th, *ante*), whence her expression, "indifferent" to have her. It is worthy of remark that their children intermarried; Lord Hinchingbroke's son married Lady Rochester's daughter. — B.

[4] Seventh son of the Duke of Ormond, created in 1676 Baron of Aghrim, Viscount of Clonmore, and Earl of Gowran. Died 1677, s.p. (see February 4th, *post*). — B.

[5] Of the lady thus sought after, whom Pepys calls "a beauty" as well as a fortune, and who shortly afterwards, about the 4th February, 1667, became the wife of the Earl of Rochester, then not twenty years old, no authentic portrait is known to exist. When Mr. Miller, of Albemarle Street, in 1811, proposed to publish an edition of the "Mémoires de Grammont," he sent an artist to Windsor to copy there the portraits which he could find of those who figure in that work. In the list given to him for this purpose was the name of Lady Rochester. Not finding amongst the "Beauties," or elsewhere, any genuine portrait of her, but seeing that by Hamilton she is absurdly styled "une triste héritière," the artist made a drawing from some unknown portrait at Windsor of a lady of a sorrowful countenance, and palmed it off upon the bookseller. In the edition of "Grammont" it is not actually called Lady Rochester, but "La Triste Héritière." A similar falsification had been practised in Edward's edition of 1793, but a different portrait had been copied. It is needless, almost, to remark how ill applied is Hamilton's epithet. — B.

[6] Probably Sir Francis Popham, K.B. — B.

and there to enquire after my tallies, which I shall get this week. Thence to the Swan, having sent for some burnt claret, and there by and by comes Doll Lane, and she and I sat and drank and talked a great while, among other things about her sister's being brought to bed, and I to be godfather to the girle. I did tumble Doll, and do almost what I would with her, and so parted, and I took coach, and to the New Exchange, buying a neat's tongue by the way, thinking to eat it out of town, but there I find Burroughs in company of an old woman, an aunt of hers, whom she could not leave for half an hour. So after buying a few baubles to while away time, I down to Westminster, and there into the House of Parliament, where, at a great Committee, I did hear, as long as I would, the great case against my Lord Mordaunt,[1] for some arbitrary proceedings of his against one Taylor, whom he imprisoned, and did all the violence to imaginable, only to get him

[1] John Mordaunt, younger son to the first, and brother to the second Earl of Peterborough, having incurred considerable personal risk in endeavouring to promote the king's restoration, was, in 1659, created Baron Mordaunt of Reigate, and Viscount Mordaunt of Avalon. He was brought to trial and acquitted but by one voice just before Cromwell's death ("Quarterly Review," vol. xix., p. 31). He was soon afterwards made K.B., Lord-Lieutenant of Surrey, and Constable of Windsor Castle; which offices he held till his death in 1675. In January, 1666-67, Lord Mordaunt was impeached by the House of Commons for forcibly ejecting William Tayleur and his family from the apartments which they occupied in Windsor Castle, where Tayleur held some appointment, and imprisoning him, for having presumed to offer himself as a candidate for the borough of Windsor. Lord M. was also accused of improper conduct towards Tayleur's daughter. He, however, denied all these charges in his place in the House of Lords, and put in an answer to the articles of impeachment, for hearing which a day was absolutely fixed; but the parliament being shortly afterwards prorogued, the inquiry seems to have been entirely abandoned, notwithstanding the vehemence with which the House of Commons had taken the matter up. Perhaps the king interfered in Lord Mordaunt's behalf; because Andrew Marvell, in his "Instructions to a Painter," after saying

> "Now Mordaunt may within his castle tower
> Imprison parents and the child deflower,"

observes,

> "Each does the other blame, and all distrust,
> But Mordaunt, *new obliged*, would sure be just." — B.

to give way to his abusing his daughter. Here was Mr. Sawyer,[1] my old chamber-fellow, a counsel against my Lord; and I am glad to see him in so good play. Here I met, before the committee sat, with my cozen Roger Pepys, the first time I have spoke with him this parliament. He hath promised to come, and bring Madam Turner with him, who is come to towne to see the City, but hath lost all her goods of all kinds in Salisbury Court, Sir William Turner[2] having not endeavoured, in her absence, to save one penny, to dine with me on Friday next, of which I am glad. Roger bids me to help him to some good rich widow; for he is resolved to go, and retire wholly, into the country; for, he says, he is confident we shall be all ruined very speedily, by what he sees in the State, and I am much in his mind. Having staid as long as I thought fit for meeting of Burroughs, I away and to the 'Change again, but there I do not find her now, I having staid too long at the House, and therefore very hungry, having eat nothing to-day. Home, and there to eat presently, and then to the office a little, and to Sir W. Batten, where Sir J. Minnes and Captain Cocke was; but no newes from the North at all to-day; and the newes-book makes the business nothing, but that they are all dispersed. I pray God it may prove so. So home, and, after a little, to my chamber to bed.

27th. Up, and to the office, where we sat all the morning, and here I had a letter from Mr. Brisband on another occasion, which, by the by, intimates my Lord Hinchingbroke's intention to come and dine with me to-morrow. This put me into a great surprise, and therefore endeavoured all I could to hasten over our business at the office, and so home at noon and to dinner, and then away by coach, it being a very foul day, to White Hall, and there at Sir G. Carteret's find my Lord Hinchingbroke, who promises to dine with me to-morrow, and bring Mr. Car-

1 Afterwards Sir Robert Sawyer, Attorney-General from 1681 to 1687. Died 1692. He had been admitted a Pensioner at Magdalene College, Cambridge, June, 1648. He was turned out of office by James II. on account of his refusal to confirm Obadiah Walker in his headship of University College, Oxford, after he had turned Roman Catholic (see Reresby's "Memoirs").

2 Sir William Turner, Lord Mayor, 1668–69, was father of Serjeant John Turner, Mrs. Turner's husband (see December 11th, *post*).

teret along with him. Here I staid a little while talking with him and the ladies, and then away to my Lord Crew's, and then did by the by make a visit to my Lord Crew, and had some good discourse with him, he doubting that all will break in pieces in the kingdom; and that the taxes now coming out, which will tax the same man in three or four several capacities, as for lands, office, profession, and money at interest, will be the hardest that ever come out; and do think that we owe it, and the lateness of its being given, wholly to the unpreparedness of the King's own party, to make their demand and choice; for they have obstructed the giving it by land-tax, which had been done long since. Having ended my visit, I spoke to Sir Thomas Crew, to invite him and his brother John to dinner to-morrow, at my house, to meet Lord Hinchingbroke; and so homewards, calling at the cook's, who is to dress it, to bespeak him, and then home, and there set things in order for a very fine dinner, and then to the office, where late very busy and to good purpose as to dispatch of business, and then home. To bed, my people sitting up to get things in order against to-morrow. This evening was brought me what Griffin had, as he says, taken this evening off of the table in the office, a letter sealed and directed to the Principal Officers and Commissioners of the Navy. It is a serious and just libel against our disorder in paying of our money, making ten times more people wait than we have money for, and complaining by name of Sir W. Batten for paying away great sums to particular people, which is true. I was sorry to see this way of reproach taken against us, but more sorry that there is true ground for it.

28th. Up, and with Sir W. Pen to White Hall (setting his lady and daughter down by the way at a mercer's in the Strand, where they are going to lay out some money), where, though it blows hard and rains hard, yet the Duke of York is gone a-hunting. We therefore lost our labour, and so back again, and by hackney coach to secure places to get things ready against dinner, and then home, and did the like there, and to my great satisfaction: and at noon comes my Lord Hinchingbroke, Sir Thomas Crew, Mr. John Crew, Mr. Carteret, and Brisband. I had six noble dishes for them, dressed by a man-cook, and commended, as indeed they deserved, for exceeding well done. We eat with great pleasure, and I enjoyed myself in it with reflections upon the pleasures which I at best can expect, yet not to exceed this; eating in silver plates, and all things mighty rich and handsome about me. A great deal of fine discourse, sitting almost till dark at dinner, and then broke up with great pleasure, especially to myself; and they away, only Mr. Carteret and I to Gresham College, where they meet now weekly again, and here they had good discourse how this late experiment of the dog, which is in perfect good health, may be improved for good uses to men,[1] and other pretty things, and then broke up. Here was Mr. Henry Howard,[2] that will hereafter be Duke of Norfolke, who is admitted this day into the Society, and being a very proud man, and one that values himself upon his family, writes his name, as he do every where, Henry Howard of Norfolke. Thence home and there comes my Lady Pen, Pegg, and Mrs. Turner, and played at cards and supped with us, and were pretty merry, and Pegg with me in my closet a good while, and did suffer me a la baiser mouche et toucher ses cosas upon her breast, wherein I had great pleasure, and so spent the evening and then broke up, and I to bed, my mind mightily pleased with the day's entertainment.

29th. Up, and to the office, where busy all the morning. At noon home to dinner, where I find Balty come out to see us, but looks like death, and I do fear he is in a con-

[1] See note, November 14th, *ante*.

[2] Henry Howard of Norfolk (1628–1684), second son of Henry, Earl of Arundel, was a considerable benefactor to the Royal Society, largely through the influence of John Evelyn. At the meeting of the society on November 27th, "It was ordered that Mr. Oldenburg attend Mr. Henry Howard of Norfolk at Arundel House, and acquaint him with the sense, which the Royal Society had of his great civilities and respects to them, which they intended also to acknowledge publicly when he should honour them with a visit at a meeting of the society." On the following day, November 28th, "Mr. Henry Howard of Norfolk was elected and admitted, who also received the public thanks of the society for his respects to them" (Birch's "History of the Royal Society," vol. ii., p. 128). He was created Baron Howard of Castle Rising in 1669, and advanced to the earldom of Norwich in 1672. He succeeded his brother Thomas as sixth duke of Norfolk in 1677.

sumption; he has not been abroad many weeks before, and hath now a well day, and a fit day of the headake in extraordinary torture. After dinner left him and his wife, they having their mother hard by and my wife, and I a wet afternoon to White Hall to have seen my Lady Carteret and Jemimah, but as God would have it they were abroad, and I was well contented at it. So my wife and I to Westminster Hall, where I left her a little, and to the Exchequer, and then presently home again, calling at our man-cooke's for his help to-morrow, but he could not come. So I home to the office, my people all busy to get a good dinner tomorrow again. I late at the office, and all the newes I hear I put into a letter this night to my Lord Bruncker at Chatham, thus: —

"I doubt not of your lordship's hearing of Sir Thomas Clifford's succeeding Sir H. Pollard[1] in the Comptrollership of the King's house; but perhaps our ill, but confirmed, tidings from the Barbadoes may not [have reached you] yet, it coming but yesterday; viz., that about eleven ships, whereof two of the King's, the Hope and Coventry, going thence with men to attack St. Christopher's, were seized by a violent hurricane, and all sunk — two only of thirteen escaping, and those with loss of masts, &c. My Lord Willoughby[2] himself is involved in the disaster, and I think two ships thrown upon an island of the French, and so all the men, to 500, become their prisoners. 'Tis said, too, that eighteen Dutch men-of-war are passed the Channell, in order to meet with our Smyrna ships; and some, I hear, do fright us with the King of Sweden's seiz-

[1] Sir Hugh Pollard, Bart., M.P. for Devonshire, died November 27th, 1666. The "order for a warrant to the Duke of Ormond, Lord Steward, or in his absence to Lord Fitzharding and the clerks of the Greencloth, to swear in Sir Thomas Clifford as Comptroller of the Household in the room of Sir H. Pollard," is dated November 28th ("Calendar of State Papers," 1666–67, p. 298).

[2] Francis Willoughby, fourth Lord Willoughby of Parham, who was drowned. A letter from D. Grosse to Williamson, dated from Plymouth, November 27th, contains the following information: "A Barbadoes ship reports that Lord Willoughby embarked thence last July with 5,000 men and 11 ships to retake St. Christopher's, but ten ships were cast away in a violent storm; 400 or 500 men got ashore at Santa Tour, and are detained prisoners by the French" ("Calendar of State Papers," 1666–67, p. 292).

ing our mast-ships at Gottenburgh. But we have too much ill newes true, to afflict ourselves with what is uncertain. That which I hear from Scotland is, the Duke of York's saying, yesterday, that he is confident the Lieutenant-Generall there hath driven them into a pound, somewhere towards the mountains."

Having writ my letter, I home to supper and to bed, the world being mightily troubled at the ill news from Barbadoes, and the consequence of the Scotch business, as little as we do make of it. And to shew how mad we are at home, here, and unfit for any troubles: my Lord St. John did, a day or two since, openly pull a gentleman in Westminster Hall by the nose, one Sir Andrew Henly,[1] while the Judges were upon their benches, and the other gentleman did give him a rap over the pate with his cane, of which fray the Judges, they say, will make a great matter: men are only sorry the gentleman did proceed to return a blow; for, otherwise, my Lord would have been soundly fined for the affront, and may be yet for his affront to the Judges.

30th. Up, and with Sir W. Batten to White Hall, and there we did attend the Duke of York, and had much business with him; and pretty to see, it being St. Andrew's day, how some few did wear St. Andrew's crosse; but most did make a mockery at it, and the House of Parliament, contrary to practice, did sit also: people having no mind to observe the Scotch saints' days till they hear better newes from Scotland. Thence to Westminster Hall and the Abbey, thinking as I had appointed to have met Mrs. Burroughs there, but not meeting her I home, and just overtook my cozen Roger Pepys, Mrs. Turner, Dicke, and Joyce Norton, coming by invitation to dine with me. These ladies I have not seen since before the plague. Mrs. Turner is come to towne to look after her things in her house, but all is lost. She is quite weary of the country, but cannot get her husband to let her live here any more, which troubles her mightily. She was mighty angry with me, that in all this time I never writ to her, which I do think and take to myself as a fault, and which I have promised to mend. Here I had a noble and costly dinner

[1] Of Hartshill, Hants; and of Henley, Somersetshire. He was created a baronet in June, 1660, and died about 1675.—B.

for them, dressed by a man-cooke, as that the other day was, and pretty merry we were, as I could be with this company and so great a charge. We sat long, and after much talk of the plenty of her country in fish, but in nothing also that is pleasing, we broke up with great kindness, and when it begun to be dark we parted, they in one coach home, and I in another to Westminster Hall, where by appointment Mrs. Burroughs and I were to meet, but did not after I had spent the whole evening there. Only I did go drink at the Swan, and there did meet with Sarah, who is now newly married, and there I did lay the beginnings of a future amour con elle. . . . Thence it being late away; called at Mrs. Burroughs' mother's door, and she come out to me, and I did hazer whatever I would. . . . and then parted, and home, and after some playing at cards with my wife, we to supper and to bed.

December 1st. Up, and to the office, where we sat all the morning. At home to dinner, and then abroad walking to the Old Swan, and in my way I did see a cellar in Tower Streete in a very fresh fire, the late great winds having blown it up.[1] It seemed to be only of log-wood, that hath kept the fire all this while in it. Going further, I met my late Lord Mayor Bludworth, under whom the City was burned, and went with him by water to White Hall. But, Lord! the silly talk that this fellow had, only how ready he would be to part with all his estate in these difficult times to advance the King's service, and complaining that now, as every body did lately in the fire, every body endeavours to save himself, and let the whole perish: but a very weak man he seems to be. I left him at White Hall, he giving *6d.* towards the boat, and I to Westminster Hall, where I was again defeated in my expectation of Burroughs. However, I was not much sorry for it, but by coach home, in the evening, calling at Faythorne's, buying three of my Lady Castlemayne's heads, printed this day,[2] which indeed is, as to the head,

[1] The fire continued burning in some cellars of the ruins of the city for four months, though it rained in the month of October ten days without ceasing (Rugge's "Diurnal"). — B.

[2] See November 7th. A fine impression of this now very rare print was purchased for the Duke of Buckingham, at Bindley's

I think, a very fine picture, and like her. I did this afternoon get Mrs. Michell to let me only have a sight of a pamphlet lately printed, but suppressed and much called after, called "The Catholique's Apology";[1] lamenting the severity of the Parliament against them, and comparing it with the lenity of other princes to Protestants; giving old and late instances of their loyalty to their princes, whatever is objected against them; and excusing their disquiets in Queen Elizabeth's time, for that it was impossible for them to think her a lawfull Queen, if Queen Mary, who had been owned as such, were so; one being the daughter of the true, and the other of a false wife: and that of the Gunpowder Treason, by saying that it was only the practice of some of us, if not the King, to trepan some of their religion into it, it never being defended by the generality of their Church, nor indeed known by them; and ends with a large Catalogue, in red letters, of the Catholiques which have lost their lives in the quarrel of the late King and this. The thing is very well writ indeed. So home to my letters, and then to my supper and to bed.

2nd (Lord's day). Up, and to church, and after church home to dinner, where I met Betty Michell and her husband, very merry at dinner, and after dinner, having borrowed Sir W. Pen's coach, we to Westminster, they two and my wife and I to Mr. Martin's, where find the company almost all come to the christening of Mrs. Martin's child, a girl. A great deal of good plain company. After sitting long, till the church was done, the Parson comes, and then we to christen the child. I was God-

sale, in 1819, for £79; and resold at the Stowe sale, in 1849, for £33.—B.

[1] "The Catholique Apology" was written by Roger Palmer, Earl of Castlemaine. In 1667 Dr. William Lloyd (afterwards successively Dean of Bangor, Bishop of St. Asaph, Lichfield and Coventry, and Worcester) published an answer, entitled, "The late Apology in behalf of the Papists reprinted and answered in behalf of the Royalists;" a fourth edition of which appeared in 1675. Lord Castlemaine and Robert Pugh, a secular priest, wrote "A Reply to the Answer of the Catholique Apology," which was published in 1668. A third edition of the "Catholique Apology with a Reply to the Answer" was published in 1674. Lord Castlemaine's pamphlets were seized by order of the House of Commons.

father, and Mrs. Holder (her husband, a good man, I know well), and a pretty lady, that waits, it seems, on my Lady Bath,[1] at White Hall, her name, Mrs. Noble, were Godmothers. After the christening comes in the wine and the sweetmeats, and then to prate and tattle, and then very good company they were, and I among them. Here was old Mrs. Michell and Howlett, and several married women of the Hall, whom I knew mayds. Here was also Mrs. Burroughs and Mrs. Bales, the young widow, whom I led home, and having staid till the moon was up, I took my pretty gossip[2] to White Hall with us, and I saw her in her lodging, and then my owne company again took coach, and no sooner in the coach but something broke, that we were fain there to stay till a smith could be fetched, which was above an hour, and then it costing me *6s.* to mend. Away round by the wall and Cow Lane,[3] for fear it should break again, and in pain about the coach all the way. But to ease myself therein Betty Michell did sit at the same end with me. . . . Being very much pleased with this, we at last come home, and so to supper, and then sent them by boat home, and we to bed. When I come home I went to Sir W. Batten's, and there I hear more ill newes still: that all our New England fleete, which went out lately, are put back a third time by foul weather, and dispersed, some to one port and some to another; and their convoys also to Plymouth; and whether any of them be lost or not, we do not know. This, added to all the rest, do lay us flat in our hopes and courages, every body prophesying destruction to the nation.

3rd. Up, and, among a great many people that come to speak with me, one was my Lord Peterborough's gentleman, who comes to me to dun me to get some money advanced for my Lord; and I demanding what newes, he tells me that at Court they begin to fear the business of Scotland more and more, and that the Duke of York

[1] Lady Bath was Rachel, daughter of Francis, Earl of Westmoreland, widow of Henry Bourchier, Earl of Bath. She afterwards married Lionel Cranfield, third Earl of Middlesex. — B.

[2] Mrs. Noble, the godmother.

[3] Cow Lane, West Smithfield (now named King Street), was famous for its coachmakers.

intends to go to the North to raise an army, and that the King would have some of the nobility and others to go and assist; but they were so served the last year, among others his Lord, in raising forces at their own charge, for fear of the French invading us, that they will not be got out now, without money advanced to them by the King, and this is like to be the King's case for certain, if ever he comes to have need of any army. He and others gone, I by water to Westminster, and there to the Exchequer, and put my tallys in the way of doing for the last quarter. But my not following it the last week has occasioned the clerks some trouble, which I am sorry for, and they are mad at. Thence at noon home, and there find Kate Joyce, who dined with me. Her husband and she are weary of their new life of being an Innkeeper, and will leave it, and would fain get some office; but I know none the foole is fit for, but would be glad to help them, if I could, though they have enough to live on, God be thanked! though their loss hath been to the value of £3,000. W. Joyce now has all the trade, she says, the trade being come to that end of the towne. She dined with me, my wife being ill of her months in bed. I left her with my wife, and away myself to Westminster Hall by appointment and there found out Burroughs, and I took her by coach as far as the Lord Treasurer's and called at the cake house by Hales's, and there in the coach eat and drank and then carried her home. . . . So having set her down in the palace I to the Swan, and there did the first time baiser the little sister of Sarah that is come into her place, and so away by coach home, where to my vyall and supper and then to bed, being weary of the following of my pleasure and sorry for my omitting (though with a true salvo to my vowes) the stating my last month's accounts in time, as I should, but resolve to settle, and clear all my business before me this month, that I may begin afresh the next yeare, and enjoy some little pleasures freely at Christmasse. So to bed, and with more cheerfulness than I have done a good while, to hear that for certain the Scott rebells are all routed; they having been so bold as to come within three miles of Edinburgh, and there given two or three repulses to the King's forces, but at last were mastered. Three or four hundred killed or taken, among which their leader, one Wallis, and seven ministers, they having all taken the Covenant a few days before, and sworn to live and die in it, as they did; and so all is likely to be there quiet again. There is also the very good newes come of four New-England ships come home safe to Falmouth with masts for the King; which is a blessing mighty unexpected, and without which, if for nothing else, we must have failed the next year. But God be praised for thus much good fortune, and send us the continuance of his favour in other things! So to bed.

4th. Up, and to the office, where we sat all the morning. At noon dined at home. After dinner presently to my office, and there late and then home to even my Journall and accounts, and then to supper much eased in mind, and last night's good news, which is more and more confirmed with particulars to very good purpose, and so to bed.

5th. Up, and by water to White Hall, where we did much business before the Duke of York, which being done, I away home by water again, and there to my office till noon busy. At noon home, and Goodgroome[1] dined with us, who teaches my wife to sing. After dinner I did give him my song, "Beauty retire," which he has often desired of me, and without flattery I think is a very good song. He gone, I to the office, and there late, very busy doing much business, and then home to supper and talk, and then scold with my wife for not reckoning well the times that her musique master hath been with her, but setting down more than I am sure, and did convince her, they had been with her, and in an ill humour of anger with her to bed.

6th. Up, but very good friends with her before I rose, and so to the office, where we sat all the forenoon, and then home to dinner, where Harman dined with us, and great sport to hear him tell how Will Joyce grows rich by the custom of the City coming to his end of the towne, and how he rants over his brother and sister for their keeping

[1] John Goodgroome, musical composer, was one of the king's twenty-four fiddlers in 1674 (see list in North's "Memoires of Musick," ed. Rimbault, 1846, p. 99, note). He was probably a relation of Theodore Goodgroome, the singing-master referred to at an earlier date (see *ante*, June 25th, 1661).

an Inne, and goes thither and tears like a prince, calling him hosteller and his sister hostess. Then after dinner, my wife and brother, in another habit,[1] go out to see a play; but I am not to take notice that I know of my brother's going. So I to the office, where very busy till late at night, and then home. My wife not pleased with the play, but thinks that is it because she is grown more critical than she used to be, but my brother she says is mighty taken with it. So to supper and to bed. This day, in the Gazette, is the whole story of defeating the Scotch rebells, and of the creation of the Duke of Cambridge, Knight of the Garter.[2]

7th. Up, and by water to the Exchequer, where I got my tallys finished for the last quarter for Tangier, and having paid all my fees I to the Swan, whither I sent for some oysters, and thither comes Mr. Falconbridge and Spicer and many more clerks, and there we eat and drank, and a great deal of their sorry discourse, and so parted, and I by coach home, meeting Balty in the streete about Charing Crosse walking, which I am glad to see and spoke to him about his mustering business, I being now to give an account how the several muster-masters have behaved themselves, and so home to dinner, where finding the cloth laid and much crumpled but clean, I grew angry and flung the trenchers about the room, and in a mighty heat I was: so a clean cloth was laid, and my poor wife very patient, and so to dinner, and in comes Mrs. Barbara Sheldon, now Mrs. Wood, and dined with us, she mighty fine, and lives, I perceive, mighty happily, which I am glad [of] for her sake, but hate her husband for a block-head in his choice. So away after dinner, leaving my wife and her, and by water to the Strand, and so to the King's playhouse, where two acts were almost done when I come in; and there I sat with my cloak about my face, and saw the remainder of "The Mayd's Tragedy;" a

[1] *i.e.* without his canonicals. — B.

[2] James, Earl and Duke of Cambridge, second son of the Duke of York, and one of the five boys who all died infants. He was given the title which his elder brother Charles had previously held. At the time when he was created K.G. he was only three years and five months old. He died seven months afterwards (June 20th, 1667).

good play, and well acted, especially by the younger Marshall, who is become a pretty good actor, and is the first play I have seen in either of the houses since before the great plague, they having acted now about fourteen days publickly. But I was in mighty pain lest I should be seen by any body to be at a play. Soon as done I home, and then to my office awhile, and then home and spent the night evening my Tangier accounts, much to my satisfaction, and then to supper, and mighty good friends with my poor wife, and so to bed.

8th. Up, and to the office, where we sat all the morning, and at noon home to dinner, and there find Mr. Pierce and his wife and Betty, a pretty girle, who in discourse at table told me the great Proviso passed the House of Parliament yesterday; which makes the King and Court mad, the King having given order to my Lord Chamberlain to send to the playhouses and bawdy houses, to bid all the Parliament-men that were there to go to the Parliament presently. This is true, it seems; but it was carried against the Court by thirty or forty voices. It is a Proviso to the Poll Bill, that there shall be a Committee of nine persons that shall have the inspection upon oath, and power of giving others, of all the accounts of the money given and spent for this warr. This hath a most sad face, and will breed very ill blood. He tells me, brought in by Sir Robert Howard,[1] who is one of the King's servants, at least hath a great office, and hath got, they say, £20,000 since the King come in. Mr. Pierce did also tell me as a great truth, as being told it by Mr. Cowly,[2] who was by, and heard it,

[1] Sixth son of Thomas Howard, first Earl of Berkshire, educated at Magdalene College, Cambridge, born January, 1625–26. During the Civil Wars he adhered to Charles I., and suffered with his family. Knighted at the Restoration, and chosen M.P. for Stockbridge, and afterwards for Castle Rising. He was Auditor of the Exchequer, and considered to be a creature of Charles II., who employed him in cajoling the parliament for money. He was ridiculed by Shadwell as Sir Positive At-All in the "Sullen Lovers." "Four New Plays," by Sir R. Howard, was published in 1665, and "Five New Plays" in 1692. His "Dramatic Works" were published in 1722. He died September 3rd, 1698.

[2] Abraham Cowley, the poet, who died July 28th, 1667, and was buried in Westminster Abbey, August 3rd.

that Tom Killigrew should publiquely tell the King that his matters were coming into a very ill state; but that yet there was a way to help all, which is, says he, "There is a good, honest, able man, that I could name, that if your Majesty would employ, and command to see all things well executed, all things would soon be mended; and this is one Charles Stuart, who now spends his time in employing his lips . . . about the Court, and hath no other employment; but if you would give him this employment, he were the fittest man in the world to perform it." This, he says, is most true; but the King do not profit by any of this, but lays all aside, and remembers nothing, but to his pleasures again; which is a sorrowful consideration. Very good company we were at dinner, and merry, and after dinner, he being gone about business, my wife and I and Mrs. Pierce and Betty and Balty, who come to see us to-day very sick, and went home not well, together out, and our coach broke the wheel off upon Ludgate Hill. So we were fain to part ourselves and get room in other people's coaches, and Mrs. Pierce and I in one, and I carried her home and set her down, and myself to the King's playhouse, which troubles me since, and hath cost me a forfeit of 10*s.*, which I have paid, and there did see a good part of "The English Monsieur,"[1] which is a mighty pretty play, very witty and pleasant. And the women do very well; but, above all, little Nelly,[2] that I am mightily pleased with the play, and much with the House, more than ever I expected, the women doing better than ever I expected, and very fine women. Here I was in pain to be seen, and hid myself; but, as God would have it, Sir John Chichly[3] come, and sat just by me. Thence to Mrs. Pierce's, and there took up my wife and away home, and to the office and Sir W. Batten's, of whom I hear that this Proviso in Parliament is mightily ill taken

[1] A comedy by the Hon. James Howard, son of the Earl of Berkshire, printed in 4to., 1674.

[2] Nell Gwyn played Lady Wealthy, a rich widow. Her first appearance on the stage is supposed to have taken place in 1665 in the character of Cydaria, in Dryden's "Indian Emperor."

[3] Captain (afterwards Sir John) Chicheley commanded the "Antelope," of fifty guns, in the Duke of York's squadron in the victory of the 3rd of June, 1665 (Charnock's "Biographia Navalis," vol. i., p. 84).

by all the Court party as a mortal blow, and that, that strikes deep into the King's prerogative, which troubles me mightily. Home, and set some papers right in my chamber, and then to supper and to bed, we being in much fear of ill news of our colliers. A fleete of two hundred sail, and fourteen Dutch men-of-war between them and us: and they coming home with small convoy; and the City in great want, coals being at £3 3*s.* per chaldron, as I am told. I saw smoke in the ruines this very day.

9th (Lord's day). Up, not to church, but to my chamber, and there begun to enter into this book my journall of September, which in the fire-time I could not enter here, but in loose papers. At noon dined, and then to my chamber all the afternoon and night, looking over and tearing and burning all the unnecessary letters, which I have had upon my file for four or five years backward, which I intend to do quite through all my papers, that I may have nothing by me but what is worth keeping, and fit to be seen, if I should miscarry. At this work till midnight, and then to supper and to bed.

10th. Up, and at my office all the morning, and several people with me, Sir W. Warren, who I do every day more and more admire for a miracle of cunning and forecast in his business, and then Captain Cocke, with whom I walked in the garden, and he tells me how angry the Court is at the late Proviso brought in by the House. How still my Lord Chancellor is, not daring to do or say any thing to displease the Parliament; that the Parliament is in a very ill humour, and grows every day more and more so; and that the unskilfulness of the Court, and their difference among one another, is the occasion of all not agreeing in what they would have, and so they give leisure and occasion to the other part to run away with what the Court would not have. Then comes Mr. Gawden, and he and I in my chamber discoursing about his business, and to pay him some Tangier orders which he delayed to receive till I had money instead of tallies, but do promise me consideration for my victualling business for this year, and also as Treasurer for Tangier, which I am glad of, but would have been gladder to have just now received it. He gone, I alone to dinner at home, my wife and her people being gone down the river to-day for pleasure, though a cold day and dark night to come up. In the afternoon I to the Excise Office[1] to enter my tallies, which I did, and come presently back again, and then to the office and did much business, and then home to supper, my wife and people being come well and hungry home from Erith. Then I to begin the setting of a Base to "It is decreed," and so to bed.

11th. Up, and to the office, where we sat, and at noon home to dinner, a small dinner because of a good supper. After dinner my wife and I by coach to St. Clement's Church, to Mrs. Turner's lodgings, hard by, to take our leaves of her. She is returning into the North to her children, where, I perceive, her husband hath clearly got the mastery of her, and she is likely to spend her days there,[2] which for her sake I am a little sorry for, though for his it is but fit she should live where he hath a mind. Here were several people come to see and take leave of her, she going to-morrow: among others, my Lady Mordant,[3] which was Betty Turner, a most homely widow, but young, and pretty rich, and good natured. Thence, having promised to

[1] After the Great Fire the Excise Office for a time found a site in Southampton Fields, at the back of Southampton House (afterwards Bedford House), on the north side of Bloomsbury Square.

[2] John Turner, here alluded to, was the eldest son and heir of Sir William Turner, Lord Mayor of London in 1669, better known as the munificent founder of Kirkleatham Hospital, in Yorkshire, and whose monument is still to be seen in Kirkleatham Church, and in the hospital a likeness of him in wax-work, with the identical wig and band that he wore. In the east window of the hospital chapel also is a stained glass portrait of him in his mayoralty robes, and one of his eldest son. John Turner was brought up to the bar, and became a serjeant-at-law, and purchased an estate in the district of Cleveland. Besides his daughter Theophila, mentioned so often, he had issue two sons, Charles and William, from the eldest of whom descended the late Sir Charles Turner, of Kirkleatham, the second baronet of the family, and the last heir male of his race. He died in 1810. See an account of the family in "The Genealogist and Topographer," part vi. — B.

[3] Sir George Mordaunt, of Massingham, Norfolk, the fourth baronet of his family, espoused Elizabeth, daughter and co-heir of Nicholas Johnson, of London, niece to Sir W. Turner above-mentioned, who is the person here alluded to by Pepys. She re-married Francis Godolphin, of Colston, Wilts (Wotton's "Baronetage") — B

write every month to her, we home, and I to my office, while my wife to get things together for supper. Dispatching my business at the office. Anon come our guests, old Mr. Batelier, and his son and daughter, Mercer, which was all our company. We had a good venison pasty and other good cheer, and as merry as in so good, innocent, and understanding company I could be. He is much troubled that wines, laden by him in France before the late proclamation was out, cannot now be brought into England, which is so much to his and other merchants' loss. We sat long at supper and then to talk, and so late parted and so to bed. This day the Poll Bill was to be passed, and great endeavours used to take away the Proviso.

12th. Up, and to the office, where some accounts of Mr. Gawden's were examined, but I home most of the morning to even some accounts with Sir H. Cholmly, Mr. Moone, and others one after another. Sir H. Cholmly did with grief tell me how the Parliament hath been told plainly that the King hath been heard to say, that he would dissolve them rather than pass this Bill with the Proviso; but tells me, that the Proviso is removed, and now carried that it shall be done by a Bill by itself. He tells me how the King hath lately paid about £30,000[1] to clear debts of my Lady Castlemayne's; and that she and her husband are parted for ever, upon good terms, never to trouble one another more. He says that he hears £400,000 hath gone into the Privy purse since this warr; and that that hath consumed so much of our money, and makes the King and Court so mad to be brought to discover it. He gone, and after him the rest, I to the office, and at noon to the 'Change, where the very good newes is just come of our four ships from Smyrna, come safe without convoy even into the Downes, without seeing any enemy; which is the best, and indeed only considerable good newes to our Exchange, since the burning of the City; and it is strange to see how it do cheer up men's hearts. Here I saw shops now come to be in this Exchange, and met little Batelier,

[1] Two thousand pounds of this sum went to Alderman Edward Bakewell for two diamond rings, severally charged £1,100 and £900, bought March 14th, 1665–66 (Second addenda to Steinman's "Memoir of the Duchess of Cleveland," privately printed, 1878, p. 4).

who sits here but at £3 per annum, whereas he sat at the other at £100, which he says he believes will prove of as good account to him now as the other did at that rent. From the 'Change to Captain Cocke's, and there, by agreement, dined, and there was Charles Porter,[1] Temple,[2] Fenn,[3] Debasty, whose bad English and pleasant discourses was exceeding good entertainment, Matt. Wren, Major Cooper, and myself, mighty merry and pretty discourse. They talked for certain, that now the King do follow Mrs. Stewart wholly, and my Lady Castlemayne not above once a week; that the Duke of York do not haunt my Lady Denham so much; that she troubles him with matters of State, being of my Lord Bristoll's faction, and that he avoids; that she is ill still. After dinner I away to the office, where we sat late upon Mr. Gawden's accounts, Sir J. Minnes being gone home sick. I late at the office, and then home to supper and to bed, being mightily troubled with a pain in the small of my back, through cold, or (which I think most true) my straining last night to get open my plate chest, in such pain all night I could not turn myself in my bed. Newes this day from Brampton, of Mr. Ensum, my sister's sweetheart, being dead: a clowne.

13th. Up, and to the office, where we sat. At noon to the 'Change and there met Captain Cocke, and had a second time his direction to bespeak £100 of plate, which I did at Sir R. Viner's, being twelve plates more, and something else I have to choose. Thence home to dinner, and there W. Hewer dined with me, and showed me a Gazette,[4] in April last, which I wonder should never be

[1] Charles Porter was brother to Thomas Porter, who killed Sir H. Bellasis in a duel in 1667 (see note, May 15th, 1663).

[2] Probably John Temple, Sir R. Viner's chief clerk.

[3] John Fenn, who is frequently referred to in the Diary.

[4] The "Gazette" of April 23rd–26th, 1666, which contains the following remarkable passage: "At the Sessions in the Old Bailey, John Rathbone, an old army colonel, William Saunders, Henry Tucker, Thomas Flint, Thomas Evans, John Myles, Will. Westcot, and John Cole, officers or soldiers in the late Rebellion, were indicted for conspiring the death of his Majesty and the overthrow of the Government. Having laid their plot and contrivance for the surprisal of the Tower, the killing his Grace the Lord General, Sir John Robin-

remembered by any body, which tells how several persons were then tried for their lives, and were found guilty of a design of killing the King and destroying the Government; and as a means to it, to burn the City; and that the day intended for the plot was the 3rd of last September. And the fire did indeed break out on the 2nd of September, which is very strange, methinks, and I shall remember it. At the office all the afternoon late, and then home to even my accounts in my Tangier book, which I did to great content in all respects, and joy to my heart, and so to bed. This afternoon Sir W. Warren and Mr. Moore, one after another, walked with me in the garden, and they both tell me that my Lord Sandwich is called home, and that he do grow more and more in esteem everywhere, and is better spoken of, which I am mighty glad of, though I know well enough his deserving the same before, and did foresee that it will come to it. In mighty great pain in my back still, but I perceive it changes its place, and do not trouble me at all in making of water, and that is my joy, so that I believe it is nothing but a strain, and for these three or four days I perceive my overworking of my eyes by candlelight do hurt them as it did the last winter, that by day I am well and do get them right, but then after candlelight they begin to be sore and run, so that I intend to get some green spectacles.

son, Lieutenant of the Tower, and Sir Richard Brown; and then to have declared for an equal division of lands, &c. *The better to effect this hellish design, the City was to have been fired*, and the portcullis let down to keep out all assistance; and the Horse Guards to have been surprised in the inns where they were quartered, several ostlers having been gained for that purpose. The Tower was accordingly viewed, and its surprise ordered by boats over the moat, and from thence to scale the wall. One Alexander, not yet taken, had likewise distributed money to these conspirators; and, for the carrying on the design more effectually, they were told of a Council of the great ones that sat frequently in London, from whom issued all orders; which Council received their directions from another in Holland, who sat with the States; and that *the third of September* was pitched on for the attempt, as being found by Lilly's Almanack, and a scheme erected for that purpose, to be a lucky day, a planet then ruling which prognosticated the downfall of Monarchy. The evidence against these persons was very full and clear, and they were accordingly found guilty of High Treason." See November 10th, 1666. — B.

14th. Up, and very well again of my pain in my back, it having been nothing but cold. By coach to White Hall, seeing many smokes of the fire by the way yet, and took up into the coach with me a country gentleman, who asked me room to go with me, it being dirty — one come out of the North to see his son, after the burning his house: a merchant. Here endeavoured to wait on the Duke of York, but he would not stay from the Parliament. So I to Westminster Hall, and there met my good friend Mr. Evelyn, and walked with him a good while, lamenting our condition for want of good council, and the King's minding of his business and servants. I out to the Bell Taverne, and thither comes Doll to me . . ., and after an hour's stay, away and staid in Westminster Hall till the rising of the house, having told Mr. Evelyn, and he several others, of my Gazette which I had about me that mentioned in April last a plot for which several were condemned of treason at the Old Bayly for many things, and among others for a design of burning the city on the 3rd of September. The house sat till three o'clock, and then up: and I home with Sir Stephen Fox to his house to dinner, and the Cofferer[1] with us. There I find Sir S. Fox's lady, a fine woman, and seven the prettiest children of their's that ever I knew almost. A very genteel dinner, and in great state and fashion, and excellent discourse; and nothing like an old experienced man and a courtier, and such is the Cofferer Ashburnham. The House have been mighty hot to-day against the Paper Bill, showing all manner of averseness to give the King money; which these courtiers do take mighty notice of, and look upon

[1] William Ashburnham, younger brother of John Ashburnham, and first cousin of the Duke of Buckingham. He was an officer of distinction in the king's army during the Civil War; and, after the Restoration, made Cofferer of the Household to Charles II. Died s.p. 1671. He married the "young, beautiful, and rich widow" of James Ley, Earl of Marlborough, Lord High Treasurer of England, to whom she was third wife. She was daughter of John, Lord Butler, of Bramfield, by Elizabeth Villiers, sister of the first Duke of Buckingham, and therefore nearly related to William Ashburnham. A splendid monument to William Ashburnham, and to the Countess of Marlborough, with whom he lived happily for nearly forty-five years, is in Ashburnham Church. — B.

the others as bad rebells as ever the last were. But the courtiers did carry it against those men upon a division of the House, a great many, that it should be committed; and so it was: which they reckon good news. After dinner we three to the Excise Office, and there had long discourse about our monies, but nothing to satisfaction, that is, to shew any way of shortening the time which our tallies take up before they become payable, which is now full two years, which is 20 per cent. for all the King's money for interest, and the great disservice of his Majesty otherwise. Thence in the evening round by coach home, where I find Foundes his present, of a fair pair of candlesticks, and half a dozen of plates come, which cost him full £50, and is a very good present; and here I met with, sealed up, from Sir H. Cholmly, the lampoone, or the Mocke-Advice to a Paynter,[1] abusing the Duke of York and my Lord

[1] The bibliography of the various "Advices" and "Instructions" to a Painter is somewhat extensive, and can only be shortly alluded to here. The poet Waller commenced the series with his "Instructions to a Painter for the drawing of the posture and progress of His Maties forces at sea under command of his Highness Royal. Together with the battel and victory obtained over the Dutch, June 3, 1665. London, 1666." In the following year appeared "Directions to a Painter for describing our Navall Business in imitation of Waller," "The second Advice to a Painter for drawing the History of our Navall Business, in imitation of Mr. Waller," "The second and third Advice to a Painter for drawing the History of our Navall Actions, in answer to Mr. Waller." These were attributed to Sir John Denham, but it is doubtful whether he had anything to do with them. In "Poems on Affairs of State," vol. i. (1703), where the "Directions" are printed, we find this note in the list of contents, "said to be written by Sir John Denham, but believed to be writ by Mr. Milton." Andrew Marvell's "Last Instructions to a Painter" is dated 1667, and his "Further Instructions to a Painter," 1670. The constant issue of "Instructions" and "Advices" attracted special attention, and "The Answer of Mr. Waller's Painter to his many new Advisers" was published in 1667. Marvell wrote an "Advice to a Painter" on the Popish Plot, and a "Second Advice to a Painter" was written in imitation of Marvell. In a broadside (1680), quoted by Mr. G. T. Drury in his edition of Waller's Poems, 1893, satirical reference is made to the fashionable form of advice to the painters:

"Each puny brother of the rhyming trade
At every turn implores the Painter's aid,
And fondly enamoured of own foul brat
Cries in an ecstacy, Paint this, draw that."

Sandwich, Pen, and every body, and the King himself, in all the matters of the navy and warr. I am sorry for my Lord Sandwich's having so great a part in it. Then to supper and musique, and to bed.

15th. Up and to the office, where my Lord Bruncker newly come to town, from his being at Chatham and Harwich to spy enormities: and at noon I with him and his lady Williams, to Captain Cocke's, where a good dinner, and very merry. Good news to-day upon the Exchange, that our Hamburgh fleete is got in; and good hopes that we may soon have the like of our Gottenburgh, and then we shall be well for this winter. Very merry at dinner. And by and by comes in Matt. Wren[1] from the Parliament-house; and tells us that he and all his party of the House, which is the Court party, are fools, and have been made so this day by the wise men of the other side; for, after the Court party had carried it yesterday so powerfully for the Paper-Bill,[2] yet now it is laid aside wholly, and to be supplied by a land-tax; which it is true will do well, and will be the sooner finished, which was the great argument for the doing of it. But then it shews them fools, that they would not permit this to have been done six weeks ago, which they might have had. And next, they have parted with the Paper Bill, which, when once begun, might have proved a very good flower in the Crowne, as any there. So do really say that they are truly outwitted by the other side. Thence away to Sir R. Viner's, and there chose some plate besides twelve plates which I purpose to have with Captain Cocke's gift of £100, and so home and there busy late, and then home and to bed.

16th (Lord's day). Lay long talking with my wife in bed, then up with great content and to my chamber to set right a picture or two, Lovett having sent me yesterday

The series was continued, for we find "Advice to a Painter upon the Defeat of the Rebels in the West and the Execution of the late Duke of Monmouth" ("Poems on Affairs of State," vol. ii., p. 148); "Advice to a Painter, being a Satire on the French King," &c., 1692, and "Advice to a Painter," 1697 ("Poems on Affairs of State," vol. ii., p. 428).

[1] See March 7th, 1666.

[2] It was called "A Bill for raising part of the supply for his Majesty by an imposition on Sealed Paper and Parchment." — B.

Sancta Clara's head varnished, which is very fine, and now my closet is so full stored, and so fine, as I would never desire to have it better. Dined without any strangers with me, which I do not like on Sundays. Then after dinner by water to Westminster to see Mrs. Martin, whom I found up in her chamber and ready to go abroad. I sat there with her and her husband and others a pretty while, and then away to White Hall, and there walked up and down to the Queen's side, and there saw my dear Lady Castlemayne, who continues admirable, methinks, and I do not hear but that the King is the same to her still as ever. Anon to chapel, by the King's closet, and heard a very good anthemne. Then with Lord Bruncker to Sir W. Coventry's chamber; and there we sat with him and talked. He is weary of anything to do, he says, in the Navy. He tells us this Committee of Accounts will enquire sharply into our office. And, speaking of Sir J. Minnes, he says he will not bear any body's faults but his own. He discoursed as bad of Sir W. Batten almost, and cries out upon the discipline of the fleete, which is lost, and that there is not in any of the fourth rates and under scarce left one Sea Commander, but all young gentlemen; and what troubles him, he hears that the gentlemen give out that in two or three years a Tarpaulin shall not dare to look after being better than a Boatswain. Which he is troubled at, and with good reason, and at this day Sir Robert Holmes is mighty troubled that his brother do not command in chief, but is commanded by Captain Hannum,[1] who, Sir W. Coventry says, he believes to be at least of as good blood, is a longer bred seaman, and elder officer, and an elder commander, but such is Sir R. Holmes's pride as never to be stopt, he being greatly troubled at my Lord Bruncker's late discharging all his men and officers but the standing officers at Chatham, and so are all other Commanders, and a very great cry hath been to the King from them all in my Lord's absence. But Sir W. Coventry do undertake to defend it, and my Lord Bruncker got ground I believe by it, who is angry at Sir W. Batten's and Sir W. Pen's bad words concerning it,

[1] Captain Willoughby Hannam or Hanham (see note, July 27th, 1666).

and I have made it worse by telling him that they refuse to sign to a paper which he and I signed on Saturday to declare the reason of his actions, which Sir W. Coventry likes and would have it sent him and he will sign it, which pleases me well. So we parted, and I with Lord Bruncker to Sir P. Neale's chamber, and there sat and talked awhile, Sir Edward Walker being there, and telling us how he hath lost many fine rowles of antiquity in heraldry by the late fire, but hath saved the most of his papers. Here was also Dr. Wallis,[1] the famous scholar and mathematician; but he promises little. Left them, and in the dark and cold home by water, and so to supper and to read and so to bed, my eyes being better to-day, and I cannot impute it to anything but by my being much in the dark to-night, for I plainly find that it is only excess of light that makes my eyes sore. This afternoon I walked with Lord Bruncker into the Park and there talked of the times, and he do think that the King sees that he cannot never have much more money or good from this Parliament, and that therefore he may hereafter dissolve them, that as soon as he has the money settled he believes a peace will be clapped up, and that there are overtures of a peace, which if such as the Lord Chancellor can excuse he will take. For it is the Chancellor's interest, he says, to bring peace again, for in peace he can do all and command all, but in war he cannot, because he understands not the nature of the war as to the management thereof. He tells me he do not believe the Duke of York will go to sea again, though there are a great many about the King that would be glad of any occasion to take him out of the world, he standing in their ways; and seemed to mean the Duke of Monmouth, who spends his time the most viciously and idly of any man, nor will be fit for any thing; yet he speaks as

[1] John Wallis, born November 23rd, 1616, at Ashford, educated at Felsted School, Essex, and Emmanuel College, Cambridge, from which he removed to a fellowship in Queen's College. In 1648 he was appointed Savilian Professor of Geometry at Oxford, where he took the degree of D.D., 1654. He was one of the most distinguished Fellows of the Royal Society, and his "Arithmetic of Infinites" is said to contain the germ of future discoveries. He died at Oxford, October 28th, 1703.

if it were not impossible but the King would own him for his son, and that there was a marriage between his mother and him; which God forbid should be if it be not true, nor will the Duke of York easily be gulled in it.[1] But this put to our other distractions makes things appear very sad, and likely to be the occasion of much confusion in a little time, and my Lord Bruncker seems to say that nothing can help us but the King's making a peace soon as he hath this money; and thereby putting himself out of debt, and so becoming a good husband, and then he will neither need this nor any other Parliament, till he can have one to his mind: for no Parliament can, as he says, be kept long good, but they will spoil one another, and that therefore it hath been the practice of kings to tell Parliaments what he hath for them to do, and give them so long time to do it in, and no longer. Harry Kembe, one of our messengers, is lately dead.

17th. Up, and several people to speak with me, and then comes Mr. Cæsar, and then Goodgroome, and, what with one and the other, nothing but musique with me this morning, to my great content; and the more, to see that God Almighty hath put me into condition to bear the charge of all this. So out to the 'Change, and did a little business, and then home, where they two musicians and Mr. Cooke come to see me, and Mercer to go along with my wife this afternoon to a play. To dinner, and then our company all broke up, and to my chamber to do several things. Among other things, to write a letter to my Lord Sandwich, it being one of the burdens upon my mind that I have not writ to him since he went into Spain, but now I do intend to give him a brief account of our whole year's actions since he went, which will make amends. My wife well home in the evening from the play; which I was glad of, it being cold and dark, and she having her necklace of pearl on, and none but Mercer with her. Spent the evening in fitting my books, to have the number set upon each, in order to my having an alphabet of my whole, which will be of great ease to me. This day Captain Batters come from sea in his fireship and come to see me, poor man, as

[1] See note, May 15th, 1663, *ante*.

his patron, and a poor painful wretch he is as can be. After supper to bed.

18th. Up, and to the office, where I hear the ill news that poor Batters,[1] that had been born and bred a seaman, and brought up his ship from sea but yesterday, was, going down from me to his ship, drowned in the Thames, which is a sad fortune, and do make me afeard, and will do, more than ever I was. At noon dined at home, and then by coach to my Lord Bellasses, but not at home. So to Westminster Hall, where the Lords are sitting still, I to see Mrs. Martin, who is very well, and intends to go abroad to-morrow after her childbed. She do tell me that this child did come la meme jour that it ought to hazer after my avoir eté con elle before her marid did venir home. . . . Thence to the Swan, and there I sent for Sarah, and mighty merry we were. . . . So to Sir Robert Viner's about my plate, and carried home another dozen of plates, which makes my stock of plates up 2½ dozen, and at home find Mr. Thomas Andrews, with whom I staid and talked a little and invited him to dine with me at Christmas, and then I to the office, and there late doing business, and so home and to bed. Sorry for poor Batters.

19th. Up, and by water down to White Hall, and there with the Duke of York did our usual business, but nothing but complaints of want of money with[out] success, and Sir W. Coventry's complaint of the defects of our office (indeed Sir J. Minnes's) without any amendment, and he tells us so plainly of the Committee of Parliament's resolution to enquire home into all our managements that it makes me resolve to be wary, and to do all things betimes to be ready for them. Thence going away met Mr. Hingston[2] the organist (my old acquaintance) in the Court, and I took him to the Dog Taverne and got him to set me a

[1] Captain Christopher Batters, of the "Joseph" fire-ship, was drowned in the Thames, and his body found some time afterwards (see "Calendar of State Papers," 1666–67, pp. 505, 506).

[2] John Hingston, composer and organist, pupil of Orlando Gibbons. In the service successively of Charles I., Cromwell, and Charles II. Gentleman of the Chapel Royal, and in 1663 keeper of the organs. He is said by Hawkins to have been Blow's earliest master. He died in 1683, and was buried in St. Margaret's, Westminster, December 17th. His portrait was in the Music School at Oxford.

bass to my "It is decreed," which I think will go well, but he commends the song not knowing the words, but says the ayre is good, and believes the words are plainly expressed. He is of my mind against having of 8ths unnecessarily in composition. This did all please me mightily. Then to talk of the King's family. He says many of the musique are ready to starve, they being five years behindhand for their wages; nay, Evens,[1] the famous man upon the Harp, having not his equal in the world, did the other day die for mere want, and was fain to be buried at the almes of the parish, and carried to his grave in the dark at night without one linke, but that Mr. Hingston met it by chance, and did give 12*d.* to buy two or three links. He says all must come to ruin at this rate, and I believe him. Thence I up to the Lords' House to enquire for Lord Bellasses; and there hear how at a conference this morning between the two Houses about the business of the Canary Company, my Lord Buckingham leaning rudely over my Lord Marquis Dorchester,[2] my Lord Dorchester removed his elbow. Duke of Buckingham asked him whether he was uneasy; Dorchester replied, yes, and that he durst not do this were he any where else: Buckingham replied, yes he would, and that he was a better man than himself; Dorchester answered that he lyed. With this Buckingham struck off his hat, and took him by his periwigg, and pulled it aside, and held him. My Lord Chamberlain and others interposed, and, upon coming into the

[1] The "Warrant to the Treasurer of the Chamber to pay to Henry Brookwell, musician on the lute, in place of Lewis Evans, deceased, £16 2*s.* 6*d.* a year for life for his livery," is dated December 20th, 1666 ("Calendar of State Papers," 1666–67, p. 362).

[2] Henry Pierrepoint, second Earl of Kingston, created Marquis of Dorchester, 1645. Died December 1st, 1680. See an account of this quarrel in Lord Clarendon's "Life," vol. iii., p. 153, edit. 1827. — B.

"The Commons being in the Painted Chamber ready for the Conference appointed concerning the Canary Company, the House was adjourned during Pleasure, and the Lords went to the Conference, which being ended the House was resumed." The Lord Chamberlain acquainted the House, "That there was an ill accident fell out when the Lords were at the Conference this day in the Painted Chamber, by reason of a quarrel between the Duke of Bucks and the Marquis of Dorchester." Explanations were made by both lords, who were sent to the Tower ("Journals of the House of Lords," vol. xii., pp. 52, 53).

House, the Lords did order them both to the Tower, whither they are to go this afternoon. I down into the Hall, and there the Lieutenant of the Tower[1] took me with him, and would have me to the Tower to dinner; where I dined at the head of his table, next his lady,[2] who is comely and seeming sober and stately, but very proud and very cunning, or I am mistaken, and wanton, too. This day's work will bring the Lieutenant of the Tower £350. But a strange, conceited, vain man he is that ever I met withal, in his own praise, as I have heretofore observed of him. Thence home, and upon Tower Hill saw about 3 or 400 seamen get together; and one, standing upon a pile of bricks, made his sign, with his handkercher, upon his stick, and called all the rest to him, and several shouts they gave. This made me afeard; so I got home as fast as I could. And hearing of no present hurt did go to Sir Robert Viner's about my plate again, and coming home do hear of 1,000 seamen said in the streets to be in armes. So in great fear home, expecting to find a tumult about my house, and was doubtful of my riches there. But I thank God I found all well. But by and by Sir W. Batten and Sir R. Ford do tell me, that the seamen have been at some prisons, to release some seamen, and the Duke of Albemarle is in armes, and all the Guards at the other end of the town; and the Duke of Albemarle is gone with some forces to Wapping, to quell the seamen; which is a thing of infinite disgrace to us. I sat long talking with them; and, among other things, Sir R. Ford did make me understand how the House of Commons is a beast not to be understood, it being impossible to know beforehand the success almost of any small plain thing, there being so many to think and speak to any business, and they of so uncertain minds and interests and passions. He did tell me, and so did Sir W. Batten, how Sir Allen Brodericke[3]

[1] Sir John Robinson.

[2] Anne, daughter of Sir George Whitmore.

[3] Sir Alan Broderick died on the 28th November, 1680, and was interred at Wandsworth on the 3rd December, when his funeral sermon was preached by Nathaniel Resbury, D.D., incumbent of the parish. The following extracts from the discourse, which, though printed, is very scarce, may throw some light on the knight's character,

and Sir Allen Apsly did come drunk the other day into the House, and did both speak for half an hour together, and could not be either laughed, or pulled, or bid to sit down and hold their peace, to the great contempt of the King's servants and cause; which I am grieved at with all my heart. We were full in discourse of the sad state of our times, and the horrid shame brought on the King's service by the just clamours of the poor seamen, and that we must be undone in a little time. Home full of trouble on these considerations, and, among other things, I to my chamber, and there to ticket a good part of my books, in order to the numbering of them for my easy finding them to read as I have occasion. So to supper and to bed, with my heart full of trouble.

20th. Up, and to the office, where we sat all the morning, and here among other things come Captain Cocke, and I did get him to sign me a note for the £100 to pay for the plate he do present me with, which I am very glad of.

and, from their quaintness, are interesting. "In the first place, therefore, I might be very well allow'd to begin with that usual head of panegyrick, where the subject could well bear it, viz., the quality of his birth and extract, and so give you his lineage in a long series of worthy and honourable ancestry, who from time immemorial had liv'd in the Registry of Honour in the Northern parts, till his own father, by the occasion of a noble trust, viz., the Lieutenancy of the Tower of London, came to add warmth to our Southern clime, and bless'd this place not only with his own and his religious Lady's presence and vertues (whose names and memories are still fragrant in those odours of goodness wherein they have been so plentifully scented in life), but with a numerous and valuable progeny, amongst whom was this wonder both of greatness and goodness. . . . I will readily acknowledge (and why, indeed, should I scruple to own what himself with such repeated contrition and brokenness of spirit would to all sober ears so freely and heartily condemn himself for?) that a long scene of his life had been acted off in the sports and follies of sin. If I may use his own words, it was a pagan and abandoned way he had sometime pursu'd, scepticism itself not excepted. . . . He had for many years practis'd in the politicks of this nation, and having so nearly attacht himself to one of the greatest Ministers of State [Lord Chancellor Clarendon] that this kingdom ever knew (whose mistaken wisdom and integrity perhaps hath been since better understood by the want of him), made himself no small figure in the administration." The Lords Middleton are descended from Sir St. John Broderick, a younger brother of Sir Alan. — B.

[1] See July 4th, 1663.

At noon home to dinner, where was Balty come, who is well again, and the most recovered in his countenance that ever I did see. Here dined with me also Mrs. Batters, poor woman! now left a sad widow by the drowning of her husband the other day. I pity her, and will do her what kindness I can; yet I observe something of ill-nature in myself more than should be, that I am colder towards her in my charity than I should be to one so painful as he and she have been and full of kindness to their power to my wife and I. After dinner out with Balty, setting him down at the Maypole in the Strand, and then I to my Lord Bellasses, and there spoke with Mr. Moone about some business, and so away home to my business at the office, and then home to supper and to bed, after having finished the putting of little papers upon my books to be numbered hereafter.

21st. Lay long, and when up find Mrs. Clerk of Greenwich and her daughter Daniel, their business among other things was a request her daughter was to make, so I took her into my chamber, and there it was to help her husband to the command of a little new pleasure boat building, which I promised to assist in. And here I had opportunity para baiser elle, and toucher ses mamailles. . . . Then to the office, and there did a little business, and then to the 'Change and did the like. So home to dinner, and spent all the afternoon in putting some things, pictures especially, in order, and pasting my Lady Castlemayne's print on a frame, which I have made handsome, and is a fine piece. So to the office in the evening to marshall my papers of accounts presented to the Parliament, against any future occasion to recur to them, which I did do to my great content. So home and did some Tangier work, and so to bed.

22nd. At the office all the morning, and there come news from Hogg that our shipp hath brought in a Lubecker to Portsmouth, likely to prove prize, of deals, which joys us. At noon home to dinner, and then Sir W. Pen, Sir R. Ford, and I met at Sir W. Batten's to examine our papers, and have great hopes to prove her prize, and Sir R. Ford I find a mighty yare[1] man in this business, making exceed-

[1] Quick or ready, a naval term frequently used by Shakespeare.

ing good observations from the papers on our behalf. Hereupon concluded what to write to Hogg and Middleton, which I did, and also with Mr. Oviatt (Sir R. Ford's son, who is to be our solicitor), to fee some counsel in the Admiralty, but none in town. So home again, and after writing letters by the post, I with all my clerks and Carcasse and Whitfield[1] to the ticket-office, there to be informed in the method and disorder of the office, which I find infinite great, of infinite concernment to be mended, and did spend till 12 at night to my great satisfaction, it being a point of our office I was wholly unacquainted in. So with great content home and to bed.

23rd (Lord's day). Up and alone to church, and meeting Nan Wright at the gate had opportunity to take two or three baisers, and so to church, where a vain fellow with a periwigg preached, Chaplain, as by his prayer appeared, to the Earl of Carlisle.[2] Home, and there dined with us Betty Michell and her husband. After dinner to White Hall by coach, and took them with me. And in the way I would have taken su main as I did the last time, but she did in a manner withhold it. So set them down at White Hall, and I to the Chapel to find Dr. Gibbons, and from him to the Harp and Ball to transcribe the treble which I would have him to set a bass to. But this took me so much time, and it growing night, I was fearful of missing a coach, and therefore took a coach and to rights to call Michell and his wife at their father Howlett's, and so home, it being cold, and the ground all snow. . . . They gone I to my chamber, and with my brother and wife did number all my books in my closet, and took a list of their names, which pleases me mightily, and is a jobb I wanted much to have done. Then to supper and to bed.

24th. Up, and to the office, where Lord Bruncker, [Sir] J. Minnes, [Sir] W. Pen, and myself met, and there I did use my notes I took on Saturday night about tickets, and did come to a good settlement in the business of that

[1] Nathaniel Whitfield was one of the four clerks of the Ticket Office, and was detailed to attend to Sir William Batten.

[2] Charles Howard, created Earl of Carlisle, 1661, employed on several embassies, and Governor of Jamaica. Died February 24th, 1684-85. — B.

office, if it be kept to, this morning being a meeting on purpose. At noon to prevent my Lord Bruncker's dining here I walked as if upon business with him, it being frost and dry, as far as Paul's, and so back again through the City by Guildhall, observing the ruines thereabouts, till I did truly lose myself, and so home to dinner. I do truly find that I have overwrought my eyes, so that now they are become weak and apt to be tired, and all excess of light makes them sore, so that now to the candlelight I am forced to sit by, adding, the snow upon the ground all day, my eyes are very bad, and will be worse if not helped, so my Lord Bruncker do advise as a certain cure to use greene spectacles, which I will do. So to dinner, where Mercer with us, and very merry. After dinner she goes and fetches a little son of Mr. Backeworth's, the wittiest child and of the most spirit that ever I saw in my life for discourse of all kind, and so ready and to the purpose, not above four years old. Thence to Sir Robert Viner's, and there paid for the plate I have bought to the value of £94, with the £100 Captain Cocke did give me to that purpose, and received the rest in money. I this evening did buy me a pair of green spectacles, to see whether they will help my eyes or no. So to the 'Change, and went to the Upper 'Change, which is almost as good as the old one; only shops are but on one side. Then home to the office, and did business till my eyes began to be bad, and so home to supper. My people busy making mince pies, and so to bed. No newes yet of our Gottenburgh fleete; which makes [us] have some fears, it being of mighty concernment to have our supply of masts safe. I met with Mr. Cade to-night, my stationer; and he tells me that he hears for certain that the Queene-Mother is about and hath near finished a peace with France, which, as a Presbyterian, he do not like, but seems to fear it will be a means to introduce Popery.

25th (Christmas day). Lay pretty long in bed, and then rose, leaving my wife desirous to sleep, having sat up till four this morning seeing her mayds make mince-pies. I to church, where our parson Mills made a good sermon. Then home, and dined well on some good ribbs of beef roasted and mince pies; only my wife, brother, and Barker, and plenty of good wine of my owne, and my heart full of true joy; and thanks to God Almighty for the goodness of my condition at this day. After dinner, I begun to teach my wife and Barker my song, "It is decreed," which pleases me mightily as now I have Mr. Hinxton's base.[1] Then out and walked alone on foot to the Temple, it being a fine frost, thinking to have seen a play all alone; but there, missing of any bills, concluded there was none, and so back home; and there with my brother reducing the names of all my books to an alphabet, which kept us till 7 or 8 at night, and then to supper, W. Hewer with us, and pretty merry, and then to my chamber to enter this day's journal only, and then to bed. My head a little thoughtfull how to behave myself in the business of the victualling, which I think will be prudence to offer my service in doing something in passing the pursers' accounts, thereby to serve the King, get honour to myself, and confirm me in my place in the victualling, which at present yields not work enough to deserve my wages.

26th. Up, and walked all the way (it being a most fine frost), to White Hall, to Sir W. Coventry's chamber, and thence with him up to the Duke of York, where among other things at our meeting I did offer my assistance to Sir J. Minnes to do the business of his office, relating to the Pursers' accounts, which was well accepted by the Duke of York, and I think I have and shall do myself good in it, if it be taken, for it will confirm me in the business of the victualling office, which I do now very little for. Thence home, carrying a barrel of oysters with me. Anon comes Mr. John Andrews and his wife by invitation from Bow to dine with me, and young Batelier and his wife with her great belly, which has spoiled her looks mightily already. Here was also Mercer and Creed, whom I met coming home, who tells me of a most bitter lampoone now out against the Court and the management of State from head to foot, mighty witty and mighty severe. By and by to dinner, a very good one, and merry. After dinner I put the women into a coach, and they to the Duke's house, to a play which was acted, "The ——." It was indifferently done, but was not pleased with the song, Gosnell not

[1] John Hingston, see note, *ante*, December 19th.

singing, but a new wench, that sings naughtily. Thence home, all by coach, and there Mr. Andrews to the vyall, who plays most excellently on it, which I did not know before. Then to dance, here being Pembleton come, by my wife's direction, and a fiddler; and we got, also, the elder Batelier to-night, and Nan Wright, and mighty merry we were, and I danced; and so till twelve at night, and to supper, and then to cross purposes, mighty merry, and then to bed, my eyes being sore. Creed lay here in Barker's bed.

27th. Up; and called up by the King's trumpets, which cost me 10*s.* So to the office, where we sat all the morning. At noon, by invitation, my wife, who had not been there these 10 months, I think, and I, to meet all our families at Sir W. Batten's at dinner, whither neither a great dinner for so much company nor anything good or handsome. In the middle of dinner I rose, and my wife, and by coach to the King's playhouse, and meeting Creed took him up, and there saw "The Scornfull Lady" well acted; Doll Common[1] doing Abigail most excellently, and Knipp the widow very well, and will be an excellent actor, I think. In other parts the play not so well done as used to be, by the old actors. Anon to White Hall by coach, thinking to have seen a play there to-night, but found it a mistake, so back again, and missed our coach[man], who was gone, thinking to come time enough three hours hence, and we could not blame him. So forced to get another coach, and all three home to my house, and there to Sir W. Batten's, and eat a bit of cold chine of beef, and then staid and talked, and then home and sat and talked a little by the fireside with my wife and Creed, and so to bed, my left eye being very sore. No business publick or private minded all these two days. This day a house or two was blown up with powder in the Minorys, and several people spoiled, and many dug out from under the rubbish.

28th. Up, and Creed and I walked (a very fine walk in the frost) to my Lord Bellasses, but missing him did find him at White Hall, and there spoke with him about some Tangier business. That done, we to Creed's lodgings,

[1] Mrs. Corey. See January 15th, 1668-69. Knipp is not mentioned by Genest as having acted in the play ("English Stage," vol. i., p. 66).

which are very pretty, but he is going from them. So we to Lincoln's Inne Fields, he to Ned Pickering's, who it seems lives there, keeping a good house, and I to my Lord Crew's, where I dined, and hear the newes how my Lord's brother, Mr. Nathaniel Crew, hath an estate of 6 or £700 per annum, left him by the death of an old acquaintance of his, but not akin to him at all. And this man is dead without will, but had, above ten years since, made over his estate to this Mr. Crew, to him and his heirs for ever, and given Mr. Crew the keeping of the deeds in his own hand all this time; by which, if he would, he might have taken present possession of the estate, for he knew what they were. This is as great an act of confident friendship as this latter age, I believe, can shew. From hence to the Duke's house, and there saw "Macbeth" most excellently acted, and a most excellent play for variety. I had sent for my wife to meet me there, who did come, and after the play was done, I out so soon to meet her at the other door that I left my cloake in the playhouse, and while I returned to get it, she was gone out and missed me, and with W. Hewer away home. I not sorry for it much did go to White Hall, and got my Lord Bellasses to get me into the playhouse; and there, after all staying above an hour for the players, the King and all waiting, which was absurd, saw "Henry the Fifth" well done by the Duke's people, and in most excellent habits, all new vests, being put on but this night. But I sat so high and far off, that I missed most of the words, and sat with a wind coming into my back and neck, which did much trouble me. The play continued till twelve at night; and then up, and a most horrid cold night it was, and frosty, and moonshine. But the worst was, I had left my cloak at Sir G. Carteret's, and they being abed I was forced to go home without it. So by chance got a coach and to the Golden Lion Taverne in the Strand, and there drank some mulled sack, and so home, where find my poor wife staying for me, and then to bed mighty cold.

29th. Up, called up with newes from Sir W. Batten that Hogg[1] hath brought in two prizes more: and so I thither,

[1] Captain Hogg wrote to Sir William Penn on December 27th that he had "sailed from Cowes on the 23rd, chased several vessels, and

and hear the particulars, which are good; one of them, if prize, being worth £4,000: for which God be thanked! Then to the office, and have the newes brought us of Captain Robinson's[1] coming with his fleete from Gottenburgh: dispersed, though, by foul weather. But he hath light of five Dutch men-of-war, and taken three, whereof one is sunk; which is very good newes to close up the year with, and most of our merchant-men already heard of to be safely come home, though after long lookings-for, and now to several ports, as they could make them. At noon home to dinner, where Balty is and now well recovered. Then to the office to do business, and at night, it being very cold, home to my chamber, and there late writing, but my left eye still very sore. I write by spectacles all this night, then to supper and to bed. This day's good news making me very lively, only the arrears of much business on my hands and my accounts to be settled for the whole year past do lie as a weight on my mind.

30th (Lord's day). Lay long, however up and to church, where Mills made a good sermon. Here was a collection for the sexton; but it come into my head why we should be more bold in making the collection while the psalm is singing, than in the sermon or prayer. Home, and, without any strangers, to dinner, and then all the afternoon and evening in my chamber preparing all my accounts in good condition against to-morrow, to state them for the whole year past, to which God give me a good issue when I come to close them! So to supper and to bed.

31st. Rising this day with a full design to mind nothing

was chased by twenty sail, consisting of four Holland men-of-war, three merchant ships, &c., but escaped, and took a galliot hoy of their fleet" ("Calendar of State Papers," 1666–67, p. 373). On the previous November 25th Commissioner Thomas Middleton reported to Pepys that Captain Hogg had brought into Portsmouth a privateer bound for France, laden with deals (p. 288 of the same).

[1] Captain Robert Robinson was sent in December as commodore of a squadron of six sail (the "Warspight," the "Jersey," the "Diamond," the "St. Patrick," the "Nightingale," and the "Oxford") to convoy the fleet home from Gottenburgh. On the 25th they fell in with a squadron of five Dutch men-of-war, of which three, including the admiral, were after a short action taken. Captain Robinson was knighted on December 12th, 1673 (Charnock's "Biographia Navalis," vol. i., p. 63).

else but to make up my accounts for the year past, I did take money, and walk forth to several places in the towne as far as the New Exchange, to pay all my debts, it being still a very great frost and good walking. I staid at the Fleece Tavern in Covent Garden while my boy Tom went to W. Joyce's to pay what I owed for candles there. Thence to the New Exchange to clear my wife's score, and so going back again I met Doll Lane (Mrs. Martin's sister), with another young woman of the Hall, one Scott, and took them to the Half Moon Taverne and there drank some burnt wine with them, without more pleasure, and so away home by coach, and there to dinner, and then to my accounts, wherein, at last, I find them clear and right; but, to my great discontent, do find that my gettings this year have been £573 less than my last: it being this year in all but £2,986; whereas, the last, I got £3,560. And then again my spendings this year have exceeded my spendings the last by £644: my whole spendings last year being but £509; whereas this year, it appears, I have spent £1,154, which is a sum not fit to be said that ever I should spend in one year, before I am master of a better estate than I am. Yet, blessed be God! and I pray God make me thankful for it, I do find myself worth in money, all good, above £6,200; which is above £1,800 more than I was the last year. This, I trust in God, will make me thankfull for what I have, and carefull to make up by care next year what by my negligence and prodigality I have lost and spent this year. The doing of this, and entering of it fair, with the sorting of all my expenses, to see how and in what points I have exceeded, did make it late work, till my eyes become very sore and ill, and then did give over, and supper, and to bed. Thus ends this year of publick wonder and mischief to this nation, and, therefore, generally wished by all people to have an end. Myself and family well, having four mayds and one clerk, Tom, in my house, and my brother, now with me, to spend time in order to his preferment. Our healths all well, only my eyes with overworking them are sore as candlelight comes to them, and not else; publick matters in a most sad condition; seamen discouraged for want of pay, and are become not to be governed: nor, as matters are now, can any fleete go out next year. Our enemies, French and Dutch, great, and grow more by our poverty. The Parliament backward in raising, because jealous of the spending of the money; the City less and less likely to be built again, every body settling elsewhere, and nobody encouraged to trade. A sad, vicious, negligent Court, and all sober men there fearful of the ruin of the whole kingdom this next year; from which, good God deliver us! One thing I reckon remarkable in my owne condition is, that I am come to abound in good plate, so as at all entertainments to be served wholly with silver plates, having two dozen and a half.

1666-67.

January 1st. Lay long, being a bitter, cold, frosty day, the frost being now grown old, and the Thames covered with ice. Up, and to the office, where all the morning busy. At noon to the 'Change a little, were Mr. James Houblon and I walked a good while speaking of our ill condition in not being able to set out a fleet (we doubt) this year, and the certain ill effect that must bring, which is lamentable. Home to dinner, where the best powdered goose that ever I eat. Then to the office again, and to Sir W. Batten's to examine the Commission going down to Portsmouth to examine witnesses about our prizes, of which God give a good issue! and then to the office again, where late, and so home, my eyes sore. To supper and to bed.

2nd. Up, I, and walked to White Hall to attend the Duke of York, as usual. My wife up, and with Mrs. Pen to walk in the fields to frost-bite themselves. I find the Court full of great apprehensions of the French, who have certainly shipped landsmen, great numbers, at Brest; and most of our people here guess his design for Ireland. We have orders to send all the ships we can possible to the Downes. God have mercy on us! for we can send forth no ships without men, nor will men go without money, every day bringing us news of new mutinies among the seamen; so that our condition is like to be very miserable. Thence to Westminster Hall, and there met all the Houblons, who do laugh at this discourse of the French, and say they are verily of opinion it is nothing but to send to their plantation in the West Indys, and that we at Court do blow up a design of invading us, only to make the Parliament make more haste in the money matters, and perhaps it may be so, but I do not believe we have any such plot in our heads. After them, I, with several people, among others Mr. George Montagu, whom I have not seen long, he mighty kind. He tells me all is like to go ill, the King displeasing the House of Commons by evading their Bill for examining Accounts, and putting it into a Commission, though therein he hath left out Coventry and ———,[1] and named all the rest the Parliament named, and all country Lords, not one Courtier: this do not please them. He tells me he finds the enmity almost over for my Lord Sandwich, and that now all is upon the Vice-Chamberlain, who bears up well and stands upon his vindication, which he seems to like well, and the others do construe well also. Thence up to the Painted Chamber, and there heard a conference between the House of Lords and Commons about the Wine Patent; which I was exceeding glad to be at, because of my hearing exceeding good discourses, but especially from the Commons; among others, Mr. Swinfen,[2] and a young man, one Sir Thomas Meres:[3] and do outdo the Lords infinitely. So down to the Hall and to the Rose Taverne, while Doll Lane come to me, and we did biber a good deal de vino, et je did give elle twelve soldis para comprare elle some gans for a new anno's gift. . . . Thence to the Hall again, and with Sir W. Pen by coach to the Temple, and there 'light and eat a bit at an ordinary by, and then alone to the King's House, and there saw "The Custome of the Country,"[4] the second time of its being acted, wherein Knipp

[1] A blank in the MS.

[2] John Swinfen, M.P. for Tamworth.

[3] M.P. for Lincoln, made a Commissioner of the Admiralty, 1679. —B.

[4] This tragi-comedy, which refers to the feudal custom styled the *droit du seigneur*, was acted in 1628, and printed in Beaumont and Fletcher's Works, 1647. Dryden, in the preface to his "Fables," says "there is more indecency in the 'Custom of the Country' than in all our plays together, yet this has been often acted on the stage in my remembrance."

does the Widow well; but, of all the plays that ever I did see, the worst — having neither plot, language, nor anything in the earth that is acceptable; only Knipp sings a little song admirably. But fully the worst play that ever I saw or I believe shall see. So away home, much displeased for the loss of so much time, and disobliging my wife by being there without her. So, by link, walked home, it being mighty cold but dry, yet bad walking because very slippery with the frost and treading. Home and to my chamber to set down my Journal, and then to thinking upon establishing my vows against the next year, and so to supper and to bed.

3rd. Up, and to the office, where we sat all the morning. At noon by invitation to dinner to Sir W. Pen's, where my Lord Bruncker, Sir W. Batten, and his lady, myself, and wife, Sir J. Minnes, and Mr. Turner and his wife. Indifferent merry, to which I contributed the most, but a mean dinner, and in a mean manner. In the evening a little to the office, and then to them, where I found them at cards, myself very ill with a cold (the frost continuing hard), so eat but little at supper, but very merry, and late home to bed, not much pleased with the manner of our entertainment, though to myself more civil than to any. This day, I hear, hath been a conference between the two Houses about the Bill for examining Accounts, wherein the House of Lords their proceedings in petitioning the King for doing it by Commission is, in great heat, voted by the Commons, after the conference, unparliamentary. The issue whereof, God knows.

4th. Up, and seeing things put in order for a dinner at my house to-day, I to the office awhile, and about noon home, and there saw all things in good order. Anon comes our company; my Lord Bruncker, Sir W. Pen, his lady, and Pegg, and her servant, Mr. Lowther,[1] my Lady Batten (Sir W. Batten being forced to dine at Sir R. Ford's, being invited), Mr. Turner and his wife. Here I had good room for ten, and no more would my table have held well, had Sir J. Minnes, who was fallen lame, and his sister, and niece, and Sir W. Batten come, which was a

[1] See January 11th, 1665-66.

great content to me to be without them. I did make them all gaze to see themselves served so nobly in plate, and a neat dinner, indeed, though but of seven dishes. Mighty merry I was and made them all, and they mightily pleased. My Lord Bruncker went away after dinner to the ticket-office, the rest staid, only my Lady Batten home, her ague-fit coming on her at table. The rest merry, and to cards, and then to sing and talk, and at night to sup, and then to cards; and, last of all, to have a flaggon of ale and apples, drunk out of a wood cupp,[1] as a Christmas draught, made all merry; and they full of admiration at my plate, particularly my flaggons (which, indeed, are noble), and so late home, all with great mirth and satisfaction to them, as I thought, and to myself to see all I have and do so much outdo for neatness and plenty anything done by any of them. They gone, I to bed, much pleased, and do observe Mr. Lowther to be a pretty gentleman, and, I think, too good for Peg; and, by the way, Peg Pen seems mightily to be kind to me, and I believe by her father's advice, who is also himself so; but I believe not a little troubled to see my plenty, and was much troubled to hear the song I sung, "The New Droll"[2]—it touching him home. So to bed.

5th. At the office all the morning, thinking at noon to have been taken home, and my wife (according to appointment yesterday), by my Lord Bruncker, to dinner and then to a play, but he had forgot it, at which I was glad, being glad of avoyding the occasion of inviting him again, and being forced to invite his doxy, Mrs. Williams. So home, and took a small snap of victuals, and away, with my wife, to the Duke's house, and there saw "Mustapha," a most excellent play for words and design as ever I did see. I

[1] A mazer or drinking-bowl turned out of some kind of wood, by preference of maple, and especially the spotted or speckled variety called "bird's-eye maple" (see W. H. St. John Hope's paper, "On the English Mediæval Drinking-bowls called Mazers," "Archæologia," vol. 50, pp. 129–93).

[2] There is a song called "The New Droll," in a rare volume entitled "The Loyal Garland, or a Choice Collection of Songs highly in request . . . . fifth edition," printed for T. Passinger, at the Three Bibles, on London Bridge, 1686, referred to in Beloe's "Anecdotes of Literature," 1812, vol. vi., p. 90, and Halliwell's "Catalogue of Chap-Books, Garlands, &c.," 1849, p. 106.

had seen it before but forgot it, so it was wholly new to me, which is the pleasure of my not committing these things to my memory. Home, and a little to the office, and then to bed, where I lay with much pain in my head most of the night, and very unquiet, partly by my drinking before I went out too great a draught of sack, and partly my eyes being still very sore.

6th (Lord's day). Up pretty well in the morning, and then to church, where a dull doctor, a stranger, made a dull sermon. Then home, and Betty Michell and her husband come by invitation to dine with us, and she I find the same as ever (which I was afraid of the contrary). . . . Here come also Mr. Howe to dine with me, and we had a good dinner and good merry discourse with much pleasure, I enjoying myself mightily to have friends at my table. After dinner young Michell and I, it being an excellent frosty day to walk, did walk out, he showing me the baker's house in Pudding Lane,[1] where the late great fire begun; and thence all along Thames Street, where I did view several places, and so up by London Wall, by Blackfriars, to Ludgate; and thence to Bridewell, which I find to have been heretofore an extraordinary good house, and a fine coming to it, before the house by the bridge[2] was built; and so to look about St. Bride's church and my father's house, and so walked home, and there supped together, and then Michell and Betty home, and I to my closet, there to read and agree upon my vows for next year, and so to bed and slept mighty well.

7th. Lay long in bed. Then up and to the office, where busy all the morning. At noon (my wife being gone to Westminster) I with my Lord Bruncker by coach as far as the Temple, in the way he telling me that my Lady Denham is at last dead. Some suspect her poisoned, but it will be best known when her body is opened, which will be to-day, she dying yesterday morning. The Duke of York is troubled for her; but hath declared he will never have another public mistress again; which I shall be glad of, and would the King would do the like. He tells me

[1] Belonging to Farryner, the king's baker.

[2] This must be a landing-place, as no actual bridge existed at Blackfriars until 1760-69.

how the Parliament is grown so jealous of the King's being unfayre to them in the business of the Bill for examining Accounts, Irish Bill, and the business of the Papists, that they will not pass the business for money till they see themselves secure that those Bills will pass; which they do observe the Court to keep off till all the Bills come together, that the King may accept what he pleases, and what he pleases to reject, which will undo all our business and the kingdom too. He tells me how Mr. Henry Howard, of Norfolke, hath given our Royal Society all his grandfather's library:[1] which noble gift they value at £1,000; and gives them accommodation to meet in at his house, Arundell House, they being now disturbed at Gresham College. Thence 'lighting at the Temple to the ordinary hard by and eat a bit of meat, and then by coach to fetch my wife from her brother's, and thence to the Duke's house, and saw "Macbeth," which, though I saw it lately, yet appears a most excellent play in all respects, but especially in divertisement, though it be a deep tragedy; which is a strange perfection in a tragedy, it being most proper here, and suitable. So home, it being the last play now I am to see till a fortnight hence, I being from the last night entered into my vowes for the year coming on. Here I met with the good newes of Hogg's bringing in two prizes more to Plymouth, which if they prove but any part of them, I hope, at least, we shall be no losers by them. So home from the office, to write over fair my vowes for this year, and then to supper, and to bed. In great peace of mind having now done it, and brought myself into order again

[1] Thomas, Earl of Arundel. The library was presented to the Royal Society on the advice of John Evelyn. Mr. Howard gave the Society all the printed books, of which a catalogue was printed; but the MSS. he divided between the Society and the College of Arms. Of the latter portion a catalogue has been privately printed by Sir Charles George Young, Garter King of Arms. In the year 1831 an arrangement was made between the Trustees of the British Museum and the Royal Society, the consent of the then Duke of Norfolk having been obtained, by which the Society's portion of the MSS. was transferred to the Museum, where they are now preserved for public use, and known as the Arundel MSS. A very full catalogue of them has been published by the Trustees. About twenty years ago the Society sold the principal portion of the Arundel Library.

and a resolution of keeping it, and having entered my journall to this night, so to bed, my eyes failing me with writing.

8th. Up, and to the office, where we sat all the morning. At noon home to dinner, where my uncle Thomas with me to receive his quarterage. He tells me his son Thomas is set up in Smithfield, where he hath a shop — I suppose, a booth. Presently after dinner to the office, and there set close to my business and did a great deal before night, and am resolved to stand to it, having been a truant too long. At night to Sir W. Batten's to consider some things about our prizes, and then to other talk, and among other things he tells me that he hears for certain that Sir W. Coventry hath resigned to the King his place of Commissioner of the Navy,[1] the thing he hath often told me that he had a mind to do, but I am surprised to think that he hath done it, and am full of thoughts all this evening after I heard it what may be the consequences of it to me. So home and to supper, and then saw the catalogue of my books, which my brother had wrote out, now perfectly alphabeticall, and so to bed. Sir Richard Ford did this evening at Sir W. Batten's tell us that upon opening the body of my Lady Denham[2] it is said that they found a vessel about her matrix which had never been broke by her husband, that caused all pains in her body. Which if true is excellent invention to clear both the Duchesse from poison or the Duke from lying with her.

9th. Up, and with Sir W. Batten and Sir W. Pen in a hackney-coach to White Hall, the way being most horribly bad upon the breaking up of the frost so as not to be passed almost. There did our usual [business] with the Duke of York, and here I do hear, by my Lord Bruncker, that for

[1] His salary was paid to March 25th, 1667.

[2] H. Muddiman, writing to George Powell on November 15th, 1666, says: "Lady Denham is recovering; some have raised strange discourse about the cause of her sickness, but the physicians affirm it to have been *iliaco passio*" ("Calendar of State Papers," 1666-67, pp. 262, 263). The popular idea that she was poisoned is alluded to in the "Grammont Memoirs," chap. ix. Lord Orrery, writing to the Duke of Ormond, January 25th, 1666-67, says: "My Lady Denham's body, at her own desire, was opened, but no sign of poison was found" ("Orrery State Papers," 1742, p. 219).

certain Sir W. Coventry hath resigned his place of Commissioner; which I believe he hath done upon good grounds of security to himself, from all the blame which must attend our office this next year; but I fear the King will suffer by it. Thence to Westminster Hall, and there to the conference of the Houses about the word "Nuisance,"[1] which the Commons would have, and the Lords will not, in the Irish Bill. The Commons do it professedly to prevent the King's dispensing with it; which Sir Robert Howard and others did expressly repeat often: viz., "the King nor any King ever could do any thing which was hurtful to their people." Now the Lords did argue, that it was an ill precedent, and that which will ever hereafter be used as a way of preventing the King's dispensation with acts; and therefore rather advise to pass the Bill without that word, and let it go, accompanied with a petition, to the King, that he will not dispense with it; this being a more civil way to the King. They answered well, that this do imply that the King should pass their Bill, and yet with design to dispense with it; which is to suppose the King guilty of abusing them. And more, they produce precedents for it; namely, that against new buildings and about leather, wherein the word "Nuisance" is used to the purpose: and further, that they do not rob the King of any right he ever had, for he never had a power to do hurt to his people, nor would exercise it; and therefore there is no danger, in the passing this Bill, of imposing on his prerogative; and concluded, that they think they ought to do this, so as the people may really have the benefit of it when it is passed, for never any people could expect so reasonably to be indulged something from a King, they having already given him so much money, and are likely to give more. Thus they broke up, both adhering to their opinions; but the Commons seemed much more full of judgment and reason than the Lords. Then the Commons made their Report to the Lords of their vote, that their

[1] In the "Bill against importing Cattle from Ireland and other parts beyond the Seas," the Lords proposed to insert "Detriment and Mischief" in place of "Nuisance," but the Commons stood to their word, and gained their way. The Lords finally consented that "Nuisance" should stand in the Bill.

Lordships' proceedings in the Bill for examining Accounts were unparliamentary; they having, while a Bill was sent up to them from the Commons about the business, petitioned his Majesty that he would do the same thing by his Commission. They did give their reasons: viz., that it had no precedent; that the King ought not to be informed of anything passing in the Houses till it comes to a Bill; that it will wholly break off all correspondence between the two Houses, and in the issue wholly infringe the very use and being of Parliaments. Having left their arguments with the Lords they all broke up, and I by coach to the ordinary by the Temple, and there dined alone on a rabbit, and read a book I brought home from Mrs. Michell's, of the proceedings of the Parliament in the 3rd and 4th year of the late King, a very good book for speeches and for arguments of law.[1] Thence to Faythorne, and bought a head or two; one of them my Lord of Ormond's, the best I ever saw, and then to Arundell House, where first the Royall Society meet,[2] by the favour of Mr. Harry Howard, who was there, and has given us his grandfather's library, a noble gift, and a noble favour and undertaking it is for him to make his house the seat for this college. Here was an experiment shown about improving the use of powder for creating of force in winding up of springs and other uses of great worth. And here was a great meeting of worthy noble persons; but my Lord Bruncker, who pre-

[1] Professor Samuel R. Gardiner has kindly enabled the editor to identify this book. A copy of "Ephemeris Parliamentaria, or a faithful Register of the Transactions in Parliament in the third and fourth years of the reign of our late sovereign lord King Charles. London, Printed for John Williams and Francis Eglesfield, 1654," is in the British Museum, and in the catalogue it is said to be edited by Thomas Fuller. A MS. note on the inside of the cover says that it was republished in 1657 under the title of "The Sovereign's Prerogative and the Subject's Privilege."

[2] "Jan. 9. The Society meeting the first time in Arundel House, the president took notice again of the great favour, which Mr. Henry Howard of Norfolk had shewn to the Society, not only in accommodating them with convenient room for their meetings, but also in presenting them with the library of the said house. The experiments appointed for the next meeting were (1) That of applying the strength of [gun]powder to the bending of springs" (Birch's "History of the Royal Society," vol. ii., pp. 138, 139).

tended to make a congratulatory speech upon their coming hither, and in thanks to Mr. Howard, do it in the worst manner in the world, being the worst speaker, so as I do wonder at his parts and the unhappiness of his speaking. Thence home by coach and to the office, and then home to supper, Mercer and her sister there, and to cards, and then to bed. Mr. Cowling did this day in the House-lobby tell me of the many complaints among people against Mr. Townsend in the Wardrobe, and advises me to think of my Lord Sandwich's concernment there under his care. He did also tell me upon my demanding it, that he do believe there are some things on foot for a peace between France and us, but that we shall be foiled in it.

10th. Up, and at the office all the morning. At noon home and, there being business to do in the afternoon, took my Lord Bruncker home with me, who dined with me. His discourse and mind about the bad performances of the Controller's and Surveyor's places by the hands they are now in, and the shame to the service and loss the King suffers by it. Then after dinner to the office, where we and some of the chief of the Trinity House met to examine the occasion of the loss of The Prince Royall,[1] the master and mates being examined, which I took and keep, and so broke up, and I to my letters by the post, and so home and to supper with my mind at pretty good ease, being entered upon minding my business, and so to bed. This noon Mrs. Burroughs come to me about business, whom I did baiser. . . .

11th. Up, being troubled at my being found abed adays by all sorts of people, I having got a trick of sitting up later than I need, never supping, or very seldom, before 12 at night. Then to the office, there busy all the morn-

[1] The "Prince Royal," which bore the flag of Sir George Ayscu, Admiral of the White, grounded on the Galloper. "Examination of George Purvis, master, and four other officers named, touching the surrender of their ship, the 'Prince,' to the Dutch, on June 3, 1666; tending to prove that she was steering in according to orders when she ran aground; that Tromp brought a fire-boat on each side to compel her to surrender, but that the flag was struck without the knowledge of the captain, Sir G[eorge] A[yscu], though one witness affirmed that he consented to its being struck. Jan. 10, 1667" ("Calendar of State Papers," 1666–67, p. 445).

ing, and among other things comes Sir W. Warren and walked with me awhile, whose discourse I love, he being a very wise man and full of good counsel, and his own practices for wisdom much to be observed, and among other things he tells me how he is fallen in with my Lord Bruncker, who has promised him most particular inward friendship and yet not to appear at the board to do so, and he tells me how my Lord Bruncker should take notice of the two flaggons[1] he saw at my house at dinner, at my late feast, and merrily, yet I know enviously, said, I could not come honestly by them. This I am glad to hear, though vexed to see his ignoble soul, but I shall beware of him, and yet it is fit he should see I am no mean fellow, but can live in the world, and have something. At noon home to dinner, and then to the office with my people and very busy, and did dispatch to my great satisfaction abundance of business, and do resolve, by the grace of God, to stick to it till I have cleared my heart of most things wherein I am in arrear in public and private matters. At night, home to supper and to bed. This day ill news of my father's being very ill of his old grief the rupture, which troubles me.

12th. Up, still lying long in bed; then to the office, where sat very long. Then home to dinner, and so to the office again, mighty busy, and did to the joy of my soul dispatch much business, which do make my heart light, and will enable me to recover all the ground I have lost (if I have by my late minding my pleasures lost any) and assert myself. So home to supper, and then to read a little in Moore's "Antidote against Atheisme,"[2] a pretty book, and so to bed.

13th (Lord's day). Up, and to church, where young Lowther[3] come to church with Sir W. Pen and his Lady and daughter, and my wife tells me that either they are

[1] Presented by Mr. Gauden; see July 28th, 1664.

[2] The work of Henry More the Platonist, entitled, "An Antidote against Atheisme, or an appeal to the natural faculties of the mind of man, whether there be not a God. London, 1653." Second edition, 1655.

[3] Anthony Lowther did not marry Margaret Penn until February (see February 15th, *post*). The marriage license is dated February 12th.

married or the match is quite perfected, which I am apt to believe, because all the peoples' eyes in the church were much fixed upon them. At noon sent for Mercer, who dined with us, and very merry, and so I, after dinner, walked to the Old Swan, thinking to have got a boat to White Hall, but could not, nor was there anybody at home at Michell's, where I thought to have sat with her. . . . So home, to church, a dull sermon, and then home at my chamber all the evening. So to supper and to bed.

14th. Up, and to the office, where busy getting before hand with my business as fast as I can. At noon home to dinner, and presently afterward at my office again. I understand my father is pretty well again, blessed be God! and would have my Br[other] John come down to him for a little while. Busy till night, pleasing myself mightily to see what a deal of business goes off of a man's hands when he stays by it, and then, at night, before it was late (yet much business done) home to supper, discourse with my wife, and to bed. Sir W. Batten tells me the Lords do agree at last with the Commons about the word "Nuisance" in the Irish Bill,[1] and do desire a good correspondence between the two Houses; and that the King do intend to prorogue them the last of this month.

15th. Up, and to the office, where busy all the morning. Here my Lord Bruncker would have made me promise to go with him to a play this afternoon, where Knipp acts Mrs. Weaver's great part in "The Indian Emperour,"[2] and he says is coming on to be a great actor. But I am so fell to my business, that I, though against my inclination, will not go. At noon, dined with my wife and were pleasant, and then to the office, where I got Mrs. Burroughs sola cum ego, and did toucher ses mamailles. . . . She gone, I to my business and did much, and among other things to-night we were all mightily troubled how to prevent the sale of a great deal of hemp, and timber-deals, and other good goods to-morrow at the candle by the Prize

[1] See note, January 9th, *ante*.

[2] "The Indian Emperor, or the Conquest of Mexico by the Spaniards," by J. Dryden, intended as a sequel to "The Indian Queen." It was entered at Stationer's Hall on May 26th, 1665, but not published until 1667.

Office, where it will be sold for little, and we shall be found to want the same goods and buy at extraordinary prices, and perhaps the very same goods now sold, which is a most horrid evil and a shame. At night home to supper and to bed with my mind mighty light to see the fruits of my diligence in having my business go off my hand so merrily.

16th. Up, and by coach to White Hall, and there to the Duke of York as usual. Here Sir W. Coventry come to me aside in the Duke's chamber, to tell that he had not answered part of a late letter of mine, because *littera scripta manet.* About his leaving the office, he tells me, [it is] because he finds that his business at Court will not permit him to attend it; and then he confesses that he seldom of late could come from it with satisfaction, and therefore would not take the King's money for nothing. I professed my sorrow for it, and prayed the continuance of his favour; which he promised. I do believe he hath [done] like a very wise man in reference to himself; but I doubt it will prove ill for the King, and for the office. Prince Rupert, I hear to-day, is very ill; yesterday given over, but better to-day. This day, before the Duke of York, the business of the Muster-Masters was reported, and Balty found the best of the whole number, so as the Duke enquired who he was, and whether he was a stranger by his two names, both strange, and offered that he and one more, who hath done next best, should have not only their owne, but part of the others' salary, but that I having said he was my brother-in-law, he did stop, but they two are ordered their pay, which I am glad of, and some of the rest will lose their pay, and others be laid by the heels. I was very glad of this being ended so well. I did also, this morning, move in a business wherein Mr. Hater hath concerned me, about getting a ship, laden with salt from France, permitted to unload, coming in after the King's declaration was out, which I have hopes by some dexterity to get done. Then with the Duke of York to the King, to receive his commands for stopping the sale this day of some prize-goods at the Prize-Office, goods fit for the Navy; and received the King's commands, and carried them to the Lords' House, to my Lord Ashly, who was angry much thereat, and I am sorry it fell to me to carry the order, but I cannot help it. So, against his will, he signed a note I writ to the Commissioners of Prizes, which I carried and delivered to Kingdone,[1] at their new office in Aldersgate Streete. Thence a little to the Exchange, where it was hot that the Prince was dead, but I did rectify it. So home to dinner, and found Balty, told him the good news, and then after dinner away, I presently to White Hall, and did give the Duke of York a memorial of the salt business, against the Council, and did wait all the Council for answer, walking a good while with Sir Stephen Fox, who, among other things, told me his whole mystery in the business of the interest he pays as Treasurer for the Army They give him 12*d*. per pound quite through the Army, with condition to be paid weekly. This he undertakes upon his own private credit, and to be paid by the King at the end of every four months. If the King pay him not at the end of the four months, then, for all the time he stays longer, my Lord Treasurer, by agreement, allows him eight per cent. per annum for the forbearance. So that, in fine, he hath about twelve per cent. from the King and the Army, for fifteen or sixteen months' interest; out of which he gains soundly, his expense being about £130,000 per annum; and hath no trouble in it, compared, as I told him, to the trouble I must have to bring in an account of interest. I was, however, glad of being thus enlightened, and so away to the other council door, and there got in and hear a piece of a cause, heard before the King, about a ship deserted by her fellows (who were bound mutually to defend each other), in their way to Virginy, and taken by the enemy, but it was but meanly pleaded. Then all withdrew, and by and by the Council rose, and I spoke with the Duke of York, and he told me my business was done, which I found accordingly in Sir Edward Walker's books. And so away, mightily satisfied, to Arundell House, and there heard a little good discourse, and so home, and there to Sir W. Batten, where I heard the examinations in two of our prizes, which do make but little for us, so that

[1] Captain Richard Kingdon (or Kingdom), Commissioner of Prizes and Governor of Excise.

I do begin to doubt their proving prize, which troubled me. So home to supper with my wife, and after supper my wife told me how she had moved to W. Hewer the business of my sister for a wife to him, which he received with mighty acknowledgements, as she says, above anything; but says he hath no intention to alter his condition: so that I am in some measure sorry she ever moved it; but I hope he will think it only come from her. So after supper a little to the office, to enter my journall, and then home to bed. Talk there is of a letter to come from Holland, desiring a place of treaty; but I do doubt it. This day I observe still, in many places, the smoking remains of the late fire: the ways mighty bad and dirty. This night Sir R. Ford told me how this day, at Christ Church Hospital, they have given a living over £200 per annum to Mr. Sanchy, my old acquaintance, which I wonder at, he commending him mightily; but am glad of it. He tells me, too, how the famous Stillingfleete [1] was a Bluecoat boy. The children at this day are provided for in the country by the House,[2] which I am glad also to hear.

17th. Up, and to the office, where all the morning sitting. At noon home to dinner, and then to the office busy also till very late, my heart joyed with the effects of my following my business, by easing my head of cares, and so home to supper and to bed.

18th. Up, and most of the morning finishing my entry of my journall during the late fire out of loose papers into this book, which did please me mightily when done, I writing till my eyes were almost blind therewith to make an end of it. Then all the rest of the morning, and, after a mouthful of dinner, all the afternoon in my closet till night, sorting all my papers, which have lain unsorted for all the time we were at Greenwich during the plague, which did please me also, I drawing on to put my office into a good posture, though much is behind. This morning come Captain Cocke to me, and tells me that the King comes to

[1] Dr. Edward Stillingfleet, Prebendary of St. Paul's, 1672; Dean of St. Paul's, 1678; and Bishop of Worcester, 1689. He died March 27th, 1699. His biographer sets down Cranborne, in Dorsetshire, and Ringwood, in Hampshire, as the sites of his schools.

[2] The preparatory school at Hertford was not founded until 1683.

the House this day to pass the Poll Bill and the Irish Bill; he tells me too that, though the Faction is very froward in the House, yet all will end well there. But he says that one had got a Bill ready to present in the House against Sir W. Coventry, for selling of places, and says he is certain of it, and how he was withheld from doing it. He says, that the Vice-chamberlaine is now one of the greatest men in England again, and was he that did prevail with the King to let the Irish Bill go with the word "Nuisance." He told me, that Sir G. Carteret's declaration of giving double to any man that will prove that any of his people have demanded or taken any thing for forwarding the payment of the wages of any man (of which he sent us a copy yesterday, which we approved of) is set up, among other places, upon the House of Lords' door. I do not know how wisely this is done. This morning, also, there come to the office a letter from the Duke of York, commanding our payment of no wages to any of the muster-masters of the fleete the last year, but only two, my brother Balty, taking notice that he had taken pains therein, and one Ward, who, though he had not taken so much as the other, yet had done more than the rest. This I was exceeding glad of for my own sake and his. At night I, by appointment, home, where W. Batelier and his sister Mary, and the two Mercers, to play at cards and sup, and did cut our great cake lately given us by Russell: a very good one. Here very merry late. Sir W. Pen told me this night how the King did make them a very sharp speech in the House of Lords to-day, saying that he did expect to have had more Bills;[1] that he purposes to prorogue them on Monday come se'nnight; that whereas they have unjustly conceived some jealousys of his making a peace, he declares he knows of no such thing or treaty: and so left them. But with so little effect, that as soon as he come into the

[1] On this day "An Act for raising Money by a Poll and otherwise towards the maintenance of the present War," and "An Act prohibiting the Importation of Cattle from Ireland and other parts beyond the Sea, and Fish taken by Foreigners," were passed. The king complained of the insufficient supply, and said, "'Tis high time for you to make good your promises, and 'tis high time for you to be in the country" ("Journals of the House of Lords," vol. xii., p. 81).

House, Sir W. Coventry moved, that now the King hath declared his intention of proroguing them, it would be loss of time to go on with the thing they were upon, when they were called to the King, which was the calling over the defaults of Members appearing in the House; for that, before any person could now come or be brought to town, the House would be up. Yet the Faction did desire to delay time, and contend so as to come to a division of the House; where, however, it was carried, by a few voices, that the debate should be laid by. But this shews that they are not pleased, or that they have not any awe over them from the King's displeasure. The company being gone, to bed.

19th. Up, and at the office all the morning. Sir W. Batten tells me to my wonder that at his coming to my Lord Ashly, yesterday morning, to tell him what prize-goods he would have saved for the Navy, and not sold, according to the King's order on the 17th, he fell quite out with him in high terms; and he says, too, that they did go on to the sale yesterday, even of the very hempe, and other things, at which I am astonished, and will never wonder at the ruine of the King's affairs, if this be suffered. At noon dined, and Mr. Pierce come to see me, he newly come from keeping his Christmas in the country. So to the office, where very busy, but with great pleasure till late at night, and then home to supper and to bed.

20th (Lord's day). Up betimes and down to the Old Swan, there called on Michell and his wife, which in her night linen appeared as pretty almost as ever to my thinking I saw woman. Here I drank some burnt brandy. They shewed me their house, which, poor people, they have built, and is very pretty. I invited them to dine with me, and so away to White Hall to Sir W. Coventry, with whom I have not been alone a good while, and very kind he is, and tells me how the business is now ordered by order of council for my Lord Bruncker to assist Sir J. Minnes in all matters of accounts relating to the Treasurer, and Sir W. Pen in all matters relating to the victuallers' and pursers' accounts, which I am very glad of, and the more for that I think it will not do me any hurt at all. Other discourse, much especially about the heat the House was in yesterday about the ill management of the Navy, which I was sorry to hear; though I think they were well answered, both by Sir G. Carteret and [Sir] W. Coventry, as he informs me the substance of their speeches. Having done with him, I home mightily satisfied with my being with him, and coming home I to church, and there, beyond expectation, find our seat, and all the church crammed, by twice as many people as used to be: and to my great joy find Mr. Frampton[1] in the pulpit; so to my great joy I hear him preach, and I think the best sermon, for goodness and oratory, without affectation or study, that ever I heard in my life. The truth is, he preaches the most like an apostle that ever I heard man; and it was much the best time that ever I spent in my life at church. His text, Ecclesiastes xi., verse 8th — the words, "But if a man live many years, and rejoice in them all, yet let him remember the days of darkness, for they shall be many. All that cometh is vanity." He done, I home, and there Michell and his wife, and we dined and mighty merry, I mightily taken more and more with her. After dinner I with my brother away by water to White Hall, and there walked in the Parke, and a little to my Lord Chancellor's, where the King and Cabinet met, and there met Mr. Brisband, with whom good discourse, to White Hall towards night, and there he did lend me "The Third Advice to a Paynter," a bitter satyre upon the service of the Duke of Albemarle the last year.[2] I took it home with me, and will copy it, having the former, being also mightily pleased with it. So after reading it, I to Sir W. Pen to discourse a little with him about the business of our prizes, and so home to supper and to bed.

21st. Up betimes, and with Sir W. Batten, [Sir] W. Pen, [Sir] R. Ford, by coach to the Swede's Resident's[3] in the Piatza, to discourse with him about two of our prizes, wherein he puts in his concernment as for his coun-

[1] See October 10th, 1666.

[2] See note, December 14th.

[3] Sir James Barkman Leyenberg, many years the Swedish Resident in this country. He is the person mentioned in the note to November 18th, 1660, as having in 1671 married the widow of Sir W. Batten (see November 18th, 1660). — B.

trymen. We had no satisfaction, nor did give him any, but I find him a cunning fellow. He lives in one of the great houses there, but ill-furnished; and come to us out of bed in his furred mittens and furred cap. Thence to Exeter House to the Doctors Commons, and there with our Proctors to Dr. Walker, who was not very well, but, however, did hear our matters, and after a dull seeming hearing of them read, did discourse most understandingly of them, as well as ever I heard man, telling us all our grounds of pretence to the prize would do no good, and made it appear but thus, and thus, it may be, but yet did give us but little reason to expect it would prove, which troubled us, but I was mightily taken to hear his manner of discourse. Thence with them to Westminster Hall, they setting me down at White Hall, where I missed of finding Sir G. Carteret, up to the Lords' House, and there come mighty seasonably to hear the Solicitor about my Lord Buckingham's pretence to the title of Lord Rosse.[1] Mr. Atturny Montagu[2] is also a good man, and so is old Sir P. Ball;[3] but the Solicitor[4] and Scroggs[5] after him are

[1] The ancient barony of De Ros, created by writ in 1264, was carried, with Belvoir Castle and other great possessions, into the family of Manners, by the marriage of Eleanor, sister and heir of Edmund, Lord De Ros (who died in 1508), to Sir Robert Manners. Katharine, only daughter and heir of Francis, sixth Earl of Rutland, married, first, George Villiers, Duke of Buckingham, and, secondly, Randal Macdonnal, Marquis of Antrim. On her death her son, the second Duke of Buckingham, became eighteenth Baron De Ros. He died without issue in 1687, and the barony remained in abeyance until the year 1806, when it was determined by the Crown in favour of Charlotte Boyle (Lady Henry Fitzgerald), who became third Baroness De Ros. The present Lord De Ros is the twenty-fourth baron.

[2] Sir William Montagu, second son of Edward, first Baron Montagu of Boughton, born about 1619, Attorney-General to the Queen, 1662 to 1676, when he was appointed Lord Chief Baron of the Exchequer. Removed by James II. in 1686, and died August 20th, 1706. The Duke of Buckingham's claim to the title of Lord Rosse was opposed by the Earl of Rutland. On January 31st "Mr. Montagu made a long argument to maintain the claim of the Earl of Rutland, and Mr. Solicitor made an answer on behalf of the claim of the Duke of Bucks" ("Journals of the House of Lords," vol. xii., p. 97).

[3] Sir Peter Ball was Queen's Attorney-General in 1662.

[4] Sir Heneage Finch, Solicitor-General, 1660-70.

[5] Sir William Scroggs, King's Serjeant, 1669; Chief Justice of the King's Bench, 1678-81. He died October 25th, 1683.

excellent men. Here spoke with my Lord Bellasses about getting some money for Tangier, which he doubts we shall not be able to do out of the Poll Bill, it being so strictly tied for the Navy. He tells me the Lords have passed the Bill for the accounts with some little amendments. So down to the Hall, and thence with our company to Exeter House, and then did the business I have said before, we doing nothing the first time of going, it being too early. At home find Lovett, to whom I did give my Lady Castlemayne's head to do. He is talking of going into Spayne to get money by his art, but I doubt he will do no good, he being a man of an unsettled head. Thence by water down to Deptford, the first time I have been by water a great while, and there did some little business and walked home, and there come into my company three drunken seamen, but one especially, who told me such stories, calling me Captain, as made me mighty merry, and they would leap and skip, and kiss what mayds they met all the way. I did at first give them money to drink, lest they should know who I was, and so become troublesome to me. Parted at Redriffe, and there home and to the office, where did much business. and then to Sir W. Batten's, where [Sir] W. Pen, [Sir] R. Ford, and I to hear a proposition [Sir] R. Ford was to acquaint us with from the Swedes Embassador, in manner of saying, that for money he might be got to our side and relinquish the trouble he may give us. Sir W. Pen did make a long simple declaration of his resolution to give nothing to deceive any poor man of what was his right by law, but ended in doing whatever any body else would, and we did commission Sir R. Ford to give promise of not beyond £350 to him and his Secretary, in case they did not oppose us in the Phœnix (the net profits of which, as [Sir] R. Ford cast up before us, the Admiral's tenths, and ship's thirds, and other charges all cleared, will amount to £3,000) and that we did gain her. [Sir] R. Ford did pray for a curse upon his family, if he was privy to anything more than he told us (which I believe he is a knave in), yet we all concluded him the most fit man for it and very honest, and so left it wholly to him to manage as he pleased. Thence to the office a little while longer, and so home, where W. Hewer's mother was, and Mrs. Turner, our neighbour, and supped with us. His mother a well-favoured old little woman, and a good woman, I believe. After we had supped, and merry, we parted late, Mrs. Turner having staid behind to talk a little about her lodgings, which now my Lord Bruncker upon Sir W. Coventry's surrendering do claim, but I cannot think he will come to live in them so as to need to put them out. She gone, we to bed all. This night, at supper, comes from Sir W. Coventry the Order of Councill[1] for my Lord Bruncker to do all the Comptroller's part relating to the Treasurer's accounts, and Sir W. Pen, all relating to the Victualler's, and Sir J. Minnes to do the rest. This, I hope, will do much better for the King than now, and, I think, will give neither of them ground to over-top me, as I feared they would; which pleases me mightily. This evening, Mr. Wren and Captain Cocke called upon me at the office, and there told me how the House was in better temper to-day, and hath passed the Bill for the remainder of the money, but not to be passed finally till they have done some other things which they will have passed with it; wherein they are very open, what their meaning is, which was but doubted before, for they do in all respects doubt the King's pleasing them.

22nd. Up, and there come to me Darnell the fiddler, one of the Duke's house, and brought me a set of lessons,

[1] The order in council is dated January 16, 1666-67, and commences as follows: "Whereas it is found by experience that the office of Comptroller of his Majesty's Navy, which being of ancient institution and exercised by a single person in times of less business, and when his Majesty's Navy was much less, hath in these times of action so much business depending upon it, and many times in places far distant the one from the other, that it is not possible for one person to manage it as it ought to be for the good of his Majesty's service; in consideration whereof, his Majesty hath pleased to direct that two assistants be added to Sir John Minnes, Knt., the present Comptroller of his Majesty's Navy, and that the work and employment of that office be so divided as that each may manage a distinct part thereof, and be able to render an exact account of his performance, that so it may appear where the default is, in case his Majesty's service suffer detriment through the undue execution of that office." The order is printed in "Memoires relating to the Conduct of the Navy," 1729, p. 59, and in Penn's "Memorials of Sir Wm. Penn," vol. ii., p. 435.

all three parts, I heard them play to the Duke of York after Christmas at his lodgings, and bid him get me them. I did give him a crowne for them, and did enquire after the musique of the "Siege of Rhodes," which, he tells me, he can get me, which I am mighty glad of. So to the office, where among other things I read the Councill's order about my Lord Bruncker and Sir W. Pen to be assistants to the Comptroller, which quietly went down with Sir J. Minnes, poor man, seeming a little as if he would be thought to have desired it, but yet apparently to his discontent; and, I fear, as the order runs, it will hardly do much good. At noon to dinner, and there comes a letter from Mrs. Pierce, telling me she will come and dine with us on Thursday next, with some of the players, Knipp, &c., which I was glad of, but my wife vexed, which vexed me; but I seemed merry, but know not how to order the matter, whether they shall come or no. After dinner to the office, and there late doing much business, and so home to supper, and to bed.

23rd. Up, and with Sir W. Batten and Sir W. Pen to White Hall, and there to the Duke of York, and did our usual business. Having done there, I to St. James's, to see the organ Mrs. Turner told me of the other night, of my late Lord Aubigney's; and I took my Lord Bruncker with me, he being acquainted with my present Lord Almoner, Mr. Howard,[1] brother to the Duke of Norfolke; so he and I thither and did see the organ, but I do not like it, it being but a bauble, with a virginall joining to it: so I shall not meddle with it. Here we sat and talked with him a good while, and he seems a good-natured gentleman: here I observed the deske which he hath, [made] to remove, and is fastened to one of the armes of his chayre. I do also observe the counterfeit windows there was, in the form of doors with looking-glasses instead of windows, which makes the room seem both bigger and lighter, I think; and I have some thoughts to have the like in one of my rooms. He discoursed much of the goodness of the

[1] Philip Howard, Lord Almoner to Queen Catherine, and third son of Henry Howard, Earl of Arundel, who died in 1652. He was made a cardinal by Clement X. in 1675, and died at Rome in 1694. He was generally styled the Cardinal of Norfolk. — B.

musique in Rome, but could not tell me how long musique had been in any perfection in that church, which I would be glad to know. He speaks much of the great buildings that this Pope,[1] whom, in mirth to us, he calls Antichrist, hath done in his time. Having done with the discourse, we away, and my Lord and I walking into the Park back again, I did observe the new buildings: and my Lord, seeing I had a desire to see them, they being the place for the priests and fryers, he took me back to my Lord Almoner; and he took us quite through the whole house and chapel, and the new monastery, showing me most excellent pieces in wax-worke: a crucifix given by a Pope to Mary Queen of Scotts, where a piece of the Cross is;[2] two bits set in the manner of a cross in the foot of the crucifix: several fine

[1] Fabio Chigi, of Siena, succeeded Innocent X. in 1655 as Alexander VII. He died May, 1667, and was succeeded by Clement IX.

[2] Pieces of "the Cross" were formerly held in such veneration, and were so common, that it has been often said enough existed to build a ship. Most readers will remember the distinction which Sir W. Scott represents Louis XI. (with great appreciation of that monarch's character), as drawing between an oath taken on a false piece and one taken on a piece of the *true* cross. Sir Thomas More, a very devout believer in relics, says ("Works," p. 119), that "Luther wished, in a sermon of his, that he had in his hand all the pieces of the Holy Cross; and said that if he so had, he would throw them there as never sun should shine on them: — and for what worshipful reason would the wretch do such villainy to the cross of Christ? Because, as he saith, that there is so much gold now bestowed about the garnishing of the pieces of the Cross, that there is none left for poore folke. Is not this a high reason? As though all the gold that is now bestowed about the pieces of the Holy Cross would not have failed to have been given to poor men, if they had not been bestowed about the garnishing of the Cross! and as though there were nothing lost, but what is bestowed about Christ's Cross!" Wolsey, says Cavendish, on his fall, gave to Norris, who brought him a ring of gold, as a token of good will from Henry, "a little chaine of gold, made like a bottle chain, with a cross of gold, wherein was a piece of the Holy Cross, which he continually wore about his neck, next his body; and said, furthermore, 'Master Norris, I assure you, when I was in prosperity, although it seem but small in value, yet I would not gladly have departed with the same for a thousand pounds.'" — *Life*, ed. 1852, p. 167. Evelyn mentions, "Diary," November 17th, 1664, that he saw in one of the chapels in St. Peter's a crucifix with a piece of the true cross in it. Amongst the jewels of Mary Queen of Scots was a cross of gold, which had been pledged to Hume of Blackadder for £1,000 (Chalmers's "Life," vol. i., p. 31). — B.

pictures, but especially very good prints of holy pictures. I saw the dortoire[1] and the cells of the priests, and we went into one; a very pretty little room, very clean, hung with pictures, set with books. The Priest was in his cell, with his hair clothes to his skin, bare-legged, with a sandall only on, and his little bed without sheets, and no feather bed; but yet, I thought, soft enough. His cord about his middle; but in so good company, living with ease, I thought it a very good life. A pretty library they have. And I was in the refectoire, where every man his napkin, knife, cup of earth, and basin of the same; and a place for one to sit and read while the rest are at meals. And into the kitchen I went, where a good neck of mutton at the fire, and other victuals boiling. I do not think they fared very hard. Their windows all looking into a fine garden and the Park; and mighty pretty rooms all. I wished myself one of the Capuchins. Having seen what we could here, and all with mighty pleasure, so away with the Almoner in his coach, talking merrily about the difference in our religions, to White Hall, and there we left him. I in my Lord Bruncker's coach, he carried me to the Savoy, and there we parted. I to the Castle Tavern, where was and did come all our company, Sir W. Batten, [Sir] W. Pen, [Sir] R. Ford, and our Counsel Sir Ellis Layton, Walt Walker,[2] Dr. Budd, Mr. Holder, and several others, and here we had a bad dinner of our preparing, and did discourse something of our business of our prizes, which was the work of the day. I staid till dinner was over, and there being no use of me I away after dinner without taking leave, and to the New Exchange, there to take up my wife and Mercer, and to Temple Bar to the Ordinary, and had a dish of meat for them, they having not dined, and thence to the King's house, and there saw "The Humerous Lieutenant:" a silly

[1] Dormitory. The French word was commonly used, and it was also anglicized as *dorter* and *dortour*. The latter word was used by Spenser ("Faerie Queene," VI., xii., 24). "This is a very fine convent with a very fine dortoire."—M. Leister, *Journey to Paris*, 1699, p. 131.

[2] Sir Walter Walker is referred to in the "Calendar of State Papers," 1666-67, p. 463.

play, I think; only the Spirit in it that grows very tall, and then sinks again to nothing, having two heads breeding upon one, and then Knipp's singing, did please us. Here, in a box above, we spied Mrs. Pierce; and, going out, they called us, and so we staid for them; and Knipp took us all in, and brought to us Nelly,[1] a most pretty woman, who acted the great part of Cœlia to-day very fine, and did it pretty well: I kissed her, and so did my wife; and a mighty pretty soul she is. We also saw Mrs. Hall,[2] which is my little Roman-nose black girl, that is mighty pretty: she is usually called Betty. Knipp made us stay in a box and see the dancing preparatory to to-morrow for "The Goblins," a play of Suckling's,[3] not acted these twenty-five years; which was pretty; and so away thence, pleased with this sight also, and specially kissing of Nell. We away, Mr. Pierce and I, on foot to his house, the women by coach. In our way we find the Guards of horse in the street, and hear the occasion to be news that the seamen are in a mutiny, which put me into a great fright; so away with my wife and Mercer home preparing against to-morrow night to have Mrs. Pierce and Knipp and a great deal more company to dance; and, when I come home, hear of no disturbance there of the seamen, but that one of them, being arrested to-day, others do go and rescue him. So to the office a little, and then home to supper, and to my chamber awhile, and then to bed.

24th. Up, and to the office, full of thoughts how to order the business of our merry meeting to-night. So to the office, where busy all the morning. [While we were sitting in the morning at the office, we were frightened with news of fire at Sir W. Batten's by a chimney taking fire, and it put me into much fear and trouble, but with a great many hands and pains it was soon stopped.][4] At noon home to dinner, and presently to the office to despatch my business, and also we sat all the afternoon to examine the

[1] Nell Gwynn.

[2] Betty Hall. She was Sir Philip Howard's mistress. Compare March 30th, 1667, and December 19th, 1668.—B.

[3] Sir John Suckling's play was first published in 1646, having been acted at the Blackfriars.

[4] The passage between brackets is written in the margin of the MS.

loss of The Bredagh,[1] which was done by as plain negligence as ever ship was. We being rose, I entering my letters and getting the office swept and a good fire made and abundance of candles lighted, I home, where most of my company come of this end of the town — Mercer and her sister, Mr. Batelier and Pembleton (my Lady Pen, and Pegg, and Mr. Lowther, but did not stay long, and I believe it was by Sir W. Pen's order; for they had a great mind to have staid), and also Captain Rolt. And, anon, at about seven or eight o'clock, comes Mr. Harris,[2] of the Duke's playhouse, and brings Mrs. Pierce with him, and also one dressed like a country-mayde with a straw hat on; which, at first, I could not tell who it was, though I expected Knipp: but it was she coming off the stage just as she acted this day in "The Goblins;" a merry jade. Now my house is full, and four fiddlers that play well. Harris I first took to my closet; and I find him a very curious and understanding person in all pictures and other things, and a man of fine conversation; and so is Rolt. So away with all my company down to the office, and there fell to dancing, and continued at it an hour or two, there coming Mrs. Anne Jones, a merchant's daughter hard by, who dances well, and all in mighty good humour, and danced with great pleasure; and then sung and then danced, and then sung many things of three voices — both Harris and Rolt singing their parts excellently. Among other things, Harris sung his Irish song — the strangest in itself, and the prettiest sung by him, that ever I heard. Then to supper in the office, a cold, good supper, and wondrous merry. Here was Mrs. Turner also, but the poor woman sad about her lodgings, and Mrs. Markham: after supper to dancing again and singing, and so continued till almost three in the morning, and then, with extraordinary pleasure, broke up — only towards morning, Knipp fell a little ill, and so my wife home with her to put her to bed,

[1] The report of "Examinations on oath of Capt. Page, commander, Barth. Peartree, master, Nich. Churchwood, chief mate, and two other officers named, as to the loss of their ship the Breda, by striking on the shoals off the Texel," dated January 24th, 1667, is preserved among the State Papers ("Calendar," 1666–67, p. 469).

[2] Henry Harris; see note, July 22nd, 1663.

and we continued dancing and singing; and, among other things, our Mercer unexpectedly did happen to sing an Italian song I know not, of which they two sung the other two parts to, that did almost ravish me, and made me in love with her more than ever with her singing. As late as it was, yet Rolt and Harris would go home to-night, and walked it, though I had a bed for them; and it proved dark, and a misly night, and very windy. The company being all gone to their homes, I up with Mrs. Pierce to Knipp, who was in bed; and we waked her, and there I handled her breasts and did baiser la, and sing a song, lying by her on the bed, and then left my wife to see Mrs. Pierce in bed to her, in our best chamber, and so to bed myself, my mind mightily satisfied with all this evening's work, and thinking it to be one of the merriest enjoyment I must look for in the world, and did content myself therefore with the thoughts of it, and so to bed; only the musique did not please me, they not being contented with less than 30*s.*

25th. Lay pretty long, then to the office, where Lord Bruncker and Sir J. Minnes and I did meet, and sat private all the morning about dividing the Controller's work according to the late order of Council, between them two and Sir W. Pen, and it troubled me to see the poor honest man, Sir J. Minnes, troubled at it, and yet the King's work cannot be done without it. It was at last friendlily ended, and so up and home to dinner with my wife. This afternoon I saw the Poll Bill, now printed; wherein I do fear I shall be very deeply concerned, being to be taxed for all my offices, and then for my money that I have, and my title, as well as my head. It is a very great tax; but yet I do think it is so perplexed, it will hardly ever be collected duly. The late invention of Sir G. Downing's is continued of bringing all the money into the Exchequer; and Sir G. Carteret's three pence is turned for all the money of this act into but a penny per pound, which I am sorry for. After dinner to the office again, where Lord Bruncker, [Sir] W. Batten, and [Sir] W. Pen and I met to talk again about the Controller's office, and there [Sir] W. Pen would have a piece of the great office cut out to make an office for him, which I opposed to the making him very angry, but I think I shall carry it against him, and then I care not. So a little troubled at this fray, I away by coach with my wife, and left her at the New Exchange, and I to my Lord Chancellor's, and then back, taking up my wife to my Lord Bellasses, and there spoke with Mr. Moone, who tells me that the peace between us and Spayne is, as he hears, concluded on, which I should be glad of, and so home, and after a little at my office, home to finish my journall for yesterday and to-day, and then a little supper and to bed. This day the House hath passed the Bill for the Assessment, which I am glad of; and also our little Bill, for giving any one of us in the office the power of justice of peace, is done as I would have it.

26th. Up, and at the office. Sat all the morning, where among other things I did the first unkind [thing] that ever I did design to Sir W. Warren, but I did it now to some purpose, to make him sensible how little any man's friendship shall avail him if he wants money. I perceive he do nowadays court much my Lord Bruncker's favour, who never did any man much courtesy at the board, nor ever will be able, at least so much as myself. Besides, my Lord would do him a kindness in concurrence with me, but he would have the danger of the thing to be done lie upon me, if there be any danger in it (in drawing up a letter to Sir W. Warren's advantage), which I do not like, nor will endure. I was, I confess, very angry, and will venture the loss of Sir W. Warren's kindnesses rather than he shall have any man's friendship in greater esteem than mine. At noon home to dinner, and after dinner to the office again, and there all the afternoon, and at night poor Mrs. Turner come and walked in the garden for my advice about her husband and her relating to my Lord Bruncker's late proceedings with them. I do give her the best I can but yet can lay aside some ends of my own in what advice I do give her. So she being gone I to make an end of my letters, and so home to supper and to bed, Balty lodging here with my brother, he being newly returned from mustering in the river.

27th (Lord's day). Up betimes, and leaving my wife to go by coach to hear Mr. Frampton preach, which I had a mighty desire she should, I down to the Old Swan, and there to Michell and staid while he and she dressed themselves, and here had a baiser or two of her, whom I love mightily; and then took them in a sculler (being by some means or other disappointed of my own boat) to White Hall, and so with them to Westminster, Sir W. Coventry, Bruncker and I all the morning together discoursing of the office business, and glad of the Controller's business being likely to be put into better order than formerly, and did discourse of many good things, but especially of having something done to bring the Surveyor's matters into order also. Thence I up to the King's closet, and there heard a good Anthem, and discourse with several people here about business, among others with Lord Bellasses, and so from one to another after sermon till the King had almost dined, and then home with Sir G. Carteret and dined with him, being mightily ashamed of my not having seen my Lady Jemimah so long, and my wife not at all yet since she come, but she shall soon do it. I thence to Sir Philip Warwicke, by appointment, to meet Lord Bellasses, and up to his chamber, but find him unwilling to discourse of business on Sundays; so did not enlarge, but took leave, and went down and sat in a low room, reading Erasmus "de scribendis epistolis,"[1] a very good book, specially one letter of advice to a courtier most true and good, which made me once resolve to tear out the two leaves that it was writ in, but I forebore it. By and by comes Lord Bellasses, and then he and I up again to Sir P. Warwicke and had much discourse of our Tangier business, but no hopes of getting any money. Thence I through the garden into the Park, and there met with Roger Pepys, and he and I to walk in the Pell Mell. I find by him that the House of Parliament continues full of ill humours, and he seems to dislike those that are troublesome more than needs, and do say how, in their late Poll Bill, which cost so much time, the yeomanry, and indeed two-thirds of the nation, are left out to be taxed, that there is not effectual provision enough made for collecting of the money; and then, that after a man his goods are

[1] The essay of Erasmus "de Conscribendis Epistolis" is printed in the first volume of his collected works, published at Leyden in 1703.

distrained and sold, and the over-plus returned, I am to have ten days to make my complaints of being over-rated if there be cause, when my goods are sold, and that is too late. These things they are resolved to look into again, and mend them before they rise, which they expect at furthest on Thursday next. Here we met with Mr. May,[1] and he and we to talk of several things, of building, and such like matters; and so walked to White Hall, and there I shewed my cozen Roger the Duchesse of York sitting in state, while her own mother stands by her; he had a desire, and I shewed him my Lady Castlemayne, whom he approves to be very handsome, and wonders that she cannot be as good within as she is fair without. Her little black boy came by him; and a dog being in his way, the little boy called to the dog: "Pox of this dog!" "Now," says he, blessing himself, "would I whip this child till the blood come, if it were my child!" and I believe he would. But he do by no means like the liberty of the Court, and did come with expectation of finding them playing at cards to-night, though Sunday; for such stories he is told, but how true I know not.[2] After walking up and down the Court with him, it being now dark and past six at night, I walked to the Swan in the Palace yard and there with much ado did get a waterman, and so I sent for the Michells, and they come, and their father Howlett and his wife with them, and there we drank, and so into the boat, poor Betty's head aching. We home by water, a fine moonshine and warm night, it having been also a very summer's day for warmth. I did get her hand to me under my cloak. . . . So there we parted at their house, and

[1] Hugh May.

[2] There is little reason to doubt that it was such as Evelyn describes it at a later time. "I can never forget the inexpressible luxury and prophaneness, gaming and all dissoluteness, and, as it were, total forgetfulness of God (it being Sunday evening) which this day se'nnight I was witness of; the King sitting and toying with his concubines, Portsmouth, Cleveland, Mazarin, &c. A French boy singing love songs in that glorious gallery, whilst about twenty of the great courtiers and other dissolute persons were at basset round a large table, a bank of at least £2,000 in gold before them; upon which two gentlemen who were with me made reflections with astonishment. Six days after was all in the dust." — *Diary*, February, 1685. — B.

he walked almost home with me, and then I home and to supper, and to read a little and to bed. My wife tells me Mr. Frampton[1] is gone to sea, and so she lost her labour to-day in thinking to hear him preach, which I am sorry for.

28th. Up, and down to the Old Swan, and there drank at Michell's and saw Betty, and so took boat and to the Temple, and thence to my tailor's and other places about business in my way to Westminster, where I spent the morning at the Lords' House door, to hear the conference beween the two Houses about my Lord Mordaunt, of which there was great expectation, many hundreds of people coming to hear it. But, when they come, the Lords did insist upon my Lord Mordaunt's having leave to sit upon a stool uncovered within their barr, and that he should have counsel, which the Commons would not suffer, but desired leave to report their Lordships' resolution to the House of Commons; and so parted for this day, which troubled me, I having by this means lost the whole day. Here I hear from Mr. Hayes that Prince Rupert is very bad still, and so bad, that he do now yield to be trepanned. It seems, as Dr. Clerke also tells me, it is a clap of the pox which he got about twelve years ago, and hath eaten to his head and come through his scull, so his scull must be opened, and there is great fear of him. Much work I find there is to do in the two Houses in a little time, and much difference there is between the two Houses in many things to be reconciled; as in the Bill for examining our accounts; Lord Mordaunt's; Bill for building the city, and several others. A little before noon I went to the Swan and eat a bit of meat, thinking I should have had occasion to have stayed long at the house, but I did not, but so home by coach, calling at Broad Street and taking the goldsmith home with me, and paid him £15 15*s.* for my silver standish. He tells me gold holds up its price still, and did desire me to let him have what old 20*s.* pieces I have, and he would give me 3*s.* 2*d.* change for each. He gone, I to the office, where business all the afternoon, and at night comes Mr. Gawden at my desire to me, and to-

[1] See note, October 10th, 1666.

morrow I shall pay him some money, and shall see what present he will make me, the hopes of which do make me to part with my money out of my chest, which I should not otherwise do, but lest this alteration in the Controller's office should occasion my losing my concernment in the Victualling, and so he have no more need of me. He gone, I to the office again, having come thence home with him to talk, and so after a little more business I to supper. I then sent for Mercer, and began to teach her "It is decreed," which will please me well, and so after supper and reading a little, and my wife's cutting off my hair short, which is grown too long upon my crown of my head, I to bed. I met this day in Westminster Hall Sir W. Batten and [Sir] W. Pen, and the latter since our falling out the other day do look mighty reservedly upon me, and still he shall do so for me, for I will be hanged before I seek to him, unless I see I need it.

29th. Up to the office all the morning, where Sir W. Pen and I look much askewe one upon another, though afterward business made us speak friendly enough, but yet we hate one another. At noon home to dinner, and then to the office, where all the afternoon expecting Mr. Gawden tc come for some money I am to pay him, but he comes not, which makes me think he is considering whether it be necessary to make the present he hath promised, it being possible this alteration in the Controller's duty may make my place in the Victualling unnecessary, so that I am a little troubled at it. Busy till late at night at the office, and Sir W. Batten come to me, and tells me that there is newes upon the Exchange to-day, that my Lord Sandwich's coach and the French Embassador's at Madrid, meeting and contending for the way, they shot my Lord's postilion and another man dead;[1] and that we have killed 25 of theirs, and that my Lord is well. How true this is I cannot tell, there being no newes of it at all at Court, as I am told late by one come thence, so that I hope it is not so. By and by comes Mrs. Turner to me, to make her complaint of her sad usage she receives from my Lord Bruncker, that he thinks much she hath not already got

[1] Intended as retaliation, perhaps, for the humiliation experienced by D'Estrades in London. See October 4th, 1661. — B.

another house, though he himself hath employed her night and day ever since his first mention of the matter, to make part of her house ready for him, as he ordered, and promised she should stay till she had fitted herself; by which and what discourse I do remember he had of the business before Sir W. Coventry on Sunday last I perceive he is a rotten-hearted, false man as any else I know, even as Sir W. Pen himself, and, therefore, I must beware of him accordingly, and I hope I shall. I did pity the woman with all my heart, and gave her the best council I could; and so, falling to other discourse, I made her laugh and merry, as sad as she came to me; so that I perceive no passion in a woman can be lasting long;[1] and so parted and I home, and there teaching my girle Barker part of my song "It is decreed," which she will sing prettily, and so after supper to bed.

30th. Fast-day for the King's death. I all the morning at my chamber making up my month's accounts, which I did before dinner to my thorough content, and find myself but a small gainer this month, having no manner of profits, but just my salary, but, blessed be God! that I am able to save out of that, living as I do. So to dinner, then to my chamber all the afternoon, and in the evening my wife and I and Mercer and Barker to little Michell's, walked, with some neats' tongues and cake and wine, and there sat with the little couple with great pleasure, and talked and eat and drank, and saw their little house, which is very pretty; and I much pleased therewith, and so walked home, about eight at night, it being a little moonshine and fair weather, and so into the garden, and, with Mercer, sang till my wife put me in mind of its being a fast day; and so I was sorry for it, and stopped, and home to cards awhile, and had opportunity para baiser Mercer several times, and so to bed.

31st. Up, and to the office, where we met and sat all the morning. At noon home to dinner, and by and by Mr. Osborne[2] comes from Mr. Gawden, and takes money and notes for £4,000, and leaves me acknowledgment for

[1] Pepys might be thinking of Francis I.'s

"Souvent femme varie,
Bien fol est qui s'y fie." — B.

[2] Nicholas Osborne.

£4,800 and odd; implying as if D. Gawden would give the £800 between Povy and myself, but how he will divide it I know not, till I speak with him, so that my content is not yet full in the business. In the evening stept out to Sir Robert Viner's to get the money ready upon my notes to D. Gawden, and there hear that Mr. Temple is very ill. I met on the 'Change with Captain Cocke, who tells me that he hears new certainty of the business of Madrid, how our Embassador and the French met, and says that two or three of my Lord's men, and twenty-one of the French men are killed, but nothing at Court of it. He fears the next year's service through the badness of our counsels at White Hall, but that if they were wise, and the King would mind his business, he might do what he would yet. The Parliament is not yet up, being finishing some bills. So home and to the office, and late home to supper, and to talk with my wife, with pleasure, and to bed. I met this evening at Sir R. Viner's our Mr. Turner, who I find in a melancholy condition about his being removed out of his house, but I find him so silly and so false that I dare not tell how to trust any advice to him, and therefore did speak only generally to him, but I doubt his condition is very miserable, and do pity his family. Thus the month ends: myself in very good health and content of mind in my family. All our heads full in the office at this dividing of the Comptroller's duty, so that I am in some doubt how it may prove to intrench upon my benefits, but it cannot be much. The Parliament, upon breaking up, having given the King money with much ado, and great heats, and neither side pleased, neither King nor them. The imperfection of the Poll Bill, which must be mended before they rise, there being several horrible oversights to the prejudice of the King, is a certain sign of the care anybody hath of the King's business. Prince Rupert very ill, and to be trepanned on Saturday next. Nobody knows who commands the fleete next year, or, indeed, whether we shall have a fleete or no. Great preparations in Holland and France, and the French have lately taken Antego[1] from us, which

[1] Antigua, one of the West India Islands (Leeward Islands), discovered by Columbus in 1493, who is said to have named it after a church at Seville called Santa Maria la Antigua. It was first settled by

vexes us. I am in a little care through my at last putting a great deal of money out of my hands again into the King's upon tallies for Tangier, but the interest which I wholly lost while in my trunk is a temptation while things look safe, as they do in some measure for six months, I think, and I would venture but little longer.

February 1st. Up, and to the office, where I was all the morning doing business, at noon home to dinner, and after dinner down by water, though it was a thick misty and rainy day, and walked to Deptford from Redriffe, and there to Bagwell's by appointment, where the mulier etoit within expecting me venir. . . . By and by su marido come in, and there without any notice taken by him we discoursed of our business of getting him the new ship building by Mr. Deane, which I shall do for him. Thence by and by after a little talk I to the yard, and spoke with some of the officers, but staid but little, and the new clerk of the 'Chequer, Fownes, did walk to Redriffe back with me. I perceive he is a very child, and is led by the nose by Cowly and his kinsman that was his clerk, but I did make him understand his duty, and put both understanding and spirit into him, so that I hope he will do well. [Much surprised to hear this day at Deptford that Mrs. Batters is going already to be married to him, that is now the Captain of her husband's ship. She seemed the most passionate mourner in the world. But I believe it cannot be true.][1] Thence by water to Billingsgate; thence to the Old Swan, and there took boat, it being now night, to Westminster Hall, there to the Hall, and find Doll Lane, and con elle I went to the Bell Taverne, and ibi je did do what I would con elle as well as I could, she sedendo sobre thus far and making some little resistance. But all with much content, and je tenai much pleasure cum ista. There parted, and I by coach home, and to the office, where pretty late doing business, and then home, and merry with

a few English families in 1632, and in 1663 another settlement was made under Lord Willoughby, to whom the entire island was granted by Charles II. In 1666 it was invaded by a French force, which laid waste all the settlement. It was reconquered by the English, and formally restored to them by the treaty of Breda.

[1] The passage between brackets is written in the margin of the MS.

my wife, and to supper. My brother and I did play with the base, and I upon my viallin, which I have not seen out of the case now I think these three years, or more, having lost the key, and now forced to find an expedient to open it. Then to bed.

2nd. Up, and to the office. This day I hear that Prince Rupert is to be trepanned. God give good issue to it. Sir W. Pen looks upon me, and I on him, and speak about business together at the table well enough, but no friendship or intimacy since our late difference about his closet, nor do I desire to have any. At noon dined well, and my brother and I to write over once more with my own hand my catalogue of books, while he reads to me. After something of that done, and dined, I to the office, where all the afternoon till night busy. At night, having done all my office matters, I home, and my brother and I to go on with my catalogue, and so to supper. Mrs. Turner come to me this night again to condole her condition and the ill usage she receives from my Lord Bruncker, which I could never have expected from him, and shall be a good caution to me while I live. She gone, I to supper, and then to read a little, and to bed. This night comes home my new silver snuffe-dish, which I do give myself for my closet, which is all I purpose to bestow in plate of myself, or shall need, many a day, if I can keep what I have. So to bed. I am very well pleased this night with reading a poem I brought home with me last night from Westminster Hall, of Dryden's[1] upon the present war; a very good poem.

3rd (Lord's day). Up, and with Sir W. Batten and [Sir] W. Pen to White Hall, and there to Sir W. Coventry's chamber, and there staid till he was ready, talking, and among other things of the Prince's being trepanned, which was in doing just as we passed through the Stone Gallery, we asking at the door of his lodgings, and were told so. We are all full of wishes for the good success; though I dare say but few do really concern ourselves for him in our hearts. Up to the Duke of York, and with him did our business we come about, and among other things resolve

[1] "Annus Mirabilis; the Year of Wonders, 1666, an historical Poem."

upon a meeting at the office to-morrow morning, Sir W. Coventry to be there to determine of all things necessary for the setting of Sir W. Pen to work in his Victualling business. This did awake in me some thoughts of what might in discourse fall out touching my imployment, and did give me some apprehension of trouble. Having done here, and after our laying our necessities for money open to the Duke of York, but nothing obtained concerning it, we parted, and I with others into the House, and there hear that the work is done to the Prince[1] in a few minutes without any pain at all to him, he not knowing when it was done. It was performed by Moulins.[2] Having cut the outward table, as they call it, they find the inner all corrupted, so as it come out without any force; and their fear is, that the whole inside of his head is corrupted[3] like that, which do yet make them afeard of him; but no ill accident appeared in the doing of the thing, but all with all imaginable success, as Sir Alexander Frazier did tell me himself, I asking him, who is very kind to me. I to the Chapel a little, but hearing nothing did take a turn into the Park, and then back to Chapel and heard a very good Anthem to my heart's delight, and then to Sir G. Carteret's to dinner, and before dinner did walk with him alone a good while, and from him hear our case likely for all these acts to be bad for money, which troubles me, the year speeding so fast, and he tells me that he believes the Duke of York will go to sea with the fleete, which I am sorry for in respect to his person, but yet there is no person in condition to com-

[1] Rupert.

[2] James Molines, Moleyns, or Mullins, one of a family of distinguished surgeons, born 1628. He was elected November 8th, 1665, in compliance with a recommendation from Charles II., surgeon to St. Thomas's Hospital as to ordinary avocations, and joint-surgeon with Mr. Hollyer for the cutting of the stone. He was afterwards appointed Surgeon in Ordinary to Charles II. and James II., and received the degree of M.D. from the University of Oxford, September 28th, 1681. He died February 8th, 1686, and was buried in St. Bride's Church, Fleet Street, where his monumental tablet still exists. This information is obtained from a valuable article by Dr. J. F. Payne on the various surgeons bearing the name of Molines in the "Dictionary of National Biography."

[3] See January 15th, 1664-65.

mand the fleete, now the Captains are grown so great, but him, it being impossible for anybody else but him to command any order or discipline among them. He tells me there is nothing at all in the late discourse about my Lord Sandwich and the French Embassador meeting and contending for the way, which I wonder at, to see the confidence of report without any ground. By and by to dinner, where very good company. Among other discourse, we talked much of Nostradamus[1] his prophecy of these times, and the burning of the City of London,[2] some of whose verses are put into Booker's[3] Almanack this year; and Sir

[1] Michael Nostradamus, a physician and astrologer, born in the diocese of Avignon, 1503. Amongst other predictions, one was interpreted as foreshowing the singular death of Hen. II. of France, by which his reputation was increased. In the 49th quatrain of his ninth century, the lines

"Gand et Bruxelles marcheront contre Anvers,
Sénat de Londres mettront à mort leur roi,"

may well be applied to the death of Charles I. Some coincidences in modern times are also curious. He speaks of the "renovation de siècle," in 1792, in which year, in fact, the French revolutionary kalendar took its rise. The landing of Bonaparte from Elba, at Fréjus, was supposed to be predicted in cent. x., quatrain xxiii.:

"Au peuple ingrat faites les remonstrances,
Par lors l'armée se saisera d'Antibe,
Dans l'arc Monech feront les doléances,
Et à Frejus l'un l'autre prendra ribe."

Jodelle's clever distich on Nostradamus is worthy of a place:

"Nostra damus, cum falsa damus, nam fallere nostrum est,
Et cum falsa damus, nil nisi nostra damus."

As well as the reply by Nostradamus's followers:

"Nostra damus, cum verba damus, quæ Nostradamus dat,
Nam quæcumque dedit, nil nisi vera dedit."

He succeeded too in rendering assistance to the inhabitants of Aix, during the plague, by a powder of his own invention. He died at Salon, July, 1566.— B.

[2] Roger L'Estrange, whose office it was to license the Almanacks, told Sir Edward Walker, "that most of them did foretel the fire of London last year, but hee caused itt to bee put out."— Ward's *Diary*, p. 94.— B.

[3] John Booker, an eminent astrologer and writing-master at Hadley. The words quoted by him from Nostradamus are (cent. ii., quatrain li.):

G. Carteret did tell a story, how at his death he did make the town swear that he should never be dug up, or his tomb opened, after he was buried; but they did after sixty years do it, and upon his breast they found a plate of brasse, saying what a wicked and unfaithful people the people of that place were, who after so many vows should disturb and open him such a day and year and hour; which, if true, is very strange. Then we fell to talking of the burning of the City; and my Lady Carteret herself did tell us how abundance of pieces of burnt paper were cast by the wind as far as Cranborne;[1] and among others she took up one, or had one brought her to see, which was a little bit of paper that had been printed, whereon there remained no more nor less than these words: "Time is, it is done."[2] After dinner I went and took a turn into the Park, and then took boat and away home, and there to my chamber and to read, but did receive some letters from Sir W. Coventry, touching the want of victuals to Kempthornes'[3] fleete going to the Streights and now in the Downes: which did trouble me, he saying that this disappointment might prove fatal; and the more, because Sir W. Coventry do intend to come to the office upon business to-morrow morning, and I shall not know what answer to give him. This did mightily trouble my mind; however, I fell to read a little in Hakewill's Apology,[4] and did satisfy myself mighty fair in the truth of the saying that the world do not grow old at all, but is in as good condition in all respects as ever it was as

"Le sang du juste à Londres fera faute,
Bruslez par foudre de vingt trois les six,
La dame antique cherra de place haute,
De mesme secte plusieurs seront occis." — B.

[1] In Windsor Forest.

[2] Sir C. Wren, it is well known, took up a stone from the ruins of St. Paul's having the word "Resurgam" inscribed, which he adopted. — B.

[3] Rear-Admiral John Kempthorne, a distinguished and gallant officer. His squadron was still in port on February 12th ("Calendar of State Papers," 1666-67, p. 509). He was knighted in 1670, and in 1675 made Commissioner at Portsmouth, which place he represented in parliament. Died 1679.

[4] "An Apology or Declaration of the Power and Providence of God in the Government of the World." By George Hakewill, a learned divine. Oxford, 1627. The work was frequently reprinted. — B.

to nature. I continued reading this book with great pleasure till supper, and then to bed sooner than ordinary, for rising betimes in the morning to-morrow. So after reading my usual vows to bed, my mind full of trouble against to-morrow, and did not sleep any good time of the night for thoughts of to-morrow morning's trouble.

4th. I up, with my head troubled to think of the issue of this morning, so made ready and to the office, where Mr. Gawden comes, and he and I discoursed the business well, and thinks I shall get off well enough; but I do by Sir W. Coventry's silence conclude that he is not satisfied in my management of my place and the charge it puts the King to, which I confess I am not in present condition through my late laziness to give any good answer to. But here do D. Gawden give me a good cordiall this morning, by telling me that he do give me five of the eight hundred pounds on his account remaining in my hands to myself, for the service I do him in my victualling business, and £100 for my particular share of the profits of my Tangier imployment as Treasurer. This do begin to make my heart glad, and I did dissemble it the better, so when Sir W. Coventry did come, and the rest met, I did appear unconcerned, and did give him answer pretty satisfactory what he asked me; so that I did get off this meeting without any ground lost, but rather a great deal gained by interposing that which did belong to my duty to do, and neither [Sir] W. Coventry nor [Sir] W. Pen did oppose anything thereunto, which did make my heart very glad. All the morning at this work, Sir W. Pen making a great deal of do for the fitting him in his setting out in his employment, and I do yield to any trouble that he gives me without any contradiction. Sir W. Coventry being gone, we at noon to dinner to Sir W. Pen's, he inviting me and my wife, and there a pretty good dinner, intended indeed for Sir W. Coventry, but he would not stay. So here I was mighty merry and all our differences seemingly blown over, though he knows, if he be not a fool, that I love him not, and I do the like that he hates me. Soon as dined, my wife and I out to the Duke's playhouse, and there saw "Heraclius,"[1] an excel-

[1] See note to March 8th, 1664.

lent play, to my extraordinary content; and the more from the house being very full, and great company; among others, Mrs. Steward, very fine, with her locks done up with puffs, as my wife calls them: and several other great ladies had their hair so, though I do not like it; but my wife do mightily — but it is only because she sees it is the fashion. Here I saw my Lord Rochester and his lady, Mrs. Mallet, who hath after all this ado married him; and, as I hear some say in the pit, it is a great act of charity, for he hath no estate. But it was pleasant to see how every body rose up when my Lord John Butler, the Duke of Ormond's son,[1] come into the pit towards the end of the play, who was a servant to Mrs. Mallet,[2] and now smiled upon her, and she on him. I had sitting next to me a woman, the likest my Lady Castlemayne that ever I saw anybody like another; but she is a whore, I believe, for she is acquainted with every fine fellow, and called them by their name, Jacke, and Tom, and before the end of the play frisked to another place. Mightily pleased with the play, we home by coach, and there a little to the office, and then to my chamber, and there finished my Catalogue of my books with my own hand, and so to supper and to bed, and had a good night's rest, the last night's being troublesome, but now my heart light and full of resolution of standing close to my business.

5th. Up, and to the office, where all the morning doing business, and then home to dinner. Heard this morning that the Prince is much better, and hath good rest. All the talk is that my Lord Sandwich hath perfected the peace with Spayne, which is very good, if true. Sir H. Cholmly was with me this morning, and told me of my Lord Bellasses's base dealings with him by getting him to give him great gratuities to near £2,000 for his friendship in the business of the Mole, and hath been lately underhand endeavouring to bring another man into his place as Governor, so as to receive his money of Sir H. Cholmly for

[1] Lord John Butler was born in 1643, and in January, 1676, married Anne, only daughter of Arthur Chichester, Earl of Donegal. In April, 1676, he was created Earl of Gowran. Died s. p., 1677 (see November 25th, 1666). — B.

[2] See November 25th, *ante*.

nothing. Dined at home, and after dinner come Mrs. Daniel and her sister and staid and talked a little, and then I to the office, and after setting my things in order at the office I abroad with my wife and little Betty Michell, and took them against my vowes, but I will make good my forfeit, to the King's house, to show them a play, "The Chances."[1] A good play I find it, and the actors most good in it; and pretty to hear Knipp sing in the play very properly, "All night I weepe;"[2] and sung it admirably. The whole play pleases me well: and most of all, the sight of many fine ladies — among others, my Lady Castlemayne and Mrs. Middleton: the latter of the two hath also a very excellent face and body, I think. Thence by coach to the New Exchange, and there laid out money, and I did give Betty Michell two pair of gloves and a dressing-box; and so home in the dark, over the ruins with a link. I was troubled with my pain, having got a bruise on my right testicle, I know not how. But this I did make good use of to make my wife shift sides with me, and I did come to sit avec Betty Michell, and there had her main, which elle did give me very frankly now, and did hazer whatever I voudrais avec la, which did plaisir me grandement, and so set her at home with my mind mighty glad of what I have prevailed for so far; and so home, and to the office, and did my business there, and then home to supper, and after to set some things right in my chamber, and so to bed. This morning, before I went to the office, there come to me Mr. Young and Whistler, flagg-makers, and with mighty earnestness did present me with, and press me to take a box, wherein I could not guess there was less than £100 in gold: but I do wholly refuse it, and did not at last take it. The truth is, not thinking them safe men to receive such a gratuity from, nor knowing any considerable courtesy that ever I did do them, but desirous to keep myself free from their reports, and to have it in my power to say I had refused their offer.

[1] A comedy by Beaumont and Fletcher, of which an alteration was produced by the Duke of Buckingham. The play which Pepys saw was probably the duke's revised version, although it was not published until 1682.

[2] This song is not in Beaumont and Fletcher, as printed, nor in the alteration of the play by the duke. — B.

6th. Up, lying a little long in bed, and by water to White Hall, and there find the Duke of York gone out, he being in haste to go to the Parliament, and so all my Brethren were gone to the office too. So I to Sir Ph. Warwicke's about my Tangier business, and then to Westminster Hall, and walked up and down, and hear that the Prince do still rest well by day and night, and out of pain; so as great hopes are conceived of him: though I did meet Dr. Clerke and Mr. Pierce, and they do say they believe he will not recover it, they supposing that his whole head within is eaten by this corruption, which appeared in this piece of the inner table. Up to the Parliament door, and there discoursed with Roger Pepys, who goes out of town this week, the Parliament rising this week also. So down to the Hall and there spied Betty Michell, and so I sent for burnt wine to Mrs. Michell's, and there did drink with the two mothers, and by that means with Betty, poor girle, whom I love with all my heart. And God forgive me, it did make me stay longer and hover all the morning up and down the Hall to busquer occasions para ambulare con elle. But ego ne pouvoir. So home by water and to dinner, and then to the office, where we sat upon Denis Gawden's accounts, and before night I rose and by water to White Hall, to attend the Council; but they sat not to-day. So to Sir W. Coventry's chamber, and find him within, and with a letter from the Downes in his hands, telling the loss of the St. Patricke coming from Harwich in her way to Portsmouth; and would needs chase two ships (she having the Malago fire-ship in company) which from English colours put up Dutch, and he would clap on board the Vice-Admirall; and after long dispute the admirall comes on the other side of him, and both together took him. Our fire-ship (Seely)[1] not coming in to fire all three, but come away, leaving her in their possession, and carried away by them: a ship[2] built at Bristoll the last

[1] "Captain Seely, captain of the fire-ship that deserted the Patrick, was this day (March 7th) shot to death on board his own vessel." — Pointer's *Chronological Hist. of Engl.*, vol. i., p. 216. — B.

[2] February 7th, "Hugh Salesbury to Williamson. A fire-ship which left Harwich with the St. Patrick, reports that she met off North Foreland two Dutch privateers; the commander of the St. Patrick indis-

year, of fifty guns and upwards, and a most excellent good ship. This made him very melancholy. I to talk of our wants of money, but I do find that he is not pleased with that discourse, but grieves to hear it, and do seem to think that Sir G. Carteret do not mind the getting of money with the same good cheer that he did heretofore, nor do I think he hath the same reason. Thence to Westminster Hall, thinking to see Betty Michell, she staying there all night, and had hopes to get her out alone, but missed, and so away by coach home, and to Sir W. Batten's, to tell him my bad news, and then to the office, and home to supper, where Mrs. Hewer was, and after supper and she gone, W. Hewer talking with me very late of the ill manner of Sir G. Carteret's accounts being kept, and in what a sad condition he would be if either Fenn or Wayth should break or die, and am resolved to take some time to tell Sir G. Carteret or my Lady of it, I do love them so well and their family. So to bed, my pain pretty well gone.

7th. Lay long with pleasure with my wife, and then up and to the office, where all the morning, and then home to dinner, and before dinner I went into my green dining room, and there talking with my brother upon matters relating to his journey to Brampton to-morrow, and giving him good counsel about spending the time when he shall stay in the country with my father, I looking another way heard him fall down, and turned my head, and he was fallen down all along upon the ground dead, which did put me into a great fright; and, to see my brotherly love! I did presently lift him up from the ground, he being as pale as death; and, being upon his legs, he did presently come to himself, and said he had something come into his stomach very hot. He knew not what it was, nor ever had such a fit before. I never was so frighted but once, when my wife was ill at Ware upon the road, and I did continue trembling a good while and ready to weepe to see him, he continuing mighty pale all dinner and melancholy, that I was loth to let him take his journey to-morrow; but he

creetly boarded one of them, the other boarded the St. Patrick, and both grappled him so that he yielded, and was carried to Holland. The fire-ship, instead of boarding one of them, only looked on" ("Calendar of State Papers," 1666-67, p. 499).

began to be pretty well, and after dinner my wife and Barker fell to singing, which pleased me pretty well, my wife taking mighty pains and proud that she shall come to trill and indeed I think she will. So to the office, and there all the afternoon late doing business, and then home, and find my brother pretty well. So to write a letter to my Lady Sandwich for him to carry, I having not writ to her a great while. Then to supper and so to bed. I did this night give him *20s.* for books, and as much for his pocket, and *15s.* to carry him down, and so to bed. Poor fellow! he is so melancholy, and withal, my wife says, harmless, that I begin to love him, and would be loth he should not do well.

8th. This morning my brother John come up to my bedside, and took his leave of us, going this day to Brampton. My wife loves him mightily as one that is pretty harmless, and I do begin to fancy him from yesterday's accident, it troubling me to think I should be left without a brother or sister, which is the first time that ever I had thoughts of that kind in my life. He gone, I up, and to the office, where we sat upon the Victuallers' accounts all the morning. A noon Lord Bruncker, Sir W. Batten, [Sir] W. Pen, and myself to the Swan in Leadenhall Street to dinner, where an exceedingly good dinner and good discourse. Sir W. Batten come this morning from the House, where the King hath prorogued this Parliament to October next. I am glad they are up. The Bill for Accounts was not offered, the party being willing to let it fall; but the King did tell them he expected it. They are parted with great heart-burnings, one party against the other. Pray God bring them hereafter together in better temper! It is said that the King do intend himself in this interval to take away Lord Mordaunt's government,[1] so as to do something to appease the House against they come together, and let them see he will do that of his own accord which is fit, without their forcing him; and that he will have his Commission for Accounts go on: which will be good things. At dinner we talked much of Cromwell; all saying he was

[1] As constable of Windsor Castle. See note, November 26, 1666

a brave fellow, and did owe his crowne he got to himself as much as any man that ever got one. Thence to the office, and there begun the account which Sir W. Pen by his late employment hath examined, but begun to examine it in the old manner, a clerk to read the Petty warrants, my Lord Bruncker upon very good ground did except against it, and would not suffer him to go on. This being Sir W. Pen's clerk he took it in snuff, and so hot they grew upon it that my Lord Bruncker left the office. He gone [Sir] W. Pen ranted like a devil, saying that nothing but ignorance could do this. I was pleased at heart all this while. At last moved to have Lord Bruncker desired to return, which he did, and I read the petty warrants all the day till late at night, that I was very weary, and troubled to have my private business of my office stopped to attend this, but mightily pleased at this falling out, and the truth is [Sir] W. Pen do make so much noise in this business of his, and do it so little and so ill, that I think the King will be little the better by changing the hand. So up and to my office a little, but being at it all day I could not do much there. So home and to supper, to teach Barker to sing another piece of my song, and then to bed.

9th. To the office, where we sat all the morning busy. At noon home to dinner, and then to my office again, where also busy, very busy late, and then went home and read a piece of a play, "Every Man in his Humour,"[1] wherein is the greatest propriety of speech that ever I read in my life: and so to bed. This noon come my wife's watchmaker, and received £12 of me for her watch; but Captain Rolt coming to speak with me about a little business, he did judge of the work to be very good work, and so I am well contented, and he hath made very good, that I knew, to Sir W. Pen and Lady Batten.

10th (Lord's day). Up and with my wife to church, where Mr. Mills made an unnecessary sermon upon Original Sin, neither understood by himself nor the people. Home, where Michell and his wife, and also there come Mr. Carter,[2] my old acquaintance of Magdalene College,

[1] Ben Jonson's well-known play.

[2] Charles Carter, who had a cure in Huntingdonshire. See February 8th, 1659–60, and December 23rd, 1660.

who hath not been here of many years. He hath spent his time in the North with the Bishop of Carlisle[1] much. He is grown a very comely person, and of good discourse, and one that I like very much. We had much talk of our old acquaintance of the College, concerning their various fortunes; wherein, to my joy I met not with any that have sped better than myself. After dinner he went away, and awhile after them Michell and his wife, whom I love mightily, and then I to my chamber there to my Tangier accounts, which I had let run a little behind hand, but did settle them very well to my satisfaction, but it cost me sitting up till two in the morning, and the longer by reason that our neighbour, Mrs. Turner, poor woman, did come to take her leave of us, she being to quit her house to-morrow to my Lord Bruncker, who hath used her very unhandsomely. She is going to lodgings, and do tell me very odde stories how Mrs. Williams[2] do receive the applications of people, and hath presents, and she is the hand that receives all, while my Lord Bruncker do the business, which will shortly come to be loud talk if she continues here, I do foresee, and bring my Lord no great credit. So having done all my business, to bed.

11th. Up, and by water to the Temple, and thence to Sir Ph. Warwicke's about my Tangier warrant for tallies, and there met my Lord Bellasses and Creed, and discoursed about our business of money, but we are defeated as to any hopes of getting [any] thing upon the Poll Bill, which I seem but not much troubled at, it not concerning me much. Thence with Creed to Westminster Hall, and there up and down, and heard that Prince Rupert is still better and better; and that he did tell Dr. Troutbecke[3] expressly that my Lord Sandwich is ordered home. I hear, too, that Prince Rupert hath begged the having of all the stolen prize-goods which he can find, and that he is looking out anew after them, which at first troubled me;

[1] Edward Rainbow, S.T.P., Bishop of Carlisle, 1664–84. He died March 26th, 1684, aged seventy-six years.

[2] Granger ("Biog. Hist. of Engl.," vol. iv., p. 190) describes an engraved portrait by Cooper, after Lely, of the Lady (Mrs.) Williams; but he describes her as the mistress of the Duke of York.

[3] John Troutbecke. See March 21st, 1665–66.

but I do see it cannot come to anything, but is done by Hayes, or some of his little people about him. Here, among other newes, I bought the King's speech at proroguing the House the other day, wherein are some words which cannot but import some prospect of a peace, which God send us! After walking a good while in the Hall, it being Term time, I home by water, calling at Michell's and giving him a fair occasion to send his wife to the New Exchange to meet my wife and me this afternoon. So home to dinner, and after dinner by coach to Lord Bellasses', and with him to Povy's house, whom we find with Auditor Beale and Vernatty about their accounts still, which is never likely to have end. Our business was to speak with Vernatty, who is certainly a most cunning knave as ever was born. Having done what we had to do there, my Lord carried me and set me down at the New Exchange, where I staid at Pottle's shop till Betty Michell come, which she did about five o'clock, and was surprised not to trouver my muger[1] there; but I did make an excuse good enough, and so I took elle down, and over the water to the cabinet-maker's, and there bought a dressing-box for her for *20s.*, but would require an hour's time to make fit. This I was glad of, thinking to have got elle to enter to a casa de biber, but elle would not, so I did not much press it, but suffered elle to enter à la casa de uno de sus hermanos, and so I past my time walking up and down, and among other places, to one Drumbleby, a maker of flageolets, the best in towne. He not within, my design to bespeak a pair of flageolets of the same tune, ordered him to come to me in a day or two, and so I back to the cabinet-maker's and there staid; and by and by Betty comes, and here we staid in the shop and above seeing the workman work, which was pretty, and some exceeding good work, and very pleasant to see them do it, till it was late quite dark, and the mistresse of the shop took us into the kitchen and there talked and used us very prettily, and took her for my wife, which I owned and her big belly, and there very merry, till my thing done, and then took coach and home. . . . But now comes our trouble, I did begin to fear that su marido might go to my

[1] **Muger = wife in Spanish.**

house to enquire pour elle, and there, trouvant my muger at home, would not only think himself, but give my femme occasion to think strange things. This did trouble me mightily, so though elle would not seem to have me trouble myself about it, yet did agree to the stopping the coach at the streete's end, and je allois con elle home, and there presently hear by him that he had newly sent su mayde to my house to see for her mistresse. This do much perplex me, and I did go presently home (Betty whispering me behind the tergo de her mari, that if I would say that we did come home by water, elle could make up la cose well satis), and there in a sweat did walk in the entry ante my door, thinking what I should say à my femme, and as God would have it, while I was in this case (the worst in reference à my femme that ever I was in in my life), a little woman comes stumbling to the entry steps in the dark; whom asking who she was, she enquired for my house. So knowing her voice, and telling her su donna is come home she went away. But, Lord! in what a trouble was I, when she was gone, to recollect whether this was not the second time of her coming, but at last concluding that she had not been here before, I did bless myself in my good fortune in getting home before her, and do verily believe she had loitered some time by the way, which was my great good fortune, and so I in a-doors and there find all well. So my heart full of joy, I to the office awhile, and then home, and after supper and doing a little business in my chamber I to bed, after teaching Barker a little of my song.

12th. Up, and to the office, where we sat all the morning, with several things (among others) discoursed relating to our two new assistant controllers, but especially Sir W. Pen, who is mighty troublesome in it. At noon home to dinner, and then to the office again, and there did much business, and by and by comes Mr. Moore, who in discourse did almost convince me that it is necessary for my Lord Sandwich to come home and take his command at sea this year, for that a peace is like to be. Many considerations he did give me hereupon, which were very good both in reference to the publick and his private condition. By and by with Lord Bruncker by coach to his house, there to hear some Italian musique: and here we met Tom Killigrew, Sir Robert Murray, and the Italian Signor Baptista,[1] who hath composed a play in Italian for the Opera, which T. Killigrew do intend to have up; and here he did sing one of the acts. He himself is the poet as well as the musician; which is very much, and did sing the whole from the words without any musique prickt, and played all along upon a harpsicon most admirably, and the composition most excellent. The words I did not understand, and so know not how they are fitted, but believe very well, and all in the recitativo very fine. But I perceive there is a proper accent in every country's discourse, and that do reach in their setting of notes to words, which, therefore, cannot be natural to any body else but them; so that I am not so much smitten with it as, it may be, I should be, if I were acquainted with their accent. But the whole composition is certainly most excellent; and the poetry, T. Killigrew and Sir R. Murray, who understood the words, did say was excellent. I confess I was mightily pleased with the musique. He pretends not to voice, though it be good, but not excellent. This done, T. Killigrew and I to talk: and he tells me how the audience at his house is not above half so much as it used to be before the late fire. That Knipp is like to make the best actor that ever come upon the stage, she understanding so well: that they are going to give her £30 a-year more. That the stage is now by his pains a thousand times better and more glorious than ever heretofore. Now, wax-candles, and many of them; then, not above 3 lbs. of tallow: now, all things civil, no rudeness anywhere; then, as in a bear-garden: then, two or three fiddlers; now, nine or ten of the best: then, nothing but rushes upon the ground, and every thing else mean; and now, all otherwise: then, the Queen seldom and the King never would come; now, not the King only for state, but all civil people do think they may come as well as any. He tells me that he hath gone several times, eight or ten times, he tells me, hence to Rome to hear good musique; so much he loves it, though he never did sing or play a

[1] Giovanni Baptista Draghi, an Italian musician in the service of Queen Catherine, and a composer of merit. He joined with Matthew Lock in composing the music to Shadwell's opera of "Psyche," produced in 1673.

note. That he hath ever endeavoured in the late King's time, and in this, to introduce good musique, but he never could do it, there never having been any musique here better than ballads. Nay, says, "Hermitt poore" and "Chevy Chese"[1] was all the musique we had; and yet no ordinary fiddlers get so much money as ours do here, which speaks our rudenesse still. That he hath gathered our Italians from several Courts in Christendome, to come to make a concert for the King, which he do give £200 a-year a-piece to: but badly paid, and do come in the room of keeping four ridiculous gundilows,[2] he having got the King to put them away, and lay out money this way; and indeed I do commend him for it, for I think it is a very noble undertaking. He do intend to have some times of the year these operas to be performed at the two present theatres, since he is defeated in what he intended in Moorefields on purpose for it; and he tells me plainly that the City audience was as good as the Court, but now they are most gone. Baptista tells me that Giacomo Charissimi[3] is still alive at Rome, who was master to Vinnecotio, who is one of the Italians that the King hath here, and the chief composer of them. My great wonder is, how this man do to keep in memory so perfectly the musique of the whole act, both for the voice and the instrument too. I confess I do admire it: but in recitativo the sense much helps him, for there is but one proper way of discoursing and giving the accents. Having done our discourse, we

[1] "Like hermit poor in pensive place obscure" is found in "The Phœnix Nest," 1593, and in Harl. MS. No. 6910, written soon after 1596. It was set to music by Alfonso Ferrabosco, and published in his "Ayres," 1609. The song was a favourite with Izaak Walton, and is alluded to in "Hudibras" (Part I., canto ii., line 1169). See Rimbault's "Little Book of Songs and Ballads," 1851, p. 98. Both versions of the famous ballad of "Chevy Chase" are printed in Percy's "Reliques."

[2] The gondolas mentioned before, as sent by the Doge of Venice. See September 12th, 1661.—B.

[3] "The name which is foremost in one's mind, if one speaks of Italian music in the second half of the seventeenth century, is Carissimi, the last great representative of the Roman school, and himself the precursor and model of a number of great musicians in his own country, of Lulli in France, and through him of Humphreys and Purcell in England." — F. Hueffer, *Italian and other Studies*, 1883, p. 296.

all took coaches, my Lord's and T. Killigrew's, and to Mrs. Knipp's chamber, where this Italian is to teach her to sing her part. And so we all thither, and there she did sing an Italian song or two very fine, while he played the bass upon a harpsicon there; and exceedingly taken I am with her singing, and believe that she will do miracles at that and acting. Her little girl is mighty pretty and witty. After being there an hour, and I mightily pleased with this evening's work, we all parted, and I took coach and home, where late at my office, and then home to enter my last three days' Journall; and so to supper and to bed, troubled at nothing, but that these pleasures do hinder me in my business, and the more by reason of our being to dine abroad to-morrow, and then Saturday next is appointed to meet again at my Lord Bruncker's lodgings, and there to have the whole quire of Italians; but then I do consider that this is all the pleasure I live for in the world, and the greatest I can ever expect in the best of my life, and one thing more, that by hearing this man to-night, and I think Captain Cooke to-morrow, and the quire of Italians on Saturday, I shall be truly able to distinguish which of them pleases me truly best, which I do much desire to know and have good reason and fresh occasion of judging.

13th. Up, and by water to White Hall, where to the Duke of York, and there did our usual business; but troubled to see that, at this time, after our declaring a debt to the Parliament of £900,000, and nothing paid since, but the debt increased, and now the fleete to set out; to hear that the King hath ordered but £35,000 for the setting out of the fleete, out of the Poll Bill, to buy all provisions, when five times as much had been little enough to have done any thing to purpose. They have, indeed, ordered more for paying off of seamen and the Yards to some time, but not enough for that neither. Another thing is, the acquainting the Duke of York with the case of Mr. Lanyon,[1] our agent at Plymouth, who has trusted us to £8,000 out of purse; we are not in condition, after so many promises, to obtain him a farthing, nor though a message was carried by Sir G.

[1] There are several letters from John Lanyon to the Navy Commissioners among the State Papers, in some of which he asks for money ("Calendar," 1666–67).

Carteret and Sir W. Coventry to the Commissioners for Prizes, that he might have £3,000 out of £20,000 worth of prizes to be shortly sold there, that he might buy at the candle and pay for the goods out of bills, and all would [not] do any thing, but that money must go all another way, while the King's service is undone, and those that trust him perish. These things grieve me to the heart. The Prince, I hear, is every day better and better. So away by water home, stopping at Michell's, where Mrs. Martin was, and I there drank with them and whispered with Betty, who tells me all is well, but was prevented in something she would have said, her marido venant just then, a news which did trouble me, and so drank and parted and home, and there took up my wife by coach, and to Mrs. Pierce's, there to take her up, and with them to Dr. Clerke's, by invitation, where we have not been a great while, nor had any mind to go now, but that the Dr., whom I love, would have us choose a day. Here was his wife, painted, and her sister Worshipp, a widow now and mighty pretty in her mourning. Here was also Mr. Pierce and Mr. Floyd,[1] Secretary to the Lords Commissioners of Prizes, and Captain Cooke, to dinner, an ill and little mean one, with foul cloth and dishes, and everything poor. Discoursed most about plays and the Opera, where, among other vanities, Captain Cooke had the arrogance to say that he was fain to direct Sir W. Davenant in the breaking of his verses into such and such lengths, according as would be fit for musick, and how he used to swear at Davenant, and command him that way, when W. Davenant would be angry, and find fault with this or that note — but a vain coxcomb I perceive he is, though he sings and composes so well. But what I wondered at, Dr. Clerke did say that Sir W. Davenant is no good judge of a dramatick poem, finding fault with his choice of Henry the 5th,[2] and others, for the stage, when I do think, and he confesses, "The Siege of Rhodes" as good as ever was writ. After dinner Captain Cooke and two of his boys to sing, but it was indeed both in performance and composition most plainly

[1] Thomas Lloyd or Floyd.

[2] This must refer to Lord Orrery's play of "Henry V.," acted at the Duke's House on August 13th, 1664.

below what I heard last night, which I could not have believed. Besides overlooking the words which he sung, I find them not at all humoured as they ought to be, and as I believed he had done all he had sett. Though he himself do indeed sing in a manner as to voice and manner the best I ever heard yet, and a strange mastery he hath in making of extraordinary surprising closes, that are mighty pretty, but his bragging that he do understand tones and sounds as well as any man in the world, and better than Sir W. Davenant or any body else, I do not like by no means, but was sick of it and of him for it. He gone, Dr. Clerke fell to reading a new play, newly writ, of a friend's of his; but, by his discourse and confession afterwards, it was his own. Some things, but very few, moderately good; but infinitely far from the conceit, wit, design, and language of very many plays that I know; so that, but for compliment, I was quite tired with hearing it. It being done, and commending the play, but against my judgment, only the prologue magnifying the happiness of our former poets when such sorry things did please the world as was then acted, was very good. So set Mrs. Pierce at home, and away ourselves home, and there to my office, and then my chamber till my eyes were sore at writing and making ready my letter and accounts for the Commissioners of Tangier to-morrow, which being done, to bed, hearing that there was a very great disorder this day at the Ticket Office, to the beating and bruising of the face of Carcasse very much. A foul evening this was to-night, and I mightily troubled to get a coach home; and, which is now my common practice, going over the ruins in the night, I rid with my sword drawn in the coach.

14th. Up and to the office, where Carcasse comes with his plaistered face, and called himself Sir W. Batten's martyr, which made W. Batten mad almost, and mighty quarrelling there was. We spent the morning almost wholly upon considering some way of keeping the peace at the Ticket Office; but it is plain that the care of that office is nobody's work, and that is it that makes it stand in the ill condition it do. At noon home to dinner, and after dinner by coach to my Lord Chancellor's, and there a meeting: the Duke of York, Duke of Albemarle, and several other

Lords of the Commission of Tangier. And there I did present a state of my accounts, and managed them well; and my Lord Chancellor did say, though he was, in other things, in an ill humour, that no man in England was of more method, nor made himself better understood than myself. But going, after the business of money was over, to other businesses, of settling the garrison, he did fling out, and so did the Duke of York, two or three severe words touching my Lord Bellasses: that he would have no Governor come away from thence in less than three years; no, though his lady were with child. "And," says the Duke of York, "there should be no Governor continue so, longer than three years." "Nor," says Lord Arlington, "when our rules are once set, and upon good judgment declared, no Governor should offer to alter them." "We must correct the many things that are amiss there; for," says the Lord Chancellor, "you must think we do hear of more things amisse than we are willing to speak before our friends' faces." My Lord Bellasses would not take notice of their reflecting on him, and did wisely, but there were also many reflections on him. Thence away by coach to Sir H. Cholmly and Fitzgerald and Creed, setting down the two latter at the New Exchange. And Sir H. Cholmly and I to the Temple, and there walked in the dark in the walks talking of newes; and he surprises me with the certain newes that the King did last night in Council declare his being in treaty with the Dutch: that they had sent him a very civil letter, declaring that, if nobody but themselves were concerned, they would not dispute the place of treaty, but leave it to his choice; but that, being obliged to satisfy therein a Prince of equal quality with himself, they must except any place in England or Spayne. And so the King hath chosen the Hague, and thither hath chose my Lord Hollis and Harry Coventry[1] to go Embassadors to treat;

[1] Henry, third son of Thomas, first Lord Coventry, Lord Keeper; after the Restoration he was made a Groom of the Bedchamber, and elected M.P. for Droitwich in 1661. In 1664 he was sent Envoy Extraordinary to Sweden, where he remained two years, and was again employed on an embassy to the same court in 1671. He also succeeded (with Lord Holles) in negotiating the peace at Breda here alluded to, and in 1672 became Secretary of State, which office he

which is so mean a thing, as all the world will believe, that we do go to beg a peace of them, whatever we pretend. And it seems all our Court are mightily for a peace, taking this to be the time to make one, while the King hath money, that he may save something of what the Parliament hath given him to put him out of debt, so as he may need the help of no more Parliaments, as to the point of money: but our debt is so great, and expence daily so encreased, that I believe little of the money will be saved between this and the making of the peace up. But that which troubles me most is, that we have chosen a son of Secretary Morris,[1] a boy never used to any business, to go Embassador [Secretary] to the Embassy, which shows how little we are sensible of the weight of the business upon us. God therefore give a good end to it, for I doubt it, and yet do much more doubt the issue of our continuing the war, for we are in no wise fit for it, and yet it troubles me to think what Sir H. Cholmly says, that he believes they will not give us any reparation for what we have suffered by the war, nor put us into any better condition than what we were in before the war, for that will be shamefull for us. Thence parted with him and home through the dark over the ruins by coach, with my sword drawn, to the office, where dispatched some business; and so home to my chamber and to supper and to bed. This morning come up to my wife's bedside, I being up dressing myself, little Will Mercer to be her Valentine; and brought her name writ upon blue paper in gold letters, done by himself, very pretty; and we were both well pleased with it. But I am also this year my wife's Valentine, and it will cost me £5; but that I must have laid out if we had not been Valentines. So to bed.

15th. Up and with Sir W. Batten and [Sir] J. Minnes by coach to White Hall, where we attended upon the Duke of York to complain of the disorders the other day among the seamen at the Pay at the Ticket Office, and that it arises from lack of money, and that we desire, unless better provided for with money, to have nothing more to do with

resigned in 1679, on account of ill-health. He died unmarried, December 7th, 1686.—B.

[1] Sir William Morris had several sons.

the payment of tickets, it being not our duty; and the Duke of York and [Sir] W. Coventry did agree to it, so that I hope we shall be rid of that trouble. This done, I moved for allowance for a house for Mr. Turner, and got it granted. Then away to Westminster Hall, and there to the Exchequer about my tallies, and so back to White Hall, and so with Lord Bellasses to the Excise Office, where met by Sir H. Cholmly to consider about our business of money there, and that done, home and to dinner, where I hear Pegg Pen is married[1] this day privately; no friends, but two or three relations on his side and hers. Borrowed many things of my kitchen for dressing their dinner. So after dinner to the office, and there busy and did much business, and late at it. Mrs. Turner come to me to hear how matters went; I told her of our getting rent for a house for her. She did give me account of this wedding to-day, its being private being imputed to its being just before Lent, and so in vain to make new clothes till Easter, that they might see the fashions as they are like to be this summer; which is reason good enough. Mrs. Turner tells me she hears [Sir W. Pen] gives £4,500 or £4,000 with her. They are gone to bed, so I wish them much sport, and home to supper and to bed. They own the treaty for a peace publickly at Court, and the Commissioners providing themselves to go over as soon as a passe comes for them.

16th. Up, and to the office, where all the morning. Among other things great heat we were all in on one side or other in the examining witnesses against Mr. Carcasse about his buying of tickets, and a cunning knave I do believe he is, and will appear, though I have thought otherwise heretofore. At noon home to dinner, and there find Mr. Andrews, and Pierce and Hollyard, and they dined with us and merry, but we did rise soon for saving of my wife's seeing a new play this afternoon, and so away by coach, and left her at Mrs. Pierce's, myself to the Excise Office about business, and thence to the Temple to

[1] The marriage licence of Anthony Lowther, of Marske, co. York, bachelor, 24, and Margaret Pen, spinster, 15, is dated February 12th, 1666-67 (Chester's "London Marriage Licences," ed. Foster, 1887, col. 865).

walk a little only, and then to Westminster to pass away time till anon, and here I went to Mrs. Martin's to thank her for her oysters. . . . Thence away to my Lord Bruncker's, and there was Sir Robert Murray, whom I never understood so well as now by this opportunity of discourse with him, a most excellent man of reason and learning, and understands the doctrine of musique, and everything else I could discourse of, very finely. Here come Mr. Hooke, Sir George Ent, Dr. Wren, and many others; and by and by the musique, that is to say, Signor Vincentio,[1] who is the master-composer, and six more, whereof two eunuches, so tall, that Sir T. Harvey said well that he believes they do grow large by being gelt as our oxen do, and one woman very well dressed and handsome enough, but would not be kissed, as Mr. Killigrew, who brought the company in, did acquaint us. They sent two harpsicons before; and by and by, after tuning them, they begun; and, I confess, very good musique they made; that is, the composition exceeding good, but yet not at all more pleasing to me than what I have heard in English by Mrs. Knipp, Captain Cooke, and others. Nor do I dote on the eunuches; they sing, indeed, pretty high, and have a mellow kind of sound, but yet I have been as well satisfied with several women's voices and men also, as Crispe of the Wardrobe. The women sung well, but that which distinguishes all is this, that in singing, the words are to be considered, and how they are fitted with notes, and then the common accent of the country is to be known and understood by the hearer, or he will never be a good judge of the vocal musique of another country. So that I was not taken with this at all, neither understanding the first, nor by practice reconciled to the latter, so that their motions, and risings and fallings, though it may be pleasing to an Italian, or one that understands the tongue, yet to me it did not, but do from my heart believe that I could set words in English, and make musique of them more agreeable to any Englishman's eare (the most judicious) than any Italian musique set for the voice, and performed

[1] Perhaps the person called Vinnecotio, February 12th, 1666–67. There was a German organist and composer named Gasparus Vincentius, who lived about this time.

before the same man, unless he be acquainted with the Italian accent of speech. The composition as to the musique part was exceeding good, and their justness in keeping time by practice much before any that we have, unless it be a good band of practised fiddlers. So away, here being Captain Cocke, who is stole away, leaving them at it, in his coach, and to Mrs. Pierce's, where I took up my wife, and there I find Mrs. Pierce's little girl is my Valentine, she having drawn me; which I was not sorry for, it easing me of something more that I must have given to others. But here I do first observe the fashion of drawing of mottos as well as names; so that Pierce, who drew my wife, did draw also a motto, and this girl drew another for me. What mine was I have forgot; but my wife's was, "Most virtuous and most fair;" which, as it may be used, or an anagram made upon each name, might be very pretty. Thence with Cocke and my wife, set him at home, and then we home. To the office, and there did a little business, troubled that I have so much been hindered by matters of pleasure from my business, but I shall recover it I hope in a little time. So home and to supper, not at all smitten with the musique to-night, which I did expect should have been so extraordinary, Tom Killigrew crying it up, and so all the world, above all things in the world, and so to bed. One wonder I observed to-day, that there was no musique in the morning to call up our new-married people, which is very mean, methinks, and is as if they had married like dog and bitch.

17th (Lord's day). Up, and called at Michell's, and took him and his wife and carried them to Westminster, I landing at White Hall, and having no pleasure in the way con elle; and so to the Duke's, where we all met and had a hot encounter before the Duke of York about the business of our payments at the Ticket Office, where we urged that we had nothing to do to be troubled with the pay, having examined the tickets. Besides, we are neglected, having not money sent us in time, but to see the baseness of my brethren, not a man almost put in a word but Sir W. Coventry, though at the office like very devils in this point. But I did plainly declare that, without money, no fleete could be expected, and desired the Duke of York to take notice of it, and notice was taken of it, but I doubt will do no good. But I desire to remember it as a most prodigious thing that to this day my Lord Treasurer hath not consulted counsel, which Sir W. Coventry and I and others do think is necessary, about the late Poll act, enough to put the same into such order as that any body dare lend money upon it, though we have from this office under our hands related the necessity thereof to the Duke of York, nor is like to be determined in, for ought I see, a good while had not Sir W. Coventry plainly said that he did believe it would be a better work for the King than going to church this morning, to send for the Atturney Generall to meet at the Lord Treasurer's this afternoon and to bring the thing to an issue, saying that himself, were he going to the Sacrament, would not think he should offend God to leave it and go to the ending this work, so much it is of moment to the King and Kingdom. Hereupon the Duke of York said he would presently speak to the King, and cause it to be done this afternoon. Having done here we broke up, having done nothing almost though for all this, and by and by I met Sir G. Carteret, and he is stark mad at what has passed this morning, and I believe is heartily vexed with me. I said little, but I am sure the King will suffer if some better care be not taken than he takes to look after this business of money. So parted, and I by water home and to dinner, W. Hewer with us, a good dinner and very merry, my wife and I, and after dinner to my chamber, to fit some things against the Council anon, and that being done away to White Hall by water, and thence to my Lord Chancellor's, where I met with, and had much pretty discourse with, one of the Progers's that knows me; and it was pretty to hear him tell me, of his own accord, as a matter of no shame, that in Spayne he had a pretty woman, his mistress, whom, when money grew scarce with him, he was forced to leave, and afterwards heard how she and her husband lived well, she being kept by an old fryer who used her as his whore; but this, says he, is better than as our ministers do, who have wives that lay up their estates, and do no good nor relieve any poor — no, not our greatest prelates, and I think he is in the right for my part. Staid till the Council was up, and attended the King and Duke of York round the Park, and was asked several questions by both; but I was in pain, lest they should ask me what I could not answer; as the Duke of York did the value of the hull of the St. Patrick[1] lately lost, which I told him I could not presently answer; though I might have easily furnished myself to answer all those questions. They stood a good while to see the ganders and geese tread one another in the water, the goose being all the while kept for a great while quite under water, which was new to me, but they did make mighty sport of it, saying (as the King did often) "Now you shall see a marriage between this and that," which did not please me. They gone, by coach to my Lord Treasurer's, as the Duke of York told me, to settle the business of money for the navy, I walked into the Court to and again till night, and there met Colonell Reames, and he and I walked together a great while complaining of the ill-management of things, whereof he is as full as I am. We ran over many persons and things, and see nothing done like men like to do well while the King minds his pleasures so much. We did bemoan it that nobody would or had authority enough with the King to tell him how all things go to rack and will be lost. Then he and I parted, and I to Westminster to the Swan, and there staid till Michell and his wife come. Old Michell and his wife come to see me, and there we drank and laughed a little, and then the young ones and I took boat, it being fine moonshine. I did to my trouble see all the way that elle did get as close a su marido as elle could, and turn her mains away quand je did endeavour to take one. . . . So that I had no pleasure at all con elle ce night. When we landed I did take occasion to send him back à the bateau while I did get a baiser or two, and would have taken la by la hand, but elle did turn away, and quand I said shall I not toucher te answered ego no love touching, in a slight mood. I seemed not to take notice of it, but parted kindly; su marido did aller with me almost a my case, and there we parted, and so I home troubled at this, but I

[1] See note, February 6th, *ante*.

think I shall make good use of it and mind my business more. At home, by appointment, comes Captain Cocke to me, to talk of State matters, and about the peace; who told me that the whole business is managed between Kevet, Burgomaster of Amsterdam, and my Lord Arlington, who hath, by the interest of his wife[1] there, some interest. We have proposed the Hague, but know not yet whether the Dutch will like it; or, if they do, whether the French will. We think we shall have the help of the information of their affairs and state, and the helps of the Prince of Orange his faction; but above all, that De Witt, who hath all this while said he cannot get peace, his mouth will now be stopped, so that he will be forced to offer fit terms for fear of the people; and, lastly, if France or Spayne do not please us, we are in a way presently to clap up a peace with the Dutch, and secure them. But we are also in treaty with France, as he says: but it must be to the excluding our alliance with the King of Spayne or House of Austria; which we do not know presently what will be determined in. He tells me the Vice-Chamberlaine is so great with the King, that, let the Duke of York, and Sir W. Coventry, and this office, do or say what they will, while the King lives, Sir G. Carteret will do what he will; and advises me to be often with him, and eat and drink with him; and tells me that he doubts he is jealous of me, and was mighty mad to-day at our discourse to him before the Duke of York. But I did give him my reasons that the office is concerned to declare that, without money, the King's work cannot go on. From that discourse we ran to others, and among the others he assures me that Henry Bruncker is one of the shrewdest fellows for parts in England, and a dangerous man; that if ever the Parliament comes again Sir W. Coventry cannot stand, but in this I believe him not; that, while we want money so much in the Navy, the Officers of the Ordnance have at this day £300,000 good in tallys, which they can command money upon, got by their over-estimating their charge in getting it reckoned as a fifth part of the expense of the Navy; that Harry Coventry, who is to go upon this treaty with

[1] See July 12th, 1666.

Lord Hollis (who he confesses to be a very wise man) into Holland, is a mighty quick, ready man, but not so weighty as he should be, he knowing him so well in his drink as he do; that, unless the King do do something against my Lord Mordaunt and the Patent for the Canary Company, before the Parliament next meets, he do believe there will be a civil war before there will be any more money given, unless it may be at their perfect disposal; and that all things are now ordered to the provoking of the Parliament against they come next, and the spending the King's money, so as to put him into a necessity of having it at the time it is prorogued for, or sooner. Having discoursed all this and much more, he away, and I to supper and to read my vows, and to bed. My mind troubled about Betty Michell, pour sa carriage this night envers moy, but do hope it will put me upon doing my business. This evening, going to the Queen's side [1] to see the ladies, I did find the Queene, the Duchesse of York, and another or two, at cards, with the room full of great ladies and men; which I was amazed at to see on a Sunday, having not believed it; but, contrarily, flatly denied the same a little while since to my cozen Roger Pepys.[2] I did this day, going by water, read the answer to "The Apology for Papists,"[3] which did like me mightily, it being a thing as well writ as I think most things that ever I read in my life, and glad I am that I read it.

18th. Up, and to my bookbinder's, and there mightily pleased to see some papers of the account we did give the Parliament of the expense of the Navy sewed together, which I could not have conceived before how prettily it was done. Then by coach to the Exchequer about some tallies, and thence back again home, by the way meeting Mr. Weaver,[4] of Huntingdon, and did discourse our business of law together, which did ease my mind, for I was afeard I have omitted doing what I in prudence ought to have done. So home and to dinner, and after dinner to the office, where je had Mrs. Burrows all sola à my closet, and did there baiser and toucher ses mamelles. . . .

[1] Her Majesty's apartments, at Whitehall Palace.

[2] See January 27th, *ante*. [3] See December 1st, 1666.

[4] Pepys records Mr. Weaver's death on April 10th, 1667.

Thence away, and with my wife by coach to the Duke of York's play-house, expecting a new play, and so stayed not no more than other people, but to the King's house, to "The Mayd's Tragedy;" but vexed all the while with two talking ladies and Sir Charles Sedley; yet pleased to hear their discourse, he being a stranger. And one of the ladies would, and did sit with her mask on, all the play, and, being exceeding witty as ever I heard woman, did talk most pleasantly with him; but was, I believe, a virtuous woman, and of quality. He would fain know who she was, but she would not tell; yet did give him many pleasant hints of her knowledge of him, by that means setting his brains at work to find out who she was, and did give him leave to use all means to find out who she was, but pulling off her mask. He was mighty witty, and she also making sport with him very inoffensively, that a more pleasant rencontre I never heard. But by that means lost the pleasure of the play wholly, to which now and then Sir Charles Sedley's exceptions against both words and pronouncing were very pretty. So home and to the office, did much business, then home, to supper, and to bed.

19th. Up, and to the office, where all the morning doing little business, our want of money being so infinite great. At noon home, and there find old Mr. Michell and Howlett come to desire mine and my wife's company to dinner to their son's, and so away by coach with them, it being Betty's wedding-day a year, as also Shrove Tuesday. Here I made myself mighty merry, the two old women being there also, and a mighty pretty dinner we had in this little house, to my exceeding great content, and my wife's, and my heart pleased to see Betty. But I have not been so merry a very great while as with them, every thing pleasing me there as much as among so mean company I could be pleased. After dinner I fell to read the Acts about the building of the City[1] again; and indeed the laws seem to be very good, and I pray God I may live to see it built in

[1] Burnet wrote ("History of his Own Time," book ii.): "An act passed in this session for rebuilding the city of London, which gave Lord Chief Justice Hale a great reputation, for it was drawn with so true a judgment, and so great foresight, that the whole city was raised out of its ashes without any suits of law."

that manner! Anon with much content home, walking with my wife and her woman, and there to my office, where late doing much business, and then home to supper and to bed. This morning I hear that our discourse of peace is all in the dirt; for the Dutch will not like of the place, or at least the French will not agree to it; so that I do wonder what we shall do, for carry on the war we cannot. I long to hear the truth of it to-morrow at Court.

20th. Up, with Sir W. Batten and Sir W. Pen by coach to White Hall, by the way observing Sir W. Pen's carrying a favour to Sir W. Coventry, for his daughter's wedding, and saying that there was others for us, when we will fetch them, which vexed me, and I am resolved not to wear it when he orders me one. His wedding hath been so poorly kept, that I am ashamed of it; for a fellow that makes such a flutter as he do. When we come to the Duke of York here, I heard discourse how Harris of his play-house is sick, and everybody commends him, and, above all things, for acting the Cardinall. Here they talk also how the King's viallin, Bannister,[1] is mad that the King hath a Frenchman[2] come to be chief of some part of the King's musique, at which the Duke of York made great mirth. Then withdrew to his closett, all our business, lack of

[1] John Banister, who had been bred up, under his father, one of the waits in St. Giles's-in-the-Fields, was sent by Charles II. to France for improvement; but soon after his return he was dismissed the king's service for saying that the English violins were better than the French. He afterwards kept a music school in Whitefriars, and died in 1679 (Hawkins's "History of Music"). There were many complaints against Banister. Among the State Papers is a "Remonstrance (dated March 29th, 1667) of the king's band of violins under M. Grabu, master of his music, against the fraudulent conduct of John Banister, who receives £600 a year for extraordinary services of the violins, and keeps most of it himself, compelling them to submit by threats of having them turned out of their places; several have been turned out without orders from the king or Lord Chamberlain" ("Calendar," 1666-67, p. 593).

[2] Louis Grabut or Grebus, Master of the King's Music. The "Warrant to Edward, Earl of Manchester, to swear in — Grabu as Master of the English Chamber Music," is dated November 12th, 1666 ("Calendar of State Papers," 1666-67, p. 256). On the death of Charles II. Dryden brought out a piece entitled "Albion and Albanius," with machinery and decorations by Betterton, and music by Grebus. Mr. Lowe found a dramatic cutting at the Guildhall Library, consisting of verses, each stanza ending with the name of Grabu. Here is one:

money and prospect of the effects of it, such as made Sir W. Coventry say publickly before us all, that he do heartily wish that his Royal Highness had nothing to do in the Navy, whatever become of him; so much dishonour, he says, is likely to fall under the management of it. The Duke of York was angry, as much as he could be, or ever I saw him, with Sir G. Carteret, for not paying the masters of some ships on Monday last, according to his promise, and I do think Sir G. Carteret will make himself unhappy by not taking some course either to borrow more money or wholly lay aside his pretence to the charge of raising money, when he hath nothing to do to trouble himself with. Thence to the Exchequer, and there find the people in readiness to dispatch my tallies to-day, though Ash Wednesday. So I back by coach to London to Sir Robt. Viner's and there got £100, and come away with it and pay my fees round, and so away with the 'Chequer men to the Leg in King Street, and there had wine for them; and here was one in company with them, that was the man that got the vessel to carry over the King from Bredhemson,[1] who hath a pension of £200 per annum,[2] but ill paid, and the man is looking after getting of a prize-ship

"Each actor on the stage his luck bewailing,
Finds that his loss is infallibly true;
Smith, Nokes, and Leigh in a fever with railing
Curse poet, painter, and Monsieur Grabu."

(Lowe's "Life of Betterton," p. 135.) See also North's "Memoirs of Musick," by Rimbault, p. 110.

[1] Brighthelmstone, or Brighton.

[2] This was Francis Mansell of Ovingdean, and not Nicholas Tettersell, as stated in former editions of the Diary. The former was appointed "Customer Inward" in the port of Southampton, from which he received £60 a year. He petitioned the king about 1661 for relief, stating that he "was forced to fly for life, being one of the instruments of his Majesty's happy escape, and has spent more in solicitation than the £60 per annum he receives from his small office." After this he was granted a pension of £200, but this was allowed to fall into arrear. Mr. F. E. Sawyer, in his paper on "Captain Nicholas Tettersell and the Escape of Charles II." ("Sussex Archæological Collections," vol. xxxii.), says, "As Mansell's pension was £200 a year, whilst Tettersell's was only £100, it would appear that the services of the former were considered by the king of more value than those of the latter." See also Diary, May 23rd, 1660.

to live by; but the trouble is, that this poor man, who hath received no part of his money these four years, and is ready to starve almost, must yet pay to the Poll Bill for this pension. He told me several particulars of the King's coming thither, which was mighty pleasant, and shews how mean a thing a king is, how subject to fall, and how like other men he is in his afflictions. Thence with my tallies home, and a little dinner, and then with my wife by coach to Lincoln's Inn Fields, sent her to her brother's, and I with Lord Bellasses to the Lord Chancellor's. Lord Bellasses tells me how the King of France hath caused the stop to be made to our proposition of treating in The Hague; that he being greater than they, we may better come and treat at Paris: so that God knows what will become of the peace! He tells me, too, as a grand secret, that he do believe the peace offensive and defensive between Spayne and us is quite finished, but must not be known, to prevent the King of France's present falling upon Flanders. He do believe the Duke of York will be made General of the Spanish armies there, and Governor of Flanders, if the French should come against it, and we assist the Spaniard: that we have done the Spaniard abundance of mischief in the West Indys, by our privateers at Jamaica, which they lament mightily, and I am sorry for it to have it done at this time. By and by, come to my Lord Chancellor, who heard mighty quietly my complaints for lack of money, and spoke mighty kind to me, but little hopes of help therein, only his good word. He do prettily cry upon Povy's account with sometimes seeming friendship and pity, and this day quite the contrary. He do confess our streights here and every where else arise from our outspending our revenue. I mean that the King do do so. Thence away, took up my wife, who tells me her brother hath laid out much money upon himself and wife for clothes, which I am sorry to hear, it requiring great expense. So home and to the office a while, and then home to supper, where Mrs. Turner come to us, and sat and talked. Poor woman, I pity her, but she is very cunning. She concurs with me in the falseness of Sir W. Pen's friendship, and she tells pretty stories of my Lord Bruncker since he come to our end of the town, of people's applications to Mrs. Williams. So, she gone, I back to my accounts of Tangier, which I am settling, having my new tallies from the Exchequer this day, and having set all right as I could wish, then to bed.

21st. Up, and to the Office, where sat all the morning, and there a most furious conflict between Sir W. Pen and I, in few words, and on a sudden occasion, of no great moment, but very bitter, and stared on one another, and so broke off, and to our business, my heart as full of spite as it could hold, for which God forgive me and him! At the end of the day come witnesses on behalf of Mr. Carcasse; but, instead of clearing him, I find they were brought to recriminate Sir W. Batten, and did it by oath very highly, that made the old man mad, and, I confess, me ashamed, so that I caused all but ourselves to withdraw, being sorry to have such things declared in the open office, before 100 people. But it was done home, and I do believe true, though [Sir] W. Batten denies all, but is cruel mad, and swore one of them, he or Carcasse, should not continue in the Office, which is said like a fool. He gone, for he would no stay, and [Sir] W. Pen gone a good while before, Lord Bruncker, Sir T. Harvy, and I, staid and examined the witnesses, though amounting to little more than a reproaching of Sir W. Batten. I home, my head and mind vexed about the conflict between Sir W. Pen and I, though I have got, nor lost any ground by it. At home was Mr. Daniel and wife and sister, and dined with us, and I disturbed at dinner, Colonell Fitzgerald coming to me about tallies, which I did go and give him, and then to the office, where did much business and walked an hour or two with Lord Bruncker, who is mightily concerned in this business for Carcasse and against Sir W. Batten, and I do hope it will come to a good height, for I think it will be good for the King as well as for me, that they two do not agree, though I do, for ought I see yet, think that my Lord is for the most part in the right. He gone, I to the office again to dispatch business, and late at night comes in Sir W. Batten, [Sir] W. Pen, and [Sir] J. Minnes to the office, and what was it but to examine one Jones, a young merchant, who was said to have spoke the worst against Sir W. Batten, but he do deny it wholly, yet

I do believe Carcasse will go near to prove all that was sworn in the morning, and so it be true I wish it may. That done, I to end my letters, and then home to supper, and set right some accounts of Tangier, and then to bed.

22nd. Up, and to the office, where I awhile, and then home with Sir H. Cholmly to give him some tallies upon the business of the Mole at Tangier, and then out with him by coach to the Excise Office, there to enter them, and so back again with him to the Exchange, and there I took another coach, and home to the office, and to my business till dinner, the rest of our officers having been this morning upon the Victuallers' accounts. At dinner all of us, that is to say, Lord Bruncker, [Sir] J. Minnes, [Sir] W. Batten, [Sir] T. Harvy, and myself, to Sir W. Pen's house, where some other company. It is instead of a wedding dinner for his daughter, whom I saw in palterly clothes, nothing new but a bracelet that her servant[1] had given her, and ugly she is, as heart can wish. A sorry dinner, not anything handsome or clean, but some silver plates they borrowed of me. My wife was here too. So a great deal of talk, and I seemingly merry, but took no pleasure at all. We had favours given us all, and we put them in our hats, I against my will, but that my Lord and the rest did. I being displeased that he did carry Sir W. Coventry's himself several days ago, and the people up and down the town long since, and we must have them but to-day. After dinner to talk a little, and then I away to my office, to draw up a letter of the state of the Office and Navy for the Duke of York against Sunday next, and at it late, and then home to supper and to bed, talking with my wife of the poorness and meanness of all that Sir W. Pen and the people about us do, compared with what we do.

23rd. This day I am, by the blessing of God, 34 years old, in very good health and mind's content, and in condition of estate much beyond whatever my friends could expect of a child of their's, this day 34 years. The Lord's name be praised! and may I be ever thankful for it. Up betimes to the office, in order to my letter to the Duke of York to-morrow, and then the office met and spent the

[1] Anthony Lowther, before the marriage. — B.

greatest part about this letter. At noon home to dinner, and then to the office again very close at it all the day till midnight, making an end and writing fair this great letter and other things to my full content, it abundantly providing for the vindication of this office, whatever the success be of our wants of money. This evening Sir W. Batten come to me to the office on purpose, out of spleen (of which he is full to Carcasse!), to tell me that he is now informed of many double tickets now found of Carcasse's making which quite overthrows him. It is strange to see how, though I do believe this fellow to be a rogue, and could be contented to have him removed, yet to see him persecuted by Sir W. Batten, who is as bad himself, and that with so much rancour, I am almost the fellow's friend. But this good I shall have from it, that the differences between Sir W. Batten and my Lord Bruncker will do me no hurt.

24th (Lord's day). Up, and with [Sir] W. Batten, by coach; he set me down at my Lord Bruncker's (his feud there not suffering him to 'light himself), and I with my Lord by and by when ready to White Hall, and by and by up to the Duke of York, and there presented our great letter and other papers, and among the rest my report of the victualling, which is good, I think, and will continue my pretence to the place, which I am still afeard Sir W. Coventry's employment may extinguish. We have discharged ourselves in this letter fully from blame in the bad success of the Navy, if money do not come soon to us, and so my heart is at pretty good rest in this point. Having done here, Sir W. Batten and I home by coach, and though the sermon at our church was begun, yet he would 'light to go home and eat a slice of roast beef off the spit, and did, and then he and I to church in the middle of the sermon. My Lady Pen there saluted me with great content to tell me that her daughter and husband are still in bed, as if the silly woman thought it a great matter of honour, and did, going out of the church, ask me whether we did not make a great show at Court to-day, with all our favours in our hats. After sermon home, and alone with my wife dined. Among other things my wife told me how ill a report our Mercer hath got by her keeping of company, so that she will not send for her to dine with us or be with us as heretofore; and, what is more strange, tells me that little Mis. Tooker hath got a clap as young as she is, being brought up loosely by her mother. . . . In the afternoon away to White Hall by water, and took a turn or two in the Park, and then back to White Hall, and there meeting my Lord Arlington, he, by I know not what kindness, offered to carry me along with him to my Lord Treasurer's, whither, I told him, I was going. I believe he had a mind to discourse of some Navy businesses, but Sir Thomas Clifford coming into the coach to us, we were prevented; which I was sorry for, for I had a mind to begin an acquaintance with him. He speaks well, and hath pretty slight superficial parts, I believe. He, in our going, talked much of the plain habit of the Spaniards; how the King and Lords themselves wear but a cloak of Colchester bayze,[1] and the ladies mantles, in cold weather, of white flannell: and that the endeavours frequently of setting up the manufacture of making these stuffs there have only been prevented by the Inquisition: the English and Dutchmen that have been sent for to work, being taken with a Psalm-book or Testament, and so clapped up, and the house pulled down by the Inquisitors; and the greatest Lord in Spayne dare not say a word against it, if the word Inquisition be but mentioned. At my Lord Treasurer's 'light and parted with them, they going into Council, and I walked with Captain Cocke, who takes mighty notice of the differences growing in our office between Lord Bruncker and [Sir] W. Batten, and among others also, and I fear it may do us hurt, but I will keep out of them. By and by comes Sir S. Fox, and he and I walked and talked together on many things, but chiefly, want of money, and the straits the King brings himself and affairs into for want of it. Captain Cocke did tell me what I must not forget: that the answer of the Dutch, refusing The Hague for a place of treaty, and proposing the Boysse,[2] Bredah, Bergen-op-Zoome, or Mastricht, was

[1] "Bays, and says, and serges, and several sorts of stuffs, which I neither can nor do desire to name, are made in and about Colchester." — Fuller's *Worthies*. — B.

[2] Bois-le-Duc or 's Hertogenbosch.

seemingly stopped by the Swede's Embassador (though he did show it to the King, but the King would take no notice of it, nor does not) from being delivered to the King; and he hath wrote to desire them to consider better of it: so that, though we know their refusal of the place, yet they know not that we know it, nor is the King obliged to show his sense of the affront. That the Dutch are in very great straits, so as to be said to be not able to set out their fleete this year. By and by comes Sir Robert Viner and my Lord Mayor to ask the King's directions about measuring out the streets according to the new Act[1] for building of the City, wherein the King is to be pleased.[2] But he says that the way proposed in Parliament, by Colonel Birch, would have been the best, to have chosen some persons in trust, and sold the whole ground, and let it be sold again by them, with preference to the old owner, which would have certainly caused the City to be built where these Trustees pleased; whereas now, great differences will be, and the streets built by fits, and not entire till all differences be decided. This, as he tells it, I think would have been the best way. I enquired about the Frenchman[3] that was said to fire the City and was hanged for it, by his own confession, that he was hired for it by a Frenchman of Roane, and that he did with a stick reach in a fire-ball in at a

[1] Entitled "An Act for Rebuilding the City of London," 19 Car. II., cap. 3. — B.

[2] See Sir Christopher Wren's "Proposals for rebuilding the City of London after the great fire, with an engraved Plan of the principal Streets and Public Buildings," in Elmes's "Memoirs of Sir Christopher Wren," Appendix, p. 61. The originals are in All Souls' College Library, Oxford. — B.

[3] "One Hubert, a French papist, was seized in Essex, as he was getting out of the way in great confusion. He confessed he had begun the fire, and persisted in his confession to his death, for he was hanged upon no other evidence but that of his own confession. It is true he gave so broken an account of the whole matter that he was thought mad. Yet he was blindfolded, and carried to several places of the city, and then his eyes being opened, he was asked if that was the place, and he being carried to wrong places, after he looked round about for some time, he said that was not the place, but when he was brought to the place where it first broke out, he affirmed that was the true place." — Burnet's *Own Time*, book ii. Archbishop Tillotson, according to Burnet, believed that London was burned by design.

window of the house: whereas the master of the house, who is the King's baker, and his son, and daughter, do all swear there was no such window, and that the fire did not begin thereabouts. Yet the fellow, who, though a mopish besotted fellow, did not speak like a madman, did swear that he did fire it: and did not this like a madman; for, being tried on purpose, and landed with his speaker at the Tower Wharf, he could carry the keeper to the very house. Asking Sir R. Viner what he thought was the cause of the fire, he tells me, that the baker, son, and his daughter, did all swear again and again, that their oven was drawn by ten o'clock at night; that, having occasion to light a candle about twelve, there was not so much fire in the bake-house as to light a match for a candle, so that they were fain to go into another place to light it; that about two in the morning they felt themselves almost choked with smoke, and rising, did find the fire coming upstairs; so they rose to save themselves; but that, at that time, the bavins[1] were not on fire in the yard. So that they are, as they swear, in absolute ignorance how this fire should come; which is a strange thing, that so horrid an effect should have so mean and uncertain a beginning. By and by called in to the King and Cabinet, and there had a few insipid words about money for Tangier, but to no purpose. Thence away walked to my boat at White Hall, and so home and to supper, and then to talk with W. Hewer about business of the differences at present among the people of our office, and so to my Journall and to bed. This night going through bridge by water, my waterman told me how the mistress of the Beare tavern, at the bridge-foot, did lately fling herself into the Thames, and drowned herself; which did trouble me the more, when they tell me it was she that did live at the White Horse tavern in Lumbard Streete, which was a most beautiful woman, as most I have seen. It seems she hath had long melancholy upon her, and hath endeavoured to make away with herself often.

25th. Lay long in bed, talking with pleasure with my poor wife, how she used to make coal fires, and wash my foul clothes with her own hand for me, poor wretch! in our

[1] Brushwood, or small faggots, used for lighting fires.

little room at my Lord Sandwich's; for which I ought for ever to love and admire her, and do; and persuade myself she would do the same thing again, if God should reduce us to it. So up and by coach abroad to the Duke of Albemarle's about sending soldiers down to some ships, and so home, calling at a belt-maker's to mend my belt, and so home and to dinner, where pleasant with my wife, and then to the office, where mighty busy all the day, saving going forth to the 'Change to pay for some things, and on other occasions, and at my goldsmith's did observe the King's new medall,[1] where, in little, there is Mrs. Steward's face as well done as ever I saw anything in my whole life, I think: and a pretty thing it is, that he should choose her face to represent Britannia by. So at the office late very busy and much business with great joy dispatched, and so home to supper and to bed.

26th. Up, and to the office, where all the morning. And here did receive another reference from Sir W. Coventry about the business of some of the Muster-Masters, concerning whom I had returned their small performances, which do give me a little more trouble for fear [Sir] W. Coventry should think I had a design to favour my brother Balty, and to that end to disparage all the rest. But I shall clear all very well, only it do exercise my thoughts more than I am at leisure for. At home find Balty and his wife very fine, which I did not like, for fear he do spend too much of his money that way, and lay [not] up anything. After dinner to the office again, where by and by Lord Bruncker, [Sir] W. Batten, [Sir] J. Minnes and I met about receiving Carcasse's answers to the depositions against him. Wherein I did see so much favour from my Lord to him that I do again begin to see that my Lord is not right at the bottom, and did make me the more earnest against him, though said little. My Lord rising, declaring his judgement in his behalf, and going away, I did hinder our arguing it by ourselves, and so broke up the meeting, and myself went full of trouble to my office, there to write over the deposition and his answers side by side, and then home to supper and to bed with some trouble of mind to think of the issue of this, how it will breed ill blood among us here.

[1] By Philip Rotier (see note, March 9th, 1662–63).

27th. Up by candle-light, about six o'clock, it being bitter cold weather again, after all our warm weather, and by water down to Woolwich rope-yard, I being this day at a leisure, the King and Duke of York being gone down to Sheerenesse this morning to lay out the design for a fortification there to the river Medway;[1] and so we do not attend the Duke of York as we should otherwise have done, and there to the Dock Yard to enquire of the state of things, and went into Mr. Pett's; and there, beyond expectation, he did present me with a Japan cane, with a silver head, and his wife sent me by him a ring, with a Woolwich stone,[2] now much in request; which I accepted, the values not being great, and knowing that I had done them courtesies, which he did own in very high terms; and then, at my asking, did give me an old draught of an ancient-built ship,[3] given him by his father, of the Beare, in Queen Elizabeth's time. This did much please me, it being a thing I much desired to have, to shew the difference in the build of ships now and heretofore. Being much taken with this kindness, I away to Blackwall and Deptford, to satisfy myself there about the King's business, and then walked to Redriffe, and so home about noon; there find Mr. Hunt, newly come out of the country, who tells me the country[4] is much impoverished by the greatness of taxes:

[1] The first fortification at Sheerness was erected by Sir Bernard de Gomme. The original draft is in the British Museum; see March 24th, 1667, note. — B.

[2] Woolwich stones, still collected in that locality, are simply water-worn pebbles of flint, which, when broken with a hammer, exhibit on the smooth surface some resemblance to the human face; and their possessors are thus enabled to trace likenesses of friends, or eminent public characters. The late Mr. Tennant, the geologist, of the Strand, had a collection of such stones. In the British Museum is a nodule of globular or Egyptian jasper, which, in its fracture, bears a striking resemblance to the well-known portrait of Chaucer. It is engraved in Rymsdyk's "Museum Britannicum," tab. xxviii. A flint, showing Mr. Pitt's face, used once to be exhibited at the meetings of the Pitt Club. — B.

[3] In "A Complete List of the Royal Navy in England in 1599" ("Archæologia," vol. xiii., p. 30), No. 11 is described as "The Beare, of two sakers, of cast iron," and No. 12 as "The White Beare, of three cannon, six demi-cannon, seven culverins, seven demi-culverins, two portpeece halls and seven fowler halls, all of brass, with five demi-cannon and three demi-culverins, all of cast iron."

[4] Cambridgeshire.

the farmers do break every day almost, and £1,000 a-year become not worth £500. He dined with us, and we had good discourse of the general ill state of things, and, by the way, he told me some ridiculous pieces of thrift of Sir G. Downing's, who is his countryman, in inviting some poor people, at Christmas last, to charm the country people's mouths; but did give them nothing but beef, porridge, pudding, and pork, and nothing said all dinner, but only his mother[1] would say, "It's good broth, son." He would answer, "Yes, it is good broth." Then, says his lady, Confirm all, and say, "Yes, very good broth." By and by she would begin and say, "Good pork:" "Yes," says the mother, "good pork." Then he cries, "Yes, very good pork." And so they said of all things; to which nobody made any answer, they going there not out of love or esteem of them, but to eat his victuals, knowing him to be a niggardly fellow; and with this he is jeered now all over the country. This day just before dinner comes Captain Story, of Cambridge, to me to the office, about a bill for prest money, for men sent out of the country and the countries about him to the fleete the last year;[2] but, Lord! to see the natures of men; how this man, hearing of my name, did ask me of my country, and told me of my cozen Roger, that he was not so wise a man as his father; for that he do not agree in Parliament with his fellow burgesses and knights of the shire, whereas I know very well the reason; for he is not so high a flyer as Mr. Chichley and others, but loves the King better than any of them, and to better purpose. But yet, he says that he is a very honest gentleman, and thence runs into a hundred stories of his own services to the King, and how he at this day brings in the taxes before anybody here thinks they are collected: discourse very absurd to entertain a stranger with. He being gone, and I glad of it, I home then to

[1] Sir George Downing's mother was Margaret, daughter and coheir of Robert Brett, D.D. His wife, Lady Downing, was Francis, fourth daughter of William Howard, of Naworth, and sister of Charles Howard, the first Earl of Carlisle of that family. — B.

[2] Money paid to men who enlist into the public service; press money. So called because those who receive it are to be prest or ready when called on ("Encyclopædic Dictionary").

dinner. After dinner with my wife by coach abroad, and set Mr. Hunt down at the Temple and her at her brother's, and I to White Hall to meet [Sir] W. Coventry, but found him not, but met Mr. Cooling, who tells me of my Lord Duke of Buckingham's being sent for last night, by a Serjeant at Armes,[1] to the Tower, for treasonable practices, and that the King is infinitely angry with him, and declared him no longer one of his Council. I know not the reason of it, or occasion. To Westminster Hall, and there paid what I owed for books, and so by coach, took up my wife to the Exchange, and there bought things for Mrs. Pierce's little daughter, my Valentine, and so to their house, where we find Knipp, who also challengeth me for her Valentine. She looks well, sang well, and very merry we were for half an hour. Tells me Harris is well again, having been very ill, and so we home, and I to the office; then, at night, to Sir W. Pen's, and sat with my Lady, and the young couple[2] (Sir William out of town) talking merrily; but they make a very sorry couple, methinks, though rich. So late home and to bed.

28th. Up, and there comes to me Drumbleby with a flageolet, made to suit with my former and brings me one Greeting, a master, to teach my wife. I agree by the whole with him to teach her to take out any lesson of herself for £4. She was not ready to begin to-day, but do to-morrow. So I to the office, where my Lord Bruncker and I only all the morning, and did business. At noon to the Exchange and to Sir Rob. Viner's about settling my accounts there. So back home and to dinner, where Mr. Holliard dined with us, and pleasant company he is. I love his company, and he secures me against ever having the stone again. He gives it me, as his opinion, that the City will never be built again together, as is expected, while any restraint is laid upon them. He hath been a great loser, and would be a builder again, but, he says, he knows not what restrictions there will be, so as it is unsafe for him to begin. He gone, I to the office, and there busy till night doing much business, then home and to my accounts, wherein, beyond

[1] Bearcroft. See March 3rd, *post*.

[2] Anthony Lowther and his wife Margaret Penn.

expectation, I succeeded so well as to settle them very clear and plain, though by borrowing of monies this month to pay D. Gawden, and chopping and changing with my Tangier money, they were become somewhat intricate, and, blessed be God, upon the evening my accounts, I do appear £6,800 creditor. This done, I to supper about 12 at night, and so to bed. The weather for three or four days being come to be exceeding cold again as any time this year. I did within these six days see smoke still remaining of the late fire in the City; and it is strange to think how, to this very day, I cannot sleep at night without great terrors of fire, and this very night I could not sleep till almost two in the morning through thoughts of fire. Thus this month is ended with great content of mind to me, thriving in my estate, and the affairs in my offices going pretty well as to myself. This afternoon Mr. Gawden was with me and tells me more than I knew before — that he hath orders to get all the victuals he can to Plymouth, and the Western ports, and other outports, and some to Scotland, so that we do intend to keep but a flying fleete this year; which, it may be, may preserve us a year longer, but the end of it must be ruin. Sir J. Minnes this night tells me, that he hears for certain, that ballads are made of us in Holland for begging of a peace; which I expected, but am vexed at. So ends this month, with nothing of weight upon my mind, but for my father and mother, who are both very ill, and have been so for some weeks: whom God help! but I do fear my poor father will hardly be ever thoroughly well again.

March 1st. Up, it being very cold weather again after a good deal of warm summer weather, and to the office, where I settled to do much business to-day. By and by sent for to Sir G. Carteret to discourse of the business of the Navy, and our wants, and the best way of bestowing the little money we have, which is about £30,000, but, God knows, we have need of ten times as much, which do make my life uncomfortable, I confess, on the King's behalf, though it is well enough as to my own particular, but the King's service is undone by it. Having done with him, back again to the office, and in the streets, in Mark Lane, I do observe, it being St. David's day, the picture of a man dressed like a Welchman, hanging by the neck upon one of the poles that stand out at the top of one of the merchants' houses, in full proportion, and very handsomely done; which is one of the oddest sights I have seen a good while, for it was so like a man that one would have thought it was indeed a man.[1] Being returned home, I find Greeting, the flageolet-master, come, and teaching my wife; and I do think my wife will take pleasure in it, and it will be easy for her, and pleasant. So I, as I am well content with the charge it will occasion me. So to the office till dinner-time, and then home to dinner, and before dinner making my wife to sing. Poor wretch! her ear is so bad that it made me angry, till the poor wretch cried to see me so vexed at her, that I think I shall not discourage her so much again, but will endeavour to make her understand sounds, and do her good that way; for she hath a great mind to learn, only to please me; and, therefore, I am mighty unjust to her in discouraging her so much, but we were good friends, and to dinner, and had she not been ill with those and that it were not Friday (on which in Lent there are no plays) I had carried her to a play, but she not being fit to go abroad, I to the office, where all the afternoon close examining the collection of my papers of the account of the Navy since this war to my great content, and so at night home to talk and sing with my wife, and then to supper and so to bed with great pleasure. But I cannot but remember that just before dinner one of my people come up to me, and told me a man come from Huntingdon would speak with me, how my heart come into my mouth doubting that my father, who has been long sicke, was dead. It put me into a trembling, but, blessed be [God]! it was no such thing, but a countryman come about ordinary business to me, to receive £50 paid to my father in the country for the Perkins's for their legacy, upon

[1] From "Poor Robin's Almanack" for 1757 it appears that, in former times in England, a Welshman was burnt in effigy on this anniversary. Mr. W. C. Hazlitt, in his edition of Brand's "Popular Antiquities," adds: "The practice to which Pepys refers . . . was very common at one time; and till very lately bakers made gingerbread Welshmen, called taffies, on St. David's day, which were made to represent a man skewered" (vol. i., pp. 60, 61).

the death of their mother, by my uncle's will. So though I get nothing at present, at least by the estate, I am fain to pay this money rather than rob my father, and much good may it do them that I may have no more further trouble from them. I hear to-day that Tom Woodall, the known chyrurgeon, is killed at Somerset House by a Frenchman, but the occasion Sir W. Batten could not tell me.

2nd. Up, and to the office, where sitting all the morning, and among other things did agree upon a distribution of £30,000 and odd, which is the only sum we hear of like to come out of all the Poll Bill for the use of this office for buying of goods. I did herein some few courtesies for particular friends I wished well to, and for the King's service also, and was therefore well pleased with what was done. Sir W. Pen this day did bring an order from the Duke of York for our receiving from him a small vessel for a fireship, and taking away a better of the King's for it, it being expressed for his great service to the King. This I am glad of, not for his sake, but that it will give me a better ground, I believe, to ask something for myself of this kind, which I was fearful to begin. This do make Sir W. Pen the most kind to me that can be. I suppose it is this, lest it should find any opposition from me, but I will not oppose, but promote it. After dinner, with my wife, to the King's house to see "The Mayden Queene," a new play of Dryden's, mightily commended for the regularity of it, and the strain and wit; and, the truth is, there is a comical part done by Nell,[1] which is Florimell, that I never can hope ever to see the like done again, by man or woman. The King and Duke of York were at the play. But so great performance of a comical part was never, I believe, in the world before as Nell do this, both as a mad girle, then most and best of all when she comes in like a

[1] "Her skill increasing with her years, other poets sought to obtain the recommendations of her wit and beauty to the success of their writings. I have said that Dryden was one of the principal supporters of the King's House, and ere long in one of his new plays a principal character was set apart for the popular comedian. The drama was a tragi-comedy called 'Secret Love, or the Maiden Queen,' and an additional interest was attached to its production from the king having suggested the plot to its author, and calling it 'his play.'" — Cunningham's *Story of Nell Gwyn*, ed. 1892, pp. 38, 39.

young gallant; and hath the motions and carriage of a spark the most that ever I saw any man have. It makes me, I confess, admire her. Thence home and to the office, where busy a while, and then home to read the lives of Henry 5th and 6th, very fine, in Speede,[1] and so to bed. This day I did pay a bill of £50 from my father, it being so much out of my own purse gone to pay my uncle Robert's legacy to my aunt Perkins's child.

3rd (Lord's day). Lay long, merrily talking with my wife, and then up and to church, where a dull sermon of Mr. Mills touching Original Sin, and then home, and there find little Michell and his wife, whom I love mightily. Mightily contented I was in their company, for I love her much; and so after dinner I left them and by water from the Old Swan to White Hall, where, walking in the galleries, I in the first place met Mr. Pierce, who tells me the story of Tom Woodall, the surgeon, killed in a drunken quarrel, and how the Duke of York hath a mind to get him [Pierce] one of his places in St. Thomas's Hospitall. Then comes Mr. Hayward, the Duke of York's servant, and tells us that the Swede's Embassador hath been here to-day with news that it is believed that the Dutch will yield to have the treaty at London or Dover, neither of which will get our King any credit, we having already consented to have it at The Hague; which, it seems, De Witt opposed, as a thing wherein the King of England must needs have some profound design, which in my conscience he hath not. They do also tell me that newes is this day come to the King, that the King of France is come with his army to the frontiers of Flanders, demanding leave to pass through their country towards Poland, but is denied, and thereupon that he is gone into the country. How true this is I dare not believe till I hear more. From them I walked into the Parke, it being a fine but very cold day; and there took two or three turns the length of the Pell Mell: and there I met Serjeant Bearcroft, who was sent for the Duke of Buckingham, to have brought him prisoner to the Tower. He come to towne this day, and brings word that, being

[1] John Speed's Chronicle ("The History of Great Britaine under the Conquests of ye Romans, Saxons, Danes, and Normans").

overtaken and outrid by the Duchesse of Buckingham within a few miles of the Duke's house of Westhorp,[1] he believes she got thither about a quarter of an hour before him, and so had time to consider; so that, when he come, the doors were kept shut against him. The next day, coming with officers of the neighbour market-town to force open the doors, they were open for him, but the Duke gone; so he took horse presently, and heard upon the road that the Duke of Buckingham was gone before him for London: so that he believes he is this day also come to towne before him; but no newes is yet heard of him. This is all he brings. Thence to my Lord Chancellor's, and there, meeting Sir H. Cholmly, he and I walked in my Lord's garden, and talked; among other things, of the treaty: and he says there will certainly be a peace, but I cannot believe it. He tells me that the Duke of Buckingham his crimes, as far as he knows, are his being of a caball with some discontented persons of the late House of Commons, and opposing the desires of the King in all his matters in that House; and endeavouring to become popular, and advising how the Commons' House should proceed, and how he would order the House of Lords. And that he hath been endeavouring to have the King's nativity calculated; which was done, and the fellow now in the Tower about it; which itself hath heretofore, as he says, been held treason, and people died for it; but by the Statute of Treasons, in Queen Mary's times and since, it hath been left out. He tells me that this silly Lord hath provoked, by his ill-carriage, the Duke of York, my Lord Chancellor, and all the great persons; and therefore, most likely, will die. He tells me, too, many practices of treachery against this King; as betraying him in Scotland, and giving Oliver an account of the King's private councils; which the King knows very well, and hath yet pardoned him.[2] Here I passed away a little time more talking with him and Creed,

[1] Westhorpe, in Suffolk, originally the magnificent residence of Charles Brandon, Duke of Suffolk; it was probably afterwards granted by the Crown to the Duke of Buckingham. The house has long since been demolished. — B.

[2] Two of our great poets have drawn the character of the Duke of Buckingham in brilliant verse, and both have condemned him to infamy.

whom I met there, and so away, Creed walking with me to White Hall, and there I took water and stayed at Michell's to drink. I home, and there to read very good things in Fuller's "Church History," and "Worthies," and so to supper, and after supper had much good discourse with W. Hewer, who supped with us, about the ticket office and the knaveries and extortions every day used there, and particularly of the business of Mr. Carcasse, whom I fear I shall find a very rogue. So parted with him, and then to bed.

4th. Up, and with Sir J. Minnes and [Sir] W. Batten by barge to Deptford by eight in the morning, where to the King's yard a little to look after business there, and then to a private storehouse to look upon some cordage of Sir W. Batten's, and there being a hole formerly made for a drain for tarr to run into, wherein the barrel stood still, full of stinking water, Sir W. Batten did fall with one leg into it, which might have been very bad to him by breaking a leg or other hurt, but, thanks be to God, he only sprained his foot a little. So after his shifting his stockings at a strong water shop close by, we took barge again, and so to Woolwich, where our business was chiefly to look upon

There is enough in Pepys's reports to corroborate the main features of Dryden's magnificent portrait of Zimri in "Absolom and Achitophel":

"In the first rank of these did Zimri stand;
A man so various that he seemed to be
Not one, but all mankind's epitome;
Stiff in opinions, always in the wrong;
Was everything by starts, and nothing long,
But, in the course of one revolving moon,
Was chymist, fiddler, statesman, and buffoon;
Then all for women, painting, rhyming, drinking,
Besides ten thousand freaks that died in thinking,
* * * * * *
He laughed himself from Court, then sought relief
By forming parties, but could ne'er be chief."

Pope's facts are not correct, and hence the effect of his picture is impaired. In spite of the duke's constant visit to the Tower, Charles II. still continued his friend; but on the death of the king, expecting little from James, he retired to his estate at Helmsley, in Yorkshire, to nurse his property and to restore his constitution. He died on April 16th, 1687, at Kirkby Moorside, after a few days' illness, caused by sitting on the damp grass when heated from a fox chase. The scene of his death was the house of a tenant, not "the worst inn's worst room" ("Moral Essays," epist. iii.). He was buried in Westminster Abbey.

the ballast wharfe there, which is offered us for the King's use to hire, but we do not think it worth the laying out much money upon, unless we could buy the fee-simple of it, which cannot be sold us, so we wholly flung it off. So to the Dockyard, and there staid a while talking about business of the yard, and thence to the Rope-yard, and so to the White Hart and there dined, and Captain Cocke with us, whom we found at the Rope-yard, and very merry at dinner, and many pretty tales of Sir J. Minnes, which I have entered in my tale book. But by this time Sir W. Batten was come to be in much pain in his foot, so as he was forced to be carried down in a chair to the barge again, and so away to Deptford, and there I a little in the yard, and then to Bagwell's, where I find his wife washing, and also I did hazer tout que je voudrais con her, and then sent for her husband, and discoursed of his going to Harwich this week to his charge of the new ship building there, which I have got him, and so away, walked to Redriffe, and there took boat and away home, and upon Tower Hill, near the ticket office, meeting with my old acquaintance Mr. Chaplin, the cheesemonger, and there fell to talk of news, and he tells me that for certain the King of France is denied passage with his army through Flanders, and that he hears that the Dutch do stand upon high terms with us, and will have a promise of not being obliged to strike the flag to us before they will treat with us, and other high things, which I am ashamed of and do hope will never be yielded to. That they do make all imaginable preparations, but that he believes they will be in mighty want of men; that the King of France do court us mightily. He tells me too that our Lord Treasurer is going to lay down, and that Lord Arlington is to be Lord Treasurer, but I believe nothing of it, for he is not yet of estate visible enough to have the charge I suppose upon him. So being parted from him I home to the office, and after having done business there I home to supper, and there mightily pleased with my wife's beginning the flagellette, believing that she will come to very well thereon. This day in the barge I took Berckenshaw's translation[1] of Alsted his Templum,

[1] The translation of the work of Joannes Henricus Alstedius is entitled: "Templum Musicum; the Musical Synopsis; being a com-

but the most ridiculous book, as he has translated it, that ever I saw in my life, I declaring that I understood not three lines together from one end of the book to the other.

5th. Up, and to the office, where met and sat all the morning, doing little for want of money, but only bear the countenance of an office. At noon home to dinner, and then to the office again, and there comes Martin my purser, and I walked with him awhile in the garden, I giving him good advice to beware of coming any more with high demands for supernumeraries or other things, for now Sir W. Pen is come to mind the business, the passing of his accounts will not be so easy as the last. He tells me he will never need it again, it being as easy, and to as much purpose to do the same thing otherwise, and how he do keep his Captain's table, and by that means hath the command of his Captains, and do not fear in a 5th-rate ship constantly employed to get a £1,000 in five years time, and this year, besides all his spendings, which are I fear high, he hath got at this day clear above £150 in a voyage of about five or six months, which is a brave trade. He gone I to the office, and there all the afternoon late doing much business, and then to see Sir W. Batten, whose leg is all but better than it was, and like to do well. I by discourse do perceive he and his Lady are to their hearts out with my Lord Bruncker and Mrs. Williams, to which I added something, but, I think, did not venture too far with them. But, Lord! to see to what a poor content any acquaintance among these people, or the people of the world, as they now-a-days go, is worth; for my part I and my wife will keep to one another and let the world go hang, for there is nothing but falseness in it. So home to supper and hear my wife and girle sing a little, and then to bed with much content of mind.

6th. Up, and with [Sir] W. Pen to White Hall by coach, and by the way agreed to acquaint [Sir] W. Coventry with the business of Mr. Carcasse, and he and I spoke to Sir W. Coventry that we might move it to the Duke of York,

pendium of the rudiments both of the mathematical and practical part of musick. Translated out of Latin by J. Birchensha." London, 1664, 8vo. (with frontispiece).

which I did in a very indifferent, that is, impartial manner,[1] but vexed I believe Lord Bruncker. Here the Duke of York did acquaint us, and the King did the like also, afterwards coming in, with his resolution of altering the manner of the war this year; that is, we shall keep what fleete we have abroad in several squadrons: so that now all is come out; but we are to keep it as close as we can, without hindering the work that is to be done in preparation to this. Great preparations there are to fortify Sheernesse and the yard at Portsmouth, and forces are drawing down to both those places, and elsewhere by the seaside; so that we have some fear of an invasion; and the Duke of York himself did declare his expectation of the enemy's blocking us up here in the River, and therefore directed that we should send away all the ships that we have to fit out hence. Sir W. Pen told me, going with me this morning to White Hall, that for certain the Duke of Buckingham is brought into the Tower, and that he hath had an hour's private conference with the King before he was sent thither. To Westminster Hall. There bought some newsbooks, and, as every where else, hear every body complain of the dearness of coals, being at £4 per chaldron, the weather, too, being become most bitter cold, the King saying to-day that it was the coldest day he ever knew in England. Thence by coach to my Lord Crew's, where very welcome. Here I find they are in doubt where the Duke of Buckingham is; which makes me mightily reflect on the uncertainty of all history, when, in a business of this moment, and of this day's growth, we cannot tell the truth. Here dined my old acquaintance, Mr. Borfett, that was my Lord Sandwich's chaplain, and my Lady Wright and Dr. Boreman,[2] who is

[1] This explanation of the word would appear even now to be necessary for those who are unacquainted with the Liturgy of the Church of England. In 1888 the following passage occurred in a leading article in the "Times": "We have no doubt whatever that Scotch judges and juries will administer indifferent justice." A correspondent in Glasgow, who supposed *indifferent* to mean *inferior*, wrote to complain at the insinuation that a Scotch jury would not do its duty.

[2] Robert Boreman, D.D. (or Bourman), brother of Sir William Boreman, Clerk of the Green Cloth to Charles II., rector of St. Giles's in the Fields from 1663 till his death, November 15th, 1675. He was installed Prebendary of Westminster Abbey in December, 1667.

preacher at St. Gyles's in the Fields, who, after dinner, did give my Lord an account of two papist women lately converted, whereof one wrote her recantation, which he shewed under her own hand mighty well drawn, so as my Lord desired a copy of it, after he had satisfied himself from the Doctor, that to his knowledge she was not a woman under any necessity. Thence by coach home and staid a very little, and then by water to Redriffe, and walked to Bagwell's, where la moher was defro, sed would not have me demeurer there parce que Mrs. Batters and one of my ancillas, I believe Jane (for she was gone abroad to-day), was in the town, and coming thither; so I away presently, esteeming it a great escape. So to the yard and spoke a word or two, and then by water home, wondrous cold, and reading a ridiculous ballad made in praise of the Duke of Albemarle,[1] to the tune of St. George, the tune being printed, too; and I observe that people have some great encouragement to make ballads of him of this kind. There are so many, that hereafter he will sound like Guy of Warwicke. Then abroad with my wife, leaving her at the 'Change, while I to Sir H. Cholmly's, a pretty house, and a fine, worthy, well-disposed gentleman he is. He and I to Sir Ph. Warwicke's, about money for Tangier, but to little purpose. H. Cholmley tells me, among other things, that he hears of little hopes of a peace, their demands being so high as we shall never grant, and could tell me that we shall keep no fleete abroad this year, but only squadrons. And, among other things, that my Lord Bellasses, he believes, will lose his command of Tangier by his corrupt covetous ways of endeavouring to sell his command, which I am glad [of], for he is a man of no worth in the world but compliment. So to the 'Change, and there bought 32*s*. worth of things for Mrs. Knipp, my Valentine, which is pretty to see how my wife is come to convention with me, that, whatever I do give to anybody else, I shall give her as much, which I am not much displeased with. So home and to the office and Sir W. Batten, to tell him what I had done to-day about Carcasse's business, and God forgive me I am not

[1] Mr. Chappell, in his account of the ballad of "St. George for England," refers to this passage ("Popular Music of the Olden Time," vol. i., p. 286).

without design to give a blow to Sir W. Batten by it. So home, where Mr. Batelier supped with us and talked away the evening pretty late, and so he gone and we to bed.

7th. So up, and to the office, my head full of Carcasse's business; then hearing that Knipp is at my house, I home, and it was about a ticket for a friend of hers. I do love the humour of the jade very well. So to the office again, not being able to stay, and there about noon my Lord Bruncker did begin to talk of Carcasse's business. Only Commissioner Pett, my Lord, and I there, and it was pretty to see how Pett hugged the occasion of having anything against Sir W. Batten, which I am not much troubled at, for I love him not neither. Though I did really endeavour to quash it all I could, because I would prevent their malice taking effect. My Lord I see is fully resolved to vindicate Carcasse, though to the undoing of Sir W. Batten, but I believe he will find himself in a mistake, and do himself no good, and that I shall be glad of, for though I love the treason I hate the traitor.[1] But he is vexed at my moving it to the Duke of York yesterday, which I answered well, so as I think he could not answer. But, Lord! it is pretty to see how Pett hugs this business, and how he favours my Lord Bruncker, who to my knowledge hates him, and has said more to his disadvantage, in my presence, to the King and Duke of York than any man in England, and so let them thrive one with another by cheating one another, for that is all I observe among them. Thence home late, and find my wife hath dined, and she and Mrs. Hewer going to a play. Here was Creed, and he and I to Devonshire House,[2] to a burial of a kinsman of Sir R. Viner's; and there I received a ring, and so away presently to Creed, who staid for me at an alehouse hard by, and thence to the Duke's playhouse, where he parted, and I in and find my wife and Mrs. Hewer, and sat by them and saw "The English Princesse, or Richard the Third;"[3] a most sad, melan-

[1] "Many men love the treason, though they hate the traitor" is attributed to Anthony Sadler, D.D. (1619–1680), in Day's "Collacon: an Encyclopædia of Prose Quotations."

[2] Devonshire House (the town house of the Earls of Devonshire) was in Bishopsgate Street, where Devonshire Square now stands.

[3] A tragedy by J. Caryl. Betterton acted King Richard; Harris, the Earl of Richmond; and Smith, Sir William Stanley.

choly play, and pretty good; but nothing eminent in it, as some tragedys are; only little Mis. Davis[1] did dance a jig after the end of the play, and there telling the next day's play; so that it come in by force only to please the company to see her dance in boy's clothes; and, the truth is, there is no comparison between Nell's dancing the other day[2] at the King's house in boy's clothes and this, this being infinitely beyond the other. Here was Mr. Clerke and Pierce, to whom one word only of "How do you," and so away home, Mrs. Hewer with us, and I to the office and so to [Sir] W. Batten's, and there talked privately with him and [Sir] W. Pen about business of Carcasse against to-morrow, wherein I think I did give them proof enough of my ability as well as friendship to [Sir] W. Batten, and the honour of the office, in my sense of the rogue's business. So back to finish my office business, and then home to supper and to bed. This day, Commissioner Taylor come to me for advice, and would force me to take ten pieces in gold of him, which I had no mind to, he being become one of our number at the Board. This day was reckoned by all people the coldest day that ever was remembered in England; and, God knows! coals at a very great price.[3]

[1] Mary Davis, some time a comedian in the Duke of York's troop, and one of those actresses who boarded with Sir W. Davenant, was, according to Pepys, a natural daughter of Thomas Howard, first Earl of Berkshire. She captivated the king by the charming manner in which she sang a ballad beginning, "My lodging it is on the cold ground," when acting Celania, a shepherdess mad for love in the play of "The Rivals." Charles took her off the stage, and she had by him a daughter named Mary Tudor, married to Francis, second Earl of Derwentwater; and their son James, the third earl, was attainted and beheaded for high treason. Miss Davis was also a fine dancer; see Hawkins's "History of Music," vol. iv., p 525, where the ballad alluded to will be found; which, as Downes quaintly observes, "raised the fair songstress from her bed on the cold ground to the bed royal." According to another account, she was the daughter of a blacksmith at Charlton, in Wiltshire, where a family of the name of Davis had exercised that calling for many generations, and has but lately become extinct. There is a beautiful whole-length portrait of Mary Davis, by Kneller, at Audley End, in which she is represented as a tall, handsome woman; and her general appearance ill accords with the description given of her by our journalist. — B.

[2] As Florimel in "Secret Love, or the Maiden Queen." See 2nd of this month.

[3] £4 the chaldron. On November 26th, *post*, Pepys speaks of them

8th. Up, and to the Old Swan, where drank at Michell's, but not seeing her whom I love I by water to White Hall, and there acquainted Sir G. Carteret betimes what I had to say this day before the Duke of York in the business of Carcasse, which he likes well of, being a great enemy to him, and then I being too early here to go to Sir W. Coventry's chamber, having nothing to say to him, and being able to give him but a bad account of the business of the office (which is a shame to me, and that which I shall rue if I do not recover), to the Exchequer about getting a certificate of Mr. Lanyon's entered at Sir R. Long's office, and strange it is to see what horrid delays there are at this day in the business of money, there being nothing yet come from my Lord Treasurer to set the business of money in action since the Parliament broke off, notwithstanding the greatness and number of the King's occasions for it. So to the Swan, and there had three or four baisers of the little ancilla there, and so to Westminster Hall, where I saw Mr. Martin, the purser, come through with a picture in his hand, which he had bought, and observed how all the people of the Hall did fleer and laugh upon him, crying, "There is plenty grown upon a sudden;" and, the truth is, I was a little troubled that my favour should fall on so vain a fellow as he, and the more because, methought, the people do gaze upon me as the man that had raised him, and as if they guessed whence my kindness to him springs. So thence to White Hall, where I find all met at the Duke of York's chamber; and, by and by, the Duke of York comes, and Carcasse is called in, and I read the depositions and his answers, and he added with great confidence and good words, even almost to persuasion, what to say; and my Lord Bruncker, like a very silly solicitor, argued against me and us all for him; and, being asked first by the Duke of York his opinion, did give it for his being excused. I next did answer the contrary very plainly, and had, in this dispute, which vexed and will never be forgot by my Lord, many occasions of speaking severely, and did, against his bad practices. Commissioner Pett, like a fawning rogue,

as being £5 10*s.* In 1812, "Napoleon's winter," £6 6*s.* were paid in the suburbs of London; an extraordinary price; but, the difference of money considered, cheap, when compared with 1667.— B.

sided with my Lord, but to no purpose; and [Sir] W. Pen, like a cunning rogue, spoke mighty indifferently, and said nothing in all the fray, like a knave as he is. But [Sir] W. Batten spoke out, and did come off himself by the Duke's kindness very well; and then Sir G. Carteret, and Sir W. Coventry, and the Duke of York himself, flatly as I said; and so he[1] was declared unfit to continue in, and therefore to be presently discharged the office; which, among othei good effects, I hope, will make my Lord Bruncker not alloquer so high, when he shall consider he hath had such a publick foyle as this is. So home with [Sir] W. Batten, and [Sir] W. Pen, by coach, and there met at the office, and my Lord Bruncker presently after us, and there did give order to Mr. Stevens for securing the tickets in Carcasse's hands, which my Lord against his will could not refuse to sign, and then home to dinner, and so away with my wife by coach, she to Mrs. Pierce's and I to my Lord Bellasses, and with him to [my] Lord Treasurer's, where by agreement we met with Sir H. Cholmly, and there sat and talked all the afternoon almost about one thing or other, expecting Sir Philip Warwicke's coming, but he come not, so we away towards night, Sir H. Cholmly and I to the Temple, and there parted, telling me of my Lord Bellasses's want of generosity, and that he [Bellasses] will certainly be turned out of his government, and he [Cholmley] thinks himself stands fair for it. So home, and there found, as I expected, Mrs. Pierce and Mr. Batelier; he went for Mrs. Jones, but no Mrs. Knipp come, which vexed me, nor any other company. So with one fidler we danced away the evening, but I was not well contented with the littleness of the room, and my wife's want of preparing things ready, as they should be, for supper, and bad. So not very merry, though very well pleased. So after suppei to bed, my wife and Mrs. Pierce, and her boy James and I. Yesterday I began to make this mark (√) stand instead of three pricks, thus (.·.), which therefore I must observe every where, it being a mark more easy to make.

9th. Up, and to the office, where sat all the morning busy. At noon home to dinner, where Mrs. Pierce did

[1] Carcasse's dismissal from office is clearly alluded to in his verses. See note, August 17th, 1665.

continue with us and her boy (who I still find every day more and more witty beyond his age), and did dine with us, and by and by comes in her husband and a brother-in-law of his, a parson, one of the tallest biggest men that ever I saw in my life. So to the office, where a meeting extraordinary about settling the number and wages of my Lord Bruncker's clerks for his new work upon the Treasurer's accounts, but this did put us upon running into the business of yesterday about Carcasse, wherein I perceive he is most dissatisfied with me, and I am not sorry for it, having all the world but him of my side therein, for it will let him know another time that he is not to expect our submitting to him in every thing, as I think he did heretofore expect. He did speak many severe words to me, and I returned as many to him, so that I do think there cannot for a great while be any right peace between us, and I care not a fart for it; but however, I must look about me and mind my business, for I perceive by his threats and enquiries he is and will endeavour to find out something against me or mine. Breaking up here somewhat brokenly I home, and carried Mrs. Pierce and wife to the New Exchange, and there did give her and myself a pair of gloves, and then set her down at home, and so back again straight home and there to do business, and then to Sir W. Batten's, where [Sir] W. Pen and others, and mighty merry, only I have got a great cold, and the scolding this day at the office with my Lord Bruncker hath made it worse, that I am not able to speak. But, Lord! to see how kind Sir W. Batten and his Lady are to me upon this business of my standing by [Sir] W. Batten against Carcasse, and I am glad of it. Captain Cocke, who was here to-night, did tell us that he is certain that yesterday a proclamation was voted at the Council, touching the proclaiming of my Lord Duke of Buckingham a traytor, and that it will be out on Monday. So home late, and drank some buttered ale, and so to bed and to sleep. This cold did most certainly come by my staying a little too long bare-legged yesterday morning when I rose while I looked out fresh socks and thread stockings, yesterday's having in the night, lying near the window, been covered with snow within the window which made me I durst not put them on.

10th (Lord's day). Having my cold still grown more upon me, so as I am not able to speak, I lay in bed till noon, and then up and to my chamber with a good fire, and there spent an hour on Morly's Introduction to Musique,[1] a very good but unmethodical book. Then to dinner, my wife and I, and then all the afternoon alone in my chamber preparing a letter for Commissioner Taylor to the City about getting his accounts for The Loyal London,[2] by him built for them, stated and discharged, they owing him still about £4,000. Towards the evening comes Mr. Spong to see me, whose discourse about several things I proposed to him was very good, better than I have had with any body a good while. He gone, I to my business again, and anon comes my Lady Pen and her son-in-law and daughter, and there we talked all the evening away, and then to supper; and after supper comes Sir W. Pen, and there we talked together, and then broke up, and so to bed. He tells me that our Mr. Turner has seen the proclamation against the Duke of Buckingham,[3] and that therefore it is true what we heard last night. Yesterday and to-day I have been troubled with a hoarseness through cold that I could not almost speak.

11th. Up, and with my cold still upon me and hoarseness, but I was forced to rise and to the office, where all the morning busy, and among other things Sir W. Warren come to me, to whom of late I have been very strange, partly from my indifference how more than heretofore to get money, but most from my finding that he is become great with my Lord Bruncker, and so I dare not trust him as I used to do, for I will not be inward with him that is open to another. By and by comes Sir H. Cholmly to me about Tangier business, and then talking of news he tells me how yesterday the King did publiquely talk of the King of France's dealing with all the Princes of Christendome. As to the States of Holland, he [the King of France] hath

[1] Thomas Morely's work is entitled, "A Plaine and Easie Introduction to Practicall Musicke, set downe in forme of a dialogue deuided into three parties." London, 1597, folio; other editions, 1608, 1771.

[2] The "Loyal London" was the ship given to the king by the City It was launched at Deptford on June 10th, 1666.

[3] The proclamation "to apprehend George Duke of Buckingham for Treason" is dated "8 March 1666[-67]" ("Bibliotheca Lindesiana: Handlist of Proclamations," vol. i., 1509-1714).

advised them, on good grounds, to refuse to treat with us at the Hague, because of having opportunity of spies, by reason of our interest in the House of Orange; and then, it being a town in one particular province, it would not be fit to have it, but in a town wherein the provinces have equal interest, as at Mastricht, and other places named. That he advises them to offer no terms, nor accept of any, without his privity and consent, according to agreement; and tells them, if not so, he hath in his power to be even with them, the King of England being come to offer him any terms he pleases; and that my Lord St. Albans[1] is now at Paris, Plenipotentiary, to make what peace he pleases; and so he can make it, and exclude them, the Dutch, if he sees fit. A copy of this letter of the King of France's the Spanish Ambassador here gets, and comes and tells all to our King; which our King denies, and says the King of France only uses his power of saying anything. At the same time, the King of France writes to the Emperor, that he is resolved to do all things to express affection to the Emperor, having it now in his power to make what peace he pleases between the King of England and him, and the States of the United Provinces; and, therefore, that he would not have him to concern himself in a friendship with us; and assures him that, on that regard, he will not offer anything to his disturbance, in his interest in Flanders, or elsewhere. He writes, at the same time, to Spayne, to tell him that he wonders to hear of a league almost ended between the Crown of Spayne and England, by my Lord Sandwich, and all without his privity, while he was making a peace upon what terms he pleased with England: that he is a great lover of the Crown of Spayne, and would take the King and his affairs, during his minority, into his protection, nor would offer to set his foot in Flanders, or any where else, to disturb him; and, therefore, would not have him to trouble himself to make peace with any body; only he hath a desire to offer an exchange, which he thinks may be of moment to both sides: that is, that he [France] will enstate the King of Spayne in the kingdom of Portugall,

[1] Henry Jermyn, Earl of St. Albans, was appointed Envoy Extraordinary to treat for peace with France on January 25th, 1666–67.

and he and the Dutch will put him into possession of Lisbon; and, that being done, he [France] may have Flanders: and this, they say, do mightily take in Spayne, which is sensible of the fruitless expence Flanders, so far off, gives them; and how much better it would be for them to be master of Portugall; and the King of France offers, for security herein, that the King of England shall be bond for him, and that he will counter-secure the King of England with Amsterdam; and, it seems, hath assured our King, that if he will make a league with him, he will make a peace exclusive to the Hollander. These things are almost romantique, but yet true, as Sir H. Cholmly tells me the King himself did relate it all yesterday; and it seems as if the King of France did think other princes fit for nothing but to make sport for him: but simple princes they are, that are forced to suffer this from him. So at noon with Sir W. Pen by coach to the Sun in Leadenhall Streete, where Sir R. Ford, Sir W. Batten, and Commissioner Taylor (whose feast it was) were, and we dined and had a very good dinner. Among other discourses Sir R. Ford did tell me that he do verily believe that the city will in few years be built again in all the greatest streets, and answered the objections I did give to it. Here we had the proclamation this day come out against the Duke of Buckingham, commanding him to come in to one of the Secretaries, or to the Lieutenant of the Tower. A silly, vain man to bring himself to this: and there be many hard circumstances in the proclamation of the causes of this proceeding of the King's, which speak great displeasure of the King's, and crimes of his. Then to discourse of the business of the day, that is, to see Commissioner Taylor's accounts for his ship he built, The Loyall London, and it is pretty to see how dully this old fellow makes his demands, and yet plaguy wise sayings will come from the man sometimes, and also how Sir R. Ford and [Sir] W. Batten did with seeming reliance advise him what to do, and how to come prepared to answer objections to the Common Council. Thence away to the office, where late busy, and then home to supper, mightily pleased with my wife's trill, and so to bed. This night Mr. Carcasse did come to me again to desire favour, and that I would mediate that he might be restored, but I did give him no kind answer at all, but was very angry, and I confess a good deal of it from my Lord Bruncker's simplicity and passion.

12th. Up, and to the office, where all the morning, and my Lord Bruncker mighty quiet, and no words all day, which I wonder at, expecting that he would have fallen again upon the business of Carcasse, and the more for that here happened that Perkins, who was the greatest witness of all against him, was brought in by Sir W. Batten to prove that he did really belong to The Prince, but being examined was found rather a fool than anything, as not being able to give any account when he come in nor when he come out of her, more than that he was taken by the Dutch in her, but did agree in earnest to Sir W. Pen's saying that she lay up all the winter before at Lambeth. This I confess did make me begin to doubt the truth of his evidence, but not to doubt the faults of Carcasse, for he was condemned by many other better evidences than his, besides the whole world's report. At noon home, and there find Mr. Goodgroome, whose teaching of my wife only by singing over and over again to her, and letting her sing with him, not by herself, to correct her faults, I do not like at all, but was angry at it; but have this content, that I do think she will come to sing pretty well, and to trill in time, which pleases me well. He dined with us, and then to the office, when we had a sorry meeting to little purpose, and then broke up, and I to my office, and busy late to good purpose, and so home to supper and to bed. This day a poor seaman, almost starved for want of food, lay in our yard a-dying. I sent him half-a-crown, and we ordered his ticket to be paid.

13th. Up, and with [Sir] W. Batten to the Duke of York to our usual attendance, where I did fear my Lord Bruncker might move something in revenge that might trouble me, but he did not, but contrarily had the content to hear Sir G. Carteret fall foul on him in the Duke of York's bed chamber for his directing people with tickets and petitions to him, bidding him mind his Controller's place and not his, for if he did he should be too hard for him, and made high words, which I was glad of. Having done our usual business with the Duke of York, I away; and meeting Mr. D. Gawden in the presence-chamber, he and I to talk; and among other things he tells me, and I do find every where else, also, that our masters do begin not to like of their councils in fitting out no fleete, but only squadrons, and are finding out excuses for it; and, among others, he tells me a Privy-Councillor did tell him that it was said in Council that a fleete could not be set out this year, for want of victuals, which gives him and me a great alarme, but me especially: for had it been so, I ought to have represented it; and therefore it puts me in policy presently to prepare myself to answer this objection, if ever it should come about, by drawing up a state of the Victualler's stores, which I will presently do. So to Westminster Hall, and there staid and talked, and then to Sir G. Carteret's, where I dined with the ladies, he not at home, and very well used I am among them, so that I am heartily ashamed that my wife hath not been there to see them; but she shall very shortly. So home by water, and stepped into Michell's, and there did baiser my Betty, que ægrotat a little. At home find Mr. Holliard, and made him eat a bit of victuals. Here I find Mr. Greeten,[1] who teaches my wife on the flageolet, and I think she will come to something on it. Mr. Holliard advises me to have my father come up to town, for he doubts else in the country he will never find ease, for, poor man, his grief is now grown so great upon him that he is never at ease, so I will have him up at Easter. By and by by coach, set down Mr. Holliard near his house at Hatton Garden and myself to Lord Treasurer's, and sent my wife to the New Exchange. I staid not here, but to Westminster Hall, and thence to Martin's, where he and she both within, and with them the little widow that was once there with her when I was there, that dissembled so well to be grieved at hearing a tune that her late husband liked, but there being so much company, I had no pleasure here, and so away to the Hall again, and there met Doll Lane coming out, and par contrat did hazer bargain para aller to the cabaret de vin, called the Rose, and ibi I staid two hours, sed she did not venir, lequel troubled me, and so away by coach and took up my wife, and away home, and so to Sir

[1] Thomas Greeting, musician, published, in 1675, "The Pleasant Companion, or new Lessons and Instructions for the Flagelet."

W. Batten's, where I am told that it is intended by Mr. Carcasse to pray me to be godfather with Lord Bruncker to-morrow to his child, which I suppose they tell me in mirth, but if he should ask me I know not whether I should refuse it or no. Late at my office preparing a speech against to-morrow morning, before the King, at my Lord Treasurer's, and the truth is it run in my head all night. So home to supper and to bed. The Duke of Buckingham is concluded gone over sea, and, it is thought, to France.

14th. Up, and with Sir W. Batten and [Sir] W. Pen to my Lord Treasurer's, where we met with my Lord Bruncker an hour before the King come, and had time to talk a little of our business. Then come much company, among others Sir H. Cholmly, who tells me that undoubtedly my Lord Bellasses will go no more as Governor to Tangier, and that he do put in fair for it, and believes he shall have it, and proposes how it may conduce to his account and mine in the business of money. Here we fell into talk with Sir Stephen Fox, and, among other things, of the Spanish manner of walking, when three together, and shewed me how, which was pretty, to prevent differences. By and by comes the King and Duke of York, and presently the officers of the Ordnance were called; my Lord Berkeley, Sir John Duncomb, and Mr. Chichly; then we, my Lord Bruncker, [Sir] W. Batten, [Sir] W. Pen, and myself; where we find only the King and Duke of York, and my Lord Treasurer, and Sir G. Carteret; where I only did speak, laying down the state of our wants, which the King and Duke of York seemed very well pleased with, and we did get what we asked, £500,000, assigned upon the eleven months' tax: but that is not so much ready money, or what will raise £40,000 per week, which we desired, and the business will want. Yet are we fain to come away answered, when, God knows, it will undo the King's business to have matters of this moment put off in this manner. The King did prevent my offering any thing by and by as Treasurer for Tangier, telling me that he had ordered us £30,000 on the same tax; but that is not what we would have to bring our payments to come within a year. So we gone out, in went others; viz., one after another, Sir Stephen Fox for the army,

Captain Cocke for sick and wounded, Mr. Ashburnham[1] for the household. Thence [Sir] W. Batten, [Sir] W. Pen, and I, back again; I mightily pleased with what I had said and done, and the success thereof. But, it being a fine clear day, I did, en gayeté de cœur, propose going to Bow for ayre sake, and dine there, which they embraced, and so [Sir] W. Batten and I (setting [Sir] W. Pen down at Mark Lane end) straight to Bow, to the Queen's Head, and there bespoke our dinner, carrying meat with us from London; and anon comes [Sir] W. Pen with my wife and Lady Batten, and then Mr. Lowder with his mother and wife. While [Sir] W. Batten and I were alone, we had much friendly discourse, though I will never trust him far; but we do propose getting "The Flying Greyhound,"[2] our privateer, to us and [Sir] W. Pen at the end of the year when we call her home, by begging her of the King, and I do not think we shall be denied her. They being come, we to oysters and so to talk, very pleasant I was all day, and anon to dinner, and I made very good company. Here till the evening, so as it was dark almost before we got home (back again in the same method, I think, we went), and spent the night talking at Sir W. Batten's, only a little at my office, to look over the Victualler's contract, and draw up some arguments for him to plead for his charges in transportation of goods beyond the ports which the letter of one article in his contract do lay upon him. This done I home to supper and to bed. Troubled a little at my fear that my Lord Bruncker should tell Sir W. Coventry of our neglecting the office this afternoon (which was intended) to look after our pleasures, but nothing will fall upon me alone about this.

15th. Up, and pleased at Tom's teaching of Barker something, to sing a 3rd part to a song, which will please mightily. So I to the office all the morning, and at noon to the 'Change, where I do hear that letters this day come to Court do tell us that we are likely not to agree, the Dutch demanding high terms, and the King of France the like, in a most braving manner. The merchants do give them-

[1] William Ashburnham, the Cofferer (see December 14th, 1666).

[2] Among the Rawlinson MSS. (Bodleian) are "Accounts with Sir W. Batten and others relating to the 'Flying Greyhound' privateer, 1667," A. 174.

selves over for lost, no man knowing what to do, whether to sell or buy, not knowing whether peace or war to expect, and I am told that could that be now known a man might get £20,000 in a week's time by buying up of goods in case there should be war. Thence home and dined well, and then with my wife, set her at Unthanke's and I to Sir G. Carteret, where talked with the ladies a while, and my Lady Carteret talks nothing but sorrow and afflictions coming on us, and indeed I do fear the same. So away and met Dr. Fuller, Bishop of Limricke, and walked an hour with him in the Court talking of newes only, and he do think that matters will be bad with us. Then to Westminster Hall, and there spent an hour or two walking up and down, thinking para avoir got out Doll Lane, sed je ne could do it, having no opportunity de hazer le, ainsi lost the tota afternoon, and so away and called my wife and home, where a little at the office, and then home to my closet to enter my Journalls, and so to supper and to bed. This noon come little Mis. Tooker, who is grown a little woman; ego had opportunity para baiser her. . . . This morning I was called up by Sir John Winter, poor man! come in his sedan from the other end of the town, before I was up, and merely about the King's business, which is a worthy thing of him, and I believe him to be a worthy good man, and I will do him the right to tell the Duke of it, who did speak well of him the other day. It was about helping the King in the business of bringing down his timber to the sea-side, in the Forest of Deane.

16th. Up, and to the office, where all the morning; at noon home to dinner, and then to the office again in the afternoon, and there all day very busy till night, and then, having done much business, home to supper, and so to bed. This afternoon come home Sir J. Minnes, who has been down, but with little purpose, to pay the ships below at the Nore. This evening, having done my letters, I did write out the heads of what I had prepared to speak to the King the other day at my Lord Treasurer's, which I do think convenient to keep by me for future use. The weather is now grown warm again, after much cold; and it is observable that within these eight days I did see smoke remaining, coming out of some cellars, from the late great fire, now above six months since. There was this day at the office (as he is most days) Sir W. Warren, against whom I did manifestly plead, and heartily too, God forgive me! But the reason is because I do find that he do now wholly rely almost upon my Lord Bruncker, though I confess I have no greater ground of my leaving him than the confidence which I perceive he hath got in my Lord Bruncker, whose seeming favours only do obtain of him as much compensation as, I believe (for he do know well the way of using his bounties), as mine more real. Besides, my Lord and I being become antagonistic, I do not think it safe for me to trust myself in the hands of one whom I know to be a knave, and using all means to become gracious there.

17th (Lord's day). Up betime with my wife, and by coach with Sir W. Pen and Sir Thomas Allen to White Hall, there my wife and I the first time that ever we went to my Lady Jemimah's chamber at Sir Edward Carteret's lodgings. I confess I have been much to blame and much ashamed of our not visiting her sooner, but better now than never. Here we took her before she was up, which I was sorry for, so only saw her, and away to chapel, leaving further visit till after sermon. I put my wife into the pew below, but it was pretty to see, myself being but in a plain band, and every way else ordinary, how the verger took me for her man, I think, and I was fain to tell him she was a kinswoman of my Lord Sandwich's, he saying that none under knights-baronets' ladies are to go into that pew. So she being there, I to the Duke of York's lodging, where in his dressing-chamber he talking of his journey to-morrow or next day to Harwich, to prepare some fortifications there; so that we are wholly upon the defensive part this year, only we have some expectations that we may by our squadrons annoy them in their trade by the North of Scotland and to the Westward. Here Sir W. Pen did show the Duke of York a letter of Hogg's[1] about a prize he drove in within the Sound at Plymouth, where the Vice-Admiral claims her. Sir W. Pen would have me speak to the latter, which I did,

[1] Thomas Waltham, muster-master at Plymouth, writes to the Navy Commissioners, January 11th, 1666-67, "Captain Hogg with his prize is ready to sail the first opportunity" ("Calendar of State Papers," 1666-67, p. 447).

and I think without any offence, but afterwards I was sorry for it, and Sir W. Pen did plainly say that he had no mind to speak to the Duke of York about it, so that he put me upon it, but it shall be the last time that I will do such another thing, though I think no manner of hurt done by it to me at all. That done I to walk in the Parke, where to the Queene's Chapel, and there heard a fryer preach with his cord about his middle, in Portuguese, something I could understand, showing that God did respect the meek and humble, as well as the high and rich. He was full of action, but very decent and good, I thought, and his manner of delivery very good. Then I went back to White Hall, and there up to the closet, and spoke with several people till sermon was ended, which was preached by the Bishop of Hereford,[1] an old good man, that they say made an excellent sermon. He was by birth a Catholique, and a great gallant, having £1,500 per annum, patrimony, and is a Knight Barronet; was turned from his persuasion by the late Archbishop Laud. He and the Bishop of Exeter, Dr. Ward, are the two Bishops that the King do say he cannot have bad sermons from. Here I met with Sir H. Cholmly, who tells me, that undoubtedly my Lord Bellasses do go no more to Tangier, and that he do believe he do stand in a likely way to go Governor; though he says, and showed me, a young silly Lord, one Lord Allington,[2] who hath offered a great sum of money to go, and will put hard

[1] Bishop Herbert Croft, who was previously Dean of Hereford (1644), was not a Romanist by birth, but entangled by the Jesuits while on his travels, and converted to Popery. It would appear, from Godwin ("De Præsulibus"), that his return to the Protestant faith is not attributable to Laud, but to the efforts of another prelate. "In patriam vero redux et in Thomæ Mortoni Episcopi Dunelmensis familiaritatem adductus melioribus consiliis adhibitis ad se quoque rediit et Ecclesiam Anglicanam." Croft, says Burnet, was a devout man, but of no discretion in his conduct. He was born 1603, and survived his elevation to the see of Hereford, in 1661, thirty years. The bishop's father, Sir Herbert, was a knight, and his son, of the same name, a baronet. See Sir Walter Scott's preface to "The Naked Truth," in "Somers' Tracts," vol. vii., p. 268. — B.

[2] William Allington, second Baron Allington, of Killard, Ireland, created an English Baron, 1682, by the title of Baron Allington, of Wymondley, Hertfordshire. He died 1684, and was succeeded by his son, Giles, who died 1691, when the title became extinct.

for it, he having a fine lady,[1] and a great man would be glad to have him out of the way. After Chapel I down and took out my wife from the pew, where she was talking with a lady whom I knew not till I was gone. It was Mrs. Ashfield of Brampton, who had with much civility been, it seems, at our house to see her. I am sorry I did not show her any more respect. With my wife to Sir G. Carteret's, where we dined and mightily made of, and most extraordinary people they are to continue friendship with for goodness, virtue, and nobleness and interest. After dinner he and I alone awhile and did joy ourselves in my Lord Sandwich's being out of the way all this time. He concurs that we are in a way of ruin by thus being forced to keep only small squadrons out, but do tell me that it was not choice, but only force, that we could not keep out the whole fleete. He tells me that the King is very kind to my Lord Sandwich, and did himself observe to him (Sir G. Carteret), how those very people, meaning the Prince and Duke of Albemarle, are punished in the same kind as they did seek to abuse my Lord Sandwich. Thence away, and got a hackney coach and carried my wife home, and there only drank, and myself back again to my Lord Treasurer's, where the King, Duke of York, and Sir G. Carteret and Lord Arlington were and none else, so I staid not, but to White Hall, and there meeting nobody I would speak with, walked into the Park and took two or three turns all alone, and then took coach and home, where I find Mercer, who I was glad to see, but durst [not] shew so, my wife being displeased with her, and indeed I fear she is grown a very gossip. I to my chamber, and there fitted my arguments which I had promised Mr. Gawden in his behalf in some pretences to allowance of the King, and then to supper, and so to my chamber a little again, and then to bed. Duke of Buckingham not heard of yet.

18th. Up betimes, and to the office to write fair my paper for D. Gawden against anon, and then to other business, where all the morning. D. Gawden by and by comes, and I did read over and give him the paper, which I think I

[1] His second wife, Juliana, daughter of Baptist Noel, Viscount Campden. She died in the September following. — B.

have much obliged him in. A little before noon comes my old good friend, Mr. Richard Cumberland,[1] to see me, being newly come to town, whom I have not seen almost, if not quite, these seven years. In his plain country-parson's dress. I could not spend much time with him, but prayed him come with his brother, who was with him, to dine with me to-day; which he did do: and I had a great deal of his good company; and a most excellent person he is as any I know, and one that I am sorry should be lost and buried in a little country town, and would be glad to remove him thence; and the truth is, if he would accept of my sister's fortune, I should give £100 more with him than to a man able to settle her four times as much as, I fear, he is able to do; and I will think of it, and a way how to move it, he having in discourse said he was not against marrying, nor yet engaged. I shewed him my closet, and did give him some very good musique, Mr. Cæsar being here upon his lute. They gone I to the office, where all the afternoon very busy, and among other things comes Captain Jenifer to me, a great servant of my Lord Sandwich's, who tells me that he do hear for certain, though I do not yet believe it, that Sir W. Coventry is to be Secretary of State, and my Lord Arlington Lord Treasurer. I only wish that the latter were as fit for the latter office as the former is for the former, and more fit than my Lord Arlington. Anon Sir W. Pen come and talked with me in the garden, and tells me that for certain the Duke of Richmond is to marry Mrs. Stewart, he having this day brought in an account of his estate and debts to the King on that account. At night home to supper and so to bed. My father's letter this day do tell me of his own continued illness, and that my mother grows so much worse, that he fears she cannot long continue, which troubles me very much. This day, Mr. Cæsar told me a pretty experiment of his, of angling with a minikin, a gut-string varnished over, which keeps it from swelling, and is beyond any hair for strength and smallness. The secret I like mightily.

19th. Up, and to the office, where we sat all the morn-

[1] Richard Cumberland, afterwards Bishop of Peterborough (see note, February 5th, 1659–60).

ing. At noon dined at home very pleasantly with my wife, and after dinner with a great deal of pleasure had her sing, which she begins to do with some pleasure to me, more than I expected. Then to the office again, where all the afternoon close, and at night home to supper and to bed. It comes in my mind this night to set down how a house was the other day in Bishopsgate Street blowed up with powder; a house that was untenanted, and between a flax shop and a ——, both bad for fire; but, thanks be to God, it did no more hurt; and all do conclude it a plot. I would also remember to my shame how I was pleased yesterday to find the righteous maid of Magister Griffin sweeping of nostra office, elle con the Roman nariz and bonne body which I did heretofore like, and do still refresh me to think que elle is come to us, that I may voir her aliquando. This afternoon I am told again that the town do talk of my Lord Arlington's being to be Lord Treasurer, and Sir W. Coventry to be Secretary of State; and that for certain the match is concluded between the Duke of Richmond and Mrs. Stewart, which I am well enough pleased with; and it is pretty to consider how his quality will allay people's talk; whereas, had a meaner person married her, he would for certain have been reckoned a cuckold at first dash.

20th. Up pretty betimes, and to the Old Swan, and there drank at Michell's, but his wife is not there, but gone to her mother's, who is ill, and so hath staid there since Sunday. Thence to Westminster Hall and drank at the Swan, and baiserais the petite misse; and so to Mrs. Martin's. . . . I sent for some burnt wine, and drank and then away, not pleased with my folly, and so to the Hall again, and there staid a little, and so home by water again, where, after speaking with my wife, I with Sir W. Batten and [Sir] J. Minnes to our church to the vestry, to be assessed by the late Poll Bill, where I am rated as an Esquire, and for my office, all will come to about £50. But not more than I expected, nor so much by a great deal as I ought to be, for all my offices. So shall be glad to escape so. Thence by water again to White Hall, and there up into the house, and do hear that newes is come now that the enemy do incline again to a peace, but could hear no particulars, so do not believe it. I had a great mind to have spoke with the King about a business proper enough for me, about the French prize man-of-war, how he would have her altered, only out of a desire to show myself mindful of business, but my linen was so dirty and my clothes mean, that I neither thought it fit to do that, nor go to other persons at the Court, with whom I had business, which did vex me, and I must remedy [it]. Here I hear that the Duke of Richmond and Mrs. Stewart were betrothed last night. Thence to Westminster Hall again, and there saw Betty Michell, and bought a pair of gloves of her, she being fain to keep shop there, her mother being sick, and her father gathering of the tax. I aimais her de toute my corazon. Thence, my mind wandering all this day upon mauvaises amours which I be merry for. So home by water again, where I find my wife gone abroad, so I to Sir W. Batten to dinner, and had a good dinner of ling and herring pie, very good meat, best of the kind that ever I had. Having dined, I by coach to the Temple, and there did buy a little book or two, and it is strange how "Rycaut's[1] Discourse of Turky," which before the fire I was asked but 8*s*. for, there being all but twenty-two or thereabouts burned, I did now offer 20*s*., and he demands 50*s*., and I think I shall give it him, though it be only as a monument of the fire. So to the New Exchange, where I find my wife, and so took her to Unthanke's, and left her there, and I to White Hall, and thence to Westminster, only out of idleness, and to get some little pleasure to my mauvais flammes, but sped not, so back and took up my wife, and to Polichinelli at Charing Crosse, which is prettier and prettier, and so full of variety that it is extraordinary good entertainment. Thence by coach home, that is, my wife home, and I to the Exchange, and there met with Fenn, who tells me they have yet no orders out of the Exchequer for money upon the Acts, which is a thing not to be borne by any Prince of understanding or care, for no money can be got advanced upon the Acts only from the weight of orders in form out of the Exchequer so long time after the passing of the Acts. So home to the office a little, where I met with a sad letter from my brother,

[1] Sir Paul Rycaut (see note, October 15th, 1666).

who tells me my mother is declared by the doctors to be past recovery, and that my father is also very ill every hour: so that I fear we shall see a sudden change there. God fit them and us for it! So to Sir W. Pen's, where my wife was, and supped with a little,[1] but yet little mirth, and a bad, nasty supper, which makes me not love the family, they do all things so meanly, to make a little bad show upon their backs. Thence home and to bed, very much troubled about my father's and my mother's illness.

21st. Up, and to the office, where sat all the morning. At noon home to dinner, and had some melancholy discourse with my wife about my mother's being so ill and my father, and after dinner to cheer myself, I having the opportunity of Sir W. Coventry and the Duke of York's being out of town, I alone out and to the Duke of York's play-house, where unexpectedly I come to see only the young men and women of the house act; they having liberty to act for their own profit on Wednesdays and Fridays this Lent: and the play they did yesterday, being Wednesday, was so well-taken, that they thought fit to venture it publickly to-day; a play of my Lord Falkland's[2] called "The Wedding Night," a kind of a tragedy, and some things very good in it, but the whole together, I thought, not so. I confess I was well enough pleased with my seeing it: and the people did do better, without the great actors, than I did expect, but yet far short of what they do when they are there, which I was glad to find the difference of. Thence to rights home, and there to the office to my business hard, being sorry to have made this scape without my wife, but I have a good salvo to my oath in doing it. By and by, in the evening, comes Sir W. Batten's Mingo to me to pray me to come to his master and Sir Richard Ford, who have very ill news to tell me. I knew what it was, it was about

[1] Sir William Penn was at Sheerness on this day, and his "Memorandum of a Consultation held at Sheerness, March 20th, 1666–67, for the security of the said places, &c.," is printed in Penn's "Life of Sir W. Penn," vol. ii., p. 437.

[2] Henry Cary, third Viscount Falkland, M.P., Oxford City, 1660, and Oxfordshire, 1661. Sir Henry Cary, first Viscount Falkland, in the peerage of Scotland, was Lord Deputy of Ireland from 1622 to 1629. The title of the play was really "The Marriage Night." It was published in 1664. The author died in the same year.

our trial for a good prize to-day, "The Phœnix,"[1] worth two or £3,000. I went to them, where they told me with much trouble how they had sped, being cast and sentenced to make great reparation for what we had embezzled, and they did it so well that I was much troubled at it, when by and by Sir W. Batten asked me whether I was mortified enough, and told me we had got the day, which was mighty welcome news to me and us all. But it is pretty to see what money will do. Yesterday, Walker[2] was mighty cold on our behalf, till Sir W. Batten promised him, if we sped in this business of the goods, a coach; and if at the next trial we sped for the ship, we would give him a pair of horses. And he hath strove for us to-day like a prince, though the Swedes' Agent was there with all the vehemence he could to save the goods, but yet we carried it against him. This put me in mighty good heart, and then we go to Sir W. Pen, who is come back to-night from Chatham, and did put him into the same condition, and then comforted him. So back to my office, and wrote an affectionate and sad letter to my father about his and my mother's illness, and so home to supper and to bed late.

22nd. Up and by coach to Sir Ph. Warwicke about business for Tangier about money, and then to Sir Stephen Fox to give him account of a little service I have done him about money coming to him from our office, and then to Lovett's and saw a few baubling things of their doing which are very pretty, but the quality of the people, living only by shifts, do not please me, that it makes me I do no more care for them, nor shall have more acquaintance with them after I have got my Lady Castlemayne's picture home. So to White Hall, where the King at Chapel, and I would not stay, but to Westminster to Howlett's, and there, he being not well, I sent for a quart of claret and burnt it and drank,

[1] There are references to the "Phœnix," a Dutch ship taken as a prize, among the State Papers (see "Calendar," 1666–67, p. 404). Pepys appears to have got into trouble at a later date in respect to this same ship, for among the Rawlinson MSS. (A. 170) are "Papers relating to the charge brought against him in the House of Commons in 1689 with reference to the ship Phœnix and the East India Company in 1681–86."

[2] Sir William Walker (see August 23rd, 1660).

and had a basado or three or four of Sarah, whom je trouve ici, and so by coach to Sir Robt. Viner's about my accounts with him, and so to the 'Change, where I hear for certain that we are going on with our treaty of peace, and that we are to treat at Bredah. But this our condescension people do think will undo us, and I do much fear it. So home to dinner, where my wife having dressed herself in a silly dress of a blue petticoat uppermost, and a white satin waistcoat and white hood, though I think she did it because her gown is gone to the tailor's, did, together with my being hungry, which always makes me peevish, make me angry, but when my belly was full were friends again, and dined and then by water down to Greenwich and thence walked to Woolwich, all the way reading Playford's "Introduction to Musique," wherein are some things very pretty. At Woolwich I did much business, taking an account of the state of the ships there under hand, thence to Blackwall, and did the like for two ships we have repairing there, and then to Deptford and did the like there, and so home. Captain Perriman with me from Deptford, telling me many particulars how the King's business is ill ordered, and indeed so they are, God knows! So home and to the office, where did business, and so home to my chamber, and then to supper and to bed. Landing at the Tower to-night I met on Tower Hill with Captain Cocke and spent half an hour walking in the dusk of the evening with him, talking of the sorrowful condition we are in, that we must be ruined if the Parliament do not come and chastize us, that we are resolved to make a peace whatever it cost, that the King is disobliging the Parliament in this interval all that may be, yet his money is gone and he must have more, and they likely not to give it, without a great deal of do. God knows what the issue of it will be. But the considering that the Duke of York, instead of being at sea as Admirall, is now going from port to port, as he is at this day at Harwich, and was the other day with the King at Sheernesse, and hath ordered at Portsmouth how fortifications shall be made to oppose the enemy, in case of invasion, [which] is to us a sad consideration, and as shameful to the nation, especially after so many proud vaunts as we have made against the Dutch, and all from the folly of the Duke of

Albemarle, who made nothing of beating them, and Sir John Lawson he always declared that we never did fail to beat them with lesser numbers than theirs, which did so prevail with the King as to throw us into this war.

23rd. At the office all the morning, where Sir W. Pen come, being returned from Chatham, from considering the means of fortifying the river Medway, by a chain at the stakes, and ships laid there with guns to keep the enemy from coming up to burn our ships; all our care now being to fortify ourselves against their invading us. At noon home to dinner, and then to the office all the afternoon again, where Mr. Moore come, who tells me that there is now no doubt made of a peace being agreed on, the King having declared this week in Council that they would treat at Bredagh. He gone I to my office, where busy late, and so to supper and to bed. Vexed with our mayde Luce, our cook-mayde, who is a good drudging servant in everything else, and pleases us, but that she will be drunk, and hath been so last night and all this day, that she could not make clean the house. My fear is only fire.

24th (Lord's day). With Sir W. Batten to White Hall, and there I to Sir G. Carteret, who is mighty cheerful, which makes me think and by some discourse that there is expectation of a peace, but I did not ask [him]. Here was Sir J. Minnes also: and they did talk of my Lord Bruncker, whose father,[1] it seems, did give Mr. Ashburnham

[1] Sir William Brouncker (born 1585) had been Commissary-General of the Musters in the Scotch expedition in 1639, Vice-Chamberlain to Prince Charles, and one of the gentlemen of the Privy Chamber to Charles I. He was the son of Sir Henry Brouncker, President of Munster, by Anne, sister to Henry Lord Morley, and was created Viscount Brouncker of Castle Lyons, in Ireland, and Baron Brouncker of Newcastle, co. Dublin, September 12th, 1645. He died in November following at Wadham College, Oxford, and was buried in Christ Church Cathedral, leaving issue by his wife, Winifred, daughter of Sir William Leigh, of Newenham, Warwickshire, two sons, William, and Henry, third and last Viscount Brouncker, who died in 1688, and was buried in Richmond Church, leaving no issue by his wife Rebecca, widow of the Hon. Thomas Jermyn, mother, by her first husband, of Thomas, Lord Jermyn, and Henry, Lord Dover. Henry Brouncker, who had been Groom of the Bedchamber to the Duke of York, had succeeded to the office of Cofferer on the death of William Ashburnham in 1671. The Lords Brouncker were descended from Henry Brouncker, who, in

and the present Lord Digby £1,200 to be made an Irish lord, and swore the same day that he had not 12*d.* left to pay for his dinner: they make great mirth at this, my Lord Bruncker having lately given great matter of offence both to them and us all, that we are at present mightily displeased with him. By and by to the Duke of York, where we all met, and there was the King also; and all our discourse was about fortifying of the Medway and Harwich, which is to be entrenched quite round, and Portsmouth: and here they advised with Sir Godfry Lloyd[1] and Sir Bernard de Gum,[2] the two great engineers, and had the plates drawn before them; and indeed all their care they now take is to fortify themselves, and are not ashamed of it: for when by and by my Lord Arlington come in with letters, and seeing the King and Duke of York give us and the officers of the Ordnance directions in this matter, he did move that we might do it as privately as we could, that it might not come into the Dutch Gazette presently, as the King's and Duke of York's going down the other day to Sheerenesse was, the week after, in the Harlem Gazette. The King and Duke of York both laughed at it, and made no matter, but said, "Let us be safe, and let them talk, for there is nothing will trouble them more, nor will prevent their coming more,

1544, bought lands at Melksham and Erlestoke, in Wilts; and his arms, and those of his two wives, are described by Aubrey as being on the window of a house at Erlestoke. There are lives of the Brounckers by Mr. Sidney L. Lee in the "Dictionary of National Biography."

[1] Sir Godfrey Lloyd had been a captain in Holland, and was knighted by Charles at Brussels in 1657. — B.

[2] Sir Bernard de Gomme was born at Lille in 1620. When young he served in the campaigns of Frederick Henry, Prince of Orange, and afterwards entered the service of Charles I., by whom he was knighted. Under Charles II. and James II. he filled the offices of Engineer in Chief of all the King's Castles and Fortifications in England and Wales, Quarter-Master-General, and Surveyor-General of the Ordnance. He died November 23rd, 1685, and was buried in the Tower of London on the 30th. He first fortified Sheerness, Liverpool, &c., and he strengthened Portsmouth. His plans of these places and others, and of some of Charles I.'s battles, are in the British Museum, where also is preserved a miniature portrait of him in oil. Mr. G. Laurence Gomme, ex-President of the Folk Lore Society, is a member of the same family as Sir Bernard, and possesses a curious carved desk with Cromwell's arms upon it. It is a tradition in the family that this was presented by the Protector to Sir Bernard de Gomme.

than to hear that we are fortifying ourselves." And the Duke of York said further, "What said Marshal Turenne, when some in vanity said that the enemies were afraid, for they entrenched themselves? 'Well,' says he, 'I would they were not afraid, for then they would not entrench themselves, and so we could deal with them the better.'" Away thence, and met with Sir H. Cholmly, who tells me that he do believe the government of Tangier is bought by my Lord Allington for a sum of money to my Lord Arlington, and something to Lord Bellasses, who (he did tell me particularly how) is as very a false villain as ever was born, having received money of him here upon promise and confidence of his return, forcing him to pay it by advance here, and promising to ask no more there, when at the same time he was treating with my Lord Allington to sell his command to him, and yet told Sir H. Cholmly nothing of it, but when Sir H. Cholmly told him what he had heard, he confessed that my Lord Allington had spoken to him of it, but that he was a vain man to look after it, for he was nothing fit for it, and then goes presently to my Lord Allington and drives on the bargain, yet tells Lord Allington what he himself had said of him, as [though] Sir H. Cholmly had said them. I am glad I am informed hereof, and shall know him for a Lord, &c. Sir H. Cholmly tells me further that he is confident there will be a peace, and that a great man did tell him that my Lord Albemarle did tell him the other day at White Hall as a secret that we should have a peace if anything the King of France can ask and our King can give will gain it, which he is it seems mad at. Thence back with Sir W. Batten and [Sir] W. Pen home, and heard a piece of sermon, and so home to dinner, where Balty come, very fine, and dined with us, and after dinner with me by water to White Hall, and there he and I did walk round the Park, I giving him my thoughts about the difficulty of getting employment for him this year, but advised him how to employ himself, and I would do what I could. So he and I parted, and I to Martin's, where I find her within, and su hermano and la veuve Burroughs. Here I did demeurer toda the afternoon. . . . By and by come up the mistress of the house, Crags, a pleasant jolly woman. I staid all but a little, and away home by water through bridge, a brave evening, and so home to read, and anon to supper, W. Hewer with us, and then to read myself to sleep again, and then to bed, and mightily troubled the most of the night with fears of fire, which I cannot get out of my head to this day since the last great fire. I did this night give the waterman who uses to carry me 10*s*. at his request, for the painting of his new boat, on which shall be my arms.

25th. (Ladyday.) Up, and with Sir W. Batten and [Sir] W. Pen by coach to Exeter House to our lawyers' to have consulted about our trial to-morrow, but missed them, so parted, and [Sir] W. Pen and I to Mr. Povy's about a little business of [Sir] W. Pen's, where we went over Mr. Povy's house, which lies in the same good condition as ever, which is most extraordinary fine, and he was now at work with a cabinet-maker, making of a new inlaid table. Having seen his house, we away, having in our way thither called at Mr. Lilly's,[1] who was working; and indeed his pictures are without doubt much beyond Mr. Hales's, I think I may say I am convinced: but a mighty proud man he is, and full of state. So home, and to the office, and by and by to dinner, a poor dinner, my wife and I, at Sir W. Pen's, and then he and I before to Exeter House, where I do not stay, but to the King's playhouse; and by and by comes Mr. Lowther and his wife and mine, and into a box, forsooth, neither of them being dressed, which I was almost ashamed of. Sir W. Pen and I in the pit, and here saw "The Mayden Queene" again;[2] which indeed the more I see the more I like, and is an excellent play, and so done by Nell, her merry part, as cannot be better done in nature, I think. Thence home, and there I find letters from my brother, which tell me that yesterday when he wrote my mother did rattle in the throat so as they did expect every moment her death, which though I have a good while expected did much surprise me, yet was obliged to sup at Sir W. Pen's and my wife, and there counterfeited some little mirth, but my heart

[1] Sir Peter Lely (1618-1680) was knighted January 11th, 1678-79. His house was in Drury Lane. He died November 30th, 1680, and was buried by torchlight in St. Paul's Church, Covent Garden, December 7th.

[2] See March 2nd, 1666-67.

was sad, and so home after supper and to bed, and much troubled in my sleep of my being crying by my mother's bedside, laying my head over hers and crying, she almost dead and dying, and so waked, but what is strange, methought she had hair over her face, and not the same kind of face as my mother really hath, but yet did not consider that, but did weep over her as my mother, whose soul God have mercy of.

26th. Up with a sad heart in reference to my mother, of whose death I undoubtedly expect to hear the next post, if not of my father's also, who by his pain as well as his grief for her is very ill, but on my own behalf I have cause to be joyful this day, it being my usual feast day, for my being cut of the stone this day nine years, and through God's blessing am at this day and have long been in as good condition of health as ever I was in my life or any man in England is, God make me thankful for it! But the condition I am in, in refeıence to my mother, makes it unfit for me to keep my usual feast. Unless it shall please God to send her well (which I despair wholly of), and then I will make amends for it by observing another day in its room. So to the office, and at the office all the morning, where I had an opportunity to speak to Sir John Harman about my desire to have my brother Balty go again with him to sea as he did the last year, which he do seem not only contented but pleased with, which I was glad of. So at noon home to dinner, where I find Creed, who dined with us, but I had not any time to talk with him, my head being busy, and before I had dined was called away by Sir W. Batten, and both of us in his coach (which I observe his coachman do always go now from hence towards White Hall through Tower Street, and it is the best way) to Exeter House, where the Judge was sitting, and after several little causes comes on ours, and while the several depositions and papers were at large reading (which they call the preparatory), and being cold by being forced to sit with my hat off close to a window in the Hall, Sir W. Pen and I to the Castle Tavern hard by and got a lobster, and he and I staid and eat it, and drank good wine; I only burnt wine, as my whole custom of late hath been, as an evasion, God knows, for my drinking of wine (but it is an evasion which will not serve me now hot weather is coming, that I cannot pretend, as indeed I really have done, that I drank it for cold), but I will leave it off, and it is but seldom, as when I am in women's company, that I must call for wine, for I must be forced to drink to them. Having done here then we back again to the Court, and there heard our cause pleaded; Sir [Edward] Turner, Sir W. Walker, and Sir Ellis Layton being our counsel against only Sir Robert Wiseman[1] on the other. The second of our three counsel was the best, and indeed did speak admirably, and is a very shrewd man. Nevertheless, as good as he did make our case, and the rest, yet when Wiseman come to argue (nay, and though he did begin so sillily that we laughed in scorn in our sleeves at him), yet he did so state the case, that the Judge[2] did not think fit to decide the cause to-night, but took to to-morrow, and did stagger us in our hopes, so as to make us despair of the success. I am mightily pleased with the Judge, who seems a very rational, learned, and uncorrupt man, and much good reading and reason there is heard in hearing of this law argued, so that the thing pleased me, though our success doth shake me. Thence Sir W. Pen and I home and to write letters, among others a sad one to my father upon fear of my mother's death, and so home to supper and to bed.

27th. [Sir] W. Pen and I to White Hall, and in the coach did begin our discourse again about Balty, and he promises me to move it this very day. He and I met my Lord Bruncker at Sir G. Carteret's by appointment, there to discourse a little business, all being likely to go to rack for lack of money still. Thence to the Duke of York's lodgings, and did our usual business, and Sir W. Pen telling me that he had this morning spoke of Balty to Sir W. Coventry, and that the thing was done, I did take notice

[1] D.C.L., King's Advocate, 1669; Judge of the High Court of Admiralty in 1673, in succession to Sir Leoline Jenkins.

[2] Sir Leoline Jenkins, Principal of Jesus College, Oxford, and afterwards made Judge of the Admiralty and the Prerogative Court. He was subsequently employed on several embassies, and succeeded Henry Coventry as Secretary of State, 1680. Died 1685, aged sixty-two. His State Papers have been published. Burnet says of him, "He was a man of an exemplary life and considerably learned, but he was dull and slow; he was suspected of leaning to popery, though very unjustly."

of it also to [Sir] W. Coventry, who told me that he had both the thing and the person in his head before to have done it, which is a double pleasure to me. Our business with the Duke being done, [Sir] W. Pen and I towards the Exchequer, and in our way met Sir G. Downing going to chapel, but we stopped, and he would go with us back to the Exchequer and showed us in his office his chests full and ground and shelves full of money, and says that there is £50,000 at this day in his office of people's money, who may demand it this day, and might have had it away several weeks ago upon the late Act, but do rather choose to have it continue there than to put it into the Banker's hands, and I must confess it is more than I should have believed had I not seen it, and more than ever I could have expected would have arisen for this new Act in so short a time, and if it do so now already what would it do if the money was collected upon the Act and returned into the Exchequer so timely as it ought to be. But it comes into my mind here to observe what I have heard from Sir John Bankes, though I cannot fully conceive the reason of it, that it will be impossible to make the Exchequer ever a true bank to all intents, unless the Exchequer stood nearer the Exchange, where merchants might with ease, while they are going about their business, at all hours, and without trouble or loss of time, have their satisfaction, which they cannot have now without much trouble, and loss of half a day, and no certainty of having the offices open. By this he means a bank for common practise and use of merchants, and therein I do agree with him. Being parted from Sir W. Pen and [Sir] G. Downing, I to Westminster Hall and there met Balty, whom I had sent for, and there did break the business of my getting him the place of going again as Muster-Master with Harman this voyage to the West Indys, which indeed I do owe to Sir W. Pen. He is mighty glad of it, and earnest to fit himself for it, but I do find, poor man, that he is troubled how to dispose of his wife, and apparently it is out of fear of her and his honour, and I believe he hath received some cause of this his jealousy and care, and I do pity him in it, and will endeavour to find out some way to do it for him. Having put him in a way of preparing himself for the voyage, I did go to the

Swan, and there sent for Jervas, my old periwig maker, and he did bring me a periwig, but it was full of nits, so as I was troubled to see it (it being his old fault), and did send him to make it clean, and in the mean time, having staid for him a good while, did go away by water to the Castle Taverne, by Exeter House, and there met Sir W. Batten, [Sir] W. Pen, and several others, among the rest Sir Ellis Layton, who do apply himself to discourse with me, and I think by his discourse, out of his opinion of my interest in Sir W. Coventry, the man I find a wonderful witty, ready man for sudden answers and little tales, and sayings very extraordinary witty, but in the bottom I doubt he is not so. Yet he pretends to have studied men, and the truth is in several that I do know he did give me a very inward account of them. But above all things he did give me a full account, upon my demand, of this Judge of the Admiralty, Judge Jenkins; who, he says, is a man never practised in this Court, but taken merely for his merit and ability's sake from Trinity Hall, where he had always lived; only by accident the business of the want of a Judge being proposed to the present Archbishop of Canterbury that now is, he did think of this man and sent for him up: and here he is, against the *gré* and content of the old Doctors, made Judge, but is a very excellent man both for judgment and temper, yet majesty enough, and by all men's report, not to be corrupted. After dinner to the Court, where Sir Ellis Layton did make a very silly motion in our behalf, but did neither hurt nor good. After him Walker and Wiseman; and then the Judge did pronounce his sentence; for some —a part of the goods and ship, and the freight of the whole, to be free, and returned and paid by us; and the remaining, which was the greater part, to be ours. The loss of so much troubles us, but we have got a pretty good part, thanks be to God! So we are not displeased nor yet have cause to triumph, as we did once expect. Having seen the end of this, I being desirous to be at home to see the issue of my country letters about my mother, which I expect shall give me tidings of her death, I directly home and there to the office, where I find no letter from my father or brother, but by and by the boy tells me that his mistress sends me word that she hath opened my letter, and that she is loth to send me any more news. So I home, and there up to my wife in our chamber, and there received from my brother the newes of my mother's dying on Monday, about five or six o'clock in the afternoon, and that the last time she spoke of her children was on Friday last, and her last words were, "God bless my poor Sam!" The reading hereof did set me a-weeping heartily, and so weeping to myself awhile, and my wife also to herself, I then spoke to my wife respecting myself, and indeed, having some thoughts how much better both for her and us it is than it might have been had she outlived my father and me or my happy present condition in the world, she being helpless, I was the sooner at ease in my mind, and then found it necessary to go abroad with my wife to look after the providing mourning to send into the country, — some to-morrow, and more against Sunday, for my family, being resolved to put myself and wife, and Barker and Jane, W. Hewer and Tom, in mourning, and my two under-mayds, to give them hoods and scarfs and gloves. So to my tailor's, and up and down, and then home and to my office a little, and then to supper and to bed, my heart sad and afflicted, though my judgment at ease.

28th. My tailor come to me betimes this morning, and having given him directions, I to the office and there all the morning. At noon dined well. Balty, who is mighty thoughtful how to dispose of his wife, and would fain have me provide a place for her, which the thoughts of what I should do with her if he should miscarry at sea makes me avoid the offering him that she should be at my house. I find he is plainly jealous of her being in any place where she may have ill company, and I do pity him for it, and would be glad to help him, and will if I can. Having dined, I down by water with Sir W. Batten, [Sir] W. Pen, and [Sir] R. Ford to our prize, part of whose goods were condemned yesterday—"The Lindeboome"—and there we did drink some of her wine, very good. But it did grate my heart to see the poor master come on board, and look about into every corner, and find fault that she was not so clean as she used to be, though methought she was very clean; and to see his new masters come in, that had nothing to do with her, did trouble me to see him. Thence to

Blackwall and there to Mr. Johnson's, to see how some works upon some of our repaired ships go on, and at his house eat and drank and mighty extraordinary merry (too merry for me whose mother died so lately, but they know it not, so cannot reproach me therein, though I reproach myself), and in going home had many good stories of Sir W. Batten and one of Sir W. Pen, the most tedious and silly and troublesome (he forcing us to hear him) that ever I heard in my life. So to the office awhile, troubled with Sir W. Pen's impertinences, he being half foxed at Johnson's, and so to bed.

29th. Lay long talking with my wife about Balty, whom I do wish very well to, and would be glad to advise him, for he is very sober and willing to take all pains. Up and to Sir W. Batten, who I find has had some words with Sir W. Pen about the employing of a cooper about our prize wines, [Sir] W. Batten standing and indeed imposing upon us Mr. Morrice, which I like not, nor do [Sir] W. Pen, and I confess the very thoughts of what our goods will come to when we have them do discourage me in going any further in the adventure. Then to the office till noon, doing business, and then to the Exchange, and thence to the Sun Taverne and dined with [Sir] W. Batten, [Sir] R. Ford, and the Swede's Agent to discourse of a composition about our prizes that are condemned, but did do little, he standing upon high terms and we doing the like. I home, and there find Balty and his wife got thither both by my wife for me to give them good advice, for her to be with his father and mother all this time of absence, for saving of money, and did plainly and like a friend tell them my mind of the necessity of saving money, and that if I did not find they did endeavour it, I should not think fit to trouble myself for them, but I see she is utterly against being with his father and mother, and he is fond of her, and I perceive the differences between the old people and them are too great to be presently forgot, and so he do propose that it will be cheaper for him to put her to board at a place he is offered at Lee, and I, seeing that I am not like to be troubled with the finding a place, and having given him so much good advice, do leave them to stand and fall as they please, having discharged myself as a friend, and not likely to be accountable for her nor be troubled with her, if he should miscarry I mean, as to her lodging, and so broke up. Then he and I to make a visit to [Sir] W. Pen, who hath thought fit to show kindness to Balty in this business, indeed though he be a false rogue, but it was he knew a thing easy to do. Thence together to my shoemaker's, cutler's, tailor's, and up and down about my mourning, and in my way do observe the great streets in the city are marked out with piles drove into the ground; and if ever it be built in that form with so fair streets, it will be a noble sight. So to the Council chamber, but staid not there, but to a periwigg-maker's of his acquaintance, and there bought two periwiggs, mighty fine; indeed, too fine, I thought, for me; but he persuaded me, and I did buy them for £4 10*s.* the two. Then to the Exchange and bought gloves, and so to the Bull-Head Taverne, whither he brought my French gun; and one Truelocke, the famous gunsmith, that is a mighty ingenious man, and he did take my gun in pieces, and made me understand the secrets thereof: and upon the whole I did find it a very good piece of work, and truly wrought; but for certain not a thing to be used much with safety: and he do find that this very gun was never yet shot off. I was mighty satisfied with it and him, and the sight of so much curiosity of this kind. Here he brought also a haberdasher at my desire, and I bought a hat of him, and so away and called away my wife from his house, and so home and to read, and then to supper and to bed, my head full in behalf of Balty, who tells me strange stories of his mother. Among others, how she, in his absence in Ireland, did pawne all the things that he had got in his service under Oliver, and run ot her own accord, without her husband's leave, into Flanders, and that his purse, and 4*s.* a week which his father receives of the French church, is all the subsistence his father and mother have, and that about £20 a year maintains them; which, if it please God, I will find one way or other to provide for them, to remove that scandal away.

30th. Up, and the French periwigg maker of whom I bought two yesterday comes with them, and I am very well pleased with them. So to the office, where all the morning. At noon home to dinner, and thence with my wife's knowledge and leave did by coach go see the silly play of my Lady Newcastle's,[1] called "The Humourous Lovers;" the most silly thing that ever come upon a stage. I was sick to see it, but yet would not but have seen it, that I might the better understand her. Here I spied Knipp and Betty,[2] of the King's house, and sent Knipp oranges, but, having little money about me, did not offer to carry them abroad, which otherwise I had, I fear, been tempted to. So with [Sir] W. Pen home (he being at the play also), a most summer evening, and to my office, where, among other things, a most extraordinary letter to the Duke of York touching the want of money and the sad state of the King's service thereby, and so to supper and to bed.

31st (Lord's day). Up, and my tailor's boy brings my mourning clothes home, and my wife hers and Barker's, but they go not to church this morning. I to church, and with my mourning, very handsome, and new periwigg, make a great shew. After church home to dinner, and there come Betty Michell and her husband. I do and shall love her, but, poor wretch, she is now almost ready to lie down. After dinner Balty (who dined also with us) and I with Sir J. Minnes in his coach to White Hall, but did nothing, but by water to Strand Bridge and thence walked to my Lord Treasurer's, where the King, Duke of York, and the Caball, and much company without; and a fine day. Anon come out from the Caball my Lord Hollis and Mr. H. Coventry,[3] who, it is conceived, have received their instructions from the King this day; they being to begin their journey towards their treaty at Bredagh speedily, their passes being come. Here I saw the Lady Northumberland[4] and her daughter-in-law, my Lord Treasurer's daughter, my Lady Piercy,[5] a beautiful lady indeed. So

1 Margaret, daughter of Sir Thomas Lucas, of Colchester, and sister to John, Lord Lucas, married William Cavendish, Marquis of Newcastle, created Duke of Newcastle, 1665. The play was written by the husband, and not by the wife.

2 Betty Hall. See January 23rd, 1666-67.

3 See February 14th, 1666-67.

4 Lady Elizabeth Howard, daughter of Theophilus Howard, second Earl of Suffolk, wife of Algernon, tenth Earl of Northumberland. — B.

5 Lady Elizabeth Wriothesley, third and youngest daughter to the last Earl of Southampton, half sister to Rachel, Lady Russell, married

away back by water, and left Balty at White Hall and I to Mrs. Martin . . . and so by coach home, and there to my chamber, and then to supper and bed, having not had time to make up my accounts of this month at this very day, but will in a day or two, and pay my forfeit for not doing it, though business hath most hindered me. The month shuts up only with great desires of peace in all of us, and a belief that we shall have a peace, in most people, if a peace can be had on any terms, for there is a necessity of it; for we cannot go on with the war, and our masters are afraid to come to depend upon the good will of the Parliament any more, as I do hear.

April 1st. Up, and with Sir J. Minnes in his coach, set him down at the Treasurer's Office in Broad-streete, and I in his coach to White Hall, and there had the good fortune to walk with Sir W. Coventry into the garden, and there read our melancholy letter to the Duke of York, which he likes. And so to talk: and he flatly owns that we must have a peace, for we cannot set out a fleete;[1] and, to use his own words, he fears that we shall soon have enough of fighting in this new way, which we have thought on for this year. He bemoans the want of money, and discovers himself jealous that Sir G. Carteret do not look after, or concern himself for getting, money as he used to do, and did say it is true if Sir G. Carteret would only do his work, and my Lord Treasurer would do his own, Sir G. Carteret hath nothing to do to look after money, but if he will undertake my Lord Treasurer's work to raise money of the Bankers, then people must expect that he will do it, and did further say, that he [Carteret] and my Lord Chancellor do at this very day labour all they can to villify this new way of raising money, and making it payable, as it now is, into the Exchequer; and expressly said that in pursuance hereof,

to Josceline, Lord Percy, who succeeded as eleventh Earl of Northumberland in 1668. She was mother of Lady Elizabeth Percy, afterwards Duchess of Somerset.

[1] Evelyn ("Diary," July 29th, 1667) says that it was owing to Sir William Coventry that no fleet was fitted out in 1667. His unpopularity after the burning of the fleet at Chatham by the Dutch was great. "Those who advised His Majesty to prepare no fleet this spring, deserved — I know what — but!" (Evelyn's "Diary," June 28th, 1667). — B.

my Lord Chancellor hath prevailed with the King, in the close of his last speech to the House, to say, that he did hope to see them come to give money as it used to be given, without so many provisos, meaning, as Sir W. Coventry says, this new method of the Act. While we were talking, there come Sir Thomas Allen[1] with two ladies, one of which was Mrs. Rebecca Allen, that I knew heretofore, the clerk of the rope-yard's daughter at Chatham, who, poor heart! come to desire favour for her husband, who is clapt up, being a Lieutenant [Jowles[2]], for sending a challenge to his Captain, in the most saucy, base language that could be writ. I perceive [Sir] W. Coventry is wholly resolved to bring him to punishment; for, "bear with this," says he, "and no discipline shall ever be expected." She in this sad condition took no notice of me, nor I of her. So away we to the Duke of York, and there in his closett [Sir] W. Coventry and I delivered the letter, which the Duke of York made not much of, I thought, as to laying it to heart, as the matter deserved, but did promise to look after the getting of money for us, and I believe Sir W. Coventry will add what force he can to it. I did speak to [Sir] W. Coventry about Balty's warrant, which is ready, and about being Deputy Treasurer, which he very readily and friendlily agreed to, at which I was glad, and so away and by coach back to Broad-streete to Sir G. Carteret's, and there found my brother passing his accounts, which I helped till dinner, and dined there, and many good stories at dinner, among others about discoveries of murder, and Sir J. Minnes did tell of the discovery of his own great-grandfather's murder, fifteen years after he was murdered. Thence, after dinner, home and by water to Redriffe, and walked (fine weather) to Deptford, and there did business and so back again, walked, and pleased with a jolly femme that I saw going and coming in the way, which je could

[1] If this is not a mistake it implies that there was some relationship between Sir Thomas Allen and Captain John Allen, the father of Rebecca.

[2] Henry Jowles, of Chatham, was married to Rebecca, daughter of John Alleyn of the same place, in 1662 (see Chester's "London Marriage Licences," ed. Foster, col. 779).

avoir been contented pour avoir staid with if I could have gained acquaintance con elle, but at such times as these I am at a great loss, having not confidence, no alcune ready wit. So home and to the office, where late, and then home to supper and bed. This evening Mrs. Turner come to my office, and did walk an hour with me in the garden, telling me stories how Sir Edward Spragge hath lately made love to our neighbour, a widow, Mrs. Hollworthy, who is a woman of estate, and wit and spirit, and do contemn him the most, and sent him away with the greatest scorn in the world; she tells me also odd stories how the parish talks of Sir W. Pen's family, how poorly they clothe their daughter so soon after marriage, and do say that Mr. Lowther was married once before, and some such thing there hath been, whatever the bottom of it is. But to think of the clatter they make with his coach, and his owne fine cloathes, and yet how meanly they live within doors, and nastily, and borrowing everything of neighbours is a most shitten thing.

2nd. Up, and to the office, where all the morning sitting, and much troubled, but little business done for want of money, which makes me mighty melancholy. At noon home to dinner, and Mr. Deane with me, who hath promised me a very fine draught of the Rupert, which he will make purposely for me with great perfection, which I will make one of the beautifullest things that ever was seen of the kind in the world, she being a ship that will deserve it. Then to the office, where all the afternoon very busy, and in the evening weary home and there to sing, but vexed with the unreadiness of the girle's voice to learn the latter part of my song, though I confess it is very hard, half notes. So to supper and to bed.

3rd. Up, and with Sir W. Batten to White Hall to Sir W. Coventry's chamber, and there did receive the Duke's order for Balty's receiving of the contingent money to be paymaster of it, and it pleases me the more for that it is but £1,500, which will be but a little sum for to try his ability and honesty in the disposing of, and so I am the willinger to trust and pass my word for him therein. By and by up to the Duke of York, where our usual business, and among other things I read two most dismal letters of the straits we are in (from Collonell Middleton and Commissioner Taylor) that ever were writ in the world, so as the Duke of York would have them to shew the King, and to every demand of money, whereof we proposed many and very pressing ones, Sir G. Carteret could make no answer but no money, which I confess made me almost ready to cry for sorrow and vexation, but that which was the most considerable was when Sir G. Carteret did say that he had no funds to raise money on; and being asked by Sir W. Coventry whether the eleven months' tax was not a fund, and he answered, "No, that the bankers would not lend money upon it." Then Sir W. Coventry burst out and said he did supplicate his Royal Highness, and would do the same to the King, that he would remember who they were that did persuade the King from parting with the Chimney-money to the Parliament, and taking that in lieu which they would certainly have given, and which would have raised infallibly ready money; meaning the bankers and the farmers of the Chimney-money, whereof Sir G. Carteret, I think, is one; saying plainly, that whoever did advise the King to that, did, as much as in them lay, cut the King's throat, and did wholly betray him; to which the Duke of York did assent; and remembered that the King did say again and again at the time, that he was assured, and did fully believe, the money would be raised presently upon a land-tax. This put as all into a stound; and Sir W. Coventry went on to declare, that he was glad he was come to have so lately[1] concern in the Navy as he hath, for he cannot now give any good account of the Navy business; and that all his work now was to be able to provide such orders as would justify his Royal Highness in the business, when it shall be called to account; and that he do do, not concerning himself whether they are or can be performed, or no; and that when it comes to be examined, and falls on my Lord Treasurer, he cannot help it, whatever the issue of it shall be. Hereupon Sir W. Batten did pray him to keep also by him all our letters that come from the office that may justify us, which he says he do do, and, God knows, it is an ill sign when we are once to come to

[1] Little?

study how to excuse ourselves. It is a sad consideration, and therewith we broke up, all in a sad posture, the most that ever I saw in my life. One thing more Sir W. Coventry did say to the Duke of York, when I moved again, that of about £9,000 debt to Lanyon,[1] at Plymouth, he might pay £3,700 worth of prize-goods, that he bought lately at the candle, out of this debt due to him from the King; and the Duke of York, and Sir G. Carteret, and Lord Barkeley, saying, all of them, that my Lord Ashly would not be got to yield to it, who is Treasurer of the Prizes, Sir W. Coventry did plainly desire that it might be declared whether the proceeds of the prizes were to go to the helping on of the war, or no; and, if it were, how then could this be denied? which put them all into another stound; and it is true, God forgive us! Thence to the chappell, and there, by chance, hear that Dr. Crew[2] is to preach; and so into the organ-loft, where I met Mr. Carteret, and my Lady Jemimah, and Sir Thomas Crew's two daughters, and Dr. Childe played; and Dr. Crew did make a very pretty, neat, sober, honest sermon; and delivered it very readily, decently, and gravely, beyond his years: so as I was exceedingly taken with it, and I believe the whole chappell, he being but young; but his manner of his delivery I do like exceedingly. His text was, "But seeke ye first the kingdom of God, and his righteousness, and all these things shall be added unto you." Thence with my Lady to Sir G. Carteret's lodgings, and so up into the house, and there do hear that the Dutch letters are come, and say that the Dutch have ordered a passe to be sent for our Commissioners, and that it is now upon the way, coming with a trumpeter blinded, as is usual. But I perceive every body begins to doubt the success of the treaty, all their hopes being only that if it can be had on any terms, the Chancellor will have it; for he dare not come before a Parliament, nor a great many more of the courtiers, and the King himself do declare he do not desire it, nor intend it but on a strait; which God defend him from! Here I

[1] John Lanyon, one of the contractors for victualling Tangier.

[2] Nathanael Crewe, afterwards Bishop of Durham, and last Lord Crewe (1633–1722). He was the founder of the noble Bamborough charities. At this time he was thirty-four years of age.

hear how the King is not so well pleased of this marriage between the Duke of Richmond and Mrs. Stewart, as is talked; and that he [the Duke] by a wile did fetch her to the Beare, at the Bridge-foot,[1] where a coach was ready, and they are stole away into Kent,[2] without the King's leave; and that the King hath said he will never see her more; but people do think that it is only a trick. This day I saw Prince Rupert abroad in the Vane-room, pretty well as he used to be, and looks as well, only something appears to be under his periwigg on the crown of his head. So home by water, and there find my wife gone abroad to her tailor's, and I dined alone with W. Hewer, and then to the office to draw up a memorial for the Duke of York this afternoon at the Council about Lanyon's business. By and by we met by appointment at the office upon a reference to Carcasse's business to us again from the Duke of York, but a very confident cunning rogue we have found him at length. He carried himself very uncivilly to Sir W. Batten this afternoon, as heretofore, and his silly Lord [Bruncker] pleaded for him, but all will not nor shall not do for ought he shall give, though I love the man as a man of great parts and ability. Thence to White Hall by water (only asking Betty Michell by the way how she did), and there come too late to do any thing at the Council. So by coach to my periwigg maker's and tailor's, and so home, where I find my wife with her flageolet master, which I wish she would practise, and so to the office, and then to Sir W. Batten's, and then to Sir W. Pen's, talking and spending time in vain a little while, and then home up to my chamber, and so to supper and to bed, vexed at two or three things, viz.: that my wife's watch proves so bad as it do; the ill state of the office; and Kingdom's business; at the charge which my mother's death for mourning will bring me when all paid.

4th. Up, and going down found Jervas the barber with a periwigg which I had the other day cheapened at Westminster, but it being full of nits, as heretofore his work used to be, I did now refuse it, having bought elsewhere.

[1] The Bear at the Bridge Foot was a famous tavern in Southwark (see note, September 10th, 1660).

[2] To Cobham Hall, near Gravesend. See April 26th, *post*. — B.

So to the office till noon, busy, and then (which I think I have not done three times in my life) left the board upon occasion of a letter of Sir W. Coventry, and meeting Balty at my house I took him with me by water, and to the Duke of Albemarle to give him an account of the business, which was the escaping of some soldiers for the manning of a few ships now going out with Harman to the West Indies, which is a sad consideration that at the very beginning of the year and few ships abroad we should be in such want of men that they do hide themselves, and swear they will not go to be killed and have no pay. I find the Duke of Albemarle at dinner with sorry company, some of his officers of the Army; dirty dishes, and a nasty wife at table, and bad meat, of which I made but an ill dinner. Pretty to hear how she talked against Captain Du Tell,[1] the Frenchman, that the Prince and her husband put out the last year; and how, says she, the Duke of York hath made him, for his good services, his Cupbearer; yet he fired more shot into the Prince's ship, and others of the King's ships, than of the enemy. And the Duke of Albemarle did confirm it, and that somebody in the fight did cry out that a little Dutchman, by his ship, did plague him more than any other; upon which they were going to order him to be sunk, when they looked and found it was Du Tell, who, as the Duke of Albemarle says, had killed several men in several of our ships. He said, but for his interest, which he knew he had at Court, he had hanged him at the yard's-arm, without staying for a Court-martiall. One Colonel Howard,[2] at the table, magnified the Duke of Albemarle's fight in June last, as being a greater action than ever was done by Cæsar. The Duke of Albemarle did say it had been no great action, had all his number fought, as they should have done, to have beat the Dutch; but of his 55 ships, not above 25 fought. He did give an account that it was a fight he was forced to: the Dutch being come in his way, and he being ordered to the buoy of the Nore, he could not pass by them without fighting, nor avoid them without great disadvantage and dishonour; and this Sir G.

[1] See note, June 13th, 1666.

[2] Son of the Earl of Berkshire.

Carteret, I afterwards giving him an account of what he said, says that it is true, that he was ordered up to the Nore. But I remember he said, had all his captains fought, he would no more have doubted to have beat the Dutch, with all their number, than to eat the apple that lay on his trencher. My Lady Duchesse, among other things, discoursed of the wisdom of dividing the fleete;[1] which the General said nothing to, though he knows well that it come from themselves in the fleete, and was brought up hither by Sir Edward Spragge. Colonel Howard, asking how the Prince did, the Duke of Albemarle answering, "Pretty well;" the other replied, "But not so well as to go to sea again." — "How!" says the Duchess, "what should he go for, if he were well, for there are no ships for him to command? And so you have brought your hogs to a fair market," said she. [It was pretty to hear the Duke of Albemarle himself to wish that they would come on our ground, meaning the French, for that he would pay them, so as to make them glad to go back to France again; which was like a general, but not like an admiral.][2] One at the table told an odd passage in this late plague: that at Petersfield, I think, he said, one side of the street had every house almost infected through the town, and the other, not one shut up. Dinner being done, I brought Balty to the Duke of Albemarle to kiss his hand and thank him for his kindness the last year to him, and take leave of him, and then Balty and I to walk in the Park, and, out of pity to his father, told him what I had in my thoughts to do for him about the money — that is, to make him Deputy Treasurer of the fleete, which I have done by getting Sir G. Carteret's consent, and an order from the Duke of York for £1,500 to be paid to him. He promises the whole profit to be paid to my wife, for to be disposed of as she sees fit, for her father and mother's relief. So mightily pleased with our walk, it being mighty pleasant weather, I back to Sir G. Carteret's, and there he had newly dined, and talked, and find that he do give every thing over for lost, declaring no money to be raised, and let Sir W. Coventry name

[1] See November 1st, 1667, *post*.

[2] The passage between brackets is written in the margin of the MS.

the man that persuaded the King to take the Land Tax on promise of raising present money upon it. He will, he says, be able to clear himself enough of it. I made him merry, with telling him how many land-admirals we are to have this year: Allen at Plymouth, Holmes at Portsmouth, Spragge for Medway, Teddiman at Dover, Smith to the Northward, and Harman to the Southward. He did defend to me Sir W. Coventry as not guilty of the dividing of the fleete the last year, and blesses God, as I do, for my Lord Sandwich's absence, and tells me how the King did lately observe to him how they have been particularly punished that were enemies to my Lord Sandwich. Mightily pleased I am with his family, and my Lady Carteret was on the bed to-day, having been let blood, and tells me of my Lady Jemimah's being big-bellied. Thence with him to my Lord Treasurer's, and there walked during Council sitting with Sir Stephen Fox, talking of the sad condition of the King's purse, and affairs thereby; and how sad the King's life must be, to pass by his officers every hour, that are four years behindhand unpaid. My Lord Barkeley [of Stratton], I met with there, and fell into talk with him on the same thing, wishing to God that it might be remedied, to which he answered, with an oath, that it was as easy to remedy it as anything in the world; saying, that there is himself and three more would venture their carcasses upon it to pay all the King's debts in three years, had they the managing his revenue, and putting £300,000 in his purse, as a stock. But, Lord! what a thing is this to me, that do know how likely a man my Lord Barkeley of all the world is, to do such a thing as this. Here I spoke with Sir W. Coventry, who tells me plainly that to all future complaints of lack of money he will answer but with the shrug of his shoulder; which methought did come to my heart, to see him to begin to abandon the King's affairs, and let them sink or swim, so he do his owne part, which I confess I believe he do beyond any officer the King hath, but unless he do endeavour to make others do theirs, nothing will be done. The consideration here do make me go away very sad, and so home by coach, and there took up my wife and Mercer, who had been to-day at White Hall to the Maundy,[1]

[1] The practice of giving alms on Maundy Thursday to poor men and

it being Maundy Thursday; but the King did not wash the poor people's feet himself, but the Bishop of London did it for him, but I did not see it, and with them took up Mrs. Anne Jones at her mother's door, and so to take the ayre to Hackney, where good neat's tongue, and things to eat and drink, and very merry, the weather being mighty pleasant; and here I was told that at their church they have a fair pair of organs, which play while the people sing, which I am mighty glad of, wishing the like at our church at London, and would give £50 towards it. So very pleasant, and hugging of Mercer in our going home, we home, and then to the office to do a little business, and so to supper at home and to bed.

5th. Up, and troubled with Mr. Carcasse's coming to speak with me, which made me give him occasion to fall into a heat, and he began to be ill-mannered to me, which made me angry. He gone, I to Sir W. Pen about the business of Mrs. Turner's son to keep his ship in employment, but so false a fellow as Sir W. Pen is I never did nor hope shall ever know again. So to the office, and there did business till dinner-time, and then home to dinner, wife and I alone, and then down to the Old Swan, and drank

women equal in number to the years of the sovereign's age is a curious survival in an altered form of an old custom. The original custom was for the king to wash the feet of twelve poor persons, and to give them a supper in imitation of Christ's last supper and his washing of the Apostle's feet. James II. was the last sovereign to perform the ceremony in person, but it was performed by deputy so late as 1731. The Archbishop of York was the king's deputy on that occasion. The institution has passed through the various stages of feet washing with a supper, the discontinuance of the feet washing, the substitution of a gift of provisions for the supper, and finally the substitution of a gift of money for the provisions. The ceremony took place at the Chapel Royal, Whitehall; but it is now held at Westminster Abbey. Maundy is derived from the Latin word *mandatum*, which commences the original anthem sung during the ceremony, in reference to Christ's command; but Spelman supposed it to be connected with the maunds or baskets to contain the gifts — as will be seen from what has been said of the original institution, this is an impossible explanation. Professor Skeat has settled the question conclusively by proving beyond doubt that Maundy is really the French *mandé*, which is the regular phonetic form of Latin *mandatum*, a command (see his "Etymological Dictionary" and note to "Piers Plowman," E. E. Text Soc. edition, part. iv., p. 379). He points out that Spelman's guess about *maund*, a basket, "is as false as it is readily believed."

with Betty and her husband, but no opportunity para baiser la. So to White Hall to the Council chamber, where I find no Council held till after the holidays. So to Westminster Hall, and there bought a pair of snuffers, and saw Mrs. Howlett after her sickness come to the Hall again. So by coach to the New Exchange and Mercer's and other places to take up bills for what I owe them, and to Mrs. Pierce, to invite her to dinner with us on Monday, but staid not with her. In the street met with Mr. Sanchy, my old acquaintance at Cambridge, reckoned a great minister here in the City, and by Sir Richard Ford particularly, which I wonder at; for methinks, in his talk, he is but a mean man. I set him down in Holborne, and I to the Old Exchange, and there to Sir Robert Viner's, and made up my accounts there, to my great content; but I find they do not keep them so regularly as to be able to do it easily, and truly, and readily, nor would it have been easily stated by any body on my behalf but myself, several things being to be recalled to memory, which nobody else could have done, and therefore it is fully necessary for me to even accounts with these people as often as I can. So to the 'Change, and there met with Mr. James Houblon, but no hopes, as he sees, of peace whatever we pretend, but we shall be abused by the King of France. Then home to the office, and busy late, and then to Sir W. Batten's, where Mr. Young was talking about the building of the City again; and he told me that those few churches that are to be new built are plainly not chosen with regard to the convenience of the City; they stand a great many in a cluster about Cornhill; but that all of them are either in the gift of the Lord Archbishop, or Bishop of London, or Lord Chancellor, or gift of the City. Thus all things, even to the building of churches, are done in this world! And then he says, which I wonder at, that I should not in all this time see, that Moorefields have houses two stories high in them, and paved streets, the City having let leases for seven years, which he do conclude will be very much to the hindering the building of the City; but it was considered that the streets cannot be passable in London till a whole street be built; and several that had got ground of the City for charity, to build sheds on, had got the trick presently to sell that for £60, which did not cost them £20 to put up; and so the City, being very poor in stock, thought it as good to do it themselves, and therefore let leases for seven years of the ground in Moorefields; and a good deal of this money, thus advanced, hath been employed for the enabling them to find some money for Commissioner Taylor, and Sir W. Batten, towards the charge of "The Loyall London," or else, it is feared, it had never been paid. And Taylor having a bill to pay wherein Alderman Hooker was concerned it was his invention to find out this way of raising money, or else this had not been thought on. So home to supper and to bed. This morning come to me the Collectors for my Poll-money; for which I paid for my title as Esquire and place of Clerk of Acts, and my head and wife's, and servants' and their wages, £40 17*s.*; and though this be a great deal, yet it is a shame I should pay no more; that is, that I should not be assessed for my pay, as in the Victualling business and Tangier; and for my money, which, of my own accord, I had determined to charge myself with £1,000 money, till coming to the Vestry, and seeing nobody of our ablest merchants, as Sir Andrew Rickard, to do it, I thought it not decent for me to do it, nor would it be thought widsom to do it unnecessarily, but vain glory.

6th. Up, and betimes in the morning down to the Tower wharfe, there to attend the shipping of soldiers, to go down to man some ships going out, and pretty to see how merrily some, and most go, and how sad others — the leave they take of their friends, and the terms that some wives, and other wenches asked to part with them: a pretty mixture. So to the office, having staid as long as I could, and there sat all the morning, and then home at noon to dinner, and then abroad, Balty with me, and to White Hall, by water, to Sir G. Carteret, about Balty's £1,500 contingent money for the fleete to the West Indys, and so away with him to the Exchange, and mercers and drapers, up and down, to pay all my scores occasioned by this mourning for my mother; and emptied a £50 bag, and it was a joy to me to see that I am able to part with such a sum, without much inconvenience; at least, without any trouble of mind So to Captain Cocke's to meet Fenn, to talk about this money for Balty, and there Cocke tells me that he is confident there will be a peace, whatever terms be asked us, and he confides that it will take because the French and Dutch will be jealous one of another which shall give the best terms, lest the other should make the peace with us alone, to the ruin of the third, which is our best defence, this jealousy, for ought I at present see. So home and there very late, very busy, and then home to supper and to bed, the people having got their house very clean against Monday's dinner.

7th (Easter day). Up, and when dressed with my wife (in mourning for my mother) to church both, where Mr. Mills, a lazy sermon. Home to dinner, wife and I and W. Hewer, and after dinner I by water to White Hall to Sir G. Carteret's, there to talk about Balty's money, and did present Balty to him to kiss his hand, and then to walk in the Parke, and heard the Italian musique at the Queen's chapel, whose composition is fine, but yet the voices of eunuchs I do not like like our women, nor am more pleased with it at all than with English voices, but that they do jump most excellently with themselves and their instrument, which is wonderful pleasant; but I am convinced more and more, that, as every nation has a particular accent and tone in discourse, so as the tone of one not to agree with or please the other, no more can the fashion of singing to words, for that the better the words are set, the more they take in of the ordinary tone of the country whose language the song speaks, so that a song well composed by an Englishman must be better to an Englishman than it can be to a stranger, or than if set by a stranger in foreign words. Thence back to White Hall, and there saw the King come out of chapel after prayers in the afternoon, which he is never at but after having received the Sacrament: and the Court, I perceive, is quite out of mourning; and some very fine; among others, my Lord Gerard, in a very rich vest and coat. Here I met with my Lord Bellasses: and it is pretty to see what a formal story he tells me of his leaving his place upon the death of my Lord Cleveland,[1] by which

[1] Thomas Wentworth, fourth Baron Wentworth of Nettlestead, advanced, February 7th, 1625–26, to the earldom of Cleveland. In 1660 he was again appointed Captain of the Band of Pensioners, an office he

he is become Captain of the Pensioners; and that the King did leave it to him to keep the other or take this; whereas, I know the contrary, that they had a mind to have him away from Tangier. He tells me he is commanded by the King to go down to the Northward to satisfy the Deputy Lieutenants of Yorkshire, who have desired to lay down their commissions upon pretence of having no profit by their places but charge, but indeed is upon the Duke of Buckingham's being under a cloud (of whom there is yet nothing heard), so that the King is apprehensive of their discontent, and sends him to pacify them, and I think he is as good a dissembler as any man else, and a fine person he is for person, and proper to lead the Pensioners, but a man of no honour nor faith I doubt. So to Sir G. Carteret's again to talk with him about Balty's money, and wrote a letter to Portsmouth about part of it, and then in his coach, with his little daughter Porpot (as he used to nickname her), and saw her at home, and her maid, and another little gentlewoman, and so I walked into Moore Fields, and, as is said, did find houses built two stories high, and like to stand; and it must become a place of great trade, till the City be built; and the street is already paved as London streets used to be, which is a strange, and to me an unpleasing sight. So home and to my chamber about sending an express to Portsmouth about Balty's money, and then comes Mrs. Turner to enquire after her son's business, which goes but bad, which led me to show her how false Sir W. Pen is to her, whereupon she told me his obligations to her, and promises to her, and how a while since he did show himself dissatisfied in her son's coming to the table and applying himself to me, which is a good nut, and a nut I will make use of. She gone I to other business in my chamber, and then to supper and to bed. The Swede's Embassadors and our Commissioners are making all the haste they can over to the treaty for peace, and I find at Court, and particularly Lord Bellasses, says there will be a peace, and it is worth remembering what Sir W. Coventry did tell me (as a secret though) that whereas we are afeard

had held before the Civil Wars. He died March 25th, 1667, s.p.m., when the barony devolved upon his daughter, Henrietta, Baroness Wentworth, afterwards mistress of the Duke of Monmouth.

Harman's fleete to the West Indys will not be got out before the Dutch come and block us up, we shall have a happy pretext to get out our ships under pretence of attending the Embassadors and Commissioners, which is a very good, but yet a poor shift.

8th. Up, and having dressed myself, to the office a little, and out, expecting to have seen the pretty daughter of the Ship taverne at the hither end of Billiter Lane (whom I never yet have opportunity to speak to). I in there to drink my morning draught of half a pint of Rhenish wine; but à ma doleur elle and their family are going away thence, and a new man come to the house. So I away to the Temple, to my new bookseller's; and there I did agree for Rycaut's late History of the Turkish Policy,[1] which costs me 55*s.*; whereas it was sold plain before the late fire for 8*s.*, and bound and coloured as this is for 20*s.*; for I have bought it finely bound and truly coloured, all the figures, of which there was but six books done so, whereof the King and Duke of York, and Duke of Monmouth, and Lord Arlington, had four. The fifth was sold, and I have bought the sixth. So to enquire out Mrs. Knipp's new lodging, but could not, but do hear of her at the Playhouse, where she was practising, and I sent for her out by a porter, and the jade come to me all undressed, so cannot go home to my house to dinner, as I had invited her, which I was not much troubled at, because I think there is a distance between her and Mrs. Pierce, and so our company would not be so pleasant. So home, and there find all things in good readiness for a good dinner, and here unexpectedly I find little Mis. Tooker, whom my wife loves not from the report of her being already naught; however, I do shew her countenance, and by and by come my guests, Dr. Clerke and his wife, and Mrs. Worshipp,[2] and her daughter; and then Mr. Pierce and his wife, and boy, and Betty; and then I sent for Mercer; so that we had, with my wife and I, twelve at table, and very good and pleasant company, and a most neat and excellent, but dear dinner; but, Lord! to see with what envy they looked upon all my fine plate was

[1] Sir Paul Rycaut's "Present State of the Ottoman Empire" is in the Pepysian Library. See note, October 15th, 1666.

[2] The sister of Mrs. Clerke.

pleasant; for I made the best shew I could, to let them understand me and my condition, to take down the pride of Mrs. Clerke, who thinks herself very great. We sat long, and very merry, and all things agreeable; and, after dinner, went out by coaches, thinking to have seen a play, but come too late to both houses, and then they had thoughts of going abroad somewhere; but I thought all the charge ought not to be mine, and therefore I endeavoured to part the company, and so ordered it to set them all down at Mrs. Pierce's; and there my wife and I and Mercer left them in good humour, and we three to the King's house, and saw the latter end of the "Surprisall,"[1] wherein was no great matter, I thought, by what I saw there. Thence away to Polichinello,[2] and there had three times more sport than at the play, and so home, and there the first night we have been this year in the garden late, we three and our Barker singing very well, and then home to supper, and so broke up, and to bed mightily pleased with this day's pleasure.

9th. Up, and to the office a while, none of my fellow officers coming to sit, it being holiday, and so towards noon I to the Exchange, and there do hear mighty cries for peace, and that otherwise we shall be undone; and yet I do suspect the badness of the peace we shall make. Several do complain of abundance of land flung up by tenants out of their hands for want of ability to pay their rents; and by name, that the Duke of Buckingham hath £6,000 so flung up. And my father writes, that Jasper Trice,[3] upon this pretence of his tenants' dealing with him, is broke up housekeeping, and gone to board with his brother, Naylor, at Offord; which is very sad. So home to dinner, and after dinner I took coach and to the King's house, and by and by comes after me my wife with W. Hewer and his mother and Barker, and there we saw "The Tameing of a Shrew," which hath some very good pieces in it, but generally is but a mean play; and the best part, "Sawny,"[4] done

[1] A comedy by Sir Robert Howard, published in 1665.

[2] Probably in Moorfields. See August 22nd, 1666. It was also exhibited at Bartholomew Fair and at Charing Cross.

[3] Jasper Trice, gent., died 27th October, 1675. — *Monumental Inscription in Brampton Church, Hunts.* — B.

[4] This play was entitled "Sawney the Scot, or the Taming of a Shrew,"

by Lacy, hath not half its life, by reason of the words, I suppose, not being understood, at least by me. After the play was done, as I come so I went away alone, and had a mind to have taken out Knipp to have taken the ayre with her, and to that end sent a porter in to her that she should take a coach and come to me to the Piatza in Covent Garden, where I waited for her, but was doubtful I might have done ill in doing it if we should be visit ensemble, sed elle was gone out, and so I was eased of my care, and therefore away to Westminster to the Swan, and there did baiser la little missa . . . . and drank, and then by water to the Old Swan, and there found Betty Michell sitting at the door, it being darkish. I staid and talked a little with her, but no once baiser la, though she was to my thinking at this time une de plus pretty mohers that ever I did voir in my vida, and God forgive me my mind did run sobre elle all the vespre and night and la day suivante. So home and to the office a little, and then to Sir W. Batten's, where he tells me how he hath found his lady's jewels again, which have been so long lost, and a servant imprisoned and arraigned, and they were in her closet under a china cup, where he hath servants will swear they did look in seaching the house; but Mrs. Turner and I, and others, do believe that they were only disposed of by my Lady, in case she had died, to some friends of hers, and now laid there again. So home to supper, and to read the book I bought yesterday

and consisted of an alteration of Shakespeare's play by John Lacy. Although it had long been popular it was not printed until 1698. In the old "Taming of *a* Shrew" (1594), reprinted by Thomas Amyot for the Shakespeare Society in 1844, the hero's servant is named Sander, and this seems to have given the hint to Lacy, when altering Shakespeare's "Taming of *the* Shrew," to foist a Scotsman into the action. Sawney was one of Lacy's favourite characters, and occupies a prominent position in Michael Wright's picture at Hampton Court. Evelyn, on October 3rd, 1662, "visited Mr. Wright, a Scotsman, who had liv'd long at Rome, and was esteem'd a good painter," and he singles out as his best picture, "Lacy, the famous Roscius, or comedian, whom he has painted in three dresses, as a gallant, a Presbyterian minister, and a Scotch Highlander in his plaid." Langbaine and Aubrey both make the mistake of ascribing the third figure to Teague in "The Committee;" and in spite of Evelyn's clear statement, his editor in a note follows them in their blunder. Planché has reproduced the picture in his "History of Costume" (vol. ii., p. 243).

of the Turkish policy,[1] which is a good book, well writ, and so owned by Dr. Clerke yesterday to me, commending it mightily to me for my reading as the only book of the subject that ever was writ, yet so designedly. So to bed.

10th. Up, and to my office a little, and then, in the garden, find Sir W. Pen; and he and I to Sir W. Batten, where he tells us news of the new disorders of Hogg and his men in taking out of 30 tons of wine out of a prize of ours, which makes us mad; and that, added to the unwillingness of the men to go longer abroad without money, do lead us to conclude not to keep her abroad any longer, of which I am very glad, for I do not like our doings with what we have already got, Sir. W. Batten ordering the disposal of our wines and goods, and he leaves it to Morrice the cooper, who I take to be a cunning proud knave, so that I am very desirous to adventure no further. So away by water from the Old Swan to White Hall, and there to Sir W. Coventry's, with whom I staid a great while longer than I have done these many months, and had opportunity of talking with him, and he do declare himself troubled that he hath any thing left him to do in the Navy, and would be glad to part with his whole profits and concernments in it, his pains and care being wholly ineffectual during this lack of money; the expense growing infinite, the service not to be done, and discipline and order not to be kept, only from want of money. I begun to discourse with him the business of Tangier, which by the removal of my Lord Bellasses, is now to have a new Governor; and did move him, that at this season all the business of reforming the garrison might be considered, while nobody was to be offended; and I told him it is plain that we do overspend our revenue: that the place is of no more profit to the King than it was the first day, nor in itself of better credit; no more people of condition willing to live there, nor any thing like a place likely to turn his Majesty to account: that it hath been hitherto, and, for aught I see, likely only to be used as a job to do a kindness to some Lord, or he that can get to be Governor. Sir W. Coventry agreed with me, so as to say, that unless the King hath the wealth of

[1] See *ante*, October 15th, 1666.

the Mogul, he would be a beggar to have his businesses ordered in the manner they now are: that his garrisons must be made places only of convenience to particular persons: that he hath moved the Duke of York in it; and that it was resolved to send no Governor thither till there had been Commissioners sent to put the garrison in order, so as that he that goes may go with limitations and rules to follow, and not to do as he please, as the rest have hitherto done. That he is not afeard to speak his mind, though to the displeasure of any man; and that I know well enough; but that, when it is come, as it is now, that to speak the truth in behalf of the King plainly do no good, but all things bore down by other measures than by what is best for the King, he hath no temptation to be perpetually fighting of battles, it being more easy to him on those terms to suffer things to go on without giving any man offence, than to have the same thing done, and he contract the displeasure of all the world, as he must do, that will be for the King. I did offer him to draw up my thoughts in this matter to present to the Duke of York, which he approved of, and I do think to do it. So away, and by coach going home saw Sir G. Carteret going towards White Hall. So 'light and by water met him, and with him to the King's little chapel; and afterwards to see the King heal the King's Evil, wherein no pleasure, I having seen it before;[1] and then to see him and the Queene and Duke of York and his wife, at dinner in the Queene's lodgings; and so with Sir G. Carteret to his lodgings to dinner; where very good company; and after dinner he and I to talk alone how things are managed, and to what ruin we must come if we have not a peace. He did tell me one occasion, how Sir Thomas Allen, which I took for a man of known courage and service on the King's side, was tried for his life in Prince Rupert's fleete, in the late times, for cowardice, and condemned to be hanged, and fled to Jersey; where Sir G. Carteret received him, not knowing the reason of his coming thither: and that thereupon Prince Rupert wrote to the Queen-Mother his dislike of Sir G. Carteret's receiving a person that stood condemned; and so Sir G.

[1] See June 23rd, 1660.

Carteret was forced to bid him betake himself to some other place. This was strange to me. Our commissioners are preparing to go to Bredah to the treaty, and do design to be going the next week.[1] So away by coach home, where there should have been a meeting about Carcasse's business, but only my Lord and I met, and so broke up, Carcasse having only read his answer to his charge, which is well writ, but I think will not prove to his advantage, for I believe him to be a very rogue. So home, and Balty and I to look Mr. Fenn at Sir G. Carteret's office in Broad Streete, and there missing him and at the banker's hard by, we home, and I down by water to Deptford Dockyard, and there did a little business, and so home back again all the way reading a little piece I lately bought, called "The Virtuoso, or the Stoicke,"[2] proposing many things paradoxical to our common opinions, wherein in some places he speaks well, but generally is but a sorry man. So home and to my chamber to enter my two last days' journall, and this, and then to supper and to bed. Blessed be God! I hear that my father is better and better, and will, I hope, live to enjoy some cheerful days more; but it is strange what he writes me, that Mr. Weaver, of Huntingdon, who was a lusty, likely, and but a youngish man, should be dead.

11th. Up, and to the office, where we sat all the morning, and (which is now rare, he having not been with us twice I think these six months) Sir G. Carteret come to us upon some particular business of his office, and went away again. At noon I to the 'Change, and there hear by Mr. Hublon of the loss of a little East Indiaman, valued at about £20,000, coming home alone, and safe to within ten leagues of Scilly, and there snapt by a French Caper.[3] Our merchants do much pray for peace; and he tells me that

[1] Secretary Morice writes, "Whitehall, April 16"—"The King wishes the £200 a week allowed to the Ambassadors extraordinary appointed to treat at Breda to begin from April 16" ("Calendar of State Papers," 1667, p. 37).

[2] Sir George Mackenzie (1636–91), King's Advocate for Scotland, published at Edinburgh, anonymously, in 1663, "Religio Stoici; the Virtuoso or Stoick, with a friendly Address to the Fanatics of all Sects and Sorts."

[3] A light-armed vessel of the seventeenth century, used by the Dutch for privateering.—Smith's *Sailor's Word Book.*

letters are come that the Dutch have stopped the fitting of their great ships, and the coming out of a fleete of theirs of 50 sayle, that was ready to come out; but I doubt the truth of it yet. Thence to Sir G. Carteret, by his invitation to his office, where my Lady was, and dined with him, and very merry and good people they are, when pleased, as any I know. After dinner I to the office, where busy till evening, and then with Balty to Sir G. Carteret's office, and there with Mr. Fenn despatched the business of Balty's £1,500 he received for the contingencies of the fleete, whereof he received about £253 in pieces of eight at a goldsmith's there hard by, which did puzzle me and him to tell; for I could not tell the difference by sight, only by bigness, and that is not always discernible, between a whole and half-piece and quarter-piece. Having received this money I home with Balty and it, and then abroad by coach with my wife and set her down at her father's, and I to White Hall, thinking there to have seen the Duchess of Newcastle's coming this night to Court, to make a visit to the Queene, the King having been with her yesterday, to make her a visit since her coming to town. The whole story of this lady is a romance, and all she do is romantick. Her footmen in velvet coats, and herself in an antique dress, as they say; and was the other day at her own play, "The Humourous Lovers;" the most ridiculous thing that ever was wrote, but yet she and her Lord mightily pleased with it; and she, at the end, made her respects to the players from her box, and did give them thanks. There is as much expectation of her coming to Court, that so people may come to see her, as if it were the Queen of Sweden;[1] but I lost my labour, for she did not come this night. So, meeting Mr. Brisband, he took me up to my Lady Jemimah's chamber, who is let blood to-day, and so there we sat and talked an hour, I think, very merry and one odd thing or other, and so away, and I took up my wife at her tailor's (whose wife is brought to bed, and my wife must be godmother), and so with much ado got a coach to carry us home, it being late, and so to my chamber, having little left to do at my office, my eyes being a little

[1] The celebrated ex-Queen Christina, whose extraordinary character and conduct were then attracting the attention of all Europe.

sore by reason of my reading a small printed book the other day after it was dark, and so to supper and to bed. It comes in my head to set down that there have been two fires in the City, as I am told for certain, and it is so, within this week.

12th. Up, and when ready, and to my office, to do a little business, and coming homeward again, saw my door and hatch open, left so by Luce, our cookmayde, which so vexed me, that I did give her a kick in our entry, and offered a blow at her, and was seen doing so by Sir W. Pen's footboy, which did vex me to the heart, because I know he will be telling their family of it; though I did put on presently a very pleasant face to the boy, and spoke kindly to him, as one without passion, so as it may be he might not think I was angry, but yet I was troubled at it. So away by water to White Hall, and there did our usual business before the Duke of York; but it fell out that, discoursing of matters of money, it rose to a mighty heat, very high words arising between Sir G. Carteret and [Sir] W. Coventry, the former in his passion saying that the other should have helped things if they were so bad; and the other answered, so he would, and things should have been better had he been Treasurer of the Navy. I was mightily troubled at this heat, and it will breed ill blood, I fear; but things are in that bad condition that I do daily expect when we shall all fly in one another's faces, when we shall be reduced, every one, to answer for himself. We broke up: and I soon after to Sir G. Carteret's chamber, where I find the poor man telling his lady privately, and she weeping. I went into them, and did seem, as indeed I was, troubled for this; and did give the best advice I could, which, I think, did please them: and they do apprehend me their friend, as indeed I am, for I do take the Vice-chamberlain for a most honest man. He did assure me that he was not, all expences and things paid, clear in estate £15,000 better than he was when the King come in; and that the King and Lord Chancellor did know that he was worth, with the debt the King owed him, £50,000, I think, he said, when the King come into England. I did pacify all I could, and then away by water home, there to write letters and things for the dispatch of Balty away this day to sea; and after dinner he did go, I having given him much good counsell; and I have great hopes that he will make good use of it, and be a good man, for I find him willing to take pains and very sober. He being gone, I close at my office all the afternoon getting off of hand my papers, which, by the late holidays and my laziness, were grown too many upon my hands, to my great trouble, and therefore at it as late as my eyes would give me leave, and then by water down to Redriffe, meaning to meet my wife, who is gone with Mercer, Barker, and the boy (it being most sweet weather) to walk, and I did meet with them, and walked back, and then by the time we got home it was dark, and we staid singing in the garden till supper was ready, and there with great pleasure. But I tried my girles Mercer and Barker singly one after another, a single song, "At dead low ebb," etc., and I do clearly find that as to manner of singing the latter do much the better, the other thinking herself as I do myself above taking pains for a manner of singing, contenting ourselves with the judgment and goodness of eare. So to supper, and then parted and to bed.

13th. Up, and to the office, where we sat all the morning, and strange how the false fellow Commissioner Pett was eager to have had Carcasse's business brought on to-day that he might give my Lord Bruncker (who hates him, I am sure, and hath spoke as much against him to the King in my hearing as any man) a cast of his office in pleading for his man Carcasse, but I did prevent its being brought on to-day, and so broke up, and I home to dinner, and after dinner with a little singing with some pleasure alone with my poor wife, and then to the office, where sat all the afternoon till late at night, and then home to supper and to bed, my eyes troubling me still after candle-light, which troubles me. Wrote to my father, who, I am glad to hear, is at some ease again, and I long to have him in town, that I may see what can be done for him here; for I would fain do all I can that I may have him live, and take pleasure in my doing well in the world. This afternoon come Mrs. Lowther to me to the office, and there je did toker ses mammailles and did baiser them and su bocca, which she took fort willingly. . . .

14th (Lord's day). Up, and to read a little in my new History of Turkey, and so with my wife to church, and then home, where is little Michell and my pretty Betty and also Mercer, and very merry. A good dinner of roast beef. After dinner I away to take water at the Tower, and thence to Westminster, where Mrs. Martin was not at home. So to White Hall, and there walked up and down, and among other things visited Sir G. Carteret, and much talk with him, who is discontented, as he hath reason, to see how things are like to come all to naught, and it is very much that this resolution of having of country Admirals should not come to his eares till I told him the other day, so that I doubt who manages things. From him to Margaret's Church, and there spied Martin, and home with her . . . . but fell out to see her expensefullness, having bought Turkey work, chairs, &c. By and by away home, and there took out my wife, and the two Mercers, and two of our mayds, Barker and Jane, and over the water to the Jamaica House,[1] where I never was before, and there the girls did run for wagers over the bowling-green; and there, with much pleasure, spent little, and so home, and they home, and I to read with satisfaction in my book of Turkey, and so to bed.

15th. Lay long in bed, and by and by called up by Sir H. Cholmly, who tells me that my Lord Middleton is for certain chosen Governor of Tangier; a man of moderate understanding, not covetous, but a soldier of fortune, and poor. Here comes Mr. Sanchy with an impertinent business to me of a ticket, which I put off. But by and by comes Dr. Childe by appointment, and sat with me all the morning making me bases and inward parts to several songs that I desired of him, to my great content. Then dined, and then abroad by coach, and I set him down at Hatton Garden, and I to the King's house by chance, where a new play: so full as I never saw it; I forced to stand all the while close to the very door till I took cold, and many people went away for want of room. The King and

[1] Jamaica House and Tea Gardens, Bermondsey, are marked in Horwood's map as situated at the end of Cherry Garden Street. The name survives in Jamaica Road. There is an illustration of the house in Rendle and Norman's "Inns of Old Southwark," 1888, p 400.

Queene, and Duke of York and Duchesse there, and all the Court, and Sir W. Coventry. The play called "The Change of Crownes;"[1] a play of Ned Howard's,[2] the best that ever I saw at that house, being a great play and serious; only Lacy did act the country-gentleman come up to Court, who do abuse the Court with all the imaginable wit and plainness about selling of places, and doing every thing for money. The play took very much. Thence I to my new bookseller's, and there bought "Hooker's Polity,"[3] the new edition, and "Dugdale's History of the Inns of Court,"[4] of which there was but a few saved out of the fire, and Playford's new Catch-book, that hath a great many new fooleries in it. Then home, a little at the office, and then to supper and to bed, mightily pleased with the new play.

16th. Up, and to the office, where sat all the morning, at noon home to dinner, and thence in haste to carry my wife to see the new play I saw yesterday, she not knowing it. But there, contrary to expectation, find "The Silent Woman." However, in; and there Knipp come into the pit. I took her by me, and here we met with Mrs. Horsley, the pretty woman—an acquaintance of Mercer's, whose house is burnt. Knipp tells me the King was so angry at the liberty taken by Lacy's part[5] to abuse him to his face, that he commanded they should act no more, till Moone[6]

[1] This play was entered on the Register of the Stationers' Company, but never printed.

[2] Edward Howard, fifth son of Thomas Howard, first Earl of Berkshire, and brother of Sir Robert Howard, baptized at St. Martin's-in-the-Fields, November 2nd, 1624. His play, the "United Kingdoms," was satirized in "The Rehearsal." Lacy's opinion of his abilities was shared by many of his contemporaries.

[3] The edition of 1666, containing *eight* books instead of *five*, edited by Dr. J. Gauden, Bishop of Exeter, and printed by Andrew Crooker, with the Life by Izaak Walton added for the first time.

[4] Sir William Dugdale's "Origines Juridiciales" was published in 1666, and a second edition appeared in 1671.

[5] In "The Change of Crownes."

[6] See November 20th, 1660, where the note requires revision. Michael Mohun (1620 ?-84) acted before the Civil War under Beeston at the Cockpit, in Drury Lane. He fought on the royalist side, and attained the rank of captain. Subsequently he went to Flanders, and there became a major. He lived in 1665 on the south side of Russell Street,

went and got leave for them to act again, but not this play. The King mighty angry; and it was bitter indeed, but very true and witty. I never was more taken with a play than I am with this "Silent Woman," as old as it is, and as often as I have seen it. There is more wit in it than goes to ten new plays. Thence with my wife and Knipp to Mrs. Pierce's, and saw her closet again, and liked her picture. Thence took them all to the Cake-house, in Southampton Market-place,[1] where Pierce told us the story how, in good earnest, [the King] is offended with the Duke of Richmond's marrying, and Mrs. Stewart's sending the King his jewels again. As she tells it, it is the noblest romance and example of a brave lady that ever I read in my life. Pretty to hear them talk of yesterday's play, and I durst not own to my wife to have seen it. Thence home and to [Sir] W. Batten's, where we have made a bargain for the ending of some of the trouble about some of our prizes for £1,400. So home to look on my new books that I have lately bought, and then to supper and to bed.

17th. Up, and with the two Sir Williams by coach to the Duke of York, who is come to St. James's, the first time we have attended him there this year. In our way, in Tower Street, we saw Desbrough[2] walking on foot: who is now

Covent Garden, and from 1671 to 1676 in a house on the east side of Bow Street. He died in Brownlow Street (now Betterton Street), Drury Lane, in October, 1684, and was buried in the church of St. Giles-in-the-Fields (see life by Mr. Joseph Knight in the "Dictionary of National Biography"). He is described as Major in the *Dramatis Personæ* of Dryden's "Assignation" as late as 1673.

[1] Afterwards called Bloomsbury Market. The following advertisement was inserted in "The Intelligencer" of May 23rd, 1664: "These are to give notice to all persons, that the King's most excellent Majesty hath granted to the Right Hon. the Earl of Southampton, one market to be held by the said Earl, his heirs, and assignes for ever, on Tuesdays, Thursdays, and Saturdays, in every week, at Bloomsbury, in the parish of St. Giles-in-the-Fields, in the county of Middlesex." — B.

[2] John Desborough, Desborow, or Disbrowe (1608–80), major-general, second son of James Desborough of Ettisley, Cambridgeshire. On June 23rd, 1636, he married Jane, sixth daughter of Robert Cromwell of Huntingdon, and sister of Oliver. After the Restoration he was imprisoned, and passed through several adventures; but after a judicial examination in 1667 he was set at liberty, and appears to have been allowed to reside quietly in England for the rest of his life. He died at Hackney in 1680.

no more a prisoner, and looks well, and just as he used to do heretofore. When we come to the Duke of York's I was spoke to by Mr. Bruncker on behalf of Carcasse. Thence by coach to Sir G. Carteret's, in London, there to pass some accounts of his, and at it till dinner, and then to work again a little, and then go away, and my wife being sent for by me to the New Exchange I took her up, and there to the King's playhouse (at the door met with W. Joyce in the street, who come to our coach side, but we in haste took no notice of him, for which I was sorry afterwards, though I love not the fellow, yet for his wife's sake), and saw a piece of "Rollo,"[1] a play I like not much, but much good acting in it: the house very empty. So away home, and I a little to the office, and then to Sir Robert Viner's, and so back, and find my wife gone down by water to take a little ayre, and I to my chamber and there spent the night in reading my new book, "Origines Juridiciales," which pleases me. So to supper and to bed.

18th. Up, and to read more in the "Origines," and then to the office, where the news is strong that not only the Dutch cannot set out a fleete this year, but that the French will not, and that he hath given the answer to the Dutch Embassador, saying that he is for the King of England's having an honourable peace, which, if true, is the best news we have had a good while. At the office all the morning, and there pleased with the little pretty Deptford woman I have wished for long, and she hath occasion given her to come again to me. After office I to the 'Change a little, and then home and to dinner, and then by coach with my wife to the Duke of York's house, and there saw "The Wits,"[2] a play I formerly loved, and is now corrected and enlarged: but, though I like the acting, yet I like not much in the play now. The Duke of York and [Sir] W. Coventry gone to Portsmouth, makes me thus to go to plays. So home, and to the office a little and then home, where I find Goodgroome, and he and I did sing several

1 "Rollo, Duke of Normandy," a tragedy by John Fletcher, published in 1640. It was previously published in 1639 under the title of "The Bloody Brother." Hart, Kynaston, Mohun, and Burt all acted in this play.

2 See August 15th, 1661.

things over, and tried two or three grace parts in Playford's new book, my wife pleasing me in singing her part of the things she knew, which is a comfort to my very heart. So he being gone we to supper and to bed.

19th. Up, and to the office all the morning, doing a great deal of business. At noon to dinner betimes, and then my wife and I by coach to the Duke's house, calling at Lovett's, where I find my Lady Castlemayne's picture not yet done, which has lain so many months there, which vexes me, but I mean not to trouble them more after this is done. So to the playhouse, not much company come, which I impute to the heat of the weather, it being very hot. Here we saw "Macbeth,"[1] which, though I have seen it often, yet is it one of the best plays for a stage, and variety of dancing and musique, that ever I saw. So being very much pleased, thence home by coach with young Goodyer and his own sister, who offered us to go in their coach. A good-natured youth I believe he is, but I fear will mind his pleasures too much. She is pretty, and a modest, brown girle. Set us down, so my wife and I into the garden, a fine moonshine evening, and there talking, and among other things she tells me that she finds by W. Hewer that my people do observe my minding my pleasure more than usual, which I confess, and am ashamed of, and so from this day take upon me to leave it till Whit-Sunday. While we were sitting in the garden comes Mrs. Turner to advise about her son, the Captain, when I did give her the best advice I could, to look out for some land employment for him, a peace being at hand, when few ships will be employed and very many, and these old Captains, to be provided for. Then to other talk, and among the rest about Sir W. Pen's being to buy Wansted House of Sir Robert Brookes, but has put him off again, and left him the other day to pay for a dinner at a tavern, which she

[1] See November 5th, 1664. Downes wrote: "The Tragedy of Macbeth, alter'd by Sir William Davenant; being drest in all it's finery, as new cloaths, new scenes, machines as flyings for the Witches; with all the singing and dancing in it. The first compos'd by Mr. Lock, the other by Mr. Channell and Mr. Joseph Preist; it being all excellently perform'd, being in the nature of an opera, it recompenc'd double the expence; it proves still a lasting play."

says our parishioner, Mrs. Hollworthy,[1] talks of; and I dare be hanged if ever he could mean to buy that great house, that knows not how to furnish one that is not the tenth part so big. Thence I to my chamber to write a little, and then to bed, having got a mighty cold in my right eare and side of my throat, and in much trouble with it almost all the night.

20th. Up, with much pain in my eare and palate. To the office out of humour all the morning. At noon dined, and with my wife to the King's house, but there found the bill torn down and no play acted, and so being in the humour to see one, went to the Duke of York's house, and there saw "The Witts" again, which likes me better than it did the other day, having much wit in it. Here met with Mr. Rolt, who tells me the reason of no play to-day at the King's house. That Lacy had been committed to the porter's lodge for his acting his part in the late new play, and that being thence released he come to the King's house, there met with Ned Howard, the poet of the play, who congratulated his release; upon which Lacy cursed him as that it was the fault of his nonsensical play that was the cause of his ill usage. Mr. Howard did give him some reply; to which Lacy [answered] him, that he was more a fool than a poet; upon which Howard did give him a blow on the face with his glove; on which Lacy, having a cane in his hand, did give him a blow over the pate. Here Rolt and others that discoursed of it in the pit this after noon did wonder that Howard did not run him through, he being too mean a fellow to fight with. But Howard did not do any thing but complain to the King of it; so the whole house is silenced, and the gentry seem to rejoice much at it, the house being become too insolent. Here were many fine ladies this afternoon at this house as I have at any time seen, and so after the play home and there wrote to my father, and then to walk in the garden with my wife, resolving by the grace of God to see no more plays till Whitsuntide, I having now seen a play every day this week till I have neglected my business, and that I am

[1] The death of Mr. Hollworthy is recorded on November 10th, 1665.

ashamed of, being found so much absent; the Duke of York and Sir W. Coventry having been out of town at Portsmouth did the more embolden me thereto. So home, and having brought home with me from Fenchurch Street a hundred of sparrowgrass,[1] cost 18*d.* We had them and a little bit of salmon, which my wife had a mind to, cost 3*s.* So to supper, and my pain being somewhat better in my throat, we to bed.

21st (Lord's day). Up, and John, a hackney coachman whom of late I have much used, as being formerly Sir W. Pen's coachman, coming to me by my direction to see whether I would use him to-day or no, I took him to our backgate to look upon the ground which is to be let there, where I have a mind to buy enough to build a coach-house and stable; for I have had it much in my thoughts lately that it is not too much for me now, in degree or cost, to keep a coach, but contrarily, that I am almost ashamed to be seen in a hackney, and therefore if I can have the conveniency, I will secure the ground at least till peace comes, that I do receive encouragement to keep a coach, or else that I may part with the ground again. The place I like very well, being close to my owne house, and so resolve to go about it, and so home and with my wife to church, and then to dinner, Mercer with us, with design to go to Hackney to church in the afternoon. So after dinner she and I sung "Suo Moro," which is one of the best pieces of musique to my thinking that ever I did hear in my life; then took coach and to Hackney church, where very full, and found much difficulty to get pews, I offering the sexton money, and he could not help me. So my wife and Mercer ventured into a pew, and I into another. A knight and his lady very civil to me when they come, and the like to my wife in hers, being Sir G. Viner[2] and his lady — rich in jewells, but most in beauty — almost the finest woman that ever I saw. That which we went chiefly to see was the

[1] A form once so commonly used for asparagus that it has found its way into dictionaries.

[2] Sir George Viner in 1665 succeeded his father, Sir Thomas, who had been Lord Mayor in 1653, and created a baronet in 1660. Sir George died in 1673. His wife was Abigail, daughter of Sir John Lawrence, Lord Mayor in 1665. — B.

young ladies of the schools,[1] whereof there is great store, very pretty; and also the organ, which is handsome, and tunes the psalm, and plays with the people; which is mighty pretty, and makes me mighty earnest to have a pair at our church, I having almost a mind to give them a pair, if they would settle a maintenance on them for it. I am mightily taken with them. So, church done, we to coach and away to Kingsland and Islington, and there eat and drank at the Old House, and so back, it raining a little, which is mighty welcome, it having not rained in many weeks, so that they say it makes the fields just now mighty sweet. So with great pleasure home by night. Set down Mercer, and I to my chamber, and there read a great deal in Rycaut's Turkey book with great pleasure, and so eat and to bed. My sore throat still troubling me, but not so much. This night I do come to full resolution of diligence for a good while, and I hope God will give me the grace and wisdom to perform it.

22nd. Up pretty betimes, my throat better, and so drest me, and to White Hall to see Sir W. Coventry, returned from Portsmouth, whom I am almost ashamed to see for fear he should have been told how often I have been at plays, but it is better to see him at first than afterward. So walked to the Old Swan and drank at Michell's, and then to White Hall and over the Park to St. James's to [Sir] W. Coventry, where well received, and good discourse. He seems to be sure of a peace; that the King of France do not intend to set out a fleete, for that he do design Flanders. Our Embassadors set out this week. Thence I over the Park to Sir G. Carteret, and after him by coach to the Lord Chancellor's house, the first time I have been therein;[2] and it is very noble, and brave pictures of the ancient and present nobility, never saw better. Thence with him to London, mighty merry in the way. Thence home, and find the boy out of the house and office, and by and by comes in and hath been to Mercer's. I did pay his coat for him. Then to my chamber, my wife comes home with linen she hath been buying of. I then to dinner,

[1] Hackney was long famous for its boarding schools.

[2] Clarendon House, Piccadilly. See February 20th, 1664-65.

and then down the river to Greenwich, and the watermen would go no further. So I turned them off, giving them nothing, and walked to Woolwich; there did some business, and met with Captain Cocke and back with him. He tells me our peace is agreed on; we are not to assist the Spanyard against the French for this year, and no restitution, and we are likely to lose Poleroone.[1] I know not whether this be true or no, but I am for peace on any terms. He tells me how the King was vexed the other day for having no paper laid him at the Council-table, as was usual; and Sir Richard Browne[2] did tell his Majesty he would call the person[3] whose work it was to provide it: who being come, did tell his Majesty that he was but a poor man, and was out £400 or £500 for it, which was as much as he is worth; and that he cannot provide it any longer without money, having not received a penny since the King's coming in. So the King spoke to my Lord Chamberlain; and many such mementos the King do now-a-days meet withall, enough to make an ingenuous man mad. I to Deptford, and there scolded with a master for his ship's not being gone, and so home to the office and did business till my eyes are sore again, and so home to sing, and then to bed, my eyes failing me mightily.

23rd (St. George's-day). The feast being kept at White Hall, out of design, as it is thought, to make the best countenance we can to the Swede's Embassadors,[4] before their leaving us to go to the treaty abroad, to shew some jollity. We sat at the office all the morning. Word is brought me that young Michell is come to call my wife to his wife's labour, and she went, and I at the office full of expectation what to hear from poor Betty Michell. This morning much to do with Sir W. Warren, all whose appli-

[1] Among the State Papers is a document dated July 8th, 1667, in which we read: "At Breda, the business is so far advanced that the English have relinquished their pretensions to the ships Henry Bonaventure and Good Hope. The matter sticks only at Poleron; the States have resolved not to part with it, though the English should have a right to it" ("Calendar," 1667, p. 278).

[2] Clerk of the Council.

[3] Wooly.

[4] See November 15th, 1666.

cations now are to Lord Bruncker, and I am against him now, not professedly, but apparently in discourse, and will be. At noon home to dinner, where alone, and after dinner to my musique papers, and by and by comes in my wife, who gives me the good news that the midwife and she alone have delivered poor Betty of a pretty girl, which I am mighty glad of, and she in good condition, my wife as well as I mightily pleased with it. Then to the office to do things towards the post, and then my wife and I set down at her mother's, and I up and down to do business, but did little; and so to Mrs. Martin's, and there did hazer what I would con her, and then called my wife and to little Michell's, where we saw the little child, which I like mightily, being I allow very pretty, and asked her how she did, being mighty glad of her doing well, and so home to the office, and then to my chamber, and so to bed.

24th. Up, and with [Sir] W. Pen to St. James's, and there the Duke of York was preparing to go to some further ceremonies about the Garter, that he could give us no audience. Thence to Westminster Hall, the first day of the Term, and there joyed Mrs. Michell, who is mightily pleased with my wife's work yesterday, and so away to my barber's about my periwigg, and then to the Exchange, there to meet Fenn about some money to be borrowed of the office of the Ordnance to answer a great pinch. So home to dinner, and in the afternoon met by agreement (being put on it by Harry Bruncker's frighting us into a despatch of Carcasse's business) [Lord] Bruncker, T. Harvey, [Sir] J. Minnes, [Sir] W. Batten, and I (Sir W. Pen keeping out of the way still), where a great many high words from Bruncker, and as many from me and others to him, and to better purpose, for I think we have fortified ourselves to overthrow his man Carcasse, and to do no honour to him. We rose with little done but great heat, not to be reconciled I doubt, and I care not, for I will be on the right side, and that shall keep me. Thence by coach to Sir John Duncomb's[1] lodging in the Pell Mell, in order to the money spoken of in the morning; and there awhile sat and discoursed: and I find him that he is a very proper

[1] See November 8th, 1664.

man for business, being very resolute and proud, and industrious. He told me what reformation they had made in the office of the Ordnance, taking away Legg's[1] fees: and have got an order that no Treasurer after him shall ever sit at the Board; and it is a good one: that no master of the Ordnance here shall ever sell a place. He tells me they have not paid any increase of price for any thing during this war, but in most have paid less; and at this day have greater stores than they know where to lay, if there should be peace, and than ever was any time this war. That they pay every man in course, and have notice of the disposal of every farthing. Every man that they owe money to has his share of every sum they receive; never borrowed all this war but £30,000 by the King's express command, but do usually stay till their assignments become payable in their own course, which is the whole mystery, that they have had assignments for a fifth part of whatever was assigned to the Navy. They have power of putting out and in of all officers; are going upon a building that will cost them £12,000; that they out of their stock of tallies have been forced to help the Treasurer of the Navy at this great pinch. Then to talk of newes: that he thinks the want of money hath undone the King, for the Parliament will never give the King more money without calling all people to account, nor, as he believes, will ever

[1] William Legge, eldest son of Edward Legge, sometime Vice-President of Munster, born 1609 (?). He served under Maurice of Nassau and Gustavus Adolphus, and held the rank of colonel in the Royalist army. He closely attached himself to Prince Rupert, and was an active agent in affecting the reconciliation between that prince and his uncle Charles I. Colonel Legge distinguished himself in several actions, and was wounded and taken prisoner at the battle of Worcester; it was said that he would have "been executed if his wife had not contrived his escape from Coventry gaol in her own clothes." He was Groom of the Bedchamber to Charles I., and also to Charles II.; he held the offices of Master of the Armories and Lieutenant-General of the Ordnance. He refused honours (a knighthood from Charles I. and an earldom from Charles II.), but his eldest son George was created Baron Dartmouth in 1682. He died October 13th, 1672, at his house in the Minories, and was buried in Trinity Church, Minories, where there is a Monument to his memory. A portrait of Colonel Legge, by Huysman, is in the possession of the Earl of Dartmouth. There is an excellent life of Legge, by Mr. C. H. Firth, in the "Dictionary of National Biography."

make war again, but they will manage it themselves: unless, which I proposed, he would visibly become a severer inspector into his own business and accounts, and that would gain upon the Parliament yet: which he confesses and confirms as the only lift to set him upon his legs, but says that it is not in his nature ever to do. He says that he believes but four men (such as he could name) would do the business of both offices, his and ours, and if ever the war were to be again it should be so, he believes. He told me to my face that I was a very good clerk, and did understand the business and do it very well, and that he would never desire a better. He do believe that the Parliament, if ever they meet, will offer some alterations to the King, and will turn some of us out, and I protest I think he is in the right that either they or the King will be advised to some regulations, and therefore I ought to beware, as it is easy for me to keep myself up if I will. He thinks that much of our misfortune hath been for want of an active Lord Treasurer, and that such a man as Sir W. Coventry would do the business thoroughly. This talk being over, comes his boy and tells us [Sir] W. Coventry is come in, and so he and I to him, and there told the difficulty of getting this money, and they did play hard upon Sir G. Carteret as a man moped and stunned, not knowing which way to turn himself. Sir W. Coventry cried that he was disheartened, and I do think that there is much in it, but Sir J. Duncomb do charge him with mighty neglect in the pursuing of his business, and that he do not look after it himself, but leaves it to Fenn, so that I do perceive that they are resolved to scheme at bringing the business into a better way of execution, and I think it needs, that is the truth of it. So I away to Sir G. Carteret's lodgings about this money, and contrary to expectation I find he hath prevailed with Legg on his own bond to lend him £2,000, which I am glad of, but, poor man, he little sees what observations people do make upon his management, and he is not a man fit to be told what one hears. Thence by water at 10 at night from Westminster Bridge, having kissed little Frank, and so to the Old Swan, and walked home by moonshine, and there to my chamber a while, and supper and to bed.

25th. Received a writ from the Exchequer this morning of distrain for £70,000, which troubled me, though it be but matter of form. To the office, where sat all the morning. At noon my wife being to Unthanke's christening, I to Sir W. Batten's to dinner, where merry, and the rather because we are like to come to some good end in another of our prizes. Thence by coach to my Lord Treasurer's, and there being come too soon to the New Exchange, but did nothing, and back again, and there found my Lord Bruncker and T. Harvy, and walked in a room very merrily discoursing. By and by comes my Lord Ashly and tells us my Lord Treasurer is ill and cannot speak with us now. Thence away, Sir W. Pen and I and Mr. Lewes, who come hither after us, and Mr. Gawden in the last man's coach. Set me down by the Poultry, and I to Sir Robert Viner's, and there had my account stated and took it home to review. So home to the office, and there late writing out something, having been a little at Sir W. Batten's to talk, and there vexed to see them give order for Hogg's further abroad, and so home and to bed.

26th. Up, and by coach with Sir W. Batten and [Sir] W. Pen to White Hall, and there saw the Duke of Albemarle, who is not well, and do grow crazy. Thence I to St. James's, to meet Sir G. Carteret, and did, and Lord Berkely, to get them (as we would have done the Duke of Albemarle) to the meeting of the Lords of Appeale in the business of one of our prizes. With them to the meeting of the Guinny Company, and there staid, and went with Lord Berkely. While I was waiting for him in the Matted Gallery, a young man was most finely working in Indian inke the great picture of the King and Queen[1] sitting, by Van Dyke; and did it very finely. Thence to Westminster Hall to hear our cause, but [it] did not come before them to-day, so went down and walked below in the Hall, and there met with Ned Pickering, who tells me the ill newes of his nephew Gilbert, who is turned a very rogue, and then I took a turn with Mr. Evelyn, with whom I walked two hours, till almost one of the clock: talking of the badness of the Government, where nothing but wickedness, and

[1] Charles I. and Henrietta Maria.

wicked men and women command the King: that it is not in his nature to gainsay any thing that relates to his pleasures; that much of it arises from the sickliness of our Ministers of State, who cannot be about him as the idle companions are, and therefore he gives way to the young rogues; and then, from the negligence of the Clergy, that a Bishop shall never be seen about him, as the King of France hath always: that the King would fain have some of the same gang to be Lord Treasurer, which would be yet worse, for now some delays are put to the getting gifts of the King, as that whore my Lady Byron,[1] who had been, as he called it, the King's seventeenth whore abroad, did not leave him till she had got him to give her an order for £4,000 worth of plate to be made for her; but by delays, thanks be to God! she died before she had it. He tells me mighty stories of the King of France, how great a prince he is.[2] He hath made a code to shorten the law; he hath put out all the ancient commanders of castles that were become hereditary; he hath made all the fryers subject to the bishops, which before were only subject to Rome, and so were hardly the King's subjects, and that none shall become *religieux* but at such an age, which he thinks will in a few years ruin the Pope, and bring France into a patriarchate. He confirmed to me the business of the want of paper at the Council-table the other day, which I have observed; Wooly being to have found it, and did, being called, tell the King to his face the reason of it; and Mr. Evelyn tells me several of the menial servants of the Court lacking bread, that have not received a farthing wages since the King's coming in. He tells me the King of France hath his mistresses, but laughs at the foolery of our King, that makes his bastards princes,[3] and loses his revenue upon them, and makes his mistresses his masters: and the King

[1] Eleanor, daughter of Robert Needham, Viscount Kilmurrey, and widow of Peter Warburton, became in 1644 the second wife of John Byron, first Lord Byron. Died 1663. — B.

[2] All these assertions respecting the King of France must be received cautiously. Pepys was very ignorant of foreign matters, and very credulous. — B.

[3] Louis made his own bastards dukes and princes, and legitimatized them as much as he could, connecting them also by marriage with the real blood-royal. — B.

of France did never grant Lavalliere[1] any thing to bestow on others, and gives a little subsistence, but no more, to his bastards. He told me the whole story of Mrs. Stewart's going away from Court, he knowing her well; and believes her, up to her leaving the Court, to be as virtuous as any woman in the world: and told me, from a Lord that she told it to but yesterday, with her own mouth, and a sober man, that when the Duke of Richmond did make love to her, she did ask the King, and he did the like also; and that the King did not deny it, and [she] told this Lord that she was come to that pass as to resolve to have married any gentleman of £1,500 a-year that would have had her in honour; for it was come to that pass, that she could not longer continue at Court without prostituting herself to the King,[2] whom she had so long kept off, though he had liberty more than any other had, or he ought to have, as to dalliance.[3] She told this Lord that she had reflected upon the occasion she had given the world to think her a bad woman, and that she had no way but to marry and leave the Court, rather in this way of discontent than otherwise, that the world might see that she sought not any thing but her honour; and that she will never come to live at Court more than when she comes to town to come to kiss the Queene her Mistress's hand: and hopes, though she hath little reason to hope, she can please her Lord so as to reclaim him, that they may yet live comfortably in the country on his estate. She told this Lord that all the jewells she ever had given her at Court, or any other pres-

[1] Louise Françoise de la Baume le Blanc de la Vallière had four children by Louis XIV., of whom only two survived — Marie Anne Bourbon, called Mademoiselle de Blois, born in 1666, afterwards married to the Prince de Conti, and the Comte de Vermandois, born in 1667. In that year (the very year in which Evelyn was giving this account to Pepys), the Duchy of Vaujour and two baronies were created in favour of La Vallière, and her daughter, who, in the deed of creation, was legitimatized, and styled princess. — B.

[2] Even at a much later time Mrs. Godolphin well resolved "not to talk foolishly to men, *more especially* THE KING," — "be sure *never to talk to* THE KING" ("Life," by Evelyn). These expressions speak volumes as to Charles's character. — B.

[3] Evelyn evidently believed the Duchess of Richmond to be innocent; and his testimony, coupled with her own declaration, ought to weigh down all the scandal which Pepys reports from other sources. — B.

ents, more than the King's allowance of £700 per annum out of the Privy-purse for her clothes, were, at her first coming the King did give her a necklace of pearl of about £1,100,[1] and afterwards, about seven months since, when the King had hopes to have obtained some courtesy of her, the King did give her some jewells, I have forgot what, and I think a pair of pendants. The Duke of York, being once her Valentine, did give her a jewell of about £800; and my Lord Mandeville, her Valentine this year, a ring of about £300; and the King of France would have had her mother,[2] who, he says, is one of the most cunning women in the world, to have let her stay in France, saying that he loved her not as a mistress, but as one that he could marry as well as any lady in France; and that, if she might stay, for the honour of his Court he would take care she should not repent. But her mother, by command of the Queen-mother, thought rather to bring her into England; and the King of France did give her a jewell: so that Mr. Evelyn believes she may be worth in jewells about £6,000, and that that is all that she hath in the world: and a worthy woman; and in this hath done as great an act of honour as ever was done by woman. That now the Countesse Castlemayne do carry all before her: and among other arguments to prove Mrs. Stewart to have been honest to the last, he says that the King's keeping in still with my Lady Castlemayne do show it; for he never was known to keep two mistresses in his life, and would never have kept to her had he prevailed any thing with Mrs. Stewart. She is gone yesterday with her Lord to Cobham.[3] He did tell me of

[1] Which she returned to the king. — B.

[2] This lady's name nowhere appears. She was the wife of the Hon. Walter Stewart, third son of Walter, first Lord Blantyre. The Duchess of Richmond, Frances Theresa, was her elder daughter. The younger, Sophia, married the Hon. Henry Bulkeley, master of the household to Charles II. and James II. — B.

[3] Cobham Hall, in Kent, after the attainder of Henry Brooke, Lord Cobham, was granted by James I. to Ludovic Stuart, Duke of Lennox, and his brother George, Lord Aubigney, from whom it descended to Charles Stuart, Duke of Richmond and Lennox, in 1660. This duke dying, s. p., in 1672, when ambassador to Denmark, the estates, together with the English barony of Clifton, passed, through his sister, Lady Catherine O'Brien, to the ancestor of the Earl of Darnley, the present possessor. Lady Catherine O'Brien married Sir Joseph Williamson,

the ridiculous humour of our King and Knights of the Garter the other day, who, whereas heretofore their robes were only to be worn during their ceremonies and service, these, as proud of their coats, did wear them all day till night, and then rode into the Parke with them on. Nay, and he tells me he did see my Lord Oxford and the Duke of Monmouth in a hackney-coach with two footmen in the Parke, with their robes on; which is a most scandalous thing, so as all gravity may be said to be lost among us. By and by we discoursed of Sir Thomas Clifford,[1] whom I took for a very rich and learned man, and of the great family of that name. He tells me he is only a man of about seven-score pounds a-year, of little learning more than the law of a justice of peace, which he knows well: a parson's son, got to be burgess in a little borough in the West, and here fell into the acquaintance of my Lord Arlington, whose creature he is, and never from him; a man of virtue, and comely, and good parts enough; and hath come into his place with a great grace, though with a great skip over the heads of a great many, as Chichly and Duncum, and some Lords that did expect it. By the way, he tells me, that of all the great men of England there is none that endeavours more to raise those that he takes into favour than my Lord Arlington; and that, on that score, he is much more to be made one's patron than my Lord Chancellor, who never did, nor never will do, any thing, but for money.[2] After having this long discourse we parted, about one of the clock, and so away by water home, calling upon Michell, whose wife and girle are pretty well, and I home to dinner, and after dinner with Sir W. Batten

who repurchased the Cobham estates, when sold, and preserved them to the family. — B.

[1] Sir Thomas Clifford was the eldest son of Hugh Clifford, of Ugbrook, near Exeter, where he was born, August 1st, 1630. He attached himself to Lord Arlington, and acted as that statesman's confidential agent when with the fleet. On April 22nd, 1672, he was created Baron Clifford, of Chudleigh, co. Devon; and he supplanted his patron when on November 28th following he was appointed Lord High Treasurer, an office which Arlington desired. He was ruined by the passing of the Test Act, and resigning his office, he retired to Devonshire, and died September, 1673, not without suspicion of suicide.

[2] See September 9th, 1665.

to White Hall, there to attend the Duke of York before council, where we all met at his closet and did the little business we had, and here he did tell us how the King of France is intent upon his design against Flanders, and hath drawn up a remonstrance of the cause of the war, and appointed the 20th of the next month for his rendezvous, and himself to prepare for the campaign the 30th, so that this, we are in hopes, will keep him in employment. Turenne is to be his general. Here was Carcasse's business unexpectedly moved by him, but what was done therein appears in my account of his case in writing by itself. Certain newes of the Dutch being abroad on our coast with twenty-four great ships. This done Sir W. Batten and I back again to London, and in the way met my Lady Newcastle going with her coaches and footmen all in velvet: herself, whom I never saw before, as I have heard her often described, for all the town-talk is now-a-days of her extravagancies, with her velvet-cap, her hair about her ears; many black patches, because of pimples about her mouth; naked-necked, without any thing about it, and a black just-au-corps.[1] She seemed to me a very comely woman: but I hope to see more of her on May-day. My mind is mightily of late upon a coach. At home, to the office, where late spending all the evening upon entering in long hand our late passages with Carcasse for memory sake, and so home in great pain in my back by the uneasiness of Sir W. Batten's coach driving hard this afternoon over the stones to prevent coming too late. So at night to supper in great pain, and to bed, where lay in great pain, not able to turn myself all night.

27th. Up with much pain, and to the office, where all the morning. At noon home to dinner, W. Hewer with us. This noon I got in some coals at 23*s*. per chaldron, a good hearing, I thank God — having not been put to buy a coal all this dear time, that during this war poor people have

[1] "A sort of jacket called a *justacorps* came into fashion in Paris about 1650. M. Quicherat informs us that a pretty Parisienne, the wife of a *maître de comptes* named Belot, was the first who appeared in it. In a ballad called 'The New-made Gentlewoman,' written in the reign of Charles II., occurs the line, 'My justico and black patches I wear.' Mr. Fairholt suggested that *justico* may be a corruption of *juste au corps*." — Planché's *Cyclopædia of Costume*, vol. i., p. 318.

been forced to give 45*s*. and 50*s*., and £3. In the afternoon (my wife and people busy these late days, and will be for some time, making of shirts and smocks) to the office, where late, and then home, after letters, and so to supper and to bed, with much pleasure of mind, after having dispatched business. This afternoon I spent some time walking with Mr. Moore, in the garden, among other things discoursing of my Lord Sandwich's family, which he tells me is in a very bad condition, for want of money and management, my Lord's charging them with bills, and nobody, nor any thing provided to answer them. He did discourse of his hopes of being supplied with £1,900 against a present bill from me, but I took no notice of it, nor will do it. It seems Mr. Sheply doubts his accounts are ill kept, and every thing else in the family out of order, which I am grieved to hear of.

28th (Lord's day). Lay long, my pain in my back being still great, though not so great as it was. However, up and to church, where a lazy sermon, and then home and to dinner, my wife and I alone and Barker. After dinner, by water — the day being mighty pleasant, and the tide serving finely, I up (reading in Boyle's book of colours),[1] as high as Barne Elmes, and there took one turn alone, and then back to Putney Church, where I saw the girls of the schools, few of which pretty; and there I come into a pew, and met with little James Pierce, which I was much pleased at, the little rogue being very glad to see me: his master, Reader to the Church. Here was a good sermon and much company, but I sleepy, and a little out of order, for my hat falling down through a hole underneath the pulpit, which, however, after sermon, by a stick, and the helpe of the clerke, I got up again, and then walked out of the church with the boy, and then left him, promising him to get him a play another time. And so by water, the tide being with me again, down to Deptford, and there I walked down the Yard, Shish[2] and Cox[3] with me, and discoursed

[1] "Experiments and Considerations touching Colours" was published by the Hon. Robert Boyle in 1664 (London).

[2] Jonas Shish, master builder at Deptford dockyard. See note, July 22nd, 1664.

[3] Captain John Cox, master attendant at Deptford.

about cleaning of the wet docke, and heard, which I had before, how, when the docke was made, a ship of near 500 tons was there found; a ship supposed of Queene Elizabeth's time, and well wrought, with a great deal of stone-shot in her, of eighteen inches diameter, which was shot then in use: and afterwards meeting with Captain Perriman[1] and Mr. Castle at Half-way Tree, they tell me of stone-shot of thirty-six inches diameter, which they shot out of mortar-pieces.[2] Thence walked to Half-way Tree, and there stopt and talk with Mr. Castle and Captain Perriman, and so to Redriffe and took boat again, and so home, and there to write down my Journall, and so to supper and to read, and so to bed, mightily pleased with my reading of Boyle's book of colours to-day, only troubled that some part of it, indeed the greatest part, I am not able to understand for want of study. My wife this night troubled at my leaving her alone so much and keeping her within doors, which indeed I do not well nor wisely in.

29th. Up, being visited very early by Creed newly come from Hinchingbrooke, who went thither without my knowledge, and I believe only to save his being taxed by the Poll Bill. I did give him no very good countenance nor welcome, but took occasion to go forth and walked (he with me) to St. Dunstan's, and thence I to Sir W. Coventry's, where a good while with him, and I think he pretty kind, but that the nature of our present condition affords not matter for either of us to be pleased with any thing. We discoursed of Carcasse, whose Lord, he tells me, do make complaints that his clerk should be singled out, and my Lord Berkeley do take his part. So he advises we would sum up all we have against him and lay it before the Duke of York; he condemned my Lord Bruncker. Thence to Sir G. Carteret, and there talked a little while about office business, and thence by coach home, in several places

[1] Among the State Papers is an "Account by Captain J. Perriman of work doing on and the movements of 13 ships named, lying in the Thames," dated April, 1667 ("Calendar," 1667, p. 66).

[2] At the passage of the Dardanelles, in 1807, a stone shot, fired by the Turks from the Castle of Sestos, entered the "Lion," of sixty-four guns, and killed and wounded a great many men. It weighed 770 pounds. — B.

paying my debts in order to my evening my accounts this month, and thence by and by to White Hall again to Sir G. Carteret to dinner, where very good company and discourse, and I think it my part to keep it there now more than ordinary because of the probability of my Lord's coming soon home. Our Commissioners for the treaty set out this morning betimes down the river.[1] Here I hear that the Duke of Cambridge,[2] the Duke of York's son, is very sick; and my Lord Treasurer very bad of the stone, and hath been so some days. After dinner Sir G. Carteret and I alone in his closet an hour or more talking of my Lord Sandwich's coming home, which, the peace being likely to be made here, he expects, both for my Lord's sake and his own (whose interest he wants) it will be best for him to be at home, where he will be well received by the King; he is sure of his service well accepted, though the business of Spain do fall by this peace. He tells me my Lord Arlington hath done like a gentleman by him in all things. He says, if my Lord [Sandwich] were here, he were the fittest man to be Lord Treasurer of any man in England; and he thinks it might be compassed; for he confesses that the King's matters do suffer through the inability of this man, who is likely to die, and he will propound him to the King. It will remove him from his place at sea, and the King will have a good place to bestow. He says to me, that he could wish, when my Lord comes, that he would think fit to forbear playing, as a thing below him, and which will lessen him, as it do my Lord St. Albans, in the King's esteem: and as a great secret tells me that he hath made a match for my Lord Hinchingbroke to a daughter[3] of my Lord Burlington's, where there is a great alliance, £10,000 portion; a civil family, and relation to my Lord Chancellor, whose son hath married one of the daughters;[4] and that my Lord Chancellor do take it with

[1] See *ante*, April 10th.

[2] James Stuart, second son of the Duke of York, born July 12th, 1663; created Duke of Cambridge, August 23rd, 1664; died June 20th, 1667.

[3] Lady Mary Boyle, fourth daughter of Richard, first Earl of Burlington, married to Viscount Hinchingbroke, 1668.

[4] Lawrence Hyde, afterwards Earl of Rochester, married Lady Henrietta Boyle, fifth daughter of the Earl of Burlington, 1665.

very great kindness, so that he do hold himself obliged by it. My Lord Sandwich hath referred it to my Lord Crew, Sir G. Carteret, and Mr. Montagu, to end it. My Lord Hinchingbroke and the lady know nothing yet of it. It will, I think, be very happy. Very glad of this discourse, I away mightily pleased with the confidence I have in this family, and so away, took up my wife, who was at her mother's, and so home, where I settled to my chamber about my accounts, both Tangier and private, and up at it till twelve at night, with good success, when news is brought me that there is a great fire in Southwarke: so we up to the leads, and then I and the boy down to the end of our lane, and there saw it, it seeming pretty great, but nothing to the fire of London, that it made me think little of it. We could at that distance see an engine play—that is, the water go out, it being moonlight. By and by, it begun to slacken, and then I home and to bed.

30th. Up, and Mr. Madden[1] come to speak with me, whom my people not knowing have made to wait long without doors, which vexed me. Then comes Sir John Winter to discourse with me about the forest of Deane, and then about my Lord Treasurer, and asking me whether, as he had heard, I had not been cut for the stone, I took him to my closet, and there shewed it to him, of which he took the dimensions and had some discourse of it, and I believe will shew my Lord Treasurer it. Thence to the office, where we sat all the morning, but little to do, and then to the 'Change, where for certain I hear, and the News book declares, a peace between France and Portugal. Met here with Mr. Pierce, and he tells me the Duke of Cambridge is very ill and full of spots about his body, that Dr. Frazier knows not what to think of it. Then home and to dinner, and then to the office, where all the afternoon; we met about Sir W. Warren's business and accounts, wherein I do rather oppose than forward him, but not in declared terms, for I will not be at enmity with him, but I will not have him find any friendship so good as mine. By and by rose and by water to White Hall, and then called my wife at

[1] Probably John Madden, surveyor of the woods on this side Trent (see "Calendar of State Papers," 1667, p. 83).

Unthanke's. So home and to my chamber, to my accounts, and finished them to my heart's wishes and admiration, they being grown very intricate, being let alone for two months, but I brought them together all naturally, within a few shillings, but to my sorrow the Poll money I paid this month and mourning have made me £80 a worse man than at my last balance, so that I am worth now but £6,700, which is yet an infinite mercy to me, for which God make me thankful. So late to supper, with a glad heart for the evening of my accounts so well, and so to bed.

May 1st. Up, it being a fine day, and after doing a little business in my chamber I left my wife to go abroad with W. Hewer and his mother in a Hackney coach incognito to the Park, while I abroad to the Excise Office first, and there met the Cofferer and Sir Stephen Fox about our money matters there, wherein we agreed, and so to discourse of my Lord Treasurer, who is a little better than he was of the stone, having rested a little this night. I there did acquaint them of my knowledge of that disease, which I believe will be told my Lord Treasurer. Thence to Westminster; in the way meeting many milk-maids with their garlands upon their pails, dancing with a fiddler before them;[1] and saw pretty Nelly standing at her lodgings'

[1] On the 1st of May milkmaids used to borrow silver cups, tankards, &c., to hang them round their milkpails, with the addition of flowers and ribbons, which they carried upon their heads, accompanied by a bagpipe or fiddle, and went from door to door, dancing before the houses of their customers, in order to obtain a small gratuity from each of them.

"In London thirty years ago,
When pretty milkmaids went about,
It was a goodly sight to see
Their May-day pageant all drawn out.

* * * * *

"Such scenes and sounds once blest my eyes
And charm'd my ears; but all have vanish'd,
On May-day now no garlands go,
For milkmaids and their dance are banish'd."

Hone's *Every-Day Book*, vol. i., pp. 569, 570.

May-day customs have nearly died out, but the editor saw a jack-in-the-green with men dressed as milkmaids dancing round it on May 1st of the present year (1895) in one of the streets near Primrose Hill. There has been a great revival of May-day decoration on cart-horses within the last few years.

door in Drury-lane[1] in her smock sleeves and bodice, looking upon one: she seemed a mighty pretty creature. To the Hall and there walked a while, it being term. I thence home to the Rose, and then had Doll Lane venir para me. . . . . To my Lord Crew's, where I found them at dinner, and among others Mrs. Bocket, which I have not seen a long time, and two little dirty children, and she as idle a prating and impertinent woman as ever she was. After dinner my Lord took me alone and walked with me, giving me an account of the meeting of the Commissioners for Accounts, whereof he is one. How some of the gentlemen, Garraway,[2] Littleton, and others, did scruple at their first coming there, being called thither to act, as Members of Parliament, which they could not do by any authority but that of Parliament, and therefore desired the King's direction in it, which was sent for by my Lord Bridgewater,[3] who brought answer, very short, that the King expected they should obey his Commission. Then they went on, and observed a power to be given them of administering and framing an oath, which they thought they could not do by any power but Act of Parliament; and the whole Commission did think fit to have the Judges' opinion in it; and so, drawing up their scruples in writing, they all attended the King, who told them he would send to the Judges to be answered, and did so; who have, my Lord tells me, met three times about it, not knowing what answer to give to it; and they have met this week, doing nothing but expecting the solution of the judges in this point. My Lord tells me he do believe this Commission will do more hurt than good; it may undo some accounts, if these men shall think fit; but it can never clear an account, for he must come into the Exchequer for

[1] The old house in Drury Lane where Nell Gwyn is believed to have lived was pulled down in 1891. It was situated on the west side of the lane, nearly opposite Wych Street. There is a view of it in Peter Cunningham's "Story of Nell Gwyn."

[2] William Garway, M.P. for Chichester (see October 3rd, 1666). Timothy Littleton, or Lyttelton, Serjeant-at-Law, M.P. for Ludlow.

[3] John Egerton, second Earl of Bridgewater, Lord-Lieutenant of the counties of Bucks and Hertford, and High Steward of the University of Oxford. Died October 26th, 1686.

all this. Besides, it is a kind of inquisition that hath seldom ever been granted in England; and he believes it will never, besides, give any satisfaction to the People or Parliament, but be looked upon as a forced, packed business of the King, especially if these Parliament-men that are of it shall not concur with them: which he doubts they will not, and, therefore, wishes much that the King would lay hold of this fit occasion, and let the Commission fall. Then to talk of my Lord Sandwich, whom my Lord Crew hath a great desire might get to be Lord Treasurer if the present Lord should die,[1] as it is believed he will, in a little time; and thinks he can have no competitor but my Lord Arlington, who, it is given out, desires it: but my Lord thinks it is not so, for that the being Secretary do keep him a greater interest with the King than the other would do: at least, do believe, that if my Lord would surrender him his Wardrobe place, it would be a temptation to Arlington to assist my Lord in getting the Treasurer's. I did object to my Lord [Crew] that it would be no place of content, nor safety, nor honour for my Lord, the State being so indigent as it is, and the [King] so irregular, and those about him, that my Lord must be forced to part with any thing to answer his warrants; and that, therefore, I do believe the King had rather have a man that may be one of his vicious caball, than a sober man that will mind the publick, that so they may sit at cards and dispose of the revenue of the kingdom. This my Lord was moved at, and said he did not indeed know how to answer it, and bid me think of it; and so said he himself would also do. He do mightily cry out of the bad management of our monies, the King having had so much given him; and yet, when the Parliament do find that the King should have £900,000 in his purse by the best account of issues they have yet seen, yet we should report in the Navy a debt due from the King of £900,000; which, I did confess, I doubted was true in the first, and knew to be true in the last, and did believe that there was some great miscarriages in it: which he owned to believe also, saying, that at this rate it is not in the power of the kingdom to make a war, nor answer the King's wants.

[1] The Earl of Southampton died May 16th, 1667.

Thence away to the King's playhouse, by agreement met Sir W. Pen, and saw "Love in a Maze:"[1] but a sorry play: only Lacy's clowne's part, which he did most admirably indeed; and I am glad to find the rogue at liberty again. Here was but little, and that ordinary, company. We sat at the upper bench next the boxes; and I find it do pretty well, and have the advantage of seeing and hearing the great people, which may be pleasant when there is good store. Now was only Prince Rupert and my Lord Lauderdale, and my Lord ——,[2] the naming of whom puts me in mind of my seeing, at Sir Robert Viner's, two or three great silver flagons, made with inscriptions as gifts of the King to such and such persons of quality as did stay in town the late great plague, for the keeping things in order in the town,[3] which is a handsome thing. But here was neither Hart, Nell, nor Knipp; therefore, the play was not likely to please me. Thence Sir W. Pen and I in his coach, Tiburne way, into the Park, where a horrid dust, and number of coaches, without pleasure or order. That which we, and almost all went for, was to see my Lady Newcastle; which we could not, she being followed and crowded upon by coaches all the way she went, that nobody could come near her; only I could see she was in a large black coach, adorned with silver instead of gold, and so white curtains, and every thing black and white, and herself in her cap, but other parts I could not make [out]. But that which I did see, and wonder at with reason, was to find Pegg Pen in a new coach, with only her husband's

[1] The second title of Shirley's play of "The Changes" (see May 22nd, 1662).

[2] Probably Craven. — B.

[3] In reference to this passage, Mr. R. Jacomb Hood wrote to "Notes and Queries" (4th series, vol. xii., p. 471), as follows: "I have an old silver tankard, which has been in my family for several generations, and which, from the inscription upon it, seems to have been given by the king to Sir Edmund Berry Godfrey, who was murdered in 1678. The inscriptions show, not only that a tankard was given in 1665 for services during the Plague, but that the recipient was further knighted by the king in September, 1666, for his efforts to preserve order in the Great Fire. The tankard is quite plain, weighs 38 oz., and holds about two quarts." Mr. Hood adds, however, that "the hall mark appears from the trade register to belong to the years 1675-76, *i.e.*, at least eight years later than the notice by Pepys."

pretty sister[1] with her, both patched and very fine, and in much the finest coach in the park, and I think that ever I did see one or other, for neatness and richness in gold, and everything that is noble. My Lady Castlemayne, the King, my Lord St. Albans, nor Mr. Jermyn, have so neat a coach, that ever I saw. And, Lord! to have them have this, and nothing else that is correspondent, is to me one of the most ridiculous sights that ever I did see, though her present dress was well enough; but to live in the condition they do at home, and be abroad in this coach, astonishes me. When we had spent half an hour in the Park, we went out again, weary of the dust, and despairing of seeing my Lady Newcastle; and so back the same way, and to St. James's, thinking to have met my Lady Newcastle before she got home, but we staying by the way to drink, she got home a little before us: so we lost our labours, and then home; where we find the two young ladies come home, and their patches off, I suppose Sir W. Pen do not allow of them in his sight, and going out of town to-night, though late, to Walthamstow. So to talk a little at Sir W. Batten's, and then home to supper, where I find Mrs. Hewer and her son, who have been abroad with my wife in the Park, and so after supper to read and then to bed. Sir W. Pen did give me an account this afternoon of his design of buying Sir Robert Brooke's fine house at Wansted; which I so wondered at, and did give him reasons against it, which he allowed of: and told me that he did intend to pull down the house and build a less, and that he should get £1,500 by the old house, and I know not what fooleries. But I will never believe he ever intended to buy it, for my part;[2] though he troubled Mr. Gawden to go and look upon it, and advise him in it.

2nd. To the office, where all the morning. At noon home to dinner, and then abroad to my Lord Treasurer's, who continues so ill as not to be troubled with business.

[1] Margaret Lowther, afterwards the wife of Captain Sir John Holmes. —B.

[2] Pepys's conjecture proved right. The house was not sold till Sir R. Brookes's death, when his heirs alienated it to Sir Josiah Child. Sir R. Child rebuilt it in 1715, and the Earl of Mornington took it down in 1823.

So Mr. Gawden and I to my Lord Ashly's and spoke with him, and then straight home, and there I did much business at the office, and then to my own chamber and did the like there, to my great content, but to the pain of my eyes, and then to supper and to bed, having a song with my wife with great pleasure, she doing it well.

3rd. Up, and with Sir J. Minnes, [Sir] W. Batten, and [Sir] W. Pen in the last man's coach to St. James's, and thence up to the Duke of York's chamber, which, as it is now fretted at the top, and the chimney-piece made handsome, is one of the noblest and best-proportioned rooms that ever, I think, I saw in my life, and when ready, into his closet and did our business, where, among other things, we had a proposition of Mr. Pierce's, for being continued in pay, or something done for him, in reward of his pains as Chyrurgeon-Generall; forasmuch as Troutbecke,[1] that was never a doctor before, hath got £200 a year settled on him for nothing but that one voyage with the Duke of Albemarle. The Duke of York and the whole company did shew most particular kindness to Mr. Pierce, every body moving for him, and the Duke himself most, that he is likely to be a very great man, I believe. Here also we had another mention of Carcasse's business, and we directed to bring in a report of our opinion of his case, which vexes us that such a rogue shall make us so much trouble. Thence I presently to the Excise Office, and there met the Cofferer and [Sir] Stephen Fox by agreement, and agreed upon a method for our future payments, and then we three to my Lord Treasurer, who continues still very ill. I had taken my stone with me on purpose, and Sir Philip Warwicke carried it in to him to see, but was not in a condition to talk with me about it, poor man. So I with them to Westminster by coach; the Cofferer[2] telling us odd stories

[1] John Troughtback (or Troutbeck) served as a surgeon in Lambert's army, but joined Monk in Scotland in 1659. He was appointed chief-surgeon to the king in 1660, was also surgeon to the Duke of Albemarle's troop of His Majesty's Life Guard, and was granted in 1667 a pension of £200 a year for his services. He married in 1665 (second wife), Frances Wray, widow of Sir Christopher Wray, fourth baronet of Glentworth (Dalton's "English Army Lists," 1661–1714, vol. i., p. 3).

[2] William Ashburnham (died 1679). See December 14th, 1666.

how he was dealt with by the men of the Church at Westminster in taking a lease of them at the King's coming in,[1] and particularly the devilish covetousness of Dr. Bushby.[2] Sir Stephen Fox, in discourse, told him how he is selling some land he hath, which yields him not above three per cent., if so much, and turning it into money, which he can put out at ten per cent.; and, as times go, if they be like to continue, it is the best way for me to keep money going so, for aught I see. I to Westminster Hall, and there took a turn with my old acquaintance Mr. Pechell, whose red nose, makes me ashamed to be seen with him, though otherwise a good-natured man. So away, I not finding of Mr. Moore, with whom I should have met and spoke about a letter I this day received from him from my Lord Hinchingbroke, wherein he desires me to help him to £1,900 to pay a bill of exchange of his father's, which troubles me

[1] The lease here mentioned was that of the famous Ashburnham House in the Cloisters. The lease was purchased by the Crown of John, Earl of Ashburnham, in 1730, and the Cottonian Library was deposited in the house. In 1731 the disastrous fire occurred there which consumed so many treasures, and injured others. Ashburnham House passed to Westminster School in 1881 in fee simple, in pursuance of the Public Schools Act, 31 and 32 Vict., cap. 118. A view of the fine staircase, still existing in old Ashburnham House, is given in Britton and Brayley's "Public Buildings."

[2] Richard Busby, D.D. (1606–1695), the famous head-master of Westminster School. In July, 1660, he was installed as Prebendary of Westminster, and in the following August he became canon residentiary and treasurer of Wells. It would be impossible to find a more inappropriate expression to apply to Busby than "devilish covetousness." He was one of the most charitable of men; and as one instance of this out of many, Mr. J. Sargeaunt, Master at Westminster School, tells the editor that he finds from Busby's accounts that between February, 1656–57, and the end of the following October, out of a total expenditure of about £670, more than £200 went in direct charity and in repairing the school buildings and the houses which he occupied as prebendary and master. In another year he spent at least a tenth of total expenditure in direct charity. Mr. Sargeaunt adds, "His benefactions to Christ Church were large, and to Wells Cathedral not small. Some works in the Abbey he did at his own expense, as well as works at Willen and in other places. By his will he left practically the whole of his property for charitable uses." It must be remembered in respect to the Cofferer's scandalous charge that buyer and seller are seldom of one mind, and that the Dean and Chapter of Westminster Abbey might quite justly take a different view from that held by William Ashburnham.

much, but I will find some way, if I can do it, but not to bring myself in bonds or disbursements for it, whatever comes of it. So home to dinner, where my wife hath ceux là upon her and is very ill with them, and so forced to go to bed, and I sat by her a good while, then down to my chamber and made an end of Rycaut's History of the Turks, which is a very good book. Then to the office, and did some business, and then my wife being pretty well, by coach to little Michell's, and there saw my poor Betty and her little child, which slept so soundly we could hardly wake it in an hour's time without hurting it, and they tell me what I did not know, that a child (as this do) will hunt and hunt up and down with its mouth if you touch the cheek of it with your finger's end for a nipple, and fit its mouth for sucking, but this hath not sucked yet, she having no nipples. Here sat a while, and then my wife and I, it being a most curious clear evening, after some rain to-day, took a most excellent tour by coach to Bow, and there drank and back again, and so a little at the office, and home to read a little, and to supper and bed mightily refreshed with this evening's tour, but troubled that it hath hindered my doing some business which I would have done at the office. This day the newes is come that the fleete of the Dutch, of about 20 ships, which come upon our coast upon design to have intercepted our colliers, but by good luck failed, is gone to the Frith,[1] and there lies, perhaps to trouble the Scotch privateers, which have galled them of late very much, it may be more than all our last year's fleete.

4th. Up and to the office, where sat all the morning, among other things a great conflict I had with Sir W. Warren, he bringing a letter to the Board, flatly in words charging them with their delays in passing his accounts, which have been with them these two years, part of which I said was not true, and the other undecent. The whole Board was concerned to take notice of it, as well as myself, but none of them had the honour to do it, but suffered me to do it alone, only Sir W. Batten, who did what he did out of common spite to him. So I writ in the margin of the letter, "Returned as untrue," and, by consent of the

[1] Frith of Forth. See 5th of this month.

Board, did give it him again, and so parted. Home to dinner, and there came a woman whose husband I sent for, one Fisher, about the business of Perkins and Carcasse, and I do think by her I shall find the business as bad as ever it was, and that we shall find Commissioner Pett a rogue, using foul play on behalf of Carcasse. After dinner to the office again, and there late all the afternoon, doing much business, and with great content home to supper and to bed.

5th (Lord's day). Up, and going down to the water side, I met Sir John Robinson, and so with him by coach to White Hall, still a vain, prating, boasting man as any I know, as if the whole City and Kingdom had all its work done by him. He tells me he hath now got a street ordered to be continued, forty feet broad, from Paul's through Cannon Street to the Tower, which will be very fine. He and others this day, where I was in the afternoon, do tell me of at least six or eight fires within these few days; and continually stirs of fires, and real fires there have been, in one place or other, almost ever since the late great fire, as if there was a fate sent people for fire. I walked over the Park to Sir W. Coventry's. Among other things to tell him what I hear of people being forced to sell their bills before September for 35 and 40 per cent. loss, and what is worst, that there are some courtiers that have made a knot to buy them, in hopes of some ways to get money of the King to pay them, which Sir W. Coventry is amazed at, and says we are a people made up for destruction, and will do what he can to prevent all this by getting the King to provide wherewith to pay them. We talked of Tangier, of which he is ashamed; also that it should put the King to this charge for no good in the world: and now a man going over that is a good soldier, but a debauched man, which the place need not to have. And so used these words: "That this place was to the King as my Lord Carnarvon [1] says of wood, that it is an excrescence of the earth provided by God for the payment of debts." Thence away to Sir

[1] Charles Dormer, second Earl of Carnarvon. Died, s. p., November 29th, 1709. His father, Robert, first earl, was killed at the battle of Newbury, September 20th, 1643, fighting under the royal banner.

G. Carteret, whom I find taking physic. I staid talking with him but a little, and so home to church, and heard a dull sermon, and most of the best women of our parish gone into the country, or at least not at church. So home, and find my boy not there, nor was at church, which vexed me, and when he come home I enquired, he tells me he went to see his mother. I send him back to her to send me some token that he was with her. So there come a man with him back of good fashion. He says he saw him with her, which pacified me, but I did soundly threaten him before him, and so to dinner, and then had a little scolding with my wife for not being fine enough to go to the christening to-day, which she excused by being ill, as she was indeed, and cried, but I was in an ill humour and ashamed, indeed, that she should not go dressed. However, friends by and by, and we went by water to Michell's, and there his little house full of his father and mothers and the kindred, hardly any else, and mighty merry in this innocent company, and Betty mighty pretty in bed, but, her head akeing, not very merry, but the company mighty merry, and I with them, and so the child was christened; my wife, his father, and her mother, the witnesses, and the child's name Elizabeth. So we had gloves and wine and wafers, very pretty, and talked and tattled, and so we away by water and up with the tide, she and I and Barker, as high as Barne Elmes, it being a fine evening, and back again to pass the bridges at standing water between 9 and 10 at night, and then home and to supper, and then to bed with much pleasure. This day Sir W. Coventry tells me the Dutch fleete shot some shot, four or five hundred, into Burnt-Island in the Frith, but without any hurt; and so are gone.[1]

[1] Burntisland, a seaport of Fife on the Frith of Forth, five miles north of Granton. April 30th, 1667: "The Dutch sounded the coast, but Gen. Dalziell cut the beacon at the extreme of Leith harbour, so that they were confused, and battered Burntisland with 1,000 shot, the town returned it from 20 pieces of cannon, and in less than two hours 10,000 were in arms at Burntisland, and as many at Leith, whither more than 6,000 citizens of Edinburgh are gone; the citadel is planted with 30 pieces of cannon, which fired to invite the enemy; the country came up in multitudes. The magistrates of Leith sunk a ship in the mouth of the harbour, and planted 20 cannon on high, whereby a fire-ship that

6th. Up and angry with my mayds for letting in watermen, and I know not who, anybody that they are acquainted with, into my kitchen to talk and prate with them, which I will not endure. Then out and by coach to my Lord Treasurer's, who continues still very ill, then to Sir Ph. Warwicke's house, and there did a little business about my Tangier tallies, and so to Westminster Hall, and there to the Exchequer to consult about some way of getting our poor Creditors of the Navy (who served in their goods before the late Session of Parliament) paid out of the 11 months tax, which seems to relate only for goods to be then served in, and I think I have found out a way to bring them into the Act, which, if it do, I shall think a good service done. Thence by coach home with Captain Cocke, in our way talking of my Lord Bruncker and his Lady, who are mighty angry with us all of the office, about Carcasse's business, but especially with me, and in great confidence he bids me have a care of him, for he hath said that he would wound me with the person where my greatest interest is. I suppose he means Sir W. Coventry, and therefore I will beware of him, and am glad, though vexed to hear it. So home to dinner, where Creed come, whom I vexed devilishly with telling him a wise man, and good friend of his and mine, did say that he lately went into the country to Hinchingbroke; and, at his coming to town again, hath shifted his lodgings, only to avoid paying to the Poll Bill, which is so true that he blushed, and could not in words deny it, but the fellow did think to have not had it discovered. He is so devilish a subtle false rogue, that I am really weary and afeard of his company, and therefore after dinner left him in the house, and to my office, where busy all the afternoon despatching much business, and in the evening to Sir R. Viner's to adjust accounts there, and so home, where some of our old Navy creditors come to me by my direction to consider of what I have invented for their help as I have said in the morning, and like it mighty well, and so I to the office, where busy late, then home to supper and sing with my wife, who do begin to give me real pleasure with her singing, and so to bed.

tried to slip in was prevented. They are now gone, it is supposed to Shetland" ("Calendar of State Papers," 1667, p. 62).

7th. Up betimes, and by coach to St. James's; but there find Sir W. Coventry gone out betimes this morning, on horseback, with the King and Duke of York, to Putney-heath, to run some horses, and so back again to the office, where some witnesses from Chatham which I sent for are come up, and do give shrewd testimonies against Carcasse, which put my Lord into a new flame, and he and I to high words, and so broke up. Then home to dinner, where W. Hewer dined with us, and he and I after dinner to discourse of Carcasse's business, wherein I apparently now do manage it wholly against my Lord Bruncker, Sir W. Pen, like a false rogue, shrinking out of the collar, Sir J. Minnes, a fool, being easily led either way, and Sir W. Batten, a malicious fellow that is not able to defend any thing, so that the whole odium must fall on me, which I will therefore beware how I manage that I may not get enemies to no purpose. It vexes me to see with what a company I am mixed, but then it pleases me to see that I am reckoned the chief mover among them, as they do confess and esteem me in every thing. Thence to the office, and did business, and then by coach to St. James's again, but [Sir] W. Coventry not within, so I wrote something to him, and then straight back again and to Sir W. Batten's, and there talked with him and [Sir] J. Minnes, who are mighty hot in Carcasse's business, but their judgment's not to be trusted. However, I will go through with it, or otherwise we shall be all slaves to my Lord Bruncker and his man's impudence. So to the office a little, and then home to supper and to bed, after hearing my wife sing, who is manifestly come to be more musical in her eare than ever I thought she could have been made, which rejoices me to the heart, for I take great delight now to hear her sing.

8th. Up pretty betimes and out of doors, and in Fen Church street met Mr. Lovett going with a picture to me, but I could not stand to discourse or see it, but on to the next hackney coach and so to Sir W. Coventry, where he and I alone a while discoursing of some businesses of the office, and then up to the Duke of York to his chamber with my fellow brethren who are come, and so did our usual weekly business, which was but little to-day, and I was glad that the business of Carcasse was not mentioned because our report was not ready, but I am resolved it shall against the next coming to the Duke of York. Here was discourse about a way of paying our old creditors which did please me, there being hopes of getting them comprehended within the 11 months Tax, and this did give occasion for Sir G. Carteret's and my going to Sir Robert Long to discourse it, who do agree that now the King's Council do say that they may be included in the Act, which do make me very glad, not so much for the sake of the poor men as for the King, for it would have been a ruin to him and his service not to have had a way to have paid the debt. There parted with Sir G. Carteret and into Westminster Hall, where I met with Sir H. Cholmly, and he and I to Sir Ph. Warwicke's to speak a little about our Tangier business, but to little purpose, my Lord Treasurer being so ill that no business can be done. Thence with Sir H. Cholmly to find out Creed from one lodging to another, which he hath changed so often that there is no finding him, but at last do come to his lodging that he is entering into this day, and do find his goods unlading at the door, by Scotland Yard, and there I set down Sir H. Cholmly, and I away to the 'Change, where spoke about several things, and then going home did meet Mr. Andrews our neighbour, and did speak with him to enquire about the ground behind our house, of which I have a mind to buy enough to make a stable and coach-house; for I do see that my condition do require it, as well as that it is more charge to my purse to live as I do than to keep one, and therefore I am resolved before winter to have one, unless some extraordinary thing happens to hinder me. He promises me to look after it for me, and so I home to dinner, where I find my wife's flageolette master, and I am so pleased with her proceeding, though she hath lost time by not practising, that I am resolved for the encouragement of the man to learn myself a little for a month or so, for I do foresee if God send my wife and I to live, she will become very good company for me. He gone, comes Lovett with my little print of my dear Lady Castlemayne varnished, and the frame prettily done like gold, which pleases me well. He dined with me, but by his discourse I do still see that he is a man of good wit but most strange experience, and acquaintance with all manner of subtleties and tricks, that I do think him not fit for me to keep any acquaintance with him, lest he some time or other shew me a slippery trick. After dinner, he gone, I to the office, where all the afternoon very busy, and so in the evening to Sir R. Viner's, thinking to finish my accounts there, but am prevented, and so back again home, and late at my office at business, and so home to supper and sing a little with my dear wife, and so to bed.

9th. Up, and to the office, and at noon home to dinner, and then with my wife and Barker by coach, and left them at Charing Cross, and I to St. James's, and there found Sir W. Coventry alone in his chamber, and sat and talked with him more than I have done a great while of several things of the Navy, how our debts and wants do unfit us for doing any thing. He tells me he hears stories of Commissioner Pett, of selling timber to the Navy under other names,[1] which I told him I believe is true, and did give him an instance. He told me also how his clerk Floyd[2] he hath put away for his common idlenesse and ill company, and particularly that yesterday he was found not able to come and attend him, by being run into the arme in a squabble, though he pretends it was done in the streets by strangers, at nine at night, by the Maypole in the Strand. Sir W. Coventry did write to me this morning to recommend him another, which I could find in my heart to do W. Hewer for his good; but do believe he will not part with me, nor have I any mind to let him go. I would my brother were fit for it, I would adventure him there. He insists upon an unmarried man, that can write well, and hath French enough to transcribe it only from a copy, and may write shorthand, if it may be. Thence with him to my Lord Chancellor at Clarendon House,[3] to a Committee for

[1] Commissioner Pett wrote from Chatham, on May 24th, to the Navy Commissioners in answer to some of these charges respecting the sale of timber ("Calendar of State Papers," 1667, p. 116).

[2] Phil. Lloyd styles himself servant to Sir William Coventry, April, 1667 ("Calendar," 1667, p. 10).

[3] See note, vol. iv., p. 334. "One unpopular act of his [Clarendon] is not to be forgot, because it had a great influence in a short time, and this was the building a very stately large house by the *Park*, called *Clarendon House*, which, in a little time, obtained the name of *Dunkirk House*, as though it had been built by the money taken for the

Tangier, where several things spoke of and proceeded on, and particularly sending Commissioners thither before the new Governor goes, which I think will signify as much good as any thing else that hath been done about the place, which is none at all. I did again tell them the badness of their credit by the time their tallies took before they become payable, and their spending more than their fund. They seem well satisfied with what I said, and I am glad that I may be remembered that I do tell them the case plain; but it troubled me that I see them hot upon it, that the Governor shall not be paymaster, which will force me either to the providing one there to do it (which I will never undertake), or leave the employment, which I had rather do. Mightily pleased with the noblenesse of this house, and the brave furniture and pictures, which indeed is very noble, and, being broke up, I with Sir G. Carteret in his coach into Hide Park, to discourse of things, and spent an hour in this manner with great pleasure, telling me all his concernments, and how he is gone through with the purchase for my Lady Jemimah and her husband; how the Treasury is like to come into the hands of a Committee; but that not that, nor anything else, will do our business, unless the King himself will mind his business, and how his servants do execute their parts; he do fear an utter ruin in the state, and that in a little time, if the King do not mind his business soon; that the King is very kind to him, and to my Lord Sandwich, and that he doubts not but at his coming home, which he expects about Michaelmas, he will be very well received. But it is pretty strange how he began again the business of the intention of a marriage of my Lord Hinchingbroke to a daughter of my Lord Burlington's[1] to my Lord Chancellor, which he now tells me as a great secret, when he told it me the last Sunday

sale of that place. This house was built in the Chancellor's absence in the plague year, principally at the charge of the Vintners' Company, who, designing to monopolize his favour, made it abundantly more large and magnificent than ever he intended or desired. And I have been assured by an unquestionable hand, that when he came to see the case of that house, he rather submitted than consented, and, with a sigh, said, 'This house will one day be my ruin.'" — Echard, vol. iii., p. 192.

[1] See *ante*, April 29th.

but one; but it may be the poor man hath forgot, and I do believe he do make it a secret, he telling me that he has not told it to any but myself, and this day to his daughter my Lady Jemimah, who looks to lie down about two months hence. After all this discourse we turned back and to White Hall, where we parted, and I took up my wife at Unthanke's, and so home, and in our street, at the Three Tuns' Tavern[1] door, I find a great hubbub; and what was it but two brothers have fallen out, and one killed the other. And who should they be but the two Fieldings; one whereof, Bazill, was page to my Lady Sandwich; and he hath killed the other,[2] himself being very drunk, and so is sent to Newgate. I to the office and did as much business as my eyes would let me, and so home to supper and to bed.

10th. Up and to the office, where a meeting about the Victuallers' accounts all the morning, and at noon all of us to Kent's, at the Three Tuns' Tavern, and there dined well at Mr. Gawden's charge; and there the constable of the parish did show us the picklocks and dice that were found in the dead man's pocket, and but 18*d.* in money; and a table-book, wherein were entered the names of several places where he was to go; and among others Kent's house, where he was to dine, and did dine yesterday: and after dinner went into the church, and there saw his corpse with the wound in his left breast; a sad spectacle, and a broad wound, which makes my hand now shake to write of it. His brother intending, it seems, to kill the coachman, who did not please him, this fellow stepped in, and took away his sword; who thereupon took out his knife, which was of the fashion, with a falchion blade, and a little cross at the hilt like a dagger; and with that stabbed him. So to the office again, very busy, and in the evening to Sir Robert Viner's, and there took up all my notes and evened our balance to the 7th of this month, and saw it

[1] There are two tokens of "The Three Tuns Tavern in Crutched Friars" ("Boyne's Tokens," ed. Williamson, vol. i., p. 581).

[2] It was Basil who was killed. He was the fourth son of George Fielding, Earl of Desmond, whose eldest son William succeeded his father as second Earl of Desmond in 1666, and his uncle Basil as third Earl of Denbigh in 1675.

entered in their ledger, and took a receipt for the remainder of my money as the balance of an account then adjusted. Then to my Lord Treasurer's, but missed Sir Ph. Warwicke, and so back again, and drove hard towards Clerkenwell,[1] thinking to have overtaken my Lady Newcastle, whom I saw before us in her coach, with 100 boys and girls running looking upon her: but I could not: and so she got home before I could come up to her. But I will get a time to see her. So to the office and did more business, and then home and sang with pleasure with my wife, and to supper and so to bed.

11th. Up, and being called on by Mr. Commander, he and I out to the ground behind Sir W. Pen's, where I am resolved to take a lease of some of it for a stable and coach [house], and so to keep a coach, unless some change come before I can do it, for I do see it is a greater charge to me now in hackneys, and I am a little dishonoured by going in them. We spoke with him that hath the letting it, and I do believe when I can tell how much it will be fit for me to have we shall go near to agree. So home, and there found my door open, which makes me very angry with Nell, and do think to put her away for it, though it do so go against me to part with a servant that it troubles me more than anything in the world. So to the office, where all the morning. At noon home to dinner, where Mr. Goodgroome and Creed, and I have great hopes that my wife will come to sing to my mind. After dinner my wife and Creed and I being entered a hackney coach to go to the other end of the town, we espied The. Turner coming in her coach to see us, which we were surprised at, and so 'light and took her and another young lady home, and there sat and talked with The., she being lately come out of the North after two or three years absence. She is come to put out her sister and brothers to school at Putney. After a little talk, I over Tower Hill with them to a lady's they go to visit, and so away with my wife, whose being dressed this day in fair hair did make me so mad, that I

[1] At Newcastle House, Clerkenwell Close, the duke and duchess lived in great state. The house was divided, and let in tenements in the eighteenth century.

spoke not one word to her in our going, though I was ready to burst with anger. So to White Hall to the Committee of Tangier, where they were discoursing about laws for the civil government of the place, but so dull and so little to the purpose that I fell to slumber, when the fear of being seen by Sir W. Coventry did trouble me much afterwards, but I hope he did not. After that broke up. Creed and I into the Park, and walked, a most pleasant evening, and so took coach, and took up my wife, and in my way home discovered my trouble to my wife for her white locks,[1] swearing by God, several times, which I pray God forgive me for, and bending my fist, that I would not endure it. She, poor wretch,[2] was surprized with it, and made me no answer all the way home; but there we parted, and I to the office late, and then home, and without supper to bed, vexed.

12th (Lord's day). Up, and to my chamber, to settle some accounts there, and by and by down comes my wife to me in her night-gown, and we begun calmly, that upon having money to lace her gown for second mourning, she would promise to wear white locks no more in my sight, which I, like a severe fool, thinking not enough, begun to except against, and made her fly out to very high terms and cry, and in her heat told me of keeping company with Mrs. Knipp, saying, that if I would promise never to see her more — of whom she hath more reason to suspect than I had heretofore of Pembleton — she would never wear white locks more. This vexed me, but I restrained myself from saying anything, but do think never to see this woman — at least, to have her here more, but by and by I did give

[1] Randle Holmes says the ladies wore "false locks set on wyres, to make them stand at a distance from the head," and accompanies the information with the figure of a lady "with a pair of locks and curls which were in great fashion in 1670" (Planché's "Cyclopædia of Costume," vol. i., p. 248).

[2] A new light is thrown upon this favourite expression of Pepys's when speaking of his wife by the following quotation from a Midland word-book: "Wretch, *n.*, often used as an expression of endearment or sympathy. *Old Woman to Young Master:* 'An' 'ow is the missis to-day, *poor wretch?*' Of a boy going to school a considerable distance off: 'I met 'im with a bit o' bread in 'is bag, *poor wretch*'" ("A Glossary of Words and Phrases used in S.E. Worcestershire," by Jesse Salisbury. Published by the English Dialect Society, 1894).

her money to buy lace, and she promised to wear no more white locks while I lived, and so all very good friends as ever, and I to my business, and she to dress herself. Against noon we had a coach ready for us, and she and I to White Hall, where I went to see whether Sir G. Carteret was at dinner or no, our design being to make a visit there, and I found them set down, which troubled me, for I would not then go up, but back to the coach to my wife, and she and I homeward again, and in our way bethought ourselves of going alone, she and I, to go to a French house to dinner, and so enquired out Monsieur Robins, my perriwigg-maker, who keeps an ordinary, and in an ugly street in Covent Garden, did find him at the door, and so we in; and in a moment almost had the table covered, and clean glasses, and all in the French manner, and a mess of potage first, and then a couple of pigeons a la esterve, and then a piece of bœuf-a-la-mode, all exceeding well seasoned, and to our great liking; at least it would have been anywhere else but in this bad street, and in a perriwigg-maker's house; but to see the pleasant and ready attendance that we had, and all things so desirous to please, and ingenious in the people, did take me mightily. Our dinner cost us 6*s*., and so my wife and I away to Islington, it being a fine day, and thence to Sir G. Whitmore's house, where we 'light, and walked over the fields to Kingsland, and back again; a walk, I think, I have not taken these twenty years; but puts me in mind of my boy's time, when I boarded at Kingsland, and used to shoot with my bow and arrows in these fields. A very pretty place it is; and little did any of my friends think I should come to walk in these fields in this condition and state that I am. Then took coach again, and home through Shoreditch; and at home my wife finds Barker to have been abroad, and telling her so many lies about it that she struck her, and the wench said she would not stay with her: so I examined the wench, and found her in so many lies myself, that I was glad to be rid of her, and so resolved having her go away to-morrow. So my wife and W. Hewer and I to supper, and then he and I to my chamber to begin the draught of the report from this office to the Duke of York in the case of Mr. Carcasse, which I sat up till midnight to do, and then to bed, believing it necessary to have it done, and to do it plainly, for it is not to be endured the trouble that this rascal hath put us to, and the disgrace he hath brought upon this office.

13th. Up, and when ready, to the office (my wife rising to send away Barker, according to our resolution last night, and she did do it with more clothes than have cost us £10, and 20*s*. in her purse, which I did for the respect I bear Mr. Falconbridge, otherwise she had not deserved half of it, but I am the more willing to do it to be rid of one that made work and trouble in the house, and had not qualities of any honour or pleasure to me or my family, but what is a strange thing did always declare to her mistress and others that she had rather be put to drudgery and to wash the house than to live as she did like a gentlewoman), and there I and Gibson all the morning making an end of my report against Carcasse, which I think will do our business, but it is a horrid shame such a rogue should give me and all of us this trouble. This morning come Sir H. Cholmly to me for a tally or two; and tells me that he hears that we are by agreement to give the King of France Nova Scotia, which he do not like: but I do not know the importance of it.[1] Then abroad with my wife to my Lord Treasurer's, and she to her tailor's. I find Sir Philip Warwicke, who I perceive do give over my Lord Treasurer for a man of this world, his pain being grown great again upon him, and all the rest he hath is by narcotiques, and now Sir Philip Warwicke do please himself, like a good man, to tell some of the good ejaculations of my Lord Treasurer concerning the little worth of this world, to buy it with so much pain, and other things fit for a dying man. So finding no business likely to be done here for Tangier, I having a warrant for tallies to be signed, I away to the New Exchange, and there staid a little, and then to a looking-glass shop to

[1] Nova Scotia and the adjoining countries were called by the French Acadie. Pepys is not the only official personage whose ignorance of Nova Scotia is on record. A story is current of a prime minister [Duke of Newcastle] who was surprised at hearing Cape Breton was an island. "Egad, I'll go tell the King Cape Breton is an island!" Of the same it is said, that when told Annapolis was in danger, and ought to be defended: "Oh! certainly Annapolis must be defended, — where is Annapolis?" — B.

consult about covering the wall in my closet over my chimney, which is darkish, with looking-glasses, and then to my wife's tailor's, but find her not ready to go home, but got to buy things, and so I away home to look after my business and finish my report of Carcasse, and then did get Sir W. Batten, Sir J. Minnes, and [Sir] W. Pen together, and read it over with all the many papers relating to the business, which they do wonder at, and the trouble I have taken about it, and like the report, so as that they do unanimously resolve to sign it, and stand by it, and after a great deal of discourse of the strange deportment of my Lord Bruncker in this business to withstand the whole board in behalf of such an impudent rogue as this is, I parted, and home to my wife, and supped and talked with her, and then to bed, resolving to rise betimes to-morrow to write fair the report.

14th. Up by 5 o'clock, and when ready down to my chamber, and there with Mr. Fist, Sir W. Batten's clerk, who writes mighty well, writing over our report in Mr. Carcasse's business, in which we continued till 9 o'clock, that the office met, and then to the office, where all the morning, and so at noon home to dinner, where Mr. Holliard come and eat with us, who among other things do give me good hopes that we shall give my father some ease as to his rupture when he comes to town, which I expect to-morrow. After dinner comes Fist, and he and I to our report again till 4 o'clock, and then by coach to my Lord Chancellor's, where I met Mr. Povy, expecting the coming of the rest of the Commissioners for Tangier. Here I understand how the two Dukes, both the only sons of the Duke of York, are sick even to danger, and that on Sunday last they were both so ill, as that the poor Duchess was in doubt which would die first: the Duke of Cambridge of some general disease; the other little Duke,[1] whose title I know not, of the convulsion fits, of which he had four this morning. Fear that either of them might be dead, did make us think that it was the occasion that the Duke of York and others were not come to the meeting of the Commission which was designed, and my Lord Chancellor did expect. And

[1] Charles Stuart, third son of the Duke of York, born July 4th, 1666; created Duke of Kendal, October 31st, 1666; and died May 22nd, 1667.

it was pretty to observe how, when my Lord sent down to St. James's to see why the Duke of York come not, and Mr. Povy, who went, returned, my Lord (Chancellor) did ask, not how the Princes or the Dukes do, as other people do, but "How do the children?" which methought was mighty great, and like a great man and grandfather. I find every body mightily concerned for these children, as a matter wherein the State is much concerned that they should live. At last it was found that the meeting did fail from no known occasion, at which my Lord Chancellor was angry, and did cry out against Creed that he should give him no notice. So Povy and I went forth, and staid at the gate of the house by the streete, and there stopped to talk about the business of the Treasury of Tangier, which by the badness of our credit, and the resolution that the Governor shall not be paymaster, will force me to provide one there to be my paymaster, which I will never do, but rather lose my place, for I will not venture my fortune to a fellow to be employed so far off, and in that wicked place. Thence home, and with Fist presently to the finishing the writing fair of our report. And by and by to Sir W. Batten's, and there he and I and [Sir] J. Minnes and [Sir] W. Pen did read and sign it with great good liking, and so away to the office again to look over and correct it, and then home to supper and to bed, my mind being pretty well settled, having this report done, and so to supper and to bed.

15th. [This morning my wife had some things brought home by a new woman of the New Exchange, one Mrs. Smith, which she would have me see for her fine hand, and indeed it is a fine hand, and the woman I observed is a mighty pretty looked woman.[1]] Up, and with Sir W. Batten and [Sir] J. Minnes to St. James's, and stopt at Temple Bar for Sir J. Minnes to go into the Devil's Taverne to shit, he having drunk whey, and his belly wrought. Being come, we up to the Duke of York's chamber, who, when ready, we to our usual business, and being very glad, we all that signed it, that is, Sir J. Minnes, W. Batten, W. Pen, and myself, and then Sir G. Carteret and [Sir] W. Coventry, Bruncker, and T. Harvy, and the officers of the Ordnance,

[1] The passage between brackets is written in the margin of the MS.

Sir J. Duncombe, and Mr. Cholmely presented our report about Carcasse, and did afterwards read it with that success that the Duke of York was for punishing him, not only with turning him out of the office, but with what other punishment he could, which nobody did forward, and so he escaped, only with giving security to secure the King against double tickets of his and other things that he might have wronged the King or subject in before his dismission. Yet, Lord! to see how our silly Lord Bruncker would have stood to have justified this rogue, though to the reproach of all us who have signed, which I shall never forget to have been a most malicious or a most silly act, and I do think it is as much the latter as the other, for none but a fool could have done as this silly Lord hath done in this business. So the Duke of York did like our report, and ordered his being secured till he did give his security, which did fully content me, and will I hope vindicate the office. It happened that my Lord Arlington coming in by chance was at the hearing of all this, which I was not sorry for, for he did move or did second the Duke of York that this roguery of his might be put in the News-book that it might be made publique to satisfy for the wrong the credit of this office hath received by this rogue's occasion. So with utmost content I away with Sir G. Carteret to London, talking all the way; and he do tell me that the business of my Lord Hinchingbroke his marriage with my Lord Burlington's daughter is concluded on by all friends; and that my Lady is now told of it, and do mightily please herself with it; which I am mighty glad of. So home, and there I find that my wife hath been at my desire at the Inne, thinking that my father might be come up with the coach, but he is not come this week, poor man, but will be here the next. At noon to dinner, and then to Sir W. Batten's, where I hear the news how our Embassadors were but ill received at Flushing, nor at Bredah itself, there being only a house and no furniture provided for them, though it be said that they have as much as the French. Here we staid talking a little, and then I to the office about my business, and thence to the office, where busy about my own papers of my office, and by and by comes the office full to examine Sir W. Warren's account, which I do appear mighty fierce in against him, and indeed am, for his accounts are so perplexed that I am sure he cannot but expect to get many a £1,000 in it before it passes our hands, but I will not favour him, but save what I can to the King. At his accounts, wherein I very high against him, till late, and then we broke up with little done, and so broke up, and I to my office, where late doing of business, and then home to supper and to bed. News still that my Lord Treasurer is so ill as not to be any man of this world; and it is said that the Treasury shall be managed by Commission. I would to God Sir G. Carteret, or my Lord Sandwich, be in it! But the latter is the more fit for it. This day going to White Hall, Sir W. Batten did tell me strange stories of Sir W. Pen, how he is already ashamed of the fine coach which his son-in-law and daughter have made, and indeed it is one of the most ridiculous things for people of their low, mean fashion to make such a coach that ever I saw. He tells me how his people come as they do to mine every day to borrow one thing or other, and that his Lady hath been forced to sell some coals (in the late dear time) only to enable her to pay money that she hath borrowed of Griffin to defray her family expense, which is a strange story for a rogue that spends so much money on clothes and other occasions himself as he do, but that which is most strange, he tells me that Sir W. Pen do not give £6,000, as is usually [supposed], with his daughter to him, and that Mr. Lowder is come to use the tubb, that is to bathe and sweat himself, and that his lady is come to use the tubb too, which he takes to be that he hath, and hath given her the pox, but I hope it is not so, but, says Sir W. Batten, this is a fair joynture, that he hath made her, meaning by that the costs the having of a bath.

16th. Up, and to the office, where we sat all the morning, and, among other things, comes in Mr. Carcasse, and after many arguings against it, did offer security as was desired, but who should this be but Mr. Powell, that is one other of my Lord Bruncker's clerks, and I hope good use will be made of it. But then he began to fall foul upon the injustice of the Board, which when I heard I threatened him with being laid by the heels, which my Lord Bruncker took up as a thing that I could not do upon the occasion he had given, but yet did own that it was ill said of him. I made not many words of it, but have let him see that I can say what I will without fear of him, and so we broke off, leaving the bond to be drawn by me, which I will do in the best manner I can. At noon, this being Holy Thursday, that is, Ascension Day, when the boys go on procession round the parish, we were to go to the Three Tuns' Tavern, to dine with the rest of the parish; where all the parish almost was, Sir Andrew Rickard and others; and of our house, J. Minnes, W. Batten, W. Pen, and myself; and Mr. Mills did sit uppermost at the table. Here we were informed that the report of our Embassadors being ill received in their way to Bredah is not true, but that they are received with very great civility, which I am glad to hear. But that that did vex me was that among all us there should come in Mr. Carcasse to be a guest for his money (5*s*. a piece) as well as any of us. This did vex me, and I would have gone, and did go to my house, thinking to dine at home, but I was called away from them, and so we sat down, and to dinner. Among other things Sir John Fredericke[1] and Sir R. Ford did talk of Paul's School, which, they tell me, must be taken away; and then I fear it will be long before another place, as they say is promised, is found; but they do say that the honour of their company[2] is concerned in the doing of it, and that it is a thing that they are obliged to do. Thence home, and to my office, where busy; anon at 7 at night I and my wife and Sir W. Pen in his coach to Unthanke's, my wife's tailor, for her to speak one word, and then we to my Lord Treasurer's, where I find the porter crying, and suspected it was that my Lord is dead; and, poor Lord! we did find that he was dead just now; and the crying of the fellow did so trouble me, that considering I was not likely to trouble him any more, nor have occasion to give any more anything, I did

[1] Alderman Sir John Frederick, elected M.P. for the City of London, March, 1662–63; Lord Mayor of London, 1662, and President of Christ's Hospital. His eldest son, John, was created a baronet, 1723.

[2] The Mercers' Company, under whose superintendence St. Paul's School was placed by Dean Colet, the founder. The school remained in its old locality until 1880, when it was removed to West Kensington, and the schoolhouse pulled down.

give him 3*s.*; but it may be, poor man, he hath lost a considerable hope by the death of his Lord, whose house will be no more frequented as before, and perhaps I may never come thither again about any business. There is a good man gone: and I pray God that the Treasury may not be worse managed by the hand or hands it shall now be put into; though, for certain, the slowness, though he was of great integrity, of this man, and remissness, have gone as far to undo the nation, as anything else that hath happened; and yet, if I knew all the difficulties that he hath lain under, and his instrument Sir Philip Warwicke, I might be brought to another mind. Thence we to Islington, to the Old House, and there eat and drank, and then it being late and a pleasant evening, we home, and there to my chamber, and to bed. It is remarkable that this afternoon Mr. Moore come to me, and there, among other things, did tell me how Mr. Moyer,[1] the merchant, having procured an order from the King and Duke of York and Council, with the consent of my Lord Chancellor, and by assistance of Lord Arlington, for the releasing out of prison his brother, Samuel Moyer, who was a great man in the late times in Haberdashers'-hall, and was engaged under hand and seal to give the man that obtained it so much in behalf of my Lord Chancellor; but it seems my Lady Duchess of Albemarle had before undertaken it for so much money, but hath not done it. The Duke of Albemarle did the next day send for this Moyer, to tell him, that notwithstanding this order of the King and Council's being passed for release of his brother, yet, if he did not consider the pains of some friends of his, he would stop that order. This Moyer being an honest, bold man, told him that he was engaged to the hand that had done the thing to give him a reward; and more he would not give, nor could own any kindness done by his Grace's interest; and so parted. The next day Sir Edward Savage did take the said Moyer in tax about it, giving ill words of this Moyer and his brother; which he not being

[1] Lawrence Moyer, of Low Leyton, in Essex, whose son, of the same name, was afterwards Sir Samuel Moyer, Bart., and High Sheriff of Essex, in 1698. He had also been one of the Council of State. His widow, Rebecca, daughter of Alderman Sir William Joliffe, founded the well-known Lady Moyer's Lectures. — B.

able to bear, told him he would give to the person that had engaged him what he promised, and not any thing to any body else; and that both he and his brother were as honest men as himself, or any man else; and so sent him going, and bid him do his worst. It is one of the most extraordinary cases that ever I saw or understood; but it is true. This day Mr. Sheply is come to town and to see me, and he tells me my father is very well only for his pain, so that he is not able to stir, but is in great pain. I would to God that he were in town that I might have what help can be got for him, for it troubles me to have him live in that condition of misery if I can help it.

17th. Up, and to the office, where all the morning upon some accounts of Mr. Gawden's, and at noon to the Three Tuns to dinner with Lord Bruncker, Sir J. Minnes, W. Batten, W. Pen, and T. Harvy, where very merry, and my Lord Bruncker in appearance as good friends as ever, though I know he has a hatred to me in heart. After dinner to my house, where Mr. Sheply dined, and we drank and talked together. He, poor man, hath had his arm broke the late frost, slipping in going over Huntingdon Bridge. He tells me that Jasper Trice and Lewes Phillips and Mr. Ashfield are gone from Brampton, and he thinks chiefly from the height of Sir J. Bernard's carriage, who carries all things before him there, which they cannot bear with, and so leave the town, and this is a great instance of the advantage a man of the law hath over all other people, which would make a man to study it a little. Sheply being gone, there come the flageolet master, who having had a bad bargain of teaching my wife by the year, she not practising so much as she should do, I did think that the man did deserve some more consideration, and so will give him an opportunity of 20*s.* a month more, and he shall teach me, and this afternoon I begun, and I think it will be a few shillings well spent. Then to Sir R. Viner's with 600 pieces of gold to turn into silver, for the enabling me to answer Sir G. Carteret's £3,000; which he now draws all out of my hand towards the paying for a purchase he hath made for his son and my Lady Jemimah, in Northamptonshire,[1]

[1] An error for Bedfordshire. The place was Hawnes, which belonged to the Lukes of Cople, who, about 1654, had sold it to Sir Humphrey

of Sir Samuel Luke,[1] in a good place; a good house, and near all her friends; which is a very happy thing. Thence to St. James's, and there spoke with Sir W. Coventry, and give him some account of some things, but have little discourse with him, there being company with him, and so directly home again and then to my office, doing some business, and so to my house, and with my wife to practice on the flageolet a little, and with great pleasure I see she can readily hit her notes, but only want of practice makes her she cannot go through a whole tune readily. So to supper and to bed.

18th. Up, and all the morning at the office, and then to dinner, and after dinner to the office to dictate some letters, and then with my wife to Sir W. Turner's to visit The., but she being abroad we back again home, and then I to the office, finished my letters, and then to walk an hour in the garden talking with my wife, whose growth in musique do begin to please me mightily, and by and by home and there find our Luce drunk, and when her mistress told her of it would be gone, and so put up some of her things and did go away of her accord, nobody pressing her to it, and the truth is, though she be the dirtiest, homeliest servant that ever I kept, yet I was sorry to have her go, partly through my love to my servants, and partly because she was a very drudging, working wench, only she would be drunk. But that which did a little trouble me was that I did hear her tell her mistress that she would tell her master something before she was aware of her that she would be sorry to have him know; but did it in such a silly, drunken manner, that though it trouble me a little, yet not knowing what to suspect she should know, and not knowing well whether she said it to her mistress or Jane, I did not much think of it. So she gone, we to supper and to bed, my study being made finely clean.

Winch, from whom, and not directly from Sir Samuel Luke, Sir George Carteret purchased it in 1667. The son by this marriage was created Lord Carteret of Hawnes in 1681.—B.

[1] Sir Samuel Luke, eldest son of Sir Oliver Luke, of Woodend, Beds. He belonged to the Presbyterian party, and appears to have been a stout soldier. He was referred to by a contemporary as "Great-spirited little Sir Samuel Luke." He was knighted in 1624, and died in 1670; buried at Cople, in Beds, on the 30th August. His fame has been injured by the supposed fact that he was the hero of "Hudibras."

19th (Lord's day). Up, and to my chamber to set some papers in order, and then to church, where my old acquaintance, that dull fellow, Meriton, made a good sermon, and hath a strange knack of a grave, serious delivery, which is very agreeable. After church to White Hall, and there find Sir G. Carteret just set down to dinner, and I dined with them, as I intended, and good company, the best people and family in the world I think. Here was great talk of the good end that my Lord Treasurer made; closing his owne eyes and setting his mouth, and bidding adieu with the greatest content and freedom in the world; and is said to die with the cleanest hands that ever any Lord Treasurer did. After dinner Sir G. Carteret and I alone, and there, among other discourse, he did declare that he would be content to part with his place of Treasurer of the Navy upon good terms. I did propose my Lord Belasses as a man likely to buy it, which he listened to, and I did fully concur and promote his design of parting with it, for though I would have my father live, I would not have him die Treasurer of the Navy, because of the accounts which must be uncleared at his death, besides many other circumstances making it advisable for him to let it go. He tells me that he fears all will come to naught in the nation soon if the King do not mind his business, which he do not seem likely to do. He says that the Treasury will be managed for a while by a Commission, whereof he thinks my Lord Chancellor for the honour of it, and my Lord Ashly, and the two Secretaries will be, and some others he knows not. I took leave of him, and directly by water home, and there to read the life of Mr. Hooker, which pleases me as much as any thing I have read a great while, and by and by comes Mr. Howe to see us, and after him a little Mr. Sheply, and so we all to talk, and, Mercer being there, we some of us to sing, and so to supper, a great deal of silly talk. Among other things, W. Howe told us how the Barristers and Students of Gray's Inne rose in rebellion against the Benchers the other day, who outlawed them, and a great deal of do; but now they are at peace again. They being gone, I to my book again, and made an end of Mr. Hooker's Life,[1] and so to bed.

[1] Izaac Walton's "Life of Mr. Richard Hooker," "London, by J. G. for Ric. Marriott," was first published in 1665.

20th. Up betimes, and comes my flagelette master to set me a new tune, which I played presently, and shall in a month do as much as I desire at it. He being gone, I to several businesses in my chamber, and then by coach to the Commissioners of Excise, and so to Westminster Hall, and there spoke with several persons I had to do with. Here among other news, I hear that the Commissioners for the Treasury were named by the King yesterday; but who they are nobody could tell: but the persons are the Lord Chancellor, the two Secretaries, Lord Ashly, and others say Sir W. Coventry and Sir John Duncomb, but all conclude the Duke of Albemarle; but reports do differ, but will be known in a day or two. Having done my business, I then homeward, and overtook Mr. Commander; so took him into a coach with me, and he and I into Lincoln's Inne Fields, there to look upon the coach-houses to see what ground is necessary for coach-house and horses, because of that that I am going about to do, and having satisfied myself in this he and I to Mr. Hide's to look upon the ground again behind our house, and concluded upon his going along with us to-morrow to see some stables, he thinking that we demand more than is necessary. So away home, and then, I, it being a broken day, and had power by my vows, did walk abroad, first through the Minorys, the first time I have been over the Hill to the postern-gate, and seen the place, since the houses were pulled down about that side of the Tower, since the fire, to find where my young mercer with my pretty little woman to his wife lives, who lived in Lumbard streete, and I did espy them, but took no notice now of them, but may do hereafter. Thence down to the Old Swan, and there saw Betty Michell, whom I have not seen since her christening. But, Lord! how pretty she is, and looks as well as ever I saw her, and her child (which I am fain to seem very fond of) is pretty also, I think, and will be. Thence by water to Westminster Hall, and there walked a while talking at random with Sir W. Doyly, and so away to Mrs. Martin's lodging, who was gone before, expecting me, and there je hazer what je vellem cum her and drank, and so by coach home (but I have forgot that I did in the morning go to the Swan, and there tumbling of la little fille, son uncle did trouver her cum su neckcloth off, which I was ashamed of, but made no great matter of it, but let it pass with a laugh), and there spent the evening with my wife at our flagelets, and so to supper, and after a little reading to bed. My wife still troubled with her cold. I find it everywhere now to be a thing doubted whether we shall have peace or no, and the captain of one of our ships that went with the Embassadors do say, that the seamen of Holland to his hearing did defy us, and called us English dogs, and cried out against peace, and that the great people there do oppose peace, though he says the common people do wish it.

21st. Up and to the office, where sat all the morning. At noon dined at home with my wife and find a new girle, a good big girle come to us, got by Payne to be our girle, and his daughter Nell we make our cook. This wench's name is Mary, and seems a good likely maid. After dinner I with Mr. Commander and Mr. Hide's brother to Lincolne's Inne Fields, and there viewed several coach-houses, and satisfied ourselves now fully in it, and then there parted, leaving the rest to future discourse between us. Thence I home; but, Lord! how it went against my heart to go away from the very door of the Duke's play-house, and my Lady Castlemayne's coach, and many great coaches there, to see "The Siege of Rhodes." I was very near making a forfeit, but I did command myself, and so home to my office, and there did much business to my good content, much better than going to a play, and then home to my wife, who is not well with her cold, and sat and read a piece of Grand Cyrus in English by her, and then to my chamber and to supper, and so to bed. This morning the Captain come from Holland did tell us at the board what I have said he reported yesterday. This evening after I come from the office Mrs. Turner come to see my wife and me, and sit and talk with us, and so, my wife not being well and going to bed, Mrs. Turner and I sat up till 12 at night talking alone in my chamber, and most of our discourse was of our neighbours. As to my Lord Bruncker, she says how Mrs. Griffin, our housekeeper's wife, hath it from his maid, that comes to her house often, that they are very poor; that the other day Mrs. Williams was fain to send a jewell to pawn; that their maid hath said herself that she hath got £50 since she come thither, and £17 by the payment of one bill; that they have a most lewd and nasty family here in the office, but Mrs. Turner do tell me that my Lord hath put the King to infinite charge since his coming thither in alterations, and particularly that Mr. Harper at Deptford did himself tell her that my Lord hath had of Foly, the ironmonger, £50 worth in locks and keys for his house, and that it is from the fineness of them, having some of £4 and £5 a lock, such as is in the Duke's closet; that he hath several of these; that he do keep many of her things from her of her own goods, and would have her bring a bill into the office for them; that Mrs. Griffin do say that he do not keep Mrs. Williams now for love, but need, he having another whore that he keeps in Covent Garden; that they do owe money everywhere almost for every thing, even Mrs. Shipman for her butter and cheese about £3, and after many demands cannot get it. Mrs. Turner says she do believe their coming here is only out of a belief of getting purchase by it, and that their servants (which was wittily said of her touching his clerks) do act only as privateers, no purchase, no pay. And in my conscience she is in the right. Then we fell to talk of Sir W. Pen, and his family and rise. She [Mrs. Turner] says that he was a pityfull [fellow] when she first knew them; that his lady was one of the sourest, dirty women, that ever she saw; that they took two chambers, one over another, for themselves and child, in Tower Hill; that for many years together they eat more meals at her house than at their own; did call brothers and sisters the husbands and wives; that her husband was godfather to one, and she godmother to another (this Margaret) of their children, by the same token that she was fain to write with her own hand a letter to Captain Twiddy, to stand for a godfather for her; that she brought my Lady, who then was a dirty slattern, with her stockings hanging about her heels, so that afterwards the people of the whole Hill did say that Mrs. Turner had made Mrs. Pen a gentlewoman, first to the knowledge of my Lady Vane,[1] Sir Henry's lady, and him to the knowledge of most of the great people

[1] Lady Vane was Frances, daughter of Sir Christopher Wray, Bart., of Ashby, Lincolnshire. — B.

that then he sought to, and that in short his rise hath been his giving of large bribes, wherein, and she agrees with my opinion and knowledge before therein, he is very profuse. This made him General; this got him out of the Tower when he was in; and hath brought him into what he is now, since the King's coming in: that long ago, indeed, he would drink the King's health privately with Mr. Turner; but that when he saw it fit to turn Roundhead, and was offered by Mr. Turner to drink the King's health, he answered "No;" he was changed, and now he that would make him drink the King's health, or any health but the Protector's and the State's, or to that purpose, he would be the first man should sheath his sword in his guts. That at the King's coming in, he did send for her husband, and told him what a great man Sir W. Coventry was like to be, and that he having all the records in his hands of the Navy, if he would transcribe what was of most present use of the practice of the Navy, and give them him to give Sir W. Coventry from him, it would undoubtedly do his business of getting him a principal officer's place; that her husband was at £5 charge to get these presently writ; that Sir W. Pen did give them Sir W. Coventry as from himself, which did set him up with W. Coventry, and made him what he is, and never owned any thing of Mr. Turner in them; by which he left him in the lurch, though he did promise the Duke of Albemarle to do all that was possible, and made no question of Mr. Turner's being what he desired; and when afterwards, too, did propose to him the getting of the Purveyor's place for him, he did tell Mr. Turner it was necessary to present Sir W. Coventry 100 pieces, which he did, and W. Coventry took 80 of them: so that he was W. Coventry's mere broker, as Sir W. Batten and my Lady did once tell my Lady Duchess of Albemarle, in the case of Mr. Falconer, whom W. Pen made to give W. Coventry £200 for his place of Clerk of the Rope Yard of Woolwich, and to settle £80 a year upon his daughter Pegg, after the death of his wife, and a gold watch presently to his wife. Mrs. Turner do tell me that my Lady and Pegg have themselves owned to her that Sir W. Coventry and Sir W. Pen had private marks to write to one another by, that when they in appearance writ a fair letter in behalf of anybody, that they had a little mark to show they meant it only in shew: this, these silly people did confess themselves of him. She says that their son, Mr. William Pen, did tell her that his father did observe the commanders did make their addresses to me and applications, but they should know that his father should be the chief of the office, and that she hath observed that Sir W. Pen never had a kindness to her son, since W. Pen told her son that he had applied himself to me. That his rise hath been by her and her husband's means, and that it is a most inconceivable thing how this man can have the face to use her and her family with the neglect that he do them. That he was in the late war a most devilish plunderer, and that got him his estate, which he hath in Ireland, and nothing else, and that he hath always been a very liberal man in his bribes, that upon his coming into this part of the Controller's business wherein he is, he did send for T. Willson and told him how against his knowledge he was put in, and had so little wit as to say to him, "This will make the pot boyle, will it not, Mr. Willson? will it not make the pot boyle?" and do offer him to come in and do his business for him, and he would reward him. This Mr. Willson did come and tell her presently, he having been their servant, and to this day is very faithful to them. That her husband's not being forward to make him a bill for Rere Admirall's pay and Generall's pay both at the same time after he was first made Generall did first give him occasion of keeping a distance from him, since which they have never been great friends, Pen having by degrees been continually growing higher and higher, till now that he do wholly slight them and use them only as servants. Upon the whole, she told me stories enough to confirm me that he is the most false fellow that ever was born of woman, and that so she thinks and knows him to be.

22nd. Up, and by water to White Hall to Sir G. Carteret, who tells me now for certain how the Commission for the Treasury is disposed of: viz., to Duke of Albemarle, Lord Ashly, Sir W. Coventry, Sir John Duncomb,[1] and Sir

[1] Burnet says of Sir John Duncomb, that "he was a judicious man, but very haughty, and apt to raise enemies. He was an able Parliament-man, but could not go into all the designs of the Court; for he had a

Thomas Clifford: at which, he says, all the whole Court is disturbed; it having been once concluded otherwise into the other hands formerly mentioned in yesterday's notes, but all of a sudden the King's choice was changed, and these are to be the men; the first of which is only for a puppet to give honour to the rest. He do presage that these men will make it their business to find faults in the management of the late Lord Treasurer, and in discouraging the bankers: but I am, whatever I in compliance do say to him, of another mind, and my heart is very glad of it, for I do expect they will do much good, and that it is the happiest thing that hath appeared to me for the good of the nation since the King come in. Thence to St. James's, and up to the Duke of York; and there in his chamber Sir W. Coventry did of himself take notice of this business of the Treasury, wherein he is in the Commission, and desired that I would be thinking of any thing fit for him to be acquainted with for the lessening of charge and bettering of our credit, and what our expence hath been since the King's coming home, which he believes will be one of the first things they shall enquire into: which I promised him, and from time to time, which he desires, will give him an account of what I can think of worthy his knowledge. I am mighty glad of this opportunity of professing my joy to him in what choice the King hath made, and the hopes I have that it will save the kingdom from perishing: and

sense of religion, and a zeal for the liberty of his country" ("Own Time," vol. i., p. 437, ed. 1833). Duncomb's removal from the Ordnance to the Treasury is not overlooked by Marvell ("Works," vol. iii., p. 391):

"*Southampton* dead, much of the treasure's care
And place in council fell to *Duncomb's* share.
All men admired, he to that pitch could fly,
Powder ne'er blew man up so soon, so high;
But, sure his late good husbandry in petre [saltpetre],
Showed him to manage the Exchequer meeter;
And who the forts would not vouchsafe a corn,
To lavish the King's money more with scorn,
Who hath no chimneys to give all is best;
And ablest speaker who of law hath least,
Who less estate for Treasurer most fit,
And for a Chancellor he that has least wit.
But the true cause was, that in's brother *May*,
Th' exchequer might the privy-purse obey." — B.

how it do encourage me to take pains again, after my having through despair neglected it! which he told me of himself that it was so with him, that he had given himself up to more ease than ever he expected, and that his opinion of matters was so bad, that there was no publick employment in the kingdom should have been accepted by him but this which the King hath now given him; and therein he is glad, in hopes of the service he may do therein; and in my conscience he will. So into the Duke of York's closet; and there, among other things, Sir W. Coventry did take notice of what he told me the other day, about a report of Commissioner Pett's dealing for timber in the Navy, and selling it to us in other names; and, besides his own proof, did produce a paper I had given him this morning about it, in the case of Widow Murford and Morecocke,[1] which was so handled, that the Duke of York grew very angry, and commanded us presently to fall into the examination of it, saying that he would not trust a man for his sake that lifts up the whites of his eyes. And it was declared that if he be found to have done so, he should be reckoned unfit to serve the Navy; and I do believe he will be turned out; and it was, methought, a worthy saying of Sir W. Coventry to the Duke of York, "Sir," says he, "I do not make this complaint out of any disrespect to Commissioner Pett, but because I do love to do these things fairly and openly." Thence I to Westminster Hall with Sir G. Carteret to the Chequer Chamber to hear our cause of the Lindeboome prize there before the Lords of Appeal, where was Lord Ashly, Arlington, Barkely, and Sir G. Carteret, but the latter three signified nothing, the former only either minding or understanding what was said. Here was good pleading of Sir Walter Walker's and worth hearing, but little done in our business. Thence by coach to the Red Lyon, thinking to meet my father, but I come too soon, but my wife is gone out of town to meet him. I am in great pain, poor man, for him, lest he should come up in pain to town. So I staid not, but to the 'Change, and there staid a little, where most of the newes is that the

[1] Commissioner Pett, in his communication to the Navy Commissioners (May 24th), states that "Murford and Moorcock went two-third in Newhall timber" ("Calendar of State Papers," 1667, p. 117).

Swedes are likely to fall out with the Dutch, which we wish, but how true I know not. Here I met my uncle Wight, the second day he hath been abroad, having been sick these two months even to death, but having never sent to me even in the greatest of his danger. I do think my Aunt had no mind I should come, and so I never went to see him, but neither he took notice of it to me, nor I made any excuse for it to him, but past two or three How do you's, and so parted and so home, and by and by comes my poor father, much better than I expected, being at ease by fits, according as his truss sits, and at another time in as much pain. I am mighty glad to see him come well to town. So to dinner, where Creed comes. After dinner my wife and father abroad, and Creed and I also by water, and parted at the Temple stairs, where I landed, and to the King's house, where I did give 18*d.*, and saw the two last acts of "The Goblins,"[1] a play I could not make any thing of by these two acts, but here Knipp spied me out of the tiring-room, and come to the pit door, and I out to her, and kissed her, she only coming to see me, being in a country-dress, she and others having, it seemed, had a country-dance in the play, but she no other part: so we parted, and I into the pit again till it was done. The house full, but I had no mind to be seen, but thence to my cutler's, and two or three other places on small errands, and so home, where my father and wife come home, and pretty well my father, who to supper and betimes to bed at his country hours. I to Sir W. Batten's, and there got some more part of my dividend of the prize-money. So home and to set down in writing the state of the account, and then to supper, and my wife to her flageolet, wherein she did make out a tune so prettily of herself, that I was infinitely pleased beyond whatever I expected from her, and so to bed. This day coming from Westminster with W. Batten, we saw at White Hall stairs a fisher-boat, with a sturgeon that he had newly catched in the River; which I saw, but it was but a little one; but big enough to prevent my mistake of that for a colt, if ever I become Mayor of Huntingdon.[2]

[1] See January 23rd, 1666–67.

[2] During a very high flood in the meadows between Huntingdon and Godmanchester, something was seen floating, which the Godmanchester

23rd. Up, and to the office, where we sat all the morning. At noon home, and with my father dined, and, poor man! he hath put off his travelling-clothes to-day, and is mighty spruce, and I love to see him cheerful. After dinner I to my chamber, and my wife and I to talk, and by and by they tell Mrs. Daniel would speak with me, so I down to the parlour to her, and sat down together and talked about getting her husband a place. . . . I do promise, and mean to do what kindness I can to her husband. After having been there hasti je was ashamed de peur that my people pensait τὸ πρᾶγμα de it, or lest they might espy us through some trees, we parted and I to the office, and presently back home again, and there was asked by my wife, I know not whether simply or with design, how I come to look as I did, car ego was in much chaleur et de body and of animi, which I put off with the heat of the season, and so to other business, but I had some fear hung upon me lest alcuno had sidi decouvert. So to the office, and then to Sir R. Viner's about some part of my accounts now going on with him, and then home and ended my letters, and then to supper and my chamber to settle many things there, and then to bed. This noon I was on the 'Change, where I to my astonishment hear, and it is in the Gazette, that Sir John Duncomb is sworn yesterday a Privy-councillor. This day I hear also that last night the Duke of Kendall, second son of the Duke of York, did die; and that the other, Duke of Cambridge, continues very ill still. This afternoon I had opportunity para jouer with Mrs. Pen, tokendo her mammailles and baisando elle, being sola in the casa of her pater, and she fort willing.

24th. Up, and to the office, where, by and by, by appointment, we met upon Sir W. Warren's accounts, wherein I do appear in every thing as much as I can his enemy, though not so far but upon good conditions from him I may return to be his friend, but I do think it necessary to do what I do

people thought was a black *pig*, and the Huntingdon folk declared it was a *sturgeon;* when rescued from the waters, it proved to be *a young donkey.* This mistake led to the one party being styled "Godmanchester black pigs," and the other "Huntingdon sturgeons," terms not altogether forgotten at this day. Pepys's *colt* must be taken to be the *colt of an ass.*—B.

at present. We broke off at noon without doing much, and then home, where my wife not well, but yet engaged by invitation to go with Sir W. Pen. I got her to go with him by coach to Islington to the old house, where his lady and Madam Lowther, with her exceeding fine coach and mean horses, and her mother-in-law,[1] did meet us, and two of Mr. Lowther's brothers,[2] and here dined upon nothing but pigeon-pyes, which was such a thing for him to invite all the company to, that I was ashamed of it. But after dinner was all our sport, when there come in a juggler, who, indeed, did shew us so good tricks as I have never seen in my life, I think, of legerdemaine, and such as my wife hath since seriously said that she would not believe but that he did them by the help of the devil. Here, after a bad dinner, and but ordinary company, saving that I discern good parts in one of the sons, who, methought, did take me up very prettily in one or two things that I said, and I was so sensible of it as to be a caution to me hereafter how I do venture to speak more than is necessary in any company, though, as I did now, I do think them incapable to censure me. We broke up, they back to Walthamstow, and only my wife and I and Sir W. Pen to the King's playhouse, and there saw "The Mayden Queene,"[3] which, though I have often seen, yet pleases me infinitely, it being impossible, I think, ever to have the Queen's part, which is very good and passionate, and Florimel's part, which is the most comicall that ever was made for woman, ever done better than they two are by young Marshall and Nelly. Home, where I spent the evening with my father and wife, and late at night some flagillette with my wife, and then to supper and to bed.

25th. Up, and to the office, where all the morning. At

[1] Mary, widow of Morgan Davis, Esq., the third wife of Alderman Robert Lowther, was the lady here referred to. — B.

[2] According to Collins, Anthony Lowther had but one brother, John, a merchant at Dantzic, and one of the Commissioners of Revenue in Ireland. See Collins, vol. v., p. 702. Anthony Lowther, who married Margaret Penn, was the son of Elizabeth, daughter of William Holcroft, Esq., *second* wife of Robert Lowther, of Marske, co. York, and Alderman of London, who died 1655. — B.

[3] See March 2nd, 1666–67.

noon dined at home, and there come Mr. Pierce, the surgeon, and dined with me, telling me that the Duke of Cambridge continues very ill, so as they do despair of his living. So to the office again, where all the afternoon. About 4 o'clock comes Mrs. Pierce to see my wife, and I into them, and there find Pierce very fine, and in her own hair, which do become her, and so says my wife, ten times better than lighter hair, her complexion being mighty good. With them talked a little, and was invited by her to come with my wife on Wednesday next in the evening, to be merry there, which we shall do. Then to the office again, where dispatched a great deal of business till late at night, to my great content, and then home and with my wife to our flageolets a little, and so to supper and to bed, after having my chamber a little wiped up.

26th (Lord's day). Up sooner than usual on Sundays, and to walk, it being exceeding hot all night (so as this night I begun to leave off my waistcoat this year) and this morning, and so to walk in the garden till toward church time, when my wife and I to church, where several strangers of good condition come to our pew, where the pew was full. At noon dined at home, where little Michell come and his wife, who continues mighty pretty. After dinner I by water alone to Westminster, where, not finding Mrs. Martin within, did go towards the parish church,[1] and in the way did overtake her, who resolved to go into the church with her that she was going with (Mrs. Hargrave, the little crooked woman, the vintner's wife of the Dog) and then go out again, and so I to the church, and seeing her return did go out again myself, but met with Mr. Howlett, who, offering me a pew in the gallery, I had no excuse but up with him I must go, and then much against my will staid out the whole church in pain while she expected me at home, but I did entertain myself with my perspective glass up and down the church, by which I had the great pleasure of seeing and gazing at a great many very fine women; and what with that, and sleeping, I passed away the time till sermon was done, and then to Mrs. Martin, and there staid with her an hour or two, and there did what I would with her, and after been here so long I away to my boat, and up

[1] St. Margaret's.

with it as far as Barne Elmes, reading of Mr. Evelyn's late new book against Solitude,[1] in which I do not find much excess of good matter, though it be pretty for a bye discourse. I walked the length of the Elmes, and with great pleasure saw some gallant ladies and people come with their bottles, and basket, and chairs, and form, to sup under the trees by the waterside, which was mighty pleasant. I to boat again and to my book, and having done that I took another book, Mr. Boyle's of Colours, and there read, where I laughed, finding many fine things worthy observation, and so landed at the Old Swan, and so home, where I find my poor father newly come out of an unexpected fit of his pain, that they feared he would have died. They had sent for me to White Hall and all up and down, and for Mr. Holliard also, who did come, but W. Hewer being here did I think do the business in getting my father's bowel, that was fallen down, into his body again, and that which made me more sensible of it was that he this morning did show me the place where his bowel did use to fall down and swell, which did trouble me to see. But above all things the poor man's patience under it and his good heart and humour, as soon as he was out of it, did so work upon me, that my heart was sad to think upon his condition, but do hope that a way will be found by a steel truss to relieve him. By and by to supper, all our discourse about Brampton, and my intentions to build there if I could be free of my engagement to my Uncle Thomas and his son, that they may not have what I have built, against my will, to them whether I will or no, in case of me and my brothers being without heirs male; which is the true reason why I am against laying out money upon that place, together with my fear of some inconvenience by being so near Hinchingbroke; being obliged to be a servant to that family, and subject to what expence they shall cost me; and to have all that I shall buy, or do, esteemed as got by the death of my

[1] "15th February, 1666-67. My little book in answer to Sir George Mackenzie was now published, entitled, 'Public Employment and an Active Life, with its Appenages, preferred to Solitude.'" — Evelyn's *Diary*. Soon afterwards Evelyn wrote to Cowley, the poet, and excused himself for writing in this strain, and in truth his opinions were divided on this question.

uncle, when indeed what I have from him is not worth naming. After supper to read and then to bed.

27th. Up, and there comes Greeting my flagelette master, and I practised with him. There comes also Richardson, the bookbinder, with one of Ogilby's Bibles in quires for me to see and buy, it being Mr. Cade's, my stationer's; but it is like to be so big that I shall not use it, it being too great to stir up and down without much trouble, which I shall not like nor do intend it for. So by water to White Hall, and there find Sir G. Carteret at home, and talked with him a while, and find that the new Commissioners of the Treasury did meet this morning. So I to find out Sir W. Coventry, but missed, only I do hear that they have chosen Sir G. Downing for their Secretary; and I think in my conscience they have done a great thing in it; for he is a business active man, and values himself upon having of things do well under his hand; so that I am mightily pleased in their choice. Here I met Mr. Pierce, who tells me that he lately met Mr. Carcasse, who do mightily inveigh against me, for that all that has been done against him he lays on me, and I think he is in the right and I do own it, only I find what I suspected, that he do report that Sir W. Batten and I, who never agreed before, do now, and since this business agree even more, which I did fear would be thought, and therefore will find occasion to undeceive the world in that particular by promoting something shortly against [Sir] W. Batten. So home, and there to sing with my wife before dinner, and then to dinner, and after dinner comes Carcasse to speak with me, but I would not give him way to enlarge on anything, but he would have begun to have made a noise how I have undone him and used all the wit I could in the drawing up of his report, wherein he told me I had taken a great deal of pains to undo him. To which I did not think fit to enter into any answer, but dismissed him, and so I again up to my chamber, vexed at the impudence of this rogue, but I think I shall be wary enough for him. So to my chamber, and there did some little business, and then abroad, and stopped at the Bear-garden-stairs,[1] there to see a prize fought. But the house so full there was no getting in there,

[1] At Bankside.

so forced to go through an alehouse into the pit, where the bears are baited; and upon a stool did see them fight, which they did very furiously, a butcher and a waterman. The former had the better all along, till by and by the latter dropped his sword out of his hand, and the butcher, whether not seeing his sword dropped I know not, but did give him a cut over the wrist, so as he was disabled to fight any longer. But, Lord! to see how in a minute the whole stage was full of watermen to revenge the foul play, and the butchers to defend their fellow, though most blamed him; and there they all fell to it to knocking down and cutting many on each side. It was pleasant to see, but that I stood in the pit, and feared that in the tumult I might get some hurt. At last the rabble broke up, and so I away to White Hall and so to St. James's, but I found not Sir W. Coventry, so into the Park and took a turn or two, it being a most sweet day, and so by water home, and with my father and wife walked in the garden, and then anon to supper and to bed. The Duke of Cambridge very ill still.

28th. Up, and by coach to St. James's, where I find Sir W. Coventry, and he desirous to have spoke with me. It was to read over a draught of a letter which he hath made for his brother Commissioners and him to sign to us, demanding an account of the whole business of the Navy accounts; and I perceive, by the way he goes about it, that they will do admirable things. He tells me they have chosen Sir G. Downing their Secretary, who will be as fit a man as any in the world; and said, by the by, speaking of the bankers being fearful of Sir G. Downing's being Secretary, he being their enemy, that they did not intend to be ruled by their Secretary, but do the business themselves. My heart is glad to see so great hopes of good to the nation as will be by these men; and it do me good to see Sir W. Coventry so cheerfull as he now is on the same score. Thence home, and there fell to seeing my office and closet there made soundly clean, and the windows cleaned. At which all the morning, and so at noon to dinner. After dinner my wife away down with Jane and W. Hewer to Woolwich, in order to a little ayre and to lie there to-night, and so to gather May-dew [1] to-morrow morning, which Mrs.

[1] If we are to credit the following paragraph, extracted from the

Turner hath taught her as the only thing in the world to wash her face with; and I am contented with it. Presently comes Creed, and he and I by water to Fox-hall, and there walked in Spring Garden. A great deal of company, and the weather and garden pleasant: that it is very pleasant and cheap going thither, for a man may gc to spend what he will, or nothing, all is one. But to heai the nightingale and other birds, and here fiddles, and there a harp, and here a Jew's trump, and here laughing, and there fine people walking, is mighty divertising. Among others, there were two pretty women alone, that walked a great while, which being discovered by some idle gentlemen, they would needs take them up; but to see the poor ladies how they were put to it to run from them, and they after them, and sometimes the ladies put themselves along with other company, then the other drew back; at last, the last did get off out of the house, and took boat and away. I was troubled to see them abused so; and could have found in my heart, as little desire of fighting as I have, to have protected the ladies. So by water, set Creed down at White Hall, and I to the Old Swan, and so home. My father gone to bed, and wife abroad at Woolwich, I to Sir W. Pen, where he and his Lady and Pegg and pretty Mrs. Lowther her sister-in-law at supper, where I sat and talked, and Sir W. Pen, half drunk, did talk like a fool and vex his wife, that I was half pleased and half vexed to see so much folly and rudeness from him, and so late home to bed.

29th. Up, and by coach to St. James's, where by and by up to the Duke of York, where, among other things, our parson Mills having the offer of another benefice[1] by Sir Robert Brookes, who was his pupil, he by my Lord Barkeley [of Stratton] is made one of the Duke's Chaplains, which qualifies him for two livings. But to see how slightly such

"Morning Post" of May 2nd, 1791, the virtues of May dew were then still held in some estimation; for it records that "on the day preceding, according to annual and superstitious custom, a number of persons went into the fields, and bathed their faces with the dew on the grass, under the idea that it would render them beautiful" (Hone's "Every Day Book," vol. ii., p. 611). Aubrey speaks of May dew as "a great dissolvent" ("Miscellanies," p. 183). — B.

[1] The rectory of Wanstead, in Essex, to which he was presented.

things are done, the Duke of York only taking my Lord Barkeley's word upon saying, that we the officers of the Navy do say he is a good man and minister of our parish, and the Duke of York admits him to kiss his hand, but speaks not one word to him; but so a warrant will be drawn from the Duke of York to qualify him, and there's an end of it. So we into the Duke's closett, where little to do, but complaint for want of money and a motion of Sir W. Coventry's that we should all now bethink ourselves of lessening charge to the King, which he said was the only way he saw likely to put the King out of debt, and this puts me upon thinking to offer something presently myself to prevent its being done in a worse manner without me relating to the Victualling business, which, as I may order it, I think may be done and save myself something. Thence home, and there settle to some accounts of mine in my chamber I all the morning till dinner. My wife comes home from Woolwich, but did not dine with me, going to dress herself against night, to go to Mrs. Pierce's to be merry, where we are to have Knepp and Harris and other good people. I at my accounts all the afternoon, being a little lost in them as to reckoning interest. Anon comes down my wife, dressed in her second mourning, with her black moyre waistcoat, and short petticoat, laced with silver lace so basely that I could not endure to see her, and with laced lining, which is too soon, so that I was horrid angry, and went out of doors to the office and there staid, and would not go to our intended meeting, which vexed me to the blood, and my wife sent twice or thrice to me, to direct her any way to dress her, but to put on her cloth gown, which she would not venture, which made me mad: and so in the evening to my chamber, vexed, and to my accounts, which I ended to my great content, and did make amends for the loss of our mirth this night, by getting this done, which otherwise I fear I should not have done a good while else. So to bed.

30th. Up, and to the office, where all the morning. At noon dined at home, being without any words friends with my wife, though last night I was very angry, and do think I did give her as much cause to be angry with me. After dinner I walked to Arundell House, the way very nasty, the day of meeting of the Society being changed from Wednesday to Thursday, which I knew not before, because the Wednesday is a Council-day, and several of the Council are of the Society, and would come but for their attending the King at Council; where I find much company, indeed very much company, in expectation of the Duchesse of Newcastle,[1] who had desired to be invited to the Society; and was, after much debate, *pro* and *con.*, it seems many being against it; and we do believe the town will be full of ballads of it. Anon comes the Duchesse with her women attending her; among others, the Ferabosco,[2] of whom so much talk is that her lady would bid her show her face and kill the gallants. She is indeed black, and hath good black little eyes, but otherwise but a very ordinary woman I do think, but they say sings well. The Duchesse hath been a good, comely woman; but her dress so antick, and her deportment so ordinary, that I do not like her at all, nor did I hear her say any thing that was worth hearing, but that she was full of admiration, all admiration. Several fine experiments were shown her of colours, loadstones, microscopes, and of liquors: among others, of one that did, while she was there, turn a piece of roasted mutton into pure blood, which was very rare. Here was Mrs. Moore of Cambridge, whom I had not seen before, and I was glad to see her; as also a very pretty black boy that run up and down the room, somebody's child in Arundell House. After they had shown her many experiments, and she cried still she was full of admiration, she departed, being led out and in by several Lords that were there; among others Lord George Barkeley and Earl of Carlisle, and a very pretty young man,

[1] May 30th. "The duchess of Newcastle coming in, the experiments appointed for her entertainment were made: first that of weighing the air . . . ; next were made several experiments of mixing colours; then two cold liquors by mixture made hot; then the experiments of making water bubble up in the rarefying engine, by drawing out the air, and that of making an empty bladder swell in the same engine; then the experiment of making a body swim in the middle of the water; and that of two well-wrought marbles, which were not separated but by the weight of forty-seven pounds." — Birch's *History of the Royal Society*, vol. ii., p. 178.

[2] This may either have been the wife or daughter of Alfonso Ferrabosco the younger or of John Ferrabosco.

the Duke of Somerset.[1] She gone, I by coach home, and there busy at my letters till night, and then with my wife in the evening singing with her in the garden with great pleasure, and so home to supper and to bed.

31st. Up, and there came young Mrs. Daniel in the morning as I expected about business of her husband's. I took her into the office to discourse with her about getting some employment for him. . . . By water to White Hall to the Lords Commissioners of the Treasury, the first time I ever was there and I think the second that they have met at the Treasury chamber there. Here I saw Duncomb look as big, and take as much state on him, as if he had been born a lord. I was in with him about Tangier, and at present received but little answer from them, they being in a cloud of business yet, but I doubt not but all will go well under them. Here I met with Sir H. Cholmly, who tells me that he is told this day by Secretary Morris that he believes we are, and shall be, only fooled by the French; and that the Dutch are very high and insolent, and do look upon us as come over only to beg a peace; which troubles me very much, and I do fear it is true. Thence to Sir G. Carteret at his lodgings; who, I perceive, is mightily displeased with this new Treasury; and he hath reason, for it will eclipse him; and he tells me that my Lord Ashly says they understand nothing; and he says he believes the King do not intend they shall sit long. But I believe no such thing, but that the King will find such benefit by them as he will desire to have them continue, as we see he hath done, in the late new Act that was so much decried about the King; but yet the King hath since permitted it, and found good by it. He says, and I believe, that a great many persons at Court are angry at the rise of this Duncomb,[2] whose father, he tells me, was a long-Parliament-

[1] George, Lord Berkeley of Berkeley (created Earl of Berkeley in 1679), died October 10th, 1698. Charles Howard, first Earl of Carlisle, born 1629; died February 24th, 1685. William Seymour, third Duke of Somerset, born 1650; died December 12th, 1671. In the Paston MSS. he is described as "a youth of great beauty and hope."

[2] Sir John Duncombe. See November 8th, 1664. Mr. J. Biddulph Martin says, "The assertion that Duncombe's father had been a Long Parliament man is not confirmed by reference to the roll of the

man, and a great Committee-man; and this fellow used to carry his papers to Committees after him: he was a kind of an atturny: but for all this, I believe this man will be a great man, in spite of all. Thence I away to Holborne to Mr. Gawden, whom I met at Bernard's Inn gate, and straight we together to the Navy Office, where we did all meet about some victualling business, and so home to dinner and to the office, where the weather so hot now-a-days that I cannot but sleep before I do any business, and in the evening home, and there, to my unexpected satisfaction, did get my intricate accounts of interest, which have been of late much perplexed by mixing of some moneys of Sir G. Carteret's with mine, evened and set right: and so late to supper, and with great quiet to bed; finding by the balance of my account that I am creditor £6,900,[1] for which the Lord of Heaven be praised!

June 1st. Up; and there comes to me Mr. Commander, whom I employ about hiring of some ground behind the office, for the building of me a stable and coach-house: for I do find it necessary for me, both in respect to honour and the profit of it also, my expense in hackney-coaches being now so great, to keep a coach, and therefore will do it. Having given him some instructions about it, I to the office, where we sat all the morning; where we have news that our peace with Spayne, as to trade, is wholly concluded, and we are to furnish him with some men for Flanders against the French. How that will agree with the French, I know not; but they say that he also hath liberty to get what men he pleases out of England. But for the Spaniard, I hear that my Lord Castlehaven is raising a regiment of 4,000 men, which he is to command there; and several young gentlemen are going over in commands with him: and they say the Duke of Monmouth is going over only as a traveller, not to engage on either side, but only to see the campagne, which will be becoming him much more than to live whoreing and rogueing as he now do. After dinner to the office, where, after a little nap, I

Long Parliament" ("The Grasshopper in Lombard Street," 1892, p. 29).

[1] Pepys's Private Accounts, made up to May 31st, 1667, are amongst the Rawlinson MSS., A. 174 (Bodleian).

fell to business, and did very much with infinite joy to myself, as it always is to me when I have dispatched much business, and therefore it troubles me to see how hard it is for me to settle to it sometimes when my mind is upon pleasure. So home late to supper and to bed.

2nd (Lord's day). Up betimes, and down to my chamber without trimming myself, or putting on clean linen, thinking only to keep to my chamber and do business to-day, but when I come there I find that without being shaved I am not fully awake, nor ready to settle to business, and so was fain to go up again and dress myself, which I did, and so down to my chamber, and fell roundly to business, and did to my satisfaction by dinner go far in the drawing up a state of my accounts of Tangier for the new Lords Commissioners. So to dinner, and then to my business again all the afternoon close, when Creed come to visit me, but I did put him off, and to my business, till anon I did make an end, and wrote it fair with a letter to the Lords to accompany my accounts, which I think will be so much satisfaction and so soon done (their order for my doing it being dated but May 30) as they will not find from any hand else. Being weary and almost blind with writing and reading so much to-day, I took boat at the Old Swan, and then up the river all alone as high as Putney almost, and then back again, all the way reading, and finishing Mr. Boyle's book of Colours, which is so chymical, that I can understand but little of it, but understand enough to see that he is a most excellent man. So back and home, and there to supper, and so to bed.

3rd. Up, and by coach to St. James's, and with Sir W. Coventry a great while talking about several businesses, but especially about accounts, and how backward our Treasurer is in giving them satisfaction, and the truth is I do doubt he cannot do better, but it is strange to say that being conscious of our doing little at this day, nor for some time past in our office for want of money, I do hang my head to him, and cannot be so free with him as I used to be, nor can be free with him, though of all men, I think, I have the least cause to be so, having taken so much more pains, while I could do anything, than the rest of my fellows. Parted with him, and so going through the Park met Mr. Mills, our parson, whom I went back with to bring him to [Sir] W. Coventry, to give him the form of a qualification for the Duke of York to sign to, to enable him to have two livings: which was a service I did, but much against my will, for a lazy, fat priest. Thence to Westminster Hall, and there walked a turn or two with Sir William Doyly, who did lay a wager with me, the Treasurership would be in one hand, notwithstanding this present Commission, before Christmas: on which we did lay a poll of ling, a brace of carps, and a pottle of wine; and Sir W. Pen and Mr. Scowen[1] to be at the eating of them. Thence down by water to Deptford, it being Trinity Monday, when the Master is chosen,[2] and there, finding them all at church, and thinking they dined, as usual, at Stepny, I turned back, having a good book in my hand, the Life of Cardinal Wolsey, wrote by his own servant,[3] and to Ratcliffe; and so walked to Stepny, and spent my time in the churchyard,[4] looking over the grave-stones, expecting when the company would come by. Finding no company stirring, I sent to the house to see; and, it seems, they dine not there, but at Deptford: so I back again to Deptford, and there find them just sat down. And so I down with them; and we had a good dinner of plain meat, and good company at our table: among others, my good Mr.

[1] Robert Scawen, at one time Receiver-General for the office of Receiver-General for Hants, Wilts, and Gloucestershire.

[2] Sir William Penn was elected Master of the Trinity House, Monday, June 3rd, 1667.

[3] George Cavendish (1500–61?), elder son of Thomas Cavendish, Clerk of the Pipe in the Exchequer. He entered the service of Cardinal Wolsey in 1526 or 1527 as gentleman-usher, and remained with his master till the latter's death, when he retired into private life, and lived quietly. He wrote the life of Wolsey in 1557, but it was not published, and remained long in MS. For some time there was uncertainty as to the authorship, and the book was attributed to William Cavendish. The question was settled in 1814, when the Rev. Joseph Hunter published his pamphlet entitled, "Who wrote Cavendish's Life of Wolsey." Singer published the life in 1815, and a second edition appeared in 1827. It has since been frequently reprinted.

[4] The churchyard of St. Dunstan's (Old Stepney Church) is referred to both in the "Tatler" and the "Spectator." In the latter we read (No. 518), "I have made discovery of a churchyard in which I believe you might spend an afternoon with great pleasure to yourself and to the public."

Evelyn, with whom, after dinner, I stepped aside, and talked upon the present posture of our affairs; which is, that the Dutch are known to be abroad with eighty sail of ships of war, and twenty fire-ships; and the French come into the Channell with twenty sail of men-of-war, and five fire-ships,[1] while we have not a ship at sea to do them any hurt with; but are calling in all we can, while our Embassadors are treating at Bredah; and the Dutch look upon them as come to beg peace, and use them accordingly; and all this through the negligence of our Prince, who hath power, if he would, to master all these with the money and men that he hath had the command of, and may now have, if he would mind his business. But, for aught we see, the Kingdom is likely to be lost, as well as the reputation of it is, for ever; notwithstanding so much reputation got and preserved by a rebell that went before him. This discourse of ours ended with sorrowful reflections upon our condition, and so broke up, and Creed and I got out of the room, and away by water to White Hall, and there he and I waited in the Treasury-chamber an hour or two, where we saw the Country Receivers and Accountants for money come to attend; and one of them, a brisk young fellow, with his hat cocked like a fool behind, as the present fashion among the blades is,[2] committed to the Serjeant. By and by, I, upon desire, was called in, and delivered in my report of my Accounts. Present, Lord Ashly, Clifford, and Duncomb, who, being busy, did not read it; but committed it to Sir George Downing, and so I was dismissed; but, Lord! to see how Duncomb do take upon him is an eyesore, though I think he deserves great honour, but only the sud-

[1] Richard Watts, writing from Deal to Williamson, June 3rd, says: "Governor Titus of Deal Castle is said to have received a packet from Whitehall at 3 a.m. that the Duke of Beaufort, with 60 sail, is at the Isle of Wight, and the Dutch, with 40 sail, at the Gunfleet. Preparations are made to receive the enemy if they attempt to land" ("Calendar of State Papers," 1667, p. 146).

[2] It was called the Monmouth cock, which, according to "The Spectator," No. 129, was still worn in the west of England by country squires in 1711: "During our progress through the most western parts of the kingdom, we fancied ourselves in King Charles the Second's reign, the people having made little variations in their dress since that time. The smartest of the country squires *appear still in the Monmouth cock.*" — B.

denness of his rise, and his pride. But I do like the way of these lords, that they admit nobody to use many words, nor do they spend many words themselves, but in great state do hear what they see necessary, and say little themselves, but bid withdraw. Thence Creed and I by water up to Fox Hall, and over against it stopped, thinking to see some Cock-fighting; but it was just being done, and, therefore, back again to the other side, and to Spring Garden, and there eat and drank a little, and then to walk up and down the garden, reflecting upon the bad management of things now, compared with what it was in the late rebellious times, when men, some for fear, and some for religion, minded their business, which none now do, by being void of both. Much talk of this and other kinds, very pleasant, and so when it was almost night we home, setting him in at White Hall, and I to the Old Swan, and thence home, where to supper, and then to read a little, and so to bed.

4th. Up, and to the office, and there busy all the morning putting in order the answering the great letter sent to the office by the new Commissioners of the Treasury, who demand an account from the King's coming in to this day, which we shall do in the best manner we can. At noon home to dinner, and after dinner comes Mr. Commander to me and tells me, after all, that I cannot have a lease of the ground for my coach-house and stable, till a suit in law be ended, about the end of the old stable now standing, which they and I would have pulled down to make a better way for a coach. I am a little sorry that I cannot presently have it, because I am pretty full in my mind of keeping a coach; but yet, when I think on it again, the Dutch and French both at sea, and we poor, and still out of order, I know not yet what turns there may be, and besides, I am in danger of parting with one of my places, which relates to the Victualling, that brings me by accident in £800 a year, that is, £300 from the King and £500 from D. Gawden. I ought to be well contented to forbear awhile, and therefore I am contented. To the office all the afternoon, where I dispatched much business to my great content, and then home in the evening, and there to sing and pipe with my wife, and that being done, she fell all of a sudden to discourse about her clothes and my humours in not suffering her to wear them as she pleases, and grew to high words between us, but I fell to read a book (Boyle's Hydrostatiques[1]) aloud in my chamber and let her talk, till she was tired and vexed that I would not hear her, and so become friends, and to bed together the first night after 4 or 5 that she hath lain from me by reason of a great cold she had got.

5th. Up, and with Mr. Kenasten by coach to White Hall to the Commissioners of the Treasury about getting money for Tangier, and did come to, after long waiting, speak with them, and there I find them all sat; and, among the rest, Duncomb lolling, with his heels upon another chair, by that, that he sat upon, and had an answer good enough, and then away home, and (it being a most windy day, and hath been so all night, South West, and we have great hopes that it may have done the Dutch or French fleets some hurt) having got some papers in order, I back to St. James's, where we all met at Sir W. Coventry's chamber, and dined and talked of our business, he being a most excellent man, and indeed, with all his business, hath more of his employed upon the good of the service of the Navy, than all of us, that makes me ashamed of it. This noon Captain Perriman brings us word how the Happy Returne's[2] [crew] below in the Hope, ordered to carry the Portugal Embassador to Holland (and the Embassador, I think, on board), refuse to go till paid; and by their example two or three more ships are in a mutiny: which is a sad consideration, while so may of the enemy's ships are at this day triumphing in the sea. Here a very good and neat dinner, after the French manner, and good discourse, and then up after dinner to the Duke of York and did our usual business, and

[1] "Hydrostatical Paradoxes made out by New Experiments" was published by the Hon. Robert Boyle in 1666 (Oxford).

[2] Captain Francis Courtenay wrote to the Navy Commissioners ("Happy Return," Hope, June 3rd): "Hopes they will not account him too great an offender in stopping the incessant requests of some necessitated persons for relief of their families. Has granted tickets to 13 men named, and commends them to favour. Is setting sail with the Portugal Ambassador, who came on board this morning" ("Calendar of State Papers," 1667, p. 147). The "Happy Return" carried the Portuguese ambassador to Holland, and was back at Plymouth on the 14th June ("Calendar," p. 187).

are put in hopes by Sir W. Coventry that we shall have money, and so away, Sir G. Carteret and I to my Lord Crew to advise about Sir G. Carteret's carrying his accounts to-morrow to the Commissioners appointed to examine them and all other accounts since the war, who at last by the King's calling them to him yesterday and chiding them will sit, but Littleton and Garraway much against their wills. The truth of it is, it is a ridiculous thing, for it will come to nothing, nor do the King nor kingdom good in any manner, I think. Here they talked of my Lord Hinchingbroke's match with Lord Burlington's daughter, which is now gone a pretty way forward, and to great content, which I am infinitely glad of. So from hence to White Hall, and in the streete Sir G. Carteret showed me a gentleman coming by in his coach, who hath been sent for up out of Lincolneshire, I think he says he is a justice of peace there, that the Council have laid by the heels here, and here lies in a messenger's hands, for saying that a man and his wife are but one person, and so ought to pay but 12*d.* for both to the Poll Bill; by which others were led to do the like: and so here he lies prisoner. To White Hall, and there I attended to speak with Sir W. Coventry about Lanyon's business, to get him some money out of the Prize Office from my Lord Ashly, and so home, and there to the office a little, and thence to my chamber to read, and supper, and to bed. My father, blessed be God! finds great ease by his new steel trusse, which he put on yesterday. So to bed. The Duke of Cambridge past hopes of living still.

6th. Up, and to the office all the morning, where (which he hath not done a great while) Sir G. Carteret come to advise with us for the disposing of £10,000, which is the first sum the new Lords Treasurers have provided us; but, unless we have more, this will not enable us to cut off any of the growing charge which they seem to give it us for, and expect we should discharge several ships quite off with it. So home and with my father and wife to Sir W. Pen's to dinner, which they invited us to out of their respect to my father, as a stranger; though I know them as false as the devil himself, and that it is only that they think it fit to oblige me; wherein I am a happy man, that all my fellow-officers are desirous of my friendship. Here as merry as in so false a place, and where I must dissemble my hatred, I could be, and after dinner my father and wife to a play, and I to my office, and there busy all the afternoon till late at night, and then my wife and I sang a song or two in the garden, and so home to supper and to bed. This afternoon comes Mr. Pierce to me about some business, and tells me that the Duke of Cambridge is yet living, but every minute expected to die, and is given over by all people, which indeed is a sad loss.

7th. Up, and after with my flageolet and Mr. Townsend, whom I sent for to come to me to discourse about my Lord Sandwich's business; for whom I am in some pain, lest the Accounts of the Wardrobe may not be in so good order as may please the new Lords Treasurers, who are quick-sighted, and under obligations of recommending themselves to the King and the world, by their finding and mending of faults, and are, most of them, not the best friends to my Lord, and to the office, and there all the morning. At noon home to dinner, my father, wife, and I, and a good dinner, and then to the office again, where busy all the afternoon, also I have a desire to dispatch all business that hath lain long on my hands, and so to it till the evening, and then home to sing and pipe with my wife, and then to supper and to bed, my head full of thoughts how to keep if I can some part of my wages as Surveyor of the Victualling, which I see must now come to be taken away among the other places that have been occasioned by this war, and the rather because I have of late an inclination to keep a coach. Ever since my drinking, two days ago, some very coole drink at Sir W. Coventry's table I have been full of wind and with some pain, and I was afraid last night that it would amount to much, but, blessed be God! I find that the worst is past, so that I do clearly see that all the indisposition I am liable to-day as to sickness is only the Colique. This day I read (shown me by Mr. Gibson) a discourse newly come forth of the King of France, his pretence to Flanders, which is a very fine discourse, and the truth is, hath so much of the Civil Law in it, that I am not a fit judge of it, but, as it appears to me, he hath a good pretence to it by right of his Queene. So to bed.

8th. Up, and to the office, where all the news this morning is, that the Dutch are come with a fleete of eighty sail to Harwich, and that guns were heard plain by Sir W. Rider's people at Bednall-greene, all yesterday even. So to the office; we all sat all the morning, and then home to dinner, where our dinner a ham of French bacon, boiled with pigeons, an excellent dish. Here dined with us only W. Hewer and his mother. After dinner to the office again, where busy till night, and then home and to read a little and then to bed. The news is confirmed that the Dutch are off of Harwich, but had done nothing last night. The King hath sent down my Lord of Oxford to raise the countries there; and all the Westerne barges are taken up to make a bridge over the River, about the Hope, for horse to cross the River, if there be occasion.

9th (Lord's day). Up, and by water to White Hall, and so walked to St. James's, where I hear that the Duke of Cambridge, who was given over long since by the Doctors, is now likely to recover; for which God be praised! To Sir W. Coventry, and there talked with him a great while; and mighty glad I was of my good fortune to visit him, for it keeps in my acquaintance with him, and the world sees it, and reckons my interest accordingly. In comes my Lord Barkeley, who is going down to Harwich also to look after the militia there: and there is also the Duke of Monmouth, and with him a great many young Hectors, the Lord Chesterfield, my Lord Mandeville, and others: but to little purpose, I fear, but to debauch the country women thereabouts. My Lord Barkeley wanting some maps, and Sir W. Coventry recommending the six maps[1] of England that are bound up for the pocket, I did offer to present my Lord with them, which he accepted: and so I will send them him. Thence to White Hall, and there to the Chapel, where I met Creed, and he and I staid to hear who preached, which was a man who begun dully, and so we away by water and landed in Southwarke, and to a church in the street where we take water beyond the bridge, which

[1] This was Hollar's map, published in 1644, and entitled, "The Kingdom of England and Principality of Wales, exactly described with every Sheere, and the small towns in every one of them, in six maps" This is generally known as the Quartermasters' map.

was so full and the weather hot that we could not stand there. So to my house, where we find my father and wife at dinner, and after dinner Creed and I by water to White Hall, and there we parted, and I to Sir G. Carteret's, where, he busy, I up into the house, and there met with a gentleman, Captain Aldrige, that belongs to my Lord Barkeley, and I did give him the book of maps for my Lord, and so I to Westminster Church and there staid a good while, and saw Betty Michell there. So away thence, and after church time to Mrs. Martin's, and then hazer what I would with her, and then took boat and up, all alone, a most excellent evening, as high as Barne Elmes, and there took a turn; and then to my boat again, and home, reading and making an end of the book I lately bought — a merry satyr, called "The Visions," translated from Spanish[1] by L'Estrange, wherein there are many very pretty things; but the translation is, as to the rendering it into English expression, the best that ever I saw, it being impossible almost to conceive that it should be a translation. Being come home I find an order come for the getting some fire-ships presently to annoy the Dutch, who are in the King's Channel and expected up higher. So [Sir] W. Batten and [Sir] W. Pen being come this evening from their country houses to town we did issue orders about it, and then home to supper and to bed.

10th. Up; and news brought us that the Dutch are come up as high as the Nore; and more pressing orders for fire-ships. W. Batten, W. Pen, and I to St. James's; where the Duke of York gone this morning betimes, to send away some men down to Chatham. So we three to White Hall, and met Sir W. Coventry, who presses all that is possible for fire-ships. So we three to the office presently; and thither comes Sir Fretcheville Hollis,[2] who is to command

[1] "The Visions of Quevedo, made English by Roger L'Estrange," was published in 1668, and reprinted 1671, 1673, 1689, 1702, 1710, 1715, 1795.

[2] Grandson of Fretcheville Hollis, of Grimsby. His father, Gervase Hollis, the antiquary, most of whose collections came into the British Museum, was an officer in the king's service. Sir Fretcheville Hollis, embracing the naval profession, lost an arm in the sea-fight of 1665, and afterwards served as Rear-Admiral under Sir Robert Holmes, when

them all in some exploits he is to do with them on the enemy in the River. So we all down to Deptford, and pitched upon ships and set men at work: but, Lord! to see how backwardly things move at this pinch, notwithstanding that, by the enemy's being now come up as high as almost the Hope, Sir J. Minnes, who has gone down to pay some ships there, hath sent up the money; and so we are possessed of money to do what we will with. Yet partly ourselves, being used to be idle and in despair, and partly people that have been used to be deceived by us as to money, won't believe us; and we know not, though we have it, how almost to promise it; and our wants such, and men out of the way, that it is an admirable thing to consider how much the King suffers, and how necessary it is in a State to keep the King's service always in a good posture and credit. Here I eat a bit, and then in the afternoon took boat and down to Greenwich, where I find the stairs full of people, there being a great riding[1] there to-day for

they attacked the Smyrna fleet. He fell in the battle of Southwold Bay, 1672, on board the "Cambridge." Although Pepys speaks slightly of him, he was a man of high spirit and enterprise, and is thus eulogized by Dryden in his "Annus Mirabilis":

"Young Hollis on a Muse by Mars begot,
Born, Cæsar-like, to write and act great deeds,
Impatient to revenge his fatal shot,
His right hand doubly to his left succeeds." — B.

[1] It was an ancient custom in Berkshire, when a man had beaten his wife, for the neighbours to parade in front of his house, for the purpose of serenading him with kettles, and horns and hand-bells, and every species of "rough music," by which name the ceremony was designated. Perhaps the *riding* mentioned by Pepys was a punishment somewhat similar. Malcolm ("Manners of London") quotes from the "Protestant Mercury," that a porter's lady, who resided near Strand Lane, beat her husband with so much violence and perseverance, that the poor man was compelled to leap out of the window to escape her fury. Exasperated at this virago, the neighbours made a "riding," *i.e.*, a pedestrian procession, headed by a drum, and accompanied by a chemise, displayed for a banner. The manual musician sounded the tune of "You round-headed cuckolds, come dig, come dig!" and nearly seventy coalheavers, carmen, and porters, adorned with large horns fastened to their heads, followed. The public seemed highly pleased with the nature of the punishment, and gave liberally to the vindicators of injured manhood (page 211, 4to ed., 1811). — B.

a man, the constable of the town, whose wife beat him. Here I was with much ado fain to press two watermen to make me a galley, and so to Woolwich to give order for the dispatch of a ship I have taken under my care to see dispatched, and orders being so given, I, under pretence to fetch up the ship, which lay at Grays (the Golden Hand),[1] did do that in my way, and went down to Gravesend, where I find the Duke of Albemarle just come, with a great many idle lords and gentlemen, with their pistols and fooleries; and the bulwarke[2] not able to have stood half an hour had they come up; but the Dutch are fallen down from the Hope and Shell-haven as low as Sheernesse, and we do plainly at this time hear the guns play. Yet I do not find the Duke of Albemarle intends to go thither, but stays here to-night, and hath, though the Dutch are gone, ordered our frigates to be brought to a line between the two block-houses; which I took then to be a ridiculous thing. So I away into the town and took a captain or two of our ships (who did give me an account of the proceedings of the Dutch fleete in the river) to the taverne, and there eat and drank, and I find the townsmen had removed most of their goods out of the town, for fear of the Dutch coming up to them; and from Sir John Griffen,[3] that last night there was not twelve men to be got in the town to defend it: which the master of the house tells me is not true, but that the men of the town did intend to stay, though they did indeed,

[1] The "Golden Hand" was to have been used for the conveyance of the Swedish Ambassadors' horses and goods to Holland. In August, 1667, Frances, widow of Captain Douglas and daughter of Lord Grey, petitioned the king "for a gift of the prize ship Golden Hand, now employed in weighing the ships sunk at Chatham, where her husband lost his life in defence of the ships against the Dutch" ("Calendar of State Papers," 1667, p. 430).

[2] That is, the block-house. There were formerly considerable fortifications at Gravesend, and about the year 1778 they were greatly extended under the superintendence of Sir Thomas Hyde Page; a few years since, however, a great portion was dismantled, the ground was sold, and the "Terrace Pier," and other works *ejusdem generis* erected. —B.

[3] An error for Sir John Griffith, Governor of Gravesend and captain of West Tilbury Blockhouse, who was knighted at Whitehall, January 2nd, 1665. His name appears in the State Papers almost as often as Griffin as Griffith.

and so had he, at the Ship, removed their goods. Thence went off to an Ostend man-of-war, just now come up, who met the Dutch fleete, who took three ships that he come convoying hither from him: says they are as low as the Nore, or thereabouts. So I homeward, as long as it was light reading Mr. Boyle's book of Hydrostatics, which is a most excellent book as ever I read, and I will take much pains to understand him through if I can, the doctrine being very useful. When it grew too dark to read I lay down and took a nap, it being a most excellent fine evening, and about one o'clock got home, and after having wrote to Sir W. Coventry an account of what I had done and seen (which is entered in my letter-book), I to bed.

11th. Up, and more letters still from Sir W. Coventry about more fire-ships, and so Sir W. Batten and I to the office, where Bruncker come to us, who is just now going to Chatham upon a desire of Commissioner Pett's, who is in a very fearful stink for fear of the Dutch, and desires help for God and the King and kingdom's sake. So Bruncker goes down, and Sir J. Minnes also, from Gravesend. This morning Pett writes us word that Sheernesse is lost last night, after two or three hours' dispute. The enemy hath possessed himself of that place; which is very sad, and puts us into great fears of Chatham. Sir W. Batten and I down by water to Deptford, and there Sir W. Pen and we did consider of several matters relating to the dispatch of the fire-ships, and so [Sir] W. Batten and I home again, and there to dinner, my wife and father having dined, and after dinner, by W. Hewer's lucky advice, went to Mr. Fenn, and did get him to pay me above £400 of my wages, and W. Hewer received it for me, and brought it home this night. Thence I meeting Mr. Moore went toward the other end of the town by coach, and spying Mercer in the street, I took leave of Moore and 'light and followed her, and at Paul's overtook her and walked with her through the dusty street almost to home, and there in Lombard Street met The. Turner in coach, who had been at my house to see us, being to go out of town to-morrow to the Northward, and so I promised to see her to-morrow, and then home, and there to our business, hiring some fire-ships, and receiving every hour almost letters from Sir W. Coventry, calling for more fire-ships; and an order from Council to enable us to take any man's ships; and Sir W. Coventry, in his letter to us, says he do not doubt but at this time, under an invasion, as he owns it to be, the King may, by law, take any man's goods. At this business late, and then home; where a great deal of serious talk with my wife about the sad state we are in, and especially from the beating up of drums this night for the trainbands upon pain of death to appear in arms to-morrow morning with bullet and powder, and money to supply themselves with victuals for a fortnight; which, considering the soldiers drawn out to Chatham and elsewhere, looks as if they had a design to ruin the City and give it up to be undone; which, I hear, makes the sober citizens to think very sadly of things. So to bed after supper, ill in my mind. This afternoon Mrs. Williams sent to me to speak with her, which I did, only about news. I had not spoken with her many a day before by reason of Carcasse's business.

12th. Up very betimes to our business at the office, there hiring of more fire-ships; and at it close all the morning. At noon home, and Sir W. Pen dined with us. By and by, after dinner, my wife out by coach to see her mother; and I in another, being afraid, at this busy time, to be seen with a woman in a coach, as if I were idle, towards The. Turner's; but met Sir W. Coventry's boy; and there in his letter find that the Dutch had made no motion since their taking Sheernesse; and the Duke of Albemarle writes that all is safe as to the great ships against any assault, the boom and chaine[1] being so fortified; which put my heart into great joy. When I come to Sir. W. Coventry's chamber, I find him abroad; but his clerk, Powell, do tell me that ill newes is come to Court of the Dutch breaking the Chaine at Chatham;[2] which struck me to the heart. And to White

[1] There had been correspondence with Pett respecting this chain in April and May. On the 10th May Pett wrote to the Navy Commissioners, "The chain is promised to be dispatched to-morrow, and all things are ready for fixing it." On the 11th June the Dutch "got twenty or twenty-two ships over the narrow part of the river at Chatham, where ships had been sunk; after two and a half hours' fighting one guard-ship after another was fired and blown up, and the enemy master of the chain" ("Calendar of State Papers," 1667, pp. 58, 87, 215).

[2] The account of this national disgrace is very characteristic, in "Poems

Hall to hear the truth of it; and there, going up the back-stairs, I did hear some lacquies speaking of sad newes come to Court, saying, that hardly anybody in the Court but do look as if he cried, and would not go into the house for fear of being seen, but slunk out and got into a coach, and to The. Turner's to Sir W. Turner's, where I met Roger Pepys, newly come out of the country. He and I talked aside a little, he offering a match for Pall, one Barnes, of whom we shall talk more the next time. His father married a Pepys; in discourse, he told me further that his grandfather, my great grandfather, had £800 per annum, in Queen Elizabeth's time, in the very town of Cottenham; and that we did certainly come out of Scotland with the Abbot of Crowland.[1] More talk I had, and shall have more with him, but my mind is so sad and head full of this ill news that I cannot now set it down. A short visit here, my wife coming to me, and took leave of The., and so home, where all our hearts do now ake; for the newes is true, that the Dutch have broken the chaine and burned our ships, and particularly "The Royal Charles:"[2] other particulars I know not, but most sad to be sure. And, the truth is, I do fear so much that the whole kingdom is undone, that I do this night resolve to study with my father and wife what to do with the little that I have in money by me, for I give [up] all the rest that I have in the King's hands, for Tangier, for lost. So God help us! and God knows what disorders we may fall into, and whether any violence on this office, or perhaps some severity on our persons, as being reckoned by the silly people, or perhaps may, by policy of State, be thought fit to be condemned by the King and Duke of York, and so put to trouble; though, God knows! I have, in my own person, done my full duty, I am sure. So having with much ado finished

on State Affairs," vol. i., p. 48, in the "Advice to a Painter," ascribed to Sir John Denham. — B.

[1] Samuel's uncle William told him that William Pepys was born at Dunbar, in Scotland, brought up by the Abbot of Crowland, placed by him at Cottenham, and made "bayliffe of all his lands in Cambridgeshire." He died in 1519, leaving issue three sons and three daughters. There were, however, earlier Pepyses at Cottenham.

[2] Vandervelde's drawings of the conflagration of the English fleet, made by him on the spot, are in the British Museum. — B.

my business at the office, I home to consider with my father and wife of things, and then to supper and to bed with a heavy heart. The manner of my advising this night with my father was, I took him and my wife up to her chamber, and shut the door; and there told them the sad state of the times how we are like to be all undone; that I do fear some violence will be offered to this office, where all I have in the world is; and resolved upon sending it away — sometimes into the country — sometimes my father to lie in town, and have the gold with him at Sarah Giles's, and with that resolution went to bed full of fear and fright, hardly slept all night.

13th. No sooner up but hear the sad newes confirmed of the Royall Charles being taken by them, and now in fitting by them — which Pett should have carried up higher by our several orders, and deserves, therefore, to be hanged for not doing it — and turning several others; and that another fleete is come up into the Hope. Upon which newes the King and Duke of York have been below[1] since four o'clock in the morning, to command the sinking of ships at Barking-Creeke, and other places, to stop their coming up higher: which put me into such a fear, that I presently resolved of my father's and wife's going into the country; and, at two hours' warning, they did go by the coach this day, with about £1,300 in gold in their night-bag. Pray God give them good passage, and good care to hide it when they come home! but my heart is full of fear. They gone, I continued in fright and fear what to do with the rest. W. Hewer hath been at the banker's, and hath got £500 out of Backewell's hands of his own money; but they are so called upon that they will be all broke, hundreds coming to them for money: and their answer is, "It is payable at twenty days — when the days are out, we will pay you;" and those that are not so, they make tell over their money, and make their bags false, on purpose to give cause to retell it, and so spend time. I cannot have my 200 pieces of gold again for silver, all being bought up last night that were to be had, and sold for 24 and 25*s.* a-piece.[2] So I

[1] Below London Bridge.

[2] After the Bank Restriction Act, in 1797, guineas were sold for 27*s.* — B.

must keep the silver by me, which sometimes I think to fling into the house of office, and then again know not how I shall come by it, if we be made to leave the office. Every minute some one or other calls for this or that order; and so I forced to be at the office, most of the day, about the fire-ships which are to be suddenly fitted out: and it's a most strange thing that we hear nothing from any of my brethren at Chatham; so that we are wholly in the dark, various being the reports of what is done there; in so much that I sent Mr. Clapham [1] express thither to see how matters go. I did, about noon, resolve to send Mr. Gibson away after my wife with another 1,000 pieces, under colour of an express to Sir Jeremy Smith; who is, as I hear, with some ships at Newcastle; which I did really send to him, and may, possibly, prove of good use to the King; for it is possible, in the hurry of business, they may not think of it at Court, and the charge of an express is not considerable to the King. So though I intend Gibson no further than to Huntingdon I direct him to send the packet forward. My business the most of the afternoon is listening to every body that comes to the office, what news? which is variously related, some better, some worse, but nothing certain. The King and Duke of York up and down all the day here and there: some time on Tower Hill, where the City militia was; where the King did make a speech to them, that they should venture themselves no further than he would himself. I also sent, my mind being in pain, Saunders after my wife and father, to overtake them at their night's lodgings, to see how matters go with them. In the evening, I sent for my cousin Sarah [Gyles] and her husband, who come; and I did deliver them my chest of writings about Brampton, and my brother Tom's papers, and my journalls, which I value much; and did send my two silver flaggons [2] to Kate Joyce's: that so, being scattered what I have, something might be saved. I have also made a girdle, by which, with some trouble, I do carry about me £300 in gold about

[1] On June 14th John Clapham wrote from Chatham a letter to Pepys describing the doings of the Dutch fleet ("Calendar of State Papers," 1667, p. 185).

[2] See July 28th, 1664, and January 11th, 1667.

my body, that I may not be without something in case I should be surprised: for I think, in any nation but our's, people that appear (for we are not indeed so) so faulty as we, would have their throats cut. In the evening comes Mr. Pelling, and several others, to the office, and tell me that never were people so dejected as they are in the City all over at this day; and do talk most loudly, even treason; as, that we are bought and sold — that we are betrayed by the Papists, and others, about the King; cry out that the office of the Ordnance hath been so backward as no powder to have been at Chatham nor Upnor Castle till such a time, and the carriages all broken; that Legg is a Papist; that Upnor, the old good castle built by Queen Elizabeth, should be lately slighted; that the ships at Chatham should not be carried up higher. They look upon us as lost, and remove their families and rich goods in the City; and do think verily that the French, being come down with his army to Dunkirke, it is to invade us, and that we shall be invaded. Mr. Clerke, the solicitor, comes to me about business, and tells me that he hears that the King hath chosen Mr. Pierpont[1] and Vaughan[2] of the West, Privy-councillors; that my Lord Chancellor was affronted in the Hall this day, by people telling him of his Dunkirke house;[3] and that there are regiments ordered to be got together, whereof to be commanders my Lord Fairfax, Ingoldsby, Bethell, Norton, and Birch, and other Presbyterians; and that Dr. Bates will have liberty to preach. Now, whether this be true or not, I know not; but do think that nothing but this will unite us together. Late at night comes Mr. Hudson, the cooper,

[1] William Pierrepont, called "wise Pierrepont," younger son of the first Earl of Kingston, and brother to the Marquis of Dorchester. His grandson, Robert, succeeded as third Earl of Kingston. — B.

[2] See March 28th, 1664.

[3] See February 20th, 1664–65. Evelyn's "Diary," September 18th, 1683: "After dinner I walked to survey the sad demolition of Clarendon House, that costly and only sumptuous palace of the late Lord Chancellor Hyde. . . . The Chancellor gone, and dying in exile, the Earl his successor sold that which cost £50,000 building to the young Duke of Albemarle for £25,000. . . . He sold it to the highest bidder, and it fell to certain rich bankers and mechanics who gave for it and the ground about it £35,000; they design a new town, as it were, and a most magnificent piazza (*i.e.* square)." — B.

my neighbour, and tells me that he come from Chatham this evening at five o'clock, and saw this afternoon "The Royal James," "Oake," and "London," burnt by the enemy with their fire-ships: that two or three men-of-war come up with them, and made no more of Upnor Castle's shooting, than of a fly; that those ships lay below Upnor Castle, but therein, I conceive, he is in an error; that the Dutch are fitting out "The Royall Charles;" that we shot so far as from the Yard thither, so that the shot did no good, for the bullets grazed on the water; that Upnor played hard with their guns at first, but slowly afterwards, either from the men being beat off, or their powder spent.[1] But we hear that the fleete in the Hope is not come up any higher the last flood; and Sir W. Batten tells me that ships are provided to sink in the River, about Woolwich, that will prevent their coming up higher if they should attempt it. I made my will also this day, and did give all I had equally between my father and wife, and left copies of it in each of Mr. Hater and W. Hewer's hands, who both witnessed the will, and so to supper and then to bed, and slept pretty well, but yet often waking.

14th. Up, and to the office; where Mr. Fryer comes and tells me that there are several Frenchmen and Flemish ships in the River, with passes from the Duke of York for carrying of prisoners, that ought to be parted from the rest of the ships, and their powder taken, lest they do fire themselves when the enemy comes, and so spoil us; which is good advice, and I think I will give notice of it; and did so. But it is pretty odd to see how every body, even at

[1] The want of ammunition when the Dutch burnt the fleet, and the revenge of the deserter sailors, are well described by Marvell:

"Our Seamen, whom no danger's shape could fright,
Unpaid, refuse to mount their ships, for spite:
Or to their fellows swim, on board the Dutch,
Who show the tempting metal in their clutch.
Oft had he [Monk] sent, of *Duncombe* and of *Legge*,
Cannon and powder, but in vain, to beg;
And *Upnor's Castle's ill-deserted wall*,
Now needful does for ammunition call,
He finds, where'er he succour might expect,
Confusion, folly, treachery, fear, neglect."

Instructions to a Painter. — B.

this high time of danger, puts business off of their own hands! He says that he told this to the Lieutenant of the Tower, to whom I, for the same reason, was directing him to go; and the Lieutenant of the Tower bade him come to us, for he had nothing to do with it; and yesterday comes Captain Crew, of one of the fire-ships, and told me that the officers of the Ordnance would deliver his gunner's materials, but not compound them,[1] but that we must do it; whereupon I was forced to write to them about it; and one that like a great many come to me this morning by and by comes — Mr. Wilson,[2] and by direction of his, a man of Mr. Gawden's; who come from Chatham last night, and saw the three ships burnt, they lying all dry, and boats going from the men-of-war and fire them. But that, that he tells me of worst consequence is, that he himself, I think he said, did hear many Englishmen on board the Dutch ships speaking to one another in English; and that they did cry and say, "We did heretofore fight for tickets; now we fight for dollars!" and did ask how such and such a one did, and would commend themselves to them: which is a sad consideration. And Mr. Lewes, who was present at this fellow's discourse to me, did tell me, that he is told that when they took "The Royall Charles," they said that they had their tickets signed, and showed some, and that now they come to have them paid, and would have them paid before they parted. And several seamen come this morning to me, to tell me that, if I would get their tickets paid, they would go and do all they could against the Dutch; but otherwise they would not venture being killed, and lose all they have already fought for: so that I was forced to try what I could do to get them paid. This man tells me that the ships burnt last night did lie above Upnor Castle, over against the Docke; and the boats come from the ships of

[1] Meaning, apparently, that the Ordnance would deliver the charcoal, sulphur, and saltpetre separately, but not mix them as gunpowder — a distinction which has been brought prominently forward lately in the war-rocket case. — B.

[2] Apparently Thomas Wilson, who was appointed gunner in Upnor Castle, July, 1667, "in consideration of his good service in defence of the river at Chatham against the late attempt of the Dutch" ("Calendar of State Papers," 1667, p. 322).

war and burnt them: all which is very sad. And masters of ships, that we are now taking up, do keep from their ships all their stores, or as much as they can, so that we can despatch them, having not time to appraise them nor secure their payment; only some little money we have, which we are fain to pay the men we have with, every night, or they will not work. And indeed the hearts as well as affections of the seamen are turned away; and in the open streets in Wapping, and up and down, the wives have cried publickly, "This comes of your not paying our husbands; and now your work is undone, or done by hands that understand it not." And Sir W. Batten told me that he was himself affronted with a woman, in language of this kind, on Tower Hill publickly yesterday; and we are fain to bear it, and to keep one at the office door to let no idle people in, for fear of firing of the office and doing us mischief. The City is troubled at their being put upon duty: summoned one hour, and discharged two hours after; and then again summoned two hours after that; to their great charge as well as trouble. And Pelling, the Potticary, tells me the world says all over, that less charge than what the kingdom is put to, of one kind or other, by this business, would have set out all our great ships. It is said they did in open streets yesterday, at Westminster, cry, "A Parliament! a Parliament!" and I do believe it will cost blood to answer for these miscarriages. We do not hear that the Dutch are come to Gravesend; which is a wonder. But a wonderful thing it is that to this day we have not one word yet from Bruncker, or Peter Pett, or J. Minnes, of any thing at Chatham. The people that come hither to hear how things go, make me ashamed to be found unable to answer them: for I am left alone here at the office; and the truth is, I am glad my station is to be here, near my own home and out of danger, yet in a place of doing the King good service. I have this morning good news from Gibson; three letters from three several stages, that he was safe last night as far as Royston, at between nine and ten at night. The dismay that is upon us all, in the business of the kingdom and Navy at this day, is not to be expressed otherwise than by the condition the citizens were in when the City was on fire, nobody knowing which way to turn themselves, while every thing concurred to greaten the fire; as here the easterly gale and spring-tides for coming up both rivers, and enabling them to break the chaine. D. Gawden did tell me yesterday, that the day before at the Council they were ready to fall together by the ears at the Council-table, arraigning one another of being guilty of the counsel that brought us into this misery, by laying up all the great ships. Mr. Hater tells me at noon that some rude people have been, as he hears, at my Lord Chancellor's, where they have cut down the trees before his house and broke his windows; and a gibbet either set up before or painted upon his gate, and these three words writ: "Three sights to be seen; Dunkirke, Tangier, and a barren Queene."[1] It gives great matter of talk that it is said there is at this hour, in the Exchequer, as much money as is ready to break down the floor. This arises, I believe, from Sir G. Downing's late talk of the greatness of the sum lying there of people's money, that they would not fetch away, which he shewed me and a great many others. Most people that I speak with are in doubt how we shall do to secure our seamen from running over to the Dutch; which is a sad but very true consideration at this day. At noon I am told that my Lord Duke of Albemarle is made Lord High Constable; the meaning whereof at this time I know not, nor whether it be true or no.[2] Dined, and Mr. Hater and W. Hewer with me; where they do speak very sorrowfully of the posture of the times, and how people do cry out in the streets of their being bought and sold; and both they, and every body that come to me, do tell me that people make nothing of talking treason in the streets openly: as, that we are bought and sold, and governed by Papists, and that we are

[1] "Pride, Lust, Ambition, and the People's Hate,
The kingdom's broker, ruin of the State,
Dunkirk's sad loss, divider of the fleet,
Tangier's compounder for a barren sheet:
This shrub of gentry, married to the crown,
His daughter to the heir, is tumbled down."
Poems on State Affairs, vol. i., p. 253. — B.

[2] The report was not true. The Lord High Constable at the coronation of Charles II. in 1661 was Algernon, Earl of Northumberland. The next holder of this office was Henry, Duke of Grafton, who officiated at the coronation of James II. in 1685.

betrayed by people about the King, and shall be delivered up to the French, and I know not what. At dinner we discoursed of Tom of the Wood, a fellow that lives like a hermit near Woolwich, who, as they say, and Mr. Bodham,[1] they tell me, affirms that he was by at the Justice's when some did accuse him there for it, did foretell the burning of the City, and now says that a greater desolation is at hand. Thence we read and laughed at Lilly's prophecies this month, in his Almanack this year.[2] So to the office after dinner; and thither comes Mr. Pierce, who tells me his condition, how he cannot get his money, about £500, which, he says, is a very great part of what he hath for his family and children, out of Viner's hand: and indeed it is to be feared that this will wholly undo the bankers. He says he knows nothing of the late affronts to my Lord Chancellor's house, as is said, nor hears of the Duke of Albemarle's being made High Constable; but says that they are in great distraction at White Hall, and that every where people do speak high against Sir W. Coventry:[3] but he agrees with me, that he is the best Minister of State the King hath, and so from my heart I believe. At night come home Sir W. Batten and W. Pen, who only can tell me that they have placed guns at Woolwich and Deptford, and sunk some ships below Woolwich and Blackewall, and are in hopes that they will stop the enemy's coming up.

[1] William Bodham was attached to Woolwich Ropeyard.

[2] Probably the following prognostications amused Pepys and his friends: "The several lunations of this month do rather portend sea-fights, wars, &c., than give hopes of peace, particularly the several configurations do very much threaten Holland with a most strange and unusual loss at sea, if they shall dare to fight His Majesty's forces. Still poor Poland is threatened either by the Muscovites or wandering Cossacks. Strange rumours dispersed in London, some vain people abuse His Majesty's subjects with untruths and ill-grounded suggestions. Much division in London about building; perhaps that may occasion those vain and idle reports. Strange news out of Holland, as if all were in an uproar; we believe they are now in a sad and fearful condition." —B.

[3] Evelyn ("Diary," July 29th, 1667) says it was owing to Sir W. Coventry that no fleet was sent out in 1667: "It is well known who of the Commissioners of the Treasury gave advice that the charge of setting forth a fleet this year might be spared, Sir W. C. (William Coventry) by name."

But strange our confusion! that among them that are sunk they have gone and sunk without consideration "The Franakin,"[1] one of the King's ships, with stores to a very considerable value, that hath been long loaden for supply of the ships; and the new ship at Bristoll, and much wanted there; and nobody will own that they directed it, but do lay it on Sir W. Rider. They speak also of another ship, loaden to the value of £80,000, sunk with the goods in her, or at least was mightily contended for by him, and a foreign ship, that had the faith of the nation for her security: this Sir R. Ford tells us. And it is too plain a truth, that both here and at Chatham the ships that we have sunk have many, and the first of them, been ships completely fitted for fire-ships at great charge. But most strange the backwardness and disorder of all people, especially the King's people in pay, to do any work, Sir W. Pen tells me, all crying out for money; and it was so at Chatham, that this night comes an order from Sir W. Coventry to stop the pay of the wages of that Yard; the Duke of Albemarle having related, that not above three of 1,100 in pay there did attend to do any work there. This evening having sent a messenger to Chatham on purpose, we have received a dull letter from my Lord Bruncker and Peter Pett, how matters have gone there this week; but not so much, or so particularly, as we knew it by common talk before, and as true. I doubt they will be found to have been but slow men in this business; and they say the Duke of Albemarle did tell my Lord Bruncker to his face that his discharging of the great ships there was the cause of all this; and I am told that it is become common talk against my Lord Bruncker. But in that he is to be justified, for he did it by verbal order from Sir W. Coventry, and with good intent; and it was to good purpose, whatever the success be, for the men would have but spent the King so much the more in wages, and yet not attended on board to have done the King any service; and as an evidence of that, just now, being the 15th day in the morning that I am writing yesterday's passages, one is with me, Jacob

[1] The "Franakin" was raised, and soon afterwards restored to its former state ("Calendar of State Papers," 1667, pp. 401, 436).

Bryan, Purser of "The Princesse," who confesses to me that he hath about 180 men borne at this day in victuals and wages on that ship lying at Chatham, being lately brought in thither; of which 180 there was not above five appeared to do the King any service at this late business. And this morning also, some of the Cambridge's men come up from Portsmouth, by order from Sir Fretcheville Hollis, who boasted to us the other day that he had sent for 50, and would be hanged if 100 did not come up that would do as much as twice the number of other men: I say some of them, instead of being at work at Deptford, where they were intended, do come to the office this morning to demand the payment of their tickets; for otherwise they would, they said, do no more work; and are, as I understand from every body that has to do with them, the most debauched, damning, swearing rogues that ever were in the Navy, just like their prophane commander. So to Sir W. Batten's to sit and talk a little, and then home to my flageolet, my heart being at pretty good ease by a letter from my wife, brought by Saunders, that my father and wife got well last night to their Inne and out again this morning, and Gibson's being got safe to Caxton[1] at twelve last night. So to supper, and then to bed. No news to-day of any motion of the enemy either upwards towards Chatham or this way.

15th. All the morning at the office. No newes more than last night; only Purser Tyler[2] comes and tells me that he being at all the passages in this business at Chatham, he says there have been horrible miscarriages, such as we shall shortly hear of: that the want of boats hath undone us; and it is commonly said, and Sir J. Minnes under his hand tells us, that they were employed by the men of the Yard to carry away their goods; and I hear that Commissioner Pett will be found the first man that began to remove; he is much spoken against, and Bruncker is complained of and reproached for discharging the men of the great ships heretofore. At noon Mr. Hater dined with me; and tells

[1] Caxton is a town in Cambridgeshire, nine and a half miles west of Cambridge.

[2] Richard Tyler.

me he believes that it will hardly be the want of money alone that will excuse to the Parliament the neglect of not setting out a fleete, it having never been done in our greatest straits, but however unlikely it appeared, yet when it was gone about, the State or King did compass it; and there is something in it. In like manner all the afternoon busy, vexed to see how slowly things go on for want of money. At night comes, unexpectedly so soon, Mr. Gibson, who left my wife well, and all got down well with them, but not with himself, which I was afeard of, and cannot blame him, but must myself be wiser against another time. He had one of his bags broke, through his breeches, and some pieces dropped out, not many, he thinks, but two, for he 'light, and took them up, and went back and could find no more. But I am not able to tell how many, which troubles me, but the joy of having the greatest part safe there makes me bear with it, so as not to afflict myself for it. This afternoon poor Betty Michell, whom I love, sent to tell my wife her child was dying, which I am troubled for, poor girle! At night home and to my flageolet. Played with pleasure, but with a heavy heart, only it pleased me to think how it may please God I may live to spend my time in the country with plainness and pleasure, though but with little glory. So to supper and to bed.

16th (Lord's day). Up, and called on by several on business of the office. Then to the office to look out several of my old letters to Sir W. Coventry in order to the preparing for justifying this office in our frequent foretelling the want of money. By and by comes Roger Pepys and his son Talbot, whom he had brought to town to settle at the Temple, but, by reason of our present stirs, will carry him back again with him this week. He seems to be but a silly lad. I sent them to church this morning, I staying at home at the office, busy. At noon home to dinner, and much good discourse with him, he being mighty sensible of our misery and mal-administration. Talking of these straits we are in, he tells me that my Lord Arlington did the last week take up £12,000 in gold, which is very likely, for all was taken up that could be. Discoursing afterwards with him of our family he told me, that when I come to his house he will show me a decree in Chancery, wherein there was twenty-six men all housekeepers in the town of Cottenham, in Queene Elizabeth's time, of our name. He to church again in the afternoon, I staid at home busy, and did show some dalliance to my maid Nell, speaking to her of her sweetheart which she had, silly girle. After sermon Roger Pepys comes again. I spent the evening with him much troubled with the thoughts of the evils of our time, whereon we discoursed. By and by occasion offered for my writing to Sir W. Coventry a plain bold letter touching lack of money; which, when it was gone, I was afeard might give offence: but upon two or three readings over again the copy of it, I was satisfied it was a good letter; only Sir W. Batten signed it with me, which I could wish I had done alone. Roger Pepys gone, I to the garden, and there dallied a while all alone with Mrs. Markham, and then home to my chamber and to read and write, and then to supper and to bed.

17th. Up, and to my office, where busy all the morning, particularly setting my people to work in transcribing pieces of letters publique and private, which I do collect against a black day to defend the office with and myself. At noon dined at home, Mr. Hater with me alone, who do seem to be confident that this nation will be undone, and with good reason. Wishes himself at Hambrough, as a great many more, he says, he believes do, but nothing but the reconciling of the Presbyterian party will save us, and I am of his mind. At the office all the afternoon, where every moment business of one kind or other about the fire-ships and other businesses, most of them vexatious for want of money, the commanders all complaining that, if they miss to pay their men a night, they run away; seamen demanding money of them by way of advance, and some of Sir Fretcheville Hollis's men, that he so bragged of, demanding their tickets to be paid, or they would not work: this Hollis, Sir W. Batten and W. Pen say, proves a very . . ., as Sir W. B. terms him, and the other called him a conceited, idle, prating, lying fellow. But it was pleasant this morning to hear Hollis give me the account what, he says, he told the King in Commissioner Pett's presence, whence it was that his ship was fit sooner than others, telling the King how he dealt with the several Commissioners and agents of the Ports where he comes, offering Lanyon to carry him a Ton or two of goods to the streights, giving Middleton an hour or two's hearing of his stories of Barbadoes, going to prayer with Taylor, and standing bare and calling, "If it please your Honour," to Pett, but Sir W. Pen says that he tells this story to every body, and believes it to be a very lie. At night comes Captain Cocke to see me, and he and I an hour in the garden together. He tells me there have been great endeavours of bringing in the Presbyterian interest, but that it will not do. He named to me several of the insipid lords that are to command the armies that are to be raised. He says the King and Court are all troubled, and the gates of the Court were shut up upon the first coming of the Dutch to us, but they do mind the business no more than ever: that the bankers, he fears, are broke as to ready-money, though Viner had £100,000 by him when our trouble begun: that he and the Duke of Albemarle have received into their own hands, of Viner, the former £10,000, and the latter £12,000, in tallies or assignments, to secure what was in his hands of their's; and many other great men of our masters have done the like; which is no good sign, when they begin to fear the main. He and every body cries out of the office of the Ordnance, for their neglects, both at Gravesend and Upnor, and everywhere else. He gone, I to my business again, and then home to supper and to bed. I have lately played the fool much with our Nell, in playing with her breasts. This night, late, comes a porter with a letter from Monsieur Pratt, to borrow £100 for my Lord Hinchingbroke, to enable him to go out with his troop in the country, as he is commanded; but I did find an excuse to decline it. Among other reasons to myself, this is one, to teach him the necessity of being a good husband, and keeping money or credit by him.

18th. Up, and did this morning dally with Nell . . . which I was afterward troubled for. To the office, and there all the morning. Peg Pen come to see me, and I was glad of it, and did resolve to have tried her this afternoon, but that there was company with elle at my home, whither I got her. Dined at home, W. Hewer with me, and then to the office, and to my Lady Pen's, and did find occasion for Peg to go home with me to my chamber, but there being an idle gentleman with them, he went with us, and I lost my hope. So to the office, and by and by word was brought me that Commissioner Pett is brought to the Tower,[1] and there laid up close prisoner; which puts me into a fright, lest they may do the same with us as they do with him. This puts me upon hastening what I am doing with my people, and collecting out of my papers our defence. Myself got Fist, Sir W. Batten's clerk, and busy with him writing letters late, and then home to supper and to read myself asleep, after piping, and so to bed. Great newes to-night of the blowing up of one of the Dutch greatest ships, while a Council of War was on board: the latter part, I doubt, is not so, it not being confirmed since; but the former, that they had a ship blown up, is said to be true. This evening comes Sir G. Carteret to the office, to talk of business at Sir W. Batten's; where all to be undone for want of money, there being none to pay the Chest at their publique pay the 24th of this month, which will make us a scorn to the world. After he had done there, he and I into the garden, and walked; and the greatest of our discourse is, his sense of the requisiteness of his parting with his being Treasurer of the Navy, if he can, on any good terms. He do harp upon getting my Lord Bruncker to take it on half profit, but that he is not able to secure him in paying him so much. But the thing I do advise him to do by all means, and he resolves on it, being but the same counsel which I intend to take myself. My Lady Jem goes down to Hinchingbroke to lie down, because of the troubles of the times here. He tells me he is not sure that the King of France will not annoy us this year, but that the Court seems [to] reckon upon it as a thing certain, for that is all that I and most people are afeard of this year. He tells me now the great question

[1] "June 17th. This day, Commissioner Pett, to whom was committed the care of the Yard at Chatham, with the affairs of the Navy there, was committed close prisoner to the Tower, in order to his farther examination." — *The London Gazette*, No. 166. "Warrants to [John] Bradley to seize [Peter] Pett, Commissioner at Chatham, and bring him to the Tower; and to the Lieutenant of the Tower to keep him close prisoner, for dangerous practices and misdemeanours," dated June 16th ("Calendar of State Papers," 1667, p. 196).

is, whether a Parliament or no Parliament; and says the Parliament itself cannot be thought able at present to raise money, and therefore it will be to no purpose to call one. I hear this day poor Michell's child is dead.

19th. Up, and to the office, where all the morning busy with Fist again, beginning early to overtake my business in my letters, which for a post or two have by the late and present troubles been interrupted. At noon comes Sir W. Batten and [Sir] W. Pen, and we to [Sir] W. Pen's house, and there discoursed of business an hour, and by and by comes an order from Sir R. Browne, commanding me this afternoon to attend the Council-board, with all my books and papers touching the Medway. I was ready [to fear] some mischief to myself, though it appears most reasonable that it is to inform them about Commissioner Pett. I eat a little bit in haste at Sir W. Batten's, without much comfort, being fearful, though I shew it not, and to my office and get up some papers, and found out the most material letters and orders in our books, and so took coach and to the Council-chamber lobby, where I met Mr. Evelyn, who do miserably decry our follies that bring all this misery upon us. While we were discoursing over our publique misfortunes, I am called in to a large Committee of the Council: present the Duke of Albemarle, Anglesey, Arlington, Ashly, Carteret, Duncomb, Coventry, Ingram, Clifford, Lauderdale, Morrice, Manchester, Craven, Carlisle, Bridgewater. And after Sir W. Coventry's telling them what orders His Royal Highness had made for the safety of the Medway, I told them to their full content what we had done, and showed them our letters. Then was Peter Pett called in, with the Lieutenant of the Tower. He is in his old clothes, and looked most sillily. His charge was chiefly the not carrying up of the great ships, and the using of the boats in carrying away his goods; to which he answered very sillily, though his faults to me seem only great omissions. Lord Arlington and Coventry very severe against him; the former saying that, if he was not guilty, the world would think them all guilty.[1] The latter urged, that

[1] Pett was made a scapegoat. This is confirmed by Marvell:

> "After this loss, to relish discontent,
> Some one must be accused by Parliament;

there must be some faults, and that the Admiral must be found to have done his part. I did say an unhappy word, which I was sorry for, when he complained of want of oares for the boats: and there was, it seems, enough, and good enough, to carry away all the boats with from the King's occasions. He said he used never a boat till they were all gone but one; and that was to carry away things of great value, and these were his models of ships; which, when the Council, some of them, had said they wished that the Dutch had had them instead of the King's ships, he answered, he did believe the Dutch would have made more advantage of the models than of the ships, and that the King had had greater loss thereby; this they all laughed at. After having heard him for an hour or more, they bid him withdraw. I all this while showing him no respect, but rather against him, for which God forgive me! for I mean no hurt to him, but only find that these Lords are upon their own purgation, and it is necessary I should be so in behalf of the office. He being gone, they caused Sir

All our miscarriages on Pett must fall,
His name alone seems fit to answer all.
Whose counsel first did this mad war beget?
Who all commands sold through the Navy? *Pett.*
Who would not follow when the Dutch were beat?
Who treated out the time at Bergen? *Pett.*
Who the Dutch fleet with storms disabled met,
And, rifling prizes, them neglected? *Pett.*
Who with false news prevented the Gazette,
The fleet divided, writ for *Rupert? Pett.*
Who all our seamen cheated of their debt?
And all our prizes who did swallow? *Pett.*
Who did advise no navy out to set?
And who the forts left unprepared? *Pett.*
Who to supply with powder did forget
Languard, Sheerness, Gravesend, and Upnor? Pett.
Who all our ships exposed in Chatham net?
Who should it be but the fanatick *Pett?*
Pett, the sea-architect, in making ships,
Was the first cause of all these naval slips.
Had he not built, none of these faults had been;
If no creation, there had been no sin:
But his great crime, one boat away he sent,
That lost our fleet, and did our flight prevent."

Instructions to a Painter. — B.

Richard Browne[1] to read over his minutes; and then my Lord Arlington moved that they might be put into my hands to put into form, I being more acquainted with such business; and they were so. So I away back with my books and papers; and when I got into the Court it was pretty to see how people gazed upon me, that I thought myself obliged to salute people and to smile, lest they should think I was a prisoner too; but afterwards I found that most did take me to be there to bear evidence against P. Pett; but my fear was such, at my going in, of the success of the day, that at my going in I did think fit to give T. Hater, whom I took with me, to wait the event, my closet-key and directions where to find £500 and more in silver and gold, and my tallys, to remove, in case of any misfortune to me. Thence to Sir G. Carteret's to take my leave of my Lady Jem, who is going into the country to-morrow; but she being now at prayers with my Lady and family, and hearing here by Yorke, the carrier, that my wife is coming to towne, I did make haste home to see her, that she might not find me abroad, it being the first minute I have been abroad since yesterday was se'ennight. It is pretty to see how strange it is to be abroad to see people, as it used to be after a month or two's absence, and I have brought myself so to it, that I have no great mind to be abroad, which I could not have believed of myself. I got home, and after being there a little, she come, and two of her fellow-travellers with her, with whom we drunk: a couple of merchant-like men, I think, but have friends in our country. They being gone, I and my wife to talk, who did give me so bad an account of her and my father's method in burying of our gold, that made me mad: and she herself is not pleased with it, she believing that my sister knows of it. My father and she did it on Sunday, when they were gone to church, in open daylight, in the midst of the garden; where, for aught they knew, many eyes might see them: which put me into such trouble, that I was almost mad about it, and presently cast about, how to have it back again to secure it here, the times being a little better now; at least at White Hall they seem as if they were, but one

[1] Clerk of the Council.

way or other I am resolved to free them from the place if I can get them. Such was my trouble at this, that I fell out with my wife, that though new come to towne, I did not sup with her, nor speak to her to-night, but to bed and sleep.

20th. Up, without any respect to my wife, only answering her a question or two, without any anger though, and so to the office, where all the morning busy, and among other things Mr. Barber come to me (one of the clerks of the Ticket office) to get me to sign some tickets, and told me that all the discourse yesterday, about that part of the town where he was, was that Mr. Pett and I were in the Tower; and I did hear the same before. At noon, home to dinner, and there my wife and I very good friends; the care of my gold being somewhat over, considering it was in their hands that have as much cause to secure it as myself almost, and so if they will be mad, let them. But yet I do intend to send for it away. Here dined Mercer with us, and after dinner she cut my hair, and then I into my closet and there slept a little, as I do now almost every day after dinner; and then, after dallying a little with Nell, which I am ashamed to think of, away to the office. Busy all the afternoon; in the evening did treat with, and in the end agree, but by some kind of compulsion, with the owners of six merchant ships, to serve the King as men-of-war. But, Lord! to see how against the hair it is with these men and every body to trust us and the King; and how unreasonable it is to expect they should be willing to lend their ships, and lay out 2 or £300 a man to fit their ships for new voyages, when we have not paid them half of what we owe them for their old services! I did write so to Sir W. Coventry this night. At night my wife and I to walk and talk again about our gold, which I am not quiet in my mind to be safe, and therefore will think of some way to remove it, it troubling me very much. So home with my wife to supper and to bed, miserable hot weather all night it was.

21st. Up and by water to White Hall, there to discourse with [Sir] G. Carteret and Mr. Fenn about office business. I found them all aground, and no money to do anything with. Thence homewards, calling at my Tailor's to bespeak some coloured clothes, and thence to Hercules Pillars, all alone, and there spent *6d.* on myself, and so home and busy all the morning. At noon to dinner, home, where my wife shows me a letter from her father, who is going over sea, and this afternoon would take his leave of her. I sent him by her three Jacobuses in gold, having real pity for him and her. So I to my office, and there all the afternoon. This day comes news from Harwich that the Dutch fleete are all in sight, near 100 sail great and small, they think, coming towards them; where, they think, they shall be able to oppose them; but do cry out of the falling back of the seamen, few standing by them, and those with much faintness. The like they write from Portsmouth, and their letters this post are worth reading. Sir H. Cholmly come to me this day, and tells me the Court is as mad as ever; and that the night the Dutch burned our ships the King did sup with my Lady Castlemayne, at the Duchess of Monmouth's, and they were all mad in hunting a poor moth. All the Court afraid of a Parliament; but he thinks nothing can save us but the King's giving up all to a Parliament. Busy at the office all the afternoon, and did much business to my great content. In the evening sent for home, and there I find my Lady Pen and Mrs. Lowther, and Mrs. Turner and my wife eating some victuals, and there I sat and laughed with them a little, and so to the office again, and in the evening walked with my wife in the garden, and did give Sir W. Pen at his lodgings (being just come from Deptford from attending the dispatch of the fire-ships there) an account of what passed the other day at Council touching Commissioner Pett, and so home to supper and to bed.

22nd. Up, and to my office, where busy, and there comes Mrs. Daniel. . . . At the office I all the morning busy. At noon home to dinner, where Mr. Lewes Phillips, by invitation of my wife, comes, he coming up to town with her in the coach this week, and she expected another gentleman, a fellow-traveller, and I perceive the feast was for him, though she do not say it, but by some mistake he come not, so there was a good dinner lost. Here we had the two Mercers, and pretty merry. Much talk with Mr. Phillips about country business, among others that there is no way for me to purchase any severall lands in Brampton, or making any severall that is not so, without much trouble and cost, and, it may be, not do it neither, so that there is no more ground to be laid to our Brampton house. After dinner I left them, and to the office, and thence to Sir W. Pen's, there to talk with Mrs. Lowther, and by and by we hearing Mercer and my boy singing at my house, making exceeding good musique, to the joy of my heart, that I should be the master of it, I took her to my office and there merry a while, and then I left them, and at the office busy all the afternoon, and sleepy after a great dinner. In the evening come Captain Hart[1] and Haywood to me about the six merchant-ships now taken up for men-of-war; and in talk they told me about the taking of "The Royal Charles;" that nothing but carelessness lost the ship, for they might have saved her the very tide that the Dutch come up, if they would have but used means and had had but boats: and that the want of boats plainly lost all the other ships. That the Dutch did take her with a boat of nine men, who found not a man on board her, and her laying so near them was a main temptation to them to come on; and presently a man went up and struck her flag and jacke, and a trumpeter sounded upon her "Joan's placket is torn:"[2] that they did carry her down at a time, both for tides and wind, when the best pilot in Chatham would not have undertaken it, they heeling her on one side to make her draw little water: and so carried her away safe. They being gone, by and by comes Sir W. Pen home, and he and I together talking. He hath been at Court; and in the first place, I hear the Duke of Cambridge is dead;[3] which is a great loss to the nation, having, I think, never an heyre male now of the King's or Duke's to succeed to the Crown. He tells me that they do begin already to damn the Dutch, and call them cowards at White Hall, and think of them and their business no better than they used to do; which is very sad. The King did tell him himself, which is so,

[1] The warrant of the Earl of Sandwich, appointing John Hart captain of the "Revenge," September 13th, 1665, is among the loose papers in Rawlinson, A. 289. — B.

[2] This was the earliest notice of the air so named that Mr. William Chappell had come across. He was unable to discover the original words. ("Popular Music of the Olden Time," p. 518.)

[3] He died on June 20th at Richmond.

I was told, here in the City, that the City hath lent him £10,000, to be laid out towards securing of the River of Thames; which, methinks, is a very poor thing, that we should be induced to borrow by such mean sums. He tells me that it is most manifest that one great thing making it impossible for us to have set out a fleete this year, if we could have done it for money or stores, was the liberty given the beginning of the year for the setting out of merchant-men, which did take up, as is said, above ten, if not fifteen thousand seamen: and this the other day Captain Cocke tells me appears in the Council-books, that is the number of seamen required to man the merchant ships that had passes to go abroad. By and by, my wife being here, they sat down and eat a bit of their nasty victuals, and so parted and we to bed.

23rd (Lord's day). Up to my chamber, and there all the morning reading in my Lord Coke's Pleas of the Crowne,[1] very fine noble reading. After church time comes my wife and Sir W. Pen his lady and daughter, and Mrs. Markham and Captain Harrison (who come to dine with them), by invitation and dined with me, they as good as inviting themselves. I confess I hate their company and tricks, and so had no great pleasure in [it], but a good dinner lost. After dinner they all to church, and I by water alone to Woolwich, and there called on Mr. Bodham: and he and I to see the batterys newly raised; which, indeed, are good works to command the River below the ships that are sunk, but not above them. Here I met with Captain Cocke and Matt. Wren, Fenn, and Charles Porter, and Temple and his wife. Here I fell in with these, and to Bodham's with them, and there we sat and laughed and drank in his arbour, Wren making much and kissing all the day of Temple's wife. It is a sad sight to see so many good ships there sunk in the River, while we would be thought to be masters of the sea. Cocke says the bankers cannot, till peace returns, ever hope to have credit again; so that they can pay no more money, but people must be

1 "The Third Part of the Institutes of the Laws of England concerning High Treason and other Pleas of the Crown and Criminall Cases," by Sir Edward Coke; London, 1644, folio.

contented to take publick security such as they can give them; and if so, and they do live to receive the money thereupon, the bankers will be happy men. Fenn read me an order of council passed the 17th instant, directing all the Treasurers of any part of the King's revenue to make no payments but such as shall be approved by the present Lords Commissioners; which will, I think, spoil the credit of all his Majesty's service, when people cannot depend upon payment any where. But the King's declaration [1] in behalf of the bankers, to make good their assignments for money, is very good, and will, I hope, secure me. Cocke says, that he hears it is come to it now, that the King will try what he can soon do for a peace; and if he cannot, that then he will cast all upon the Parliament to do as they see fit: and in doing so, perhaps, he may save us all. The King of France, it is believed, is engaged for this year; [2]

[1] "I shall draw towards a conclusion of this section with a case of very recent memory and of singular notoriety throughout the whole kingdom. I mean that of the conflagration of our ships by the Dutch (June, 1667) not many years past in the river of Chatham. There prevailed at that time an universal jealousie among the people that upon this occasion some suddain stop might be put upon the Exchequer, and thereupon the Bankers were exercised with restless solicitations for the speedy payment of their debts. The king for the sedation of these fears and apprehensions is advised (and to the eternal honour of the persons who gave the advice I write it) to issue forthwith his declaration (see the Declaration at the end of this treatise), to preserve inviolate the course of payments in the Exchequer, which was accordingly done" ("The Case of the Bankers and their Creditors Stated and Examined; the third impression with additions amounting to a third part more than hath been at any time before printed," London, 1675, 8vo., pp. 105, 106). This curious little work, written to show the enormity of shutting up the Exchequer, is composed by Thomas Turnor, as appears by the preliminary letter and by the postscript at the end. The "Declaration" alluded to, which was issued in 1667, is printed in pp. 135-137.—Buckle's *Miscel. and Posth. Works*, vol. ii., p. 215.—M. B.

[2] Louis XIV. was at this time in Flanders, with his queen, his mistresses, and all his Court. Turenne commanded under him. Whilst Charles was hunting moths at Lady Castlemaine's, and the English fleet was burning, Louis was carrying on the campaign with vigour. Armentières was taken on the 28th May; Charleroi on the 2nd June, St. Winox on the 6th, Furnes on the 12th, Ath on the 16th, Tournay on the 24th; the Escarpe on the 6th July, Courtray on the 18th, Audenarde on the 31st; and Lisle on the 27th August.—B.

so that we shall be safe as to him. The great misery the City and kingdom is like to suffer for want of coals[1] in a little time is very visible, and, is feared, will breed a mutiny; for we are not in any prospect to command the sea for our colliers to come, but rather, it is feared, the Dutch may go and burn all our colliers at Newcastle; though others do say that they lie safe enough there. No news at all of late from Bredagh[2] what our Treaters do. By and by, all by water in three boats to Greenwich, there to Cocke's, where we supped well, and then late, Wren, Fenn, and I home by water, set me in at the Tower, and they to White Hall, and so I home, and after a little talk with my wife to bed.

24th. Up, and to the office, where much business upon me by the coming of people of all sorts about the dispatch of one business or other of the fire-ships, or other ships to be set out now. This morning Greeting come, and I with him at my flageolet. At noon dined at home with my wife alone, and then in the afternoon all the day at my office. Troubled a little at a letter from my father, which tells me of an idle companion, one Coleman, who went down with him and my wife in the coach, and come up again with my wife, a pensioner of the King's Guard, and one that my wife, indeed, made the feast for on Saturday last, though he did not come; but if he knows nothing of our money I will prevent any other inconvenience. In the evening comes Mr. Povy about business; and he and I to walk in the garden an hour or two, and to talk of State matters. He tells me his opinion that it is out of possibility for us to escape being undone, there being nothing in our power to do that is necessary for the saving us: a lazy Prince, no Council, no money, no reputation at home or abroad. He says that to this day the King do follow the women as much as ever he did; that the Duke of York hath not got Mrs. Middleton, as I was told the other day: but says that he wants not her, for he hath others, and hath always had, and that he [Povy] hath known them brought through the Matted Gallery at White Hall into his [the

[1] See June 26th, *post.*
[2] See August 9th, *post.*

Duke's] closet; nay, he hath come out of his wife's bed, and gone to others laid in bed for him: that Mr. Bruncker is not the only pimp, but that the whole family is of the same strain, and will do any thing to please him: that, besides the death of the two Princes lately, the family is in horrible disorder by being in debt by spending above £60,000 per annum, when he hath not £40,000: that the Duchesse is not only the proudest woman in the world, but the most expensefull; and that the Duke of York's marriage with her hath undone the kingdom, by making the Chancellor so great above reach, who otherwise would have been but an ordinary man, to have been dealt with by other people; and he would have been careful of managing things well, for fear of being called to account; whereas, now he is secure, and hath let things run to rack, as they now appear. That at a certain time Mr. Povy did carry him an account of the state of the Duke of York's estate, showing in faithfullness how he spent more than his estate would bear, by above £20,000 per annum, and asked my Lord's opinion of it; to which he answered that no man that loved the King or kingdom durst own the writing of that paper; at which Povy was startled, and reckoned himself undone for this good service, and found it necessary then to show it to the Duke of York's Commissioners;[1] who read, examined, and approved of it, so as to cause it to be put into form, and signed it, and gave it the Duke. Now the end of the Chancellor was, for fear that his daughter's ill housewifery should be condemned. He [Povy] tells me that the other day, upon this ill newes of the Dutch being upon us, White Hall was shut up, and the Council called and sat close; and, by the way, he do assure me, from the mouth of some Privy-councillors, that at this day the Privy-council in general do know no more what the state of the kingdom as to peace and war is, than he or I; nor knows who manages it, nor upon whom it depends; and there my Lord Chancellor did make a speech to them, saying that they knew well that he was no friend to the war from the

[1] The Commissioners for regulating the Duke of York's affairs, in May, 1667, were John, Lord Berkeley of Stratton, Colonel Robert Werden, and Colonel Anthony Eyre. — *Household Book*, at Audley-End. — B.

beginning, and therefore had concerned himself little in, nor could say much to it; and a great deal of that kind, to discharge himself of the fault of the war. Upon which my Lord Anglesey rose up and told his Majesty that he thought their coming now together was not to enquire who was, or was not, the cause of the war, but to enquire what was, or could be, done in the business of making a peace, and in whose hands that was, and where it was stopped or forwarded; and went on very highly to have all made open to them: and, by the way, I remember that Captain Cocke did the other day tell me that this Lord Anglesey hath said, within few days, that he would willingly give £10,000 of his estate that he was well secured of the rest, such apprehensions he hath of the sequel of things, as giving all over for lost. He tells me, speaking of the horrid effeminacy of the King, that the King hath taken ten times more care and pains in making friends between my Lady Castlemayne and Mrs. Stewart, when they have fallen out, than ever he did to save his kingdom; nay, that upon any falling out between my Lady Castlemayne's nurse and her woman, my Lady hath often said she would make the King to make them friends, and they would be friends and be quiet; which the King hath been fain to do: that the King is, at this day, every night in Hyde Park with the Duchesse of Monmouth, or with my Lady Castlemayne: that he [Povy] is concerned of late by my Lord Arlington in the looking after some buildings that he is about in Norfolke,[1] where my Lord is laying out a great deal of money; and that he, Mr. Povy, considering the unsafeness of laying out money at such a time as this, and, besides, the enviousness of the particular county, as well as all the kingdom, to find him building and employing workmen, while all the ordinary people of the country are carried down to the sea-sides for securing the land, he thought it becoming him to go to my

[1] At Buston Hall, in Suffolk, on the borders of Norfolk, which afterwards came into the Grafton family by the marriage of the first duke with Lord Arlington's only child. Among Pepys's papers (Rawlinson, A. 195, fol. 58) is a document, entitled "Considerations touching the purchase of the Park and Woods near Euston, drawn and presented by Mr. Povy, as his advice to my Lord Arlington, at this time (Oct. 28, 1668) in treaty for the purchase of Euston." — B.

Lord Arlington (Sir Thomas Clifford by), and give it as his advice to hold his hands a little; but my Lord would not, but would have him go on, and so Sir Thomas Clifford advised also, which one would think, if he were a statesman worth a fart should be a sign of his foreseeing that all shall do well. But I do forbear concluding any such thing from them. He tells me that there is not so great confidence between any two men of power in the nation at this day, that he knows of, as between my Lord Arlington and Sir Thomas Clifford; and that it arises by accident only, there being no relation nor acquaintance between them, but only Sir Thomas Clifford's coming to him, and applying himself to him for favours, when he come first up to town to be a Parliament-man. He tells me that he do not think there is anything in the world for us possibly to be saved by but the King of France's generousnesse to stand by us against the Dutch, and getting us a tolerable peace, it may be, upon our giving him Tangier and the islands he hath taken, and other things he shall please to ask. He confirms me in the several grounds I have conceived of fearing that we shall shortly fall into mutinys and outrages among ourselves, and that therefore he, as a Treasurer, and therefore much more myself, I say, as being not only a Treasurer but an officer of the Navy, on whom, for all the world knows, the faults of all our evils are to be laid, do fear to be seized on by some rude hands as having money to answer for, which will make me the more desirous to get off of this Treasurership as soon as I can, as I had before in my mind resolved. Having done all this discourse, and concluded the kingdom in a desperate condition, we parted; and I to my wife, with whom was Mercer and Betty Michell, poor woman, come with her husband to see us after the death of her little girle. We sat in the garden together a while, it being night, and then Mercer and I a song or two, and then in (the Michell's home,) my wife, Mercer, and I to supper, and then parted and to bed.

25th. Up, and with Sir W. Pen in his new chariot (which indeed is plain, but pretty and more fashionable in shape than any coach he hath, and yet do not cost him, harness and all, above £32) to White Hall; where staid a very little: and thence to St. James's to [Sir] W. Coventry, whom

I have not seen since before the coming of the Dutch into the river, nor did indeed know how well to go to see him, for shame either to him or me, or both of us, to find ourselves in so much misery. I find that he and his fellow-Treasurers are in the utmost want of money, and do find fault with Sir G. Carteret, that, having kept the mystery of borrowing money to himself so long, to the ruin of the nation, as [Sir] W. Coventry said in words to [Sir] W. Pen and me, he should now lay it aside and come to them for money for every penny he hath, declaring that he can raise no more: which, I confess, do appear to me the most like ill-will of any thing that I have observed of [Sir] W. Coventry, when he himself did tell us, on another occasion at the same time, that the bankers who used to furnish them money are not able to lend a farthing, and he knows well enough that that was all the mystery [Sir] G. Carteret did use, that is, only his credit with them. He told us the masters and owners of the two ships that I had complained of, for not readily setting forth their ships, which we had taken up to make men-of-war, had been yesterday with the King and Council, and had made their case so well understood, that the King did owe them for what they had earned the last year, that they could not set them out again without some money or stores out of the King's Yards; the latter of which [Sir] W. Coventry said must be done, for that they were not able to raise money for them, though it was but £200 a ship: which do shew us our condition to be so bad, that I am in a total despair of ever having the nation do well. After talking awhile, and all out of heart with stories of want of seamen, and seamen's running away, and their demanding a month's advance, and our being forced to give seamen 3*s*. a-day to go hence to work at Chatham, and other things that show nothing but destruction upon us; for it is certain that, as it now is, the seamen of England, in my conscience, would, if they could, go over and serve the King of France or Holland rather than us. Up to the Duke of York to his chamber, where he seems to be pretty easy, and now and then merry; but yet one may perceive in all their minds there is something of trouble and care, and with good reason. Thence to White Hall, and with Sir W. Pen, by chariot; and there in the

Court met with my Lord Anglesey: and he to talk with [Sir] W. Pen, and told him of the masters of ships being with the Council yesterday, and that we were not in condition, though the men were willing, to furnish them with £200 of money, already due to them as earned by them the last year, to enable them to set out their ships again this year for the King: which he is amazed at; and when I told him, "My Lord, this is a sad instance of the condition we are in," he answered, that it was so indeed, and sighed: and so parted: and he up to the Council-chamber, where I perceive they sit every morning, and I to Westminster Hall, where it is Term time. I met with none I knew, nor did desire it, but only past through the Hall and so back again, and by coach home to dinner, being weary indeed of seeing the world, and thinking it high time for me to provide against the foul weather that is certainly coming upon us. So to the office, and there [Sir] W. Pen and I did some business, and then home to dinner, where my wife pleases me mightily with what she can do upon the flageolet, and then I to the office again, and busy all the afternoon, and it is worth noting that the King and Council, in their order of the 23rd instant, for unloading three merchant-ships taken up for the King's service for men-of-war, do call the late coming of the Dutch "an invasion." I was told, yesterday, that Mr. Oldenburg,[1] our Secretary at Gresham College, is put into the Tower, for writing newes to a virtuoso in France, with whom he constantly corresponds in philosophical matters; which makes it very unsafe at this time to write, or almost do any thing. Several captains come to the office yesterday and to-day, complaining that their men come and go when they will, and will not be commanded, though they are paid every night, or may be. Nay, this afternoon comes Harry Russell from Gravesend, telling us that the money carried down yesterday for the Chest at Chatham had like to have been seized upon yesterday, in the barge there by seamen, who did beat our watermen: and what men should these be but the boat's crew of Sir Fretcheville Hollis, who used to brag so much

[1] Henry Oldenburgh, secretary to the Royal Society. The warrant for his arrest is dated June 20th, 1667. The warrant for his discharge is dated August 26th.

of the goodness and order of his men, and his command over them. Busy all the afternoon at the office. Towards night I with Mr. Kinaston to White Hall about a Tangier order, but lost our labour, only met Sir H. Cholmly there, and he tells me great newes; that this day in Council the King hath declared that he will call his Parliament in thirty days: which is the best newes I have heard a great while, and will, if any thing, save the kingdom. How the King come to be advised to this, I know not; but he tells me that it was against the Duke of York's mind flatly, who did rather advise the King to raise money as he pleased; and against the Chancellor's, who told the King that Queen Elizabeth did do all her business in eighty-eight without calling a Parliament, and so might he do, for anything he saw. But, blessed be God! it is done; and pray God it may hold, though some of us must surely go to the pot, for all must be flung up to them, or nothing will be done. So back home, and my wife down by water, I sent her, with Mrs. Hewer and her son, W. Hewer, to see the sunk ships, while I staid at the office, and in the evening was visited by Mr. Roberts the merchant by us about the getting him a ship cleared from serving the King as a man of war, which I will endeavour to do. So home to supper and to bed.

26th. Up, and in dressing myself in my dressing chamber comes up Nell, and I did play with her. . . . So being ready I to White Hall by water, and there to the Lords Treasurers' chamber, and there wait, and here it is every body's discourse that the Parliament is ordered to meet the 25th of July, being, as they say, St. James's day; which every creature is glad of. But it is pretty to consider how, walking to the Old Swan from my house, I met Sir Thomas Harvy, whom, asking the newes of the Parliament's meeting, he told me it was true, and they would certainly make a great rout among us. I answered, I did not care for my part, though I was ruined, so that the Commonwealth might escape ruin by it. He answered, that is a good one, in faith; for you know yourself to be secure, in being necessary to the office; but for my part, says he, I must look to be removed; but then, says he, I doubt not but I shall have amends made me; for all the world knows upon what terms I come in, which is a saying that a wise man would not unnecessarily have said, I think, to any body, meaning his buying his place of my Lord Barkely [of Stratton]. So we parted, and I to White Hall, as I said before, and there met with Sir Stephen Fox and Mr. Scawen, who both confirm the news of the Parliament's meeting. Here I staid for an order for my Tangier money, £30,000, upon the 11 months' tax, and so away to my Lord Arlington's office, and there spoke to him about Mr. Lanyon's business, and received a good answer, and thence to Westminster Hall and there walked a little, and there met with Colonell Reames, who tells me of a letter come last night, or the day before, from my Lord St. Albans, out of France, wherein he says, that the King of France did lately fall out with him, giving him ill names, saying that he had belied him to our King, by saying that he had promised to assist our King, and to forward the peace; saying that indeed he had offered to forward the peace at such a time, but it was not accepted of, and so he thinks himself not obliged, and would do what was fit for him; and so made him to go out of his sight in great displeasure: and he hath given this account to the King, which, Colonell Reymes tells me, puts them into new melancholy at Court, and he believes hath forwarded the resolution of calling the Parliament. Wherewith for all this I am very well contented, and so parted and to the Exchequer, but Mr. Burgess was not in his office; so alone to the Swan, and thither come Mr. Kinaston to me, and he and I into a room and there drank and discoursed, and I am mightily pleased with him for a most diligent and methodical man in all his business. By and by to Burgess, and did as much as we could with him about our Tangier order, though we met with unexpected delays in it, but such as are not to be avoided by reason of the form of the Act and the disorders which the King's necessities do put upon it, and therefore away by coach, and at White Hall spied Mr. Povy, who tells me, as a great secret, which none knows but himself, that Sir G. Carteret hath parted with his place of Treasurer of the Navy, by consent, to my Lord Anglesey, and is to be Treasurer of Ireland in his stead; but upon what terms it is I know not, but Mr. Povy tells it is so, and that it is in his power to bring me to as great a friendship and confidence in my Lord Anglesey as ever I was with [Sir] W. Coventry, which I am glad of, and so parted, and I to my tailor's about turning my old silk suit and cloak into a suit and vest, and thence with Mr. Kinaston (whom I had set down in the Strand and took up again at the Temple gate) home, and there to dinner, mightily pleased with my wife's playing on the flageolet, and so after dinner to the office. Such is the want already of coals, and the despair of having any supply, by reason of the enemy's being abroad, and no fleete of ours to secure, that they are come, as Mr. Kinaston tells me, at this day to £5 10*s.* per chaldron. All the afternoon busy at the office. In the evening with my wife and Mercer took coach and to Islington to the Old House, and there eat and drank and sang with great pleasure, and then round by Hackney home with great pleasure, and when come home to bed, my stomach not being well pleased with the cream we had to-night.

27th. Wakened this morning, about three o'clock, by Mr. Griffin with a letter from Sir W. Coventry to W. Pen, which W. Pen sent me to see, that the Dutch are come up to the Nore again, and he knows not whether further or no, and would have, therefore, several things done — ships sunk, and I know not what — which Sir W. Pen (who it seems is very ill this night, or would be thought so) hath directed Griffin to carry to the Trinity House; so he went away with the letter, and I tried and with much ado did get a little sleep more, and so up about six o'clock, full of thought what to do with the little money I have left and my plate, wishing with all my heart that that was all secured. So to the office, where much business all the morning, and the more by my brethren being all out of the way; Sir W. Pen this night taken so ill cannot stir; [Sir] W. Batten ill at Walthamstow; Sir J. Minnes the like at Chatham, and my Lord Bruncker there also upon business. Horrible trouble with the backwardness of the merchants to let us have their ships, and seamen's running away, and not to be got or kept without money. It is worth turning to our letters this day to Sir W. Coventry about these matters. At noon to dinner, having a haunch of venison boiled; and all my clerks at dinner with me; and mightily taken with Mr. Gibson's discourse of the faults of this war in its management compared [with] that in the last war, which I will get him to put into writing. Thence, after dinner, to the office again, and there I saw the proclamations[1] come out this day for the Parliament to meet the 25th of next month; for which God be praised! and another to invite seamen to bring in their complaints, of their being ill-used in the getting their tickets and money, there being a Committee of the Council appointed to receive their complaints. This noon W. Hewer and T. Hater both tell me that it is all over the town, and Mr. Pierce tells me also, this afternoon coming to me, that for certain Sir G. Carteret hath parted with his Treasurer's place, and that my Lord Anglesey is in it upon agreement and change of places, though the latter part I do not think. This Povy told me yesterday, and I think it is a wise act of [Sir] G. Carteret. Pierce tells me that he hears for certain fresh at Court, that France and we shall agree; and more, that yesterday was damned at the Council, the Canary Company; and also that my Lord Mordaunt hath laid down his Commission, both good things to please the Parliament, which I hope will do good. Pierce tells me that all the town do cry out of our office, for a pack of fools and knaves; but says that everybody speaks either well, or at least the best of me, which is my great comfort, and think I do deserve it, and shall shew I have; but yet do think, and he also, that the Parliament will send us all going; and I shall be well contented with it, God knows! But he tells me how Matt. Wren should say that he was told that I should say that W. Coventry was guilty of the miscarriage at Chatham, though I myself, as he confesses, did tell him otherwise, and that it was wholly Pett's fault. This do trouble me, not only as untrue, but as a design in some [one] or other to do me hurt; for, as the thing is false, so it never entered into my mouth or thought, nor ever shall. He says that he hath rectified Wren in his belief of this, and so all is well. He gone, I to business till the evening, and then by chance home, and find the fellow that come up with my

[1] A proclamation by the Privy Council "Concerning the Pay of the Navy and Army" was issued on June 25th, 1667, and a proclamation for "Reassembling of Parliament" on June 26th, 1667 ("Bibliotheca Lindesiana," "Hand List of Proclamations," vol. i., 1893).

wife, Coleman, last from Brampton, a silly rogue, but one that would seem a gentleman; but I did not stay with him. So to the office, where late, busy, and then to walk a little in the garden, and so home to supper and to bed. News this tide, that about 80 sail of the Dutch, great and small, were seen coming up the river this morning; and this tide some of them to the upper end of the Hope.

28th. Up, and hear Sir W. Batten is come to town: I to see him; he is very ill of his fever, and come to town only for advice. Sir J. Minnes, I hear also, is very ill all this night, worse than before. Thence I going out met at the gate Sir H. Cholmly coming to me, and I to him in the coach, and both of us presently to St. James's, by the way discoursing of some Tangier business about money, which the want of I see will certainly bring the place into a bad condition. We find the Duke of York and [Sir] W. Coventry gone this morning, by two o'clock, to Chatham, to come home to-night: and it is fine to observe how both the King and Duke of York have, in their several late journeys to and again, done them in the night for coolnesse. Thence with him to the Treasury Chamber, and then to the Exchequer to inform ourselves a little about our warrant for £30,000 for Tangier, which vexes us that it is so far off in time of payment. Having walked two or three turns with him in the Hall we parted, and I home by coach, and did business at the office till noon, and then by water to White Hall to dinner to Sir G. Carteret, but he not at home, but I dined with my Lady and good company, and good dinner. My Lady and the family in very good humour upon this business of his parting with his place of Treasurer of the Navy, which I perceive they do own, and we did talk of it with satisfaction. They do here tell me that the Duke of Buckingham hath surrendered himself to Secretary Morrice, and is going to the Tower. Mr. Fenn, at the table, says that he hath been taken by the watch two or three times of late, at unseasonable hours, but so disguised that they could not know him: and when I come home, by and by, Mr. Lowther tells me that the Duke of Buckingham do dine publickly this day at Wadlow's, at the Sun Tavern; and is mighty merry, and sent word to the Lieutenant of the Tower, that he would come to him as soon as he had dined. Now, how sad a thing it is, when we come to make sport of proclaiming men traitors, and banishing them, and putting them out of their offices, and Privy Council, and of sending to and going to the Tower: God have mercy on us! At table, my Lady and Sir Philip Carteret have great and good discourse of the greatness of the present King of France — what great things he hath done, that a man may pass, at any hour in the night, all over that wild city [Paris], with a purse in his hand and no danger: that there is not a beggar to be seen in it, nor dirt lying in it; that he hath married two of Colbert's daughters to two of the greatest princes of France, and given them portions — bought the greatest dukedom in France, and given it to Colbert;[1] and ne'er a prince in France dare whisper against it, whereas here our King cannot do any such thing, but everybody's mouth is open against him for it, and the man that hath the favour also. That to several commanders that had not money to set them out to the present campagne, he did of his own accord send them £1,000 sterling a-piece, to equip themselves. But then they did enlarge upon the slavery of the people — that they are taxed more than the real estates they have; nay, it is an ordinary thing for people to desire to give the King all their land that they have, and themselves become only his tenants, and pay him rent to the full value of it: so they may have but their earnings. But this will not be granted; but he shall give the value of his rent, and part of his labour too. That there is not a petty governor of a province — nay, of a town, but he will take the daughter from the richest man in the town under him, that hath got anything, and give her to his footman for a wife if he pleases, and the King of France will do the like to the best man in his kingdom — take his daughter from him, and give her to his footman, or whom

[1] The Carterets appear to have mystified Pepys, who eagerly believed all that was told him. At this time Paris was notoriously unsafe, infested with robbers and beggars, and abominably unclean. Colbert had three daughters, of whom the eldest was just married when Pepys wrote, viz., Jean Marie Therèse, to the Duc de Chevreuse, on the 3rd February, 1667. The second daughter, Henriette Louise, was not married to the Duc de St. Aignan till January 21st, 1671; and the third, Marie Anne, to the Duc de Mortemart, February 14th, 1679. Colbert himself was never made a duke. His highest title was Marquis de Seignelay. — B.

he pleases. It is said that he do make a sport of us now; and says, that he knows no reason why his cozen, the King of England, should not be as willing to let him have his kingdom, as that the Dutch should take it from him, which is a most wretched thing that ever we should live to be in this most contemptible condition. After dinner Sir G. Carteret come in, and I to him and my Lady, and there he did tell me that the business was done between him and my Lord Anglesey; that himself is to have the other's place of Deputy Treasurer of Ireland, which is a place of honour and great profit, being far better, I know not for what reason, but a reason there is, than the Treasurer's, my Lord of Corke's,[1] and to give the other his, of Treasurer of the Navy; that the King, at his earnest entreaty, did, with much unwillingness, but with owning of great obligations to him, for his faithfulness and long service to him and his father, and therefore was willing to grant his desire. That the Duke of York hath given him the same kind words, so that it is done with all the good manner that could be, and he I perceive do look upon it, and so do I, I confess, as a great good fortune to him to meet with one of my Lord Anglesey's quality willing to receive it at this time. Sir W. Coventry he hath not yet made acquainted with it, nor do intend it, it being done purely to ease himself of the many troubles and plagues which he thinks the perverseness and unkindness of Sir W. Coventry and others by his means have and is likely every day to bring upon him, and the Parliaments' envy, and lastly to put himself into a condition of making up his accounts, which he is, he says, afeard he shall never otherwise be. My Lord Chancellor, I perceive, is his friend in it. I remember I did in the morning tell Sir H. Cholmly of this business: and he answered me, he was sorry for it; for, whatever Sir G. Carteret was, he is confident my Lord Anglesey is one of the greatest knaves in the world, which is news to me, but I shall make my use of it. Having done this discourse with Sir G. Carteret, and signified my great satisfaction in it, which they seem to look upon as something, I went away

[1] Richard Boyle, eldest son of the great Earl of Cork (1612–1698), succeeded his father as second Earl of Cork in 1643, created Baron Clifford of Lanesborough in 1644, and Earl of Burlington in 1664.

and by coach home, and there find my wife making of tea; a drink which Mr. Pelling, the Potticary, tells her is good for her cold and defluxions. I to the office (whither come Mr. Carcasse to me to sue for my favour to him), and Sir W. Pen's, where I find Mr. Lowther come to town after the journey, and after a small visit to him, I to the office to do much business, and then in the evening to Sir W. Batten's, to see how he did; and he is better than he was. He told me how Mrs. Lowther had her train held up yesterday by her page,[1] at his house in the country; which is so ridiculous a piece of pride as I am ashamed of. He told me also how he hears by somebody that my Lord Bruncker's maid hath told that her lady Mrs. Williams had sold her jewels and clothes to raise money for something or other; and indeed the last night a letter was sent from her to me, to send to my Lord, with about five pieces of gold in it, which methought at the time was but a poor supply. I then to Sir W. Pen, who continues a little ill, or dissembles it, the latter of which I am apt to believe. Here I staid but little, not meaning much kindness in it; and so to the office, and dispatched more business; and then home at night, and to supper with my wife, and who should come in but Mr. Pelling, and supped with us, and told us the news of the town; how the officers of the Navy are cried out upon, and a great many greater men; but do think that I shall do well enough; and I think, if I have justice, I shall. He tells me of my Lord Duke of Buckingham, his dining to-day at the Sun, and that he was mighty merry; and, what is strange, tells me that really he is at this day a very popular man, the world reckoning him to suffer upon no other account than that he did propound in Parliament to have all the questions that had to do with the receipt of the taxes and prizes; but they must be very silly that do think he can do any thing out of good intention. After a great deal of tittle-tattle with this honest man, he gone we to bed. We hear that the Dutch are gone down again; and thanks be to God! the trouble they give us this second time is not very considerable.

29th. Up, having had many ugly dreams to-night of my fa-

[1] See July 14th, *post*.

ther and my sister and mother's coming to us, and meeting my wife and me at the gate of the office going out, they all in laced suits, and come, they told me, to be with me this May day. My mother told me she lacked a pair of gloves, and I remembered a pair of my wife's in my chamber, and resolved she should have them, but then recollected how my mother come to be here when I was in mourning for her, and so thinking it to be a mistake in our thinking her all this while dead, I did contrive that it should be said to any that enquired that it was my mother-in-law, my wife's mother, that was dead, and we in mourning for. This dream troubled me and I waked. . . . These dreams did trouble me mightily all night. Up, and by coach to St. James's, and there find Sir W. Coventry and Sir W. Pen above stairs, and then we to discourse about making up our accounts against the Parliament; and Sir W. Coventry did give us the best advice he could for us to provide for our own justification, believing, as everybody do, that they will fall heavily upon us all, though he lay all upon want of money, only a little, he says (if the Parliament be in any temper), may be laid upon themselves for not providing money sooner, they being expressly and industriously warned thereof by him, he says, even to the troubling them, that some of them did afterwards tell him that he had frighted them. He says he do prepare to justify himself, and that he hears that my Lord Chancellor, my Lord Arlington, the Vice Chamberlain and himself are reported all up and down the Coffee houses to be the four sacrifices that must be made to atone the people. Then we to talk of the loss of all affection and obedience now in the seamen, so that all power is lost. He told us that he do concur in thinking that want of money to do the most of it, but that that is not all, but the having of gentlemen Captains, who discourage all Tarpaulins, and have given out that they would in a little time bring it to that pass that a Tarpaulin should not dare to aspire to more than to be a Boatswain or a gunner. That this makes the Sea Captains to lose their own good affections to the service, and to instil it into the seamen also, and that the seamen do see it themselves and resent it; and tells us that it is notorious, even to his bearing of great ill will at Court, that he hath been the opposer of gentlemen Captains; and Sir W. Pen did put in, and said that he was esteemed to have been the man that did instil it into Sir W. Coventry, which Sir W. Coventry did owne also, and says that he hath always told the Gentlemen Captains his opinion of them, and that himself who had now served to the business of the sea 6 or 7 years should know a little, and as much as them that had never almost been at sea, and that yet he found himself fitter to be a Bishop or Pope than to be a Sea-Commander, and so indeed he is. I begun to tell him of the experience I had of the great brags made by Sir F. Hollis the other day, and the little proof either of the command or interest he had in his men, which Sir W. Pen seconded by saying Sir Fr. Hollis had told him that there was not a pilot to be got the other day for his fire-ships, and so was forced to carry them down himself, which Sir W. Coventry says, In my conscience, he knows no more to do and understand the River no more than he do Tiber or Ganges. Thence I away with Sir W. Pen to White Hall, to the Treasury Chamber, but to no purpose, and so by coach home, and there to my office to business, and then home to dinner, and to pipe with my wife, and so to the office again, having taken a resolution to take a turn to Chatham to-morrow, indeed to do business of the King's, but also to give myself the satisfaction of seeing the place after the Dutch have been here. I have sent to and got Creed to go with me by coach betimes to-morrow morning. After having done my business at the office I home, and there I found Coleman come again to my house, and with my wife in our great chamber, which vexed me, there being a bed therein. I staid there awhile, and then to my study vexed, showing no civility to the man. But he comes on a compliment to receive my wife's commands into the country, whither he is going, and it being Saturday my wife told me there was no other room for her to bring him in, and so much is truth. But I staid vexed in my closet till by and by my cozen Thomas Pepys,[1] of Hatcham, come to see me, and he up to my closet, and there sat talking an hour or two of the sad state of the times, whereof we did talk very freely,

[1] See May 12th, 1665.

and he thinks nothing but a union of religious interests will ever settle us; and I do think that, and the Parliament's taking the whole management of things into their hands, and severe inquisitions into our miscarriages, will help us. After we had bewailed ourselves and the kingdom very freely one to another (wherein I do blame myself for my freedom of speech to anybody), he gone, and Coleman gone also before, I to the office, whither Creed come by my desire, and he and I to my wife, to whom I now propose the going to Chatham, who, mightily pleased with it, sent for Mercer to go with her, but she could not go, having friends at home, which vexed my wife and me; and the poor wretch would have had anybody else to have gone, but I would like nobody else, so was contented to stay at home, on condition to go to Epsum next Sunday, which I will do, and so I to the office to dispatch my business, and then home to supper with Creed, and then Creed and I together to bed, very pleasant in discourse. This day talking with Sir W. Batten, he did give me an account how ill the King and Duke of York was advised to send orders for our frigates and fire-ships to come from Gravesend, soon as ever news come of the Dutch being returned into the river, wherein no seamen, he believes, was advised with; for, says he, we might have done just as Warwicke[1] did, when he, W. Batten,[2] come with the King and the like fleete, in the late wars, into the river: for Warwicke did not run away from them, but sailed before them when they sailed, and come to anchor when they come to anchor, and always kept in a small distance from them: so as to be able to take any opportunity of any of their ships running aground, or change of wind, or any thing else, to his advantage. So might we have done with our fire-ships, and we have lost an opportunity of taking or burning a good ship of their's, which was run aground about Hole-haven, I think he said, with the wind so as their ships could not get her away; but we might have done what we would

[1] Robert Rich, Earl of Warwick, Lord High Admiral 1643–45, 1648–49.

[2] See May 25th, 1660. Clarendon's assertion that Batten was an "obscure fellow," there quoted, is disputed by Professor Laughton in the "Dictionary of National Biography."

with her, and, it may be, done them mischief, too, with the wind. This seems very probable, and I believe was not considered.

30th (Lord's day). Up about three o'clock, and Creed and I got ourselves ready, and took coach at our gate, it being very fine weather, and the cool of the morning, and with much pleasure, without any stop, got to Rochester about ten of the clock, all the way having mighty pleasant talk of the fate that is over all we do, that it seems as if we were designed in every thing, by land by sea, to undo ourselves. At the foot of Rochester bridge, at the landing-place, I met my Lord Bruncker and my Lord Douglas,[1] and all the officers of the soldiers in the town, waiting there for the Duke of York, whom they heard was coming thither this day; by and by comes my Lord Middleton, the first time I remember to have seen him, well mounted, who had been to meet him, but come back without him; he seems a fine soldier, and so every body says he is; and a man, like my Lord Teviott, and indeed most of the Scotch gentry, as I observe, of few words. After staying here by the water-side and seeing the boats come up from Chatham, with them that rowed with bandeleeres about their shoulders, and muskets in their boats, they being the workmen of the Yard, who have promised to redeem their credit, lost by their deserting the service when the Dutch were there, my Lord Bruncker went with Lord Middleton to his inne, the Crowne, to dinner, which I took unkindly, but he was slightly invited. So I and Creed down by boat to Chatham-yard (our watermen having their bandeleeres about them all the way), and to Commissioner Pett's house, where my Lord Bruncker told me that I should meet with his dinner two dishes of meat, but did not, but however by the help of Mr. Wiles had some beer and ale brought me, and a good piece of roast beef from somebody's table, and eat well at two, and after dinner into the garden to shew Creed, and I must confess it must needs be thought a sorrowful thing for a man that hath taken so much pains to make a place neat to lose it as Commissioner Pett must now this. Thence

[1] James, second Marquis of Douglas, and nephew to the Duke of Hamilton. — B.

to see the batteries made; which, indeed, are very fine, and guns placed so as one would think the River should be very secure. I was glad, as also it was new to me, to see so many fortifications as I have of late seen, and so up to the top of the Hill, there to look, and could see towards Sheerenesse, to spy the Dutch fleete, but could make [out] none but one vessel, they being all gone. But here I was told, that, in all the late attempt, there was but one man that they knew killed on shore: and that was a man that had laid himself upon his belly upon one of the hills, on the other side of the River, to see the action; and a bullet come, took the ground away just under his belly, and ripped up his belly, and so was killed. Thence back to the docke, and in my way saw how they are fain to take the deals of the rope-house to supply other occasions, and how sillily the country troopers look, that stand upon the passes there; and, methinks, as if they were more willing to run away than to fight, and it is said that the country soldiers did first run at Sheerenesse, but that then my Lord Douglas's men did run also; but it is excused that there was no defence for them towards the sea, that so the very beach did fly in their faces as the bullets come, and annoyed them, they having, after all this preparation of the officers of the ordnance, only done something towards the land, and nothing at all towards the sea. The people here everywhere do speak very badly of Sir Edward Spragge, as not behaving himself as he should have done in that business, going away with the first, and that old Captain Pyne, who, I am here told, and no sooner, is Master-Gunner of England, was the last that staid there. Thence by barge, it raining hard, down to the chaine; and in our way did see the sad wrackes of the poor "Royall Oake," "James," and "London;"[1] and several other of our ships by us sunk, and several of the enemy's, whereof three men-of-war that they could not get off, and so burned. We did also see several dead bodies lie by the side of the water. I do not

[1] "The bottom of the 'Royal James is got afloat, and those of the 'Loyal London' and 'Royal Oak' soon will be so. Many men are at work to put Sheerness in a posture of defence, and a boom is being fitted over the river by Upnor Castle, which with the good fortifications will leave nothing to fear." — *Calendar of State Papers*, 1667, p. 285.

see that Upnor Castle hath received any hurt by them, though they played long against it; and they themselves shot till they had hardly a gun left upon the carriages, so badly provided they were: they have now made two batteries on that side, which will be very good, and do good service. So to the chaine, and there saw it fast at the end on Upnor side of the River; very fast, and borne up upon the several stages across the River; and where it is broke nobody can tell me. I went on shore on Upnor side to look upon the end of the chaine; and caused the link to be measured, and it was six inches and one-fourth in circumference. They have burned the Crane House that was to hawl it taught. It seems very remarkable to me, and of great honour to the Dutch, that those of them that did go on shore to Gillingham, though they went in fear of their lives, and were some of them killed; and, notwithstanding their provocation at Schelling,[1] yet killed none of our people nor plundered their houses, but did take some things of easy carriage, and left the rest, and not a house burned; and, which is to our eternal disgrace, that what my Lord Douglas's men, who come after them, found there, they plundered and took all away; and the watermen that carried us did further tell us, that our own soldiers are far more terrible to those people of the country-towns than the Dutch themselves. We were told at the batteries, upon my seeing of the field-guns that were there, that, had they come a day sooner, they had been able to have saved all; but they had no orders, and lay lingering upon the way, and did not come forward for want of direction. Commissioner Pett's house was all unfurnished, he having carried away all his goods. I met with no satisfaction whereabouts the chaine was broke, but do confess I met with nobody that I could well expect to have satisfaction [from], it being Sunday; and the officers of the Yard most of them abroad, or at the Hill house, at the pay of the Chest, which they did make use of to-day to do part in. Several complaints, I hear, of the Monmouth's coming away too soon from the chaine, where she was placed with the two guard-ships to secure

[1] The island near the entrance of the Zuyder Zee, on which Sir Robert Holmes had landed. See August 15th, 1666. — B.

it; and Captain Robert Clerke, my friend, is blamed for so doing there, but I hear nothing of him at London about it; but Captain Brookes's running aground with the "Sancta Maria," which was one of the three ships that were ordered to be sunk to have dammed up the River at the chaine, is mightily cried against, and with reason, he being the chief man to approve of the abilities of other men and the other two ships did get safe thither and he run aground; but yet I do hear that though he be blameable, yet if she had been there, she nor two more to them three would have been able to have commanded the river all over. I find that here, as it hath been in our river,[1] fire-ships, when fitted, have been sunk afterwards, and particularly those here at the Mussle,[2] where they did no good at all. Our great ships that were run aground and sunk are all well raised but the "Vanguard," which they go about to raise to-morrow. "The Henery," being let loose to drive up the river of herself, did run up as high as the bridge, and broke down some of the rails of the bridge, and so back again with the tide, and up again, and then berthed himself so well as no pilot could ever have done better; and Punnet says he would not, for his life, have undertaken to have done it, with all his skill. I find it is true that the Dutch did heele "The Charles"[3] to get her down, and yet run aground twice or thrice, and yet got her safe away, and have her, with a great many good guns in her, which none of our pilots would ever have undertaken. It is very considerable the quantity of goods, which the making of these platforms and batterys do take out of the King's stores: so that we shall have little left there, and, God knows! no credit to buy any; besides, the taking away and spending

[1] The Thames.

[2] Muscle Bank, in the Medway.

[3] John Conny, writing to Williamson from Chatham, June 17th, 1667, says: "The 'Royal Charles' is got away. The Dutch are all drawn down the river; there are not many within Sheerness, yet enough to secure their men, who are said to be fortifying the Ness. They have fired what they can of the ships sunk to prevent their approach, and cleared the river except weighing those vessels. The 'St. George' is got afloat. Hopes this high water to recover the 'Monmouth,' 'Rainbow,' 'Triumph,' 'Unicorn,' and 'Henry'" ("Calendar of State Papers," 1667, p. 200).

of (it is possible) several goods that would have been either rejected or abatement made for them before used. It is a strange thing to see that, while my Lords Douglas and Middleton do ride up and down upon single horses, my Lord Bruncker do go up and down with his hackney-coach and six horses at the King's charge, which will do, for all this time, and the time that he is likely to stay, must amount to a great deal. But I do not see that he hath any command over the seamen, he being affronted by three or four seamen before my very face, which he took sillily, methought; and is not able to do so much good as a good boatswain in this business. My Lord Bruncker, I perceive, do endeavour to speak well of Commissioner Pett, saying that he did exercise great care and pains while he was there, but do not undertake to answer for his not carrying up of the great ships. Back again to Rochester, and there walked to the Cathedral as they were beginning of the service, but would not be seen to stay to church there, besides had no mind, but rather to go to our inne, the White Hart, where we drank and were fain (the towne being so full of soldiers) to have a bed corded for us to lie in, I being unwilling to lie at the Hill house for one night, being desirous to be near our coach to be gone betimes to-morrow morning. Here in the streets, I did hear the Scotch march beat by the drums before the soldiers, which is very odde. Thence to the Castle, and viewed it with Creed, and had good satisfaction from him that showed it us touching the history of it. Then into the fields, a fine walk, and there saw Sir Francis Clerke's house, which is a pretty seat, and then back to our inne and bespoke supper, and so back to the fields and into the Cherry garden, where we had them fresh gathered, and here met with a young, plain, silly shopkeeper, and his wife, a pretty young woman, the man's name Hawkins, and I did kiss her, and we talked (and the woman of the house is a very talking bawdy jade), and eat cherries together, and then to walk in the fields till it was late, and did kiss her, and I believe had I had a fit time and place I might have done what I would with her. Walked back and left them at their house near our inne, and then to our inne, where, I hear, my Lord Bruncker hath sent for me to speak with me before I go: so I took his coach, which stands there with two horses, and to him and to his bedside, where he was in bed, and hath a watchman with a halbert at his door; and to him, and did talk a little, and find him a very weak man for this business that he is upon; and do pity the King's service, that is no better handled, and his folly to call away Pett before we could have found a better man to have staid in his stead. So took leave of him, and with Creed back again, it being now about 10 at night, and to our inne to supper, and then to bed, being both sleepy, but could get no sheets to our bed, only linen to our mouths, and so to sleep, merrily talking of Hawkins and his wife, and troubled that Creed did see so much of my dalliance, though very little.

END OF VOL. VI.